THE PASTOR AND THE MATRIARCH OF THE GERMAN UNDERGROUND AND THEIR TIMES

A Polish Perspective
By Vince Barwinski

Printed in Taiwan, Republic of China by
Elephant White Cultural Enterprise Ltd. Press,
8F.-2, No.1, Keji Rd., Dali Dist., Taichung City 41264, Taiwan (R.O.C.)
Distributed by Elephant White Cultural Enterprise Co., Ltd.

ISBN: 978-626-7018-12-5
Suggested Price: NT$900

To my dear father Stanisław

1923 — 2010

CONTENTS

Preface[i]

Birth and Memory upon the Lesser Known Fault Line of History

On a miserable mid-afternoon in February 2005,[i] in Wrocław, the historical capital of the Silesian region located in modern-day south-western Poland, outside the Gothic and now Catholic church of Saint Elisabeth, I photographed a bronze cross monument. At its foot were tablets in Polish and German describing and honouring the life of the German Lutheran pastor Dietrich Bonhoeffer.

POLISH:

DIETRICH BONHOEFFER
URODZIŁ SIĘ 4 LUTEGO 1906
WE WROCŁAWIU-
EWANGELICKI KSIĄDZ
TEOLOG UCZESTNIK
NIEMIECKIEGO RUCHU OPORU
PRZECIW NARODOWEMU
SOCJALIZMOWI ORĘDOWNIK
EKUMENIZMU I MĘCZENNIK
ZA WIARĘ CHRZEŚCIJAŃSKA
ZAMORDOWANY W OBOZIE
KONCENTRACYJNYM
WE FLOSSENBÜRGU
9 KWIETNIA 1945 ROKU

KOMITET ORGANIZACYJNY
„Dla Dietricha Bonhoeffera"

GERMAN:

DIETRICH BONHOEFFER
WURDE AM 4 FEBRUAR 1906
IN BRESLAU GEBOREN.
EVANGELISHER PASTOR

---

[i] Saturday February 12, 2005 to be exact.

UND THEOLOGE MITGLEID
DES DEUTSCHEN
WIDERSTANDS GEGEN
DEN NATIONALSOZIALIZMUS,
VORKAMPFER DER ÖKUMENE
UND MÄRTYRER
FÜR DEN CHRISTLICHEN
GLAUBEN. ERMORDET
IM KONCENTRATIONSLAGER
FLOSSENBÜRGU AM 9.APRIL 1945

ORGANISATIONSKOMITEE
„Für Dietrich Bonhoeffer"

Which translates to:

DIETRICH BONHOEFFER
BORN ON 4th FEBRUARY 1906
IN BRESLAU/WROCŁAW.
EVANGELICAL PRIEST
THEOLOGIAN AND MEMBER OF THE
GERMAN RESISTANCE MOVEMENT
AGAINST NATIONAL SOCIALISM. (NAZISM)
SPOKESMAN FOR
ECUMENISM AND MARTYR FOR
THE CHRISTIAN FAITH.
MURDERED IN THE
CONCENTRATION CAMP
OF FLOSSENBÜRG
ON 9th APRIL 1945.

ORGANISING COMMITTEE
"For Dietrich Bonhoeffer"

When Dietrich was born, a year shy of one century before my visit, modern-day Polish Wrocław was German Breslau. Poland had official-ly ceased to exist since its third partitioning of 1795, between the em-pires of Germanic Prussia, Austria, and Tsarist Russia.[2] With the col-lapse of these three empires in the wake of the Great War in November 1918, and the subsequent power vacuum, a fully independent Poland was reborn as the Second Republic,[3] only to be extinguished in late

September 1939 in the wake of Hitler and Stalin's dual invasion, precipitating the second world conflict.[4]

The newly independent Poland came very close to being wiped from existence after less than two years, when, in August 1920, during the Polish-Soviet War of 1919-20, the Poles, thanks to the risky but brilliant counter attack conceived by Poland's father of modern-day independence, Józef Piłsudski, repelled Lenin's Bolsheviks in the Battle of Warsaw; this became known as the *Cud na Wisła* (Miracle on the Vistula). It not only saved Poland from the terror of Bolshevik occupation, but also saved a chronically chaotic and weak Germany.[5] Curiously, this fascinating Polish epoch was to play a most significant part in the post-WWII upheaval of Breslau, and in Old Prussia in general. Both lay in what would become known in Stalinist parlance as the "Recovered Territories."[6]

The body of this book primarily focuses on the Pastor of the anti-Nazi German Resistance, Dietrich Bonhoeffer, and the matriarch, Ruth von Kleist-Retzow, a native Silesian of the Old Prussian Junkers (pronounced YUN-kers).[7] She shared the same birthday as Dietrich,[8] and came to regard him like a son; she will become part of the story from Chapter 6 onwards. Indeed, Jane Pejsa titled her book about this remarkable lady most aptly as *Matriarch of Conspiracy*, as much of the German Resistance, was in some way, linked to her. As a fellow native Silesian of Ruth, Dietrich was only six years old when the family left Breslau in 1912, yet he retained very fond memories of his birthplace.[9] Nevertheless, given the history of Wrocław/Breslau over the centuries, and the centuries of bad blood between these great nations of Poland and Germany, the existence of a monument to a German in this modern-day Polish city is remarkable.

The name of this city on the Odra (German: Odor) has many variants amongst the languages of Europe, such as Vratislav in Czech, Vratislav or Vroclav in Slovak, вроцлав (Vroclav) in Serbian, Вроцлав (Vrotslav) in Ukrainian and Russian, and Vratislavia in Latin.[10] But in German it was called Breslau up until the end of World War II in Europe, when *Festung* Breslau (Fortress Breslau) fell to the Soviet Army on May 6 1945, just a couple of days before the end of the war in Europe, and four days following the surrender of Berlin.[11] Its origins at the intersection of two great trade routes, the Via Regia and the Amber Road, are strongly debated by historians;[12] however, the majority argue that the dukes of the Czech Přemyslid dynasty, especially Boleslav I the Cruel of Bohemia (915—967) and Boleslav II the Pious of Bohemia

(967—999), were the first sovereigns of the Odra (German: Oder) region.[13]

In 966, Mieszko I, the first historic ruler of the Polish Piast dynasty, was baptised at age thirty-six,[14] in the name of the Roman church, and would pass away in 992, to be succeeded by his twenty-five-year-old son Bolesław I the Brave.[ii] It's not certain which of these two early Piast monarchs annexed these territories of the Odra late that century, but Bolesław I incorporated them into his realm in 1000 with the establishment of the Bishopric in Wrocław as one of the dioceses of the Archdiocese in Gniezno, the original Polish capital, upon Ostrów Tumski (Island of the Cathedral).[15] The Přemyslids, however, did not accept that they had lost control over Wrocław, and reclaimed the Odra region after invading Poland in 1038. The province was again annexed in 1050 by the Piast monarch Casimir I the Restorer (1034—1058),[16] and remained under formal control of the Piasts until 1335. Almost a century before that year, the ethnic balance of Wrocław was transformed when the city was devastated in 1241 during the Mongol invasion of Europe, although not directly by the Mongols. In a bizarre, draconian and extreme but successful measure to persuade the Mongols to withdraw, the townspeople burnt their city to the ground.[17]

When the city was repopulated, it was mostly with Germans, who ultimately became the dominant ethnic group. For the first time, the Germanised name of the city, Breslau, appeared in written records, with the city council using Latin and German languages in the town, and adopting German town law in the following year of 1242 in the expanding city. However, in spite of the city's German ethnic dominance, formal Polish sovereignty did not cease until 1335, when, under the mediation of the Hungarian king Charles Robert (Charles I) at a meeting in Visegrád, on the northern frontier of modern Hungary, Casimir the Great (Kazimierz Wielki) purchased the Czech rights to the Polish crown from John of Bohemia for a huge sum, which amounted to twice the annual income of the famous Wieliczka[18] salt mines just east of Kraków. However, on top of the monetary price for the Polish crown, Casimir the Great had to relinquish Polish control of almost all of Silesia, which naturally included its regional capital of Wrocław.[19]

This arrangement was formalised in the treaties of Trenčín, in modern-day western Slovakia, and of Visegrád in Hungary; both were

---

[ii] As opposed to Boleslav I the Cruel of Bohemia (915—967). Hence, by 992, Boleslav I the Cruel of Bohemia had been dead for 25 years — the age by then of the Polish Piast monarch Bolesław I the Brave.

ratified in 1339,[20] but not finalised until 1372.[21] While the city lost its political ties to the Polish state, it remained connected to Poland by religious links and the existence of an ethnic Polish population within it.[22] Nevertheless, it was well over half a millennia before formal Polish sovereignty would be restored to the city and region, when the Third Reich collapsed at the end of World War II in Europe — albeit under the puppet rule of the Soviet-sponsored Communist regime of the People's Republic of Poland. Regardless of sovereignty, throughout the fourteenth century, fires were commonplace, and floods were a perennial menace. On at least four occasions, in 1344, 1349, 1360, and 1379, fires devastated large sections of the city centre, while in 1464, the city suffered major flooding.[23] Furthermore, leprosy and the plague were a constant menace.[24]

Eleven years before the flood in 1464, the Jewish community of Breslau suffered a massacre of unspeakable horror at the hands of the 67-year-old Franciscan and former governor of Perugia, Brother John Capistrano (1386—1456), who had been sent to Bohemia as "Inquisitor General" to stamp out heresy.[25] Between February 14 and April 27 1453, Capistrano preached three times daily in Breslau (Bohemian Vretslav), probably speaking in Latin with the help of a German interpreter.[26] In May 1453, with the siege and the ultimate fall of Orthodox Christian Constantinople (now modern-day Turkish Istanbul, but then capital of the crumbling relic of the Eastern Roman Empire) to the Ottoman Turks,[27] Brother John unleashed his fanatical zeal upon the Jews of Breslau. With the absence of both the heretical Muslim Ottoman Turks and the Hussites — the movement of Bohemian Jan Huss that preceded Europe's Reformation[28] — the Jews became his third target.[29]

That terrible month, Jews were rounded up and their property seized on various trumped-up charges, which included the poisoning of the water supply and the "desecration of the host."[30] Torture was used to extract the desired confessions, with Brother John taking an active interest. This was merely the entrée for the unspeakable horrors to come, when the first fourteen victims sentenced were tied to wooden boards on the Market Square, and their flesh removed with red-hot tongs and thrown into pans over hot coals. Finally, they were quartered alive. For the remainder of the condemned, their choice was to convert or be burned; some, such as the Rabbi, committed suicide. Six weeks later, on July 4 in the Salt Market, another 41 Jews were burned.[31]

Two years later in 1455, the Jewish community of Breslau officially ceased to exist. It was a legal prohibition destined to remain in force for three centuries.[32] While not amounting to an absolute ban, it was only various categories of privileged Jews who were allowed to take up residence.[33] For instance, Isaak Meyer, a Jew from Prague, was the Breslauer Münzer or leaseholder/coiner of the mint. Others, such as rich merchants, were only permitted to visit for limited periods on certain business.[34] The punishments for failing to leave on time could be severe.[35]

During Breslau's three annual fairs, Jews were free to enter the city and ply their trade, but they were under strict supervision, and in 1577 were compelled to wear yellow discs for identification.[36] This precursor to the Star of David armbands almost four centuries later[37] was indicative of centuries of fermented European anti-Semitic sentiment, as exemplified by the horrors of May and July 1453. Such toxic sentiment was exploited by Hitler from around 1919 onwards, in the wake of the Great War and Germany's signing of the humiliating Treaty of Versailles, to ferment his absolutist agenda.[38] As Robert Gellately comments:"

> Growing up in Austria, Hitler likely did not differ from many of his generation in tending toward anti-Jewish attitudes, though it was not until after the Great War that he became the type of rabid anti-Semite we associate with the Nazi movement."[39]

According to Michael Berenbaum, in 1919 Adolf Hitler wrote: "Rational anti-Semitism, however, must lead to systematic legal opposition....Its final objective must unswervingly be the removal of the Jews altogether."[40]   By 1925, this would evolve into *Mein Kampf* (My Struggle), further developing the idea of the Jews as an evil race struggling for world domination.[41]

Back in 1526, with the Reformation in full swing, and in spite of Johann Heß, a fervent follower of Martin Luther, publicly professing the Lutheran faith for Breslau in 1524,[42] Silesia came under the rule of the Catholic House of Habsburg (also known as the house of Austria).[43] Given that relations between Breslau's Protestant majority and the Catholic Habsburgs always ranged from lukewarm to openly hostile, it is little wonder that for the vast majority of the city's Protestant inhabitants, its annexation by the Protestant Germanic Kingdom of Prussia, along with most of Silesia during the War of the Austrian Succession in the 1740s, was viewed as a liberation.[44]

In January 1762, contemplating suicide in his firewood-bereft, freezing Breslau Spaetgen Palace, Frederick the Great received news of the remarkable political providence of what would be dubbed the "Miracle of Brandenburg," saving Prussia from virtual political and military annihilation.[45] This was the death of the Messalina[46] of the North — the hostile Tsarina Elizabeth Petrovna,[47] daughter of Peter the Great — and the succession of her nephew Peter, who was a great admirer of Frederick. Then in the following year of 1763, the Habsburg empress Maria Theresa formally ceded Silesia.[48] The history of Wrocław/Breslau thus far had been one of Bohemian, Polish, Austrian and Prussian sovereignty, with periods of Saxon and Swedish occupation thrown in during the devastating Thirty Years' War from 1618 to 1648.[49]

While the Thirty Years' War took its inevitable toll on the city, by the 1670s, when many of its Silesian neighbours were still depressed, Breslau's population had recovered to its pre-war levels and was at the forefront in reviving the local trade in wool and linen.[50] The Silesian poet Friedrich von Logau, whose family estate at Nimptsch (Niemcza) had been destroyed by enemy troops, summed up the utter futility of this conflict that was only nominally related to the schism between Protestant and Catholic: "

> Die Welt hat Krieg geführt weit über zwanzig Jahr,
> Nunmehr soll Friede sein, soll werden, wie es war.
> Sie hat gekriegt um dass, o lachenswerte Tat!
> Was sie, eh sie gekriegt, zuvor besessen hat.

> The world has warred for twenty years and more,
> Peace will now prevail, all will be as was before,
> The joke is this: all that it's been fighting for,
> It already owned before it went to war."[51]

From 1861-88, Kaiser Wilhelm I (the grandfather of Kaiser Wilhelm II who would lead Germany into the Great War)[52] reigned, and in concert with his "Iron Chancellor" Otto von Bismarck, Prussia seized the initiative and led Germany to its holy grail of unification in January 1871.[53] Predictably however, wars were fought; three in all, against Denmark in 1864, Austria in 1866, and France (Franco-Prussian) in 1870—1. Ultimately, victory in all three secured Prussia's unquestionable supremacy among the German states, with Breslau's role most prominent in the campaign of 1866 against the Austrians.[54]

With the eager approval of the city, invoking its "spirit of 1813"[55] from the Napoleonic Wars, and mindful that Breslau and the Silesian province were primary Austrian objectives, Wilhelm dispatched the strongest of his three armies facing the Austrians to central Silesia; his son, Crown Prince Frederick William, established his headquarters in the city on May 28 1870.[56] As the summer fighting wore on, the Austrians, weakened by their concurrent conflict against Italy, were compelled to abandon all hope of invading Silesia. At the conclusion of the campaign, both Kaiser and the Crown Prince stood as one in Breslau to take the salute at a parade of the Silesian Corps, and to thank the Breslauers for their resolute loyalty to the Prussian cause.[57] Indeed, it was this "spirit of 1813," embodying Breslau as the birthplace of the War of Liberation against Napoleon, that led to the city becoming the birthplace of the Iron Cross, the most famous German military decoration, and of Germany's national colours, black, red and gold.[58]

However, while the 1866 campaign was undoubtedly crucial to the Prussian holy grail of the unified German state, it was not until the victorious conclusion of the Franco-Prussian War that this came to pass in the Hall of Mirrors at Versailles near Paris, in January 1871. There, the Kaiser and Crown Prince stood together once again, declaring the united German Empire.[59] This was witnessed by Ruth von Kleist-Retzow's father Robert Gräfin von Zedlitz-Trützschler, and future Pomeranian father-in-law Hans Hugo von Kleist-Retzow,[60] four years after her birth. Given the humiliating indemnities France was compelled to pay Prussia,[61] the question arises: was this pivotal to France choosing the same venue in June 1919 for Germany to sign the harsh and humiliating peace to conclude the Great War?

On February 4 1906, the 39th birthday of Ruth von Kleist-Retzow, Dietrich and his twin sister Sabine, the sixth and seventh children in their family, were born in a prosperous and thriving Breslau. This state of prosperity was shared by all cities in Germany at the time, including of course Berlin,[62] where the family moved in 1912. Two years later, however, a prosperous Germany entered into a devastating war triggered by the assassination of Archduke Franz Ferdinand of Austria, heir to the throne of Austria-Hungary, by Bosnian-Serbian nationalist Gavrilo Princip in Sarajevo on June 28, 1914.[63] Initially, it seemed nothing more than a minor localised spat when Austria-Hungary delivered an ultimatum to the Kingdom of Serbia.[64] However, the complex web of alliances forged over the previous decades, supposedly to avert major war, precipitated what they were intended to avoid. All warring parties were optimistic about their boys being home for Christmas. Yet this war lasted from late July 1914 to November 11, 1918, and became the most devastating war of all time. The unresolved issues in its aftermath led to another world conflict, two decades later, lasting almost six years, and dwarfing the first in unbridled devastation, cruelty, misery and upheaval.

In the wake of the first world conflict, Germany was descending into chaos amidst the humiliation of defeat. This humiliation was even more acute for Germans in the east of the Reich, such as Breslau;[65] here, by the winter of 1914—15, with German defences in the east dangerously undermanned, the Russian Imperial army was camped barely eighty kilometres to the east of the city.[66] It was pushed back 1,600 kilometres east[67] by the time Russia pulled out of the war in December 1917 following the Bolshevik October Revolution, and was compelled to sign the humiliating peace treaty of Brest-Litovsk four months later in March.[68] This virtual total victory over the Russian bear, after it came so close to Breslau in the early stages of the war, made the humiliating armistice of November 1918 an especially bitter pill for Breslauers to swallow. This, followed by the signing of the Treaty of Versailles in late June 1919, is a theme frequently revisited in this book; Hitler repeatedly exploited it in his rise to power, in concert with the perception of the Dolchstosslegende,[69] the "stab in the back myth" to the German military, alleged to have been committed by Germany's political left-wing, perceived as synonymous to the Jews.[70]

The Kaiser fled into Dutch exile in early November 1918,[71] to the disgust and sense of betrayal of Ruth and her fellow Junkers in the east of the Reich.[72] The political chaos in post-war Germany centred around the conflict between extreme left- and right-wing factions, with moderate centrist politicians desperately trying to preserve the fledgling democratic republic. Berlin was in the midst of revolution and the Democratic Republic was declared in the relative tranquillity of the Saxon city of Weimar.[73] Thus, the much-maligned Weimar Republic was born, but despite its impressive democratic credentials, it was constantly under threat in the maelstrom of post-war German political turmoil and chaos.

On the radical right wing of the Freikorps (Volunteer or Free Corps), the myth of the *Dolchstosslegende* was born. Conversely, on the extreme left wing, radical Socialists of the Spartacist League eagerly anticipated a quintessential Soviet-style overthrow of the fledgling bourgeois Weimar Republic and the defeat of all far-right elements. In the centre, politicians such as Matthias Erzberger, a warmonger turned pacifist, strove to keep the opposing extremists apart. However, his signing of the armistice placed him in the crosshairs of the *Dolchstosslegende*, and he was assassinated in 1921.[74] It was not the first, nor the last political assassination in Germany's post-WWI chaos, that plagued Weimar in the first five or so years of its existence.

Clearly, Weimar had few champions of its own, and survived its infancy only because militants on either side didn't want power falling into their opponents' hands.[75] The political party that Dietrich's father Karl supported was the moderate, left-leaning Social Democrats, who had come to power following the November 1918 revolution in the death throes of the Great War.[76] Neither the violent, extreme left-wing Spartacists, nor the radical right wing, would gain the support of Karl or any of his family. The following letter, written by Dietrich to his Oma (Grandmother) in Tübingen before his thirteenth birthday in January 1919,[77] makes this clear. It describes the fighting between government troops and Spartacists, after the latter had made two night-time attacks on the Halensee station: "

> Early today we heard gunfire. There are some bangs going on now. Karl-Friedrich [the eldest of the Bonhoeffer siblings — he was wounded but survived both wars] has at last been discharged from the Charité [the hospital where father Karl worked]. He would like to be part of this somehow, but Mama and Papa do not yet agree. At present, thank heaven, the government troops are getting the better of it. Our holidays have been extended to 17 January. Either because of the unrest or because of the coal shortage."[78]

As Robert Gellately commented: "

> Worries about a 'Red scare' did not go away in Germany, and even if popular support for far-left radicals was minimal, that did not mean there was no basis for concern. After all, the Bolsheviks had little backing in Russia and never intended to wait for a majority to claim all power.

> Lenin wanted the world. His idea of a vanguard party, which was to 'enlighten' and direct the workers, was not meant to be restricted to the Soviet Union. In March 1919 he created the Communist International (Comintern). He said that the Russian Revolution could not stand on its own and pleaded for the world proletariat to support it. This was the rationale for spreading Russian-style Communism, including by force of arms. At the second annual meeting of the Comintern in July—

August 1920, he stipulated that Communist parties everywhere had to agree to twenty-one conditions, accepting 'iron proletarian centralism,' that is, subordinating themselves completely to Moscow."[79]

Weimar was, for almost all Germans, synonymous with betrayal and humiliation, and never had any real friends. This was so even during the so-called golden years from around 1924, in the wake of the republic's recovery from hyper-inflation of the early 1920s, to October 1929, just preceding the Wall Street crash.[80] The latter ushered in the Great Depression with its political and economic turmoil, which was what the extremist parties had been waiting for during Weimar's golden years. Now their moment to seize power and eliminate opponents, both extreme and moderate, had presented itself.

Amidst the immediate post-Great War chaos, tensions in Breslau were now especially acute, given that it was now only forty kilometres or so from the border of a newly independent enemy of Poland. Silesia was a veritable powder keg, with three uprisings taking place in August 1919, August 1920, and March 1921.[81] The first and last were pro-Polish, but the second, pro-German one occurred during the Battle of Warsaw of the 1919-20 Polish-Soviet War.[82] Then it appeared inevitable that Lenin's Bolshevik horde would seize the capital of the fledgling Polish state, with the rest of the country soon to follow.

Western opinion across the entire political spectrum was divided on the "merits" of the Bolsheviks. Nevertheless, there was a common belief that the territory of the former Russian (Tsarist) Great War ally should remain intact. So when the Poles in early May 1920 joined the independent government of Ukraine in driving the Bolsheviks from the Ukrainian capital of Kiev, with the Bolsheviks having planned an invasion of Poland,[83] there were angry shouts of "Hands off Russia!" from Western Europe.

The Communist propaganda skilfully exploited German sensitivities, even though the Bolsheviks were no less hostile to the "bourgeois" Weimar Republic than they had been to Imperial Germany and the newly independent Poland.[84] They espoused the notion that the Red Army was marching to Berlin in order to "liberate" it and overthrow the yoke of oppression of the Versailles Treaty. Thus many Germans cheered them, and ethnic German dock workers in Danzig[85] (Gdańsk) refused to unload shipments of weapons bound for Poland. Such was the enthusiasm for anti-Polish feeling that German newspapers, including some in Silesia, announced in August 1920 that Warsaw had fallen, even though it had not.[86]

In Breslau, motivated by German anger over the Allied terms of the carve-up of Upper Silesia with Poland,[iii] there was widespread rioting, directed mainly against the Inter-Allied Plebiscite Commission, and specifically the French. The Polish Consulate was damaged, the French Consulate looted, eight of the Commission's ten cars were destroyed, and the French Consul was forced to flee.[87] The "Breslau Incident" soon escalated into a full-scale diplomatic incident, with terse cables being transmitted between Berlin, Paris and Warsaw. Already, the notion of the "war to end all wars" was proving to be an illusion in the post-war power vacuum.

The third, pro-Polish Silesian rising proved by far the most serious. In the Upper Silesian plebiscite of March 1921, 59.4% of the vote was for Germany and 40.5% for Poland.[88] However, outraged voices protested that the voting had been distorted by a mass influx of Germans from outside Silesia. The Polish Silesian leader, Wojciech Korfanty, raised a force of 40,000 Polish volunteers to contest the result. The Freikorps, the sole German military force available after the withdrawal of Reichswehr units from the plebiscite zone, faced the Poles. Two months of skirmishing followed, including the inconclusive pitched battle of Annaberg (Góry Swięty Anny), until the Freikorps were dissolved by the Weimar Chancellor, Ebert, in June.[89] In October 1921, a new carve-up of Upper Silesia was decreed by the Allied Powers,[iv] with 61% of the province to remain in Germany, while four-fifths of the industrial installations, most of the coal fields and the cities of Königshütte (Królewska Huta) and Kattowitz (Katowice) were to be ceded to Poland.[90]

These borders would remain until September 1, 1939, when Hitler's army invaded Poland. However, before the Third Reich invaded Poland and precipitated the second world conflict, there were two chilling events that were co-ordinated nationally, following Hitler's rise to power on January 30 1933.[91] These events chillingly illustrated the regime's readiness to go outside the law and norms of civilised society

---

[iii] Upper Silesia is upstream on the Odor (Polish: Odra) River from Lower Silesia. Breslau/Wrocław is in Lower Sielsia. See footnote [xlvi] for Polish WWII Supplement II "The Gleiwitz (Gliwice) Incident" for further clarification.
[iv] Upper Silesia is upstream on the Odor (Polish: Odra) River from Lower Silesia. Breslau/Wrocław is in Lower Sielsia. See footnote [xlvi] for Polish WWII Supplement II "The Gleiwitz (Gliwice) Incident" for further clarification.

and to use murder and intimidation as political tools. The first event became known as the *Nacht der Langen Messer* "Night of the Long Knives" or "*Röhm Putsch*" in 1934. Silesia witnessed the nationwide slaughter of Ernst Röhm's SA (Sturmabteilung, meaning Storm Troopers) at first hand,[92] during Dietrich's eighteen month London pastorate, from October 1933 until April 1935.

This purge occurred in the summer of 1934, but already in April 1933, less than three months after Hitler ascended to power, ideological cracks were surfacing within the Brown Shirts. For example, SPD (Socialist Party) sources reported a gun battle on the streets of Breslau between rival units of the SA.[93] The SPD considered it to be a reflection of the fundamental social split in the National Socialist membership and Hitler's betrayal of working-class interests; in other words, his disregard for the socialist implication in the official name of the National Socialist Party, Nationalsozialistische Deutsche Arbeiterpartei (National-Socialist German Workers' Party). Of course, the implication was not explicit and not meant to be taken too seriously.[94] By the following year, with its naïve insistence on taking the socialist element in National Socialism seriously, it was clear that the working-class faction of the SA's days were numbered.

The thuggish SA were proving to be a serious impediment to Hitler gaining the backing of the Reichswehr (Regular Army). Indeed, President Hindenburg had warned Hitler's defence minister Werner von Blomberg, in early June 1934, that unless Hitler did something to end the growing political tension in Germany, he would declare martial law and turn over control of the government to the army. Blomberg, who had been known to oppose the growing power of the SA, was chosen to inform Hitler of this decision on Hindenburg's behalf.[95] So it was, on the morning of Saturday June 30, 1934, that the purge of Ernst Röhm's SA began. It was to last forty-eight hours.

Silesia, a bastion of SA power, was to observe some of the worst of the nationwide slaughter led by Udo von Woyrsch (1895—1983), SS-Oberführer, and Himmler's Sonderkommissar for Silesia.[96] Having been ordered to arrest certain SA leaders and occupy the Breslau police headquarters, von Woyrsch went much further, summarily executing the Breslau Police President and Silesian SA chief Edmund Heines, who had been appointed in February 1933. His deputy, Hans Engels, was taken to the nearby woods and blasted with a shotgun.[97] In a scene of black comedy, the one-armed former Silesian Freikorps leader, Peter von Heydebreck, died proclaiming "Long live the Führer!" to the very individual, Hitler, who authorised his execution.[98] The Gauleiter[v] Brückner, also, like Heines, appointed in early February 1933,[99] was stripped of his office and expelled from the province. He seems to have been one of the "lucky" ones.

In the end, the protracted "clean-up" operation against the Silesian SA was only terminated by Göring's personal intervention.[100] While the SA continued its existence, with its leadership taken over by Viktor Lutze, its previous prestige and influence was usurped by Himmler's SS (Schutzstaffel — Protection Squadron), helped by the purge, not just of the SA, but also of other "unreliable" conservative elements such as the members of the German nationalist right[101] and the Catholic Centre Party.[102] Indeed, Ruth von-Kleist Retzow's cousin, Ewald von-Kleist Schmenzin, had been earmarked for assassination, but was forewarned and managed to find shelter in Berlin's Swedish Embassy, until the putsch ran out of steam.[103] As did Franz von Papen,[104] former member of the Catholic Centre party, so instrumental in Hitler's rise to power in late January 1933.

Certainly, the "*Röhm Putsch*" or purge exceeded its scope or definition. Disturbingly, President Hindenburg, Germany's revered military hero, sent a telegram expressing his "profoundly felt gratitude" and congratulations to Hitler for "nipping treason in the bud."[105] About one month later, on August 2, the ailing president died,[106] along with any semblance of government accountability. The 1934 purge set a precedent that would be used by Himmler during the war when justifying the heinous "Final Solution."[107]

The second of these nationally co-ordinated, disturbing acts was the *Reichskristallnacht* (National Crystal Night or Night of Broken Glass) of November 1938,[108] which underlined the fact that the new Germany had no place for Jews.[109] In Breslau and the surrounding Silesian region, it was particularly rampant. Usually, *Reichskristallnacht* was described as a purely urban phenomenon. However, in Silesia, the SS were more virulent; they targeted every single village and hamlet where Jews were living. In the village of Trebnitz (Trzebnica), they even forced the Jews to set their own synagogue alight, before cutting the beards of the men and arresting them.[110]

While the SS released the women, another SS squad from Breslau, under Criminal Commissar Schubert, headed for the Zionist Auswandererlehrgut (Emigration Training Farm) at Gross Breesen (Brzeźno), which trained candidates in agriculture and crafts before

---

[v] Gauleiter: The leader or chief official of a political district under Nazi control. See https://www.dictionary.com/browse/gauleiter.

sending them to Palestine. There the staff were arrested, and the buildings destroyed and looted. SS-Oberführer Katzmann proudly reported his "achievements" to Berlin: In Breslau alone: 1 synagogue (burned), 2 synagogues (demolished), 1 building of the 'Society of Joy' (demolished), at least 500 shops (completely destroyed), 10 Jewish inns (demolished), 35 other Jewish enterprises (demolished) and 600 men arrested.[111] As was the case in the 1934 purge,[112] Heinrich Himmler's second in command, Reinhard Heydrich, was at the forefront of the planning for *Reichskristallnacht*.[113]

A month or so before *Reichskristallnacht*, with the blessing of Great Britain and France, the ethnic German Sudetenland was annexed by the Third Reich at the infamous Munich conference in late September 1938. Five months later, in March 1939, in violation of the Munich agreement, and with the natural barrier of the Giant Mountains now in his hands,[114] as well as most of Czech industry,[115] Hitler annexed the remainder of what was now a virtually indefensible Czech rump state. This was done without a shot being fired, and with Britain and France looking the other way.[116] For Breslau and the Silesian region as well, the Sudeten annexation was of special significance because of its bordering proximity.

Breslau, which lay immediately to the north-east of the Sudetenland, was pivotal in aiding and abetting the disintegration of Czechoslovakia, not least with the pumping of propaganda into the Sudetenland and the transformation of Henlein's Sudetendeutsche Partei into an instrument of Nazi policy.[117] During the 1930s, at all of the city's Nazi-inspired events, Sudeten delegations, parades and costumes were everywhere. The Sudeten Germans, who lived on the Bohemian side of the Giant Mountains, were indistinguishable from their ethnic brethren on the Silesian side, and their leader, Konrad Henlein, came from the town of Maffersdorf near Reichenberg, less than twenty kilometres from the Silesian border.[118]

Moreover, they had genuine grievances, which Hitler exploited to the utmost. Among these was the fact that they experienced the highest rate of unemployment in the country, coupled with the fact that in the aftermath of the Great War, regions with an ethnic German minority, such as the Sudetenland, which was part of the Austro-Hungarian Hapsburg Empire pre-WWI,[119] were incorporated into the newly born Czechoslovakia.[120] This amounted to over three million ethnic Germans.[121] On the other hand, Hugh LeCaine Agnew, who delves deeply into the dual Germanic and Czech ancestry of Charles IV,[122] defined what was known as the Sudetenland in 1938 as being part of the traditional Bohemian lands.[123] In any event, Hitler's March 1939 occupation of Prague and the remainder of the Czech rump state signifies that in Hitler's mind, the Czech homeland had no right to exist.[124]

Unlike Czechoslovakia, Poland was never going to acquiesce to Hitler's bullying. Even when Hitler conquered it by the end of September 1939, it still formed the largest underground in Nazi-occupied Europe, surpassing even the French.[125] Breslau was only forty kilometres from the Polish border; it became a launch pad for von Rundstedt's Army Group South and was no less important for the operations of the Luftwaffe.[126] Before the invasion, five special units, numbered I—V of around 500 SS[127] and SD men of the SS Totenkopf (Death's Head) Units or Einsatzgruppen,[128] were created and attached to one of the German armies. They were named after the cities in which they were mustered: Vienna, Oppeln, Dramburg (Drawsko), Allenstein (Olsztyn) and Breslau. Heinrich Himmler, head of the SS, summed up their purpose as "the radical suppression of Polish resistance ... using all available means."[129] Naturally, "resistance" was defined broadly, and less than two years later, with the launch of the Barbarossa invasion of the Soviet Union, such units were resurrected.[130] In the wake of advancing Wehrmacht or regular army units they "cleaned" the conquered area of all resistance or any perceived "racial undesirables."

At the time of the invasion of Poland, one of the most brutal of the Einsatzgruppen commanders was Udo von Woyrsch (1895-1983),[131] who had been a Reichstag member for Breslau in the early 1930s, and organised the bloody 1934 suppression of the Silesian SA (Brown Shirts).[132] In 1939 however, von Woyrsch was given command of an additional Einsatzgruppe, which was to operate in Upper Silesia,[vi] more or less, the region granted to Poland following the last of the Silesian uprisings in 1921. On September 7, six days following the invasion's launch, his unit moved into the area of the city of Kattowitz (in Polish, Katowice); he subsequently gave brutally succinct descriptions of his operations, such as "insurgents arrested ... rebels shot ... synagogue set on fire ... more on-the-spot executions ... 4 Jews and 3 Poles shot ... 18 Jews shot ..." etc.[133]

Through his brother-in-law Hans von Dohnányi, Dietrich, unlike the German population in general, was made aware of the atrocities committed in Poland, chronicled by Dohnányi in his secret "Chronicle

---

[vi] Upper Silesia is upstream on the Odor (Polish: Odra) River from Lower Silesia. Breslau/Wrocław is in Lower Sielsia. See footnote [xlvi] for Polish WWII Supplement II "The Gleiwitz (Gliwice) Incident" for further clarification.

of Shame" files.[134] As notorious as these acts were, it was with Hitler's launch of Operation Barbarossa in June 1941 — the invasion of the Soviet Union — that the Einsatzgruppen committed greater and more barbarous acts, in accordance with the dictates of National Socialist racial dogma.

Up until February 1945, just three months before Germany's official unconditional surrender, Breslau, unlike most German cities, being outside western Allied bombing range,[135] and with the Soviet Air Force not possessing the capacity for extensive bombing, escaped the second world conflict virtually unscathed. However, by February 9 1945, with the sighting of Soviet T34 tanks at Schöngarten airport in Breslau's west, and the capture six days later of the Sudeten mountain passes to pre-war Czechoslovakia in the south, all routes of supply were cut.[136] Breslau had become, in its *Götterdämmerung*[137] (Twilight of the Gods), "*Festung* Breslau," a fortress that would ultimately rival that of the capital Berlin, both in the implacable fighting, and the unparalleled, often ideologically-driven brutality of both sides, not infrequently inflicted on their very own people.

Breslau was not the only city other than Berlin to be declared a fortress by Hitler. Danzig (Gdańsk), Frankfurt an der Oder, Kolberg (Kołobrzeg), Königsberg (Kaliningrad), Küstrin (Kostrzyn), Glogau (Głogów), Graudenz (Grudziądz), Oppeln (Opole), Posen (Poznań), Ratibor (Racibórz) and Thorn (Toruń)[138] all were designated "*Festung-en*."[139] Hitler had hoped that by desperately holding out for as long as possible, the animosity or uneasy alliance between the Western allies of Britain and the US and the eastern ally of the Soviet Union would manifest itself in such a way as to enable his regime to make a negotiated peace. In his Berlin bunker, he harboured visions that a miracle,[140] akin to the "Miracle of Brandenburg,"[141] that saved his idol King Frederick II (Frederick the Great) and Prussia 183 years earlier in January 1762, would now save his Third Reich. But the ideological friction between the western Allies and the Soviet Union only emerged strongly post-war amongst the ashes of the Third Reich, in the soon-to-follow Cold War.

The brutality that each side committed on its own people was exemplified by SS officers executing any Germans on the slightest suspicion of treachery to the Fatherland,[142] while Soviet soldiers indiscriminately raped women regardless of ethnicity or nationality. German women, along with female Russian and Polish forced labourers and the like, all were victims of the "Soviet Liberation."[143] Given Stalin's contempt for Soviet soldiers taken prisoner by the Germans earlier in the war, it can be assumed that Stalin fully condoned and encouraged such acts. These women, in his eyes, would have been traitors to the Soviet State.[144]

With the Third Reich fighting the war on two fronts, no amount of slave labour, wanton SS brutality and fanatical racial hatred was going to save it. The giant of Soviet industry was established much further east, and the industrial might of the US was in a league of its own. Hitler's irrational notion of Aryan will overcoming all was in tatters. *Festung* Breslau would indeed live up to its name, with its *Götterdämmerung*[145] outlasting by six days the lives of Hitler and Eva Braun — his wife of less than two days. Hitler and his wife were terrified of Stalinist Soviet retribution, coupled with the recent news of Mussolini's gruesome fate at the hands of Italian partisans,[146] and on April 30 1945, took the action of last resort. On Sunday May 6, 1945, Breslau was the last major German city to capitulate.[147] The capital had already done so four days earlier,[148] and less than an hour later on that same evening, General Jodl signed the unconditional surrender of the Third Reich at Rheims in northern France.[149]

Two days later, on Tuesday May 8 1945, the declaration of "Peace in Europe" (V—E Day — Victory in Europe Day) throughout the continent was made. In Breslau, amidst the continuing Soviet plundering, rape and murder, it was a mocking irrelevance.[150] The following day, an advance party of thirteen Polish administrators, at Stalin's behest, arrived without warning, and took over an undamaged house at 25/7 Blücherstrasse, now ulica Józefa Poniatowskiego, where they ceremonially fixed the Polish state emblem over the door.[151] This was the first step towards the usurpation of two-centuries-old German Breslau by the return of Polish Wrocław after six centuries and a decade. A day later, a further group of administrators arrived, headed by Bolesław Drobner.[152] Typical of Stalin, the move had everything to do with illegitimacy, and nothing to do with formal legalities.[153]

For one thing, the Potsdam conference near Berlin to decide the post-war carve-up of Europe was still three months ahead.[154] For another, Breslau had hardly been an aspiration of the Poles and their Underground as they fought their Nazi oppressors throughout the war.[155] This was a Stalinist contrivance; its questionable legal basis hinged upon an obscure July 1920 telegram, known as the Spa—London—Moscow telegram (or Curzon Line telegram).[156] It was sent initially from Spa in Belgium, following a meeting there between the Polish emissary Grabski and the British PM Lloyd George. With the dire military situation for Poland in its conflict with Lenin's Bolsheviks, the purpose of this meeting at Polish request was to sort out possible peace terms that Lenin's regime might accept, and/or possible Anglo-French military support.[157] Grabski was hoping for possible British and French intervention, but since they had sacrificed the flower of their youth during the four years of the Great War, Grabski only received vague assurances from Lloyd George. Indeed, George seemed not to interpret Soviet aggression to Poland until the fall of Warsaw, which left a virtually prostrate Poland.[158]

The proposed ceasefire line was well east of the Polish city of Lwów[159] (modern Ukrainian Lviv — Львів), pending a proposed London conference.[160] However, this telegram was not sent directly from Spa to Moscow, but rather via London.[161] On the face of it, this seems benign, but curiously, the text of the telegram, while in transit in London, was changed, placing Lwów well on the Soviet side of the proposed demarcation line.[162] At the time, this seemed of little or no consequence when Lenin, now perceiving a total Bolshevik victory in Poland,[163] and onwards into a chaotic and weak Germany,[164] blithely dismissed the ceasefire proposal. One month later, Lenin would regret this decision when the Pole's achieved their miraculous victory in Warsaw,[165] seemingly consigning the Spa—London—Moscow telegram to an obscure footnote in history.

In between the wars, this indeed seemed the case. But when Stalin invaded Poland on September 17 1939, sixteen days following Hitler's invasion, he regarded this obscure and dormant telegram as a justification for Soviet seizure of then eastern Polish lands. In the midst was the city of Lwów. Moreover, in 1943, Soviet diplomats pointed to the tampered July 1920 cable from London to Moscow, as now compelling the British, and hence all the Western Allies, to agree to the Soviet annexation of Lwów post-war,[166] even though it was never intended as a permanent border settlement.[167] Now, with the fall of Breslau at war's end in Europe, the fate of these two cities would become inextricably linked.

From February 4 to 11, 1945, in the Black Sea resort city of Yalta (modern-day Russia since 2014), on the Crimean Peninsula, the three chief Allied leaders, Roosevelt, Churchill and Stalin, met to discuss the final defeat of Nazi Germany, and the post-war order for Europe.[168] It was at this conference, in Poland's absence, that the uprooting of Poles from Lwów was agreed upon.[169] However, at Potsdam in July, just five months later in the immediate aftermath of the war in Europe, "The Big Three" of the USA, Britain and the Soviet Union, saw the need for Poland to be "compensated" in some way.[170] Thus was born the dubious concept of the so-called "Recovered Territories," with a defeated Germany the obvious sacrificial lamb for Polish western territorial "compensation." German guilt associated with Nazi war-time atrocities would furnish the "legitimacy" or justify the means. For Poland, however, even with the "compensation" of territory from pre-war Germany's east, there was an overall loss of 80,000 square kilometres in its westward post-war translation.[171] In the territorial upheaval, four centuries of national history were erased in Germanic Breslau and Polish Lwów, with the attendant human suffering.

Before the outbreak of war, Poland had made no serious claim in regard to Breslau. Yet now it was to be the jewel for communist Poland in the so called "Recovered Territories" to the west of pre-war Poland. Put another way, Wrocław, in May 1945 was a Soviet aspiration, not a truly Polish one.[172] This is a relevant point in a balanced appraisal of the claims of some ill-informed commentators who maintained that the Poles seized Breslau, and were responsible for many of the serious offences and injustices that followed on the German population.[173] Bolesław Drobner and most of his associates were certainly Polish, and always thought of themselves as such. Drobner had once fought with Piłsudski's Legions in Poland's pre-independence era, and had served the left wing of the Polish Socialist Party (PPS) for decades, and worked for years in the local government of his native Kraków. However, in post-war Poland, all political entities such as those Drobner ran were devoid of popular support.[174]

Drobner had been a prisoner in the Soviet Gulag two years earlier. So too was his close colleague, Alexander Zawadzki, who had been put in charge of Upper Silesia (more or less Polish Silesia pre-war)[vii] and who, in 1952, would become President of the Polish "People's" Republic. In order to avoid a repeat of this terrible fate, they and others like them resorted to unscrupulous opportunists or the dregs of society to do the bidding of their Stalinist overlords.[175] Drobner had even proposed the purest implementation of the Socialist system by suggesting a moneyless economy, along with dividing the city into German and Polish sections. It was colloquially dubbed "The Drobner Republic,"[176] but with the ultimate Soviet objective of evicting the entire German population from Wrocław and Silesia in general, the Soviets would not have found this proposal appealing. Moreover, even in the Soviet Union

---

[vii] Upper Silesia is upstream on the Odor (Polish: Odra) River from Lower Silesia. Breslau/Wrocław is in Lower Sielsia. See footnote [xlvi] for Polish WWII Supplement II "The Gleiwitz (Gliwice) Incident" for further clarification.

at the height of Stalinist rule, and at the zenith of its 1917 to early 1920s revolutionary fervour, money was still essential in its planned economy. Hence, Drobner's days in Silesia were numbered.[177] While superficially, the moneyless system seems utopian, in practice, one only has to look at the heinous Khmer Rouge regime imposed on Cambodia in the mid to late 1970s.[178]

In the very early post-war years, the formation of a fully-fledged Polish communist regime was nigh on impossible; Stalin likened the task to "putting a saddle on a cow."[179] For one thing, Communism had always been repugnant to the overwhelming majority of deeply Catholic Poles, with the still recent memory of Bolshevik-perpetrated massacres in the 1919-20 Polish-Soviet war,[180] including Polish prisoners being used by the Bolsheviks for "sabre practice."[181] Moreover, this feeling was greatly magnified after the Soviet atrocities of 1939—41, such as the April 1940 Katyń Wood massacre[182] among numerous others, before the Barbarossa campaign. Coupled with this was the murder of Polish communists in the Soviet Union during Stalin's Great Purge of 1937-39.[183] This meant that by the end of World War II, there were not enough trained Polish Communists around to run a factory, let alone a country of thirty million people.[184] Hence, Stalin had to make do with an almost interminable series of fake front organisations, which professed to be "Polish" and representative of the aspirations of the Polish people, but were anything but.

Arguments in favour of the Stalinist-perpetrated mass evictions of eastern Germans and eastern Poles have been put forward. From the exclusively Polish perspective, it has been argued that Poland acquired much more advanced German infrastructure for the loss of much poorer and backward regions in the east.[185] This notion, however, is questionable, given the mass devastation in the wake of the Soviet advance. The other argument put forward is the elimination of centuries of ethnic tensions between Poles, Ukrainians, Lithuanians and Belorussians that existed in Poland's pre-war eastern Borderlands. Certainly, post-war Poland is much less ethnically and culturally diverse,[186] and thus, free of the old eastern ethnic violence.[187]

Moreover, it has been stated that the borders of post-war Poland closely resemble those of 966 AD,[188] at the founding of the Polish Christian nation. After centuries of Polish borders moving east, they had reverted back to their frontiers almost a millennia earlier. However, was this worth the human suffering and upheaval for both eastern Poles and Germans in the aftermath of the world's most devastating conflict? And do these arguments justify or legitimise the German loss of

100,000 square kilometres of eastern territory? Both questions will be examined from both the German and Polish perspectives.

In the summer of 1945, somewhat counter-intuitively, the percentage of Germans in Breslau increased. However, this was only due to an influx of pre-war Breslauers hoping to salvage something of their pre-war possessions. By the end of 1945, Germans still outnumbered the 33,297 registered Poles by more than five to one; nine months later this figure was reversed, with 152,898 Poles compared to 28,274 Germans.[189] In other words, about 140,000 Breslauers were removed from the pre-war German "Recovered Territories" in just nine months, at a rate that would average approximately 500 a day. By March 1947, Wrocław numbered 196,814 Poles out of a total population 214,310, leaving 17,496 Germans remaining. While these remaining Germans were eventually evicted, their rate of expulsion was much slower, due to the need for skilled labour. When one considers the mass genocide of Polish intelligentsia by both Hitler[190] and Stalin[191] during the war, this is not surprising.

From towns surrounding Wrocław in the Lower Silesian region,[viii] people had to make their way to the regional capital, usually by foot, and often in the middle of a freezing cold winter.[192] Once in Wrocław they faced an indefinite wait for trains to take them to the Soviet, or in the case of the more fortunate, the British-occupied zone of Germany. With an average daily transport of 500 people a day in the first nine months of 1946, their comfort was not a priority to the Stalinist and Polish mindset.

The rail cars, all locked from the outside, were best described as cattle wagons, with men, women, and children all crammed in for days on end. When they were finally opened at an intermediate station, coffins would be on hand to throw in the inevitable dead corpses, while the still living would be covered in excrement.[193] The British military authorities, who accepted more than a million deportees into their zone, called it "Operation Swallow,"[194] and by April 1946, they formally protested at the treatment of the German deportees. Ruth von Kleist's daughter-in-law Mieze and their entire village of Kieckow in Pomerania to the north were deported that month.[195] By August, the British scaled down their intake, and by December, they would accept no

---

[viii] Upper Silesia is upstream on the Odor (Polish: Odra) River from Lower Silesia. Breslau/Wrocław is in Lower Sielsia. See footnote [xlvi] for Polish WWII Supplement II "The Gleiwitz (Gliwice) Incident" for further clarification.

more.[196] From that point on, no deportation trains could go beyond the Soviet occupied zone.

While the Germans' ordeal lasted a matter of days, for the Poles, it was more a matter of weeks.[197] Furthermore, the majority of these unfortunates had already been ravaged and terrorised by the hideous experiences of World War II throughout its duration. Breslauers experienced the horror of the war as well, but this was essentially in the war's concluding months when the city was declared *Festung* Breslau, around the commencement of the Soviet siege in February 1945. The eastern Polish provinces from whence the evictees came were in the process of being absorbed into Lithuania, and the west of Belorussia and the Ukraine. Evictees from Wilno, the city destined to become the Lithuanian Soviet Republic's capital of Vilnius, were mostly sent to Gdańsk or Toruń, in the north of the "Recovered Territories."[198] Poles from Lwów and the surrounding eastern Galician region were sent to Wrocław and the surrounding Silesian region to the south.

The regions the eastern Poles were coming from were referred to as the "Borders" by professor Norman Davies in *White Eagle Red Star*, his book on the 1919-20 Polish Soviet War. He states it was neither definitively Polish nor Russian; the major cities of Wilno and Lwów were islands of Polish ethnic majorities in an alien sea.[199] This "sea" however was far from uniform, being made up of Lithuanians in the north, Belorussians in the centre, and Ukrainians in the south. In this multi-ethnic spread, religion was another dividing factor. Many of the peasants, in particular Belorussians, identified themselves more by religion than by language. "I am a Catholic," or "I am an Orthodox," they would answer when questioned on their "nationality." Moreover, this region had been the pale of Jewish settlement in the Tsarist Empire, and they were likely to define themselves more by their faith than by any notion of nationalism.[200]

In this multi-ethnic and religious "sea," Davies states that the people most culturally and socially identifiable by their nationhood and language in the borders, despite their overall numerical minority, were the Poles. For well over a century of official non-existence, they held on strongly to their national and cultural identity. For one thing, the Poles among the Tsars' subjects had the most recent memories of a separate and independent national existence, whereas national movements of the Western Ukraine, Belarus and Lithuania were directed by a handful of intellectuals — as Lewis Bernstein Namier, the Polish born Professor of Modern History at the University of Manchester in the 1930s, quipped, "they could have all sat together on a small sofa."[201]

The Polish presence in the Borders was a consequence of the centuries of Polish eastward expansion under the landed *szlachta* (magnates or nobility).[202] From October 1610 to November 1612, during the reign of King Zygmunt III Wasa, the Poles, who had moved the capital from Kraków to Warsaw in 1596, even occupied Moscow when Russia was racked by civil war.[203] Hence the exaggerated Bolshevik and Stalinist notion that all eastern Poles were landed bourgeois elite, which supposedly legitimised the deportation of 1.7 million[204] to the Siberian gulags from September 1939 until June 1941 — the month of the launch of Hitler's invasion of the Soviet Union. The truth was that by 1939, the majority of the six million Borders Poles were peasants,[205] and that deportations proceeded regardless of class, profession, age, health or gender. Even cripples were not spared.[206]

The Borders, ravaged by the 1919-20 Polish-Soviet war, were butchered and displaced many times over in the next world conflict two decades or so later. They were subjected to Soviet occupation, with the requisite gulag deportations from September 1939 to June 1941, coupled with the April 1940 massacres of Poland's officer elite at Katyń and elsewhere.[207] Then there was the Nazi terror from 1941-44, when around two million Jews and others were murdered in cold blood by the SS Einsatzgruppen[208] as they followed behind the advancing Wehrmacht, and several hundred thousand Poles were butchered or displaced by terrorist bands of the nationalist and Nazi collaborationist Ukrainian UPA.[209]

In accordance with secret protocols of the August 1939 Molotov-Ribbentrop pact,[210] ethnic German settlements were uprooted to the eastern area of German-occupied Poland under the Nazi administered General Government. They may have welcomed this rather than face life under Stalinist rule. Many of these people would have spent months in Breslau in transition to their resettlement in those areas whence the original Polish population was evicted.[211]

From around the middle of 1944 came the return of the Soviet terror in the guise of Red Army "Liberation," directed against so-called "nationalists," "saboteurs," "recidivists" and "collaborators." The unfortunates thus labelled were those unwelcoming of rule by Stalin, not working with the requisite enthusiasm, denigrating the previous period of brutal Soviet rule, and finally, people who could not legitimately explain to the NKVD how they had avoided Nazi execution. Once again, the convoys of cattle wagons rolled eastwards to Siberian gulags. Such was the nature of Soviet "liberation."[212]

Even with the westward retreat of the Germans, many Border communities, already ravaged by years of war, still lay in areas of conflict between the Soviet army and anti-Soviet partisans, such as those of the nationalist, Nazi collaborationist Ukrainian UPA.[213] Hence, for many of the Border people, fortunate enough not to be condemned to the convoys of cattle wagons bound east for the gulags, boarding a convoy west out of this cursed region that was being absorbed into the Soviet Union may have seemed like manna from Heaven. From 1944-48, official statistics state that the overseeing Soviet authorities processed about 1.5 million people among the exodus west from the Borders, but realistically, the total number, whether legal or illegal, was undoubtedly much higher[214]

Between the wars, during the time of the Second Polish Republic, a significant number of Polish citizens of the Borders were ethnically not Polish, but of the other ethnicities of the Borders, namely Ukrainian, Belorussian or Lithuanian. Many would intermarry with ethnic Poles despite the racial turmoil.[215] Nevertheless, in spite of pre-WWII Polish citizenship, these people were not permitted on the convoys to the so-called German "Recovered Territories."[216] They became instead, something they had never been previously, citizens of the USSR. This in spite of the vast majority being born in pre-1939 Poland or pre-1918 Tsarist Russia or Austria. For the new Soviet overlords, the basis for Polish identity was not pre-war Polish citizenship, but rather the twin criteria of the Polish language and Catholicism.[217] Officially, by these criteria, Jews were not normally eligible, but by joining Polish Communist organisations, they could possibly make it on the westward convoys.

For the ethnic Poles granted passage west out of the eastern Borderlands ravaged by years of war and ethnic strife, the ordeal was far from over. Their journey westwards commenced by foot or on carts to collecting centres, where they frequently had to wait for weeks, easy prey to local robbers and thugs. Brutal soldiers were supposed to "guard" the collecting centres, but their dedication to this role was a token one. These soldiers, along with Soviet bureaucrats, treated the request to leave the workers' "utopia" of the Soviet Union as a crime, and scorned the Polish migrants for being permitted to depart.[218] On top of the interminable delays, the collecting centres were places of filth, hunger, thirst, overcrowding, and the spectre of death. Five years earlier, their compatriots had experienced even more terrible and inhumane conditions on their eastern journeys to the hell of Siberia and Kazakhstan, with the sole prospect of the frigid gulag hell to greet them at journey's end.[219]

Highlighting the scale and unanswered questions about the post-war "migration" of eastern Germans and Poles, Norman Davies and Roger Moorhouse write: "

> From the historian's viewpoint, several large question marks hang over the post-war migration of Germans and Poles. The first issue is purely technical and concerns railway freight. The movement of about six million human beings from the USSR to Poland and from Poland to Germany required administrative expertise of the sort attributed to Adolf Eichmann, and logistical planning on a scale at least twice as large as anything attempted during the Holocaust. Where, in 1945—7, did the rolling stock come from? Where, and by whom, was the operation coordinated? And were the two parts of the operation separate or linked? In the particular case of Wrocław, one could pose the last question in a more specific way. Were the cattle trucks that rolled into Wrocław from the East sent straight back to the USSR for more repatriants? Or were those same trucks emptied of their Polish cargo at one of the stations of the eastern suburbs and then sent round (westwards) to Wrocław-Świebodzice to collect their German cargo?"[220]

This, a displacement of six million people, was legitimised in the Stalinist mindset by an obscure and dormant July 1920 telegram.

Unlike Warsaw, Wrocław's post-war reconstruction did not begin until 1956.[221] This followed the mysterious death of the notorious Polish Stalinist Bolesław Bierut that year in Moscow, during his attendance of the Soviet Communist Party's 20th Congress, at which Nikita Khrushchev presented his famous *Crimes of the Stalin Era* report.[222] Moreover, this was three years following the death in 1953 of Stalin himself.[223] Preceding Bierut's death, reconstruction of Wrocław played third fiddle to communist indoctrination and de-Germanisation. Warsaw, designated as the capital of the newly formed "Polish worker's paradise," required undamaged bricks for its reconstruction; these were acquired from Wrocław in the infamous and cynical episode that became known as the "exploitation of the bricks." Any usable bricks from the lingering rubble were not to be used;[224] only those from any buildings that somehow escaped major wartime damage, in the spirit of de-Germanisation, were acceptable. In 1949, these buildings included the

Renaissance Wlast Gateway, near the Salt Market, the magnificent General Post Office, and hundreds of modern villas in the outer suburbs. The "exploitation of the bricks" served a twofold purpose: the reconstruction of the capital of the "Polish worker's paradise," and removal of all historical traces of Germanic Breslau.[225]

In post-war Wrocław, the displaced Borderland Poles from the east, with their still fresh and terrible memories of the war and the even more recent ordeal of their Stalinist perpetrated displacement, were unwilling to acknowledge the history of German Breslau; they wanted to declare that every brick in their newly Polish Wrocław only lived and spoke Polish.[226] To the north, in Oma Ruth's Pomeranian village of Kieckow, now Polish Kikowo, while the church remained to be used for Catholic services, all German headstones in the cemetery were removed.[227] For the displaced Borderland Poles, historical nuances were irrelevant as they tried to preserve a true Polish consciousness[228] amidst the squalor[229] of Soviet oppression.[230] By the 1960s, however, long after the deaths of the mass murderers, Stalin and his faithful Polish stooge Bolesław Bierut,[231] the economy of Wrocław was modernised and diversified; by early the following decade, Wrocław was producing 2.8% of Poland's GDP. This was a slice twice as large as its population justified. At the same time, its population was still growing; from 400,000 in 1958, it passed 600,000 in the late seventies.[232]

With the subsequent collapse of the Communist regime in August 1989,[233] a Polish acknowledgement of Germanic Breslau has finally surfaced. A symbol of this is the building of the bronze cross monument to Dietrich Bonhoeffer,[234] acknowledging the gentle but yet resilient Lutheran pastor and son of Breslau, who died, like so many Poles, in resisting the terrible evil that was the Third Reich. Upon this lesser known fault-line in history, it is to him and his fellow countrymen and women, including the extraordinary matriarch and fellow native Silesian, Ruth von Kleist-Retzow and her kin, who dared to uphold everything that was decent in an a world of indecency and injustice,[235] that this story is dedicated.

Chapter 1

Roots, Genesis and Moulding of the Pastor

The illustrious family of Bonhoeffer could trace their roots back to 1403, to the annals of Nymwegen on the Waal River in the Netherlands near the German border. In 1513, Caspar van den Boenhoff left the Netherlands to settle in the German city of Schwäbisch Hall. Soon after, their name was Germanised to Bonhöffer, literally meaning "bean farmer," but in 1800, they replaced the umlaut "ö" with "oe." Buildings around Schwäbisch Hall still bear pictures of a lion holding a beanstalk on a blue background, and on more than one occasion, Dietrich would wear a signet ring with this family crest.[236]

When he was born on the February 4 1906, he was followed ten minutes later by his twin sister Sabine. Naturally, Dietrich constantly enjoyed reminding Sabine of being her elder,[237] although she ended up outliving him by fifty-four years, passing away in 1999.[238] They were born into a prominent and very close-knit upper-class family, the sixth and seventh of eight children, all born in Breslau in the decade from 1899-1909. Six years later in 1912, the family left Breslau for Berlin, where the father, Karl Bonhöffer became one of the most distinguished neurologists in Germany, employed as the professor of neurology and psychiatry at the University of Berlin and the director of the psychiatric clinic at Charité Hospital in Berlin, posts which he held until his death in 1948. Their mother, Paula née von Hase was a daughter of Clara von Hase, born Countess Kalkreuth, and her father Karl had for two years been a chaplain in the court of Kaiser Wilhelm II,[239] who led Germany into the First World War.

Karl's appointment could have lasted far longer, if not for Karl's non-compliant and belligerent nature. Karl resisted the inclination of the Kaiser to have his chaplains preach the way he dictated. Things came to a head when Karl dared to contradict the Kaiser, referring to the proletariat as "rabble."[240] When one considers Dietrich Bonhoeffer's brave and dangerously belligerent attitude towards the Nazis decades later, one can assume he inherited it, at least in part, from his maternal grandfather.

Upon departure from the Kaiser's court in Potsdam, Karl von Hase became an official in the consistory (church council) in the church province of Silesia, and an honorary professor in the theological faculty of the University of Breslau. Clara made their home a regular meeting place for scholars and artists. A junior doctor named Karl Bonhoeffer visited their home one day, and saw their daughter Paula for the first time. The young physician later said that he knew he would marry her.[241]

However, in spite of the impressive pastoral credentials of Paula's father, and her giving each of her eight children three years of serious religious instruction,[242] the Bonhoeffer family was not notably devout; Sunday church going was not practised.[243] Paula was a college graduate and trained teacher, and home-schooled the five eldest of her children in their early years, as well as some of the neighbours' children. The children's education hardly suffered, as they performed brilliantly in final yearly examinations and even ended up skipping years. In this multi-talented family, Dietrich, played the piano from the age of twelve, with Mozart sonatas among his repertoire; later he played the guitar on family hikes. He played diverse games such as tennis and chess with like fervour. Sadly, during the First World War, the second eldest, Walter, an officer cadet, was severely wounded during an advance on April 23 1918, and died five days later. His death utterly devastated his mother.[244]

In 1920, when Dietrich turned fourteen, he announced to his family that his ambition was to become a theologian. While not openly hostile to the idea, his parents were not convinced this was the path for their youngest son, given his musical ability. His siblings expressed feelings bordering on shock, most of all the eldest, Karl-Friedrich, by now acknowledged as a brilliant physical chemist.[245] Nevertheless, the cocky younger sibling would not be intimidated by his elders. When brother Klaus, destined to become a top lawyer at Lufthansa, told him not to waste his life in such a "poor, feeble, boring, petty bourgeois institution as the Church," fourteen-year-old Dietrich retorted: "If what you say is true, I shall reform it!"[246] What Dietrich was implying in this defiant rebuff to his elder sibling was a clear assertion of his independence. When Dietrich was confirmed in March of the following year, his mother gave him the bible of her deceased son Walter. For the rest of his life, Dietrich used it for his daily devotions.[247]

In 1923, like his fathers and brothers before him, Dietrich enrolled at Tübingen University just south of Stuttgart in the south-west of the country. At the time, German hyper-inflation was at its peak. Their father Karl, after cashing in a matured life insurance policy, was able to bring home a small basket of strawberries.[248] If not for his foreign patients paying him in their own currencies, there would have been no way for him to keep four of his children simultaneously at university. By the end of the first semester, a meal at the student dining hall cost a billion Reichsmarks.

Dietrich studied at Tübingen for a year, but on his eighteenth birthday in February 1924, he was severely concussed in an ice-skating accident. On their way to Italy, his concerned parents visited him. Dietrich expressed his desire to go with them, but they declined his request. However, when Klaus passed his bar exams, and asked for an Italian trip to celebrate, Dietrich was allowed to go with him. By now, the German currency had been stabilised,[249] which would have greatly relieved father Karl's hyper-inflation cash flow stress, albeit with the loss of "billionaire" status.

As you might expect, chaos and political assassination were both part of the Weimar political landscape during the years of hyper-inflation in the early 1920s, preceding the Golden Age of Weimar from 1924 until the Wall Street crash of October 1929. The assassination of Walthau Rathenau on June 24 1922 deeply disturbed Dietrich; he and his classmates, from their classroom on the *Königsallee*, heard the shots. One of Dietrich's classmates recalled: "

> I particularly remember Bonhoeffer on the day of Rathenau's murder. The average age in our class in the Grunewald high school was seventeen, but he and G.S., who ended up committing suicide in exile, were only sixteen. I remember the shots we heard during the lesson, and then, on the playground during the break, we heard what had happened... I still recall my friend Bonhoeffer's passionate indignation, his deep and spontaneous anger... I remember his asking what would become of Germany if its best leaders were killed. I remember it because I was surprised at the time someone could know so exactly where he stood."[250]

A niece of the victim, Ursula Andreae, who, like Dietrich was interested in theology, also attended that class, which included a number of children from prominent families, in the main, Jewish.[251] A few days later, when Dietrich left on the train for his final school holiday, he wrote to his parents that while on the train he found himself sitting opposite "a man wearing a swastika." He spent the trip arguing with him, and described him as being bigoted and right-wing.[252]

The political party that Dietrich's father Karl supported was the moderate, left-leaning Social Democrats, who had come to power following the November 1918 revolution in the wake of the war's end. The violent, extreme left-wing Spartacists were never going to gain the support of Karl or any of his family. The following letter, written by Dietrich to his Oma[253] in Tübingen before his thirteenth birthday in January 1919, makes this clear. It describes the fighting between government troops and radical left-wing Spartacists, after the latter had made two night-time attacks on the Halensee station: "

> Early today we heard gunfire. There are some bangs going on now. Karl-Friedrich [the eldest of the Bonhoeffer siblings — he was wounded but survived both wars] has at last been discharged from the Charité [the hospital where father Karl worked]. He would like to be part of this somehow, but Mama and Papa do not yet agree. At present, thank heaven, the government troops are getting the better of it. Our holidays have been extended to 17 January. Either because of the unrest or because of the coal shortage [....or perhaps due to both.]."[254]

Italy had long been a much-desired holiday destination for the Bonhoeffer family, and indeed, Great Grandfather Hase had visited it twenty times in his lifetime.[255] Dietrich loved Italy and its people; he had a great command of languages, and his elementary Italian improved dramatically over the months of this trip, unlike his brother. By chance they would meet Walther Kranz, their old history teacher from the Grunewald Gymnasium (High School) in Berlin on a trip to the top of Mount Vesuvius, but it was Rome that most captured Dietrich's heart.

More than anything else, it was Catholic Rome with its magnificent Saint Peter's Basilica which kept drawing him back, compelling him to attend every service of the Holy week. He found that these services, in particular the Palm Sunday service of 1924, with its *Sanctorum Communio* (Communion of Saints), marvellously illustrated the universality of the church,[256] with the gathering of races from all over the world. While he thought that it would, in all probability, be impossible for Catholicism and Protestantism to ever unite, at the same time he thought it would benefit both parties. That said, having witnessed Catholicism first-hand in its heartland and the devotion of its worshippers, he also said that Catholicism can exist for a long time without Protestantism, and that in comparison to the church of Rome, Protestantism seemed like just a small sect.[257]

Yet four centuries earlier, in the spring of 1511, when the young and utterly devout Catholic and Augustinian monk Martin Luther visited Rome for the first time,[ix] he expressed his disillusionment with the Eternal City and its Vatican, with its overt cynicism and rampant corruption, manifested more than anything by the dubious practice of the sale of indulgences.[258] If someone was of sufficient financial and earthly means, they could purchase absolution for almost all manner of sin and debauchery. In 1567, the devout and reformist Pope Pius V, in the period that would become known as the "Counter Reformation," abolished this practice.[259]

Dietrich, during his time in Rome, met the royal family, Mussolini, and even Pope Pius XI. However, he did not regard these meetings as the highlight of his visit to the Eternal city.[260] Rather, it was Saint Peter's that held that distinction. This is reflected in the title of his brilliant and ground-breaking doctoral thesis, *Sanctorum Communio* (Communion of Saints) when he graduated from the University of Berlin in 1927. On his return from Italy, he enrolled there at the last moment for the 1924 summer semester in mid-June. At that time, Berlin's university was a centre of liberal theology under such distinguished church historians as Adolf von Harnack, who would become one of the many teachers to witness the great promise of the young Dietrich. No doubt, Harnack's discussions with Dietrich on the tram to the university gave him notice of this promise.

Dietrich always stated his view rationally and coherently, not always in agreement with his teacher; but Harnack acknowledged this gifted student, and marked his work accordingly. Moreover, post-WWII fellow students who witnessed such discussions would most ardently agree.[261] With an astonishing academic workload, aged just twenty-one, Dietrich Bonhoeffer graduated from Berlin's Friedrich Wilhelm University on December 17 1927 as the sole student awarded *"summa cum laude"*[262] — highest honours. During his studies in Berlin from 1924-27, Dietrich lived in the family home on Berlin's Wangenheimstrasse. When he first arrived back there from his Italian visit, he discovered that his twin sister Sabine had left and was now studying in the siblings' birthplace of Breslau; she had become engaged to a young lawyer, Gerhard Leibholz.[263] Her fiancée, though baptised as a child, was of Jewish

---

[ix] As a young monk Luther was obsessed with atoning for his sins and went to ridiculous lengths to punish himself. This ranged from extreme self denial and physical and mental tests to self flagellation. One such punishment consisted of lying in the snow, through the night at the height of winter until he would have to be carried back inside. See the *10 things you didn't know about Martin Luther* PBS web page at https://www.pbs.org/empires/martinluther/cheats.html.

descent; the Leibholz family had to flee to England in 1938. Dietrich used his London contacts to facilitate their escape. In 1947, they returned to Germany, where Gerhard became a prominent jurist.[264]

Dietrich was obliged, as a theological candidate, to perform parish work as a curate or vicar's assistant, in order to become a pastor. Initially he took on a Sunday school class with typical diligence in the local Grunewald parish. On his graduation in December 1927, he received a phone call from the Catalan capital of Barcelona, directing him to serve as a curate for the expatriate German community there. Naturally, Dietrich was advised to turn this offer down for more prestigious cities such as London, Paris or Rome. However, he opted for the relative backwater of Barcelona, as he thought he would benefit from experiencing a whole new environment.[265]

By February, Dietrich received an official copy of his order dispatching him to Barcelona. From the Pyrenees border, Dietrich boarded a train for Barcelona; the train journey hugged the Mediterranean coast through the beautiful Catalan countryside, where, upon his arrival at the station, he was greeted by his new mentor, Pastor Olbricht. Dietrich's relationship to his new mentor was cordial, but they never became friends. Privately, Dietrich stated that Pastor Olbricht preferred a good glass of wine and a good cigar to a bad sermon, and did not have a dynamic pulpit presence.[266] However, Pastor Olbricht gave Dietrich virtually a free hand. This was exemplified in the way Dietrich implemented the Sunday school class, which soon grew to forty students from an initial number of one.

His accommodation was spartan, in a house of three impoverished Spanish ladies who couldn't speak a word of German. The language barrier didn't concern Dietrich; with his gift for languages, he wished to learn Spanish as soon as possible. Dietrich soon struck a good rapport with his two fellow German boarders, and went with them on his first outings to the beautiful surrounding countryside of the Catalan.[267] He found the German expatriate congregation rather staid and conservative, and markedly different to the liberal and intellectually sophisticated world of Berlin.[268] Moreover, they seemed untouched by the dramatic events of the previous decade in Germany. That said, ever mindful that he had chosen the backwater of Barcelona for new experiences, he adapted to the local lifestyle and was committed to becoming effective in his role as pastor. One example of his adaptation to the local lifestyle was the appreciation he gained for bull fighting. Dietrich found Barcelona to be blessed with an unusual charm, exemplified in its beautiful harbour.[269]

However, he was not blind to its poverty. Several times he asked his father for help for people in need, and around Christmas, he would arrange loans for his impoverished landladies. The German expatriate community was not immune to poverty either, as German businesses were having difficulty in competing with Western countries, even before the onset of the Great Depression.[270] In Pastor Olbricht's absence, he had to arrange the burial for a respected businessman who had committed suicide because of sudden financial ruin. Sometimes people would approach him for help; but he would often greet them rather coldly, as he had become aware that in many instances, they were not truly in need, and he had to be prudent in the granting of limited church funds.

In Barcelona, Dietrich conversed with characters such as vagrants, escaped criminals, deserting legionnaires and German gangster murderers on the run; they would tell him their life stories.[271] When food shortages in Germany had started to make themselves felt during the Great War, Dietrich's father Karl had praised his very young son's unexpected but most welcome ability as a "messenger" and "food scout," for he knew the black market prices for all the delicacies and the nature of the queues outside the shops. So, he was able to direct the servants to the least troublesome queues.[272]

One year later in February 1929, Dietrich returned to Berlin; in his final report, Pastor Olbricht was unstinting in his praise of the young curate.[273] From July that year to the same month of the following year, he was an academic assistant to Professor Wilhelm Lütgert, by which time he had completed his post-doctoral degree, in the midst of the Great Depression.[274] While back in Berlin, he resumed his acquaintance with Franz Hildebrandt, whom he first met back in December 1927.[275] Franz, a fellow theological student, was three years Dietrich's junior, and like Dietrich's brother-in-law Gerhard Leibholz, was a baptised Christian of Jewish descent — albeit from his mother's side.[276] Like Dietrich, he was raised in Berlin's Grunewald district. They became lifelong friends, forever enjoying interminable arguments with each other.

Just three or so months later, still too young to be ordained, he commenced a one-year postgraduate study at the Union Theological Seminary in New York City, and youth work at the Abyssinian Baptist Church in Harlem. There he taught Sunday school and formed a lifelong love for African-American spiritual music, a collection of which he took back to Germany.[277] Dietrich had life-changing experiences, brought on in no small part by the deep friendships formed. One in particular was with fellow student Albert Franklin ("Frank") Fisher, raised in Alabama, who introduced him to the Abyssinian Baptist Church and the African American church experience. Another friendship was with the preacher at the Abyssinian church, Adam Clayton Powell Senior.[278]

At the end of the American Civil War, General Robert E. Lee, on Sunday April 9, 1865, surrendered at the Appomattox Court House in Virginia.[279] Just three weeks later, Powell was born, the son of slaves, although not quite of the bloodlines you would expect. His father was African American, and his mother was a full-blooded Cherokee.[280] In his early years, he was brought up in an environment of heavy drinking, violence, and gambling. The turning point came during a week-long series of revival meetings in Rendville, Ohio, from which Powell never looked back; in 1908, he became the senior pastor of the Abyssinian church.[281] One century earlier, during the presidency of Thomas Jefferson, the Abyssinian Baptist Church was founded; it broke away from the First Baptist Church of New York City because of its segregated seating policy. In 1920, Powell won a contentious battle to move the church to 138th Street in Harlem.[282] It was the passionate faith and dedication of such committed and extraordinary people as Adam that captured Dietrich's loyalty and admiration.

During his American experience, the idea that real piety and power only developed in churches where there was a present reality and history of suffering took hold.[283] The present reality was graphically illustrated with the infamous March 1931 case of the Scottsboro Boys, which Dietrich followed closely, indicating the interest he had in American racial issues in general. Put another way, he began to see things "from below," from the perspective of those who suffer oppression. He observed, "Here one can truly speak and hear about sin and grace and the love of God... the Black Christ is preached with rapturous passion and vision."[284] Years later, in a letter from prison in April 1944 to his dear friend and first biographer Eberhard Bethge, Dietrich would write that this was the critical point where "I turned from phraseology to reality."[285] In his time in America, it was his experience of the "Black Christ" that made an indelible impression, contrasting radically with the "theological desert" of the Union Theological Seminary, where he could easily have been the teacher rather than the student. In describing his time at Union, he would state unequivocally, "There is no theology here."[286]

At the beginning of December 1930, on a visit to Washington DC with Frank Fisher, a white student and another black student, he would write to his parents of experiencing the segregation at first hand, in a way hardly any whites would experience, when he and his companions were refused service in a restaurant just south of the national capital.[287] In letters to his eldest brother Karl-Friedrich, Dietrich lamented the racism inherent in American society, to which, it seems, he found no analogous situation in Germany. Karl-Friedrich, having already witnessing it first hand on his earlier visit there, wrote back to Dietrich on January 24 1931: "

> I am delighted you have the opportunity of studying the Negro question so thoroughly. I had the impression when I was over there that it is really the problem, at any rate for people with a conscience and, when I was offered an appointment at Harvard, [as a physical chemist] it was the very basic reason for my disinclination to go to America for good, because I did not want either to take on that legacy myself or to pass it on to my hypothetical children. It seems impossible to see the right way to tackle the problem."[288]

But Karl-Friedrich did not dream that such a dubious legacy would ever affect his country: "In any case, our Jewish question is a joke by comparison; there won't be many people who claim they are oppressed here. At any rate, not in Frankfurt."[289]

With present-day hindsight into Nazi atrocities, in particular with regard to the Jews, this statement by Dietrich's brother seems naive. However, this letter was written in late Janaury 1931, just over two years before Hitler's ascent to power in late January 1933. Moreover, Karl-Friedrich and Dietrich grew up in the affluent Berlin neighbourhood of Grunewald, dominated by academics and cultural elites, of which a third were Jewish. In general, Jews had economic parity with the Gentile population.[290]

What is most disturbing in the episode of Dietrich being refused service in a segregated restaurant in early December 1930 is that it was so close to the national capital. It may have been in the bordering state of Maryland, which was, during the Civil War of 1861-5, one of the four so-called "Border states," which included Delaware, Missouri and Lincoln's birth state of Kentucky. Equally disturbingly, while these states ultimately decided upon the non-secessionist path of remaining loyal to Abraham Lincoln's Union, they did so by forcing Lincoln to concede to the same right of slave ownership as was maintained in the deep south states.[291] Given the history of Maryland and the Border states in general, Dietrich's segregation episode in early December

1930, so near to the nation's capital, should come as no surprise. More-over, slavery had existed even in the national capital from the very be-ginning of the city's history in 1790, when Congress created the federal territory from lands formerly held by the slave states of Virginia and Maryland.[292]

Dietrich's big agnostic brother Karl-Friedrich, who derided Dietrich as a young fourteen-year-old for committing himself to a life of theology, rose to prominence as a brilliant physical chemist,[293] even as several of his relatives, such as Klaus and Dietrich, became involved in the resistance against Hitler, ultimately leading to their executions. Karl-Friedrich was nominated for the Nobel Prize and was an expert on heavy water, which was a critical source of heavy hydrogen for the hy-drogen bomb. While he reluctantly advised German nuclear scientists, he also collaborated with Paul Rosbaud, a British spy, while torn by his love of chemistry, his family and his country.[294]

Dietrich took every opportunity to explore New York City and experience all it had to offer, mostly with four fellow Union students — the Frenchman Jean Lasserre, the Swiss, Erwin Sutz, the white Ameri-can, Paul Lehmann, and Frank Fisher; the city was not the limit of his American sojourn. He made international trips to Cuba during the New York winter of December 1930 with Erwin Sutz, and a road trip to Mexico in May-June 1931 with Jean Lasserre. Before and after Cuba, he visited the American South and remarked on the ludicrously pedan-tic segregation that took place there. At the time he wrote: "

> The separation of whites from blacks in the southern states real-ly does make a rather shameful impression. In railways that separation extends to even the tiniest details. I found that the cars of the negroes generally look cleaner than the others. It al-so pleased me when the whites had to crowd into their railway cars while often only a single person was sitting in the entire railway car for negroes. The way the southerners talk about the negroes is simply repugnant, and in this regard the pastors are no better than the others. I still believe that the spiritual songs of the southern negroes represent some of the greatest artistic achievements in America. It is a bit unnerving that in a country with inordinately so many slogans about brotherhood, peace, and so on, such things still continue completely uncorrected."[295]

While in Cuba, Dietrich met up with his childhood governess Käthe van Horn, then a teacher at a German school in Havana, and celebrated

Christmas mass. After the ice of the North American winter, he found the luxuriant tropical vegetation and sun of Cuba most alluring, almost succumbing as he put it, to "sun worship." The road trip with Laserre to Mexico, where they camped out like proverbial hoboes at night, went only as far as the Texas border town of Laredo. There, due to obscure visa regulations in regard to re-entering the US, they left the Oldsmobile they had driven there in and entered Mexico after several days of delay. On the way to the Mexican border, Lasserre recalled: "

> Once at night, we had pitched our tent in a quiet grove of trees, without suspecting that we were taking over the dormitory of a herd of pigs. We had a hard time driving them away and discouraging these angry and noisy animals from reclaiming their bedrooms. After finally settling the matter we were worn out with fatigue and Dietrich fell quickly asleep. I was not so sure and I slept badly. At dawn I awoke with a start, because of a regular but ferocious snoring quite near to me. Thinking Dietrich quite ill, I threw myself towards him, only to find that he was sleeping peacefully as a child. The snoring which had terrified me was that of a huge pig who had stretched out against the whole side of the tent. . . . Dietrich was undisturbed, apparently quite unflappable, whatever happened. He had an extraordinarily even temperament, capable of ignoring anger, anxiety and discouragement. He seemed unable to despise anyone."[296]

While in Mexico, they travelled 1900 kilometres (1200 miles) by train. In Victoria City, where there was a teachers' training college, Lasserre had arranged through a Quaker friend for himself and Dietrich to give a joint address. Because the two came from the so-called "eternal enemies" of France and Germany, their appearance together was more than a passing novelty. Before returning to New York, just south of Mexico City, Dietrich and Lasserre visited Aztec ruins. Atop one of the pyramids, Dietrich talked at length with an indigenous shepherd boy who could neither read nor write, but had a great deal to tell. He wrote of how poor but friendly the people were, and the beauty of the scenery atop the two thousand metre elevation, sparing one from the heat at sea-level. On their return journey, they were refused entry at the US border. Only after telegrams were sent by Paul Lehmann and the German ambassador to Mexico, with tickets waiting in New York for their passage to Bremen Germany, were the immigration officials convinced they would not be a burden on the American labour market.[297]

By June 17, 1931, Dietrich and Lasserre arrived back in the sweltering summer heat of New York, and three days later, with many a fond memory, minus the tedious farce of Prohibition,[x] [298] Dietrich boarded a ship back home to Germany. Almost immediately upon arrival in his homeland, Dietrich, with powers of perception beyond that of many of his fellows, could sense the ominous clouds on the horizon of the Weimar political landscape.

---

[x] Amen to that Dietrich!

Chapter 2

Ominous Clouds on the Horizon

When Dietrich arrived home in Berlin, just a few days passed before he left Germany again for the neighbouring country of Switzerland. This was because one of his fellow students in New York, Erwin Sutz, had arranged for him to meet one of his most admired contemporary theological figures, Swiss Reformed theologian Karl Barth (1886-1968, born and died in Basel).[299] On July 23 1931, Barth, who was twenty years Dietrich's senior, invited him to dinner. Alone with Doctor Barth, Dietrich was finally able to ask him the questions he so long desired. At evening's end, Dietrich was even more impressed with him than by any of his earlier writings and lectures, and as a result, would often visit Barth over the next two years.

While Dietrich had only been across the Atlantic for nine months, in some respects it seemed like a lifetime. In the May 1928 Reichstag elections, with Weimar still in its so-called Golden Age, the Nazis only garnered a pathetic 2.6% of the national vote, while in the Silesian province, it was just a miserable 1%. However, two or so years later, on September 14 1930, just two days after Dietrich arrived in New York, the first threatening grey clouds of Nazi rule began to appear on the horizon. In the wake of the 1928 elections, the Nazi Party had been relegated to the ninth and smallest party in Germany and was regarded as little more than a joke. Just over two years later, with the Great Depression in full swing, they had become the second largest political party in the land, having secured 18% of the national vote, while in Breslau, they secured almost a quarter of the vote (24.2%).[300]

On August 1 1931, just nine days after his meeting with Barth, Dietrich was appointed adjunct lecturer in systematic theology in Berlin. However, around the same time, Dietrich wrote to Sutz that he sensed an exceptionally grim outlook at a tumultuous turning point in history. He was not yet certain what it was exactly, but he felt certain that the integrity of the church would be threatened, and wondered if it would even survive.[301] Eric Metaxas likened it to him imagining a beautiful mighty oak tree, with families picnicking under its seemingly invincible branches, with children climbing and swinging upon them, blissfully and fatally unaware that they were rotting and about to crush and kill them all.[302] For those around him, the change in him was obvious; his sermons became much harsher, and it seems, not so palatable to his congregations in general.

Four or so months after his return from New York, on November 15, 1931, aged 25, Dietrich was ordained at the Old Prussian United Saint Matthew's Church (St. Matthäikirche) in Berlin.[303] Almost a year later, on Reformation Sunday, November 6 1932[304] — the day Germany celebrated Martin Luther and the great cultural heritage of the Reformation,[305] and less than three months before Hitler took power — Dietrich was asked to preach in Berlin's famous Kaiser Wilhelm Memorial Church. Today, only a damaged hulk of a bell tower now remains,[306] but back then, the Berlin congregation of that day might, like American Protestants on July 4, expect an uplifting patriotic sermon. Moreover, there is every reason to expect that President von Hindenburg,[307] Germany's famous national icon, was also present, as this was the very church he attended. Thus, the stage was set for a wonderful sermon to stroke and pamper nationalist and Reformationist pride.

However, influenced in no small part, one would imagine, by his American racial relations experience, Dietrich delivered a perfect example of his more recent severe sermons. It was like pouring a bucket of freezing cold water on his congregation. With the thuggery and intimidation of Hitler and Röhm's Brown Shirts (SA) running rampant,[308] Dietrich proclaimed that the German church was dying or was already dead, and condemned his congregation for the grotesquely inappropriate act of conducting a celebration in the midst of a funeral. "A fanfare of trumpets is no comfort to a dying man,"[309] he cried! It was not the last of such sermons delivered by Dietrich that year.

The previous chapter mentioned the indelible impression made on Dietrich when he attended the 1924 Palm Sunday service in Rome. Its universality, epitomised by the transcendence of race and national identity, would have played no small part in fermenting his interest in the ecumenical movement.[310] Hence his attendance at the International Conference of the World Alliance in Cambridge England from September 1 to 5 in 1931. This organisation was a forerunner to the post WWII World Council of Churches, and it was at this conference that Dietrich was appointed one of their three European youth secretaries.[311] Inevitably, Dietrich's philosophy of the universal church, synonymous with the ecumenical movement, would put him at odds with the National Socialist philosophy of a church defined solely and violently by racial identity and blood.

The idea of wedding the German Protestant church to a dangerous and bigoted national consciousness had a genesis that pre-dated

Hitler's Reich by three years. However, Hitler and his other dyed-in-the-wool pure Nazi cohorts such as Himmler, Goebbels, Göring, Heydrich, and the like, did not really care much for Christianity, even in a bastardised form made more palatable and consistent with National Socialist doctrine. Himmler in particular, in nostalgic awe of the Germanic victory over the Roman legions in the Teutoburg Forest in 9AD,[312] longed for a reversion to the old pagan traditions, and found the Christian concepts of forgiveness, tolerance and mercy utterly banal, interpreting Christ's death on the cross as a symbol of insipid weakness and Jewish victory. Now in his mind, and that of his fellow cronies, they would save the world from the Jews and thereby redeem humanity, something that Christ on the cross had been unable to do.[313]

In between the wars, Christianity in Germany was in crisis. For one thing, after the humiliation of Versailles, what relevance did Jerusalem and a document nearly two millennia old hold for Germany? A new Reformation, in the eyes of many German Christians, was desperately needed to restore German pride and prestige. This was, as it turned out, the German Christian movement, founded in Thuringia on radical German nationalism and racism. On May 26 1932, they issued their *Guiding Principles*, which included a prohibition on "racial mixing," thus making racial purity of the German *Volk* sacred, an anathema to the philosophy of Dietrich. In a dubious parallel to the New Testament conversion of Saint Paul on the road to Damascus, they likened it to Hitler's temporary blindness suffered on the front during the Great War, proclaiming: "

> We put our trust in our God-sent Führer who was almost blinded when he heard God's call: 'You must save Germany.' And who, once his sight was restored, began that great work which led to the wonderful day of 30th January 1933."[314]

If one were to replace four words in the above with Satan, destroy, evil and terrible, you would at least have a proclamation much closer to the truth. For Dietrich, the National Socialist ideology and Christianity were profoundly incompatible; this was one point at least which found these bitter antagonists in total agreement. However, in a curious twist, the German Christians, while certainly an anathema to Dietrich's ideas of universality and ecumenism, were also disagreeable to the fascist megalomaniacs they were attempting to court.

Hitler did not care for them, but they, numbering around 600,000 by early 1933, certainly wanted Hitler, a man they had elevated to idolatrous reverence.[315] While they were useful in such numbers in bringing the Nazis to power, Hitler felt no obligation to prop up any form of Christianity, no matter how much it was bastardised to appeal to the National Socialist dogma. On the other hand, they were certainly no threat to his power base, and since their sons were willing to fight for the glorious Aryan Fatherland, and not stand in the way of the agenda of mass engineered genocide, and yes, even encourage it, the regime viewed them as nothing more than mildly annoying.

Dietrich, however, saw them as much more insidious and destructive. He rightly viewed them as bastardising Christianity in Germany, even to the point of disowning the Old Testament, with their obsequious and idolatrous courting of Hitler, the most nominal of Catholics. By early November 1932, when Dietrich delivered his controversial Reformation Sunday sermon, their dubious *Guiding Principles* issued six months earlier, followed eleven days later in Berlin by their "set of public guidelines," were no doubt greatly troubling and repugnant to Dietrich. In Point 9, they forbade the marriage of Germans and Jews; worse still was Point 7: "We see in race, national heritage (*Volkstum*) and the nation an order of life that has been given and entrusted to us by God....Therefore the mingling of races is to be opposed."[316]

Given the above, and his recent memories of racial relations in the US, Dietrich, a man of courageous integrity, must have felt compelled to deliver his less than patriotic and nationalist sermon. Moreover, that same month, in the church elections, the German Christians had already garnered enough support to create a serious schism in the church. In early 1933, a chair in theology opened at Berlin University, which prompted Dietrich to use his family's connections in the Prussian Ministry of Culture to push for the appointment of Karl Barth. However, Hitler had just taken power, and anyone who scorned Hitler's views had no hope of attaining any academic positions of real significance. Instead, the chair went to the ideologically compliant Georg Wobbermin.[317] Now, before his very eyes, what Dietrich had sensed with the greatest foreboding upon his return from New York was coming to pass.

Chapter 3

Evil's Storm Descends

On Wednesday February 1 1933, just two days after Hitler had taken power in a then minority government,[318] Dietrich gave a radio address at the Potsdamerstrasse radio station. It was entitled "The Younger Generation's Altered Concept of Leadership" and it dealt with the fundamental problems of leadership by a Führer, explaining how such a leader inevitably becomes an idol and a "mis-leader" or seducer (Verführer). However, just as he stated the concept of the Verführer, the speech was cut off.[319]

It would seem that Hitler's henchmen ordered the termination of the broadcast. That may have been the case, but there is nothing that conclusively points to this. For one thing, it's unclear whether or not the Nazis, after barely a couple of days in power as a minority government, had the authority or ability to control the airwaves, as they most certainly would in the not too distant future. Given the strict schedules radio stations always have to adhere to, an alternative and much more benign possibility has been suggested — that Dietrich simply ran out of time.[320]

One important aspect of Dietrich's address was that it was not specifically about Hitler, but about the popular concept of the so-called Führer Principle (Leader Principle); this was at the heart of Dietrich's objection to Hitler, and had, curiously enough, been around for decades. It had its genesis in the popular German Youth Movement of the early twentieth century; at the time of Dietrich's radio address, the Führer and Adolf Hitler were not yet the same thing. Moreover, Dietrich's address was not a response to Hitler's recent election, as it had already been planned for some time. In the speech, there was no mention of politics or current events. Rather it was a philosophy lecture, but as Metaxas stated, "it spoke more clearly about the political situation than a thousand political speeches."[321] "It was everything a ranting Hitler speech was not,"[322] being most measured, sedate and precise.

In elaborating his thoughts and ideas on the Führer Principle, Dietrich began by explaining the reasons why the nation was looking for a Führer. In the chaotic aftermath of the Great War and the subsequent chronic unemployment of the Great Depression, the younger generation had lost all faith in traditional authority.[323] In their mind, the

Kaiser had led them into a disastrous war, and the democracy of the Weimar Republic in his place merely delivered the humiliation of Versailles; further, the Republic was impotent to deal with the crisis of the Depression. The strong-arm dictatorship embodied by the Führer Principle seemed the only solution to restore full employment and national pride.

The reason that a Führer inevitably becomes a Verführer, making the two virtually synonymous, as Dietrich explained, is that real leadership derives its legitimate authority from God, the supreme altruistic and just being. Parents, for example, in raising their children, have legitimate authority to do so, because it is derived from and submitted to the legitimate authority of God.[324] However, in stark contrast, the authority of the Führer was submitted to nothing, and derived from pure megalomania. The episode the following year of the Night of the Long Knives is a perfect case in point; Hitler, certainly by then the Verführer, had no qualms in abandoning any pretence of legal due process to serve the whims of a diabolical agenda. As Dietrich put it, a true, legitimate leader knows the limits of his or her authority.

Dietrich was naturally upset that his speech was terminated prematurely,[325] and so he had the speech copied and sent it to many of his influential friends and relatives, along with a note explaining that the speech's conclusion had been cut off. The speech was published in the *Kreuzzeitung*, a politically conservative newspaper, and in early March, upon the invitation of the College of Political Science in Berlin, Dietrich delivered an extended version of the speech. Yes, in early 1933, in the Third Reich's infancy, such things were still possible.

Hitler himself never publicly denounced God,[326] and this was because he, the most nominal of Catholics, was a practical and cynical opportunist. As mentioned, at the time of his rise to power, the German Christians alone numbered 600,000,[327] but he of course realised that there were many more churchgoing Christians that he would need to placate, at least in the very early days of his reign. Thus, on the very same day that Dietrich delivered his prematurely terminated radio address, and barely 48 hours in power, Hitler delivered a speech of the most practical expediency, infused with unparalleled cynicism. "We are determined, as leaders of the nation, to fulfil as a national government the task which has been given to us, swearing fidelity only to God, our conscience, and our *Volk*."[328] This by a man whose conscience had long since been a corpse! He declared that his government would make Christianity "the basis of our collective morality." The conclusion, in unparalleled cynicism, was: "May God Almighty take our work into his grace, give true form to our will, bless our insight, and endow us with the trust of our *Volk!*"[329]

Late that same month of February 1933, at 9 pm on Monday 27th,[330] the burning of Berlin's Reichstag, whether a Nazi contrivance or otherwise, precipitated a chain of events of untold political "manna from heaven" (or perhaps hell!) for the still precarious minority regime. Today, there seems to be a fragile consensus amongst historians in general that a recently arrived Dutch communist, Marinus Van der Lubbe, born in 1909, was the sole perpetrator of the arson. However, there is enough evidence to at least view this conclusion with scepticism. William L. Shirer, in his book *Rise And Fall of the Third* Reich, quotes the testimony at the Nuremberg trials of General Franz Halder, Chief of the German General Staff during the early part of WWII: "

> At a luncheon on the birthday of the Fuehrer in [April 20] 1942 the conversation turned to the topic of the Reichstag building and its artistic value. I heard with my own ears when Göring interrupted the conversation and shouted: 'The only one who really knows about the Reichstag is I, because I set it on fire!' With that he slapped his thigh with the flat of his hand."[331]

At the time of the fire, Hitler was dining at Joseph Goebbels' home when his host received the call that the Reichstag was on fire. According to Metaxas, quoting Shirer's book, Goebbels was not at first convinced, as the caller was Ernst "Putzi" Hanfstaengl. While he was Harvard educated, and his money and connections had greatly helped Hitler's rise to power, he was also known as a bit of a clown, and thus Goebbels' first impression was that Hanfstaengl was pulling his leg. However, when he and Hitler arrived, they found that for once, Hanfstaengl was deadly serious, and were greeted by the first at the scene, the rotund Hermann Göring.[332]

Puffing and panting, the most corpulent of the Nazi elite professed that this was the beginning of the communist revolution, and that no mercy must be shown in shooting and/or stringing up every communist official that could be found. If Göring was in on the possible Nazi plot, now of course was not the time for honesty! The removal of their communist rivals from the dying Weimar political landscape was resoundingly called for. Could it be that Goebbels and Hitler were not in on the plot, but Göring was? In any event, at the scene, the shirtless Dutchman, who had supposedly used his shirt for tinder, was arrested on the spot.

55

Suddenly, the Bonhoeffer family was thrust into the centre of the national crisis.[333] Firstly, Dietrich's father Karl, Berlin's premier psychiatrist, was summoned to assess Van der Lubbe, while Dietrich's brother-in-law, Hans von Dohnányi, with whom Dietrich and brother Klaus became close friends during their gymnasium days in Grunewald,[334] was appointed as an official observer at the trial. It did not commence until seven months after the fire, in Leipzig on September 21 1933, and on October 10 it moved to Berlin to observe the Reichstag premises. There, court proceedings were carried out in the Reichstag's budget committee room. However, for the last month, from November 23 to the reading of the verdict on December 23 by presiding Judge Bünger, the court returned to Leipzig.[335]

Van der Lubbe was only one of the five defendants on trial; the others were Ernst Torgler, leader of the Communist Party group in the Reichstag, and three Bulgarian Communists, Georgi Dimitrov, Simon Popov, and Vassili Tanev, all agents of the Comintern (Communist International) founded in Moscow in March 1919, and dissolved in May 1943.[336] Dimitrov would become Bulgaria's first communist leader post-war, and in 1929 he settled in Berlin to direct the West European Bureau of the Comintern, where he was known to German authorities under the assumed identity of Doctor Hediger. During the trial, he acted as his own lawyer and took prodigious delight in ridiculing the vain and red-faced Göring. Since the whole world was watching, the Nazis could not yet do as they liked, and it seems this fact did not escape the attention of the brilliant Dimitrov. Torgler, when he heard that Göring had implicated him, gave himself up on the day following the fire (February 28),[337] and just nine days later, the Bulgarian communists were arrested.[338]

Many people believed Göring's henchmen were behind the fire and hoped the incorruptible Karl Bonhoeffer, in his assessment of the troubled Dutchman, would present evidence to support that belief. After all, he and his family loathed the Nazis. However, the Bonhoeffer family were not the type to manufacture evidence simply to suit their view or any political agenda. Karl Bonhoeffer, in his official report published in *Monatsschrift für Psychiatrie und Neurologie* was unbiased, lucid and objective, making no implication about the Dutchman's guilt or innocence. In the process, he angered both sides, who wasted no time in writing him irate letters. The affair weighed heavily on the family that year.[339]

Karl Bonhoeffer visited Van der Lubbe twice in March and then six times in the autumn during the course of the trial. In his official report, he stated that the Dutchman, while violently ambitious and capable of unwavering determination, was at the same time a modest and friendly scatterbrain, closed minded to any contradictory arguments, and inherently rebellious to all authority. While admitting his early conversion to communistic ideas had contributed to the mindset which led the Dutchman on this disastrous path, Karl Bonhoeffer concluded that it was unlikely that Van der Lubbe was going to follow a quiet and orderly pattern throughout his life. However, Karl Bonhoeffer stated that he was not to be regarded as mentally ill.[340]

When the verdict was handed down on December 23 by Judge Bünger, Marinus van der Lubbe, the most forlorn and pathetic figure imaginable, was sentenced to death. The Dutch Ambassador in Berlin appealed for clemency, and countless petitions from all over the world poured into Germany, all to no avail.[341] On January 9 1934, Van der Lubbe was informed by the Public Prosecutor of the rejection of his appeal, and that he was to be beheaded the following morning. With commendable composure, the condemned man replied; "Thank you for telling me; I shall see you tomorrow." He wrote no letters to family or friends, and was to die a forlorn and lonely death, a tragic mirror image of his painful life.[342]

His fellow defendants, however, were far more fortunate, as there was no evidence to link them to the fire. Hence, much to the embarrassment of Göring and the regime in general, they were acquitted and exiled to the Soviet Union as heroes, after eleven or so months of Nazi rule.[343] As in the lead-up to and during the 1936 Berlin Olympics, with the eyes of the world again upon them, the regime moderated their anti-Jewish measures. This case was heard in a court where the rule of law in concert with hard evidence still applied, regardless of the intensity of raving, bellicose Nazi propaganda. Tragically, however, this was one of the last cases to be conducted independent of the Nazi party agenda until post-war.[344]

Enraged by the acquittal of the other defendants, Hitler and Göring took action just a few months later in a cabinet meeting on March 23, 1934.[345] Its participants included Doctor Wilhelm Frick, the minister of the interior, and ironically, Ernst Röhm, head of the Sturmabteilung (SA) (aka Brown Shirts or Stormtroopers), who would be murdered in the Night of the Long Knives just a matter of months later, along with his SA cronies. For now, however, this meeting's focus was on initiating measures, in cases of "treason" at least, to replace the "irritating and annoying" Reichgericht (National Court), which conducted the Reichstag Fire trial, with a court much more amenable to the National Socialist agenda. Just one month later, on April 24, 1934, the Volksgerichtshof (People's Court) was officially founded.[346] It is likely that the Volksgerichtshof possessed ultimate discretion in ascertaining whether or not a case was one of treason. Indeed, in July 1944, in the aftermath of the failed Valkyrie assassination attempt on Hitler, it was the SS judges of the Volksgerichtshof that conducted the trial of brutal mass retribution. Their most conspicuous member, the infamous Roland Freisler, will be discussed in depth later in this book.[xi]

Due to the precarious minority status of Hitler's government, Weimar Germany still had one more "free" election of sorts to run, which took place on Sunday March 5, 1933, just six days after the fire. Hitler hoped it would give him the holy grail of an absolute majority, and in this regard, the Reichstag Fire was opportune for the Nazis. The day after the fire, Hitler predictably used the perceived threat of communist revolution to pressure the ageing and ailing 85-year-old President Hindenburg to sign the "Decree for the Protection of the People and the State," which would become popularly known as the "Reichstag Fire Decree." This decree suspended those sections of the German constitution that guaranteed individual liberties and civil rights. The Weimar democracy was going up in smoke, and was an ominously apt symbol of the charred and empty husk of the gutted parliament.[347]

Emboldened with this decree, Röhm's Brown Shirts ran amok in the streets, arresting and beating their political opponents; torture and killings became commonplace. To assemble publicly against them was now illegal, and the press was gagged. But in spite of all the intimidation and thuggery, while attaining just over 50% in Breslau and even 54% in the neighbouring Silesian region of Liegnitz, the Nazi Party was still not able to gain its absolute majority nationally, with only 43.2% of the vote.[348] Dietrich's dear friend Franz Hildebrandt voted for the Christian People's Party, but while they walked together to the polling booths, Dietrich told Franz that the only party that offered any promise of stability and independence, due to its "international ties," was the Catholic Centre Party. Given that Dietrich was a devout Protestant minister, his vote was a radical and most unusual step at the time.[349]

This was only going to prove a minor annoyance to Hitler. Röhm's aptly coloured brown shirt pit bulls worked in concert with the police to continue their agenda of terror and arrests. Their dubious legitimacy was authorised by the rump Reichstag. In servile compliance, it

---

[xi] Roland Freisler and his People's Court will be discussed at length in Chapter 20 "Valkyrie II."

passed the suppressive "Malicious Practices" and "Enabling" acts on March 21 and 23, just sixteen and eighteen days following the last "free" election. The former furnished the judicial means to prosecute anyone who, "with malicious afterthought" put forward reports that might impair the welfare of the Reich; the latter, officially the "Law to Remove the Crisis of the People and the State," was the constitutional means by which the Reichstag of Weimar,[350] like a snake swallowing its tail, passed the law that obliterated its existence.[351]

While the acquittal of all the defendants bar Van der Lubbe in the fire trial was somewhat of an embarrassment for Hitler and Göring, and perhaps a minor propaganda coup for the Soviet regime, over-whelmingly, the fire, whether contrived or otherwise by the regime, became the National Socialists' political and propaganda weapon, paving their pathway to unbridled absolute power. Moreover, for anyone outspoken like Dietrich, who refused to declare his loyalty to Hitler's Reich, the passing of the Malicious Practices Act meant that in the wake of the last vestiges of Weimar, he was now walking a dangerously thin line.[352] However, not one to shy away from the challenge of a just cause, Dietrich's theological battle with the Third Reich would now commence in earnest.

Chapter 4

The Aryan Paragraph

Soon after the passing of the Malicious Practices and Enabling acts came the Aryan Paragraph, which took effect on April 7 1933.[353] The Bonhoeffers always had access to privileged information, but as the spectre of the Third Reich encroached more and more into German life, most of it came from Christine's husband and lawyer Hans von Dohnányi at the German Supreme Court. The Aryan Paragraph was, for Dietrich, of grave concern, and with advanced notice, he started to write his essay, *The Church and the Jewish Question* in March; he delivered it in early April to a group of pastors who met regularly at the home of Gerhard Jacobi, pastor of the Kaiser Wilhelm Memorial Church.

The Aryan Paragraph would result in a set of disturbing new laws, by which all government employees had to be of Aryan stock. Cynically packaged as the "Restoration of the Civil Service," all Jewish employees would, among other "racially impure" ethnicities, have their employment terminated. In the case of the German Church, which was essentially a state church, compliance with this directive would mean that all pastors of Jewish blood, including Dietrich's dear friend Franz Hildebrandt, would be excluded from the ministry. It was under this intense pressure on institutions all over the country to fall in line with the tsunami of National Socialist dogma that Dietrich wrote his essay.[354]

For the members of the German Christian Movement, the implications of the Aryan Paragraph in general, but in particular for the church, were endorsed with rapturous enthusiasm. However, what Dietrich found even more disturbing was the willingness of more mainstream Protestant leaders to consider adopting the Aryan Paragraph.[355] While not necessarily harbouring any ill will to Jews in general, they could see no real problem with Christians of Jewish heritage being compelled to form their own Christian church, as was the case for example with negroes in the American South. This pragmatic appeasement of Hitler, before the coming of future horrors, seemed on the surface rather benign, and they reasoned that appeasement of the Nazi state would bear the fruits of restoring the church to its glory before the Treaty of Versailles and the chaos and humiliation of the last twenty years. After all, was not the moral degeneration of Weimar Germany self-evident?[356]

Dietrich, however, had seen first-hand the negative consequences of such thinking during his visit to America, especially in the South. At the time, in his letters back home to Germany, he had written that he saw no analogous situation in Germany. However, with the passing of the Aryan Paragraph, this was now becoming a stark reality. For Dietrich, the Aryan Paragraph would have been an unequivocal violation of the book of *Galations*, Chapter 3, verse 28: "there is neither Jew nor Greek, bond nor free, male nor female, for you are all one in Christ Jesus."[357]

As such, a church that excluded Jews was not a church of Christ, but a heresy. However, in his address, he went further by stating that the church still had an obligation to act, even when victims of institutionalised injustice were not Christian. Naturally, everyone knew he was talking about the Jews, and with the church's existence thus threatened, it was not enough for the church to "bandage the victims under the wheel, but to put a spoke in the wheel itself."[358]

In this regard, Dietrich's grandmother Julie Bonhoeffer was a perfect example.[359] On April 1 1933, Hitler declared a national boycott of Jewish stores. The pretext was to stop the perceived Jewish dominated international press from printing lies about the National Socialist regime. In effect, they were again justifying an act of unconstitutional aggression as an act of defence against actions against them and the German Volk. Goebbels ranted and raved at a rally in Berlin, and across the nation, SA men intimidated shoppers who tried to enter Jewish-owned stores, along with the offices of lawyers and doctors. Their windows were defaced in black or yellow paint with the Star of David and the word "Jude" (Jew), while SA thugs handed out pamphlets and held placards proclaiming *Deutsche Wehrt Euch! Kauft Nicht Bei Juden!"* (Germans, protect yourselves! Don't buy from Jews!).[360] Strangely, perhaps for the benefit of the "Jewish dominated international press," some signs were in English: "Germans, defend yourselves from Jewish Atrocity Propaganda — buy only at German shops!"[361]

It was on this day, in this atmosphere of bigotry and intimidation, that Dietrich's ninety-year-old grandmother decided she would nevertheless shop wherever she wanted to shop. Moreover, she was forthright in telling the brown shirt thugs of her intentions when they tried to restrain her from entering. Later that same day, she did the same at the famous Kaufhaus des Westens, the largest department store in the world at the time. For the Bonhoeffer family, the story of their brave and defiant granny blithely marching past Nazi gorillas became the embodiment of the values they sought to live by.[362]

Just before this time, in late March, Paul and Marion Lehmann, whom Dietrich knew from his time at the Union Seminary in New York, came to visit. Witnessing the April 1 boycott first hand, they also saw the spectacle of the German Christians' conference, at which Göring gave an address, extolling the dubious virtues of the "Führer Principal" and admonishing them "to expect their Führer to lead in every aspect of German life, including the church." Göring later stated Hitler's proposal for the office of Reichsbischof (Nation's Bishop) to "bring all the disparate elements in the German church together."[363] Ludwig Müller, a rather unrefined former naval chaplain, was ultimately appointed in this "unifying" role.

For the Lehmanns, the Bonhoeffer home on Wangenheimstrasse was like a sanctuary utterly removed from the surrounding madness that Germany was spiralling into. Although they did occasionally notice big brother Klaus tiptoeing to the door in the room in which they were speaking, to check if any servants were listening.[364] Such was the rapidity with which the Nazis were implementing their agenda that just two months following Hitler's appointment as Chancellor, they did not know who they could trust. The Lehmanns noticed a change in Dietrich from his more flamboyant and carefree days in New York two years ago. Institutionalised discrimination in Germany was now, to his horror, becoming a reality.

This reality would have played no small part in prompting Dietrich, in collaboration with Paul Lehmann, to write a letter to Rabbi Stephen Wise in New York, an honorary president of the American Jewish committee with connections to President Franklin Roosevelt. Since the passing of the Reichstag Fire Edict, the writing of such a letter was a treasonable offence, and Dietrich knew full well that he could end up in a concentration camp for his troubles. Nevertheless, he felt honour bound to co-author the letter.[365]

This environment led to Dietrich making a decision he would later regret. On April 11, just ten days after the Jewish boycott, Dietrich was approached to preach a sermon for a funeral. On the surface, this seems benign enough, but it was for the ethnically Jewish father of Gerhard Leibholz, who, unlike his son, had not been baptised into the Christian church. As a man who had been passionately campaigning against the Nazis on the so-called Jewish question, Dietrich was aware that the preaching of such a sermon for one who had not been baptised into the Christian church would be construed as incendiary and provocative.

On the other hand, the fact that Gerhard was his brother-in-law and husband of his twin sister Sabine meant that Dietrich was emotionally conflicted.[366] After consulting with his district superintendent, who was overly sensitive to the uproar it would cause, Dietrich declined the invitation to preach at the funeral. It was a decision he would later regret, and one he was not likely to have felt comfortable with at any time. Seven or so months later, on Reformation Sunday, even though Gerhard and Sabine had never said anything to him, Dietrich would write to them, expressing his abject regret about the weakness in his decision.

Gerhard was a popular professor of law at Göttingen, and Sabine would often attend his lectures. On the day of the boycott, Sabine made a point of attending her husband's scheduled lectures.[367] When Gerhard and Sabine walked down the street, the atmosphere was toxic; people who recognised them would suddenly cross over the street. When Sabine arrived, she was greeted by students dressed in SA uniforms with the words, "Leibholz must not lecture, he is a Jew. The lectures are not taking place."[368] Theologian Walter Bauer and a certain professor met them there, expressing their disgust with the Nazis. Worse still, many of Gerhard's relatives lost their jobs, and one of his Jewish school friends committed suicide. By now, such instances were commonplace.

At the German Christians' conference, Göring declared that everything in German society was compelled to fall in line with Nazi doctrine.[369] This included books and ideas, and on the night of Thursday May 11 1933 at 11pm, thousands of students gathered in every university town across Germany to perform a chillingly symbolic implementation of this objective. From Heidelberg to Tübingen to Freiburg to Göttingen, where the Leibholzes lived, mobs of student "intellectuals" marched in torchlight parades to huge bonfires, into which they hurled thousands of books declared "degenerate" in the infamous literary *Säuberung* (cleansing). In Berlin, at the stroke of midnight, addressing the mob of thirty thousand, Joseph Goebbels, of club foot and short stature, ranted into the darkness with characteristic Aryan "super-race" zeal: "

> German men and women! The age of arrogant Jewish intellectualism is now at an end!…You are doing the right thing at this midnight hour — to consign to the flames the unclean spirit of the past. This is a great, powerful, and symbolic act… Out of

these ashes the phoenix of a new age will arise... O Century! O Science! It is a joy to be alive!"[370]

Goebbels, the ultimate propagandist, saw the staging of a torchlight parade, followed by a bonfire at the stroke of midnight in the nation's capital, as something ancient, tribal and pagan, evoking the pagan gods of the German Volk of antiquity, melded with the memory of the great victory of the Germanic tribes in 9 AD over the Romans, symbols of strength, ruthlessness, blood and soil. While certainly the antithesis of Christianity, this was never explicitly declared, due to the major support base of the German Christians. However, the ominous summoning of forces, counter to the perceived "weak virtues"[371] of traditional Christianity, was palpable. Works of famous writers and scholars such as Albert Einstein, the author of *Relativity* — one of the two great pillars of modern physics, Helen Keller, Jack London, H. G. Wells, Erich Maria Remarque, and Thomas Mann, to name just a handful, were consigned to the National Socialist heap of degenerate works.

Two or so months later, with just one week's notice, Hitler announced new church elections in a mirage of choice, to take place on July 23 1933.[372] In spite of the odds stacked against them, Dietrich and his students in the Young Reformation movement threw themselves into the task of writing and duplicating their campaign leaflets. However, on the night of the 17th, barely twenty-four hours after Hitler announced the elections, the Gestapo broke into the offices of the Young Reformation movement and confiscated them. The "legal" premise under which this was authorised centred around the German Christians objecting to the title by which the candidates for the Young Reformers were listed, the "List of the Evangelical Church." In the minds of the German Christians, *they* were the true Evangelical Church, regardless of how they bastardised Christianity to suit their agenda and that of the National Socialists.

Dietrich, however, would not be cowered into submission. With his regret over not performing the funeral sermon for Gerhard Leibholz's father ever present, Dietrich confronted the Gestapo head on. Driving in his father's Mercedes, accompanied by senior pastor Gerhard Jacobi, resplendent in his two Iron Crosses awarded for bravery in the Great War, they stormed into Gestapo Headquarters on Prinz-Albrecht-Strasse, demanding to see Rudolf Diels, the head of the Gestapo.[373]

Nine months later, on April 20 1934, about two months before the Nacht der Langen Messer (Night of the Long Knives), Göring handed over control of the Gestapo to Heinrich Himmler, the head of the SS, as Göring had major concerns that Diels was not ruthless enough to carry the forthcoming purge to its completion.[374] Diels, fortunate not to be one of the 1934 purge's victims, a decade later in July 1944, would become one of the Gestapo's "guests" in the wake of the failed Valkyrie assassination plot on Hitler, and would survive post-war.[375] But for now, as Eric Metaxas wrote, Dietrich exuded the "confidence of someone who knew his rights and was bold enough to claim them"[376] in spite of Gestapo intimidation. Dietrich pointed out to Diels that Hitler himself had guaranteed free elections, thus compelling Diels to concede that it was a case of blatant election interference. While the leaflets were returned, he and Jacobi had to agree to a change in the title of the leaflets from the "Evangelical Church" to the more neutral "Gospel and Church." If any of the original leaflets were distributed or found, they would be paying a prolonged visit to a concentration camp.

Three days later on July 20, Hitler had achieved a major diplomatic coup involving the other main religion of Germany. Hitler announced that a Concordat had been forged with the Vatican in Rome, guaranteeing the freedom of profession and public practice of the Catholic faith, and ensuing friendly relations between the German Reich and the Holy See.[377] Of course in time, these assurances of Hitler would prove to be cynical, but for the time being they portrayed a benign face to the outside world. This came in the midst of a rigged election process of the state church. Three days later, the German Christians won in a predictable landslide, receiving about 70% of the votes.[378] One disturbing consequence of this result was the election of Ludwig Müller, widely regarded as a half-educated buffoon, as Reichsbischof (National Bishop). Back in early April at the German Christians' conference, Göring had mentioned Hitler's proposal of Müller for that very office, and now in the wake of the rigged July elections, this became a reality.

In a disturbing recent parallel to the 1933 Vatican-National Socialist Concordat, in September 2018, the Vatican signed a provisional agreement in Beijing with the Communist government of the People's Republic of China (PRC). The Vatican had hailed the agreement as a major diplomatic breakthrough;[379] however, as part of the deal, Pope Francis recognised seven Chinese bishops who were appointed by Beijing without the Vatican's approval, and had been excommunicated as illegitimate.[380] The accord reportedly gave the Vatican a say in the naming of bishops and supposedly granted the pope veto power over candidates, but the appointment of the seven bishops puts this assertion into serious question. China's Catholics are split between an underground church swearing loyalty to the Vatican, and the state-supervised Catholic "Patriotic" Association (CPA).[xii][381]

For critics of the deal, it is a sell-out to the Chinese Communist Party (CCP), given its litany of human rights abuses. Cardinal Joseph Zen, born in Shanghai, the former archbishop of Hong Kong and participant in the Hong Kong Democracy protests,[382] has led the opposition to the deal. He observes:

> "The consequences will be tragic and long lasting, not only for the church in China but for the whole church because it damages credibility ...."[383] And "The deal 'sends the flock into the mouths of the wolves' and is a 'betrayal'."[384]

In 1933, Dietrich was commencing his fight against the National Socialist bastardisation of his faith. Eight to nine decades later, Chinese President Xi Jinping introduced a programme to "Sinicise" all religious practice, insisting that it must be "Chinese in orientation." The government must "provide active 'guidance' to religions so that they can 'adapt' themselves to socialist society," he said.[385]

Beijing's increasingly horrific pogrom against ethnic Muslim Uyghurs in the north-west province of Xinjiang, as much Central Asia as it is China, casts a huge human rights and religious persecution shadow over the deal. Surveillance techniques used in Xinjiang have already emerged elsewhere; the government has installed closed-circuit TV cameras in some Catholic and Protestant churches. Uyghurs, since 2009, have been subjected to extreme repression that has seen the banning of many traditional Islamic practices, mass disappearances, thousands jailed, and hundreds sentenced to death in stadium trials. In the eighteen months preceding September 2018, the pogrom culminated in concentration camps that human rights agencies estimate hold up to a million Uyghurs.[386] As Drew Pavlou, the young University of Queensland (UQ)[xiii] philosophy student, suspended in mid-2020 for daring to lead protests against the CCP on campus, commented: "This is the largest internment of a people based on their ethnicity since the Holocaust."[387]

[xii] The Catholic "Patriotic" Association (CPA) seems to be a modern-day Chinese Communist Party (CCP) parallel of the pro-Hitler German Christians.
[xiii] The University of Queensland is located in Queensland's state capital of Brisbane, approximately 750 kilometres north of Sydney.

According to Drew Pavlou's pro bono Queen's Counsel (QC), Tony Morris, UQ students who organise protests against the democratic state of Israel are always left unhindered on campus to exercise their democratic rights.[388] Israel however, is not so critical to the financial bottom line for UQ.[389] According to the final report released on March 1, 2020 by the UK based China Tribunal, chaired by UK Queen's Counsel (QC) Sir Geoffrey Nice: "Hospitals in the PRC have had access to a population of donors whose organs could be extracted according to demand for them."[390]

Prime targets for this heinous practice, are members of the Falun Gong spiritual movement.[391] For the Uyghurs, the CCP are implementing programmes of forced sterilisation and abortion to curb China's Muslim population, while at the same time, encouraging some of the country's ethnic Han majority to have more children.[392] The Vatican's provisional agreement, openly "blessed" by Pope Francis, who refuses to meet with the legitimate Tibetan spiritual leader the Dalai Lama,[393] is due to expire in September 2020. In June 2020, according to the pro-Beijing Italian Archbishop Claudio Maria Celli, it will be renewed.[394] However, in late July 2020, it was revealed by the U.S. cybersecurity firm Recorded Future that hackers linked to the Chinese government had infiltrated Vatican computer networks. The attacks began in May. A Chinese delegation had been due to visit the Vatican as part of continuing talks, but there was no indication if or when they would travel because of the coronavirus outbreak, as reported by a senior Vatican source.[395]

Earlier that summer of 1933, Dietrich received an invitation from Theodor Heckel to become a pastor of a German speaking congregation in London. Heckel knew Dietrich through ecumenical contacts, and was the head of the German church's Foreign Office, which oversaw the diaspora of German speaking parishes around the world. Understandably, the idea of leaving the political troubles of Germany behind had its appeal for Dietrich. Moreover, his close friend Franz Hildebrandt, ordained on June 18 in the midst of this turmoil, was thinking of moving there. Thus, just one week after the rigged July 23rd election, Dietrich preached to two of the congregations considering him. They were the Church of Saint Paul's in the East End, and another in the southern suburb of Sydenham where the parsonage was located. Both congregations were impressed with him, and Heckel glowingly recommended him.[396] However, Heckel's fondness for Dietrich would not last.

It was not till autumn that Dietrich accepted the appointment in London.[397] In the meantime, he visited Friedrich von Bodelschwingh's Bethel community in Biesenthal, just thirty or so kilometres north-east of Berlin. The man and his community were the classical antithesis of National Socialist dogma; the community had been founded in the 1860s by Friedrich's father as a Christian community for people with epilepsy. By the turn of the century, it included several facilities caring for 1,600 people, and upon the death of his father in 1910, Friedrich continued and indeed greatly expanded on his father's legacy. Dietrich witnessed the degree to which this legacy was enriched during his August 1933 visit; by then it was a town in itself, with schools, churches, farms, factories, shops and the like. At its centre were numerous hospitals and care facilities, among which were orphanages. As Eric Metaxas wrote, "It was the gospel made visible, a fairy-tale landscape of grace, where the weak and helpless were cared for in a palpably Christian atmosphere."[398]

As already mentioned, Hitler had proposed the creation of the office of Reichsbischof, which Göring had confirmed during the German Christian's conference in April. Their recommendation was the bull-headed sycophant and former naval chaplain Ludwig Müller. However, during the following month of May, Bodelschwingh, the antithesis of Müller, was legitimately elected by the nation's bishops, much to the displeasure of the German Christians. With the apparatus of the Nazi state behind them, the German Christians were greatly emboldened to put extreme pressure on Bodelschwingh, and forced him to resign in late June. Their catch cry was that the "will of the people," not that of the lofty high-minded bishops, should be heard. For Dietrich's closest friend from university days in the 1920s, Franz Hildebrandt, the fact that he, a man of Jewish heritage was ordained just days before the resignation of Bodelschwingh was significant.[399]

Bethel is actually Hebrew for "House of God," and the community, founded by the father of Friedrich von Bodelschwingh in the 1860s, and enhanced by the son, was aptly named. Moreover, for the rest of the decade and throughout the war, unlike almost all other church social service institutions, Friedrich would valiantly resist Nazi orders for them to give up their permanently disabled patients, who were deemed by the regime as "useless eaters" and "life unworthy of life"[400] in accordance with the infamous T-4 euthanasia programme.[401] In 1940, while some patients in other institutions, in response to protests of Friedrich von Bodelschwingh and others, were "spared" from death by gassing, most would still die by lethal injection or by simply being left to die by starvation. In the madness and barbarity of the entire twelve years of the Third Reich, Bethel would remain as an oasis of peace and the very best of German Christian culture.[402]

It also seemed the most fitting place for Dietrich to spend three weeks, with Hermann Sasse, drafting the so-named "Bethel Confession," a repudiation of the theology of Ludwig Müller and his German Christians.[403] However, after it was sent to twenty prominent theologians throughout the country, it was so watered down, that to Dietrich's horror, it became nothing more than an insipid document compliant with National Socialist dogma.[404] About two months earlier in late June, Dietrich and Franz Hildebrandt, newly ordained, had proposed the churches go on strike against the state to assert their independence. In their minds, if the state would not allow the church to be the church, it would cease functioning like the church, among other things, refuse to perform funerary functions. However, as would become typical, such proposals were deemed too dramatic, unsettling and confronting for the timid church hierarchy.[405]

On September 5-6, 1933, a fortnight or so after Dietrich's three or so week stay at Bethel, the General Synod of the Evangelical Church of the Old Prussian Union Church was held in Berlin.[406] It was dominated by the German Christians, but the reason why it became known as the "Brown Synod" was because eighty percent of the delegates wore the Brown Shirts of the SA, giving it more the look of an SA rally than of a synod.[407] While opposition voices were shouted down, the minor victory of denying the passing of the motion to exclude already ordained non-Aryans such as Franz Hildebrandt was achieved. Further, the similar motion to remove spouses of non-Aryans from their posts was also blocked.[408]

That said, the Aryan Paragraph was fundamentally left unchanged, in that all future non-Aryans were barred from the state church. This prompted Dietrich and Franz to call for a schism in the state church, with pastors standing up to be counted by resigning from office. Again, they were voices in the wilderness; even the great theologian Karl Barth was most disapproving, stating that if a schism were to occur, it must come from the other side, precipitated by an issue more central than the current issue of the Aryan Paragraph. Dietrich and Franz quite rightly thought, "What could be more central than the Aryan Paragraph?"[409] Moreover, Barth's response so disturbed Dietrich that he did not inform Barth of his eventual move to London until well after he left.

With the failure of the proposed schism, Dietrich, Franz, and pastor Martin Niemöller, an Iron Cross decorated U-boat captain from the Great War,[410] decided to compose a statement protesting against the Brown Synod. It contained four main points, which included protecting the fidelity of the church to the scriptures, the lending of financial aid to those persecuted by the new Nazi laws and violence, and the outright rejection of the Aryan Paragraph. For Niemöller, this was a drastic change in position, as he had at first welcomed the Nazis as the Messiah for restoring German pride. This feeling was reinforced during a personal meeting with Hitler in 1932, where he received assurances, which would of course prove empty and cynical, that the National Socialist regime would respect the independence of the Reichskirche (State Church) and never initiate pogroms against the Jews.[411]

The statement was entitled "To the National Synod," since late in September 1933, a national synod would be held in Wittenberg; surprisingly, it received a positive response. By October 20, 1933, the pastors across Germany who had signed the document formed an official organisation called the "Pfarrernotbund" (Pastors' Emergency League), and by the end of the year, six thousand pastors joined its ranks.[412] This would become the pre-cursor to the Confessing Church.

In September, Dietrich attended two international Ecumenical conferences. The later conference was the ecumenical conference of the World Alliance, which took place in the Bulgarian capital of Sofia from September 15 to 20 in 1933. It was the earlier conference, of the organisation named "Life and Work" at Novi Sad in Yugoslavia from September 9 to 12, 1933, which was more revealing and productive for Dietrich. This was because, on the day after the conference, Dietrich had his first personal meeting with the Bishop of Chichester, George Bell,[413] in which it is likely that he informed Bell in no uncertain terms of the distorted and rosy picture that Theodor Heckel, the head of the German church's Foreign Office, had painted of the state church in Germany.[414]

Although Heckel had approached Dietrich in the summer to take up the position of pastor of a German speaking congregation in London, and spoke glowingly of the sermons he delivered there during his short London visit, it appears that from Novi Sad onwards, his fondness for Dietrich rapidly evaporated. Furthermore, Bell and the Novi Sad delegates did not regard Heckel's account as credible. For years to come, Dietrich would be the irrepressible voice informing Bell, and thus the world, of the truth of what was happening to the church in Germany. This of course, was a major annoyance and in direct contradiction to the warped accounts of "official" representatives such as Heckel. One compelling reason why George Bell would have been receptive to Dietrich's true account of the German State Church or Reichkirche, in concert with his dismissal of Heckel's distorted version, was the account that Bell received from his neighbour Arthur Stuart Duncan-Jones, the Dean of Chichester, who flew to Berlin on July 1 1933, just three or so weeks before the German Church elections called by Hitler.[415]

During his flight, Duncan-Jones struck up a conversation with Hitler's confidant, Ernst "Putzi" Hanfstaengel, and in so doing, was able to secure a brief but captivating meeting with Hitler himself. During it, the nominal Catholic, Hitler, insisted that he merely desired a united Protestant church so that he himself could "deal" with religious matters in an orderly manner.[416] In the face of such seemingly benign and reasonable logic, Duncan-Jones was somewhat receptive to the new regime, but he realised that in the drastically altered political landscape of Germany in the wake of the Reichstag Fire decrees, further and more in-depth investigation was required.

Days later, at the Kaiser Friedrich Gedächtniskirche, Duncan-Jones found a crowded congregation gathered to listen to the head of the German Christians, Joachim Hossenfelder, surrounded by the ubiquitous swastika flags. But as Hossenfelder's oratory proceeded with the requisite ranting and shouting of National Socialist dogma, there was no sense of spiritual cohesion. That evening, Duncan-Jones returned to hear one of the leading voices of the opposition, Gerhard Jacobi, again preaching to a packed church, but with a palpable "unity of feeling"[417] and a powerful sense of prayer.

At the end of his sermon, Jacobi told of the arrest that morning of a pastor in Berlin's south-western district of Dahlem; he had refused to allow Nazi flags to be hung in his church. Duncan-Jones continued to meet as many church people as he could, finding that those who held an independent or critical view were fearful of what was now coming to pass in the new Germany. Furthermore, they spoke of the grim consequences for anyone publicly expressing sympathy for those oppressed or persecuted by the regime. Upon Duncan-Jones's return, George Bell almost immediately set about making known to the British media the plight of non-Aryans in the new Germany, as well as making plans to settle refugees in his diocese and all across Great Britain.[418]

The conference in Sofia had unequivocally condemned the Aryan Paragraph. Nevertheless, upon Dietrich's return to Germany to attend the National Synod with Franz Hildebrandt and Martin Niemöller in Wittenberg on September 27, the synod, again seemingly more akin to a Nazi rally, elected the half-educated toady Ludwig Müller as Reichsbischof.[xiv] The irony was that this synod was held in the very Castle Church where Martin Luther, over four centuries earlier, had possibly nailed his ninety-five theses,[419] in contradiction, among other issues, to the Catholic Church's corrupt practice of indulgences; and so the Reformation was precipitated with all its incalculable historical and political consequences. Moreover, Müller's election, coupled with the election of other German Christians unopposed as regional bishops, took place right beside the tomb where Luther was buried. This prompted Franz Hildebrandt to whisper to Dietrich that he now believed in the doctrine of the "real rotation"[420] of Luther's bones in his grave.

At the synod, Dietrich, along with Franz Hildebrandt and Martin Niemöller, distributed leaflets of the declaration "To the National Synod" to the various delegates, as well as nailing them to trees. But in the end, in the quintessential totalitarian farce of an election with candidates of one sole party, the "rotation of Luther's bones" was inevitable. Later, flanked by dozens of saluting SA thugs outside the town's council chambers, Müller, in bishop's dress, returned the Nazi salute. On December 3, in Berlin Cathedral, Ludwig Müller would officially be consecrated as Reichsbischof.[421]

Greatly dismayed with the course of events in Germany, in October, Dietrich turned his attention to the possibility of accepting the post in London.[422] However, with Heckel's former fondness of Dietrich all but evaporated, the transfer to London was not a certainty. Heckel had decided to make the transfer conditional on Dietrich recanting entirely his anti-Reichkirche agenda, and on his refraining from ecumenical activities in London. Dietrich remained as defiant and resolute as ever, demanding a meeting, or perhaps more to the point, a confrontation with Ludwig Müller.

At this meeting, Dietrich reiterated what he told Heckel. Müller nevertheless asked Dietrich to retract his signature on the Pastors' Emergency League statement. Dietrich obdurately refused, reciting the Augsburg Confession in Latin at great enough length for Müller to become uncomfortable and cut the lengthy recital short. Nevertheless, more than likely fearing the trouble Dietrich would cause if refused

---

[xiv xxi] Ludwig Müller is not to be confused later on with his namesake Josef Müller. As will be discussed later, it would be hard to find two individuals of more contrasting character.

unconditional permission to accept the London post, Müller relented. As Eric Metaxas put it: "

> Bonhoeffer had declared his loyalty to Germany, but he would not declare his loyalty to the 'National Socialist state.' That summed up Bonhoeffer's attitude going forward: he would be fiercely loyal to the church and to Germany, but would not pledge one atom of himself to Müller's pseudochurch or to the dictatorship that claimed to represent the great country and culture he cherished."[423]

Dietrich would commence his London ministry on October 17 1933. However, just three days earlier on the 14th, when Dietrich was preparing to leave for London, Hitler announced that Germany was leaving the League of Nations. Only recently, Hitler had asked the League for "equality of status,"[424] meaning they should grant the right for Germany to build up its military to the level equivalent to other major powers. When the League predictably refused, Hitler found the pretext to exit it, and correctly predicted they would never have the will to physically block any Nazi military expansion. Hitler, in tune with the majority of Germans still feeling the humiliation of Versailles, found overwhelming popular support which, much to the anger of Franz Hildebrandt and Dietrich, included Martin Niemöller.

Like so many Germans at the time, and especially for the Iron Cross decorated former Great War U-boat captain-come pastor, this was a great moment in the restoration of German pride. While Niemöller had opposed Hitler since his election, with his quintessential empty promises of church independence, for Niemöller, German pride, including the right of Germany to build up its military to the strength of other major powers, was an entirely different matter. Moreover, it seemed that Hitler's empty 1932 promise to Niemöller was of no consequence, since he sent Hitler a congratulatory telegram in the name of the Pastors' Emergency League, swearing their loyalty and gratitude.[425] Little wonder then that Dietrich and Franz Hildebrandt reacted angrily; for Niemöller's swearing of unconditional support for Hitler was in itself a violation of church independence.

In these early stages of the Third Reich, one could have been forgiven for having no idea of the horrors to come. The feeling of the humiliation of Versailles included Germans who were by no means pro-Nazi, with even the upper echelons of the Weimar regime of the very early 1930s pushing hard for a revision of their eastern frontier with

Poland. Moreover, France, which Poland held a formal alliance with, was sympathetic to such revisions in the name of "preserving peace in Europe."[426] Hitler, all too well aware of this at the time, saw future political opportunities under the pretext of "the restoration of German pride," to garner crucial support from the more moderate sectors of the German political spectrum. Challenging the League of Nations in October 1933 was one such opportunity, and Martin Niemöller, a staunch opponent of Hitler at the National Synod in Wittenberg just two to three weeks earlier on September 27, was a perfect example of how brilliantly Hitler exploited the very broad national resonance of "the restoration of German pride."

Given these alarming developments, it appears that Dietrich and Franz became lone voices even among their "allies" in the Pastors' Emergency League. What at first seemed to be some sort of coherent opposition to Hitler became a weak opposition divided by the wedge of national pride. Hildebrandt's legitimate grievance of a church not granting all of its people equal status was engulfed in the tsunami of newly discovered patriotic zeal. Years later, some would come to regret this embrace of the Verführer, and Martin Niemöller would be among them. As a concentration camp inmate from 1938-1945, he wrote: "

> First they came for the Socialists, and I did not speak out — because I was not a Socialist.
> Then they came for the Trade Unionists, and I did not speak out — because I was not a Trade Unionist. Then they came for the Jews, and I did not speak out — because I was not a Jew. And then they came for me — and there was no one left to speak for me."[427]

Originally incarcerated at the Sachsenhausen camp near Berlin, Niemöller would be transferred to Dachau in 1941, where he would stay until almost war's end, before being liberated in Niederdorf in the German speaking South Tyrol region of northern Italy in late April 1945.[428] Born in 1892, he would live out his life post-war in West Germany, becoming, for some time, the vice-chairman of War Resisters International,[429] before passing away in 1984.

In a clever and cynical move, Hitler decided to "democratically" ratify the exit from the League of Nations by taking the issue to the people in a plebiscite scheduled for November 12.[430] November 11 1918 had been declared as the day the German people lost their honour;

one day and fifteen years later, November 12 was recorded in the history of the German people as a day of national salvation.

On the following day, in the euphoria of the plebiscite outcome, the German Christians decided to stage a massive rally of twenty thousand in their favourite arena of the Berlin Sportpalast, resplendent in National Socialist flags and banners, declaring "One Reich. One People. One Church." For Reinhard Krause, a zealously patriotic high school teacher, his moment in the glorious limelight of a proud and reborn Germany had arrived.[431] However, unaware that his speech would be heard beyond the ideologically devoted audience in the Sportpalast, Krause let fly with radical rhetoric that only the most extreme disciples of the German Christian movement dared to utter amongst themselves.

In crude and bellicose language, he announced that the German church must purge itself of all vestiges of Judaism,[432] commencing with, but not stopping with, the unequivocal revocation of the Old Testament.[433] Next, the New Testament needed to be radically revised, to present a Jesus in line with all tenets of National Socialism.[434] Foremost in this regard was his mocking of the crucified Christ as a symbol of banal and defeatist weakness and all too "Jewish" in a time when Germany needed hope and victory.[435] In advocating the unbridled implementation of the Aryan Paragraph with the expulsion of every ethnic Jew from the church,[436] he demanded that every pastor swear an oath of personal allegiance to Hitler.[437] Krause gave the performance of his life, spurred on by profuse and sustained applause.[438]

The morning after, following the release of press reports, most Germans outside the Sportpalast were shocked and disgusted by his diatribe. It was one thing to advocate the restoration of German pride, but his mockery of the Bible, Saint Paul, Jesus, and so much else, had gone too far.[439] For mainstream Protestants, the German Christians became a band of heretical and fanatical Nazi thugs, while most of the Nazis who were overtly anti-Christian, such as Heinrich Himmler, and others who were nominal Christians only, such as Hitler, thought of them as a harmless joke.[440]

The German Christians had been useful to Hitler, firstly in garnering 600,000 votes[441] for him during the January 1933 election, and then in attempting to create a truly unified but bastardised German Church in the National Socialist image. However, after Reinhold Krause's indiscreet rant, all efforts to this end were in vain. Instead, a schism formed in the church when, at a synod held in Barmen in late May 1934, the Barmen declaration opposing the German Christian movement was published;[442] a few days later on June 4, it was published in the *London Times*.[443]

Its principle author was Karl Barth,[444] and Dietrich's close ties with Bishop George Bell were instrumental in the declaration's London publishing; Dietrich was then in the middle of his eighteen-month London pastorate. Born out of this document was the Bekennende Kirche — Confessing Church, which publicly announced its opposition to the pro-Nazi Reichskirche. However, its wording was clever in that it made it clear that they were not the ones causing the schism. Rather, it was the German Christians with their blatant bastardising of the church who were the real perpetrators, and thus devoid of any legitimacy. As a result, the star of Reichsbischoff Ludwig Müller would slowly wane over the years, culminating with his suicide soon after the Nazi capitulation in July 1945.[445]

A month or so before Reinhold Krause's embarrassment, Dietrich's decision to leave for his ministry in London was brought about in great part by his disillusionment with the direction that the German church was heading.[446] With the opportunity for regular contact with Bishop Bell, it was in mid-October 1933, that Dietrich commenced his eighteen-month London pastorate.

Chapter 5

London Pastorate and the Fanø Conference

When Dietrich moved into the parsonage of the German congregation in south London on October 17 1933, it meant a radical change in his life. To begin with, up until that day, he had lived in his parents' home, or, as was the case in Barcelona and New York, people kept house for him. While the Barcelona accommodation had been rather spartan, there in the more benign Catalan climate, he had not had to contend with anything like an English winter. The English accommodation, unlike what he had become accustomed to in Germany, was bereft of central heating and hot water. Until long after World War II's end, hardly any English private homes had central heating. Moreover, the windows wouldn't close properly and the wooden doors were warped. While there was a gas fire, it made no difference unless one sat directly in front of it, with mice scurrying around everywhere.[447]

In the first few months, Dietrich was often ill with colds and fever. But when spring came he could see that this house in Forest Hill was in an especially attractive part of London. There was a large garden with old trees, and just a short walk away was a famous park on a hill with a wonderful panorama, stretching deep into the Kentish countryside in the south, and to the north, offering a view of the world-renowned skyline of London. Visitors, too, would offer solace; from November, he had the company of Franz Hildebrandt, who stayed for three months. To him and other visitors, he offered meals and lodging without a great deal of bother. Indeed, in spite of the modest accommodation, all guests, in testament to Dietrich's welcoming and easygoing personality, gave glowing reports of their stay. Among them was the physicist Herbert Jehle, who had attended Dietrich's lectures on "Creation and Fall"; he often came over from Oxford, and would later turn up at Dietrich's underground Finkenwalde seminary.[448]

One man whose friendship meant as much to him as would his relationship with the English bishop George Bell was Karl Barth. After the latter had not backed Dietrich's proposed schism in response to the passing of the Aryan Paragraph at the Brown Synod in early September, a rift had developed between the two. Thus Dietrich only informed Barth by letter of his arrival in London on October 24 one week later. In the letter, Dietrich explained the isolation and fear he now felt even among friends he still felt personally close to, but was divided from by an ever widening ideological gap. Barth did not accept this as an excuse to leave Germany, but rather as the act of somebody running away from the real battle, wasting his "splendid theological armoury" while "the house of your church is on fire." In urging Dietrich to return to Berlin post-haste, he wrote that it was only because he felt so attached to Dietrich that he had "let fly" with his feelings on the matter.[449]

In context, Barth's rebuke appears unfair and overly harsh. Eighteen months later, upon Dietrich's return to Germany, this was emphasised unequivocally.[450] Dietrich had proven himself time and time again not to be the type to run away from a fight he saw as a just cause. The case of his storming into Berlin's Gestapo headquarters to confront its chief over blatant election interference was still only three months recent, and a perfect case in point. More to the point, if Müller, Heckel and company envisioned keeping Dietrich off the continent in Britain, where he would supposedly cause no "trouble" to the fascist regime, then they had chronically miscalculated.[451] The key factor was the much greater freedom Dietrich had to operate in London, and he exploited this to the full.

Beginning with deepening his relationships with the ecumenical world, assisted in no small part by Bishop George Bell, Dietrich used his charismatic influence to enlighten other expatriate German pastors in London in regard to the true nature of the Third Reich. His great success in doing so is indicated by the fact that, of all countries with expatriate German congregations, England was the only nation where German pastors joined the Pastors' Emergency League, and later, the Confessing Church.[452] In February 1934, Heckel travelled to London to meet seven German pastors, of whom Dietrich was one, to instruct them to refrain from ecumenical activity not directly authorised by Berlin. Dietrich's reply and subsequent actions were predictable. On March 5 1934, Dietrich was summoned to meet Heckel in Berlin. Heckel again demanded that Dietrich cease his agitation and sign the required document. Now in Berlin, Dietrich had the sense not to be openly defiant, but to stall by saying that he needed time to consider the document. On his return to London, Dietrich wrote to Heckel with his refusal to sign the document.[453]

Dietrich's trips back to Berlin were quite frequent, every few weeks or so. Moreover, he ran up a huge telephone bill, keeping in regular contact with Gerhard Jacobi, Martin Niemöller, and his mother, who was as immersed in the church struggle as anyone else. At one stage, the local Post Office reduced the phone bill,[454] whether out of disbelief or pity. However, one thing is clear: Dietrich didn't use the post in England, to avoid trouble at home.

Of all the friendships Dietrich formed in London, that with Bishop George Bell was the closest, and politically the most significant. From 1933 onwards, Hitler tried to curry favour with the international community, and had many friends and allies in English aristocratic circles, including King Edward VIII (King from January 1936 to December 1936),[455] who abdicated his throne to marry the American divorcee Wallis Simpson. Bishop George Bell was certainly not among Hitler's friends. Like Karl Barth, he was two decades plus Dietrich's senior, sharing with Dietrich a February 4th birthday. Bell had been a student at Christ Church Oxford and became involved in the ecumenical movement following the Great War. In 1935, while Dean of Canterbury, he commissioned T. S. Eliot to write the play *Murder in the Cathedral*; it dramatised the murder of Thomas à Becket, which had taken place in that very cathedral in 1170. The play, an obvious criticism of the Third Reich, had its première on the June 15 1935, likewise in that same cathedral.[456]

In later years, Dietrich would be Bell's principal source of news from inside the Third Reich. In 1938, Bell received a seat in the House of Lords,[457] and his standing and prestige carried a great deal of weight when he conveyed this news to the British public, often with letters to the *London Times*. Ultimately, Dietrich Bonhoeffer and Bishop George Bell were critical in galvanising British opinion against the Third Reich.[458] Moreover, it seems that Bell's influence was not lost on Hitler. On November 6, 1934, Joachim von Ribbentrop, Hitler's foreign minister, would meet with Bell, and would do so again in 1935, as would Rudolf Hess[459] later that same year.

Amongst the German pastors in London was Pastor Julius Rieger, then in his early thirties. In the years to come, Julius Rieger would work closely with Dietrich and George Bell, and upon Dietrich's permanent return to Germany in 1935, he would become Bell's main German contact. Rieger was the pastor of St. George's Church in London's East End, which quickly became the epicentre for refugees from Germany. In becoming so involved in the plight of the German refugees, Bishop Bell would be dubbed the "bishop to refugees."[460] When Sabine and Gerhard Leibholz were forced to leave Germany in 1938, Bell, Rieger, and St. George's Church were of critical importance, as they would also be for Franz Hildebrandt, when he too was forced to leave Germany in 1937. Most appropriately, Franz would become a pastor at St. George's.

On August 2 1934, in the middle of Dietrich's London ministry, the German president Paul von Hindenburg died. This was only a month after the bloody purge of Röhm's SA,[461] and just eight days following the assassination of Austria's Federal Chancellor Engelbert Dollfuß by Austrian Nazis. But public sentiment in Germany was overwhelmingly preoccupied with the death at age 86 of their great war hero at his home in Neudeck in East Prussia,[462] now Ogrodzieniec in Poland.[463] Hitler's cabinet, aware Hindenburg was on his death bed, had agreed upon a law to come into force from the very moment of the Reich President's death, in which the joint responsibilities of President and Chancellor were amalgamated into the single office of "Der Führer."[464] Or as Dietrich would have put it, Der Verführer.

When Hindenburg was buried in Prussian military style in the Tannenberg Mausoleum, the memorial to Germany's victory over Russia in the Great War, Hitler's farewell cry, "Departed Chief, now enter into Valhalla!" was regarded by many as being in bad taste.[465] While Hitler presented himself as a loyal follower and now the successor of Hindenburg, when he assumed the office of Reich President, he took great care never to be addressed by that title, but rather, as "Führer and Reich Chancellor." School children were being taught at the time that this was out of respect for the great Field Marshal Hindenburg, but of course, this personal title of Hitler's was intended to make it clear that with the last relic of the vanquished Weimar Republic gone, the country was now governed by one single and indomitable will.[466]

With Hindenburg's passing, coupled with the unrest in Austria provoked by Hitler, Dietrich realised that the ominous possibility of another major war was one step closer; in this critical context, the Ecumenical Conference was held on the Danish island of Fanø from the 18th to the 30th of August.[467] One of the pivotal issues for the conference was the Ascension Day[468] pastoral letter which Bishop Bell had sent to all World Alliance and Universal Council member churches. The German question almost immediately took centre stage in the discussions of whether to approve or reject Bell's letter, with Heckel, the head of the German church's Foreign Office, trying desperately to have it rejected. The resolution was passed in favour of Bell's letter, which condemned the use of force by Müller and August Jäger, their autocratic government, the ban on free discussion, and the loyalty oath, instituted by Müller, which German pastors had to swear to Hitler after Hindenburg's death.[469]

Dietrich did not take part in these discussions, but he had already said all that was necessary to those who would discuss it, including Bishop Bell, the Swedish Bishop Ammundsen, and Dr. Henry Smith Leiper, whom he knew casually while in the Union Seminary in New York. Leiper recalled their conservation as follows: "

> When I asked what his reply had been to the Bishop's order, he said with a grim smile: 'Negative.' Amplifying that laconic remark he said: 'I told him he would have to come to London to get me if he wanted me out of that church.' With utter candour and fearless scorn he talked of what the followers of Christ must be prepared to do in resisting Nazi Caesarism and its penetration of spiritual domains. From that it was quite plain to me that he was prepared to fight the régime of Ludwig Müller. Yet at no point in our conversation did he show any concern for what might be the consequences of his decision to oppose openly the whole effort of Hitlerism to take over the control of the Church in Germany. Nor did he show the least doubt that the discerning Christians would have to deal realistically with the most dangerous and unscrupulous dictator who believed that he could achieve his plan for making what he called 'practical Christianity" a source of power and influence for his political platform."[470]

Sadly, however, what seemed at the time a major victory for the Confessing Church would in the long term prove to be short-lived. Heckel was able to have inserted into the resolution a seemingly insignificant amendment stating that the council wanted to stay in "friendly contact with all of the groups in the German Evangelical Church." The word "group" was the operative word, as it implied an equal footing in the world council for both the Reichskirche and the Confessing Church. Heckel's deft political manoeuvre had effectively defused Dietrich's valid claim that the German Christians and their Reichskirche were heretical and as such could not be recognised as the German church.[471] In time, the council's staff in Geneva would come to regret not making a clean break with Heckel and the Reichskirche.[472] As Eberhard Bethge, Dietrich's future great friend and first biographer wrote, the ecumenical movement would never go any further in its commitment to the Confessing Church. "Fanø," he wrote, "did not represent a first step, but a short-lived climax."[473]

Today, Fanø is most remembered for Dietrich's speeches, which he delivered with commanding presence. In particular, two of them related to "The Churches and Peace," which was apt in the context of the assassination of the Austrian chancellor Engelbert Dollfuß. It had thrown Austria into turmoil, with Germany threatening to invade at any moment, while at the same time, Mussolini was threatening to invade Ethiopia.[474] In his speech on Tuesday morning August 28, 1934, Dietrich espoused the concept of obedience and faith in Christ as the means to true peace, counter to the political demands of nationalism and internationalism: "

> Let me hear what God the Lord will speak: for he will speak peace to his people, and to his faithful (Psalm 85:8). Between the twin crags of nationalism and internationalism, ecumenical Christendom calls upon its Lord and asks for guidance. Nationalism and internationalism have to do with political necessities and possibilities. The ecumenical church movement, however, does not concern itself with these things, but with the commandments of God, and regardless of consequences it transmits these commandments to the world... Peace on earth is not a problem, but a commandment given at Christ's coming. There are two ways of reacting to this command from God: the unconditional, blind obedience of action, or the hypocritical question of the Serpent: 'Did God say... ?' This question is the mortal enemy of obedience, and therefore the mortal enemy of all real peace... Has God not understood human nature well enough to know that wars must occur in this world, like laws of nature? Must God not have meant that we should talk about peace, to be sure, but that it is not to be literally translated into action? Must God not really have said that we should work for peace, of course, but also make ready tanks and poison gas for security? And then perhaps the most serious question: Did God say you should not protect your own people? Did God say you should leave your own a prey to the enemy?

> No, God did not say all that. What God has said is that there shall be peace among all people — that we shall obey God without further question, that is what God means. Anyone who questions the commandment of God before obeying has already denied God...

> Why do we fear the fury of the world powers? Why don't we take the power from them and give it back to Christ? We can still do it today. The Ecumenical Council is in session; it can

send out to all believers this radical call to peace. The nations are waiting for it in the East and in the West. Must we be put to shame by non-Christian peoples in the East?... We want to give the world a whole word, not half a word — a courageous word, a Christian word. We want to pray that this word may be given us, today. Who knows if we shall see each other again another year?"[475]

During the twelve days of Fanø, a youth conference also took place, where Dietrich's hope that it would result in some bold resolutions of real substance was not in vain. In the true spirit of Dietrich's speech, the fifty delegates drew up two resolutions. The first was that God's commandments emphatically overruled any claims by state; it was passed with the barest of margins, with Dietrich's Berlin students registering contrary votes. The second condemned Christian support for "any war whatsoever"; Polish and Hungarian delegates,[476] understandably, suggested an amendment to a condemnation of "aggressive war" rather than "any war whatsoever." This, however, was not accepted by the other delegates, perhaps being mindful of all nations claiming they were fighting a "defensive war" in the previous world conflict. Furthermore, there was a lively debate on conscientious objection; one must commend the bravery of the German students to discuss such matters,[477] given, for one thing, the presence of Heckel and his cronies at Fanø.

During the days between formal sessions, Dietrich and the youth conference participants gathered on the Fanø beaches for informal discussions, still dressed as they were during the official meetings. During one such seaside conversation, a Swede asked Dietrich what he would do if war came. Considering the fact that Dietrich had three brothers who took up arms in the Great War, which led to the death of his brother Walter in April 1918, this question was relevant. Moreover, Dietrich had served a brief two-week stint as an Igel ("Hedgehog" Fraternity that Dietrich was a member of during his university days in Tübingen in 1923)[478] with the Ulm Rifles, and was acutely aware of the disastrous path to conquest and war that Hitler intended to lead Germany along. According to those present, Dietrich quietly scooped up a handful of sand and let it run out between his fingers as he pondered the question and his answer. Then looking calmly at the young man, he replied, "I pray that God will give me the strength then not to take up a weapon."[479]

Dietrich's pause before answering may have been because he was speculating on the consequences of being a conscientious objector in the Third Reich. In the first year of the war, 112 German soldiers were executed, most for conscientious objection; of these, the great majority were Jehovah's witnesses. Among the German Protestants, there was only one, Hermann Stöhr; among the Catholics, there was only the Austrian priest Franz Reinisch, who in turn persuaded the farmer Franz Jägerstätte to do likewise.[480] When one looks past the German Jehovah's witnesses, the number of conscientious objectors in the Third Reich was minimal. Hence the dearth of sources on them.

Certainly, the resolutions passed at Fanø were idealistic. As the thirties rolled by, ever closer to the inevitable outbreak of war, it would become clear that their words of idealism could not match with the dire political and strategic reality of Europe at the time. In May 1939, seven or so months following Britain and France's humiliating peace/appeasement in the 1938 Czech-Sudeten crisis, a few months before the outbreak of war, and just days before Dietrich's second sojourn in the US, he would pose to his students the question: "Would you grant absolution to the murderer of a tyrant?"[481] By that time, Dietrich had realised that any negotiated peace with Hitler was pointless,[482] a manifestation of "cheap grace,"[483] as Dietrich would write during the thirties in his famous work *Nachfolge* (*Discipleship*). On September 1 1939,[484] with the invasion of Poland, Hitler would violate the peace resolutions of Fanø, but at the same time, in rightly taking up arms in its defence, so too would Poland.

Before returning to London in 1934, Dietrich spent time in Göttingen with his twin sister Sabine and brother-in-law Gerhard Leibholz, and then in Würzburg, where he met with some of the Confessing Church leaders. Lastly, he visited Jean Lasserre at his mining village church in the north of France.[485] At Fanø, Dietrich had caught up with him for the first time since they left New York in June 1931. Dietrich was moved by Lasserre's solidarity with the poor people in his congregation, and like other guests in his village, he took part in street preaching as part of an evangelisation drive.

However, his visit to Göttingen was rather disturbing. The daughters Marianne and Christiane were being subjected to ridicule; for example, one of Christiane's friends called out over the fence "Your father is a Jew." A few days later, a noticeboard was fixed to one of the trees in front of the school; on it was written "The Father of the Jew is the Devil." Every day their daughters had to pass under this notice with taunts from the mob. Opposite the school was a box with the Nazi newspaper *Der Stürmer*, resplendent with anti-Semitic propaganda claiming fabricated instances of sexual crimes of the most obscene kind, and sadistic ritual acts allegedly practised by Jews.[486] Here at this box, the more senior school children would throng to consume the offal of state-sanctioned racism and character assassination. On the Herzberger Landstrasse, where Gerhard and Sabine lived alongside many other Göttingen professors, the SA often marched down it on Sunday mornings, singing "Soldiers, comrades, hang the Jews, shoot the Jews"; years later after the war, this memory would still send shudders down Sabine's spine.[487]

Over the years, Dietrich had expressed his desire to visit Mahatma Gandhi at his ashram in India; he was attracted to his philosophy of passive resistance. He had already considered doing so when he left America in June 1931.[488] In May 1934, just three or so months before Fanø, he had written to his paternal grandmother Julie of his wish to visit India. As he wrote to her, it sometimes felt to him that there was more Christianity in their "heathenism than in the whole of our Reich Church"; he alluded to the origins of Christianity in the East, which had in the modern era become "so westernised and so permeated by purely civilised thought," it had been "almost lost to us."[489] Upon his return to London, Bishop Bell wrote to Gandhi in India on Dietrich's behalf, seeking to finalise plans for Dietrich's long-delayed trip there, and on the first day of November 1934, about two months after his return to London, Dietrich received a letter of invitation from the great man himself.[490]

So Dietrich made plans to travel to the exotic east of India, to become a pupil of Gandhi. Julius Rieger expressed his desire to accompany Dietrich, and the two friends searched for the cheapest and most expeditious means of travel, and read whatever they could find about India and its culture. For various reasons, these plans were abandoned, beginning with the considerable follow-up work after Fanø, and later because Dietrich was needed back in Germany to set up the intended preacher's seminary in Pomerania. Post-war, pastor Gerhard Jacobi, the highly decorated Great War hero, who in July 1933 had accompanied Dietrich to confront the Gestapo, said with some pride that he was the one who had thwarted Dietrich's trip to India. As Jacobi put it: "At my instigation, the Confessing Church called Bonhoeffer to a preachers' seminary which was to be set up ... I also wanted to keep Bonhoeffer away from India by directing him towards a serious task to be done with young Germans."[491]

Karl Barth also had reservations about Dietrich's admiration for Gandhi.[492] Remembering Barth's rebuke back in October 1933, Dietrich had, by now, little choice other than to return to Germany. In Britain, Dietrich had, through his close friendship with Bishop George Bell, played a major role in swaying British opinion against Hitler, and indeed, that of his German expatriate congregation. India, however, was far removed from the scene in Europe, and it was more important for Dietrich to return to the theological fight in Germany.

Before his return to Berlin in mid-April, the Saar Plebiscite was carried out in accordance with the terms of the Versailles Treaty in January 1935.[493] This coal rich region of 2,500 square kilometres[494] in Germany's south-west was ceded to France in 1920 to compensate the nation for the destruction of its northern coal mines during the war.[495] However, unlike the permanent secession of Alsace-Lorraine to the French, after fifteen years, the ethnic German inhabitants of Saar had the opportunity to vote in a plebiscite for the sovereignty they so desired.

The significance of this plebiscite was that by January 1935, numerous German refugees had fled there from Germany following Hitler's rise to power in January 1933, and their fear was that if the ethnic German population of Saar voted to be incorporated into the Third Reich, their political asylum would be terminated, thus precipitating, as Julius Rieger and Dietrich foresaw, a flood of refugees to London.[496] Indeed, ominously, and in the true spirit of a step towards "vanquishing the humiliation of Versailles," the vote was a resounding vindication for Hitler, with over ninety percent voting for the Saar region's incorporation into the Third Reich.[497] With Dietrich's forewarning of the flood of refugees from the Saar region, Bishop Bell, with his assistance, was able to make the first preparations for aiding the refugees himself before Dietrich's return to Germany. Julius Rieger ably took over the mantle of George Bell's assistant in these matters.

Admittedly, there was one minor price Hitler had to pay for this otherwise significant political coup. This was the dismissal of August Jäger, the legal counsel for the Reichkirche, in which Dietrich played a significant role. He did this through his contact with George Bell, who visited the German embassy in London before he persuaded the Archbishop of Canterbury to summon the German Ambassador to Lambeth Palace. Earlier, Hitler received warnings from several sources that if further measures were taken against the Church in Germany, the Saar vote would go against him, and thus in response, Hitler had August Jäger immediately dismissed from all the offices he held.[498]

In 1938, Jäger left the church, and during the war was involved in serious war crimes in Poland. After the war he was condemned to death and hanged on June 17, 1949 in Poznań.[499] Overall, however, the Saar plebiscite was a resounding political coup for Hitler. An article in Kalgoorlie's[xv] *Western Argus* on January 29, 1935 clearly illustrates the naive perception held by many in the international community about Germany's vertically challenged, brown haired demagogue. "

> It will be a great thing for Europe if the return of the Saar to Germany leads to a reconciliation between France and Germany and the re-entry of the Reich to the League of Nations. Upon hearing the result of the plebiscite, Herr Hitler stated:
>
> 'With the return of the Saar there will be no more territorial claims by Germany against France. I declare, no more claims will be raised by us. We are now certain that the time has come for appeasement and reconciliation. I want to express my gratitude and satisfaction for the loyal help other countries have given through difficult days by guaranteeing orderly procedure during the plebiscite. We want to assure the world of our deep desire for the preservation of peace, just as we are determined to win back our equality of rights in the fullest measure, and afterwards co-operate fully in the creation and preservation of that international solidarity which is essential to the welfare of the peoples of the world.'
>
> If France can be brought to agree to a reasonable measure of re-armament by Germany, which really means agreeing to an accomplished fact, and if Hitler is sincere in his peaceful protestations, there should be a period of tranquillity ahead of the sorely troubled peoples of Europe."[500]

We read this today with hindsight. But the thuggery and intimidation of the Brown Shirts during Hitler's ascent to power, their subsequent bloody purge in June 1934, the infamous literary *Säuberung* (cleansing/book burning) on the night of May 11 1933, the oppressive acts passed in the wake of the highly suspicious Reichstag fire of late February 1933, and the countless anti-Jewish measures already embodied

---

[xv] Kalgoorlie is a gold mining town in Western Australia about 550 kilometres east-north-east of the state capital Perth.

by the Aryan Paragraph, should have given clear warnings of what was to come. However, with all too recent memories of the slaughter and general horrors of the Great War, in which Australia, with a population of fewer than five million, enlisted 416,809 men, and lost 60,000 of the cream of its youth, with a further 156,000 wounded, gassed or taken prisoner,[501] the author's hope that the Saar Plebiscite and the words of Herr Hitler would be a watershed for European peace and for peace for the youth of his country, is understandable.

Chapter 6

Old Prussia — Birth of Ruth to Precarious Survival

In the heyday of Old Prussia, on February 4, 1867, Ruth Ehrengard Gräfin von Zedlitz-Trützschler, was born and christened on the grand Lower Silesian estate of Grossenborau,[xvi] with none other than the illustrious Otto von Bismarck present at the christening.[502]

Post-World War II, Germany's history is virtually bereft of any mention of Prussia — the nation state that had dominated the proud and unified Germany or Second Reich, founded in January 1871,[503] in the wake of its glorious victory over the French in the Franco-Prussian War.[504] Wilhelm I, then King of Prussia, a title which he retained, was adorned with the additional title of Emperor or "Kaiser" of the newly unified Germany. However, the true architect of German unification was the politically astute and adept Prussian Prime Minister Otto von Bismarck (1815-1898), who now became the Chancellor of the newly united Germany.[505] As if to accentuate French humiliation, the ceremony witnessed by the father and future father-in-law of the young child Ruth, was held in the most grand of all French palaces — Versailles.[506] Decades later, in 1914, Kaiser Wilhelm I's grandson, Kaiser Wilhelm II (1859-1941), led the Second Reich into the Great War, but by early November 1918, was forced into abdication and subsequent exile in Holland,[507] until his death in 1941.[508] Seven months later, in June 1919, in the same palace of Versailles, Germany, rather than celebrating the dawn of a grand new era, was compelled to sign the humiliating treaty of Versailles.

In spite of Prussia's dominant position in 1871, not all of the Prussian landed gentry embraced this notion of Otto von Bismarck's unified Reich. One such dissenter was Ruth's future father-in-law and Bismarck's oldest friend and bachelor roommate, Hans Hugo von Kleist-Retzow.[509] However, Prussia remained the most dominant state in Germany until 1945, before it was formally dissolved by the Allied powers on February 25, 1947.[510]

[xvi] Upper Silesia is upstream on the Odor (Polish: Odra) River from Lower Silesia. Breslau/Wrocław is in Lower Sielsia. See footnote [xlvi] for Polish WWII Supplement II "The Gleiwitz (Gliwice) Incident" for further clarification.

In April 1882, Ruth's father Robert first pointed out the young Jürgen von Kleist-Retzow to the impressionable fifteen-year-old Ruth from his governor's box.[511] This was during a concert outside Oppeln in the military compound; Ruth was instantly enchanted by his dashing presence. However, until Jürgen's formal written proposal to Ruth in October 1885,[512] their meetings were fleeting. Before writing his letter, as was the custom, Jürgen had asked Ruth's father for permission. Ruth had yearned for Jürgen, and was resigned that she would never see him again, much less marry him. Upon reading Jürgen's letter, Ruth's reply was: "tausendmal ja!" — "a thousand times yes!"[513] Now, as a young wife, she had an inordinate fear that she would lose him again, during his overnight absences in performing his duties as the district Landrat. Only death, years later in 1897,[514] would permanently separate them. After which, Ruth never married again.

In 1885, Charlotte, the wife of Jürgen's father Hans Hugo von Kleist, passed away. Her death left her husband so distraught, that he could not bear the thought of burying his wife,[515] and so had her laid in a casket in the church crypt. Seven years later, when Hans Hugo passed away, he was also laid in a casket in the church crypt next to his wife. When Ruth's husband Jürgen first showed her the crypt of his deceased mother in February 1886,[xvii] just days after their marriage at Grossenborau, Ruth, a native Silesian, incorrectly perceived this as a bizarre Pomeranian tradition, since only in the extreme depths of winter would the Silesians not immediately bury their own.[516]

Five or so years later in November 1897, when Hans Hugo's son and Ruth's dear husband Jürgen died at age 43,[517] Ruth decided to have him laid to rest beside his parents in the crypt; Jürgen's unmarried brother and sister had been reluctant to bury their parents in the Kieckow cemetery.[518] For months, Ruth dressed and was veiled in black. Ruth's father, Robert senior, visited seven or so months later in June 1898, and insisted that his daughter must put the past and her grief to bed, under the responsibility that she now bore as the widowed mistress of the grand estate of Kieckow.[519] Ruth conceded to her father the need to move on and accept the responsibility thrust upon her by her husband's death. At the burial, the priest accordingly declared the time for

---

[xvii] Jürgen was Ruth's husband. Hans Jürgen was Jürgen and Ruth's first child. See the family tree on page 394 of *Matriarch of Conspiracy : Ruth von Kleist 1867-1945* by Jane Pejsa, originally published by Kenwood Publishing, Minneapolis, Minnesota 1991 and in 1992 by The Pilgrim Press, Cleveland Ohio 44115, ISBN 0829809317.

mourning at Kieckow over, while the weekly ritual of Ruth taking her children below into the ancestral crypt likewise ceased forthwith.[520] Nevertheless, the caskets of Hans Hugo and his wife Charlotte remained in the crypt until the cataclysm of 1945.xviii

Having now, in the second-half of 1898, put the grief of her husband's death behind her, the widowed Ruth realised that the modern and increasingly industrial times at the cusp of the twentieth century meant that local schooling was inadequate for her children's future, so she decided, late that year, to leave the Kieckow estate in the capable hands of her cousin Fritz von Wödtke, and moved to a large town house in Stettin (now modern-day Polish Szczecin)[521] to mind the children during their gymnasium education.[522]

That year as well, Ruth's elder brother, Robert junior, started serving in the Imperial Court in Berlin. Until 1903, he would serve as the personal adjutant to Prince Joachim of Prussia, born in 1890[523] as the sixth and youngest son of Kaiser Wilhelm II.[524] As impressive as this may sound, the down-to-earth nobleman, Robert, regarded his role as nothing more than playing nursemaid to a petulant boy, insistent on embarrassing the royal family.[525] However, in 1903, he would be promoted to the office of *Hofmarschall* (Court Marshall — chief administrator) for the Kaiser's court, and serve there until his resignation in 1910.[526] In spite of the promotion to the Kaiser's inner circle, his opinion of the Kaiser's court did not change. Throughout his twelve years in the Kaiser's court, he was frustrated in his efforts to bring about any sort of reform in what he believed to be a Byzantine circle of hangers-on, who distracted, misled and even infected the Kaiser with their gossip and petty intrigues.[527]

During the reception in Stettin in October 1908 for the wedding of Ruth's first daughter Spes to the local industrial magnate Walter Stahlberg, Ruth's father, Robert senior, expressed his agreement with his son's view of a vainglorious Kaiser who only listened to the worst advice.[528] As they were conversing in what they thought was a secluded corner of the resplendent Hotel Preussenhof, Robert senior peered over his son's shoulder to notice his daughter Ruth had been listening to every word. Brother Robert junior implored his sister not to allow the Kaiser to come between himself and her.[529] While Ruth seemed to heed his plea then, it was not so sixteen years later, when Robert junior's book

---

xviii The cataclysm of 1945 will be discussed in Chapter 25 "Old Prussia Gone With The Wind."

was published, documenting the litany of petty intrigues in the Kaiser's court.[530]

In February 1912, Robert senior saw the Kaiser as indecisive to the point of being dangerous, pontificating in domestic politics while threatening in matters of foreign policy, yet incapable of acting consistently in either.[531] In 1890, just two years into the reign of Kaiser Wilhelm II, Chancellor Otto von Bismarck, the architect of German unification, resigned after a major fall-out.[532] Eight years later in 1898, the year Robert junior entered the Kaiser's court, Bismarck passed away in his estate near Hamburg.[533]

Throughout Prussia, there was the sense that the Kaiser and his chancellor did not possess political acumen, such as Bismarck had shown, to ensure the survival of Old Prussia, and a united Imperial Germany in general.[534] Intellectual naysayers in Berlin, and even Gertrud von Bismarck, a fellow Pomeranian Junker and great niece of Otto von Bismarck, were predicting the downfall of the Kaiser and the monarchy within Ruth's lifetime.[535] Such talk was depressing for the proud Ruth, in spite of her admission, deep down, of the shortcomings of her Kaiser, as previously elaborated by her brother. As Jane Pejsa commented: "

> Still, one man's reign is nothing in comparison to the five centuries that have gone into the building of an orderly system in which every man and woman has a designated place and set of responsibilities and privileges to go with it. Besides, it is all part of God's plan, a secular order in parallel with, yet subservient to, the spiritual order in which Jesus Christ reigns supreme. Whatever the future holds, if the monarchy is threatened and duty calls, Ruth will be there, and she has absolute confidence that all her children, from Hans Jürgen to Ruthchen, will be there too."[536]

On July 28, 1914, the fears of a now ailing Robert senior and his son, and the call to arms of Ruth's family, were realised when the empire of Austria-Hungary declared war on Serbia.[537] On the face of it, this should have just been a minor localised spat,[538] but the intricate web of European alliances, supposedly fostered to avert war, precipitated what would become the most cataclysmic war so far. A domino effect of mobilisation orders and declarations of war by Europe's major powers, starting with Russia's declaration of war on Austria in solidarity with their fellow Serbian Slavic brethren,[xix] [539] then Germany entering the fight in solidarity with their Germanic Austrian kinsmen, triggered a war that far exceeded what they had planned or desired.[540]

Germany's subsequent invasion of neutral Luxembourg on August 2 and Belgium on August 4, as the "back door" to France, in accordance with the Schlieffen Plan, compelled Britain's entry.[541] The original conflict between Austria and Serbia that triggered this war was brought about by the assassination of Archduke Franz Ferdinand of Austria, heir to the throne of Austria-Hungary, by Bosnian-Serbian nationalist Gavrilo Princip in Sarajevo on June 28 1914.[542] Ironically, in terms of the worldwide scenario that became World War I, it would devolve into little more than a side show.[543] By October 1914, a despondent Robert senior, passed away.[544]

When war broke out, Ruth was living at her flat in Stettin, as her youngest, Ruthchen, was still completing her Gymnasium (senior high school) education.[545] Now, with the call to war, Ruth and her youngest daughter headed back to Kieckow to take charge of affairs at their Kieckow estate. The call to arms of all young men in Germany left their estate with a major shortfall in manpower. Before long, they would have the company of the rest of the von Kleist children and their mothers.[546] At this stage, they felt confident their boys would be home by Christmas. This is certainly what Ruth prayed for. But for the time being, the Oma (grandmother), aged forty-seven, felt honoured to be called upon to protect the family bastion and hold down the eastern flank of the Hohenzollern (Kaiser's dynasty) kingdom.[547] As the war dragged on well past the Christmas of 1914, Ruth's youngest would be pivotal in keeping the estate afloat and functioning, as Ruth had assigned her the task of balancing the ledgers.[548] The young Ruthchen would usually appear for morning and evening prayer, but rarely any time in between. Her sisters speculated that Ruthchen would be the unmarried one, like Ruth's dour sister-in-law, Elisabeth von Kleist.[549]

Ruth's two boys, the eldest Hans Jürgen and third child Konstantin, her favourite and most gifted,[550] naturally honoured their call to arms. The latter initially served in the trenches, firstly on the eastern front against the Imperial Russian army, but in 1916,[551] he was transferred west to fight in the iconic and bitter Battle of Verdun against the French, and to a lesser extent, the British, in 1916. For most of that year,

---

[xix] Slavs include Russians, Ukrainians, Belorussians, Czechs, Slovakians, Serbs, Croats and Poles, all categorised as *Untermensch* (sub-human) in the National Socialist dogma. See the endnote [539] from this chapter for more information.

from February 21—December 18, the French endured a major German offensive before finally repelling it. It was one of the longest, bloodiest, and most ferocious battles of the war: French casualties amounted to about 400,000, German ones to about 350,000. Some 300,000 were killed.[552] In December 1916, as the Battle of Verdun finally drew to a bitter close, there was a civilian death that, for the young survivor of Verdun, Konstantin, felt like a death in the family. He was Wilhelm Merton, the Jewish founder of a prosperous metallurgical firm in Frankfurt am Main, and close friend of Robert senior. This friendship had led to Konstantin's employment at the firm in the pre-war years. Konstantin regarded Merton more as a second father than a boss.[553]

In 1917, there were two revolutions in Russia. In February, the Tsarist regime fell.[554] The Tsar and his family were initially detained within the Tsarist capital, Petrograd (pre-war Saint Petersburg), but in August 1917 were deported to Tobolsk in western Siberia.[555] The new regime, however, was still committed to Russia's participation in the war. Then, in November (October by the Julian calendar still in use in Russia), Lenin's Bolsheviks seized power. Among other items on their agenda was the withdrawal of Russia from the war, culminating with the signing of the peace treaty, humiliating for Russia, of Brest-Litovsk in modern-day Belarus in March 1918.[556] This "dictated peace" compelled Russia to concede eighteen provinces and nearly 30 percent of its pre-war population.[557] This included vast swathes of land such as the three Baltic states (Lithuania, Lativa and Estonia) and virtually the entire territory of the modern-day Ukraine.[558] In June 1918, near Ekaterinburg in western Siberia, the entire Tsarist royal family was executed by the Bolsheviks.[559]

Normally, for the Junkers, a collapse of a neighbouring monarchy to the Bolsheviks would trigger alarm bells. But with the war now ending against Russia, thousands of troops that were committed to fighting pre-Bolshevik Russia were now free to engage the enemy on the Western Front. In March 1918, the sound of steam whistles was ubiquitous in the von Kleist lands, as battle hardened troops from the east made their way west.[560] On the other hand, the super-power[561] of the USA had officially entered the war in April 1917, and by now, were amassing in great numbers on the Western Front.[562]

Ruth no doubt found the end of the war on the Eastern Front welcome news. But in early October 1917, as the second revolution in Russia was brewing, she received a dreaded telegram. Since it was not addressed to her daughter-in-law Mieze, the wife of Hans Jürgen, she knew that it was to inform her of the death of her favourite and most gifted child,[563] the unmarried Konstantin.[564] By this time, Konstantin was no longer fighting in the trenches, as he had become a pilot. On October 7, his plane was shot down near Verdun. Initially, he survived the crash, but later succumbed to his wounds. Within hours of learning the tragic news on the 8th, Ruth, for the first time in twenty years since the death of her husband Jürgen, was dressed in her blackest gown. On Wednesday 10, she received a personal telegram dated the 9th from the German Crown Prince, Wilhelm, the eldest child and heir to the Kaiser; this offered the proud Junker matriarch some comfort. For her, it was a reminder that for the Fatherland, some must die.[565] Unlike the death of her husband twenty years earlier, Ruth realised there was now no time for prolonged morbid self-pity. In the following month of November, Ruth gathered with five women and six children of her clan to pray and dedicate the newly laid headstone:

Konstantin von Kleist-Retzow
1891-1917
"With wings like eagles"

There were no tears.[566]

In 1918, the character of the war transformed from one of trench stalemate to one of mobile warfare.[567] In the spring, the German Army on the Western Front, reinvigorated with battle-hardened rein-forcements from the east, turned this to their advantage, and at one stage, were even threatening Paris.[568] However, as their supply lines became over-extended, coupled with the US Army now making its presence felt, the fortunes of war turned against the Germans. The Aus-tralian General John Monash was one of the first and most prominent to grasp the significance of the new mobile warfare, where the use of tanks gave great force and mobility.[569]

Nevertheless, as dire as Imperial Germany's plight was in the late summer of 1918, the Prussian aristocracy was still determined to find ways to perpetuate itself.[570] In late August, the dashing Hans von Wedemeyer, in the quest for a wife, visited Kieckow. For all the women present, the matriarch and Ruthchen included,[571] he possessed a com-pelling charm as he recalled his early war years in France,[572] and later in Palestine under Franz von Papen,[573] who would, in the early 1930s, figure prominently in Hitler's rise to power.[574] Weeks later, in October 1918, with the German monarchy now on the brink of collapse following more than four years of bitter war and a British naval blockade that led to dire food shortages,[575] an appeal was made to the US government for an armistice.[576] There were hopes for the killing on the Western Front to end, but also, grave fears that a bloody Bolshevik revolution would follow in its wake.[577] Nevertheless, the hunt at Kieckow still took place. Hans von Wedemeyer, staying at nearby Köslin, where he was undergoing pilot training,[578] was invited as the principal guest.

After breakfast one morning, Hans asked to speak privately to the matriarch. When he requested her permission to marry her youngest, Ruth naturally asked him; "Do you love my daughter?," to which he replied with candid honesty, "No, but I do know that I would like to marry her and that I must marry her; I believe that this assurance is the most important basis for a marriage." To which Ruth replied, "Do you believe then that my daughter loves you?"[579] Hans replied, "I have no idea whether or not she loves me. Why, I have hardly spoken a word to her!"[580]

When Ruth discussed the matter with her two older daughters, Spes and Maria, and daughter-in-law Mieze, they were all incensed. Just because their mother and mother-in-law was enchanted by this young officer in uniform, did not mean she should hand over her youngest on a silver platter.[581] The following day, Ruth arranged a wagon ride with Hans at the reins, Ruthchen seated next to him, and Ruth riding in the wagon behind. Hans did most of the talking. The following morning, after a curious exchange between the couple in the corridor before breakfast, the two become betrothed. The matriarch was happy; she firmly believed, in spite of the intransigence of her elder daughters and daughter-in-law, that Hans was Ruthchen's prince charming, just as Jürgen was for her over three decades earlier.[582]

A fortnight later, Hans was back at Kieckow, temporarily relieved of his military duties owing to a bout of influenza. War or no war, Junker tradition dictated the obligation of every young man to introduce his betrothed to his mother within three days of the engagement. Although this time had passed, the couple boarded a southbound train at Gross Tychow to travel to the estate of Hans's widowed mother in the Neumark region.[583] Unlike her mother a generation before, who found the Pomeranian estate of Kieckow spartan in comparison to the opulence of her childhood home of Grossenborau in Lower Silesia, the young Ruthchen was in awe of her future husband's childhood home. She was pleasantly surprised with the warmth and open affection of Hans's elegant mother. From this point, all doubt that Ruthchen may have had in regard to this marriage vanished like the late morning mist.[584] In turn, her mother was vindicated. This union would give birth to the future fiancée of Dietrich.

The following month of November, the unthinkable event for the Junkers took place—the abdication and flight of their Kaiser on the 9th[585] under cover of darkness from his military headquarters in Spa in Belgium to neutral Holland.[586] Their sense of betrayal was palpable.[587] For the families of the von Kleists, Wedemeyers, von Tresckows and Bismarcks, their most bitter memory of the death throes and aftermath of this war would be their abandonment by their Kaiser, for whom all would have gladly given their lives.[588] When the former Kaiser finally passed away in 1941 in Nazi-occupied Holland, his death, among the Junkers, hardly registered a murmur.[589]

In part, pressure for the Kaiser to abdicate was due to Germany's peace overtures to the Americans leading to demands for an armistice and the creation of a democratic Republic of Germany.[590] Revolution had spread to most of Germany's cities, and Friedrich Ebert, a socialist, became chancellor of a chaotic Germany.[591] In the wake of the Kaiser's abdication and flight, a mob carrying bright red banners and armed with clubs and pitchforks attacked the military base at Köslin. Lieutenant Hans von Wedemeyer was prepared to respond with gunfire, but his commander refrained from giving the order because of the news that the Kaiser had fled the country. In short, if the people in the new republic of Germany wanted the air base, let them have it.[592]

Hans, disgusted with his superior, decided to quit his post. He feared for his mother's life, which prompted him to board a train for home. However, in the chaos now enveloping Germany, the train was overrun by left-wing revolutionaries, accosting military officers and tearing their epaulettes and insignia off their uniforms. When they got to Hans von Wedemeyer, he dared the thug to touch the uniform of the Kaiser. His assailant hesitated, and Hans jumped from the train.[593] He was still thirty kilometres from home. When he made his way there by foot, he was relieved to find his mother safe, thanks to the protection of loyal villagers.[594]

A day later, at 5:15 a.m. on Monday November 11, 1918, in a rail car in the Compiègne Forest, within the Rethondes Clearing, the Armistice was signed between the Allied commanders of France and Great Britain and the German civilian plenipotentiaries.[595] At 11 a.m., the guns fell silent for the first time in over four years on the European continent.[596] However, in accordance with orders from the US supreme commander, General John J. Pershing, American soldiers died needlessly from German machine-gun fire in the final minutes before the Armistice.[597] Pershing reasoned that if the Germans were not forced into unconditional surrender, they would believe they never truly lost the war.[598] This pointless act prompted a congressional committee investigation, in which Pershing remained unapologetic, and escaped any form of punishment.[599]

That day, in a hastily written letter to Ruthchen, Hans pleaded with her to make her way to the Neumark post-haste for their wedding. If there was to be a Bolshevik style revolution, at least, Hans reasoned, they "should hang from the same tree."[600] However, while Oma Ruth agreed that an immediate wedding was called for, she insisted it should take place at Kieckow. Hence, on November 17, 1918, just six days following the armistice, Hans and Ruthchen were married in the Kieckow church.[601] In the following month of December, by train, wagon, or foot, the men of the manor house and the men of the villages returned to the land and their families. Among them was Ruth's eldest and master of the estate, Hans Jürgen. Ruth's eldest daughter, Spes, the wife of the magnate Walter Stahlberg, came home to Stettin to her returning husband, as did the second daughter, Maria von Bismarck. For Walter, there was the pressing issue of restoring his mills, which were in dismal disrepair.[602]

Upon Hans Jürgen's return, Ruth proposed that she move back to her flat in Stettin, but her son would have none of it. He proposed the renovation of the former bailiff's house, on the edge of the forest near the village of Klein Krössin, as a retirement home for his mother. The village of Kieckow had more than enough skilled craftsmen to perform such a task. For Ruth, the offer was too good to refuse, as she was given great freedom in planning it to her needs. In 1923, Ruth moved into the renovated bailiff's house, and found great joy in tending the garden,[603] and engaging in deep Bible and theological study.[604] At the same time, frequent visitors, ensured she never felt alone.[605]

On June 28, 1919, five years to the day of the assassination of Austrian Archduke Franz Ferdinand in Sarajevo,[606] the Versailles Treaty was signed by the Allied and associated powers and Germany in the Hall of Mirrors in the Palace of Versailles. It came into force on January 10, 1920.[607] As discussed at the beginning of this chapter, it was less than fifty years earlier, in that same palace, in January 1871, that Wilhelm I, then King of Prussia (a title which he retained) was adorned with the additional title of Emperor or Kaiser of the newly unified Germany, in the wake of their famous victory over France in the Franco-Prussian war.[608] This event had been witnessed by Ruth's father

Robert and future father-in-law Hans Hugo, and they had already re-counted it to Ruth many times.[609]

However, in late June 1919, a humiliated Germany was forced to cede the long disputed region of Alsace Lorraine to France,[610] and the Rhine River's west bank became demilitarised.[611] In January 1923, Germany's industrial Ruhr heartland was occupied by French and Belgian troops in response to the German government's default in war reparations and France's own coal shortage.[612] Germany's pre-war coal-rich Saarland was now governed by the League of Nations, with the French given control of the coal mines as part of Germany's war reparations. After fifteen years, a plebiscite in 1935 was planned, in which the inhabitants of the Saarland would be given the opportunity to choose between France and Germany.[613] In the east, as part of the post-Great War rebirth of the independent Polish nation, a Slavic state now lay just a few kilometres east of the von Kleist lands. Finally, the German army would be limited to just 100,000 men, with military aircraft and other modern weaponry forbidden.[614]

As much as this was humiliating and repugnant to Junker pride, Ruth and her clan were sheltered somewhat from the anarchy enveloping post-Great War Germany. However, in August to September 1919, just weeks after the signing of the Versailles Treaty, something previously unheard of in Prussian history took place — a strike of agricultural workers, leading to the ruination of the crops.[615] This was, perhaps, an omen of what would follow in 1945. But for the time being, at least, Oma Ruth and her fellow Junkers' way of life would survive the storm of post-Great War revolution and chaos.

This was in part due to the Germans on the Eastern Front defeating the Russian Bear in early 1918, compelling the fledgling Bolshevik regime to sign the humiliating treaty of Brest Litovsk in modern-day Belarus.[616] For the Germans, even in the face of the humiliation of Versailles, their victory in the east became a face-saving propaganda coup of sorts. The monument near Tannenberg, in East Prussia, now Stębark in modern-day Poland,[617] was modelled on Stonehenge,[618] and was unveiled in 1927 by Reich President Paul von Hindenburg, the victorious Field Marshal at the Battle of Tannenberg thirteen years earlier in late August 1914.[619]

When Hindenburg died in 1934, he and his wife, who had already died in 1921,[620] were interred at Tannenberg.[621] But as Soviet troops approached in January 1945, German soldiers removed the Hindenburgs' remains,[622] and they were eventually interred in Marburg, Germany.[623] In 1949, the Polish communist regime commenced the complete dismantling of the memorial. Today, among the weeds, shrubs and bushes, hardly any vestiges remain of the old "monument to German glory."[624] For Oma Ruth and her fellow Junkers, at least from its unveiling in 1927 to the final cataclysm in 1945, it became a symbol of the survival of their way of life.

However, amidst the post-Great War chaos, the continuance of Old Prussia was, in large part, owing to the Poles having repelled the Bolsheviks from the gates of Warsaw in August 1920. Indeed, former Tsarist officer[625] and now Soviet General, Mikhail Tukhachevsky, who would die in Stalin's 1937 purge,[626] issued the order of the day for July 2, 1920: "To the West! Over the corpse of White Poland lies the road to worldwide conflagration. March upon Vilna, Minsk, Warsaw! … and onward to Berlin over the corpse of Poland!"[627]

If Warsaw fell in August 1920, a democratic but chronically weak and chaotic Weimar Germany was there for the taking by Lenin's Bolsheviks, to spread his dream of world-wide proletarian revolution.[628] Moreover, Lenin desired the Bolshevik Revolution to reach Germany with the added objective of procuring German industrial technology to modernise a still backward Russia.[629] In short, the Junkers owed their existence post-Great War to their old Slavic enemy of Poland. Of course, such an admission would not support the notion of face-saving German pride after the humiliation of Versailles.

On the other hand, the memory of the victorious Battle of Tannenberg in late August 1914 certainly did. This battle was so-named on Hindenburg's insistence, as it drowned the memory of the humiliating defeat over half a millennium earlier in July 1410 against Slavic Polish and Lithuanian forces.[630] For Erich Ludendorff, Hindenburg's second-in-command, the real mastermind behind the victory in August 1914, this was poignant, as his Teutonic Knight ancestors had fought in this medieval battle.[631] For the Germans, this battle was also known as the Battle of Tannenberg,[632] and while the 1914 battle was not exactly in Tannenberg, but rather in nearby Allenstein,[633] and against Russians rather than Poles and Lithuanians, it still satisfied the theme of a grand Germanic victory over the Slavic menace at the time—namely, Tsarist Russia.[634] Hence the 1914 Battle of Tannenberg, avenging the old memory of medieval defeat, embodying the Slavic-inflicted humiliation of Germanic pride.

In April 1924, Weimar Germany was at the start of its "Golden Years," from that year until the Wall Street crash in October 1929,[635] following its recovery from the post-Great War chaos and hyperinflation. Ruth's brother, Robert junior, was excommunicated from the family clan. This was due to his explosive book published in April 1924,[636] chronicling his years in the court of Kaiser Wilhelm II from 1898 to 1910, discussed earlier this chapter.[637] In it, he spoke freely of its intrigue, petty gossip and so on, as the vainglorious Kaiser and Imperial Germany trod the path to war. Oma Ruth was instrumental in this estrangement, for she perceived the Kaiser, appointed in God's name, as beyond all reproach. Only upon the death and funeral in 1926 of her sister Anni,[638] mother of Henning von Tresckow, did Oma Ruth briefly relent; she rushed and embraced her estranged brother as he arrived unexpectedly amid the grief of Anni's death.[639] In 1942, brother Robert junior, at age 79, passed away.[640]

The Junkers, now in Weimar's Golden Years, had weathered the storm of post-Great War chaos and upheaval. However, in 1925, a turgid literary work was published, and in hindsight, become a portent for a cataclysm that would, in every respect, surpass the Great War and its aftermath. As a consequence, the proud Junkers way of life, unlike post 1918, would not survive.

Chapter 7

Zingst and Finkenwalde

On April 15 1935, Dietrich left London for Berlin,[641] and almost immediately upon arrival, he and Franz Hildebrandt set about finding premises for the underground seminary training of Confessing Church pastors. For the first couple of months, it was located at temporary facilities near the German Baltic resort village of Zingst, before moving onto Finkenwalde, near Stettin (now modern-day Szczecin in Poland).[642]

The daily routine at Zingst and Finkenwalde was a strict one laid down by Dietrich.[643] One student from Finkenwalde, Albrecht Schönherr,[644] recalled the morning service beginning within minutes of awakening, not in the chapel, but at the large dinner table. Dietrich requested that the students not speak a word when they awoke until after the service, which was rather difficult, given that they bunked six to eight a room on old feather beds atop dusty mattresses that had been used for generations. However, this strict code was not like those of the demagogic leader or Verführer, but that of a servant leader following Christ's example to his disciples.[645]

A perfect example of this humility was an occasion in the early days at Zingst, when Dietrich requested someone to help in the kitchen. When no one responded, Dietrich locked the door and started to wash the dishes. When others knocked to come in and help, he would not answer and simply continued until the job was done. Later, Dietrich did not mention a word about it, because his point was made.[646] In his seminary, as in his upbringing as a child, there was to be no place for selfishness, laziness, self-pity, poor sportsmanship and the like.[647]

One may ask why, in such a strict seminarian environment, the quality of sportsmanship was relevant. Dietrich was an avid sportsman and bush walker himself, and was no stranger to the simple concept of "fun." As Eric Metaxas put it: "

> One may ask why, in such a strict seminarian environment, the quality of sportsmanship was relevant. Dietrich was an avid sportsman and bush walker himself, and was no stranger to the simple concept of 'fun.' Most afternoons and evenings a time was set aside for hiking or sports. Bonhoeffer was forever or-

ganizing games, just as his mother had done in their family. There was a lot of table tennis, and anyone looking for Bonhoeffer would try the table tennis room first. They also played soccer. Schönherr recalled that 'Bonhoeffer was always at the head of the pack because he was such a fantastic runner.' He had always been competitive, and Bethge remembered that 'he hated to lose when we tried shot-putting—or stone-putting—down the beach.' Albrecht Schönherr remembered that after dinner and recreation, around ten o'clock, there was another service of about three-quarters of an hour, 'as the last note of a day with God.' After that, silence and sleep. That was the way the day went."[648]

Moreover, Dietrich a lover of Beethoven,[649] Mozart, Brahms and the like,[650] brought his musical passions and talents to the routine, amazing his students.[651] Hardly any seminaries any Germany could be found where music was such an integral aspect of daily life.[652]

In the very early days of the seminary, at the temporary location of Zingst, a significant announcement by Hitler was made on May 1, May Day — a day celebrated by organised labour. It was in regard to a new law for military conscription that had just come into effect. Unlike Dietrich, most of the ordinands at the time had few qualms about it; most didn't think of Hitler as Dietrich did.[653] For them, just as in the time of the Kaiser, the church's obedience to the state was sacrosanct and self-evident. Hence, the much-maligned Weimar state, with its acquiescence to the humiliating Versailles Treaty and the consequent chaos and unemployment, coupled with its undermining of this perceived fundamental relationship, was a blight to German pride. Moreover, accusations by the German Christians of a lack of patriotism among members of the Confessing Church needed to be proven unwarranted. Hitler, unlike other high ranking Nazis like Himmler and Bormann,[654] was adept at not appearing openly hostile to the church. At least, not until a more favourable moment. Thus, even among most of Dietrich's ordinands in the Confessing Church, few had any qualms about serving their country in the military. Put another way, serving their country could not possibly conflict in their minds with any tenets of the church.

Dietrich explained his position, but most were taken aback. That said, there never was any thought of mutiny amongst the ordinands, and their respect for Dietrich as their religious mentor never wavered. They and students in the seminary's four subsequent six-month courses would end up serving in the military, and Dietrich would never try and stop them; he did not wish his classes or the seminary to become a cult of personality centred on him. He would only persuade by reason, as imposing his thoughts on others was an anathema to him, appropriate only for a Verführer.

In June, Dietrich and his ordinands had to leave the temporary premises in Zingst for the more permanent site at Finkenwalde near Stettin on the Odor River in the heart of the Pomeranian region.[655] This site was the former location for a private school ,which was among the countless types of institutions the Third Reich disapproved of and subsequently closed. When Dietrich and his ordinands arrived, they found buildings on the site in a state of gross disrepair. Some of the ordinands were forced to use hostel accommodation while they cleaned and repaired the premises. As the repairs and clean-up continued, Dietrich and the ordinands donated to the fledgling enterprise; Dietrich donated his entire theological library, including his great-grandfather von Hase's invaluable Erlangen edition of Martin Luther's works. As music was to become an integral part of the seminary, he brought along his gramophone and many of his recordings, the most prized and exotic of which were the Negro spirituals he had purchased in Manhattan.[656]

The Pomeranian region encompasses the land from northeastern Germany's River Recknitz in the west to Poland's great River Vistula in the east, and almost as far south as the River Noteć to its northern bounds by the Baltic Sea.[657] This region has, over the centuries, had more than its fair share of territorial disputes between two nations. In the midst of the so-called "Recovered Territories" in the aftermath of World War II, German Stettin became the western Polish border city of Szczecin; similarly, Breslau in the Silesian region to the south became Wrocław; both cases were more a consequence of Stalinist-Soviet policy than by Polish design or intentions.[658]

For Dietrich, it was of crucial assistance that the landed gentry or Junkers[659] of Pomerania at the time, in contrast to the south of Germany like Bavaria and Silesia,[660] were staunch opponents of Hitler and his Third Reich. While Berlin's metropolitan climate of liberal intellectualism was absent here, in the conservative and almost feudal world of landed estates of centuries past, the traditional values and devotion to high standards of culture bore a striking similarity to Dietrich's infant upbringing in Breslau and later childhood in Berlin.[661] Dietrich almost instantly felt at home with them. Most of the families were members of the Prussian military officers' class, from whom virtually all the conspirators against Hitler would come. Furthermore, in time, he would announce his engagement to one of their daughters.[662] However, the greatest benefactor for the Finkenwalde seminary was a Silesian native, Ruth von Kleist-Retzow. Following Dietrich's first meeting with Tante (Aunt) Ruth in 1935, he spent many weeks at Kieckow and Klein-Krössin over the next few years, even stretching into the Second World War. It was there that, in the thirties, he worked on his famous work, *Nachfolge* (Discipleship), and in the forties, wrote his next book *Ethics*.[663]

Although Ruth had moved into her renovated cottage at Klein-Krössin following the Great War, circumstances[664] following Hitler's rise to power again led to her taking up residence in her Stettin flat, this time to look after her grandchildren during their gymnasium education. This in turn led to Oma Ruth's first meeting with Pastor Bonhoeffer during one of Finkenwalde's Sunday services in 1935, to which the public were invited. Soon Pastor Bonhoeffer became affectionately known to her as Dietrich.[665]

Because Dietrich and Tante Ruth became so close, he often addressed her as Oma (the diminutive of Grandmother), mainly because he spent so much time with her grandchildren; at her insistence, he personally oversaw several of their confirmations.[666] To Eberhard Bethge, perhaps his most prominent student at Finkenwalde, he sometimes referred to her affectionately as *Tante* (Aunt), just as he referred to George Bell as Uncle to Franz Hildebrandt. At Finkenwalde, Dietrich introduced the practice of confession, which had been dismissed by most Lutherans as too overtly Catholic.

However, Dietrich's implementation of it was in the spirit of Martin Luther, where people confessed to one another rather than to a priest.[667] Dietrich chose Eberhard Bethge as his confessor; post-war, Bethge wrote Dietrich's biography, *Dietrich Bonhoeffer: Man of Vision, Man of Courage* (1970).[668] Eberhard was well qualified as confessor and biographer, with his gift of entering into Dietrich's mindset, opening him up with the right questions.[669]

Eberhard soon became Dietrich's closest friend. This intimacy could have had a negative effect on the sense of community in Finkenwalde, especially as there was a group from Berlin who had known him longer and could have asserted their entitlement to a special relationship with their revered teacher. But no one could resist the charm of this "country boy."[670] Years later, Dietrich wrote to Eberhard: "

I don't know a single person who can't stand you, whereas I know quite a few who can't stand me. I don't have a hard time with that; wherever I find opponents, I also find friends, and that's enough for me. But it's due to your being open and modest by nature, whereas I'm reserved and more demanding."[671]

Finkenwalde's greatest benefactor, Tante Ruth, would write to Eberhard in September 1942: "you are less complicated than he."[672]

The matriarch, a strong willed and assertive woman of compassion, found the brilliant, cultured and heroic Dietrich Bonhoeffer an answer to her prayers in the crude, brutal and maniacal regime of Hitler's Reich. She lobbied families in the region to support Finkenwalde in any way they were capable of, and her efforts were not in vain.[673] Much of the seminary's food was supplied by the region's families, and thanks to their advocacy, many of the ordinands would find posts as pastors in the region's churches. This was because the old system by which families were able to select the pastors of their local church still held sway.[674]

One of Tante Ruth's grandchildren, Ruth-Alice, remembered how many of the young, seduced by Hitler, would boldly proclaim that this darkly charismatic leader was their future. Ruth-Alice, on the other hand, although she found Dietrich somewhat detached, felt his compelling and positive charisma was devoted wholly and utterly to God whenever he preached, prompting her to think, "Here is our future."[675]

Chapter 8

Institutionalised Hatred — The Nuremberg Laws

On September 15 1935, just three or so months after the seminary moved from Zingst to Finkenwalde, the infamous Nuremberg Laws came into effect. In particular, The Law for the Protection of German Blood and German Honour was proclaimed by Hitler at Nuremberg during the Rally of Freedom (*Reichsparteitag der Freiheit*), held as part of the 7th Party Congress from September 10 to 16.[676] The "freedom" referred to the reintroduction of compulsory military service and hence German "liberation" from the Treaty of Versailles — manifested in the National Socialist mindset by the Dolchstosslegende (the "stab in the back legend" of the Jews and the socialists and communists being responsible for Germany's humiliating defeat in November 1918.)[677] Thus the law "legitimised" the legal sanction of hatred and revenge: "

> Thoroughly convinced by the knowledge that the purity of German blood is essential for the further existence of the German people and animated by the inflexible will to safeguard the German nation for the entire future, the Reichstag has resolved upon the following law unanimously, which is promulgated herewith:
>
> **Section One**
>
> 1. Marriages between Jews and nationals of German or kindred blood are forbidden. Marriages concluded in defiance of this law are void, even if, for the purpose of evading this law, they are concluded abroad.
>
> 2. Proceedings for annulment may be initiated only by the Public Prosecutor.
>
> **Section Two**
>
> Relations outside marriage between Jews and nationals of German or kindred blood are forbidden.

Section Three

Jews will not be permitted to employ female nationals of German or kindred blood in their households.

Section Four

1. Jews are forbidden to hoist the Reich and national flag and to present the colours of the Reich.

2. On the other hand they are permitted to present the Jewish colours. The exercise of this authority is protected by the State.

Section Five

1. A person who acts contrary to the prohibition of Section One will be punished with hard labour.

2. A person who acts contrary to the prohibition of Section Two will be punished with imprisonment or with hard labour.

3. A person who acts contrary to the provisions of Section Three or Four will be punished with imprisonment up to a year and with a fine or with one of these penalties.

Section Six

The Reich Minister of the Interior in agreement with the Deputy of the Führer will issue the legal and administrative regulations which are required for the implementation and supplementation of this law.

Section Seven

The law will become effective on the day after the promulgation, however, section 3 will become effective January 1st 1936."[678]

Nuremberg held great significance for the Third Reich;[679] with its location in the centre of Germany, it was relevant to the Holy Roman Empire or First Reich founded by Charlemagne in the year 800 AD.[680]

Hence the regime's decision to make Nuremberg the city to hold the huge Nazi Party conventions which became known as the Nuremberg rallies, held annually from 1927 to 1938.[681] While the Final Solution was still some way from its implementation and genocidal climax, the Nuremberg Laws, in particular, The Law for the Protection of German Blood and German Honour, was a critical step on the path to organised and industrial scale mass murder. While discriminatory measures against the Jews had been promoted almost from the outset, such as the April 1933 attempted boycott of Jewish shops and exclusion from the Civil Service and other professions, the Nuremberg Laws would henceforth become the institutionalised and formal basis of anti-Semitic discrimination.

In particular, they formally decreed racial and genealogical definitions of "Jewishness," and the attendant denial of legal rights. Marriage and any form of sexual relations between Jews and Gentiles entailed criminal penalties, similar to laws that existed in apartheid South Africa. Families were compelled to verify beyond all doubt that they had no Jewish blood going 200 years.[682] To carry out this work, the Nazi regime required two things which they did not have when they ascended to power: automated machines that were capable of extracting and cross-referencing detailed genealogical information from millions of census returns, and skilled demographers. The former were punch card machines, like primitive computers supplied by the American firm IBM, while the skilled demographers were found by trial and error. Both, like the Nuremberg Laws, would be absolutely critical in the Third Reich's preparations for their campaign of genocide against the Jews.[683]

In April 1935, five months or so before the announcement of the Nuremberg Laws, a Breslau woman was ridiculed for her relationship with a Jewish man.[684] Such a relationship became a criminal act, with Jews classified as "non-persons." However, with the eye of the world upon the regime in the weeks leading up to and during the 1936 Berlin Olympics, the Nazi regime moderated its anti-Jewish attacks and even removed some of the signs saying "Jews Unwelcome" from public places.[685] Of course, once the Olympics had delivered the regime another propaganda coup, this façade of tolerance was discarded.

When these laws were passed, Dietrich felt that the Confessing Church had to act. As he put it, one must speak for those who could not speak, as to outlaw slavery inside the church was right, but to allow it to exist outside the church would be evil. The Confessing Church, in its timidity, invoked Paul's letter to the Romans 13:1—5 in a literal and superficial interpretation: "

> Everyone must submit himself to the governing authorities, for there is no authority except that which God has established. The authorities that exist have been established by God. Consequently, he who rebels against the authority is rebelling against what God has instituted, and those who do so will bring judgement on themselves. For rulers hold no terror for those who do right, but for those who do wrong. Do you want to be free from fear of the one in authority? Then do what is right and he will commend you. For he is God's servant to do you good. But if you do wrong, be afraid, for he does not bear the sword for nothing. He is God's servant, an agent of wrath to bring punishment on the wrongdoer. Therefore, it is necessary to submit to the authorities, not only because of possible punishment but also because of conscience."[686]

As Metaxas put it, Lutherans had never been forced to deal with the boundary or literal limits of this scriptural idea of obedience to worldly authorities,[687] citing for example the early Christians standing up to Caesar and the Romans; this history should have guided the Confessing Church to publicly condemn the Nuremberg Laws. As Dietrich declared in the first months following Hitler's rise to power in late January 1933, it was not enough for the church to "bandage the victims under the wheel, but to put a spoke in the wheel itself,"[688] while in the wake of these infamous laws, Dietrich declared, "Only he who cries out for the Jews may sing Gregorian chants."[689]

The timid acquiescence of the Church came to the notice of Franz Hildebrandt, who wasted no time in calling Finkenwalde from his church in the Berlin locality of Dahlem, and informing Dietrich that the Confessing Synod was proposing a resolution conceding the state's right to enact the Nuremberg legislation.[690] For Franz, it was the final straw, and as such, he was ready to resign from the Pastors' Emergency League and the Confessing Church. Dietrich, true friend as he was, arranged for himself and a group of ordinands to travel to Berlin in an attempt to influence the deliberations of the synod, which would be held in Berlin's Steglitz locality.

Since Dietrich was not a delegate, he could not speak at the synod, and as such could only attempt to embolden those who saw things as he did. But the Synod was a resounding success for the regime's strategy of dividing and conquering its weak opponents. Dietrich realised that the reluctance of the Confessing Church to speak out boldly had a lot to do with money, as the state provided financial security for the pastors of Germany. As a result, Confessing Church pastors would only go so far in opposing the regime.[691]

Before 1935, Hitler and his cronies had noticed, much to their annoyance, that the Confessing Church had not only gained respect and influence, but that in court it was almost always found to be in the right. Thus, from March to July 1935, in order to rid themselves of this perceived irritant, they enacted three new laws which ostensibly were meant to ensure the state's care for the Church's welfare, but in truth, were to muzzle it. The first was signed by Hermann Göring as prime minister of Prussia and provided "finance departments" for the Prussian provincial churches, which were to "guarantee" local church assets and contributions.[692]

In reality this meant that local confessing pastors in the Old Prussian Union could no longer take up their usual collections without risking prison. The other two laws were signed by Hitler himself, because they applied to the entire Reich, creating a "Legislative Authority for [the administration of] Legal Matters in the German Evangelical Church."[693] In effect, this law prohibited access by the Confessing Church to regular public courts, and was another of Hitler's countless violations of German law. It contributed to the repressive climate that led, months later, to the Confessing Synod's humiliating acquiescence to the Nuremberg Laws.

Little wonder, then, that Dietrich's struggles with depression continued. Moreover, with the passing of the monstrous Nuremberg Laws, Sabine and Gert's suffering as a non-pure-Aryan family had been exacerbated even further. Many women who had worked for them were now dismissed by them, as they had been harried for working for a Jewish household. SA men making deliveries to the home would say things to them like; "What? Are you still working with Jews?" while some professors who had been family friends distanced themselves from them in fear of their jobs.[694] The more Sabine heard through her sister Christine von Dohnányi, the more she knew that she, Gert, and the girls would have to do the unthinkable — leave Germany. When Christine told Sabine of what was happening in the concentration camps, long before most knew, she couldn't bear to hear any more and asked her to stop.[695]

Dietrich's grandmother Julie, who, back in April 1933, had defied the SA boycott of Jewish stores, now aged ninety-three, wrote to

Dietrich of her concern for her granddaughter Gertrud Wedell, whose Jewish husband was forced to give up a legal practice in Düsseldorf as a result of the new laws. In what would end up being her last letter to Dietrich, she asked for his help: "

> This fifty-four-year-old man is travelling around the world looking for work so that he can finish raising his children... A family's life destroyed! ... Everything is affected, down to the smallest details. Can you actively advise or help us here? ... I hope you can give some energetic thought to this and perhaps know some way out."[696]

In October 1935, the month following the passing of the Nuremberg Laws, Dietrich's parents moved from their vast home on Wangenheimstrasse in Grunewald to a new house that they had built in Charlottenburg. It was smaller, but still large enough for guests, and Dietrich would always have a room on the top floor. At the same time, Dietrich's grandmother, Julie née Tafel Bonhoeffer, moved in with them, but after Christmas, she contracted pneumonia and died in January. On January 15 1936, Dietrich, delivered a eulogy at her funeral which reflected her great influence on Karl Bonhoeffer and his children: "

> A refusal to compromise over the right principle, free speech for the free individual, the fact that one's word once given is binding, clarity and common sense in one's opinions, candour and simplicity of life in private and in public — these were factors that went to her very heart ... She could not bear to see these values despised or to see the rights of an individual violated. For this reason, her last years were clouded with the great sorrow that she bore for the fate of the Jews among our people, a burden which she shared with them and a suffering which she, too, felt. She stemmed from another age, from another spiritual world, and this world does not descend with her into the grave.... This heritage for which we thank her lays duties upon us."[697]

Chapter 9

The von Kleists and the Prophecy

By the beginning of 1936, the Confessing Church's position as a bulwark against the National Socialist assimilation of the Protestant church was under attack not just from within the Reich, with its tactic of divide and conquer in concert with draconian "legal" measures, but also from abroad. Dietrich had been dumbfounded by international church organisations, such as The World Alliance, Life and Work, and Faith and Order,[698] in which the leadership constantly sought to accommodate both the Confessing Church and the Reichkirche. This was in spite of the latter's promotion of an Aryan Christianity centred around Führer idolatry that virtually usurped Christ. Now, the victory that Dietrich and the Confessing Church thought they had won over Heckel and his Reichkirche at Fanø was proving to be hollow; Heckel's insidious last-moment clause of "maintaining friendly relations with both churches" came back to haunt them. Accordingly, Dietrich resolved to refuse all speaking invitations at gatherings to which German Christians were invited.[699]

On Tuesday February 4, Ruth von Kleist's sixty-ninth birthday was celebrated in her Stettin flat. This flat had been leased in September the previous year for the matriarch to look after all her grandsons of gymnasium age who had been withdrawn from the boarding school in Templin in 1934. This was a response to the public humiliation of her grandson Hans Otto von Bismarck, great great nephew of the famous Otto von Bismarck, on the parade grounds of the school in 1934.[700] In a display of Pomeranian clan solidarity, Hans Jürgen, Ruth's surviving son from the Great War, withdrew his two sons from the school.

For almost four decades, since the death of her husband Jürgen in 1897 from what seemed to be a kidney disorder,[701] Ruth's birthday had been bitter-sweet, as it was also her wedding anniversary.[702] Now in 1936, her fiftieth anniversary of marriage, February 4 took on a new dimension for Ruth, as this day was also the thirtieth birthday for Dietrich, whom she had come to regard like a son. His presence at her birthday tea party projected a charisma which even the children responded to.[703] Five days later on the Sunday, there was a large birthday celebration for Dietrich at Finkenwalde, with Frau von Kleist and her brood present. Motivated by Dietrich's accounts of his times abroad, his ordinands presented their director with a birthday wish. Namely, that he use his ecumenical connections to organise a trip to Sweden.[704] Their spokesman was Eberhard Bethge, whose friendship with Dietrich was by now every bit as close as that with Franz Hildebrandt. Jane Pejsa, in her book *Matriarch of Conspiracy*, described Bethge as Dietrich's closest friend, if not his alter ego.[705]

The trip, Eberhard reasoned, would enhance international support for their seminary as well as boost their morale. Moreover, Sweden was a stronghold of the Lutheran faith but unencumbered with state harassment, and so free to remain a church truly representative of Christ. Dietrich it seems, did not need convincing, and began to evaluate all the possibilities and hurdles to overcome. The most immediate and obvious was limited funds, which meant that not all the ordinands could go. This, however, was not the only obstacle to confront.

Dietrich and the ordinands had to reach Sweden before officials of the Reichkirche became aware of it and reported it to the Reich authorities. They could not have Confessing Church pastors travelling abroad and spouting anti-Reich propaganda. It was not permitted to take cash out of Germany,[706] and so all the arrangements for the trip had to be made in Sweden. These included land transport, tickets, accommodation and most problematically, visas. Nevertheless, the party of ordinands, together with their director, made it to Sweden, unbeknownst to officials of the Reichkirche. While they were away, nothing unusual or untoward occurred at Finkenwalde.

On Saturday March 7, Hitler made his first territorial and military violation of the Versailles Treaty when his troops marched into the Rhineland, the region of Germany located west of the River Rhine which had been demilitarised under the terms of the treaty. This demilitarisation, which Germany had acquiesced to for the past sixteen years or so, was a constant source of irritation, if not humiliation for Germans of all political persuasions,[707] not least the old Prussians descended from the landed feudal gentry. This included Frau Ruth von Kleist, born and christened in that era's heyday in 1867 on the grand Lower Silesian estate of *Grossenborau*, with none other than the illustrious Otto von Bismarck present at the christening.[708]

The image of a German army, after sixteen long humiliating years, once again marching through these German lands stirred the old Junker heart of Ruth with pride. Ruth, who would have seen the swastika as an abomination, would have imagined German troops marching in under the flag of the old Kaiser's Imperial Germany. The Kaiser had been in exile in Holland for the past seventeen years, and the matriarch still felt a sense of betrayal from the death throes of the Great War, when he abdicated his crown and abandoned his homeland for a benign existence in then neutral Holland. The Kaiser's death in then German-occupied Holland in 1941 hardly raised a murmur among the proud Junkers.[709]

Nevertheless, when Ruth heard the news of a parade in Berlin on the following day of Sunday to celebrate another shedding of the shackles of Versailles, she phoned her daughter Spes (Latin for "hope") and invited herself for a weekend stay in the capital. Much to her delight, her grandsons of her Kieckow estate, Konstantin and Jürgen Christoph, were there to enhance the experience for Oma Ruth. On their Oma's suggestion, they took a chair from the flat on the tram, and walked with it down Berlin's famous Unter den Linden to near the Brandenburg Gate.[710] There Ruth, a sixty-nine-year-old Junker lady in an outdated gown reminiscent of her bygone heyday, stood to attention upon her chair, flanked either side by her teenage grandsons.

For Oma Ruth von Kleist, too many years had passed since she last witnessed a parade that stirred her old Prussian heart. In Berlin, over four decades earlier in 1892, her husband Jürgen, as an army reserve officer, tilted his sword ever so slightly to acknowledge the proud gaze of his wife.[711] Oma Ruth blotted out the swastika flags by imagining the black, red, and white of the Hohenzollern flag and the uniforms of the old Kaiser's guard. Moreover, the music was the same, the precision of the marchers obvious; the sheer numbers of proud young men presenting "eyes left" as they marched by was a feast for Ruth von Kleist.[712]

From a modern-day western perspective, it is disturbing that a patron of Dietrich's seminary would so eagerly embrace a parade "resplendent" with flags of swastikas, the symbol of the evil that was the Third Reich. However, Ruth was born into a proud feudal society, humiliated in a world conflict where all parties, rightly or wrongly, perceived they were fighting a war of defence or even survival, fought on two fronts by Germany, from France to Imperial Russia. The other side of this picture is that she gave haven to Jews at her Stettin flat and estate at Klein Krössin while Dietrich arranged visas for them to Sweden, assisted by the Swedish contacts he had made on his trip there with his ordinands.[713]

Back in 1925, Oma Ruth and her son Hans Jürgen were called to a private meeting by the latter's dear friend from childhood, Ewald von Kleist of Schmenzin, master of the nearby Schmenzin estate. Ewald was related by blood to Hans Jürgen and Ruth, a distant cousin.

The friendship that had developed over the years transcended the remote bloodline, or perhaps was enhanced by it. Although Ewald was a Unitarian Christian for most of his life (not believing in the Holy Trinity of the Father, Son and Holy Spirit), upon his death in 1945, he embraced the Holy Trinity.[714] He and Ruth often debated this theological point, but it never detracted from their bond, as Ewald indicates in his account of calling this private meeting with them.

The point of the meeting was to discuss a book already published that year. Ruth also had a book of hers published in 1925;[715] it discussed the role of the Junkers in the modern-day democracy of Weimar Germany, now experiencing the relative prosperity of its "golden years" from 1924-1929, following the recovery from the chaos and hyper-inflation of the immediate post-war years, and just preceding the October 1929 Wall Street crash. Her book prompted a rather large gathering of friends and family in August at her cottage at Klein Krössin, although it would only reach a limited circle of readers in Germany. Many would dismiss it as the sentimental meanderings of an old Pomeranian aristocratic woman — she was fifty-eight at the time, although twenty years later, her statement, "Thus we are obligated to fight and to suffer together —for ourselves, for the German nation and for this land that God has given us!"[716] would prove rather prophetic. Like the Confederate South in the wake of the American Civil War,[717] the final vestiges of her way of life would be destroyed in the state that was to become the "People's" Republic of Poland.

Ewald von Kleist of Schmenzin was prophetic in their private meeting in Ruth's cottage in September 1925. He had just completed the most disturbing read of his life — *Mein Kampf* (My Struggle) by Adolf Hitler. Ewald stated:[718] "

> Everyone now knows about the National Socialist German Workers' Party in Bavaria. It is a nest of radicals; its leaders are ruffians and goons at best; and its spokesman, Adolf Hitler, is a demagogue. We conservatives at least have seen beyond their seductive rhetoric. We know them for what they are — proletarians of the worst kind."

As Ruth and her son Hans Jürgen nodded in unison, Ewald continued: "And now that the economy is recovering we ought to have more influence politically; isn't that so?" (Four or so years later in October 1929, the Wall Street crash would change all that)."

Once again, there was agreement, upon which Ewald laid open *Mein Kampf* on his lap. "

> I received a great jolt last night. I read this diatribe, and I cannot rest until I share it with you to whom I am bound so closely. This book has the potential for great evil, precisely because in many ways it speaks to the longings of us all. Until last night I had some concern that the masses, under certain conditions, might succumb to this man's rhetoric. But now it is clear that the situation is more critical than that."

It "speaks to the longings of us all": this indeed it did to Oma Ruth, albeit briefly, over a decade later in March 1936 at the parade. Then, as Ewald continued: "

> This man has taken our Prussian history and corrupted it; he has stolen our heroes — the great Friedrich[719] and Bismarck[720] — and turned them to his own ends. Hans Jürgen, Cousin Ruth, we must pray for stability and for prosperity — and you, Ruth, know how to pray better than I — else our kind too is in danger of being seduced."

Ewald then stated that after speaking to various members of the local agricultural council and conservative politicians, he was disturbed to find that many had read at least parts of *Mein Kampf* and been enamoured with the seductive vision it projected of a rebirth of the spirit of the Fatherland, an emphasis on family and decency, and in the true spirit of the Dolchstosslegende,[721] the purging of Bolsheviks, socialists, Jews and other "undesirable" elements from the land. As Ewald described it:
"The devil himself could not construct a more seductive thesis than the obscenities of this Austrian bastard."

Hans Jürgen spoke up, wanting to declare a united front with his cousin and friend. But Ewald, eager not to be interrupted, started quoting passages he had marked from the book. He began with a passage that espouses the virtues of the Old Prussia. Ruth remarked that while it was a little obscure, it was not far removed from her own thinking. To which Ewald replied that he could find dozens of such passages from *Mein Kampf* to which they could all say "Amen."

Then Ewald quoted passages that were progressively more disturbing: "

In general the art of all truly great national leaders at all times consists among other things primarily in not dividing the attention of a people, but in concentrating it upon a single foe... It belongs to the genius of a great leader to make even adversaries far removed from one another seem to belong to a single category, [eg: Jews, Socialists and Bolsheviks, as embodied in the Dolchstosslegende] because in weak and uncertain characters the knowledge of having different enemies can only too readily lead to the beginning of doubts in their own right.

...

All propaganda must be popular and its intellectual level must be adjusted to the most limited intelligence among those it is addressed to. Consequently, the greater the mass it is intended to reach, the lower its purely intellectual level will have to be....

The purpose of propaganda is ... to convince the masses. But the masses are slow-moving, and they always require a certain time before they are ready even to notice a thing, and only after the simplest ideas are repeated thousands of times will the masses finally remember them....

When there is a change, it must not alter the content of what the propaganda is driving at, but in the end must always say the same thing. For instance, a slogan must be presented from different angles, but the end of all remarks must always and immutably be the slogan itself. Only in this way can the propaganda have a unified and complete effect."

As Ewald read each passage, Ruth and Hans Jürgen became ever more uncomfortable as they grasped the insidious nature of this work. Ewald was not finished; he wished to point out the ethnic scapegoat Hitler had chosen: "

If the Jews were alone in this world, they would stifle in filth and offal; they would try to get ahead of one another in hate filled struggle and exterminate one another, in so far as the absolute absence of all sense of self-sacrifice, expressing itself in their cowardice, did not turn battle into comedy here too."

Ewald's quotations of the rants about the Jews did not end there; Ruth and her son were not able to get a word in until Cousin Ruth broke in after the following passage: "Protestantism combats with all the greatest hostility any attempt to rescue the nation from the embrace of its most mortal enemy, since its attitude toward the Jews just happens to be more or less dogmatically established."

"Well I should hope so!" Ruth became increasingly agitated as Ewald continued to read without giving her the chance to speak. She rose to her feet: "Stop it, Ewald, what you are reading is all nonsense, if not blasphemy."[722] Ewald had achieved his goal. He had made his close friends aware of how Hitler and his cronies would operate and what they were capable of.[723]

Back in Chapter 2, "Ominous Clouds on the Horizon," mention was made of how Dietrich, upon his return from America in June 1931, sensed that Germany was at a turning point in history. He was not yet sure what it was, but in one respect he was certain: the integrity of the church would be threatened, and he wondered if it would even survive.[724] This, he wrote in a letter in August of that year to the Swiss friend he made in New York, Erwin Sutz. This was six years after Ewald's meeting with Hans Jürgen and Ruth. Both cases illustrate how perceptive these two men were, more so than most mere mortals, albeit with similar conclusions drawn from rather divergent paths. Indeed, Jane Pejsa in her book on Ruth von Kleist, *Matriarch of Conspiracy*, implies just that. "

> Ewald von Kleist and Dietrich Bonhoeffer both possess a special knack for seeing through the obvious to life's hidden dangers, long before these dangers are visible to ordinary eyes. Ewald's domain of course is politics and the secular state, though his judgements are handed down in a manner not unlike those of the Old Testament prophets. [Perhaps in part, due to Ewald being a Unitarian Christian]. Dietrich on the other hand, is a theologian, and his domain is the organised church of Germany. Here his vision is no less keen."[725]

If Dietrich had read Hitler's diatribe in September 1925 as a mature and scholarly nineteen-year-old theological student in Berlin, albeit sixteen or so years Ewald's junior, it is likely that he too would have sensed the peril for Germany that this demagogue represented. As far as I am aware, there is no evidence to suggest that Dietrich had yet foreseen this future; he was a theologian who focussed on religious writings and the classics, both ancient and more recent. Unlike the German Christians, Dietrich was never going to entertain any concept of a führer, or more to the point, a verführer virtually usurping Christ. By mid 1931, while Dietrich had indeed sensed the ominous political and theological clouds on the horizon, he had not yet recognised the evil of their central protagonist, even though his true identity, from that point on, would reveal itself.

After the 1928 election, Hitler and his cronies were not taken seriously when they secured 2.6% of the national vote; in the Silesian province, it was 1%.[726] But following the Wall Street collapse of October 1929, in September 1930, as Dietrich arrived in New York, the National Socialists were getting the second most votes among the multitude of parties in the Weimar political landscape. The ideal scenario for extremist parties of all persuasions was now set — a weak succession of governments, products of a fractious democracy beset by the economic chaos of the Great Depression. Choice may be the cornerstone of democracy, but in the political landscape of Weimar, literally dozens[727] of political parties were unable to form a robust coalition to counter the seductive rhetoric of the Nationalist Socialists. The party backed by the von Kleists, the Bismarcks, the Wedemeyers and the Tresckows, was the German National People's Party (Deutschnationale Volkspartei (DNVP)).[728] In all, however, there were about thirty parties in the Weimar Republic, all with their divergent agendas. Some would come to align themselves with the communists, and some with the National Socialists.

In February 1931, amidst the growing turmoil and chaos of post Wall Street Weimar, Oma Ruth's first grandchild, the stunningly beautiful but headstrong Raba,[729] born in 1909 to Oma Ruth's equally headstrong first daughter Spes,[730] was seduced by the rhetoric of the increasingly popular National Socialist Party.[731] Raba was the first female of the von Kleist family to attend University,[732] and in identifying with this party, she was following a trend among the university students around the country. For example, ninety percent of Protestant theology students at one university wore their party badges to class.[733] Months later, in September that year, Raba and her mother spent a week at Oma Ruth's cottage at Klein Krössin near Kieckow. The matriarch hoped that her headstrong daughter Spes would find fulfilment through her children and music, and that her granddaughter's flirtation with the National Socialists was merely a passing phase.[734]

However, as the morning passed, Raba prepared a speech she was to give the following week at a Nazi Party student rally to be held in Berlin's Sport Palace. She saw this as a great honour and a challenge, as she had never spoken publicly before.[735] Serendipitously, there was a gathering that Saturday afternoon of the local Agricultural Council at the estate of Jürgen von Wödtke, a relative whose father Fritz had helped Ruth to maintain and run her estate upon the death of her husband in 1897.[736] On this afternoon, the younger Wödtke opened the meeting with exhortations to his listeners for all to come aboard and help implement the "*new*" Germany. He made no explicit reference to Hitler.[737] There was polite applause as the young female guest asked for a chance to speak. She saw this as an opportunity to practise her speech among the less sophisticated and discerning Junkers.[738]

Rarely, if ever, was a female allowed to speak at such gatherings;[739] but as the cordial and respected Jürgen von Wödtke called for order, silence descended as Raba stepped onto the raised platform where the Wödtke grand piano stood. Without making any references to the Jews,[740] she extolled the benefits of joining the National Socialists, to redeem the last twelve years of humiliation post Versailles. She questioned how one could remain loyal to a government that lacked the courage to stand up to international treachery and Bolshevism.[741] As her speech concluded amidst rapturous applause, including from her dear Oma, she stepped down to be congratulated by everyone — minus the figure she spied behind the hall curtain, who, up until now, had been conspicuous in his apparent absence, but had heard every word.

"Raba," rather than inviting her, Ewald commanded her, "I would like a moment with you in the garden."[742] Raba quickly disentangled herself from her numerous well-wishers, and followed her mother's cousin through the terrace door and onto the bench beneath the huge maple tree, well out of earshot of her new admirers, who were blind to the dire events boded for their beloved Germany under Hitler's National Socialists.[743] Ewald outlined what was likely to come to Raba and cautioned her against quoting Hitler's writings without examining them in full; he made her aware of the penchant for thuggery and intimidation, in particular, of the thugs of the Sturmabteilung (SA or Brown Shirts).[744] Ewald was stern, but as he stood and helped Raba to her feet, he warmly embraced her, declaring his devotion to her, her mother, and her grandmother, all of whom were Kleists like himself.[745]

Upon her return to Berlin, Raba told Doctor Josef Goebbels that speech making was not her forte, and begged him to excuse her from giving it. Goebbels agreed, but she still joined the Nazi students in the cabaret following the rally, where the wine and beer flowed freely. When they expressed their true feelings about the Jews: "*Wenn das Judenblut vom Messer spritzt, dann geht es nochmal so gut,*" ...which translates to: "When Jewish blood spills from my knife, so much better is my life."[746]

Chapter 9

Raba felt ill; she raced to the toilet to spew forth the beer, sausages and most of all, abject feelings of guilt.[747] Raba rushed home, dispensing with all "*Auf Wiedersehen*(s)" to her former National Socialist "friends." Her life, apart from the immediate question of "where do I belong?,"[748] would soon take another twist. Her home was located in the Grunewald district,[749] a Berlin enclave of culture and tolerance, where Jews and Gentiles from various professions, including the Bonhoeffers,[750] lived in a harmony that seemed to be immune to the madness that was descending on Germany. She pondered her future, in the light of Ewald's warning a few days before.[751]

On the first Sunday morning of October 1931, Raba was woken from her sleep by the phone ringing, changing her life forever. The caller was Baldur von Schirach, the Nazi Party student leader: "

> Raba, I have bad news for you. Doctor Goebbels gave me a report yesterday showing that you are one-fourth Jewish blood, on your father's side... Of course, you know what this means; you must give up your post. You know the rules as well as I. But as far as I'm concerned, you may certainly stay in the party."[752]

Raba kept her self-control, but when the call ended, she burst into tears.[753] While she had been on the brink of quitting the party in any case, this revelation, in the midst of rising National Socialist power, was, for her, a seismic shock. Ten years earlier, Raba's parents divorced, but now there erupted an acrimonious spat of finger pointing.[754] Spes accused her former husband Walter Stahlberg of hiding his ancestry, while Walter, in turn, accused Spes of bigotry.[755] However, before long, these two intelligent and decent people came to realise that their children's futures were at stake.[756] Walter promised to look into the state birth and marriage records, and see to it that any "incriminating" evidence was removed.[757] Such was the atmosphere of fear and suspicion during the social and economic chaos of the crumbling Weimar Republic fifteen or so months before Hitler's rise to power. Spes phoned her mother at Klein Krössin to tell her about the skeleton in the cupboard.[758]

Oma Ruth, realising there is a time for prayer and a time for action, decided upon the latter. She wrote to the journalist in Hamburg with whom she had made contact when her book was published in 1925.[759] She asked, would he please investigate? Oma Ruth needed to know if her former son-in-law, Walter Stahlberg, was half-Jewish.[760] Some weeks later, on a rainy Sunday afternoon in November, Walter Stahlberg made an unannounced visit to his former wife's Berlin apartment. It was their first face-to-face contact for almost a decade.[761]

After their first greeting and handshake, the atmosphere was tense, but when their eyes met, a long -lost tenderness was reborn.[762] Walter took from his pocket the three documents that were the reason for his visit. They were certified documents direct from the Stettin Provincial Registry, one for each of their three children; Raba, Alla, and Hans Conrad, each "documenting" the names of paternal ancestors going back four generations. As Spes carefully read through them, she found no mention of any Jewish ancestry.[763] Puzzled, Spes looked up at Walter; he assured her, as he took her hand, that any Jewish blood in the Stahlberg family had been purged from the Provincial Registry. "In Stettin," declared Walter, "we Stahlbergs still count for something!"[764] As Walter turned to go, Spes stammered "thank you"; when the door closed behind Walter, she sat down with her head in her hands and wept.[765] Deep down, she realised, you cannot truly undo the past.

Meanwhile, Raba made two phone calls to Goebbels and to Baldur von Schirach to resign from the Nazi Party. The confidence and composure she displayed in dealing with the matter surprised even herself.[766] She adopted a new family name and started to attend church for the first time in years, a Catholic church in Berlin. She didn't tell her mother about this, nor her devoutly Lutheran Oma.[767]

In the following month of December, the matriarch at Klein Krössin received a phone call from her journalist contact in Hamburg. Having examined the Stahlberg family records in Stettin and Hamburg for traces of Jewish descent, he advised Madam von Kleist to leave the affair alone, as it was worse than she thought![768]

Walter's maternal grandfather was Wihelm Moritz Heckscher, the Justice minister for a brief period during the 1848 German Revolt, while his father had been the president of the Hamburg synagogue.[769] This fact was not lost on Raba, when in 1986, at the age of 76, she emigrated to Israel; in 1989, she converted to Judaism and adopted the family name of her Jewish forebears — Heckscher. In the process she took the full formal title of Ruth Roberta Stahlberg Heckscher, and every Friday, she worked as a volunteer at Jerusalem's Yad Vashem Holocaust Museum.[770]

In April 1932, Hindenburg, in a second round of voting for the office of President, won with 53% of the vote, thanks to all the democratic parties urging their supporters to back the 84-year-old war hero as the defender of the constitution. While 10% of the vote went to rather inconsequential candidates, Hitler achieved 37% of the vote.[771] It was an ominous portent that the solidarity shown in the Presidential election would not even last the month.

The incumbent chancellor was Heinrich Brüning of the Catholic Centre Party, backed by a weak Weimar coalition that excluded the Social Democrats on the left and the German Nationals on the right. In the Reichstag, the left and right mainstream parties aligned themselves with the two most extreme parties, the Communist party and the National Socialists, to form a hostile majority to the incumbent government. Brüning, powerless to deal with the imploding economy and untenable government, made a move which his detractors called a betrayal of German democracy. He declared a state of national emergency.[772] This move alienated Brüning from many parties in the Weimar political landscape. One of them was the party of the Pomeranian Junkers, the German National People's Party (DNVP), with its agenda of resurrecting the old Hohenzollern monarchy. The DNVP were themselves deeply divided as to who should replace Brüning. Twenty years later, Hans Jürgen[773] would look back with regret when he said to his son that they all erred by not supporting Brüning in what turned out to be the critical final months of Weimar's existence.

Weimar still had another nine or so months to run before President Hindenburg would be pressured into allowing a National Socialist minority government to form in January 1933. Every political machination in that period leading to Hitler's rise to power repeated a pattern of bargaining and compromise. The numerous parties and individuals were too preoccupied with their own petty agendas and some didn't hesitate to make deals with the demagogue to out-manoeuvre more benign rivals. Franz von Papen[774] of the ultra-right wing of the Catholic Centre Party, who would take power in June 1932 with the assistance of Kurt von Schleicher, made a deal with the Nazis to tolerate their SA thugs in return for their support of Papen's cabinet.[775] Papen outdid Brüning in the abuse of emergency powers. More than once he dissolved parliament. In October, in the town of Belgard (now Białogard in modern-day Poland) near the von Kleist estates, multiple bloody clashes took place between the communists and the SA. The landowners, astonished by the utter lawlessness, blamed the police for their failure to maintain law and order.[776]

In November 1932, elections were held; surprisingly the National Socialists lost a substantial number of seats to their opposing extremist rivals. Papen was then forced to resign, as he had lost the support of Hindenburg and his old friend Hans von Wedemeyer. The following month, Hindenburg reluctantly appointed Kurt von Schleicher, the general of the Reichswehr, as chancellor. Oskar von der Osten, Ewald's choice as chancellor over Papen back in May,[777] lamented Schleicher's appointment as a descent into military dictatorship; in contrast, Hans von Wedemeyer applauded it.[778] In nearby Wartenburg, the aging Osten's young friends, Gert and Henning von Tresckow, the sons of Ruth's deceased sister Anni, perceived Hitler as Germany's sole saviour. However, after Hitler took power, their favourable perceptions of him faded.

In early January 1933, Papen had not forgotten Schleicher usurping him as chancellor the month before. If it took a deal with the evil incarnate to remove Kurt von Schleicher, then so be it — "I can control him!"[779] This idea horrified Ewald,[780] and he had intended to discuss this matter with both Hindenburg and Papen. If Papen could not be persuaded to desist from bargaining with Hitler, Ewald intended to meet with Alfred Hugenberg, the leader of the DNVP, which was the party of the Kleists. Before doing so however, Ewald, himself a member of the DNVP, decided to arrange a meeting with the Hitler. Hitler was much less accessible than Hindenburg for the Junkers, but Ewald was able to prevail on Papen to arrange a meeting.[781] As leader of a party represented in the Reichstag, Hitler was entitled to an office in the Chancery, where most party leaders vied for the largest windows and best views of the Wilhelmstrasse. Hitler had chosen an interior office with no windows and just two pieces of furniture — a comfortable chair and a footstool. As Ewald's meeting with him progressed, the reason for this arrangement would become clear.

When Ewald took the seat, he expected Hitler to sit on the cushioned footstool. Instead, Hitler began to rant as he paced back and forth across the room. As the rant progressed, he became more agitated and his pace quickened. Ewald, who had expected a productive two-way dialogue, was subjected to a recital of *Mein Kampf,* with special emphasis on Lebensraum in the east and his plans for Poland, Ukraine and Russia. Two hours later, having hardly spoken a word, Ewald bade his haranguer *"auf wiedersehen."* That night, from cousin Herbert von Bismarck's apartment, Ewald phoned his wife Anning: "There is no chance for compromise; the rest of my life will be dedicated to the destruction of that man before he destroys our nation and our history."[782]

Over the phone, Ewald took care not to mention the name, for even before Hitler took power, you had to be careful in those treacherous times.[783] Seventeen months later, in late June 1934, Ewald, like von

Papen, was fortunate to survive the *Nacht der Langen Messer* (Night of the Long Kives or Röhm purge), thanks to being forewarned by Oma Ruth's future grandson-in-law and young lawyer, Fabian von Schlabrendorff. Ewald remained in hiding for three weeks until the Gestapo lost interest in his pursuit; the purge had run its course, and all its prime targets were liquidated. Ewald's first week of hiding was with a left-wing contact of Fabian's in Berlin; the last two weeks he took shelter in the Swedish Embassy.[784]

In contrast to Hitler's one-way rant, a genuine dialogue with Hindenburg proved much easier for Ewald to arrange. The following day, the two Junker aristocrats were seated alone in the plush presidential office overlooking the Wilhelmstrasse. Ewald brought up the widespread rumour that Papen was only interested in ousting Schleicher, and in order to achieve this he would propose a cabinet that included Alfred Hugenberg, leader of the DNVP, and members of the Nazi Party, possibly with Hitler as chancellor. Ewald expressed his horror at this, to which Hindenburg replied that he had already heard from Papen himself that he wished to have Hitler installed as Reich chancellor. However, Hindenburg was quick to "assure" Ewald that his "sense of duty" would never allow Hitler to become Reich chancellor, as he regarded the Austrian as no statesman and fit only for the role of the Postal Ministry at best.[785]

Believing initially in Hindenburg's integrity as a fellow Junker, Ewald spent the next week in conversations with Papen, pleading with him to see past his personal grievance for the good of his country. But Ewald, now fearing his fellow Junker might falter, met with him again and attempted to make him realise the dire consequences of installing the "Austrian Bastard" as chancellor.[786] Neither man, however, heeded Ewald's warnings, as they could not envisage a minority of crass Nazis prevailing over a majority of "refined" and "noble" conservatives. About a fortnight later, Hindenburg dismissed Schleicher and appointed Hitler as chancellor of Germany, with Franz von Papen appointed as vice-chancellor and Reich Commissioner of Prussia. Papen had earlier declared, and may have been thinking then: "In two months' time we will have squeezed Hitler into a corner until he squeaks."[787]

In spite of Papen's major political miscalculation in regard to Hitler, predisposed by his petty revenge for being usurped by Kurt von Schleicher in November 1932, his survival instincts were razor-sharp. He survived the 1934 SA purge, unlike Kurt von Schleicher,[788] before being appointed as ambassador to Austria from 1934 to 1938; he helped bring to fruition Austria's annexation to Germany. This was followed by his next diplomatic appointment as ambassador to Turkey from 1939 to 1944, where he succeeded in keeping Turkey from signing any alliance with the Allies. In April 1945 he was arrested by the Allies and placed on trial as a war criminal, and while he was found not guilty by the Nuremberg tribunal of "conspiracy to prepare aggressive war," he was sentenced to eight years' imprisonment by a German court as a major Nazi. However, in 1949, he was released on appeal and fined. His story, *Der Wahrheit eine Gasse* [the truth an alley] was first published under the title *Memoirs* in the UK in 1952. He died in 1969 aged eighty-nine[789]

In a partial defence of Papen, it should be mentioned that he was not alone, even in western democracies, in fatally underestimating Hitler and his henchmen such as Joseph Goebbels, whose masterful manipulation of propaganda elevated Hitler to god-like status. A perfect example is an article written on Tuesday January 31 1933, just the day after Hitler took power, in the *Broken Hill Barrier Miner*, based in the far west of New South Wales in eastern Australia: "

> This is a swift dramatic result of the political and constitutional crisis precipitated by the resignation of General Von Schleicher. Though several powerful subordinates of Hitler are included in the Cabinet, the fact that it is a coalition will probably prevent the adoption of an undiluted Nazi programme."[790]

After Hindenburg's treacherous appointment of the new cabinet, Ewald had one last visit to make to the German Chancery, where he confronted Papen and Alfred Hugenberg, the leader of the DNVP. He declared them both to be traitors to the Fatherland.[791] Harsh words from a gentleman of the honoured Pomeranian Junkers, but warranted. Such words should also have been directed at his fellow Junker Paul von Hindenburg, but perhaps his honoured position as a war hero on the Eastern Front during the Great War deterred Ewald from labelling him a traitor. As later events would prove, von Papen's petty treachery, in unison with Hindenburg's complacency and Hugenberg's self-serving political short-sightedness, were more than a betrayal of Germany — ultimately, they were implicated in the betrayal of an entire continent.

Chapter 10

Swedish trip and the Brethren Houses

When Oma Ruth returned to Pomerania following the Berlin parade in early March 1936, she was having second thoughts over her attendance there, which had substituted for her normal attendance at the Sunday Finkenwalde service. She resolved not to tell Dietrich of her Berlin excursion,[792] knowing that he wouldn't harbour any notions of restored national pride embodied by waving swastikas.

For Britain and France, a tremendous opportunity was missed in the Rhineland to stop Hitler in his tracks; the marching of troops into the demilitarised Rhineland, unlike the January 1935 Saar Plebiscite, was a blatant violation of the Versailles Treaty. Moreover, Hitler's army at the time was still no match for Britain or France, making it difficult to envisage Hitler surviving for much longer in power. However, at the time, Britain and France were pre-occupied with the issue of Benito Mussolini's invasion of Ethiopia:[793] "

> ...in March 1936, Britain and France were given their last chance to halt, without the risk of a serious war, the rise of a militarised, aggressive, totalitarian Germany and, in fact — as we have seen Hitler admitting — bring the Nazi dictator and his regime tumbling down."[794]

When William C. Bullit, the American Ambassador to France, called on the German Foreign minister von Neurath in Berlin on May 18 1936, about two months following Hitler's military occupation of the Rhineland, Bullit wrote the following to the US State Department: "

> Von Neurath said that it was the policy of the German Government to do nothing active in foreign affairs until "the Rhineland had been digested." He explained that he meant that until the German fortifications had been constructed on the French and Belgian frontiers, the German Government would do everything possible to prevent rather than encourage an outbreak by the Nazis in Austria and would pursue a quiet line with regard to Czechoslovakia. "As soon as our fortifications are constructed and the countries of Central Europe realise that France can-

not enter German Territory at will, all these countries will begin to feel very differently about their foreign policies and a new constellation will develop," he said."[795]

The Austrian chancellor Dr. Kurt von Schuschnigg wrote in his memoirs: "

> As I stood at the grave of my predecessor [Engelbert Dollfuss, murdered in 1934 during the failed Austrian Nazi Party coup],[796] I knew that in order to save Austrian independence I had to embark on a course of appeasement... Everything had to be avoided which could give Germany a pretext for intervention and everything had to be done to secure in some way Hitler's toleration of the status quo."[797]

This sense of powerlessness was manifested in the construction of the fortress line, later dubbed in the west the Siegfried Line, but in Germany called the Westwall;[798] it dramatically altered the strategic map of Europe in Hitler's favour.[799] As is shown in multiple instances throughout this book, if your only hope against Hitler is appeasement, then you have no hope. Ironically, unbeknown to the French, Hitler had given the order for German troops to retreat in the event of French troops invading the Rhineland.[800]

In 1938, the Austrian Anschluss [annexation into Nazi Germany][801] and annexation of the ethnic German Sudetenland of Czechoslovakia took place.[802] For Oma Ruth, this pre-war territorial expansion by Hitler did not represent the restoration of German pride. Nor, it is likely, would she have welcomed the absorption of the defenceless remaining Czech rump state as a Reich "protectorate" in March 1939.[803] Indeed, following the Austrian Anschluss in March 1938, in contravention of a nationwide order, no swastika was flown at Kieckow or Klein Krössin; this disobedience resulted in Hans Jürgen spending a week as a guest in the local gaol. However, the swastika flag did wave on Ewald's Schmenzin estate, albeit with its pole standing in the middle of the appropriate heap of manure![804]

Months later, following the Sudetenland annexation in September to October 1938, when, in Stettin, there was a tumultuous celebration culminating in a torchlight parade, Oma Ruth remained in her apartment playing dice with three of her grandchildren and two Jewish house guests.[805] The latter were awaiting the issue of visas to Sweden, thanks to the contacts Dietrich had forged during his trip to Sweden with his ordinands in March 1936.[806]

Early that month, thanks in part to Birger Forell, the chaplain at the Swedish embassy in Berlin, Dietrich received an official invitation from the Church of Sweden, which included free board and lodgings for himself and his ordinands. This was for the trip the ordinands had requested at Dietrich's birthday celebration the previous month. Before long they boarded the boat from Stettin. Upon their arrival in Sweden, they were warmly welcomed, as they would be throughout the country, with the main Swedish newspapers covering their visits on the front page. The Archbishop and the widow of his predecessor, the great ecumenicist Nathan Söderblum, at whose grave an impressive memorial service was held, invited ordinands to stay in their homes, as did many other members of local churches.[807]

Inevitably however, the extensive coverage in the Swedish newspapers had its downside. The news was relayed to Heckel and his cronies within the Reichkirche. The warm Swedish reception that was afforded Dietrich and his ordinands, all of whom were members of the "renegade" Confessing Church, evoked great jealousy and disdain. Heckel was quick to write to Archbishop Eidem in Uppsala, asking whether his invitation to the Finkenwaldians should be understood as a statement by the Church of Sweden against the leadership of the German Evangelical Church. While the Swedish Archbishop hastened to reply that it was purely a private invitation, he later had to concede Heckel's point when his secretary pointed out to him that the trip had been arranged through official channels in Sweden.[808] Moreover, the seemingly innocuous concession won by Heckel at Fanø in 1934, was once again making itself felt. Heckel felt empowered to write to the Prussian church committee accusing Dietrich of being a pacifist and an enemy of the state; he recommended Dietrich have his *venia legendi*, his right to lecture at the University of Berlin, revoked.[809]

Dietrich had failed to notice, it seems, that since June 1935, university lecturers were not permitted to travel abroad without official permission. The Minister of Education wrote to him informing him of this violation, and stating that the seminary he directed, under the Fifth Decree on the Implementation of the Law for the "Protection" of the German Evangelical Church, no longer had the right to exist. Thus Finkenwalde now came under closer scrutiny by the Reich authorities.[810] At this time, the Reichkirche had been pursuing a nationwide theological revival. It was reaping extraordinary results. Ever since the humiliation of Versailles, this seemed to be the answer to the prayers of the Pomeranian Junkers, that the spirit of God would enter the hearts of their people and fill the churches as they were filled in the glory days of the Hohenzollerns. Certainly, the pews of churches which, ever since Versailles, had only drawn two or three people to a Sunday service, were now filled with parishioners, both young and old, brimming with a new-found pride.

This pride, embodied in the idolatrous worship of the verführer, was a restored and vainglorious national pride, rather than any sort of rebirth or renewal of faith in Christ. For the German Christians, this bastardisation of the church was its necessary "second reformation" to make it relevant in a resurgent Germany. Pastors, with the Nazi badge often resplendent upon their robes,[811] preached the revised interpretation of New Testament passages, removing all references to Jerusalem and Israel, coupled with a virtual rejection of the Old Testament.[812] These developments were not lost on Dietrich, who had formulated a decisive plan of action to counter the insidious corruption of church doctrine by the German Christians. Yet the Confessing Church was riddled with internal doubts and almost bankrupt, due to the never-ending legal battles with the relatively unlimited resources of the state.[813]

Dietrich's plan was to prevail upon the Pomeranian Council of Brethren to establish a Brethren House that would share facilities with the Finkenwalde seminary. Once established, newly graduated seminarians and other pastors would be trained in evangelism to go about the countryside and establish mission parishes within the Confessing Church. In this region of once feudal estates, the mission parishes would meet in the homes of sympathetic landowners such as Hans Jürgen and Ewald von Kleist, who were still patrons of the village churches, and in village homes of supportive parishioners.[814] Dietrich had resolved that if there was to be a church revival in Germany, then at least in Pomerania, it would be one truly in the image of Christ.

The Pomeranian Council of Brethren was supportive of Dietrich's undertaking, but promised nothing in the way of financial support. However, with the hand of Dietrich's Tante Ruth evident, the decision was unanimous that the first mission would be established in Belgard,[815] the home of the Kleists. As a result, in June 1936, the entire Finckenwalde seminary of twenty-five students and faculty moved to Belgard, with six village churches selected as missionary targets. Three were under the patronage of Ewald von Kleist, and one under Hans Jürgen; four brethren were assigned to each church, spending five days of the week in their respective assigned villages. A major obstacle was that the pastors of all the churches had been appointed by the Reichkirche;

the one at Ewald's Schmenzin church was the most militant, totally avoiding the Old Testament and editing the New Testament to avoid all references to Jerusalem and Israel; this was accompanied by his interminable denunciation of the Jews. It was only Ewald's church at Naseband that was blessed with a man of the cloth from the Confessing Church — the irrepressible pastor Reimer, who would later be jailed repeatedly but never silenced.[816]

The potential of conflict with the Reichkirche-appointed pastors was avoided by the brethren conducting their activities on weekdays when they were free to visit homes and to conduct Bible discussions with school-age children. In the evening, the village families were invited to the church, where each of the four visiting brethren spoke for no longer than ten minutes from the pulpit, filling the pews to capacity. Dietrich, being well cared for by Mieze and Hans Jürgen at the Kieckow manor house, visited each of the village church meetings on alternate evenings. The only disappointment was that Oma Ruth had to stay in Stettin to look after the six grandchildren of gymnasium age, thus missing out on the entire venture.[817]

Ruth and her family had committed all the resources they could towards Dietrich's endeavour. Nevertheless, this was not enough, making it evident that a broader and more organised system of support for Finkenwalde and the Brethren Houses was required sooner rather than later. Accordingly, on the last day of the Belgard mission, Hans Jürgen invited family, friends, neighbours and patrons of the district to Kieckow to a meeting with Dietrich. The families of the Bismarcks, Wödtkes, Braunschweigs and of course the Kleists of Schmenzin were among those present, as was Fabian von Schlabrendorff, instrumental in Ewald's fortunate escape from execution in the 1934 Röhm purge,[818] and now often seen in the company of Herbert von Bismarck's daughter and Ruth's granddaughter, Luitgarde. This was Dietrich's first meeting with both Fabian and Ewald and certainly not the last.[819] Dietrich gave a sobering assessment of the deepening church struggle, but he at least left with pledges of support that would guarantee the existence of Finkenwalde for another year.[820]

Moreover, in spite of the National Socialist propaganda surrounding the Olympics, another small victory of sorts for the Confessing Church would play out before year's end, thanks in part to the world's focus on Hitler's Third Reich.

Chapter 11

Memo to Hitler and his Olympics

In Dietrich's mind, Steglitz Synod, held in the wake of the infamous declaration of the anti-Jewish Nuremberg Laws in September
1935, had been far too much about preserving the existence of the Confessing Church at all costs.[821] However, around the time he established
the Brethren Houses in Pomerania, he heard that the Confessing Church
administration was preparing a memorandum to be presented to Hitler.
Moreover, one of the members of the three committees preparing the
draft was Franz Hildebrandt;[822] he worked on the final version and
asked Dietrich for advice several times during the process. While the
memo was a clear statement of the Confessing Church's position
against the policies of the Third Reich, it was not originally intended to
be published. Rather, it was handed in to the Reich Chancellery on
Thursday June 4 1936; its aim was to offer Hitler an opportunity for a
"discussion" of the facts. It seems that they had not consulted Ewald
von Kleist of Schmenzin in regard to the one-way nature of "discussions" with Hitler.

In any event, the memo addressed seven main points, of which
points five and seven were the most poignant: "

> Point 5: Protestant members of National Socialist organisations
> are being required to commit themselves without reservation to
> the [Nazi] world view. This world view is very frequently pro-
> posed as a positive replacement for Christianity, which has to
> be given up. But while blood, race, national heritage and hon-
> our are elevated to the status of eternal values, a Protestant
> Christian, according to the First Commandment, cannot accept
> this. While people of the Aryan race are glorified, God's Word
> testifies that all human beings are sinful. While the [Nazi] view
> imposes on Christians an anti-Semitism which commits them to
> hatred of the Jews, Christians are commanded to love our
> neighbours. This lays an especially heavy burden on the con-
> science of our Protestant church members, since it is their duty
> as Christian parents to combat this anti-Christian thinking in
> their children.

Point 7: [in addressing the idolatrous cult of the verführer]: We, however, ask that the people of our nation be free to go forward into the future following the cross of Christ as their standard, that their grandchildren may not curse them some day .."[823]

Even if Hitler received the memo, he would have had no intention of replying to it,[824] and no evidence of any reply exists. It seems more likely that he never saw it. In any event, the Reich Chancellery office passed it on to the Ministry of Church Affairs, from which it was passed on to the Evangelical High Church Council, where it remained dormant for six weeks. The memo's resurrection from its dormancy had nothing to do with any action by the Reich bureaucracy.

It was at this point that the *Morning Post* in England reported the existence of such a document, and on Thursday July 23, the entire text, word for word, appeared in the Swiss paper *Basler Nachrichten*. For those who had sent it to Hitler, this was the very outcome they wanted to avoid; for while it was regarded abroad as a courageous sign of resistance, opponents of the Confessing Church would spin it as an act of disloyalty or even treason, not as a genuine but naive attempt for dialogue with Hitler over their grievances. The Lutheran Council distanced themselves in every way from the authors of the memo, prompting the administration of the Confessing Church to assert their intention of a private dialogue with Hitler. They suspected a government department may have been responsible for the leak, and visited the Presidential Office of the Reich Chancellery and asking for an investigation.[825] At this moment in time, this seems a brave but pointless gesture.

Dietrich soon succeeded in discovering the informers; they were two of his former students, Werner Koch and Ernst Tillich.[826] The latter had been one of Dietrich's students in Berlin before 1933, but had since then ceased all contact. Werner Koch on the other hand had taken part in the second course at Finkenwalde and in the trip to Sweden, and when he first met Dietrich in 1931, he too had taken a most critical view of the ominous political developments.[827]

He was a gifted journalist and would, on Karl Barth's recommendation, write articles to prominent foreign news outlets. However, Barth's enthusiasm for Koch's articles was not shared by several Confessing Church staff members, and Koch was transferred as a pastoral assistant in Wuppertal to isolate him from his sources in Berlin. Friedrich Weißler, the Jewish Christian head of the Provisional Administration office of the Confessing Church, had one of the only three copies of the memo in his safe, which Ernst Tillich had been able to borrow overnight, ostensibly to take a few notes. Instead, without Weißler's knowledge, Tillich had copied the full text word for word, before he made contact with the *Basler Nachrichten* through Koch.[828]

At the time, the Third Reich's potential propaganda gold mine of the eleventh[829] Olympiad, where the eyes of the entire world would be watching, had yet to run its course in the first half of August. Hence Hitler, wishing to appear magnanimous and tolerant, delayed any action for now. While he must have been irritated by the black American Jessie Owens winning the most gold medals for any athlete at the games, Germany topped the all-important gold medal count and overall medal count by nations.[830] So in all, the games were a resounding propaganda coup for his regime. As Barbara Burstin, history lecturer at the University of Pittsburgh and Carnegie Mellon University, wrote: "

> It provided Hitler with a showcase. It was a propaganda bonanza for him... It kind of dulled the opposition to [Hitler] that clearly had been quite evident up to 1936. A lot of people felt he was clearly heading in the wrong direction, and by going to the Olympics we gave him the opportunity to appear sane, rational and tolerant."[831]

David Clay Large, author of *Nazi Games: The Olympics of 1936*, wrote: "

> The Berlin Olympics were the first to host the torch relay and the first to be broadcast on television—and some of its deeper-seated elements have continued as well... Those games really set the stage for the Olympics as we know them today. That injection of politics and extreme nationalism, that's continued. There's no question that nationalism is a very fundamental part of it all."[832]

Many Jewish athletes who either competed in the Olympics prior to 1936 or in the 1936 Olympics itself would become concentration camp inmates during the Holocaust. Among them were Ilja Szraibman, a Polish swimmer, and Roman Kantor, a Polish fencer, both of whom competed in 1936 and later died in the Majdanek camp near Lublin. One survivor was Alfred Nakache, a French swimmer and competitor in the 1936 games; he competed again in the 1948 Games in London, after surviving Auschwitz,[833] and towards the end of the war, Buchenwald.[834]

In London, Nakache swam in the 200m breaststroke, reaching the semi-finals, as well as playing in France's water polo team.

Before the games commenced, there had been widespread talk of a boycott by several European countries as well as in the US, were the debate was most heated, due in part to its significant Jewish contingent. However, Avery Brundage, then president of the American Olympic Committee, opposed a boycott, arguing that "the Olympic Games belong to the athletes and not to the politicians." In reality, however, he felt that America should applaud the new Germany for halting Communist gains in Western Europe (in the Spanish Civil War from 1936 to 1939), while at the same time perceiving that Jewish interests were in league with both a misguided liberal establishment and a sinister and deadly Communist conspiracy to undermine traditional American values.[835]

Of course, aside from the dubious perception of all Jews as being in league with communists, the notion that Nazi Germany had at the time stemmed westward expansion of the Soviet Union is questionable as well. Hitler, and to a greater degree Mussolini,[836] supported the Francoist forces in overthrowing a republican socialist government democratically elected in 1931. Indeed, within the first two weeks of the war, from July 17 1936, just preceding the Olympic opening ceremony, Berlin sent twenty planes and pilots to the Nationalists to assist them with flying in 3,000 troops stationed in Morocco. This was in response to control of the eastern and southern coasts of Spain by naval forces loyal to the leftist republican government.[837]

Poland was more in the spirit of stemming the Bolshevik tide westwards, after its victory over Lenin's autocratic Bolsheviks in the 1919-20 Polish-Soviet War. During this time, Germany was in a state of chaos in the aftermath of its catastrophic defeat in the Great War; this was coupled with the fact that France and Britain, so soon after the Great War, had no stomach or will for further armed conflict.

Admittedly, the US, France, and Britain supplied Poland with arms. And 2,000 French officers (no non-commissioned men) arrived in Warsaw in the spring of 1919,[838] including Charles de Gaulle, attached briefly to a Polish combat unit in July to August 1920.[839] The volunteer American Kościuszko Squadron, which included Merian Cooper,[840] the creator of *King Kong,* and the Ukrainian nationalist force of Semyon Petlura,[841] also took part. But most of the blood spilt in fighting the Bolsheviks in that conflict was undoubtedly that of Poles fighting for their newly independent Second Republic. Indeed, when the French General Weygand arrived in Warsaw in August 1920, with the Bolsheviks virtually at the gates of Warsaw, an agitated Piłsudksi asked him in perfect French; *"Combien de divisions m'apportez-vous?"* Weygand had no divisions to offer — only the counsel of abandoning Warsaw.[842]

In any event, with the eyes of the world now upon them, to protect their potential gold mine of propaganda, the Nazis took down anti-Jewish propaganda and did what they could to clean up Germany's image prior to the games. Ultimately, the US would send several Jewish athletes to the games, with many journalists covering the games in a most positive light. In particular, *TIME Magazine* reported that most newspapers focused on "the ceremonious procession" of the Olympics' first modern torch relay rather than "other goings on in Berlin."[843]

It seems one member of the US coaching staff shared Avery Brundage's disturbingly sympathetic view of the New Germany. As Jesse Owens was running to victory, two Jewish runners for the US team, Marty Glickman and Sam Stoller, had been suspiciously withdrawn by their coach from the 4×100 metre relay the day before the event, in what was believed by Glickman to be an attempt not to embarrass Germany. After the games, William E. Dodd, the US ambassador to Germany, said that Jews, upon games' end, awaited with dread the restoration of anti-Semitic Nazi actions.[844]

These fears were more than justified when the popular head of the Olympic village, Captain Wolfgang Fürstner, killed himself just two days after the games upon his dismissal from military service in accordance with the 1935 anti-Jewish Nuremberg Laws. The Nazis claimed that Fürstner's death was the result of a car accident.[845] However, it was not long before word of the cover-up was leaked to foreign journalists, including the *Sydney Morning Herald* in Australia, which reported that Fürstner had been found dead with a gun by his side.[846] The article mentioned that his percentage of Jewish blood was minimal.

Consequences for Werner Koch, Ernst Tillich and most of all for Friedrich Weißler, the Jewish Christian head of the Provisional Administration office of the Confessing Church, followed. Tillich and Weißler were arrested on October 6, and Koch's day of reckoning came on November 13 1936. On February 1937, all three of them were sent to the concentration camp at Sachsenhausen, where Weißler died just six days later, after being tortured as a Jew. Koch was released in December 1938, as was Tillich in 1939.[847] Emil Fackenheim, a surviving Jewish fellow prisoner of theirs in Sachsenhausen, found out long after the war why Ernst Tillich had been sent to the camp, when he read Bethge's biography of Dietrich. Tillich had told his fellow prisoners that he had circulated an anti-Nazi pamphlet. Fackenheim, upon reading

Bethge's biography of his dear friend all those years after the war, was stunned by the naivety of the memo's authors.[848]

Werner Koch had a close association with Ruth von Kleist. At her Stettin pension, Koch had for some time been the seminarian who always presided at their table on French speaking evenings. However, by October he had taken up a position as a journalist for the Confessing Church periodical, so Ruth, who had maintained an exemplary level of French throughout her life, continued to lead the conversations without her charming partner.[849] Upon hearing of his arrest the following month, Ruth prayed fervently for his release. She believed that when he was finally released in December 1938 upon an order signed by none other than Heinrich Himmler himself, it was due to a combination of fervent prayer and divine intervention. Dietrich, however, knew it also had a lot to do with good connections to the Nazis who now sat in places most high.[850]

Werner Koch was not the only one whom Oma Ruth prayed for. A year or so earlier, there may have been a detention here, a questioning there, an arrest, or maybe even an imprisonment, but not for long if one had friends with connections. Now however, one by one, here and there, seminarians, pastors and minor church officials were being picked up by the Gestapo on charges of spreading "false" propaganda at home and abroad. Dietrich, with his superb organisational skills, kept track of them all, with relevant details such as dates of arrest, locations, accusations, prisons and when possible, dates of release. At first there were only eight names on the list; but now it ballooned to seventy.[851]

Dietrich kept on top of it all, delegating tasks such as who should contact authorities, visit the prisoner, write letters to his parents, and provide support for his wife. As well, Dietrich kept a second list of pastors of Jewish descent or who had wives of like descent, as he envisioned that they would soon require special care. Each Sunday, following the Finkenwalde service, Dietrich presented Ruth with an updated carbon copy of the litany of arrests, and a list of those just released. Before supper, Ruth prayed aloud for all those arrested, then read aloud those names recognised by the children, before closing with the names of ones just newly released, whereupon she and the children would rejoice as if they were one of their own kin.[852]

In June 1936, before the leaking of the memo on July 23, Dietrich noticed in a Berlin bookshop a placard bearing the following lines of intimidating National Socialist rhetoric:

After the end of the Olympiade
we'll beat the CC to marmalade,
Then we'll chuck out the Jew,
the CC will end too.[853]
[CC: Confessing Church]

With the Olympiad pending, there was still, as Bethge put it in his biography of his dear friend, no lack of intimidation by party speakers and their press. On the other hand, it was clear that the influx of foreign visitors had compelled the state to act more cautiously. Dietrich felt that a pulpit proclamation of the memorandum could be made without any dire consequences of violence or arrest. On August 3 1936, two days following the opening ceremony of the Olympiad, it was decided that a modified version of the memo should be read on the 23rd, just a week following the end of the Olympiad. Moreover, one million pamphlet copies of the memo were printed and issued in a year where everything had seemingly gone right for Hitler, such as the occupation of the Rhineland, the Rome-Berlin axis, Francisco Franco's recognition as the Generalissimo and Chief of State of the Nationalist zone just two-and-a-half months into the Spanish Civil War on October 1,[854] the anti-Comintern pact with Japan, and most recently, the crowning jewel of propaganda that was the Eleventh Olympiad.[855]

As such, the Confessing Church was risking open criticism which could portray its proclamation to most Germans as that of disloyal whining or even outright treason, given the aforementioned string of glowing successes for the Führer's foreign policy. When the decision to make the proclamation was made public, the Reich minister Kerrl instructed the church committee to discipline anyone who did so, whereupon the committee then sent telegrams to its superintendents warning them of the consequences for their clergy. It was at this point that the Provisional Administration of the Confessing Church urged that Dietrich, come what may, must attend the summer Life and Work conference from the 20th to the 25th, accompanied by Werner Koch and superintendent Otto Dibelius[856] in the Swiss village of Chamby, near the eastern edge of Lake Geneva. He would also be accompanied by Eberhard Bethge.[857]

Originally, Dietrich had no intention of attending; early in the year, frustrated by foreign ecumenical organisations always sitting on the fence in order to accommodate both the Reichkirche and the Confessing Church, he resolved to never again attend such conferences with

Reichkirche officials present.[858] However, Dietrich realised that the present situation overrode his early year resolution: "

> At the moment, I can only say this, we should try to remain in Switzerland beyond the time of the conference. This can be very important .. It might be that we must stay another ten days... Please don't speak to anyone about this... It's just a matter of having someone there at this time. It's connected to the memorandum..."[859]

Dietrich's suggestion of a prolonged stay in Switzerland, and indeed the order itself for his attendance at Chamby, was a contingency plan in the event that the state took drastic action against the authors and those pastors making the proclamation from their pulpits. In short, Dietrich, with his intimate knowledge of the history of the memorandum, and his foreign ecumenical contacts, which included Bishops Bell and Ammundsen[860] among those to be present, made him the ideal candidate to be the Confessing Church's spokesman to the foreign ecumenical movement. In the worst case scenario, he could assist in possible measures from abroad, which could perhaps include the formation of a foreign delegation to hold the Reichkirche to account. At least, that was the theory.

As Sunday August 23 1936 arrived, a number of courageous pastors made the proclamation from their respective pulpits. Among this brave number were most of the Finkenwalde pastors in their isolated villages, including Gerhard Vibrans, a former ordinand from the first Finkenwalde course. A local sycophantic schoolmaster, following the service, hailed the passing village policeman, demanding "Arrest this traitor!" To which the policeman casually replied, "Can't. No orders." Indeed, one week following the closing ceremony for the Olympiad,[861] this was the case. The Gestapo had been ordered to avoid all violent intervention and arrest. The only action they took was to register the names of all the proclaimers, and later to implement a press campaign against the so-called "fellows without a fatherland."[862]

Thus, as no consequences came to pass, Dietrich and Eberhard, probably in celebratory moods, took a few days after the conference in Switzerland for a brief trip to Rome. This was the city that Dietrich loved more than any other since his stay there twelve years previously as an eighteen-year-old first year university graduate.[863]

Weeks later, however, came the arrests of Tillich, Koch and Friedrich Weißler, the Jewish Christian head of the Provisional Administration office of the Confessing Church. He would die within just a week of arrival at Sachsenhausen on February 13 1937, after days of torture for being Jewish, while Tillich and Koch, as mentioned earlier, were eventually released.[864] This was happening while the eyes of the world gradually turned away from Germany and Hitler's Olympics faded into history.

Chapter 12

The Sammelvikariats

While the meeting on the final day of the Belgard mission in June 1936 had, with its pledges, secured the existence of Finkenwalde for another year or so, by the middle of 1937, with an ever-tightening Gestapo noose, its existence was under serious threat. In September 1937, while Dietrich was on summer vacation with Eberhard Bethge, Hitler's henchmen sealed its doors. Dietrich explored every possibility to appeal its closure, but it was clear by the end of that year that its closure was irrevocable.[865]

Two or so months earlier on July 1 1937, again indicative of the ever tightening noose of the Gestapo, Martin Niemöller was arrested in Berlin; he was released eight months later. However, characteristically, they promptly re-arrested him, and he remained a so-called "personal prisoner of the Führer" almost until war's end,[866] before being liberated in Niederdorf in the German speaking South Tyrol region of northern Italy.[867] Around this time, Franz Hildebrandt, following an early release thanks to extraordinary efforts by the Bonhoeffer family, especially by Dietrich's brother-in-law Hans von Dohnányi, was able to use this fleeting respite to make his flight unnoticed to Switzerland, and ultimately to London.[868] As mentioned earlier, Franz became assistant pastor to his and Dietrich's old friend Julius Rieger at St. George's, where he continued to work with refugees, and Bishop Bell along with other ecumenical contacts. Of course, Dietrich would sorely miss one of his closest friends.

With the irrevocable closure of Finkenwalde, Dietrich realised that its spirit would now have to continue in a more covert fashion in an increasingly hostile totalitarian environment. The plan was for *Sammelvikariats* or collective pastorates. To begin with, Dietrich had to find a church whose senior pastor was sympathetic to the Confessing Church, then register the ordinands through the local police as "assistant vicars" under him. The ordinands would live in groups of seven to ten and would receive an education in the Finkenwalde mode. Finkenwalde would effectively continue to operate, but in a decentralised and much more mobile and covert mode, which included operation in much more remote areas of eastern German Pomerania.[869] From this point on,

Dietrich taught, reflected and wrote with no settled place to work, and without his book collection, which had always been readily on hand.[870]

Although he would never admit it to anyone inside Germany, he would at times yearn for a more settled existence; he wrote to Erwin Sutz in Switzerland in September 1938 that it was a pity that Sutz could not have got him for a year in Zurich as a substitute. His second sojourn in New York in the middle of 1939 was in part motivated by this desire for a more settled existence. But after less than a month, with a safe, comfortable existence in the New World there for the taking, Dietrich could not help but return to the responsibilities and dangerous existence in his beloved Germany.[871]

In 1938, two collective pastorates commenced operation at Köslin and Schlawe (now Polish Koszalin and Sławno).[872] The former was about 160 kilometres north-east of Stettin, while the latter was even more remote, about fifty kilometres farther east. The superintendent of the Köslin church district was the father of Fritz Onnasch, a Finkenwalde graduate, and he placed ten ordinands with five Confessing Church pastors in his area. The superintendent in Schlawe was Eduard Block, who employed Bethge and Dietrich as assistant ministers under him. This group of ordinands lived east of Schlawe in what Bethge described as "the rambling, wind-battered parsonage in Gross-Schlönwitz [now Polish Słonowice[873]], at the boundary of the church district."[874]

Dietrich split his time between Köslin and Schlawe, travelling between them on his motorcycle when weather permitted. Often, he travelled over 300 kilometres to Berlin and was on the phone almost every day, more often than not to his mother who continued to be his principal source of news from the national capital. As primitive as the conditions were at Gross-Schlönwitz, they seemed relatively luxurious when Eberhard Bethge and his group had to vacate them by the end of April 1939. For once, the reason was not Gestapo harassment, but that the local pastor was now in need of the parsonage.[875]

Their "new" accommodation, still in the vicinity of the town of Schlawe, was put at their disposal by the landowner von Kleist of Wendisch Tychow.[876] It was the Sigurdshof house near the village of Tychow (now Polish Tychowo[877]), backing onto the idyllic Wipper River[878] (now Polish Rzeka Wieprza).[879] It was even more spartan than Gross-Schlönwitz, as they had to fetch their water from a pump on the edge of the forest, while their food and coal for heating had to be brought in from afar. Moreover, the house had no electricity.[880] Nevertheless, Bethge, though concerned about the impending Pomeranian winter, which would be one of the worst on record, was complimentary about the area's secluded beauty; Dietrich's impressions were similar — he was enchanted with its wild beauty. For him, even in the midst of this most severe of Pomeranian winters, it was the ideal utopian escape from the machinations of Berlin. He felt that life in the country, especially in times like these, had much more human dignity than it did in towns.[881]

Moreover, it was thanks to the secluded beauty of Sigurdshof, in concert with the severe winter of 1939-40, that the *Sammelvikariat* was able to survive six months into the war.[882] This allowed for the fifth collective pastorate course to be completed on March 15 1940. But with the passing of winter, it was the faithful Erna Struwe, the housekeeper at Finkenwalde who had moved with the community to the Sigurdshof house, that handed Dietrich the police order to close the house.[883]

For almost five years from its very beginnings in Zingst, the underground seminary of the Confessing Church existed in its various manifestations. However, its end didn't mean that Dietrich was now unemployed as a pastor, as many pastors of Confessing Church congregations had been conscripted into military service, and somehow the void of pastorates without pastors had to be filled. As a result, "visiting pastorates" were set up, and Dietrich, with his experience of regular motorcycling to Berlin and around the various *Sammelvikariats* during their existence, was ideally suited to the task. He was assigned to the parishes of East Prussia.[884]

Chapter 13

Flight and the Tumultuous Appeasement of Evil

During the five years of the Underground Seminaries' existence, from April 1935 until March 1940, tumultuous events took place, not the least of which was during the year of 1938. These years were also tumultuous for Dietrich and his immediate family.

Apart from the Austrian Anschluss and Hitler's annexation of the ethnic German Sudetenland in Czechoslovakia, other notable events took place in 1938. There were proposed coup attempts on the Nazi regime, which never took place because, as Metaxas put it: "... the *fumfering* [dithering] inaction of the German army officer corps, bound and gagged by their misplaced scruples. In time the bloodthirsty devils with whom they were playing patty-cake would strangle them with the guts of their quaint scruples."[885]

At year's beginning, while attending a meeting of the Confessing Church in Dahlem in the south-west of Berlin on Tuesday January 11, Dietrich and his fellow ministers were paid a visit by the Gestapo. All thirty people were arrested and interrogated for seven hours at the Alexanderplatz Headquarters. While all were released, the bad news for Dietrich was that he was henceforth banned from Berlin and put on a train bound for Stettin with Fritz Onnasch that evening.[886]

The first term of collective pastorates had begun, and Dietrich was greatly relieved that he was able to continue his work there. However, by this time, via information conveyed by brother-in-law Hans von Dohnányi, who worked in the Ministry of Justice, hopes were raised that Hitler and his regime may have been on the way out. To be cut off from Berlin, with such a joyful possibility imminent, was bitterly disappointing. However, in early February, his parents met with him and the underground seminary's greatest patron, Tante Ruth, in Stettin, and on their return to Berlin, father Karl was able to bring his eminence to bear by somehow persuading the Gestapo to limit the ban to purely work matters. As a result, Dietrich was now free again to regularly commute to Berlin to at least see his parents and family.[887]

Back in the previous autumn, in late November 1937, Hitler suffered a blow when his Minister for Economics and architect of Germany's rearmament and economic recovery, Hjalmar Schacht, resigned. This was due in a great part to his simmering rivalry with Hermann Göring, who, in 1936, had become virtual dictator of the German economy.[888] Schacht, along with Gustave Stresemann, had helped engineer Weimar Germany's recovery from the rampant inflation of the early 1920s. He was concerned that Göring was leading the country into bankruptcy, and would testify at the Nuremberg Trials post-war that, in regard to economics, Göring was an incompetent fool.[889] Schacht had supported Hitler in violating the humiliating Versailles Treaty, but only in so far as to rearm Germany to the point where it would be back on an equal footing with the major powers such as Britain and France. He was adamant that rearmament should not be undertaken by placing Germany deeper and deeper into debt. Clearly, however, Göring had other ideas — that the basic tenets of "Görinomics" would address this shortfall via the plunder of future conquered nations.[890]

Hitler apologists and Holocaust deniers constantly point to the "economic recovery" supposedly engineered by Hitler and his regime. However, based on the testimony of Schacht, it is evident that the National Socialist-engineered economic recovery was based on the prospective plunder of future conquered nations. Much to the chagrin of the Soviets at the Nuremberg trials, Schacht was acquitted.[891] But soon after, upon visiting a friend outside Bavaria, where the Nuremberg writ was not valid, he was arrested in Stuttgart, placed in gaol, and sentenced by a de-Nazification court to eight years. However, on appeal, he was released in 1948, but when he entered the British Occupation Zone, he was again imprisoned to face further de-Nazification proceedings. It was not until the end of 1950 that Schacht was given final, unequivocal acquittal.[892] He lived on until 1970, passing away in Munich.

Earlier that same month, on November 5 1937, Hitler summoned his generals to a meeting where he made clear his plans for war.[893] In a four-hour rant, he outlined the plan to invade Austria and Czechoslovakia and to mollify Britain, his most powerful and immediate military threat for the time being. Nearly two years later, war with Britain and France did come to pass, and it was just sixteen months later, without a shot being fired, that all of Austria and Czechoslovakia[894] fell under the Nazi jackboot. Austria's fall was four years after the failed coup attempt by Austrian Nazis in July 1934, preceding the Fanø conference.[895]

When the generals left the November 5 meeting, they were in various states of shock and fury. The foreign minister, Baron Von Neurath, had several heart attacks. Chief of the elite General Staff, Ludwig Beck, upon witnessing and hearing this Hitlerite rant, was set on his mutinous course. In the following year, he would send Ewald von

Kleist of Schmenzin to London to seek British assurances that they would not allow Hitler to get away with marching into Czechoslovakia.[896] But more significantly, Beck would lead the conspiracy to assassinate Hitler, in which Dohnányi and Dietrich would also become involved. The problem was that Beck and the other generals were gentlemen from the old Prussian officer tradition, too refined to know how to deal with Hitler. Almost all of them loathed and hated Hitler, convinced he was leading their nation to its doom, but on the other hand, they had all sworn an oath to him as the undisputed leader of their beloved Germany. For them, Hitler was an obscene conundrum.[897]

Beck had done all he could to get the generals to stage a coup, but when this failed, he resigned.[898] This should have shaken the nation to its roots, but again, true to the refined and gentlemanly old Prussian officer traditions, he did it in such a way as not to draw attention to himself. He was caught between hate and loathing for a common swine he was convinced was leading his beloved Germany to its doom on the one hand, and on the other, the old Prussian officer tradition of unquestioning loyalty to the state. The latter, as was always the case with officers of this tradition at the time, won out. What they could not grasp, or perhaps were unwilling to grasp in their blinkered vision, was that their old honourable traditions had been trampled on and buried by Hitler and his inner circle. Nothing illustrated this more graphically than the Fritsch Affair of January 1938.[899]

Commander in Chief of the Army, General Wilhelm von Fritsch, had made the mistake of trying to talk Hitler out of his war plans. Thus, Hitler or one of his cronies needed to contrive some scandal to force his resignation. Indeed, Göring, who had been eyeing the top position in the military for some time, had already been successful in getting rid of the previous head of the army, Field Marshal Blomberg, by accusing his new wife of being a prostitute, which she had in fact been.[900] Fritsch, however, free of any potential scandal, wasn't going to be so easy to remove. Enter SS leader Himmler, a key player in eliminating Göring's most feared rival, Ernst Röhm, during the SA purge.[901] Himmler provided the incriminating evidence of a questionable eyewitness who claimed that Fritsch had a homosexual liaison in a dark alley near the Potsdam railway station with an underworld character named "Bavarian Joe."

Confronted with this allegation, Fritsch, with his sense of Old Prussian officer's honour, was speechless, and vowed to defend it. Dohnányi was determined to get to the bottom of it, and soon discovered that General Wilhelm von Fritsch had been "confused" with a retired bedridden cavalry officer named Frisch.[902] Himmler, Heydrich and the Gestapo were of course aware of this, but their desire to be rid of General Wilhelm von Fritsch was behind their attempt to frame him with a typographical error. They nearly succeeded, but thanks to the diligence of Dietrich's brother-in-law in the Ministry of Justice, they were caught red handed.

Initially, once he was made aware of the frame-up, General Fritsch vowed to fight the charge. It was envisaged that the military court would exonerate Fritsch, and that Himmler, Heydrich and Hitler, along with the Gestapo and SS in general, would be exposed for what they truly were. Plans were being made for a coup, and Dietrich and Dohnányi both waited with jubilant anticipation. The problem was that, at the last moment, General Fritsch, as was so typical of the Prussian officer class, allowed himself to get caught up in the conundrum of conflicting values. He now thought that fighting this charge publicly in court was beneath the dignity of a German officer. Incredibly, with the encouragement of Beck, he decided to challenge Himmler to the traditional "gentleman's duel"![903] As Metaxas wrote, "he may as well have challenged a shark to a game of chess!"[904]

A golden opportunity to save Germany from the apocalypse had been wasted. On the morning of February 4, Dietrich's thirty-second birthday, Hitler announced a drastic restructuring of the German military, starting with himself assuming control of the entire armed forces. In a stroke, the whole problem of Fritsch and more was eliminated by the dissolution of the War Ministry, replaced by the Oberkommando der Wehrmacht (OKW — High Command of the Wehrmacht), with Wilhelm Keitel appointed as its chief, due to his lack of leadership qualities.[905] The obsequious Keitel could be relied upon to be Hitler's proverbial rubber stamp. Incredibly, this would not be the final golden opportunity of that year, or before the outbreak of war, to stage a coup. But the inertia of the old Prussian officer class caught in the Hitler conundrum would not be the culprit.

It was out of the abject disappointment in the aftermath of the Fritsch Affair that much of the underground resistance to Hitler would emerge.[906] Its principal figure from the military would be Oberstleutnant (Lieutenant Colonel) Hans Oster, who became the head of the Central Division of the Abwehr (German Military Intelligence). Among the civilians, the former belligerent mayor of Leipzig, Carl Goerdeler, was a key figure. While mayor, in 1933 he refused to raise the swastika in the city hall; in 1937, he refused to remove a public statue of the Jewish composer Felix Mendelssohn.[907] When he was absent from the city, they had removed it in any case, but this did not weaken Goerdeler's commitment to the fight against Hitler.

During the following month of March, Hitler's troops marched into Austria without a shot being fired; this followed Hitler's bullying of the Austrian chancellor Kurt von Schuschnigg during a meeting in Hitler's Berghof in Bavaria the previous month.[908] Later, Schuschnigg repudiated the agreement, announcing a plebiscite on the question of the Anschluss, but was again intimidated. He cancelled the plebiscite and resigned from office, ordering Austrian troops not to resist the German troops crossing over the frontier. On Sunday April 10, a plebiscite did indeed take place in Austria, but by then, with the implementation of the Anschluss, it was no more than a token formality.[909]

Hitler's rejection of the humiliating Versailles Treaty had already resonated powerfully with many Germans from that era. Now, after a major territorial gain without a shot being fired, under the pretext of uniting the Germanic peoples and giving the union a façade of legitimacy, the Führer or Verführer worship was rising in a crescendo. As such, there was no shortage of public figures eager to curry sycophantic favour. Sadly but predictably, religious figures were among them.

The first of them was Bishop Sasse of Thuringia, (not to be confused with Hermann Sasse who co-authored the Bethel Confession with Dietrich in August 1933) demanding that all pastors under him take, as an "inner command," a joyful personal oath of loyalty to the Führer and Reich, synonymous to "One God—one obedience in the faith."[910] Other bishops, seizing the opportunity to express their sycophantic gratitude, ordered their own pastors to do likewise. The new head of the Reichskirche, the obsequious Dr. Friedrich Werner, decided he would not be outdone. He chose Hitler's birthday of April 20 to publish a sweeping directive in the *Legal Gazette*, ordering every single pastor in Germany to take an oath of obedience to the Führer.[911] Failure or refusal to do so would mean that pastor's immediate dismissal.

For many Confessing Church pastors, this was akin to bowing down to a false god. Just as early Christians and Jews of the time had refused to worship images of Caesar and the like, these modern- day pastors refused to swear this oath to Adolf Hitler. Other pastors within the Confessing Church thought of it merely as a formality not worth losing their careers over; another group, who felt they had taken this oath under extortion, did so with the guilt of a torn and heartsick conscience. Dietrich, seeing it as a cynical political move on Werner's part, urged the Confessing Church to oppose it.

However, the oppressive totalitarian state grew in power and popularity by the day. In April, Dietrich was in Thuringia and passed by the famous Wartburg castle in Eisenach. There, in 1521, following his excommunication by Pope Leo X, Martin Luther translated the New Testament into German.[912] Now, in the aftermath of the Anschluss, Dietrich noticed its great cross had been eclipsed by the hideous floodlit swastika.[913] Karl Barth, forced to leave Germany in 1935 and now writing from Switzerland,[914] expressed his dismay.[915] For Dietrich, the only bright spot at the time was in Pomerania, where he ministered the confirmation of three of Ruth von Kleist-Retzow's grandchildren in April—Spes von Bismarck, Hans-Friedrich von Kleist-Retzow, and Max von Wedemeyer.[916] The service was held in the church at Kieckow, and among the congregation was Maria von Wedemeyer (1924-77),[917] to whom he would propose marriage four years later. Both the young men confirmed that day would be killed during the war—Hans-Friedrich in 1941, and Max in 1942; so also was Max's father.[918]

Late in the following month of May, on the 28th, Hitler confirmed to his generals his intention to invade Czechoslovakia and ultimately end its existence, with the words; "It is my unshakeable will that Czechoslovakia be wiped off the map!"[919] With Germany leaning towards war, the next golden opportunity for a coup arose, as the German military did not possess the capability to wage a successful full-scale invasion of the Czech lands. At least, not in the event of a probable French and British intervention on the Czechs' behalf.

In August, Ewald von Kleist-Schmenzin travelled to England and met with Winston Churchill[920] to discuss the possibility of Britain assisting Germany to set up a new government.[921] With no one from the Wehrmacht, Abwehr or German Foreign Office willing to make this trip to London, which could be construed as treasonous by the Reich, Ewald saw himself in the role of an obscure German conservative, unknown abroad, but able to talk the language of the British Conservatives in power.[922] While Hitler's generals would be hoping for Hitler to march into Czechoslovakia, this hope was not based on the belief that it was wise for the expansion of Hitler's Reich. Rather, they saw it as a perfect opportunity for them to launch the coup they so longed for in the aftermath of the failed invasion they envisaged.[923] They of course, did not count on Neville Chamberlain's capacity for appeasement, which came weeks later at the infamous Munich conference in late September.

In the meantime, the clock was ticking for Dietrich's twin sister Sabine and her husband of Jewish descent, Gerhard Leibholz. They had already travelled to Italy and Switzerland on holiday and had experienced the freedom of being outside the Third Reich. When they returned, especially as they approached Göttingen, Sabine would recall how they felt an iron band tightening around their hearts.[924] Stories of Jews being abducted at night and humiliated abounded, and whenever their doorbell rang, they were terrified of what trouble might lie behind it. Laws were about to take effect making it compulsory for a Jewish man to amend his passport to contain the middle name Israel if his name was not obviously Jewish, and in the equivalent case for women, to Sarah.[925] Now if war were to break out, which seemed likely by September 1938, Germany's borders would be sealed, making a successful flight from the Reich impossible. Little wonder then, that by early September, Hans Von Dohnányi, with his insider information, was urging the Leibholzes to flee.[926]

They finally made their heartbreaking decision. In Berlin, prior to their flight from their beloved homeland, they discussed the final details with family. Phone conversations had to be spoken in code, and letters, likewise, written in it.[927] At the time, with news from von Dohnányi of an imminent coup to follow the envisaged failed invasion of Czechoslovakia, the Leibholzes hoped that their exodus from Germany would only be for a matter of weeks; but come what may, the present situation demanded their painful departure from Germany.[928]

On Thursday September 8, Sabine and Gerhard arrived back in Göttingen, closely followed by Dietrich driving his car, accompanied by Bethge, his assistant minister. The plan was for them to accompany the Leibholzes part of the way to the Swiss border the following day. Secrecy was paramount; the girls' nanny, even as she was getting the girls ready for school the following morning around six-thirty, was left in the dark as to their real intentions. Sabine told the girls they were going to Wiesbaden, and then she informed the nanny they would return on Monday.[929] Fortunately, while eleven-year-old Marianne suspected something was afoot, she had the presence of mind to conceal this fact. This was critical, when her best friend Sybille arrived as usual for them to walk together to school. At this moment, it occurred to Sabine that she and the family might never see Sybille again, and she felt compelled to remember what Sybille looked like. This is a poignant reminder of the pain of leaving their beloved country.[930]

Dietrich and Bethge followed the Leibholzes as far as the town of Giessen, where they parted ways at dusk.[931] On the way, the girls were told the truth. Late at night they finally crossed the Swiss frontier, with the girls Marianne and Christiane feigning anger at being awoken from a deep sleep, in order to discourage the German frontier guards from being too diligent in their search of the vehicle. The daughters' ruse was successful, but any hope of returning to Germany soon would be dashed at the Munich appeasement conference at the end of the month. In the meantime, with expectations of an imminent coup, Dietrich and Bethge returned to the Leibholzes' home in Göttingen, where they stayed during the final days of September.[932] There, Dietrich resumed his work on the manuscript *Life Together*, after having first dictated it to his ordinand Hans-Werner Jensen at Gross Schlönwitz. This work would become a classic of devotional literature, concerned not with teaching theology, but written for the faithful with the intention to develop or heighten feelings of devotion toward God or the saints.[933]

Czechoslovakia and its ethnic German Sudetenland remained dominant in the news.[934] The Anschluss of Austria had been portrayed by Hitler not as an act of aggression, which it truly was, but in the guise of the benevolent father welcoming his children home.[935] A modern-day parallel can be seen in Vladimir Putin's attempt to legitimise Russian aggression in the Ukraine by claiming the peoples of the Ukraine and Russia as the same people. In the Sudeten crisis, Hitler was using the same logic, but this was not going to be quite as straightforward as in the Austrian instance.

For one thing, unlike Austria, the majority of the Czech nation didn't speak German, and the Sudetenland still possessed within it a substantial Czech minority. Furthermore, considering the major strategic defensive significance of the Sudetenland for the Czechs, with the natural barrier of the Giant Mountains coupled with its vast fortifications, its concession would leave Czechoslovakia a sitting duck for invasion at Hitler's whim, as indeed it would be six or so months later. Moreover, the Sudetenland was the Czech industrial heartland.[936]

The Sudeten Germans living in the industrial heartland of Czechoslovakia prospered quite well as ethnic minorities went, at least in comparison to ethnic German minorities in Poland and Italy, for example, and better than Czechoslovakia's ethnic Slovak minority, which was, linguistically and ethnically, related more closely to the Czechs.[937] It was in the interests of Hitler, with his aim of wiping Czechoslovakia from the map, to exaggerate any perceived discrimination against Sudeten Germans by the Czechs. In this plan, Konrad Henlein, the leader of the Sudeten German Party (SDP), formed in 1933, the year of Hitler's rise to power, was crucial. This is evident in the fact that from 1935 onwards, Henlein's Sudeten German Party was secretly subsidised to the tune of 15,000 Reichmarks a month by the German Foreign Office.[938]

Within a couple of years, the SDP had secured the majority of the Sudeten vote, and by the time of the Austrian Anschluss, it was perfectly placed to do Hitler's bidding. That was, as Henlein summarised Hitler's objective upon meeting with him in Berlin just a fortnight after the Anschluss, to "… always demand so much that we can never be satisfied." In so doing, Henlein would provide the undermining from within, while Hitler would confuse, mislead and divide Czechoslovakia's allies to conceal his real purpose.[939] For the German generals however, it was clear that the Sudetenland was merely a pretext for blind and naked aggression that would lead Germany into a world war it could not win. Around this time, Karl Barth wrote in a letter to a friend: "

> Every Czech soldier who fights and suffers will be doing so for us too, and I say this without reservation—he will also be doing it for the church of Jesus, which in the atmosphere of Hitler and Mussolini must become the victim of either ridicule or extermination."[940]

Somehow the letter was made public and triggered a huge furore. Sadly, many in the Confessing Church thought he went too far, and distanced themselves from him.

As the month of September was drawing to its close, the coup was keenly anticipated by all involved. However, they needed Hitler to make the first move, the foolhardy invasion of Czechoslovakia. Germany was simply not prepared for this action on the scale that would be required when Britain and France intervened. Moreover, the Czech fortifications in the Giant Mountains, the natural barrier between Silesia and the Sudetenland, were the most formidable in Europe, with the possible exception of the French Maginot Line.[941] The German Generals had Churchill's letter of assurance, delivered on Ewald's visit in August, that Britain would not abandon the Czech nation. In this letter, Churchill had written: "

> I am sure that the crossing of the frontier of Czechoslovakia by German armies or aviation in force will bring about renewal of the World War. I am as certain as I was at the end of July, 1914, that England will march with France … Do not, I pray you, be misled upon this point."[942]

Ultimately, however, in a tragic irony, the German coup plotters *would* be misled on "this point," but not in any way that they or Churchill could have imagined. Such were the terms of Chamberlain's appeasement, rendering Hitler's Sudeten military conquest superfluous.

As the German generals waited in the wings for the envisioned "first move," they considered their options upon Hitler's arrest. One prime option involved declaring Hitler insane and hence unfit for leadership, and the invasion of Czechoslovakia certain to bring disaster and ruin to Germany. Eventual war, precipitated by the invasion of Poland a year later, would in time prove beyond any shadow of a doubt that Hitler was a pathological madman. But for the Bonhoeffers, war was not necessary for them to be convinced of this fact. The testimony of Dietrich's father and esteemed psychiatrist, Karl, to this fact would be critical in the coup's envisaged aftermath.[943] Hitler's popularity had soared following the Anschluss, and it was essential that he should not be transformed into a martyr. Rather, by going through legal means to expose his crimes and psychopathic behaviour, they hoped to avoid plunging the country into civil war.

For the Bonhoeffers, the most immediate benefit would be the return of the Leibholzes to Germany. Dohnányi's news that the coup was imminent was the reason why Dietrich and Bethge had stayed in the Leibholzes' home in Göttingen for most of September. At this time, all European leaders thought it inevitable that Hitler would march into Czechoslovakia even though he was not ready to wage war on a such a scale. His psychotic mindset could not consider a humiliating last-minute back-down, leaving him the only option of playing "bluff-poker."

Tragically, Hitler's mastery of the bluff, and Chamberlain's ineptitude and lack of nerve, meant that Czechoslovakia was doomed to be sacrificed for the fool's gold of "Peace for our time."[944] Instead of an immediate war on favourable terms, the bitter fruit was humiliation and war one year later on vastly inferior terms, when Hitler, now much better armed, marched into Poland, laughing contemptuously at Chamberlain. Hitler was surprised by Chamberlain's appeasement, while the coup plotters were aghast. The sixty-nine-year-old Prime Minister met at Hitler's beck and call, even flying seven hours from London to Berchtesgaden on the far side of Germany, although he had never before flown in an aircraft.[945] In the most superficial sense, at Munich, Chamberlain had achieved, on the night of September 29th—30th 1938, a "bloodless" solution to the Sudeten crisis. But the consequences far outweighed what the consequences of forcing Hitler's hand would have been.

The Munich appeasement agreement, with Czechoslovakia's absence the elephant in the room, was signed by Germany, Italy, Great Britain, and France; it compelled Czechoslovakia to surrender the Sudeten region to Nazi Germany, with German troops occupying the region between the 1st and 10th of October. Hitler again used the pretext of the benevolent father reuniting the Germanic peoples, in this case 198 years after the Prussian annexation of Silesia had separated the Silesian Germans in 1740 from their kin in Austrian-occupied Sudetenland on the opposite side of the Giant Mountains.[946] (Polish: Karkonosze, Czech: Krkonošich, German: Riesengebirge).[947]

The consequences for Czechoslovakia of this disgraceful pact went light years beyond simple or benign territorial concession. The final settlement of November 20 1938 compelled Czechoslovakia to concede to the Third Reich 28,500 square kilometres of territory, in which dwelt 2.8 million ethnic Germans and 0.8 million Czechs.[948] Whatever grievances the Sudeten Germans had under a Czech regime were small in comparison to those of the ethnic Czechs, part of what the National Socialists perceived as Slavic *Untermenschen* (subhuman);[949] they made up almost a quarter of this disputed territory's population under Hitler's rule. Militarily, this territorial concession was catastrophic for Czechoslovakia, as the vast Czech fortifications lay within it. However, the devastating consequences for the Czechs, upon which lay the dubious foundations of "Peace for our time," did not end there.

The effects on the Czech infrastructure and economy were crippling. Their entire system of rail, road, telephone and telegraph communications was disrupted, and they lost 66% of their coal, 80% of lignite, 86% of chemical works, 80% of cement, 80% of textiles, 70% of iron and steel, 70% of electric power, and 40% of timber.[950] For Carl Goerdeler, the former mayor of Leipzig, the concession was nothing short of "outright capitulation."[951] Another disturbing aspect of this affair was that, while Nazi Germany was far and away the prime predator in the Czech nation's dismemberment, it had company — Hungary and to a lesser extent, Poland. Moreover, Hitler was not shy in expressing his encouragement to these nations' leaders.[952] Not out of generosity towards Hungary or the perceived Slavic *Untermensch* of the Poles, but to sow disunity and antipathy between the nations of Europe, while at the same time masking his ultimate intentions. His next target was Poland.

On November 2, Hungary was given almost 19,500 square kilometres of Czech territory, made up of 0.5 million ethnic Hungarians and 272,000 Slovaks. Poland, upon the insistence of its foreign minister Józef Beck, would annex almost 1700 square kilometres around the coal-rich Teschen district (Polish: *Cieszyn* and Czech: *Těšín*),[953] which they had lost to Czechoslovakia in the one-week Polish-Czech war in January 1919,[954] when Europe was in the chaotic Great War aftermath of what Churchill termed the "War of the Pygmies."[955] This district was made up of 228,000 inhabitants, of which 133,000 were Czech and the remainder nearly all ethnic Poles.[956] In this whole sordid episode, and not for the last time, Hitler was able to exploit petty fringe ethnic and nationalist squabbles to his utmost advantage.

Stalinist apologists may wish to apply the dubious concept of "moral equivalence," as neo-Nazis do in using the February 1945 British firebombing of Dresden to absolve The Third Reich of all guilt at Auschwitz and other camps of the Konzentrationslager (KZ).[957] Such reasoning, however, does not absolve Stalin, of the following litany: the deportation of 1.7 million Borderland Poles in 1939-41 to Siberia;[958] the murder of 20,000 plus Polish officers in Katyń Wood in April 1940;[959] the August 1939 Molotov-Ribbentrop pact,[960] with its secret protocols for cooperating with Hitler in the effort to wipe Poland from existence;[961] the Soviet's virtual inaction during the 1944 Warsaw General Uprising, while camped on the east bank of the Vistula in Warsaw's Praga district, leading to the deaths of 0.2 million Poles;[962] the post-war Sovietisation of Poland; the loss of 80,000 square kilometres of territory overall in the Stalinist-imposed post-war western translation;[963] and finally, the round-up, torture and execution of Polish Home Army veterans near war's end and post-war.[964]

In a lecture at Georgetown University in October 2002, Norman Davies stated the following: "The death and destruction of Warsaw during [the Uprising] August and September 1944 was equivalent to the 9/11 World Trade Centre attack repeated every day for 63 days."[965]

While Poland may well have had a legitimate claim to the Cieszyn district, given that the Czechs seized it from Poland in January 1919, the circumstances of the mass dismemberment of the Czech state in 1938 made Poland's acceptance of Hitler's poisoned chalice of 1700 square kilometres of Czech territory deplorable. However, one must not lose sight of the fact that among all of Nazi-occupied Europe throughout the war, Poland had by far the largest armed underground resistance movement.[966]

That the appeasement of Munich 1938 was unnecessary would be confirmed at the Nuremberg Trials post-war, with the testimony of both pro and anti-Hitler generals. In the case of the former, the testimony of General Keitel, Chief of the High Command of the armed forces (OKW) in the wake of the Fritsch Affair was most enlightening: "

> We were extraordinarily happy that it had not come to a military operation because… we had always been of the opinion that our means of attack against the frontier fortifications of Czechoslovakia were insufficient. From a purely military point of view we lacked the means for an attack which involved the piercing of the frontier fortifications."[967]

… and that of fellow OKW General Jodl: "

> It was out of the question with five fighting divisions and seven reserve divisions in the western fortifications, which were nothing but a large construction site, to hold out against 100 French divisions. That was militarily impossible."[968]

Field Marshal von Manstein, who became one of the most brilliant of Germany's field commanders, confirmed the testimony of Keitel and Jodl at Nuremberg; unlike them, he was not on trial for his life. "

> If war had broken out, neither our western border nor our Polish frontier could really have been effectively defended by us, and there is no doubt whatsoever that had Czechoslovakia defended herself, we would have been held up by her fortifications, for we did not have the means to break through."[969]

Even more damning is an assessment by Hitler himself, post-Munich, to Doctor Carl Burckhardt, the League of Nations High Commissioner to Danzig (Gdańsk). "

> When after Munich we were in a position to examine Czechoslovak military strength from within, what we saw of it greatly disturbed us; we had run a serious danger. The plan prepared by the Czech generals was formidable. I now understand why my generals urged restraint."[970]

"Peace for our time," with its dangerous equating of appeasement with peace, would last less than a year. One could argue that this period gave Britain and France time to rearm. The truth however belies this argument; Nazi Germany was the real beneficiary. Not the least of their advantages was the loss for the Czechs of thirty-five well trained and well-armed divisions.[971] As Churchill stated: "The year's breathing space said to be 'gained' by Munich left Britain and France in a much worse position compared to Hitler's Germany than they had been at the Munich crisis."[972]

He stated, more succinctly than anyone else, the consequences of Munich in his speech to the Commons on October 5 1938: "

> We have sustained a total and unmitigated defeat ... We are in the midst of a disaster of the first magnitude. The road down the Danube ... the road to the Black Sea has been opened ... countries of Mittel Europa and the Danube valley, one after another, will be drawn into the vast system of Nazi politics ... radiating from Berlin ... And do not suppose that this is the end. It is only the beginning ..."[973]

But Churchill, perhaps the only British politician (or then former politician) to have read Hitler's *Mein Kampf*,[974] was not in the government and his words went unheeded.[975] Years earlier, in 1935,[976] after reading Hitler's diatribe, Churchill summarised it as follows: "

> Hitler's sentence was reduced from four years to thirteen months. These months in the Landsberg fortress were however sufficient to enable him to complete in outline *Mein Kampf*, a treatise on his political philosophy inscribed to the dead of the recent *Putsch*. [Hitler's failed November 1923 Munich Beer Hall Putsch.] When eventually he came to power there was no book which deserved more careful study from the rulers, political and military, of the Allied Powers. All was there — the programme of German resurrection, the technique of party propaganda; the plan for combating Marxism; the concept of a National Socialist State; the rightful position of Germany at the summit of the world. Here was the new Koran of faith and war: turgid, verbose, shapeless, but pregnant with its message.

Hitler's sentence was reduced from four years to thirteen months. These months in the Landsberg fortress were however sufficient to enable him to complete in outline *Mein Kampf*, a treatise on his political philosophy inscribed to the dead of the recent *Putsch*. [Hitler's failed November 1923 Munich Beer Hall Putsch.][977] When eventually he came to power there was no book which deserved more careful study from the rulers, political and military, of the Allied Powers. All was there — the programme of German resurrection, the technique of party propaganda; the plan for combating Marxism; the concept of a National Socialist State; the rightful position of Germany at the summit of the world. Here was the new Koran of faith and war: turgid, verbose, shapeless, but pregnant with its message."[978]

Thus, upon the sacrificial pyre of Czechoslovakia, evaporated the final real opportunity to overthrow Hitler and avert the forthcoming apocalypse and all its consequences. Auschwitz, synonymous with the final solution, need never have existed. A whole continent need never have been devastated upon the whim of a mass murdering fascist lunatic. No Molotov-Ribbentrop Pact,[979] meaning 1.7 million eastern Poles need never have been deported to the Siberian Gulags,[980] where half would die from cold, overwork and starvation in the frigid hell. One of the costs of appeasement was the sacrifice of Poland and the rest of Eastern Europe to post-war Stalinist terror and decades of Soviet direct and indirect collaborationist oppression. Moreover, Germany need never have been divided.

A significant factor in the hypothetical scenario of a successful 1938 overthrow of Hitler would be that Imperial Japan, with its litany of horrors in China such as the December 1937 Nanking massacre,[981] would have continued. For Australia, the massive post-war continental European migration, with its incalculable influence on its cultural landscape and identity, may never have happened, or been greatly delayed. Would the mass migration of European Jewry to Palestine with all its consequences still have taken place?

By October 1938, it was mandatory for every Jew to have a "J"[982] stamped on their passport. It was obvious, at least for the foreseeable future, that the Leibholzes could not return to their beloved Germany. They moved to London, where Dietrich put them in contact with Bishop Bell and Julius Rieger, who welcomed them as they had welcomed so many Jewish refugees before them from Hitler's Reich. Franz Hildebrandt, whom they knew very well, was also on hand to help them get established, and ultimately, Gerhard was able to secure a lectureship at Oxford's Magdalen College,[983] where C. S. Lewis was at the time.[984] Moreover, further vindication of their difficult decision to flee Germany would be forthcoming.

Chapter 14

Reichskristallnacht

In early November 1938, an infamous chain of events was triggered on Monday the 7[985]th, when a seventeen-year-old *Ostjuden* (Eastern Jew) shot Ernst vom Rath, the third secretary of the Germany Embassy in Paris.[985] The latter would die from his wounds two days later.

It was revenge for the youth's father, who had recently been placed in a crowded carriage and deported to Poland. Since Poland didn't want these people either, they became stateless, and were dumped in a no-man's-land on the German-Polish border near the town of Zbaszyn.[986] This, among other abuses, was now commonplace against the Jews. There is a contention that the young assassin, Herschel Grynszpan, actually intended to kill the ambassador, Count Johannes von Welczeck, but this has now been discredited as a Nazi fabrication of evidence.[987]

Grynszpan was born in 1921 in Hanover, Germany, to Polish Jews who never at any stage attained German citizenship. The Jews from the Bonhoeffers' affluent Grunewald district in Berlin, such as Franz Hildebrandt, mostly regarded themselves as German first and Jewish second;[988] Grynszpan, however, was an Eastern Jew. They usually spoke Yiddish and tended to be more religiously devout, as well as impoverished and less well educated than German Jews.[989] As with the Reichstag Fire, the pretext that Hitler and the Nazi leaders needed to launch new infamy had now presented itself.

History does not tell us whether the assassination was engineered by the Nazis, but they exploited it to its utmost. A series of "spontaneous" and violent demonstrations began, unleashing evils against the Jews on a massive scale all over the country. Such a program required meticulous co-ordination, and the man Hitler looked to, as he did in the 1934 "Nacht der Langen Messer" (Night of the long knives or Röhm putsch),[990] the Fritsch affair earlier that year, and later in 1942 in formalising the "Final Solution,"[991] was Himmler's second in the SS, Reinhard Heydrich.[992] Metaxas likened this man of icy mien to a creature from the light-less nautical depths of the Marianas Trench.[993]

At around 1:00 a.m. on the morning of Thursday the 10th, following the death on the 9th of vom Rath[994] from fatal gun shot wounds inflicted on the 7[985]th, Heydrich sent an urgent teletype message to every

Gestapo station across the country. The text contained explicit instructions on how to perpetrate acts of destruction, looting, intimidation, beatings and murder of all things Jewish in what became known as the Kristallnacht (Night of Broken Glass), or Reichskristallnacht (National Crystal Night).[995]

In Breslau and the surrounding Silesian region, it was particularly rampant and destructive, with details on how the Breslau SS received and executed their orders being obtained from post-war trials in Germany and from the Polish Consul, Leon Koppens.[996] According to his report, by 8 p.m. on Wednesday November 9 1938, he was already aware that the SS had orders for so-called "*Aktion*" (Action), with a very high degree of planning involved. According to German records, by 1.09 a.m. the following early morning of the 10th, the Breslau SS received a message from Berlin ordering their commanding officer, Erich von dem Bach-Zelewski, to place a call to Reinhard Heydrich in Munich.[997] Heydrich would then simply give the final command to execute the orders prepared well in advance, and within twenty or so minutes, uniformed SS and surviving SA from the 1934 purge were on the move to wreak destruction of all things in Breslau Jewish.[998]

At 2 a.m., Wehrmacht sappers placed the first explosive charges under the New Synagogue, with dutiful journalists present to take notes.[999] These were used the following day in two of the *Schlesische Tageszeitung* (*Silesian Daily)* articles; one being, "*Wie* Breslau *mit den* Juden *abrechnete*" ("How Breslau got even with the Jews") and the other, "Demonstrationen auch in ganz *Schlesien*" ("Demonstrations throughout Silesia"). An onlooker remarked, "I was in the Middle Ages,"[1000] — as if to recall Brother John Capistrano's inquisition of May to July 1453.[1001]

Usually in the Reich, "Crystal Night" was described as a purely urban phenomenon. However, in Silesia, the SS were more virulent as they targeted every single village and hamlet where Jews were living.[1002] In the village of Trebnitz (Trzebnica), they even forced the Jews to set their own synagogue alight, before cutting the beards of the men and arresting them.[1003] While the SS released the women, another SS squad from Breslau, under Criminal Commissar Schubert, headed for the Zionist *Auswandererlehrgut* (Emigration Training Farm) at Gross Breesen (Brzeźno), which trained candidates in agriculture and crafts before sending them to Palestine. There the staff were arrested, with the buildings being destroyed and looted.[1004] SS-Oberführer Katzmann dutifully and proudly reported his "achievements" to Berlin: In Breslau alone: 1 synagogue (burned), 2 synagogues (demolished), 1 building of the 'Society of Joy' (demolished), at least 500 shops (completely destroyed), 10 Jewish Inns (demolished), 35 other Jewish enterprises (demolished) and 600 men arrested.[1005]

When it all began, Dietrich was on his way to Gross-Schlönwitz in the far eastern wilds of Pomerania to commence the second half of his teaching week. So it was not until the next day, Friday the 11th, that he received news of the burning of the synagogue in Köslin, and the nationwide program of destruction, looting, beatings, murder and intimidation.[1006] When he heard the news, he sent Eberhard to Göttingen to check on the Leibholzes' house; Eberhard found it undamaged.[1007] Next day, Dietrich discussed the events with his ordinands. They did not condone what had happened and were genuinely upset about it, but they seriously suggested that the reason for the evils must be the "curse" that the Jews bore for rejecting Christ.[1008] Looking to the Bible itself to refute such notions, Dietrich found it in David's Psalm 74, verse 8. Dietrich wrote in pencil next to the second half of it, "9.11.38," the date of vom Rath's death and the infamy of the Reichskristallnacht: *"Sie verbrennen alle Häuser Gottes im Lande."* — "They burn all of God's houses in the land."[1009]

This psalm, referring it seems to the destruction of Solomon's temple and others by the Babylonians in the late sixth century,[1010] was for Dietrich proof that the synagogues burned in Germany were God's own. To lift one's hand against the Jews was to lift one's hand against God himself. Reflecting further on Psalm 74, in a circular a few days later to all the *Sammelvikariats* (Collective Pastorates), Dietrich quoted passages respectively from Old and New Testament Jewish prophets:

> "For thus said the Lord of hosts, after his glory sent me to the nations who plundered you, for he who touches you touches the apple of his eye" (Zechariah 2:8).

And

> "They are Israelites, and to them belong the adoption, the glory, the covenants, the giving of the law, the worship, and the promises. To them belong the patriarchs, and from their race, according to the flesh, is the Christ who is God over all, blessed forever. Amen." (Paul to the Romans 9:4f.; English Standard Version ESV).[1011]

Dietrich was using the words of the Jews, David, Zechariah, and Paul,[1012] from across both the *Old* and *New Testaments*, to make the point that the Jews are God's people, and that the Messiah came from them and came *for* them first. Hence, for Dietrich, the horror of Kristallnacht: an evil committed against the Jews was an evil committed against God and his people. For Bethge, it was significant that Dietrich, for the first and last time, wrote anything about contemporary events in his Bible. No doubt, the words of David, Zechariah, and Paul were the positive antithesis to the events of Kristallnacht. Jesus was born and raised a Jew, and the ultimate act of crucifixion was committed with sadistic relish, not by Jews, but by the Gentile Romans. It is believed that this was when he proclaimed the words that so resonated with his students: "Only he who cries out for the Jews may sing Gregorian chants."[1013]

Dietrich had already spoken these words years earlier in 1935,[1014] in the wake of the infamous anti-Jewish Nuremberg Laws.[1015] The government-sanctioned "revenge of the German people," perpetrated by SS and SA militia dressed as civilians,[1016] had set synagogues on fire and devastated Jewish homes and businesses. In the process, numerous Jews were tortured, with around 100 murdered and 30,000 deported to concentration camps.[1017] The Confessing Church no longer had the strength to protest, having been plunged into virtual impotency by the decrees issued earlier that year by the Reichkirche head, Dr. Friedrich Werner, in the wake of the Austrian Anschluss.[1018] Only a few brave and isolated individuals had the courage to speak out.

One of them was Pastor Julius von Jan in Oberlenningen, Württemberg. In a courageous sermon the following Sunday, he proclaimed:
"

Who would have thought that this single crime in Paris could result in so many crimes committed here in Germany? Now we are facing the consequences of our great apostasy, our falling away from God and Christ, of organised anti-Christianity. Passions are being unleashed and the commandments of God ignored. Houses of God which were sacred for others are being burnt down, the property of others is being plundered or destroyed. Men who have served our nation loyally and conscientiously fulfilled their duties have been thrown into concentration camps, merely because they belong to another race. Those in authority may not admit to any injustice, but to the healthy good sense of our people it is quite clear, even though no one dares speak of it."[1019]

How dangerous this sermon was became clear when he was hauled out of his parsonage by 500 demonstrators from outside his village, and beaten without mercy. Later he was dragged through a raging crowd to the town hall, where he was interrogated and thrown into prison, and remained there until the US Army liberated him in 1945.[1020]

In Bonn, the now old West German capital, the wife and sons of the internationally known expert in ancient Near Eastern studies, Paul Kahle, had been aiding Jewish business people on the morning following the pogrom. When a policeman appeared while they were doing so, he noticed the eldest son Wilhelm helping in what must have been an "illegal" clean-up; Wilhelm had to appear before the university's court, where he was expelled from the university "because of the seriousness of his offence." The backlash did not stop there, as vitriolic hate articles appeared in the press, such as the *Westdeutschen Beobachter* (*West German Observer*), while the family received numerous threats. Fortunately, they were able to flee Germany just in time.[1021]

The decline of moral values and courage among large sections of the population is shown in a letter to Paul Kahle, dated around that time, from one of his former students, who held the chair in Oriental Studies at the University of Göttingen. Addressing him as "My dear and honoured colleague," he said:

> You surely remember the case of a former rector of Bonn University, who got into bad trouble because his wife shopped at a Jewish butcher shop; that could actually have been a warning ... We younger colleagues regret that, due to the insensitive behaviour of Frau Kahle, it has been made impossible for you to conclude your university career with due honour.[1022] (Paul Kahle's wife, with her sons, had been aiding Jewish business people on the morning following the pogrom.)

Such was the prevalent distorted notion of "honour."

In all, 1938 was, for the Bonhoeffers, the Confessing Church, Germany, and the world in general, a year as tumultuous as it was disappointing. The flight of the Leibholzes to England, the arrest of twenty-seven pastors, and the annexation of Austria and the Sudetenland took place against the background of the Fritsch Affair in March, and Chamberlain's appeasement in late September, which extinguished the hopes for Hitler's removal from power. Dietrich was disheartened by the inability of the Confessing Church to stand up to Hitler. In his Advent letter before Christmas, he criticised the tendency for Confessing Church pastors to question if their cause was right; he pointed out that the prophet Paul and reformer Luther never did so, even in the face of great opposition and suffering.[1023] In short, the failure of a just cause will never make it unjust.

Post WWII, the Commandant of the Polish *Armia Krajowa* (Home Army) in the Wilno Region during that conflict, Alexander Krzyżanowski ("*Wilk*" — Wolf), personified courage in a just cause when, tortured by thugs of the UB (*Urząd Bezpieczeństwa*, Polish Communist post-war secret police) at Warsaw's notorious Mokotów Prison in Rakowiecka, he never admitted to trumped-up charges brought against him.[1024] As the Wilno native, Józef Piłsudski, the father of modern-day Polish independence, put it decades earlier, at the end of Great War: "To be defeated and not yield is victory. To win and to rest on one's laurels is defeat."[1025]

Chapter 15

New York — Troubled Revisiting

Early the following year, 1939, Dietrich's response to possible military call-up was forced. His mother had seen a notice ordering all men born in 1906 and 1907 to register with the military, and informed Dietrich on January 23.[1026] Declaring himself a conscientious objector was out of the question, as that would lead to his imprisonment in a concentration camp or possible execution,[1027] and the Confessing Church would be portrayed as cowards. On the other hand, Dietrich found the idea of fighting for a regime he despised morally unconscionable. One possible solution was to have his military call-up deferred for a year. In the meantime, Dietrich could speak with the German born theologian Reinhold Niebuhr, who had been his professor at the Union Seminary in New York; he was giving the prestigious Gifford Lectures in Edinburgh that year, and would soon be in Sussex, England. Dietrich dearly wished to visit Sabine and Gert, for whom living in England was difficult, as well as to see Bishop Bell.[1028]

On March 10, Dietrich and Bethge took a night train to Ostend on the Belgian coast.[1029] Because of the tense political situation, with Hitler threatening to invade the practically indefensible remainder of Czechoslovakia, Dietrich didn't sleep until they crossed the border, as the train would have been stopped at the border in the event of an outbreak of war. The following day, they made the Channel crossing, and by the 15th,[1030] Hitler had violated Chamberlain's assurance of "Peace for our time." To salvage some modicum of dignity, Chamberlain "vowed" to declare war if Hitler invaded Poland;[1031] and while, technically, this was honoured when Hitler invaded in early September 1939, the Polish defence counted on a promised immediate French invasion of the Reich. However, this did not materialise, beyond a token advance of eight kilometres in September 1939, followed by the rapid withdrawal that was known as the Saar Offensive.[1032]

From the end of the Polish campaign to the German invasion of Norway at 2315 hours on April 8 1940,[1033] more than six months would pass in the "Phoney War," with Chamberlain clinging to hopes of a possible overthrow of Hitler,[1034] or some kind of appeasement. Of course, the horse had long since bolted, thanks to Chamberlain's appeasement in 1938. In France, Polish soldiers, who managed miraculous escapes via Romania and Hungary, were desperate to engage the Germans, but were frustrated by France's reluctance to do so.[1035] When France was finally compelled to engage the Wehrmacht in May 1940, followed by the French surrender in late June, they were willing to detain and even arrest Polish soldiers at their ports, rather than allow them escape to England.[1036] Only with the German invasions of Norway, France and the low countries, and Chamberlain's resignation, did meaningful British engagement of the Germans commence.

In England, Dietrich was overjoyed to see Franz Hildebrandt again.[1037] But meetings with the ecumenical movement on how Confessing Church members could take part in ecumenical conferences without having to go through Heckel's Foreign Office were fruitless and disappointing for Dietrich.[1038] On the other hand, his counsel with George Bell in Chichester was pleasing and satisfying. As was his trip on April 3 to Sussex, with Julius Rieger and Gerhard Leibholz, to see Niebuhr about a teaching position in America. Dietrich explained to Niebuhr that he saw this as the solution to his dilemma, and emphasised his urgent need for it. Niebuhr didn't need much convincing and agreed to pull what strings he could on his return.[1039]

The following day, the Reichskirche published the infamous Godesberg Declaration,[1040] signed by Dr. Friedrich Werner, who, a year or so earlier, had ordered all pastors to take an oath of loyalty to the Führer. The document declared that National Socialism was the natural continuation of "the work of Martin Luther," emphasising the church's current position, that Christianity was the "unbridgeable religious opposite to Judaism." Moreover, it attacked the universality of Catholicism and any notion of a world-Protestant church as the epitome of the degeneration of Christianity.

In response, at the request of the World Council of Churches, Karl Barth drafted a manifesto rejecting the notion of race, national identity, or ethnicity having anything to do with Christian faith. The principal advocate for the manifesto was Willem A. Visser 't Hooft,[1041] a Dutchman whom Dietrich had known in ecumenical circles, and who was now the head of the Council's Geneva office, having studied under Barth. When Dietrich learned that 't Hooft would be in London, he requested Bell to arrange a meeting at Paddington Station. Many years later, Visser 't Hooft would recall their conversation and the remarkable impression Dietrich left upon him: "

We had heard a great deal about each other, but it was surprising how quickly we were able to get beyond the first stage of merely feeling our way into the deeper realm of real conversation—that, in fact, he was soon treating me as an old friend … We walked up and down the platform for a long time. He described the situation of his church and country. He spoke in a way that was remarkably free from illusions, and sometimes almost clairvoyantly, about the coming war … Had not the time now come to refuse to serve a government that was heading straight for war and breaking all the commandments? But what consequences would this position have for the Confessing Church? I remember his acute questions better than his answers; but I think I learned more from his questions than he did from my answers. In the impenetrable world between "Munich" and "Warsaw," in which hardly anyone ventured to formulate the actual problems clearly, this questioning voice was a liberation."[1042]

Clearly, among Dietrich's ecumenical meetings during this trip, this one was to prove a positive exception.

On April 18, Dietrich returned to Berlin,[1043] realising he could be called up any day.[1044] While he hoped and prayed, Niebuhr started pulling strings, which included a letter to Henry Leiper in New York, extolling Dietrtich's virtues and stressing the need to act urgently.[1045] Dietrich knew Henry Leiper from ecumenical circles, and they had in fact met at Fanø in 1934.[1046] This was only one of many letters written by Niebuhr on Dietrich's behalf in a flurry of activity across the Atlantic, with phone calls made, meetings hastily arranged, and more letters written. Dietrich was unaware of the great efforts made on his behalf,[1047] and was becoming ambivalent about a possible move back to America.

Finally, on May 11, Leiper wrote a formal letter to Dietrich, offering him a dual position with the Union Theological Seminary and his organisation, the Central Bureau of Interchurch Aid, serving as pastor to German refugees in New York. During Union's summer break, he would lecture in the theological summer school of Union and Columbia.[1048] Leiper had created this position just for him, and it was envisaged Dietrich would occupy it for at least two to three years. Paul Lehmann was overjoyed at the prospect of having his old friend back, and promptly wrote and sent letters to more than thirty colleges enquiring as to whether they would be interested in one of Germany's most courageous younger pastors lecturing at their institutions.[1049]

Pushing Dietrich towards America was the seemingly hopeless situation of the Confessing Church, with its antagonism to Karl Barth following Barth's statement, written from Switzerland in 1938, that; "

> Every Czech soldier who fights and suffers will be doing so for us too, and I say this without reservation—he will also be doing it for the church of Jesus, which in the atmosphere of Hitler and Mussolini must become the victim of either ridicule or extermination."[1050]

The church's position greatly disturbed Dietrich; add to that, the arrest that year of twenty-seven Confessing Church pastors, the flight of the Leibholzes, the failed hopes of coups in that year, and the imminent military call-up, all influencing Dietrich's leaning towards America. Yet, in spite of all this, Dietrich was far from feeling certain that he should go.

Before embarking for America, the issue of how to continue the work of Finkenwalde, his own creation, needed to be discussed. While the seminary had officially been closed since the end of 1937, it continued to exist via the underground seminaries of Sammelvikariats (collective pastorates) in the eastern wilds of Pomerania. Hence Dietrich's meeting in Berlin. It was held in the apartment of Otto Dudzus, one of his long-time students since his return from America in 1931, along with nine other students and friends, among whom were Albrecht Schönherr and Eberhard Bethge. Dietrich challenged them by asking if they would "grant absolution to the murderer of a tyrant."[1051]

At that time, Bethge was the only one among them that knew Dietrich was involved in the Resistance.[1052] As the conversation continued, Dietrich used an example of a drunken driver killing pedestrians on a main street in Berlin, compelling everyone to do literally anything they could to stop the rampant drunk.[1053] In more recent times, the July 2016 attack on the *Promenade des Anglais* in Nice, France, is a perfect example of what Dietrich was talking about; the French police had no option but to shoot the terrorist dead.[1054] A year or two later, Dietrich found out, via his brother-in-law Hans von Dohnányi in the resistance, what very few knew: that the killing of the Jews was beyond anything they had imagined possible. This compelled him to act. At that meeting in May 1939, he may well have seen it coming, but before he left for his second visit to America, he was just starting to grapple with these gruesome future possibilities.[1055]

On May 22, Dietrich received notice to report for military duty. Now, it seemed, Henry Leiper's offer from New York had arrived just in time. Dietrich informed the requisite authorities of his official invitations from Union and Leiper, and on June 2, at Berlin's Tempelhof Airport, he boarded the evening flight to London with eldest brother Karl-Friedrich,[1056] who had been invited to lecture in Chicago.[1057] By the 8th, they were seaward bound on the *Bremen*[1058] from Southampton for New York.[1059]

One of the authorities Dietrich had to inform was the Council of the Confessing Church. Understandably, they were reluctant to do without him as a teacher of theology, and Dietrich had to convince them that his intended trip was necessary without revealing its true purpose.[1060] Moreover, the rushed preparations meant that no replacement could be found for Dietrich as director of the collective pastorates before his departure. In Sigurdshof, Eberhard Bethge was holding the fort as best he could, but the latest of Dr. Friedrich Werner's decrees was obliterating the last remnants of courage for many of his friends, students, and the like.[1061]

On Monday June 12, 1939,[1062] Dietrich and Karl-Friedrich's ship entered New York harbour, which Dietrich had left eight years before. Then, the Manhattan skyline held positive memories for him, but now, he was weighed down by homesickness and the feeling he was deserting the sinking ship of his German brethren.[1063] These doubts grew as he disembarked with Karl-Friedrich and entered the great metropolis of the world for the second time. The next morning, Dietrich met Henry Leiper for breakfast, and shocked him by telling him of his intention to go to back to Germany in a year's time at the latest. Leiper had expected Dietrich to be around for much longer, even permanently. In fact, he would only be there for twenty-six days.[1064]

Dietrich was given the star treatment,[1065] with accommodation in the Prophet's Chamber at Union, a large, well furnished suite with a view from its east window across Broadway. Later that day, he met Dr. Henry Sloane Coffin, the acclaimed liberal theologian who featured on the cover of *TIME Magazine* back in 1926.[1066] He invited Dietrich to his country estate in the Berkshires, near the Massachusetts border.[1067] On the two-and-a-half-hour train ride north, the two theologians, the liberal fifty-nine-year-old American and the more fundamentalist thirty-three-year-old German, discussed the church situation in America.

As they spoke, Dietrich's mind was in turmoil over the situation back home and how long he should stay in America, or whether he should have come at all. He didn't betray any of his inner turmoil to his host or his family, on the train or over the three days he stayed at their country home. He unburdened himself privately, in his diary entry on the third day: "

> 15th June, 1939 — Since yesterday evening I haven't been able to stop thinking of Germany. I would not have thought it possible that at my age, after so many years abroad, one could get so dreadfully homesick. What was in itself a wonderful motor expedition this morning to a female acquaintance in the country, i.e., in the hills, became almost unbearable. We sat for an hour and chattered, not in a silly way, true, but about things which left me completely cold—whether it is possible to get a good musical education in New York, about the education of children, etc., etc., and I thought how usefully I could be spending these hours in Germany. I would gladly have taken the next ship home. This inactivity, or rather activity in unimportant things, is quite intolerable when one thinks of the brethren and of how precious time is. The whole burden of self-reproach because of a wrong decision comes back again and almost overwhelms one. I was in utter despair."[1068]

Back in Rome in 1924, Dietrich had met the royal family, Mussolini, and even Pope Pius XI. However, these meetings were not the highlight for Dietrich.[1069] Rather, they were the sideshow to Saint Peter's with its Palm Sunday service, which captivated him. Star treatment, to Dietrich, was an indulgence in vanity. Moreover, the sense of isolation Dietrich felt was heightened in an unexpected way. When he spent time in the library to prepare lectures, he found his English utterly inadequate, in spite of the fact that everyone found it perfectly fluent. It seems everyday conversation was one thing, but when it came to contemplative theology and prayer, he found his thoughts nowhere near as fluent as in his native tongue.[1070] This suggests how greatly he missed his ordinands at the collective pastorates in the wilds of Pomerania. On the morning of Tuesday 20th, a letter arrived from his parents, but not from the brethren;[1071] the absence of news from them was becoming unbearable. It was due in part to no replacement being found for him before he left Germany.

While in America, Dietrich attended one service at the Riverside church, which Rockefeller had built for Harry Emerson Fosdick, opening it to great fanfare in 1930. While it was largely out of a sense of obligation, in that it was just a hundred metres away from where he lived at Union, Dietrich also desperately needed to hear something from God. However, remembering its tepid preaching from his last visit in 1930-31, he didn't expect anything inspiring, and his low expectations were confirmed. Dietrich was aware, but not impressed that Fosdick was the most famous liberal preacher in America, and that Riverside was America's premier pulpit of theological liberalism; it's debatable whether he was aware that Fosdick was one of the premier advocates for appeasing Hitler.[1072] Later that day, he left Union and walked seven blocks south on Broadway to the Presbyterian church, where the fundamentalist preacher, Dr. McComb, reviled by the liberal theologians at Union and Riverside, gave a sermon that answered Dietrich's prayer to hear God's word preached.[1073]

Two days later, just hours after receiving the letter from his parents, he had a critical luncheon with Henry Leiper at the exclusive National Arts Club on Gramercy Park. While both would have been in agreement as to its importance, they had quite different motives. Leiper looked forward to it as much as Dietrich dreaded it.[1074] Years later, Leiper recalled his disappointment when Dietrich, just eight days after arriving in New York, informed him that he had "received an urgent appeal from his colleagues in Germany to return at once for important tasks which they felt he alone could perform."[1075] Since Dietrich had not yet received any word from the brethren, the reason he gave Leiper for now leaving America appears to have been contrived. However, Leiper considered it possible that Dietrich's parents' letter included a coded reference to the conspiracy,[1076] thus compelling his return to Germany. In any event, Leiper considered it prudent not to press Dietrich for details.

While Leiper was shocked, Dietrich was now at peace. On the evening of the following day, he met with the Bewers,[1077] German friends he had known from his year at Union. Among them was Julius August Bewer,[1078] a long serving professor at Union, lecturer at Columbia University's Teachers' College, and Old Testament scholar. Dietrich felt the freedom of thinking and speaking again in German, and the peace of mind of his imminent homecoming. The following Saturday, the 24th, he received with great relief his long-awaited letter from the brethren in the Pomeranian wilds.[1079] Four days later, he had a letter from Paul Lehmann, writing from Chicago, who was still under the impression that Dietrich was staying permanently, and made joyful references to their first prospective meeting since Lehmann's visit to Germany in 1933. Dietrich wrote a postcard back, briefly explaining he would be going back on August 2 or even earlier, to continue the "fight in the trenches,"[1080] but stated his desire to speak with Lehmann before returning to Germany.

Dietrich's last morning in New York was just twenty-six days after his arrival in America. On July 7, Paul Lehmann tried to talk Dietrich out of leaving, knowing the great dangers that awaited him.[1081] Karl-Friedrich, in spite of lucrative offers of the safety of a professorship in Chicago,[1082] decided to join his brother, before arriving in New York on Saturday the 1st.[1083] On the evening of the 7th, just before midnight, Paul took Dietrich to his ship and bade him a sad farewell.[1084] They would be his final words to his dear friend as he boarded one of the last ships to return to Germany before the outbreak of war. In Dr. Coffin's garden, just days before sailing, Dietrich wrote to Reinhold Niebuhr his reasons for returning to Germany. "

> I have had the time to think and to pray about my situation and that of my nation and to have God's will for me clarified. I have come to the conclusion that I have made a mistake in coming to America. I must live through this difficult period of our national history with the Christian people of Germany. I shall have no right to participate in the reconstruction of Christian life in Germany after the war if I do not share the trials of this time with my people. My brothers in the Confessing Synod wanted me to go. They may have been right in urging me to do so; but I was wrong in going. Such a decision each man must make for himself. Christians in Germany will face the terrible alternative of either willing the defeat of their nation in order that Christian civilization may survive, or willing the victory of their nation and thereby destroying our civilization. I know which of these alternatives I must choose; but I cannot make that choice in security."[1085]

Karl-Friedrich, in spite of being the most vocal critic of Dietrich's chosen career path, now in all likelihood, concurred that it was not a choice that could be made in security.[1086]

Seven to eight days later, Dietrich and Karl-Friedrich's ship berthed in Southampton. They boarded the train to London, whence Karl-Friedrich immediately flew home.[1087] Dietrich, however, stayed a further ten days or so in England. While unable to visit George Bell, he met with Franz Hildebrandt and Julius Rieger,[1088] before spending time with Sabine, Gerhard, and their daughters. With war imminent, the dangers that Dietrich was returning to were to become more obvious.

During a brief interlude when Dietrich was enjoying teaching his nieces English nursery rhymes, he was called outside by Julius Rieger and informed that Pastor Paul Schneider from the Rhineland, upon refusal to leave his church in Hunsrück in spite of government expulsion orders, had been executed in Buchenwald on July 18.[1089] On July 25, Sabine and family farewelled Dietrich from London's Victoria Station.[1090] Like Paul Lehmann's farewell in New York, they were the last words they ever spoke with him as he returned to Germany, with war now imminent.

Chapter 16

Homecoming to Outbreak of War

Upon making the channel crossing, Dietrich spent some time, first in Dortmund with Hans Joachim Iwand, and then in Elberfeld with Hermann Albert Hesse. The latter, along with his four sons, were members of a small group of German theologians and pastors who spurned any accord with the Third Reich — men after Dietrich's own heart. Later, as if further confirmation of the "safety" he left behind in New York was required, Hermann and his youngest son Helmuth were imprisoned in Dachau because of their protests against the deportation of Jews; ten days later, Helmuth died, more than likely by execution.[1091]

Dietrich finally arrived back in Berlin on July 27, but immediately left for Sigurdshof to resume his duties as its director, only to find that Hellmut Traub had ably taken over where he had left off.[1092] Traub had been happy to think that Dietrich was safe in America from the reign of terror that was to follow. His surprise was mixed with indignation at the cost and trouble it had been to get Dietrich to safety, which was now all for nothing.[1093] Calmly lighting a cigarette, Dietrich explained the mistake of his move to America, and his inability to understand why he had gone.[1094]

While life at the eastern Pomeranian Sammelvikariats continued throughout most of August, their close proximity to the Polish border and the sense of imminent war led Dietrich to think that it was too dangerous to remain there. As a result, the Köslin and Sigurdshof terms were prematurely terminated, with Dietrich back in Berlin on August 26,[1095] just six days before Hitler's invasion of Poland on the first day of September, and five days before the infamous Gleiwitz incident at the German radio station in Upper Silesia near the border.[1096] This was masterminded by Reinhard Heydrich and invoked by his SD (the intelligence arm of the SS), creating a shallow pretext for German "retaliation." The pretext was more for German consumption, to portray the notion of Germany merely responding to Polish aggression.

With the outbreak of war, the issue of conscientious objection, which had led to his brief sojourn in America, was of no immediate concern for Dietrich, as that trip had secured him a one-year deferral of military service. Naturally, though, he was concerned with what to do once that time was up, and so, in the first weeks of the war, he looked into the possibility of a military chaplaincy. However, he discovered that only a pastor with a record of active military service could be considered for such a role.[1097]

In the middle of October, following Poland's surrender, he drove to Schlawe and from there, on to Sigurdshof. As mentioned in Chapter 11,[1098] and as Bethge reported, Dietrich oversaw the fifth and the last term of the Pomeranian Sammelvikariats in one of the most severe winters on record. Eight ordinands had arrived, but one of them would be conscripted into the military during that time. However, in the period prior to the final Pomeranian term and just following the outbreak of war, Dietrich received the news that Theodor Maaß, the first pastor in Pomerania to go to prison,[1099] was killed in action in Poland on September 3.[1100] On the 20th, Dietrich informed the brethren in a circular letter of the war's first Finkenwalden casualty; Maaß would not be the last, as by war's end, eighty of the 150 Finkenwalden graduates would be killed.[1101]

As hard as this news was for Dietrich, he received troubling news from his brother-in-law, Hans Von Dohnányi. Previously, Dohnányi had held a privileged position in the Ministry of Justice, but on August 25, 1939, just days before the outbreak of war, Dohnányi was inducted into the military as a special aide to the chief of staff, Colonel Hans Oster, in the foreign office of Military Intelligence (Abwehr).[1102] In the aftermath of the Fritsch Affair of March 1938, Oster, a pastor's son from Dresden,[1103] had been instrumental in creating much of the underground resistance to Hitler, and became its leading military figure. Through Oster's privileged access to military intelligence, the barbarism of SS atrocities during the invasion of Poland was revealed to Dietrich.

The SS units, known as the Einsatzgruppen,[1104] did the dirty work in the wake of the Wehrmacht advance in Poland. Later, at the launch of Operation Barbarossa in June 1941, they dealt in the same way with the Slavic and Jewish Untermensch in the Soviet Union. This was in accordance with a meeting on August 22 at the Obersalzberg, where Hitler stated to his Wehrmacht generals that things would happen "which would not be to the taste of German generals" and that they "should not interfere in such matters, but restrict themselves to their military duties."[1105]

On September 10 1939, the Einsatzgruppen oversaw the forced labour of fifty Polish Jews in a day's repair of a bridge. Upon completion of the repair, the Jews were herded into the synagogue and murdered. This was only one of a list of Polish civilians who were murdered in a widespread and calculated program. Following this incident, the local Wehrmacht commander insisted on trying them by court martial; the prosecuting officer pushed for the death sentence, but the perpetrators only received token sentences for manslaughter, which, upon strong pressure from Himmler, were dropped.[1106]

Incidents of incarceration, forced labour, and executions were disturbing for even hardened military leaders, and even more so for the average soldier experiencing a battlefield for the first time. Field commander Colonel General Johannes Blaskowitz remarked on this in a memo to his superior Walther von Brauchitsch. "

> What the foreign radio stations have broadcast up to now is only a tiny fraction of what has actually happened ..... The only possibility of fending off this pestilence lies in bringing the guilty parties and their followers under military command and military justice with all possible speed."[1107]

Hitler, upon eventually reading this, blithely labelled Blaskowitz's concerns as "childish."[1108] As news leaked out, Admiral Wilhelm Canaris, the ultimate head of the Abwehr, troubled by these revelations, demanded a meeting with Wilhelm Keitel, the Oberkommando der Wehrmacht (OKW), which took place in Hitler's private armoured train in Upper Silesia[xx] on September 12.[1109] However, Keitel, appointed head of OKW in the wake of the Fritsch Affair, brushed aside Canaris's concerns: "The Führer has already decided on this matter." He also told General Franz Halder that "if the military wanted no part in such actions, they should stand aside and let the Einsatzgruppen do their work."[1110] Moreover, around the time of Hitler dismissing Blaskowitz's memo, Brauchitsch, in his meeting with Himmler, received platitudes, such as "mistakes were made in carrying out the ethnic policy in Poland" and it would in future be carried out in a much more "considerate" manner.[1111] The Barborossa campaign less than two years later made a lie of his feigned promise.

This SS show of contrition was motivated by Himmler's uncertainty of Hitler's support if it came to a full-blown showdown between the Wehrmacht and the SS;[1112] at the time, the vast arsenal of Hitler's military came under the Wehrmacht. In any event, Brauchitsch was ra-

---

[xx] Upper Silesia is upstream on the Odor (Polish: Odra) River from Lower Silesia. Breslau/Wrocław is in Lower Sielsia. See footnote [xlvi] for Polish WWII Supplement II "The Gleiwitz (Gliwice) Incident" for further clarification.

ther indifferent to the whole question. If the SS were willing to do the dirty work, then the "good name" of the Wehrmacht would not be sullied. In this regard, he and Keitel were agreed in their indifference.[1113] For Dietrich, it was abundantly clear that any "peace" with Hitler was no better than war.[1114] The Czechoslovakian episode testified to this fact. Any naive, meaningless, or humiliating peace deal would imply that Poland would be wiped off the map of Europe amidst the orgy of ethnically based and co-ordinated mass genocide. As Metaxas put it: "

> What seemed so offensive to the international community—that Hitler would take the territory of the Polish people by force— was nothing compared to what the Nazis were doing. Their racial ideologies demanded more than territory; Poland must become a giant slave labor camp. The Poles were to be treated as Untermenschen (sub-humans). Their lands would not merely be occupied; they themselves would be terrorized and broken into utter docility, would be dealt with as beasts. The Germans would not tolerate the possibility of failure or the slightest manifestation of mercy. Brutality and mercilessness would be aggressively cultivated as virtues."[1115]

... while compassion and mercy would be trampled on as weakness.

Canaris wrote in his diary that he pointed out to Keitel that he knew of extensive executions being planned for Poland, most particularly for the nobility and the clergy. This was what the SS termed the "housecleaning of Jews, intelligentsia, clergy and the nobility." The implication was that all Poles with leadership abilities, Jewish and otherwise, were to be exterminated, thus reducing the nation of the Vistula to illiterate serfs. If confirmation of this is required, soon after his appointment as governor general of Poland, Hans Frank declared that "The Poles shall be the slaves of the German Reich."[1116] From Friday September 1 1939, what Hitler had written about the necessity for *lebensraum* (living space) in the east in *Mein Kampf*, written in the mid 1920s while he was imprisoned in Bavaria following the ill-fated 1923 Beer Hall Putsch, was becoming a heinous reality.[1117]

Canaris was not yet aware that from this civilised but fruitless meeting with Keitel, the atrocities would not only continue, but worsen with time. It was as if the dark horsemen of Sauron from Tolkien's *Lord of the Rings* had plunged through a wormhole of the present, coming from way back in space-time to obliterate the history and culture of

Germany that Dietrich, Dohnányi, Oster, and Canaris had loved. Their fear was that future generations would perceive that nothing good could ever have existed in a country that perpetrated such evil.[1118] The news that Dohnányi divulged to Dietrich was beyond anything Dietrich could have thought possible; indeed, for the average German, it would have beggared belief.[1119] To convey such explosive revelations was fraught with danger and a foreboding sense of loneliness. Dietrich's sense of isolation was increasing in church and ecumenical circles,[1120] as useless and convoluted efforts were being made to end the war, with Hitler still in power.

A perfect example was the peace proposals that Norwegian Bishop Eivind Berggrav conveyed, first to the British Foreign Minister Lord Halifax in London, then to the rotund Hermann Göring in Berlin. Berggrav returned to Halifax before his second visit to Göring. While in Berlin, Berggrav also met with Heckel, the head of the Reichkirche Foreign Office, but made no contact with members of the Confessing Church.[1121] Hence Dietrich's scepticism and cynicism towards Berggrav's overtures. Six or so months later, any notion of Norway as a neutral peacemaker was erased. Indeed, as soon as September 27, the day of Warsaw's surrender, Hitler ordered his generals to plan invasions of the Netherlands and the back door of Belgium through to France.[1122]

Around this time, just before the outbreak of war in August, the infamous T-4 euthanasia program commenced after years of preparation.[1123] For dedicated Nazis, it was convenient to implement this program with war imminent. As they reasoned, physically and mentally disabled patients were taking up medical facilities and beds that should be used for soldiers wounded while fighting for the Fatherland.[1124] At first, lethal injection was used, but then it was carbon monoxide gas,[1125] which was later utilised in the death camps. Following the victims' cremation, a letter was sent to the families informing them of their loved one's death by pneumonia or some fictional cause.[1126] Soon after, the family would receive the ashes of their murdered loved one. T-4 was another outcome of the so-called "peace" with Hitler. While some patients were "spared" from gassing, thanks to the brave protests of Frederick von Bodelschwing and others in 1940, they nearly always faced death later through execution by lethal injection or enforced starvation.[1127]

Hence, by early October 1939, the illusion that peace would follow Hitler getting what he wanted, namely Poland, was lost. The generals talked of another putsch, with Beck asking Dohnányi to update the chronicle of the regime's crimes, for which the perpetrators would one day hang, and which would explain to the German people why the conspirators were compelled to overthrow it. To that end, Dohnányi obtained film footage of numerous SS atrocities in Poland.[1128] At many meetings, although he was not yet officially part of the conspiracy, Dietrich was a major participant.[1129]

Sadly, but somewhat predictably, however, from a much weaker position than the golden opportunities in 1938, this proposed putsch would also fail. At the same time, Hitler concealed his true intentions to the outside world, by extending, in a speech to the Reichstag on October 6, the most withered of duplicitous olive branches.[1130] It was full of false platitudes of ridding relations with France of all traces of ill will and the fostering, not just of Anglo-German understanding, but of friendship.[1131] Of course, no mention was made of the continuing atrocities in Poland, or the cartographic obliteration of Czechoslovakia, and as such, the overture was rejected, even by the supine Chamberlain, one week later on the 13th.[1132]

The generals realised they had to act promptly before the invasion in the west was implemented, if the British and French were to take them seriously. However, they needed the help of an intermediary. Dr Josef Müller,[xxi] a lawyer from Munich who had close ties to the Vatican, was appointed by Dohnányi and Oster. He succeeded around January 1940 in getting Pope Pius XII to affirm to the Western powers the German conspirators' commitment to the removal of Hitler from power before the launch of any western offensive.[1133] In return, France and Britain would agree to peace negotiations based on Germany's 1937 borders, which existed before the Austrian Anschluss and dismemberment of Czechoslovakia. But soon after Josef Müller's meeting with the Pope, Reinhard Heydrich, now chief of the Reich Main Security Office (Reichssicherheitshauptamt or RSHA),[1134] intercepted Vatican radio broadcasts revealing detailed intelligence of German attack plans for the west. It appeared that Canaris, Oster, Dohnányi and co from the Abwehr, the German military intelligence service, would inevitably be implicated, but they escaped such scrutiny.[1135]

Unfortunately, the putsch came to naught when Franz Halder, Chief of the General Staff in the High Command headquarters, approached Walther von Brauchitsch, the Army commander-in-chief, with

---

xxi xlviii As stated in an earlier footnote, Josef Müller is not to be confused with his previously mentioned pure namesake Ludwig Müller (See Chapter 4 "The Aryan Paragraph"). As will become clear, it would be hard to find two individuals of more contrasting character.

a memo authored by Dohnányi, proposing the coup. Brauchitsch was indifferent to SS atrocities in Poland, but had already stated his opposition to Hitler's western invasion. Nevertheless, for Brauchitsch, Dohnányi's memo was tantamount to treason, and he reprimanded Halder for revealing it to him, demanding that he have its author and others associated with it arrested. Halder, however, insisted that if anyone was to be arrested, it should be him alone.[1136]

Ultimately, no one was arrested. But in the process, another coup attempt had evaporated, and with it, the last real chance the German conspirators would have for a negotiated peace. When the July 1944 assassination/coup attempt failed, the west, and the Soviets, especially, were in no mood for any negotiated peace with Germany. Unconditional surrender, even in the event of a successful coup, was the only term on the table for Germany. Canaris and the Abwehr had put out feelers to the British for peace in 1942 and 1943, but they were rejected. Moreover, by July 1944, the Soviet Army had already crossed the pre-war eastern Polish frontier. The frontline was, by then, just 160 kilometres or so from the Wolfsschanze (Wolf's Lair — Military Headquarters) in East Prussia, where the assassination attempt took place.[1137] For the conspirators at the time, however, it was still of paramount importance to preserve their credibility for possible future coup attempts, in view of the blessing of the Pope. Hence, Josef Müller's third trip to Rome with news that the coup had failed, or more to the point, had been aborted, and that attacks on the Netherlands, Belgium, and France were imminent.[1138]

In 1967, Eberhard Bethge had his critically acclaimed biography of Dietrich Bonhoeffer *Dietrich Bonhoeffer — Eine Biographie* published in Munich, then three or so years later in London and New York as *Dietrich Bonhoeffer: Man of Vision, Man of Courage*.[1139] While he was writing the biography, heated discussions were going on in Germany about the question of "treason" of the conspirators.[1140] Outside Germany, the debate was more about how culpable the German elite were in their prolonged obedience to a regime which committed such heinous crimes. Brauchitsch, who scuttled the 1940 coup attempt with full knowledge of and indifference to Einsatzgruppen atrocities in Poland, was a case in point.

Among the 1940 conspirators, Hans Oster went one step further when he arranged a meeting with a Dutch military attaché who was a friend of his. At this meeting, Oster revealed Hitler's plans to invade the Netherlands, including the exact date, pleading with the attaché to hinder the German advance by destroying all bridges strategic to it. However, the government in The Hague did not do so, or perhaps more to the point, they didn't want to believe this. Rather, they fooled themselves with Hitler's empty assurances,[1141] coupled perhaps with the memory of the neutrality they were able to maintain during the Great War.[1142]

Before making this revelation, Oster, the son of a Dresden pastor,[1143] confided in Dietrich. Oster was troubled that he was about to put the lives of fellow German soldiers at risk, perhaps commit an act of treason. Bethge, in his biography, quoted Dietrich's counsel to Oster in regard to this question: "

> Bonhoeffer regarded Oster's action on the eve of the Western offensive as a step taken on his own final responsibility ..... 'Treason' had become true patriotism, and what was normally 'patriotism' had become treason. An officer saw [Hitler's] diabolical reversal of all values, and acted entirely alone to prevent new outrages in other countries, such as those he had experienced in Poland — and the pastor approved of what he did."[1144]

While Dietrich knew about the early coup attempts, and was in Berlin on the crucial days, he was not yet a member of the Military Intelligence resistance group. His double life as a Confessing Church pastor alongside that as a Military Intelligence staff member only came about following Hitler's surprisingly rapid victory over France in June 1940.[1145] From early April to the end of June, Denmark, Norway, Holland, Belgium, Luxembourg, and finally France, fell to the Nazi blitzkrieg juggernaut, on the pretext of Reich protection from British invasion. Hitler, in retribution for the humiliating November 11th Armistice of 1918 signed by German officials in the rail car in the forest of Compiègne, would compel the French to sign a more humiliating one in the same rail car in the same forest on Saturday June 22 1940.[1146]

The terms involved France being split between German occupied France, including Paris, and the so-called "neutral" but collaborationist Vichy France in the south-eastern two-fifths of the country under their World War I hero Marshall Petain.[1147] However, by World War II's end, he, along with the rest of the Vichy regime, embodied the collaboration. The Marshall was sentenced to death in August 1945, but it was commuted to life imprisonment due to his advanced age of almost ninety years. Six years later, he would die in the fortress on the Île d'Yeu off the Atlantic coast at the age of ninety-five.[1148]

For Hitler's regime, the signing of the symbolic armistice in Compiègne in June 1940, nearly twenty-two years after the armistice of November 1918, was a joyful event of Germanic retribution and vindication of their Führer. Hitler was able to become executor of this dubious justice, largely thanks to Britain and France granting him numerous concessions from 1933 on, ones which they had denied the maligned Weimar Republic.[1149] Ecumenically, this was reflected during Dietrich's March 1939 visit to England. Then, Dietrich had tried to get ecumenical circles to allow the Confessing Church to take part in ecumenical conferences without having to go through Theodore Heckel's Reichkirche Foreign Office. Sadly, he only received lukewarm responses,[1150] as England, influenced by the loyalty of broad church circles in Germany toward Hitler, took the side of Hitler against his domestic opposition.[1151] With Germanic retribution for Versailles complete after Compiègne, Hitler personified the deception of "Satan appearing in the form of an angel of light," as written by the prophet Paul in his second letter to the Corinthians, Chapter 11, verse 14.[1152]

During the first half of 1940, the last of the collective pastorates in the Pomeranian wilds was closed on March 18, following one of the worst winters on record.[1153] Dietrich still had some months remaining of his deferral from military call-up, so he was not unemployed as a pastor. Many ministers had been conscripted into military service, leaving their parishes without formal pastoral care. The void was often filled by their wives conducting religious education, and in one instance, a farmer, in his capacity as a local church elder, conducting services. These measures could never be more than stop-gap, and so "Visiting Pastorates"[1154] were created — to which no one was better suited for the circuit than Dietrich, who had performed the same duties during the years of the Pomeranian Sammelvikariats. He was appointed further east to the Confessing Church parishes in East Prussia, which had been separated from Germany proper between the wars by the Polish Corridor in order for Poland to have its sole access to the sea.[1155]

Before embarking on the first of his East Prussian visitations, he waited anxiously in Berlin[1156] for news of the Allied evacuation at Dunkirk. As the French army rapidly disintegrated, a critical Allied victory materialised with the miraculous escape of 198,000 British/Canadian and 140,000 French and Belgian troops across the Channel over nine days from May 26 to June 4. This was in no small part thanks to the bravery of civilian seamen.[1157] Dietrich's concern was for his twin sister Sabine and her family, as he feared that Hitler would launch an immediate invasion of Britain.[1158] When this didn't eventuate, on the day following the successful Dunkirk evacuation, he and Bethge set off eastwards for Tilsit and Memel.[1159]

There they found churches overflowing with devoted congregations and met the faithful who were filling the void left by the conscription of their pastors. This prompted Dietrich and Bethge to propose the creation of training courses for lay preachers within the Confessing Church on their return to Berlin. However, while they sat in the garden of a café on the peninsula opposite Memel, enjoying the early summer sunshine of mid-June, their joy and excitement at the overflowing congregations faltered. News of France's surrender came booming across loudspeakers, with patrons singing "Deutschland, Deutschland *über alles*" and the song of SA militia leader, Horst Wessel, the icon for the Hitler Youth. Dietrich and Bethge stood up, but Bethge, in a dazed state, didn't immediately raise his right arm in the Nazi salute, prompting Dietrich's whispered rebuke:

"Raise your arm! Are you crazy?" followed later by: "We shall have to run risks for very different things now, but not for that salute!"[1160]

This suggests that Dietrich's alert mind was well suited for his forthcoming role in the shadowy world of espionage. As Eric Metaxas put it: "

> It was then, Bethge realised, that Bonhoeffer crossed a line. He was behaving conspiratorially. He didn't want to be thought of as an objector. He wanted to blend in. He didn't want to make an anti-Hitler statement; he had bigger fish to fry. He wanted to be left alone to do the things he knew God was calling him to do, and these things required him to remain unnoticed. Bethge said that one cannot fix a date when Bonhoeffer passed into being a part of the conspiracy in any official way. But he knew at that café in Memel, when Bonhoeffer was saluting Hitler, that his friend was already on the other side of the border. He had crossed from 'confession' to 'resistance.'"[1161]

Bethge would write: "

> It was then that Bonhoeffer's double life began: the involvement as a pastor in the political underground movement, which he wrote in 1943 [from Berlin's Tegel prison], 'may prevent me from taking up my ministry again later on.' That passage in a letter from Tegel was not an expression of secret uncertainty about the way that was beginning; on the contrary, he meant

that he was acting out of an inner necessity for which his church as yet had no formulas. By normal standards everything had been turned upside down."[1162]

And finally, Jane Pejsa: "

Dietrich Bonhoeffer is now fully committed to a conspiracy that is only waiting for the right moment to set aside the government of Germany. He is also of one mind with the inner circle of conspirators in that he believes a coup cannot succeed without the death of Hitler. Still he will continue to maintain his very visible ties with the pastors and the brethren who have taken their stance against the state church [Reichkirche] — both out of inner conviction and as an outward mask."[1163]

Chapter 17

Pastor and Spy

On the second weekend of July 1940, during Dietrich's second journey to East Prussia, which he made on his own, he met some students from the East Prussian capital of Königsberg (literally "King's mountain," now modern-day Kaliningrad in the Russian enclave),[1164] at a nearby weekend retreat in Bloestau. During this gathering, the Gestapo appeared and asked questions, writing down the names and addresses of the participants before breaking it up.[1165] Meanwhile, Hans von Dohnányi met with Colonel Hans Oster, the chief of staff of Military Intelligence (Abwehr). His aim was to gain Canaris's approval for his brother-in-law to be admitted to the Abwehr.[1166] It was not long in forthcoming, and Dietrich's third visit to East Prussia had the cover of a Military Intelligence assignment.

While in Königsberg on his third visit, Dietrich reported to the local Military Intelligence officer. But Superintendent Block telephoned him from Schlawe in Pomerania, stating that he had to report to the police there immediately. Upon arrival, a Gestapo officer informed him that, in accordance with orders from the Reich SS Headquarters, he was now banned from public speaking throughout Germany, on the grounds of "activity subverting the people."[1167] Moreover, he was to report regularly to the authorities in the town where he resided, and inform them beforehand of any travel. Upon the collapse of communist East Germany half a century later, it was discovered in their archives that one of the students Dietrich met at the retreat in Bloestau was a Gestapo informant.[1168]

By late July 1940, upon Dohnányi's recommendation, the decision was made for Dietrich to serve as a V-Mann (*Verbindungsmann* or confidential agent) under Admiral Canaris.[1169] Eventually, following a nervous six month wait, he would be granted the classification of "*unabkömmlich — UK*" or indispensable,[1170] which ruled out any possibility of his conscription into the army.[1171] However, in view of his recent problems with the Gestapo, it was seen as prudent to transfer him to the Military Intelligence office in Munich in the south of the country, where other antagonists of the Reich, most notably his friend and Vatican contact, Josef Müller, were based.[1172]

Curiously, however, Dietrich was never on the Abwehr payroll, and would have refused any such income as an agent.[1173] He did continue to receive income from the Confessing Church, but 30 to 50 percent less, due to the increasing difficulties the Confessing Church had in meeting its financial obligations to the pastors who had been suspended without pay from their pastorates. Fortunately, his twin sister Sabine and her husband still had a bank account in Germany which the Gestapo had not yet discovered; the remaining shortfall was met by Dohnányi, who maintained a special account for the benefit of the Confessing Church. It was funded periodically by Carl Friedrich Goerdeler, the former mayor of Leipzig, who collected the required funds from among his extensive contacts.

It may seem puzzling, given that the Reich Main Security Office had labelled Dietrich as subversive, that he was able to be recruited by the Abwehr, which for all outward appearances, was an instrument of Hitler's Reich. In the shadowy world of espionage, however, appearances are everything. The highest echelons of the Abwehr, from its head Admiral Canaris to Hans Oster and Dietrich's brother-in-law Hans von Dohnányi, had to portray a façade of unquestioning loyalty to the Third Reich on the one hand, while, on the other, plotting its demise — which included Hitler's assassination. In the event of his arrest and subsequent interrogation, Dietrich was told by Oster's office to tell his interrogators that "Military Intelligence works with everyone, with Communists and with Jews; why not also with people of the Confessing Church?"[1174]

While this seems like a very strange comment, there is the story of the German Jew Paul Ernst Fackenheim. To the outsider, Fackenheim was just another faceless prisoner, No. 26,336. But this loyal German, who had distinguished himself in World War I and had become a friend of Hermann Göring,[1175] would soon become "the only Jew to be willingly released by the Nazis" during WWII. A man whom the Abwehr had specific plans for. He was to be trained as a spy and ultimately parachuted into Palestine, to learn what he could of the British effort to stop Field Marshal Erwin Rommel from taking control of the Suez Canal.[1176] On the night of October 10 1941, Paul Fackenheim, now assigned the code name Paul Koch, boarded a Heinkel bomber and took off for Palestine. His jump was successful, and he landed safely in an orange grove. But his troubles were just beginning. Unbeknownst to Abwehr officials, in a classic case of bitter inter-agency rivalry within the Reich, in concert with National Socialist dogma, the SS leaked the mission to the British, informing them that a dangerous agent named Koch would be parachuted into Palestine.[1177]

British troops, tipped off about Fackenheim's arrival, swarmed to the drop zone, but he used the skills he had learned on the battlefields of World War I to evade capture. The next morning he joined a group of civilians and boarded a bus for Haifa. With British soldiers still searching for their quarry, Fackenheim was convinced that his best chance of survival was to turn himself in. He entered a British camp and told the officer that he was a Jewish immigrant from Europe who had landed on the beach the night before. When the officer saw the name "Koch" on the papers, Fackenheim was immediately arrested and sent to Cairo. There he was interrogated by British intelligence services, who were certain that he was a dangerous German spy.[1178] Fackenheim tried to tell them the truth about his release from Dachau, but they responded with considerable scepticism. He was placed on trial and faced the spectre of a firing squad, but he had a stubborn lawyer. Somehow, the lawyer was able to locate a woman from his hometown in Germany who vouched for his true identity. Fackenheim had dodged the bullet once again, but he remained in prison until the war's end. Sadly, his mother was deported in 1943 to Theresienstadt, where she died.[1179]

Another example of the double dealing demanded of the Abwehr in this environment was the use of British made plastic explosives, of the type that had been dropped all over Europe by the RAF (Royal Air Force) to equip the burgeoning resistance movements in countries occupied by the Nazis. Some of this plastic explosive was seized by the Abwehr, and used in the failed assassination plots of March 1943 and the July 1944 Valkyrie plot, because it was extremely powerful, yet easy to conceal, since its fuse functioned silently without a tell-tale hiss.[1180]

Hitler's SS (Shutzstaffel — Protection Squadron)[1181] did have its own intelligence arm, namely the Sicherheitsdienst (SD) and there was of course Hitler's secret police — the Gestapo. While in a sense, the Gestapo was separate from the SS, they both came under the Reichssicherheitshauptamt (RSHA — Reich Main Security Office), ultimately answerable to its head Heinrich Himmler. The RHSA was the all-encompassing body responsible for the concentration camps, Einsatzgruppen, and ultimately the Final Solution, which embodied the Holocaust.[1182] The Abwehr, on the other hand, was the intelligence arm of the regular military, including the Wehrmacht — the German regular army, the Luftwaffe — the German Air Force, and the Kriegsmarine — the German Navy.[1183] The vast majority of the military members of the conspirators came from the Wehrmacht, with hardly any coming from the SS or RHSA in general; the opportunistic Arthur Nebe[1184] was one of the very few, or perhaps the only one.

While Admiral Canaris was not a member of the Wehrmacht, he had served in the German Imperial Navy in the Great War;[1185] in the war's aftermath, up until 1935, he had served in the Reichsmarine, which had that year, two years after Hitler's rise to power, been superseded by the Kriegsmarine.[1186] They were nevertheless still part of the regular military, and so never subordinate to the SS or Gestapo. On January 2 1935, Canaris was made head of the Abwehr,[1187] and in 1933, was seduced by Hitler, and was loyal to him well into 1936. Then, in a major intelligence coup for the Abwehr, Canaris had audaciously contradicted other intelligence agencies of the Reich, correctly advising Hitler that the French and British would not intervene militarily in the March 1936 Rhineland crisis.[1188] Canaris' perception of Hitler, however, had changed by early 1938, preceding the Austrian Anschluss in March, and in the wake of the Fritsch Affair in January.[1189]

Now an agent of the Abwehr, Dietrich, in the "twilight zone"[1190] of a double life, continued his life as no less a pastor.[1191] He still conducted funerals, kept in contact with former students at the front, and the few who still worked as pastors in remote villages. He still wrote personal letters to the families of students and friends who died at the front, and despite the ban from public speaking, he still held discussions in small groups, and continued to work on his book *Ethics*. None of them could know the other side of his new double life. From October 1940 until his arrest on April 5 1943, during frantic weeks of carrying out assignments for the conspiracy, travelling on overcrowded trains that were blacked-out at night, and on planes, ferries and the like, mingled with periods of working undisturbed on his theology in the home of Ruth von Kleist-Retzow in Pomerania, at the Benedictine monastery in Ettal in Bavaria, or in his attic room in Berlin, he traversed in all well over 50,000 kilometres, or one-and-a-quarter times the world's circumference.[1192]

That Dietrich had successfully concealed his double life from the Confessing church, is supported by what occurred at a meeting of the Confessing Church's Old Prussian Council of Brethren in early July 1940 at Nowawes (today Babelsberg; it was a remote site they often used for meetings) near Potsdam. There, Kurt Scharf, Wilhelm Niesel and others post-war, claimed that Dietrich had acknowledged Hitler's stunning victory in France as if it were the very will of God.[1193] They claimed that Dietrich appeared there and surprised his friends by indicating that he, like virtually everyone else, was capitulating before Hitler's incredible success as before a divine judgement, and recommended a new attitude toward the National Socialist state.

As Bethge put it, Dietrich had revised his views, but some at the meeting had entirely misunderstood this revision.[1194] This however, did not include younger members of the Confessing Church's Provisional Church Administration, also present, such as Pastor Wilhem Rott and Dr. Herbert Werner, who stated: "It would be beyond me to imagine how anyone could turn what was said [by Dietrich] in Babelsberg into a sudden enthusiasm for National Socialism and a confession of loyalty to Hitler."[1195]

Dietrich was attempting to make his colleagues understand that in the wake of Hitler's stunning success in France and the Low Countries, they would have to accept the fact, regardless of how unpalatable it was, that the regime of Hitler's Third Reich was bound to ensure its existence for far longer than they, and the resistance movement in general, had anticipated. In this context the contrast between the hopes that were still cherished and the consolidation of the regime was much sharper for Dietrich than for his less well informed audiences.[1196]

Moreover, Dietrich wanted to impress on himself and others that after June 17, 1940, there could no longer be a simple return to things as they had been before. The relationship to neighbouring countries, the social structure, the political status-quo — everything from now on would be irrevocably influenced by Hitler's actions, and would remain so. The goal of eliminating Hitler could no longer be a restoration of the past. The road to something new would be infinitely more lengthy and costly; the form that the goal would take was unknown.[1197]

Dietrich's official entry into the anti-Hitler conspiracy clearly refutes any notion of him suddenly professing Hitler's staggering success in the west to be a divine vindication of the National Socialist agenda. However, at the time, Scharf and Niesel were not privy to this intelligence. Two excerpts of Dietrich's book *Ethics*, which Dietrich was writing at the time, read in their entirety but not in isolation, clearly illustrate that Dietrich never interpreted Hitler's success as the divine will of God: "

> The successful create facts that cannot be reversed. What they destroy cannot be restored. What they construct has, at least in the following generation, the right of existence. No condemnation can make good the wrong that the successful commit .... The judges of history play a sad role alongside those who make history; history rolls over them."[1198]

This excerpt on its own may be construed as Dietrich contending that success is always the judge of what is right or the true will of God. The following however, cancels out this interpretation: "

> Where the figure of a successful person becomes especially prominent, the majority fall into idolising success. They become blind to right and wrong, truth and lie, decency and malice .... Success per se is the good. This attitude is only genuine and excusable while one is intoxicated by events. After sobriety returns it can be maintained only at the cost of deep inner hypocrisy, with conscious self-deception."[1199]

Back in mid-June, at the café in Memel after the announcement of France's surrender, Dietrich and Bethge had witnessed first-hand the mass intoxication of idolising success, manifested by "Satan appearing in the form of an angel of light."[1200] Moreover, Dietrich's alertness in contrast to his dear friend's bewilderment illustrated his suitability for the parallel roles of pastor and spy, contradicting the claims of Scharf and Niesel. Dietrich's Hitler salute in Memel[1201] can hardly be seen as his acceptance of the legitimacy of Hitler's Third Reich.

While Dietrich accepted the necessity for the move to Bavaria, he had hoped he could continue theological work there. Dietrich's mother Paula had asked Josef Müller if the Benedictine Monastery in Ettal, south-west of Munich and near the modern-day Austrian border, could become Dietrich's new home. To Dietrich's delight, Müller found the 14th century Catholic monastery the ideal solution; not the least of which was the opposition of the monks to the Nazi regime; among them was Father Johannes, who was in close contact with the conspirators.[1202] Later, the abbot, extending a formal invitation, was accepted into the conspirators' confidence. While Dietrich was given a room in the hotel Ludwig der Bayer opposite the monastery, he was invited to meals with the monks, and even given a key to the restricted area of the monastery where guests were usually not permitted.

Moreover, he could work in the library any time he liked. The endless discussions he had with the Catholic monks reminded the Protestant pastor of the idyllic nostalgia of Finkenwalde. As well as writing the chapter "Ultimate and Penultimate Things" for his book *Ethics*[1203] while in Ettal, he found the peaceful setting there ideal for contemplation and preparation for his work with the Abwehr. Dietrich would stay at Ettal for three months during the winter of 1940-41.[1204]

During the early phase of his imprisonment in 1943, nothing consoled Dietrich more than his nostalgia for the experience of the monastic life in Finkenwalde and Ettal.[1205]

Dietrich's usefulness to the conspiracy was in great part due to the ecumenical contacts he had in the English-speaking world. In Geneva, there was the Dutch national Willem A. Visser 't Hooft, the Ecumenical General Secretary.[1206] Dietrich had met him at Paddington station in London in April 1939. He also had ready contact with Bishop George Bell in England, who had access to key figures in the British government. In addition, Karl Barth, whom Visser 't Hooft studied under, was called upon by Dietrich more than once. The first such occasion was on February 24 1941,[1207] when the Abwehr sent Dietrich to Switzerland on his first assignment. In the eyes of the American historian Klemens von Klemperer: "

> This trip marked the beginning of the "war behind the war"[1208] or the "the war of the churches against the 'great Counter-Churches',"[1209] in which not only the conspirators in Germany, but also a number of influential Christians in Western countries [such as George Bell] tried to get people to realise that, in contrast to the First World War, the Second World War was not just a conflict between opposing nations, but involved a battle of life and death between two irreconcilable world views."[1210]

Dietrich's objective was to make contact with Protestant leaders outside Germany, informing them of the anti-Hitler conspiracy within the Third Reich, with possible peace terms upon the coup's hoped-for success. At the same time, Josef Müller was having similar conversations at the Vatican.[1211] However, an unforeseen problem for Dietrich occurred when the Swiss border police insisted that someone within Switzerland vouch for him as his guarantor. That was Karl Barth, albeit with perplexing misgivings.[1212] After all, how could a Confessing Church pastor come to Switzerland in the midst of war? Had the incorruptible Bonhoeffer made peace with the Nazis?

Barth was not alone in asking himself such questions. But while it may have appeared that Dietrich was living a privileged life while others of his generation were suffering or risking their lives at the front, Dietrich could not confide his situation to anyone outside the conspiracy's inner-circle. The exception, on his way back to Germany in Basel, was when Dietrich had a long and open conversation with his guarantor for entry into Switzerland. Dietrich was able to allay Barth's fears that he had turned to the dark side.[1213] But before doing so, Dietrich had spent a month in Switzerland, which included extensive meetings with Visser 't Hooft, informing him personally of the situation in Germany.

Issues such as the monstrous T-4 euthanasia program,[1214] persecution of Confessing Church ministers, and the reasons for the failure of various assassination attempts on Hitler[1215] were discussed. In many circles in Britain, Churchill included,[1216] the failed attempts were casting serious doubt on the credibility of the German Underground or their commitment to eliminating Hitler and his regime.[1217] Up until this point, hardly any word of the T-4 program had reached the outside world,[1218] implying that in all probability, Dietrich had, on his first visit to Switzerland as an Abwehr operative, leaked the first comprehensive reports of this heinous program outside Germany.

Other issues were discussed daily, with one day devoted entirely to assistance for persecuted Jews.[1219] Visser 't Hooft invited people such as Adolf Freudenberg to these meetings. He was the former counsellor to the German Legation in London, and was later removed in accordance with Nazi racial laws, before arriving in Geneva to co-ordinate aid for Jewish refugees under the auspices of the Provisional World Council of Churches. Charles Guillon informed Dietrich about the efforts of the French Resistance to help Jews. This would have included the story of the village of Chambon-sur-Lignon, a centre of the French Protestant Church, which became famous after the war for bravely rendering assistance, co-ordinated by its pastors, André Trocmé and Édouard Théis. Jews fleeing for Switzerland would be sheltered among the village inhabitants before their flight across the border to Switzerland.[1220]

The significance of these discussions didn't cease in Geneva. When Dietrich returned to Berlin, he met with close friends in Bethge's apartment. The most significant of them was the brave lady Gertrud Staewen.[1221] By now, Heinrich Grüber, who had been directing the Confessing Church's aid office for Jewish Christians, had been incarcerated in a concentration camp for protesting against the persecutions.[1222] The same fate was met by his colleague, Werner Sylten, who was murdered in the camp by the SS.[1223] Dietrich put a request to Gertrud Staewen before his second visit to Switzerland, one which carried great risk. Gertrud accepted the great danger of continuing the work of Grüber and Sylten.[1224] Together with other brave Berliners, she helped Jews to go underground. Other women who assisted her ending up serving long prison sentences, but it seems they never betrayed her, as miraculously, even with Jews going in and out of her house, Gertrud never roused the unwelcome scrutiny of the Gestapo.[1225] Up until his own imprisonment, Dietrich, with stringent precautions, maintained contact with Gertrud.

Dietrich returned to Germany on March 24 1941, but not before visiting his friend Erwin Sutz. They had met during their time at New York's Union seminary in 1930-31, and it was Sutz that facilitated the Bonhoeffers' contact with the Leibholz family since the outbreak of war.[1226] On his way back to Berlin, Dietrich stopped by in Munich, where two letters from the Reich Writers' Guild were waiting for him. The earlier one informed him that he was fined because he had published work without being a member of the Guild, but it was the latter that would have concerned him the most. It stated that his application of November 1940 for membership in the Guild had been rejected, since he was already banned from public speaking owing to acts of "subverting the people,"[1227] and was henceforth forbidden from all written activity.

Dietrich had mentioned in his membership application that specialists writing in their field were exempt from having to become members, but predictably, this loophole had been closed.[1228] When Dietrich made the side trip to Halle to consult with Ernst Wolf, the publisher of several of his works, on his way back to Berlin, he was left in no doubt that his present work, *Ethics*, would never be published while the Third Reich was in existence. Nevertheless, Dietrich did not hesitate to continue his work on the manuscript secretly;[1229] it would become one of the most famous of all his written works post-war, even though, it was never finished, with fragments arranged posthumously.[1230]

Around this time, Hitler issued an order that would have cataclysmic consequences. On Sunday March 30 1941,[1231] Hitler issued the notorious "Commissar Order," in which the Einsatzgruppen, as they did in Poland, would play a pivotal role in implementing Lebensraum (living space) in the east, as espoused in *Mein Kampf*. Operation Barbarossa, Hitler's invasion of the Soviet Union, would take place less than three months later on June 22 1941.[1232] As in Poland in fighting the Slavic Untermensch, and in the ideological war of "righteous" National Socialism against the scourge of Bolshevism, all measures of genocide and summary execution were legalised on the basis of fulfilling the "unquestionable" racial and ideological agenda embodied in *Mein Kampf*. In accordance with its designation, the "Commissar Order" directed that when Soviet political officers or "commissars" fell into German hands, they were to be summarily liquidated. This directive went much further, demanding that the invasion overall be implemented with the utmost cruelty.[1233] The most barbaric theatre of World War II, and perhaps of all wars in human history, had begun.

As commander of the armed forces, Brauchitsch was flooded with pleas from within to challenge Hitler or to resign.[1234] However, once again, he was incapable of committing himself to a definite position. Publicly, only a few commanders condemned Hitler's directive, but privately, more were coming around to the conspirators' view. Six days before Barbarossa, General Beck held a meeting in regard to another planned coup.[1235] However, the invasion six days later was followed by its staggering success in the months preceding the Russian winter.

Curiously, however, unlike the fall of France a year earlier, the conspirators did not become discouraged.[1236] They may have felt that the Russian winter, exacerbated by chronically stretched supply lines never experienced in Poland and Western Europe, coupled with seemingly unlimited Soviet manpower, would, in time, prove Hitler's undoing. However, the conspirators' hope for a future negotiated peace was complicated much further by having to deal with an additional power — the giant of the Soviet Union. Atrocities in France and the Low Countries would demand much harsher peace terms than immediately following the Polish invasion. But after Barbarossa, in the wake of Einsatzgruppen-perpetrated genocide, and with Stalin now at any likely future negotiation table, it's hard to see how Germany, even with the removal of Hitler and his regime in a successful coup, could hope for anything better than unconditional surrender.[1237]

At the time, however, Hitler's advance into the vast eastern Slavic lands seemed inexorable. Moreover, there seemed to be nothing to halt their march into Asia. In its late summer midst, Dietrich made his second visit to Switzerland on August 29. Upon entering Visser 't Hooft's office, he declared: "Well, now it's all over, isn't it?"[1238] However, on seeing how taken aback his Dutch friend was, he clarified his position: "No, I mean, this is the beginning of the end; Hitler will never get out of there."[1239]

While in Geneva, Dietrich was handed Bishop George Bell's book *Christianity and World Order,* published the previous year. In this book, the author understood the disastrous consequences of a victory for the Third Reich, and demanded that no effort be spared to defeat them and remove them from power. However, Bell also wished for a recognition that not all Germans were pro-Hitler, with members of the German Underground, such as Dietrich and Gertrud Staewen, among others, risking their lives day in and day out against this criminal regime. Bell urged his readers "not to let slip any genuine chance of a negotiated peace which observes the principles of Order and justice ..."[1240] This dovetailed perfectly with Dietrich's hopes and aspirations.

However, in spite of George Bell's prominence in religious and political circles in England, this was far from being the majority view in all walks of British society. That being, as Churchill put it, only "Hitler's Germany."[1241] This position was reinforced further with the Barbarossa invasion which brought the Soviet giant over to the Allied side, although not in the cause of freedom and democracy, as the Iron Curtain post-war would attest to. If Dietrich was buoyed by Bell's written words, this optimism was crushed upon visiting Siegmund-Schulze in Zürich. There, Dietrich received the depressing news that the British embassy in Bern, in accordance with orders from London, had just refused to accept a document from Goerdeler containing peace proposals in the event of a successful coup.[1242]

Dietrich, it seems, was of the opinion that Germany could not escape the consequences for the crimes committed up to that point by the Third Reich. During his time in Zürich, he spent an evening at the city's famous Pestalozzi Bibliotek, among a group of people with whom he could safely express his truest and deepest feelings.[1243] Among them was his Dutch friend Visser 't Hooft, who had arrived from Geneva especially for this gathering. While there, he asked Dietrich: "What do you pray for in the present situation?" To which, Visser' t Hooft reported, Dietrich's reply was: "

> Since you ask me, I must say that I pray for the defeat of my country, for I believe that this is the only way in which it can pay for the suffering which it has caused in the world."

Eberhard Bethge's thoughts, as written in his 1960s biography of Dietrich, were: "

> This was a statement people did not like to hear repeated in post-war Germany, but its essential content can hardly be denied ..... More than anything, it proved how absurd and extraordinary the situation was under Hitler, when the true patriot had to speak unpatriotically to show his patriotism. It is a reaction that defies normal feelings in normal times; it may be a good thing that it has been passed on without defence or explanation, so that one confronts it directly and relives the incredible sen-

timents in those days. It is abundantly true that the best people of that era lived with the constant thought that they had to wish for Germany's defeat to end the injustice."[1244]

In September 2014, I was with my wife in a tour group in Nuremberg. While visiting the now abandoned Nazi Rally grounds, our German guide recalled a story his father had told him of a conversation, or more to the point, a confrontation he had with his father (the guide's grandfather). It was 1969, and the then young man desired to know about the war, as German history of that time in schools and society in general was hardly ever spoken about. It seemed that the Germans consigned that period to an historical vacuum. However, the generation post-war, now grown up, much to the chagrin of their parents, could not leave this epoch of German history consigned to the vacuum of repressed memories. When the son pressed his father on this subject once too often, the father exploded and told him if he ever raised this topic again, he would be thrown out of the house.

Just two years preceding this incident, in Munich in 1967, Bethge first published his biography of Dietrich Bonhoeffer.[1245] It was only then that German people seemed willing to admit the truth of Hitler's Germany. Even then, given the account of our guide in Nuremberg by the city's infamous Nazi rally grounds, it was more the younger generation born around or soon after the war's end that was willing to hear the confronting and uncomfortable truth of the infamous Third Reich. Our guide, the second generation post-war, was forthright in his criticism of Hitler's Germany. While we were standing at the rally grounds, he spent time describing the rallies to us, regularly holding up a folder of copies of photos from the rallies. He admitted they had a kind of spectacular magnificence, but of the darkest colour. He did not waste the opportunity to quote the old joke: "as slim as Göring, as tall as Goebbels, and as blond as Hitler." At the time of our visit, the state of the old rally grounds was one of abandonment, indicating the dilemma of local authorities. Some advocated their demolition, while others wished to maintain them as a reminder of their nation's dark Nazi epoch, so as to ensure that history is not repeated.

Dietrich spent about a month in Switzerland on his second visit, not arriving back in Germany until the end of September. What greeted him upon his arrival greatly disturbed him, in spite of Dohnányi having prepared him for it some time before. On the train back to Berlin, he saw German Jews who were forced to wear the Star of David.[1246] The decree had been issued on September 2 1941, and came into effect on the 19th. Dietrich soon discovered that deportations of Jews were imminent, with "evacuation notices" sent to large numbers of Jewish families. On October 16 and 17,[1247] these families were taken from their homes and deported to areas in the newly occupied Lebensraum (living space) in the east.

In the winter of 1936-37, during the early days of Finkenwalde, a close friendship between Dietrich and Friedrich Justus Perels, the legal adviser to the Confessing Church, had developed.[1248] Now, like Dietrich, Perels was in on of the plans of the anti-Hitler conspiracy, and together they now collaborated on gathering as much information as possible on the deportations to the east.[1249] Since asking about this on the telephone or in a letter would have been foolhardy,[1250] the Abwehr had sent one of them on a brief trip to the Rhineland where the deportations had already begun, and through the discreet grapevine of trusted friends, a report was compiled on October 18 1941, with another more detailed one to follow two days later.

It was around this time that the operation codenamed Unternehmen Sieben (Operation 7) was conceived, with the initial objective of having seven German Jews removed from the deportation lists on the pretext of being used by the Abwehr.[1251] Ultimately, that figure would double, thanks to the persistence, energy and cunning of Hans von Dohnányi, acting with the consent of Admiral Canaris. This strategy was well over a year in the making,[1252] much in the spirit of the old Jewish proverb, "Whoever saves one life, saves the whole world."[1253]

In Canaris's office, they were assisted by the lawyer Count Helmuth James von Moltke, head of the Silesian Kreisauer Kreis or "Kreisau circle" and great grandnephew and grandnephew of two past Field Marshals (the latter was the commander of Imperial Germany's campaign in Belgium and France at the outbreak of the Great War).[1254] Dietrich, in collaboration with Wilhelm Rott, whom he knew from Finkenwalde, and Perels, the legal adviser, arranged for their Swiss Christian contacts, such as Karl Barth and the president of the country's Church Federation, Alphons Koechlin,[1255] to insist that Swiss entry visas be granted these Jews. Such visas were only issued at that time if travellers could prove they were merely travelling through the country. Among those saved, and indeed the first, largely through Dietrich's efforts, was Charlotte Friedenthal, a staff member of the Confessing Church. A month later, the rest of the group followed, but not before Hans von Dohnányi deposited a substantial sum of foreign money into a Swiss bank account to assist the rescued Jews.[1256]

Following the conception of Operation 7, Dietrich become ill with severe pneumonia at the beginning of November 1941. Before the advent of antibiotics, it was only after weeks of much needed rest in Pomerania at the Kleist family estate in Kieckow that he made a full recovery. As his condition improved, he made use of the time to complete another chapter of his work *Ethics*.[1257] Meantime, in the east, the Wehrmacht offensive stalled in the unrelenting Russian winter.

In the previous month of October, Colonel Henning von Tresckow, the General Staff officer of the Central Army group in Russia, advancing on Moscow, had sent his adjutant, Fabian von Schlabrendorff, from Smolensk[1258] to Berlin to discuss with Colonel Oster the possibility of another joint coup attempt.[1259] Tresckow felt that the atrocities committed by the SS Einsatzgruppen units in the wake of the German advance, coupled with Hitler's constant interference in operational plans, with gruesome consequences for the troops, had brought many of the German High command around to considering his overthrow. By late November, in the midst of one of the worst Russian winters on record, the Wehrmacht was forced into its first significant withdrawal of the campaign. Their exhausted and hypothermic Army Group South was routed at Rostov, the gateway to the Caucasus with its prodigious oil fields.[1260] General Gerd von Rundstedt, the commander of Army Group South, ordered the withdrawal from Rostov. Hitler's predictable rage compelled his resignation.[1261] He would not be the only one.

By early December, with the spires of the Kremlin just twenty or so kilometres distant and visible to the most advanced German units of the Army Group Centre, commanded by General von Bock,[1262] Hitler's advance on Moscow stalled.[1263] Thousands of soldiers, minus winter clothing due to Hitler's expectation of a quick and easy victory in the summer, were dying from severe frostbite, and winter was claiming more German casualties than in battle.[1264] With fuel freezing, the traditional horse and sleigh became a common sight, as did fires being started under tanks to get their engines to kick in. Oil used to grease German sub-machine guns would often freeze, in stark contrast to the equivalent Soviet weapons.[1265]

With all this, a number of General Staff officers began to view the invasion as a lost cause, and even the Army commander-in-chief, Walther von Brauchitsch, gave the impression that he now had grave reservations about Hitler's continued leadership of the Reich because of his constant interference in military operations and the toll on the troops. The conspirators were no doubt cautiously optimistic that Brauchitsch would be ready to issue orders to the army for the coup's consolidation.[1266]

Any such hopes were quashed when, on December 19, news broke that Hitler had dismissed Brauchitsch and appointed himself the supreme commander of the army. Coup plans were again in a state of collapse, and had to be rebuilt from scratch.[1267] On December 7 1941, with the German army being routed outside Moscow, came a ray of strategic sunshine for Hitler at his Wolf's Lair, when the Japanese, akin to the Barbarossa invasion, bombed Pearl Harbour without any formal declaration of war.[1268] The world was being plunged into conflict on two parallel but unconnected fronts.

One was an Anglo-Soviet alliance against Nazi Germany in Europe, and the other an Anglo-American one fighting the Japanese in South-East Asia and the Pacific. While Germany, Italy, and Japan had signed the Tripartite Pact in Berlin on September 27 1940, Article Three only compelled one party to assist the other if it was attacked by a power not involved in the European war or in the Chinese-Japanese conflict.[1269] Clearly, however, at Pearl Harbour, Japan was the aggressor, so Germany was not honour bound by this pact to declare war on the US for Japan's sake. Not that pacts or agreements on paper meant anything to Hitler.

Nevertheless, Hitler, in a conversation with the Japanese ambassador Hiroshi Ōshima, stated that the Japanese had given the "right declaration of war."[1270] This reflected how Hitler viewed the propaganda diversion that Pearl Harbour offered in the midst of the winter rout of German armies in Russia, with their 0.75 million casualties.[1271] America was weakened and wounded in the wake of Pearl Harbour, precipitated in part by the misguided American and British complacency[1272] about Japan's unpreparedness and lack of will for war. Hitler, now in jubilant agreement with his naval commander Grand Admiral Raeder and Rear Admiral Dönitz,[1273] commander of the U-boat arm, saw a perfect opportunity to unleash their U-boats on the American east coast and the Atlantic.

Indeed, in the first half of 1942, Britain's lifeline with the US navy was in danger of being permanently severed by the U-boat threat. While the US was officially neutral, American shipping was for the most part immune from U-boat attacks. But now, with the US officially at war with Japan and Germany, Raeder and Dönitz, after months of entreating Hitler, were free to unleash their fleet and threaten the destruction of Britain's Atlantic lifeline. Churchill stated that the "U-boat peril" was the only thing that ever really frightened him during World War Two.[1274]

The first wave of these attacks, known as Operation Drumbeat (Paukenschlag), had returned to base in France in early February. By then they had inflicted losses on US merchant and naval shipping exceeding Pearl Harbour, which prompted the U-boat fleet to dub it "die Nacht der Langen Messer"[1275] in reference to Hitler's 1934 purge of the SA. However, as the year wore on and US industrial might asserted itself, together with the eventual adoption of anti-submarine seaplanes, starting with the sinking of U-158 by PBM (VP74) west of Bermuda on June 30 1942,[1276] the party for the U-boats was coming to an end. Hitler now had to confront the almost unlimited industrial might of the US, coupled with the boundless manpower of the Russians. Any short term benefit or propaganda effect of the ill-conceived declaration of war on America was lost.

Hitler had formally announced Germany's declaration of war on the world's foremost industrial power in the Reichstag on Thursday December 11 1941, just four days following Pearl Harbor.[1277] It was the usual Hitler rant, claiming Roosevelt was "the main culprit of this war" and a stooge for the "entire satanic insidiousness" and "diabolical evil of the Jews."[1278] In his book, *Hitler: A Study in Tyranny*, the British historian Sir Alan Bullock states that Hitler's lack of knowledge about the US and its industrial and demographic capacity for mounting a war on two fronts against Germany and Japan played a great part in his miscalculation. Bullock points out that Hitler's deeply-held racial prejudices, in keeping with the mantra of Aryan racial purity and his perception of absolute authority which had led to the Russian winter catastrophe of 1941-42, made him see the US as: "

> ...a decadent bourgeois democracy, filled with people of mixed race, a population heavily under the influence of Jews and Negroes, with no history of authoritarian discipline to control and direct them, interested only in luxury and living the "good life" while dancing, drinking and enjoying negrofied music."[1279]

Hence, such a country, in Hitler's monolithic mindset, would never be willing to make the economic and human sacrifices necessary to threaten National Socialist Germany.

Polls taken in America in July 1940, ten months after WWII began in Europe, and four months before the election which Roosevelt won in a landslide for an unprecedented third term, had shown that only eight percent of Americans supported war against Germany.[1280] In the weeks prior to Pearl Harbour, albeit with a reduced majority, the isolationists still held an overwhelming sway, with 75% of Americans remaining opposed to a repeat war with Germany.[1281] The majority of the nation of immigrants, with German-Americans representing a fifth of the population, hoped and prayed that Old World rivalries and grudges had been abandoned on the other side of the Atlantic. Their immediate priorities revolved around surviving the Great Depression, and securing their Great American Dream.[1282]

Meanwhile Dietrich, when he received the news of Brauchitsch's dismissal and Hitler's declaration of war upon the US, was still in Kieckow working on his book *Ethics*. With the entry of the US into the war against Germany, Dietrich now regarded the defeat of Germany as just a matter of time, and envisaged the burning question that would be asked of the collective guilt which had led to mass murder and war. For him, the church had to take this guilt upon itself, without any ifs or buts or sidelong glances at others who were also guilty. As Dietrich put it: "

> The Church is the place where each person who counts himself or herself a member can give up looking to the left or the right at neighbours in the pews and confess that "We have left undone those things which we ought to have done; and we have done those things which we ought not to have done."[1283]

Moreover… "

> The church confesses that it has witnessed the arbitrary use of brutal force, the suffering in body and soul of countless innocent people, that it has witnessed oppression, hatred and murder without raising its voice for the victims and without finding ways of rushing to help them. It has become guilty of the lives of the Weakest and most Defenceless Brothers and Sisters of Jesus Christ."[1284]

Hitler and his cronies were obviously guilty, but their program of mass genocide of virtually an entire continent would not have been possible without the compliance of some, or in the case of the church, the pretence of ignorance. Dietrich does not allow the church the excuse to look sideways at Hitler, Göring, Goebbels, Heydrich and Himmler, but rather compels it to confront its passive acceptance of organised and industrial scale mass murder.

Early the following year, Dietrich received a letter from Erich Klapproth. He had been one of the most gifted of Dietrich's Finkenwalde ordinands, but was now serving in the frigid hell of the Russian front line. In the bitter cold of minus forty-five degrees Celsius, he wrote of clothes sticking to their bodies, and for days at a time, not being able to wash their hands, and going from dead bodies to a meal and back to their rifles, while all the while summoning all their energy, even in a state of total exhaustion, to keep warm. When away from the mess hall for extended periods, he wrote that it was common for them to raid farmhouses for geese, hens, sheep, pigs and the like, stealing them from starving peasants. Acts Erich Klapproth would have thought unthinkable for himself pre-war, were now commonplace in the extreme ideologically charged horror of the Eastern Front. His company of 150 men had now been reduced to forty; just days after writing, it was reduced by one more when Klapproth died in action.[1285]

Klapproth's letter was mild when compared to a letter Dietrich received from another of his former Finkenwalde ordinands. In mid-January 1942, the letter spoke of a unit of their detachment shooting fifty prisoners in one day, justifying it on the grounds that they were on the march and unable, for whatever reason, to take them along. In districts where women and children were suspected of supplying food to Soviet partisans, they were murdered by being shot in the back of the neck; otherwise, it was reasoned, the lives of German soldiers would be lost.[1286] This ordinand was later killed in action, consumed by the horror of WWII's most devastating theatre. In the context of these letters, it might seem that Dietrich was leading a privileged and safe existence. But his brother-in-law Hans von Dohnányi, in mid-February 1942, received a tip-off from friends that his mail and telephone were under surveillance.[1287] Dietrich and others in the conspiracy would have been aware that they had enemies close by, and lived each day knowing, like those on the front, that it could be their last.

Around early April 1942, Dietrich spent Holy Week and Easter again with Ruth von Kleist in Pomerania. When Dohnányi called him back to Berlin on the following Wednesday, he was expecting to make a third trip to Switzerland. But he was informed that he would be going to the Norwegian capital of Oslo with Helmuth James von Moltke.[1288] At the time, Norway was under the collaborationist regime of Prime Minister Vidkun Quisling (1887-1945), who first rose to international prominence as a close collaborator of Fridtjof Nansen in organising humanitarian relief during the Russian-Ukrainian famine of 1921.[1289] It was estimated his efforts saved 200,000 lives out of a million saved by international efforts; the dominant relief agency was the American Relief Administration of Herbert Hoover.[1290]

Quisling had served in Russia as a diplomat, even managing British diplomatic affairs there until 1929, when, it was clear that the newly elected Labour government of Ramsay MacDonald wished to resume diplomatic ties with Moscow.[1291] Upon his return to Norway, leaving behind Stalin's mass purge of the kulaks,[1292] he served as Minister of Defence in the Agrarian government of Peder Kolstad (1931—32),[1293] and upon Kolstad's death,[1294] was retained by Jens Hundseid (1932—33).[1295] Moreover, Quisling had been awarded the Romanian Crown Order and the Yugoslav Order of Santa Sava for his earlier humanitarian efforts, as well as, in recognition of his diplomatic services to Britain, being appointed a Commander of the Order of the British Empire (CBE).[1296]

In 1933, the year of Hitler's rise to power, Quisling left the Agrarian Party and founded the fascist party *Nasjonal Samling* (National Union).[1297] Never, at any stage however, either pre-war or during wartime, did the *Nasjonal Samling* enjoy anywhere near the popular support of its equivalent in Germany, and on June 24 1940, in the wake of the Norwegian capitulation on the 10th,[1298] Quisling's CBE was revoked by King George VI.[1299] When the invasion of Norway was launched at the beginning of April that year,[1300] the *London Times* coined the new term "quisling," and by the spring of 1942, the essence of the new term became even clearer.[1301]

When Provost Fjellbu of Trondheim Cathedral made statements against the occupation, Quisling had him deposed.[1302] This triggered appeals and protests, but when it became clear the collaborationist regime was not prepared to listen, all the bishops and local pastors in Norway resigned. The crowning piece of collaboration was when the regime set up a Norwegian Nazi youth organisation, much along the lines the Hitler Youth, leading to the resignation of a thousand Norwegian teachers.[1303] Clearly, the Norwegian people were proving nowhere near as compliant as German authorities and institutions in general were during the Nazi rise to power in the previous decade. Quisling's hope that his regime would win the hearts and minds of the people was proving naïve.

As the leader of the church resistance movement, Bishop Eivind Berggrav was interrogated and placed under house arrest before being taken to prison.[1304] As mentioned earlier in Chapter 16, "Homecoming to Outbreak of War," following the fall of Poland in October 1939, Berggrav was making naïve and convoluted overtures of peace to Lord Halifax in London and Hermann Göring in Berlin, under the misguided notion that meaningful peace was possible with Hitler remaining in power. While in Berlin, Berggrav also met with Heckel, the head of the Reichkirche Foreign Office, but made no contact with members of the Confessing Church, which led to Dietrich's scepticism about Berggrav's overtures.[1305] In a neutral country holding a misguided belief in peace with Hitler, but now living under the Nazi jackboot following Hitler's invasion of neutral Norway, it appears that in 1942 Berggrav, as the leader of the Norwegian church resistance, finally abandoned all futile hope.

Moreover, it now appeared that Berggrav would be tried before the "People's" Court (Volksgerichtshof) in Berlin, and as the charges against him were "incitement to insurrection and contacts with the enemy," it was expected he would be sentenced to death.[1306] Theodor Steltzer, a close friend of the Kreisau circle, was a lieutenant colonel in the occupation army in Norway, and telegraphed Moltke immediately upon hearing the news of Berggrav's arrest. Upon receipt, Moltke arranged with the Military Intelligence central office to send him and Dietrich to Norway, on the official pretence of assessing the Norwegian church struggle and the possible threat it represented to the occupying German troops.[1307] Naturally, this was a front for their true intention to aid the Norwegian Resistance and to save Berggrav's life. Dietrich's role was critical, as he was known to the Norwegian bishops and thus assured them that they could speak freely and openly with Moltke.

For Count Moltke, the prime objective of his role in the Abwehr was to ensure that prisoners of war were treated in accordance with international treaties that Germany was a signatory to.[1308] Closely related to this work were the efforts he made to reduce the ever-increasing incidents of the shooting of hostages, which was in violation of international law.[1309] He constantly travelled to occupied countries, where his first move involved gaining the cooperation of officers he knew personally, upon which he would attempt to persuade the commanders of the occupying forces. This is where his illustrious military ancestry came to bear, especially in regard to his famous grand-uncle Field Marshal Helmuth von Moltke the elder who won three wars for Bismarck, leading to the creation of the united German Empire in 1871.

Moltke persuaded many commanders by stating that the shooting of hostages constituted a grave violation of international law. To the many who were not moved by this argument, Moltke warned that such acts might provoke revenge against German occupation troops by resistance groups. While he did not always succeed, it is plausible to assume that by the end of the war, thousands of people owed their lives to the brave count, without realising he had been their saviour.[1310] Dietrich and the count had significant similarities; they were reserved and solitary, they loathed idle chatter, they were shrewd judges of human character,[1311] and were indispensable for intelligence work. Yet they had only met once before and had not formed a close bond.[1312]

Some found the tall count to be taciturn, although not his friends, and the letters he left behind indicate otherwise.[1313] Perhaps only people engaging in idle chatter found him to be so, which would suggest that Dietrich would be comfortable in his company. Like Dietrich, Moltke had dependable and influential friends in the English-speaking world, having studied law both in England and Germany. Moreover, his mother's father had presided over the highest court in South Africa.[1314] His closest friend at that time was Count Peter Yorck von Wartenburg, to whom Dietrich was related through his mother, and whose wife, Countess Marion Yorck, had been a classmate of Dietrich's in Grunewald.[1315] In 1933, Dietrich had written *The Church and the Jewish Question*, and from around that time, the count had been an attorney working tirelessly on behalf of Jews who were being more ostracised each day in the new Reich. [1316]

In the late 1920s, Moltke had become associated with an eclectic group of friends, including intellectual Jews, socialists, writers and scholars, and the like; most of them believed that Christianity had outlived its relevance in the building of a new society. From 1933, Moltke changed his stance, as he stated in a letter written to Lionel Curtis in England whilst in transit in neutral Swedish Malmö, on his return with Dietrich to Berlin from Oslo: "

> Perhaps you will remember that in a conversation before the war I argued that belief in God was not essential in order to come to where we are now. Today I know that I was wrong, wholly and utterly wrong. You know that from the first day I have struggled against the Nazis, but the level of danger, and the readiness for self-sacrifice which is demanded of us today, and perhaps tomorrow, demands more than good ethical principles, especially when we know that the success of our struggle will probably mean the total collapse of national unity. But we are ready to face this."[1317]

On April 10 1942, at Saßnitz on the German island of Rügen in the Baltic Sea, they missed their ferry to Trelleborg in Sweden. The following morning, due to drifting sea ice, there was no ferry crossing, so they took the time to walk for hours in the woods, only coming across a sole woodsman; they discussed their assignment in Oslo among other issues. Moltke had written to his wife Freya that they had discussed which of them would do what task in Oslo. From Dietrich, in Bethge's biography, there is only one comment: "Stimulating, but we are not of the same opinion."[1318]

While their mission to Oslo was a great success,[1319] with Bishop Berggrav able to see out the war under house arrest in a remote mountain forest chalet near Asker,[1320] there seemed to be a widening gulf between the two most prominent Protestant Christians in the German Underground. One bone of contention centred around the former Leipzig mayor Goerdeler and the older members of the German Resistance in general. Moltke and his Kreisau circle faction of the resistance considered Goerdeler's ideas would only lead to further failure post-war, while Dietrich considered Goerdeler an integral part of the resistance and Germany's future post-war.[1321]

The Kreisau Circle was more for planning Germany's future, while the faction around Oster and Dohnányi, of which Dietrich was part, kept its focus on the coup d'état itself. However, the core difference between the factions was that Dietrich and the coup plotters in general were for the assassination of Hitler, while Moltke and his circle were opposed to it.[1322] This difference had led Moltke to cease contact with Dietrich's brother-in-law Hans von Dohnányi,[1323] and it must have been a topic raised in the woods of Rügen, as the lack of unity between the different factions in the Resistance endangered all.

Dietrich, in his book *Ethics*, took the line: "Here it is apt to cite Goethe's statement that the person who acts is without conscience."[1324] This implies, as Ferdinand Schlingensiepen put it:[1325] "If you let your scruples tempt you into brooding about it, you will miss the moment that calls for action."[1326] Certainly, the Fritsch affair in 1938,[1327] with Fritsch's naïve honourable inaction, was a case in point. As Dietrich also wrote: "It is the advantage and the essence of the strong that they are able to pose the great decisive questions and take clear positions on them. The weak must always decide between alternatives that are not their own."[1328] This prompted Schlingensiepen to write: "In the face of the innumerable victims of Hitler's arbitrary state, all conscientious reservations about assassination were silenced. There was nothing more to re-examine, only the deed to be done."[1329]

However, during the 1920s, the young Moltke read the following words from a German politician: "The fate of a nation might really be decided for the better by a single murder. The historical justification for believing this could be, for instance, that a people is languishing under the tyranny of some prodigious oppressor."[1330] These words made the young Moltke, Dietrich's junior by one year, a determined adversary of Nazism, as the book was none other than Hitler's *Mein Kampf*.[1331] Thus lay the core and critical defining difference between these brave men. This debate may have taken up the greater part of their "stimulating" walk through the Baltic woods of Rügen.

Without having seen the bishop, their mission succeeded, whereupon they flew back to Berlin from Malmö in neutral Sweden by way of Copenhagen.[1332] Bishop Berggrav, seeing out the war in a remote mountain chalet under house arrest, lived on until January 14 1959, forever remembered in honour.[1333] However, Vidkun Quisling suffered a traitor's execution, just months after the end of the war in Europe, on October 24 1945.[1334] Unlike the Bishop, who was honoured with a service in Oslo Cathedral six days after his death,[1335] Quisling's name lived on as a traitor.

In the book *Memories of Kreisau and the German Resistance*[1336] by Moltke's wife Freya, she wrote that Helmuth always felt that the chances of a successful coup were slim, and that he had no trust in the people who were capable of carrying it out. Freya wrote that he considered the generals hopeless, even those who hated Hitler and his regime. Certainly, given the number of bungled and abortive coups he had witnessed, this view makes sense. Freya wrote that Helmuth believed that Hitler had to destroy himself, which he would indeed ultimately do. Helmuth did not want a repeat of the radical right-wing myth of the Dolchstosslegende, or "stab in the back" that was alleged to have been dealt by the Socialist politicians and Jews to the German military in the death throes of the Great War.[1337] As Schlingensiepen put it, the need was for the German people to confront, at last, the truth of their history.[1338]

Freya wrote about her husband's primary work, to convince occupying German armies to cease shooting hostages, even raising the subject with SS officers. While not always successful, she states, many were undoubtedly saved by his tireless efforts.[1339] She spoke too of Helmuth's two visits to Istanbul, the capital of neutral Turkey in 1943; following his return from the second visit, he was despondent after failing to convince the Allies to relinquish their demand for unconditional German surrender.[1340] On January 19 1944, he was arrested in Berlin, although not in relation to any operations related to the Kreisau circle, but rather for tipping off an acquaintance who openly spoke out against the Nazi regime about his imminent arrest.[1341]

One year later in January 1945, about six months after the Valkyrie plot, Helmuth stood before the dreaded Volksgerichtshof, being mercilessly grilled by the infamous SS judge Roland Freisler. It had become clear to Freisler that Helmuth had no part in the Valkyrie assassination plot, so in order to obtain a conviction, Freisler contended that Helmuth's meetings with Protestant and Catholic clergymen were treasonous. Helmuth, in a letter to his wife, just days before his execution later that month, wrote that as he stood before the court: "

> The trial proved all concrete accusations to be untenable, and they were dropped accordingly.... But what the Third Reich is so terrified of ... is ultimately the following: a private individual, your husband, of whom it is established that he discussed with two clergymen of both denominations [Protestant and Catholic] ... questions of the practical, ethical demands of Christianity. Nothing else; for that alone we are condemned.... I just wept a little, not because I was sad or melancholy ... but because I am thankful and moved by this proof of God's presence."[1342]

To his sons, he wrote: "

> Since National Socialism came to power, I have striven to make its consequences milder for its victims and to prepare the way for a change. In that, my conscience drove me — and in the end, that is a man's duty."[1343]

Freisler was not long in following Helmuth to his maker when he died in court during an Allied bombing raid on Berlin on February 3 1945.[1344] Helmuth's wife survived the war, passing away in Vermont on January 1 2010, aged 98, but not before founding the Freya von Moltke Foundation for the New Kreisau in 1990. A memorial to the Kreisau circle, it is located on the site of the pre-war Moltke estate, but having been located in Silesia, it's now in the Polish village of Krzyżowa in Świdnica County, less than fifty kilometres south-west of Wrocław. The Moltke estate was naturally absorbed into the Polish communist state in the aftermath of the war, but with its collapse in 1989, Freya's lifetime dream has become a reality.[1345]

In Freya's book, a curious aspect is that there is no mention whatsoever of Dietrich Bonhoeffer, and furthermore, no mention of the April 1942 mission to Oslo.[1346] This is in spite of Dietrich and Helmuth being two of the most prominent civilian members of the resistance, and as we have seen, devoted Christians, to the point of constantly risking their lives for a better future for their beloved country, and Europe in general. However, it seems the point of difference in regard to the assassination plot on Hitler was indicative of a fundamental rift in the resistance, and thus the two could never be friends. That said, when it came to cooperation in an endeavour where they were of like mind, they were able to put this aside to achieve their common objective. Bishop Berggrav would surely testify to this fact.

In regard to Helmuth belatedly agreeing to the Valkyrie assassination plot, sources do seem to differ. Certainly, at the outset, he was opposed to it. However, one book, *Traitors or Patriots?: A Story of the German Anti-Nazi Resistance* by Louis R. Eltscher,[1347] claims that in late 1943 Helmuth had begun working with the military establishment to create conditions for a coup. Schlingensiepen, however, claims in a footnote that Helmuth was always against the use of force, and backs this up with what took place in the Volksgerichtshof, where even the zealous SS judge Freisler seemed to change tack.[1348] Certainly, many members of the Kreisau Circle did become involved in the implementation of the Valkyrie plot, but in Helmuth's case, it seems he would have known of the plot, but was never directly involved.

That said, while the split in the resistance was to a great extent, at least for the first three to four years of the war, over the question of Hitler's assassination, it wasn't the only issue. When Dietrich spoke at length with Helmuth on the Baltic isle of Rügen, Helmuth raised his concerns over the former Leipzig mayor Carl Goerdeler, whom Dietrich approved of. As Louis R. Eltscher put it: "

> From beginning to end, the civilian resistance suffered a debilitating lack of unity. It remained "a motley collection of individuals who differed greatly in their social origins, habits of thought, political attitudes and methods of action." These differences created insurmountable barriers. Vital questions remained unanswered, such as: What exactly must be done to actually bring about the changes they all so fervently desired? Is assassination acceptable or not? Once it is decided what should be done, the next question was, how should it be done? What form should it take? What should replace the Nazi state?

Should there be a social democracy, a monarchy, or something in between? These two civilian resistance groups—namely, the Kreisau Cirlce and the coalition that formed under the leadership of Ludwig Beck and Carl Goerdeler—never provided adequate answers to these questions."[1349]

One may wonder why democracy was not the unanimous choice to replace the Nazi state among the resistance. However, for many, the abject failure of the Weimar democracy, perceived as synonymous with the humiliation of Versailles, was all too recent a memory. This may be indicative that Weimar did not have enough real friends to sustain it, with parties like the Communist Party (KPD), the German Nationalist People's Party (DNVP — the party of the von Kleists)[1350] and of course the Nazis (NSDAP) all running on autocratic platforms, that only stood candidates in elections to undermine the Weimar democracy. The Dolchstosslegende was used by militarists and hard-line nationalists with their unshakeable faith in authoritarianism to explain Germany's post WWI demise,[1351] but there seemed no inclination to blame the types who led Germany into this disastrous war. The "old days of empire" under Bismarck and the authoritarian monarchy were often romanticised and recalled as proud memories of the peak of German power and pride, but of course, the empire pre-1914 never had the daunting list of challenges which confronted Weimar. One of these Weimar indeed confronted and solved with remarkable resilience—hyper-inflation.[1352]

Soon after returning from Oslo, Dietrich left on his third Abwehr-authorised visit to Switzerland; he had originally planned to make it straight after Easter. He arrived in Zürich on May 12 1942, and two days later in Geneva, but was disappointed not to find the people he wished to see. In particular, Visser 't Hooft was in England, after receiving a memorandum from Adam von Trott in the German Resistance requesting that Visser 't Hooft recommend it to His Majesty's government. Thus Dietrich was only able to take action on a matter in regard to Operation 7; the visa for Charlotte Friedenthal had not yet been received. She did not make it into Switzerland until September; four weeks later, the rest of the group also successfully made their way south over the Alps.[1353]

While he was not able to see the people he wished to see in Geneva, Dietrich heard that Bishop Bell had flown to Stockholm, planning to be there for three weeks.[1354] Dietrich proposed to Dohnányi a visit to Stockholm post-haste, albeit, with discretion. Travel to German-occupied Norway was one thing; travel to neutral Switzerland could, it seems, still be veiled fairly easily as intelligence matters for the Reich. However, meeting with a member of the British House of Lords went into the realms of high treason.

It would take three days to arrange the trip to Stockholm. In the meantime, on May 25, Dietrich made his final visit to his dear friend Karl Barth. As they conversed into the afternoon, any hope the German Underground had of coming to an arrangement with the British came to seem all the more implausible. The news came over the radio waves that Molotov, the Soviet defence minister, had arrived in London to sign the Anglo—Soviet treaty; one of its key terms was the preclusion of either country from making a separate peace with Germany.[1355] For Dietrich, this news was depressing, prompting him to remark, "Well, now it's all over!" since one of the major objectives of a successful coup was to secure in its aftermath some notion of a negotiated peace with the West. Two days later on the 27th, one of the Nazi inner circle, Reinhard Heydrich, was ambushed by members of the Czech Underground in Prague, and just a few days later, in hospital, it was all over for him. This precipitated mass retaliatory executions and the obliteration of the Czech village of Lidice.[1356]

For Dietrich, there were deep personal reasons to meet again with his dear "Uncle" George, Bishop Bell, for the first time since the spring of 1939, prior to his departure for New York. For the conspirators, the opportunity to personally meet with a prominent member of the House of Lords and British Clergy who was sympathetic to their cause could not be missed,[1357] especially in the wake of Molotov's signing of the Anglo—Soviet treaty. It was only through Bell that a glimmer of hope of a negotiated peace with the West for post-coup Germany hung by a thread.[1358]

General Beck authorised the visit, instructing Dietrich to give the names of key figures to be involved in the coup, such as Beck himself, the still active Field Marshals Günther von Kluge, Fedor von Bock and Georg von Küchler, as well as civilian figures such as former Leipzig mayor Carl Goerdeler and union leaders Wilhelm Leuschner and Jakob Kaiser. Dietrich mentioned Hjalmar Schacht, the former Reich Economics minister, albeit with a note of caution, since he saw Schacht as an opportunist,[1359] although it was Kluge who would prove to be the most untrustworthy.[1360] Upon reiterating the plotters' intention to sue for a negotiated peace, Dietrich was to request the Allied powers not to attack Germany in the aftermath of the coup so as to enable the new regime to restore order and firmly establish itself.[1361]

Upon flying into Stockholm, on May 30, 1942,[1362] Dietrich found that Bell was staying in the ancient royal city of Sigtuna, which had become the centre of Sweden's church renewal movement. Before meeting Bell, he found that Hans Schönfeld, a former adversary and supporter of Heckel in the Church's Foreign Office, had preceded him. Fortunately, following the revelations of Nazi atrocities in Poland, Schönfeld changed sides;[1363] from this point, he and Dietrich gradually built a firm trust. Schönfeld had already had two conversations with Bell,[1364] raising the possibility that the putsch might be preceded by a mutiny of the SS,[1365] with the conspirators' coup to then follow. With the new Germany ready to respect human rights, Schönfeld expected that the conspirators' Germany could simply be accepted back into the world community.

Of course, both premises of Schönfeld were naive. To begin with, while Wehrmacht or regular Army officers were participating in the conspiracy, the staging of a mutiny by SS personnel indoctrinated with blind loyalty to their Verführer's agenda was unthinkable. The notion that the new Germany could just be accepted back into the international community as if WWII had never taken place was equally so. Indeed, Dietrich contradicted Schönfeld on this point in their first joint discussion with Bell; he emphasised the need for God to pass judgement on Germany and its people.[1366] Rather than Germany hoping for a seamless transition to peace, Dietrich reiterated the need for repentance and for assuming the guilt for all the atrocities committed by Hitler's regime.

In Sigtuna, the ecumenical visitors were hosted by the theologian Harry Johansson. He was present for part of the conversations taking place and had offered his services as an intermediary between the German conspirators and Great Britain. However, owing to the precarious strategic location of Sweden, with its neighbour Norway assimilated to the Nazi cause, his superiors decided that such a role for a Swede was too risky, and Johansson withdrew his offer.[1367] The need for Sweden, militarily much weaker, to present a face of strict neutrality to Nazi Germany was deemed paramount. There was already great risk for the conspirators and Sweden itself in this meeting between agents of German Military Intelligence and a member of the House of Lords in neutral Sweden, a haven for foreign spies.[1368]

Moreover, the highest ranking of Johansson's superiors was Bishop Manfred Björquist (1884-1985), head and founder of Sigtuna's Nordic Ecumenical Institute, and the first bishop of the newly formed diocese of Stockholm in November 1942. In February to March 1936, during his ten-day trip to Sweden in 1936 with his Finkenwalde ordinands, Dietrich had met Björquist, but the meeting was hardly a cordial or happy one. For one thing, Björquist was close to the Reichskirche and Heckel, and an advocate of the Volkskirche theology of the German Christians. During this visit, Dietrich and his ordinands had attended a lecture in Sigtuna by Björquist, and Albert Schonherr's newsletter report stated that Björquist saw the Volkskirche as "the perfect example and crown of a completely Christian culture."[1369]

Dietrich's arrival had come as a complete but wonderful surprise to Bell, as the last thing he heard about Dietrich was that he was in Norway fighting in the campaign there.[1370] Bell gave Dietrich welcome news about Sabine and Gert, and they caught up after three years of no contact due to the war. While it seemed that several lifetimes had passed by, they could still converse as if they had just met yesterday.[1371] As for Churchill responding favourably to their peace overtures, Bell noted that with the recent signing of the Anglo-Soviet pact, the odds had lengthened dramatically.[1372] For one thing, Churchill saw all the conspirators as types who wished Britain to allow Germany to retain all the territory it conquered. Territory in which it had committed the most barbaric acts. To a certain extent, Schönfeld did fit this perception, at least in wanting the west to go easy on Germany post-war.

Many of the conspirators, including men such as Ludwig Beck, recalling Versailles and Germany's economic morass, had initially welcomed the "revolution" of January 1933, and Hitler and his National Socialists' commitment to abolishing the German humiliation, the Treaty of Versailles. However, in August 1938, Beck had realised there had to be a limit to blind military obedience when Hitler committed himself irrevocably to the Czech adventure.[1373] Some, of course, had no illusions from the outset about Hitler. Dietrich for one, as well as Helmuth James von Moltke and the former Leipzig mayor, Carl Goerdeler.

For His Majesty's government, there was another consideration. With the Soviet Union now compelled to bear the brunt of the Nazi juggernaut,[1374] appeasement of Stalin was the order of the day. This included what would become the western Allies' whitewashing of the Stalinist perpetrated April 1940 Katyń Wood massacre, where they conveniently accepted Stalin's lie, in April 1943, that the massacre had been committed by the Germans.[1375] In London's Grand Victory Parade on Saturday June 8 1946, it was upon Stalin's petulant insistence that Polish soldiers were not allowed to march![1376] Moreover, 1.7 million eastern Poles were imprisoned in Siberian Gulags,[1377] where, even after the launch of Barbarossa in June 1941, hundreds of thousands of Poles remained incarcerated in the freezing gulag hell.[1378] Ultimately, if the western Allies were so readily inclined to appease and turn a blind eye to Stalinist perpetrated atrocities upon such a loyal ally as Poland, the First Ally[1379] and fourth largest of all members in the Allied coalition,[1380] then German conspirators were hardly going to fare any better.

Back in England, George Bell made every effort on behalf of the conspirators, but two months later, in early August, when Bell received a letter from the Foreign Minister Anthony Eden,[1381] it was clear that it was all to no avail. Almost two years later, on July 29 1944, when Britain's Special Operations Executive (SOE) gave the Polish Government in Exile all assurances that top priority would be given for support of the forthcoming Warsaw Uprising, Eden's Foreign Office countermanded the order.[1382]

Curiously, Jane Pejsa wrote of Fabian von Schlabrendorff postwar visit to Winston Churchill, where he inquired about the numerous messages relayed to Churchill via Dietrich and others by way of Switzerland and Sweden.[1383] To which Churchill replied that he never heard of any such messages. Moreover, years later, they would be found in Eden's effects, archived with his private papers, having never reached the Foreign Office, let alone Churchill himself.[1384] As Norman Davies summed it up in his award winning book *Rising '44*: "

> As viewed from Warsaw and elsewhere, the Second World War can be seen to have been a three-sided struggle, in which the centrepiece was provided by the duel of two totalitarian monsters, fascism and communism, and in which the Western democracies frequently featured as a third party of only moderate importance. Whether one likes it or not, the Soviet Union made the largest military contribution to the defeat of Nazi Germany. But it was not interested in the least in the ideals of Freedom, Justice, Self-determination, and Democracy that inspired the West. As a result, the Western powers could not fairly claim to have been the all-conquering liberators of their own legends. In reality, they were repeatedly obliged to pander to Stalin's ambitions in order to keep the Coalition intact. But that is not the whole story. For in the process of cosying up to Stalin, many Westerners assumed a strange state of self-deception, a form of near-mesmerization, where principles could be forgotten and loyal friends [such as Poland and the German conspirators] could be deserted. The smouldering ruins of Warsaw illustrated the consequences."[1385]

Chapter 18

Romance, Plots and Arrest

While Ruth was unaware of Dietrich's involvement in the conspiracy, as the war wore on, she had noticed him becoming more dour and serious. No doubt he was haunted by the realisation that any day could be his last.[1386] At Easter time that year, Dietrich and Eberhard were present at Kieckow, but Ruth was absent; the doctor insisted that with her heart condition, she must stay at the hospital in Stettin where she could be closely monitored.[1387]

In the week of early June 1942, following his visit to Stockholm, Dietrich returned to Klein-Krössin in Pomerania to continue working on his *Ethics*. As always, he had long conversations with Ruth.[1388] They were not aware that these were their last opportunities for intimate exchanges. Ruth's 18-year-old granddaughter, Maria von Wedemeyer, was also there, having just completed her university entrance exams at her boarding school in Wieblingen, near Heidelberg. The headmistress of Maria's school, Elisabeth von Thadden, was the sister of Reinhold Thadden, one of the staunchest supporters of the Confessing Church in Pomerania, and since she ardently supported her brother, she would later be executed.[1389]

Maria was not at Klein-Krössin long; she left the following morning. She and Dietrich had strolled in the garden the day before. Dietrich's earlier perception of her was of a thirteen-year-old girl too young to take on as a confirmand in August 1937, when he had agreed to teach her elder brother Max and two cousins.[1390] His feelings towards her now transformed to a fledgling romantic enchantment for a beautiful and intelligent eighteen-year-old woman.[xxii] Seven or so months later, in January 1943, albeit with much emotional trauma, squabbling and misunderstandings, they were engaged.[1391] This was in spite of his declaration, when he broke off with his then girlfriend (possibly fiancée) of nine years, Elisabeth Zinn, in 1936, that his pastoral life, now dedicated to saving the church from the Nazis, ruled out marriage.[1392]

[xxii] Maria was born on the Wedemeyer Pätzig estate on April 23, 1924. See the website of the Dietrich Bonhoeffer portal at https://www.dietrich-bonhoeffer.net/bonhoeffer-umfeld/maria-von-wedemeyer-weller/ accessed on Wednesday August 5, 2020.

In September 1942, following the death of Ruth's son-in-law, Hans von Wedemeyer, Dietrich was only able to make the briefest of visits to Kieckow to express his condolences in person to Ruth.[1393] She did not know that Dietrich's visit was not just social but was also to discuss his proposed trip to Switzerland with Hans Jürgen and Ewald. At the last minute, this was changed to his trip to Oslo with Helmuth James von Moltke to save the life of the Norwegian Bishop Eivind Josef Berggrav.[1394]

Oma Ruth was burdened by old age and ill health,[1395] and Dietrich's visit in September 1942 seemed all too brief, as Ruth said in her letter to Eberhard Bethge, to whom she was almost as close: "

My dear Eberhard….

What must you have thought when I did not write on your birthday. Probably Dietrich told you already that I am so overwhelmed these days I have forgotten dates and anniversaries. But subsequently I did remember your birthday and I asked God for his blessing on you….

In hindsight I have real regrets about Dietrich's visit here. It is as if I said too much and, even without words, made judgements on what ought or ought not to be. May God forgive me if I conducted myself badly. I hope Dietrich will not be influenced by my behaviour. With you, there is not so much at stake because you are less complicated than he.

So many questions have turned up and they all need to be answered. How happy I would be if you could resolve them for me. Even if a happy marriage is cut asunder too soon [by death], still one is rewarded for an entire lifetime. Marriage is a mystery. Not every marriage is entered into as God would have it. I am too inclined to take my own marriage as the standard.

I thank you for the dear words at the time of my son-in-law's death. It is so hard for me to realise that my daughter must tread the same road that I once travelled; I know the way too well. But she is older and much more mature than I was. Still the overwhelming sense of loss will be the same. No doubt she has a foreboding as to what this broken tie means though she is only at the beginning of it.

I talked much too much with Dietrich about this; I told him everything that weighed upon me…. May God keep you.

Faithfully, Your RvK."[1396]

Ruth's belief that her youngest child Ruthchen was much more mature than she was at the same age may have been in reference to the early years of her marriage, when she felt distraught at Jürgen's overnight absences, when he visited towns within the Belgard district in accordance with his duties as the district's Landrat.[1397]

In 1944, when Dietrich was imprisoned at Berlin's Tegel prison, having been engaged to Maria for well over a year, Dietrich told Maria in a letter about his early love affair with Elisabeth Zinn: "

> I was once in love with a girl; she became a theologian, and our paths ran parallel for many years; she was almost my age. I was 21 [in 1927] when it began. We didn't realise we loved each other. More than eight years went by. Then we discovered the truth from a third person, who thought he was helping us. We then discussed the matter frankly, but it was too late. We had evaded and misunderstood each other for too long. We could never be entirely in sympathy again, and I told her so. Two years later she married, and the weight on my mind gradually lessened. We never saw or wrote to each other again. I sensed at the time that, if I ever did get married, it could only be to a much younger girl, but I thought that impossible, both then and thereafter. Being totally committed to my work for the Church in the ensuing years, I thought it not only inevitable but right that I should forgo marriage altogether."[1398]

Dietrich opened the next paragraph with: "Do you understand my beloved Maria, that a man who has undergone such experiences is not what he was at twenty-one?"[1399] Eric Metaxas commented: "

> From this letter and from other clues we can ascertain that Bonhoeffer's relationship with Elisabeth Zinn was an important part of his life from 1927 until 1936, although he spent a year in Barcelona, nine months in New York, and eighteen months in London. [Over three years in total]. Even when living in Berlin, he was often travelling on behalf of the ecumenical movement. After his year in Barcelona, things seem to have cooled some-

what, but the relationship survived that separation. It was after his return from London in late 1935 that a well-meaning third party told them of their feelings for each other. But as he explained in his letter, it was then too late. Bonhoeffer had changed greatly over the years, and by then he had dedicated his heart and soul to the battle to save the church from the Nazis. He was running the Confessing Church's seminary at Finkenwalde. It wasn't until the beginning of 1936 that he made things clear to Elisabeth, and the chapter between them was closed. He wrote her a letter, telling her of the change in him and dramatically explaining that God had called him to devote himself completely to the work of the church: 'My calling is quite clear to me. What God will make of it I do not know … I must follow the path. Perhaps it will not be such a long one … Sometimes we wish that it were so (Philippians 1:23 — where Paul expressed his desire to "depart, and to be with Christ.") But it is a fine thing to have realised my calling … I believe that the nobility of this calling will become plain to us only in the times and events to come. If only we can hold out.'[1400]

In 1938, Dietrich's third cousin Elisabeth married the New Testament theologian Günther Bornkamm.[1401]

Now, however, in the midst of war, much of the trauma associated with Dietrich's burgeoning love affair with a much younger Maria revolved around two tragic family deaths. Maria's father Hans, aged 54, died on the night of August 21, 1942, following a Soviet shell attack near Stalingrad.[1402] This followed Hans's reassignment, at his request, from the relative safety of staff headquarters to an active unit, in protest over staff decisions regarding the treatment of enemy civilians and captured enemy soldiers.[1403] Hans had, during the Great War, served under Franz von Papen,[1404] the penultimate Reich chancellor before Hitler, and one of the leading figures deluded into thinking he could control Hitler.[1405] Hans was under no such illusion; his wife, Ruth, clearly recalled his despair.[1406] Von Papen became Hitler's vice chancellor; Hans initially remained on his staff, but after three months, he quit. One year later, during the Night of the Long Knives, Han's successor, Herr von Bose, was murdered at his desk.[1407]

In 1935, because Hans had refused to fly the swastika flag upon his estate, the regime attempted to "legally" bar him from managing his Pätzig estate. During the kangaroo court proceedings, Hans was forced to stand for three-quarters of an hour to listen to the judge's Nazi diatribe against him before the predictable verdict was reached. An appeal seemed pointless, and his friends advised him not to bother. However, with the counsel of his cousin Fabian von Schlabrendorff, who became a central figure in the plot against Hitler, and after one year of Fabian's meticulous preparation, the appeal succeeded.[1408]

Hans and his wife were leaders of the renewal Berneuchen movement, attempting to breathe life into what they saw as staid Lutheran churches, hosting annual gatherings at Pätzig. Although this movement was anti-Nazi, Dietrich was not attracted to it; he saw it as tending too much to avoid confrontation on key issues.[1409] However, because of his deep friendship with the family matriarch, he confirmed Maria's elder brother Max in August 1937,[1410] and wrote a heartfelt letter of condolence to Max's mother, Ruth von Wedemeyer.[1411] When the news arrived of Max's death at Demyansk, about 400 kilometres northwest of Moscow, on October 26, Dietrich and the von Wedemeyer family were devastated. Dietrich expected to minister the funeral service, but was shocked when he received a call from Maria's mother requesting that he not attend Max's funeral.[1412]

Back in early June, as brief as their contact was, Ruth von Kleist had noticed the chemistry between her close friend Dietrich and her granddaughter. In late September, she travelled to Berlin's St Francis Hospital accompanied by Maria, as she had long been afflicted with a serious eye disease, and now feared she was going blind.[1413] Dietrich, a native Berliner, in his first meeting with Maria since early June, played the polite and cordial host, performing his regular pastoral duties of morning devotions to the matriarch, coupled with moral support for her and Maria in this time of loss. For the time being at least, Dietrich understood the need to put any thoughts of romance aside. Moreover, when Maria's brother Max died late that month, the need to do so would have been all the more paramount, except it seems, to the much loved but not so discreet matriarch.

Ruth von Kleist had been watching them from her hospital bed for weeks, and noticing feelings beyond plain friendship, decided to share her joy with her daughter Ruth. Whereupon Maria's mother sent a letter to Dietrich requesting that he not attend the funeral. Her daughter was too young to be engaged to the pastor, and she considered any discussion of a match inappropriate, given the two recent family deaths. She felt that her daughter needed to be left in peace to grieve the recent deaths of her father and brother. Maria was unhappy that Dietrich had been barred from the funeral because of her dear but indiscreet Oma's gossip.[1414]

Fortunately, by November 24, Frau Ruth had calmed sufficiently to agree to a meeting with Dietrich at the family's Pätzig estate. Dietrich found Frau Ruth calm, friendly, and not overwrought. While not opposed to the match, she proposed a yearlong separation. Dietrich had concerns, but since Frau Ruth had been so recently widowed, he decided not to push the issue. As he put it in a letter to Eberhard Bethge three days later, "

> I think that if I wanted to, I could prevail. I can argue better than the others and could probably talk them into it. But that seems dreadful to me; it strikes me as evil, like an exploitation of the others' weakness."[1415]

At the end of the discussion, Frau Ruth asked Dietrich to explain to her mother how things stood. The feisty matriarch blew up on hearing the news, but reluctantly accepted it.[1416] On this visit, Dietrich did not see Maria, and it was not until January 10 1943 that Maria was able to get permission from her mother and guardian, uncle Hans Jürgen (eldest child of Oma Ruth), to write to Dietrich and answer "yes" to his as yet unasked question. This was on the condition that they should not announce their engagement, and put off setting a date for their wedding.[1417] Dietrich replied, for the first time addressing Maria as "Dear Maria" rather than "Miss von Wedemeyer."[1418] They would look back on January 17 1943 as the official date of their engagement. However, unbeknownst to Dietrich and other members of the conspiracy, the Gestapo were hot on their trail. They were arrested in early April, but not before two unsuccessful assassination attempts had been made on Hitler in March.

The first attempt was codenamed "Operation Spark" (or sometimes in translation, "Flash" or "Blitz"),[1419] because its intended climax was the detonation of a bomb aboard Hitler's plane as it flew west over the Belarussian city of Minsk on its way from Smolensk in western Russia to the Wolf's Lair in East Prussia. The key protagonists were General Friedrich Olbricht, General Henning von Tresckow, nephew of Oma Ruth, and his aide-de-camp and second cousin by marriage, Fabian von Schlabrendorff, who was in turn, married to Maria von Wedemeyer's first cousin Luitgarde née von Bismarck.[1420] Olbricht had been helpful in obtaining military exemptions for many Confessing Church pastors.[1421]

The plan involved Schlabrendorff planting a bomb on Hitler's plane in Smolensk, where he would be on March 13 for a brief visit to the troops on the Russian front. If it succeeded, Hitler's death, so far removed from his assassins, would have seemed like an accident, allowing time for the conspirators to overwhelm the centres of power in the Nazi apparatus before they realised what was truly afoot. Moreover, as Schlabrendorff explained years later, the semblance of an accident would avoid the political fallout of an obvious murder.[1422] During the preparation for the plot, Schlabrendorff and Tresckow had experimented with numerous bombs, but in the end settled for a silent English made plastic explosive, seized from captured British SOE agents,[1423] since the relatively noisy clockwork mechanisms and fuses of German equivalents greatly increased the likelihood of their discovery. Upon Schlabrendorff pressing a button, the vial holding a corrosive chemical would be broken, releasing it to eat away the wire holding back the spring, which once sprung, would strike the detonator cap, thus exploding the bomb and scattering Hitler's remains over Minsk and its surrounds.

But before this could happen, there was the problem of covertly transporting the explosive to Smolensk. Hans von Dohnányi was to take it by train from Berlin to Smolensk. Eberhard Bethge, who by now, like Dietrich, had been recruited by Dohnányi to work for the Abwehr so that he too would avoid military service, drove Dohnányi in Karl Bonhoeffoer's car to Berlin's station, unaware of the explosive Dohnányi was carrying in his case, as was Doctor Karl.[1424] For Bethge, the avoidance of military service was opportune for another reason — his imminent marriage to Dohnányi's young niece Renate Schleicher.

On March 13 1943 in Smolensk, Tresckow and Schlabrendorff, now in possession of the bomb, were so close to Hitler on two occasions that they were tempted to explode the bomb prematurely, even though that would mean their certain death. But they decided to adhere to the original plan of placing the bomb in Hitler's plane because the generals meant to lead the coup were also present.[1425] Of course, this now left the problem of getting the bomb onto the plane. In the meantime, they lunched with the Führer. Schlabrendorff recalled, years later, the revolting spectacle of Hitler at the officer's mess dining table: "

> Watching Hitler eat was a most revolting spectacle. His left hand was placed firmly on his thigh; with his right hand he shovelled his food, which consisted of various vegetables, into his mouth. He did this without lifting his right arm, which he kept flat on the table throughout the entire meal; instead, he brought his mouth down to the food."[1426]

As horrified aristocratic generals engaged in polite chatter, trying to ignore the Führer's culinary habits, General Tresckow casually asked a favour of his table mate and member of Hitler's entourage, Lieutenant Colonel Heinz Brandt. It involved Brandt taking a gift of brandy to Rastenburg to give to Tresckow's old friend, General Stieff, with the implication that the brandy was payment for a gentleman's wager. Brandt agreed, and within an hour or two, as Brandt, Hitler and the rest of the entourage headed for the airfield, Schlabrendorff handed Colonel Brandt the "brandy," but not before he pressed the button to release the corrosive liquid that would gradually eat away the wire holding back the spring, and trigger the detonator thirty or so minutes later. With the deadly package placed in the cargo hold, the plane took off, accompanied by its squadron of fighter aircraft, which (it was planned) would break the news of the Führer's death.[1427]

Hitler was forever aware of the possibility of assassination, and meticulously planned his movements and activities accordingly; for instance, a chef that travelled with him prepared all his meals. Each dish prepared by his chef was taste-tested by his personal physician Dr. Theodor Morrell,[xxiii] while he watched on. The hat he wore was incredibly heavy, as it was lined with three pounds of steel, which Schlabrendorff could attest to when he wore it on the sly while Hitler and the generals were meeting at Kluge's quarters.[1428] As for Hitler's plane, as Schlabrendorff recalled, it was divided into several compartments, with Hitler's personal cabin armour-plated, holding a contraption for descent by parachute. In spite of this, Schlabrendorff and his cousin and superior, General Henning von Tresckow, were confident the bomb would destroy the entire aircraft including Hitler's cabin.[1429]

Less than thirty minutes should have passed after take-off before the fighter aircraft transmitted the message of the Führer's demise. But after two hours, they heard nothing until the news of the flight's safe arrival in East Prussia! The conspirators were now terrified that the bomb would be discovered. However, General Tresckow, with remarkable composure, phoned Hitler's headquarters, asking to speak with Brandt. When Brandt came on the line, Tresckow asked whether the "brandy" had been delivered to Stieff, to which Brandt answered in the negative. Tresckow then said that he had given Brandt the wrong package, and asked if Schlabrendorff could stop by the following day to exchange it for the "correct" one.[1430] Conveniently, it turned out that Schlabrendorff was headed for East Prussia on official business. So

---

xxiii This will not be the last mention of this "doctor" that mesmerised Hitler.

with great courage, he took the train to Rastenburg (now Kętrzyn in modern-day Poland)[1431] to pay the dreaded visit to the Wolfsschanze (Wolf's Lair). No one had realised he was there to retrieve an unexploded bomb, and all seemed well until a grinning Brandt, juggling the package back and forth,[1432] handed him the bomb. In the end, there was no "ka-boom," but a cordial exchange of packages, with Brandt receiving the brandy, and Schlabrendorff, with heart pounding, the defective bomb.

On the train to Berlin, Schlabrendorff locked the door of his sleeper car and opened the package to analyse what had gone wrong. It seemed everything had worked perfectly, with the vial being broken to release the corrosive liquid to dissolve the wire and release the spring, which ultimately struck the detonator cap. But the detonator cap, for whatever reason, had not ignited the explosive. Hitler thus survived this assassination attempt, while none of the conspirators were arrested, nor was the plot discovered.[1433]

On the morning of March 15, Schlabrendorff showed Dohnányi and Oster the dud bomb. However, there was hardly time for regret; six days later on Sunday March 21 in Berlin, a golden and rare opportunity presented itself. Hitler was to be in Berlin, accompanied in a rare public gathering by Himmler and Göring. The opportunity to send the most powerful figures of the Third Reich into the next world was too good to pass up. The infamous trio were scheduled to attend ceremonies for Heldengedenktag (Heroes' Memorial Day) at the Zeughaus on Unter den Linden, followed by the viewing of captured Soviet weaponry.[1434]

Naturally there were difficulties to overcome. The most glaring was that it would have to be a suicide mission. Nevertheless, the Silesian noble, Major Rudolf-Christoph von Gersdorff on Kluge's staff, bravely volunteered. He would meet Hitler and his entourage after the ceremony and lead them through the exhibit of captured weaponry. In his overcoat, von Gersdorff would carry two bombs of the same type that had failed to detonate in Hitler's plane, but with shorter fuses. Initially, they considered rigging them with much faster fuses, but since Hitler was supposed to be there for thirty minutes or so, they settled for ones that would take up to ten minutes to break the vials; in another ten minutes the wire would be dissolved, to finally release the spring and instantly detonate the bombs. In these twenty minutes Gersdorff would calmly describe the displayed weaponry to the Führer and his entourage.[1435] The Saturday night before, Gersdorff met Schlabrendorff in his room in the Eden Hotel to collect the bombs. Everything was prepared. What could go wrong?

The following day of Sunday March 21 1943, most of the Bon-hoeffer clan was assembled at the Schleicher home at 41 Marien-burgerallee. Karl Bonhoeffer's 75th birthday was ten days hence, thus the need for the rehearsal of their musical performance of Walcha's can-tata "Lobe den Herrn" ("Praise the Lord") to honour Doctor Karl's birthday. Dietrich played piano, Rüdiger Schleicher the violin, and Hans von Dohnányi sang in the choir.[1436] In a remarkable act of Ger-manic self-discipline, they kept their focus on the music in spite of the three conspirators and Hans von Dohnányi's wife Christine being aware of what was unravelling ten kilometres away in the Zeughaus. At any moment it would happen or had already happened...or...perhaps not!

When the phone call to herald a new future where they could harness their great energies and talents for a Germany they could all once again be proud of didn't arrive on time, they continued to rehearse with Germanic diligence. Unbeknownst to them, the ceremony at the Zeughaus had been delayed by an hour, thus prolonging Gersdorff's wait and concealment of the bombs in his military overcoat. Finally, Hitler arrived, giving the requisite, albeit brief and benign speech, be-fore proceeding to the exhibition with his entourage of Göring, Himm-ler, General Keitel, and the head of the navy, Admiral Karl Dönitz.[1437] The latter became the one to briefly succeed Hitler upon his suicide in late April 1945.[1438] Thus was set the golden opportunity to eliminate Hitler and four of his foremost vassals.

When Hitler approached him, Gersdorff reached inside his coat and pressed the buttons, breaking the vials to release the acid which in turn gradually corroded the wires. He feigned diligence in describing the captured Soviet weaponry to the Führer as they proceeded.[1439] However, the brevity of Hitler's speech, while benign to the plan, was mirrored in his unexpectedly brief viewing of the weaponry. It seemed he did not have a great interest in the weaponry of the Slavic *Unter-mensch*, and suddenly decided to end his visit, promptly exiting a side door onto Unter den Linden. What was to have taken half an hour or so had taken just a few minutes. Gersdorff was still wearing the overcoat laden with explosives and about to go off, with no "shut off" switch. The acid was dissolving the wire further with every second. As soon as Hitler was gone, Gersdorff rushed into a toilet and ripped the fuses from the two bombs.[1440] Instead of dying that afternoon as planned, this brave man lived on until 1980,[1441] and just the following month, made the initial report to Berlin of the discovery of the graves of the April 1940, Stalinist-perpetrated Katyń Wood massacre.[1442] Not only had Hitler escaped another assassination attempt, the conspirators escaped discovery.

Back at the Marienburgerallee, they finally received the long-awaited phone call.[1443] But while all the conspirators had escaped any implication in the plot, the Gestapo were closing in. But not before Karl Bonhoeffer's 75th birthday was grandly celebrated on the last day of March 1943.[1444] Five days later, the Gestapo paid a visit to the Marienburgerallee.[1445] The birthday celebration was the last one for the Bonhoeffer family, and a crowning moment for this most extraordinary of families for whom such performances had been a long and cherished tradition over the decades. Upon the Gestapo's visit, their lives would change forever, and they would never gather like this again.[1446]

But for now, they sang "Praise the Lord" with the whole family present, except for the Leibholzes, who were exiled in England. Thanks to a congratulatory telegram relayed by Erwin Sutz in Switzerland,[1447] they made their spirits felt. Among others present were their former governess Maria Czeppan, and Eberhard Bethge, who would officially become a member of the family in a month's time. To cap off the grand gathering, for his lifetime of service to Germany, Karl Bonhoeffer was awarded the nation's coveted Goethe medal by an official from the Reich's Ministry of Culture. It was adorned with the special certificate:
"

In the name of the German people I bestow on Professor Emeritus Bonhoeffer the Goethe medal for art and science, instituted by the late Reichspräsident Hindenburg. The Führer, Adolf Hitler."[1448]

Five days later on the morning of Monday April 5, 1943, the arrests commenced with the arrival of Colonel Manfred Roeder at Canaris's office. He was the investigating judge in the Reichskriegsgericht[1449] (War Court), and was accompanied by Criminal Commissioner Franz-Xaver Sonderegger. Roeder informed Canaris that he came to arrest Dohnányi; Canaris showed him the way.[1450] Dohnányi's office could only be accessed through Oster's office, which led to Oster demanding Roeder arrest him as well, as Dohnányi had not done anything without his knowledge. While Dohnányi had already partly cleared his office of sensitive material just days earlier, including a substantial sum of money belonging to the Confessing Church, it was a terrible shock to him when Roeder, Sonderegger, Oster and Canaris appeared in his office unannounced.

Among the folders found by Roeder and placed by him on Dohnányi's desk was a grey one containing, among other items, the application for authorisation by Canaris of Josef Müller's and Dietrich's trip to Rome, planned for four days later.[1451] Its true purpose, to inform the Vatican that the assassination plots had failed, was documented in a vague cover story of supposedly influencing the Pope's worldwide Christmas message. Dohnányi, anxious not to let it fall into Roeder's hands, tried to slip it from the pile, which Roeder could not fail to notice.[1452]

This seemingly innocuous *Zettel* (brief note) had its genesis on the day of the assassination attempt by Tresckow and Schlabrendorff, just over three weeks earlier on the March 13 1943 at the airport in Smolensk. It was then that a new order arrived from the Munich recruiting station for Dietrich to report for military service. This had been precipitated by the early February 1943 military disaster in Stalingrad, leading to all German state offices being scrutinised for physically fit men who had been exempted due to their jobs being designated as indispensable.[1453] Dietrich, having been granted the classification of "*un-abkömmlich — UK*" — indispensable in January 1942,[1454] was naturally in the recruiting office's sights, and ordered to report to the Seidlstrasse recruitment station in Munich with all his papers on the 22nd of March.

With the utmost urgency, this prompted Oster, in cooperation with Dohnányi, in the week between the assassination attempts of March 1943, to have Dietrich released from his obligation to report in Munich. This was to be by arranging a visit for Dietrich to the Balkans, Italy and Switzerland during the first half of April 1943.[1455] What the conspirators did not know, however, was that the SS had finally prevailed over the military and gained the consent of Keitel, chief of OKW (Army High Command), for an investigation into the Schmidhuber case.[1456]

Now, just two to three weeks later, on April 5, 1943, this Zettel would be a disastrous factor in Dohnányi's arrest.[1457] Oster, who earlier heard Dohnányi whisper something to him about a Zettel, interpreted that it was a life or death matter to take a "note" from the folder pile. Sonderegger noticed and promptly informed Roeder. This risk, which led to Oster's house arrest,[1458] turned out to be utterly pointless, as Dohnányi was only asking Oster to send his wife a Zettel. This came to be known post-war as the Zettel Affair, and without Roeder and Sonderegger knowing it, it paralysed the centre of the German Resistance.[1459] Eleven days later, Oster was officially dismissed as chief of staff for Military Intelligence and transferred to the officer reserves.[1460]

Dohnányi's fate was more severe. He was taken to the military officers' prison next to the Lehrter Railway Station,[1461] under top secret arrangements which included him being confined under a false name. Likewise, the proceedings against him were classified. With the seized Zettel, Roeder was confident he had proof of Dohnányi's high treason.[1462] Moreover, when Oster stated during an interrogation that he had never seen these notes, and had never signed the one he had tried to take, despite it having the initial "O" on the back, Roeder was smelling blood.

The arrests that day were not confined to Dohnányi and Oster. Later that day at noon, Dietrich attempted to phone his sister Christine from his parent's home, when he heard a strange voice answer. He correctly surmised that her house was being searched. Without telling his parents anything, he went next door, where his sister Ursula prepared his final hearty home cooked *Mittagessen* (lunch).[1463] Then he went back next door to his study in the attic to get all his documents in order, including leaving some of the more innocuous ones lying around for the "benefit" of the Gestapo when they commenced their search.[1464] Once he completed this task to his satisfaction, he waited with Ursula, Rüdiger Schleicher and Eberhard Bethge.[1465] A few hours later, at around four o'clock, his father came over to inform Dietrich they had arrived; two men up in his room wished to "speak" to him. They were Roeder and Sonderegger, who had already arrested Christine and her husband von Dohnányi and Oster in the morning.[1466]

Naturally, their conversation with Dietrich was brief, as arrest and interrogation in prison was their agenda. With bible in hand, never to return, they escorted Dietrich to their black Mercedes.[1467] The same day, in Munich, Josef and Anni Müller were also arrested, leaving the backbone of the German resistance in tatters.[1468] Like Dohnányi, Josef Müller was sent to the Wehrmacht prison, next to the Lehrter Railway Station, while his wife and Dietrich's sister Christine were sent to the women's prison in Charlottenburg. Dietrich alone was taken to the Tegel Military prison. All were inside the Berlin metro area.[1469]

Maria von Wedemeyer, meanwhile, was training as a nurse with the Red Cross in Hanover. Soon after that day she sealed the diary she had been keeping, and it was not opened again until after her death from cancer in November 1977, when her correspondence with Dietrich, the *Love Letters from Cell 92*, was being prepared for publication. As if sensing something ominous, she had on that terrible day written as her final diary entry; "Has something bad happened? I'm afraid it must be something very bad."[1470] On April 18 she had to leave Hanover to attend the confirmation of her brother Hans-Werner in Pätzig. While out for a walk with her brother-in-law Klaus von Bismarck, she told him that despite the promise to her mother, she was determined to see Dietrich.[1471]

When they returned to the house, Maria's uncle and the eldest son of Oma Ruth, Hans-Jürgen von Kleist, informed them of the terrible news, which Maria had felt in her bones, that Dietrich had been arrested.[1472] Maria insisted that her engagement to Dietrich now be made public. Her mother agreed. It was too late for her to see Dietrich again, at least for the next couple of months as it turned out; at the time, it seemed like she might never see him again. Her regret over not defying her mother's wishes earlier was palpable. Her mother came to regret her actions in this regard, and Maria went to great pains to forgive her.[1473]

The remaining conspirators were all too aware that their fate hung on how the prisoners would stand up to the ordeal of interrogation. With the impressive legal skills of Hans von Dohnányi and Josef Müller, they felt relatively confident, and they foresaw that their wives could plausibly assert that they themselves had known nothing. However, they regarded Dietrich as the weak link.[1474] In fact, in his meeting with George Bell in Stockholm on Beck's approval, Dietrich had given the names of all the Resistance leaders to the English bishop.[1475] They feared for how Dietrich would fare when grilled by a ruthless and cunning interrogator like Roeder, who was certainly not averse to the use of torture. However, their fears would prove to be unfounded when Dietrich invoked his subtle resilience and prodigious intellect to outwit his tormentor.

Chapter 19

The Tormentor Tormented

For the time being, military Judge General Roeder and the Gestapo were ignorant of all assassination and coup attempts by the conspirators against Hitler. It was the so-called Schmidhuber affair[1476] that had put the Gestapo on their trail back in October 1942; this was an unfortunate side effect of the successful Operation 7, when a customs officer in Prague discovered a currency irregularity that led to Wilhelm Schmidhuber,[1477] a member of the Abwehr who visited Dietrich at the Ettal monastery in December 1940.[1478] Wasting no time in finding Schmidhuber, the Gestapo interrogated him about the smuggling of foreign currency abroad. In a typical case of Nazi double standards, this was commonplace among party members, but was a grave crime otherwise during wartime, even if done under the authorisation of the Abwehr.[1479] Schmidhuber, it seems, like the vast majority of people, did not possess the resilience of those arrested in April 1943. Before long, Josef Müller was implicated, and when Schmidhuber was transferred to the infamous Gestapo prison on Prinz-Albrecht-Strasse in Berlin, he gave up with information implicating Dohnányi, Oster, and Dietrich.[1480]

The baby-faced Manfred Roeder, a Luftwaffe officer and regular visitor to Göring's country palace of Karinhall,[1481] was known to be clever and brutal, and it was with him that the prisoners would have to fight their case. Already he had achieved major notoriety as the chief prosecutor of the Rote Kapelle (Red Orchestra), a resistance group that had contacted the Soviet Union in the hope of their assistance in overthrowing Hitler; it was only by mentioning Roeder's name that Göring had been able to get Hitler's consent to holding their trial in the War Court instead of the People's Court. For the SS, it was only a peripheral issue to be rid of these men as "enemies of the State," and ultimately to assimilate Canaris's office into the SS. To this end, Roeder, who already had ties to several high-ranking SS officers, was assigned a room at the SS Headquarters. Moreover, Sonderegger, who had investigated the Schmidhuber case in Munich, had been assigned to work for him.[1482]

Baby-faced Roeder may have been, but in reality, he rivalled the chief judge of the People's court, Roland Freisler, for callous, cynical and unscrupulous brutality. Post-war, he was still proud of securing 45 death sentences in the trial of the Rote Kapelle; these included Liane

Berkowitz being decapitated just a few days following the birth of her first child. He even had pregnant women put to death, prompting Adolf Grimme, the ex-Prussian Minister of Culture and the future director of Northwest German Radio, to state that Roeder was "one of the most inhuman, cynical and brutal Nazis"[1483] he had ever encountered.

Since the Rote Kapelle had maintained contacts with the Soviet Union, it was not until the end of the Cold War that it was recognised as a Resistance group.[1484] With the obvious exception of the fascist far right, its members actually encompassed a wide political spectrum. Eva-Maria Buch (January 31 1921 - August 5 1943) for example, who grew up in a devout Catholic family in Berlin, remained so until she was murdered in Berlin's Plötzensee prison.[1485] In her book *Resisting Hitler: Mildred Harnack and the Red Orchestra*, Shareen Blair Brysac stated that during the Cold War, the American-born and raised Mildred Harnack nee Fish, the only American woman to be tried and executed in Nazi Germany, and her German husband Arvid, were viewed by West Germany as little more than Soviet spies, whereas in East Germany, they were hailed as the heroic epitome of a future worldwide Marxist state. However, with the termination of the Cold War and the declassification of former Eastern-bloc intelligence documents, this narrative documents the still heroic but much more complicated truth.[1486]

Moreover, the Harnacks had close links to the Bonhoeffers. For example, when writing about her meeting with Falk Harnack, the brother of Arvid, Shareen Blair Brysac recalls Falk stating: "

There were these big scholarly families, four families—the Bonhoeffers, Dohnányis, Delbrücks[1487] and Harnacks—all intermarried. We're all cousins. And the pride of these scholarly families is that they fought against Hitler, that they fought Nazi Germany. Arvid and Mildred, Hans von Dohnányi, Justus Delbrück, Ernst von Harnack, Klaus Bonhoeffer … the pastor [Dietrich Bonhoeffer]. All have been executed. All of our elite. This is more important than anything else I can say. They all stood for a moral principle. They all had very good positions. They felt responsible for the moral principle and they fought to the last minute until they were executed by the Nazi criminals. And I am one of the few survivors—and Hitler wanted to murder me too. I am proud of these moral principles that the family stood for."[1488]

In regard to Mildred, Falk Harnack stated: "

It is important for the Americans to recognize that she was the only American woman executed by the Nazis in Germany. She was a fighter, for the Americans, for the Allies! Mildred fought for the Allied front. America owes her the highest honors and should not forget her."[1489]

The Rote Kapelle was not the name by which its activists identified themselves. Rather, it was a term created within German Counter-Intelligence circles; the Abwehr typically designated radio networks as kapelle, translated variously as chapels, bands or orchestras, while rote translated most literally as red, meaning, in the intelligence context, Communist. Hence the Abwehr designation of Rote Kapelle, which was readily adopted by the Gestapo. Extending this nomenclature further, the organisers of the orchestras were dubbed conductors, the short wave transmitters as pianos, and the operators as pianists.[1490] During 1941, about five hundred radiograms from secret transmitters were picked up in the West by the Funkabwehr (The Abwehr's radio counter-intelligence arm) and the Orpo (Ordungspolizei — Order Police — the uniformed police force in Nazi Germany between 1936 and 1945).[1491]

However, picking up radio transmissions was one thing; locating the transmitter and decoding the signal was another matter entirely. While the Abwehr and Gestapo became aware of the Red Orchestra just after Hitler launched Barbarossa in June 1941,[1492] it was only after a year of painstaking detective work, lucky breaks and betrayal, in concert with the requisite application of "intensified interrogation," that German counter-intelligence finally cracked open the Red Orchestra. Thus, beginning in June 1942 with the arrest of the pianist Johann Wenzel,[1493] there followed in quick succession the arrest of the 33-year-old Luftwaffe officer, Lieutenant Harro Schulze-Boysen, on August 30 1942,[1494] and eight days later, Mildred Harnack and her husband while on their summer vacation in East Prussia.[1495]

By December 19 that year, the first dozen death sentences were announced.[1496] Three days later, at Berlin's Plötzensee Prison, the executions were carried out at the rate of one every three minutes.[1497] Initially, Mildred and Countess Erika Brockdorff, much to the chagrin of Hitler, escaped death sentences. Hitler ordered their retrial by another panel of judges in Roeder's War Court, inevitably leading to Mildred's execution on February 16 1943,[1498] seven weeks before Dietrich's arrest, and a fortnight following the surrender of 91,000 frozen and starving men of the German Sixth Army in Stalingrad.[1499]

Given these events, a comparison of the Red Orchestra with the resistance group within the Abwehr suggests that women were far more prominent in the former than in the latter; indeed, this was the case. For example, among the 108 individuals pictured in the Gestapo file, 90 of the Orchestra were listed as "active members," among which 54 were men and 36 were women. While the leaders Arvid Harnack and Schulze-Boysen were males making the strategic decisions, the women were recruiters, gatherers of information, and translators of texts, arranging and holding illicit meetings, often running the greater risks when acting as couriers and transporting radios and duplicating machines.[1500] Thus, given the sadistic nature of Roeder, it was inevitable that pregnant women would be among his victims.

Another question that arises, given the Abwehr's prominent role in concert with the Gestapo in breaking the Red Orchestra spy ring, is: "were Dohnányi, Oster and Canaris involved in such an operation?" It is relevant that aside from the arrests of Dohnányi and Oster, and their complicity in the assassination attempts on the Führer, there were bitter rivalries within the Abwehr itself. Put another way, the Abwehr were by no means an entirely united front in regard to removing Hitler from power. Firstly, within the Abwehr were fanatical party members, many of whom didn't trust Oster, much less Dohnányi. Moreover, zealous party members perceived that they had a politically questionable Confessing Church pastor working for them. Secondly, many of these Nazi zealots hated Dohnányi as an outsider who had been brought in over their heads,[1501] rather than rising through the ranks. Hence their motivation in attempting to leak documents pertaining to Operation 7 to SS Headquarters.[1502] In view of all this, it seems likely that it would have been party zealots within the Abwehr who collaborated with the Gestapo in cracking the Red Orchestra.

According to V. E. Tarrant, author of *The Red Orchestra: The Soviet Spy Network Inside Nazi Europe*, the arrests and cracking apart of the Red Orchestra came too late for the Nazi regime;[1503] "too late" in the context of perhaps the most critical battle of World War II, for Stalingrad. This city, now the modern-day industrial city of Volgograd[1504] on the River Volga about 460 kilometres north-west of that river's delta that drains into the great inland Caspian Sea,[1505] became, in the summer of 1942, Hitler's obsession.

Initially, Stalin had expected Hitler's 1942 main summer offensive to target Moscow, as had been the case back in December 1941. The first indication that this was not the case came on the morning of June 19, when the operations officer of the 23rd Panzer Division, Major

Reichel, was shot down in a two-seat Fieseler Storch reconnaissance aircraft behind the Russian Front at Nezhegol, located on the banks of the River Oskol east of Kharkov. In violation of Hitler's personal instructions, Reichel was carrying in his briefcase the operational orders of the 40th Panzer Corps, which was part of the northern thrust, and more critically, the outlines of the first phase of Hitler's planned operation Case Blue — Fall Blau. Both Reichel and his pilot were killed, but Soviet infantrymen who came upon the wreck retrieved Reichel's briefcase with its 1:100,000 scale map and documents.[1506]

These documents clearly indicated that for the summer of 1942, Hitler's target was not Moscow, but Stalingrad and the capture of the badly needed and prized oilfields further south in the Caucasus. Yet Stalin angrily dismissed it as a decoy to draw Soviet reserves from the Central front, where he expected the main German thrust. However, the pianists were able to relay information which established the authenticity of the contents of Reichel's briefcase by providing the full details of Case Blue, which had been obtained from sources in the German High Command. This intelligence, which included all ten pages of Hitler's Directive No 41 issued on April 5 1942 and set out the strategic intentions of the summer offensive, was transmitted to Moscow by a pianist in the GRU (Glavno Razvedyvatelno Upravlenie or Soviet Military Intelligence) apparat operating in Switzerland, known as Die Rote Drei (The Red Three), better known in the West as the Lucy Ring after its base in Lucerne.[1507]

The arrests of the Red Orchestra leaders, namely Harro Schulze-Boysen on August 30 1942,[1508] and eight days later, Arvid Harnack and his wife,[1509] were two or so months after the launch of Case Blue on June 28 1942.[1510] This gives plausible time for its true objective to be transmitted to Moscow. However, what seems to be in dispute amongst various authors is whether Stalin at any stage acted upon this intelligence. Shareen Blair Brysac thinks not, downplaying the perception that the Red Orchestra may have had a role in the outcome of the Battle of Stalingrad.[1511] Tarrant, however is unequivocal in his opinion that the Red Orchestra were critical in the defeat of the Axis forces at Stalingrad.[1512] He contends that Stalin eventually came around to acting upon such intelligence, acknowledging that Stalingrad was Hitler's primary strategic and ideological objective. By early September, British Intelligence were aware of this; Tarrant contends that the Allied Chiefs of Staff were informed by the Soviet High Command.[1513] If Tarrant is correct, then the arrests and sadism of Manfred Roeder, of which he was so proud of even post-war, were too late in the historical context.

In her footnotes, Brysac concedes that this question needs further close analysis.[1514]

With the prosecution of other members of the Red Orchestra continuing, Dohnányi and Dietrich realised they faced a long and dire struggle. Fortunately, long beforehand, they had prepared a contingency plan; one crucial aspect of this was that when Dietrich was interrogated and the subject was on dangerous ground, he would simply say that it was Dohnányi's responsibility. The idea was that Dohnányi, with his brilliant legal mind, was better armed with the skills to deflect such questions. Indeed, Roeder saw Dohnányi as his real opponent, and saw Dietrich as a "meek and mild" clergyman who was no credible or worthwhile match.[1515] As Bethge alluded to, Dietrich cleverly exploited his tormentor's misguided perception that he was naive and unworldly: "

> Bethge: Formally Bonhoeffer appeared to be far more coopera-tive than he actually was. He portrayed himself as a pastor un-familiar with military and Abwehr matters.[1516]

> Dietrich, in a letter to Roeder: I am the last person to deny that I might have made mistakes in work so strange, so new and so complicated as that of the Abwehr. I often find it hard to follow the speed of your questions, probably because [as a naive and unworldly simple pastor] I am not used to them."[1517]

Contrast this to a letter Dietrich wrote to Eberhard on November 27, 1942, in regard to his meeting with Ruth von Wedemeyer three days earlier concerning his turbulent engagement to Maria: "

> I think that if I wanted to, I could prevail. *I can argue better than the others and could probably talk them into it.* But that seems dreadful to me; it strikes me as evil, like an exploitation of the others' weakness."[1518]

In this way, Roeder played into the hands of both prisoners. When writ-ing letters to family, both prisoners knew how to write in a way that would be literally interpreted by Roeder's censoring eyes but read be-tween the lines by family. A perfect case in point was when, on April 23, Good Friday, Dohnányi forfeited his right to write a letter to his imme-diate family and penned the following letter to Dietrich:

"My dear Dietrich, I don't know if I'll be allowed to send you this greeting, but I'll try. The bells are ringing outside for the service … You can't imagine how unhappy I am to be the reason why you, Christel, the children, and my parents should have to suffer like this, and that my dear wife and you should have your freedom taken away. *Socios habuisse malorum* (Latin for "Misery loves company") may be a comfort, but the *habere* (Latin for "company") is a terribly heavy burden … If I knew that you all — and you personally — did not think hardly of me, I'd feel so relieved. What wouldn't I give to know that you were all free again; what wouldn't I take on myself if you could be spared this affliction."[1519]

A letter as much for Dietrich as it was for Roeder's censoring eyes, fostering the latter's erroneous notion that Dietrich was a naive and unworldly pastor.

On April 30, Christine von Dohnányi, feeling wretched and ill, was released from the female prison.[1520] Being her husband's closest confidante, she had an intimate knowledge of his affairs and could summon help most promptly when required. Upon her release, she realised that the most pressing and immediate matter was the accursed "Zettel" affair.[1521] In particular, how Oster should handle the questions being asked of him. Since protocols had already been established for secret communications in such circumstances, it wasn't long before Oster was informed by Hans von Dohnányi why it was imperative that he admit to the content of the notes about Dietrich's intended trip to Rome on April 9.[1522] This meant he had to retract his original statement and now acknowledge the Zettel with the "O" on the back was bearing his initial. On the face of it, such a move might appear suicidal, but with the legal brilliance of Dohnányi and the influence of Canaris, they were able to make Roeder accept the story that the Zettel was a routine encoded Military Intelligence document.[1523]

While Dietrich wasn't treated quite as brutally as Dohnányi was by Roeder, since Dietrich had no legal experience, the interrogations would still have been an ordeal for him. Roeder treated Dietrich like a common criminal. This attitude was self-defeating for the interrogator,[1524] as Roeder never gained any insight into the true nature and resilience of the pastor, whose devout faith no doubt sustained him. Dietrich confounded every attempt by his tormentor to catch him out out in serious contradictions, thanks in part to his observance of Dohnányi's warning to plead ignorance and assign all responsibility to him.

Perhaps Dietrich, from the weaker and more vulnerable position, tormented his cunning but less intelligent tormentor. Eventually, Dietrich was permitted visits from his parents; their concealed messages revealed Roeder's strategy to him, and enabled the dovetailing of his accounts with Dohnányi's line of defence. Critical in this regard was Christine von Dohnányi, who would ascertain from her husband how Dietrich should conduct himself, and transmit the answer to him without arousing suspicion. The method was ingenious in its simplicity; she used books that were allowed to be sent to him, with his name on the flyleaf.[1525]

If his name was underlined, this meant that the book contained a cleverly encoded and hidden message for him to decode. Starting from the back of the book, every tenth page would contain a single letter marked very lightly with a pencil, and when one noted the so marked letters in that order, a coherent message would be formed, such as *"Oster erkennt jetzt Zettel an"* ("Oster now acknowledges Zettel.").[1526] Likewise, Dietrich could return books in which he concealed replies or questions. Would Roeder have been so proud post-war if he'd known this was occurring under his very nose?

Dietrich recalled his first night in Tegel prison when he was locked in a holding cell. The blankets on the cot had such a wretched stench[1527] that in spite of the cold, he found it impossible to cover himself with them. The following morning, he had a piece of bread thrown into his cell, and soon afterwards he heard the curses inflicted on people detained for interrogation by the prison staff, lasting from morning until night. In all, there were at the time 800 prisoners awaiting trial in Tegel; about twenty a week were being condemned to death, mostly on convictions of "undermining Germany's defences," which amounted to no more than speaking against the regime.[1528] New prisoners would promptly arrive to take their place, with those condemned to death confined on the top floor where Dietrich was initially assigned.[1529]

During the day, the prison was permeated with the noise of cursing guards and the pain and terror of prisoners; at night Dietrich could hear the occasional weeping of prisoners facing death, and could tell when they would be led away for execution. Dietrich was overwhelmed by "prison shock" and at the most vulnerable point in his life, with Roeder hovering like the proverbial vulture. Ever mindful of not betraying his family, friends and fellow conspirators, he was possessed by thoughts of suicide;[1530] at first, he doubted his ability to withstand the gruelling and constant interrogation he would have to face from Roeder.[1531]

During this early phase of his prison life, Dietrich drew great strength from his experience with the monastic life both at Protestant Finkenwalde and Catholic Ettal.[1532] By the third day, his Bible was returned to him, so he could go back to reading it regularly as he had done in the monasteries. He found further solace in saying aloud the hymns of the great German poet Paul Gerhardt, which he already knew by heart.[1533] This was his spiritual means of overcoming prison shock. He also realised the importance of less spiritual practices, such as observing carefully what went on around him and how this affected his mindset. He devised a daily schedule, including physical exercises, which he maintained with an iron will.[1534] By preparing himself in spirit and body, he gradually perceived equality with his tormentors, and indeed, surpassed this. Perhaps when Dietrich was going through this vulnerable early stage, Roeder's insistence on treating Dietrich like a common criminal had a fair chance of succeeding.[1535] However, as time passed, this approach became self-defeating, and it seems Roeder hadn't the ability to adapt to a more subtle approach. Perhaps, given the fact that Roeder post-war was proud of executing pregnant women close to giving birth,[1536] one should not be overly surprised.

Further solace lay in the books Dietrich received and returned, as they were, for him, not solely carriers for important coded messages, but literature to be read voraciously, allowing him to escape mentally from Tegel into a better world. In the first months of his imprisonment he read more novels, stories, and plays than at any other time in his life.[1537] He was allowed to borrow a few books, even as early as April, from the prison library. In letters which were read by Roeder, and in conversations with visitors monitored by prison officials, the exchange of opinion on literature became a non-incriminating and stimulating respite from the grim reality of Tegel Prison.[1538]

Family connections were also able to make prison conditions more bearable for Dietrich. It turned out that General Paul von Hase, the city commander of Berlin who was to be a key figure in the Valkyrie plot, was a cousin of Dietrich's mother; she asked him to ring up the prison and ask how his nephew was getting along.[1539] Since the prison was under Hase's command, this phone call turned Dietrich into a celebrity overnight.[1540] The prison commander extended his visitation rights as far as they would go, and all packages delivered by his family were received by him, greatly improving his diet. Dietrich was now allowed to go to the infirmary and seek needed treatment; later, he did so in a pastoral capacity — more like a prison pastor than a prisoner.

Moreover, Dietrich would serve as a medical orderly for his section. The prison commandant Captain Maertz, upon learning of Dietrich's medical talent, spoke to him in regard to improving air raid precautions. Two days following the air raid of November 26 1943, Dietrich submitted a "Report on Experiences during Alarms" recommending new counter-measures and procedures to be implemented.[1541] During the winter of 1943-44, when air raids started to upset the order of the prison, many people found that being close to Dietrich gave them a welcome sense of safety, especially as Dietrich never asked for more than could be reasonably expected of them.[1542]

Much to his disgust, the guards who had treated him badly now tried to ingratiate themselves with him. But he met at least three guards, the closest of which became Corporal Knobloch, who were honest and trustworthy anti-Nazis, prepared to help him in any way they could. It was through them that, from November 1943, he was able to have an "illegal correspondence"[1543] with Eberhard Bethge, which contained his theological reflections while in Tegel. At further risk to their lives, the friendly guards carried news back and forth between him and his family. This was in contrast to the early days of his imprisonment, when Dietrich, on orders from Roeder, was only allowed a one-page letter every ten days to his parents.[1544]

While Dietrich's distinguished uncle no doubt helped to ease his prison conditions, his character was a central factor in the respect and privileges he enjoyed.[1545] Others in the grim environment found him a source of comfort, and gravitated towards him to speak with him, to tell him their problems, to confess things to him, and simply to be near him. Dietrich was also allowed time alone in his cell with others, contrary to explicit prison orders.[1546] In all, he spent quite a significant amount of time working pastorally at Tegel.[1547] Condemned prisoners and some guards, especially Corporal Knobloch, became so charmed by the gentle pastor, that they would later go to great risk to help him escape, two or so months after the failed Valkyrie assassination plot.[1548] However, as there was not a clear plan for his escape out of Germany, although a false passport was ready for flight to Sweden, on September 24 1944, Dietrich refused the chance, owing to fear of Gestapo reprisals.[1549] One week later, his brother Klaus was arrested by the Gestapo.[1550]

His brother-in-law Hans von Dohnányi had no such good fortune.[1551] His suffering began with a bad case of phlebitis in both legs. His family requested he see the leading Berlin physician Dr Ferdinand Sauerbruch, but Roeder refused. Months later, during the air raid on

November 26, 1943[1552] that Dietrich wrote his report on, Roeder's court files were destroyed in a fire. Dohnányi's cell was struck by a fire-bomb, causing an embolism in his brain.[1553] When Justice Karl Sack of the General Staff, whom Dohnányi had worked with on the 1938 Fritsch case, and Rudolf Lehmann, head of the army legal department and Roeder's immediate superior, could not reach Roeder by phone, they decided to have Dohnányi taken to the Charité Hospital under Sauerbruch's care. Two days later, in a bullying rage, Roeder demanded to have his victim returned to him, but Sauerbruch steadfastly refused, stating that Dohnányi could well suffer further embolisms in his present condition.[1554]

Roeder then ordered that no one but Dohnányi's wife and children were permitted to see or speak to him. Nevertheless, Sauerbruch and his assistant allowed all visitors who were important to the patient to visit him at night during blackouts. Roeder almost certainly suspected this and sent an ambulance with medical orderlies to move Dohnányi to a prison hospital, but Sauerbruch emphatically sent them on their way. But in January 1944, when Sauerbruch was out of town, Roeder turned up at the Charité Hospital to take Dohnányi to the prison hospital in Buch on the north side of Berlin. There, Roeder obtained General Keitel's permission for Professor Max de Crinis to make a token examination of Dohnányi before certifying the patient as fit for normal imprisonment and interrogations.[1555] De Crinis was the natural choice for Roeder; he was the successor to Karl Bonhoeffer, who had retired as head of the Charité Hospital's Psychiatric department in 1938. His first act as the new chief was to have a large bust of the Führer installed in the foyer. He was a civilian SS member with numerous friends among its leaders. The report he submitted was exactly as Roeder ordered.[1556]

In spite of all this, under the brunt of Roeder's interrogations, Dohnányi's brilliant legal mind never wavered or cracked. The pastor stayed resolute too, prompting Schlingensiepen to write that his ability to withstand months of interrogation was his last but greatest contribution to the German Resistance.[1557] On January 1 1944, after Dohnányi filed an official complaint against Roeder to the war department, supporting many complaints from others about Roeder and his conduct, the baby-faced interrogator was "kicked upstairs" as "judge with the rank of general" to Air Fleet Four at Lemberg (Lwów now Lviv in the Ukraine)[1558] in then occupied Poland.[1559]

Roeder had set out to have Dietrich and Hans von Dohnányi condemned to death, and clearly he had failed, to his chagrin.[1560] When Roeder had Dohnányi transferred out of the Charité Hospital in January while its administrator Ferdinand Sauerbruch was out of town, it seemed to be an act of petty revenge for being outmanoeuvred from a position of obvious strength by brave men much smarter than he could ever hope to be. Perhaps his "fond" and "proud" memories of executing pregnant women helped him escape from the embarrassing memory of his failure to extract information from Dohnányi and Dietrich.

Roeder was succeeded by a prosecutor named Kutzner, who conducted Dohnányi's case without ideological zeal, much to the distaste of the SS, whom Kutzner refused to be swayed by.[1561] During this time, Dohnányi and Dietrich, emboldened by withstanding months of interrogation by Roeder, were both pushing for their day in court, confident in their ultimate acquittal. Their friends, however, did not want their case to be turned over to the dreaded SS, as it would be if they lost. They thought it more prudent that they wait it out and let the case "run out of steam,"[1562] especially with renewed hopes for a coup. The latest concept for a coup was another suicide attack involving one of several young officers who were modelling new uniforms for Hitler. Two of them were Axel von dem Bussche and Ewald Heinrich von Kleist, the eldest son of Ewald von Kleist-Schmenzin. However, shortly before Busshe's presentation, after multiple postponements by Hitler, the uniforms were burnt during an air raid.[1563] These plots and others will be covered in more detail in Chapter 20, "Valkyrie II."

In early June 1943, with the interrogations over, Roeder granted Dietrich permission to write to Maria. Later that month, on the 24th,[1564] Maria finally received visitation privileges, and for the first time since November 1942, she met with Dietrich in Roeder's presence, not at Tegel, but in his office at the War Court. Roeder informed Dietrich of her visit only a minute beforehand. Years later, Maria wrote: "

> I found myself being used as a tool by the prosecutor, Roeder...I was brought into the room with practically no forewarning, and Dietrich was visibly shaken. He first reacted with silence, but then carried on a normal conversation; his emotions showed only in the pressure with which he held my hand."[1565]

Since their engagement in January 1943, they had not met or spoken to each other until then; Roeder's unwelcome presence made it an awkward meeting. "Chaperones" would be required for all of Maria's sixteen visits at Tegel. The final one was on August 23 1944, about a month after the failed Valkyrie assassination plot.[1566] Even before Dietrich's arrest in early April 1943, their last meeting had been four to five months earlier in November 1942, prompting Maria at meeting's end in June 1943, to break away from the men leading her out, to embrace her Dietrich one last time before leaving.[1567]

Initially Dietrich had concerns about his family accepting Maria.[1568] This was because she came from a landed nobility east of the Oder River, now of course in modern-day Poland. Their sons grew up to be military officers or to farm their inherited estates, while their daughters married elite men, in what may have seemed like a bygone era for the more sophisticated elite of Berlin's Grunewald district. Then there was the eighteen-year age difference, coupled with Maria being fifteen years younger than Dietrich's youngest sister Sausanne. Dietrich was aware how critical his family could be — his siblings in particular. He recalled their scorn when he announced his ambition to become a pastor when he was a teenager in 1920.[1569]

But he need not have worried. His eldest brother Karl-Friedrich wrote a letter to him in prison on April 23, professing his joy at Dietrich's now not so "secret" engagement.[1570] From the first moment, Dietrich's mother Paula got on famously with Maria; she was impressed that Maria quickly learned the names of all eighteen of her grandchildren.[1571] Soon both women were marshalling friends, relatives, and acquaintances to improve the situation for their imprisoned family members. Maria untiringly provided food for her Dietrich and future brother-in-law Hans. As time passed by, however, the strain of him being in prison gradually made itself felt, and she suffered bouts of dizziness and fainting.[1572]

Letters sent and received were undoubtedly Dietrich's "elixir of life" during his imprisonment at Tegel.[1573] The lively exchanges with his parents, siblings, fiancée, and with his dearest friend Eberhard Bethge, transformed his imprisonment, though with Bethge, it was only from November 1943 onwards.[1574] On February 1 1944, Dietrich jokingly[1575] wrote to Bethge: "

> Carpe diem — in this case that means I use every opportunity to write you a letter. First, I could go on writing for weeks without coming to the end of everything I have to tell you, and second, one never knows how long it will still be possible. And since you will some day be called upon to write my biography, I want to make sure the material you have is as complete as possible!"[1576]

This desire became a reality when Bethge had his work *Dietrich Bonhoeffer - Eine Biographie* published in Munich in 1967. Three years later, the English version, entitled *Dietrich Bonhoeffer: Man of Vision, Man of Courage* would follow.[1577] Eberhard Bethge would dedicate the rest of his life to the works of his friend; without his tireless work, only a few traces of it would be left. Moreover, Eberhard Bethge was much more than Dietrich's biographer, but this fact would only come to light in 1951, when Bethge first had *Letters and Papers from Prison* published. The letters Bethge submitted to the publisher only contained Dietrich's side of the correspondence. It was not until an enlarged edition appeared years later in 1967,[1578] that it was revealed that Dietrich developed his ideas through his dialogue with Bethge.[1579] Their written and verbal dialogue began in 1935, and lasted right up until late September 1944, just two to three weeks before Dietrich's transfer from Tegel to the dreaded cellar prison of the Reich SS Headquarters on Prinz-Albrecht-Strasse in October 1944.

Dietrich's arrest didn't lead to Bethge's ties to the Resistance being discovered. He was still an agent for the Abwehr, and from July 8 to 10 1943, Bethge was sent to Switzerland as an "expert on India" due to his work for the Goßner Mission.[1580] While there he saw Visser 't Hooft and Karl Barth. The latter gave him a cigar as a present for Dietrich, which Dietrich received among other presents[1581] on November 26 1943, when he had the joy of a visit from the four people most dear to him —Maria, his parents, and Eberhard.[1582]

However, by the end of July 1943, Bethge's deployment in the Abwehr was terminated.[1583] He was then conscripted into the military and sent to a training camp at Lissa (Leszno) in south-west Poland. The hideous prospect of being posted to a front-line role on the Russian Front loomed, but thanks to the influence of family members via military contacts, he ended up being posted to the Italian front in January 1944. There, as a corporal, he served in a small Military Intelligence unit of sixteen men in the 10th Army; he was a clerk for its commanding officer, thus being spared front-line combat.[1584] Also, since he wasn't sent to Italy until January 1944, he had the opportunity for the visit to Dietrich on November 26 1943.

As a clerk, he had ready access to a typewriter, and was able to use it for his correspondence with Dietrich. However, with the noose tightening after the failed Valkyrie plot, his final letter to Dietrich was in late September 1944. Soon after, he was ordered back to Berlin under guard.[1585] This was around the same time as Dietrich's transfer on October 8 to the Gestapo's central high security prison on Prinz-Albrecht-

Strasse under the Reich Security Head Office. Before his return, Bethge prudently burnt all of Dietrich's letters that he still had, since he had not yet sent them as usual to his wife for safekeeping.[1586]

On Dietrich's 38th birthday on February 4 1944, he was visited by Maria, who was unknowingly the bearer of bad news in a coded message contained in one of the books she passed to her fiancé.[1587] It read that Admiral Canaris had been dismissed from office. The same day, Canaris was summoned by an angry Hitler due to the defection of the Abwehr operative, Erich Vermehren to the British in Istanbul, in neutral Turkey.[1588] Two weeks later on the 18th, Hitler issued a decree setting up Reinhard Heydrich's old dream of a unified German intelligence service under Himmler and Kaltenbrunner's control. Two years earlier, just months before his assassination by the Czech Underground in Prague,[1589] Heydrich had struggled in vain to achieve such an end. Now, in February 1944, perhaps his ghost was celebrating.[1590] If so, war's end would ensure his celebration was, in the big scheme of things, little more than fleeting.

However, as the Abwehr dissolved into the SD (Sicherheitsdienst — Intelligence arm of the SS),[1591] a new assassination plot was being hatched. This final attempt, out of the dozens made came the closest to killing their target, and was also the first plot to reveal itself to the whole world. The retribution unleashed by Hitler, who felt himself vindicated by providence, was unparalleled in its brutality and sadistic vengeance.[1592]

Chapter 20

Valkyrie II

The central figure in the final but most tumultuous assassination plot on Hitler was the charismatic Colonel Count Claus Schenk von Stauffenberg.[1593] He was born on November 15 1907, the surviving child of a second set of twins in Swabia in south-western Germany,[1594] born to a noble family whose unbroken lineage could be traced as far back as 1382. The family produced many distinguished soldiers, of which Claus was one, having enlisted in the 17th Cavalry Regiment garrisoned in the small cathedral city of Bamberg on April 1 1926.[1595] However, they could also count many scholars and religious clerics among their progeny throughout the centuries.[1596] A devout Catholic, Stauffenberg inherited his handyman father's practicality and his mother's dreamy literary nature, and had, as Nigel Jones put it in his book *Countdown to Valkyrie: The July Plot to Assassinate Hitler*, "a commanding and towering personality."[1597]

Around the time of Reinhard Heydrich's death in early June 1942,[1598] following the assassination attempt on him in late May in Prague by the Czech Underground, and Dietrich's mission to Stockholm,[1599] then Captain von Stauffenberg, working in OKW (Army High Command),[1600] learned the full truth of what was being perpetrated behind the lines on the Eastern Front. A Foreign Office diplomat, Hans von Bittenfeld, was involved in administering the regions of Russia occupied by the Wehrmacht; he informed Stauffenberg that the rounding-up and mass murder of Jews was now official policy.[1601] Indeed, Heydrich himself had chaired the infamous Wannsee Conference in January of that year, which had given the authorisation for the implementation of the "Final Solution."[1602]

Bittenfeld described how, following the Wannsee directive, SS men had rounded up the Jewish population of a Ukrainian town and forced them to dig their own graves in a field, then shot them.[1603] Stauffenberg, already frustrated by Hitler's meddling and incompetence in military matters, stated emphatically the need for Hitler's removal, and declared it was the duty of senior commanders to act against him. His remarks that summer were not just for von Bittenfeld's ears, but were made to several different acquaintances. As a devout Catholic, he began to quote the medieval theologian St Thomas Aquinas's justification for

tyrannicide, and one of the poems of his spiritual mentor Stefan George, "The Antichrist," in an obvious reference to its modern version, Hitler:
"

> The High Priest of Vermin extends his domain;
> No pleasure eludes him, no treasure or gain.
> And down with the dregs of rebellion!
>
> You cheer, mesmerised by demonic sheen,
> Exhaust what remains of the honey of dawn,
> And only then sense the debacle.
>
> You then stretch your tongues to the now arid trough
> Mill witless as kine through a pasture aflame
> While fearfully brazens the trumpet."[1604]

Already it seems, two years before Valkyrie, and given his superiors' unwillingness to act, Stauffenberg believed that the responsibility of ridding Germany of its "High Priest of Vermin" would fall on him.

Another aspect of Stauffenberg's contempt for the tyrant was the latter's zealous refusal, based on his racial dogma, to enlist the peoples of the occupied Soviet Union to fight on Germany's side.[1605] Stauffenberg, like most of his fellow officers, was all too painfully aware that Germany's finite resources were strained to the limit, and needed all the material and manpower they could get, regardless of National Socialist racial dogma. Instead, an almost limitless supply of manpower was spurned by the dreaded SS Einstazgruppen, following in the wake of the Wehrmacht's initial advances into the Soviet Union. There, the local populace often greeted the Wehrmacht as liberators from Stalin's arbitrary and brutal rule,[1606] especially in the Ukraine, with the memory of the Stalinist-orchestrated famine of the early 1930s still relatively fresh in their minds. Nigel Jones wrote that if the Ukrainians and the thousands of Russian soldiers who surrendered without a fight had been put into German uniforms, given guns, turned eastwards and told to boot out the Bolsheviks, the eventual outcome of the war may well have been very different.[1607]

Stauffenberg's many duties included the investigation of the possibility of raising and equipping such volunteer units; he was astonished that Hitler appeared not merely indifferent, but overtly hostile to the idea. It did not take long for the initial enthusiasm of Stalin's subjects for their new German masters to dissolve into bitter resentment and then fury. Stauffenberg's rage was heightened when, on September 24 1942, Hitler's clashes with his commanders came to a head, and Franz Halder, his Chief of Staff,[1608] was sacked for issuing one too many warnings that disaster was looming on the Eastern Front. The following day, at a meeting of staff officers, Stauffenberg sprang to his feet and cried, "Hitler is responsible. No fundamental change is possible until he is removed. I am ready to do it!" As Nigel Jones wrote, for Stauffenburg, a Rubicon had been crossed.[1609] For Dietrich, this Rubicon had been crossed even before Hitler and his cronies came to power in January 1933 ... perhaps before that, when Dietrich arrived back from America in June 1931.

Stauffenburg's concerns that Hitler was dangerously overextending his Sixth Army were well founded; he had already visited the army's commander Friedrich von Paulus in May of that year at the front.[1610] So when, on September 1 1942,[1611] von Paulus entered Stalingrad on Hitler's order, Stauffenberg must have had a sense of foreboding, and clearly was not alone. The Sixth Army's vulnerable northern and southern flanks were only defended by ill-equipped and inferior Romanian units, whom the Germans regarded with unconcealed contempt — a contempt matched by Romanian officers for their own rank and file. The Germans regarded the Romanians as barely one step above the Slavs on the racial hierarchy.[1612]

Unlike Dietrich, in January 1933, Stauffenburg was among those seduced by the Verführer in the economic and political malaise of the Weimar Republic in its death throes. Hoping like many other Germans that the Nazis would give a desperate and demoralised nation a renewed sense of discipline and purpose, he dismissed the 1934 "Nacht der Langen Messer,"[1613] as did so many of his colleagues in the Army, as a purge of thugs long overdue. In 1938, he praised Hitler's "tough" diplomacy in annexing Austria and the Sudetenland to the Reich without a shot being fired. Then in 1939 and 1940 he had taken "professional" pride in the Blitzkrieg conquests of Poland, Norway, Denmark, the Low Countries, and finally France. Even at the beginning of 1942, in the wake of the winter disaster at Moscow, when Hitler assumed supreme personal command of the army, Stauffenberg felt optimistic that this would simplify the chain of command.[1614]

As 1942 wore on, with the disaster at Stalingrad emerging in the final quarter of that year, it was on January 14 1943, seventeen days before von Paulus surrendered the city that had mesmerised Hitler with its name, that Stauffenberg informed his military colleague, Werner Reerink, of a conference in November.[1615] Then, army chiefs believed they were on the verge of persuading their supreme commander to order a breakout from Stalingrad while there was still time. What had come to pass at this meeting was the straw that broke the camel's back for Stauffenberg.

The obvious wisdom of a breakout from Stalingrad was even conceded by the short, club-footed propaganda minister Josef Goebbels. Then, according to Stauffenberg,[1616] the corpulent Göring "lumbered" in, and with boastful abandon, assured Hitler that the Luftwaffe alone could keep the Sixth Army supplied indefinitely, even in the event of them being cut off. Stauffenberg naturally saw this as a betrayal of the army, as it had effectively condemned 300,000 men to a lingering death by starvation, hypothermia and disease. Such criminal irresponsibility could no longer be borne, he decided. His conversion to the conspirators' cause soon spread among the select few, and by late January 1943, General Friedrich Olbricht told his aide, Hans Bernd Gisevius, "Stauffenberg has now seen the light and is participating."[1617]

Unlike Stauffenberg, Olbricht, born in 1888,[1618] was a quietly efficient, mild-mannered and bespectacled officer who had been a long-standing opponent of the Third Reich, never having been seduced by its cult of the Verführer. He had concluded as early as 1940 that Hitler would have to be removed by force, and quietly started planning for the putsch to usurp the National Socialists. However, lacking Stauffenberg's obvious charisma, Olbricht served more as the conspiracy's man behind the scenes.[1619] This work included getting military exemptions for many Confessing Church pastors.[1620]

However, before Stauffenberg could take the step of formally entering the conspiracy, he was transferred to Northern Africa, where Germany was facing another devastating defeat. As on the Eastern front, the days when Erwin Rommel's Afrika Korps had vanquished all before it for German conquest almost to the banks of the Suez Canal and the gates of Cairo were long gone. Now British Commonwealth forces were advancing westwards from Egypt through to Libya, while at the end of 1942, newly arrived Anglo-American forces had landed in Algeria and were advancing towards German positions in Tunisia. In this dire situation, Kurt Zeitzler, who had replaced Franz Halder as Chief of Staff, personally chose Stauffenberg, who had been promoted to lieutenant-colonel on New Years' day 1943, to be the senior staff officer of operations in the 10th Panzer Army. On February 11 1943, flying via Naples, Stauffenberg arrived in the Tunisian capital of Tunis,[1621] not before unnerving several people in Berlin with his forthright but often unwise and overtly public statements in support of Hitler's forced removal from power.[1622]

On February 2, at the fashionable Berlin restaurant of Kempinskis, while Stauffenberg, his wife, and a family friend, Frau Bremme, dined with Colonel and Frau Burker,[1623] the conversation inevitably turned to the debacle of Stalingrad. This followed the grim briefing that Colonel Burker gave Stauffenberg on the situation in Tunisia, as he had just been recalled to Berlin from there. As the conversation progressed, according to Frau Bremme, Stauffenberg left no one within earshot in ignorance of his views on the disaster. This prompted a nervous waiter to insist they speak softly, which provoked Stauffenberg, and indeed the others, to speak even louder.[1624]

A few days earlier, Stauffenberg was no less indiscreet when he urged Field Marshal Manstein to take action against Hitler while there was still an army and nation left to save. In Stauffenberg's eyes, a military victory was now impossible, leaving only the forced removal of Hitler followed by a diplomatic solution as the only course left for saving Germany from outright destruction. Stauffenberg was so insistent that Manstein threatened his arrest. Stauffenberg bluntly expressed his contempt for the generals to his friend Dietz von Thungen: *"Diese Jungs haben ihre Hosen voller Scheiße und ihre Schädel voller Stroh. Sie wollen nichts tun."* Which translates to: "These guys have their pants full of shit and their skulls full of straw. They don't want to do anything."[1625]

Upon arrival in Tunis, his first duty was to visit his badly wounded predecessor, Major Wilhelm Burklin, in hospital. He later recalled Stauffenberg's visit, remarking that he had warned his successor to beware of strafing by low-flying enemy aircraft.[1626] Three days later on February 14, Stauffenberg arrived at his forward post; while he was inexperienced in desert warfare, he nevertheless felt he was now in his element among real soldiers on the front-line. This feeling was reinforced when he formed a close bond with his divisional commander, Brigadier Baron Friedrich von Broich, who was appointed at the same time as Stauffenberg and similarly inexperienced in desert warfare.[1627] In great part, this bond was fostered by their common and intense contempt for Hitler; Stauffenberg was as indiscreet about this as he had been back in Berlin.[1628] Around the time of their arrival, Rommel had received reinforcements and was confident of success with his battle-hardened Afrika Corps veterans against the green and ill-trained Americans in his planned "Operation Spring Breeze," which was a series of offensives in different directions designed to disrupt the Allied grip that was tightening around Tunisia.[1629]

During February, Rommel achieved some notable success with the defeat of the Americans in the battles of Sidi Bou Zid and the Kasserine and Faid Passes over the Atlas Mountains in central Tunisia, in which Stauffenberg and von Broich were actively involved.[1630] During any periods of inactivity, the two friends wasted no time in venting their contempt for Hitler. In their mobile command post, a captured British bus, as they sat well into the night over a bottle or two of heavy Tunisian red wine, their judgement that "That guy [Hitler] ought to be shot" was frequently made within earshot of the lower ranks.[1631]

However, as March passed into early April, the Allied command of the Mediterranean started to make itself felt as supplies began to dwindle, stalling the German offensive.[1632] When Rommel became ill, he was evacuated from Africa, while the Allied air forces, virtually unimpeded by the Luftwaffe, asserted their dominance over the clear desert skies.[1633] By now, the Americans, after licking their wounds in the aftermath of Spring Breeze, had learned their lessons of defeat, and the experienced British Commonwealth Eighth Army moved in to attack the Germans entrenched behind the Mareth Line. As in the east, the tide of war was turning against Germany, confirming the end of the offensive war for Germany.[1634]

Allied air dominance was to have terrible personal consequences for Stauffenberg. On the morning of April 7 1943, two days following Dietrich's arrest, he was on duty in a gorge near a range of hills known as Sebkhet en Noual, supervising a tactical withdrawal eastwards towards the Tunisian coast as they were being strafed by American fighter bombers.[1635] Diving from his jeep, he was shot and lay in agony with his left eye and both hands mutilated, while the rest of his body was riddled with splinters of shrapnel. A passing medical officer, Second Lieutenant Dr Hans Keysser, dressed his wounds before an ambulance appeared out of nowhere and took him to No. 200 Field Hospital at Sfax on Tunisia's eastern coast, where his condition was stabilised. From there he was taken on a pain-wracked journey north to a hospital outside Tunis near ancient Carthage, where the remains of his left eye were removed, his right hand amputated, and all but three fingers cut from his left hand. After another fortnight passed he was stable enough to be evacuated by sea to the Italian port city of Livorno, where he was placed on a hospital train for Munich.[1636]

Once in Munich, strings were pulled to get him admitted to the First General Military Hospital in Lazarettstrasse, where Germany's greatest surgeons, Ferdinand Sauerbruch[1637] and Max Lebsche, operated. While his left eye and hands had already been operated on, critical surgery to remove splinters of steel and rock from his scalp and middle ear still had to be carried out. These procedures were excruciatingly painful, as Stauffenberg stubbornly refused to use opiates such as morphine to alleviate the pain.[1638] His resilience during these ordeals astonished his doctors, as did his rapid recovery from the gruesome injuries.

Within weeks, Stauffenberg, sporting an eye-patch, was back on his feet and learning to write and dress himself using just the three remaining fingers of his left hand in concert with his teeth. Both family and fellow officers were impressed by his determination and courage, including Kurt Zeitzler, the Chief of Staff. Soon, Stauffenberg's keen interest in current events was revived; in particular, in the "White Rose,"[1639] which was a small group of Munich University students who had recently been beheaded for openly distributing leaflets calling for the end of the regime. To his maternal uncle Nikolaus von Üxküll, or "Uncle Nux," a fierce opponent of Hitler, he remarked, "If the generals won't do anything, then it's up to us colonels to take action."[1640] He added that he did not think of his survival as a mere matter of chance, but rather that his life had been spared for a purpose. Amid the bouts of high fever that he suffered as his post-operative infections came and went, he muttered in delirium, "We must save Germany."[1641]

In early July, the month of the failed Kursk offensive (one of the greatest tank battles in history),[1642] Stauffenberg was well enough to leave hospital and join his family to convalesce at his old family summer retreat in the Swabian Alps.[1643] With its fond childhood memories, it was the ideal place to do so. In spite of his injuries, he told enquirers that he was anxious to get back to the front![1644] He even joked "that he did not know what he had done with all ten fingers when he had had the full set!"[1645] Unbeknownst to Stauffenberg, General Olbricht, the conspirators' man behind the scenes and head of the General Army Office in Berlin's Bendlerstrasse, had already mapped out his future.

As maimed as Stauffenberg was, Olbricht had been greatly impressed by the young officer's calmness, efficiency, and air of natural authority. Olbricht saw that Stauffenberg was a man of principle, a Christian and an idealist, and recognised that Germany was spiralling downwards on Hitler's insane and destructive path. Having already been appointed as Olbricht's Chief of Staff,[1646] on August 10, Stauffenberg was introduced at Olbricht's Berlin home to the man who had preceded him as the mainstay of the conspiracy — Henning von Tresckow,[1647] Oma Ruth's nephew.[1648] Tresckow, now removed at least for the time being from the Eastern Front due to a transfer to Berlin's Reserve Army, and one of the masterminds of the bungled "brandy" package plot in March to scatter Hitler's body parts over the skies of Belarus, had lost none of his zeal for plotting against Hitler.[1649] Furthermore, he had recently recruited General Stieff, the unwitting decoy recipient of Schlabrendorff's "brandy-bottle" bomb, to the conspiracy's ranks.[1650]

In spite of their mutual loathing, Hitler recognised Stieff's administrative genius by appointing him as the head of the organisational section of his headquarters staff. When asked by Tresckow if he would kill Hitler in person at one of their numerous meetings, Stieff had initially accepted. However, this acceptance must have been reluctant, since, after much vacillation, he ultimately declined the honour.[1651] The more resilient Stauffenberg did not vacillate when he was called upon for this dangerous duty.

When he met the maimed young colonel, Tresckow instantly recognised a man after his own heart. Stauffenberg's debilitating injuries hardly diminished his energy, enthusiasm and radiant charisma, which put other tired and dispirited members of the conspiracy to shame.[1652] In the wake of that demoralising spring, with its dud-bomb plots and the collapse of Oster's Abwehr network, Stauffenberg's presence came like a breath of fresh alpine air to revitalise the conspiracy. Even before he officially took up his post with the Reserve Army on October 1 1943, he set to work.[1653]

Officially, Stauffenberg's job was to revise and update Olbricht's approved and codenamed plan, "Operation Valkyrie." Throughout the Reich, there were foreign workers, both volunteer, and more commonly, forced labour of various hierarchical levels from all around the Reich and its conquered territories. Since the Slavs were considered *Untermensch* in Nazi ideology, most of the minority volunteer labour was from western countries such as France. Conversely, the vast majority from the east, such as Poland, were almost invariably slave labour, forced to work on a range of duties from housework to hard labour on starvation rations in the concentration camps (KZ — Konzentration Lager).[1654]

Life for the top class of forced labourers seemed relatively benign compared with that of the less fortunate, with shelter, food and pay (though very poor) being guaranteed. Yet, as a Polish woman, from Jarocin, working in Breslau recalled, the list of prohibitions was endless:
"

We were obliged to wear an armband marked 'P', and we were not allowed to ride on the trams, to enter a church, theatre, restaurant, opera or circus, or even to visit the zoo or botanical garden. We could not participate in any sports, speak Polish in the street, listen to the radio, or read the press. We were not even free to sit on the park benches, which were marked with the words: "*Für* Polen *und* Juden *sitzen verboten.*" [For Poles and Jews sitting is forbidden] We were not permitted to study, or to get married …"[1655]

Any transgression of these rules was treated as a "breach of contract" and risked immediate investigation by the Gestapo.[1656]

As the war dragged on, with its extreme demands on the Reich's manpower, especially for cannon fodder on the Eastern Front, the number of discontented foreign workers conscripted to alleviate this chronic shortfall rose to over one million;[1657] the shortage of workers was exacerbated by the Nazi regime's insane refusal to allow women to perform factory work.[1658] Now in such numbers, the possibility of an uprising by these discontented workers gave rise to the emergency contingency plan codenamed Valkyrie,[1659] named after the ancient Norse/Germanic female deities who decided who should die in battle.[1660]

Under this official plan, already drawn up by Olbricht and personally approved by Hitler,[1661] scattered groups of paramilitaries, trainees, front-line soldiers on leave, guards at prisoner-of-war camps, anti-aircraft defence units, and similar varied groups would be amalgamated as emergency fighting units to quash any revolt within the foreign workforce. For the conspirators, this official plan would be designated as "Valkyrie I," under the cover of which Tresckow and Stauffenberg would conceive "Valkyrie II,"[1662] in which officers privy to it would take charge and mobilise the emergency units in the wake of a successful assassination of Hitler. The units, rather than suppressing a foreign workers' revolt, would seize key points throughout the Reich and crush opposition from loyal and fanatical Nazis such as the SS and whatever was left of the SA. With the key vassals of Nazi power suppressed, the way would be open for a new government headed by Beck, Witzleben, and Goerdeler to smoothly assume power.[1663]

There were glaring flaws in the plan, three of which were ultimately fatal. The first
was that given the repeated past failures, the successful assassination of Hitler was problematic. The second was that the putsch's central pillar

rested on a deception that seemed impossible to maintain long enough to ensure a successful conclusion. This was the pretence that the putsch would be spawned by the Nazis, such as Himmler's SS, rather than the anti-Hitler conspirators. Thus, the Berlin Reserve Army, most of whom were still loyal to Hitler and his cronies, would unknowingly be acting against their own side. How they would react when they realised the deception was a question that the conspirators never addressed.[1664]

The third problem was that Olbricht and Stauffenberg were the number two and three men in the command structure of the Reserve Army, while their superior, General Friedrich Fromm, was the quintessential "flipflopper" who always prided himself on being able to end up on the "winning side."[1665] Hitler reputedly trusted Fromm, having dubbed him "the strong man in the homeland,"[1666] based on Fromm's deceptively strong and oak-like appearance. Having participated in the Polish campaign at the start of the war, this unremarkable officer had been assigned to the Reserve Army in the wake of Poland's surrender. Nevertheless, Fromm was aware of what Olbricht and Stauffenberg were planning, and they had indeed approached him. He merely assured them that he would only join them after Hitler died and they looked like winners.[1667]

Undeterred by Fromm's fence sitting, they proceeded to plan. Remembering the fate that befell the Oster group, they entrusted the written documentation to Tresckow's wife Erika and a trusted secretary in the War Ministry, Margarete von Oven. When handling these documents, both women wore gloves so as not to leave fingerprints for the Gestapo to discover.[1668] By November 1943 all the plans were signed and sealed, with Field Marshal Witzleben, designated Commander-in-Chief of the post-Hitler regime, putting his hand to the proclamation of martial law.[1669]

Tresckow was now unexpectedly ordered back to the Eastern Front, where he attempted to secure a post on the staff of Manstein, the commander of Army Group South. Tresckow hoped to persuade the militarily talented but timid field marshal to join the conspiracy.[1670] It seems Manstein guessed as much, and assigned Tresckow to command an infantry regiment instead. Along with Olbricht, Stauffenberg was left in Berlin to see Valkyrie through with his characteristic vigour and energy. While hardly a left winger himself, he realised that a post-Nazi regime must be drawn from the widest possible spectrum of society, from socialists and trade unionists on the left, to ultra-conservative nationalists on the right.[1671]

Accordingly, he met with representatives of both wings of the conspiracy, such as the monarchist/nationalist and friend of Dietrich, Carl Goerdeler, who now harboured the illusion that Hitler could somehow be persuaded to change his ways,[1672] and Julius Leber, a former Social Democratic Reichstag deputy, who had survived a spell in a concentration camp in the regime's early days, and maintained his opposition to it.[1673] After meeting both men, Stauffenberg was unimpressed with Goerdeler, whom he found verbose, and recommended that Leber serve as vice-Chancellor to represent the left in the post-putsch regime.[1674]

Now the search had begun in earnest for an assassin to eliminate Hitler, and if possible, other elite Nazis as well. By now Stauffenberg had decided against the hesitant General Stieff, whom he described as "nervy as a racing jockey."[1675] His attention now turned to less senior officers. This was in line with his dictum that if the field marshals and generals wore pants full of Scheiße, it was up to less senior officers such as colonels, even down to lieutenants, to do what was needed to save Germany.[1676] Through his friend, the lawyer Count Fritz-Dietlof von der Schulenberg, whose job in the Army Reserve gave him access to all army units, Stauffenberg was introduced to a young Wehrmacht captain. He was 24-year-old Baron Axel von dem Bussche-Streithorst, who resolved to join the underground after witnessing the mass shooting of Jewish civilians at Dubno in eastern Poland in 1942 by the Einsatzgruppe C, with the Ukrainian militia acting as their willing auxiliaries.[1677]

To be fair to von dem Bussche, the failure of this suicide assassination attempt, initially scheduled to take place in November 1943 at the gloomy Wolfsschanze at Rastenburg, deep in the forests of East Prussia, wasn't due to any lack of courage on his part. Rather, it seems it was Hitler's uncanny sixth sense that foiled the plot; time and time again the inspection of new greatcoats to be modelled by von dem Bussche was scheduled, only to be postponed. Finally, when the consignment of new greatcoats was stored in an army goods train, they were destroyed during one of the numerous and increasingly heavy and frequent Allied bombing raids on Berlin. With replacements not available until around January, the dejected von dem Bussche returned to the Eastern Front with the expectation of being recalled as soon as the new consignment was ready.[1678]

But again, fate would not smile upon the conspirators; in December, von dem Bussche was, not for the first time, severely wounded — this time losing a leg. He spent the rest of the war in hospital and played no further part in the conspiracy, although he was left with some potentially damning evidence in his suitcase as he was moved around from hospital to hospital. That was the bomb itself! Not until the autumn of 1944, months after Stauffenberg's attempt, was he able rid himself of it, when a fellow officer of similar mind tossed it into a lake for him.[1679] Like the suicide bomber before him, von Gersdorff, he would live on long after the war, until 1993, serving, among other roles, as a diplomat from 1954 to 1958.[1680]

On December 23 1943, Stauffenberg made his first visit to the fateful Wolfsschanze.[1681] While he was waiting in Hitler's antechamber, it suddenly occurred to him that in spite of his injuries, he could perform the assassin's task and blow himself up along with the increasingly demented and irrational dictator. For one thing, the lair's several two-metre-plus thick windowless concrete fortifications would be ideal to contain and concentrate the blast, rendering impossible the survival of any of its occupants. Indeed, Hitler's architect and armaments minister Albert Speer described Hitler's Führerbunker in unflattering but accurate terms: "

> From the outside it looked like an ancient Egyptian tomb. It was actually nothing but a great windowless block of concrete, without direct ventilation, in cross section a building whose masses of concrete far exceeded the usable cubic feet of space. It seemed as if the concrete walls sixteen and a half feet thick that surrounded Hitler separated him from the outside world in a figurative as well as a literal sense, and locked him up inside his delusions."[1682]

Little wonder then that General Alfred Jodl described the forbidding forest clearing of the Wolfsschanze as "a cross between a monastery and a concentration camp."[1683] He would become one of the surviving victims of the July 20th blast, but would face prosecution and subsequent execution in the Nuremberg trials. This was in part due to his issuing of the notorious order on the behalf of the Führer on July 23 1941, about a month after the launch of Barbarossa, to eradicate all Soviet resistance — not legally, but by the explicit use of terror.[1684]

Upon his return to Berlin, Stauffenberg proposed the plan to both Beck and Olbricht, but they objected on the grounds that the sacrifice of such a brilliant mind and charismatic personality would be too great a waste for Germany, as it needed Stauffenberg alive.[1685] Hence the continuation of the search for another viable assassin. Meantime, the disaster of Stalingrad was followed months later by the failed Kursk offensive 660 kilometres west of the city. In the northern sector of the Eastern Front, the terrible 900 day siege of Leningrad, which had reduced the population of Russia's second city to eating dogs, cats, and each other,[1686] had been broken. In the Mediterranean, the Allies had landed in Italy, and while bitter fighting still lay ahead in its mountainous terrain, it was only heading in only one direction — northwards towards the Reich. Moreover, Allied bombing of German cities continued unabated.[1687]

As December 1943 passed into January 1944, the next candidate von der Schulenberg produced for the assassination was Ewald Heinrich von Kleist-Schmenzin, a young infantry lieutenant and son of Ewald von Kleist-Schmenzin. The latter was the Pomeranian Junker, conservative lawyer, and cousin of Oma Ruth who had travelled twice to London in 1938 as Beck's emissary, seeking in vain British support before the implementation of Oster's aborted coup in the wake of Chamberlain's Sudeten back-down.[1688] Ewald was the one who had summoned Oma Ruth and her son Hans Jürgen to the prophetic September 1925 meeting at Klein Krössin cottage to discuss *Mein Kampf*.[1689]

As this was to be another suicide greatcoat presentation, Stauffenberg asked the young lieutenant if he was willing to commit the deed.[1690] After counsel from his illustrious father, the young man decided to offer himself up for the suicide mission.[1691] But again, the final scene, for whatever reason, never came to pass. Now desperate, Stauffenberg asked his adjutant Werner von Haeften, assigned to him in November, whether he would be prepared to do the deed. At first Haeften agreed, but when he consulting his older brother Hans-Bernd,[1692] who was a member of the conspiracy, but had strong Christian ethical objections to assassination, he was persuaded to withdraw his offer. Nevertheless, Werner von Haeften would later be at Stauffenberg's side throughout the events of July 20 1944.

Still one more candidate was to be tried before Stauffenberg finally accepted the poisoned chalice. He was Eberhard von Breitenbuch, a young cavalry captain and protégé of von Tresckow, who had initially recruited the young captain to the staff of Army Group Centre. When Tresckow departed temporarily for assignment to the Berlin Reserve Army around August 1943, and Field Marshal Günther von Kluge was seriously injured in a car crash two or so months later, Breitenbuch would stay on to become aide-de-camp to the new commander and overly promoted Hitler "yes man,"[1693] Field Marshal Ernst

Busch. Like von dem Bussche, the candidate before him, Breitenbuch had been converted to the conspiracy by the atrocities he had witnessed on the Eastern Front.[1694]

By early March 1944, Breitenbuch was given the opportunity to finally rid Germany of its leader, who was spiralling the country to its inexorable destruction. Breitenbuch told Tresckow, who had been chosen to accompany Busch on a briefing mission at Hitler's Bavarian mountain retreat of the Berghof near Berchtesgaden, that he would be willing to attempt an assassination with his trusty Browning pistol rather than use what had proved to be unreliable explosives. Tresckow replied that this could be a "a unique chance to end with his own hands the war with all its horrors."[1695]

So it was on Saturday March 11 1944 that Busch and Breitenbuch flew in to Salzburg airport, before driving up the winding mountain roads to the heavily guarded Berghof.[1696] By this time, the security surrounding Hitler had been significantly increased. All visitors were required to remove their caps, uniform belts, and side-arms before they were permitted to meet the Führer. Before leaving for Salzburg, Breitenbuch had already removed his watch and wedding ring, having sent them with a farewell letter to his wife. What he still kept, however, was his Browning pistol with its safety-catch off, in his trouser pocket.[1697] Considering the heightened security around Hitler, the fact that it was never discovered by any of the SS guards at the Berghof is remarkable.

While waiting for Hitler, Göring kept company with Busch and Breitenbuch, along with others of the top Nazi brass, and entertained them with his characteristic rendition of coarse jokes. Amid the laughter, Breitenbuch, unable to feign the sycophantic laughter, could feel the beating of his heart in his throat as he pondered his imminent death within the next thirty minutes or so.[1698] The rich array of Nazi elite in the entourage included Göring, Goebbels, and Hitler's two top military aides, Generals Keitel and Jodl. As Breitenbuch pondered the possibility of firing enough shots to kill almost the entire Nazi elite, with his own death bound to follow, the doors to the Berghof's grand hall swung open, and the SS officer indicated that the Führer was at last ready to receive them.[1699]

As the entourage proceeded obediently to the open doors, the SS guard informed Busch that his aide was of too lowly a rank to take part in the discussions.[1700] In vain, Busch argued that he would be required, but the guard was adamant that Breitenbuch, along with another lowly ranked adjutant, could not be allowed in. Outside, in the fresh, crisp early spring Bavarian mountain air, Breitenbuch's companion noticed him sweating profusely. Fearing he was sick, he asked if the young captain needed to be taken to the hospital in nearby Berchtesgaden. Shaking his head, Breitenbuch said he would be fine in a minute or two.[1701]

The abortive few minutes as assassin in waiting had shattered his nerves more than any experience on the Eastern Front. Hence his refusal to accept this poisoned chalice again: "You only do something like that once!"[1702] Remarkably, like his predecessors Rudolf-Christoph von Gersdorff and the most recent would-be assassin, Axel von dem Bussche-Streithorst, the young cavalry captain would live on long after the war, passing away in the same year as von Gersdorff, in 1980 in Göttingen.[1703]

By the beginning of 1944, whatever remained of any civilian resistance had been liquidated by the Gestapo. Beginning on September 10 1943 at an apparently innocuous tea party held in Heidelberg, members of the Solf Circle discussed plans for a post-Hitler Germany. Unbeknownst to them, the Swiss doctor and Gestapo informant Rieske carefully noted the names of all those present and the subversive subjects they discussed. Rieske reported his findings, but in order to lure more into the net, the arrests did not come until January 12 1944. Helmuth von Moltke, the Prussian aristocrat whose Silesian estate at Kreisau lent its name to the so-named group, was aware that the Solf Circle had been infiltrated, but was unable to inform its leader Otto Kiep in time, as he was arrested at what would be Kiep's final tea party.[1704] A week later, the Gestapo came for Moltke himself. Finally, on February 11, the Abwehr lost all pretence of independence when Admiral Canaris was dismissed and taken for a cordial Gestapo interview at the medieval castle of Lauenstein in Saxony.[1705]

The Allied landings in Normandy on D-Day on June 6 1944 opened up the long awaited second front on the Reich; Stauffenberg was reduced to despair. Defeat was now not just likely, but inevitable, crushing any strategic hope of forcing the Allies to a negotiated peace. Stauffenberg began to question if there was now any point to further assassination attempts. He sought counsel with his admired and respected friend Henning von Tresckow, now serving back at his old post as Chief of Staff of the Second Army in the southern sector of Army Group Centre.

While Tresckow, in his almost immediate reply, conceded that Germany was now facing certain conquest with unconditional surrender, he asserted that this fact was no longer relevant: "

The assassination must be attempted, come what may. Even if it fails, we must take action in Berlin [to launch a coup]. For the practical purpose no longer matters; all that counts now is that the German resistance movement must take the plunge before the eyes of the world and of history. Compared to that, nothing else matters."[1706]

That Valkyrie went ahead regardless, with Stauffenberg accepting the poisoned chalice of assassin, speaks volumes for the respect he had for Henning von Tresckow. Clearly he saw, in him, one senior officer with "*keine Scheiße*" (no excrement) in his pants. His hesitation was only momentary.[1707]

While Stauffenberg's contempt for Hitler was complete, his professional reports on the state of the Reserve Army had attracted the attention and praise of Hitler himself, who is said to have remarked; "Finally, a General Staff officer with imagination and intelligence."[1708] So it was that on the afternoon of June 7, the day after the D-Day landings, their very first meeting took place when Stauffenberg and Fromm were summoned to the Berghof to report on the readiness of the Reserve Army. Certainly, given the opening of the Second Front in Normandy, this was now a question becoming more practical than theoretical. As usual, Hitler had the company of fellow elites such as Göring, Himmler, Keitel, and his armaments minister Albert Speer.[1709]

Stauffenberg made these remarks to his wife on the weekend of June 24—25 at their town-house in Bamberg.[1710] The Countess Stauffenberg was busy with her plans to take the children with her to their Schloss at Lautlingen, Stauffenberg's own childhood country home, for their annual summer holidays. This year, she had been looking forward to the break more than usual. In the idyllic rural setting of Lautlingen, she hoped it might be possible to forget that a war was going on. Certainly, even in the small city of Bamberg, this was impossible, as there were constant air-raid alarms, compelling the elder Stauffenberg children to complete their end of summer term tests in underground shelters. Her husband was unenthusiastic about his family's holiday plans, which prompted her in hindsight to realise that he was worried about them being stranded in such a remote location in the aftermath of what he hoped would be his successful assassination of Hitler.[1711]

Nina was aware of her husband's extreme contempt for the regime, which she shared, but she was unaware of how deeply her husband was involved in plotting Hitler's assassination. Clearly, Stauffenberg operated on the prudent "need to know" principle to protect his family. When they parted, the countess had no idea that she had seen her husband for the last time. It seems her husband's "need to know" principle[1712] achieved its objective, for she and her children would live on long after the war. She passed away in 2006, in spite of having been imprisoned by the Gestapo, while heavily pregnant, under the invocation of the ancient Sippenhaft law.[1713] Less than a week after his final parting from his wife,[1714] and nineteen days before the plot's ultimate implementation, on July 1, Stauffenberg was promoted to full colonel and confirmed as Chief of Staff to the commander of the Reserve Army, General Fromm.[1715] Thus Stauffenberg now had regular access to Hitler at his daily military conferences,[1716] which meant that out of all the plotters, in spite of his obvious handicaps, he was now best placed to execute an assassination attempt. Typically, he wasted no time in setting about to achieve that end.

The need for Stauffenberg to act was dire. In part, this was due to the Gestapo tightening its noose in the first half of 1944, while at the same time, the conspirators disregarded the intelligence axiom, "need to know." By July 4 and 5, two prominent socialists within the conspiracy, Julius Leber, much admired by Stauffenberg, and Adolf Reichwein, a former Kreisau member, were arrested;[1717] this weighed heavily on Stauffenberg's mind.[1718] They were trying to make contact with a communist cell that the Gestapo had cracked (much to the concern of the more conservative members of the conspiracy). The thinking was that, with communists in the new regime and an appeal to a broader base of the general German population, a negotiated peace with the Soviets would be more plausible, given the utter intransigence of the west.[1719] In reality of course, the conspirators were clutching at straws.

In regard to careless talk, neither Stauffenberg nor his adjutant were guiltless. Werner von Haeften was telling people that his boss had "decided to do the job himself," while Stauffenberg had incautiously told at least two people that "he was engaged in high treason, and would be branded a traitor to Germany before history"; he added that he would be "committing treason to his own conscience if he failed to act."[1720]

Before the unaborted plot on July 20 finally came to pass, there was still time for several more abortive attempts in the nineteen-day period between Stauffenberg's promotion on the 1st and the tumultuous day at the Wolfsschanze. On the 6th and 8th, accompanied by his new superior General Fromm, Stauffenberg flew to Salzburg to again brief Hitler at the Berghof, this time in relation to the latest modifications to the Valkyrie plan. These changes looked perfectly reasonable, as since the Normandy landings, the High Command were increasingly concerned that the Allies might launch a landing on the unprotected northern German coastline.[1721] Stauffenberg was ordered to tweak Valkyrie to enable the 300,000 German soldiers who were at home on leave at any given time to be rapidly formed into new units called "shell detachments" to meet any such threat.[1722] As one would expect, Hitler approved Stauffenberg's plan, which gave military commanders "executive powers" encompassing authority over Nazi Party officials in the event of such an invasion. In reality, such powers would mask the army takeover of the state in the wake of the Führer's assassination. This was the essence of Valkyrie II.[1723]

It was at the second of these briefings on July 8 that Stauffenberg saw his fellow conspirator General Stieff, the diminutive administrative genius who, in spite of his constant access to the Führer as chief of operations, lacked the audacity required to attempt the assassination himself. Upon crossing paths with Stieff, Stauffenberg patted his briefcase, remarking:, "I have got the whole bag of tricks with me."[1724] It seems Stieff interpreted this as meaning that Stauffenberg was already carrying a bomb, rather than as a heavy hint that Stieff should place the bomb himself. For whatever reason, no attempt was made; Stieff testified at his post-war trial that he had dissuaded Stauffenberg from carrying out the attempt that day. Given the circumstances, this seems questionable.[1725]

The pressure to act was becoming unbearable. The Gestapo noose was tightening, and the leaky conspirators were playing their part in the building tension, but so too was the worsening strategic situation on all fronts. Stauffenberg was very aware of this, since his duties included supervising the supply of reserve troops to these crumbling fronts, and he witnessed the consequences of the ever-worsening Allied bombing raids.[1726] Three days later on the 11th,[1727] the penultimate abortive attempt took place, when Stauffenberg flew back to the Berghof for another afternoon briefing with Hitler. Once again, he was carrying the bomb in his trusty briefcase. However, before leaving Berlin, Beck and other conspirators had impressed upon Stauffenberg the great allure of having Göring and Himmler meet their maker with their Führer. Göring was assigned to take over command of all military forces in such an event, while Himmler's ever-growing SS would be the chief armed body to overcome in any post-assassination aftermath.

But when Stauffenberg arrived at the Berghof, Stieff, more than likely with relief, informed him that Göring and Himmler would not be present. Stauffenberg cried; "shouldn't we go ahead anyway?" Stauffenberg had ordered his fellow conspirators in Berlin to stand by to initiate Valkyrie, and had his aide for the day, Captain Friedrich Klausing (Haeften was ill), have a Heinkel aircraft on standby at Salzburg to fly him back to Berlin to take command of the putsch. So his frustration when Stieff outranked him was great. Back in Berlin, upon hearing the news, Carl Goerdeler, half laughing, half crying, shook his head and predicted, "They'll never do it."[1728]

The following day of the 12th, the Abwehr's Hans Bernd Gisevius returned to Berlin from Switzerland. There, he had been, on behalf of the plotters, in contact with Allen Dulles, the local chief of America's secret service, the OSS. The news was predictably bad: the Western Allies would not make a separate peace with Germany against their Soviet ally.[1729] In desperation, Stauffenberg asked Gisevius whether there was any hope of making an "eastern peace" with the Soviets alone. This was an outcome the Western powers had been desperate to avoid, as evidenced in their never-ending appeasement in the conferences of Casablanca and Teheran. Gisevius, who had resented Stauffenberg's role as the new leading light in the conspiracy in spite of Oster's virtual house arrest,[1730] tersely replied that all Allied powers demanded no less than Germany's unconditional surrender, regardless of the plotters' success or failure.

Now, on the 14th, only six days before the ultimate Valkyrie, Hitler abruptly moved his headquarters from the Berghof among the beautiful backdrop of the Alps to the grim and now sweltering Wolfsschanze near Rasternburg in the East Prussian forest. This was in spite of it now being less than one hundred kilometres from the advancing Red Army.[1731] Fromm and Stauffenberg were summoned to an urgent lunchtime conference with Hitler on the 15th to discuss the allocation of Reserve Army reinforcements on that front. This news precipitated a frenzy of activity among the conspirators. At a meeting of Beck, Goerdeler, Olbricht, and Stauffenberg that afternoon, it was agreed that Stauffenberg would attempt the assassination regardless of the presence or absence of Göring or Himmler. Back in Berlin, the conspirators would activate Valkyrie, which included Olbricht issuing orders to move troops into the centre of Berlin at 11am, without Fromm's authority, and two hours before Stauffenberg was due to explode his bomb.[1732]

Meanwhile, in France, at his headquarters in the riverside château of La Roche-Guyon, Rommel, urged on by his fellow Swabian and Chief of Staff Speidel, drafted an ultimatum to Hitler insisting that the position in the west was now hopeless and that peace terms must be sought.[1733] Speidel was a conspirator himself, and had already tried unsuccessfully to enlist Rommel into the conspiracy. Rommel, it seems, was a simple soldier who always avoided politics,[1734] but he acknowledged that the strategic situation in the west was lost and never at any stage betrayed the conspirators. On July 15, Fromm and Stauffenberg, again accompanied by Captain Klausing, flew out on an early morning flight from Berlin before having breakfast at the Wolfsschanze, and meeting with Keitel for a preparatory briefing.[1735] Later, Stauffenberg also met with the main conspirators there, Stieff and Fellgiebel, before meeting with Hitler, where a photographer took the only photograph of Hitler with his would-be assassin.[1736]

Standing to the left of the photo is Stauffenberg, his injuries hidden from view while he rigidly stands to attention with characteristic resolute calm, betraying no hint of the incredible tension he must have been under. Hitler, a shrunken figure with his cap pulled low over his eyes, shakes hands with General Karl von Bodenschatz, Göring's Luftwaffe liaison man at Hitler's headquarters.[1737] This all took place before 1 p.m., when the party proceeded to the briefing hut, which was a one-storey wooden structure, reinforced by brick supports and a concrete ceiling, with large steel-shuttered windows. This was to be the eventual location for the explosion of Stauffenberg's bomb five days later on July 20, but here on the 15th, it should have gone off but didn't. Why?

No definitive answer exists among the varying accounts.[1738] One report claims that Stieff and Fellgiebel were insistent that no attempt must be made without Himmler being present. The timid Stieff, being worried that Stauffenberg would go ahead anyway, sabotaged the attempt by removing the briefcase bomb while Stauffenberg was phoning Berlin to acquaint the plotters in Berlin as the situation was unfolding. More benign versions claim that Stauffenberg was unexpectedly called to present his report early in the conference before he had a chance to prime the bomb, while another states that Hitler unexpectedly ended the conference early while Stauffenberg was phoning Berlin. When one looks closely at the aforementioned photo, you notice that Stauffenberg, so close to the time of the briefing, is minus his briefcase, prompting the author in the description to ask the question, "had a nervous Stieff already hidden it?"xxiv

---

xxiv Position 409.4 of Nigel Jones describes the photo taken at the Wolfsschanze on July 15 1944, where Stauffenberg and Hitler are both present. The only such photo. This being just before the planned conference where Stauffenberg was to detonate the bomb in his briefcase. Strangely, as the author alludes to, Stauffenberg is seemingly not carrying or has his briefcase with him, prompt-

As Stauffenberg and Klausing walked disconsolately to Keitel's special train for lunch, Stauffenberg rued another abortive attempt. While he had managed to phone Olbricht to inform him of yet another failed attempt, it was too late for Olbricht to call off Valkyrie's preliminary troop movements, as the codeword had been issued at 11 a.m. as per the plan.[1739] Hastily countermanding the orders, Olbricht even drove to Potsdam and Gleinicke, but of course, the movements could not be concealed from his superiors; Olbricht lamely justified them as a test of the efficiency and readiness of the troops. This excuse did not stop Fromm venting his rage on Olbricht for the unauthorised command. Clearly, the next time Olbricht dared issue such an order, he had to be certain that the attempt had been carried out to its planned conclusion.[1740]

The following day, the 16th, was spent by the conspirators in another lengthy autopsy of a failed coup. Stauffenberg, even with his reserves of courage and nerve, was understandably but uncharacteristically tired, irritable, and nervous. General Beck, who earlier that year had been operated on for stomach cancer, was, according to his housekeeper, waking up every morning with his sheets soaked in sweat.[1741] That evening at Stauffenberg's home in the Tristranstrasse, the core of younger conspirators from Stauffenberg's closest circle met.[1742] They included his brother Berthold and Albrecht Mertz von Quirnheim, who, under Olbricht, would initiate Valkyrie in Berlin. In Paris, Cäsar von Hofacker, Stauffenberg's cousin, was the plotters' man, while another cousin, Peter Yorck von Wartenburg, and Fritz-Dietlof von der Schulenburg and Adam von Trott zu Solz were also present.

The following day, the 17th, the Americans in France were breaking out of their bridgehead,[1743] while in the east, the Soviets, having unleashed Operation Bagration on June 23,[1744] had crossed the River Bug, which would become part of the eastern frontier of Poland post-war. That same day, the Normandy commander Rommel was seriously hurt when his staff car was strafed by an American fighter, inflicting serious head injuries which required hospitalisation back in Germany.[1745] These wounds would be put to great use by Goebbels in covering up Rommel's forced suicide.[1746] On July 18 more bad news confirmed the tightening noose within which the plotters were now operating, when the president of Berlin's police, Count von Helldorf, a former ardent if corrupt Nazi, tipped Stauffenberg off that a warrant had been

___

ing the author's question; *had a nervous Stieff already hidden it?* For full details of this book, see endnote [1594] for this chapter.

issued for the immediate arrest of Carl Goerdeler.[1747] Having been nominated by the conspirators for the post of Chancellor in the post-putsch government, Goerdeler went into hiding when Stauffenberg warned him.

A naval officer, Lieutenant Commander Alfred Kranzfelder, informed Stauffenberg that he had heard from a Hungarian nobleman that Hitler's headquarters were to be blown sky-high over the next few days. In turn, the young Hungarian had heard the report from the daughter of General Bredow, murdered by the Nazis in the Night of the Long Knives purge,[1748] who in turn had apparently heard it from Stauffenberg's own indiscreet adjutant, Werner von Haeften.[1749] So aside from the fact that the Gestapo were now breathing down the conspirators' necks, their own plans were about to become common Berlin street gossip. Stauffenberg knew that he must act quickly, and as if to answer his call, he received another summons from Rastenburg to attend a conference on July 20.[1750]

News of this latest opportunity, while welcome in many respects, had the critical disadvantage of allowing less than twenty-four hours for the conspirators to plan their plot.[1751] Hence, the 19th was spent making frantic checks of numerous ad-hoc arrangements, although the basic rudiments of the plot were in place, thanks to Olbricht's and Stauffenberg's tireless and patient work.[1752] Dangerously, much still had to be left to chance, such as whether or not individual commanders, amongst them Fromm the flip-flopper, would remain loyal to the regime or support the coup. Another of the key plotters, Dietrich's uncle, Major-General Paul von Hase, who greatly alleviated Dietrich's prison time at Tegel, was also taking a grave risk.

As the military commander of Berlin, an absolutely critical element in Hase's command was the Grossdeutschland Guard Battalion, commanded by Major Otto Remer, a much-decorated veteran of the Eastern Front. Incredibly, Hase neglected to ascertain where Remer's loyalties would lie on the day of the putsch, although he could well have guessed when it was pointed out to him that Remer, among his numerous medals, proudly displayed a Hitler Youth gold badge on his army uniform![1753] Hase, ignoring the obvious implication, assumed that Remer would obey his orders without question. Hence, Hase's dismissal of the suggestion to have Remer sent out of the way on assignment in Italy.[1754]

This complacency, perhaps fostered by the fawning of guards over him that Dietrich reported at Tegel Prison, would prove fatal. Dietrich's distinguished uncle visited him in Tegel on June 30 1944.[1755] He presented Dietrich with a bottle of Sekt (German Champagne); the visit lasted an unprecedented five hours.[1756] This fact was not lost on Dietrich, and neither was the clear implication, confirmed by this visit, that another attempted putsch was in the air. Indeed, in the next twenty days, there would be three. There were two aborted plots on the 11th and 15th July at the Obersalzburg and Wolfsschanze respectively,[1757] and finally, again at the Wolfsschanze on the 20th, when the bomb that finally blew but without killing Hitler led to all hell breaking loose, and the elimination of virtually all vestiges of the German Underground.

On July 7 1944, thirteen days before the final aborted plot, Dietrich wrote to Bethge an obliquely phrased and fateful message: "

> Who knows—it may be that it will not have to be too often now, and that we shall see each other sooner than we expect ... We shall very soon now have to be thinking a great deal about our journey together in the summer of 1940, and my last sermons."[1758]

Dietrich was writing in coded language, just as he and his friends and family had been writing to each other for over a decade. This in spite of the fact that Dietrich's letters to Eberhard had bypassed the official censor, thanks to the trusted guard Corporal Knobloch. His "last sermons" given in the collective pastorates of East Prussia in 1940 just before he joined the Abwehr, were here used as an oblique reference to Hitler's Wolfsschanze headquarters,[1759] where indeed, the bomb would go off thirteen days hence. Nine days later on the 16th, just four days before the plot's execution, in another letter to Bethge, Dietrich would be even more direct. There, his reference to his brother Klaus meant simply that the conspiracy had achieved its objective: "I am glad that Klaus is in such good spirits; he was so depressed for some time. I think all his worries will soon be over; I very much hope for his own and the entire family's sake."[1760]

On the morning of Thursday July 20 1944, Stauffenberg arose at five, and before leaving, he told his brother Berthold, "We have crossed the Rubicon."[1761] While driving on the way to the now abandoned Rangsdorf Airport just south of Berlin,[1762] with his adjutant Werner von Haeften, they stopped at a Catholic chapel where Father Wehrle let Stauffenberg in to pray. Just ten days earlier, according to Pierre Galante and Eugene Silianoff, joint authors of *Operation Valkyrie: The German Generals' Plot Against Hitler*, Stauffenberg had asked Father Wehrle the burning and poignant question that had been on his mind for years. Namely, "Can the Church grant absolution to a murderer who has taken the life of a tyrant?"[1763]

This question had been posed by Dietrich to his students five or so years earlier in May 1939, just before he left for his second visit to New York: "Would you grant absolution to the murderer of a tyrant?"[1764] The difference between the questions regards who takes the onus of forgiveness; the identical theme is whether or not tyrannicide can be justified. Father Wehrle, while not categorically ruling out such a justification, qualified his response by stating that only the Pope could grant absolution in such a case, but promised he would look into it further. Moreover, twenty months earlier, in November 1942, Haeften had broached this very question to Dietrich, about four to five months before the latter's arrest.[1765]

In the aftermath of the plot, Father Wehrle was hauled before the dreaded People's Court and sentenced to be hung. According to Pierre Galante and Eugene Silianoff, Stauffenberg's question, in the eyes of the People's court, provided ample evidence of Stauffenberg's treasonable intent. Father Wehrle's defence hinged on the church's doctrine of the confidentiality of the confessional, but of course, this argument was dismissed with contempt by the People's Court.[1766] However, considering the fact that neither Stauffenberg nor Werner von Haeften were to survive the night of July 20-21, the question arises of how the People's court supposedly became aware of Father Hermann Wehrle's conversation with Stauffenberg.

In the autumn of 1943, Stauffenberg told a German cavalry officer, Major Ludwig Freiherr (Baron) von Leonrod, his comrade from the Bamberg cavalry regiment,[1767] about the plans for a coup. Leonrod was designated in the plans as liaison officer in military district VII (Munich). According to other sources, Leonrod came to Father Wehrle in December 1943[1768] for spiritual counsel and confession, in regard to tyrannicide. To which, according to the Roman Christendom blogspot, Father Wehrle gave him open spiritual counsel and advised him that it was moral if the tyrant had no legal right to be leader.[1769] On July 21 1944, the day following Valkyrie, Ludwig Freiherr von Leonrod was arrested by the Gestapo, sentenced to death by the People's Court on August 21 1944, and murdered five days later in Berlin-Plötzensee.[1770] Three weeks later,[1771] Father Wehrle would follow the Baron to the gallows.

Upon arrival at the airport, Stauffenberg proclaimed: "

> This is more than we dared hope for … Fate has offered us this opportunity, and I would not refuse it for anything in the world. I have searched my conscience, before God and before myself. This man is evil incarnate."[1772]

In the aftermath of the plot, Father Wehrle and all present would be among thousands to experience the vindictive retribution of the evil incarnate.

Their flight lasted three hours, arriving at Rastenburg at 10:15 a.m.,[1773] before they were picked up in a staff car and driven into the gloomy East Prussian woods surrounding Hitler's Lair. The gloom of the woods was matched as they drove past the foreboding barriers of the Lair — the pillbox fortifications, mine-fields, and electrified barbed wire fence, before passing the SS guards patrolling the area. Now in the so-called "safe" zone, all that remained was to assemble the bomb, arm it, then place it near the Führer at the conference, before slipping out of the room on some contrived excuse of needing to take an urgent phone call from Berlin, before it blew up. Then slip past the devoted SS guards, electrified fence, mine fields and pillbox fortifications. All these things Stauffenberg would indeed do, but one loose end, which he would not discover to his horror until hours after arriving back in Berlin, would be left hanging.

Right now, however, there were still two hours or more until the conference, allowing time for a late breakfast before Stauffenberg met with Fellgiebel, who was to inform the conspirators in Berlin when the bomb went off. As the chief of signals at OKW,[1774] he was able to effectively seal off the Wolfsschanze from the outside world by cutting off all communications such as phone, radio, and telegraph, to allow just enough time for the execution of the Valkyrie plans in Berlin.

After this meeting, Stauffenberg made his way to the office of General Keitel, the chief of OKW, for the routine preliminary conference briefing, where Keitel sprang some unwanted news. Mussolini, the Il Duce himself, was on his way, due at 2:30 p.m. Thus Stauffenberg's presentation to Hitler had to be brought forward thirty minutes to 12:30 p.m.[1775] Moreover, Keitel stressed that Hitler would be in a hurry, thus compelling Stauffenberg to greatly hasten things along during his presentation. Stauffenberg was now concerned that the meeting might be too brief for the fuse to detonate, and decided to trigger the fuse before his arrival at the meeting.

This was not the only nor the most unpleasant surprise that Keitel announced. Because of the sweltering heat, the conference was moved from the conference room in the underground bunker, to the above ground Lagebaracke.[1776] The underground bunker would have confined and hence greatly magnified the blast, eliminating the prospect of any survivors, including the elusive Führer.[1777] While this was certainly unwelcome news, and although he had removed one kilo of explosive while stopping the staff car in transit to the first checkpoint before tucking it under the seat,[1778] so as to lighten the load in his briefcase, Stauffenberg was still confident the bomb was powerful enough to achieve its objective,[1779] if placed close to the slippery Führer.

It was now already 12:20 p.m., just ten minutes before the revised commencement of the conference, and Stauffenberg had still not armed the bomb. He asked if he could take time to wash up, but realising that the latrine was not the most propitious place to arm the bomb, asked if it were possible for him to change his shirt in another room.[1780] Given the humid and sweltering conditions, it seemed a plausible enough request, which bought Stauffenberg barely enough time, alone with Haeften, to arm the bomb and change into the shirt that had wrapped it. When they reappeared, Keitel told them to hurry up, and they arrived at the conference a few minutes late.

As they started to walk, Keitel's adjutant John von Freyend offered to carry Stuaffenberg's briefcase. However, as von Freyend later testified, as he put out his hand and gripped its handle, Stauffenberg practically ripped the case from his grasp. Then, probably worried that his behaviour was arousing suspicion, he thought better of it and allowed von Freyend to carry it. At the same time, Stauffenberg explained that he wanted to be placed as close to the Führer as possible, since his hearing was very poor since the terrible injuries he suffered in Tunisia.[1781]

As they entered and saluted, Hitler brusquely returned their salute as General Heusinger was describing to Hitler the dire situation on the Eastern Front, minus the presence of Himmler and Göring. Stauffenberg took his place with the briefcase close to Hitler, knowing that if it were not to be moved, the blast should instantly kill his target. However, with just minutes now before detonation, Stauffenberg had to invoke the excuse to Keitel that he had to take an urgent call from Berlin in regard to revised troop reserves back in Berlin.[1782] Certainly, for someone to leave the presence of Adolf Hitler without his permission was unprecedented.

As Stauffenberg left the Lagebaracke, Colonel Brandt, the unwitting recipient of the bomb in the failed "brandy" bomb plot of March 1943[1783] to scatter Hitler's remains over the skies of Belarus, was now, again unwittingly, Hitler's saviour for perhaps his "ninth" life. As Brandt was leaning over the table to view the maps,[1784] he tipped over Stauffenberg's brief case, then placed it on the other side of one of the heavy oaken conference table's pillars, which were more than a metre-and-a-half thick.[1785] Unlike in previous botched attempts, the bomb did detonate, with many in the Lagebaracke perishing. But Hitler, now on the opposite side of one of the oaken table's heavy and thick pillars, survived with relatively minor injuries. Brandt, who had been standing right next to the bomb at the time of detonation, initially survived, but was among those who succumbed to their injuries.[1786]

When Stauffenberg, now about two hundred metres away, saw bluish-yellow flames shoot out the windows, accompanied by some of the high-ranking officers who moments earlier had been dully gazing at maps, he was in no doubt that Hitler was dead, and was only made aware of the horrible truth hours after his arrival in Berlin. For the plotters, after numerous scenarios of dud bombs enabling them to at least cover their tracks, the worst possible scenario, for which they had no contingency plans, was now confronting them.[1787] Namely, a detonating bomb with a surviving Führer made a fall-back concealment impossible, with gruesome consequences to follow. Moreover, how critical was Stauffenberg's dispensing of one kilo of explosive whilst in transit in the staff car?[1788]

What followed in Berlin was outright inaction by the plotters, although explanations for this differ. Nigel Jones states that Fellgiebel, responsible for the critical task of closing down Rastenburg's communications, saw with horror the sight of the Führer staggering out of the smoking debris of the Lagebaracke, supported by the ever-loyal Keitel, who was sobbing "My Führer; you're alive; you're alive!"[1789] While Keitel's beloved Führer was still alive, his secretary, Gertraud Junge, recalled, "The Führer looked very strange. His hair was standing on end, like quills on a hedgehog, and his clothes were in tatters. But in spite of all that he was ecstatic—after all, hadn't he survived?"[1790] As Hitler staggered away from the carnage, behind him four of his lieutenants lay dead or dying, while two others, including Brandt, had life-threatening injuries, and almost everyone else had suffered burns and/or shock and concussion.[1791] Later, Hitler, ever the romantic, had his now tattered pants sent to Eva with the following message: "I have sent you the uniform of that wretched day. Proof that Providence protects me and that we no longer have to fear our enemies."[1792]

Nigel Jones claims that the communications chief General Erich Fellgiebel, saw Hitler staggering from the scene of the bomb,[1793] and would have realised the danger of immediately cutting off communications as scheduled, since he would immediately attract attention and suspicion in this unplanned scenario. Ultimately, Hitler himself ordered a communications blackout until the perpetrators could be identified, although exceptions were made for the Nazi leadership and the Wehrmacht's higher command, including Fellgiebel himself, who could use his personal phone. It was at 1:30 p.m., Jones states,[1794] that Fellgiebel made the call to the Bendlerstrasse in Berlin: "the Führer is alive." However, according to Pierre Galante and Eugene Silianoff, Fellgiebel made the call to the Bendlerstrasse at 1 p.m.: "The bomb has exploded. Hitler is dead."[1795] This was the call the conspirators back in Berlin were hoping for, prompting Olbricht to contact Fromm's office with the order to immediately invoke Valkyrie. But Fromm stated that he was unwilling to do so merely on the grounds of one unsubstantiated report. He put a call through to Rastenburg, where Keitel answered the call and informed Fromm that the Führer was alive and barely wounded.[1796]

Whatever the reason may have been for the inaction of the plotters back in Berlin, when Stauffenberg finally arrived back at the Bendlerstrasse, after bluffing his way past several SS checkpoints at the Wolfsschanze,[1797] he was shocked to see that virtually nothing had been done in the three or so hours since the bomb exploded.[1798] It was just after 4 p.m. when Stauffenberg rang his cousin Cäsar von Hofacker in Paris with the news, which he believed was true, that Hitler was dead. When this news reached Karl Heinrich von Stülpnagel, the military governor of Occupied France, the Paris arm of Valkyrie was invoked, and by midnight, no fewer than 1200 SS, Gestapo, and SD passively submitted to arrest, upon which they were detained at the Fresnes prison and an old military fort at St Denis.[1799] Sadly, nowhere else in the Reich, nor in any other of the occupied territories, was Valkyrie as decisively implemented.[1800] As Nigel Jones stated: "

> Elsewhere in Germany and occupied Europe, the Valkyrie orders had met with more mixed results. Because the orders had gone out so belatedly from the Bendlerblock, some military commanders received the countermanding orders from Rastenburg first, causing much bewilderment. At Breslau in

the far east of Germany, the local military commanders met and decided not to support the putsch. At Hamburg, in contrast to Paris, local Nazi party and SS officers gathered at the office of the district Wehrmacht commander, General Wilhelm Wetzel, to drink mutual toasts in sherry and Martini, and assure one another that they would not be arresting each other."[1801]

There was never any doubt that the bomb exploded, and that there was no turning back for the conspirators, as they'd been able to do with all the previous botched attempts. Their only hope was to vigorously invoke Valkyrie before Stauffenberg's return, and amidst the confusion of the bomb blast's aftermath, to optimise their fleeting advantage of surprise.[1802] The consequences of such an action's failure, Hitler's retribution, would not be mitigated by any half-measures, dithering, or last-minute attempts to save their own skin. The irony of the Paris Valkyrie was that while it was invoked with the erroneous notion that Hitler was dead, it was successful, and if they had done likewise in Berlin, and arrested Fromm, regardless of Hitler's survival, the plot could have been successful in its ultimate objective — the removal of the National Socialist regime itself from power, rendered impotent by the arrest and liquidation of the SS, Gestapo and SD, its key organs of control. The conspirators' obsession over whether the Führer had survived, and their failure to plan for him surviving the bomb blast, rendered them impotent.

These were not the only shortcomings to plague the conspirators. There was also a dangerous complacency which had manifested itself in their loose talk, in which Stauffenberg's adjutant Werner von Haeften was a major culprit.[1803] Complacency was also evident in their naive notion that a subordinate would unquestioningly obey orders. In this respect, Dietrich's uncle, Major-General Paul von Hase, had his old-school Prussian officer's unshakeable faith in military discipline shattered at a critical juncture of the plot,[1804] followed by the consequences that all the plotters feared.

The conspirators, having squandered the best part of the afternoon with excessive prudence,[1805] decided, belatedly and haphazardly, to take key nerve-centres in the city centre, such as the telephone exchange, radio transmitters, the Ministry of the Interior, and the SS Barracks on the Prinz-Albrecht-Strasse. Hase entrusted Major Remer, commander of the Gross Deutschland Guards Batallion, decorated hero of the Eastern Front, and proud bearer of the Hitler Youth gold badge, to this mission, having earlier spurned the opportunity to have Remer transferred out of the way on assignment in Italy.[1806] Hase simply pointed out the objectives on a map to Remer, and explained that the Führer had met with an accident, and that at present, it was unknown whether or not the Führer was still alive. Remer raised no objections at this point, in spite of the fact that several of the buildings to be secured were not under military jurisdiction.[1807]

Upon return to his barracks, Remer assembled three companies in the courtyard and repeated Hase's instructions to his officers. However, Lieutenant Hagen, a "political education" officer and pre-war employee of the Propaganda Ministry, who was personally acquainted with Goebbels, found all this rather strange, and suggested to Remer that they confer personally with his former chief.[1808] Remer, it seems, did not require much convincing, and deployed his troops around the Propaganda Ministry, while he and Hagen went inside to confront Goebbels. Hase's complacency, beyond any shadow of a doubt, had doomed the conspirators; by now, Goebbels had spoken to Hitler on the phone. Remer was stunned by the news, and had trouble believing Goebbels, but Goebbels put a call through to Rastenburg and handed Remer the phone. Remer instantly stood to attention when he recognised Hitler's voice ordering him to take all measures to crush the plot, and promoting him to colonel.[1809] Remer immediately ordered the cordoning off of the Bendlerstrasse, and with it, the plotters' fate was sealed.

When Remer surrounded the Bendlerstrasse at around 9:15 p.m., a brief skirmish ensued, in which Stauffenberg was grazed on his right arm. At 10:30 p.m., Remer's battalion, which had made no attempt to occupy the building, was relieved by the SS. This accelerated events and ramped up the fear of the trapped conspirators; many tried to save their own skins by switching sides. In the heat of the moment, all sense of honour deserted them. One of them, Lieutenant Colonel Bodo von der Heyden, with pistol in hand, burst in upon Stauffenberg, and cried "Treason! Treason!"[1810] as he fired and wounded Stauffenberg in the back. Then he and his cohorts released Fromm from a nearby office where the conspirators had been holding him.

Fromm brandished a pistol and proclaimed, "Gentlemen, I'm going to treat you as you treated me. You are all guilty of treason and deserve to die. Put down your weapons."[1811] Later, Fromm declared that he had convened a court martial in the name of the Führer, condemning Olbricht, Stauffenberg, Haeften, and Quirnheim to death by firing squad in the Bendlerblock courtyard. In truth, Fromm convened the court martial not in the name of the Führer, but in his own name, to satisfy his proud assertion that he always ended up on the right side. While this was so for a brief time, it was not long before questions were asked of him, and it was deemed by the Gestapo that he was not energetic enough in suppressing the plot. After several sessions of torture, he was executed on March 19, 1945, in Brandenburg Prison,[1812] just three weeks before Dietrich's execution at Flossenbürg concentration camp in Bavaria.[1813]

Thus, Fromm outlived his victims by eight months. However, his name lives on as an infamous and disgraced opportunist, while Stauffenberg and his compatriots, not least his adjutant Werner von Haeften,[1814] live on as heroes in the memories of modern Germans. On July 20 1952, Eva Olbricht, the widow of General Friedrich Olbricht, laid the cornerstone for a memorial in the courtyard of the Bendlerblock, and on July 20 1968, the permanent memorial exhibit was opened; it became known as the Gedenkstätte Deutscher Widerstand (Memorial of the German Resistance). Furthermore, on July 20 1955, the former Bendlerstrasse was ceremoniously renamed "Stauffenbergstrasse."[1815]

Paris was the only place where the Valkyrie plot was completely successful.[1816] But even here, all the good work done was ruined by the vacillating conspirator Field Marshal Günther von Kluge. At the time, he was the commander of Army Group B fighting in the Normandy campaign,[1817] having just replaced Rommel following the serious injuries the latter suffered when his staff car was strafed by an Allied fighter on July 17 1944.[1818] Technically, Karl Heinrich von Stülpnagel, the military governor of Occupied France, who ultimately gave the order for the arrests, needed Kluge's authorisation.[1819] It was at this point that all his great work would be undone. At around 6 p.m., with the arrest orders already issued, Stülpnagel received a call from Kluge's headquarters at the Seine riverside chateau of La Roche-Guyon to report there by no later than 8 p.m.[1820] Stülpnagel left Colonel Hans Otfried von Linstow in charge in Paris before he and his party departed in two staff cars for their appointment at Kluge's Chateau headquarters, where they arrived at around 7:20 p.m.[1821] Kluge's reception was less than lukewarm.[1822]

While waiting for Stülpnagel's party, Kluge had been receiving conflicting reports as to whether or not Hitler was still alive. It was on this point, much in the vein of Fromm, that the stance taken by this man, a conspirator as crucial to the Paris Valkyrie as he was vacillating and weak, would be decided. General Beck had made phone calls to Kluge in the late afternoon to early evening and outlined to him the measures that had been taken in Berlin and throughout the territories. He had said,

"Kluge, listen to me, it's essential that you support the operation that's been launched in Berlin."[1823] To which the irresolute Kluge countered, "Is Hitler dead?"[1824]

At this moment Kluge was handed the text of a communiqué which had just been broadcast at 6.30 p.m. on Radio Berlin; it assured the world that although there had been a bomb explosion inside his Rastenburg headquarters, the Führer had escaped with only minor injuries. Kluge continued his conversation with Beck, asking, "What is the exact situation at GHQ [Rastenburg] right now?" To which Beck replied, "That will have little consequence as long as we take action. I'm going to put the question to you unequivocally, Kluge: do you approve of what we're doing here, and will you agree to be led by me?"[1825] Kluge, however, continued equivocating, citing the radio communiqué's assurance that Hitler was still alive. Beck continued to press him, reminding him of previous commitments he had made to their cause, and appealing for his unconditional support. Kluge made the excuse that he needed to consult with his staff, promising to call Beck back in half an hour. Kluge never called Beck back.[1826]

Before the arrival of Stülpnagel's party, more conflicting reports came in. However, it was Stieff who would prompt Kluge's final about-face. When Kluge's aide, Blumentritt, managed to get a call through to Stieff at Camp Anna, the OKH (Army High Command) Eastern Front Headquarters at Mauersee near Rastenburg, Stieff, without any thought for the consequences of the truth to a wavering Kluge,[1827] confirmed Radio Berlin's communiqué that the Führer was very much alive and exuberant. The conspirator's fate in France was now sealed. Hence Kluge's lukewarm reception for Stülpnagel's party upon their arrival.

Among Stülpnagel's entourage was Stauffenberg's cousin Cäsar von Hofacker; Stülpnagel was counting on Hofacker's eloquence and dash to win Kluge over, regardless of whether or not Hitler was dead. Hofacker's entreaties were forceful in their eloquence: "

> Since the autumn of '43, I've been acting as liason between Beck and his circle in Berlin, my cousin Stauffenberg's circle, and the movement that General Stülpnagel directed in Paris. But it doesn't much matter what happens in Berlin. [Hofacker now raises his voice and stares fixedly at Kluge.] What counts are the decisions that we're about to make here in France. I appeal to you, Marshall von Kluge, to take action on behalf of our country as Rommel would have done. I spoke to him in

this very place on the ninth. Free yourself from Hitler's spell and put yourself at the head of our movement in the west!"[1828]

But Kluge's disinterest fell far short of the degree of fortitude that the situation demanded. His response was to invite them to dinner, where he recounted stories of his time served on the Eastern Front while he ate heartily. For Stülpnagel and Hofacker it was not a pleasant dining experience, and their disinterest in Kluge's recollections of time served in the east matched Kluge's disinterest in the urgent situation at hand. When Stülpnagel asked Kluge straight out if he was aware that many officers had allowed themselves to be implicated in the conspiracy only because of the position Kluge had committed to in the past, coupled with his verbal attacks on Hitler, Kluge was dismissive and continued to eat heartily. Stülpnagel looked at Kluge, and said, "I'd like to have a word with you in private."[1829] Kluge paused, then stood up and motioned Stülpnagel to a small adjoining drawing room.

Moments later, the door was thrown open. Stülpnagel had revealed to Kluge that he had ordered the arrests in Paris in the hope that he, with Hofacker's support, could cajole Kluge into authorising the arrests without knowing that they were already authorised. Stülpnagel had ordered the Paris arrests believing that Kluge could be swayed face to face. But this gamble had backfired with dire consequences for the plotters in France, thanks to Field Marshal Günther von Kluge.

Before leaving, Hofacker made a final and desperate entreaty to Kluge:
"

> Herr Feldmarschall, your own and the army's honour are at stake and the destiny of millions of men rests in your hands."[1830]

To which Kluge replied: "

> Yes, if only the swine were dead … "[1831]

As Kluge escorted Stülpnagel down the steps to the chateau's courtyard where the general's car was waiting, he said: "

> Consider yourself suspended from duty. Get changed into civilian clothes and disappear until this has blown over."[1832]

Stülpnagel snapped a smart military salute and climbed into his car. Kluge bowed in response before the cars drove away into the night. It was 11 p.m.; the arrests in Paris were well under way.[1833] Unfortunately it would all be undone. After midnight, Stülpnagel's entourage arrived back in Paris in time to hear the triumphant Führer's radio address to the German Volk. They must have felt they were hearing their death sentences; at its end, Stülpnagel bowed to the inevitable and ordered the release of all arrested SS, SD and Gestapo personnel. Before noon, Stülpnagel was summoned to Berlin; on the way there, the car stopped some way off the main road, near the site of the famous Battle of Verdun in 1916, ostensibly for Stülpnagel to stretch his legs and have some time alone. Ten or so minutes later, the driver Schauf and the man accompanying him, Fischer, heard a gunshot. They found a body floating in a canal.

When Stülpnagel's body was retrieved from the canal, he was still alive in spite of being shot through the right temple. The rescuers thought he had been shot by French "terrorists," and required urgent medical attention at the German military hospital at Verdun. However, it was clear to the medical staff that the gunshot wound was self-inflicted, with the intention of ending his life in the very place where he had fought in the preceding Great War.[1834] Stülpnagel survived with permanent loss of his eyesight, but upon his "recovery," the SS took him to Berlin to face Freisler's People's Court and ultimately, the gallows. While he was recovering in Verdun, the bespectacled "butcher of Paris,"[1835] General Carl Oberg of the SS, paid Stülpnagel a "visit" by his bedside. Stülpnagel readily took full responsibility for his actions, conditional on his family escaping any retribution. However, with the ancient Sippenhaft law invoked,[1836] any hope that this condition would be honoured was forlorn.[1837]

Back in Paris, Hofacker hoped to get his family to safety before making his way to Switzerland or joining the French Resistance. But before there was time to do so, the Gestapo agent Maulaz arrested Hofacker on July 25, the same day that Oberg paid his visit to Stülpnagel in Verdun. Given Hofacker's elite status in the French Valkyrie, the Gestapo were counting on him as a gold mine of information, at least under torture. However, Stauffenberg's cousin remained defiantly silent until the very end, five months later, on December 20 1944, when he became the final victim of the July 20 plot in Paris.[1838] He was tried on August 30 alongside other conspirators of the French Valkyrie, such as Hans Otfried von Linstow, Eberhard Finckh and Karl Heinrich von Stülpnagel; he was the only one not executed immediately post-trial. That may have been due to his dauntless spirit, when he refused to be cowed by Freisler's rants, claiming that he had had as much right to revolt against Hitler on July 20 as Hitler had to rise against the Weimar republic in Munich on November 9 1923 (Munich Beer Hall Putsch).[1839] He proclaimed: "My only regret was that my maimed cousin, rather than I, had been chosen to place the bomb, since, had it been me, it would not have failed." When Freisler, outraged, tried to silence Hofacker, he replied: "Be quiet now, Herr Freisler, because to-day it's my neck on the block — but in a year's time, it will be yours."[1840]

Hofacker's taunt was vindicated five or so months later when Freisler died in his own court during an American bombing raid of Berlin on February 3 1945.[1841] Moreover, thanks to the stoicism of Hofacker, along with his fellow conspirators, Stülpnagel, von Linstow, and Finckh when they held out against their tormentors in Freisler's court, the rest of the conspirators in France for the most part escaped charges. The wily Swabian Hans Speidel, successively Rommel's and then Kluge's Chief of Staff, was detained, but thanks in part to protection given by his friend Guderian, he managed to talk his way out of trouble without implicating anyone. He would survive the war, where he would resume his military career in the post-war West German army as a top NATO commander.[1842]

Freisler's s attitude to the course of the war could, on the face of it, be explained as the delusion of a National Socialist zealot. This is an over-simplification. Others were less blinded, such as Adolf Heusinger, the general who briefed Hitler on the disastrous situation unravelling on the Eastern Front in the minutes before Stauffenberg's bomb exploded, surviving the blast. He was incarcerated in the aftermath in Berlin's Gestapo prison on the Prinz-Albrecht-Strasse, in spite of his arms, legs, and face being badly burned and both his eardrums pierced.[1843] He was released in September, and made his way to his family, taking refuge in the Harz Mountains. There he was kept under close surveillance by the Gestapo until the end of March 1945, by which time the Americans were already approaching. He made his way south to Lake Konstanz in an attempt to cross the border into Switzerland. It was during this trek that he met a civilian electrician in his fifties, who remarked: "It seems to me, general, that we're going to lose the war." To which Heusinger replied: "Here we are in March 1945, and it's taken you until now to figure that out?"[1844] Heusinger never made it to Switzerland, and surrendered to the Americans in May 1945. However, like Speidel, he resumed his military career post-war as a top NATO commander.[1845]

The spell of Hitler was not just confined to zealots within the National Socialist Party such as Roland Freisler. The eventual arrest of Carl Goerdeler is another case in point. In the aftermath of the plot, Goerdeler, with the help of a Protestant pastor, attempted to escape to Sweden. When this proved impossible, he set out on foot for Königsberg in East Prussia (modern-day Kaliningrad in the Baltic Russian enclave)[1846] with a price of ten million marks on his head, dead or alive. At the end of August, when he was still in his native East Prussia, a woman who had once worked for his family recognised him in a village tavern, and reported her sighting to the local police. It might seem that the ten million mark bounty on Goerdeler was her prime incentive, but post-war, this woman explained that since the Führer was always right, then Goerdeler must have been a monstrous criminal. Moreover, she had not spent a single pfennig of her blood money.[1847]

Like Stauffenberg's children, Goerdeler's younger daughter, Nina, who was not yet fourteen, and his two grandchildren, were dispatched to an SS "children's village" to be brought up under a different name, while the rest of the family was dispersed to Dachau, Buchenwald and several other camps. They were eventually liberated by the Allies, but Goerdeler himself was executed on February 2 1945, along with Johannes Popitz, former Prussian Minister of Finance, a distinguished member of Beck's Wednesday Club, and Father Delp, a Jesuit who was associated with the Moltke group.[1848]

And what of Field Marshal Günther von Kluge, supreme commander of France? To begin with, when Blumentritt phoned Kluge to inform him of Stülpnagel's summons to Berlin, Kluge simply said ,"Well, it's starting then..."[1849] before hanging up and taking care of the next order of business. Which was to send an effusive telegram to the Führer congratulating him on his providential escape. Hitler, however, saw right through it, summoning Kluge to Berlin about a month later on the evening of August 17.[1850] At dawn on the 19th, six days before the liberation of Paris,[1851] Kluge took much the same route through the battlegrounds of the Great War as Stülpnagel, where he likewise had served. Sensing the inevitable, he committed suicide by taking a cyanide pill.[1852] Thus, Kluge's vacillation and attempts at playing both sides had purchased him about a month more of life. In many respects his end mirrored the actions and fate of General Friedrich Fromm.

Hitler's wounds paled into insignificance in the euphoria of survival, which he proclaimed was a divine vindication of his work, in his radio address from Rastenburg around midnight. While listening to this address, Stülpnagel, Hofacker and co in Paris realised they were hearing the proclamation of their respective death sentences,[1853] as the final scenes at the Bendlerstrasse were still being played out:[1854] "

> My German comrades!
>
> If I speak to you today it is first in order that you should hear my voice and should know that I am unhurt and well, and secondly, that you should know of a crime unparalleled in German history.
>
> A very small clique of ambitious, irresponsible and, at the same time, senseless and stupid officers had concocted a plot to eliminate me and, with me, the staff of the High Command of the Wehrmacht.
>
> The bomb planted by Colonel Count Stauffenberg exploded two metres to the right of me. I t seriously wounded a number of my true and loyal collaborators, one of whom has died. I myself am entirely unhurt, aside from some very minor scratches, bruises and burns. I regard this as confirmation of the task imposed upon me by Providence …
>
> The circle of these usurpers is very small and has nothing in common with the spirit of the German Wehrmacht and, above all, none with the German people. It is a gang of criminal elements which will be destroyed without mercy.
>
> I therefore give orders now that no military authority … is to obey orders from this crew of usurpers. I also order that it is everyone's duty to arrest, or, if they resist, to shoot at sight, anyone issuing or handling such orders …
>
> This time, we shall settle accounts with them in the manner to which we National Socialists are accustomed."[1855]

Three or so hours after the explosion, Hitler showed Mussolini the bomb damage, to which the deposed Duce declared: "You are right, Führer. Heaven has helped protect and defend you. After this miracle, it is inconceivable that our cause could come to any harm."[1856] Present too in Rastenburg were Göring and Admiral Dönitz, the latter being the one to briefly succeed Hitler upon his suicide in late April 1945.[1857] Both were no less effusive than the Duce about divine intervention and Providence vindicating their beloved Führer.[1858] This was also affirmed by Jacques de Lesdain, the French collaborator in Paris, writing in *L'Illustration*: "

> I have always been at some pains, to implant in the minds of my readers the conviction, nay the certainty, that the armies of the Reich will be quite capable of throwing back the enemy on the day the supreme command decides to unleash their reserves. The fact that the Führer has emerged unscathed from a frightful ordeal that was actuated by the blackest treachery and perfidy cannot be explained as mere happen stance. The sort of chance which on several widely separated occasions has preserved the life of a man whose death had been envisaged by a meticulously planned conspiracy deserves the name of Providence or Destiny.
>
> ... The creation of a new Europe is even more of a certainty today than it was before the tragic events of the twentieth of July."[1859]

Thirty-six days following the Valkyrie plot, and in the midst of the heroic but tragic Warsaw General Uprising,[1860] Paris, in stark contrast, on August 25, experienced true liberation. Jacques de Lesdain, the collaborator, fled to the Sigmaringen Castle in the Swabian Alp region of Baden-Württemberg in south-western Germany with members of the like-minded Vichy French government.[1861] There he would serve as their Director of Broadcasting and survived the war, living until 1975 as a free man.

As for Stauffenberg's family, his then pregnant wife Nina was arrested on July 23, but not before explaining to her three boys and three-and-a-half-year-old daughter Valerie the reason for their father carrying out the failed assassination plot — namely, to save Germany.[1862] After she was taken into investigative custody at the Berlin Police Presidium on Alexanderplatz, she was transferred to the Nazi concentration camp for women at Ravensbrück, and incarcerated in an annex kept by the Gestapo. When the birth of her fifth child was imminent, she was taken to a maternity home at Frankfurt an der Oder, where, on January 17 1945, Konstanze was born, just days before they were forced to evacuate by hospital train before the advancing of Soviet troops.[1863]

During the evacuation, she and Konstanze contracted an infection and were thus taken under false names with Gestapo guards to a Catholic hospital in Potsdam. After they recovered, they were escorted by a military policeman to join the other Sippenhaft prisoners who were at that time in Schönberg. In transit, the policeman, considering such a duty beneath him, and wanting to go home, simply deposited Nina and Konstanze in a village near Hof in north-eastern Bavaria after obtaining from Nina a written certificate that he had more than performed his duty. This dereliction of duty worked in their favour, for when the Americans arrived in the village, Nina, quite by chance, became the first of the Sippenhaft prisoners to be liberated. However, it was not until 1953 that she and her children were able to return to their family home in Bamberg.[1864]

On August 16, following a month or so of house arrest, the order arrived that the children — Berthold, ten years old, Heimeran, eight, Franz-Ludwig, six, and Valerie, three and a half; along with their cousins, aged six and five, were to be taken to a children's home at Bad Sachsa in the southern Harz mountains.[1865] This home had been founded by the Bremen businessman Daniel Schnackenberg, but in 1936 it had been taken over by the Bremen Nazi party as the Bremen children's home.[1866] With its Black Forest style wooden houses, it seemed picturesque and idyllic, and according to the eldest child, Berthold, he and his siblings had no bad memories of the place, despite the material shortages for the general German population, and the almost daily terror of air raids in the cities.

Only fourteen children remained at the home by Christmas 1944, and they were all accommodated into just one house. There were six Stauffenbergs, including the children of Claus's brother Berthold, along with those of Claus's cousin Cäsar von Hofacker. Among those not related to the Stauffenbergs were the daughter of General Lindemann, who was the same age as Berthold, as well as two grandchildren of Carl von Goerdeler and two other little girls. Then, as they hardly had settled into their new arrangement, the home was taken over by the Wehrmacht, where it became the top-secret Unit 00400, which was the staff headquarters for the nearby V-weapons rocket program. Moreover, Bad Sachsa was very close to the notorious Mittelbau forced labour underground rocket factory and the Dora concentration camp.[1867]

At Easter, they faced the prospect of being transferred to the Buchenwald concentration camp, where they were told their families were being held. However, they never reached the camp, because after being placed in a Wehrmacht transport vehicle, and taken to the outer suburbs of Nordhausen, where they were to board a train, a terrible air raid began, destroying the town and the railway station. Fortunately, the children survived and where thus returned to Bad Sachsa, where, just days later on April 12, the Americans arrived.[1868]

Suddenly, on June 1945, with the war in Europe now over, their Great Aunt Alexandrine, who had been a prisoner, together with other Sippenhaft detainees and many other prominent prisoners of the Nazis, arrived in a car with French number plates. She wasted no time in arranging a bus to drive the children back through a devastated Germany to the Stauffenberg country home at Lautlingen, where they arrived on June 13 1945. There, they were greeted by the scene of occupying French-Moroccan troops, who were given free rein for one long day to plunder, with the local populace being given "permission" to seek sanctuary in the castle garden and in the church in order to protect themselves from assault and rape. Fortunately, just weeks later in early July, the whereabouts of their mother Nina in a village near Hof was made known to them.[1869]

Nina would live on long after the war, well into the next millennium in fact, passing away in 2006. In retrospect, while always supporting her husband, she thought the heroic failure of the plan resonated more down the years than a successful coup might have done;[1870] there are some among the surviving conspirators, and others from this era, who agree with her. My father is one. Hitler's cowardly death by his own hand to escape the consequences of his crimes was far more appropriate than a martyr's death. Perhaps this was the true fulfilment of his and his collaborators' so-called "Providence."

Nina, though born a Lutheran of German-Baltic stock, brought up her children in the Catholic faith.[1871] The eldest, Berthold, named after his uncle and father's brother and fellow conspirator who ended up in Freisler's court, would take up a career in the German military, attaining the rank of general. He mentioned that he did not take up this career because of his father, but rather, in spite of the fact that he would forever be living in his father's shadow, and bearing the repeated annoyance of the question "Are you your father's son?"[1872] While the official line of the modern-day German government is rightly to eulogise Berthold's father as a hero, he has overheard many an outspoken messroom discussion when his father was labelled a traitor.[1873] Berthold believes that, while some may have been bound to the oath to Hitler in good faith, some used it as an alibi to excuse them from taking part in the conspiracy.[1874]

In 1999, a precious family memento reappeared after five-and-a-half decades. It was Claus's Sword of Honour, awarded to him in 1929 by the Chief of Staff of the army for being the best cavalry graduate of that year. It had disappeared following the Valkyrie plot, more than likely looted by the Berlin Gestapo, from which it eventually found its way into the hands of Max Reimann, the post-war chairman of the Communist Party of Germany (KPD). By the 1960s it was in the hands of the chairman of the West German Communist Party (DKP), Herbert Mies, who had never been able to locate a single member of the Stauffenberg family until 1999, when at last, the sword found its way back to Nina, who treasured it as a precious memento until her death in 2006. [1875] It is now on display in the Stauffenberg exhibition in Stuttgart's Old Castle.

Berthold described the twelve months post-Valkyrie and beyond as follows: "

> In hindsight, the months from July 1944 to June 1945 marked me indelibly for the rest of my life, and for this reason I would not have missed them. The same goes for the materially even more difficult post-war time. Like most of my contemporaries, especially the war orphans, these times taught us the seriousness of life through our own eyes in a manner that today's younger generation — on whom I would never wish it — must fail to understand. We certainly grew up faster, and were continually aware that we had to stand on our own two feet rather earlier than normal. And that we did, yet from all of us something upright grew. I have been ever thankful since 1945 above all for one thing: that practically all our family were finally and happily re-united. We certainly mourned my grandmother who died in a concentration camp, even though she had never borne the name Stauffenberg; and also grieved for my shot-down aviator aunt, but we still came through it all. Among our regular evening prayers was the sentence: "Dear Lord, we thank thee that thou has reunited us again."[1876]

Several more of the conspirators should be mentioned. There is the timid General Hellmuth Stieff and the more resilient Henning von Tresckow, Oma Ruth's nephew, as well as his adjutant and dear friend Fabian von Schlabrendorff, married to Oma Ruth's granddaughter Luitgarde née Bismarck.[1877] Stieff, while often labelled timid, was of stronger character than Kluge, even though, when Kluge phoned him to ascertain whether or not Hitler survived the blast, he lacked the presence of mind, or perhaps the fortitude, to utter the white lie the situation demanded when dealing with such a wavering character.[1878] Stieff, the youngest general in the German army, and also probably the shortest, achieved early promotion thanks to his exceptional organisational abilities. He was arrested within hours of his phone conversation with Kulge on the evening of July 20. Despite brutal torture, Stieff was remarkably resolute in the face of his tormentors and Freisler's rants in court. He was among the first to be hanged on August 8. His letters to his wife remain as a moving testament to the German Resistance.[1879]

Two days later, Claus's brother Berthold was executed, as were General Erich Fellgiebel and Fritz-Dietlof von der Schulenberg. Fellgiebel, the Wolfsschanze communications chief, mocked Freisler's perception of the course of the war, when he "urged" Freisler to "hurry up and get on with the hangings, or he would find himself hanged first!" In similar vein, a few weeks later, when the Catholic lawyer Josef Wirmer was told by the judge that he would soon be roasting in hell, Wirmer bowed and remarked: "It will be a pleasure to welcome you there soon afterwards, your honour!"[1880]

Henning von Tresckow, the man who urged Stauffenberg on when he momentarily faltered in the wake of the D-day landings in early June 1944,[1881] ended up killing himself with a rifle grenade in the front lines. This was to feign an exchange of fire with the enemy on July 21 1944, when he became aware of the failure of the putsch. His body was disinterred by Hitler's henchmen when they realised the extent of his plotting, and cremated at Sachsenhausen concentration camp before the horrified eyes of his former adjutant Fabian von Schlabrendorff,[1882] who, by a twist of fate, would survive the war until 1980.[xxv] Upon meeting his cousin Henning for the last time, von Tresckow resolutely affirmed: "

> Now they will all fall upon us and cover us with abuse. But I am convinced, now as much as ever, that we have done the right thing. I believe Hitler to be the arch enemy, not only of Germany, but indeed of the entire world. In a few hours time, I

[xxv] Fabian's miraculous survival post-war will be described in detail in Chapter 27 "The Prominenten and Miraculous Reprieves."

shall stand before God and answer for both my actions and the things I neglected to do. I think I can, with a clear conscience, stand by all I have done in the battle against Hitler."[1883]

Tresckow's wife Erika née von Falkenhayn endured seven weeks of Gestapo interrogation at the Prinz-Albrecht-Strassse prison, but upon release on October 2 1944,[1884] a few days before Dietrich's transfer there from Tegel, she survived the war until 1974, aged 69.[1885] As already mentioned, she and Margarete von Oven had been entrusted with the written documentation for Valkyrie, but had most prudently worn gloves when handling the documents, thus denying the Gestapo any incriminating fingerprints.[1886]

Tresckow and Schlabrendorff were the masterminds behind the "brandy bottle" plot of March 1943. While eventually Schlabrendorff was put on trial at Freisler's People's Court, this delay proved to be fortunate for Schlabrendorff when Freisler was killed in the American air raid on February 3 1945,[1887] while hearing Schlabrendorff's case![1888] On the face of it, this should only have given Schlabrendorff a brief reprieve, but the replacement judge acquitted him on the grounds that he had been tortured. The torture had induced a heart attack,[1889] but Schlabrendorff only implicated his now dead cousin Henning.

Hitler had him immediately re-arrested, and rather than having him re-tried in the People's Court, had him held with other prominent prisoners in various concentration camps, while the territory of the Reich imploded. Incredibly, he survived the war; while in transit under SS guard in the idyllic town of Niederdorf in the German-speaking Tyrol region of northern Italy, his party of fellow prisoners, known as "Hostages of the SS," "Special Prisoners" or "Prominenten — Prominent Prisoners,"[1890] were liberated by Wehrmacht troops confronting the SS at gunpoint as Allies troops advanced.[1891] Post-war, he wrote one of the earliest histories of the Resistance and resumed his auspicious legal career, which included eight or so years as a judge of West Germany's constitutional court between 1967 and 1975.[1892]

Accompanying Fabian, among the 139 prisoners liberated at Niederdorf on April 30 1945, the very day Hitler performed his final act, were numerous Stauffenbergs and Goerdelers, including Alexander Schenk Graf von Stauffenberg, Claus's brother, and Jutta Tominski née Goerdeler, and her cousin Benigna Klemm née von Goerdeler, the fourteen-year-old daughter of Carl von Goerdeler, who had been executed in the wake of Valkyrie. Among the foreign prisoners were Vasily Vasilyevich Kokorin, a Lieutenant of the Soviet Air Force, prisoner since

1942 and nephew of Vyacheslav Mikhailovich Molotov, Stalin's Foreign minister. Among the British contingent were Bertram Arthur "Jimmy" James, a pilot officer of the RAF, and one of the escapees in the March 1944 "Great Escape"; upon recapture , he avoided Gestapo retribution, before becoming one of the "Hostages of the SS,"[1893] or "Prominenten — Prominent Prisoners."[1894]

As head of the SS, Heinrich Himmler's wishful plan was that the hostages could be used as bargaining chips by the Reich in any possible peace negotiations. Nevertheless, the prisoners were at the mercy of the impulsive and unpredictable SS commander Untersturmführer Ernst Bader, who gave the impression that he could execute anybody if he merely woke up on the wrong side of bed.[1895] This man, whom the Wehrmacht were forced to threaten at gunpoint as he drew his pistol upon them, survived the war as a free man, becoming a police officer.[1896]

As for Freisler, who was present at the infamous Wannsee Conference in January 1942,[1897] his idol was none other than Andrei Vyshinsky — the bespectacled legal terrorist who had presided over the show trials of Stalin's leading victims in the 1930s.[1898] Hence, Freisler making a special study of the techniques used by Vyshinsky.[1899] In the Great War, Freisler was taken prisoner by the Russians in 1915 while the Tsarist regime was still in power. However, he did not return to Germany until after the war, well after the Bolshevik October Revolution in 1917, by which time he had learned fluent Russian,[1900] and had assumed the role of camp commissar in charge of food supplies.[1901] Upon his return to Germany, he resumed his law studies, but throughout his career, he was dogged by the tag "Commissar with the Reds," or by Hitler, as that "Old Bolshevik"[1902] or "our Vyshinsky,"[1903] when Hitler overlooked him for the post as justice minister, although he had joined the Nazi Party in 1925.[1904] However, in the wake of the Valkyrie plot, Hitler appreciated Freisler more than ever before for his skills as a twisted jurist whose speciality was heaping abuse on his victims, bawled out in a raucous roar that rivalled Hitler's own,[1905] and indeed, that of Vyshinsky.[1906]

From the moment of Valkyrie's execution on July 20 1944 to the end of the war in Europe on May 8 1945, 292 days had passed, during which, it is estimated that in Europe, over ten million[1907] soldiers and civilians had died. It could be argued that over ten million lives would have been saved if Valkyrie had succeeded. Moorhouse however, suggests that even if the plotters had enjoyed better luck, and prosecuted their coup more decisively, the outcome would have been problematic.

The fact was that they enjoyed precious little popular support and even less international sympathy, and would have had to confront massed ranks of the Gestapo and SS, as well as countless regular army troops and civilians who still felt bound by their oath of loyalty.[1908] A case in point was Major Remer, commander of the Gross Deutschland Guards Batallion, whom Dietrich's distinguished uncle, Paul von Hase, mistakenly believed he could control.[1909] With a negotiated peace well and truly out of the question, the scene could have been set for a bitter civil war in the Reich homeland, against the backdrop of the oncoming fronts from east and west.[1910] The question, "what if" Valkyrie had succeeded opens a Pandora's box. Certainly, Hitler's secretary Gertraud "Traudl" Junge née Humps believed that the war would have ended if Valkyrie succeeded, declaring: "

> I don't know what would have happened if the assassination had succeeded. All I see is millions of soldiers now lying buried somewhere, gone for ever, who might instead have come home again, their guns silent and the sky quieter once more. The war would have been over."[1911]

But what terms would this peace have entailed, if it were indeed possible? Perhaps, what is more important than the success of the plot itself, as von Tresckow put it, was that it proved to the world that a part of the old and honourable Germany still existed, although the Western Allies had not recognised it at the time. This was Tresckow's message to Stauffenberg when he momentarily faltered in the wake of the successful Allied D-Day landings.[1912] Stauffenberg's wife Nina would concur with this sentiment.[1913]

Cynics may question the motivation of the conspirators, claiming, with some basis, that it was influenced by the lamentable course of the war for Germany. They would point to Stauffenberg's support of Hitler in 1933, and even until the end of 1941,[1914] when Hitler assumed supreme command of all armed forces in the wake of the Moscow winter disaster. However, it seems as 1942 wore on,[1915] with news of mass genocide in the east, culminating with the Stalingrad disaster in early 1943, Stauffenberg crossed the Rubicon, and from then on he was unfalteringly committed to the conspiracy.

Others, such as the quiet and bespectacled Friedrich Olbricht who had recruited Stauffenberg to the conspiracy,[1916] had decided upon his course in 1940,[1917] when Nazi power was riding high in the wake of the French conquest. Others such as General Ludwig Beck and Hans Oster were committed to the conspiracy well before the outbreak of war. Henning von Tresckow, awarded the Iron Cross as a seventeen year-old Lieutenant in the Great War,[1918] was initially dazzled by Hitler and his cohorts in 1933 when they revoked the humiliation of Versailles, but his eyes were opened to the true nature of the Nazi regime by its lawless Röhm purge in 1934 (Night of the Long Knives).[1919] Next, the Fritsch—Blomberg affair and Hitler's reckless gamble, threatening war with Czechoslovakia, both in 1938, shocked him deeply, and the last straw was the release of the genocidal Einsatzgruppen on the Polish population at the outbreak of war. This prompted Tresckow to declare to his friends, "Hitler is a whirling Dervish. He must be shot down."[1920]

It would be difficult to find a German military figure, especially among those who served in the Great War, who was not at least initially seduced by Hitler's decisive revocation of the humiliating Versailles Treaty. Dietrich, however, was never a military figure, and was only twelve years old in November 1918. As a dedicated young pastor whose judgement was not clouded by Versailles, he could see the dark and ominous clouds on the horizon immediately upon his return from America in June 1931,[1921] eighteen or so months before Weimar politicians such as Franz von Papen would allow Hitler to head a minority government from which they believed they could "control" the ranting Austrian and have him "squeaking" within two months.[1922] Had Dietrich not been absent for nine months in America, with the 1930 elections taking place a few days after his arrival in New York he would no doubt, have seen these ominous clouds months earlier. At home that year, the Nazi Party was elevated from an abject joke in the pre-depression year of 1928 to the party with the second largest primary national vote of 18%, with the depression in full swing.[1923]

Winston Churchill perceived the German plotters as opportunists motivated purely by the lamentable course of the war, especially by July 1944. Their only friend in the British parliament was Dietrich's close friend Bishop George Bell; Anthony Eden, the British Foreign minister, was no less hostile towards them than Churchill.[1924] Moreover, Eden's feeling of hostility towards the German conspirators was somewhat mirrored in his attitude to Britain's First Ally, the Polish Government in exile, with its more than legitimate, albeit "awkward" and "annoying" desire for true Polish independence post-war. Put another way, if the Allied governments were amenable to the betrayal of the First Ally in order to appease their giant Soviet ally, exemplified by their whitewash of the Stalinist perpetrated April 1940 Katyń Wood Massacre,[1925] it follows that the German conspirators would be treated as pariahs by the Western Allies.[1926]

In the aftermath of the plot, there was still one church newspaper operating in the Third Reich. It saw the failed plot as: "

> The frightful day. While our brave armies, courageous unto death, are struggling manfully to protect their country and to achieve final victory, a handful of infamous officers, driven by their own ambition, ventured on a frightful crime and made an attempt to murder the Führer. The Führer was saved and thus unspeakable disaster averted from our people. For this we give thanks to God with all our hearts and pray, with all our church, congregations, for God's assistance and help in the grave tasks that the Führer has to perform in the most difficult times."[1927]

On Wednesday August 9 1944, the *New York Times* declared: "

> In point of fact, the details of the plot suggest more the atmosphere of a gangsters' lurid underworld then the normal atmosphere one would expect within an officers' corps and a civilized Government. For there were some of the highest officers of the German Army ... plotting for a year to kidnap or kill the head of the German state and Commander in Chief of its army; postponing the execution of the plot repeatedly in order to kill his high executioner as well; and finally carrying it out by means of a bomb, the typical weapon of the underworld.

> All this is so contrary to all the tenets of the "Code of Potsdam" that the world is still skeptical as to whether it is all true. Yet there is no reason to doubt the essential truth of the plot itself. And the truth is merely evidence that the underworld mentality and methods which the Nazis brought from their gutters and enthroned on the highest levels of German life have begun to pervade the officers' corps as well, and were, in fact, considered to be the only effective weapons against the Nazis themselves. For, knowing that many of their number had already fallen victim to Nazi terror, the dissident officers obviously came to the

conclusion that this terror could only be met with counter-terror as the necessary preliminary to their contemplated coup d'etat. Their tragedy was that while they were willing to stoop to Nazi methods they lacked the Nazi cunning to make effective use of them. And so they were hanged."[1928]

When the truth of the death camps was revealed months later, with the liberation of Auschwitz on January 27 1945 by Soviet forces,[1929] and camps such as Dachau and others to the west opened later by American and British forces, one wonders whether the *New York Times* revised their image of the "civilised head of the German state and commander in chief of the Army"? On the other side of the Atlantic, Churchill, on Wednesday August 2 1944 in a speech to the House of Commons, referred to the plotters as: "The highest personalities in the German Reich murdering one another."[1930] Robert B. Kane, however, Chief Historian of the Air University at Maxwell Air Force Base in Alabama,[1931] in his assessment of the *New York Times* editorial, puts it this way: "

> While the editor provided some elements of truth in his assessment, he missed the psychological struggle that had to take place before these officers could even act. His comparison of the attempted coup to the American gangster underworld is most certainly an injustice to these tragic men who finally 'came to their senses' to end Hitler's crimes."[1932]

The editor of the New York Times was, like most of the world at the time, still ignorant of crimes such as the unmitigated horror of the concentration camps. Dietrich's twin sister Sabine wrote in her book postwar: "

> Nowhere in the English Press was any appreciation to be found of the events of the 20th of July. Hitler's statement that the attempt was the work of a clique of officers who were merely ambitious to seize power, was accepted without question."[1933]

Aside from Churchill and Eden's appeasement of the Soviet Union post-Barbarossa, we must remember the disgraceful 1938 Czech-Sudeten episode, where the Czechs were not the only ones betrayed by British and French appeasement led by Neville Chamberlain. Many

German generals testified in the post-war Nuremberg trials that if the French and British had stood up to Hitler, any invasion would have failed,[1934] especially given the formidable Czech mountain fortifications. Amid this failure, with Hitler's plunge in popular support, his position would have become untenable, presenting the German conspirators with an ideal opportunity to launch their putsch.

To that end, in August 1938, Ewald von Kleist-Schmenzin travelled to London to meet with representatives of His Majesty's Government. Unbeknownst to him, Sir Nevile Meyrick Henderson, the British ambassador to Germany, who was already most anxious to give Hitler whatever he wanted, advised the British Foreign Office that "it would be unwise for him [Kleist] to be received in official quarters."[1935] Indeed, according to a German Foreign Office memorandum of August 6 1938, Henderson had remarked to the Germans present at a private party "that Great Britain would not think of risking even one sailor or airman for Czechoslovakia, and that any 'reasonable solution' would be agreed to so long as it were not attempted by force."[1936] Hence, some observers believed that Henderson was more influential in implementing the appeasement policy than Chamberlain himself.[1937]

Nevertheless, Sir Robert Vansittart, chief diplomatic adviser to the Foreign Secretary, and, unlike Henderson, one of the leading opponents in London to the appeasement of Hitler, met with Ewald on the afternoon of his arrival on August 18, 1938. The following day, so did Winston Churchill, in spite of the latter still being in the political wilderness.[1938] Both men were impressed by their visitor's sobriety and sincerity, as Ewald, in accordance with his orders, stressed that Hitler had set a date for aggression against the Czechs, and that the generals, most of whom opposed him, would act, but further British appeasement of Hitler would cut the ground from under their feet (as it indeed did). If however, Britain and France would declare publicly that they would not stand idly by while Hitler threw his armies into Czechoslovakia, and if some prominent British statesman would issue a solemn warning to Germany of the consequences of Nazi aggression, then the German generals, for their part, would act to stop Hitler.[1939]

Ewald's entreaty prompted Churchill to give Ewald a ringing letter to take back to Germany to uplift the spirit of his colleagues:[1940] "

> I am certain as I was at the end of July 1914 that England will march with France, and certainly the United States is now strongly anti-Nazi. It is difficult for democracies to make precise declarations, but the spectacle of an armed attack by Ger-

many upon a small neighbour and the bloody fighting that will follow will rouse the whole British Empire and compel the gravest decisions. Do not I pray you, be misled on this point. Such a war, once started, would be fought out like the last to the bitter end, and one must consider not what might happen in the first few months, but where we should all be at the end of the third or fourth year."[1941]

But Chamberlain betrayed the Czechs and scuttled the German conspirators. Upon his arrival back in Britain, the piece of paper he waved, rather than securing "peace for our time," was the guarantor of the greatest conflict of all time. Moreover, during the aptly named "Phoney War" from the conquest of Poland in early October 1939[1942] to the invasion of Norway in early April 1940, Chamberlain based his unwillingness to engage with the Germans on a desperate hope that the German people would overthrow Hitler.[1943] This, after he had scuttled the realistic hope in 1938.

Of the many critics who have questioned the true motives of all the German conspirators, one of the more zealous is Christian Gerlach, professor of Modern History at the University of Bern in Switzerland. In a major volume published in 2000, with articles by numerous historians, Gerlach contributed Chapter 6, "Men of 20 July and the War in the Soviet Union."[1944] In it he writes that Henning von Tresckow and von Gersdorff (March 1943 bomb suicide plot) were complicit in SS perpetrated massacres while posted at Army Group Centre on the Eastern front, and implies that the Wehrmacht was not guilt free in regard to atrocities committed in the east. Gerlach's argument has been criticised by the contemporary German historian Klaus Jochen Arnold, and Peter Hoffman, the German-Canadian professor of history at McGill University in Montreal, Canada, and author of the book *German Resistance to Hitler*.[1945]

It is true that Stauffenberg was a firm supporter of Hitler until well after the Moscow winter disaster of December 1941. He had no qualms about the Austrian Anschluss and Czech Sudeten annexation in 1938, the complete obliteration of the Czech state by March 1939, the invasion of Poland in September that same year followed by Norway, France and the Low countries in 1940, topped off with the Barbarossa campaign in 1941.[1946] Many claim that it was only after or just as the Stalingrad disaster was unravelling at the critical turning point of the war that Stauffenberg felt compelled to oppose Hitler.[1947]

Moreover, as Gerlach wrote, most of the conspirators favoured a monarchy or other type of authoritarian state, given the abject failure of the Weimar Democracy.[1948] Carl Goerdeler, the planned Chancellor in the event of a successful Valkyrie putsch, was firmly in the monarchist camp.[1949] Moreover, many, albeit not all, envisaged a full restoration of the 1914 borders, which would have included the then German occupied partition of Poland. Given the Allied stance of "unconditional surrender," this was a fantasy.

On his posting to Poland in mid-September 1939, in the midst of the Nazi invasion, Stauffenberg wrote to his wife Nina of Poland as a dreary land of nothing but sand and dust. Further, he described the people as Untermensch, to be made servile to the German good: "

> *Die Bevölkerung ist ein unglaubicher Pöbel, sehr viele* Juden *und sehr viel Mischvolk. Ein Volk, welches sich nur unter der Knute wohlfühlt. Die Tausenden von Gefangenen werden unserer Landwirtschaft recht gut tun. In* Deutschland *sind sie sicher gut zu gebrauchen, arbeitsam, willig und genügsam.*"[1950]

Which translates to: "

> The population here are an unbelievable rabble; a great many Jews and mixed folk. A folk that only feels good under the knout.[xxvi] The thousands of prisoners, hard-working, willing and frugal, will be of great use in Germany for our agriculture."

Stauffenberg would be executed around midnight on July 20—21 1944 on Fromm's orders in the courtyard of Berlin's Bendlerblock. This was ten to eleven days before the outbreak of the Warsaw General Uprising on August 1; it lasted for 63 days,[1951] and in the process of obliterating Stauffenberg's notion of servile Slavs, prompted Heinrich Himmler to declare on September 21, 1944: "

[xxvi] The Russian knout, consisting of a number of dried and hardened thongs of rawhide interwoven with wire—the wires often being hooked and sharpened so that they tore the flesh. See the online *Encyclopaedia Britannica* article at https://www.britannica.com/topic/flogging#ref177594.

This is the fiercest of all our battles since the start of the war. It compares to the street battles of Stalingrad. We will finish this in the next five to six weeks. Then we will have destroyed Warsaw, the capital, the heart, the flower of the intelligentsia of the former Polish nation; this nation that for 700 years has blocked our road to the East and stood always in our way since the first battle at Tannenburg."[1952] [The Battle of Grunwald or First Battle of Tannenberg fought on July 15, 1410, which resulted in a Polish victory.]

Stauffenberg's mindset was a product of the German nobility, which had, for over a century and two decades, been a party to the tripartite partitioning of Poland, wiping it from official existence for the entire nineteenth century and into the early twentieth.[1953] It seems that the earliest Stauffenberg's perception of Hitler changed was around the time of the successful assassination of Reinhard Heydrich in Prague by the Czech Underground; he died in hospital in early June 1942, days after the attack in late May.[1954] This was when Hans von Bittenfeld, involved in administering the regions of the Soviet Union occupied by the Wehrmacht, informed Stauffenberg that the rounding-up and mass murder of Jews was now official policy.[1955]

At around the same time in the Czech village of Lidice, as retribution for Heydrich's assassination, every male, not deemed a child, was slaughtered. Even the few who chanced to be absent were run down and killed — two hundred men and boys in all. The women were driven into concentration camps. The children were shipped off to Germany. Everything above ground, all structures, were razed, and the ground was ploughed. Lidice became a blank, a field of regular brown furrows.[1956] In January of that year, Heydrich had chaired the infamous Wannsee Conference which had given the authorisation for the implementation of the "Final Solution."[1957] Bittenfeld described how, in fulfilment of the Wannsee directive, SS men rounded up the Jewish population of a Ukrainian town, forced them to dig their own graves in a field, then shot them. Stauffenberg, already frustrated by Hitler's meddling and incompetence in military matters, asserted the need for Hitler's removal, and declared it was the duty of senior commanders to act against him.[1958]

Such remarks that summer were not just for von Bittenfeld's ears, but for several different acquaintances.[1959] As a devout Catholic, he began to quote the medieval theologian St Thomas Aquinas's justification for tyrannicide, and one of the poems of his spiritual mentor

Stefan George, "The Antichrist," in an obvious reference to its modern version, Hitler.[1960] At this point, in the summer of 1942, the war against Germany was still well and truly in the balance, and Germany's ally, Japan, was in the clear ascendancy as it ran rampant throughout South-East Asia and the Pacific.[1961] When Stauffenberg finally committed to the resistance a year later in the summer of 1943, following his repatriation to Germany after suffering terrible injuries on the front in Tunisia, the war for both Germany and Japan had dramatically turned,[1962] with the Allies holding the initiative, but with the outcome still far from being a fait accompli.

If one were to seek a truly cynical or opportunistic German conspirator, it would be impossible to ignore Gruppenführer und Generalleutnant der Polizei Arthur Nebe. He had volunteered to command Einsatzgruppe B from June to November 1941,[1963] which operated behind the Army Group Centre in the wake of the launch of Barbarossa, exterminating over 45,000 Jews.[1964] On the day of Valkyrie, as one of the plotters, Nebe was to lead a team of twelve policemen to kill SS leader Heinrich Himmler, but the order to act never reached him. For a day or two after the bomb exploded at the Wolfsschanze, Nebe made a pretence of vigorously searching for Stauffenberg's accomplices, but when Helldorf, the Berlin Police President, was arrested, he had to go underground.[1965] On July 24, a warrant was issued for Nebe's arrest,[1966] but he evaded capture on the island of Wannsee,[1967] until January 16 1945.[1968] His capture was made possible through his betrayal by a former mistress.[1969] He was sentenced to to death on March 2 1945, and according to official records, was executed in Berlin at Plötzensee Prison on March 21 1945 by being hanged with piano wire from a meat hook, in accordance with Hitler's order that the bomb plotters were to be "hanged like cattle."[1970]

Guenter Lewy, author of *The Nazi Persecution of the Gypsies*, gives an assessment of Arthur Nebe by Bernhard Wehner, a German criminal inspector and Schutzstaffel (SS) officer who was flown to the Wolfsschanze in the wake of the Valkyrie plot: "

> Wehner regarded Nebe as a careerist who joined the ranks of the resistance because of the many crimes in which he had been involved. With a German military defeat becoming a near certainty, Nebe needed protection."[1971]

Lewy writes that Wehner's assessment is more than likely correct, as it would be almost impossible to ignore Nebe's gruesome record as commander of Einsatzgruppe B, and his willingness to make human guinea pigs of mental patients and Gypsies.[1972] Even if the claim that Nebe provided assistance to the resistance during these years is correct, the question remains: can an individual who has committed many and monstrous crimes to camouflage his resistance activities and to remain in the good graces of the leaders of a genocidal regime be exonerated?[1973] Nebe's proposal to Himmler to use inmates of the Gypsy camp at Auschwitz for medical experiments was submitted just a few weeks before the execution of the Valkyrie plot. Perhaps, like Fromm, the SS officer was trying to purchase insurance for all possible outcomes.[1974]

As for Bernhard Wehner, he survived the war, and while investigated for war crimes, he was never prosecuted. Indeed, post-war, he wrote sanitised articles about the Nazi Criminal Police to the *Der Spiegel* weekly news magazine, and was appointed Chief of Criminal Police in Dortmund in 1951.[1975] When asked by Hitler in the wake of the Valkyrie plot if his survival was a miracle, Wehner replied,"Yes my Führer, it is a miracle."[1976]

Whatever the judgment of Stauffenberg, there is no denying his extraordinary resilience in recovering from his horrific wounds, and his no less extraordinary courage in carrying out the plot to its conclusion regardless of the consequences of its failure, when so many among the high command lacked the courage to do so. When Stauffenberg committed to the conspiracy just months following the arrests of Dohnányi, Oster and Dietrich, the resistance was floundering and could only be rejuvenated by someone with the resilience, courage and charisma that was shown by Colonel Count Claus Schenk von Stauffenberg.

The blanket assertion that all conspirators were cynically motivated by the course of the war is simplistic, as is the notion they were all altruistic heroes. As always, the truth lies somewhere in between. In the nine or so months following Valkyrie to war's end, about 5,000 people were executed upon the judgement of the People's Court.[1977] Moreover, during the economic failure of the democratic Weimar Republic, forged in the humiliation of Versailles, support for Hitler is understandable. That Dietrich and Ewald von Kleist saw what Hitler was from the outset showed both insight and foresight. Further, the numerous conspirators, albeit perhaps years later than Dietrich and Ewald, still came to recognise Hitler's megalomania well before the outbreak of war. The 1938 plot during the Sudeten crisis, which was scuttled by Chamberlain's appeasement, is a perfect case in point.

In summing up the military resistance, it would be difficult to go past Roger Moorhouse's vindication of the men and the women who put their lives on the line to prove to the world that an honourable Germany still existed: "

> The military resistance is often viewed, in the popular mind at least, as a 'Johnny come lately', stung into action by the fear of defeat when the war on the Eastern Front turned against Germany. However, the experiences that drove Tresckow and his confederates to resist show beyond all doubt that the road to Rastenburg did not begin at Stalingrad; it had begun at Dubno and a thousand other sites like it. The men of the resistance recognised Hitler's bestial racial war for the crime that it was, and were resolved to act, if not to end it, then at the very least to testify that not all Germans had lost their moral compass. Despite their failure, they personified all that was best of Germany."[1978]

By the time of Valkyrie, Hitler was a degenerate drug addict. Theodor Morell, his obese and halitosis-ridden doctor since 1937,[1979] had Hitler on dozens of questionable medications, which multiplied over time. The British historian Hugh Redwald Trevor-Roper, collecting first hand information in 1945-46, graphically described Morell as follows: "… a gross but deflated old man of cringing manners, inarticulate speech and the hygienic habits of a pig," [1980] echoing the views of Albert Speer and Eva Braun.[1981]

Albert Speer, Hitler's architect and armaments minister, noted that while Hitler, at mass rallies, was known to mesmerise millions of his countrymen and women, in the case of Theodor Morell, this situation was reversed, with Hitler accepting all manner of ludicrous treatments and medications without question.[1982] However, from late January 1933, right up until the Wehrmacht were in sight of the spires of the Kremlin in late 1941, Hitler had known dizzying political and military success. Perhaps he had the mindset of a compulsive gambler on an incredible winning run, incapable of foreseeing its inevitable end, or a drug addict in the vain quest for the repeat of their first high. The Moscow winter disaster, his first major defeat, was followed by a rejuvenating high as the Wehrmacht advanced through the Russian and Ukrainian steppe in the summer of 1942 towards Stalingrad, but was followed by disaster by the end of that year and into early 1943.

From this point on, Hitler tried to regain the elation that he must have felt after the conquest of France in June 1940 and getting so tantalisingly close to the Kremlin in late 1941. Any fleeting highs from this point were drowned out as the military situation slowly crumbled in 1943 and accelerated to near collapse by July 1944, thanks to his military incompetence and lack of all rational thought processes. The zenith of his success, when he compelled the French to sign the humiliating armistice in the train carriage in the forest near Compiègne,[1983] never reappeared. His escape at the Wolfsschanze gave him a fleeting illusion of resurgence.

However, for Dietrich and his immediate family, Valkyrie brought dire consequences in its wake.

Chapter 21

Valkyrie's Wake

Dietrich heard the terrible news of the plot's failure while listening to the radio in the sick bay on July 21. His reaction was surprisingly calm, with little impact on his theological thoughts as he expressed them that day in his letter to Eberhard Bethge. "

Dear Eberhard

This short greeting is all I want to send you today. I think you must be so often present in spirit with us here that you will be glad for every sign of life, even if our theological discussion takes a breather for a while. To be sure, theological thoughts do preoccupy me incessantly, but then there are hours, too, when one is content with the ongoing processes of life and faith without reflecting on them. Then the Daily Texts simply make you happy, as I found especially to be the case with yesterday's and today's, for example. And then returning to the beautiful Paul Gerhardt hymns makes one glad to have them in the repertoire."[1984]

Three weeks later, during his final two months at Tegel, in another letter to Bethge, in a poem "Stations on the Way to Freedom," he spoke of four stations on the journey — Discipline, Action, Suffering and Death. Of Action, he wrote: "

Daring to do what is right, not what fancy may tell you, valiantly grasping occasions, not cravenly doubting — freedom comes only through deeds, not through thoughts taking wing. Faint not nor fear, but go out to the storm and the action, trusting in God whose commandment you faithfully follow; freedom, exultant, will welcome your spirit with joy."[1985]

"Daring to do what is right, not what fancy may tell you" is reflected in Pope John Paul II's words: "freedom consists not in doing what we like, but in having the right to do what we ought."[1986] In the wake of the Valkyrie failure, and the conspirator's resistance to the Third Reich in the face of torture and death, the message resonates with great clarity.

On July 23, two days after writing his first letter to Bethge after Valkyrie's failure, Dietrich heard that Canaris had been arrested;[1987] further terrible news followed soon after. The first was that Stauffenberg's adjutant, Werner von Haeften, died while bravely leaping into a hail of bullets intended for his leader, who himself, moments later, cried his last words: "Long live sacred Germany!"[1988] On August 8, Dietrich's uncle, General Paul von Hase, aged 59, was sentenced to death by Freisler and hanged that day at Plötzensee prison.[1989] Hase's wife was also arrested, and on August 22, Hans von Dohnányi was moved from the epidemic hospital in Potsdam,[1990] to the Sachsenhausen concentration camp.[1991]

On September 20 or 22, the "Chronicle of Shame files" (henceforth known as the Zossen files)[1992] were discovered at Zossen, just south of Berlin, by Criminal Commissioner Franz-Xaver Sonderegger; he, along with Manfred Roeder, had arrested Dietrich and Dohnányi back in April 1943. For Dietrich and Dohnányi, this was a disaster, as since 1938, Dohnányi had been documenting the crimes of the Third Reich in these files. Several times since his imprisonment, Dohnányi had enquired about the files and begged to have them destroyed, because their discovery would be catastrophic for the conspirators.[1993] However, General Beck ordered that they be preserved, as he wished to use them as evidence of the Third Reich's crimes dating back to well before the war. Dohnányi's wife Christine had expressed her husband's concerns, and had been assured that every necessary precaution had been taken to prevent their discovery. Unfortunately, with the unbridled investigative powers granted to the July 20 Commission created in the wake of Valkyrie, such measures were now inadequate. The files were discovered at a branch office of the Armed Forces High Command in Zossen,[1994] about thirty kilometres south of Berlin.[1995]

The commission was set up by SS chief Ernst Kaltenbrunner,[1996] a man who wielded great power; even Himmler himself feared him. Moreover, he often by-passed Himmler to report directly to Hitler, with whom he had had personal ties since childhood, and towards the end, he spent several hours a day with him.[1997] Kaltenbrunner had no trouble appointing a staff of 400 officials to leave no stone unturned, as he rightly suspected that Valkyrie had roots going back years, as was incontrovertibly proven by the discovery of the Zossen files.[1998] Following this, Hans von Dohanyi was transferred from Sachsenhausen to the Gestapo prison on Berlin's Prinz-Albrecht-Strasse.[1999]

The trials being heard in the People's Court were suspended, and the executions already ordered were postponed,[2000] so that the conspirators under arrest could be tortured and the names of further participants and accessories revealed. For the next three months, Kaltenbrunner's Commission carried on working in eleven groups; the commissioner then sorted through their findings and passed them on to Freisler. Summaries were sent to Hitler through the Party general secretary, Martin Bormann.[2001]

There was another reason for Hitler to postpone the trials, and when they resumed, to forbid any further reporting and public viewing of them. This centred around unfavourable propaganda in the shape of the brave and belligerent testimonies of some of the conspirators, who refused to be cowed by the rants of Freisler. The testimony of Stauffenberg's brave cousin Cäsar von Hofacker,[2002] involved in the Paris Valkyrie, is a case in point — as is Ewald von Kleist's when he declared to Freisler on February 3, 1945: *"Ich halte diesen Kampf fur ein von* Gott *verordnetes Gebot.* Got *allein wirt mein Richters sein."*[2003] Which translates to: "I consider this struggle to be a commandment ordained by God. God alone will be my judge."

The elder brother of Werner von Haeften, Hans-Bernd, who had been in the same confirmation class as Dietrich in 1922,[2004] stated that Hitler would go down in the annals of world history as a "great perpetrator of evil." Von der Schulenberg said to the court: "We resolved to take this deed upon ourselves in order to save Germany from indescribable misery. I realise that I shall be hanged for my part in it, but I do not regret what I did and only hope that someone else will succeed in luckier circumstances."[2005] Fellgiebel, the Wolfsschanze communications chief, mocked Freisler's perception of the course of the war, when he "urged" Freisler to "hurry up and get on with the hangings, or he would find himself hanged first!"[2006] In similar vein, a few weeks later, when the Catholic lawyer Josef Wirmer was told by the judge that he would soon be roasting in hell, Wirmer bowed and remarked: "It will be a pleasure to welcome you there soon afterwards, your honour!"[2007]

In short, the public trials and their reporting which Hitler and Goebbels had originally perceived as a treasure trove of propaganda were, thanks to the testimonies of multiple conspirators, becoming a poisoned chalice for the regime; hence Hitler's ban on further public trials and their reporting. Moreover, no members of the Abwehr were taken before Freisler's court, as the regime did not want to have the highly secret intelligence which conspirators such as Dohnányi, Canaris, Oster, and indeed Dietrich were privy to revealed to the public, or for that matter, to any court, public or private.[2008] The contents of the Zossen files were a case in point.

For Maria, even before Valkyrie, the stress of their uncertain future was taking its toll on her. Her letters to Dietrich had become less and less frequent as she began to suffer from headaches, insomnia, and fainting fits.[2009] According to her sister, Ruth-Alice, there were numerous indications that she was going through an emotional crisis, while her relatives in general noticed that each time she returned from Tegel, she seemed more and more depressed, she seemed more and more depressed, as if she felt that the possibility of her and Dietrich spending their lives together was vanishing. In June 1944, she wrote Dietrich a letter which has not survived. Dietrich's reply on June 27 confirm her crisis of uncertainty. In the first paragraph of his reply, Dietrich wrote: "

> My dearest, most beloved Maria,
>
> Many thanks for your letter. It didn't depress me at all; it made me happy, boundlessly happy, because I know that we couldn't speak to each other in such a way unless we loved each other very much—far more so than either of us realises today... None of what you wrote surprised or dismayed me. It was all more or less as I thought. What entitled me to believe, when we've seen so little of each other, that you could love me at all, and how could I have failed to rejoice in the smallest token of your love? ..."[2010]

That day, Maria made what would be her penultimate visit to Dietrich. He wrote to her again on August 13, when he found out she had moved to Berlin to work for the Red Cross. Not long after, Dietrich heard from his parents that Maria had moved in with them; Dietrich wrote to tell Maria how much this pleased him. No doubt, he envisaged more frequent visits from her, but Maria's final visit was made on August 23 1944. Dietrich, wrote to Bethge that day, "Maria was here today, so fresh and at the same time steadfast and tranquil in a way I've rarely seen."[2011] However, Dietrich resolved in the following month of September, upon the discovery of the Zossen files, to escape from Tegel.[2012]

With the discovery of the files, and almost every member of the underground now arrested, Dietrich's hope that the case against him would eventually run out of steam was all but obliterated. When he approached his loyal guard Corporal Knobloch, who also worked at a factory in the city's north, Knobloch agreed to disappear with Dietrich.

The plan was for Dietrich, dressed in a mechanic's uniform, to walk out the gate with the trusty guard, whereupon they would take refuge for a few days in a summer garden house, before taking flight to Switzerland or Sweden with false passports. On Sunday September 24, Dietrich's sister Ursula and her husband Rüdiger Schleicher drove to Berlin-Niedierschönhausen with their daughter Renate Bethge, now married to Eberhard, and handed Knobloch a package with clothing, including the mechanic's uniform, money and food coupons; the false passports were still to be arranged.[2013]

Unfortunately, events on the following Saturday, the 30th, put paid to this plan. Dietrich's elder brother Klaus, upon returning home from work, saw a suspicious car parked before his garden gate at Eichkamp. He immediately turned around and headed for Ursula's home on Marienburgerallee, as Dietrich had done almost eighteen months earlier. At the time, Klaus's wife Emmi was away at Schleswig-Holstein towards Denmark,[2014] visiting their children, who had been sent there because of the ever-increasing Allied bombing raids. Klaus was not the only one to take refuge that day at the Marienburgerallee; their cousin Margarete, the wife of the now executed General Paul von Hase, was released from prison and showed up at their door. Because of her husband's role in the conspiracy, none of her immediate relatives would take her in.[2015] At almost that very moment, Corporal Knobloch arrived to discuss details of the escape, false passports, and possible contacts with the chaplain to the Swedish Embassy. Unfortunately, with no time available for these measures, Ursula and Klaus had to ask Knobloch to inform Dietrich of the impending arrest of Klaus. Knobloch would return two days later on the Monday.[2016]

Klaus stayed overnight, while Ursula succeeded in talking her brother out of suicide. Ursula came to regret this when she later learned of her brother's brutal torture and death at the Gestapo's hands.[2017] The next morning, a Sunday on the first day of October, the Gestapo arrived and took Klaus away, and on the following day, Knobloch returned to the Schleichers and informed them that Dietrich had decided against escape, as he could only see it making things worse for everyone else, especially for Klaus, and feared that the Gestapo would go after his parents or Maria.[2018] Fortunately, it never came to that. However, Dietrich's selflessness was not enough to save his brother-in-law Rüdiger when the Gestapo paid another visit to Marienburgerallee on the Wednesday.[2019] Now, there were two Bonhoeffer brothers and two Bonhoeffer brothers-in-law incarcerated, and they would not live to see war's end.

From the relative safety of his eighteen-month London pastorate from October 1933 to April 1935, Dietrich had written his impressions of death: "

> Death is only dreadful for those who live in dread and fear of it. Death is not wild and terrible, if only we can be still and hold fast to God's Word. Death is not bitter, if we have not become bitter ourselves. Death is grace, the greatest gift of grace that God gives people who believe in him....It beckons to us with heavenly power, if only we realise that is the gateway to our homeland, the tabernacle of joy, the everlasting kingdom of peace."[2020]

Now a decade or so later, on Sunday October 8 1944,[2021] amidst the terrible aftermath of Valkyrie, Dietrich was transferred to the somewhat less "accommodating" residence of the cellar prison of the Reich SS Headquarters on Prinz-Albrecht-Strasse. His mostly routine eighteen-month imprisonment at Tegel, where, for the most part, he had enjoyed the protection of his distinguished, but now executed uncle, was at an end, and, he now faced the stark reality of the words of his London sermon. Dietrich again proved that he was not a pastor of mere words, but one who lived as he preached.

Chapter 22

Prinz-Albrecht-Strasse

In the book *I Knew Dietrich Bonhoeffer*, Dietrich's fellow inmate at Prinz-Albrecht-Strasse, Fabian von Schlabrendorff, spoke, not for the last time, of Dietrich as a man who indeed, 'lived as he preached.' "

> Dietrich Bonhoeffer told me of his interrogations … His noble and pure soul must have suffered deeply. But he betrayed no sign of it. He was always good-tempered, always of the same kindliness and politeness towards everybody, so that to my surprise, within a short time, he had won over his warders, who were not always kindly disposed. It was significant for our relationship that he was rather the hopeful one while I now and then suffered from depression. He always cheered me up and comforted me, he never tired of repeating that the only fight which is lost is that which we give up. Many little notes he slipped into my hands on which he had written biblical words of comfort and hope. He looked with optimism at his own situation too. He repeatedly told me the Gestapo had no clue to his real activities. He had been able to trivialise his acquaintance with Goerdeler. His connection with Perels, the justiciary of the Confessing Church, was not of sufficient importance to serve as an indictment. And as for his foreign travels and meetings with English Church dignitaries, the Gestapo did not grasp their purpose and point. If the investigations were to carry on at the present pace, years might pass till they reached their conclusions. He was full of hope, he even conjectured that he might be set free without a trial, if some influential person had the courage to intercede on his behalf with the Gestapo."[2022]

Dietrich spent four months in the Prinz-Albrecht-Strasse Gestapo prison, which made Tegel prison seem like the Ritz. In 1933, the former arts school at Prinz-Albrecht-Strasse 8 had been transformed into Gestapo headquarters, with cells underground.[2023] Of these, Dietrich's cell was only 1.5 x 2.5 metres (8 x 5 feet) in area,[2024] without any daylight, and there was no prison yard for the prisoners to exercise.[2025] Amongst the prisoners were Carl Goerdeler, Joseph Müller, General Oster, Judge Sack, Admiral Wilhelm Canaris and of course, Fabian von Schlabren-dorff, whose book gives the most detailed account of Dietrich's incarceration at Prinz-Albrecht-Strasse. It seemed that the entire Resistance was incarcerated, and even Eberhard Bethge had been arrested, although he was not held here, but at Lehrter Strasse Wehrmacht prison,[2026] along with Rüdiger Schleicher and Klaus Bonhoeffer.[2027]

While discipline was not so strict as to prevent all human contact, the prisoners were manacled, and Admiral Canaris, along with his fellow inmates, was forced to scrub the floors like a sailor on the deck of a ship, much to the amusement of his SS jailers.[2028] Nevertheless, Canaris, much like what Dietrich had achieved with Manfred Roeder in 1943, was able to use his superior intellect, in concert with his Christian outlook, to outwit his tormentors: "

> No doubt supported by his Christian outlook, he almost seemed to relish 'notching up another cross' of ill-treatment. He played a relentless war of wits with his interrogators, who did not resort to torture, [as was the case with Dietrich] and fenced brilliantly with them, exposing all their intellectual weaknesses.

> He also developed an amusing technique of prising information from the guards by asking supposedly foolish questions such as "I suppose we have pushed the Russians back over the Vistula?" [The river Warsaw is on, and Poland's greatest river, running from the mountainous frontier in the south towards the Baltic Sea in the north.] These were invariably answered with a realistic assessment of where the Russian army was at this stage. The ease with which he affected stupidity (always a useful weapon in a spy chief's armoury) astounded those who knew him. He could mislead the interrogators with secondary plots, camouflage the truth and apologetically offer the occasional half-admission of some totally irrelevant fault in order to throw his interrogators off the scent.

> In this way he kept secret the names of many who would otherwise have ended up in prison with him, notably Lahousen and Leverkuen, to name but two. Other prisoners did not possess the same moral, intellectual and nervous resources. Oster

was confounded by irrefutable evidence. Others were broken by physical torture."[2029]

The adjacent Hotel Prinz Albrecht became the SS headquarters in 1934, and that same year, the SS intelligence service, the SD, took over the Prinz Albrecht palace on nearby Wilhelm Strasse. It was from this complex of buildings that Hitler's officials administered the concentration and extermination camps, directed the deadly campaigns by the SS death squads (Einsatzgruppen) and kept an eye on the regime's opponents.[2030] In short, the Prinz Albrecht precinct was the nerve centre for the administration and co-ordination of terror throughout the Third Reich and its occupied territories. For over six decades following the war, the site was left a virtual wasteland, but on Thursday May 6 2010, Federal President Horst Köhler opened the Documentation Centre of the Topography of Terror Foundation (*Topographie des Terrors*) on an 800 square metre site, very close to remains of the Berlin Wall, to the south of the city centre.[2031] It is the new permanent exhibition on the system of terror that defined the Third Reich, located on today's Niederkirchnerstrasse, on what had been the notorious Prinz-Albrecht-Strasse.[2032]

When Dietrich was first interrogated, he was threatened with torture, and told that the fate of his parents, his other family members, and his fiancée hung on his confession. He was able to speak with von Schlabrendorff and characterised his interrogations as "frankly repulsive." While nothing suggests that Dietrich was ever tortured, his brother Klaus and most of the others were, including Schlabrendorff, who wrote of the torture he suffered in his book *They Almost Killed Hitler*.[2033]

When Dietrich was first moved to Prinz-Albrecht-Strasse, he was forbidden to write to Maria, who made several visits in vain to see her beloved. However, with Himmler and many in the SS now realising it was inevitable that Germany would lose the war, desperate feelers for peace were being extended, using prisoners with foreign contacts such as Dietrich as bargaining chips.[2034] Just before Christmas, Dietrich was allowed to write what was to be his final letter to Maria. In spite of the almost endless solitude in his claustrophobic cell, broken only during air raids and fleeting opportunities in the cold communal showers, Dietrich wrote that he never, for an instant, felt lonely or forlorn, as he regarded Maria, his parents, all his friends and students, as his constant companions. In sensing his connection with them all, he wrote, "It's as if, in solitude, the soul develops organs of which we're hardly aware in everyday life."[2035] In this letter, Dietrich enclosed his final poem from prison, "Powers of Good," which became famous throughout Germany; it is included in numerous school textbooks and is sung in churches as a hymn.

While Dietrich's health had not suffered even right up until his execution in April 1945, this was not the case for his brother-in-law Hans von Dohnányi. Before a bombing raid destroyed his cell in November 1943, inflicting an embolism to his brain, Dohnányi was suffering a bad case of phlebitis in both legs. After his connections had managed to have him moved to the benevolent care of the Charité Hospital, the vindictive Roeder, in early 1944, had Dohnányi transferred to the prison hospital in Buch on the north side of Berlin.[2036] It seems that it was from here that Dohnányi begged his wife Christine to contaminate the food she brought for him with diphtheria, in order for him to avoid further interrogation at the hands of the Gestapo. Christine finally agreed to do so, and it succeeded in as much as Dohnányi was transferred to the epidemic hospital in Potsdam.[2037]

However, when his son Christoph visited him secretly and for the last time, he noticed, while peering through a window, that his father's fingers were taped — a sure sign of torture.[2038] Upon the failure of the Valkyrie plot, Dohnányi was moved to the Sachsenhausen concentration camp. On February 1 1945, in spite of being seriously ill, he was moved to Prinz- Albrecht-Strasse because the interrogations of the former Abwehr members incarcerated in Berlin were going nowhere.[2039] It was while he was briefly there that he had a remarkable exchange with Dietrich while the jostling between prisoners was taking place during the air raid warning for the bombing on February 3. Schlabrendorff relates this in *I Knew Dietrich Bonhoeffer*: "

> When Dohnányi was also delivered to the Prinz-Albrecht-Strasse prison, Dietrich even managed to get in touch with him. When we returned after an air-raid warning from our cement shelter, his brother-in-law lay on a stretcher in his cell, paralysed in both legs. With an alacrity that nobody would have believed him capable of, Dietrich Bonhoeffer suddenly dived into the open cell of his brother-in-law. It seemed a miracle that none of the warders saw it. But Dietrich also succeeded in the more difficult part of his venture, in emerging from Dohnányi's cell unnoticed and getting into line with the column of prisoners who were filing along the corridor. That same even-

ing, he told me that he had agreed with Dohnányi upon all essential points of their further testimony."[2040]

The bombing on Saturday February 3 1945, the day before Dietrich's 39th and final birthday, was carried out by the American Eighth Air Force; they unleashed nearly one thousand B-17 Flying Fortress bombers on Berlin, and over two hours, they dropped three thousand tons of bombs from the clear blue winter sky.[2041] Amongst the buildings destroyed that morning was the Gestapo prison on Prinz-Albrecht-Strasse, and Freisler's People's Court, where Freisler himself was "conducting" Fabian von Schlabrendorff's case, moments after angrily dismissing an impudent Ewald von Kleist.[2042] While Dietrich, Fabian, Ewald and their fellow inmates, survived the ordeal, Freisler, an attendee of the January 1942 Wannsee conference which founded the infamous "Final Solution,"[2043] was not so fortunate. The day before, Freisler had sentenced Klaus Bonhoeffer and Rüdiger Schleicher to death,[2044] and was about to do likewise for Schlabrendorff as the American Eighth Air Force liberated their destructive payloads. It was at this moment or thereabouts, that Freisler's head was struck by a collapsing ceiling beam, just over five months after Cäsar von Hofacker's most apt prophecy in Freisler's very own court.[2045]

As the Eighth Air Force's destructive payload rained down on Berlin, the brother of Rüdiger Schleicher, Doctor Rolf Schleicher, a senior staff doctor in Stuttgart, was in the Potzdamer Platz subway station,[2046] having arrived in Berlin to appeal the death sentence handed down by Freisler to his brother. When the bombing ceased, Doctor Schleicher was allowed to the streets above; he passed by the wreckage of the People's Court in which Freisler had sentenced his brother the day before.[2047] As he passed, someone noticed his doctor's uniform and hailed him into the courtyard to help with one of the wounded; to Doctor Schleicher's shock, it was Freisler himself. Fortunately, his prompt assessment of Freisler's death spared him any breach of his Hippocratic oath, and later in the day, allowed him, upon arrival at his brother's house on Marienburgerallee, the satisfaction of pronouncing, "The scoundrel is dead!"[2048]

While still at the People's Court, Doctor Schleicher was pressed to write a death certificate, but refused to do so until he could see the minister of justice, Otto Thierack, who informed the doctor that the execution of his brother Rüdiger would be delayed until an official "plea for mercy" had been submitted.[2049] Unfortunately, this proved to be academic. On the night of April 22 1945, Rüdiger, aged just fifty, was shot from behind by the SS, while he was ostensibly being transferred to another prison.[2050] He was not alone, as others, including Klaus Bonhoeffer, suffered an identical fate.

The morning of the raid, Dietrich's parents, along with Klaus's wife Emmi, set out for the prison to deliver his birthday package. However, on the way there they had to wait out the air raid in the Underground below the Anhalter railway station.[2051] In the raid's aftermath, they were not permitted to approach the heavily damaged Prinz-Albrecht-Strasse prison, and with no immediate news on the welfare of the prisoners, they were terribly worried as they headed back home. It was not until the following Wednesday, the 7th, when most of the prisoners, including Dietrich, were moved out of Berlin, that they were able to deliver the parcel and receive the good news that nothing had happened to the prisoners in the bunker; however, the letter accompanying the package was refused.

In it, Karl Bonhoeffer, hiding his fears behind his usual laconic style, wrote: "

Dear Dietrich,

Our birthday letter for the fourth that we wanted to bring on Saturday did not reach you because of the bombing raid. During the raid we were sitting in the S-Bahn [railway car] in the Anhalter train station; it wasn't a very pretty sight. Apart from the fact that we looked like chimney sweeps afterward, we came away unscathed. But afterward, when we tried to get to you, we were very worried, since they wouldn't let us anywhere near you because of the unexploded bombs. The next day we heard that the prisoners were unharmed; I hope it's true.

As for the family, Maria is accompanying her Pätzig siblings as they head westward. [This epic journey will be discussed in Chapter 25 "Old Prussia Gone With The Wind"] Aunt Elisabeth is in Warmbrunn. Suse is here with her children and wants to remain here. Hans Walter is in the west.

Unfortunately I had no luck at the library. Pestalozzi is only given out for the reading room. Natorp is out. Karl Friedrich had decided to give you the Plutarch for your birthday. I hope

313

this letter reaches you. We hope for permission to visit you soon. At our age there are some things to take care of that one needs to discuss with one's children. I am typing this for the sake of legibility.

Warmest greetings
[Your Father]"[2052]

Due to the almost complete destruction of Prinz-Albrecht-Strasse, most of the prisoners, Dietrich included, were moved out of Berlin on February 7, 1945. Those not included were Hans von Dohnányi, who was moved to the city's state hospital,[2053] and those such as Fabian von Schlabrendorff who were scheduled to have their cases "heard" within the next few days.[2054] The prisoners leaving the capital were split into two groups — one for the concentration camp of Flossenbürg in northern Bavaria, and the other for Buchenwald, about 320 kilometres south of Berlin near Weimar.

Among the distinguished entourage of prisoners bound for Flossenbürg was the pre-Anschluss (March 1938) chancellor of Austria,[2055] Doctor Kurt von Schuschnigg, who was among the "Hostages of the SS,"[2056] liberated in the idyllic town of Niederdorf in the German-speaking Tyrol region of northern Italy on April 30 1945.[2057] Upon Hitler's takeover of Austria, Schuschnigg had been imprisoned in various camps throughout the Reich until his liberation on the very day of Hitler's suicide. Others bound for this not so idyllic Bavarian destination included Doctor Hjalmar Schacht,[2058] former head of the Reichsbank, who had enabled Hitler's rise to power until his resignation in 1937. He had fought in vain against the monster he had helped to empower, having been part of the 1938 plot. Now, as was the case with hundreds of others, he was arrested after the failed Valkyrie plot. Among the now defunct Abwehr were its top men Admiral Canaris and General Oster, accompanied by the jurist, Judge Karl Sack, who maintained contact throughout the war. Other notable inmates were General Franz Halder,[2059] and Oster's colleague Theodor Strünck.[2060]

The other group bound for Buchenwald and first to leave,[2061] was no less distinguished. It included General von Falkenhausen, the former governor of Belgium and northern France during Germany's occupation from late May 1940 right up until the Valkyrie plot;[2062] Count Werner von Alvensleben, nearly seventy years old, had been opposed to Hitler from the outset;[2063] the Catholic politician Doctor Hermann Pünder, who had been the secretary of state just before Hitler; Ludwig Gehre, a colleague of Hans Oster and Doctor Josef Müller, the Abwehr's conduit to the Vatican.[2064] Müller, in spite of being tortured by the Gestapo for almost two years, never yielded. Indeed, Sigismund Payne Best, a British MI6 agent kidnapped by the SS in the Dutch border town of Venlo in November 1939 before the German invasion, described Josef Müller as "one of the bravest and most determined men imaginable."[2065]

Mark Riebling, author of *Church of Spies: The Pope's Secret War Against Hitler*, a historian who made several appearances in the National Geographic documentary, *Pope Vs Hitler*, wrote that: "

> Müller was a beer-loving Bavarian of sturdy peasant stock, with sky-blue eyes, and an Iron Cross hero of the Great War, before becoming a self-made lawyer post-war. Because he worked his way through school driving an ox cart, his friends ribbed him as Ochsensepp — Joey Ox. The nickname aptly captured Müller's robust build, his rural roots, and the powerful will that brought him such good and bad fortune."[2066]

Dietrich was among the Buchenwald group. Having just celebrated his 39th birthday in a subterranean Gestapo cell, he now witnessed his first daylight in four months; for most there, it had been far longer.[2067] In spite of where they were headed, the daylight was a liberation of sorts, as was the sudden but uplifting encounter with old friends.[2068] As the Third Reich imploded from east and west, it was obvious the war was ending. Hitler was finished, but whether or not they would live to see the end was uncertain. When it was time to board the eight-seat prison van with eleven other prisoners, Dietrich protested at being handcuffed. However, Müller, who had already endured numerous instances of torture, calmed and consoled his friend and fellow prisoner: "Let us go calmly to the gallows as Christians."[2069] Only on arrival in Buchenwald were the handcuffs removed.[2070]

Thanks to the amazing resilience of Müller and others in the Canaris group, their interrogations ceased, with even Walter Huppenkothen, the chief investigator at Prinz-Albrecht-Strasse, now bereft of ideas to compel them to yield.[2071] While the latter never tortured anyone himself, he ordered it done by others, and when he appeared again afterwards, he would offer his victim a cigarette and act the perfect gentleman.[2072] Disturbingly, having served in one of the Einsatzgruppen[2073] in Poland at the outbreak of war, and directed the Gestapo in Lublin until being recalled to Berlin in June 1941,[2074] he was one of multiple Gestapo/SS to survive long after the war — in his case, until 1978, with minimal time served.[2075] Nevertheless, the immortal memory of Dietrich Bonhoeffer lives on, as that of his executioners fades into history.

Chapter 23

Buchenwald

Buchenwald (Beech Forest), as was the case with other concentration camps or KZ throughout the Reich and its occupied territories, was a place where people not only died,[2076] but their suffering and death were celebrated as a barbaric vindication of Germanic superiority over all perceived *Untermensch*. Pieces of tattooed human skin, ostensibly used for criminal investigations, had been used by SS officers to make articles such as wallets, while the heads of some prisoners were shrunk and given as gifts. As late as January 31 1945, three bales of human hair with a net weight of 208 kilos was approved for the Alex Zink Felt factory at Roth near Nuremberg.[2077] In this regard, the Auschwitz camp was the most notorious; in late June 2005, I witnessed there almost two metric tons of human hair cut from victims.

Like Auschwitz, Buchenwald had satellite camps, which included the Berga am Elster camp, about 70 kilometres to the east-southeast. Among its inmates were a group that one would not normally associate with the KZ. They were Jewish American GIs and American GIs whom their German captors considered to be of Jewish appearance. In one instance, the unfortunate victim of this logic was Tony Acevedo, a twenty-year-old GI medic of Mexican heritage, captured during the Germans' Ardennes Forest offensive (Battle of the Bulge) in Belgium on January 6 1945 — Hitler's last offensive success.[2078] There, like fellow European Jews and other peoples considered to be among the National Socialist *Untermensch*, they were subjected to brutal forced labour, which involved the building of tunnels to protect the Third Reich's new wonder weapon, the Messerschmitt-262 fighter jet, from Allied bombing. This was similar to tunnels built to protect the V2 rocket launchers that had wreaked havoc on London from the last quarter of 1944.[2079] Today, if you venture deep into the forests near Berga, you will still find the entrances to these tunnels.

While the seventeen new arrivals from Berlin were moved to Buchenwald itself, they were not in the main compound, but just outside it in the cold makeshift prison cellar of a five- to six-floor yellow tenement-style building constructed to house the camp staff. This dank cellar had previously been used as a military jail for the SS, but now it would hold all seventeen of these prominent prisoners in twelve cells.[2080] As grim, cold and foreboding as it was, they were not subjected to hard labour on starvation rations as the inmates in the main compound and the American GIs in Berga were. Nevertheless, the rations were meagre and unappetising — soup at midday, and bread with a little pork fat and jam for supper. For breakfast, part of their meagre supper from the previous evening had to be saved. Moreover, there was the terror of bombing raids to endure, during which they were locked in while their guards fled into the woods nearby, where trenches had been dug.[2081]

As the Americans advanced from the west, the guards became increasingly nervous and refused to allow the prisoners outside for fresh air. Eventually, they granted the meagre concession of allowing the prisoners a daily walk in the cellar corridor, which was divided lengthwise into three narrow passages. With some gaps in these dividing walls, the inmates were able to converse with each other during these periods, as the guards found it too much trouble to supervise the prisoners while engaged in their entrepreneurial endeavours of marketing black market tobacco.[2082] As Schlingensiepen put it, these were "really sociable times,"[2083] where prisoners could get to know one another and share any books they still had with them. Dietrich's neighbour in the adjoining cell was Catholic Rhinelander Doctor Hermann Pünder, who had been Chancellor Brüning's chief of staff before 1933.[2084] This pair greatly enjoyed political and cultural discussions, especially in regard to future relations they both hoped for between Catholics and Protestants in post-war Germany.

Dietrich's solitude in his cell lasted less than three weeks; on February 24,[2085] four more prisoners arrived. They were British MI6 agent Sigismund Payne Best; fellow countryman Hugh Falconer; Vassily Kokorin, a Soviet Air Force officer and nephew of the Soviet Foreign minister Vyacheslav Molotov; and General Friedrich von Rabenau. The latter joined Dietrich in his cramped cell. The new arrivals, except for Rabenau, ended up among the "Hostages of the SS" to be liberated in Niederdorf at the end of April.[2086] As there are no extant letters from Dietrich for the last two months of his imprisonment, the account of his fellow Buchenwald inmate Sigismund Payne Best in his book *The Venlo Incident* is enlightening.[2087] In it, Payne Best describes Rabenau as a militant churchman, never losing the authoritative bearing of the soldier he was.[2088] He retired from a distinguished military career in 1942, which had included his appointment as General Beck's Chief of General Staff in 1936 with the role of building up and directing the Army Archives.[2089] He then studied Theology in Berlin, as Dietrich had done.[2090] Payne Best perceived Rabenau as someone who expected unquestioning military-style obedience to his religious opinions.[2091]

Although Dietrich's and Rabenau's theological views were poles apart in many respects,[2092] it seems they were united in one crucial aspect — their fundamental opposition to National Socialism, and the bastardisation of the German Church by the German Christians in their attempt to render it compatible with National Socialist dogma.[2093] They had lively but rational theological discussions, which their fellow inmate in the adjoining cell, Hermann Pünder, sometimes overheard with great interest.[2094] This was not their only means of passing the time, as Payne Best had given Rabenau a chess set, which the pair put to great use.[2095] Always a devout Christian, Rabenau, a veteran of the Great War,[2096] was compelled to oppose Hitler almost from the outset. He served as a liaison between Beck and Goerdeler, and was the author of a lengthy and highly regarded biography of the German military leader Hans von Seeckt, which Dietrich had read.[2097]

During the invasion of Poland in September 1939, he was the commander of the 73rd Infantry Division, and later, among church and military resistance groups, spoke out in favour of depositing the war logs from the Polish campaign in the military archive because of the war crimes recorded in them.[2098] From Hermann Pünder, we know that Rabenau continued to work on his autobiography at Buchenwald,[2099] and it seems likely that Dietrich was writing, too, though unfortunately, nothing survived either of them.[2100] After the failed Valkyrie plot, Rabenau was arrested on July 25 1944, upon which he was imprisoned in the Ravensbrück (Fürstenberg) concentration camp for women, and then in Berlin in the Lehrterstrasse (Moabit)[2101] Prison and Gestapo Headquarters prison in Prinz-Albrecht-Strasse.[2102] From there, he was taken to the Sachsenhausen Concentration Camp in January 1945, before arriving in Buchenwald on February 24 1945.[2103]

Rabenau had introduced Payne Best to Dietrich in the washroom, whereupon Dietrich enjoyed the opportunity to speak English for the first time since his meeting with George Bell in Stockholm in 1942. Payne Best took to Dietrich immediately, and so when he noticed that Dietrich lacked warm clothes and was wearing wooden prison clogs instead of shoes, he gave him his golf shoes and a warm sweater from among his ample luggage. Describing Dietrich in comparison to Rabenau, Payne Best wrote: "

> Bonnhöfer, on the other hand, was all humility and sweetness;
> he always seemed to me to diffuse an atmosphere of happiness,

of joy in every smallest event in life, and of deep gratitude for the mere fact that he was alive. There was something dog-like in the look of fidelity in his eyes and his gladness if you showed that you liked him. He was one of the very few men that I have ever met to whom his God was real and ever close to him. Yet both these men, each of them deeply religious in his own way, had played an active role in the plot to depose Hitler, which culminated in the events of July 20, 1944. I do not know whether they were actually involved to the extent that they knew that Hitler's removal was to be effected by assassination, but they were in the confidence of all the main conspirators, and Bonnhöfer in particular had played an important role as messenger and connecting link between different parts of the country."[2104]

Of course, we now know that Dietrich was fully aware that Hitler's removal was to be effected by assassination. The aborted March 1943 attempt in Berlin was a case in point.[2105] Moreover, it's difficult to see how the distinguished Rabenau could have been ignorant of this fact.

On March 2 1951, Payne Best, in a letter to Dietrich's brother-in-law Gerhard Leibholz, husband of his twin sister Sabine, wrote: "

Just quite calm and normal; seemingly perfectly at his ease. It is a funny thing, but when I think of him I always seem to see him with a halo of light round his head — his soul really shone in the dark desperation of our prison. I don't suppose I spoke to him more than three times whilst we were at Buchenwald but when we left he sat for a time next to me in the prison van. He told me then how happy prison had made him. He had always been afraid that he would not be strong enough to stand such a test but now he knew that there was nothing in life of which one need ever be afraid. He also expressed complete agreement with my view that our warders and guards needed pity far more than we and that it was absurd to blame them for their actions."[2106]

Payne Best described the general atmosphere among the German prisoners, which was in stark contrast to his image of Dietrich's soul shining in the darkness and despair of Buchenwald: "

When I first made contact with the other prisoners what struck me most forcedly was the intense distrust of most of the Germans of each other; almost every one of them warned me to be careful of some other as he was a Gestapo spy. I paid no heed to these warnings and just took people as I found them; later on we all became good friends and none ever showed the least inclination toward treachery. This atmosphere of suspicion was typical of Nazi Germany, though it seemed to me strange that these people, imprisoned by the Gestapo, had so little inclination to form a common front and pull together. Both then and later, most of the German prisoners I met displayed an apathetic, I might say, fatalistic resignation and, as I suppose they had done all their lives, obeyed every order given to them without sign of unwillingness. I believe, that but for these two elements of mutual distrust and subservience to authority, it would have been possible to organise a mass escape in the company of our warders. These men were so badly scared that it would have required very little to convince them that their only hope of safety lay in helping us to liberty, and in accompanying us to the American lines; I tried hard to induce them to go off one night with Falconer, Kokorin, and myself, but we were after all foreigners, and I could never overcome their last instinctive distrust of us which only the whole-hearted co-operation of the distinguished Germans of our party could have perhaps done."[2107]

Payne Best's fellow Briton and RAF officer, Squadron-Leader Hugh Falconer, remarked of Dietrich and Rabenau that they were the only cell-mates to enjoy each other's company,[2108] and as already mentioned, even before the arrival of the new prisoners on February 24, Dietrich and Hermann Pünder had formed a close bond.[2109] These friendships were two exceptions to the general feeling of mistrust among the German prisoners, with Dietrich as the common thread.

No doubt, if the German inmates had had the overall spirit, camaraderie and trust that was shared by the men of the Great Escape, with the Reich imploding as it was, and the frightened guards, the opportunity was there to be taken. The only guard that may have proven a problem was Dittman, who let it be known to Best that he would fight till the last moment and would save two bullets; one for Best, whom he despised, and one for himself.[2110] Ultimately, the German prisoners' fear of the "stoolies" or "stool pigeons," of whom Alexander Solzhenitsyn wrote more than once in the Gulag Archipelago,[2111] stopped them from seriously contemplating escape.

Payne Best's favourite among all of his sixteen fellow inmates was General Freiherr von Falkenhausen,[2112] who had been the German Governor-General and Commander-in-Chief in Belgium and Northern France from 1940 to 1944.[2113] He was a member of an old family of the German nobility, and during the Great War he received the "Pour le mérite," the highest German decoration for bravery, while attached to the Turkish Ottoman Army in Palestine.[2114] In 1934, he succeeded General von Seeckt as head of the German Military Mission in China, where he remained for over four years, training the army of Generalissimo Chiang Kai-shek, and helping to modernise their arms industry.[2115]

The East, and particularly Chinese philosophy, had always held a great fascination for him, and as he found his work made significant progress over the years, he committed to making his home in China. Hitler's seemingly unstoppable rise to power was the embodiment of everything he found abhorrent; he went even further, relinquishing his German nationality and adopting that of his new home. The Third Reich attempted to woo Japan into their envisaged Axis power block, whereupon the Japanese objected that a German mission was assisting China in her fight against "divinely" sanctioned Japanese aggression.[2116] In December 1937, the infamous Nanking Massacre took place,[2117] and by 1939, before the outbreak of war in early September, Berlin ordered Falkenhausen to liquidate his organisation and return to Germany.[2118]

Upon receiving this order, Falkenhausen reported it to the Generalissimo, who told Falkenhausen that he could not allow him to return to Germany. Falkenhausen knew every detail of China's military organisation and her plans for the future; moreover, Germany's flirtation with China's arch-enemy Japan looked like developing into a close alliance. Falkenhausen replied that he had no desire to return to Germany, and asked the Generalissimo to refuse to sanction his return and to expedite his request for Chinese citizenship. All came to naught when Ribbentrop, in a lengthy and terse telegram, stated that unless Falkenhausen left for Germany by a boat due to sail in about three weeks' time, all his property would be confiscated and all members of his family would be sent to concentration camps.[2119]

Chiang Kai-shek, understanding the predicament that Falkenhausen was in, relented on the condition that he never reveal any of China's military secrets to the Nazi regime.[2120] Falkenhausen bravely lived up to his part of the bargain, greatly assisted by the fact that his return to Germany was during the recent aftermath of the 1938 Fritsch affair.[2121] Hitler, not desiring another scandal, decided against violent action against such a distinguished figure of the military. With the conquest of Belgium in late May 1940, von Falkenhausen was appointed as governor because he was well known for his liberal views, and it was thought that he might succeed in establishing a government which would reconcile the mass of the population to German occupation, and even bring it gradually into the Nazi camp. Initially he refused. During the four years he was governor, he was far from blameless, but he said to Payne Best that if he had not accepted the post in Belgium, it would have suffered far worse under the rule of some dyed-in-the-wool Nazi.[2122]

While among the liberated in Niederdorf after the fall of the Nazi regime, he was tried and sentenced by a military tribunal in Brussels in March 1951 to twelve years imprisonment for the execution of hostages and the deportation of 25,000 Belgian Jews. However, after serving just three years, he was released as an act of clemency in consideration of the Belgians he also saved. This was thanks to the remarkable Chinese-Belgian female scientist Qian Xiuling (錢秀玲), known as China's female Schindler in Belgium during WWII;[2123] she gathered Falkenhausen's beneficiaries to testify in the trial on his behalf. While not gaining a full acquittal, the appeal reduced his sentence by nine years. Falkenhausen passed away in 1966, aged 87, and Qian Xiuling in 2008, aged 95.[2124] Falkenhaus's history is not bloodless, but his conscience would have been troubled by the memory of those he had deported or sentenced to death. He clearly had a conscience, or he would not have risked his life to save the people he did, or refused to divulge Chinese military secrets to the Reich. It must be said, however, that not all the "special" prisoners at Buchenwald had such scruples, or the capability for such remorse.

When Dietrich first arrived at Buchenwald, one of the special prisoners was the former head SS doctor at Buchenwald, Hauptsturmführer (Captain) Waldemar Hoven. However, due to the shortage of doctors, he was released about three weeks later, with his place in prison taken by another SS Doctor of identical rank, Sigmund Rascher. Payne Best wrote that while Hoven was a prisoner, he was privileged, spending most of his day sitting with the warders in their room. Payne Best never found out what crime he committed to incur the angst of the SS, but discovered that before the war, he had a clinic in Freiburg near the idyllic Schwarzwald (Black Forest) in the south-west of the country, which was apparently frequented by many well-known English people. Hoven had gone to some length to curry favour with Payne Best, but the Englishman saw him as a shifty and cruel creature, and as such,[2125] was neither sorry nor surprised when he heard he was condemned to death then hanged on June 2, 1948.[2126]

Waldemar Hoven was tried at Nuremberg in the Doctors' Trial that ran from December 9 1946 until the announcement of verdicts on August 20 1947. It involved almost 140 days of proceedings, including the testimony of 85 witnesses and the submission of almost 1,500 documents to the panel of four American judges. Among the twenty-three physicians tried, sixteen were found guilty, with seven sentenced to death. Hoven was found guilty of conducting spotted fever experiments and practising euthanasia on humans.[2127]

However, when I viewed some of the transcripts from the Nuremberg Doctors' Trials, it did not seem so clear cut to me. In particular, the testimony of a former Buchenwald inmate, Leendert (Leen) Seegers, (1891—1970), a Dutch politician and long time member of the Dutch Communist Party and alderman and city councillor of Amsterdam, states:[2128] "

> I know that Dr. HOVEN only killed those of the prisoners systematically who had to be looked upon as SS and Gestapo spies or as dangerous collaborators within the camp [Stoolies or stool pigeons]. Conditions in Buchenwald, where there was a state of war practically between the inmates and the SS, permitted of no other alternative in my opinion.
>
> These killings, as far as I know, were an absolute necessity for the growing organisation of political prisoners in Buchenwald .....
>
> There were such possibilities. Many of the spies were "liquidated" also by leading prisoners or removed by transports. In many cases, however, the only safe possibility, under the conditions prevailing, was the liquidating of the spies with the help of Dr. Waldemar Hoven.
>
> To continue to exist would have meant certain death for the illegal prisoners' organisation in Buchenwald and for the leading prisoners and would have led to a catastrophe for the entire camp."[2129]

It is astonishing to find a man who had been a communist inmate of a Nazi concentration camp testifying on behalf of a Waffen SS doctor, the camp's chief physician. However, when one analyses the transcripts closely, one sees that such testimony is not isolated. During the trials, the Dutch artist and communist Henri Christiaan Pieck (1895-1972), born in Den Helder, and twin brother and fellow artist of Anton (1895-1987), was asked: "Did the defendant Hoven prevent members of the United Nations, especially French and Dutch citizens, from being transferred to Natzweiler in the Nacht and Nobel Action (Night and Fog Action)?" To which the Buchenwald artist answered: "

> I am very glad to be in a position to answer this question with yes, because had that not been the case I would not be sitting here right now. I am personally indebted to Dr. Hoven, I personally can thank him for my life, because he prevented this transport and he kept me from it."[2130]

Henri Christiaan Pieck lived to surreptitiously create his twenty-four drawings of life in the Buchenwald camp.[2131] If it is suggested that Hoven only acted mercifully when the war started going badly for Germany, the testimony of Henri Pieck was corroborated by Dr. Frederik van der Laan: "

> It is remarkable how Dr. Hoven on many occasions faked, and as an example I may mention a certain Dr. De Laan, a Dutch hostage, who was released through the aid of Dr. Hoven, and as is confirmed by this doctor himself this was only possible by faking the X-ray of his healthy lungs and exchanging it with X-rays of lungs of people with sick lungs, who were already in a progress state of tuberculosis."[2132]

Van der Laan added: "The good will of Dr. Waldemar Hoven was thus shown at a time when all Germans still believed in their victory. The risk that Dr. Waldemar Hoven then ran was in my opinion very great."[2133]

Further, Pieck testified: "

> It is a fact that contrary to every other camp we managed to maintain a Jewish hospital illegally where sick Jews were cared for. This fact alone would suffice to kill Dr. Hoven had

the SS known about any such situation. In the case of people who were beaten and were not allowed to be cared for, Dr. Hoven saw to it that an exception was made and saw to it that these people were cared for properly in the hospital."[2134]

When asked: "Would it have been possible to say that in accordance with Hoven's position in Buchenwald that he actually killed prisoners when there was no other in the community to do so?" The German national, Paul Friedrich Dorn, answered: "

> Your Honours, I can't imagine that a man who helped a Jew who had no right to live in the National Socialist state, that he killed people is possible, a man who asked him for his wishes regarding food and nursed him and aided him in the sick bay for months and even helped conceal him in the sick bay for years, that the same man arbitrarily might have carried out killings which were not necessary. I just cannot imagine such a thing."[2135]

Random killings it seems, were not Hoven's thing. The only killings he was guilty of, apparently, were of stool pigeons. When Hoven himself was asked the question; "Was there no way of doing away [with] traitors and stool pigeons?," he answered forthrightly: "

> If you had ever been in a concentration camp and knew the actual conditions there, you wouldn't ask that question. What was I to do? Should I go to the SS administration? Should I go to Koch [The camp commandant] or Lolling? To Gluecks, to Himmler, or to his Gestapo agent, Dr. Morgen, who on Himmler's orders was carrying out exterminations in the camp? And should I tell one of these people "Kuschnarev [White Russian anti-Semite stoolie], or one of those informers you have employed, has killed hundreds of prisoners, turned Russian commissars over for extermination and let the Jews be beaten to death?" They would have told me I was crazy or more, probably they would have simply shot me, and no one would have been helped by that and nothing would have been changed, because the highest representatives of justice in the camp were also at the same time the main representatives of the extermination program in the camp. Nor should it be forgotten, and I should like to emphasise again now, that a political prisoner,

whether German or foreign, was considered in the concentration camp to be the worst criminal, and his extermination from the point of view of the SS was a good deed."[2136]

Next, there is the questioning and testimony of the Dutch nobleman and philanthropist Philip Dirk, Baron van Pallandt (1889-1979), a Buchenwald inmate for nine months, from October 7 1940 to July 1941, as a hostage in retaliation for Germans held by the Dutch in the then Dutch East Indies, now Indonesia:[2137] "

> What do you think about the necessity of these killings?
>
> They were probably very necessary.
>
> Has each killing [of stoolies] saved the life of many times the number of [genuine] prisoners?
>
> Very probably.
>
> Under the existing conditions at the time at the Concentration Camp Buchenwald, was there any other way to render harmless these SS and Gestapo spies?
>
> So far as I know, no."[2138]

In regard to the character of Philip Dirk, Baron van Pallandt, it was stated in the court: "

> Regarding the affiant's character, I draw the Tribunal's attention to No. 1. This man is not a German who is making this statement to help a former camp doctor in Buchenwald. This man is a Dutchman. Let me draw your particular attention to the fact that he himself says 'I am chiefly interested in international and humanitarian movements.'
>
> In view of this, the statements made in questions 13 to 15 by this affiant should be of particular probative value. He also says under No. 1 'Since 1935 I have [had] a school for Quakers in my manor. After the war I received an official recognition of gratitude from the USA for having concealed a US airman for seven months, during the war.'"[2139]

When the Americans captured the Buchenwald camp on April 11 1945, all the SS members still inside the camp were handed over to them by the prisoners, while Hoven, who was outside the camp, was captured directly by the Americans and brought to the camp. Henri Pieck gives the following account: "

> Hoven was outside of the camp. He was captured by the American troops. I heard this, I did not see it myself. He was taken to the camp and a Jew named Cohen, and other prisoners, went to the Americans and made it clear to them that this was a mistake — "That man is in SS uniform but he belongs to us." The prisoners worked for him and in Block 50 we took Dr. Hoven in and took care of him."[2140]

Oscar Schindler was rightly made famous for saving 1,200 hundred Jews.[2141] In comparison, even prosecution witness Ferdinand Roemhild[2142] had to admit that Hoven saved around 20,000 prisoners by the actions he took in killing stool pigeons or looking the other way whenever the underground prisoner administration did as such.[2143] This figure, however, does not take into account the number Hoven saved by more principled means such as the operation of the officially illegal Jewish hospital.[2144] Nevertheless, in spite of all the testimony vindicating Waldemar Hoven, the United States Holocaust Memorial Museum simply states that: "

> Waldemar Hoven was a captain in the Waffen SS and chief doctor of the Buchenwald concentration camp. He was found guilty of conducting spotted fever experiments and practising euthanasia on humans. Hoven was given the death sentence and executed on the 2nd of June 1948."[2145]

Can a man on the one hand experiment on and kill genuine prisoners, and at the same time, be the saviour of thousands, including Jews and communists — arch-enemies of the National Socialist state? Payne Best wrote of seeing a cruel streak in Hoven, perhaps evident in the ruthless action he took against stoolies. However, in the environment that was KZ Buchenwald, would an angel have saved so many innocent lives? If that involved leaving the stoolies unhindered, then no.

It could be argued that the guilt or innocence of alleged stoolies should have been determined in a legitimate court of law, but in KZ Buchenwald, such a court was only a distant future possibility upon the annihilation of the Third Reich. Hoven, in KZ Buchenwald, had always to think of possible ways of saving the lives of genuine prisoners on the spot. A post-war court of law would have been too late for thousands of genuine prisoners that Dr. Hoven saved. Finally, there is the need to address a quote which Eric Metaxas attributes to "a witness at the Nuremberg trials, a man who was an inmate at Buchenwald and had worked with Hoven": "

> Dr. Hoven stood once together with me at the window of the pathological section and pointed to a prisoner not known to me who crossed the place where the roll calls were held. Dr. Hoven told me: "I want to see the skull of this prisoner on my writing desk by tomorrow evening." The prisoner was ordered to report to the medical section, after the physician had noted down the number of the prisoner. The corpse was delivered on the same day to the dissection room. The post-mortem examination showed that the prisoner had been killed by injections. The skull was prepared as ordered and delivered to Dr. Hoven."[2146]

In the notes at the back of the book, Metaxas gave the name of the accuser as Josef Ackermann,[2147] and did not comment on his credibility. When Hoven was questioned about this, he of course denied it.[2148] When I looked into the Nuremberg transcripts, I discovered that the accuser's statement was made in an affidavit; I found another affidavit written by German national Paul Dorn, read out to the court by Dr. Hans Gawlik, counsel for the defence: "

> I am the same Paul Dorn who testified here as a witness on 5 and 6 June 1947 before Military Tribunal I.

> Josef Ackermann's affidavit Document 2631, Exhibit 522, has been shown to me. I know Josef Ackermann. I made his acquaintance in the concentration camp Buchenwald in 1941. I know the general reputation which Josef Ackermann enjoyed in the concentration camp Buchenwald. Josef Ackermann enjoyed among the prisoners in the concentration camp a very bad reputation.

> I still remember for certainty that Josef Ackermann in about the year 1942 or 1943 betrayed a few prisoners who had stolen

some food in the camp to the SS camp management — namely, to the head of the administrative custody camp, Schober. Among the prisoners whom Josef Ackermann denounced was included the former political prisoner Heinrich Bach, a medical student by profession, from Finsterwalde. The SS camp management then carried out exhaustive investigations of the persons denounced. Heinrich Bach was to be transferred to the quarry work detail, where he very probably would have died. It is only to be attributed to Dr. Hoven's intervention that the SS camp management could not carry out this plan. Dr. Hoven first accommodated Bach in Block 46 in order to withdraw him from the clutches of the SS camp command. I think it therefore quite possible that Ackermann had a disinclination toward Dr. Hoven because Hoven helped the prisoners whom Ackermann had denounced at that time.

I state further Dr. Hoven never had a skull on his desk. This I know for certain. My statements here refer to the period from 1941 until his imprisonment in September 1943. I, therefore, consider it out of the question that Hoven asked Ackermann to give him a skull for his desk."[2149]

Hoven had been arrested and imprisoned in September 1943 because of the allegation that he had killed an incarcerated SS officer named Köhler by lethal injection. Köhler was a potential witness in the corruption case against Karl Otto Koch, the camp commandant, and his wife Ilse Koch, with whom Hoven allegedly had an affair. While the SS judge Konrad Morgen sentenced Hoven to death in the spring of 1945, Hoven remained in Buchenwald for eighteen months, until he was pardoned due to the prevailing physician shortage and released on April 2 1945.[2150]

The Nuremberg medical case testimonies suggest that Dr. Waldemar Hoven was a man capable of remorse and compassion. While horrific medical experiments undoubtedly took place in Buchenwald, the Nuremberg testimony points to the perpetrator being the infamous Doctor Ding alias Schuler,[2151] who committed suicide post-war but left a detailed diary of his diabolical experiments. Hoven, as the chief medical officer, must have been aware of these experiments, and it was probably on this basis that he was convicted. However, if Hoven had decided to issue an order banning such experiments in Buchenwald, he would probably have been overruled by the camp commandant before being incarcerated himself, and a replacement with no such annoying scruples would have been found. Many that lived to see liberation, including Dutch communists and Jews, would have become statistics in the litany of death at Buchenwald.

However, Sigmund Rascher, Hoven's replacement in his old prison cell in the cellar among the special prisoners, was devoid of any semblance of remorse and compassion. Payne Best kept getting varying accounts from him concerning how he ended up in Buchenwald,[2152] but what remained consistent were his accounts of medical experiments he carried out on prisoners with great relish,[2153] justified by the supposedly life-saving scientific data they rendered.[2154]

Three or four days after his arrival at Buchenwald, Payne Best was informed by the guard Sippach that they were expecting a new arrival who was an Englishman, and due to the shortage of space, he would probably have to share his larger cell with him. The prospect of sharing his cell with a fellow countryman delighted Payne Best. The following morning, when Payne Best went to wash, he noticed a little man with a ginger moustache who introduced himself and mentioned that he was half English and that his mother was related to the Chamberlain family.[2155] When Payne Best told him his name, Rascher told Payne Best that he knew all about his case, and that he knew Payne Best's fellow Venlo kidnap victim, Major Richard Stevens, while he was the medical officer in Dachau.[2156] At this first meeting, they did not have the opportunity to talk at length, but Best often managed to have his exercise time at the same time as Rascher. According to Payne Best, this was in a large part because Rascher was an SS officer. From these meetings and later events in this prison, he concluded that Rascher was the queerest character that had ever come his way.[2157]

At their first opportunity to speak at length, Rascher told Best that he had been on Himmler's personal staff, and that it was he who had planned and supervised the construction of the gas chambers and was responsible for the use of prisoners as guinea pigs in medical research.[2158] Rascher saw nothing wrong in this, and described it as mere expediency, as if it were nothing more sinister than performing a routine operation or experimenting on rats. In regard to the gas chambers, he described Himmler as a "very kind-hearted man," who was most anxious that prisoners be exterminated in a manner that caused them "least anxiety and suffering!"[2159]

The problem, he related, was to design a death chamber so camouflaged that its purpose would not be apparent, and to regulate the flow of the lethal gas so that the patients might painlessly fall asleep to never again awaken. Naturally, however, different prisoners would have varying degrees of resistance to the gaseous poison, and they would survive long enough to foil Himmler's grand "humanitarian" design. Moreover, Rascher elaborated that with the vast numbers to be exterminated, it was impossible to prevent the gas chambers from being overfilled, which hindered any attempts to ensure the objective of a regular and simultaneous death rate.[2160]

In regard to the medical experiments on prisoners, Rascher considered them entirely justified by the "life saving" scientific data they provided.[2161] Most of all, he was proud to claim that he had discovered a technique which would save the lives of thousands who would otherwise die of exposure.[2162] He had no qualms in exposing a couple of dozen people to intense cold, in water or air, and then attempting their resuscitation.[2163] Rascher, in one of six varying accounts to Payne Best, asserted that his imprisonment was due to the fact that he had attempted to publish the results of his research into this topic in a Swiss medical journal.[2164] His motivation was that it might benefit British seamen who, after rescue from the sea when their ships were torpedoed, frequently died without recovering consciousness.[2165]

One variation of Rascher's medical genocide, not mentioned by Payne Best, was the high altitude experiments he carried out in 1942 on prisoners in Dachau. Exploring how best to save German pilots forced to eject at high altitude, he devised another experiment. It involved placing inmates in low-pressure chambers that simulated altitudes as high as 21,000 metres (68,000 feet) and monitoring their physiological response as they succumbed and died. Rascher was said have to dissected victims' brains while they were still alive to show that high-altitude sickness resulted from the formation of tiny air bubbles in the blood vessels of a certain part of the brain. Of 200 people subjected to these experiments, 80 died outright and the remainder were executed.[2166]

Initially, Rascher was a Luftwaffe officer but was frustrated by the Christian scruples of many of its officers who baulked at his concept of using concentration camp inmates as test subjects for these diabolical experiments. Heinrich Himmler wrote a letter to the Luftwaffe's Field Marshal Erhard Milch, requesting Milch to authorise the transfer of Rascher to the SS, where he could operate free of such moral constraints.[2167] An irony here was that Milch's father was ethnically Jewish, which the Gestapo had duly investigated in 1935, only for Göring to compel the Gestapo to drop the case, and he himself issued a blood certificate stating Milch was a full blooded Aryan. Göring's generosity may have been motivated by his need to have someone competent to rebuild the Luftwaffe.[2168] Milch was forced to appear in Nuremberg in relation to these experiments, but only served time until 1954, and advised the German air industry until his death in 1972.[2169]

Payne Best was not shocked by these stories. Moreover, when they got to know Rascher, neither were Payne Best's fellow prisoners, although it's impossible to imagine Dietrich sharing this perspective.[2170] Payne Best explained his and his fellow prisoners' indifference by the fact that, day in and day out, hardened as they were to their possible sudden death, they had little energy to expend in sympathy for the sufferings of unknown people who, after all, were already dead. Furthermore, in Payne Best's mind, Rascher was apparently a good comrade to all his fellow prisoners, never hesitating to stand up to the guards who had them in their power.[2171] The question remains: can being the life and soul of a party,[2172] or standing up to brutal guards for a month or so, absolve him of years of heinous crimes, for which he felt no remorse?

The true reason for Rascher's arrest was his involvement in a bizarre child abduction scheme; his wife Nini had kidnapped a series of infants after she discovered she was unable to conceive children of her own. Her husband went along with her, portraying three of the stolen babies as his newborn sons to Himmler. However, in 1944, Munich investigators discovered the truth, and when Himmler learned of it, he dispatched Rascher's wife Nini to the Ravensbrück concentration camp for women, and Rascher to Buchenwald.[2173] Rascher ended up back in Dachau in April 1945, where he had conducted his medical experiments. Then, just days before the Americans liberated Dachau, an SS officer shot Rascher in his cell.[2174]

One prisoner with whom Payne Best forged a close friendship post-war was Oberstleutnant (Lieutenant Colonel) Horst Bernhard Kurt von Petersdorff.[2175] Payne Best described his character as adventurous. Von Petersdorff's bravery is beyond question, as were his allegiances with the Nazi Party pre-war, and with Ernst Röhm's SA or Brown Shirts. Born in 1892 in Posen, now Poznań in modern-day western Poland, he had been wounded six times in the Great War, and already in 1914, had lost the use of his right arm.[2176] After the 1918 armistice and amidst its ensuing chaos, he had joined one of the far-right Freikorps operating in the Baltic, with which he had had a number of hair-raising escapes.[2177] He would become one of the earliest members of the Nazi Party, and as a noble and wealthy man, he became one of their most valuable recruits.[2178]

Within months of Hitler's ascent to power in January 1933, von Petersdorff joined Röhm's SA. His and the SA's interpretation of Hitler's election pledges diverged from that of the Nazi Party in general.[2179] In short, many in the SA took the "socialism" in National Socialism too seriously.[2180] By June 1934, it all came to a head, with President Hindenburg demanding that Hitler rein in Röhm's band of unruly street thugs,[2181] which culminated in the Nacht der Langen Messer or Night of the Long Knives in early July 1934. All the key figures in the SA, including Ernst Röhm, were summarily shot in a two day nation wide purge. While the SA continued to exist under the leadership of the more compliant Victor Lutze, it would never regain its former prominence; it faded into insignificance as the star of Heinrich Himmler and his SS ascended.[2182]

Nevertheless, von Petersdorff somehow avoided being a victim of the bloody purge; he went underground and engaged with those most actively involved in the conspiracy against the Third Reich. This did not stop him. however, from responding to the call to arms at the outbreak of war. He took part in the Polish campaign and the invasion of France, where he commanded the armoured reconnaissance unit, which was the first to reach the coast on the English Channel near Abbeville. For this action he was awarded the Knight's Cross of the Iron Cross, being one of the first three men to receive this decoration. Almost immediately following this award, he was again in active opposition to the Reich, even though he continued to be engaged in the war, and was wounded another four times.[2183]

Involved in the failed Valkyrie plot, he was naturally among the hundreds of army officers arrested in its aftermath. He was hauled before the People's Court. A case was prepared for his prosecution, but without any firm evidence of his complicity in the plot, Freisler's court acquitted him. This verdict did not stop the Gestapo from re-arresting and incarcerating him in Berlin's Prinz-Albrecht-Strasse prison. When this was destroyed by the American Eighth Air Force's raid on February 3 1945,[2184] he was buried under debris in his cell, suffering injuries to his lungs and kidneys for which he was given no treatment. Hence, when Payne Best first met him, he was chronically ill, but his spirit, which would see him through to liberation in Niederdorf, was utterly unyielding, never flinching in the eye of danger or seeking any special favours.

Among the special prisoners, the only one Payne Best detested was Doctor Horst Hoepner, whom he regarded as an abject coward. He was the brother of Valkyrie conspirator General Erich Hoepner, who managed to talk his way out of execution at the hands of Fromm in the courtyard of the Bendlerstrasse. However, he was hanged two-and-a-half weeks later on August 8 1944, following his appearance in Freisler's court. His brother Horst, it seems, was terrified of suffering the same fate, and while occupying a cell next to Payne Best, on more than one occasion he collapsed into nervous fits whenever Payne Best got himself into heated arguments with the guards; these fits twice led to the doctor being fetched to treat him.[2185]

He nevertheless survived, to be liberated in Niederdorf among the special prisoners in late April 1945. For Payne Best, what concerned him most about what he called "this miserable worm of a man"[2186] was that fear is contagious and could provoke a general panic amongst the prisoners. However, as time passed in Buchenwald and beyond, Payne Best's concerns proved to be unfounded.

Chapter 24

Dietrich's Final Days

By Easter Sunday April 1 1945, the American Third Army of General George S. Patton crossed the Werra River, upon which, the inmates of Buchenwald heard the thunder of their artillery.[2187] One could imagine that Dietrich hoped this most important day in Christendom, celebrating Christ's resurrection, symbolised his imminent liberation after nearly two years' imprisonment. Later that day, however, the chief guard, Sippach, told the prisoners to get ready to leave. Their destination was unknown, and all except for one had very few belongings to transport. The exception was Payne Best, who had a typewriter, suitcase, and three large boxes.[2188]

That day they heard nothing more, but the next day, Dittman, the other more surly guard, told everyone they should be ready to leave on foot, prompting some to fear that they would be taken into the woods and shot. In this dire situation, with his life on a knife's edge, and with a general scarcity of food, vehicles and fuel, Payne Best's overriding concern was having to jettison some of his belongings![2189] Even with some of the prisoners sick from lack of food and constant cold, including Captain Gehre, Josef Müller, and Colonel von Petersdorff, it surprised no one that they would have to walk.

Throughout the implosion of the Reich, many would perish in the freezing cold of these death marches. Among them were American GIs who died on death marches from the Buchenwald satellite camp of Berga; of the 350 prisoners originally incarcerated there, only two groups totalling 63 lived to see liberation. The first was liberated by the 90th Infantry Division on April 20 1945, and the second by the 11th Armored Division on April 23.[2190] However, they were forbidden to tell the stories of their ordeal post-war; just days following their liberation, on April 24 1945, they were coerced into signing a "Security Certificate for Ex-Prisoners of War," which stipulated in its first clause: "Some activities of American prisoners of war within German prison camps must remain secret not only for the duration of the war against the present enemies of the United States, but in peacetime as well."[2191] Their enforced silence was only broken sixty years later, when the handful of them still alive, such as Tony Acevedo, the 20 year-old GI medic of Mexican heritage, finally spoke out.[2192] A few years later in 2009, the

US Army admitted that US soldiers had been imprisoned in a German slave labour camp.[2193]

On early Tuesday evening after Easter, Sippach announced that they would be leaving on foot within an hour. However, an hour turned into several; then at 10 p.m., they were told that they would not be leaving on foot, but in a van. However, the van was powered by a bulky wood fuelled generator at the front, leading to the passenger area becoming filled with choking smoke upon their departure.[2194] Eight days later, other starved and emaciated prisoners stormed the watchtowers and seized control of the camp, before the US Third Army entered Buchenwald in the afternoon, where soldiers from its 6th Armored Division found more than 21,000 emaciated prisoners.[2195]

The seventeen[2196] special or Prominenten (prominent) prisoners[xxvii] were a motley assortment of decorated and aristocratic army generals, a naval commander, a diplomat and his wife, a Catholic lawyer, a theologian, a mysterious and promiscuous woman, Heidi, suspected of perhaps being a spy for both sides,[2197] a depressed Russian air force officer who was infatuated with her, a RAF officer, an MI-6 agent, and a concentration camp "doctor." All managed somehow to cram themselves and their luggage into the van they came to dub the Grüne Minna (Green Minnie). However, just as the guards closed the doors, the air raid siren sounded, upon which the guards abandoned the prisoners in the Grüne Minna, and ran as far as possible from the nearby cellar with its stores of munitions.[2198] At this point, one can imagine the state of mind of Doctor Horst Hoepner.

When the all clear was finally sounded, the military personnel returned to start the engine. In this they succeeded, but after the van proceeded only a hundred metres or so, it halted, with the wood fuelled engine still idling. Within moments, the van was filled with fumes, prompting Rascher to cry, "My God, this is a death van; we are being gassed!"[2199] Certainly, having been instrumental in designing the gas chambers,[2200] rather than the less "efficient" but still monstrous predecessor of the vans, Rascher was still more qualified than most to suspect the worst. Such mobile killing units (душегубка — dushegubka), camouflaged as bread vans, were first used on a limited experimental basis by the Soviet NKVD during the Stalinist purges of the 1930s,[2201] with the victims encased in an air-tight compartment into which carbon

---

[xxvii] In regard to the Prominenten (prominent prisoners), see the beginning of Chapter 27 "The Prominenten and Miraculous Reprieves" from endnotes [2708] to [2714].

monoxide from the exhaust would be fed while they died on their way to the mass grave at Butovo on the outskirts of Moscow.

The Nazis did not use them until around August 1941, in the aftermath of the Barbarossa's launch, when Einsatzgruppe members complained of the "psychological burden caused by shooting large numbers of women and children."[2202] With the invention of the gas vans, aside from their greater and more economical efficiency, the "battle fatigue and mental anguish" for the "heroic" Einsatzgruppe members decreased. The most vocal "complainants" on their behalf were Erich von dem Bach-Zelewski, the central figure, among other incidents, in the suppression of the 1944 Warsaw General Uprising,[2203] and Arthur Nebe,[2204] then commander of Einsatzgruppe B based in the Belarusian capital of Minsk,[2205] and perhaps the most questionable member in the entire German resistance.

In the Grüne Minna, Payne Best. with the characteristic composure of an intelligence operative, noticed some light coming through what seemed to be a vent, upon which he asked Rascher whether or not such things were to be found in gas vans. Rascher, somewhat relieved, replied they were not, and so, if they perished, it would more than likely be unintentional.[2206] Eventually the van began moving again, allowing sufficient ventilation for breathing, but Rabenau and both women, Margot Heberlein, the wife of the former ambassador to Spain, and the mysterious Heidi, fainted.[2207]

At most, the van could only manage about 30 kilometres (20 miles) an hour,[2208] and every hour it had to be stopped to get its air filters cleaned and its boiler refilled with chopped wood before it was reheated. In the process, in spite of the air inside the van becoming almost unbreathable, the prisoners were not allowed to get out; they had no water and nothing to eat during these stops.[2209] Dietrich discovered the last of his tobacco in his pocket; Payne Best, a heavy smoker, was grateful when Dietrich decided to share it with everyone, declaring Dietrich to be a "good and saintly man."[2210]

Once during the night, when the prisoners banged on the sides of the van to signal the call of nature, the guards relented, allowing the prisoners out in an area almost bare of vegetation and undulations while they held their machine guns at the ready.[2211] The two women were taken across a field to a small copse in the distance for privacy. When dawn broke some hours later on Wednesday April 4, with no idea of their destination, the prisoners' spirits rose somewhat. The stock of wood had dropped, and Hugh Falconer was able to rearrange the luggage for what felt like a welcome doubling of available room. At the same time, the guards produced a couple of loaves of bread and a large sausage and drink, which the prisoners divided up between themselves.[2212] After seven to eight hours of travel, they had covered just 160 kilometres (100 miles).[2213]

One of the prisoners recognised one of the villages they passed through, and after some discussion, they came to the conclusion that they were headed south for the Flossenbürg concentration camp. Since this camp was primarily used for the extermination of unwanted prisoners, their spirits must have plummeted. By noon, after thirteen hours of travel, they arrived at the police station of Weiden, a town of 30,000 in northern Bavaria, just 16 kilometres or 10 miles east of the death camp. After talking with the police, the guards returned to inform the prisoners that no room was available at Flossenbürg to accommodate them. The prisoners' concentration camp expert,[2214] Sigmund Rascher, happily informed them that, for the time being at least, they could not be marked for execution, as places like Flossenbürg always had room for extra corpses.[2215]

With the huge influx of refugees into Weiden,[2216] space there was at a premium, so the guards had to comply with the vague order to move on further south. It was at this point that Payne Best noticed a distinct relaxation in the disposition of the three SS guards. He reasoned that this meant that whereas at Buchenwald, they were under clear orders to head for Flossenbürg, they were now simply ordered to head south until they found somewhere to deposit the prisoners. As such they had a sense that they were in part sharing the prisoners' experience into the wide blue yonder,[2217] as indicated by the next stop for refuelling, where they asked the prisoners if they would like to get out to stretch their legs, with this now becoming the norm at all further stops.

This feeling of optimism among the prisoners was tested when, soon after leaving Weiden, they were overtaken by a car from which signs were made for the prisoners' driver to stop. Two police officers then boarded the van and, according to Payne Best, called out: "Müller, Gehre, Liedig, get your things and come with us."[2218] Another report says that Dietrich, not Gehre, was called out; Bethge says that Dietrich leaned back in the van to avoid being seen, and that Gehre, after sharing a cell with Müller, wished to stay with him.[2219] As events five days later suggest, the police could well have thought they had Dietrich instead of Captain Gehre,[2220] although, if that's so, they must have been unaware that Dietrich was the pastor, and Gehre the military officer.

Ludwig Gehre had been involved in Tresckow's March 1943 brandy bomb plot, and when the Kreisau Circle's Helmuth James Graf von Moltke was arrested in January 1944, Gehre's arrest soon followed.[2221] However, he had managed to elude his guards during transport and it was not until November, in the Valkyrie aftermath, that he was rearrested. This was in the wake of Gehre shooting his second wife before turning the gun on himself in a botched suicide attempt where he seriously injured his eye.[2222] The Gestapo, before engaging in the requisite torture, "nursed" him back to health,[2223] and he ended up with the party of seventeen prisoners.

As for Commander Franz Liedig, he had been stationed in Greece and was a member of the staff of Admiral Canaris. Payne Best perceived in him a foreboding sense of approaching death.[2224] But he found conversation with him particularly interesting; he had a detailed knowledge of the German railway system, enabling him to estimate the possibility of any mass movement of troops from the north to what was already known as the Southern Redoubt. In Liedig's opinion, even by the beginning of March 1945, such a movement was no longer feasible, and for all practical military purposes, Germany had already been cut in half into a northern and a southern zone.[2225] This was relevant for the party of seventeen, as rumours were rife that their final destination was the area around Berchtesgaden in Bavaria, where Hitler intended to make his last stand, and use it as a point of exchange for hostages in return for the safe passage of important members of the Nazi hierarchy.[2226] This may explain the general southwards direction of travel for the hostages. It also suggests how far removed from reality the inner circle of the Third Reich were, even in its death throes.

Although Ludwig Gehre and Josef Müller shared cell eight in Buchenwald, it seems unlikely that, as Metaxas and Bethge propose,[2227] Gehre joined his old cell mate out of any sense of comradeship. Payne Best alluded to the suspicion that Müller held for Gehre and almost anyone in general, while he commended Müller's extraordinary bravery.[2228] Having already shot his second wife, and botched his suicide, Gehre may have had a sense of being more expendable than anyone else, and perhaps didn't wish to live out the rest of his life with the memory of that terrible episode. He may have welcomed execution and the martyr's status that it indeed conferred, as attested to by the monument now standing in Flossenbürg.

In any event, as the remaining party of fourteen restarted their trek south to nowhere in particular, Payne Best noted the plummeting spirits of his remaining fellow prisoners, all certain that the three who'd left them were on their way to certain death.[2229] However, their spirits rose when they stopped near a large farmhouse by mid to late afternoon. The farmer and his wife were friendly and accommodating, allowing the women to go inside for a wash and the men to share the pump. Before long, the farmer's wife came out with a big jug of milk and two loaves of beautiful rye bread such as none of them had tasted for years, in an idyllic setting on that beautiful day in Bavaria's Naab Valley.[2230] It was as if the war, for that hour, had granted them this fleeting enjoyment of the beauty around them and exchange of happy banter. For Dietrich and von Rabenau, this respite was in the final days of their lives on this earth, and for Rascher, his final three weeks.[2231]

Just as dusk was falling, they reached the large medieval town of Regensburg, on the confluence of the Danube, Regen and Naab rivers.[2232] Since July 13 2006,[2233] it has been listed as World Heritage, as it is one of the very few German towns to have its medieval old town largely unscathed by the destruction of World War II,[2234] and has a history that pre-dates Roman times.[2235] Between 1945 and 1949, Regensburg was the site of the largest DP (Displaced Persons) camp in Germany, and at its peak from 1946 to 1947, the workers' district of Ganghofersiedlung housed almost 5,000 Ukrainian and 1,000 non-Ukrainian refugees and displaced persons.[2236]

Upon arrival in Regensburg, one of the guards told the prisoners that if they couldn't find anywhere for them to stay, he didn't know what they could do next. As considerable time passed, they stopped every now and again at several large buildings, before they were told to get out at the entrance to the Landes Gefängnis (state prison). As they started to ascend the flight of steps, they were confronted by two or three men in uniform, more than likely warders, who started to order them about very crudely, until one of the "special" prisoners' guards explained that they were "very important people" to be treated with consideration and courtesy. To which one of the warders barked, "Oh! Some more aristocrats. Well, put them with the other lot on the second floor."[2237] Less than five days later, Dietrich would not be afforded such "courtesy."

As they dragged their luggage up the steep iron steps to the second floor, they were greeted by an amicable elderly warder, who explained that due to the cramped conditions in the prison, the men would have to sleep five to a cell, while the two women would get their own cell. Dietrich shared his cell with Pünder, von Rabenau, von Falkenhausen, and Hoepner. However, as they were all famished, they asked if they could have some food, which, the warders replied, was impossible, as the kitchen was closed. Arguments quickly ensued before the entire party joined in the chorus of "*Wir wollen Essen!*" — "We want food!,"[2238] which in no time spread to the cells on other floors. Finally, the warders relented and gave each of them a large bowl of passable vegetable soup, a hunk of bread and some coffee.

The following morning of Thursday April 5, their cell doors were opened by the warders to allow the prisoners to go and wash. However, when the Buchenwald party of fourteen got to the long corridor leading to the wash rooms, they found it packed with a mass of humanity. Many of them were familiar.[2239] In fact, as Payne Best commented, Falkenhausen and Petersdorff seemed to know everybody, and as he was on such good terms with these two, he was soon being introduced right and left, with the atmosphere more like a huge social gathering than a morning in a criminal prison. The other prisoners were the Sippenhäftlinge or "family prisoners"; the relatives of people executed for complicity in the Valkyrie plot, such as all the surviving members of the von Stauffenberg, Goerdeler, and other families, and the relatives of German officers who, as prisoners of war captured in the Soviet Union, had associated themselves with the Soviet sponsored "Nationalkomittee Freies Deutschland" — NKFD (National Free German Committee).[2240]

Among the Stauffenbergs was Alexander, the older brother of Claus and the younger surviving twin brother of Berthold, who had already been executed upon the order of Freisler's court on August 10 1944. Alexander would be among the liberated at Niederdorf; he became a professor of Ancient History at Munich University before passing away there in 1964, aged 58.[2241] Another interesting character among the Sippenhäftlinge was the likeable and extroverted Isa Vermehren,[2242] born in Lübeck in 1918, who passed away in 2009 in Bonn.[2243]

Before her arrest, she was a cabaret singer and film actress and sister of Erich,[2244] a member of the Abwehr in the Bulgarian capital of Sofia. Erich and his wife had succeeded in escaping to Turkey and thence to England in early 1944,[2245] but Isa, together with her parents and other brother Michael, were arrested in accordance with the Sippenhäft law.[2246] Post-war, from 1951 until her death, Isa became a Catholic nun, joining the order of the Society of Sisters of the Sacred Heart of Jesus, and her character figured prominently in the dramatised two-part documentary "Hostages of the SS." Like Dietrich, she was opposed to the Nazi regime from the outset. In 1933, after refusing to offer the Hitler greeting to the flag out of sympathy for a Jewish schoolmate prohibited from making the gesture, she was expelled from high school. In Isa's mind, the Third Reich was a "spiritual dictatorship."[2247]

Another of the Sippenhäftlinge in Regensburg, whose character also figured prominently in the dramatised documentary, was Fey Von Hassell, born in 1919. She passed away in 2010 — the year following Isa Vehmehren's death.[2248] She was the author of *Hostage of the Third Reich: the story of my imprisonment and rescue from the SS.*[2249] She was the daughter of Ulrich von Hassell, who had been executed in the wake of the Valkyrie plot, and the granddaughter of the ultra-nationalist Grand Admiral Alfred Peter Friedrich von Tirpitz (1849—1930).[2250] He was the German Naval commander at the outbreak of the Great War, and the German sister ship of the Bismarck was named after him.[2251] In January 1940 Fey married the anti-Fascist Italian, Ditalmo Pirzio-Biroli, and settled on his Castello di Brazzà (Castle Brazzà) family estate, near Udine in the far north-eastern corner of the country.[2252] In early September 1943, her privileged life at Castello di Brazzà took a significant turn for the worse.[2253]

On the third day of that month, at Fairfield Camp near the village of Cassibile in Sicily, Italy signed an armistice with the Allies,[2254] which was kept secret for five days until September 8.[2255] The signatories where the Italian General, Giuseppe Castellano, acting on behalf of Prime Minister Marshal Pietro Badoglio, and representing the Italian government that deposed Mussolini in July, and General Bedeli Smith, acting on behalf of General Dwight D. Eisenhower, the supreme Allied Commander.[2256] The hope was that the Allies, with the help of their newest official ally, would be able to parry any potential German threat to Italy. Unfortunately, this was a naive hope. For one thing, many Italian units only had enough ammunition to fight for twenty minutes, since the Germans had long since ceased supplying fuel and ammunition.[2257] For another, no clear orders had been issued to the Italian fleet or to the sixty army divisions totalling 1.7 million.[2258] Moreover, after the removal of Mussolini from power, Hitler and many of his advisors were extremely suspicious of the new regime's intentions, in spite of their repeated "assurances" they would fight alongside Germany until the perceived final victory.[2259]

Accordingly, the Germans had prepared Operation Alarich, later to become Achse (Axis), as a contingency plan in the event of an armistice being signed. When the armistice was publicly announced, the Wehrmacht wasted no time in implementing Achse,[2260] and by September 11, Rome was already under Wehrmacht control, not to be liberated until nine months later on June 5 1944, the day preceding the

Normandy D-day landings.[2261] With virtually the entire Italian peninsula under German control, Mussolini was rescued on the 12th by daring German glider-borne commandos, enabling Hitler to establish the fascist puppet Italian Social Republic in the country's north.[2262] Given the mountainous terrain typical throughout Italy, greatly lending itself to resilient and stubborn defence, significant German resistance was still present in its mountainous north even until its unconditional surrender in early May 1945.[2263] Little wonder then that the Wehrmacht, almost immediately upon the launch of Achse, occupied Castello di Brazzà in Italy's far north.

While the Italian armed forces virtually disintegrated on the peninsula, there were exceptions elsewhere, such as the Italian Acqui division on the Greek Ionian island of Cephalonia. This division held out until September 23, where, upon their surrender to the Wehrmacht (not SS) Alpine Division, in an act characteristic of his vindictive nature, Hitler ordered the execution of thousands of their men. This became known as the Cephalonia massacre,[2264] and with the exception the infamous Soviet-perpetrated April 1940 Katyń massacre, may have been the largest prisoner of war massacre of the Second World War.[2265]

When the Germans seized Rome, Fey's husband, Detalmo Pirzio Biroli, went underground there to serve with the Comitato di Liberazione Nazionale (National Liberation Committee) as a member of the Partito d'Azione (Action Party). Most notably, he helped liberate three thousand allied prisoners and provided false passports to Jews and anti-fascists to escape arrest.[2266] While his wife was still able to live on the estate, she now had to play permanent "host" to Wehrmacht officers. However, about a year later on September 8 1944, in the wake of the failed Valkyrie plot, and following a two day "trial" before Freisler's court, her dear father Ulrich, the ambassador to Italy from 1932-8, was sentenced before being executed in Berlin's Plötzensee prison.[2267] Upon hearing this news on the radio, the Wehrmacht commander at Castello di Brazzà denounced his hostess and had her and her two boys picked up by the SS.[2268] Fey was now one of the Sippenhäftlinge; to her horror, days later, her two young boys, aged four and two, were taken into SS custody while they were being detained in a hotel in Innsbruck in Austria.[2269] All this was unbeknownst to her husband.

From here, Fey was taken to an up-market forested hotel in what is now the Czech Republic, where she met Alexander von Stauffenberg while he was struggling over reading Dante's *Inferno*.[2270] Before long, Fey began giving Alexander Italian lessons, and during short walks in the snow-covered hotel grounds, under the watchful eyes of the guards, and united in their separation from their respective spouses and their common love of literature and poetry, an intense romantic bond formed between them. Alexander had been a professor in Munich before the war, so post-war he followed on from where he had left off. As he was the typical absent-minded professor, his brothers had decided not to let him in on the plot, and as it turned out, that was just as well.

Their respite in this idyllic captivity was abruptly terminated when they and their fellow Sippenhäftlinge were moved on to the grim KZ Stutthof near the Baltic port of Danzig (now Polish Gdańsk). While their group was somewhat more "privileged" than the general camp inmates, dysentery was common, and in Christmas 1944, typhoid swept through the camp, killing hundreds of inmates. Before long, Fey contracted the dreaded disease; during her illness, Alexander was constantly by her side, writing his first poem to her. For four weeks, Fey was at death's door, but ultimately, due in part, no doubt, to Alexander's support, she survived.[2271] By January, in the face of advancing Soviet troops, they were moved on to the camps of Buchenwald and later Dachau before being driven through the Bremer Pass to their liberation in Niederdorf. While in transit between these camps, they spent time at the prison in Regensburg; in her book, Fey described the Grüne Minna and the meeting with the party of fourteen. She commented how much more comfortable her and her fellow prisoners' trips had been than those of the unfortunate fourteen in the Grüne Minna.[2272]

When Alexander first met Fey, he was married to a remarkable woman who was not exactly in the perceived National Socialist mould of the subservient housewife. She was Melitta (Litta) von Stauffenberg, née Schiller (1903-1945),[2273] one of two whom Clare Mulley dubbed "Hitler's Valkyries." (Hitler's female pilots.)[2274] The other was Litta's bitter rival Hanna Reitsch, (1912-1979) who never married,[2275] and who lived on in total denial of the Holocaust.[2276] Curiously, while Litta's father Michael was baptised and raised a Protestant, her paternal grandfather Moses was a non-practising Jew.[2277] As Clare Mulley put it: "

> In the nineteenth century, when Posen (today Poznań in western Poland) had come under Prussian rule, a new synagogue had been built and the Jewish community developed close links with the German, mainly Protestant, population. Moses admired German culture, and when Michael was baptised, both father and son considered their Jewish roots to be behind them. They were German patriots, and either from a sense of shame, a wish to avoid discrimination or a belief in its irrele-

vance, the Schillers' Jewish ancestry was never discussed. None of Michael's friends knew that this young man was anything other than the model German Protestant that he both appeared, and considered himself, to be."[2278]

It is unclear when Melitta first became aware of her Jewish heritage. Perhaps when she was confirmed at age fourteen in 1917, or when Hitler came to power in 1933; the fact of Jewishness became politically significant when the first wave of legislation came into force limiting Jewish participation in German public life. Certainly, by the time of Hitler's proclamation of the anti-Jewish Nuremberg Laws in September 1935, the Third Reich's agenda of anti-Semitism was enshrined, stripping German Jews of their citizenship, depriving them of basic political rights, and prohibiting them from marrying or having sexual relations with "Aryans." In effect, ending any realistic hope for a tolerable existence within their country that Jews may have held on to.[2279]

However, at first, none of the Schiller family were directly affected by the Nuremberg Laws: "

> In a painful attempt to discriminate systematically, the regime identified Jews as those who had three or four "racially" Jewish grandparents, or two if they were practising Jews. Melitta and her siblings therefore fell outside the scope of the laws. Furthermore, initial exceptions were made for highly decorated veterans, people over sixty-five or those married to Aryans, meaning Michael was also exempt. There was no need for an anxious conversation about whether to register or try to disappear. Nevertheless, it was clear that the Schiller family were no longer quite the equal German citizens that they had once been, and now that the principles of racial segregation and discrimination were enshrined in German law, there could be no guarantee that they would not yet find themselves subject to persecution."[2280]

For Melitta, as it turned out, her diluted Jewish heritage never became a pressing issue, and in January 1943, she was awarded the Iron Cross. What became a real issue for her, was the invocation of the ancient Sippenhäft law in the wake of the failed Valkyrie plot owing to her marriage to a Stauffenberg. However, in the desperate and parlous state of Germany by that stage, and intense lobbying by elements in the Luftwaffe, she was considered vital to the war effort and released after six weeks incarceration on September 2, 1944.[2281]

From then on, she searched for Alexander in the concentration camps. She was able to see him in Stutthof in January, and pass on news of the children to him, before seeing him for the last time in Buchenwald in mid-March 1945.[2282] There she landed in a light Storch reconnaissance aircraft just outside the barbed wire perimeter just two weeks after Alexander and Fey had arrived, and while Dietrich and his fellow inmates were incarcerated there. Upon alighting she was overwhelmed by the camp's stench and the hideous sight of thousands of starved prisoners. This all too brief meeting would be the last with her husband, as on April 8, the day before Dietrich's execution, she was shot down by an American fighter mistaking her unarmed aircraft for a Focke Wulf 190 fighter.[2283] By this time of course, the Allies had total control of the skies over Germany. Litta survived the crash landing, but she passed away hours later, with the cause of death documented as a fracture to the base of her skull.[2284]

With the guards at Regensburg under instructions to treat the prisoners politely, it began to feel as if the latter had taken over the prison.[2285] When a warder shouted "everybody go his cell," they all just laughed, and it was only when one of the warders had the bright idea to leave the food in the cells that the inmates made their way back. In his cell, with Carl Goerdeler's widow in the neighbouring cell, Dietrich took the opportunity to tell her through the small door opening of her husband's final days at Prinz-Albrecht-Strasse.[2286] Carl Goerdeler was executed on February 2 1945, the day before the American air raid that hit the prison.[2287]

Before long, the air raid siren sounded, and the prisoners were taken to the prison basement.[2288] While Regensburg's Old Town was left largely unscathed from the destruction of World War II, this was not the case for other areas of the town. Payne Best noted the total destruction of the railway marshalling yard when he looked out from the window of the lavatory.[2289] After they returned to their floor, the guards did not attempt to lock the prisoners back in, and at 5 p.m., the old guards at Buchenwald informed the party of fourteen to get ready to move on again.[2290] The Grüne Minna was there waiting for them, and after the almost festive day with friends, everyone was feeling cheerful and upbeat. Unfortunately, unbeknownst to them on this day of Thursday April 5 1945, the gruesome fate of two of their own had already been decided. By chance on the previous day, the SS General Walter Buhle had discovered in Zossen, just south of Berlin, even further material from

Dohnányi's secret archive, which included diaries belonging to Admiral Canaris.[2291]

The man responsible for setting up the July 20th Commission, Ernst Kaltenbrunner,[2292] passed this damning content on to his drug-addicted Führer, who worked himself into one of his apoplectic fits of rage. The core reason for the failure of Hitler's beloved Third Reich is reflected in this outburst. It mirrors the thinking in his perceived Dolchstosslegende (Stab in the back myth) of November 1918.[2293] At a noon meeting, he gave the order for the "liquidation" of Canaris and other conspirators among the Abwehr.[2294] The time was now up for Wilhelm Canaris, Ludwig Gehre, Hans Oster, and Hans von Dohnányi, and from among the party of fourteen, Friedrich von Rabenau and Dietrich Bonhoeffer.

By this time, even the most delusional and fanatical National Socialist diehards did not expect a German victory. The catch phrase everywhere had become "every man for himself" — "save yourself if you can." Yet, it only took one command from a vindictive and delusional Hitler to put in motion the official mechanism of "*judicial*" murder in an isolated corner of the crumbling Reich, virtually cut-off from its capital.[2295] Hitler was still surrounded by sycophantic henchmen who shared his fury and blindly carried out their orders to the very last.[2296] Many historians believe that Hitler's mistress Eva Braun married him, before committing herself to the dual suicide on April 30 1945, so that history would perceive her as faithful to the last to her beloved Führer, the one and only true leader of the German Fatherland. In fact, history remembers her as a silly, bigoted, self-centred, narcissistic female.[2297] In early April, the SS judge Otto Thorbeck in Nuremberg was summoned to preside over a "court-martial" at Flossenbürg. On Sunday the 8th, he found an open coal train that took him as far as Weiden. From there, no motorised transport was available, so he got hold of a bicycle for the last twenty kilometres or so, intent on carrying out Hitler's judicial murders.[2298] As Metaxas put it, "The corpse of German jurisprudence must be exhumed to create the image of lawfulness."[2299]

On that evening of April 5 in Berlin, exactly two years to the day after Hans von Dohnányi's and Dietrich's arrests, Dr Tietze in the State Hospital received orders to prepare Dohnányi for transport to KZ Sachsenhausen the following morning. He immediately sent for his wife Christine, and at Hans's bedside they discussed escape plans with him, but were forced to accept that it was too late. The next morning Sonderegger, who had arrested Dohnányi and Dietrich with Roeder two years earlier, came to pick up the prisoner, and left no doubt in anyone's mind that Dohnányi's fate was sealed. At Sachsenhausen on Friday the 6th, Walter Huppenkothen, who had been the chief investigator at Prinz-Albrecht-Strasse, together with an unknown SS judge and the camp commandant, proclaimed the death sentence for Hans von Dohnányi, who was lying on a stretcher, half-conscious, before them. The sentence was carried out on April 9 — the very same day as Dietrich's execution at Flossenbürg.[2300]

At the Lehrterstrasse prison, Dietrich's brother Klaus, brother-in-law Rüdiger Schleicher, Hans John, Friedrich Justus Perels, Albrecht Haushofer, and eleven other prisoners, were told on April 22 that they were to be moved to another building where they were to be released. Instead, they were taken out that night behind Lehrter Railway Station and murdered by machine pistol shots in the back. One fortunate prisoner, H. Kosney,[2301] escaped, and was able to inform their families of their deaths on May 31. At a bomb crater in the Dorotheenstadt Cemetery, which had been used as a shallow grave for these victims and many others, Eberhard Bethge, who had been freed in the meantime by Soviet troops, held a funeral service with the families of the dead on June 11.[2302] At this time, more than one month after the war's end, the Bonhoeffers were still waiting for Dietrich to return home.[2303]

For the party of fourteen, their more immediate worry came when they had barely left Regensburg's outskirts, when the Grüne Minna violently jerked before coming to a standstill.[2304] Hugh Falconer, as an engineer, was called upon by the guards for his assessment and soon revealed that the Grüne Minna's steering had packed it in and was beyond repair.[2305] A cyclist passing by asked if he could report their predicament and ask for a relief van to be sent, but as the hours passed on this bitterly cold night, rain began to fall and became heavier and heavier, with no relief van appearing. The party had no food or drink, and to Payne Best's concern, no tobacco.[2306] Moreover, the exposed stretch of road on which they were stuck contained the burnt-out skeletons of many vehicles, while the field between them and the railway line was thickly pitted with bomb craters.[2307]

Payne Best noticed the guards becoming more and more anxious and frightened, as if they felt they were sharing the prisoners' plight in this dark scenario. When dawn broke, they opened the door and let the prisoners out to stretch their legs;[2308] hours seemed to pass by. Finally, a motor cyclist appeared, and one of the guards decided it was time to take no chances and "requisition" the motor cycle.[2309] How this was done, Payne Best didn't describe, but given that the guards were armed with machine pistols, it is likely to have been by force.

When the guard returned, he did so with the news that another van had been sent the previous evening, but the driver had stopped about 200 yards short of where they were and had gone back to say that he couldn't find them.[2310] With the multiple skeletal vehicle wrecks by the road, coupled with nearby bomb craters in the field on this dismal evening, it is likely that the driver's urge for self-preservation made his search rudimentary. At last at 11 a.m. on Friday April 6, a rarity in the crumbling Reich appeared, a majestic bus, resplendent with plate glass windows and soft upholstered seats,[2311] putting the Grüne Minna to shame.

After transferring their belongings, the party of fourteen now parted ways with their friendly guards, who were left to stay with the broken down Grüne Minna. The replacement guards, numbering ten, were SD men with automatic weapons at the ready, and probably without the friendly disposition of the former guards.[2312] Nevertheless, in their much more comfortable bus, it was a delightful drive through the north-eastern Bavarian countryside as they headed in a generally eastwards direction, hugging the south bank of the Danube until they reached Straubing, where they tried to cross.[2313] However, the bridge there was bombed and impassable, so they continued following the Danube downstream in the hope of finding a traversable bridge, until at last they found a pontoon bridge to cross one of Europe's mightiest rivers.[2314]

After crossing, they passed by the Metten Benedictine Monastery,[2315] before being hailed by some village girls asking a for a lift. Upon entry, the girls were perplexed by the sight of ten young SD men armed with tommy guns, and a band of dishevelled aristocrats. The guards informed them that they were members of a film company on their way to make a propaganda film.[2316] Payne Best observed that the country seemed to be strong on poultry, as many hens crossed the road, compelling the driver to dodge them, though he and his fellow prisoners hoped that one might meet with an accident, so they could all enjoy some nice roast fowl. Payne Best suggested to one of their guards that perhaps they might stop and see if they could beg some eggs at one of the farms, and the idea received immediate approval. However, when the guard returned with a cap full of eggs, the prisoners received none, and were left to tighten their belts and hope that they were approaching their next meal.[2317]

By early afternoon, they arrived at their destination for the day — the pretty village of Schönberg in the Bavarian forest,[2318] about thirty kilometres north of Passau on the Danube,[2319] near the modern- day border with Austria. The population of Schönberg had been just 700, but in recent months, the village had been flooded with 1,300 refugees fleeing the advancing Red Army, making food exceedingly scarce.[2320] Moreover, the special prisoners originally left behind in Regensburg had already arrived in Schönberg ahead of the party of fourteen, bringing the total number of such prisoners to 150.[2321] When Dietrich's party arrived, their bus stopped in front of the village school, a white building of four storeys which accommodated all the aristocrats, with Dietrich's group lodged on the first floor. It had beautiful views of the surrounding Ilz River Valley,[2322] which distracted them, for the time being at least, from their hunger pains as they unpacked and settled in.

The distraction, however, was not to last, as twenty-four hours had now passed since their last meal in Regensburg. Their hunger compelled them to thump on the door and call the guard, who took their demand to the SS commander Untersturmführer (Second Leiutenant) Ernst Bader; he would remain in charge of the special prisoners until their liberation by the Wehrmacht in Niederdorf at the end of the month. Payne Best described Bader as a "hard-bitten thug."[2323] Certainly, the prisoners in Niederdorf were only liberated when the Wehrmacht officers threatened this thug at gunpoint.[2324]

On hearing their plea for food, Bader explained that since there was no fuel and all telephones lines were cut, he was powerless to do anything, and they would have to go without. But Margot Herberlein, the diplomat's wife, took the initiative to ask leave for nature's calling, and found an elderly woman who looked like the school's housekeeper and told her of their plight.[2325] Luckily, this lady, unlike Bader, had compassion, and returned about half an hour later with a couple of big basins of potatoes boiled in their jackets and some jugs of coffee. This in a village where the mayor, upon hearing of the additional 150 special prisoners, refused to allow any of his scanty food reserve to be given to them, since, in his mind, "the Gestapo had brought them and the Gestapo must feed them."[2326] They were still hungry when they went to sleep on their comfortable, soft feather beds, but they had become used to this at Buchenwald, and went to sleep in relatively high spirits.[2327]

When they awoke on Saturday the 7th, there was no breakfast.[2328] Payne Best shared his electric razor around to raise spirits among the men. Later that day, the villagers, now aware of their plight, brought along a couple of loaves of country bread and some potato salad. This was probably Dietrich's final meal. That morning, Payne Best and von Petersdorf took it upon themselves to see Bader about the food situation. Bader repeated what he had said the night before. Admitting there was food to be had in nearby Passau, he said that, with no fuel, even he and his men were going without.[2329] But at least, Bader was able to get hold of a motorcycle to go to Passau and see if he could find any transports to bring food to the village.[2330]

This food did eventually arrive, but not in time for Dietrich, whose bed was beside the depression-prone Wasily Kokorin, whom Hugh Falconer saw as one of the "weaker brethren." In October that year, Falconer wrote to Dietrich's twin sister Sabine: "

> He [Dietrich] did a great deal to keep some of the weaker brethren from depression and anxiety. He spent a good deal of time with Wasily Wasiliev Kokorin, Molotov's nephew, who was a delightful young man although an atheist. I think your brother divided his time with him between instilling the foundations of Christianity and learning Russian."[2331]

Dietrich spent much time in conversation with others in front of open windows overlooking the sun-drenched Ilz Valley in early spring. Removed for the time being from the war, the prisoners' spirits rose as they considered the prospect of freedom post-war, so tantalisingly close. Indeed, this day may have been their most pleasant for months. Dietrich still had his books with him, and probably also his manuscript, which had grown considerably since he left Tegel. Unfortunately, probably on his way to or at Flossenbürg, this was lost, and has never been recovered.[2332]

The night before, Friday the 6th, having returned to Berlin from proclaiming the death sentence for Hans von Dohnányi in Sachsenhausen, Walter Huppenkothen and his wife packed several large suitcases. He was again to be the prosecutor, on this occasion at Flossenbürg, of the Abwehr group of Resistance members, and to ensure in typical "SS Drumhead fashion,"[2333] their liquidation before the arrival of American troops. The next morning, the couple joined the convoy led by SS Obersturmführer (Second Lieutenant) Gogalla; Huppenkothen had two objectives in mind: to carry out the Führer's orders, and to prepare his later flight from the capital before its capture by the dreaded Red Army. He would indeed return briefly to Berlin to be entrusted with more "Reich Secret Business" files before escaping to Austria.[2334]

Both Gogalla and Huppenkothen were carrying the secret files with them, which guaranteed them the support of the military police if their journey to the south was interrupted by accidents or other delays on the way.[2335] Curiously, Payne Best received one of these sensitive documents when he arrived in the Tyrol, and provided his translation of it in his book.[2336] The documents in general were most specific in their instructions, detailing what they were to do in Flossenbürg, Dachau and Schönberg. This suggests that Himmler hoped to the last that if he had internationally respected prisoners who had been well treated and handed over to the Allies, he could save his own life.[2337]

The document Payne Best received was illuminating. It stated that Georg Elser, who had attempted to assassinate Hitler in 1939 in the Bürgerbräu Cellar in Munich, was to be liquidated in a staged "accident," but others such as Schacht, Halder, former Austrian Chancellor Schuschnigg and his wife, and Martin Niemöller were to be treated politely and transported on towards the Alps. Gogalla, who was responsible for carrying out these orders, picked up General Falkenhausen, Payne Best and Vassily Kokorin at Schönberg on Monday morning the 9th — the very morning of Dietrich's execution.[2338] Upon execution of these orders, this letter was meant to be destroyed.[2339]

Huppenkothen arrived in Flossenbürg on Saturday evening the 7th, and together with the camp commandant, Max Kögl, prepared the summary "court-martial" or "SS Drumhead Court" that was to pass the death sentences on the Abwehr Resistance group and Army Judge Karl Sack who had acted as their legal protector.[2340] As they were doing so, one of the Reich henchmen realised that prisoner Bonhoeffer was absent. This prompted a frantic search for him. While they did so, other prisoners, including Fabian von Schlabrendorff and Josef Müller, were yelled at in their cells: "Surely you are Bonhoeffer!"[2341] Finally, the realisation dawned that by mistake, Dietrich had been driven onwards to Schönberg when the Grüne Minna was stopped at outskirts of Weiden. Although the armies of the Third Reich had abandoned their vehicles on the eastern and western fronts for lack of petrol, KZ Commander Kögl managed to dispatch two men in a car on the 160 kilometre or 100 mile journey, by way of Weiden, Cham and Regensburg, to Schönberg.[2342] While Kögl (Koegel) survived the war in hiding, in June 1946, he commited suicide in his prison cell.[2343]

In the meantime, at Schönberg, on Sunday April 8 1945, Hermann Pünder, a Catholic who had become quite close to Dietrich, suggested that Dietrich perform a morning service for Quasimodo or White Sunday — the first Sunday after Easter.[2344] At first Dietrich declined, as most of the group were Catholic and Kokorin was an atheist. However, it seems that Dietrich's conversations with Wasily Kokorin had born fruit, for Wasily joined the chorus that persuaded Dietrich to read the

Bible texts for the first Sunday after Easter, and lead them in prayer before delivering his homily on the texts.[2345]

The texts were "With his stripes we are healed" (Isaiah 53:5) and "Blessed be the God and Father of our Lord Jesus Christ! By his great mercy we have been born anew to a living hope through the resurrection of Jesus Christ from the dead" (First Epistle of Peter 1:3).[2346] Payne Best described the service, delivered less than 24 hours before Dietrich's execution: "

> Pastor Bonnhöfer held a little service and spoke to us in a manner which reached the hearts of all, finding just the right words to express the spirit of our imprisonment and the thoughts and resolutions which it had brought."[2347]

But Dietrich had barely finished his final prayer when the door opened and two evil-looking men in civilian clothes, came in and grimly announced: "Prisoner Bonnhöfer. Get ready to come with us." Those words *"Komm mit uns"* — "Come with us" — for all prisoners had come to mean one thing only—the scaffold. Payne Best added: "We bade him good-bye — he drew me aside and said — *'This is the end — for me the beginning of life.'* and then he gave me a message to give, if I could, to the Bishop of Chichester, a friend to all evangelical pastors in Germany."[2348] Six years later, in a letter to Professor Gerhard Leibholz, husband of Dietrich's twin sister Sabine, Payne Best recalled what he had written about Dietrich in his book, where he had said that he "was a good and saintly man." But in the letter, he went further: "In fact my feeling was far stronger than these words imply. He was, without exception, the finest and most lovable man I have ever met."[2349]

Since Dietrich's family had not heard of him since he had left Prinz-Albrecht-Strasse two months earlier, he decided to leave some hint of his whereabouts. With a blunt pencil he wrote his name and address in the front, middle, and back of the volume of Plutarch that one of his family had given to him for his birthday two months earlier on February 2, and left it behind, but took with him his volume of Goethe. One of Carl Goerdeler's sons who was at the schoolhouse took the volume of Plutarch and gave it to the Bonhoeffers years later.[2350] Dietrich had been with Carl Goerdeler in the last days before his execution at Prinz-Albrecht-Strasse in early February. Now, as he ran down the stairs of the schoolhouse to enter the van that would take him to his execution, he bumped into Carl Goerdeler's widow, who bade him his final friendly "Auf Wiedersehen."[2351]

That evening, with the arrival of what must have been food from Passau, there was sausage, bread, and potatoes aplenty for supper, and everyone became cheerful and noisy again.[2352] Such it was, as Payne Best remarked, when you lived knowing that every day could well be your last.[2353]

Chapter 25

Old Prussia Gone with the Wind

By February 25, 1947,[2354] following the formal dissolution of Prussia by the Allied powers, great swaths of it had been absorbed into the communist "People's" Republic of Poland, including the estates of the Kleists in the Pomeranian province in the north, and to the south, Oma Ruth's ancestral home of Grossenborau in the Lower Silesian province.[2355] These became part of the "Recovered Territories"[2356] after World War II — so dubbed by Stalinist propaganda in a deal which had catastrophic consequences for Germany and for Poland. While Poland gained these former eastern German territories, they lost more than double the amount of land in the east to the Ukrainian, Belarusian and Lithuanian Soviet Republics; this effectively translated Poland's territory and eastern Borderlands people westwards into the pre-war eastern Reich. For Borderland Poles, and Germans from the east of the pre-war Reich, numbering six million in all, this became the largest human migration in history.[2357] With it came untold misery, suffering and death.[2358] All was legitimised in the Stalinist mindset by the obscure, dormant and tampered-with Spa-London-Moscow telegram from July 1920, during the 1919-20 Polish Soviet War.[2359]

The cataclysmic death throes of the American Civil War and its aftermath from April 1865 onwards[2360] saw the end of the South's agrarian way of life that had been established upon black slavery.[2361] Just as this era was eulogised in the novel and subsequent Hollywood epic *Gone with the Wind*,[2362] so too, the Prussian agrarian way of life, the only life Oma Ruth ever knew, became just a memory, eight decades later, in 1945.[2363] The death throes and cataclysmic aftermath of a major war, a conflict on a global scale surpassing any in history, were epitomised in the barbaric theatre of the European Eastern Front.[2364] Of course, the privileged agrarian Prussian class that Oma Ruth was born into, was not based on anything like the oppressive system of Black slavery, so integral to the pre-civil war society of the Old American South. Nor was it based on the system of serfdom, no less fundamental to the society of Tsarist Russia.[2365] For example, Jane Pejsa wrote of Ruth making her monthly visit to the village in June 1899, when she visited and took time to chat and present flowers to a mother who recently gave birth. This was followed by her visiting another household where the man was facing death, with her words of great solace to he and his family. This being two years following the death of her dearly beloved husband Jürgen.[2366]

By Christmas 1943, ten months or so following the disaster for the Sixth Army at Stalingrad, with the war having turned against Germany and its Axis partner Japan on all fronts,[2367] all the young Prussian estate workers were now fighting at the front or already dead. Soviet and French prisoners of war were now working on the Prussian lands to cover the shortfall in manpower.[2368] At Kieckow, fifty Soviet prisoners were in the employ of Ruth's eldest child, Hans Jürgen, living in a converted stable and under guard at all times by a German soldier. At Oma Ruth's nearby Klein Krössin estate, there were a like number of Frenchmen guarded by German soldiers.[2369] While the guards turned out to be benign, the problem for the prisoners and Hans Jürgen was that the guards were monitored by a group of zealous civilian Nazi leaders from Gross Tychow; they were totally committed to the enforcement of Reich directives in regard to the treatment of prisoners of war of the Slavic *Untermensch*.[2370]

These included each prisoner only being allowed a single straw cover — a freezing prospect in a Pomeranian winter, as well as the prisoners' rations being limited to the bare minimum required for survival — as was the case in the concentration camps and Jewish ghettos. Yet the prisoners were expected to perform heavy manual labour every day.[2371] The reasoning was that, with the almost limitless supply of such manpower, the regime could enforce this prolonged starvation in the name of the extermination of the *Untermensch*.[2372]

However, right from the outset, Hans Jürgen insisted that every prisoner be provided with two straw mats — one to lie on and one as a blanket to survive the Pomeranian winter. Of course, this was still woefully inadequate; but he also insisted that the prisoners receive the same rations as village workers. In the village, these rations were supplemented with fruit and vegetables from the villager's gardens, and Hans Jürgen ensured that the prisoners received additional portions from the manor house larder. In the two years that Hans Jürgen had prisoners on his estate, this was how he operated. Invariably, this led to confrontations with every new Nazi official, to whom he argued that he must have healthy workers to run his estate, in spite of warnings of dire consequences. It seemed that in Pomerania at least, on his own land, a resolute landowner could still hold sway.[2373] Sadly, however, upon their "liberation," the Soviet prisoners served time in the Soviet Gulags, hav-

ing been branded as traitors to the Motherland.[2374] As Alexander Solzhenitsyn put it: "

> Capitalist England fought at our side against Hitler; Marx had
> eloquently described the poverty and suffering of the working
> class in that same [Victorian] England. Why was it that in this
> war only one traitor could be found among them, the busi-
> nessman "Lord Haw Haw" [William Joyce][2375] — but in our
> country millions?"[2376]

For the time being, however, Soviet prisoners experienced the resolute
benevolence of Hans Jürgen. At Christmas, his wife Mieze arranged
packages for the prisoners with cards containing portraits of the Virgin
Mary, obtained by scouring every town in the Belgard district. Unlike
the iconoclastic Lutherans of Pomerania,[2377] the French Catholics and
those of the Russian Orthodox faith retained icons as a cornerstone of
their veneration of Christ. Hence the diligent search throughout this
Lutheran stronghold for cards bearing images of the Mother of
Christ.[2378]

However, at Pätzig, the estate of the von Wedemeyers, Ruthchen had taken an intense dislike to the group of German soldiers
guarding the Soviet prisoners.[2379] Frustrated with the powerlessness of
his mother in the face of these bullies, Hans Werner, aged fourteen,
took to the attic stairs, from where he was able to look down at them,
spit on them, and make a hasty retreat. Over the weeks, his aim improved before he was caught, not by the guards, but by his widowed
mother. A stern lecture followed; his mother lectured him that regardless of one's opinion of the man wearing the uniform of the Fatherland,
one must never dishonour it![2380]

On the night of New Year's Eve 1943, after travelling from
Berlin, Ewald Heinrich von Kleist-Schmenzin, the eldest son of Ewald
von Kleist-Schmenzin, had sought counsel with his father about what
became the second and final abortive greatcoat suicide assassination
plot.[2381] However, with multiple cancellations by Hitler, it never came
to pass, and like his fellow greatcoat conspirator, Axel von dem
Bussche, Ewald Heinrich survived the war and became the final conspirator to pass away in Munich on March 8 2013.[2382] But seven months
after Ewald Heinrich's counsel with his father, all hell broke loose for
the Kleists and their related families, as was the case for all involved in
the conspiracy in the wake of Valkyrie.

In the very early morning of Friday July 21, 1944, Ewald was arrested, before the local police superintendent arrived at 5 a.m. at Kieckow to wake and inform Hans Jürgen's secretary that he too was under arrest.[2383] After dressing, Hans Jürgen was seated in the car alongside Ewald; they did not exchange looks or words. However, at the Gestapo headquarters in Köslin, the two conspirators and old friends found the opportunity to talk. Ewald's words proved to be, as they had been almost two decades earlier in 1925,[2384] prophetic: "You will probably be free one day. I shall not, but that doesn't matter so much. It may sound strange, but I feel exulted that it has come this far."[2385]

By noon that day, the Kleist conspirators were alone in their respective cells. Later that day, Gestapo officers arrived at Kieckow to search desks and wardrobes for incriminating evidence. By now, the names of some of the conspirators had been made public, including that of the leading figure, Colonel von Stauffenberg. However, at Hans Jürgen's estate, little was uncovered other than earlier connections to the long since prostrate Confessing Church,[2386] coupled with family connections to men and women already on the suspect list.[2387] Unfortunately, this was not the case on the Schmenzin estate, where, on Ewald's desk, a Gestapo officer (later to be "commended") discovered a handwritten letter from Winston Churchill, dated August 17, 1938: "

> I am certain as I was at the end of July 1914 that England will march with France, and certainly the United States is now strongly anti-Nazi. It is difficult for democracies to make precise declarations, but the spectacle of an armed attack by Germany upon a small neighbour and the bloody fighting that will follow will rouse the whole British Empire and compel the gravest decisions. Do not I pray you, be misled on this point. Such a war, once started, would be fought out like the last to the bitter end, and one must consider not what might happen in the first few months, but where we should all be at the end of the third or fourth year."[2388]

For Ewald, this letter was a poisoned chalice leading to his execution seven or so months later.

About one month later, on August 18, Ewald was transferred to the Moabit (Lehrterstrasse) prison in Berlin,[2389] as was his son Ewald Heinrich, brought by military police from the front. As both faced the wall next to each other, Ewald whispered to his son, "Do not lose your self-control whatever happens."[2390] By early October, the pair were transferred to the Prinz-Albrecht-Strasse prison, headquarters of the Reich Security Office.[2391] They of course were not alone, as on the 8th, Dietrich had been moved from the relatively benign environment of Tegel to this subterranean hell.[2392] Hans Jürgen was also reunited with his nephew Fabian von Schlabrendorff, married to Hans Jürgen's niece Luitgarde,[2393] completing a Kleist family reunion of sorts.[2394] They were not the only ones, as the two most senior former heads of the Abwehr, Admiral Canaris and General Oster, among many conspirators and non-conspirators, made up the list of the incarcerated.[2395] Their treatment ranged from malevolent neglect to repeated torture.[2396]

In December, during the first week of Advent,[2397] Ewald Heinrich, who was among the conspirators making their last stand in the Bendlerblock with Claus von Stauffenberg,[2398] was released from prison on the personal order of the Führer. Apparently Hitler noticed a von Kleist on the prisoner list, which he scanned from time to time, and incorrectly assumed that this Kleist was the son of Field Marshal Paul Ludwig Ewald von Kleist,[2399] who was in no way connected with the conspiracy against Hitler, but was nevertheless a distant relative of Ewald von Kleist of Schmenzin. Ewald Heinrich was subsequently ordered to return to his front-line unit.[2400]

A day later, Ewald's second wife Alice was granted her last visit with her husband.[2401] Afterwards, on the 7th, Ewald wrote to her: "

7.12.1944

> Yesterday I finally saw you and spoke with you. That was my final great wish. I had been so uneasy that something would prevent my seeing you. Such a joy this last meeting was for me, for which I thank God. And that God sheltered you from the terrible air raid. You have made me so happy through the short half-hour [we were together]. No doubt I shall not see you again in this lifetime. Our farewell was so difficult for me. I was amazed how you held yourself together and how you did not let me see your pain. God has given you so much strength. This is a great comfort for me.
>
> I thank God also that Ewald Heinrich walks free again. By mortal reckoning I shall never see you again — never. And yet: God's will be done."[2402]

For Ewald, as he had foreseen, there was no last-moment miraculous escape from death.

In the meantime, Hans Jürgen's questioning by Commissioner Habecker continued, not so much about what Hans Jürgen had done, but more about what he knew of the deeds of others. At this point, Habecker had not yet used torture, but sought to intimidate his subject by threatening it. At first, Hans Jürgen had grave fears that torture would compel him to "sing like a canary," and he made contingency plans. He stole a razor blade from the prison barbershop, and slipped it into a bar of soap to conceal it during any impromptu cell inspections; he also had hidden a steel nail in an inconspicuous nook in his cell.[2403]

On the early morning of December 9, the second Sunday of Advent, Hans Jürgen prayed for guidance — a special sign or absence of it from God. Should there not be one, he resolved to take his own life that night, as any alternative would lead to the betrayal of others. At noon, a guard delivered a Christmas package from his wife Mieze to his cell, with a change of clothing inside. On the outside of the parcel was the spiritual sign he was looking for — a tiny Christmas tree on which a little wooden angel was perched. He placed the tree on his stool and slipped the angel into his pocket. In the days of merciless interrogation that followed, during many a sleepless night, he often reached for the angel in his pocket.[2404] As each day passed, the threatened tortures never took place. They would however, come in the near future from an equally brutal regime.

Meanwhile, while Dietrich was rarely taken from his subterranean cell where he was always isolated and sometimes tormented by the guards, he was hardly ever questioned. He had acknowledged his foreign links to neutral Sweden and Switzerland, and thence to the Reich's enemy, England (George Bell), but he succeeded in withholding the most damning evidence — the messages he conveyed from the Abwehr conspirators to their contacts abroad.[2405] A perfect example is the names of key conspirators he gave to Bishop George Bell during their June 1942 meeting in Stockholm.[2406] That Advent, while Hans Jürgen resisted his interrogators, Dietrich wrote what was to be his final letter to Maria.[2407]

On December 22, Luitgarde was allowed a fifteen-minute penultimate visit to see her husband Fabian von Schlabrendorff in the Moabit prison. Their discourse was conducted more with eyes than with words. A few hours later she went into labour and gave birth to their third child, a boy. Two weeks later on January 5 1945, while still in Berlin, her new son was christened in a simple ceremony, with the baby's great-grandmother Ruth von Kleist, whose eyesight was rapidly deteriorating, deemed his godmother in absentia. In her final visit to Fabian in prison, Luitgarde held their new son in her arms before leaving for Bavaria, to be reunited with her other children.[2408]

For the last six months of 1944, the Red Army were building up their communications and supply systems east of Poland's River Vistula.[2409] This was used as an excuse for their virtual inaction during the Warsaw General Uprising from early August to early October 1944, when they were camped for months on the Vistula's east bank in Warsaw's Praga district.[2410] This inaction is further exemplified by Stalin's refusal to let Allied aircraft use Soviet controlled airfields east of Warsaw for supplying air drops to the Uprising, coupled with his blatant refusal, beyond the most token air drops, for Soviet pilots to do likewise.[2411] Moreover, there is the account of Australian aircrewman Alan McIntosh,[2412] of the RAF and South African Air Force squadrons of No. 205 Group, based in Brindisi southern Italy, where he spoke of our Russian "Friends" and "Allies" firing on his aircraft as they were on their way to making supply drops to the Warsaw Rising in September 1944.[2413]

In January 1945, following almost six months of occupation of Warsaw's districts on the east bank of the Vistula River,[2414] the Red Army finally crossed the river into the city centre and its outlying western districts. By this time, the Germans had already effected a systematic obliteration of the city west of the Vistula, leaving a virtually uninhabited city of almost pure rubble — a devastation that led to the postwar proposal that Warsaw should never be rebuilt.[2415] Hence, during the six months of virtual Soviet inactivity in the sector around Warsaw, with moments of sporadic and token Soviet "assistance" for the Uprising, the Red Army had built up an overwhelming numerical superiority over the Germans, in tanks, trucks, aircraft, and most of all, manpower.[2416]

As a result, Hitler's decision to mount a last desperate counter-offensive in the Ardennes Forest of Belgium,[2417] in what would later become known as the Battle of the Bulge, further worsened the situation for his already battered forces in the east.[2418] Initially, as Hitler's last offensive success, it made significant inroads, but once the weather cleared, allowing the Allies to assert their clear air superiority,[2419] the end was nigh. However, Hitler still held onto the vain hope that the ideological friction between the Soviets and Western Allies might see a revisitation of the Miracle of Brandenburg,[2420] which had saved Frederick the Great 183 years earlier.[2421]

Within days of the group of special prisoners from Prinz-Albrecht-Strasse arriving in Buchenwald in early February 1945, the Red Army's siege of Breslau on the Oder had commenced, cutting off the city from the outside world by February 15, creating the Festung (Fortress) Breslau.[2422] Essentially, all of Germany east of the Oder River, with the exception of the Kleist estates to the north, was under the control of the Red Army,[2423] which, by then, included the von Wedemeyer's Pätzig estate in Pomerania,[2424] and Oma Ruth's ancestral Lower Silesian home of Grossenborau.[2425] On January 26 1945, the day before the liberation of KZ Auschwitz[2426] and eight days before the bombing of Berlin by the American Eighth Air Force,[2427] Dietrich's fiancée Maria, answering the desperate pleas of her mother Ruthchen, was back at Pätzig,[2428] having lived with Dietrich's parents since August.[2429]

With temperatures below freezing, the shock waves of Soviet artillery were close enough at times to make the manor windows rattle.[2430] On the following day, Ruthchen decided that Maria would lead the three youngest children, the two oldest and most frail of her refugee guests, and the wife of her estate manager and their two children west, across the Oder River to safety. Including Maria and their Polish driver, himself an estate worker, this party of ten were to be transported in an improvised covered wagon, loaded with food and hitched to the three strongest horses on the estate.[2431] As they left before dawn, Maria jettisoned some of the non-essential cargo, which included heavy art books obviously treasured by the elderly women. By the next day, the 28th, the party had joined a seemingly endless stream of refugees hoping to cross the Oder ahead of the Red Army, whose inexorable vengeance they all feared. Like Maria's party, nobody had gasoline, but some had wagons, while others had only bikes, wheelbarrows or prams.[2432] With the roads so crowded, they had to be cleared whenever the retreating German Army required priority passage.

With great foresight and a degree of calculated risk, Maria decided to avoid the Oder River bridges, clogged with refugees and manned by SS troops, who often turned people back. Instead, she deviated north, hoping to find a spot on the river were its ice seemed firm enough to take the weight of a wagon emptied of its passengers, while the passengers crossed on foot. Her hope was not in vain; when they made it to the relative safety of the west bank, the party enjoyed a brief period of joy and relief. Their ultimate destination was not devastated Berlin, but the relative safety of the village of Opperhausen near Celle in Lower Saxony,[2433] about 220 kilometres to the west of the capital.

The village would end up in the British occupied zone post-war, and would not experience anywhere near the devastation of Berlin, Breslau, Hamburg and other cities within the Reich. However, it was only 11 miles or 18 kilometres south of the infamous Bergen-Belsen concentration camp, liberated peacefully by the British 11th Armoured Division on April 15, 1945.[2434]

After sending Maria on this dangerous trek, Ruthchen wrote to Dietrich's mother Paula to inform her that the party was making their way to family in the village of Opperhausen near Celle; she confided to Paula her unwarranted lack of faith in Maria's fortitude and foresight: "

> I need her help desperately. It is a task far beyond her strength... Pray with me that she will be equal to this hard task. If all goes well, the journey will take 14 days. But there has been a lot of snow and the winds are very strong."[2435]

By January 29, the Soviet army was almost on the threshold of the Pätzig estate, prompting Ruthchen to decide that her estate workers and the remainder of her refugee guests should prepare for flight.[2436] Unfortunately, the Gauleiter (local or regional Nazi leader) forbade all such movements, as they would jam the road that was required for "reinforcements" arriving from the west. Ruthchen asked, "What reinforcements? What front?"[2437] as everyone knew the German army was retreating behind the Oder. The Gauleiter insisted that to abandon the estate was to betray the Reich. Of course, such zealous rhetoric was not going to stop the implacable advance of the Red Army, leaving their footprint of rape, pillage and plunder,[2438] while at the same time, caravan leaders of fleeing parties were being hanged and their provisions confiscated along the Oder River by the SS.[2439]

With Ruthchen now compelled to abandon her prudent measures for evacuation, she ordered that all the food, blankets, pillows and other goods the marauding army might desire were to be gathered and placed in the main hall, in the forlorn hope of avoiding the plundering of her beloved home.[2440] By 2 p.m. on January 31, a refugee camping in the area glimpsed some Soviet tanks on the northern fringe of the village. Panic stricken, the woman cut the wrists of her mother and daughter before cutting her own. As they were bleeding to death in Ruthchen's courtyard, Ruthchen grabbed a sheet and pillowcase from a pile in the entry hall and rushed outside to tear strips and bind the potentially fatal wounds.[2441]

For the time being, the Soviets ignored the manor, as a column of tanks and other vehicles slowly crossed the estate with the aim of killing the village's Nazi spokesman, plundering anything on the way in the process.[2442] At 5 p.m., Ruthchen implored Herr Döpke, whose wife and children had left days before on the wagon with Maria, to leave immediately. He refused, as he had made up his mind to organise the village caravan after the Soviet troops had moved on.[2443] At 6 p.m., the Pätzig forester appeared at Ruthchen's back door, still dressed in the grey-green uniform that had been worn for centuries on German lands. Mindful of the imminent peril, he asked Ruthchen if he could take the sleigh and a horse to make his getaway, which Ruthchen granted without hesitation. However, he never made it to the barn, as he was over-powered by two Red Army soldiers, and died a few minutes later.[2444] It's possible that his forester's uniform was mistaken for a military one.[2445]

In any event, at 6:30 p.m., the estate manager, Herr Döpke, had a change of heart, appearing at the manor door and entreating Ruthchen to leave immediately.[2446] With a Soviet tank parked in front of the es-tate's entrance, Herr Döpke had grave fears that it would fire on the manor with people still inside. Ruth ordered all the women in the manor to exit via the French doors leading to the back of the terrace, saying that she would soon follow. It was just as well that she did so, because as she left, having first taken money from her late husband's desk, the tank began to fire on the manor.[2447]

Now huddled in the gardener's cottage, Ruthchen collected her thoughts to decide her next course of action. She and one other woman decided to escape, with the remainder staying behind to place them-selves at the "mercy" of the marauding army. As far as Ruthchen was concerned, these women were more than welcome to come along, but their fear of almost certain death if caught in the process of fleeing was uppermost,[2448] and they had heard of instances of SS men hanging car-avan leaders and confiscating provisions, treating German escapees as traitors to the Third Reich.[2449] Since the perimeter of the estate was now sealed off by enemy troops, Ruthchen and her companion left in the freezing midnight cold, illuminated by the near full moon,[2450] through a gap in the fence behind the cottage. As they fled, they looked back to see the beloved Pätzig manor house engulfed in flames.[2451]

When Maria arrived among relatives in the village of Opper-hausen near Celle, her thoughts turned almost immediately to her be-loved Dietrich. On February 12 she returned to Berlin and discovered that Dietrich was missing. With no definite idea of where he was, she left the following day for Flossenbürg. Days later on Monday February 19, after trudging seven kilometres from the railway station to the camp, she found no sign of him, as he was not yet there. Utterly dejected, she wrote to her mother of her fruitless search for her beloved. She decided to head for the relative safety of the northern Bavarian village of Bundorf, about 140 kilometres west-north-west of Flossenbürg.[2452] In her letter, Maria wrote that it was pointless to travel back to Berlin, since Dietrich was not there. There was also the imminent arrival of their "Pätzig friends" (marauding Soviet troops) and the prospect of being conscripted into the Flak — "Flug-Abwehr-Kanone" — or anti-aircraft batteries, which were now conscripting women and school-aged children.[2453] This was in spite of the fact that the regime refused to employ women in factories throughout the entire war.[2454]

Meanwhile, in Oma Ruth's ancestral land of Lower Silesia, six days before the flight west of the party led by Maria out of Pätzig, an astonishing event was taking place; it was Sunday January 21, 1945 in the mid-sized town of Oppeln (now Polish Opole),[2455] near Breslau, where the matriarch's father Robert senior, Count of Zedlitz and Trützschler, had been appointed by Otto von Bismarck as governor of the Prussian province of Silesia in the summer of 1881.[2456] Now, in this still opulent palace, Hans Conrad Stahlberg, son of Oma Ruth's headstrong first daughter Spes, was marrying Maria von Loesch, a descendant from a branch of the Zedlitz family.[2457] The wedding was a Zedlitz family reunion, oblivious, at least for the time being, to the implacable advance of the Red Army.

Among the guests were the groom's mother, Spes, who made it from Berlin in spite of all the difficulties, along with Stefan, younger brother of Oma Ruth and his wife Lene, the count and countess of Zedlitz and Trützschler, from their ancestral estate of *Grossenborau,* about 200 kilometres to the north-west. If anyone was missed that day, it was Oma Ruth herself, since travel from far to the north in Pomerania was clearly out of the question for the increasingly frail and almost blind matriarch. However, eighteen-year-old Ruthi, the fifth child of Hans Jürgen and Mieze, and first cousin of the groom, had made the trip all the way from Pomerania with a friend, to ensure that this celebration, on the brink of Armageddon, had its Kieckow connection.[2458] Hans Conrad's sister Ruth Roberta (Raba),[2459] who now lived with her physician husband near Breslau, and who had flirted dangerously with the city's left-wing conspiracy,[2460] was also present, as was brother Alexander (Alla).[2461] He was now adjutant to the illustrious but timid General Erich von Manstein,[2462] whom Claus von Stauffenberg attempted to persuade to take action against Hitler in early 1943 before his posting to Tunisia.[2463] As Manstein was an old friend of the Zedlitz clan, he too was among the guests.[2464]

As this extraordinary Silesian wedding took place on the brink of Armageddon on Sunday January 21, 1945, numerous horse-drawn wagons were ready to transport most of the guests to the Loesch family castle upon the ceremony's completion. One military vehicle was amongst the array of wagons in front of the church. It was the staff car for General von Manstein and his adjutant Alla Stahlberg,[2465] older brother of the groom.[2466] Upon arrival at the castle, there was joyous celebration in the rejoining of these ancient families, while artillery thundered in the background well within earshot.[2467] The relentless advance of the Red Army, raping and pillaging, could be put on hold as Old Prussia played out this grand wedding reception in the castle — one of the last, if not the last, of its kind.

Ruthi read Tante Spes's amusing poem, believed to be advice from the Baron of Vernezobre, a common ancestor of bride and groom, before Great-Uncle Stefan gave a moving tribute to his nephew, Hans Jürgen von Kleist, imprisoned in Berlin, unlikely to survive.[2468] At that moment, fear erupted when a German soldier burst into the banquet hall with the ominous announcement that Russian soldiers had reached the outskirts of Oppeln, and advised that all civilians leave immediately.[2469] The civilian guests abandoned the banquet table to make for their wagons and head for the railway station, while Manstein and his adjutant Alla Stahlberg raced back to their posts.[2470] At the station, panic and confusion reigned. A train had stopped to take on desperate passengers fleeing west, but it filled rapidly, and more desperate passengers tried to push themselves aboard.

Ruthi and her friend, having taken Großonkel (Great Unlce) Stefan and Großtante (Great Aunt) Lene under their care, desperately searched from carriage to carriage for space for them to board the train. When this proved fruitless, Ruthi, like her cousin Maria would do a week or so later in crossing the Oder, was able think laterally — in this instance by using her beauty and charm with the engine driver. With her elders out of view, Ruthi and her friend approached the engine driver in his cab, and without naming them, asked if he could take two passengers.[2471] The engine driver, in making the typical man's assumption, gleefully beckoned them to come aboard.[2472] But rather, the selfless young ladies raced towards their loving elders to help them board the cab, as the engine driver's wide grin vanished.[2473] Both elders would survive the war, Stefan passing away at age eighty in 1951, while his wife Helene (Lene) would outlive him by thirty years.[2474]

Now alone on the station platform, at the "mercy" of the marauding Red Army, the young ladies were saved when Alla Stahlberg turned up in a commandeered military vehicle. The girls jumped into the truck, and Alla drove them cross-country to another town, where he knew one more westward bound train was expected. As he dropped them off, he felt confident they were on their way to safety,[2475] but in doing so, did not count on the impulsive and foolhardy nature of youth.

While the young ladies waited on the platform for the train west, an earlier train, heading east and virtually empty, stopped. Foolishly,[2476] Ruthi agreed with her friend to return east and rescue her mother, but within minutes, both realised they had made a terrible mistake when they found the train was surrounded by Soviet troops.[2477] Forced to make their escape, they were shot at as they jumped out of the train, as they rushed to a bush and remained hidden until the soldiers left. When no one was in sight, they moved on and managed to escape capture for a day or so, but were eventually captured and subjected to the sexual retribution that the Red Army would become notorious for during their counter-invasion of Germany. Within a week, they were put to work in a Soviet military horse stable.[2478] Ruthi survived the war and lived on into the 1990s,[2479] working with the World Council of Churches in Geneva.[2480]

As close as the Kleists of Kieckow and Schmenzin were on their neighbouring estates near Belgard, so too were the families on the neighbouring estates in the Neumark region, south-west of Belgard — the Wedemeyers of the Pätzig estate and the Tresckows of Wartenberg.[2481] When the funeral was held for Henning von Tresckow in the wake of Valkyrie, there were the added common threads of the kinship of Ruthchen and Henning, the military careers of Henning and Ruthchen's now deceased husband Hans, and their common contempt for the regime.[2482] At Henning's funeral, the Bismarck clan, who made their way from the north, including Luitgarde née Bismarck and her husband Fabian von Schlabrendorff, were also present. The Kleists were notably absent, due to the imprisonment of Hans Jürgen and Ewald in the Gestapo prison at Köslin. As for Henning's wife Erika, she had been arrested by the Gestapo and released after seven weeks of interrogation at Prinz-Albrecht-Strasse; [2483] she survived the war, living on until 1974.[2484]

Around the time of Erika's arrest, on Monday August 7 1944, Ruthchen was visited by the Gestapo. This was after Henning von Tresckow's grave had been disinterred on account of his pivotal role in the Valkyrie plot. When a servant informed Ruthchen of a Gestapo car parked at the front of the manor house, Ruthchen rushed into the entry hall and seized the family guest book and threw it behind the curtain. Upon opening the door, one of the police officers asked her to accompany them to the study, assuring her the "discussion" would be a mere formality. Six hours later, they left, as Ruthchen knew very little and told even less.[2485] That night, after the children were asleep, Ruthchen read through the names of the guests in the Pätzig guest book for the last time, committing to memory the large assortment of family and friends, including those brave men now branded by the Reich as traitors. When she was done, she lit a match to the pages and threw the book into the fireplace.[2486] Six months later, the entire estate was in flames as she made her flight west.[2487]

Meantime, significantly further west than the Kleist estates, the marauding Red Army first appeared on the twin estates in the Neumark. The von Tresckows remained in Wartenberg, where, on Monday January 29 1945,[2488] the day after Maria and her party crossed the ice over the frozen Oder River,[2489] and two days before Ruthchen made her desperate flight from neighbouring Pätzig,[2490] the Red Terror descended upon Wartenberg. Just a week earlier, following a hunting accident, Jürgen, the master of the estate and half-brother of Henning,[2491] had died from blood poisoning.[2492] Now, at the entry hall to the manor house, his widow Hete stood alone, hoping the soldiers of the marauding army would be sufficiently satiated by its plunder. To her horror, they showed no such inclination. Hearing her screams from behind the manor house, her fourteen-year-old son Rüdiger raced to her defence, and was shot dead, as was his mother soon after. An hour later, after the requisite plundering, the manor house was set on fire.[2493]

Stalin, in an explosive response to a complaint by Yugolslav/Serbian communist Milovan Djilas, during the latter's visit to Moscow in 1944,[2494] regarding rapes committed by Red Army soldiers in Yugoslavia, asked the Serb, "Can't you understand it if a soldier who has crossed thousands of kilometres through blood and fire has fun with a woman or takes a trifle?"[2495] The "trifle" in this instance was the murder of a mother and her son while the son attempted to defend her. When Stalin made his reply, he kissed Djilas's Serbian wife while accusing the Serb of ingratitude.[2496] Little wonder that Milovan Djilas would later proclaim Stalin to be: "the greatest criminal in history,"[2497] and write: "

Every crime was possible to Stalin, for there was not one he had not committed. For in him was joined the criminal sense-lessness of a Caligula with the refinement of a Borgia and the brutality of a Czar Ivan the Terrible. I was more interested, and am more interested, in how such a dark, cunning and cruel in-dividual could ever have led one of the greatest and most pow-erful states, not just for a day or a year, but for 30 years. He was one of those rare terrible dogmatists capable of destroying nine-tenths of the human race to 'make happy' the one-tenth. Stalin's dethronement proves that the truth will come out even if only after those who fought for it have perished. The human conscience is implacable and indestructible."[2498]

By the end of the 1940s, Milovan Djilas was instrumental in Tito's break with Stalin and the international Communist movement that Moscow dominated.[2499] At first, as editor and contributor to the party's theoretical journal *Kommunist*, and to *Borba*, the party daily, he de-fended Yugoslavia's national Communism. But by the early 1950s, Dji-las had grown increasingly disenchanted with the course of Com-munism both inside and outside of Yugoslavia. This was reflected in his writings, which became increasingly critical, leading to him spending much of the period from 1954 until 1990 in and out of prison.[2500]

On Saturday February 3 1945, the day of the bombing of Berlin by the American Eighth Air Force,[2501] which delivered the death of Ro-land Freisler as he pronounced the death sentence for Fabian von Schlabrendorff in his People's Court, providence smiled on Fabian's surviving co-conspirator and relative through marriage, Hans Jürgen von Kliest of Kieckow. Just before hearing Fabian's case, the prosecu-tor read the litany of accusations against Ewald von Kleist of Schmenzin — the distant cousin but long time and childhood friend of Hans Jürgen. Freisler, at around 10 a.m., asked if Ewald had anything to add. Ewald declared: "

Yes, I have carried on high treason since the 30th of January 1933, continually and with all means available to me. I have never concealed my fight against Hitler and National Social-ism. I believe this fight to be a commandment ordered by God. God alone will be my judge."[2502]

Freisler, taken aback, but still faced with a litany of cases to hear, dismissed Ewald and called for the next case, that of Fabian. However, just at that moment, the air raid sirens blared and everyone, including the manacled accused, headed for the shelters. When the air raid by the American Eighth Air Force — the most devastating air raid ever on Berlin — was over, it was discovered that just one individual in the courthouse had perished.[2503] A steel beam plunged through the ceiling, delivering a fatal blow to Freisler's head. Initially, Freisler hastily left the courtroom with everyone else, but then unwisely returned to the courtroom to retrieve the file on Fabian that he had inadvertently left behind.[2504] Perhaps Fabian's deliverance played its role in Freisler's demise.

Significantly for Hans Jürgen, the fire that raged in the courtroom above destroyed the files of the carefully prepared cases against the von Kleist cousins.[2505] Nine days later, on February 12, and five days following the transfer of prisoners from the bombed-out Prinz-Albrecht-Strasse to Buchenwald and Flossenbürg, the Reich Security Office decided not to bother with reconstructing the case against Hans Jürgen.[2506] However, perhaps in part due to Ewald's much greater degree of involvement, fortune did not smile upon him.

When Hans Jürgen was released, conditions were imposed upon his release. They were that he refrain from political activities, plan nothing in opposition to the Third Reich, and finally, that he speak to no one about his interrogations. He had but one thought on his mind, to return east to Kieckow and lead his family and villagers in a desperate flight west, so these conditions were hardly of consequence for him. Of much greater concern was a two-day delay due to the requirement for him to report to Prinz-Albrecht-Strasse one final time in order to obtain all the required documents. For Hans Jürgen, knowing that the Red Army to the south of Pomerania had already occupied some land west of the Oder,[2507] such a wait, with his sister Spes in her Berlin apartment where the roof was gone and virtually all the windows blown out, must have been distressing.[2508] Uncertain if he would ever see his family in Kieckow ever again, Hans Jürgen took the opportunity to write to them:
"

> Even in these times our God can perform genuine miracles and he does perform them. This has been my experience in the last half year, a hundred, a thousand times. I would not have traded this experience for anything, not even for a peaceful and comfortable life. Even if we should never again see one another in

this world, still we can look forward to the priceless reunion with all our loved ones who have gone ahead to our Heavenly Father and who we know are so well taken care of there....

Let our daily prayer be from Matthew 6:10: "Thy kingdom come, Thy will be done, on earth as is in heaven." Let us also learn to sing and to pray the last verse of "A mighty Fortress is our God." ... God be with us all!"[2509]

In the meantime, sister Spes, having somehow made her return from the Silesian wedding siege, was far from idle; she was working for the German Red Cross. A few days later, on February 16, following six months in exile, Hans Jürgen made his Pomeranian homecoming. With the civilian rail service in Pomerania now non-existent, it took all the reserves of his energy and all the influence his title could muster to find a series of military vehicles that got him as far as Gross Tychow. A joyous reunion followed.[2510]

The following day, an uneasy quiet reigned over the Kleist lands.[2511] Occasionally, they could hear the sound of heavy artillery fire in the distance, aircraft flying over, and military trains making their way to and from the front. All the while, Hans Jürgen was making plans, but when he visited the crypt in the Kieckow church, two caskets remained unburied, as they had been since before the turn of the century.[2512] Whereas the Kleists of Kieckow had agonised for decades over whether or not to finally bury Hans Hugo and his wife, now in the middle of February 1945, with Old Prussia on the brink of extinction, Hans Jürgen found this decision obvious. Thus, on February 17, 1945, after more than half a century, the caskets of his grandparents were laid to rest in the Kieckow cemetery.[2513] Unfortunately, their rest there was only transitory.[2514]

Three days later, Hans Jürgen began to organise the flight of the family westward.[2515] All the villagers from Kieckow and Klein Krössin were to join his family's party, which included himself, his wife Mieze, Oma Ruth, with her rapidly fading eyesight, and the children's governess and her mother. However, none of Hans Jürgen's children was among them, as Jürgen Christoph and Hans Friedrich had died on the front in 1941, his eldest son Konstantin was safely in American captivity,[2516] and his two youngest, Elli and Heinrich, were already in the relative safety of Mecklenburg to the west.[2517] If not for foolishly agreeing to her friend's request to board the eastward bound train in the forlorn hope of rescuing her friend's mother in January, the selfless Ruthi would have been among the planned family party rather than missing somewhere in Silesia.xxviii

Hans Jürgen had naturally ordered that the preparations for the caravan west be made in secrecy. However, the inclusion of the villagers added greatly to the caravan's size, and it was inevitable, as happened in late January at the Wedemeyer estate at Pätzig,[2518] that word reached the ideologically zealous Gauleiter (local or regional Nazi leader)[2519] in Gross Tychow, forbidding the flight west. Caravan leaders of some of the fleeing German refugee parties were publicly hung and their provisions confiscated by the SS.[2520] Six days later on the 26th, it was still not too late to make the flight west. Ruth, whose eyesight had been fading for three years or more, needed the letters she still received read aloud to her, but continued to answer them with her own pen. That day she wrote to Dita Koch, the wife of Werner, who had taught her grandchildren French all those years ago in her Stettin flat.[2521] She wrote of Hans Jürgen's miraculous return, but also of his eldest daughter Ruthi now missing in Silesia, and the murder of four of her relatives in the Neumark by marauding Red Army soldiers, which included Hete and her son Rüdiger von Tresckow on the Wartenberg estate a month or so before. "

> How God puts us to the test! Four of my relatives, all landowners in the Neumark, have been murdered by the Russians. If we await the same fate, we will take it from God's hand. I am so happy that you have not been molested by the enemy. Perhaps the English do not take such severe measures as the Russians. God, however, can build walls around us, In recent times we have experienced so much protective care that would have been unthinkable if we did not put our faith in him."[2522]

For over three years during their occupation of the Soviet Union, Hitler's armies and the Einsatzgruppen had engaged in what Hitler dubbed a *Vernichtungskrieg* (war of annihilation),[2523] a war of race and ideology, where he ordered his armies to dispense with all notion of scruples and international law.[2524] By late January 1945, three and a half years or so after the launch of Barbarossa (Hitler's invasion of the Soviet Union on June 22, 1941), the Red Army was now well entrenched in the east of

---

xxviii See page 346 of Jane Pejsa and endnotes [2455] to [2458] for this chapter. Ruthi and her friend were guests at the extraordinary wedding in Silesia on Sunday January 21 1945, with the sound of artillery fire at the front line readily audible.

the pre-war Reich,[2525] and had the opportunity, with Stalin's tacit approval,[2526] of inflicting retribution on an unprecedented scale on its ideological and racial enemy.

For the Poles, acts such as the brutal Stalinist occupation of eastern Poland in September 1939,[2527] leading to the deporting of 1.7 million Poles to Siberia, where half would die,[2528] coupled with the Katyń Wood massacre in April 1940,[2529] were, given Stalin's vindictive mindset,[2530] almost certainly motivated by retribution for the Soviet defeat in the 1919-20 Polish-Soviet War.[2531] Born in 1878 into the tradition of the Georgian blood feud,[2532] with an abusive father to boot,[2533] Ioseb Dzhugashvili's[2534] memory of this defeat, in which he was personally involved, never faded. In early 1913,[2535] he dubbed himself "Stalin" — "man of steel." This became a euphemism for legitimising all manner of crimes as acts of a benevolent leader or national father figure of decisive resolve and strength.

Now, in 1945, the opportunity to dish out vengeance on Hitler's Reich for three-and-a-half years of *Vernichtungskrieg* seemed the natural thing to do. Oma Ruth's hope that "Perhaps the English do not take such severe measures as the Russians" was justified, as Norman Davies and Roger Moorhouse wrote: "

> German soldiers in the West knew that they would be reasonably treated if they surrendered. In the East, they had no such assurances. They were facing an implacable enemy, which showed no concern even for the welfare of its own men and rarely bothered to take prisoners. The nature of the war in the East was infinitely more savage than anything the Western Allies could imagine."[2536]

On the 27th of February 1945, the day after Oma Ruth wrote to Dita Koch, the eldest Wedemeyer daughter, Ruth Alice von Bismarck, pregnant with her third child, arrived with her wagon load of refugees at the relative safety of Celle in western Germany. She had left Kniephof in Pomerania the same night her mother Ruthchen barely made it out alive from Pätzig.[2537] Ruth Alice's entourage included a driver and five passengers — an elderly friend, Ruth Alice's two small children, their nursemaid, and herself. Her husband Klaus, although deeply involved in the fighting still taking place in East Prussia, was able to put a phone call through to lift the Reich authorities' prohibition on travel, due to his wife's condition.[2538]

Her party made it safely to Mecklenburg by courtesy of intelligence given by her husband; they came out of Pomerania north of Stettin, island-hopped across the Oder via little known bridges not on official maps, and rested there with relatives before completing their final leg to Celle.[2539] In the meantime, Maria had arrived back from her fruitless search for Dietrich. Later that day, Maria's mother Ruthchen arrived late in the afternoon in good spirits, in spite of the trials and tribulations of her perilous journey. Among those to greet her was the faithful Pätzig bailiff Herr Döpke,[2540] who had likewise made his successful flight from Pätzig earlier that same evening in late January.

The following and final morning of February after breakfast, Ruthchen and her family bade a heartfelt farewell to the Döpke family, including Herr Döpke, his wife, children, and parents. Ruthchen's caravan of two wagons, six horses and fifteen people was heading for the home of relatives further west in Westphalia. After hours upon the road, they came upon a rural church, where Ruthchen ordered them to halt, to enter the vacant sanctuary, pray at the altar, and sing an old Lutheran hymn of praise.[2541] While Ruthchen and her Wedemeyer clan made it to their holy grail of safety in the west, the situation at Kieckow reached a crisis point by March 2.[2542] A fortnight before, when Hans Jürgen had made his joyous homecoming, spasmodic heavy artillery fire was heard in the distance.[2543] Now it had become deafening, and the air was acrid with smoke from the burning of neighbouring estates. Belgard had already fallen and Gross Tychow, the base of the zealous Gauleiter, responsible for the prohibition on prudent travel a fortnight earlier, was under siege.[2544]

Now the wagons were once again made ready under the cover of darkness. Kieckow and Klein-Krössin were to be abandoned. The French prisoners, their guard having disappeared, begged to be among the caravan, to which Hans Jürgen had no objection. Once the entire caravan was made ready, the inhabitants of the neighbouring villages gathered in the Kieckow church, where Hans Jürgen stood before them and spoke the words of God to Abraham: "Go from your country, your people and your father's household to the land I will show you."[2545]

God told Abraham to leave the land of his ancestors for a promised new land of Canaan,[2546] later to become Israel. Now, Hans Jürgen and his caravan were likewise leaving the land of their ancestors, about to be consumed in the cataclysm, for a promised land of safety in Germany's west, where they hoped to rebuild their lives. As they finally departed, Oma Ruth was in the forward wagon, behind Mieze and next to the mother of the children's governess. Even in her now fragile state, the proud matriarch felt she had to be the one to resolutely set the example and not to look back.[2547] By the following evening of the 3rd, the caravan had traversed thirty kilometres from Kieckow, but was forced to halt, as the road ahead was blocked. They were now surrounded by the invaders, and were compelled to seek cover in the forest and wait until the advancing units passed by.[2548] Six days later, after thousands of tanks, troops, and supply trucks had passed by, oblivious to the defenceless caravan embedded in the forest, Hans Jürgen gave the order for the caravan not to resume the westward journey, but to return to Kieckow and simply hope for the best.[2549]

In the meantime, in the dead of night on the 5th, Maria von Bismarck née von Kleist Retzow (Ruth's second daughter and fourth child) and her clan,[2550] in a single horse-drawn wagon, departed from their Lasbeck estate westwards to the Oder and beyond. Among the passengers were Maria's husband Herbert and his mother Hedwig von Bismarck, who, as a fellow widow, had been of great support to Oma Ruth in her grief.[2551] As the night wore on, the sky was illuminated by the incessant pounding of artillery fire; Maria could make out seven distinct pillars of fire rising from her beloved courtyard.[2552] As she did so, her mother-in-law Hedwig threw her arms around her and said, "If we should ever come through this, then we have you to thank for it."[2553]

Hours later, with the breaking of dawn, their terror now somewhat subsided, Maria started singing the centuries-old Pomeranian hymn "Morgenglanz der Ewigkeit" ("Come, thou Bright and Morning Star" or more literally, "Dawn of Eternity").[2554] She and her siblings had sung it as children at Kieckow manor at night while the thunder and lightning raged around them.[2555] Now, Maria's entire clan joined her in singing celebration of their successful flight from the marauding Red Army. How-ever, for the caravan of the von Kleists, their goal was not reached. On the 9th, they were intercepted. Hans Jürgen, his wife, and his mother were taken to a peasant hut to be held for later questioning, while the rest of the caravan was ordered to return to Kieckow. They made it back, but not before they were ordered to pull over by another unit of Soviet soldiers, who plundered their food and horses, leaving only a threadbare party to return by foot, dragging the wagons behind.[2556]

Within hours of Hans Jürgen's arrest, a very high-ranking Soviet general, a divisional commander, arrived to interview him. He was fluent in German; the reason why such a high-ranking interrogator was sent was that they suspected that Hans Jürgen might be Field Marshal Paul Ludwig Ewald von Kleist.[2557] Back in early December, during Advent, a similar misconception led Hitler to personally authorise the release of Ewald's son Ewald Heinrich; the Führer had mistakenly taken Ewald Heinrich to be the son of the said field marshal.[2558]

Hans Jürgen assured his interrogator that this namesake general and loyal vassal of Hitler was no more than a remote relative of his. Moreover, in follow-up, Hans Jürgen informed the interrogator of his recent release from seven months' incarceration in Gestapo prisons, as clear evidence that he was anti-fascist. While the interrogator sounded sympathetic, he still ordered that the three remain in the hut with a guard posted at the entrance, ostensibly for their safety. At the same time, he assured them, that for the time being, they were safer there than in Kieckow — and more than likely, this was the case.[2559] In the ensuing fortnight, the three prisoners were well fed and not ill-treated in any way. The soldiers, it seems, were waiting for someone even higher up to arrive and question the prisoners further. Now, on the 23rd, this day arrived; Hans Jürgen was taken to another building for more rigorous questioning from far less sympathetic interrogators who were sceptical of their subject's testimony.[2560]

The consequence was that Hans Jürgen was be taken to Moscow with the empty promise of "good treatment"; he was denied the opportunity to bid his mother and wife "auf Wiedersehen."[2561] Hans Jürgen's second round of incarceration at the hands of another regime no less ruthless and sadistic was about to commence. At the same time, Mieze and the increasingly frail Oma Ruth were now "free to go," and made their way by foot, dozens of kilometres to Kieckow, uncertain of whether life or death awaited them back there.[2562] At the same time, Allied troops in the west now crossed the Rhein River in the rapidly imploding Reich.[2563]

On April 9 in Berlin, Ewald von Kleist of Schmenzin was taken from his cell in the Moabit prison annex. Since the guard seemed to be in no hurry, Ewald, as he passed by Eberhard Bethge's cell, paused for moment to speak to his fellow conspirator. "If you should come out of all this and ever meet my wife and family, tell them that I have made peace with my God. Tell them also that I leave this world in full faith and in peace."[2564] A short time later, at the nearby Plötzensee prison,[2565] under the guillotine, Ewald left this world. That same morning in the Bavarian camp of Flossenbürg, Dietrich and fellow conspirators from the Abwehr died via the hangman's noose. Two of them however, miraculously escaped their fate.[xxix]

On April 30, Hitler and his wife of a day or so, Eva Braun, committed suicide in their Berlin bunker, and Admiral Karl Dönitz, in Flensburg in the country's north near the pre-war Danish border, succeeded Hitler for the Third Reich's final week or so of existence. Hence it became known as the Flensburg government on May 3. On the 7th, General Jodl signed the unconditional surrender in a schoolroom in Rheims France, but as it was not recognised by the Soviet Union, a second was signed in the Berlin suburb of Karlshorst on the 8th, which became known as VE (Victory in Europe) Day. Officially, the world's most cataclysmic war, at least in Europe, was now over, but it was not until May 20, 1945 that hostilities finally ceased on the Dutch island of Texel. Three days later, on Wednesday May 23. 1945, the final vestige of governance in the Third Reich, the Flensburg government of Admiral Karl Dönitz, was arrested.[2566]

By early June, the special prisoners who had been liberated in late April in Niederdorf in Italy's South Tyrol, among whom was Fabian von Schlabrendorff, were not yet quite free. They were driven by jeep and then flown to Verona and on to Naples before settling for some time on the island of Capri. After their respective ordeals, the island, virtually untouched by the war, was idyllic; they were accommodated in fine hotels and provided with new clothing and fine dining.[2567] The reason for their detention was that their American liberators had to fully document every prisoner,[2568] and as mentioned, some of them were not entirely innocent. Georg Thomas, the ruthless and cynical pragmatist, is a perfect case in point. While he had toyed with the notion of opposition to Hitler, he had been deeply involved in the crafting of the Third Reich's policy for the occupied Soviet Union, which became known as the "Hunger Plan." This was designed to exploit the entire resources of the country for the benefit of Germany and its armed forces by starving millions of its people.[2569] He would not long survive the war, passing away on December 29 1946 in Frankfurt am Main.[2570]

When Fabian's release finally came, he was taken by military escort as far as Wiesbaden in western Germany. From there he borrowed an American vehicle to set about searching for his wife and children, who he assumed were settled safely somewhere in the countryside. As he drove along a narrow country road a few days later, he slowed

---

[xxix] The identity of these two miraculous survivors will be discussed in Chapter 27 "The Prominenten and Miraculous Reprieves."

down to make way for a young woman approaching on a bicycle. As they were about to pass, Fabian realised with joy that it was none other than his beloved wife Luitgarde, and that he had assumed correctly.[2571]

Meanwhile, at Kieckow in the east of the now conquered Reich, things were not so certain. Oma Ruth and her faithful daughter-in-law Mieze were living in the Kieckow's forester's house with his widow; it seems that during the invasion, his forester's uniform had been mistaken for a military one. He was arrested and died en route to a Soviet prison.[2572] The village, abandoned for a week or two in early March, was once again inhabited by the villagers who had attempted to flee and failed, as well as by refugees from as far as East Prussia and as near as Schmenzin. Mostly they were women, children and old men, but one by one the younger men returned, having been released from prisons or work camps among the Soviet conquered lands. Unfortunately, Hans Jürgen was not among that number.[2573]

In comparison with the joyous certainty of the Schlabrendorfs in their family reunion in the west, and the successful flight of Herbert, Maria and Hedwig von Bismarck, Oma Ruth and Mieze had no idea who was alive or dead. Oma Ruth believed that Ruthi, her Kieckow granddaughter, and daughter of Hans Jürgen was in heaven, as she had not been heard of since February, when she was captured by the Red Army in Silesia near Oppeln. In her dreams, Oma Ruth had seen her with the wings of an angel.[2574]

The Kieckow manor house had already been stripped of its ancestral paintings, furnishings and whatever else the invaders felt like plundering, in pay back for the devastation the Third Reich had wreaked on Soviet lands over the past four or so years. In the process, it had been converted into a dairy, with the upstairs bedrooms occupied by the commandant, three of his fellow soldiers, and a Pole. Ruth's own house at Klein Krössin had become uninhabitable, and she had given up the last of her treasures to the conquerors, including her wedding ring. Nevertheless, the women of Kieckow had been left unmolested in an island of relative peace in the eastern lands, counter to the general reign of terror there of the Red Army.[2575]

Gathered from around the countryside were six hundred head of cattle; as they grazed around Kieckow, they had eaten the meadows and horse paddocks clean. Only a small plot of land had been planted with crops, but the roses were blooming more resplendently than at any time in recent memory.[2576] The few inhabitants not directly involved with the dairy operation, male and female alike, were assigned to work parties in and around the area of the Gross Tychow and Belgard, which had suffered almost total devastation.[2577]

During the day, the children were unsupervised, but although lame and almost blind, Oma Ruth taught a kindergarten and Bible classes in the schoolhouse, thanks to one of the workers creating makeshift furnishings from scrounged lumber. In her cellar at Klein Krössin, Ruth had discovered a treasure of no interest to the conquerors — the copious amounts of paper she had stored for Dietrich's writing there over the years. For Ruth, just handling these sheets of paper brought back so many fond memories of better times, and stirred the burning questions — Where is Dietrich? Is he with Maria or with God?[2578] Indeed, whenever a newcomer or unfamiliar vehicle arrived, Ruth became feverish for news of any of her loved ones.[2579]

She expressed these sentiments in the final letter that anyone received. Unaware that her second daughter Maria, mother of Luitgarde and husband of Herbert von Bismarck, had successfully fled west from their Lasbeck estate three months earlier, she expressed her frustration at the lack of news of any of her loved ones. These included her godson Fabian and his family, Ruthchen, Ruth Alice and her husband Klaus von Bismarck, interred she thought in East Prussia, and not least of all, her son Hans Jürgen. The one positive she mentioned was that her village had mostly been spared the ordeal suffered elsewhere in the Old Prussian lands. In closing, Ruth left no doubt as to who was responsible for the cataclysm wrought on her Old Prussia, sweeping away the only way of life she had ever known: "

> Adolf Hitler! Oh how the devil possessed you! Oh how we suffered over the past years because of you and always we knew it would come to an evil end!! And now it is we who must suffer the for the delusions of those who hung onto you.[2580] God is the only assurance in the wretchedness of these times. "Thou art with me."
>
> Physically, I am remarkably well. It is only my sight that is worse and I have lost all my spectacles. Recently, a woman found a pair on the ground at Klein Krössin and she gave them to me. They help a little. It is a miracle....
>
> I greet you with so much affection, my dear beloved children. Your old Mother."[2581]

This was the last letter received from Ruth von Kleist, the last Matriarch of Kieckow, written on the last of the Kleist lands in Pomerania.[2582] In Oma Ruth's story however, there is still a remarkable and heart-warming twist.

Three or so months later in September 1945, in a village near the foot of the Thuringian mountains,[2583] Ruthchen von Wedemeyer was working as a horticultural apprentice. Accompanying her were four of her six surviving children, including her son-in-law and husband of Ruth-Alice, Klaus von Bismarck, who, one day in July, had appeared at the door of the place they now called home. After his return, their family grew to three, their latest a boy. With most of their extended clan now safe in the west, including even Ruthi, their prayers turned to Hans Jürgen, still in Soviet captivity; as for their beloved matriarch, they were convinced that she must be dead.[2584]

On the contrary, Oma Ruth was still alive. However, on the eighth day of that month, she suffered a major injury when she left the forester's cottage to continue her duty of teaching the village children about God. When she left the cottage, she stumbled and fell from the stone step. When she attempted to get up, the pain was excruciating. Four women in the cottage rushed to her side, three carrying her to the bed inside, while the fourth rushed to the old manor to get permission from the Soviet commandant to summon a doctor. Hours later, a German doctor pedalled over from Belgard and determined that the leg was badly broken. Because he had no medicines, he recommended that she be taken to the hospital at Bublitz after he applied the splint. Mieze obtained the necessary permit from the commandant, and they were allowed to use a horse and wagon to transport the last Matriarch.[2585]

Back in the American occupied zone,[2586] Ruthchen, the former mistress of Pätzig, was gathering vegetables from her garden, feeling thankful that she was able to feed her children, and hopeful that her horticultural training would lead to her earning a sustainable income. Her and her family's future now looked brighter than it had nine or so months ago, and Ruthchen now felt content. But she was suddenly gripped by a disturbing sense of unease, as if someone was calling for help. There was no voice, as she was alone in the garden. Ruthchen's first thought was of the brooding, dour older brother of Henning, Gerd von Tresckow and his fatherless children; or perhaps it was the Pätzig villagers they'd left behind, whose fate still weighed on her conscience. In any event, she came to the conclusion that she must heed this call by heading back east over the Oder River! At that time, no German or Old Prussian ever headed back voluntarily to these lands, which, in accordance with the Stalinist edict of the so called "Recovered Territories" (legitimised in Potsdam a month before),[2587] were fast becoming Polonised to compensate Poland for its far greater loss of territory in the east to the Soviet Union.[2588]

Understandably, her family, of Old Prussian stock like herself, living comfortably with her at the foot the Thuringian mountains, were in a state of disbelief, and tried to impress upon her the possibility of leaving her children orphaned.[2589] Nevertheless, the 48-year-old Ruthchen was adamant. She reasoned that she was not afraid of crossing Russian lines in wartime and would not be deterred in peacetime.[2590] And so it was, dressed in cast-off German army trousers, with a backpack full of provisions, and messages to be delivered if she ever made it to her indeterminate destination on the other side of the Oder, she embarked into the unknown. By the 17th, Ruthchen, travelling by train first to Hannover and then on to Göttingen,[2591] was on the way to her first intended stop — Berlin. As she progressed, the call became ever louder, without revealing its origin.[2592] Two days later, she arrived at the border between the British and Soviet occupied zones where the trains naturally stopped. Overnight, while she slept with other travellers in a hay shed, her backpack with all her provisions was stolen.

In spite of this, Ruthchen remained determined to find a way over the border, which was blocked by a large wooden barrier guarded by British soldiers on one side and Soviet on the other. As she wandered, carrying nothing, into some fields which straddled the border, she mingled with peasant workers digging potatoes.[2593] She joined them in their labours and learned that they were mostly members of one family who had crossed the border from the Soviet zone to harvest potatoes on their own land, now occupied by the British. Throughout the day, Ruthchen related her story to the peasants, including the loss of her backpack and her hopes of making it to Berlin. Upon hearing that Ruthchen had not eaten for a day or so, a kind peasant woman opened her bag and cut off a slice of bread, spreading it with lard and sausage; Ruthchen had hardly ever tasted anything so delicious.

As evening descended, Ruthchen urged the peasants to keep two sacks of potatoes for themselves; as she could not believe their assertion that the British would shoot them for taking some of the harvest of their own land.[2594] They finally agreed. Ruthchen, had an ulterior motive, which was revealed when she grabbed a third and empty bag. She begged the peasants to tie her into the bag and load her onto their wagon. In spite of their unease, they agreed. As the wagon passed the British checkpoint, Ruthchen's argument that British soldiers would hardly shoot them for transporting the harvest from their own land over the border rang true. Her heart and those of the brave peasants must have missed a beat or two as they crossed into the Soviet zone and the border guards counted the passengers on the wagon. They waved them on, and for the second time, but in the opposite direction, Ruthchen crossed Soviet lines. Ruth von Wedemeyer felt proud of this accomplishment,[2595] but the ordeal of this eastern sojourn had hardly begun.

After thanking the brave peasants, Ruthchen took to the road to the next station, where she was able to board a train to Nordhausen. She knew that her late husband's favourite sister Anne and her husband had taken refuge there; their reunion was joyful, but tinged with sadness. Anne was still mourning the loss of her eldest grandson, who was shot dead by the sacking Soviets as he went back to the courtyard to feed his cow before they fled the estate.[2596]

A few days later, on the 23rd, Ruthchen resumed her trek towards Berlin. In the Russian occupied zone, train travel to Berlin was hazardous. To begin with, the trains to the bombed out capital were packed to overflowing with passengers trying to make it into one of the three western (US, British and French) Allied occupied zones of West Berlin. In June 1948, to stem this tide, Stalin would implement the Berlin blockade, isolating West Berlin by road and rail, hoping to starve the western sector out. Fortunately, the West was able to supply its three sectors of Berlin by means of a continuous airlift, which, over the next eleven months, supplied West Berlin with over 2.3 million tons of food, fuel, machinery,[2597] and the like, compelling Stalin to lift his blockade.

Ruthchen found there was no available space on the carriages. Undeterred, she climbed one of them and joined others seated on the roof. However, before the train left, they were all hustled back down. Ruthchen, forty-eight years old, broke into a run as the train started to depart; she grabbed hold of one the ladders and clung on until she got off at the next station, unnoticed, it seems, by any of the train staff. This process she repeated again and again, with increasing proficiency, until she reached Gräfenhainichen, where she decided to rest and inquire after an old friend. She discovered that her friend, no longer living in her castle, was still nearby; the joy of their reunion was mixed with grief over the deaths of her friend's husband and son. After a good night's sleep, Ruthchen's friend gave her a backpack, blanket and warm jacket for the remainder of her trip.[2598]

The following day, the 24th, Ruthchen completed the final stage of her trip to Berlin, and made her way by foot to the Bonhoeffer home on the Marienburgerallee in the British occupied zone.[2599] Amidst the devastation of the capital, and their grief at the loss of two sons and two sons-in-law so near to war's end, Karl and Paula had aged dramatically. Ruthchen's primary purpose in Berlin was to search for whatever records remained in makeshift and bombed-out government buildings of the possible whereabouts of the person whose distress call she had heard. She thought again of the orphaned children of Neumark cousin Gerd von Tresckow, the brooding brother of Henning, who submitted himself to arrest in loyalty to his younger brother, before cutting his wrists in prison a year earlier in the wake of Valkyrie in September 1944,[2600] following numerous sessions of torture. Until this moment on September 26 1945, two days after arriving in Berlin, Ruthchen's mind had been closed to the possibility that was the truth.

But then, at the end of a corridor of another government office, Ruthchen could not believe her eyes when she noticed Eberhard Bethge, the dearest of friends to both Dietrich and Oma Ruth, walking towards her. Likewise, Eberhard looked at her as if he had seen a ghost. Before long he regained his composure enough to inform Ruthchen that he had just returned from the post-office where had received a letter from his sister in Köslin, in what had been Prussian Pomerania. This was the first time in seven months that Eberhard had heard anything from his sister. The letter's biggest piece of news for Ruthchen was that her mother, Ruth von Kleist, was still alive, albeit with a broken leg, in Bublitz hospital. In that moment, the youngest child of the last Matriarch was overcome with tears of joy and clarity![2601]

Two days later, at four in the morning, Ruthchen stood at the station platform in Berlin accompanied by Pan (Mister) Sukalski, a former Polish landowner, who for the previous six years, had been a forced labourer in the Third Reich.[2602] Introduced to Ruthchen through a mutual Berlin friend, his forlorn objective was to reclaim his German confiscated lands in newly Soviet occupied Poland, soon to be the communist People's Republic of Poland. Though there was no way to thwart the second confiscation, he could assist Ruthchen in her more realistic but daunting quest — to carry her mother westwards out of the "Recovered" Polish territories, even if that meant doing so on her back.[2603]

As they boarded the train to Stettin (now the Polish border city of Szczecin),[2604] Ruthchen's only possessions were her jacket, backpack, a small amount of German money, and a sturdy carrying belt. She was probably the only German crammed into this train among a sea of Poles returning to Poland, like Pan Sukalski, after years of forced labour in the Reich.[2605] It was a cold autumn day in late September, and the carriages were spartan, without glass windows. When the train stopped for the night, Ruthchen and her Polish companion took shelter and rest in the stationmaster's house. The following day, the 29th, there was no let-up to the cold, but by evening they had almost reached Stettin. They again stopped for the night on the German side of the post-war revised border. The Soviet soldiers guarding the train, feeling the cold, decided to tear down the wooden fence surrounding the station and start a giant bonfire on the platform. Ruthchen and Pan Sukalski took leave to sleep in the comfort of a nearby vacant pigsty until morning.[2606]

The morning of the 30th, they finally made their way into what had been German Stettin, now Polish Szczecin. The companions now agreed not to speak German any longer,[2607] suggesting that English, or perhaps French, should be their common tongue. Ruthchen's fluency in English later came to her aid. At the station, her Polish companion purchased tickets for them to continue their journey further east into Pomerania. By evening, they had reached Stargard, close to the old Bismarck estates, but now a Polish-manned checkpoint. Signs in the train now proclaimed *Keine Deutschen erlaubt* — No Germans allowed,"[2608] after years of signs conversely declaring *Nur für Deutsche* — Only for Germans."[2609] While at this stop, Pan Sukalski was able to pass Ruthchen off as a Pole. But at the next stop, Ruthchen was evicted from the train without the chance to say thank you to Pan Sukalski for getting her this far. Standing in the rain, she attempted in vain to board another carriage, but was unceremoniously pushed from the door.

Her next attempt was to board a freight carriage, wherein she came across two stretchers in the darkness, on which either gravely ill or dead people were lying.[2610] As she moved to a corner in the car away from the stretchers, the train started to move again. Before long, a Pole crawled over from his straw bed in the opposite corner to shine his lantern in the fugitive's face. Ruthchen let fly with English words, convincing her inquisitor she was not German,[2611] despite the strangeness of a supposedly native English speaker travelling eastwards on a freight car in the newly declared Polish lands still occupied by the Red Army. In any event, her fragile ruse succeeded in getting her as far as the formerly Prussian town of Belgard, now Polish Białogard,[2612] where she was born when her father, whom she hardly remembered, had presided as Landrat.[2613] It was now midnight on September 30/October 1, with still plenty of people on the street in the town of her birth, but now, less than five months following war's end in Europe in early May 1945, they only spoke Polish.[2614]

In desperation, Ruthchen asked if a pastor's home was present in the town, to which all replied; "*Nie rozumiem* — I don't understand." When she reached the residential section of the town, she stopped by several lit windows, in the vain hope of hearing some German words.[2615] By now, the misery of Stalinist-engineered post-war Polish-German deportations, amounting to six million people overall[2616] — the largest migration in human history — was overwhelmingly obvious to Ruthchen,[2617] but did not daunt her. With nowhere to stay, in spite of the fatigue she must have been feeling after almost a fortnight of intermittent and hazardous travel, Ruthchen decided to take to the highway towards Bublitz,[2618] about forty kilometres east-south-east of Belgard,[2619] where Eberhard's letter from his sister said that Ruth von Kleist was in hospital.

The sky, which had been clear earlier in the evening, was now clouded over. Nevertheless, Ruthchen was confidant she was walking in the right direction, and indeed, in a manner of speaking, she was. After an hour, seeing another light in a cottage, she again crept towards the window, and again to her frustration, only heard Polish. However, convinced she was walking towards Bublitz, Ruthchen ordered herself to soldier on to where mother Ruth would undoubtedly be waiting for her in hospital. As she passed through another village just after dawn, she spotted a cottage with an open window, and to her delight, heard a woman speaking German. Knocking on the door, Ruthchen asked; "How far to Bublitz?," to which the woman replied; "To Bublitz? as she pointed in the opposite direction; "You must go through Gross Tychow[2620] and circle back." Ruthchen, exhausted, realised she had became lost in the near total darkness, and was heading towards to her childhood home in Kieckow![2621]

This still German village was Grussöw, and it was the home to the sister of Hete von Tresckow,[xxx] who was murdered, along with her son Rüdiger, by the marauding Red Army.[2622] Their Wartenberg estate had been on the doorstep of the Pätzig estate of the von Wedemeyers. Ruthchen asked about the whereabouts of this old family friend, and was directed to cross the stream to a hut just outside the village. There were two doors, more than likely housing two apartments. As Ruthchen contemplated which door to open in the dim early morning light, one swung open to reveal her old family friend.[2623]

As Ruthchen raced to hug her, the friend covered her mouth with her hand, to silence her until they entered the hut. Inside, they em-

---

[xxx] I have not been able to find the name of this sister of Hete von Tresckow.

braced each other with the joy of old friends who had both survived the cataclysm. Their joy was muted by grief when Ruthchen whispered to her the terrible news that her sister Hete, brother-in-law Jürgen and nephew Rüdiger were all dead. As Ruthchen was urged to lie down and sleep in her friend's bed, she was told that her errant walk was all for the best, as her mother was now home at Kieckow! The hospital in Bublitz had no medicine or even plaster to make a cast for the matriarch's broken leg.[2624] Ruthchen's rest was brief. By nine o'clock, impatient to be reunited with her mother, after a hearty breakfast, she was off again to make the thirty kilometre walk to Kieckow. As she passed Gross Tychow to make her way into Klein Krössin, she was amazed to find the village houses there virtually undisturbed, with a herd of 150 or so young cattle grazing peacefully in the meadow and a field of potatoes alongside. While the matriarch's cottage had become uninhabitable, Klein Krössin and Kieckow had been a microcosm insulated from the Soviet scourge of retribution.

When Ruthchen met with a worker, she was told that her eldest brother Hans Jürgen was still incarcerated in Russia, but that her mother was at Kieckow, living with her daughter-in-law Mieze in the forester's cottage.[2625] Now, on the final stretch to Kieckow, just past the little monument to her niece Ferdinande, who died in 1924 in a wagon accident, Ruthchen crossed paths with a stranger on a bicycle; she was a nurse from Gross Tychow. When she informed Ruthchen that her mother was seriously ill with pneumonia, Ruthchen thanked her and broke into a run, past the cattle barns, past the road to the manor house, only acknowledging the old family coachman with the briefest of waves, not slowing down until she made it to the forester's cottage.[2626]

She entered the cottage, and with joy and astonishment, she and her sister-in-law Mieze embraced each other. "Is it really you? … Mother is dying." Ruthchen almost fainted with relief that she was not too late. Her mother had been in and out of a coma for the past two days and more. As Ruthchen knelt beside her mother and gently took her hands, the grand old lady turned her head to face her daughter. When Oma Ruth opened her eyes to gaze at her youngest child, it was without any sign of recognition. Mieze then told Ruthchen to say the words that would move her mother most: "Mother, Fabian is alive."[2627] The grand old lady, with a passing smile, slowly responded; "is alive?" Encouraged, Ruthchen added; "Klaus is with us and he is well."[2628] A fleeting smile prompted Ruthchen to continue: "Ruth-Alice has a healthy baby boy; Maria and Herbert are in the west." To which the dying matriarch, for the first time since returning from the hospital,[2629] softly spoke aloud, to the amazement of all present; "I don't seem to remember any more. It is all so far away." Oma Ruth, eyes fixed upon her baby daughter, asked of the one absent from Ruthchen's roll call of joy: "And Dietrich, is he alive?"[2630]

On hearing the sad answer to her final question, the face of the last Matriarch of Kieckow, perhaps in joyful realisation of her imminent reunion with her dear Dietrich in Heaven,[2631] betrayed no pain or sorrow. She closed her eyes in contentment for the final time as her beloved Old Prussia faded into history. Such was not the case for her prodigious and loving progeny.[2632]

Chapter 26

Oma Ruth's Progeny After Death

The grand old lady, Ruth Ehrengard von Kleist-Retzow née Gräfin von Zedlitz-Trützschler, died on Tuesday October 2 1945 — the day following Ruthchen's arrival and her sad revelation of Dietrich's execution.[2633] From this point on October 1, it seems, Oma Ruth did not come out of her coma, and passed away in contented peace the following day. She was buried in the Kieckow cemetery between her dear husband Jürgen and favourite son Konstantin,[2634] who died in action during the Great War.[2635] On what turned out to be the first day of no work in the seven months of Soviet occupation, the Kieckow workers were given an afternoon off to attend the matriarch's funeral, because, even in the words of the Soviet commandant, "the Frau Kleist was a great lady."[2636]

Ruthchen had implored her sister-in-law Mieze née von Diest to return west with her to join her children, but without the villagers, Mieze was having none of it.[2637] Ruthchen again made the trip alone; it took her more than two weeks, during which time she was jailed by Poles and put to work cleaning and mending her jailers' clothing. Fortunately, however, she managed to escape, and was back with her children by the end of October. Needless to say, there were to be no further hazardous journeys east for her! In January 1946,[2638] Ruthchen was reunited with her second son and fourth child, Hans Werner — the one she caught spitting on the bullying guards.[2639] He was not among her three youngest children, who were in the party bravely evacuated by Maria in late January 1945. By 1944, he had turned seventeen,[2640] meaning that well before war's end, he was conscripted into an army, which was becoming ever more critically short of manpower in the Reich's implosion from east and west.

Three months following this reunion, in April 1946,[2641] six months since the grand old lady's passing, the Stalinist engineered Polonisation of the Old Prussian lands finally reached Kieckow and Klein Krössin,[2642] whereupon they respectively became Kikowo and Krosinko.[2643] Mieze was forced to leave Kieckow on a Red Cross train, with her fellow villagers following soon thereafter. A few weeks later, with Mieze now settled in the west, her son Konstantin finally arrived back from his captivity in America.[2644] Then, in January of the following year, Mieze received a telegram from Frankfurt an der Oder,[2645] with the following message: "In a few days with you. Psalm 126."[2646] A week later, almost two years after his deportation to Russia in a state of terrible apprehension, Hans Jürgen returned in joy, liberated and reunited with his dear wife in her little cottage. He was frostbitten and thin after three months of torture at Moscow's infamous Lubyanka prison, followed by nineteen months of hard labour in a Siberian gulag.[2647] Ironically, he, the anti-fascist, had escaped torture at the hands of the fascists,[2648] but not from the champions of the so-called workers' anti-fascist utopia.

However, Hans Jürgen realised he was one of the lucky ones, as most of his fellow German prisoners were still incarcerated in that frigid hell, with no prospect of release any time soon. Indeed, many, even Friedrich von Paulus, the general who surrendered the Sixth Army at Stalingrad in early February 1943, and subsequently became a member of the Soviet-sponsored "Nationalkomittee Freies Deutschland" (NKFD, National Free German Committee), were not released until 1953.[2649] According to the German historian, Rüdiger Overmans, approximately 3.3 million German prisoners of war were captured by the Soviet Union during World War II,[2650] most of them during the great advances of the Red Army in the last year of the war. The POWs were employed as forced labour in the Soviet wartime economy and post-war reconstruction.

By 1950, almost all surviving POWs had been released. In September 1955, the first chancellor of West Germany, Konrad Adenauer, negotiated with Nikita Khrushchev for the release to Germany of 15,000 German interned civilians and prisoners of war;[2651] the last prisoner returned from the USSR in 1956.[2652] According to Soviet records, of 2,733,739 German POWs, 381,067 German Wehrmacht POWs died in NKVD camps.[2653] Rüdiger Overmans maintains that it is plausible, though not provable, that one million died in Soviet custody.[2654] He also believes that there were men who actually died as POWs amongst those listed as missing-in-action (MIA).[2655]

For Hans Jürgen post-war, there were two regrets. The first, which ended up affecting the fate, not just of Germany, but of an entire continent, was mentioned back in Chapter 9, The von Kleists and the Prophecy. In 1952, Hans Jürgen told his son of his deep regret that he had not supported the then incumbent chancellor, Heinrich Brüning, twenty years earlier in April 1932, when a more united front by all parties involved could still have stopped Hitler.[2656] The second regret only concerned one man, but it would nevertheless haunt Hans Jürgen for the rest of his life.

In January 1941, Oma Ruth, approaching seventy-four years of age, suffered a stroke in her Stettin flat — an omen of her declining health from this point on in her final years. The cook, upon finding her lying on the floor, summoned the doctor, and with the help of a house guest, managed to get her into bed. On arrival, the doctor diagnosed a small stroke. In the meantime, within just hours of being phoned, Hans Jürgen arrived and knocked on the door; an elderly stranger opened the door. Hans Jürgen, already distraught, bluntly interrogated the stranger. He was shocked to learn that the stranger was a Jew with no money or resources of any description, and, sixteen or so months into the war, with no prospect of flight out of Germany.

Moreover, he had been staying with Oma Ruth since around September 1940, when the deportation of Jews out of Stettin was already well under way.[2657] Up until March 1940, Oma Ruth had been playing host to Jews at both her Stettin flat and the Klein Krössin estate. In the meantime, Dietrich arranged Swedish visas for them, while at the same time, no one in either Klein Krössin or Stettin ever spoke of them. However, by March 1940, when Germany had been at war for six months, subsequently closing all its borders, it was decided by her family that Oma Ruth should cease her role as the risk-taking host.[2658] Hence Hans Jürgen's shock ten or so months later. He ordered the man's almost immediate eviction, believing that the Jew's continued presence would be a dangerous liability in his mother's fragile state of health. The stranger left within the hour, never to be heard of again. Hans Jürgen carried the memory of this man, whom he had condemned to almost certain death.[2659] A regret no less than the regret for the missed political opportunity in 1932, which had dire consequences for his beloved Germany and indeed, for almost all of Europe.

By 1985, the last of Oma Ruth's children, her youngest Ruth-chen, had passed away in Hannover West Germany, aged 87. All her children had contributed in one way or another to the rebuilding of Germany post-war. In the process, the eldest, Hans Jürgen, before his death in 1969 aged 83, along with Ruthchen and Maria von Bismarck (1893-1979), left fragmented memoirs for their children.[2660] They chronicled their feudal childhood, life under the Third Reich, the war, and its ultimate closing act.[2661] In addition, Hans Jürgen wrote a loving memoir of his faithful friend and cousin, Ewald of Schmenzin, which became a major source for Bodo Scheurig's biography *Ewald von*

Kleist-Schmenzin: ein Konservativer gegen Hitler: Biographie (Ewald von Kleist-Schmenzin: a Conservative against Hitler: Biography).[2662]

Of Oma Ruth's surviving grandchildren post-war, there was one who was outlived by one of their parents. She was none other than Dietrich's fiancée and Ruthchen's third child, Maria,[2663] for whom, post-war, life was not an altogether happy one. In part, it is reflected in her continuing grief over the loss of Dietrich, in whom she had found great solace in the wake of the deaths of her father and brother Max in 1942. After the loss of the three dearest men in her life, amid the devastation of her native Germany and virtually the entire Old World of Europe, upon her graduation from Göttingen University,[2664] she sought a new life across the Atlantic in the American New World. She lived the rest of her life in Pennsylvania, Massachusetts, and Connecticut on its eastern seaboard.[2665]

Her life in the New World began with enrolling in Pennsylvania's Bryn Mawr Women's Liberal Arts College, where she studied mathematics, as she had planned ever since her gymnasium graduation in 1942. Then, following graduation, she took up a position with Honeywell in Massachusetts, and rose to become a departmental head, which was a most significant accomplishment for a woman at that time. However, while Maria had the joy of having two sons, the great sadness of her new life was that she was twice married and divorced before dying of cancer in 1977, aged just fifty-two.[2666] For many years following Dietrich's death, his devotees and scholars wished to know more about the woman to whom he had been engaged. Such knowledge was not forthcoming; Maria was probably unwilling to publicly revisit her relationship with Dietrich. It was not until her death was approaching that Maria gave her eldest sister, Ruth-Alice, permission to publish the many love letters between her and Dietrich,[2667] which were finally published in 1992 in a volume entitled *Love Letters from Cell 92*.[2668]

In 2008, while researching his book,[2669] Eric Metaxas wrote of the privilege he had of meeting Maria's eldest sister, Ruth-Alice, in Hamburg. She was then in her eighties; she had been a young woman during the time of the Finkenwalde Seminary in the mid 1930s, Oma's Ruth's patronage, and Dietrich's numerous visits to their regal Old Prussian estates. She remembered how many of her fellow young people, being seduced by Hitler, would boldly proclaim that he was their future. However, while she found that Dietrich always seemed to have an aura of detachment, she felt his compelling, positive charisma, devoted wholly and utterly to God whenever he preached — prompting her to declare, "Here is our future."[2670] Indeed, though he did not live to be part of Germany's post-war future in the corporeal sense, Dietrich, in his martyrdom, has become part of his country's future by living on in its consciousness, outlasting the diabolical evil that was the Third Reich. Five years after Eric Metaxas's visit, Ruth-Alice passed away on December 28, 2013 at the grand old age of 93.[2671]

Maria treasured the few possessions she retained from her Old Prussian past. There were her letters of correspondence with Dietrich. There was the oriental rug that graced her Boston home and had originally protected the parquet floor of the Pätzig manor home, before covering the wagon and the pieces of silver cutlery she had impulsively thrown into it on her epic flight west in late January 1945.[2672] Maria was not alone among her siblings in emigrating to the New World. Her younger sister Christine Beshar, among those on the wagon party, practised law in New York, passing away as recently as January 11 2018, aged 88. In the 1980s, Christine successfully campaigned for the firm to become the first major one in New York to open its own child-care centre,[2673] after she became the firm's first female partner in 1971.

As one would expect, there have been many weddings post-war of the children of the Wedemeyer siblings, but in regard to the main subject of this book, one in 1986 is of particular interest. That year, Werburg Doerr, the second youngest child of Ruthchen and so among those in the wagon party, witnessed the marriage of her daughter to the grandson of Dietrich's sister Ursula Schleicher. The groom's uncle, Emeritus Eberhard Bethge, performed the ceremony of this marriage of Dietrich's grandnephew and the great-granddaughter of Oma Ruth. Thus, albeit posthumously, the dream of the last matriarch of Kieckow, Oma Ruth, of the union of her old Prussian progeny to the Bonhoeffers was fulfilled.[2674]

As mentioned in Chapter 8, Ruth Roberta Stahlberg Heckscher (Raba), the daughter of Oma Ruth's second child Spes, and the matriarch's first grandchild, emigrated to Israel in 1986, and in 1989, aged 80, converted to Judaism.[2675] In the process, she adopted the surname of her great-grandfather Wilhelm Moritz Heckscher, son of a rabbi and Hamburg delegate in the Frankfurt Church of Saint Paul in 1848,[2676] and the Justice Minister for a brief period during the German Revolt of that year.[2677] In Israel, Raba worked as a volunteer at Jerusalem's Yad Vashem Holocaust Memorial Museum every Friday, sitting at the exit table, bidding farewell to each visitor and comforting those for whom the visit was all too disturbing.[2678]

Raba's two brothers, Alexander (Alla) and Hans Conrad, who was the groom at the extraordinary Silesian wedding in January 1945, marrying Maria von Loesch, a descendant from a branch of the Zedlitz family,[2679] both had successful business careers in Germany. Hans Conrad passed away in 1987, aged 73; the handsome Alla, the first grandson of the matriarch, laid claim to being her favourite.[2680] In the early 1990s, his own memoir, was published in both German and English.[2681] Ruthi, Countess de Pourtales née von Kleist, the fifth child of Hans Jürgen and Mieze, was among the guests at the wedding; she worked with the Council of Churches in Geneva Switzerland. After the death of Ruthi's mother Mieze, Hans Jürgen bestowed upon Ruthi the famous family heirloom of the black gold-rimmed Stolberg cross,[2682] known to the Kieckow villagers as the Kaiser's magic cross. It was treasured by Ruthi with some sadness, as she knew that Oma Ruth never got to wear it, due to the strained relationship that Oma Ruth had with her spinster sister-in-law Elisabeth.[2683]

Ruthi's younger sister Elisabeth (Elli) Sittig was still, by the early 1990s, residing in Bremen. Their elder brother Konstantin, who had spent time in American captivity during the war, was also living in Germany after spending fourteen years as a Lutheran missionary and pastor in the black townships of South Africa.[2684] Heinrich, the youngest, worked for years for a large German metallurgical firm, which was the same one that his uncle Konstantin, third child and second son of Oma Ruth, worked for before dying on the front in the Great War. The owner was Wilhem Merton the Jew,[2685] who had taken Uncle Konstantin into his family, and indeed his heart.[2686]

In regard to the Kleists of Schmenzin, Ewald's widowed second wife Alice, born in 1910, survived the war along with all eight of his children. There were six to his first wife Anning, who died of scarlet fever in May 1937,[2687] and two to Alice; all, by the early 1990s, lived in Germany and Switzerland. Ewald's fourth child Reinhild Hausherr lived not far from Ruthi in Geneva; the two cousins had formed a close bond, reminiscent of that of their respective fathers.[2688] Tragically, Ewald's brother Hermann Conrad and his wife were murdered by Soviet soldiers when their estate was seized. A few weeks later, Ewald's elderly mother, the Countess Lili, while still wearing the sombre grey gown of the estate mistress, met the same fate.[2689]

The modern-day south-western Polish village of Borów Wielki,[2690] which, pre-war, was known as Grossenborau, was the childhood home of Oma Ruth; the stone church and the sturdy brick and stucco dwellings that defined it have changed little. The now unoccupied neighbouring manor house, while still standing, is sorely in need of repair. The steps at the main entrance have collapsed, and in the grand entry hall, only the remains of the marble fireplace reflect distant and fading memories of its grand past. Viewed from outside, its sheer size still gives it an imposing reminder of Oma Ruth's bygone era.[2691] Today, following the 1999 provincial boundaries revision,[2692] less than ten years after the communist regime's collapse, it lies in the Polish voivodeship (*województwo* — province) of Lubusz, but is still less than sixteen kilometres from the boundary with the neighbouring voivodeship of Dolny Śląsk (Lower Silesia, or in German, Niederschlesien, pronounced "Dolny Shlongsk" in Polish), with its capital in Wrocław.[2693] No doubt in Oma Ruth's time, she regarded herself a native of Silesia, before the regional border manipulations were implemented under various Polish administrations.

Over 250 kilometres to the north in the voivodeship of West Pomerania (*zachodniopomorskie*), in the historic region of Pomerania (Polish: Pomorze, German: Pommern), is the village and state farm of Kikowo, formerly Prussian Kieckow.[2694] Unlike most of Poland, it has changed little since war's end, with the old stone roads lined with linden, chestnut, oak and maple trees still conveying traffic throughout the Białogard,[2695] formerly Prussian Belgard district.[2696] In the early 1990s, the stone cross monument to Ferdinande, Hans Jürgen and Mieze's oldest child who died in the wagon accident in 1924 aged ten, still stood by the roadside as it had since her death.[2697] Given how little Kikowo has changed over the decades, it could well be still there today, almost a century later, in late 2019. Unlike the neglected manor house at Grossenborau, time has been kinder to its Kieckow counterpart; in 1986, the entire stucco exterior was repaired and repainted for the first time in fifty years. Today, it has a tin roof rather than the red tiles of the Old Prussian times; the old library still serves as such, in addition to being a lounge for the entire state farm.[2698]

The other notable change to Kikowo since war's end has been the cemetery, which, just as Old Prussia has gone with the wind, no longer contains any German names. Polish graves and their requisite monuments have taken their place. The paternal grandparents of Hans Jürgen and in-laws of Oma Ruth, Hans Hugo von Kleist and his wife Charlotte, both passed away in 1885 and 1892 respectively; Hans Jürgen had them removed from their Kieckow crypts and buried in the cemetery during Old Prussia's death throes in February 1945.[2699] Given the bad blood between Poles and Germans just months following war's end, with memories of German atrocities still so fresh in Polish minds, and for many, the Stalinist upheaval of being expelled from their old eastern Borderlands post-war, plus their experiences of Stalinist-perpetrated atrocities in the first two years of the war,[2700] it was not likely that they cared to preserve any remnants of one of their hated former German masters.

The Borderland Poles, who experienced the very worst from alternating and equally despised fascist and Soviet overlords during World War II, had no interest whatsoever in historical nuances after the war,[2701] as they attempted to rebuild their lives and preserve their national consciousness and identity. Such was the mindset of all Borderland Poles deported to the so called German "Recovered Territories," of which Grossenborau in the Silesian south and Kieckow in the Pomeranian north were part. Fortunately, however, the church was left intact, and just like Old Prussian times, the priest makes the weekly trip from modern-day Tychowo, formerly Gross Tychow,[2702] for services in the Catholic faith. The church had been the passion of Heinrich von Kleist-Retzow, the youngest child of Hans Jürgen and Mieze, who visited Poland every year to consult with the priest and provide the funds required to maintain the church as a symbol of reconciliation between two faiths and two nations.[2703] Heinrich passed away on August 15 2014 aged 84.[2704]

By 1985, the last of Oma Ruth's children, her youngest, the remarkable Ruthchen,[2705] passed away in Hanover.[2706] With Heinrich's passing in 2014, the youngest of Oma Ruth's eldest son Hans Jürgen, it would be difficult to imagine many of her grandchildren still alive in 2019, as the decades roll by.[xxxi] Their children today are ensuring that Oma Ruth's progeny, as well as the legacy and proud memory of her beloved Old Prussia, "in doing what's right even in the face of seemingly invincible evil," live on.[2707] As does the memory of her fellow native Silesian and dearest friend Dietrich, whom she regarded, it seems, as no less than a son.

[xxxi] Time travels faster as you get older.

Chapter 27

The Prominenten and Miraculous Reprieves

On Wednesday, February 7, 1945, following the almost complete destruction of Berlin's Prinz-Albrecht-Strasse prison four days earlier, two groups of prisoners were transferred to the concentration camps of Buchenwald near Weimar (about 225 km south-west of Berlin), and Flossenbürg in northern Bavaria.[2708] Dietrich, as already discussed, was among the group for Buchenwald, as was Captain Ludwig Gehre.[2709] On the other hand, for example, Admiral Wilhelm Canaris, General Hans Oster and Judge Karl Sack, were headed for Flossenbürg.[2710] All the prisoners from both groups were Prominenten[2711] — VIP, special or prominent prisoners, or more to the point, hostages.[2712] Hitler and Himmler hoped that their lives could be bargained for some concession in any envisaged surrender negotiations with the Allied powers.[2713] In Dietrich's case for example, his friendship with Bishop George Bell, a member of the British House of Lords,[2714] supposedly gave the Reich some sort of bargaining power with the British. Of course, such notions were fanciful.

In early April 1945, with the Americans advancing on Buchenwald,[2715] Dietrich and his group were evacuated to nowhere in particular. By Saturday April 7, 1945, Dietrich's party had arrived in the idyllic Bavarian village of Schönberg.[2716] However, at around noon the following day of the 8th, Dietrich was arrested, and taken to Flossenbürg.[2717] [xxxii] At dawn the next day, he and four others, Admiral Wilhelm Canaris, General Hans Oster, Judge Karl Sack and Captain Ludwig Gehre, were executed.[2718] This was in response to the discovery of the Canaris Diaries in Zossen, just south of Berlin, on April 4, implicating all five victims in the conspiracy.[2719] This included their role in assassination plots

---

[xxxii] Dietrich was already arrested on April 5, 1943. However, that was in relation to the Schmidhuber affair, regarding currency irregularities associated with "Operation 7" — the successful arranged flight of fourteen Jews to Switzerland. See endnotes [1449] to [1475] of Chapter 18, "Romance, Plots and Arrest" and endnotes [1476] to [1480] of Chapter 19, "The Tormentor Tormented." Whilst execution in 1943 was certainly a possible outcome, it was by no means certain. However, at noon on Sunday April 8, 1945, when he was arrested for the second time in Schönberg in relation to assassination plots on Hitler, (e.g. the March 1943 plots), his execution at Flossenbürg was beyond all doubt.

on Hitler before Valkyrie.[2720] Up until that point, Hitler and his cronies had no idea of any such plots, since, for example, in the March 1943 plots, the conspirators were able to cover their tracks.[2721] When Dietrich, Oster, Dohnányi, and Josef Müller were arrested on April 5, 1943,[2722] it was in relation to something much more benign — currency irregularities associated with the successful Abwehr Operation 7, the flight of fourteen Jews over the Alps into Switzerland in 1942.[2723]

When the contents of the Canaris Diaries were revealed to Hitler on April 5, 1945, the day following their discovery in Zossen, he flew into an apoplectic rage.[2724] Prominenten or prominent prisoners these five men may have been, but now Hitler's desire for vengeance took precedence. Seven months earlier, in September 1944, in Valkyrie's wake, it was also in Zossen that Hans von Dohnányi's secret archive, which was dubbed the *Chronicle of Shame files*,[2725] had been discovered.[2726] Dohnányi started writing them in the wake of the invasion of Poland in September 1939,[2727] and following their discovery, they became known as the Zossen Files.[2728] In September 1944, they sealed the fate of Dohnányi after he had pleaded for their destruction for months.[2729] At Sachsenhausen on Friday April 6, Walter Huppenkothen, who had been the chief investigator at Prinz-Albrecht-Strasse, together with an unknown SS judge and the camp commandant, proclaimed the death sentence for Hans von Dohnányi, who was lying half-conscious on a stretcher before them.[2730] The sentence was carried out on April 9 — the very same day as Dietrich's execution at Flossenbürg.[2731] (The fate of Dietrich and his fellow victims, and the aftermath, will be discussed in detail in the following chapter. This chapter deals with the fate of Prominenten who survived post-war.)

American troops were approaching Flossenbürg,[2732] just before dawn on Monday April 9, 1945, before the planned executions of the five victims, when the first transport of Prominenten, bound for Dachau, left Flossenbürg. It was under the charge of SS Obersturmführer (Second Lieutenant) Gogalla.[2733] The prisoners included Hjalmar Schacht, the former Reich finance minister pre-war, the Schuschnigg Family, which included Kurt, the Austrian chancellor pre-1938-Anschluss, Franz Halder, who had been Hitler's Chief of Staff, Colonel Bogislav von Bonin, who served with Rommel in Africa and was later Operations Chief under Guderian at Hitler's General Headquarters, and the ruthless and cynical pragmatist, General Georg Thomas.[2734] Later that morning of the 9th, on the way to Dachau, the transport picked up General Falkenhausen, Payne Best, and Vassily Kokorin at Schönberg.[2735] All these prisoners, unlike Dietrich and his fellow condemned, were not condemned, but still "hostages of the SS," to be kept alive for any future possible surrender negotiations with the Allied powers. Such was the mindset of the Third Reich in its death throes.

While Thomas had toyed with the notion of opposition to Hitler, he had been deeply involved in the crafting of the Third Reich's policy for the occupied Soviet Union. It was a policy which became known as the "Hunger Plan" and was designed to exploit the entire resources of the country for the benefit of Germany and its armed forces, via the starvation of millions of its people.[2736] Yet this cynical opportunist's name is on the website of Die Gedenkstätte Deutscher Widerstand (German Resistance Memorial Centre).[2737] Being among the liberated at Niederdorf, he survived the war, albeit briefly, dying in Frankfurt-am-Main in December 1946.[2738] From numerous meetings with them, Payne Best described Thomas and Halder as the type that perceived themselves in no way responsible for the cataclysm that had been World War II. In their minds, as diligent military professionals, such responsibility lay outside their scope, being in the realm of politics. In particular, they saw Hitler, who waged war outside established military doctrine, as an intrusive and incompetent amateur.[2739]

For Halder and Thomas, it seemed as though war was merely a game of chess to be played to the utmost of their professional abilities.[2740] Politics was irrelevant, and it seemed they even took a mild satisfaction in the German defeat, vindicating their notion that the German plight was solely due to the politician Hitler playing the game of war outside of its rules.[2741] True, as the war wore on, Hitler became more and more reckless and incompetent, but it seems that was their only problem with Hitler, and the concentration camps and the mass genocide were all well and good if they led to a more powerful Germany. Certainly, Thomas's major role in the "Hunger Plan" strongly suggests this.

Upon their arrival in Dachau, the cells for this group of Prominenten, Falkenhausen, Best, and Kokorin, were described by Payne Best as being "almost luxuriously appointed,"[2742] a far cry from what they had endured at Buchenwald and Flossenbürg. Moreover, they held out hope for some time that they would be liberated there when Allied troops arrived. However, on April 25,[2743] they would leave Dachau for their odyssey over the Alps through the Brenner Pass; the following day or thereabouts, Sigmund Rascher, the SS doctor proud of carrying out medical experiments on human subjects, was shot in his cell.[2744] While in Dachau, Payne Best met Martin Niemöller,[2745] the Confessing

Church pastor arrested in 1937;[2746] he was to join Payne Best and the others among the liberated in Niederdorf.

Nine days following his arrival at Dachau from Schönberg, and his subsequent meeting with Martin Niemöller, Payne Best had a most unexpected but joyful reunion.[2747] On April 18, he ran into Josef Müller and Franz Liedig,[2748] who had, with Fabian von Schlabrendorff,[2749] just arrived in Dachau from Flossenbürg. They were two of the three men taken from the Grüne Minna just outside Weiden two weeks earlier on the 4th, and along with the third man taken, Ludwig Gehre, the general feeling among the remaining prisoners was that all three were being taken to their certain death.[2750] As it turned out, of the three, only Ludwig Gehre was executed, along with Dietrich, Wilhelm Canaris, Hans Oster and Doctor Karl Sack, at Flossenbürg at dawn on April 9. Both Müller and Liedig could not understand why their lives were spared;[2751] Payne Best alluded to Liedig's foreboding sense of inevitable death.[2752] Both were among the liberated in Niederdorf and lived on until well after war's end; Liedig passed away in Munich in 1967 at age 67.[2753] Müller also passed away in Munich, but lived on a dozen years later until 1979, aged 81;[2754] he became one of the founders of the Bavarian conservative political party, the Christian Socialist Union.[2755]

As to why Müller was spared, it seems to have been due in part to his Vatican contacts, which some of the Reich's inner circle perceived as affording Germany more favourable surrender terms. Naive as this notion was, it led to them sparing the lives of 130 special prisoners.[2756] In Müller's case, on the day he was to be hanged along with the other five, and with his hangman's noose before him, a last-minute phone call from an SS adjutant in the bunker in Berlin saved him.[2757] The head of Hitler's personal security, Johann "Hans" Rattenhuber, persuaded Ernst Kaltenbrunner, who had been responsible for setting up the July 20 commission,[2758] to spare Josef Müller on the condition that he be used as the bargaining chip, due to his numerous Vatican contacts.[2759] It was not until post-war that Müller was made aware of this fateful phone call,[2760] which explains why Payne Best recalled that Müller had no idea as to why he was spared.

This conversation between Kaltenbrunner and Rattenhuber took place above Hitler's bunker in Berlin on Sunday April 8, 1945, the day before the executions in Flossenbürg. Rattenhuber had come up to get some fresh air, and found Ernst Kaltenbrunner, head of the Reich Security Office, having a smoke.[2761] Although Kaltenbrunner theoretically reported to Himmler, Himmler feared Kaltenbrunner, who often by-passed Himmler to report directly to Hitler, with whom he had had personal ties since childhood.[2762] Towards the end, Kaltenbrunner spent several hours a day with Hitler.[2763] As head of the July 20 Commission[2764] for nearly nine months, Kaltenbrunner had probed plots to kill Hitler, and since Rattenhuber had the job of protecting the Führer, he followed the findings with a kind of mortified rapture.[2765] In the first week of April 1945, Kaltenbrunner said, the story had taken a wild turn. The finding of Canaris's diaries at Zossen had confirmed what Hitler long suspected: that many of the threats to his life and his power could be traced to "the Vatican, which Hitler... regarded as the greatest centre of espionage in the world."[2766]

Johann Rattenhuber, head of Hitler's personal security, cared for Müller's fate because of the bizarre "beer brotherhood" he and Müller had formed, following an interrogation that Müller had endured from Heinrich Himmler, head of the SS and then head of all German Police units outside of Prussia,[2767] on February 9, 1934: "

> By early 1934, Müller's intrigues had riled the secret police. His name appeared on an SS list of Catholics opposed to the regime. Dachau's warden warned that Müller himself would soon "arrive" at the camp. A few weeks later, on 9 February, the Gestapo arrested Müller in Munich and charged him with "a treasonous conspiracy ... punishable by death."[2768]

However, Müller's courage confounded Himmler and had him in awe, and he was prompted to invite him to join the SS. To which Müller replied: "I am philosophically opposed to you. I am a practising Catholic, and my brother is a Catholic priest. Where could I find the possibility of a compromise there?"[2769] On this point, Josef Müller was in complete agreement with Dietrich.[2770]

Himmler, overtly anti-Christian,[2771] had hoped to get Müller to abandon his faith and be seduced by the lure of being accepted into the most elite and powerful organ of Hitler's Reich. Himmler dismissed Müller. Shortly after, Hans Rattenhuber, a thirty-seven-year-old ex-cop, now commanding Hitler's bodyguard, called on Müller. Rattenhuber was just as impressed as Himmler was with Müller's courage, but, like Kaltenbrunner, Rattenhuber saw Himmler and most of the Nazi inner-circle as corrupt sycophants.[2772] He admired Müller for standing up to Himmler, and wanted to meet *Joey der Ochse*. (Joey the Ox.)[2773] Over the traditional Bavarian pastime of sharing steins of beer, their "Beer Brotherhood" was forged."[2774] Rattenhuber cherished it because it gave him the chance, so rare in a dictatorship, to speak his mind. For Müller, Rattenhuber's rants were a treasure trove of intelligence, as they revealed the Third Reich's plans against the Church; and so, the head of Hitler's bodyguard regularly revealed SS secrets to a Vatican spy.[2775]

Johann "Hans" Rattenhuber would remain with Hitler in his bunker until Hitler's suicide on April 30. Before taking his life, Hitler signed an order permitting the remaining residents of the bunker to attempt a breakout from Berlin.[2776] On the following day of May 1, Rattenhuber led the second of the three groups escaping from the Reich Chancellery and Führerbunker.[2777] The other two were led by SS-Brigadeführer Wilhelm Mohnke[2778] and Werner Naumann.[2779] Most, including Rattenhuber, were taken prisoner by the Soviets on the same day or the following day. Rattenhuber was taken to Moscow, where on May 20 he gave a description of the last days of Hitler and the Nazi leadership in the bunker complex.[2780] The text of this was kept in the Soviet archives until it was published by V.K. Vinogradov in the Russian edition of *Hitler's Death: Russia's Last Great Secret from the Files of the KGB in 2000.*[2781]

In August 1951, Rattenhuber was charged by the Soviet Ministry of State Security that "from the early days of the Nazi dictatorship in Germany in 1933 and until the defeat of the latter in 1945, being an SS-Gruppenführer, Police Lieutenant-General and the chief of the Reich Security Service, he ensured the personal security of Hitler and other Reich leaders."[2782] Rattenhuber was sentenced by the Court Martial of the Moscow Military District on February 15, 1952, to 25 years' imprisonment. By a decree of the Presidium of the Supreme Soviet of September 28 1955,[2783] he was released from prison on October 10, 1955 and handed over to the German Democratic Republic authorities, who allowed him to go to West Germany. More than likely, this was on the previously mentioned initiative of the West German Chancellor Konrad Adenauer.[2784] Rattenhuber did not live long to enjoy his newfound freedom, as he died in Munich on June 30, 1957.[2785]

On April 20, Hitler, on his 56th and last birthday, made one of his last filmed appearances outside the subterranean Führerbunker in Berlin, where he dished out tributes of now meaningless platitudes to teenage boys from the Hitler Youth for their bravery.[2786] Kaltenbrunner was among those present, but realising the end was near, he then fled from Berlin.[2787] Three weeks later, on May 12, 1945, after a short standoff, Kaltenbrunner was apprehended along with his adjutant, Arthur Scheidler, and two SS guards in a remote cabin at the top of the Totes Gebirge mountains near Altaussee, Austria, about eighty kilometres east of Salzburg, by a search party initiated by the 80th Infantry Division of the Third U.S. Army.[2788]

Ernst Kaltenbrunner suffered a cerebral haemorrhage the night before the opening of his Nuremberg trial in November 1945. He finally appeared three weeks later on Monday December 10. Later that week, the cerebral haemorrhage recurred, and he could not return to the dock until January.[2789] For the man even Himmler feared,[2790] the hangman's noose finally accounted for him and eleven of his co-defendants on October 15, 1946, at Nuremberg.[2791] As for Josef Müller, reprieved thanks in part to Ernst Kaltenbrunner, he had a meeting with Pope Pius XII on June 1, 1945. Overwhelmed with joy, the pontiff asked Müller what he had learned, to which the latter replied, "I have unlearned to hate... even the Nazis."[2792]

When Payne Best found Liedig and Müller, he discovered they had had almost no food in the fortnight since they were taken from the Grüne Minna. Müller's face was bruised and puffy from blows received with a rubber truncheon, and after their privations at Buchenwald, they were in an appalling state.[2793] Payne Best gave them the remainder of the bottle of cod liver oil he had received the day before, and after they finished every drop, they declared it was the best drink they had ever had.[2794]

Many have dubbed the wartime pontiff "Hitler's Pope." One of these is Geoffrey Robertson QC. But their perspective is from the security of the present,[2795] and not from the utterly precarious position that Pope Pius XII had to work from, especially when Rome was occupied for nine or so months by the Germans, from September 1943 until early June 1944.[2796] At this time, with the Vatican under siege, protected only by its pike-and-axe-wielding Renaissance Swiss Guards against the twentieth-century machine gun-and-tank-wielding German troops, it sheltered thousands of Jews and Allied airmen. The Irishman, Monsignor Hugh O'Flaherty of Killarney town in County Kerry, played no small part in offering them sanctuary.[2797]

Geoffrey Robertson, and more harshly, Rabbi Shmuley Boteach, are critical of what they perceived to be Pope Pius XII's appeasing silence, especially when the Germans deported about 1,000 Jews from Rome during their occupation.[2798] Both critics, in particular the Rabbi, expected Pope Pius XII to publicly proclaim his condemnation in order to stop these deportations, while maintaining the Vatican's sovereignty. Rabbi Boteach held that the pontiff should have made use of his perceived "moral clout," to which Hitler would have yielded, rather than being the pretentious and ineffectual "head of the CIA."[2799] Robertson asserts that for the "Catholics" in the SS, such a moral statement from their leader would have led to them question their blood oath to their Führer,[2800] and the deportations would not have taken place.

However, Hitler was not one to take notice of pieces of paper or formal declarations. Witness the Czech-Sudeten debacle of September 1938, with its humiliating appeasement based upon Czech economic and strategic castration; six months later, it led to the occupation of its capital and the rest of its dismembered state.[2801] This was in direct violation of Chamberlain's piece of paper, which he had waved upon arrival on the tarmac in England six months before, in early October 1938, supposedly the guarantor of "peace for our time."[2802] Another case was Hitler's assurance he would respect Belgian, Dutch and Norwegian neutrality, which came to naught in 1940.[2803]

Furthermore, Robertson's assertion that the Pope would have held some moral sway with Catholics in the SS overlooks the deeply embedded, dark, pagan Germanic mindset of the SS. Its head, Heinrich Himmler, was overtly anti-Christian;[2804] he called for Germany to return to its ancient pagan roots,[2805] embodied in the famous Germanic victory over Emperor Augustus' legions in the Teutoburg Forest in 9 AD.[2806] For a soldier of the SS, by 1943, any notion of the Christian god had long before been usurped by their new pagan deity, the Führer. For them, "Christ was the illegitimate son of a Jewish whore";[2807] this assertion was the cornerstone of their mindset. Their victory would not be complete until all synagogues and churches were destroyed; during the invasion of France, the "Leibstandarte SS Adolf Hitler" destroyed crucifixes in their wake and ransacked churches.[2808] For Himmler's SS, the cross was a symbol of shame, weakness, and humility, and their new Germany would achieve what Christ had failed to do.[2809] Namely, to save the world from the Jews and thereby redeem humanity[xxxiii]

As the church historian, Father Peter Gumpel, puts it near the end of the documentary *Pope Vs Hitler*, "If from repeated experience you know that any protest has no positive effect for the people, but rather makes it worse, and you still protest, then you are a fool."[2810] For example, there was an instance where the Dutch Bishops, with noble intentions, issued an official protest against deportations. However, this only led to the deportations increasing. Later, the pontiff sent a letter to the Polish people to be be read by their bishop, but when the Polish bishop read it privately, he sent a note back to the pontiff stating that

---

[xxxiii] See endnotes [312] to [313] for Chapter 2 "Ominous Clouds on the Horizon."

while it was noble and profound — like the idealistic 1934 resolutions of Fanø —[2811] it would only lead to more people being killed.[2812] Bravery does not equate with stupidity, especially when you are working from a position of chronic weakness. If the pontiff did as the Rabbi and Geoffrey Robertson called for, the lives of all the Jews being sheltered in the Vatican would have been placed in dire jeopardy, and the Allied airman would have ended up in POW camps or worse. The 1,000 Jews that were deported, with only sixteen surviving post-war,[2813] would have still suffered the same terrible fate. Put another way, Pope Pius XII achieved more as "Head of the CIA"[2814] than as a naive and foolish public orator.

No less remarkable than Josef Müller's post-war survival, was that of Fabian von Schlabrendorff. On February 7, 1945,[2815] when the two transports of the Prominenten left the bombed-out ruins of Berlin's Prinz-Albrecht-Strasse prison, respectively for Flossenbürg and Buchenwald, Fabian was left behind, as his case, still had to be "heard."[2816] Before Prinz-Albrecht-Strasse was hit by the American bombing on February 3 1945,[2817] Fabian had managed to communicate several times with Dietrich,[2818] who was now on the transport bound for Buchenwald.[2819] However, as a major suspect in the Valkyrie plot, being the adjutant to Henning von Tresckow[2820] — himself Ruth's nephew[2821] and mentor to Claus von Stauffenberg[2822] — Fabian had to remain in Berlin, as his postponed case still had to be "heard."[2823]

At around 10 a.m. on the 3rd,[2824] Roland Freisler, the ranting head judge of the People's Court had announced the death sentence for Ruth's cousin Ewald von Kleist.[2825] Then Fabian was to hear Freisler's typical rant, followed by the obligatory death sentence. That was until the American Eighth Air Force unleashed the most devastating bombing raid on Berlin,[2826] compelling all those present to head for the bomb shelter. Freisler however, after initially heading for the shelter, realised he had inadvertently left Fabian's "precious" file behind, and decided to return to the bench to retrieve it. As he did, a beam fell on his head, killing him instantly.[2827]

As fortunate as Freisler's death turned out for Fabian, this fact would not become apparent to Fabian until weeks later. On March 16, 1945,[2828] with Dietrich still incarcerated in Buchenwald,[2829] Fabian's case was heard again. The presiding judge was Dr. Krohne, Vice President of the People's Court. Unlike Freisler, Krohne had not heard Fabian's name in other trials.[2830] As the proceedings started, in a desperate bid for clemency, Fabian stated that Frederick the Great had abolished torture in Prussia two centuries before, but that in spite of this edict, he had been subjected to torture in this now "modern" age.[2831] As Fabian gave a detailed account of his ordeal by torture, at one point he had to stop to regain his composure.[2832] He was surprised that he was not interrupted, and felt that the court and all present must be holding their breath.[2833]

After Fabian completed his statement, the court questioned him. Fabian expected the Police Commissioner responsible for interrogating and torturing him would be called.[2834] To Fabian's surprise, Judge Dr. Krohne declared that the court had already questioned the Commissioner in a special session during which neither Fabian or his counsel had been present, and that this questioning had confirmed Fabian's account.[2835] In view of this, the Chief Prosecutor dropped the indictment. The "People's Court" acquitted Fabian and cancelled the warrant for his arrest![2836] Crucial as this legal loophole was, courtesy of Hitler's idol Frederick the Great,[2837] Fabian was not yet in the clear.

Fabian was returned to the Gestapo prison, for there was no question of an immediate release and, as he soon found out, no hope of release at all.[2838] A few days later, there was another air raid alarm. As Fabian and his fellow inmates were taken to the shelter, Fabian heard the Gestapo Commissioner Habecker ordering the guards to keep a particularly close eye on him. Just hours later, Fabian was informed that the decision of the "People's Court" had clearly been in error. Nevertheless, Fabian had the "consolation" that the Gestapo would respect it — at least to the extent of not hanging him. Rather, he would now be shot![2839] To satisfy the bureaucratic mechanisms of the crumbling Third Reich, Fabian had to acknowledge this news with his signature![2840]

A few days later, Fabian was awakened around two o'clock in the morning and told to get ready.[2841] Several other prisoners and he were loaded into closed trucks and transported to Flossenbürg. Fabian now felt a depressing certainty that he would meet his end there, as Flossenbürg was one of the extermination camps. People murdered there had either never come before the People's Court, or, like Fabian, had been acquitted by it.[2842] Once again, Fabian found himself in solitary confinement and in chains, although this time, the chain was fastened to one wrist only and was long enough so that he could move in a half circle.[2843] By climbing on a stool, he was able to peep out of the small cell window near the ceiling, and see the bodies of those who had been murdered being carried down the hillside by other prisoners.[2844] Because the camp crematorium was out of order at the time, the bodies were burned on piles of wood out in the open.[2845] Time and again, around six o'clock in the morning, Fabian could hear prisoners in other cells being awakened, forced to undress completely, and taken past the cells to the prison courtyard, where they were either hanged or shot in the back of the head.[2846]

One of the large adjoining cells housed a number of British prisoners of war who had attempted to escape from a prison camp, and after recapture had been transferred to Flossenbürg. They were treated quite well in comparison with the German prisoners, and Fabian could often hear the sound of English songs coming from their cells.[2847]

Fabian found out that his friend Dietrich had been at Flossenbürg.[2848] One night he was awakened and asked for his name. A short while later the guard returned and accused Fabian of giving him a false name. He insisted that Fabian must be Bonhoeffer. When Fabian denied this, the guard left and did not return again.[2849] Any faint hope that the interest shown in locating Dietrich might mean that the SS had received orders to release him was shattered one morning a few days later, when an SS guard told Fabian that the night before, they had again hanged several men of the Abwehr.[2850] Fabian questioned him about the identity of these men, and soon found out that Canaris, Oster, Sack, Bonhoeffer, and Gehre had been among them.[2851] Much later Fabian heard through another guard that Dietrich had been taken to Flossenbürg on April 8.[2852] On April 9, Dietrich's few belongings, consisting mainly of the Holy Bible and a volume of Goethe's works, were left in the Guard room of the camp. It can therefore be assumed without a shadow of doubt that Dietrich was hanged by the SS on the morning of April 9 at Flossenbürg.[2853]

On April 12, three days following the execution of the five members of the Abwehr, the noise of the rapidly advancing American troops became more and more audible. From his cell, Fabian was able to differentiate the noises made by firing and the impact of the artillery shells.[2854] Around noon, a guard appeared and ordered Fabian to get ready — not that he had too much to get ready with, other than his blue convict's attire and a pair of canvas sneakers. After he had been unlocked from his chains, he was loaded on a truck together with other prisoners and taken to Dachau.[2855] Josef Müller, after his miraculous reprieve on the morning of April 9, was among them.[2856] So too was the Danish prisoner, Jørgen Lønborg Friis Mogensen, a Danish diplomat and a member of the Polish resistance during the war.[2857] In 1944 he was arrested by the Gestapo, whereupon, following prolonged sessions of interrogation, he was sent to Flossenbürg, where he remained until the 12th.[2858] This was three days following his witnessing of the executions on the 9th; his post-war account would cast grave doubts on the traditional version of events.[xxxiv]

The route took them via Munich, giving Fabian the first glimpse of a city that had suffered heavy bombing.[2859] During the night, they arrived at Dachau, and were lined up in the camp courtyard for a head count. It was a macabre spectacle: the prisoners, pale-faced and shabby, closely guarded by SS-men with their vicious, snarling police dogs, the entire scene bathed in the cold glare of the camp search-lights.[2860] Remarkably, when the names on the list had been checked off, it was found that Fabian's name was missing, invoking the SS guard in charge to fly into a rage, and hurl a torrent of abuse at Fabian.[2861] In turn, this helped to confirm Fabian's suspicion that he was alive due to a last-minute oversight, and that, unlike Josef Müller with his Vatican contacts, he was never meant to leave Flossenbürg alive![2862]

This implies that, in the strictest sense of the word, Fabian was not one of the Prominenten. Now, for the first time in many months, Fabian was not in chains, and no longer in solitary confinement. Fabian was of the opinion that the SS no longer possessed sufficient manpower or organisation to guard prisoners as strictly as before.[2863] However, by chance, he was among the Prominenten or prominent prisoners; as "very important people," the SS were under orders to treat them with consideration and courtesy[2864] — while they were perceived as useful to the crumbling regime of the Third Reich.

On April 25,[2865] with American troops approaching,[2866] they were ordered to evacuate Dachau, whereupon they commenced their trek southwards, via Innsbruck in Austria,[2867] over the Brenner Pass into the Northern Italian region of the South Tyrol.[2868] Through trials and tribulations,[2869] on Monday April 30, 1945, on the day of Hitler's suicide in the Berlin bunker,[2870] and twenty-one days following Dietrich's execution at Flossenbürg,[2871] Fabian was among the liberated in the village of Niederdorf,[2872] in the Puster Valley of the German speaking South Tyrol region.[2873] Indeed, if not for the discovery in Zossen of the Canaris diaries, Dietrich and his fellow condemned would have been among them as well. Such are the twists of fate. Among others liberated were Fabian's fellow evacuees from Flossenbürg: Josef Müller and the Danish Prominente, Jørgen Lønborg Friis Mogensen.[2874] Post-war, Mogensen continued his career in the Danish diplomatic core, returning to

---

xxxiv [2900] This will be discussed in the following chapter.

Warsaw from 1946-1952, and later to Belgium, USA, South Africa, Rhodesia, and Australia. He passed away in 2000 aged 91.[2875]

In June 1945, Fabian obtained the use of a vehicle from the Americans at Wiesbaden, just west of Frankfurt am Main, and was on his way east to locate his wife and children.[2876] After fleeing from their home in Pomerania, when it became clear that the Red Army would occupy the Old Prussian lands in Germany's east, Luitgarde and her children found refuge in the home of Fabian's mother in upper Franconia in northern Bavaria.[2877] On a road not far from there, Fabian saw a woman on a bicycle approaching — it was, amidst unbridled joy, his wife and granddaughter of Ruth, Luitgarde.[2878] Post-war, Fabian embarked upon an illustrious legal career, which included serving as a judge of West Germany's constitutional court from 1967 to 1975,[2879] and with great assistance from his wife, wrote two books on the conspiracy against Hitler[2880] before passing away in 1980, aged 73.[2881] Two decades later, in 2000, Luitgarde passed away in Wiesbaden, aged 86.[2882] With Josef Müller, the collective memory of their extraordinary defiance and survival against all odds, in the face of inexorable evil, lives on.

Chapter 28

Memory Transcending Executioners' Legal but Criminal Flights from Justice

While Flossenbürg is a place indelibly associated with Oma Ruth's dearest friend, intended son-in-law and fellow native Silesian, Dietrich Bonhoeffer, it's worth noting that he spent no more than twelve or so hours there before his execution.[2883] Dietrich arrived at Flossenbürg late that second Sunday of April 1945, while the SS Judge and sycophant, Otto Thorbeck, arrived in Flossenbürg by bicycle; he would insist post-war that he, Huppenkothen, and Kögl, had conducted a proper trial by allowing the prisoners to respond to "thorough questioning," both individually and by confronting them with each other.[2884] However, even if they were allowed to respond, this point is moot, as the verdict had already been decided before the "court" was called to order.[2885] In a totalitarian state, whether in its death throes or otherwise, appearances are everything, however superficial they are. A case in point is the Gleiwitz incident of August 31 1939,[2886] masterminded by Reinhard Heydrich, the Chief of the Security Police and Sicherheitsdienst (SD — intelligence arm of the SS) to give the imminent invasion of Poland some semblance of legitimacy.[2887] Likewise, the Stalinist show trials of the late 1930s.[2888]

After midnight on April 9, the deposed head of the Abwehr, Admiral Wilhelm Canaris,[2889] following a period of some absence, returned to his cell and signalled, via a specific sequence of knocks, that his fate was now sealed;[2890] his signal was to the Danish prisoner and former intelligence officer Colonel Lunding in the neighbouring cell, who was to be among the liberated in Neiderdorf.[2891] If Dietrich and his fellow condemned prisoners had any sleep that night of April 8 to 9 1945, it must surely have been minimal and restless at best. For Dietrich, the words of his sermon, delivered from the relative safety of his eighteen-month London pastorate (from October 1933 to April 1935), may have been foremost in his thoughts: "

> Death is only dreadful for those who live in dread and fear of it. Death is not wild and terrible, if only we can be still and hold fast to God's Word. Death is not bitter, if we have not become bitter ourselves."[2892]

In a letter to Bethge from Tegel, during the tragic aftermath of the failed Valkyrie plot, Dietrich explained a poem entitled "Stations to Freedom"; the stations were Discipline, Action, Suffering, and Death.[2893] The first two, Dietrich had fulfilled time and time again, and since his imprisonment at Tegel and Prinz-Albrecht-Strasse, separated from family and his beloved Maria, he had endured great suffering. However, he still had more to endure at this penultimate station. From this point, at 6 a.m. on Monday April 9 1945, when the farce of the SS Drumhead court martial had secured Hitler's predetermined outcome, versions now diverge markedly on how close or how distant Dietrich was from ultimately fulfilling the station of suffering.

In the original version, given by Metaxas and Bethge, the SS camp doctor at Flossenbürg, Hermann Fischer-Hüllstrung gave the following spiritually uplifting account: "

> On the morning of that day between five and six o'clock the prisoners, among them Admiral Canaris, General Oster …. and Reichgerichtsrat Sack were taken from their cells, and the verdicts of the court martial read out to them. Through the half-open door in one room of the huts I saw Pastor Bonhoeffer, before taking off his prison garb, kneeling on the floor praying fervently to his God. I was most deeply moved by the way this lovable man prayed, so devout and so certain that God heard his prayer. At the place of execution, he again said a short prayer and then climbed the steps to the gallows, brave and composed. His death ensued after a few seconds. In the almost fifty years that I worked as a doctor, I have hardly ever seen a man die so entirely submissive to the will of God."[2894]

We know Dietrich had the ability to endear himself to some of the most cynical and hardened individuals. He had done this at Tegel, and as Fabian von Schlabrendorff attested,[2895] in the much grimmer incarceration of Prinz-Albrecht-Strasse. Perhaps the idea of Dietrich being able to reach out and touch a cynical and brutal SS Totenkopf (Death's Head) doctor, Hermann Fischer-Hüllstrung, has seemed plausible and unchallenged for decades. Similarly, the perception that the deaths of Dietrich and his fellow condemned were relatively quick rather than brutal, painful and prolonged executions.

The traditional scenario, however, relies solely on the statement of an SS Totenkopf doctor, which must immediately bring into question its credibility, in spite of the case of Doctor Waldemar Hoven in Chapter 22, "Buchenwald."[2896] In the vast majority of cases (perhaps Waldemar Hoven was the only exception) these sadistic doctors practised cruelty with relish; Sigmund Rascher, among Dietrich's fellow inmates at Buchenwald, was the norm, and Hoven the rare, if not sole, exception.[2897] On page 311 of the book by Thomas Kaiser, the author gives a brutal and disturbing account of the mysterious Hermann Fischer-Hüllstrung: "

> Fischer-Hüllstrung, Hermann (1885 to ?): The SS Obersturmbannführer [Senior Storm leader — equivalent to Lieutenant Colonel] and wearer of the skull ring, Doctor Hermann Fischer-Hüllstrung issued the death certificate for Dietrich Bonhoeffer; his duties included the revival of the half strangled in order to prolong their suffering. His later statement about Bonhoeffer as a kneeling prisoner in prayer belongs to the realm of legends. The certificate of death was one of the doctor's everyday tasks, since Flossenbürg was an extermination camp. The document certifying Bonhoeffer's death had been destroyed like all the documents of evidence. The rubber hoses with which the inmates were beaten and the block of wood on which they were flogged were also removed, as were the hooks used to strangle the prisoners."[2898]

Moreover: "

> Fischer-Hüllstrung, whose nationality is stated as unknown in the Rüter Collection, was in court in 1955/56. Initially acquitted, but later sentenced to 3 years imprisonment: "Participation as a stationed physician (*Standortarzt*) of KL Flossenbürg in the killing by means of injections, of at least 40 prisoners who were ill and unfit for work. Participation in the execution of prisoners in the crematorium and on the roll-call assembly grounds."[2899]

The contention that Fischer-Hüllstrung performed the monstrous act of reviving the prisoners to prolong their torture is corroborated by Ferdinand Schlingensiepen in his last footnote before the epilogue in his book: "

> The report by the SS doctor H. Fischer-Hüllstrung, in Zimmermann (ed.), *I Knew Dietrich Bonhoeffer*, is unfortunately a

lie (DB-ER 927f.).* The doctor could not have seen Bonhoeffer kneeling in his cell, neither could Bonhoeffer have said a prayer before his execution and then climbed the steps to the gallows. There were no steps. Fischer-Hüllstrung had the job of reviving political prisoners after they had been hanged until they were almost dead, in order to prolong the agony of their dying. According to a Danish prisoner, L. F. Mogenson,[2900] the executions of Admiral Canaris and his group were drawn out from 6 a.m. until almost noon."[2901]

However, on the website of the Foundation for Research on National-Socialist Crimes, Amsterdam, it's stated that the executions of Canaris, Oster, Doctor Sack, Gehre, and Pastor Bonhoeffer took place one after another, taking in all thirty minutes to an hour in the presence of Doctor Fischer. They climbed a set of steps completely naked, and a rope was put around their necks before the steps were pulled away from underneath them, resulting in their immediate death.[2902] This contradicts Schlingensiepen's assertion and all the sources backing it. But then again, in the 2016 National Geographic documentary *Pope Vs Hitler*, when describing the execution of Wilhelm Canaris, Geoffrey Robertson, the author of *The Tyrannicide Brief*,[2903] and Nigel Jones, author of *Countdown to Valkyrie*,[2904] maintain that he was hung and revived several times. Robertson further asserts that these prolonged hangings of Canaris and the other victims were filmed in colour for Hitler's sadistic *schadenfreude* [malicious joy] viewing in his Berlin bunker.[2905]

Fischer-Hüllstrung's statement (quoted above) was given in court ten years later in 1955,[2906] and by that time, he was aged over seventy.[2907] He could well have been giving this testimony to mitigate his guilt, rather than in a perceived epiphany; proponents of the more disturbing scenario point this out. That there are so many contradictory sources, illustrates how chaotic and confusing the final weeks of the Third Reich were. Likewise, just hours before and in the immediate chaotic aftermath of Valkyrie, sources diverge on certain points.[2908] If the Danish prisoner Mogensen's account is correct, the five condemned men must have had a hideous experience of prolonged pain on the penultimate station of suffering before the final station of death — which, as Dietrich put it, was the gateway to their true homeland. I hope their arrival at the final station took the more expeditious route. Unfortunately, given Hitler's sadistic streak, especially as the Third Reich was crumbling around him, he may well have desired and so ordered the most painful death possible for ones he perceived as stabbing the Fatherland in the back, in his perceived repeat of the November 1918 Dolchstosslegende (Stab in the back myth).[2909]

When the executions of Dietrich and his four condemned companions were completed, their bodies were, according to Schlabrendorff, burned in piles, since the crematorium was no longer working.[2910] Around 10 a.m., white flecks drifted in through the barred window of Josef Müller's cell. They looked like snowflakes but smelled like fire. Abruptly the hatch in his cell door opened. A captured British secret agent, Peter Churchill, said, "Your friends have been hanged already and are now being burned behind the ridge."[2911] Müller shook with grief and wept as he realised that the flakes whirling into his nose and mouth were all that remained of his friends.[2912] Their ashes, together with those of thousands of other victims of Hitler's Reich, formed the grass-grown pyramid in the middle of the site that was KZ Flossenbürg.[2913] In the guard room that Monday morning, Prince Philip of Hesse, who had been a prisoner at Flossenbürg for years, found some books which included Dietrich's volume of Goethe, but they, too, were later taken from him and burned. A fortnight later, on April 23, regiments of the 90th US Infantry Division liberated 1,500 prisoners still in the camp, but two hundred died in the days to follow.[2914]

One week later, with the liberation of the 130 or so special prisoners in Niederdorf, Hitler performed his own execution; Germany's formal surrender followed about a week later. However, while the war in Europe was now formally over, neither Maria nor anyone in Dietrich's family knew what had become of him. It was not until May 31 that Dietrich's twin sister Sabine, in Oxford, England, became the first of his immediate family to hear about his death. Since all ties to Berlin were now broken, upon their liberation in Niederdorf, Müller and Schlabrendorff sent news of Dietrich's execution to Visser 't Hooft in Geneva, who in turn relayed it to Bishop George Bell. On May 30, Adolf Freudenberg, who co-ordinated the aid for Jewish refugees in Geneva, telegrammed the tragic news to Pastor Julius Rieger in London"

> Just received sad news that Dietrich Bonhoeffer and his Klaus have been murdered in Concentration Camp Clossburg near Neustadt about 15 April short time before liberation region by American army--Stop--Please inform family Leibholz and his friends--Stop--We are united in deep sorrow and fellowship--Freudenberg."[2915]

It was not until the following day that Rieger could bring himself to phone Sabine and Gert in Oxford to inform them that he needed to see them face to face.[2916] Rieger knocked on their door, and when Sabine opened it, she felt a terrible surge of fear as she noted the pale and withdrawn expression on Rieger's face. "It's Dietrich. He is no more — and Klaus too … "[2917] As he laid the telegram on the table, Rieger took the *New Testament* out of his pocket and read Matthew Chapter 10. Sabine found great consolation in it; one sentence speaks eloquently of Dietrich's character: "He that findeth his life shall lose it: and he that loseth his life for my sake shall find it."[2918] The likes of Fromm and Kluge, in Valkyrie's aftermath,[2919] each found a fleeting and insignificant extension of earthly life, but in turn, a dishonourable death; their memories live on in eternal disgrace — "He that findeth his life shall lose it." In stark contrast, Dietrich, in losing his life in brave and uncompromising devotion to God and his fellow man, has given a courageous legacy to history.

As Pastor Rieger finished reading the final verse of Matthew's tenth chapter, he reminded the family of Dietrich's beautiful exposition of them in one of his most famous works, *Nachfolge* — Discipleship. For the rest of the day, Sabine could remember nothing more than Gert's face streaming with tears and the children sobbing. Her grief was extreme, as she had lived so intensely for the moment that they could be reunited in a new and better Germany, when they could recount to each other their experiences amidst the tumultuous years that had left an entire continent devastated.[2920]

Sabine had held out hope that Allied paratroopers would take and liberate the concentration camps before their regular infantry arrived.[2921] Many of her English friends and acquaintances had reassured her that this would be the case, but in retrospect, Sabine thought they were merely telling her what she wanted to hear. While admitting she was hardly qualified to judge whether or not such missions were possible, she could never rid herself of the nagging suspicion that such operations were never considered, due to the cynical view that the Allies, and in particular Churchill and Anthony Eden, held of the German resistance in general.[2922] The Allies perceived that most were only motivated to oppose Hitler when the tide of war for Germany started to take a marked turn for the worse. Considering how amenable the Western Allies were to appeasing Stalin, even to the extent of betraying the First Ally, Poland, and swallowing the Soviet lie that the Germans were responsible for Katyń,[2923] and Anthony Eden's hostile line towards the insurgents in the Warsaw General Uprising of August to October

1944,[2924] it is not surprising that the west was dismissive of conspirators on the enemy's side.

Certainly, this perception of the German conspirators being motivated only by the parlous state of the war for Germany is not baseless; this view applies to officers such as Georg Thomas and Franz Halder, and perhaps the most cynical of all, Arthur Nebe.[2925] Moreover, even in Claus von Stauffenberg's case, it was not until the middle of 1942, with Germany holding the initiative but the war in the balance, that Stauffenberg finally saw Hitler for what he truly was.[2926] However, such blanket assertions are rarely the definitive truth, and there were numerous brave individuals, such as Dietrich himself, who didn't need the tide of war to turn to see Hitler for the petty, vindictive and genocidal tyrant he undoubtedly was. Indeed, as we have seen, Dietrich's perceptive mind sensed the ominous clouds on the Weimar political horizon as early as June 1931, upon return from his maiden visit to America.[2927]

In June 1945, at her cousin's in the northern Bavarian town Bundorf, Maria received the terrible news of her fiancée's execution, sooner than did Dietrich's family in Berlin. At the war's end, Dietrich's parents had heard encouraging rumours that Dietrich was alive. This was contradicted when Hans Bernd Gisevius visited them in Berlin and informed them that Dietrich was murdered by the Gestapo at Flossenbürg, just days before the camp was liberated by American troops.[2928] Gisevius had been part of the circle of Oster and Canaris, and had escaped to Switzerland in the wake of Valkyrie;[2929] nevertheless, Karl and Paula still held onto some hope that Dietrich was alive. They implied this in a letter dated July 23 1945 to Sabine and Gert; this was their first opportunity to communicate with them, as communication between the Soviet-occupied German capital and the outside world had been almost impossible since Berlin's surrender: "

> 23rd July 1945
> My dearest children,
> We have just been told that an opportunity has arisen for us to send you our greetings and news. It is now three years, I believe, since we received the last letters from you. Now we have just heard that Gert sent a telegram to Switzerland in order to obtain news of the fate of our dear Dietrich. From this we conclude that you are all still alive, and that is a great consolation for us in our deep sorrow over the fate of our dear Klaus, Dietrich and Rüdiger.

Dietrich spent eighteen months in the military prison at Tegel. Last October he was handed over to the Gestapo and transferred to the SS prison in Prinz-Albrecht-Strasse. During the early days of February he was taken from there to various concentration camps such as Buchenwald and Flossenbürg near Weiden. We did not know where he was.

His fiancée, Maria von Wedemeyer, who was living with us at this time, attempted to find out for herself where he was. But in this she was unsuccessful. After the victory of the Allies we heard that Dietrich was still alive. But later we received news that he had been murdered by the Gestapo a little before the Americans arrived."[2930]

In the meantime, Pastors Julius Rieger and Franz Hildebrandt, along with Bishop Bell, organised a memorial service for Dietrich and Klaus in consultation with Gert and Sabine. The service was to be held on Friday July 27 at London's Holy Trinity Brompton Church,[2931] and Bishop Bell asked Gert and Sabine's permission for it to be broadcast to Germany as well. The announcement of this service in an English church for a German, coupled with its public broadcast so soon after the war, made this a most unusual event; but such was the character, charisma and universal appeal of Dietrich Bonhoeffer, that the church was packed with both locals and German immigrants.[2932] Moreover, Karl and Paula Bonhoeffer heard the death of their youngest son confirmed on their radio in their home at 43 Marienburgerallee.[2933] BBC shortwave broadcasts were how Germans received most of their reliable information.[2934] Two days before the service, Bishop Bell wrote to Gert and Sabine: "

The Palace, Chichester 25th July 1945

My dear Sabine, (If I may thus call you.) I am deeply grateful for your letter. All you say, so undeserved, is a great comfort to me; and I am very happy to have Dietrich's photograph. You know something, I am sure, of what his friendship and love meant to me. My heart is full of sorrow for you, for alas, it is only too true that the gap he and Klaus leave can never be filled. I pray that God may give peace and strength to your parents, and to all who mourn, and bless them.

I am greatly looking forward to seeing you both on Friday. I do not know whether your daughters will be there; but my telegram just sent will of course include them …

Yours very sincerely, George Chichester"[2935]

The service began with the English hymn, "For All the Saints," and upon the congregation singing all seven stanzas, Bishop Bell prayed the prayer of supplication and the prayer of thanksgiving, before the hymn "Hark, a Herald Voice Is Calling" was sung in English and in German. Then Bishop Bell read from Matthew 10:17—42, as Julius Rieger had read to Gert and Sabine when he delivered the terrible news to them in Oxford. In his following sermon, Bishop Bell described the essence of Dietrich's character: "

> He was quite clear in his convictions, and for all that he was so young and unassuming, he saw the truth and spoke it out with absolute freedom and without fear. When he came to me all unexpectedly in 1942 at Stockholm as the emissary of the Resistance to Hitler, he was, as always, absolutely open and quite untroubled about his own person, his safety. Wherever he went and whoever he spoke with — whether young or old — he was fearless, regardless of himself and, with it all, devoted his heart and soul to his parents, his friends, his country as God willed it to be, to his Church and to his Master."[2936]

He ended his sermon with the words: "The blood of martyrs is the seed of the Church."[2937]

During the service, Julius Rieger and Dietrich's close and long-time friend, Franz Hildebrandt, also spoke. Dietrich first met Franz in December 1927,[2938] upon his graduation from Berlin's Friedrich Wilhelm university on December 17, the sole student awarded "summa cum laude" — highest honours, aged just twenty-one.[2939] In July 1937, after being arrested and released from the Gestapo, Franz, a Confessing Church pastor of Jewish heritage, was forced to flee Germany for Switzerland and then England.[2940] During these early years of the Third Reich, especially when it came to fighting the infamous "Aryan Paragraph" in 1933,[2941] it often appeared as if he and Dietrich were the sole voices of reason, and Dietrich missed him terribly. Franz's early release from the Gestapo in July 1937 was thanks to the great efforts of the Bonhoeffer family and Dietrich's brother-in-law and gifted jurist, Hans von Dohnányi, which gave Franz the brief respite needed to flee Germany.[2942] Dietrich would only see Franz on two more occasions, which were in England in 1939 during his March-April 1939 visit,[2943] and upon his return from America that year before the outbreak of war.[2944] Hence, Franz's grief at this moment must have been extreme.

His sermon's theme revolved around "Neither know we what to do; but our eyes are upon Thee" from the Old Testament Second Book of Chronicles, chapter 20, verse 12.[2945] This is the translation from the ancient Hebrew and Greek texts in the English Standard Version (ESV), which essentially mirrors that found in the older King James Version (KJV). However, using the New Living Translation (NLV), which translates entire thoughts, rather than just words into natural, everyday English, it is rendered; "O our God, won't you stop them? We are powerless against this mighty army that is about to attack us. We do not know what to do, but we are looking to you for help."[2946] This translation better conveys the nature of the cross borne by Dietrich when he felt compelled to fight the seemingly invincible evil and power that was the Third Reich. This was a text Franz offered to Dietrich in the 1930s, and it had produced a powerful sermon.[2947]

Hitler came to power in late January 1933, and consolidated it as the year wore on, thanks to the thuggery and intimidation perpetrated by Röhm's Brown Shirts. By October, Dietrich felt disillusioned with the compliant state church (Reichskirche) and the failure of the Bethel Confession declaration he initiated in fighting the former. This was the main reason that he left Germany in October 1933 for his eighteen-month London pastorate;[2948] the words of 2 Chronicles 20.12 in the NLV version aptly portray his mindset around that time. They express his sense of powerlessness against Hitler's clerical vassal, but then, in asking God's help, the wisdom of his eighteen month London pastorate was revealed. The lesson was not to "run away" from a church in crisis in Germany, as his decision was portrayed by Karl Barth;[2949] rather, it was to disclose the abuse of the church by Hitler's Reich to the international religious community. In those eighteen months, Dietrich, contrary to what Reichkirche stooges like the Reichsbischoff Ludwig Müller and the Foreign Office head Theodor Heckel imagined, proved to be even more of a thorn in their side than when he was in Germany.[2950] This was in part due to his close friendship with Bishop George Bell, forged the month before at the Novi Sad conference in Yugoslavia.[2951]

Years later, during the war and the early stages of Dietrich's imprisonment at Tegel, this theme again applied in a seemingly hopeless situation, when he was able to overcome his fear and apprehension with resilient composure. This not only served him admirably in the prison environment itself, but more importantly perhaps, in his interrogations by Manfred Roeder. He diligently following the instructions given to him by his brave brother-in-law, Hans von Dohnányi, enabling him, with his superior intellect in concert with his deep faith, to "torment his tormentor,"[2952] by never implicating any of his family or colleagues in the Abwehr. Dietrich's fellow victim, Admiral Canaris, did likewise.[2953]

Then, with the help of his famous uncle, Paul von Hase, and Dietrich's endearing personality, most of the eighteen months at Tegel became relatively routine.[2954] This all changed with his transfer to the dreaded Gestapo prison on Prinz-Albrecht-Strasse in the wake of Valkyrie, but by then, Dietrich had acquired the means to deal with any imprisonment or interrogation, no matter how grim or harsh. Indeed, while returning from the air raid shelter following the American Eighth Air Force bombing on February 3 1945,[2955] which virtually obliterated the prison, he calmly took time out to converse with his brother-in-law Hans von Dohnányi in order to get their respective stories straight for any future interrogations. This was in spite of the grave risk of any of the guards noticing his entry and exit from his brother-in-law's cell. Years later, Fabian von Schlabrendorf would recall Dietrich informing him that evening of February 3 1945, of his agreement with his brother-in-law on all essential points of their further testimony.[2956] Moreover, faced with his imminent death when hearing the dreaded words "*Komm mit uns*" in Schönberg, his faith gave him the strength to face it calmly.[2957]

In the spirit of Chronicles, chapter 20, verse 12, Dietrich, from a position of seemingly hopeless weakness in battling a powerful and evil regime, has triumphed posthumously. His reputation is one of everlasting honour and bravery. Reciprocally, the memory of the regime of the Third Reich, despite the distorted history of Holocaust deniers with their rhetoric of the Global Jewish Conspiracy,[2958] lives on in infamy, along with that of their Führer, creator of the Third Reich, unwilling to face justice for his countless crimes against humanity.

To return to the service held on Friday July 27 at London's Holy Trinity Brompton Church: when Franz Hildebrandt concluded his sermon in honour of his dearest friend, he expressed his and everyone's deepest and most heartfelt thoughts: "

> We know not what to do. After these anxious weeks of uncertainty through which we have lived with you, dear Sabine and

Gert, and with your parents, we know less than ever how to carry on without the counsel of our brother on whom we could lean and who was so desperately needed by the Church at this time. Today we understand what Harnack said when Holl had died: 'with him a piece of my own life is carried to the grave.' Yet: our eyes are upon Thee. We believe in the communion of saints, the forgiveness of sins, the resurrection of the body and the life everlasting. We give thanks to God for the life, the suffering, the witness of our brother whose friends we were privileged to be. We pray God to lead us, too, through his discipleship from this world into His heavenly kingdom; to fulfil in us that other word with which Dietrich concluded his obituary of Harnack: '*non potest non laetari qui sperat in Dominum*' — 'while in God confiding I cannot but rejoice.'"[2959]

When the service ended, Karl and Paula Bonhoeffer in Berlin turned off the radio.[2960] After the service, Sabine said, "No one else could have given such a lovely address," and her husband Gerhard said that Dietrich's death made Franz's friendship more precious than ever.[2961] Unlike Gert and Sabine,[2962] Franz, who had a British wife — half-English, half-Scottish — and a son David, born in 1944, never returned permanently to Germany.[2963] Franz passed away in Edinburgh in the Autumn of 1985, aged 76, following a severe stroke.[2964]

That a German, so soon after war's end in Europe, had a memorial service held in his honour in London is truly remarkable and speaks volumes for Dietrich's character. However, memorials on foreign soil for the pastor did not end there. On Thursday July 9 1998,[2965] ten new statues above the west entrance to Westminster Abbey were unveiled before Queen Elizabeth II and her husband the Duke of Edinburgh. They were carved to honour "Modern Martyrs" or "Martyrs of the 20th Century," in a formerly empty niche above the western entrance,[2966] during the Abbey's last restorative work from 1973-1995.[2967]

They include victims of Communism, such as the Chinese pastor and evangelist Wang Zhiming, executed on December 29 1973 at age 66, during Mao's Cultural Revolution; and the Orthodox nun, Grand Duchess Elizabeth, the older sister of Tsar Nicholas's wife Alexandra, the last empress of Russia; she was murdered by the Bolsheviks in Ekaterinberg western Siberia on July 18, 1918, shot down a mineshaft. Another martyr is the victim of right-wing death squads, Oscar Romero, the Salvadorean Catholic Archbishop, who was shot dead at age 62 on March 24 1980, while celebrating mass in the chapel of the hospital where he lived. Others were victims of religious prejudice, such as the black South African Manche Masemola, murdered by her parents on February 4 1928, aged just fifteen; and the Pakistani Christian woman Ester John, murdered on February 2 1960, aged thirty.[2968]

Better known among this honoured number in the US and the western world in general is the victim of racial prejudice, the famous Martin Luther King Junior, assassinated on April 4, 1968 in Memphis Tennessee, aged 39 years. Another victim is Lucian Tapiedi; he was murdered in 1942, aged around 20 years, by one of his countrymen, while leading his fellow missionaries in flight from the advancing Japanese invaders during the terror of Japanese occupation in Papua. Another martyr is the victim of the genocidal regime in Uganda during the 1970s, Anglican Archbishop Janani Luwum; he was murdered in February 1977, aged around 55 years, for daring to question the mass murder that was perpetrated by Idi Amin.[2969] Naturally, such a number would not be complete without acknowledging martyrs who opposed the most heinous regime of the twentieth century. When one looks at the statues of the ten martyrs, the first from the left is the Polish Catholic priest, Saint Maximilian Kolbe — Auschwitz Prisoner 16670,[2970] born as Raymond Kolbe on January 8, 1894, as the second son of a poor weaver at Zduńska Wola near Łódź.[2971]

When Germany invaded Poland in September 1939,[2972] Father Kolbe realised that his friary at Niepokalanów, about forty kilometres west of Warsaw,[2973] would be seized, and sent most of the friars home before he was imprisoned for about two months. Upon his release in early December,[2974] he returned to the friary, where he and the other friars founded a shelter for 3,000 Polish refugees, whom they fed, clothed, and gave sanctuary to.[2975] However, day after day, Gestapo spies had Niepokalanów under heavy surveillance, looking for anything they could report against the friars.[2976] On the morning of February 17, 1941, Father Kolbe was arrested for the second and last time, and incarcerated in Warsaw's notorious Pawiak prison.[2977] Three months later, as he left his putrid boxcar with his fellow prisoners on May 28, he arrived in Auschwitz.[2978] In June 1941, there was an alleged escape of one of the prisoners from the camp.[2979] The consequence was that ten prisoners were to be randomly selected for execution;[2980] one of them was the Polish Army Sergeant, prisoner 5659,[2981] Franciszek Gajowniczek.[2982] To the prisoner's astonishment, Father Kolbe offered himself up for execution in Franciszek Gajowniczek's place.

Soon after, Father Kolbe was thrown down the stairs of the notorious punishment Block 11,[2983] along with the other victims and simply left there to starve. As hunger and thirst in the summer heat consumed the condemned, some drank their own urine, while others licked moisture on the dank walls.[2984] Maximilian Kolbe, not regretting his sacrifice, encouraged the others with prayers, psalms, and meditations on the Passion of Christ, even after two weeks, when only four remained alive.[2985] By this time, the cell was needed for more victims, and the camp executioner, a common criminal named Bock, came in and injected a lethal dose of carbolic acid into the left arm of each of the four dying men. Kolbe was the only one still fully conscious. With a prayer on his lips, the last prisoner raised his arm for the executioner. His wait was over.[2986] xxxv

For the beneficiary of Father Kolbe's courage, time would never fade or extinguish the memory of the heroic priest who saved his life, as indicated by his pilgrimage to Auschwitz each year on August 14 until 1994, the year before his death.[2987] On several occasions, he visited Zduńska Wola[2988] — the birthplace of Father Kolbe.[2989] In accordance with his wishes, Franciszek Gajowniczek, a veteran from the 1919-20 Polish-Soviet war,[2990] was buried in the Franciscan cemetery in Niepoka-lanów.[2991]

The second figure among the haloed ten, likewise honoured for his martyrdom in defiance of Hitler's Reich, is the seventh figure from the left — the equally selfless Lutheran pastor, Dietrich Bonhoeffer.[2992] For them both, and indeed all the other martyrs of the twentieth century, the words of Matthew Chapter 10 verse 39 resonate truly: "Whoever finds their life will lose it, and whoever loses their life for my sake will find it." Their honoured memories live on for all eternity, unlike those of certain perpetrators who escaped meaningful justice, due to the invocation of morally questionable legal loopholes. Cases in point are Dietrich's Drumhead court-martial judge, Otto Thorbeck, and prosecuting accomplice Walter Huppenkothen. In 1955, both were sentenced to prison terms, but in the following year, upon appeal, they were released on the grounds that they were executing traitors to the Fatherland.[2993] This precedent ignored the true purpose of the People's Court, which

---

xxxv A terrible irony surrounds this story. After the ten condemned had died their terrible deaths, the alleged "escaped" prisoner was found drowned in a camp latrine. See the DK Holocaust website article on Father Maximilian Kolbe at http://www.auschwitz.dk/Kolbe.htm. Still, this does not detract in any way, from the story of the extraordinary heroism of the Franciscan priest and Saint, Maximilian Kolbe.

was the persecution and eradication of the Third Reich's political and racial "enemies."

In 1996, the Berlin Regional Court repudiated their 1956 acquittal; but these legal instruments of Hitler were then long gone, with Thorbeck passing away in 1976,[2994] and Huppenkothen two years later in 1978,[2995] more than three decades following the execution of Dietrich and his four fellow victims on April 9 1945. They should be remembered as obscure murderous cogs in the machinery of the Third Reich. If it were not for Roland Freisler's fatal misfortune, courtesy of the American Eighth Air Force on February 3 1945,[2996] Hitler's ranting henchman might also have escaped post-war justice and pursued a comfortable and lucrative legal career. Huppenkothen, on the heels of his 1956 release, was made to serve another three years, but upon his release on parole in 1959, he resumed his legal career as a commercial lawyer in Cologne.[2997]

It is a curious fact that Thorbeck and Dietrich both received the same classical education at the same German university; both attended many of the same classes, both read the *Iliad*,[2998] and were classmates and friends.[2999] Otto Thorbeck became a lawyer, then a judge, and a servant to the most infamous legal instrument of Hitler's Reich, the Volksgerichtshof or People's Court, and pronounced Dietrich's death sentence in Flossenbürg on Monday April 9 1945.[3000] Yet Dietrich is posthumously honoured in perpetuity upon the western portal of Westminster Cathedral, while Thorbeck's memory fades into history.

A text that epitomises Dietrich's life may be the "Death of Moses," a poem that Dietrich wrote from Tegel Prison.[3001] It relates to the Old Testament book of Deuteronomy 34:1—4, chronicling the story of Moses, who, after forty years of leading the Israelites out of captivity in Egypt and throughout the desert in search of the Promised Land, upon finally reaching it, was not allowed by God to enter it with his people. However, before his death, God showed him that land from the summit of Mount Nebo. Dietrich narrates this biblical story in simple verse: "

> Through death's veil you let me see at least this, my people, go to highest feast. They stride into freedom, God, I see, as I sink to your eternity. To punish sin, to forgive you are moved; O God, this people have I truly loved."[3002]

While it contains no overt reference to the present, it is likely that he was thinking of himself and the others who were prepared to pay with their lives for their patriotism,[3003] and could only imagine, but would not live to experience, the freedom and liberty of a prosperous post-war West Germany, and ultimate unification of East and West Germany in October 1990.

Back on that first Sunday morning after Easter, April 8, 1945,[3004] in the relatively benign environment of the school in the idyllic Bavarian village of Schönberg, Dietrich, far removed from the privations of Prinz-Albrecht-Strasse and Buchenwald, must have been almost tasting liberation as the Reich imploded, with war's end in Europe barely a month away. However, when he heard the dreaded words "*Komm mit uns*" around midday, his thoughts may have turned to a 1932 sermon he delivered before Hitler's rise to power: "

> The blood of martyrs might once again be demanded, but this blood, if we really have the courage and loyalty to shed it, will not be innocent, shining like that of the first witnesses for the faith. On our blood lies heavy guilt, the guilt of the unprofitable servant who is cast into outer darkness."[3005]

By midday April 8, 1945, Dietrich may have felt complicit, at least in sharing the knowledge of various assassination attempts on Hitler. He was a martyr guilty of renouncing his principle of non-violence, compelled by a church that was complicit in its own destruction through supporting Hitler. He had asked his students in Berlin in 1939, before his second visit to America: "Would you grant absolution to the murderer of a tyrant?"[3006] Claus von Stauffenberg, according to Pierre Galante and Eugene Silianoff, joint authors of *Operation Valkyrie: The German Generals' Plot Against Hitler*, had asked much the same question of the Catholic priest Father Wehrle, in a chapel on July 10 1944, ten days before his departure for the Wolfsschanze.[3007]

Stauffenberg, apparently, received the answer no. What is certain is that in November 1942, Stauffenberg's adjutant, Werner von Haeften, whose brother Hans-Bernd had been in Dietrich's 1922 confirmation class,[3008] had broached that question to Dietrich,[3009] about four to five months before the latter's arrest in early April 1943.[3010] Dietrich's student, Wolf-Dieter Zimmermann, co-author of *I Knew Dietrich Bonhoeffer*, recalled the conversation at his home:[3011] "

> Bonhoeffer answered that he could not decide this for him. The risk had to be taken by him, him alone. If he even spoke of guilt in not making use of a chance, there was certainly as much guilt in light-hearted treatment of the situation. No one

425

Chapter 28

could ever emerge without guilt from the situation he was in. But then that guilt was always a guilt borne in suffering.

The two men talked for hours. We others only made some marginal comments. No decision was taken. Werner von Haeften returned to his duties without being given any direction. He had to decide for himself. And later, he did decide. As aide-de-camp to Stauffenberg he was one of those who were involved in the abortive attempt on Hitler's life. He was also one of those who, in the evening of 20th July 1944, were shot in the courtyard of the Army High Command in the Bendlerstrasse. Eye-witnesses tell us that he faced death calmly and bravely."[3012]

However, the Catholic priest, Father James Wallace of Chicago's Saint Juliana's Parish, in writing of Dietrich's and Claus's (and in effect, Werner von Haeften's) moral dilemma, put it this way: "

He [Dietrich] argued an 'activist spirituality.' Being a Christian wasn't about avoiding sin and merely reacting to events, but living one's whole life in obedience to God's will through action. 'It depends on a God who demands responsible action in a bold venture of faith, and who promises forgiveness and consolation to the man who becomes a sinner in that venture.'

Killing Hitler was a bold action that, though sinful, was holy because it trusted on God's mercy and not on his judgement. It's not a theory we should invoke all the time, but here it was valid. Stauffenberg and Bonhoeffer are regarded today in Germany as heroes."[3013]

Perhaps God's judgement, for Dietrich as the guilty martyr, may have been to not quite live to witness a resurgent, prosperous, and free West Germany rise from the immediate post-war ruins that Hitler's megalomania was responsible for. Others of his family did. In 1947, Gerhard and Dietrich's twin sister Sabine returned; Sabine's husband Gerhard became a prominent jurist,[3014] living on until February 1982, aged 80, and Sabine became the longest lived of the Bonhoeffer siblings, passing away just before millennia's end in 1999, aged 93.[3015]

Dietrich's parents survived the war by a few years. Karl passed away in 1948 aged 80, and Paula three years later, aged 74. Karl-

Friedrich, the eldest sibling, was the only Bonhoeffer brother to survive the war, but passed away in 1957, aged 58. Christine, the wife of Hans von Dohnányi, passed away in 1965, aged 62, while the youngest sibling, Susanne, died in 1991, aged 82.[3016] Ursula, who had cooked brother Dietrich's final meal as a free man,[3017] and in the following year of 1944, in the wake of Valkyrie, had talked Klaus out of committing suicide just prior to his arrest (much to her later regret, given the terrible torture he suffered at the hands of the Gestapo)[3018] lived on until 1983, aged 81.[3019] Her husband, Rüdiger Schleicher, was executed on April 22 1945[3020] with Klaus and several others in Berlin,[3021] but her daughter Renate married Eberhard Bethge during the war. The latter passed away on March 18 2000.[3022]

Apart from his presence among the pantheon of Ten Martyrs of the Twentieth Century above Westminster's west portal, there is another monument outside of modern-day Germany that stands in Dietrich's honour. It is the one mentioned at the very beginning of this book, beside the now Catholic church of Saint Elisabeth in his birthplace of then German Breslau, post-war Polish Wrocław, which I had the privilege to visit in mid-February 2005; at the foot of the bronze cross monument lie tablets in Polish and German, honouring his memory.

Given the centuries of bad blood between these two great nations, this consensus is truly remarkable, especially in the context of the Stalinist-perpetrated displacement of the Borderland Poles from the east during the immediate post-war period,[3023] and their still fresh and terrible memories of the war under both fascist and Stalinist overlords.[3024] The displaced Poles from the eastern Borderlands had no will to acknowledge the history of German Breslau; in attempting to preserve their Polish consciousness, they declared that every brick in their newly Polish Wrocław only lived and spoke Polish.[3025] It was this monument that inspired me to write of this extraordinary man, who, in his death, transcended this deeply engrained ethnic mistrust and animosity. Such is the honoured legacy of this gentle, brave, resilient pastor of the German Underground, Dietrich Bonhoeffer, who, as Ferdinand Schlingensiepen said, like all true Berliners, was born in Silesia's German Breslau,[3026] but whose memory lives on today in Polish Wrocław and beyond.

Chapter 29

Dietrich and Ruth and their Times Relevance for America in 2020-21 —
Lessons of History[xxxvi]

"Who controls the past," ran the Party slogan, *"controls the future: who
controls the present controls the past."*
Part One, Chapter III of *1984* by George Orwell.[3027]

*"Hence, for the cup of liberty to be replenished, it's beholden upon the
people, by means of truth, to fervently attempt the liberation of the past,
however recent or distant, from tyrants."*
The author inspired by George Orwell and the American Founding Fathers.

Ferdinand Schlingensiepen, author of *Dietrich Bonhoeffer 1906-1945:
Martyr, Thinker, Man of Resistance*, which is one the premiere sources
for this book, wrote an English language article in 2015 on the official
Bonhoeffer website titled *Making Assumptions About Dietrich: How
Bonhoeffer was Made Fit for America*.[3028] The title can perhaps be gen-
eralised to "Made fit for the English Speaking World." Ferdinand was
born in 1929 and post-war was a close friend of Eberhard Bethge —
who was Dietrich's closest friend. Eberhard died in 2000, but Ferdinand

---

[xxxvi] Note that in this time of growing mass censorship in America and indeed
elsewhere, it's possible that some source endnote links, since the time of writing in March 2021, have been removed. For articles, it may be possible to still
retrieve them on the WayBack Machine or Web Archive at
https://archive.org/web/. Just type or paste the link into the dialogue box. In the
case of videos, especially YouTube videos, given YouTube's mass censorship, I
have as much as possible, given links to these videos on alternative platforms
such as *The Epoch Times* Youmaker platform at https://www.youmaker.com/.
Indeed, some links already given by me, are via the Web Archive. See for example, the final footnote (not endnote) for this chapter. YouTube videos might
be retrieved on the Internet Archive with the Youtube code for the video. For
example; Joshua Philipp's Question and Answer on December 19, 2020 still on
YouTube at https://youtu.be/EI4zqaRG-sk, can also be accessed on the Internet
Archive at https://archive.org/details/youtube-EI4zqaRG-sk. At 45 minutes and
30 seconds, Joshua answers a question of mine where I use the pseudonym
"kulturedyobbo."

is still alive at the time of writing, aged 91.[3029] He spent crucial years of his childhood in an illegal Confessing Church seminary that his father led until his arrest.[3030]

In the article, he is critical of the American conservative author and radio presenter Eric Metaxas who wrote *Bonhoeffer: Pastor, Martyr, Prophet, Spy A righteous Gentile vs, the Third Reich* published in 2010, and the liberal author Charles Marsh, a liberal theologian from Virginia and author of *Strange Glory, A Life of Dietrich Bonhoeffer* published in 2014. The former is the most prominent source for my book, closely followed by Ferdinand's book and then Eberhard's giant biography. After I found and read Ferdinand's 2015 article in 2016, I started to thoroughly vet my citations of Eric Metaxas, and in my book, the majority of my citations of Eric Metaxas are accompanied by other sources, often those of Ferdinand and Eberhard. Charles Marsh I never used in my book, and indeed, while Ferdinand was critical of Eric Metaxas, he was even more so for Charles Marsh. To summarise, this is how Ferdinand sees Metaxas and Marsh: "

> Marsh and Metaxas have dragged Bonhoeffer into cultural and political disputes that belong in a U.S. context. The issues did not present themselves in the same way in Germany in Bonhoeffer's time, and the way they are debated in Germany today differs greatly from that in the States. Metaxas has focused on the fight between right and left in the United States and has made Bonhoeffer into a likeable arch-conservative without theological insights and convictions of his own; Marsh concentrates on the conflict between the Conservatives and the gay rights' movement. Both approaches are equally misguided and are used to make Bonhoeffer interesting and relevant to American society. Bonhoeffer does not need this and it certainly distorts the facts."

and...

> "Unlike Metaxas, Charles Marsh does know some German. He has read Bonhoeffer's writings in the original and has carried out research in Germany. He served briefly as a 'Bonhoeffer guest professor' at Humboldt University in Berlin. Even so, his manuscript needed more substantial corrections than that of Metaxas before being published in Germany."

and...

> "The authors have received much praise from their respective admirers. Both of them write extremely well. In Germany only those readers who can compare the German version of the biography with the American version will be able to see the pictures these two Americans are painting of Bonhoeffer. Both authors are said to have included new research. Whereas Metaxas actually presents very little that is new in this respect, new findings are restricted to the chapter on Bonhoeffer's first visit to the United States in Marsh's book."

and...

> "Marsh refers to Bonhoeffer's fiancée [Maria von Wedemeyer] by surname only and deals with her almost as an irritation."

Ferdinand's concluding paragraph explains Marsh's reasons for doing so:

> "Marsh's argument rests on the assumption that Bethge knew of Bonhoeffer's secret passion. Marsh does not seem to know that homosexuals in Germany were being sent to concentration camps. The Gestapo would have taken great pleasure in incarcerating a man like Bonhoeffer. Bonhoeffer would have been under constant strain, if this had been his sexual orientation. Bethge would have sensed something. There was never any suggestion of such tensions when Bethge talked about his time with Bonhoeffer. If even Bethge did not know anything about those homosexual tendencies, then Marsh's hypothesis is completely unfounded. It does not contribute anything to the theological or political debate about Bonhoeffer in any way."

For liberals/progressives the world over, they see Joe Biden's victory in the American November 2020 election as a triumph over evil, albeit, given Biden's interminable gaffes,[3031] and their irrational hatred of Trump, they celebrated more out of relief than enthusiasm.[3032] If familiar with Dietrich's life, they may perceive of Dietrich's story as an inspiration for democracy in challenging times. In doing so, they are assuming the election was legitimate and reported by a free and diverse unbiased media. However, for conservatives the world over, including myself, the election was anything but fair and legitimate, and trust in the global pack mainstream media (MSM), masquerading as free and diverse unbiased media, has been eviscerated. At the time of writing this chapter in March 2021, unlike 2015 when Ferdinand wrote his article, the American Constitutional Republic itself is now under dire threat, whereupon disturbing parallels with the death throes of Weimar Germany from Dietrich and Ruth's time, can be drawn.

When I think of Dietrich and the November 2020 US election, I think of how Dietrich would have felt in March 1933, when in servile compliance to the thuggery of Ernst Röhm's Brown Shirt Sturmabteilung (Storm Troopers), still loyal to Hitler at the time, the Reichstag of Weimar passed the suppressive "Malicious Practices" and "Enabling" acts on the 21st and 23rd, just sixteen and eighteen days following the last "free" election on March 5th. The former furnished the judicial means to prosecute anyone who, "with malicious afterthought" put forward reports that might impair the welfare of the Reich; the latter, officially the "Law to Remove the Crisis of the People and the State," was the constitutional means by which the Reichstag of Weimar,[3033] like a snake swallowing its tail, passed the law that obliterated its existence.[3034] Likewise, following an election riddled with unaddressed irregularities, and the rampant censorship implemented in the first six weeks of the Biden-Harris regime, I see the death of the US Constitutional Republic, as the Democrats repeatedly trample on its very Constitution.

To detail in depth,[xxxvii] the vast case of electoral irregularities in the 2020 US election, would require a book in itself. Nevertheless,

---

[xxxvii] For an excellent in-depth analysis on electoral fraud, see Joshua Philipp's documentary *2020 Election Investigative Documentary: Who's Stealing America?* at https://www.youmaker.com/video/73bbe59a-0850-4b10-a132-ffdaa5beb240. Joshua Philipp is an **investigative** reporter for New York's Independent media *The Epoch Times*, which has been my main source of information in regard to the US election, to replace the leftist **pack-driven** news of the global MSM. Facebook in December 2020, most predictably censored it, to which I informed Joshua on one of his Question and Answer sessions on his *Crossroads* channel on Saturday December 19, 2020. His response can be seen and heard on YouTube at https://youtu.be/EI4zqaRG-sk?t=2747 or if YouTube take it down, on the Internet Archive at https://archive.org/details/youtube-EI4zqaRG-sk from 45 minutes and 40 seconds in. I used the pseudonym "kulturedyobbo." In regard to Tik Tok funded Facebook "fact" checkers *Lead Stories*, see endnotes [3049] and [3137] for this chapter. **NOTE:** Contrary to what main-

some context on this issue that transcends just Trump, needs to be outlined. Firstly, November 2020 isn't the first time that the legitimacy of the American electoral process has been under a cloud. According to *Newsweek*, by May 2017, a class action lawsuit alleging the Democratic National Committee worked in conjunction with Hillary Clinton's 2016 campaign to keep Bernie Sanders out of the White House had been raging on in the courtrooms for months on end. Yet, most people had no idea of its existence, in large part thanks to the mainstream media's total lack of coverage.[3035] Sanders and Clinton were contesting the Democratic nomination in the months before the 2016 federal election. Hence, according to the Sanders' camp, Bernie Sanders should have been contesting the November 2016 federal election against Trump, not Hilary Clinton.

Moreover, in an article published just nine days before the 2016 federal election on November 8th, by the progressive journalist Emily Cameron, ironically titled *OPINION: Our Elections are a Mess and Only Leftists Care Enough to Fix Them*, she opened with: "

> The vehement insistence that Hillary Clinton won the Democratic primary fair-and-square is unhealthy for democracy, and the narrative that Bernie Sanders supporters critiquing voter suppression and election fraud are 'sore losers' causes lasting damage to our elections."[3036]

And ... "

> The Clinton Foundation has received donations from Dominion Voting and H.I.G. Capital, two manufacturers of voting machines. Does this definitively prove Clinton of committing election fraud? No, but it raises a lot of questions."[3037] (More on Dominion voting machines later.)

---

land Chinese companies like Huawei assert, if the Chinese Communist Party (CCP) demand they hand over network data, they would be compelled to do so because of espionage and national security laws in the "People's" Republic of China. See https://www.cnbc.com/2019/03/05/huawei-would-have-to-give-data-to-china-government-if-asked-experts.html. This of course, is not the case in western democracies, although, given the path already taken by the Biden-Harris regime, how much longer will this be the case in the US? All links accessed on Sunday March 14, 2021.

And in November 2017, a BBC article was titled; "[Democrat Senator] Elizabeth Warren agrees Democratic race 'rigged' for Clinton."[3038]

Secondly, on February 4, 2021, the global MSM mouthpiece, TIME magazine published a bizarre article of vague double-speak titled *The Secret History of the Shadow Campaign That Saved the 2020 Election*.[3039] A key aspect of the story was to sideline the Biden-Harris campaign from the "shadow campaign" to "save" the election. But as *The Epoch Times* opinion piece by Jeff Carlson put it: "

> Although the article treats the actions taken by this "Shadow Campaign" as necessary steps towards saving our democracy, *a more objective reader of events might make the case that our democracy was actually trampled underfoot.*"[3040]

And ... "

> According to the players in this saga, the perceived threat to our democracy was so consequential that it would require 'an effort of unprecedented scale' and a measure of cooperation heretofore not seen during an election process. And one that would encompass a surprisingly broad coalition of interests that would include 'Congress, Silicon Valley [Twitter, Facebook, Google and the like] and the nation's statehouses.'
>
> As the article notes, the efforts of this cabal 'touched every aspect of the election' including our election laws. These groups [before the election] engaged in a unified legal front to 'change voting systems and laws' at the state level, often unconstitutionally bypassing state legislatures and shifting power to the states' governors in the process. Conservative efforts to fight against this process were euphemistically termed as 'voter-suppression lawsuits.'"[3041]

Flowery and idealistic language such as "fortifying" rather than "rigging" the election was used by TIME's Molly Ball to describe the "shadow campaign,"[3042] which sounded very much like electoral interference in plain language.

Thirdly, in an unprecedented move, late on election night in Wisconsin, Michigan, Pennsylvania, North Carolina, Georgia and Nevada, counting stopped with Trump well ahead — only to resume hours later in the early morning, when sudden inexplicable and huge surges for Biden ensued.[3043] At Farm Arena in Fulton County Georgia, the most damning and indeed direct evidence was video footage from that night, heard by a Georgia Senate Judiciary Subcommittee hearing in early December 2020.[3044] At around 10:30 p.m. on election night, a woman can be seen addressing the multiple Republican election observers. Soon afterwards the Republican observers and media staffers left. About one-and-a-half hours later, as I returned home from work at 3:15 p.m. in Brisbane Australia, which was just after midnight on the US east coast, I heard on *The Epoch Times* YouTube channel, that counting at Farm Arena had ceased owing to a burst water main flooding the building. This later turned out to be just a toilet leak,[3045] which was consistent with the video footage, that had not shown any evidence of flooding.

Soon after the Republican observers and media crew left, multiple large black cases were pulled from under tables. These cases were previously concealed due to large black table cloths covering the tables down to the floor. The cases were hauled several metres to desks with Dominion voting machines, whereupon, ballots from these cases were then inserted into the machines. This process was continued until 12:55 a.m.,[3046] and would have continued beyond that, if not for the fact, that when Republican observers arrived at the central tabulation centre, after leaving Farm Arena, they heard from a news crew staffer, counter to what they had been told when leaving the Arena, that counting was still taking place![3047]

In the two or so hours that this questionable counting took place, it's estimated that 18,000 ballots were processed, which alone is way above Biden's official winning margin of less than 12,000 in Georgia.[3048] In other words, if one subtracts this questionable count of ballots, caught on video, from around 11 p.m. until 12:55 a.m. on the night of November 3-4, 2020 at Farm Arena, from Biden's official vote count for Georgia, Trump is the winner in Georgia, not Biden! Facebook "fact" checkers *Lead Stories*, funded by Chinese owned *Tik Tok*,[3049] contrived the implausible story that the Republican observers and media left voluntarily, knowing that "counting" would continue after they left at 10:30 p.m.[3050] Moreover, the *Lead Stories* spin-doctoring, as alluded to by *The Epoch Times* reporter Joshua Philipp,[3051] focuses inordinately on Jackie Pick, the presenter of the video footage to the Georgia Senate Judiciary Subcommittee, calling the black cases "suitcases" when they are supposed to be "the standard container used for the ballot counting process."[3052] Of course, such an inconsequential fact has no fundamental bearing on this issue. Curiously, in February

2021, the Fulton County Board voted to fire their elections director Richard Barron.[3053]

Next, at almost the same time the TIME magazine article was published in early February 2021, self-made billionaire and CEO of "My Pillow" Mike Lindell, towards the end of his two hour documentary *ABSOLUTE PROOF Exposing Election Fraud and the Theft of America by Enemies Foreign and Domestic*, interviewed by phone, National Intelligence Researcher and Author, Mary Fanning. During the interview, just a tiny fraction of a report of thousands of pages, documenting IP addresses of foreign hacks into the US election was displayed.[3054] Overall, more than two-thirds came from the People's Republic of China,[3055] with the objective to always slash the vote count for Trump. Moreover, on Christmas day 2020, investigative reporter Simone Gao released an interview of IT expert Russell Ramsland Junior, who spoke of a tabulation server in Georgia reporting tabulation results to China.[3056] Furthermore, Ramsland's audit team found evidence that the audit logs were changed signalling a change of ballot data.[3057]

In July 2016, Jin Canrong, CCP advisor and professor and associate dean of the School of International Studies at Beijing's Renmin University of China, in a July 2016 speech on "Sino-U.S. Strategic Philosophy" given over two full days at Southern Club Hotel Business Class in south China's Guangzhou City, outlined a multi-pronged strategy involving a range of malign actions to subvert the United States while strengthening the Chinese regime. They included; interfering in U.S. elections, controlling the American market, cultivating global enemies to challenge the United States, stealing American technology, expanding Chinese territory, and influencing international organisations.[3058] In regard to manipulating elections, Jin Canrong stated: "

> The Chinese government wants to arrange Chinese investments in every single congressional district to control thousands of voters in each district."

and ... "

> Normally [within any of the 435 US congressional districts] the difference of votes between two candidates is 10,000 or less. If China has thousands of votes on hand, China will be the boss of the candidates."[3059]

Hence, now as president, how compromised is Biden by the genocidal[3060] Chinese Communist Party (CCP)?[3061]

Finally, less than a fortnight before Biden's "inauguration," and just the day following the Capitol Hill riot on January 6th, the then Director of National Intelligence (DNI) John Ratcliffe, in his report *Views on Intelligence Community Election Security Analysis*, documented the following:

> "China analysts were hesitant to access Chinese actions as undue influence or interference. These analysts appeared reluctant to have their analysis on China brought forward because they tend to disagree with the [Trump] administration's policies, saying in effect, I don't want our intelligence used to support those policies. This behavior would constitute a violation of Analytic Standard B: Independence of Political Considerations (IRTPA Section 1019)."[3062]

… and in the concluding paragraph:

> "In that same spirit, I am adding my voice of support of the stated minority view — based on all available sources of intelligence, with definitions consistently applied, and reached independent of all political considerations or undue pressure — that the People's Republic of China sought to influence the 2020 U.S. federal elections, and raising the need for the Intelligence Community to address the underlying issues with reporting outlined above."[3063]

Which again raises the question; now as president, how compromised is Biden by the genocidal[3064] CCP?[3065] And why was the release of Ratcliffe's report delayed until January 7, 2021 — the day following the storming of Capitol Hill? This was when Congress was meeting in what was usually a formality to finalise the election result. However, that day of the 6th, there was the cloud of electoral irregularities to deal with, with seven states mired in allegations of fraud, sending duelling electors to contest the result of those states, as was and is their right under the Constitution. As such, I held out some hope for this very suspicious election to be overturned, or at least have the inauguration on the 20th delayed, in order to genuinely investigate major election irregularities.

But when I heard of the storming of the Capitol Building by Trump supporters on January 6, 2021, I was in a state of shock. Before this time, Trump protests such as the Jericho marches in November and December 2020, had been peaceful. As I collected my thoughts, and discussed the incident with my mate, my heart sank. For the perpetrators of electoral fraud, and the CCP, openly hoping for a Biden "victory,"[3066] such an incident was political and propaganda manna from heaven, or perhaps hell. Further indicative of this being the CCP's desire, was when a Chinese professor Di Dongshen, associate Dean at Renmin University in China, and part of Xi Jinping's brain trust, in a video that went viral in December 2020, even boasted of how the CCP could control virtually the entire American elite, including of course, Joe Biden, but not Trump![3067] Again raising the question; how compromised is Biden, now as president, by the genocidal[3068] CCP?[3069] Then it occurred to me; how convenient the Berlin Reichstag fire of late February 1933 was for Hitler's National Socialists.

At that time, Hitler's hold on power in a then minority government, was somewhat precarious. He still required some pretext to cement absolute power. Hence in this sense, the Weimar Republic was still alive, but teetering on the edge. Franz von Papen of the Catholic Centre party,[3070] who had been instrumental in making Hitler chancellor of this minority government in late January, had declared; "In two months' time we will have squeezed Hitler into a corner until he squeaks."[3071] On February 27, 1933,[3072] the night of the fire, four weeks had now passed since Hitler took office. But now the fire ensured that Hitler would not be "squeaking" any time soon.

At the time of the fire, Hitler was dining at Joseph Goebbels' home when his host received the call that the Reichstag was on fire. According to Metaxas, quoting Shirer's book, Goebbels was not at first convinced, as the caller was Ernst "Putzi" Hanfstaengl. While he was Harvard educated, and his money and connections had greatly helped Hitler's rise to power, he was also known as a bit of a clown, and thus Goebbels' first impression was that Hanfstaengl was pulling his leg. However, when he and Hitler arrived, they found that for once, Hanfstaengl was deadly serious, and were greeted by the first at the scene, the rotund Hermann Göring.[3073]

Puffing and panting, the most corpulent of the Third Reich's elite professed that this was the beginning of the Communist revolution, and that no mercy must be shown in shooting and/or stringing up every Communist official that could be found. If Göring was in on the possible National Socialist plot, now of course was not the time for honesty! The removal of their Communist rivals from the dying Weimar political landscape was resoundingly called for. Could it be that Goebbels and

Hitler were not in on the plot, but Göring was? In any event, at the scene, the shirtless and hapless young Dutch communist, Marinus Van der Lubbe, who had supposedly used his shirt for tinder, was arrested on the spot, and the golden pretext the National Socialists required to initiate the political mechanisms to remove the Communists and other political rivals from the dying Weimar political landscape presented itself.

Almost 88 years later in Washington DC, in the early afternoon of Wednesday January 6, 2021, a parallel pretext now enabled the Deep State to crackdown on their ideological enemies, and in the process, suppress all mention of electoral fraud and thus cement their "victory" in the most questionable election in over 244 years of US history. The global MSM would deny the existence of the American Deep State, however, it's worth noting, that in the first three or so decades post-WWII, the Italian government and media denied the self-evident existence of the Cosa Nostra — Sicilian Mafia.[3074] Indeed, as to which state was or is more corrupt, the Italy of that time, or America of today, would be highly contentious to say the least.

As the Jewish American and Conservative radio talk show host and writer Dennis Prager stated: "

> In Germany, the German parliament was burned down. We're not absolutely certain who did it, but it seems that a communist did it. Anyway, it didn't matter to the Nazis who did it, what mattered was what they could use it for, and they used it for the Enabling Act, which they quickly ran through Parliament, and it enabled the Nazis to curtail civil liberties in the name of a national emergency caused by the burning of the parliament of the Reichstag."[3075]

To reiterate, the Enabling Act was the constitutional means by which the Reichstag of Weimar,[3076] like a snake swallowing its tail, passed the law that obliterated its existence. And likewise, almost 88 years later, following January 6, 2021, the American Deep State had its pretext or "Enabling Act" to enable its own suppression of civil liberties, and in particular, the Constitution's First Amendment protection of free speech.

Following the Capitol Hill breach, thousands of National Guard troops were brought in, as indeed Trump himself had suggested before January 6th.[3077] On Biden's "inauguration" day on the 20th, about 26,000 National Guard troops were deployed with barb wire fencing surrounding the Hill, and the traditional parade cancelled.[3078] Before the 20th,

National Guard troops were vetted for their political leanings, while on CNN, Democrat Congressman Stephen Cohen of Memphis to the interviewer, talked of three-quarters of the National Guard being white Trump voting males making them a threat to national security and unsuitable for deployment on "inauguration" day![3079] Such was the celebration of the "Saving of Democracy," as the Constitution of the American Constitutional Republic was trampled upon.

Or perhaps, was it more like the founding of the one party "Democratic" Socialist State? Indeed, the global MSM mouthpiece and professed voice of "fearless journalism," *The Daily Beast*, in the wake of January 6th, has even floated the idea of America forming its own secret police. Supposedly based on Britain's MI5,[3080] but given the disturbing trends in America since January 6th, it would more than likely be along the lines of secret police in other present day and bygone dictatorships, such as the Stasi of the former German "Democratic" Republic.[3081]

When a recruit to the American Armed Forces swears his or her oath, it's not to the President, nor his or her administration. Rather, it's to the Constitution,[3082] unlike countries such as the People's Republic of China, the "Democratic" People's Republic of Korea, the former German "Democratic" Republic and indeed the former Third Reich, where the recruit swears or swore allegiance to the dictator and the regime. This point seems lost or trampled upon by the new Biden-Harris regime.

The storming of Capitol Hill, was undoubtedly a horrible and reprehensible act. However, as Dennis Prager stated, it was nothing in comparison to the rampant censorship and flagrant violation of the US constitution that followed in its wake.[3083] With the memory of electoral irregularities now buried by this most convenient of neo-Reichstag pretexts, the path to the obliteration of the American Constitutional Republic to make way for the "Democracy" of the one party Socialist state, had presented itself. The Deep State coup was seemingly initiated by electoral fraud, as implied by the general intransigence of official entities to investigate or deal with it. Nevertheless, it was impeded by reporting of alleged fraud by thousands of brave people, putting their careers and reputations on the line in the face of Deep State intimidation.[3084] Sadly however, with the overwhelming propaganda reinforcement of the January 6th riot, the coup was now, seemingly complete.

Any future "elections" it seems, could be manipulated at will to preserve the illusion or pretence of Democracy if required — as was and is the case in Chavez and now Maduro's Socialist "utopia" of Venezuela.[3085] Indeed, from the early November 2020 *Epoch Times* article and video interview titled *Video: Dr. Paul Kengor: The Pennsylvania Voting Curve Doesn't Line Up*, there is the most intriguing and disturbing comment from a former Venezuelan in the forum, "danielmg007." (With grammar and spelling errors not corrected.)

> "Hi Josua.
> I am a Venezuelan american. I am pro Trump. All this that happen in the election is a flashback of what happened in Venezuela during many elections trying to put Chavez or Maduro out of the power. Is a photo copy. Many many times the opposition candidate, was winning until in the middle of the night everything stop. [As was the unprecedented case in Wisconsin, Michigan, Pennsylvania, North Carolina, Georgia and Nevada][3086] And unexpectedly the government candidate start getting more votes and more votes and finally Chavez or more recently Maduro won. Every poll said the opposition candidate will win. You can feel the intention of vote of every Venezuelan poor or rich in the streets. And the whole society was sure we will win. I do not how they do it but we need to find out how. On another hand other events happening in USA are the same events started happening in Venezuela. The black life matter movement(in Venezuela with different names of course). Everything. Really worry."[3087]

Just a couple of days following his "inauguration," Biden asked his newly appointed Director of National Intelligence, Avril Haines, to "assess" domestic extremism.[3088] The overt implication being, to only focus on right-wing extremism, real and perceived, and ignore left-wing acts of extremism being perpetrated by Antifa in Democrat run cities like Portland Oregon and Seattle in Washington state. Such acts on one hand, remind one of Hitler/Ernst Röhm's bands of Brown Shirt Sturmabteilung (Storm Troopers) from the early 1930s, but on the other hand, are chillingly reminiscent of Mao Zedong's fanatical Red Guards from the Cultural Revolution of the mid-1960s to 70s.[3089] Moreover, the monthly Harvard/Harris poll for February 2021, found that 55% Americans were more concerned over the violence that happened last summer in the aftermath of the death of George Floyd than the Capitol riot on January 6, 2021.[3090] Furthermore, 64% think the January 6 riot was "being used by politicians to suppress legitimate political movements."[3091] This, in spite of global MSM saturation bombing of their narrative of domestic far-right terrorism, being the number one threat to national security.

But of course, the agenda of the radical-left has no need for any basis in truth. Hence, following January 6, 2021 and the invoking of the "assessment" of domestic extremism, with the Biden regime barely a month old, the pretext had been set for nation wide persecution of Trump supporters, including for example, David Schoen, one of the attorneys who successfully defended Trump during the unconstitution-al[3092] February 2021 impeachment trial. Schoen had a law school cancel a civil rights law course he was going to teach and he was suspended from a civil rights lawyer email discussion list.[3093] It seems "civil rights" activists have deemed Schoen and his entire team as defenders of a so-called domestic terrorist (Trump), who based on the flimsiest evidence of words taken out of context,[3094] incited the January 6th riot.

In any case, is it not so that anybody is entitled to a defence? At the same time, in another instance of cancel culture intimidation, reminiscent of Mao's Cultural Revolution, another member of Trump's defence team, Michael van der Veen had his driveway spray-painted with the word "traitor,"[3095] and had started receiving constant death threats,[3096] for merely defending his client in an unconstitutional sham of a trial.[3097]

On April 1, 1933, thirty-three days following the Reichstag Fire[3098] and less than a fortnight after passing the suppressive "Malicious Practices" and "Enabling" acts on the 21st and 23rd March,[3099] Hitler declared a national boycott of Jewish stores. Its repercussions, naturally extended to other aspects of Jewish life. For example, Dietrich's brother-in-law of Jewish descent but converted Lutheran Gerhard Leibholz, was a popular professor of law at Göttingen, and his wife Sabine, twin sister of Dietrich, would often attend his lectures. On the day of the boycott, Sabine made a point of attending her husband's scheduled lectures.[3100] When Gerhard and Sabine walked down the street, the atmosphere was toxic; people who recognised them would suddenly cross over the street. When Sabine arrived, she was greeted by students dressed in SA (Sturmabteilung — Storm Troopers or Brown Shirts) uniforms with the words, "Leibholz must not lecture, he is a Jew. The lectures are not taking place."[3101] Theologian Walter Bauer and a certain professor met them there, expressing their disgust with the National Socialists. Worse still, many of Gerhard's relatives lost their jobs, and one of his Jewish school friends committed suicide. By then, such instances were commonplace.

To highlight how terrorism does not just spawn from the right of politics, in Portland Oregon, police made several arrests within a few hours of Biden being "inaugurated," after Antifa terrorists spray-painted anti-Biden graffiti while vandalising the headquarters of the Democratic Party of Oregon. In the streets, Antifa mobs displayed banners proclaiming "We don't want Biden. We want revenge for police murders, imperialist wars, and fascist massacres."[3102] In Washington DC on February 6, 2021, Black Lives Matter and Antifa marched chanting "burn It down" and threatened people as they ate dinner.[3103]

Curiously, Antifa-Black Lives Matter-(BLM)-Insurgence USA activist John Earle Sullivan, who in a video he himself shot while inside the Capitol Building on January 6th, could be heard saying "let's burn this [expletive] down." [3104] Later, Sullivan was respectively paid $35,000 by CNN and NBC, and $2,375 by the Australian Broadcasting Corporation (ABC) for video footage of the breach, according to invoices that were filed with the U.S. District Court for the District of Columbia.[3105] As an Aussie tax payer, in paying Sullivan the prodigious discount rate, I am pleased tens of thousands of our tax dollars have been saved by our public broadcaster. It seems, they have read Trump's book *The Art of the Deal*, but CNN and NBC have not.

For the far-left anarchists that are Antifa, the US is utterly irredeemable. [3106] In January 2021, independent Vietnamese-American journalist Andy Ngo had his book *Unmasked Inside Antifa's Radical Plan to Destroy Democracy* published before it went on sale at Powell's book store in Portland Oregon — one of the largest independent book stores in the US. However, almost immediately, the book store was surrounded by Antifa protesters calling for the book to be removed from the shelves. Unfortunately, Powell a family owned business, caved into the threats, but still kept the book in its online store.[3107] This naturally compelled me to order my own copy. In 2019, Andy Ngo was bashed by Antifa and suffered a brain bleed which required months of treatment. Unlike claims made by much of the global MSM, Andy Ngo is not far-right. For example, as an independent journalist, he has written for mainstream publications such as *Newsweek, Wall Street Journal* and *New York Post*.[3108]

More than likely, the types making such claims of Andy Ngo, would in all likelihood, say the same of me. However, it must be remembered that during the Stalinist show trials of the 1930s, all enemies of Stalin were labelled as "accomplices of fascism."[3109] Moreover, from the Antifa frame of reference embodying their "anti-fascism," anyone even the slightest bit right of their world view, is fascist. This includes even the far-left Alexandria Ocasio Cortez (AOC), Democrat House of Representative from New York's 14th district,[3110] and formal member of the far-left Democratic Socialists of America (DSA),[3111] who according to former Antifa member Gabrielle Nadales, is regarded as a capitalist![3112] Hence, given Antifa's reaction to Andy Ngo's book, and their ultra-extreme leftist anarchist agenda, it would be plausible in the event of them achieving their "utopia," to surmise their invoking of book burning, in a throwback from the infamous literary *Säuberung* (cleansing) in Hitler's Reich in May 1933.[3113] Indeed, could my book, if noteworthy enough, be burnt upon this "cleansing" anarchist pyre of so-deemed, "degenerate bourgeoisie literature?" Indeed, as reported by *The Epoch Times* in late February 2021, in a war against faith, the CCP burnt religious books and imprisoned believers.[3114]

Antifa's extreme world view has been briefly practised in so-called "autonomous" zones such as the Capitol Hill Organised Protest (CHOP) zone in Seattle. In its first days of early to mid June 2020, much of mainstream media had idealised it,[3115] while at the same time, the Democrat Seattle Mayor Jenny Durkan on the 11th, in a CNN interview, even dubbed it euphemistically as the "summer of love."[3116] In a matter of days following several serious and violent crimes, including an attempted arson, multiple assaults captured on video, and the fatal shooting of a 19-year-old, it was obvious her remark didn't age well.[3117]

In Portland Oregon, before, during and after Durkan's "summer of love," Antifa rioted for 120 consecutive days, with the tacit approval of the Democrat mayor, Ted Wheeler.[3118] In Minneapolis, in the wake of George Floyd's death, burning, looting and pillaging was perpetrated by the radical left Freedom Road Socialist Organisation (FRSO), as joyously proclaimed by its leading members and partners Steff York and Jess Sundin.[3119] Moreover, the FRSO website leaves no doubt as to their Marxist agenda, as they view the Tiananmen Square massacre in June 1989 as the defeat of counter-revolution in China![3120] Nevertheless, many such radicals in the summer of 2020 were bailed out of gaol by Biden-Harris staff.[3121] In March 2021, FRSO launched its Spring Fund raising drive of $100,000-plus required for its "great leap forward" with the following violent pitch:

> "Over the past year, Freedom Road Socialist Organization has undergone a period of dramatic growth, and we have emerged as one of the largest revolutionary organizations in the United States…

... To continue this pace of development we need your help. We are going to establish a national office and we are going to have some full-time staff who are devoted to building FRSO. We will increase our capacity to build a revolutionary movement that is capable of engaging the class enemy and waging a serious fight for working class political power: socialism.

To do this takes money and everyone can play a role in this. Urge your comrades and friends to give all that they can to the FRSO Spring Fundraising drive. Congress and the president just approved stimulus checks for most of us. Please consider contributing your stimulus check to FRSO...

... Some people say real change is impossible. **Burning police stations and millions of people in the streets this past year suggest otherwise.** We want to abolish capitalism and replace it with socialism. This is not some dream; it can be a reality if we work – and fight – for it.

To do that we need to expand the fighting capacity of FRSO. Your the contributions, the bigger the better, will help us do exactly that. Go to donate at https://frso.org/.

Great [burning] things are ahead!
The future is [burning] bright!
Contribute to the FRSO Spring Fundraising campaign!"[3122]

Hence, one could sum up Antifa, Freedom Road and the CHOP, with one of the final lines of the1848 Communist Manifesto: "

The Communists disdain to conceal their views and aims. They openly declare that their ends can be attained only by the *forcible overthrow of all existing social conditions.*"[3123]

Such are adults, indoctrinated as kids to hate their country in order to comply with a distorted "WOKE" version of American history, embodied by the toxic *1619 Project*, subservient to the ideological Marxist agenda.[3124] But they are not just rioting on the streets. They also dominate the global MSM, as implied by retired police Sergeant Betsy Smith, a 29-year veteran of a large metropolitan police department in Chicago, who now represents the National Police Association in the US. She talks of how the media are currently spending a great deal of time talking about the U.S. Capitol breach but not enough on violent riots perpetrated by Antifa and others.[3125]

> "Right now, their current obsession is, you know, white supremacy, white supremacists, and the Capitol riot. They don't want to talk about the other 99 percent of violent riots that American law enforcement has been dealing with for the past year."[3126]

Nevertheless, in the first presidential debate in late September 2020, Biden made the assertion that the decentralised[3127] Antifa entity was "only an idea."[3128] But within hours of his "inauguration," these "only an idea" leftist extremist anarchists were out of control, in spite of Biden and Harris staff repeatedly bailing them out in the summer.[3129] This of course is what happens when you think you can control pure unbridled malevolence. Indeed, it makes one think of mid-1934 in the Third Reich, when Hitler ordered the *"Nacht der Langen Messer,"* (Night of the Long Knives) to eliminate Ernst Röhm's Brown Shirt thugs or Storm Troopers, which had become uncontrollable and a threat to his hold on power, in spite of being a crucial element in his rise to power in late January 1933.[3130] As the Biden regime is presently ignoring acts of terrorism by Antifa and Freedom Road, Hitler likewise, for seventeen months, ignored the violence perpetrated by Ernst Röhm's Brown Shirts, until President Hindenburg threatened to impose martial law if Hitler didn't reign them in. After Hitler invoked and completed the forty-eight hour bloody purge in late June 1934,[3131] Hindenburg praised Hitler for "nipping treason in the bud."[3132] About one month later, on August 2, the ailing president died,[3133] along with any semblance of government accountability.

To reiterate, in one sense, the global MSM are correct, that on Wednesday January 6, 2021, "Democracy" in America was saved, or indeed, perhaps founded. Such "democracies" in the past have existed such as the German Democratic Republic (former East Germany) and today there is the Lao People's Democratic Republic and the Democratic People's Republic of Korea (North Korea.) In Biden's America, or the America of the new radical Democrats, the Constitutional Republic is under dire threat, as the Constitution of 1789, is incessantly trampled upon. Big-Tech, such as Facebook, Twitter, Google and the like have become self-appointed moral arbiters, even able to deny a sitting president his voice, on the knee-jerk hearsay of an agenda driven news media.[3134] At the same time, the self-appointed moral arbiter Twitter, implies that links to child pornography are integral to an "open Internet."[3135]

Much of Trump's speech on January 6th before the riot was taken out of context, with quotes such as "fight like hell." However before the election, when Biden let slip "We have put together I think the most extensive and inclusive voter fraud organisation in the history of American politics,"[3136] Facebook "fact" checkers, or more accurately, Chinese Tik Tok funded spin doctors *Lead Stories*,[3137] claim he was "taken out of context."[3138] Of course, this raises the question; why are global MSM and Big-Tech so quick to afford such a defence to Biden, but never to Trump?

The legal tool of impeachment, is intended to try an incumbent president. In August 1974 for example,[3139] facing impeachment, Richard Nixon resigned and the matter was finished. But even after Biden's "inauguration" on January 20, 2021, the radical left "Democrat" regime, now more akin to the far-left Democratic Socialists of America (DSA), still pursued this unconstitutional agenda, on the flimsiest of evidence that Donald Trump, in an act of alleged "sedition," incited the riot on January 6th. Nothing in his speech that day, suggested such a thing, but again, Kamala Harris and Joe Biden's staff, bailing out leftist radicals for months,[3140] involved in perpetrating months of burning, pillaging and looting of Democrat run cities, occupying court houses, declaring lawless autonomous zones such as the Seattle CHOP zone are not seditious. Moreover, Kamala Harris in an interview on Stephen Colbert's Late Show in mid-June 2020, proclaimed that:

> "They're not going to stop, they're not going to stop … before and after the election … they're not going to let up and they should not!"[3141]

Furthermore, the dubious pursuit of Trump's impeachment, was an ideal diversion from the real issue of electoral irregularities, in spite of the fact that Trump on several occasions before January 6th, offered to deploy 10,000 National Guard troops.[3142] Nevertheless, on Friday February 12, 2021 at around 6:15 p.m. on Channel 7's evening news in Brisbane Australia, I heard the news reader proclaim the Democrat propaganda of their "*blistering*" impeachment case against Trump. As Harvard Law School professor emeritus Alan Dershowitz stated; "Congressional lawmakers are violating the U.S. Constitution" in what he described as a "show trial" against former President Donald Trump.[3143]

This in spite of the fact that Dershowitz has never voted for Trump.[3144] Moreover, one of the nine Nancy Pelosi (house speaker and Democrat) appointed impeachment managers was Eric Swalwell,[3145] who had been involved in an affair with a Chinese spy,[3146] further devolving the credibility of this pseudo-impeachment to less than a joke.[3147] On February 13th, Trump was acquitted.[3148]

By the time of Biden's "inauguration" on January 20th, it tragically appeared to me that the Democrats and the Deep State had achieved total victory. They had the majority in the Senate, albeit requiring vice-president Harris' vote to break deadlocks, a clear majority in the House of Representatives, and following January 6th, a seemingly interminable pretext to suppress all discussion on voter fraud. However, the way they are acting post "inauguration," including their vindictive and fearful obsession with Trump, exemplified with their farce of an impeachment, and the speed with which they are pushing their far-left agenda forward, including, as already mentioned, the push to de-platform Conservative media networks,[3149] makes one wonder, if they truly believe they have achieved total victory. Something seems to be bugging them. Perhaps this is due to the rampant electoral irregularities, implying fraud on a like scale, not passing entirely unnoticed?

Moreover, according to Mike Lindell's documentary, on election night, Trump broke the Dominion voting machine algorithm,[3150] by attaining large unforeseen leads in battleground states, leading to the unprecedented cessation of voting in the middle of the night, to facilitate the injection of fraudulent ballots shipped in hours later. According to Mike Lindell, these injections of fake ballots, did the trick in decisively increasing Biden's "vote," but the sudden vertical surges in Biden's vote,[3151] could not go unnoticed — as would have been the case if the Dominion algorithm had not been broken by Trump's unexpectedly substantial lead that night in those critical states. Moreover, it's pertinent to note, how pollsters in both the 2016 and 2020 elections, got it so wrong,[3152] and *The Epoch Times'* team of analysts late that night, with reserved confidence, predicted a Trump victory,[3153] as did my own analysis. Furthermore, *The Epoch Times* just before the 2016 election, counter to the entire global/pack MSM, had predicted a Trump victory.[3154]

But already on election night, on the screens of CNN, in the state of Pennsylvania, in the space of just 30 seconds, Trump's vote count dropped from 1,690,589 to 1,670,631, while Biden's rose from 1,252,537 to 1,272,495. In just 30 seconds, this amounted to a drop in votes of 19,958 for Trump, but for Biden, a rise in votes matching the drop for Trump![3155] *The Epoch Times* reporter, Joshua Philipp in his documentary captures this. Given that Pennsylvania hosted the Dominion machines, and Dominion's director of product strategy and "security" is Eric Coomer,[3156] a deep admirer of the violent anarchist and leftist Antifa[3157] and Trump hater,[3158] has to raise grave concerns as to the legitimacy of this election, and hence the claim by the Clinton Foundation, of Dominion facilitating "democracy through technology."[3159]

Furthermore, Eric Coomer in late September 2020, just prior to the commencement of in-person early voting, performed last-minute software updates to thousands of machines in Georgia without the requisite recertification required by law. Coomer, a 1997 radical-left[3160] PHD nuclear engineering graduate from California's Berkeley University,[3161] a hotbed of radical left extremism,[3162] rationalised that "the change is 'minor' and doesn't require recertification."[3163]

On November 19, 2020, the head of Dominion John Poulos, cancelled at the last minute a planned appearance at the Pennsylvania House of Representatives hearing. The following day, Eric Coomer, disappeared and his biography on Dominion's website was removed. Suddenly, with world focus on Dominion and voting fraud, Dominion's offices in Toronto and Denver closed, and over one-hundred of Dominion's employees, one-third of their workforce, including all in Serbia, had their Linked-In accounts deleted.[3164]

And in this light, how suspicious is UBS Securities LLC, on October 8, 2020, less than four weeks before the election, arranging a private placement of $400 million with Staple Street Capital — the parent company of Dominion,[3165] co-run and founded by Joe Biden's brother-in-law Stephen Owens?[3166] According to Bloomberg, three of the four board members of UBS Securities LLC at the time (but not since mid-December 2020) were Chinese,[3167] with at least one of them appearing to reside in Hong Kong.[3168] This prompted Joshua Philipp in his documentary to raise the question; had the CCP, less than a month before the US election, purchased Dominion Voting? And, as raised by *The Jewish Voice*; is Dominion connected to CCP money?[3169] These questions become all the more compelling, when shortly after the election, all information pertaining to Staple Street Capital's founders and their investment portfolios, including their relationship with Dominion, was removed.[3170]

But after January 6th, conservative voices were silenced, or at least severely repressed based on the questionable notion, not fact, reminiscent of 1930s Stalinist show trials,[3171] that all conservatives are fascists, legitimising the closure of alternative social media such as Parler, supposedly being used to foment the sedition of January 6th. However, the fact that Big-Tech platforms such as Twitter, Facebook and YouTube were used almost exclusively for this purpose, is ignored.[3172] Alexandria Ocasio Cortez (AOC), Democrat House of Representative from New York's 14th district,[3173] had before the election drawn up a "list" of Trump supporters to go after post-inauguration.[3174] Clearly AOC, has no concept of the Constitution not allowing the 51% majority to persecute the 49% minority. But then again, for the new radical Democrats, in effect, the Democratic Socialists of America (DSA) — of which AOC is a formal member,[3175] their tacit objective, when one judges them by their actions, is the undermining of the 1789 Constitution. Indeed, dare one dub it a "democracy" of two wolves and a sheep voting on "what's for dinner?"

The above quip has been credited to founding father Benjamin Franklin, although there is no hard evidence to confirm this.[3176] Nevertheless, this does not detract in any way its poignancy for America in early 2021, and no less poignant, is the following from a letter by America's second president and first vice-president,[3177] John Quincy Adams, to John Taylor on December 17, 1814: "

> It is in vain to Say that Democracy is less vain, less proud, less selfish, less ambitious or less avaricious than Aristocracy or Monarchy. It is not true in Fact and no where appears in history. Those Passions are the same in all Men under all forms of Simple Government, and when unchecked, produce the same Effects of *Fraud Violence and Cruelty*. When clear Prospects are opened before Vanity, Pride, Avarice or Ambition, for their easy gratification, it is hard for the most considerate Phylosophers and the most conscientious Moralists to resist the temptation."[3178]

Such is America, just six weeks into the Biden-Harris regime.

Certainly censorship has been virulently invoked by Big-Tech and the Biden-Harris regime. However, their actions have broadened to targets such as the Republican Missouri Senator Josh Hawley, who after only hearing about it in the media, had is his publishing contract for his book *The Tyranny of Big Tech*[3179] with Simon and Schuster cancelled![3180] Hawley, *abiding by federal law*, objected to electoral votes from Arizona and Pennsylvania, pointing to alleged and proven election irregularities and moves from officials to change election processes in contravention to state Constitutions.[3181] On the last Monday night before January 6th, Hawley tweeted the following: "

> Tonight while I was in Missouri, Antifa scumbags came to our place in DC and threatened my wife and newborn daughter, who can't travel. They screamed threats, vandalized, and tried to pound open our door. Let me be clear: My family & I will not be intimidated by leftwing violence."[3182]

Which raises the question; would the Biden-Harris regime deem this incident as domestic terrorism, or just dismiss as an "idea," the violent leftist-anarchist entity that is Antifa?

On the Sunday night following Biden's "inauguration," I was watching a documentary on marine archaeology in the Black Sea on SBS Australia. Twice during advert breaks, there were short so-called "news" clips. They centred around asserting as fact, the prediction that Biden was going to heal and unite America and his presidency was the "dawn of a new era." To begin with, how can the nation heal when the infection of the festering wound, namely rampant election irregularities is ignored? And what wound has Trump inflicted in any case? Perhaps the exposure of the sewer that is the Deep State of Washington DC? Secondly, when Trump was elected in November 2016, the Democrats, at the behest of the bitter loser, Hilary Clinton, commenced a relentless four year witch hunt of Trump's supposed collusion with Russia in the election. Nevertheless, in spite of the limitless resources of the FBI, they found nothing![3183]

On the other hand, look how much evidence was uncovered on electoral fraud, in just over two months, in spite of the abject lack of will by the FBI and the Department of Justice to investigate it. As Republican Texas Attorney General Ken Paxton affirmed when filing the Texas law suit against states such as Pennsylvania, illegally and unconstitutionally changing their federal electoral laws just before the November election: "

> Our country stands at an important crossroads. Either the Constitution matters and must be followed, even when some officials consider it inconvenient or out of date, or is simply a piece of parchment on display at the National Archives. We ask the [Supreme] court to choose the former."[3184]

Regrettably, by refusing to hear the case and give a reason as to why, the feckless Supreme Court clearly implied that the Constitution, in their eyes, with America at its greatest ever crossroads in history, does not matter.[3185] [xxxviii] Hence, the Biden-Harris regime, elected under a cloud of fraud and the tacit support of extreme leftist rioters; the latter of whom, seemingly all too intimidating for a weak Supreme Court,[3186] and the contrived Russian collusion from 2016, implies that no leftist has any right to order American Patriots to move on.[3187] Moreover, Hilary Clinton back in August 2020, instructed Biden to not concede the election "under any circumstances."[3188]

Leftist "unity" of rampant censorship of Conservatives, can only mean "unity" by submission of half the population. Indeed, I have heard many liberal/progressive analysts and speakers on the global MSM, such as Katie Couric, talk of the need for Trump supporters to be deprogrammed![3189] Indeed, is this just one aspect of the "dawn of a new era?" Orwellian monitoring of our thoughts? Is Biden's executive order for America to rejoin the Paris Climate Accord,[3190] another such aspect? Well, Trump, without joining the globalist accord, has in the term of his presidency, dramatically decreased America's CO_2 emissions, while China's, as a so-called "developing" country, continue to sky rocket.[3191] Is this yet another aspect of the "dawn of a new era?" Putting America last? Given all the above, is it not more like the descent of an era of Orwellian darkness?

The extreme left in America would have one believe they are the antithesis of Hitler's National Socialism. However, both extremes have what I term "agendas of exclusion." For example, the Stalinist perpetrated Katyń Wood massacre of April 1940 in western Russia, was the calculated and deliberate murder of a nation's [Poland's] elite, simultaneously embodying classicide, with the intention of obliterating its political and creative energy for the future.[3192] One could indeed infer this as mirroring in a microcosm, the agenda of the CCP under Mao Zedong in his Cultural Revolution from the mid-1960s to mid-1970s.[3193]

Poland of course during WWII suffered to at the hands of the National Socialists, as was exemplified in the massacre in Warsaw's

---

[xxxviii] As to the possible motives of the US Supreme Court, see the transcript of an interview conducted by Attorney Lin Wood of Ryan D. White on Saturday January 9, 2021 at https://www.scribd.com/embeds/497646937/content. Search for key terms such as "Supreme," "Roberts" and "Pence" to name a few. Accessed on Sunday March 14, 2021.

south-eastern district of Wawer in late December 1939, just three months into the German occupation of Poland. Then, over a hundred Poles were massacred in response to fatal shootings of two German soldiers by two escaped common Polish criminals. The will of the Germans to track down the perpetrators was almost non-existent, but their will for indiscriminate and disproportionate retribution on the perceived Slavic Untermensch was inexorable.[3194] Then, from August 1 until October 2, 1944, during the Warsaw General Uprising, the Poles suffered at the hands of both extremes, as the Soviet Army, on the eastern doorstep of Warsaw, after encouraging the Poles to rise up, allowed the Germans virtually unhindered action in brutally suppressing the Rising of the non-communist Polish Home Army and civilian population in general.[3195]

To reiterate, just after the US 2020 election, Alexandria Ocasio Cortez (AOC), U.S. House of Representative from New York's 14th district,[3196] had drawn up a list of post-inauguration retribution for Trump supporters, "legitimised" under the leftist banner of the "Trump Accountability Project."[3197] Such is "leftist democracy," which to reaffirm, is especially so for an American "Democratic" party subverted so far left, it's now more akin to the radical left Democratic Socialists of America (DSA),[3198] of which AOC is also a formal member.[3199]

For Hitler's Third Reich, the most obvious targets for exclusion were of course the Jews, naturally extending to others deemed by the regime as not worthy of life, such as gypsies and the physically and mentally disabled. This was ramped up in August 1939, just preceding the outbreak of war, in what became known as the infamous T-4 program.[3200] Do I exaggerate for America in early 2021? Perhaps, but the Biden-Harris regime at the time of writing is just shy of two months old.

From the liberal/progressive point of view, ignoring the mountain of evidence of electoral irregularities, and the assumption of a supposedly diverse and non-agenda driven free media, there is the "self-evident" notion that Dietrich in this election, would have undoubtedly supported Biden. His support of Trump being unthinkable. However, as Ferdinand Schlingensiepen alluded to in his 2015 article, such assumptions would be presumptuous at best. From the religious aspect, I cannot see how Dietrich could turn a blind eye to Biden and his regime's support of abortion. On the political side, I cannot see how a sharp and perceptive mind like Dietrich, and indeed Ruth's cousin Ewald von Kleist,[3201] could ignore the parallel of January 6, 2021 with the Reichstag fire in late February 1933, followed by the rank intimidation of the Weimar election of March 5, 1933[3202] in parallel with the intimidation of Republican observers in the election of November 2020,[3203] and intimidation of witnesses of fraud in its aftermath.[3204] Moreover, could they ignore the rank bias of the modern-day global MSM, mirroring in so many respects, the media of Berlin and Moscow of the 1930s?

The intransigence and lack of critical thinking of liberals/progressives in the US and indeed globally, to acknowledge the self-evident violence and intimidation of radical leftist entities in the US, such as Antifa and Freedom Road; the ubiquity of rampant electoral irregularities and intimidation; the incessant violation of the US Constitution by the Biden-Harris regime in just its first six weeks in office, and the ideologically driven pack-journalism of global MSM, recalls for myself, the following.[3205] In September 2014, I was with my wife in a tour group in Nuremberg in Northern Bavaria. While visiting the now abandoned National Socialist Rally grounds, our German guide recalled a story his father had told him of a conversation, or more to the point, a confrontation he had with his father (the guide's grandfather).

It was 1969, and the then young man desired to know about the war, as German history of that time in schools and society in general was hardly ever spoken about. It seemed that the Germans consigned that period to an historical vacuum. However, the generation post-war, now grown up, much to the chagrin of their parents, could not leave this dark epoch of German history consigned to the vacuum of repressed memories. When the son pressed his father on this subject once too often, the father exploded and told him if he ever raised this topic again, he would be thrown out of the house.

Just two years preceding this incident, in Munich in 1967, Eberhard Bethge first published his biography of his dear friend Dietrich Bonhoeffer.[3206] It was only then that German people seemed willing to admit the truth of Hitler's Germany. Even then, given the account of our guide in Nuremberg by the city's infamous Third Reich rally grounds, it was more the younger generation born around or soon after the war's end that was willing to hear the confronting and uncomfortable truth of the infamous Third Reich. Our guide, the second generation post-war, was forthright in his criticism of Hitler's Germany. While we were standing at the rally grounds, he spent time describing the rallies to us, regularly holding up a folder of copies of photos from the rallies.

This modern-day liberal/progressive intransigence, in concert with the actions of the Biden-Harris regime and the global MSM, seems to imply their notion that Dietrich would only condemn or acknowledge right-wing violence. However, such a notion is dubious at best, as one need only look at the following letter written by a young Dietrich just

before his thirteenth birthday in January 1919, to his Oma (Grandmother)[3207] in Tübingen. He wrote it during the chaos in Berlin in the wake of the Great War, when equally violent right- and left-wing groups clashed among themselves, and with government troops trying to preserve some semblance of law and order. In this letter, Dietrich describes the fighting between government troops and radical leftist Spartacists, after the latter had made two night-time attacks on the Halensee station:
"

> Early today we heard gunfire. There are some bangs going on now. Karl-Friedrich [the eldest of the Bonhoeffer siblings — he was wounded but survived both wars] has at last been discharged from the Charité [the hospital where father Karl worked]. He would like to be part of this somehow, but Mama and Papa do not yet agree. *At present, thank heaven, the government troops are getting the better of it.* Our holidays have been extended to 17 January. Either because of the unrest or because of the coal shortage."[3208]

Moreover for Ruth and her Junker clan, one need just recall numerous instances from Chapter 25 "Old Prussia Gone With The Wind" and Chapter 26 "Oma Ruth's Progeny After Death" of this book to emphasise their cognisance and acknowledgement of the twin evils of both political extremes. For example, Ruth's eldest child Hans Jürgen, postwar, spent three months in Moscow's infamous Lubyanka prison, followed by nineteen months of hard labour in a Siberian gulag.[3209] Ironically, he, the anti-fascist, had escaped physical torture at the hands of the fascists,[3210] but not from the champions of the so-called workers' anti-fascist utopia. Furthermore, for liberals/progressives who may think a collective crackdown and/or deprogramming of Conservatives is imperative for the preservation of "democracy," the story of pastor and friend of Dietrich, Martin Niemöller, a concentration camp inmate from 1938-1945, is a chilling wake-up call: "

> First they came for the Socialists, and I did not speak out — because I was not a Socialist.
> Then they came for the Trade Unionists, and I did not speak out — because I was not a Trade Unionist. Then they came for the Jews, and I did not speak out — because I was not a Jew. And then they came for me — and there was no one left to speak for me."[3211]

Originally incarcerated at the Sachsenhausen camp near Berlin, Niemöller would be transferred to Dachau in Bavaria in 1941, where he would stay until almost war's end, before being liberated in Niederdorf in the German speaking South Tyrol region of northern Italy in late April 1945.[3212] Born in 1892, he would live out his life post-war in West Germany, becoming, for some time, the vice-chairman of War Resisters International,[3213] before passing away in 1984. For Jeff Stein, the author of the aforementioned Daily Beast article proposing the formation of an American Secret Police,[3214] the words of Martin Niemöller, are way beyond just essential reading. As is the following by the Spanish-American philosopher, essayist, poet, and novelist George Santayana,[3215] inscribed on a tablet at Poland's Auschwitz Concentration Camp Museum:

> "The one who does not remember history is bound to live through it again."[3216]

Moreover, on the night of May 2, 2021, near the end of the Live Q & A chat of Joshua Philipp's YouTube Crossroads channel, the Polish political refugee Zygmunt (Ziggy) Staszewski wrote: "I grew up in communist Poland, living under censorship for 29 years then became a political prisoner. Came to US as political refugee. I am scared now."[3217]

To reiterate, when I think of Dietrich in relation to America in 2020-21, I think of him in the aftermath of the passing in the Reichstag of the infamous Malicious Practices and Enabling acts, providing the judicial and constitutional means respectively, to wipe the Weimar Republic from existence. Likewise, as Biden and his leftist cabal incessantly trample on the American Constitution, including farcical impeachments of private citizens, the Constitutional Republic, is likewise being wiped from existence — unless, unlike Weimar 1933, enough people speak up! As indeed Dietrich, his family and Ruth and her brave Junker clan did. And enough people explore at least the idea of independent news media alternatives and alternative search engines such as the French search engine Qwant.xxxix

For example, after listening to the diatribe from the global MSM at my mate's place, claiming that Trump definitively incited the riot on January 6, 2021, when I got home, I listened to the truth from the independent media *The Epoch Times*. Moreover, given this distor-

---

xxxix https://www.qwant.com.

tion of the truth by the global MSM, on what Trump said on January 6th, has to bring into question, the veracity of claims by the global MSM, that electoral fraud allegations were baseless. As do their years of saturation bombing the false narrative of Trump's Russian collusion.[3218] Add to which, two House Democrats in late February 2021, pressuring TV Carriers to cease hosting Conservative channels such as Fox, OAN (One America News), and Newsmax.[3219] Indeed, what could be a clearer indication of the Biden-Harris regime's agenda of turning America into a one-party "Democratic" Socialist state? Is this the "democracy" that was "saved," or more to the point, founded on January 6, 2021? As a Newsmax spokesperson wrote by email to *The Epoch Times*: "

> The House Democrats' attack on free speech and basic First Amendment rights should send chills down the spines of all Americans. Newsmax reported fairly and accurately on allegations and claims made by both sides during the recent election contest. We did not see that same balanced coverage when CNN and MSNBC pushed for years the Russian collusion hoax, airing numerous claims and interviews with Democrat leaders that turned out to be patently false."[3220]

And in an email from FOX: "

> As the most watched cable news channel throughout 2020, FOX News Media provided millions of Americans with in-depth reporting, breaking news coverage and clear opinion. For individual members of Congress to highlight political speech they do not like and demand cable distributors engage in viewpoint discrimination sets a terrible precedent." [3221] [Such as Trump's words on January 6th "fight like hell" taken out of context.]

And by email from One America News President Charles Herring: "

> We stand by our reporting and don't let intimidation influence our newsroom. When government officials want to silence media, especially media that opposes their false narratives, it's nothing short of an attack on our democracy and freedom of press. Media shines a light on wrongdoing and helps keep our government officials in check. Discussion and debate are healthy for our country. This call by government officials for

media censorship is expected from dictators and countries such as China, but it's horrifying to see its ugly head pop up in our U.S. Congress."[3222]

As America heads to effectively one media voice, does it not mirror the death throes of Weimar Germany when the "Malicious Practices" and "Enabling" acts were passed on the 21st and 23rd March 1933?[3223] Yes, American media would still have "multiple" voices of sorts, but they would all espouse the same ideologically driven agenda. Like indeed Communist China, where multiple outlets present the façade of media diversity, such as Global Times, Xinhua, CGTN and the like,[3224] but naturally, all proclaim the very same ideologically driven agenda, subservient to the genocidal CCP.[3225] In that sense, the media of China, and the path American media is now taking, is not essentially different to the mono-voice of the former Soviet Union or the present day "Democratic" People's Republic of Korea. As Alan Dershowitz, Harvard Law School professor emeritus and lifelong Democrat supporter who has never voted for Trump[3226] stated:

> "I hope all Americans wake up to this," Dershowitz told Newsmax on Thursday. "I hope it's not just the 'shoe is on the other foot' test. Now, the conservatives are the victims of cancel culture so they're big supporters of the Constitution and constitutional rights. During McCarthyism [of the 1950s], it was the left that were the victims, and the right were the oppressors."

Going further, he stated that:

> "we need both the right, the left, and also the center to stand united against censorship, against cancel culture, and in favor of the marketplace of ideas."

> "We have the right to flip the channel if we don't like what's on Newsmax. Change the channel, but don't tell the carriers, the satellite carriers, and the cable carriers, to deny us the right to watch Newsmax. That is wrong," he remarked.[3227]

The Epoch Times were founded by Falun Gong practitioners who fled China for America on account of the heinous oppression perpetrated upon them by the CCP since July 20, 1999.[3228] Now ironically, in the "free" country of America, their multi-cultural staff report the truth in the face of an ideologically driven mass-media of pack journalism,[3229] which to reiterate, mirrors in so many respects, that of Berlin and Moscow of the 1930s, and indeed, modern-day Beijing. Mainstream media inevitably use the old foil of portraying them as far-right, but after years of studying Communism and National Socialism, and viewing with my own eyes, almost two metric tons of human hair at the Auschwitz Concentration Camp Museum in Poland in mid-2005, I do not require an agenda driven pack global media, masquerading as diverse free media, telling me what's far-right. On the other hand, feigned incognisance of far-left accountability by global MSM reporters, literally amidst the burning and devastation of the 2020 summer riots, claiming that such "protesters" were mostly peaceful, is breathtaking.[3230] As is their synonymous and inexorable hypocrisy.[3231]

Moreover, loads of *The Epoch Times* footage from the peaceful Jericho marches in Washington DC on December 12, 2020, where hundreds of thousands participated, as global MSM played down their numbers, and indeed from January 6th, among the vast majority of 0.5 million peaceful Trump supporters who did not participate in the riot, people came from all walks of life and ethnicities. During the December 12, 2020 march, I saw on the *NTD* channel, sister media of *The Epoch Times*, a black couple proudly declare they were Trump supporters and that Trump was not a racist, but Biden was,[3232] and that Black Lives Matter (BLM) were a terrorist organisation.[3233] Curiously, in mid-September 2020, BLM from their website took down their "What We Believe" page with all its overt implications of its Marxist agenda, which included disruption of the traditional nuclear family unit. However, it can still be accessed on the WayBack machine.[3234] Not to mention, one of their founding members, Patrisse Cullors stating:

> "We are trained Marxists super versed on, sort of, ideological theories."[3235]

Certainly, the black American couple from the December 2020 Jericho march, are not alone in their assessment. For example, Barbara Heineback, a black American now living in Wollongong Australia, who was a press officer to the wife of Democrat President Jimmy Carter and an advisor to Democrat President Bill Clinton, and 1960s civil rights activist,[3236] stated that; "Donald Trump is being destroyed by vested interests in Washington and Black Lives Matter is a menace."[3237][xl] On Australian Sky News on November 4, 2020[3238] she categorically stated that Trump was not racist, citing for example, the numerous contestants of varying ethnicity that appeared on his show *The Apprentice*. Of course, this is just her opinion, but her views are certainly no less valid than saturation bombing assertions of Trump's perceived racism, and as such, are not fact, as global MSM wish us to perceive them. Moreover, as affirmed by Lara Logan, the South African born and former CBS 60 Minutes and now self-professed "outlaw" journalist; "They're not journalists. They're political assassins, working on behalf of political operatives and propagandists."[3239]

Moreover, the Black American, Vernon Jones, Democrat member of the House of Representatives, likewise believes electoral fraud was rampant,[3240] and voted for Trump in the 2020 election, owing to the Democrats overt shift to the radical left, as indicated by their tacit approval of the summer riots. Clearly, America in 2020-21, is more about ideology than race.[3241]

Starting with the death of George Floyd in late May 2020, I have witnessed events unfold in America in an eerie and frightening parallel with the death throes of Weimar Germany, as documented in the Preface "Birth and Memory upon the Lesser Known Fault Line of History" (in regard to the Röhm Purge of mid-1934)[3242] and Chapter 3 "Evil's Storm Descends" and Chapter 4 "The Aryan Paragraph" of this book. Couple this with the coronavirus, as terrible as it was, raising to some extent at least, awareness of the rank despotism of the Chinese Communist Party — not just in relation to their cover-up of the virus,[3243] but the genocide, forced sterilisation and abortion of the Uyghurs, and the religious persecution and forced human organ harvesting

---

[xl] It's worth noting that contrary to the BLM/leftist/progressive agenda, slavery was not something unique to the US or western civilisation in general. See https://www.youtube.com/watch?v=CDltQlrU5nE titled *Black History MYTHS Promoted by the Left* and https://www.youtube.com/watch?v=VWrfjUzYvPo titled *THE REAL HISTORY OF SLAVERY* as told by the distinguished Black American historian Thomas Sowell. Moreover, the Muslim slave trade started long before the European slave trade and continued long after. See Larry Elder's video titled *What Most 'Experts' Aren't Telling You During Black History Month* at https://www.youtube.com/watch?v=LwUbx6Y1Zgo or https://rumble.com/vctcb9-what-most-experts-arent-telling-you-during-black-history-month-larry-elder-.html from 2 minutes and 40 seconds in.

of Falun Gong practitioners. Under Xi Jinping however, religious persecution and bastardisation of all religions in China, both western and traditional, now has a parallel with Dietrich when he commenced in early 1933, his battle with the National Socialists, over the integrity of his Lutheran faith.[3244]

In concluding this chapter, I wish to dedicate it to all the brave American men and women who came forward in attempting to alert their country, and indeed the world, to the rampant and unaddressed electoral irregularities, threatening the very fabric of their constitutional republic. Legal professionals such as Rudy Giuliani, Jenna Ellis, Lin Wood, Sidney Powell and Senators Josh Hawley and Ted Cruz who put their reputations and careers on the line for their country. Just weeks before writing, Lin Wood declared he would represent Sidney Powell in her defence against the law suite from Dominion Voting, whose voting machines have been mired in controversy from the election's fall-out. In his letter to Dominion in mid-February 2021, he affirmed the following: "

> Last night, I was honored when Sidney Powell called me and asked me to serve as lead counsel for her in defending the frivolous defamation lawsuit filed against her by Dominion.
>
> I quickly accepted. Get ready to rumble, Dominion. You made a mistake suing Sidney. You are going to pay a heavy price.
>
> Sidney and I will not be intimidated. We will not go quietly in the night.
>
> Hey Dominion, I will see you and your employees and officers soon as truth is pursued and established. I will see you across the table where you will be subjected to a thorough and sifting cross-examination under oath. I know how to deal with legal bullies like you.
>
> Check my record.
>
> I love Sidney Powell. I admired her brilliance, skills, and tenacity from a distance as I watched her fight a corrupt system to achieve justice for a great American, Lt. General Mike Flynn.

Sidney is a truth-giver. She also shares my love for God. As does General Flynn who is also a truth-giver.

I have had the privilege to work with Sidney and General Flynn over the past recent months. They are great Americans. They are role models for many.

God blessed me with their friendship."[3245]

In an article published June 22, 2010 and updated December 6, 2017, the global MSM mouthpiece the Huffington Post, wrote a damning article on Dominion.[3246] Then, in a December 2019 letter to Toronto based Dominion Voting Systems, Democrat Senators Elizabeth Warren, Ron Wyden, and Amy Klobuchar and congressman Mark Pocan warned about reports of machines "switching votes," "undisclosed vulnerabilities," and "improbable" results that "threaten the integrity of our elections."[3247] Even in the months just preceding the November 2020 election, there are documented cases of grave concerns over the Dominion machines.[3248] Nevertheless, according to the global MSM and the Democratic Party, just following the November 2020 election, Dominion machines had suddenly acquired impregnable security[3249] that according to the Cybersecurity and Infrastructure Security Agency (CISA), delivered the "most secure election in US history."[3250]

However, in the following month of December 2020, a nationwide hack, going back months of US computers using the Solar Winds platform, was revealed.[3251] When Trump mentioned the possibility that voting machines may have been breached during the election, Dominion were quick to deny ever using Solar Winds.[3252] The thing is, even though the Solar Winds logo is no longer present on the Dominion login page,[3253] it's still visible from an archived copy dated December 14, 2020.[3254] As well, Dominion still have the Solar Winds logo itself present on that server, at the time of writing in mid-May 2021.[3255] Hence, making a mockery of CISA's claim back in November 2020, that they delivered the "most secure election in US history."[3256]

Moreover, Dominion is a member of CISA's Election Infrastructure Sector Coordinating Council,[3257] and in October 2019, the Dominion machines failed to meet the standards required by the Texas Election Code.[3258] To which, it's worth noting, the trouble free counting of votes in the Lone Star state. Hence, given what one would envisage as a resolute and robust defence of Sidney Powell, coupled with a rigorous cross-examination of Dominion witnesses by Lin Wood, this case may shed much needed light on the question of changing narratives of the global MSM and Democratic Party in regard to Dominion. Namely, which of their narratives of Dominion are true? Their pre-election or post-election version? Likewise, Dominion's suit against, but still welcomed by Conservative billionaire Mike Lindell.[3259]

And of course, to the thousands of ordinary people, such as Michigan's Melissa Carone,[3260] who signed affidavits on penalty of perjury (which according to the most basic tenants of law, in spite of incessant assertions to the contrary by global MSM and Democrats, are evidence)[3261] and came forward as witnesses, in spite of intimidation, death threats, ostracism, termination of employment and the like.[3262] To *The Epoch Times*, for reasons just mentioned and people such as the independent journalist Andy Ngo, who has literally risked life and limb to report the truth of thuggery, intimidation, burning and general destruction that defines the ultra-extremist leftist/anarchist radicals that are Antifa.

To the gregarious and self-made billionaire and CEO of "My Pillow," Mike Lindell,[3263] who has stood resolute and determined in the face of censorship.[3264] And to the president who achieved the highest number of votes ever for a sitting president in the November 2020 election,[3265] Donald John Trump, the nemesis of globalists[3266] and broker of the historic peace agreements between Israel and Arab-Muslim countries, including the United Arab Emirates, the Kingdom of Bahrain, and Sudan,[3267] and architect of American energy independence from the Middle East who exposed the sewer of corruption that are the career politicians and Deep State bureaucrats of Washington DC,[xli] this chapter

---

[xli] The sewer of corruption that are many of the career politicians of Washington DC include both Democrats and Republicans — such as RINOs — "Republicans In Name Only." NOTE: Trump, unlike Biden, is not a career politician. Hence, the huge appeal of Trump for so many of the common people, but at the same time, the virulent and irrational hatred he generates for the establishment. Moreover, why has this hatred for Trump only manifested itself when he announced his intention to run for President in June 2015? See https://www.thegatewaypundit.com/2020/06/five-years-ago-today-donald-announced-historic-run-president-watch-media-mocked/, which recalls when the global MSM mocked what proved to be his successful bid for the US presidency. Curiously, I found this link on the French search engine Qwant at https://www.qwant.com — not Google. Both links accessed on Saturday March 6, 2021.

is dedicated to you, as your accomplishments transcend the attempts by the Deep State leftist-cabal to rewrite history.[xlii]

[xlii] https://web.archive.org/web/20210120151726/https://www.whitehouse.gov/trump-administration-accomplishments/ Note; the Biden administration removed this article from the White House website by January 23, 2021, just three days following Biden's "inauguration." See
https://web.archive.org/web/20210123094108/https://www.whitehouse.gov/trump-administration-accomplishments/ and
https://web.archive.org/web/*/https://www.whitehouse.gov/trump-administration-accomplishments/. In regard to the Middle East, compare it at the end of Trump's presidency in January 2021 to the chaos under the Obama administration when ISIS was running rampant. And under Biden in May 2021, the terror attacks in Israel from Iranian funded terror groups such as Hezbollah and Hamas. See for example https://www.gatestoneinstitute.org/17350/biden-upcoming-iran-deal and https://www.gatestoneinstitute.org/17364/iran-proxy-war-israel. All links accessed on Saturday May 15, 2021.

Polish WWII Supplement I

The Molotov-Ribbentrop Pact

The greatest criminal conspiracy of the 20th century.[3268]

On the evening of May 3, 1939,[3269] the commissariat building in Moscow was surrounded by NKVD (Stalin's secret police) troops. The following morning, Vyacheslav Molotov, accompanied by Lavrenti Beria, the dreaded deputy head of the NKVD[3270] and Stalin's fellow Georgian,[3271] had informed the Jew, Maxim Litvinov, that he had been removed as the commissar of foreign affairs. Litvinov would be replaced by Molotov, who later recalled Stalin telling him to "purge the ministry of Jews." In what was a violation of the official Soviet policy to reject anti-Semitism[3272] and a reflection of the rising anti-Semitism in the Soviet Union,[3273] Molotov recalled in his old age that he was more than happy to comply.[3274] For Hitler, Stalin's anti-Semitic move of removing the overtly anti-Nazi Maxim Litvinov[3275] suggested Stalin's interest in talking about an anti-aggression pact with Hitler. But Stalin had been trying to form a triple alliance with Britain and France since April 15, and so, he kept German approaches at arm's length.[3276] However, by mid-August of 1939, Stalin's patience with the democracies of Britain and France had worn thin, although he was still negotiating with a low-level Anglo-French military delegation in Moscow.[3277]

On Friday August 18, 1939, on Berlin's Wilhelmstrasse, an economic agreement had been successfully concluded with the visiting Soviet economic mission.[3278] It was to be formally signed at noon the following day.[3279] At the time, Hilter's foreign minister, Joachim von Ribbentrop, was with Hitler at his Berghof in the Obersalzberg retreat in Bavaria, and wasted no time in cabling Friedrich-Werner Graf von der Schulenburg,[3280] the German ambassador in Moscow, proposing his immediate departure for Moscow, armed with full powers from the Führer.[3281] Ribbentrop elaborated further: "

> I should also be in a position to sign a special protocol regulating the interests of both parties in questions of foreign policy of one kind or another; for instance, the settlement of spheres of interest in the Baltic area. Such a settlement will only be possible, however, in an oral discussion. Please emphasise that

German foreign policy has today reached a historic turning point.... Please press for a rapid realisation of my journey and oppose any fresh Russian objections. In this connection you must keep in mind the decisive fact that an early outbreak of open German-Polish conflict is possible and that we, therefore, have the greatest interest in having my visit to Moscow take place immediately."[3282]

The reason for Ribbentrop's urgency was Hitler's desire to invade Poland with a Soviet guarantee of non-aggression towards Germany. Hence, the Molotov-Ribbentrop pact, also known as the German-Soviet Non-aggression Pact, or other variants, highlights the theme of non-aggression between the Soviet Union and the Third Reich.[3283] It contained the controversial Secret Additional Protocol, whereby Hitler and Stalin would agree to the carve-up of Eastern Europe. Hence Ribbentrop's reference to "the settlement of spheres of interest."

By noon of Saturday August 19 1939, with the signing of the trade agreement to take place, the tension in Berlin and the Berghof was palpable. Dr. Schnurre in Berlin had reported to Hitler that while the trade agreement had already been agreed to the day before, the Soviet delegation was now stalling over signing it. When they phoned him at noon, they gave the excuse that they had to await instructions from Moscow.[3284] In Schurre's mind, it was clear that the Soviet delegation had received instructions from Moscow to delay the signing of the trade agreement for political reasons.[3285] He was proven right before the evening was out; the following telegram from Schulenburg was received at 7:10 p.m. at the Berghof. "

> The Soviet Government agree to the Reich Foreign Minister coming to Moscow one week after the announcement of the signature of the economic agreement. Molotov stated that if the conclusion of the economic agreement is made public tomorrow, the Reich Foreign Minister could arrive in Moscow on August 26 or 27. Molotov handed me a draft of a nonaggression pact. A detailed account of the two conversations I had with Molotov today, as well as the text of the Soviet draft, follows by telegram at once."[3286]

On the face of it, Hitler got what he wanted: the Soviet government would receive his foreign minister in Moscow for negotiations and finalising of a non-aggression pact. The problem was, with Hitler's invasion of Poland looming ever closer, the weekend of the 26th to 27th was too close to Y Day,[3287] the planned day of invasion. Ultimately, it was Friday September 1 1939,[3288] but on August 19, it was planned for just before dawn on Saturday 26 August,[3289] when Abwehr operatives in civilian clothes [3290] crossed into Poland in order to capture the Jablunkova (Jabłonkowski) Pass tunnel and the train station in the nearby town of Mosty,[3291] near the Czech and Slovak borders.[xliii] However, when Hitler was informed of the signing of the Anglo-Polish military alliance,[3292] with the French ambassador also indicating that his country was willing to fight with Poland,[3293] he aborted the planned invasion for the 26th, but not before the Abwehr operatives had crossed the border and engaged the Polish 21st Mountain Division (21 DPG), before beating a retreat back.[3294]

Hence, no time was wasted in cabling Schulenburg, and instructing him to request they receive Ribbentrop on Tuesday 22 August, or at the latest, the 23rd.[3295] Hitler even stepped in and wrote a personal appeal to Stalin to receive Ribbentrop in Moscow.[3296] On the 22nd, one day after the talks broke down with France and Britain,[3297] Moscow revealed that Ribbentrop would visit Stalin the next day.[3298] On the 21st, the signing of the economic agreement in Berlin was also made public.[3299] For Stalin, the trade treaty was more important than the non-aggression pact, probably because Stalin wanted benefits up front before the inevitable conflict.[3300]

Just after midday on the 23rd, a German delegation of forty in two Focke-Wulf Condors touched down at Moscow's Khodynka airfield, following a five hour flight from Königsberg (now the Russian enclave city of Kaliningrad)[3301] in East Prussia. Each aircraft contained around twenty officials, made up of advisors, translators, diplomats and photographers, including Heinrich Hoffmann, Hitler's personal photog-

---

[xliii] This region was in the coal rich Teschen (Polish: Cieszyn and Czech: Těšín) district in what had been Czech Silesia. See *Ustawa z dnia 27 października 1938 r. o podziale administracyjnym i tymczasowej organizacji administracji na obszarze Ziem Odzyskanych Śląska Cieszyńskiego* at https://www.sbc.org.pl/dlibra/show-content/publication/edition/6949?id=6949 *Dziennik Ustaw Śląskich* (Journal of Silesian Laws), Katowice, nr 18/1938, poz. 35. 31 October 1938, retrieved 28 December 2019. This territory, with a large ethnic Polish minority, was seized by Poland during the 1938 September-October Czech-Sudeten crisis, which over nineteen years earlier, in January 1919, had been seized by the Czechs from Poland in the one week Czech-Polish War. See endnotes [3397] to [3403] for this supplement for more information on this episode.

rapher.[3302] The party was led by the nervous, but vain and pompous Ribbentrop,[3303] making copious notes as he endured the flight. Meanwhile, Hoffman, the man who introduced Hitler to his mistress Eva Braun,[3304] lived up to his title of "Reichssäufer" (Reich drunkard),[3305] sleeping through the entire flight, after a night of merriment the evening before in Königsberg.

For the delegation in general, Moscow had a feel of intriguing ambivalence about it. As the Soviet capital, it was geographically and ideologically far removed from all they knew, laden with sinister political connotations as the home of proletarian revolution — the fountainhead of world communism.[3306] Now fate was leading them to the capital of a nation they had perceived as the enemy of European culture.[3307] Indeed, the enmity between Fascism and Communism had defined the thirties and twenties in Europe, but within hours of the German delegation touching down in Moscow, this alliance of strange bedfellows would be rationalised in Moscow and Berlin by dint of ideological acrobatics.[3308]

When the German delegation exited their aircraft, it became clear that a substantial welcome had been arranged, as both the airfield and its two-storey terminal building were bedecked with German and Soviet flags, the swastika juxtaposed with the hammer and sickle, a sight that Heinrich Hoffmann, like many others, had considered inconceivable only days before. The Soviet authorities had encountered considerable difficulty in finding sufficient swastika banners for the purpose; they finally requisitioned them from local film studios, where, ironically, they had recently been used for anti-National Socialist propaganda films.[3309] Unlike the inauspicious acknowledgement of the low-level Anglo-French mission, the welcome for the German delegation was resounding. As they stepped from the aircraft, a Soviet military band began to play "Deutschland, Deutschland *über alles*" (Germany, Germany above all else) followed by the "Internationale."[3310] Fervent handshakes and smiles were then exchanged, with Gestapo officers shaking hands with their counterparts from the Soviet secret police, the NKVD.[3311]

That afternoon, they got down to business. Stalin, accustomed to being treated as a toxic and malevolent outsider in world politics,[3312] relished being courted by Hitler, the Führer of a now powerful and feared Germany after the humiliation of Versailles.[3313] When Hitler, at the Berghof, received Stalin's telegram on the 22nd, agreeing to Ribbentrop's trip to Moscow, Albert Speer witnessed Hitler banging on the table so hard that the glasses rattled, and exclaiming in a voice breaking with excitement, "I have them! I have them!"[3314]

However, as Ribbentrop, Stalin, Molotov, and Ambassador Schulenburg got down to business, Stalin acted like one certain that he held all the trump cards.[3315] Since draft treaties had already been agreed upon in the preceding days, all that needed to be done was to finalise terms and draw up the necessary documents.[3316] Nevertheless, in an attempt to seize the initiative, Ribbentrop began with a "bold" or perhaps wishful suggestion, proposing on Hitler's behalf that the non-aggression pact should have a hundred-year term. Blithely dismissive, Stalin replied "If we agree to a hundred years, people will laugh at us for not being serious. I propose the agreement should last ten years."[3317] Deflated, Ribbentrop acquiesced. As events panned out, even Stalin's ten years would prove optimistic.

The public and relatively benign protocols of the non-aggression pact were revealed to the world, and only garnered the most cursory of discussions, as they had already been dealt with to the satisfaction of both parties in the drafts. They were as follows: "

> The German Reich Government and the government of the Union of Soviet Socialist Republics guided by the desire to consolidate the cause of peace between Germany and the USSR, and based on the basic provisions of the treaty of neutrality concluded between Germany and the USSR in April 1926,[3318] the following agreement has been reached:
>
> Article I.
>
> The two Contracting Parties undertake to refrain from any act of violence, aggressive action or attack against each other, both individually and in concert with other powers.
>
> Article II.
>
> In the event that one of the Contracting Parties should become the subject of acts of war by a third power, the other Contracting Party will in no way support that third power.

Article III.

The governments of the two Contracting Parties will continue to be in constant contact for consultation in order to inform each other of issues affecting their common interests.

Article IV.

Neither of the two Contracting Parties shall participate in any grouping of powers that is
directly or indirectly directed against the other Party.

Article V.

If disputes or conflicts between the Contracting Parties arise over issues of this or that nature, both parties will settle these disputes or conflicts solely by means of friendly exchange of views or, if necessary, through the appointment of arbitration commissions.

Article VI.

The current contract is concluded for a period of 10 years with the proviso that unless one of the Contracting Parties terminates it one year prior to the expiration of this period, the period of validity of this contract shall be automatically extended for another five years.

Article VII.

The current contract should be ratified within the shortest possible time. The instruments of ratification are to be exchanged in Berlin. The contract enters into force immediately upon signing.

Done in duplicate, in both German and Russian,

Moscow on August 23, 1939.

For the German Reich Government: J. Ribbentrop

In authority of the Government of the USSR: V. Molotov"[3319]

Before long, the discussions turned to the essence of the pact — the so-called "secret [additional] protocol" by which both parties were to divide the spoils of their collaboration.[3320] With the knowledge that Hitler was champing at the bit to launch his invasion of Poland, Stalin realised he was in a position to exact maximum possible territorial concessions,[3321] when he announced: "Alongside this agreement there will be an additional agreement that we will not publish anywhere else, with a clear delineation of "spheres of interest" in central and eastern Europe."[3322]

Ribbentrop, having himself made reference to "spheres of interest" in his telegram to Schulenburg on Friday the 18th,[3323] made his opening offer: "The Führer accepts that the eastern part of Poland and Bessarabia [then part of Romania] as well as Finland, Estonia and Latvia, up to the river Dvina, will all fall within the Soviet sphere of influence."[3324] As generous as this offer was, Stalin was not happy, and demanded all of Latvia. Ribbentrop, caught off balance, decided to stall by adjourning the talks to refer the question to a higher authority, even though Hitler had given him authority to agree to terms as required,[3325] with the invasion of Poland now imminent. Ribbentrop replied to Stalin that he could not accede to the Soviet demand for Latvia without consulting Hitler; he requested an adjournment so he could make a call to Germany.

That hot summer's evening, Hitler, from a terrace of his Berghof, anxiously awaited news on the negotiations, as he took in a view north across the valley to the Untersberg peak. He was accompanied by his Luftwaffe adjutant, Nicolaus von Below, who recalled in his memoir: "

> As we strolled up and down, the eerie turquoise-coloured sky to the north turned first violet and then blood red. At first we thought there must be a serious fire behind the Untersberg mountain, but then the glow covered the whole northern sky in the manner of the Northern Lights. Such an occurrence is exceptionally rare in southern Germany. I was very moved and told Hitler that it augured a bloody war. He responded that if it must be so, then the sooner the better; the more time went by, the bloodier it would be."[3326]

Shortly thereafter, the phone rang. It was Ribbentrop calling from Moscow. For once, Hitler was initially silent as he listened to Ribbentrop's summary of progress and Stalin's demand for all of Latvia. Less than thirty minutes later, after viewing a map, Hitler returned the call, consenting to Stalin's demand.[3327] By two o'clock the following morning, Ribbentrop called again and advised that the treaty, with its secret additional protocol, had been signed.[3328] The text of the latter was as follows:
"

On the occasion of the signing of the non-aggression treaty between the German Reich and the Union of Soviet Socialist Republics, the undersigned plenipotentiaries of the two parts discussed in a strictly confidential manner the question of the delimitation of the mutual spheres of interest in Eastern Europe. This debate has led to the following conclusion:

1. In the event of a territorial-political transformation in the Baltic States (Finland, Estonia, Latvia, Lithuania), the northern border of Lithuania also forms the border of the spheres of interest of Germany and the USSR. Here, the interest of Lithuania in the Vilnius [Wilno] region is recognised by both sides.[3329]

2. In the case of a territorial-political reorganisation of the territories belonging to the Polish state, the spheres of interest of Germany and the USSR are approximately delimited by the line of the Narew, Vistula and San rivers. The question of whether the mutual interests desired the maintenance of an independent Polish state and how this state could be delimited can finally be clarified only in the course of further political development.[3330] In any case, both governments will solve this question by means of friendly understanding.

3. With regard to the Southeast of Europe, the Soviet side emphasises the interest in Bessarabia.[3331] The German side explains the completely political lack of interest in these areas.

4. This protocol will be treated top secret by both sides.

Moscow, August 23, 1939.

For the German Reich Government: J. Ribbentrop

In authority of the Government of the USSR: V. Molotov"[3332]

Hitler jubilantly congratulated Ribbentrop before remarking to Nicolaus von Below and others, "That will explode in their faces."[3333] Indeed, two years later, from July to November 1941, following the launch of Operation Barbarossa — Hitler's invasion of the Soviet Union on June 22, shattering the ten year non-aggression pact — a demoralised and devastated Stalin ordered that peace feelers be put out to Hitler, conceding nearly all of European Russia.[3334] One year later, in late 1942, during the Battle of Stalingrad, Ribbentrop implored Hitler to make peace with Stalin.[3335] Hitler rejected Ribbentrop's plea.

At around midnight on August 23-24, the atmosphere became one of warm conviviality, as samovars of black tea, followed by caviar, sandwiches, vodka, and finally, Crimean champagne abounded, which Molotov recalled as being "our treat."[3336] Not to be outdone in hospitality to his guests by his subordinate, Stalin filled their glasses, as he offered them cigarettes and lights,[3337] before making the following toast: "I know how much the German nation loves its Führer. I should therefore like to drink to his health."[3338] Later, in the early morning hours of Thursday August 24, 1939, Heinrich Hoffmann and the Soviet photographers, with what Hoffmann dubbed their antediluvian equipment,[3339] were called upon to record the ceremonial signing of the pact for posterity. Stalin had one condition, however: "The empty bottles should be removed beforehand, because otherwise people might think that we got drunk first and then signed the treaty."[3340]

Certainly, in what Robert Forczyk dubbed "the greatest criminal conspiracy of the 20th century,"[3341] which precipitated untold misery on millions in eastern Europe, that would not do! Moreover, upon the glasses being cleared, the Comintern (Communist International),[3342] realising the imperative of political acrobatics extending beyond the walls of the Kremlin, almost immediately issued a worldwide directive to the faithful.[3343] Instead of being against Germany, Communists in countries engaging the "Fascists" had to take a stand against war with Germany. Even in neutral countries like the United States, Communists were instructed to come out against intervention. That is, they were now to promote the prevailing US policy of isolationism and the mindset of the population in general.[3344] The world over, Communists were instructed to "immediately correct their political line."[3345]

François Furet, once a member of the French Communist Party, wrote that the Communists, faced with Stalin's directive, showed an "extraordinary discipline, unique in the history of humanity." Communists, whether in Britain, France, America, or out in the far corners of the world, who had been screaming for war against Hitler one minute, now had to come out just as enthusiastically against it.[3346] Furthermore, Mao Zedong (毛泽东), who had been ordered by Moscow to oppose Japanese aggression in China, saw the advantages of Stalin concluding a non-aggression pact with Japan, one that would divide China. In short, as he stated in an interview with the foreign journalist Edgar Snow,[3347] a "Polish solution" for his own country.[3348] Indeed, at that time, the Kremlin signed a ceasefire with Japan, bringing to a halt to fighting that had been going on between the Soviet Red Army and the Japanese on the border of Outer Mongolia and Manchukuo (Manchuria).[3349]

His idea was that the Soviets would make him head of a puppet government for half of China, while the other half would be abandoned to the whim of Japanese occupation. The demarcation line Mao imagined, was along the Yangtse River.[3350] In this process of outright collaboration, Mao envisaged the Japanese crushing Chiang Kai-shek (蔣介石) and his Nationalist Army.[3351] At the same time, the Japanese, he reasoned, would not be disposed to wage war with him, due to his alliance with Stalin. The problem with such an arrangement, would arise if Hitler broke his pact with Stalin, as was the case almost two years later.

However, not all in China were so positive about Stalin's pact with Hitler. One such was Chen Tu-hsiu (陳獨秀), the man who had set Mao on the path of Communism, but who had been expelled from the party for being too independent.[3352] After years imprisoned by the Nationalists, he had been released with other political prisoners when the Nationalist—Communist 'United Front' was formed in 1937. Now he penned a poem expressing his "grief and anger," comparing Stalin to "a ferocious devil," who: "

> strides imperiously into his neighbouring country
> … and boils alive heroes and old friends in one fell swoop …
> Right and Wrong change like day and night,
> Black and White shift only at his bidding …"[3353]

Twenty-six days into Hitler's invasion of Poland, on September 27, 1939, the Warsaw garrison began surrender negotiations. However, the last Polish forces would not surrender until October 6, after the Battle of Kock. In the Battle of Szack on September 28, eleven days following the Soviet invasion of Poland, Polish border troops defeated the Soviet 52nd Rifle Division.[3354] Nevertheless, Poland's dismemberment was now inevitable; by this time Ribbentrop was again in Moscow to negotiate amendments to the Secret Protocol.[3355] In the terms of the Secret Protocol, signed on August 23, Lithuania still came under the German sphere of interest, even though Hitler had authorised Ribbentrop to concede Latvia to Stalin.[3356] Stalin however, really wanted all three Baltic states — Estonia, Latvia, and Lithuania, which had been part of the Tsarist Empire. Ribbentrop arrived in Moscow on the evening of the September 27, but amendments to the Secret Supplementary Protocol were not signed until the early morning hours of the 29th.[3357]

Stalin got what he wanted, with Germany conceding virtually all of Lithuania to the Soviet sphere of interest, but with Poland now on the brink of collapse, Stalin was compelled to concede substantial territory in the east of Poland. In the August agreement, Poland was virtually bisected, delineated in part, along Poland's River Vistula, putting Warsaw just west of the demarcation line.[3358] Now, it was well and truly in the German sphere. To the east of Warsaw, the city of Lublin, and its so named voivodeship,[xliv] formerly part of the Soviet sphere, now came under German control.[3359]

After September 28, the demarcation line for the soon-to-be-dismembered Polish state closely resembled the Curzon Line border settlement in the obscure, tampered-with July 1920 Spa-London-Moscow telegram in the midst of the 1919-20 Polish Soviet War.[3360] Post WWII, and indeed during it, Stalin and Molotov would claim this as a legitimisation of Soviet seizure of eastern Polish lands,[3361] displacing millions of eastern Poles in the process, to be settled in formerly eastern German lands which became known as the Recovered Territories.[3362] In turn, millions, of eastern Germans, including kin of Ruth von Kleist, were displaced west,[3363] leading to a greatly contracted Germany, even when Communist East and democratic West Germany were combined. Even with the newly seized eastern German lands, overall, Po-

---

[xliv] In the modern-day, a voivodeship is an English language term for a province of Poland. In Polish, the word translates as województwo. See the online Merrimam Webster's dictionary at
https://www.merriam-webster.com/dictionary/voivodeship and page 546 of *The CIA World Factbook 2010* by the Central Intelligence Agency, published by Skyhorse Publishing Inc., 2009, ISBN 1602397279, 9781602397279.

land post-WWII contracted in size by 80,000 square kilometres,[3364] and in the process, on Stalin and Molotov's whim, became ethnically diminished.[3365]

Eastern Poland suffered twenty-one months of Soviet occupation, from September 1939 until Hitler's obliteration of the Molotov-Ribbentrop pact in June 1941, when he launched Operation Barbarossa — the invasion of the Soviet Union.[3366] In that time, 1.7 million eastern or Borderland Poles were deported to Siberian gulags,[3367] regardless of age, gender or health — even cripples would not be spared.[3368] Moreover, hundreds of thousands of Lithuanians, Latvians and Estonians were deported after the annexation of their states in 1940 by the Soviets. Following the launch of Barbarossa, on the suspicion of collaboration with the Germans, many Tartars and Volga ethnic Germans joined them.[3369] For others, their exile was not based on their ethnicity, but rather, on their belonging to a social group, such as the *kulaks*, who were rich peasants, targeted by the Soviet regime since years before the war.[3370]

Fifty people or more were crammed like cattle in each rail car as they were transported to the gulags, often in the midst of the Russian winter, with only a tiny stove, if they were lucky, for heating, and a hole in the side of the carriage functioning as a toilet. However, this was the easy stage, since usually, the gulags were many miles from any railway line. As they trudged through snow, death from exposure, malnutrition, exhaustion, and disease was commonplace, while in the transition from winter to spring, they risked the consequences of breaking ice as they crossed icy rivers.[3371]

People of all ages, regardless of how old, frail or sick they were, as well as infants, cripples, and the blind, were all exiled into the vast abyss of the frigid Siberian hell. There they were often worked to death or died from infections and disease, covered in sores, with teeth falling out due to the almost complete absence of medical care and proper nutrition. In the twenty-one months of the Soviet occupation of eastern Poland, over half of the 1.7 million Poles deported to the Siberian wilderness died of disease and pestilence. Labour in the gulags would include working in gold mines, timber cutting in the Siberian taiga, building of airfields, roads and so forth. Conditions were atrocious. In the gold mines you would be working knee deep in mud and water for ten hours regardless of how sick you were, because if you didn't work, you would not receive the miserable daily bread allowance of seven ounces or 200 grams.[3372] Even after Hitler launched Barbarossa, many of the deported Borderland (Kresy) Poles, were still not released, having to wait until April 1946 — eleven months after the official end of the war in Europe.[3373]

Nikita Khrushchev, Stalin's successor upon his death in early March 1953,[3374] and the orator of the March 1956 "Crimes of the Stalin Era" report at the 20th Party Congress in Moscow[3375] which denounced Stalin and his legacy, appeared in the 1940 propaganda film *Liberation*, in which good was supposedly triumphing over evil, legitimising the crushing of any perceived enemies of the proletariat. When Khrushchev met leaders of the NKVD in a village near Lwów, shortly after Poland's surrender, he berated them for being "lazy": "You call this work? You haven't carried out a single execution."[3376]

The NKVD, would however, quickly make up for lost time, and when they were not executing people, they were arresting them.[3377] Meanwhile, the tiny minority of Polish Communists had hoped for politically inspired behaviour from the Red Army. They were, however, disappointed: "

> We waited for them to ask how was life under [Polish] capitalism and to tell us what it was like in Russia. But all they wanted was to buy a watch. I noticed that they were preoccupied with worldly goods, and we were waiting for ideals."[3378]

One Polish survivor described the impact of Siberian deportations: "

> I can describe this in a few words: it was murder of babies and children, banditry, theft of other people's property, the death penalty without sentencing or guilt. One lacks words to speak about the horror of this thing, and who has not lived through it could never believe what happened. Having removed from Polish territories to Siberia those whom they found uncomfortable, the Bolshevik Communists announced at meetings: 'This is how we annihilate the enemies of Soviet power. We will use the sieve until we retrieve all bourgeois and *kulaks,* not only here, but in the entire world. ...You will never see again those that we have taken away from you.'"[3379]

In spite of all this evidence, the left-wing American historian, Grover Furr, who denies Stalinist guilt in the 1940 Katyń Wood massacre,[3380] claims that the Soviet Union never invaded Poland. He bases this spurious assertion on the basis that the Polish state had collapsed by September 17 1939,[3381] as the government of Poland had by then fled to

Romania, [3382] hence rendering the May 1934 Soviet-Polish non-aggression pact, valid until December 31 1945,[3383] null and void. However, as mentioned earlier, it was not until September 27 that the Warsaw garrison began surrender negotiations with the Germans. Moreover, the last Polish forces did not surrender until October 6, after the Battle of Kock. The Battle of Szack took place on September 28, eleven days following the Soviet invasion of Poland, when Polish border troops defeated the Soviet 52nd Rifle Division.[3384]

Clearly then, in the minds of the Poles, the Soviets were not saviours of Poland — as Soviet actions, ignored by Furr in his article, would prove after Poland's eventual surrender. Furr is not alone in denying the September 1939 Soviet invasion of Poland; the Russian Supreme Court, on September 1, 2016, the 77th anniversary of Hitler's invasion of Poland, and 16 days before the anniversary of the Soviet invasion from the east, ruled that the USSR did not invade Poland in 1939.[3385] Clearly, historical revisionism is not just the domain of the far right — as is alluded to on the website of the Polish Institute of National Remembrance: "

> The fact that a state of war existed between Poland and the USSR after 17 September 1939 is certified by the fact that the Soviet authorities described Polish Army soldiers as "prisoners of war" and that a special Prisoner-of-War Administration was created inside the NKVD to handle the entire problem of prisoners. This reflects the conviction of USSR state officials that a war was being waged with Poland."[3386]

At 0315 hours on September 17, 1939, Wacław Grzybowski, the Polish ambassador in Moscow, was called to the Soviet Foreign Ministry. Once there, Molotov's deputy, Vladimir Potyomkin, began by reading the following note: "

> The Polish—German war has revealed the internal failure of the Polish state. Within ten days of military operations, Poland lost all its industrial areas and cultural centres. Warsaw as the capital of Poland does not exist any more. The Polish government fell apart and shows no signs of life. This means that the Polish state and its government have virtually ceased to exist. Thus, the agreements concluded between the USSR and Poland are terminated. ... In view of this situation, the Soviet government has ordered the High Command of the Red Army

to order its troops to cross the border and take under their protection the lives and property of the population of Western Ukraine and Western Belarus. At the same time, the Soviet government intends to take all measures to rescue the Polish people from the ill-fated war, where it was plunged by its unwise leaders, and give them the opportunity to lead a peaceful life."[3387]

For 1.7 million eastern Poles,[3388] their "peaceful life" would be spent in the Siberian gulags, while for some, in the village near Lwów, upon commissar Nikita Khrushchev's order for random executions, would "Rest In Peace."[3389]

Realising the note's cynical intent, Ambassador Grzybowski refused it and promptly refuted the spurious Soviet assertion that the Polish state had collapsed, justifying their invasion of Poland.[3390] Poland's dire straits, he argued quite rightly,[3391] had no bearing on its sovereignty.[3392] In early April 1943, following the Germans' discovery of the mass grave of Polish officers in Katyn Wood,[3393] Potyomkin, like Furr, was in charge of pushing the Soviet narrative that the Germans were responsible for the Katyń Forest massacre during their occupation of the Soviet Union.[3394]

But now, just forty-five minutes after Ambassador Grzybowski's meeting with Vladimir Potyomkin, the first Soviet troops, in violation of the May 1934 Polish-Soviet non-aggression pact, with no secret protocols,[3395] began crossing the Polish border. After this, the Soviets rejected any notion of diplomatic immunity for Polish diplomats within the Soviet Union. Ambassador Grzybowski only avoided arrest through the intervention of other senior members of the foreign diplomatic corps in Moscow, including the German ambassador, Friedrich-Werner Graf von der Schulenburg. However, the Polish consul in Kiev, Jerzy Matusiński, received no such protection — he was arrested by the NKVD and executed a month later.[3396]

Modern-day Russian rationalisation of Poland's 1939 dismemberment continues with the Russian president in late 2019; Vladimir Putin, applying the dubious principle of "moral equivalence," pointed to the Polish annexation of Czech land during the 1938 Czech-Sudeten crisis.[3397] He thus absolved the USSR of any guilt in Poland's 1939 carve-up.[3398] The region in question was the coal rich Teschen (Polish: *Cieszyn* and Czech: *Těšín*) district in Czech Silesia,[3399] which Poland had lost to Czechoslovakia in the one week Polish-Czech war in January 1919,[3400] when Europe was in the chaotic Great War aftermath of what Winston Churchill disparagingly termed the "Wars of the Pygmies."[3401] This district amounted to just under 1700 square kilometres, with 228,000 inhabitants, of which 133,000 were Czech and the remainder nearly all ethnic Poles.[3402] Poland, it could be argued, had a valid claim to the district, but the way in which it regained this small amount of territory in 1938 was reprehensible.

However, one must retain a realistic sense of scale. Polish seizure of 1700 square kilometres of Czech land in September-October 1938 hardly compares to the Soviet Union, in collaboration with Hitler, wiping Poland from the map of Europe in 1939. Moreover, many Soviet atrocities were committed during their twenty-one-month occupation in eastern Poland, and in all of Nazi-occupied Europe throughout the war, the non-Communist Polish Home Army (AK — Armia Krajowa) had by far the largest armed underground resistance movement.[3403]

Earlier, mention was made of the failure of the British and French to secure an alliance with Stalin against Hitler. Negotiations had begun in March 1939 and would drag on for five months until breaking down in mid-August, just days before the signing of the Molotov-Ribbentrop pact on August 23rd.[3404] When the overtly anti-Nazi and Jewish foreign minister Maxim Litvinov was sacked and replaced by Vyacheslav Molotov in May, reflecting rising anti-Semitism in the USSR at the time,[3405] it could be construed that Stalin was engaging in double dealing.

While Nazi Germany was the natural ideological enemy of the Soviet state, Stalin held the western democracies in contempt[3406] — a view he had in common with Hitler.[3407] Indeed, in the brutal enforcing of their "New Order," the two sides employed similar tactics of deportation, hard labour, and execution.[3408] Ruthless dictatorship was a telling common trait that led to Stalin choosing Hitler, at least for the time being, over what he perceived as weak democracies attempting to ferment war between the Soviet Union and Nazi Germany.[3409] In Stalin's mind, better to have a war between the Anglo-French alliance and Nazi Germany,[3410] and wait to choose a propitious moment for Soviet entry.

Some historians, however, both western and Soviet, have laid blame squarely on the Poles, and to a lesser extent, the Romanians, for the failure of a potential Soviet-Anglo-French alliance to materialise in 1939. One of the most vociferous in this regard, has been the American William L. Shirer, author of the critically acclaimed *The Rise and Fall of the Third Reich: A History of Nazi Germany*. The work has had its detractors, mostly in West Germany following its first publication in October 1960. In the US, its success reached stellar proportions, way beyond anything Shirer could have dreamed.[3411] As a reporter in Berlin in the 1930s, he literally watched Hitler's rise to power and his steady undermining of a democratic government until it was no more. In fact, he witnessed many of Hitler's speeches (and those of his party cronies) at various times before leaving Germany, when he began to fear for his life in late 1940[3412] — the year before America officially entered the war. These experiences, Shirer recorded in his *Berlin Diary: The JOURNAL of a Foreign Correspondent 1934-1941*.[3413]

In West Germany, however, the book revived memories of the Nazi past that many in Germany still wished to suppress.[3414] This included the first West German chancellor Konrad Adenauer.[3415] Shirer, being a journalist outside the academic mainstream, had been accused of having no better than an elementary knowledge of German history.[3416] For one thing, he explained German history before 1933 as the inevitable preparation for National Socialism,[3417] without acknowledging the phenomenon of Fascism outside Germany, such as the regimes in Italy and Spain, and the Fascist movements in France, Poland and Britain, where the British Union of Fascists was led by Oswald Mosley.[3418] In short, he espoused the notion that the rise of extremist right-wing philosophy, with all its horrors, was only ever possible in Germany.

Moreover, during his first visit to America in 1930-31,[3419] Dietrich had noted the racism there, embodied by endemic segregation and a parallel violent mindset of white supremacy, synonymous with the Klu Klux Klan.[3420] In 1940, the year before the US entered the war, the deputy Bundesführer of the pro-Hitler German-American Bund, August Klapprott, addressed a joint Bund-Klan rally in New Jersey.[3421] Moreover, in Miami Florida, a klansman extolled their parallel agendas as follows: "When Hitler has killed all the Jews in Europe, he's going to help us drive all the Jews on Miami Beach into the sea!"[3422]

Given the right conditions, political extremism in any of manifestations, has the potential to spring forth anywhere — not just in Germany. While in America, Dietrich wrote to his brother Karl-Friedrich that he could think of no analogous situation at the time in Germany, as the Jews, in the Grunewald district of Berlin, had economic parity with the Gentiles.[3423] This was before Hitler's rise to power; upon his arrival back in Germany in June 1931, after nine months in the US, he already sensed an ominous change in his beloved Germany.[3424]

From a Polish perspective, it appears that Shirer's knowledge of Polish history, in particular Poland's acrimonious relationship with Russia, is similarly "elementary" at best. He repeatedly refers to what he perceives as Polish intransigence[3425] in concert with unbelievable stupidity[3426] in the weeks leading up to the signing of the Molotov-Ribbentrop pact in Moscow on August 23, 1939, and ultimately, Hitler and Stalin's joint invasion in September.[3427] Shirer blames the failure of the British and French to reach an agreement with Stalin on the Poles' and Romanians' refusal to allow Soviet troops on their soil. This suggests Shirer's ignorance of the 1919-20 Polish-Soviet war, when the newly independent Poland came within a whisker of being wiped from existence, and the Bolsheviks' intention at that time was to ride over the corpse of Poland[3428] to a then chaotic and weak Weimar Germany.[3429]

Shirer's argument also suggests his ignorance of Stalin's fear that, if the fighting were to take place within Soviet territory, the populace might receive the foreign armies as liberators,[3430] for example, in the Ukrainian countryside, where, in the early 1930s, Stalin had engineered a mass famine which became known as the *Holodomor*.[3431] Hence, Stalin's fears of a populace, at least part of it, receiving an invading army as liberators, ran very deep,[3432] and events in the early months of Hitler's Barbarossa invasion confirmed them.[3433] During the initial onslaught, the Germans were greeted as liberators by the Baltic peoples and favourably received in many areas in the Ukraine. Even in White Russia [Belarus] and the Russian Soviet Federated Socialist Republic, many Russian communities greeted the advancing Germans as potential friends and liberators during the first three months of Barbarossa.

It took the civilian National Socialist Reich Kommissars following the Wehrmacht field armies several months to alienate the Ukrainian and Russian populace.[3434] These actions of the Reich Kommissars, were in line with Hitler's obsession to implement his vision of Lebensraum in the east, embodied in his turgid literary work; *Mein Kampf*.[3435] The interviewees for the Harvard Project on the Soviet Social System after the war said that what changed most people's minds to fight the Germans, rather than to surrender, was not love of Communism, much less loyalty to Stalin, but the barbaric treatment meted out by the Germans.[3436]

For Stalin, the loss in the 1919-20 Polish-Soviet War was a personal one, as he had been the immediate superior and friend of Semion Budionny,[3437] the commander of the Konarmia (literally Horse Army, but in effect, cavalry). From August 30 to September 2, 1920, the Battle of Komarów, or the Zamość Ring, where the Poles engaged the Konarmia, ensued. Located about 250 kilometres south-east of Warsaw, it was Europe's first cavalry battle since 1813 during the Napoleonic era, but also the last major cavalry-to-cavalry engagement in Europe's history.[3438] A fortnight earlier, Poland had achieved its miracle on the Vistula in Warsaw, repelling the forces of Soviet general Mikhail Tukhachevsky, but its position by late August, as documented by Norman Davies, was still perilous.[3439]

However, with the Poles' victory in this cavalry engagement, Polish independence in the interwar years was now assured, just as the memory of this defeat was seared into the vindictive and petty mindset of Josef Stalin, forged in the tradition of the Caucasian blood feud.[3440] Lenin was devastated, as he held the illusion that the newly independent Poles would welcome his crusaders of the proletariat as liberators.[3441] For Stalin in 1939, there were no such illusions. As Adam Zamoyski, a descendant of the founder of Zamość, wrote:[3442] "

> And when his troops marched into [eastern] Poland in support of the Germans in 1939, Stalin had showed he learnt the lessons of 1919-20. There would be no attempt to win the Poles over to communism; his previous experience had taught him that they were not amenable. So he set about extirpating not only nobles, priests and landowners, but also doctors, nurses and veterinary surgeons, and in general anyone who might show the slightest sign of independent thought or even curiosity — the scores of charges which entailed immediate arrest and deportation included possessing a stamp collection. Over 1,500,000 people were caught up in this fine net. Army officers, for whom Stalin felt a particular hatred, were murdered in the forest of Katyń and elsewhere, other ranks and civilians were despatched to the Gulag, where a majority died. After 1945, he would do his best to extend the same principles to the rest of Poland."[3443]

On September 7 1939, ten days before the Soviet invasion of Poland, Stalin left no doubt as to his intentions for Poland: "

> The destruction of this state [Poland] in the present conditions would mean one less bourgeois fascist state! What would be bad if, as a result of the defeat of Poland, we extended the socialist system to new territories and population?"[3444]

Shirer made the point that a tripartite alliance between France, Britain and the Soviet Union was only going to be effective if the Soviet Union were allowed onto Polish and Romanian soil before any envisioned engagement of the Germans took place. The validity of this notion, however, hinges on the questionable assumption that Stalin was the benevolent saviour of Polish and Romanian sovereignty. This is only credible if one ignores the Stalinist litany of terror embodied in the most arbitrary violence.[3445]

The evidence lies in the deportation of the kulaks (rich peasants) in the late 1920s to early 1930s,[3446] the Holodomor — the engineered mass famine in the Ukraine in the early 1930s,[3447] the bloody purge of the armed forces in 1937-38,[3448] the purges of the Soviet elite throughout the 1930s,[3449] or of anyone or any element perceived as an enemy of the state on Stalin's whim. This included priests, bishops and nuns, since, in a complete shock to the regime, in the 1937 census, 60% of people answered yes to the question "Are you a believer in religion?"[3450] In 1936, 20,000 churches and mosques were functioning, but by 1941, this had dropped to less than one thousand.[3451]

Both dictatorships (National Socialism and Communism) used terror, but in somewhat contrasting ways. Anyone in the Soviet Union, including those from the most elite, could run afoul of the terror, and in that sense it was completely arbitrary.[3452] How can one sum up all the suffering or even the fatalities resulting from the continuous Communist terror from 1917 to Stalin's death? Starting with all the deliberate murders in the civil war, the famines, and forced collectivisation, there are those killed in the Great Terror and during the wartime ethnic cleansing, the Red Army soldiers executed by their own on various grounds, and all those who died or were killed in the Gulag.[3453]

Aleksandr Solzhenitsyn suggested that Soviet authorities used "internal repression" from the October Revolution up to 1959 to kill an estimated sixty-six million.[3454] He admits the figure is tentative and will need adjusting by future research. He had been a "true believer" himself and for a time held on to his faith in Communism even in the Gulag. His book points an accusing finger at anyone today, in his own country or anywhere else, who might suggest there were "productive" aspects to Soviet terror.[3455] More recent estimations of the Soviet-on-Soviet killing have been more "modest" and range between ten and twenty million.[3456] In any event, Anne Applebaum, the Pulitzer Prize-winning author in 2004 of *Gulag: A History of the Soviet Camps*,[3457] is right to insist that the statistics "can never fully describe what happened."[3458]

They do suggest, however, the massive scope of the repression and the killing.[3459]

When Molotov was asked about the use of torture to extract confessions, how clearly innocent family members were killed for nothing, and why it never seemed to occur to Stalin "that we could not possibly have so many enemies of the people" inside the Soviet Union itself, Molotov's reply was: "

> It is certainly sad and regrettable that so many innocent people died. But I believe the terror of the late 1930s was necessary. Of course, if we had used greater caution, there would have been fewer victims, but Stalin was adamant on making doubly sure: spare no one, but guarantee absolute stability in the country for a long time—through the war and post-war years, which was no doubt achieved. I don't deny that I supported that view. I was simply not able to study every individual case… It was hard to draw a precise line where to stop …That policy of repression was the only hope for the people, for the Revolution. It was the only way we could remain true to Leninism and its basic principles."[3460]

Given this litany, it's impossible to harbour a notion of the benevolent Stalin. If Soviet troops were allowed onto Polish and Romanian soil, and the Germans were repelled, or convinced their invasion now had no chance of success, it seems almost certain that the Poles and Romanians would have been faced with the proverbial guests that never leave. As Adam Zamoyski commented: "With all the wisdom of hindsight, it is impossible to suggest a foreign policy that may have saved Poland."[3461] And in relation to Shirer's notion of "friendly" Soviet troops on Polish soil: "Józef Beck [Polish Foreign Minister] could not turn to the Soviet Union for a full military alliance, since no Pole who knew his history could consider allowing "friendly" Russian troops on Polish soil."[3462]

When Hitler invaded Poland, the Poles had envisaged repelling the Germans not with Soviet "assistance," but with the French launching an invasion of the Reich. Tragically, and perhaps predictably, this did not materialise beyond a token advance of eight kilometres in September 1939, followed by the rapid and timid withdrawal that was known as the Saar Offensive.[3463] At the time, no European army on its own could hope to defeat the Wehrmacht, and the Poles realised this. It had already been agreed with the British and French, that in the event of German aggression, Poland was to hold down German forces for a fortnight, allowing the French time to launch 90 divisions, 2,500 tanks and 1,400 aircraft across the virtually undefended Rhine River.[3464] For the French under Édouard Daladier, and the British, still under Neville Chamberlain, this was the commencement of six months of vacillation, that an American journalist came to dub "The Phoney War."[3465] From the end of the Polish campaign to the German invasion of Norway at 2315 hours on April 8 1940,[3466] more than six months would pass in the "Phoney War," with Chamberlain clinging to hopes of a possible over-throw of Hitler,[3467] or some kind of appeasement.

Of course, the horse had long since bolted, thanks to Chamber-lain's appeasement at Munich in September 1938.[3468] In France, Polish soldiers, who managed miraculous escapes via Romania and Hungary, were desperate to engage the Germans, but frustrated by France's reluc-tance to do so.[3469] In May 1940, France was finally compelled to en-gage the Wehrmacht, but following French surrender in late June, the French were willing to detain and even arrest Polish soldiers at their ports, rather than allow them to escape to England.[3470] Only with the German invasions of Norway, France and the Low countries, and Chamberlain's resignation, did meaningful British engagement of the Germans commence.

In 1934, for whatever it was worth, Poland had secured non-aggression pacts with Nazi Germany on January 26, and an extension of its three-year 1932 pact with the Soviet Union, in May 1934, until December 31, 1945.[3471] Unlike the August 1939 Molotov-Ribbentrop pact, there were no secret protocols,[3472] which meant that the Molotov-Ribbentrop pact was a dual violation of both the 1934 treaties Poland had secured. In the interwar years, Poland's foreign policy in dealing with both Germany and the Soviet Union, was a strict policy of even-handedness — the so-called "Doctrine of Two Enemies" — governing her relations with her two largest neighbours.[3473]

As Józef Piłsudski, Poland's father of independence in the wake of the Great War, stated, a military alliance with either power im-plied Poland becoming that power's satellite or vassal.[3474] In January 1935, an ailing but still mentally alert Piłsudski, in the final months of his life, met Hermann Göring, head of Germany's Luftwaffe and prem-ier of Prussia. When Göring steered the conversation towards Poland forming an anti-Soviet alliance with the Third Reich, Piłsudski cut him off, affirming that Poland was Russia's neighbour, and bound to con-duct a moderate policy towards it.[3475] Moreover, Piłsudski stressed the importance of Polish interests in the Baltic port of Gdańsk (Danzig), which the Reich had to respect.[3476]

Nevertheless, assertions of secret protocols, directed against the USSR in the January 1934 German-Polish non-aggression pact, persist in the modern-day Communist Party of the Russian Federation. Moreover, in an alleged[3477] documentary film shown on the Russian state-owned TV channel Rossiya on August 21, 2009, the Polish Foreign Minister Józef Beck is portrayed as a German agent.[3478] Such a claim may have been spawned by the fact that, at that time, Hitler was anxious to meet with Piłsudski to discuss a German drive into the Baltic states in conjunction with a Polish drive to the Black Sea. The Poles, however, were not going to give up their access to the Baltic Sea at Gdańsk (Danzig) in exchange for a port on the Black Sea in what would have been an ungovernable Ukraine.[3479]

In October 1938, in the wake of the Czech-Sudeten crisis, Ribbentrop had requested that the Poles relinquish all rights to the disputed Free City of Danzig/Gdańsk, offering Warsaw a twenty-five-year guarantee of the German—Polish border in return.[3480] The following January, the Polish foreign minister, Józef Beck, had been invited for talks with Hitler at the Berghof; again, German support for Polish ambitions in Ukraine was offered as an incentive to broker a deal, and Poland's role as a bulwark against communism was lauded. In short, the Germans pushed the idea of a joint German-Polish anti-Soviet alliance, with Poland the junior partner or vassal, as the now deceased Piłsudski had predicted. Ribbentrop, in the minutes of this meeting written to the German ambassador in Warsaw, wrote optimistically that: "Great possibilities exist in Polish-German co-operation, above all in the pursuit of 'a common Eastern policy' against the USSR."[3481]

Yet the Poles would not be swayed, either by German offers or by veiled threats, directed in part, at their interests in Danzig/Gdańsk. Poland's territorial integrity and independence, newly restored only a generation before after 123 years of tripartite foreign occupation,[3482] were far too precious to her to be frittered away in return for dubious promises and vassal status. Hence, the earlier mentioned strict policy of even-handedness — the so-called "Doctrine of Two Enemies" — governed her relations with her two largest and most hostile neighbours.[3483]

In May 1915, just ten months into the Great War, Józef Piłsudski foresaw Imperial Russia's defeat, but as well, the later defeat of Russia's foes — the German and Austro-Hungarian empires, at the hands of the entente powers of France and Britain (which happened eventually with US help following their entry in April 1917).[3484] Consequently, revolution first broke out in Russia, then in Austria and Germany, ending the old monarchical order that had partitioned and officially wiped Poland from the map of Europe for 120 years. In the ensuing power vacuum, the opportunity for the birth of a newly independent Poland arose. Subsequent events would prove Piłsudski correct.[3485] In the spring of 1933, just months following Hitler's rise to power in late January, when Piłsudski spoke to the first officer of his staff, Lieutenant Colonel Kazimierz Glabisz, he was again proven correct by subsequent events. Although, in this instance, he would have dearly wished he was not: "

> It is Germany's dream to achieve cooperation with Russia, as it was in the time of Bismarck. [In spite of Hitler's rhetoric of the threat of "Jewish" Bolshevism to Germany at the time, and ever since he first joined the National Socialists following the Great War.][3486] The achievement of such cooperation would be our downfall. We cannot allow it to happen. Despite the large differences between the systems and cultures of Germany and Russia, this danger must be constantly watched. Stranger alliances have existed in the world. How to work against it? Depending on the given circumstances: either by frightening the weaker one or by a successive relaxation of tensions. The game will be difficult, given the paralysis of will and short-sightedness of the west and the failure of my federation plans."[3487]

The idea of Piłsudski's federation entailed a political and military understanding between Poland and Lithuania, and then with Latvia and Estonia, with an independent Ukraine, connected not with the Soviet Union, but in an alliance with Poland, and thus with the west, to counter the Soviet threat[3488] that manifested itself in the wake of the Molotov-Ribbentrop pact. Piłsudski passed away in May 1935 to an outpouring of six weeks of national grief,[3489] so he did not live to witness the dire realisation of his prophecy for Poland, which was embodied in the Molotov-Ribbentrop pact.

For the Baltic states of Lithuania, Latvia and Estonia, their loss of independence, unlike Poland, was a case of agonising slow burn. By mid-October, all three were compelled to concede military bases to accommodate 70,000 Soviet troops on their soil, more than the standing armies of all three Baltic states.[3490] Eight months later on June 17 1940, only days after Wehrmacht troops paraded down the Champs-Elysées in

Paris, the Red Army marched on to the streets of the Latvian capital, Riga.[3491] The mood of the respective populations of both cities was one of abject fear and dismay. Two days earlier, Soviet troops marched into the new Lithuanian capital of Vilnius (Polish Wilno),[3492] given to Lithuania by the Soviets upon Poland's collapse,[3493] but now claimed as part of the Soviet sphere of influence. Estonia was soon to follow.

On June 15, at the Latvian border town of Masļenki, five Latvian border guards and civilians were ambushed and killed by NKVD troops. The day before, a Finnish civilian aircraft — the Kaleva — had been shot down by Soviet bombers en route to Helsinki from Tallinn, with the loss of all nine passengers and crew on board, as well as a bag of French diplomatic mail, which was picked up by a Soviet submarine. However, the furore that followed, both incidents were quickly silenced by the Soviet invasion.[3494] In Moscow, Molotov made Soviet intentions clear to Vincas Krėvė-Mickevičius, the Soviet-appointed new foreign minister of Lithuania: "

> You must take a good look at reality and understand that in future small nations will have to disappear. Your Lithuania, along with the other Baltic nations … will have to join the glorious family of the Soviet Union. Therefore you should begin to initiate your people into the Soviet system, which in future shall reign everywhere, throughout all Europe."[3495]

However, upon his return home, Krėvė-Mickevičius resigned in protest, exclaiming that he did not want to participate in the burial of Lithuanian independence.[3496] In July, rigged elections were arranged, and by early August, all three Baltic states were formally annexed into the USSR.[3497]

Earlier, in the autumn of 1939, when Soviet troops had been allowed into the Baltic states, Hitler had tried to convince ethnic Germans, whose families had lived there for centuries, to "*Heim ins Reich*" — "[come] home to the Reich," signalling his abandonment of the region to Stalin. By mid-October 1939, Hitler's persuasion, in part at least, proved successful when the first ship carrying ethnic Germans left Riga en route for Germany. Over the following two months, a further eighty-six vessels departed from the region's ports, carrying over 60,000 people "home" to the German Reich, or at least to the annexed region of the Warthegau,[3498] incorporated directly into the Reich from conquered Poland. From mid 1940, another wave of ethnic Germans left for the Reich. This was allowed for, in both instances, under the terms of the pact's secret protocol, but for some staunch National Socialists among the German Balts, this state of affairs was appalling: "Everything for which we had lived, everything our ethnic group had established in the course of 700 years … was to disappear, just like a melting snowman."[3499] In Lithuania, over 50,000 volunteered to leave for Germany, despite estimation of the country's remaining German population at barely 35,000. In Estonia, meanwhile, it was observed by one official that, if the Soviets had allowed it, the vast majority of the Estonian population would have asked to be resettled.[3500]

From the moment the Soviet invasion of Poland commenced in mid-September 1939, the Baltic governments had telegraphed Berlin repeatedly, requesting that Germany explain its position, especially in light of the fact that, just three months earlier, on June 7 1939, Latvia and Estonia had signed non-aggression pacts with Germany.[3501] By late September, Stalin had informed Hitler of his intentions in the Baltic, at which point, the negotiations on a "defence treaty" with the Lithuanian government had been abandoned.[3502] Ribbentrop issued a circular to all three German diplomatic missions in the region, tersely asserting that, in view of the new frontier arrangements agreed with Moscow, Lithuania, Latvia, Estonia and Finland did not belong to the German sphere of interest;[3503] hence, prompting the second exodus of ethnic Germans from the region.

Following the Barbarossa invasion in June 1941, the Baltic states initially welcomed the Germans as liberators. In the process, pogroms on Jews,[3504] some of whom welcomed the Soviet invasion, soon followed. Historians say that the percentage of Jews in the Communist party was not disproportionate to the urban population, where the party membership was concentrated, but observations by historians cannot easily reach back to alter contemporary perceptions.[3505] During 1940, Lithuanians perceived Jews as major supporters of the Soviet system and identified them with the regime,[3506] in spite of Soviet authorities persecuting Bundists and Zionists, suppressing Jewish religious institutions and expropriating their property. Moreover, Jewish authors point out that disproportionately more Jews than non-Jewish Lithuanians were deported to Siberia during the mass deportation of 1940-1; among that number was Menachem Begin,[3507] who became Prime Minister of Israel from 1977 to 1983.[3508] Similarly in Latvia, Jews had made up around 5% of the total population, but had numbered at least 12% of those deported by the Soviets in 1941.[3509]

However, the Baltic peoples' perception of the Germans as their liberators and saviours of their culture would not last. In May

1942, the SS Planning Office in its Generalplan Ost (the intended Germanisation of Central and Eastern Europe) had called for the population of the eastern Marken (frontier regions) of Estonia to be substantially Germanised within 25 years.[3510] However, Heinrich Himmler, head of the SS, demanded an amendment of the plan, to include, among other things, the complete Germanisation of Estonia and Latvia within twenty years.[3511] Their culture, like that of Poland, was slated for extinction in the coming decades.[3512]

Unlike the Baltic states, the former Tsarist province of Finland[3513] was proving most vexing for Stalin throughout the winter of 1939-1940, in what became known as the Russo-Finnish War.[3514] Finland had been consigned to the Soviet sphere of interest, but the Finns, in spite of their isolation, were proving to be anything but pushovers, as they inflicted 200,000 casualties upon the Red Army.[3515] In the process, exposing glaring weaknesses and inflexibility,[3516] that would later be exploited by the Germans in the Barbarossa invasion. After three-and-a-half months, however, the heavily outnumbered Finns made peace with the Soviets in the Treaty of Moscow on March 12, 1940, agreeing to the cession of western Karelia and to the construction of a Soviet naval base on the Hanko Peninsula.[3517]

Following the Barbarossa invasion, the Finns joined the Germans in undertaking the "War of Continuation."[3518] An armistice signed on September 19, 1944, effectively concluded the conflict between the Soviet Union and Finland, conditional on Finnish recognition of the Treaty of Moscow. The formal end of the Soviet-Finnish conflict came with the signing of a peace treaty in Paris on February 10, 1947.[3519] Unlike the Baltic states and the rest of Eastern Europe, Finland had been spared the post-war fate of becoming a Soviet satellite.

On Wednesday August 23, 1989, the fiftieth anniversary of the signing of the Molotov-Ribbentrop pact, a human chain of 650 kilometres (400 miles), from Tallinn in Estonia, via Riga in Latvia, to the Lithuanian capital, Vilnius, held hands for fifteen minutes, galvanising the Baltic push for independence.[3520] This chain of two million citizens of the Baltic republics of the USSR[3521] was indicative of the changing mood throughout Eastern Europe, with the fall of the Berlin Wall in early November 1989,[3522] and a week later in Warsaw, when Poles tore down the statue of Felix Dzerzhinsky (Dzierżyński), the Polish founder of the first Soviet secret police (Cheka).[3523] By the end of 1991, the Soviet Empire itself was no more.[3524] For five nations — the peoples of the Baltic states, Poland and Romania, the Molotv-Ribbentrop pact was a pact of "misery,"[3525] manifested by the self-serving agendas of the two greatest despots of all time.

According to the 21st century Russian rationalisation of the Molotov—Ribbentrop pact,[3526] Poland's morally questionable annexation of the tiny Teschen region from Czechoslovakia in 1938 has an infamy surpassing anything the Soviets perpetrated in eastern Poland from October 1939 until June 1941.[3527] Poland's refusal to trust the implied Soviet notion of the "benevolent" Stalin was highlighted by not allowing Soviet troops on Polish soil to counter German aggression.[3528]

From Stalin's perspective, for the temporary price of providing economic and morale support to Germany's war effort, he could mitigate Anglo-French influence in Europe and recover pieces of the old Tsarist empire in eastern Europe.[3529] In retrospect, according to Robert Forczyk, author of *Case White The Invasion of Poland, 1939*, the Molotov—Ribbentrop Pact was the greatest criminal conspiracy of the 20th century,[3530] condemning millions to death or slavery.[3531] Soviet historians denied the existence of the secret protocol for decades, but then, as part of Glasnost, released a copy of it in 1992.[3532]

However, Glasnost did not last, and the current Putin regime has returned to denying that the Soviet Union collaborated with Nazi Germany in carving up Poland in 1939, or that the secret pact acknowledged spheres of influence.[3533] However, documents from the Nuremberg trials, when the Secret Protocol was first revealed,[3534] as well as telegrams between Moscow and Hitler's Berghof in the Obersalzburg in August 1939,[3535] prove otherwise. Moreover, it is difficult to imagine that any of the two million Baltic people in the August 1989 human chain from Tallinn to Riga to Vilnius would doubt the existence of the Secret Protocol in this pact of abject misery. To the memory of all its victims, in particular, the 1.7 million Borderland Poles deported to the frigid hell of the Siberian gulags,[3536] this chapter is dedicated.

Polish WWII Supplement II

The Gleiwitz (Gliwice) Incident [3537]

Pretext of defence for the people.[3538]

At 4.45 a.m. on September 1 1939 (Y Day), the German battle-ship Schleswig-Holstein opened fire, without warning, on the Polish garrison of the Westerplatte Fort,[3539] in the Free City of Danzig/Gdańsk. The latter was created in the wake of the Versailles Treaty, as a compromise between Polish economic needs — central to which was access to the Baltic Sea — and the ethnic German majority of 89 to 95%, who wanted to maintain their autonomy from Warsaw. Ten years after its founding on November 15, 1920,[3540] few experts, whether Polish, French, or German, could agree on a legal definition of the city and its outlying villages — whether it was a sovereign state, a state with limited sovereignty, a state without sovereignty, a Polish protectorate, or a protectorate of the League of Nations.[3541]

Nevertheless, whatever the legal definition of the Free City of Danzig/Gdańsk at dawn on Friday September 1 1939, the first military engagement of the Second World War took place, followed almost simultaneously by sixty-two German divisions, supported by 1,300 aircraft,[3542] commencing *Fall Weiss* (Case White),[3543] the invasion of Poland. Contrary to numerous sources, the entire Polish Air Force was not virtually obliterated in the first twenty-four hours, and Polish cavalry never made suicidal charges on German tanks.[3544] Indeed, far from being completely destroyed on the ground in the early morning hours of September 1, though obsolete and vastly outnumbered, the Polish fighter aircraft scored at least 126 confirmed kills (aircraft shot down) during the campaign. German records state a number no less than 160, nearly ten percent of the German aerial attacking force.[3545] Many of these Polish fighter pilots would later distinguish themselves during Britain's darkest hour — the aerial Battle of Britain in 1940.[3546] Moreover, the Polish Air Force lost only seven percent of its operational aircraft on the first day of the war, and remained actively in the fight for a total of 17 days, until the Soviet invasion.[3547]

Before implementing his invasion, Hitler required a pretext, of which the emphasis was not so much on plausibility, but rather in fermenting confusion and exploiting the lack of readiness of the Poles and its dithering allies Britain and France,[3548] in the prelude to the invasion. On August 22, 1939, Hitler, in his usual diatribe of ideological hatred, addressed his commanders-in-chief: "

> When starting a war it is not right that matters, but victory … The destruction of Poland has priority. Close your hearts to pity. Act brutally. Eighty million [German] people must obtain what is their right.[3549]

> I shall give a propaganda reason for starting the war; whether it is plausible or not. The victor will not be asked whether he told the truth."[3550]

Accordingly, it was on the evening of Thursday August 31, 1939, that the SS, in concert with the Abwehr,[3551] staged "Operation Himmler,"[3552] a series of fake Polish attacks on German positions near the border with Poland; of these, the action at Gleiwitz — which became known as the "Gleiwitz incident," was but one. Early that same month, Admiral Canaris, the head of the Abwehr, had received an order from Hitler himself to deliver to Himmler and Heydrich 150 Polish uniforms and some Polish small arms. This struck Canaris as very strange, and on August 17 he asked General Keitel, the OKW (German High Command) Chief about it. While Keitel, the Hitler yes man,[3553] declared to Canaris that he did not think much of "actions of this kind," he nevertheless said that "nothing could be done," since the order had come from the Führer. Repulsed as he was, Canaris obeyed his instructions and turned the uniforms over to Heydrich.[3554]

Hitler wanted his war, come what may, but in 1939, he faced three problems. Firstly, the problem of the Soviet Union entering on the Allied side was solved on August 23, 1939, with the signing of the Molotov-Ribbentrop pact in Moscow.[3555] Secondly, there were the British and French, who had, at least on paper, pledged to stand by Poland in the event of foreign aggression. Thirdly, and perhaps most critically, even the staunchest supporters of the Third Reich, for the most part, had no stomach for another war. As Roger Moorhouse commented: "

> Hitler needed to dress up his belligerent intentions to make them appear defensive: he needed to show Poland as the aggressor and Germany as the innocent victim. In this way, he reasoned, the German people might be persuaded to support

the war, and Poland might even be detached from its international alliances."[3556]

To this end, a training centre was established at Bernau, north of Berlin, at which over 300 SS volunteers, mostly from Upper Silesia,[xlv] were prepared for infiltration operations against Poland. They were trained using Polish weapons and uniforms, and taught the essentials of the Polish language.[3557] By late August, they were ready for action and on the night of the 31st, were deployed in "raids" on the German customs post at Hochlinden (Stodoły), near Rybnik, and the foresters' lodge near Pitschen (Byczyna).[xlvi] By smashing windows, firing into the air and singing and swearing in broken Polish, they were to simulate border incursions by Polish forces. Were it not for the bodies of six concentration camp inmates, who were dressed in Polish uniforms and then shot and left at Hochlinden, about 20 kilometres south-west of Gleiwitz, to add bloody "authenticity" to the scene, it would all have been rather comical.[3558]

Given the fabrication of Polish aggression, embodied in an orgy of murderous pretence that the SS engineered on the eve of the war,[3559] it's perhaps understandable that generations of historians have persistently got the story of the Gleiwitz incident wrong. This has arisen by the conflation of it with other actions encompassed by Operation Himmler, such as Hochlinden, and erroneous reports of assailants in Polish uniforms and of multiple Polish victims. However, by analysing the original sources, it's clear that the assailants at Gleiwitz were not in uniform, and that there was only one victim.[3560]

[xlv] Upper Silesia is upstream on the Odor (Polish: Odra) River from Lower Silesia. Breslau/Wrocław is in Lower Sielsia. See the following footnote.

[xlvi iii iv vi vii viii xvi xx xlvii] Hochlinden (Stodoły) is about 20 kilometres south-west of Gleiwitz (Gliwice) and Pitschen (Byczyna) is about 100 kilometres north-north-west of Gleiwitz (Gliwice). Gleiwitz (Gliwice) in Upper Silesia, is about 150 kilometres south-east of Breslau (Wrocław) on the Odra (German: Oder) River in Lower Silesia. All these places, post-war, became part of Poland, but in August 1939, all, except for Breslau (then well inside Germany), were just inside Germany from the Polish frontier. Upper Silesia and Lower Silesia are distinguished by Upper Silesia being further upstream on the Odra River Valley than Lower Silesia. Gleiwitz is on the Kłodnica (German: Klodnitz) River, which is a short tributary of the Upper Odra River. See Google Maps.

Alfred Helmut Naujocks was central to the execution of the plot in the Upper Silesian town of Gleiwitz;[xlvii] he was a member of the SS from 1931 to 19 October 1944 and a member of the SD (Sicherheitsdienst), its intelligence arm,[3561] from its creation in 1934 to January 1941. He surrendered to the Allies in Belgium in October 1944, and it was his sworn affidavit, signed in Nuremberg on November 20, 1945,[3562] and used at the subsequent Nuremberg Trial Proceedings in December 1945, that shed significant light on the Gleiwitz incident.[3563]

Reinhard Heydrich was the Chief of the Sipo (Sicherheitspolizei — Security Police) and SD,[3564] and later the chairman of the infamous Wannsee Conference in January 1942, convened to implement the Final Solution to the so-called "Jewish question."[3565] On or about August 10 1939, he personally ordered Naujocks to simulate an attack on the radio station near Gleiwitz, just inside the Polish border. The objective was to make it appear that the attacking force consisted of Poles. Heydrich elaborated further by telling Naujocks that, "Actual proof of these attacks of the Poles is needed for the foreign press, as well as for German propaganda purposes."[3566]

Naujocks was ordered to go to Gleiwitz with five or six SD men and wait there until he received a code word from Heydrich indicating that the attack should take place. Whereupon they were to seize the radio station and to hold it long enough to permit a Polish-speaking German to broadcast a speech in Polish. Heydrich told Naujocks that the speech should state that the time had come for the conflict between the Germans and the Poles and that the Poles should get together and strike down any Germans from whom they met resistance. Heydrich also stated that he expected the attack on Poland to take place within the next few days;[3567] but as it turned out, on August 10, that was still more than three weeks away.[3568] On August 10, Naujocks travelled to Gleiwitz and waited there a fortnight. Since the invasion did not take place in that time, as Heydrich predicted, on the 24th, Naujocks requested permission from Heydrich to leave the backwater of Gleiwitz and return to Berlin. It was refused, and he was ordered to remain in Gleiwitz.[3569]

[xlvii xlvi] Upper Silesia is upstream on the Odor (Polish: Odra) River from Lower Silesia. Breslau/Wrocław is in Lower Sielsia. See footnote for this supplement for further clarification.

However, some days later, between August 25 and 31,[3570] Naujocks travelled to nearby Oppeln to meet with Heinrich Müller,[xlviii] the head of the Gestapo. In Naujock's presence, Heinrich Müller discussed the plans for another pre-invasion border incident with a man named Mehlhorn; it was to appear that a company of Polish soldiers were attacking German troops. Müller made it known that he had 12 or 13 condemned criminals who were to be dressed in Polish uniforms and left dead on the ground at the scene of the incident to show that they had been killed while attacking.[3571] Toward this end, they were to be given fatal injections by a doctor employed by Heydrich. Later they were also to be given gunshot wounds, whereupon, the press and other persons were to be taken to the location of the incident. Subsequently, a police "report" was to be prepared.[3572]

After briefing Mehlhorn, Müller turned to Naujocks and told him that he had orders from Heydrich to make one of those criminals, referred to by the codename "Canned Goods," available for the action at Gleiwitz, to be carried out on the evening preceding the German invasion of Poland. This invasion finally took place on September 1; at noon on August 31, Naujocks received a call from Heydrich to report to Müller regarding "Canned Goods" required for the attack on the Gleiwitz radio station.[3573]

Upon reporting to Müller, Naujocks gave Müller instructions to deliver the man near the radio station. When this was done, Naujocks noticed that the victim was still alive, albeit barely so, and unconscious. Naujocks noticed no bullet wounds on the body; a lot of blood was smeared across his face, and he was dressed in civilian clothes,[3574] not in a Polish military uniform, as stated erroneously in numerous sources.[3575] Naujocks concluded his affidavit[3576] with the seizure of the radio station as ordered, followed by the broadcast of a speech of 3 to 4 minutes over an emergency transmitter, before firing some pistol shots and leaving.[3577] In the Gleiwitz incident, the unfortunate individual referred to as "Canned Goods" by Heydrich and co was Franciszek Honiok, a 43-year-old unmarried Silesian Catholic farmer.[3578] Being a German citizen, he lived in a German village close to Gleiwitz, but as he was of Polish ethnicity,[3579] coupled perhaps with being a Catholic in a

---

[xlviii] Not to be confused with Josef Müller, the Abwehr's Vatican contact, and Ludwig Müller, the Nazi appointed Reichsbischof (Nation's Bishop) in 1933. See footnote [xxi] of Chapter 16 "Homecoming to Outbreak of War" in regard to Josef Müller, and footnote [xiv] of Chapter 4 "The Aryan Paragraph" in regard to Ludwig Müller.

Lutheran dominated region of Germany,[3580] he strongly sympathised with the Poles in this borderland region,[3581] in which both sides had been bickering over numerous border claims ever since Versailles.[3582]

Honiok was most vocal in expressing these sympathies, and indeed, had been involved in a number of local revolts against German rule in Silesia,[3583] which made him an ideal choice as the person to provide "proof" of Polish aggression towards the Third Reich. To this end, he was arrested on August 30 by the SS in the nearby village of Pohlam[3584] (now Polish Połomia).[3585] Contrary to numerous sources, Honiok was the only victim of the Gleiwitz incident,[3586] but in the deception, would become known as the first victim of World War II.[3587] As Roger Moorhouse commented: "

> ... Franciszek Honiok was murdered to provide the gloss on Heydrich's nefarious propaganda coup. He was expendable, disposable, anonymous; collateral damage in Nazi Germany's headlong drive to war. He would become a footnote to history, his murder demonstrating the sneering contemptuous brutality of the Nazi regime, and giving a grim foretaste of the fate that would befall Poland. His was a single death that prefaced at least fifty million others; [an estimate for the total death toll of WWII][xlix] an individual tragedy presaging a collective slaughter."[3588]

Initially, Naujocks planned for the raid to go ahead without bloodshed, but his superiors decided that the raid required a clinching piece of "evidence."[3589] To this end, rather than using concentration camp inmates, as used elsewhere along the border in Operation Himmler, Reinhard Heydrich and Heinrich Müller decided it had to be someone in the Gleiwitz district with a proven history of anti-German agitation.[3590] None met these requirements better than the 43-year-old unmarried Silesian Catholic farmer.[3591]

[xlix] Poland's death toll for WWII, among its population according to its borders in August 1939, was 5.9 to 6 million, which was just under 20% of its population. See page 683 of *Polska i Polacy w drugiej wojnie światowej (Poland and Poles in the Second World War)* by Czesław Łuczak, published by the Uniwersytet im. Adama Mickiewicza, 1993, ISBN 8323205116, 9788323205111. This is also Volume 5 of *Polska, dzieje narodu, państwa i kultury, (Volume 5 of Poland, the history of the nation, state and culture)* by Jerzy Topolski, ISBN 8323205361, 9788323205364.

Franciszek Honiok spent his final hours alive in the Gleiwitz police station,[3592] while Naujocks waited in his hotel room to receive the code words that would authorise the plot's execution. At 4 p.m., the phone rang and, on answering, Naujocks heard Heydrich's nasal, high-pitched voice demanding that he call back immediately. On doing so, he heard Heydrich give the code: *"Grossmutter (Oma) gestorben"* (Grandmother has died).[3593] Naujocks called his men together for a final briefing, reiterating their objectives and respective tasks, before they changed into their unkempt civilian clothes and climbed into two cars for the short journey north-east to the transmitter station. As planned, with dusk rapidly falling, and most people at home listening to their radios,[3594] they arrived at precisely 8 p.m.; they rushed into the building, pushing past the station manager who rose to meet them. Before long, Naujocks' men overpowered the staff and took them to the basement, where they were ordered to face the wall as their hands were tied behind their backs.[3595]

The problem now was for Naujocks and his radio technician to work out how they would make their provocative broadcast. During the operation's planning, Naujocks had considered targeting the main radio station in Gleiwitz, near the town centre.[3596] He decided against this, as aside from the logistical challenge in the more heavily populated area, it was likely that the broadcast would be shut down. Consequently, the raid was made on the transmitter station itself, where there was only a "storm microphone" used to interrupt local programmes to warn of extreme weather. Here, it was assumed that any interruption to their broadcast was far less likely.[3597]

Having dealt with the station staff, Naujocks had to locate the storm microphone and determine how to patch it into (interrupt) the main broadcast. He succeeded in the former, but not the latter, whereupon he hauled the staff one by one from the basement at gunpoint, until one of them obliged and told him what to do.[3598] It was then that the henchmen's Polish speaker, Karl Hornack, pulled a crumpled sheet of paper from his pocket and stepped forward. As he did so, a pistol was fired into the air to provide an appropriately martial atmosphere, as Hornack "proclaimed": "UWAGA! TU GLIWICE! RADIOSTACJA ZNAJDUJE SIĘ W POLSKICH RĘKACH!" (Attention! Here is Gleiwitz! The radio station is in Polish hands!)[3599]

What followed was supposed to be a call to arms from a fictional "Polish Freedom Committee," demanding that the ethnic Polish population in Germany rise up to resist the authorities and conduct sabotage operations, and promising that the Polish army would soon march in as a liberator. However, for reasons that have never been satisfactorily explained, only the first nine words were broadcast, and those were only audible in the district of Gleiwitz itself; the remainder was lost in a cacophony of static. Heydrich, listening in Berlin, heard nothing at all.[3600] One possibility given for the truncated broadcast, was that the transmission was shut down by one of the engineers standing beside the electrical equipment.[3601]

While Naujocks and his henchmen had been busying themselves in the takeover of the transmitter station shortly before 8 p.m., Franciszek Honiok was visited in his cell at the Gleiwitz police station by an SS man in a white coat, purporting to be a doctor as he injected his unfortunate subject. Now unconscious, Honiok was then driven the short distance to the transmitter station, where two of Naujocks' men carried him into the building, laying him down close to the rear entrance. It has never been ascertained who shot Honiok and when,[3602] but as Naujocks left the radio station, he stopped briefly to examine the dead man, slumped close to the door, his face smeared with his own blood. To his death in 1966, he would maintain that neither he nor his men had shot Franciszek Honiok. He knew nothing about the man, Naujocks told prosecutors, not even his name: "I was not responsible for him," he said.[3603]

In his affidavit presented as evidence in the Nuremberg Trial Proceedings on Thursday December 20, 1945, Naujocks claimed that Honiok was still alive, albeit barely so, and unconscious. Naujocks also claimed he noticed no bullet wounds on the body; but a lot of blood smeared across his face, and that Honik was dressed in civilian clothes, not in a Polish military uniform.[3604] However, to have left Honiok still alive at the scene, even barely so, and without bullet wounds, would not be desirable, one would think, for the scene's "plausibilty." On this point, Naujocks could well be lying, in attempting to mitigate his guilt, and that of his own men.

Although the truncated and spurious nine-word broadcast did not make it out of Gleiwitz and its surrounding district, the German media were already primed and ready to run the story regardless. Within hours the radios were blaring and the newspaper presses were rolling, bearing headlines about the Polish "attack" on Gleiwitz and the inevitability of a German response. By the time most Germans heard or read those words, the following morning, Hitler's tanks were already advancing into Poland. The Second World War had begun.[3605]

In London, the BBC would broadcast the following statement: "

There have been reports of an attack on a radio station in Gli-wice, which is just across the Polish border in Germany. The German News Agency reports the attack came at about eight p.m. this evening when the Poles forced their way into the studio and began broadcasting a statement in Polish. Within a quarter of an hour, say reports, the Poles were overpowered by German police who opened fire on them. Several of the Poles were reported killed but the numbers are not yet known."[3606]

Clearly, the spurious plot was already achieving its objective, as British, French and other European governments were informed that Poland had started the war, ensuring that the German army gained vital hours while ministers and leaders such as Chamberlain, and French PM Édouard Daladier, dithered.[3607] Moreover, this was not the end of German disinformation, as at 11.15 hours on Friday September 1, 1939, more than six hours after the German battleship Schleswig-Holstein opened fire, without warning, on the Polish garrison of the Westerplatte Fort,[3608] the German ambassador in London told Lord Halifax that Warsaw had not been bombed, and the only shooting along the border was being done by Polish troops.[3609] The appeasing Lord Halifax was all too ready to consider this claim as more than plausible.[3610]

Details of the Gleiwitz raid first emerged during the Nuremberg trials in 1945-46, but it was not until 1958 that the full facts were revealed, after the British writer Comer Clarke tracked down former SS-Sturmbannfuhrer Alfred Naujocks in Hamburg. Confronted by Clarke, Naujocks admitted: "Yes, I started it all. I don't think anyone will bother about me now." In the resulting article, he was identified as "The Man who Started the Last War."[3611] Naujocks passed away in 1966, and never faced a war-crimes tribunal; he was only required to submit his affidavit to the Nuremberg trials in December 1945, as mentioned above.[3612] He had been involved in the planning of the 1940 Venlo Incident,[3613] and held as a war criminal since he surrendered to the Americans in Belgium in October 1944, but made a dramatic escape from a special camp in Germany for war criminals in 1946, and thus escaped trial.[3614] He was only heard of again when Comer Clarke tracked him down in Hamburg in 1958.

Franciszek Honiok's death has never been marked with any commemoration in Poland, where his memory is virtually erased from the records. Paweł Honiok, his nephew and only remaining relative, was born in 1936; he lived in the small village of Koszecin, about an hour's drive from post-war Polish Gliwice [Gleiwitz].[1] He stated: "

> Nobody has ever wanted to talk about what happened, it's always been secret. The Germans were in control of us until 1945 and then the Russians took over and they had no interest in digging up the truth about what had happened back at the start of the war. Even my own family were too afraid to talk about it when I was a child, and it was many, many years before we started to hear anything at all about what happened to him. I know about Franz, and my father, his brother, was always proud of him. But no one in the family ever really spoke about what happened to him [Franz] or what happened to the body. No one ever mentioned what had taken place because at that time it was a time to be silent and secret. As time passed nothing really changed — until now [2009]. As a young boy, I can remember my family sitting in a room, quietly speaking about what had happened to Franz. But I was not allowed to sit in and listen, this was for the adults, not the younger ones. The only thing I know, was that it was rumoured his body was buried in the mountains. But there is no
> memorial. It was as if Poland was ashamed of the way his body was used to start the war. They never even accepted he was a victim of the war because he was killed on the evening of August 31, and officially, the war did not begin until September 1. But now, people accept he was the first person killed in that war."[3615]

As grim and lonely as Franciszek Honiok's death was, the fate of the dozen or so other unfortunates designated by Heydrich and co as "Canned Goods" at the disposal of other operations along the German-Polish border in late August 1939 is truly disturbing. Naujocks stated that the bodies were forwarded to villages where they were required, in

---

[1] German pre-war Gleiwitz became post-war Polish Gliwice in the wake of the Stalinist imposed post-war western translation of Polish territory and people. In turn, evicting pre-war eastern Germans westwards. As such, today, what was German Gleiwitz, is now well and truly inside Polish territory as Gliwice. See also, endnotes [190] to [220] of the Preface "Birth and Memory upon the Lesser Known Fault Line of History" in regard to the Stalinist perpetrated displacement post-war of eastern Poles and eastern Germans.

packing cases labelled "preserves." As was the case for Franciszek Honiok, some of the victims arrived at their destinations only half-dead, having been given inadequate injections for immediate death, leading to them being put out of their misery before they could be exploited for the spurious evidence.[3616] Hence, Naujocks's claim that he and his men never shot Honiok, barely alive and unconscious, seem questionable, since the plot was mainly perpetrated to legitimise a lunatic's war of conquest and genocide in the minds of average Germans.[3617] To the memory of a few, Franciszek Honiok and the concentration camp inmates deemed by Hitler's Reich as expendable in the prelude to the greatest mass death and suffering the world would ever know, this chapter is dedicated.

Polish WWII Supplement III

The Katyń Wood Massacre

It is difficult to shake off entirely the suspicion that Stalin's behaviour towards the Poles in the 1940s was tinged with revenge for the humiliation of 1920.[3618]
Adam Zamoyski.

Their tragic final truth will not rot in the grave of Katyń.[3619]

Katyń is not just about Katyń.
The author.

In March 1943, two failed assassination attempts on Hitler took place.[3620] The first was on the 13th and the latter just eight days later. The former involved getting Hitler to visit a military headquarters at Smolensk in western Russia, where a bomb made with seized British explosives and a time delay mechanism would be taken aboard Hitler's plane unwittingly by one of his staff, and explode as he flew back to his Wolf's Lair in East Prussia. For whatever reason, however, the bomb never exploded, but remarkably, with the quick thinking of Oma Ruth's nephew, Henning von Treskcow, his adjutant Fabian von Schlabrendorff was able to retrieve the dud bomb at the Wolf's Lair without the plot being uncovered. Smolensk, though, following a gruesome discovery just weeks later in a nearby forest in early April 1943, would become infamous.

However, before this would come to pass, on March 21, a golden opportunity in Berlin presented itself for the plotters — albeit, a suicide mission for the would be assassin, the Silesian baron, Major Rudolf-Christoph von Gersdorff — a subordinate and deep admirer of Henning von Treskcow.[3621] Hitler was to view a display of captured Soviet weaponry at the Zeughaus on Unter den Linden. Gersdorff would describe the weaponry to Hitler, but not before he set the timing mechanism, hidden under his trench coat, to detonate the explosive after twenty minutes, which was ten minutes before Hitler was scheduled to leave. Hitler, however, after just ten minutes, unexpectedly, took an exit to the Unter den Linden, prompting Gersdorff to urgently make for a toilet and disable the bomb. Again, Hitler survived without the plot being revealed. Fifteen days later, on April 5th, Dietrich, his brother-in-law Hans von Dohnányi and others, would be arrested.[3622]

Gersdorff would survive the war, and like Fabian von Schlabrendorff,[3623] did not pass away until 1980.[3624] Moreover, just a fortnight or so later, in early April 1943, upon his return to the Smolensk region in western Russia, Gersdorff, in his role as G-2 (Intelligence Officer)[3625] of the Central Army Group from 1942 to 1943,[3626] would be involved in a revelation in his zone, that would acquire worldwide significance — a mass grave of Polish prisoners captured during the September 1939 Soviet invasion of Poland.[3627] Attached to Gersdorff's section was a small Feldpolizei (Field Police) unit, headed by Feldpolizeisekretär Voss. Its primary mission was to act as a personal security detail for the field marshal. Since his section had been living in the same headquarters near Smolensk for nearly two years, they had to deal with the possibility of Soviet commando-style (or Russian partisan) operations against the Army Group staff. Gersdorff assigned Voss the task of routinely monitoring the inhabitants of the neighbouring villages, in order to learn immediately about the arrival of strangers.[3628]

In early April 1943, Voss reported to Gersdorff, informing him of what he heard from Russian peasants, with whom his people had established a good relationship.[3629] Quartered with the peasants, were Polish auxiliaries, working as volunteers in the supply units of a German division that was marching toward the front. The peasants informed Voss that these Poles were seeking out Polish prisoners of war taken by Soviet forces in September 1939, asking whether the peasants had ever seen them in the Smolensk area. It had then occurred to the peasants that three years earlier, in April 1940, fourteen months before Hitler's Barbarossa invasion, numerous transport trains carrying Polish war prisoners had been unloaded at the Gniezdowo[li] [3630] railway station

---

[li] In regard to clearing up the confusion associated with the various English spellings and other Romanised variants of this railway station's name, see endnote [3630] for this supplement. In the interest of clarity and consistency, I have decided to use the Polish spelling "Gniezdowo," as Polish and Russian, in spite of using different alphabets, have similar pronunciation for many words, owing to both being Slavic languages. For example, Polish "*prawda*," Russian "*правда*," both being pronounced as "pravda," which in English means "truth."

and that the men had been led into a small nearby forest, after which gunshots were heard from that direction for days.[3631] After hearing this news, the Polish volunteers had made excavations in the little forest, and soon located mass graves containing the remains of Polish officers, before erecting a tall birch-wood cross at the site of the discovery.[3632]

Gersdorff had the inhabitants interrogated under oath, and found their statements confirmed the time of the shootings around three years earlier in April 1940. Moreover, he personally saw many of these Russians and they repeatedly described the affair in such a way that left no doubt, that the NKVD had been responsible.[3633] Gersdorff reported this to Berlin and gave orders for the matter to be investigated. The woods lay in the immediate vicinity of the so-called "Little Castle on the Dnieper," a former NKVD (Narodnii Komisariat Vnutrennikh Del — Народный комиссариат внутренних дел or People's Commissariat of Internal Affairs)[3634] vacation resort in which the commander of his signals regiment was now billeted. Through further excavations, Gersdorff's men located more mass graves, in which clearly lay thousands of Polish officers,[3635] all murdered by a shot to the back of the neck.

In response to Gersdorff's report, OKH (Oberkommando des Heeres — Army High Command)[3636] ordered the investigation into the number and identity of the victims, and the circumstances of their murder. Directing the exhumation of the bodies, was the forensic surgeon Professor Dr. Gerhard Buhtz, Professor of Forensic Medicine and Criminology at the University of Breslau, who happened to be on the staff of Gersdorff's Chief Quartermaster's section.[3637] Joseph Goebbels' propaganda ministry perceived in this emerging truth the possibility of fracturing the Soviet-British-American alliance against the Third Reich, just two months after the catastrophe of Stalingrad.[3638] As Gersdorff commented in his autobiography: "

The Propaganda Ministry had directed that the discovery of the mass graves should be employed for propaganda purposes. Therefore I sought a suitable label for the matter. During the preparation of the initial statement, we had noticed that quite close to Gniezdowo[3639] (the nearest village to the mass burials) there were mound graves from ancient Russian history that the Soviets could use as an explanation for the discovery. [And not long afterwards, the Soviets actually did so.] I thus looked on the map for a larger place nearby with a memorable name, located the little city of Katyń about five kilometres away, and decided to designate this affair by that title.[3640]

Thus, and in no other manner, did the story of the discovery of the "Katyń Massacre" play itself out. All other descriptions are either false or completely made up, including the tale about the wolf that was supposed to have dug up the graves."[3641]

Professor Buhtz had an assistant and a commission of four or five people from the Polish Red Cross, including one or two doctors, working on the cordoned-off site guarded by Polish volunteers.[3642] Then a mass grave was opened for inspection; in it, Gersdorff estimated, there were 5000 to 6000 corpses in twelve layers, one on top of the other, with all victims having one to three bullet-holes in the back of the head. Among the bodies were two generals, a few staff officers and enlisted men who would have been orderlies for these senior officers. The bulk however, were captains and lieutenants of the Polish Army.[3643]

The corpses were all decomposed, but because of the dry sandy soil and the uniforms holding together, they could be carefully exhumed, examined, and identified.[3644] The subsequent medical examination proved beyond all doubt that the shootings took place about three years earlier, which was corroborated by the three-year-old tree-growth on the site, established indisputably by Russian and German forestry experts.[3645] Thanks, however, to the not-so-thorough NKVD executioners, the damning evidence did not end there. On the bodies were found all their papers and a large amount of money (złotys). No valuables were found except amulets under some of the shirts, a general's cigarette-case, and a few rings. However, among the papers discovered were letters from relatives which the officers had received during captivity, and, what would be most damning, numerous diaries. The letters dated from 1939 to the beginning of 1940, to which Gersdorff added: "If the Nuremberg International Tribunal wants to question the relatives of the victims of "Katyn" they can ask them when their postal contact with the prisoners was interrupted."[3646]

The diaries, uncensored by their NKVD captors, and either preserved or made legible by the application of chemicals, recounted the daily life of the victims in more revealing detail.[3647] From these diaries,[3648] it appeared that these officers were the bulk of those taken by the Soviets when they marched into Poland in 1939. After several intermediate stops they were brought to a former monastery in Kozelsk, where they thought of nothing but their hopeful release and return to Poland. By the end of March 1940 (or beginning of April), just weeks following Stalin signing their execution order on March 5th,[3649] they boarded the train and moved westward toward Smolensk.[3650] Remarkably, some of the diary entries continued until a few minutes before the shooting, stating that they stopped for a long time at a little station near Smolensk called Gniezdowo,[3651] before they were alighted from the train, and taken in black closed vehicles to the "Little Castle on the Dnieper"[3652] — the NKVD holiday resort near the wood.[3653] They still did not suspect what was in store for them until their valuables were taken from them, when diary entries show they knew they were going to be shot. All these diaries end in the first days of April 1940.[3654] Timothy Snyder, author of *Bloodlands*, documented the final diary entry of Adam Solski: "

> There, at an NKVD resort, they were searched and their valuables taken. One officer, Adam Solski, had been keeping a diary up to this moment: 'They asked about my wedding ring, which I....' The prisoners were taken into a building on the complex, where they were shot. Their bodies were then delivered, probably by truck in batches of thirty, to a mass grave that had been dug in the forest. This continued until all 4,410 prisoners sent from Kozelsk had been shot."[3655]

Before long, two more graves were discovered, by looking for places where the tree-growth was three years old. In one grave many bodies were found with the hands tied behind their backs, and others with clothing pulled around their heads. As Gersdorff commented in his affidavit: "...these men were clearly people who had been guilty of resistance."[3656]

These revelations, just two months following the Stalingrad disaster, had seemingly, for Joseph Goebbels, embodied a timely gold mine of propaganda.[3657] To this end, a propaganda detachment under Major Kost, subordinate to the commander of the communications zone behind Army Group Centre, General von Schenkendorff, was commissioned.[3658] Significantly however, deputations and commissions without any such agenda, came to Smolensk to view the sight. They included the Archbishop of Kraków, a commission of neutral news correspondents, a commission of neutral legal-medical experts, a Red Cross commission, deputations of Polish POWs of both officers, and enlisted men, and finally deputations of British and American POWs.[3659]

Ultimately, even with the suspicions of many among the multinational deputations of Nazi trickery and blatant agenda, all found it impossible to explain away the overwhelming evidence of Stalinist complicity,[3660] including the moving letters and diaries of the victims, all ending in the early days of April 1940, three years before the discovery of the mass graves, and over a year before Hitler's invasion.[3661] A unanimous verdict made by a commission comprising members from Belgium, Bulgaria, Denmark, Finland, Italy, Croatia, Netherlands, the "Protectorate" of Bohemia and Moravia (the former Czechoslovakia), Romania, Switzerland, Slovakia and Hungary.[3662]

Admittedly, it could be said that the Swiss representative, Dr. François Naville, Professor of Forensic Medicine at the University of Geneva,[3663] was the only truly neutral medical examiner at Katyń. Finland, while not occupied by Nazi Germany, was at the time, an ally of Nazi Germany, fighting alongside the German Army Group North. This was motivated by the loss of territory during the Soviet invasion of Finland in the Winter of 1939-40, as per the Secret Protocol of the infamous Molotov-Ribbentrop Pact.[3664] Bulgaria, Italy, Croatia, Romania, Slovakia and Hungary had likewise been Axis allies, with the fascist and puppet Ustaša regime in Croatia, shocking even the Germans in their brutality,[3665] while Belgium, Denmark, Netherlands and the "Protectorate" of Bohemia and Moravia (essentially the former Czechoslovakia) where under German occupation.[3666]

Hence the Stalinist assertion that these highly qualified examiners were compelled to adhere to the agenda of Goebbels' propaganda ministry. They applied this reasoning one step further to the Swiss examiner, Dr. François Naville, citing his isolation and perceived intimidation in German occupied Russia among a sea of perceived collaborationist colleagues. Indeed, post-war, Jean Vincent, a deputy of the Swiss Communist party, who dutifully claimed German perpetration of the Katyń massacre, criticised Professor Naville for having accepted participation in the mission to Katyń.[3667] Moreover, Professor Naville got no support from the CICR (International Committee of the Red Cross), who "did not want to know" who was responsible in order to avoid diplomatic complications with the Soviet Union. Only in 1989, twenty-one years after his death, was Professor Naville's discovery accepted and confirmed by the Soviet authorities[3668] under Mikhail Gorbachev.[3669] This fact was documented in 2004 by the retired Professor of Neurology and Epileptology at the University of Berne, Kazimierz Karbowski, whose Jewish mother died in the Warsaw Ghetto and father was executed at Katyń.[3670]

Post-war, Professor Naville never wavered in his conviction that the Katyń Massacre was a Stalinist perpetrated crime. As Professor Karbowski commented: "

Professor Naville continued to take a keen interest in "the Katyn affair." He gathered books, brochures and press articles, as well as iconographic material on this massacre, and even some pieces from mass graves, and has exchanged letters with Polish and foreign personalities. After his death, his daughter Madame Valentine Aubert-Naville, as well as her grandson the professor Gabriel Aubert, continued for several years, until 1995, to complete this voluminous file and then handed it over to the ICRC Archives. Other documents from the years 1943 to 1952 concerning Professor Naville can be accessed in the Swiss Federal Archives in Bern and in the State Archives of Geneva."[3671]

Most significantly, some deniers of Stalinist perpetration of Katyń, misleadingly claim that the entire international commission at Katyń consisted of twelve doctors and professors from the German-occupied areas.[3672] Clearly, however, with Professor Naville being from neutral Switzerland, this number could only be eleven at most, with some of those eleven not from German-occupied Europe, but from Axis-allied powers such as Finland.[3673] After the Barbarossa invasion in June 1941, the Finns joined the Germans in undertaking the "War of Continuation,"[3674] with the sole objective of regaining the territory lost in the 1939-40 winter war.

Among Western Allied POWs brought to Katyń were two US servicemen brought over from a POW camp in Germany. There, in April 1943, when Berlin held an international news conference to publicise the atrocity, the more senior ranking officer was Colonel John H. Van Vliet, a fourth-generation West Pointer.[3675] After returning to Washington DC on May 22, 1945,[3676] a fortnight following the official end of the war in Europe,[3677] he wrote a report concluding that the Soviets, not the Germans, were responsible. He gave the report to Major General Clayton Bissell, who was General George Marshall's assistant chief of staff for intelligence, who "deep-sixed" (discarded) it. Years later, Bissell "defended" his action before the 1951-52 Congressional Inquiry, contending that it was not in the US interest to "embarrass" an ally whose forces were still "needed" to defeat Japan.[3678]

The ally's "assistance" against Japan only happened when Stalin declared war on Japan on August 8, 1945,[3679] two days following the atomic bombing of Hiroshima, and the day before Nagasaki suffered the identical fate, three months following the end of the war in Europe.[3680] This was not the only instance of Katyń being an inconvenient truth not just for the Soviets, but for the Western Allies as well, as the importance of the Soviet giant rose, while the importance of the fourth largest[3681] but much smaller and expendable Allied power, Poland, diminished in the eyes of the British and Americans. For the Western Allies, while the war in Europe raged, Stalinist appeasement was paramount to prevent Stalin reaching a negotiated peace with Hitler, and after Germany's surrender, to secure Soviet "support" in the war against Japan. "Support," which led to the birth of the so-called "Democratic People's Republic of Korea" on the Korean peninsula's north.

From July to October 1940, Britain's darkest hour, when German-Soviet relations were most cosy in the midst of the Molotov-Ribbentrop carve-up of Europe,[3682] Polish pilots were of vital importance as bombs from the German Luftwaffe rained down on Britain.[3683] Commander-in-Chief of Fighter Command, Air Chief Marshal Sir Hugh Dowding, who once was so reluctant to allow Polish pilots into battle, summarised their contribution during the Battle of Britain in the most telling way: "Had it not been for the magnificent work of the Polish squadrons and their unsurpassed gallantry, I hesitate to say that the outcome of battle would have been the same."[3684] Now, in 1943 and beyond, the fourth largest[3685] and First Ally[3686] was deemed barely above expendable.

The Poles, even as victims of Katyń, were losers from the political fallout of Katyń, and Stalin, as the perpetrator, the political beneficiary. Most disappointingly for Goebbels, his anticipated propaganda coup proved an anti-climax. The Polish Government in Exile in London, unable to ignore the evidence, accused the Soviets of the massacre. In turn, Stalin's propagandists, in an act of gross hypocrisy, accused the Poles of being fascist collaborators in the April 19th issue of the party organ *Pravda* (правда — Truth),[3687] ignoring the Secret Protocol embedded in the August 1939 Molotov-Ribbentrop pact.[3688] At the same time, Stalin took the opportunity to sever formal diplomatic ties, forged in the wake of Hitler's June 1941 Barbarossa invasion, with the Polish Government in Exile in London.[3689] For the Western Allies, the truth of Katyń was inconvenient, as the importance of the First Ally,[3690] Poland, in the alliance was diminished in the interests of Stalinist appeasement. To swallow the pathological lie of "Uncle Joe" in Moscow was far easier and more convenient than believing the truth, for once, from a pathological liar in Berlin.

In Warsaw, packed German-run cinemas ran a grisly documentary film showing the reopened gravesite at Katyń. It was screened on the same day that SS-Brigadeführer (Major General) Jürgen Stroop launched the final assault on the heroic April-May 1943 Warsaw Jewish Ghetto Uprising.[3691] Varsovians (people of Warsaw) had proof of what they, unlike Western audiences, had long suspected. In some cases, they saw flickering pictures of the corpses and skulls of their loved ones, each with a tell-tale bullet hole. However, in another propaganda anti-climax for Goebbels, the Varsovians, and Poles in general, didn't react as he had anticipated. Rather, their sense of desolation increased, as they were not impressed by one gang of murderers exposing the crimes of another. They were simply confirmed in their long-standing belief in the "doctrine of two enemies."[3692]

During the negotiations in Moscow with Hitler's foreign minister Ribbentrop in August 1939, Stalin, rather presumptuously, acted as one who held all the trump cards.[3693] Certainly the first few months following the Barbarossa invasion in June 1941 proved this over-confidence to be misplaced, when a desperate and demoralised Stalin ordered peace feelers to be put out to Hitler,[3694] which the latter rejected. Now in 1943, Stalin again was acting like he did in August 1939. The crucial difference in 1943, unlike August 1939, was that his arrogance, was more than justified. As Robert Gellately commented: "

> It was only in 1943, Khrushchev recalled, that Stalin began to show more confidence, and only after the first big victories did he begin to strut about 'like a rooster, his chest puffed out and his nose sticking up to the sky.' Before 1943 Stalin 'walked around like a wet hen.'"[3695]

After Stalingrad, the greatly weakened German Army could only fight a defensive war — a war of survival, as the Reich gradually imploded from east and west. Moreover, the Western Allies, would be in no position to mitigate Stalin's objective of absorbing virtually all of Eastern Europe into the Soviet sphere. Central to this objective, was revenge on the Poles for the humiliation of 1920 in the Polish-Soviet War. By extension, Stalinist revenge for 1920 was just as central to Katyń.[3696] By the time Gersdorff disclosed the Katyń Massacre, Stalin knew he held all the trump cards to nullify any political fallout, such as from Katyń, with outright lies. Their plausibility was furnished from the position of clear strategic superiority on the battle field against the imploding Reich for now, and if need be, post-German surrender, against the Western Allies. He was like a shark, now smelling the blood of post-war Soviet domination of Eastern Europe. Lenin's dream of expanding the Soviet system to Eastern Europe, and perhaps beyond,[3697] was beckoning.

In his written report, before it was "deep-sixed"[3698] (discarded) by Major General Clayton Bissell, Colonel John H. Van Vliet wrote: "

> I hated the Germans. I didn't want to believe them. * * * When I became involved in the visit to Katyń I realized that the Germans would do their best to convince me that Russia was guilty. I made up my mind not to be convinced by what must be a propaganda effort."[3699]

Likewise, in his oral testimony to the 1952 Congressional Katyń committee, Van Vliet stated: "

> As a prisoner of war, I had a personal grudge against them [the Germans] and as an American army officer I had a professional grudge against them. * * * So the German story was one that I did not want to believe."[3700]

Further into his oral testimony, he elaborated: "

> If those Polish officers had been alive and in prison camp until the Germans overran the Polish prison camps, and if the Germans had in fact killed these Polish officers, then by the very virtue of the fact that their clothes had been worn and their shoes had been walked in, they would show much more wear."[3701]

Likewise, in his written report, Van Vliet explicitly said: "The sum of circumstantial evidence, impressions formed at the time of looking at the graves, what I saw in peoples' faces — all force the conclusion that Russia did it."[3702]

Van Vliet's fellow American officer at Katyń, Captain Donald Stewart, recalled in his oral testimony: "

> I was there [Katyn] under orders; I felt the matter was for a propaganda effort, and, in any event, it was a political effort. * * * I had no desire to have anything to do with a propaganda effort or a political matter."[3703]

Nevertheless, Captain Stewart later stated: "The decision I reached, I can never forget. My decision was that those [Polish] men were killed by the Russians while they were prisoners of the Russians."[3704]

Clearly, the American prisoner of war in Germany, and fourth generation West Pointer, Colonel John H. Van Vliet, and fellow American prisoner and officer Captain Donald Stewart, brought over by the Germans to Katyń in May 1943, after being taken prisoner in North Africa,[3705] were a perfect example of what Gersdorff alluded to in his 1946 affidavit to the Nuremberg Tribunal: "Even those who came fortified against being fooled by smart propaganda found it impossible to explain away the evidence as based on any possible trickery."[3706]

The US Congressional Report of December 22, 1952, elaborated on how these two American officers, arrived at equally unwanted and identical conclusions: "

> It is particularly noteworthy that both officers independently emphasized the same convincing factor, which they both stated had not been brought to their attention by the Germans but which was an independent deduction from their own observations. This was the evident fact that the clearly undisturbed corpses were clothed in winter attire which was in an excellent state of repair, showing practically no wear. The two officers also independently made these same observations about the condition of the boots of the Polish officers. In both instances the officers stated from their own personal experience as prisoners of war in a German camp that clothing could not have remained in that condition if it had been worn for a year in a prison camp."[3707] [Katyń occurred about six to seven months after the victims were taken prisoner in September 1939. The soil around Katyn was dry and sandy which meant the corpses were all decomposed, but because of the dry sandy soil and the uniforms holding together, they could be carefully exhumed, examined, and identified.][3708]

When the Polish officers were executed in early April 1940, in the early western Russian spring, according to the climatic graph for Smolensk,[3709] average temperatures would not have been much above freezing. On the other hand, when the Battle for Smolensk ended in early September 1941,[3710] the average temperature is just above 10 degrees Celsius or 54 degrees Fahrenheit. In early April 1940, it made sense that the Polish officers were wearing winter clothing, but not in the summer to very early autumn of 1941.

Gersdorff in his affidavit mentioned that if the crime had been committed during the short period between the German capture of Smolensk and the movement of the Army Group Centre to the Smolensk area, the perpetration of this crime could not have been kept a secret from the supreme military (Wehrmacht) authorities, especially if it had been the work of a German Army unit, as the Russians claim. The notorious SS police raiders (Einsatzkommandos)[3711] were, to his knowledge, withdrawn on orders from the Army Group, at the time of the capture of Smolensk.[3712]

In all, at Katyń, a total of 4000 to 5000 bodies were identified.[3713] As summer approached, it was imperative, for reasons of hygiene, to suspend the work, which was to be resumed the following autumn. However, by that time, circumstances for the Germans on the front, had taken a turn for the worse. Smolensk was then all too close to the advancing enemy and the Army Group HQ was moved to the region of Orscha.[3714] The two Polish generals were buried in two single graves, and the rest of the bodies were properly interred in new graves. Meanwhile another mass grave was discovered about as large as the first.[3715] According to Gersdorff, no National Socialist Party or SS authority had at any times any influence over the proceedings.[3716] In concluding his affidavit, Gersdorff wrote: "

> I repeat in closing that I am aware that the crime of Gniezdovo-Katyn has been surpassed many times by the murders of Jews and other Nazi crimes, but I am equally sure that the Polish officers were never shot by German hands, still less by members of the German [Wehrmacht or regular, not SS] army."[3717]

In the body of his autobiography, Gersdorff mentioned the discovery of bullet shells bearing the name of a German munitions factory. For deniers of Stalinist perpetration of Katyń, much is made of this,[3718] however, as Gersdorff states, this did not cause doubts, since it was shown, much in the spirit of Molotov-Ribbentrop,[3719] that factory had shipped pistol ammunition to the Soviet Union in 1939.[3720] Indeed, NKVD functionaries had learnt from experience that the Soviet TT pistol was unreliable for repeated use as it tended to get jammed.[3721] There was also the claim that German ropes, not supposedly available in Russia at the time,[3722] were used to tie the hands of some of the victims. According to Sanford however, the ropes were of Soviet origin.[3723] In any event, in accordance with the Molotov-Ribbentrop pact, like German ammunition and arms shipped to the Soviet Union, why not other more benign items such as rope?

In the opening to his affidavit, Gersdorff countered the assertion of the Soviet prosecutor at the Nuremberg trials that Katyń was a crime committed by the German Army: "

> It is not my purpose to cast the slightest doubt on the wealth of evidence against the Nazi terror which has been offered during this trial, since I have at all times been convinced of the guilt of the National Socialist regime. On the other hand it would depreciate the value of the evidence offered so far if an obvious untruth like the Russian account of Katyn were to remain uncontested. The Nuremberg Trial is too important an event to be burdened with an open lie."[3724]

Significantly, in his autobiography, Gersdorff alluded to the fact that he was never deposed as a witness about Katyń while he was at Nuremberg.[3725] The witnesses who were called to testify were all members of the Army Group's signals regiment or the staff of the chief signals officer — all of whom had been involved only as spectators and were hardly in a position to give solid testimony.[3726] Furthermore, again in his autobiography, Gersdorff wrote of his conversation at Katyń with the Bulgarian medical examiner Professor Marko Antonov Markov,[3727] during which, Markov asserted that there was not the slightest doubt that the murder of the Polish officers had been the work of the Soviets.[3728]

However, during the trial of major war criminals at Nuremberg, with Bulgaria now under Soviet occupation, Markov, a witness called by the Soviet prosecutor, stated the exact opposite,[3729] claiming that the International Commission had been presented with already exhumed bodies and had signed only under German pressure.[3730] A claim which was refuted later by the Swiss doctor Francois Naville and Danish doctor Helge Tramsen,[3731] leading to the Katyń allegations of the Soviets against the German army being dropped.[3732] Markov had earlier, toed the Soviet line in February 1945 in a war crimes trial in the Bulgarian capital of Sofia, as the price for having Soviet charges against him withdrawn.[3733]

Aside from Professor Markov retracting his signed assessment of Soviet guilt at Katyń, there was the Prague medical examiner Professor František Hájek;[3734] his country, like Bulgaria, became a Soviet satellite post-war. On the other hand, the Slovakian medical examiner at Katyń, František Šubík, who escaped Czechoslovakia in life threatening circumstances in April 1952, stated that at Katyń he had specifically asked Hájek if the massacre had been committed by the Russians, to which Hájek answered in the affirmative.[3735] Unlike some deniers of Stalinist perpetration of Katyń, who misleadingly claim that the Hungarian examiner, Ferenc Orsós, also withdrew his signed assessment of Soviet guilt at Katyń,[3736] professors Markov and Hájek, on pain of death, were the only ones successfully coerced by the communist authorities to revoke their signatures.[3737] Orsós had escaped the Red Army siege of Budapest in early December 1944, and post-war lived in West Berlin, and so is used by some pro-Soviet Katyń deniers as a so-called example of one who recanted his signature without Stalinist coercion.[3738]

The truth is that in 1952, the American Congress established a commission of inquiry in Washington, to which its members came to Frankfurt am Main in the spring of 1952 to interview witnesses. Orsós was interrogated there as a witness on April 21, 1952, as was the Danish examiner Helge Tramsen and the Italian examiner Vincenzo Palmieri. During witness questioning, Orsós asked that his name should not be mentioned in the newspaper, which the committee of inquiry could not promise because the press was present during the public questioning.[3739] Hence the Stalinist distortion that Orsós recanted his assessment of Soviet guilt at Katyń in 1943.

In regard to Professor Hájek and communist coercion in general in post-war Czechoslovakia, pages 8 to 9 of František Šubík's 1953 statement to the CIA are most enlightening. As is the latter's shrewd ability, without rank capitulation, to placate and stall his Stalinist-puppet post-war overlords. "

> On Sunday afternoon, 6 April 1952, a tall man called on me; he introduced himself (in Czech) as Vincent NECAS, editor of the Czech Publishing Office (Cesky Tiskovy Kancelar — CTK). He told me that the 'American Imperialists' had set up a Congressional committee to prove that the Soviets were to blame for the massacre of Polish soldiers at Katyn for propaganda purposes. He mentioned that the Czech journalist, Dr, Frantisek KOZISEK, had already written newspaper articles proving that the Germans were to blame for the Katyn mass murders. Dr. KOZISEK had gone to Katyn in his capacity as a

journalist either before or after our commission was there. He represented the Moravian-Bohemian Protectorate.[3740] I had read Dr. KOZISEK'S article which stated that the Germans had committed 'another gruesome, bestial atrocity,' and that the 'American imperialists' were trying to twist the facts for propaganda purposes. He added that Prof. Dr. HAJEK had done likewise. NECAS said that he had gotten them to write the articles. Dr. HAJEK's article was published in the newspaper, Lidova Demokracie (People's Democracy); he reiterated his statements of 1945 that the Germans had committed the atrocities at Katyn. I know, however, that after Dr. HAJEK returned to Czechoslovakia in May 1945, he was arrested by the Communists and jailed for three days; shortly after that he wrote, under duress, a brochure entitled The Truth About Katyn. Although I haven't seen Dr. HAJEK since we returned from Katyn in 1943, I am certain that he was forced to write the brochure, because at Katyn, I specifically asked him his opinion as an expert in criminal medicine. I clearly remember him saying that there was no doubt that the murders had been committed by the Russians, since they were in command of the territory at the time the murders were estimated to have taken place. NOIBERT, Czech publisher, told Dr. AMBRUS that Dr. HAJEK was coerced into writing his statement although it was prefaced by the assertion that he was voluntarily submitting his views on the subject. NECAS requested me to write the 'facts' about Katyn, strongly slanted against the 'Western Imperialists.' I told him that I was not an expert in criminal medicine[3741] and that Dr. Hajek was better qualified to give an opinion. NECAS said the reason was not adequate, I would have to write something immediately. I told him the earliest I could get it to him would be the next day. He said that if he didn't call for the material before noon the next day, I should send it special delivery to: Vincent NECAS, CTK, Praha, Na Porici. I wrote about a page and a half, double-spaced, on a typewriter. He didn't come for it so I sent it to him as requested. I stated that I was not a specialist in criminal medicine, that I had not participated in any debates at Katyn since this was not my field.[3742] I said that I had always been interested in Poland because I had translated Polish works into SLOVAK and that my interest in Katyn was general; I wanted to find out whether the bodies were actually Polish. I went on to say, in carefully couched terms, that it was common knowledge that the Germans had committed similar atrocities and that they were capable of having committed the atrocity at Katyn.[3743] I could see what NECAS was after and I felt I had to slant my story. To have done otherwise would have meant possible incarceration. I quoted the German admission (contained in a book published by the Germans) that the cartridges used in the killings at Katyn were of German manufacture.[3744] ... I also said that when we arrived at Katyn, the graves had already been opened by the Germans, and the bodies were arranged with typical German neatness. I stated that the commission had examined only some 15 bodies. I pointed out [fabricated for the benefit of Vincent NECAS] that Dr. COSTEDOAT had been dismissed as a member of the Commission because he did not want to sign the final report of the Commission,[3745] and that only three men had written the protocol which was read before a large group at a banquet which made it very inconvenient to contest any part of the report.[3746] I used these points to slant the blame for Katyn on the Germans, although certainly none of them proved anything. I tried to slant the blame in the Germans' direction without actually saying that they had really committed the atrocities. I found this difficult to do because of what I had seen at Katyn and the unamimous [actual misspelling] opinion of the experts on the scene at the time.

Up until the time I left Czechoslovakia in April 1952, nothing concerning my report on Katyn had ever been published to the best of my knowledge. About 15 April 1952, I received a letter from the Tatra Publishing House in Bratislava begging me not to stand by silently any longer and urging me to write my views on the matter and so disprove the false claims of the West. I replied that earlier in the month I had submitted my views in full and told them to whom I had sent the data. [Namely to Vincent NACAS — editor of the Czech Publishing Office (Cesky Tiskovy Kancelar — CTK.] I added that I thought it a tragedy that books of Polish poetry which I had translated had been banned in Czechoslovakia. These books had been written during the first [pre-WWII] Czechoslovak Republic and contained absolutely no political coloring [American spelling] in the least. [Albeit, containing no Socialist revolutionary fervour.] I ended my letter with 'Phooey on life! (fuj zivot!) Sincerely yours, (signature), former poet, former physician, and former human being!"[3747]

Communist harassment of members of the April-May 1943 Katyń Commission didn't end with the Soviet-imposed Iron Curtain engulfing all of Eastern Europe post-war. Earlier, mention was made of the Swiss investigator Francois Naville being pressured by Jean Vincent, deputy head of the Swiss Communist party, who dutifully claimed German perpetration of the Katyń massacre.[3748] Another however, was the Italian investigator, Vincenzo Palmieri, who from 1948 onwards, in his refusal to recant his signature given in the April-May 1943 Katyn investigation, was openly accused by the Italian Communist Party of being a Nazi collaborator. This from a party taking its instructions from Moscow,[3749] as they dutifully ignored Stalinist co-operation with Hitler, embodied in the August 1939 Molotov-Ribbentrop pact.[3750] Moreover, Professor Palmieri's former student Professor Canfora recalled those post-war years as follows: "

> I remember things had started to change especially since when in Russia, Stalin decided to eliminate all coroners who had participated in the Katyn expedition. The KGB[3751] killed several doctors, some of whom were poisoned. We knew that Palmieri risked his life, even if we didn't know these dark threats were coming from the secret services. We had no doubt that he was stalked, but we did not know if the stalking was ordered by the Italian or American governments, or if so it was simply Italian police officers charged with protecting him from the intemperance of some all to zealous [communist] militant."[3752]

The Finnish investigator, Arno Saxén (1895 — 1952), an adjunct professor of ear, nose and throat diseases at the University of Helsinki from 1928 to 1938, and a professor of pathological anatomy since 1938,[3753] among numerous other titles of great acclaim, came under intense pressure from the Allied (Soviet) Monitoring Commission, headed by Andrei Zhdanov,[3754] that came to Finland post-war. This commission had a British presence,[3755] but was dominated by the Soviets attempting to extract the most favourable terms in the armistice with Finland. Prominent of which, was the Soviet demand for Saxén to join professors Markov and Hájek, in recanting his signature of Soviet guilt at Katyń. The resolute Saxén refused.[3756]

However, in taking the only course of action allowable to his conscience, he was, like his fellow Katyń investigator, Vincenzo Palmieri, labelled a Nazi collaborator, as the Helsinki University attempted to have him dismissed.[3757] At the time, it was feared Finland, in these so-named *"Vaaran vuodet"* — "Years of Danger" from 1944-48, could become a communist state, either through occupation by the Soviet Union or through a Communist coup.[3758] Hence, Katyń was an inconvenient truth for both the Soviet Union and jittery Finns who feared Saxén's perceived intransigence would provoke a Soviet invasion and occupation. In spite of this, Saxén refused to let Katyń's truth rot in the graves of its victims,[3759] but would, in the next few years, live in Sweden, until the "Years of Danger" passed.[3760]

When back in Finland in 1952, Saxén informed the US Senate that he was ready to consult with the committee's investigation into Katyń.[3761] However, before doing so, he travelled to a conference in Zürich Switzerland, before returning to Helsinki, where at age 57, on November 19, 1952, he suddenly died of a heart attack.[3762] Just 106 days later, on March 5, 1953,[3763] Stalin followed him to the grave. Could Arno Saxén, as Vincenzo Palmieri's former student and longtime friend, Professor Canfora, suggested, have been a victim of Stalinist retribution? Indeed, many historians, such as Adam Zamoyski and the Russian historian Natalya Lebedeva, see the Katyń massacre itself as Stalin's retribution for the humiliation of 1920.[3764] As Zdzisław Mackiewicz, the son of a Katyń victim wrote: "Według źródeł polskich komisja miała zamiar przesłuchiwać Saxéna w roku 1952. Czy przeszkodzili w tym agenci KGB?"[3765] Which translates to: "According to Polish sources, the [1952 US] commission intended to interrogate Saxén in 1952. Was it prevented by KGB agents?" Mackiewicz concludes his paper thus: "

> Moje badania stały sie dla mnie niezwykłym przypadkiem. Okazało się, że prawnuk Arno Saxéna i syn mojej córki, czyli prawnuk mego ojca zamordowanego w Katyniu, są najlepszymi przyjaciółmi, nie wiedząc wcale, że ich pradziadkowie spotkali się w Katyniu. Jeden z nich to naukowiec badający groby, drugi to Polski oficer w tych grobach znaleziony!"[3766]

Which translates to: "

My research has become an extraordinary accident for me. It turned out that a great-grandson of Arno Saxén and a son of my daughter — great-grandson of my father murdered in Katyń, became best friends without knowing at all that their great-grandparents met in Katyń. One of them a scientist studying graves, the other a Polish officer found in these graves!"

... and moreover, perhaps, both victims of Stalinist retribution.

On June 6, 2007, Arno Saxén was posthumously awarded the Order of Merit of the Republic of Poland in a ceremony at the Polish embassy in Helsinki. It was received by Arno's eldest and 86 year-old son Erkki, following in his father's footsteps as a professor of pathology, from Poland's Chargè d'Affaires, Bolesław Kościuszkiewicz.[3767] That same year, Vincenzo Palmieri, who passed away on December 23, 1994, was likewise posthumously awarded the same honour "for outstanding services in discovering and documenting the truth about the Katyń massacre."[3768]

In 1947, Dr. André Costedoat, who had been sent to Katyń by the head of the Vichy French government to observe the work of the Commission,[3769] died in "unexplained"[3770] circumstances. The Danish investigator, Dr. Helge Tramsen, a specialist at the Institute of Forensic Medicine in Copenhagen, received an official written request from the director of the Danish Ministry of Foreign Affairs, Nils Svenningsen,[3771] and subsequently, permission from the anti-Nazi Danish resistance,[3772] of which he was a member. This was recorded in Tramsen's diary and dealt with in the Danish documentary film *Kraniet fra Katyn (The Skull from Katyn; 2006)*.[3773] Tramsen flew to Smolensk via Berlin, where he and the other committee members stayed in a hotel, from which they commuted to Katyń.

For Dr. Tramsen, the days of April 1940 involved autopsies of murdered Polish officers, confirming that the executions took place in the spring of 1940. Back in Denmark, Tramsen described the layout of the victims at Katyń: "they lie like sardines in neatly arranged layers, heads in the same direction."[3774] While in Katyń, the Germans, without Dr. Tramsen's consent, photographed him and subsequently published that photo in the German magazine *Signal*.[3775] On his return, while in transit in Berlin, Tramsen reported on the Katyń massacre to a Danish MP in Berlin. At the same time, he had in his possession a package for the Danish resistance — namely the skull of a murdered Polish army officer, Ludwik Szymański from Kraków, as material evidence of the Katyń massacre.[3776]

Later, for the Danish resistance movement, Dr. Tramsen wrote another report on Katyń, blaming Moscow for the crime. Not surprisingly, it made him very unpopular with the Danish communists,[3777] who less than four years earlier in late August 1939, in the wake of the signing of the Molotov-Ribbentrop pact, had themselves, been proclaiming pro-Nazi German rhetoric.[3778] The document was sent to the Danish Ministry of Foreign Affairs and hence to SOE (British Special Operations Executive). On July 28 1944, Dr. Tramsen was arrested by the Germans on the basis of a denunciation and taken to the Frøslev internment camp.[3779] There he delivered a lecture on Katyń to the prisoners.[3780] This raises the question: was Dr. Tramsen denounced by a vindictive Danish communist? Certainly, in the August to October 1944 Warsaw General Uprising, as will be dealt with in Polish WWII Supplement IV "AK and 1944 Warsaw General Uprising — Stalin's mass murder by German proxy", overwhelming evidence suggests Stalin was not beyond letting the Germans wipe out the non-communist Polish Home Army, as his Red Army lay virtually idle on the east bank of the Vistula in Warsaw's Praga district.

Upon his liberation from Frøslev in 1945, Dr. Tramsen was dismissed from the Institute of Forensic Medicine and was continually harassed. The leftist press, in ignoring the Molotov-Ribbentrop pact,[3781] constantly slandered him, accusing him of collaboration with Nazi Germany, while "unknown perpetrators" smashed windows in his apartment. Upon his dismissal, Dr. Tramsen opened a private medical practice and later worked during the Korean War (June 1950 to July 1953)[3782] as the head of medical staff aboard the hospital ship *Jutland*.[3783] The harassment suffered by Dr. Tramsen and the growing Soviet threat in the 1950s affected his health. However, despite pressure, Dr. Tramsen never revoked his statements blaming the NKVD for the Katyń massacre, and in April 1952 he took part in the hearing before the US Madden Committee in Frankfurt am Main.[3784]

On many occasions, he repeated his unwavering position, which included interviews in English with the Polish section of Radio Free Europe in the 1960s.[3785] In 1970, in mysterious circumstances, Dr. Tramsen's eldest daughter Elizabeth, the wife of Polish composer Romuald Twardowski, died in Warsaw. Years earlier, against her father's will, she left Denmark to live with her husband. In his grief, Dr. Tramsen claimed, until his death in 1979, that Elizabeth was murdered by KGB agents, to avenge his unwavering stance on the Katyń massacre.[3786] Initially, it would be plausible to maintain the position that the only truly neutral investigator at Katyń was the Swiss investigator Francois Naville, as all the other investigators were from countries either occupied by or friendly to Nazi Germany. However, the stories of František Šubík, Vincenzo Palmieri, Arno Saxén and Helge Tramsen (the latter a member of the Danish anti-Nazi resistance) refute this notion, since, in spite of intense pressure and fear for their lives post-war, none would recant their 1943 stance on Katyń. In each case, the easy way out would have been to give in to communist pressure post-war, both internal and external, rather than to hold firm to the stance, however dangerous, in their minds, of justice.

The two investigators that did recant post-war, Marko Antonov Markov of Bulgaria and František Hajek of Czechoslovakia, were living in countries that became Soviet satellites post-war, rendering their respective post-war "positions" on Katyń hardly credible. Moreover, the testimony of the US Army officers Colonel John H. Van Vliet and Captain Donald Stewart, brought over by the Germans to Katyń in May 1943, after being taken prisoner in North Africa,[3787] were hardly predisposed to German propaganda.[3788]

The Burdenko Commission was of like credibility to the recantations of professors Markov and Hájek; it was set up by the Soviets in the months following the German retreat from Smolensk in September 1943.[3789] Its sole objective was to manufacture a conclusion of German guilt for the Katyń Wood massacre, or as its brief explicitly stated: "to ascertain and investigate 'the Circumstances of the Shooting of Polish Officer Prisoners by the German-Fascist Invaders in the Katyń Forest'."[3790] As Tadeusz Wolsza commented, in part quoting professor Jacek Tebinka: "

> Tebinka has given an elegant explication of the issue: 'whereas British diplomacy wanted to hush up the matter as much as possible, the Kremlin did its best to exonerate itself.' And he adds, 'One of the items on the Soviet agenda was to invite a group of Moscow-based Western diplomats and journalists to come to Katyn round about January 21, 1944.[3791] Britain's diplomats did not participate in the project, unlike Kathleen Harriman, the daughter of the American ambassador, and John F. Melby, third secretary of the US embassy, both of whom came away convinced that the Germans had done it. But most of the British and American journalists had reservations, not to say they were skeptical about the Soviet claim. This was because

they felt that the excursion was an attempt to bribe them. Never before during the War had an excursion been organized for journalists in the Soviet Union with such splendor — luxury railcars, good cuisine and drinks ....' The most concise way of summing up British policy on the Katyn affair and the Polish government would be to say it was an attempt to get the Poles to accept the conclusions of the Soviet commission and try once more to embark on talks with Stalin."[3792]

George Sanford's assessment of the Burdenko Commission, indeed bears out the above, being none too flattering of Kathleen Harriman, the 25-year-old daughter of the millionaire Averill Harriman, who was US ambassador to the Soviet Union at the time.[3793] Her role at Katyń, according to Sanford, appeared as that of a "silly girl"[3794] being used by Roosevelt and the State Department in support of the thesis of German guilt.[3795]

Professor Nikolai Burdenko was a member of the Soviet Academy of Sciences, as was his fellow commission member, the writer and former Count Aleksei Nikolayevich Tolstoy (1882—1945),[3796] a remote relative of Leo Tolstoy.[3797] In spite of being deaf by that time, Professor Burdenko was chosen, as he still held world renown as a neuro-surgeon who had founded the Institute of the Mind. Moreover, and perhaps more importantly in the Stalinist context, he had acted as Stalin's and Molotov's personal physician.[3798] On September 27, 1943, just two days following the Red Army's capture of Smolensk, Burdenko requested permission to begin conducting fieldwork at Katyń.[3799] However, it was more than three months later that his infamous committee arrived at Katyń, as "preparation" of the crime scene was first required by the People's Commissariat for Internal Affairs (NKVD) and People's Commissariat for State Security (NKGB).[3800]

Such "preparation" was most pressing for the nervous Politburo decision-makers who approved the death order of the Polish officers in March 1940. Hence the haste of officers who carried out the death orders issued by NKVD Chief Lavrenty Beria, to camouflage their crimes at the expense of methodical and professional investigation. Even trusted members of the scientific establishment of the party, including Burdenko, were excluded, as Stalin eventually endorsed the "preparation" and manipulation of the crime scene.[3801]

As a result, the perpetrators of the Katyń crime had the first opportunity to conduct a preliminary "investigation" of the Katyn crime, which laid the groundwork for further concealment. From late September 1943 and throughout October, NKVD and NKGB officers from their headquarters in Moscow, accompanied by members of the NKVD Board of the Smolensk Oblast, arrived at the crime scene. Leonid Rajchman, a head of counter-intelligence of the NKGB, commanded the initial operations in the Katyn region, while the Deputy People's Commissar of Internal Affairs, Sergei Kruglov and People's Commissar of State Security Vsevolod Merkulov guided and oversaw the whole operation from Moscow. The latter two were members of the "troika" authorised by the NKVD to implement the Katyń order on March 5, 1940, which subsequently led to them making several on-site inspections in 1943.[3802]

From the beginning of October 1943 to January 1944, officers of the NKVD and NKGB made efforts to hide the truth about the crimes and create a false picture of the fate of Polish prisoners of war. Operational activities of the officers under Kruglov and Merkulov, partially described later as "the initial investigation into the so-called Katyn matter," involved firstly securing the site of the crime and concealment of bodies from outsiders; secondly, the opening of the grave pits between October and December 1943, and finally, preparing evidence for the future "exhumations" in order to draw manipulated conclusions about innocence and guilt.[3803] The second task involved the fabrication of documents with dates from the second half of 1940 and first half of 1941, demonstrating that the Soviet attempts to show that the Polish victims were still alive during that time frame,[3804] when dates of final entry were recorded in the diaries of the victims, suggested otherwise.[3805] The fabricated documents were slipped into the corpses to be later "discovered" by the Burdenko Commission as evidence of German guilt.[3806] All this was verified from post-Cold-War analysis of documents at the Russian archives and confirmed by the Military Prosecutor General of Russia.[3807]

However, crucial as the manufacturing of physical evidence was to the Stalinist sanitisation of events, the main focus of the Kruglov-Merkulov team was the collection of coerced live testimony. That encompassed the collection of false testimony in writing, preparing witnesses to confirm the false version of events, and ruthlessly eliminating any witnesses who would dare to proclaim the truth. Of interest were people with knowledge of the circumstances of the crime as well as those who had nothing to do with it. The favourite and frequently used method was to intimidate and blackmail the targeted persons by threatening them with accusations of collaboration with the

Germans during the occupation.[3808] Given this, it's almost certain that Russian peasants interviewed, for example, by Gersdorff and his sub-ordinates during April to May 1943,[3809] would have been among those intimidated to conform to the contrived Stalinist narrative. Certainly, as dealt with earlier, such Stalinist coercion of witnesses was used post-war to force the two international Katyń commissioners of Markov and Hájek, by then living in Soviet satellite countries, to recant their con-clusions of April-May 1943.[3810]

The findings of the Kruglov-Merkulov team known as "The Special Committee Composed of Representatives of Relevant Bodies" in the crucial period from October 5, 1943 to January 10, 1944, were summarised in the "Information on the Results of a Preliminary Inves-tigation into the So-Called Katyn Matter" (Information of a Preliminary Investigation). This document, signed by Kruglov and Merkulov, con-cluded with the following fabricated sequence of events:[3811] "

> 1. The Polish prisoners of war were working on a road con-struction project from the spring of 1940 to June 1941 (that is until Barbarossa — Hitler's invasion of the Soviet Union) west of Smolensk. [They were housed in three camps: 1-ON, 2-ON, and 3-ON, situated 25–45 kilometres west of Smolensk. These camps were a wholly fictitious NKVD invention and were never given precise locations.][3812]

> 2. The prisoners of war were captured by the Germans in late August and September 1941.

> 3. The shooting of Polish prisoners of war in the autumn of 1941 in the Katyn Forest was carried out by an "unknown German military institution" that was stationed in a dacha in "Kozy Gory" until the end of September 1943. Colonel Ahrens commanded the unit; his closest associates and accomplices in this crime were Lieutenant Rechst and Second Lieutenant Hott.

> 4. After the shooting of the prisoners of war on orders from Berlin in the autumn of 1941, Germany undertook proactive efforts to assign their despicable crimes to the Soviet pow-er."[3813]

In a further embellishment of the thesis of German guilt, the NKVD-NKGB stressed the notion that, in accordance with the German fascist ideology of "extermination of the 'inferior' Slavic nations," the Germans also killed 500 Russian prisoners of war who were digging the Katyń graves. Subsequently, the Katyń lie, made possible by the mystification of the crime by the NKVD-NKGB and the report of the Kruglov-Merkulov committee, became the official position of the Soviet state.[3814]

This contrived preliminary report was finalised on January 10, 1944, and it was not until two days later, in Moscow, more than three months after Nikolai Burdenko's request to start an investigation on the Katyń massacre, that the eight-member committee to be led by him was created. It was officially dubbed "Special Commission for the Findings and Examination of the Circumstances Surrounding the Shooting by the German Fascist Invaders in the Katyn Forest of the Prisoners of War."[3815] As already mentioned, the official name for the commission led by Burdenko, explicitly stated his commission's pre-determined outcome. Fifteen months later, an SS Drumhead court-martial would likewise have its verdict predetermined for Dietrich and four of his fellow conspirators at Flossenbürg, and his brother-in-law, Hans von Dohnányi at Sachsenhausen.[3816]

The inaugural meeting of the Burdenko Commission in Moscow, on the 13th, left no doubt as to the course of action it would take. Deputy Commissioner of Internal Affairs Sergei Kruglov, was also present to highlight the findings of his commission, as guidelines for the Burdenko commission, which were accepted without the slightest discussion, as demonstrated in the following documented exchange between Tolstoy, Kruglov, and Burdenko:[3817] "

> TOLSTOY: The most basic statement is that the Poles were still alive after our withdrawal from Smolensk.

> KRUGLOV: Very many witnesses testify that in autumn 1943 Germans escorted small groups of Poles, about 30-40 each in vehicles to the Katyń Forest.

> TOLSTOY: I think that at upon opening of the graves there should certainly be some documents, cards, notes, letters dated later than 1940.

> KRUGLOV: Later than the spring of 1940; for sure it will be representative material evidence ...

BURDENKO: As we heard from a speech by Comrade Kruglov, this matter is serious, and I propose to discuss the plan of our work."

The field work of the Burdenko Commission from the 16th to the 26th of January 1944,[3818] consisted of collecting "evidence" for developing and supporting the fabricated version of German guilt for the murder of the Poles. The Burdenko Commission did not investigate who perpetrated the crime. Rather, as obsequiously stated in the official name of this body, it only investigated the "circumstances of the shooting by the German-Fascist invaders of the Katyn Forest."[3819] Gathering evidence in practice was limited to the recording of evidence gathered and manufactured by the Kruglov committee. Typical of this was the extraction from the Katyń pits of previously prepared materials left by the NKVD-NKGB.[3820]

On January 24, 1944, the Burdenko Commission, issued its official communiqué, formally signed by all its eight members. It was subsequently released on January 26, published in *Pravda* (правда — "Truth"), and referenced by the Telegraph Agency of the Soviet Union (TASS) and other newspapers. The release of the communiqué on January 24, 1944, completed the basic work of the Commission, but Burdenko, very involved in the promotion of its product, continued his correspondence and, at least on paper, the Commission convened again many times.[3821] However, as already mentioned, two days earlier on January 22, the Burdenko Commission, recognising an urgent need to present material to the international community, organised a press conference for mostly foreign journalists, even though the Commission had yet to officially publish its findings from the investigation.[3822]

For the Soviets, having qualified western investigators involved in their examination of the Katyń crime scene was unthinkable. However, at some stage, some sort of foreign presence for international consumption of the Soviet Katyń lie, would be demanded. Hence, a group of about 20 journalists gathered, nearly all British and American except for a Frenchman and the Polish communist editor of *Wolna Polska* and subsequent PRL cultural notable, Jerzy Borejsza.[3823] Among the Americans was John Melby, the Third Secretary of the American Embassy and Kathleen Harriman, the 25-year-old daughter of the millionaire Averill Harriman, who was US ambassador to the USSR at the time.[3824]

This group was in no position to draw any substantive conclusions. Their trip was short and superficial and the atmosphere was somewhat strained. As already stated, Kathleen Harriman allowed herself to be used by Roosevelt and the State Department in support of the thesis of German guilt. John Melby, as well, was all too ready to accept [3825] what was, for himself, Roosevelt and the entire Anglo-American alliance in general, the birth of the convenient "Katyń Lie."[3826] Another participant in this visit, Alexander Werth, became a well-known Soviet specialist and journalist based in the United Kingdom. In 1966, an edited Russian translation of his massive *Russia at War* was published in the Soviet Union towards the end of its second phase of destalinisation. While Werth's criticism of the weak, shoddy and unconvincing presentation of the Soviet case by Burdenko was published in this translated work, critically, it did not directly tackle the central issue of Soviet responsibility.[3827] Hence, it fostered the persistence of the Katyń Lie.[3828]

The British embassy in Moscow reported that the journalists, while predisposed to accept the Soviet version, had not been impressed by what they saw and heard. Witnesses were clearly intimidated and "told their tale before the same people and repeated it parrot fashion." The Soviet case was based entirely on the credibility of the medical evidence which could not be challenged, and unexpected questions by the journalists caused their hosts "noticeable irritation."[3829] A quintessential case in point was when an American journalist asked if the Committee noticed that the victims were dressed too heavily in sweaters and warm underwear for the August and September weather [of 1941, when the Battle for Smolensk was raging]. Vladimir Potemkin, the People's Commissar of Education,[3830] replied that cool nights begin in September (ignoring August), and Tolstoy tortuously explained that the men had no other clothing.[3831] This had been noticed by the American prisoner of war in Germany, and fourth generation West Pointer, Colonel John H. Van Vliet, and fellow American prisoner and officer Captain Donald Stewart, brought over by the Germans to Katyń in May 1943, after being taken prisoner in North Africa.[3832] As Witold Wasilewski commented: "

> Perhaps this exchange contributed to the replacement in subsequent Soviet documents of the August and September 1941 time frame (alternatively, the end of August and September) with the phrase "autumn" of 1941."[3833]

This point it seems, was missed during the three months in late 1943 of the preparatory Kruglov-Merkulov committee. Moreover, as alluded to by Witold Wasilewski: "

It should be noted that, contrary to popular opinions, activities related to the inspection of the death pits and testing of the exhumed bodies could not — at the then existing state of knowledge — give a clear and unarguable answers to questions about the time of the murder of POWs, and so unquestionably determine the identity the perpetrators, and could be useful only when compared with data collected by other means. Earlier correct conclusions made under the auspices of the German [sponsored] investigation in 1943 stemmed more from the examination of documents [Such as the dates of final entries in the diaries of the victims.][3834] and hearing witnesses than from medical forensic testing."[3835]

Moreover, as stated by Gersdorff, after the discovery of the first mass grave, several more were discovered by looking for areas of three-year-old tree growth. This implies that the spring of 1940 was the time the executions were carried out.[3836] The age of such growth was established indisputably by Russian and German forestry experts.[3837]

In June 1950, a curious report surfaced in the Russian exile press in the US. Boris Olshanskii, a Voronezh University academic, who served with the Red Army in Stalingrad and later on the Belarusian Front, had succeeded in defecting from the Soviet Zone of Germany.[3838] Olshanskii claimed to have been a close and long-established family friend of Burdenko's and to have visited the ailing surgeon, who had suffered two strokes in Moscow, just before his death in 1946. According to Olshanskii, Burdenko stated that Mother Russia's soil was full of Katyńs.[3839] Stalin had personally ordered him to visit Katyń to refute the German accusation. Such unsupported hearsay evidence is unprovable even though it was repeated in 1952 before the US Congress committee investigating Katyń.[3840] In words reminiscent of Beria's admission at a meeting in October 1940, six or so months after Katyń,[3841] Burdenko allegedly said that "our comrades from the NKVD made a great blunder" [In committing the massacre].[3842]

Hearsay or not, the alleged statement of Burdenko "Mother Russia's soil was full of Katyńs," with emphasis on the symbolic plural for Katyń, would, in the decades following, be proven chillingly true. Around the time of the Katyń massacre, four other massacres of Polish officers took place. They were to the south-east of Katyń, near the Ukrainian city of Kharkov; to the north-east of Katyń in the western Russian town of Kalinin, now modern-day Tver;[3843] to the south of Katyń, the western Ukrainian village of Bykivnia near Kiev;[3844] and finally to the west-south-west of Katyń, the western Belarusian village of Kuropaty near Minsk.[3845] These four massacres have, in the modern-day, become synonymous with the story of Katyń, as they embody the Stalinist theme of extermination of the Polish officer class, or anyone who bore even the slightest indication of a privileged class or independent thought.[3846] Of these four additional massacres, the ones perpetrated near Kharkov and Kalinin are the best known.

East of Kharkov was the Starobelsk prison, a former nunnery, which held 3,894 prisoners, which included a lot of scholars, priests, about 100 teachers and 400 doctors, several hundred lawyers and engineers, several dozen journalists, and also eight generals. The latter group included the defender of Lwów (Lviv), Franciszek Sikorski, and Konstanty Plisowski, Stanisław Haller, Leonard Skierski, Leon Billewicz, Aleksander Kowalewski, Kazimierz Orlik-Lukoski and Piotr Skuratowicz.[3847] They would all be buried near Kharkov. West of Kalinin was the Ostashkov prison, a former monastery on Stolobny Island on Seliger Lake, 11 kilometres from Ostashkov. Among the prisoners were State Police and Military Police officials, secret service and counter-espionage officials, the soldiers of the Border Protection Corps and the employees of the Prison Guard. As well, almost the entire staff of the Military Police Education Centre, among whom was Colonel Stanislaw Sitek. This camp was the largest of the three camps, holding 6,570 prisoners of war just before it was disbanded in April 1940,[3848] around the time of the massacres. They would all be buried near Kalinin, now modern-day Tver. As stated earlier, the victims of Katyń were held at a former monastery in Kozelsk to the east of Katyń.[3849]

For the almost simultaneous Stalinist-perpetrated murders at multiple locations of mostly Polish officers (and reserves) and some civilian intelligentsia, Katyń has come to collectively embody them all. This is due to the fact, that for almost half a century after the execution of these crimes, the knowledge about people taken into captivity, or arrested and finally murdered, based on the resolution of the Political Bureau of All-Union Communist Party (Bolsheviks), was limited to the information about the executions in Katyń.[3850] Hence, the term "Katyń massacre" refers not only to that massacre itself, but also to the ones committed at Kharkov, Kalinin, Bykivnia and Kuropaty, and to their origin, the lies accompanying them, and attempts to judge those responsible for them.[3851]

Unlike the Katyń Wood massacre itself, where the crime scene had been under German control for more than three years from June 1941 to September 1944, Kalinin, where the NKVD perpetrated executions took place, and the nearby village of Mednoye, where the bodies were buried, were never at any stage, under German control. From October 17 to 20, 1941,[3852] the village was on the front line of the northernmost sector for the Battle of Moscow,[3853] but on October 21, the Wehrmacht was driven back during a Red Army counter-offensive.[3854] In one of the pro-Soviet Katyń myths, much had been made of the fact that bullets and shells consistent with the German manufactured 7.65 D Geco pistol,[3855] had been found on the Katyń Wood crime scene. However, the same types of German bullets were also found in the mass graves of Poles in Mednoye, which the Germans never occupied.[3856] Moreover, as mentioned earlier, Gersdorff in his autobiography, wrote that this did not cause doubts, since it was shown, much in the spirit of Molotov-Ribbentrop, that the factory had shipped pistol ammunition to the Soviet Union in 1939.[3857] Indeed, NKVD functionaries had learnt from experience that the Soviet TT pistol was unreliable for repeated use as it tended to get jammed.[3858]

While news of the Katyń massacre was revealed decades ago, it was only in the spring of 1988 that rumours spread about the bodies lying near Mednoye. According to Sergei Glushkov, who co-founded the Katyń Memorial's Tver branch, former officers of the KGB, the NKVD's 1954 successor agency,[3859] revealed the presence of the secret graveyard. One day, Glushkov and five other Memorial members travelled to the site to see what they could find.[3860] "We just climbed over the metal fence and started digging," said Glushkov, who, in 2019, was 72 years old. "It definitely wasn't legal, but we couldn't wait." He said a duty officer from the KGB gave him coordinates for the site.[3861] It was from the Ostashkov camp, where, according to documents signed by high-ranking NKVD operatives, more than 6,000 Poles were transferred in groups to the secret police headquarters in Kalinin in May 1940. Over a period of several months, 100 Poles were taken daily from the camp to the city.

The documents include no order to kill the prisoners, but proof that executions took place in the basement of the NKVD headquarters, came from the March 1991 testimony of Dmitry Tokarev, the former head of the NKVD's regional branch.[3862] It was then that military prosecutors twice questioned Tokarev as part of a criminal investigation into the Katyń massacre. Tokarev explained how each night, some 250 prisoners were shot in secret and later driven to Mednoye for burial. Exhumations took place at the site in 1991, 1994, and 1995. The photos from the digs show earth turned navy blue from the dye that seeped from the uniforms of Polish officers.[3863] Even if one were to consider the unlikely case that Tokarev, for whatever reason, was lying, the burning question still remains as to how the bodies of Polish police officers ended up in a mass grave on Soviet soil in Mednoye, which the Germans never reached.

Twenty-three pits were excavated, containing the remains of around 2,300 victims and various personal items that established the identities of many victims. In Mednoye today, tall wooden crosses mark the spots where the pits were dug; only the Polish part of the burial site has been studied. The names of Soviet victims of repression who may also lie there in their thousands are yet to be ascertained.[3864] Every year, since the 1990s, on October 30th, a delegation from Poland came to lay flowers at the building of the former NKVD headquarters, now a modern-day university building, beneath two metal plaques that were affixed to its façade in 1991, with inscriptions commemorating those who died in its basement: "… the 6,000 Poles estimated to have been shot, and the many other nationalities who fell victim to what became known as Stalin's Great Terror."[3865]

Yet, in spite of all the evidence, many in Russia today continue to deny that the killings ever took place, fostering a cottage industry of deniers,[3866] which includes neo-Stalinists in the west, such as Grover Furr.[3867] Propaganda films, now realising the implausibility of any contrived German guilt in and around Kalinin (modern-day Tver) for the murder of Polish prisoners, spread the message that Mednoye contains the bodies of Red Army soldiers, not Poles. Moreover, a new Tver-produced war movie depicts Tokarev as a valiant NKVD commander who roots out spies among his officers on the eve of the city's invasion by the Fascist horde.[3868] Ilya Kleymenov, head of the Tver branch of the Communists of Russia party, which is separate and much smaller than Russia's main Communist Party, initiated the campaign to get the plaques removed from the building of Tver State Medical University; he commented: "There is no direct or even circumstantial evidence that can be seen to prove that those events took place in the building on Soviet Street, in the city of Kalinin, and especially in Mednoye."[3869]

On June 14, 2019, in a letter to Tver's Mayor Aleksei Ogonkov, Kleymenov's neo-Stalinist party claimed the information on the plaques is "distorted," hence fostering "anti-patriotic feelings on the young generation." Without providing support for his claim, he called the idea that Polish officers were shot in Kalinin's NKVD building "quite simply falsified."[3870] Four months later, the prosecutor's office sent its letter to the university's rector Lesya Chichanovskaya, ordering that the plaques be removed. The letter claims that: "… crucial documents relating to the plaques' origins are missing from the archives." Their inscriptions, it said, are "not based on documented facts."[3871]

Though this order was issued in October 2019, it was not until May 7, 2020, on the eve of the 75th Anniversary of VE (Victory in Europe) day, that the plaques were finally removed.[3872]

Aleksandr Guryanov, who coordinates Memorial's Polish research team, sees the order to remove the plaques in Tver as part of a years-long effort to rewrite the history of the Katyń massacre, and indeed, moreover, sanitise the history of Russia's dark Stalinist past. In 2019, he and his colleagues at Memorial released a three-volume book listing the names and biographies of 6,287 Polish inmates of the Ostashkov camp. Over several hundred pages of meticulous research cites documents attesting to their imprisonment there, their execution in Kalinin, and their eventual burial at Mednoye.[3873] In August 2019, the State Central Museum of Contemporary Russian History in Moscow, which oversees the Mednoye Memorial Complex, announced plans to commence digs at the site in a bid to identify the Soviet citizens, including wounded Red Army soldiers believed to have received treatment at military hospitals in the area, who may possibly be buried there as well. However, while Guryanov is not in principle opposed to this, he suspects ulterior motives.[3874] "We must first find the documents, so that we don't dig blindly and at least delineate the likely burial spots prior to any digs," he said, adding, re the museum, "I don't trust them."[3875]

For Memorial, which has painstakingly researched Stalinist repressions for the past 30 years, the conflict over Mednoye now makes its existence a most precarious one. Since September 2019, Memorial has been barraged with fines associated with its status as a "foreign agent," a label applied by the Russian government to groups that receive foreign funding. With the total sum now exceeding 3 million rubles (almost US $50,000), Memorial has been forced to launch an online funding campaign for the first time in its 30-year history.[3876]

In the west, one of the most zealous neo-Stalinist revisionists is Grover Furr, an American professor of Medieval English literature at New Jersey's Montclair State University. He is best known for his books and articles on the Stalinist history of the Soviet Union from 1930 to 1953.[3877] Earlier, in Polish WWII Supplement I, I discussed "The Molotov-Ribbentrop Pact," Furr's spurious contention that the Soviet Union never invaded Poland.[3878] This notion can be easily refuted on several grounds, but the most poignant one here is the fact that a state of war existed between Poland and the USSR after September 17,

1939 due to the Soviet authorities describing Polish Army soldiers as "prisoners of war" and that a special Prisoner-of-War Administration was created inside the NKVD to handle the entire problem of prisoners. This reflects the conviction of USSR state officials that a war was being waged with Poland.[3879] Further, the official name for the contrived Burdenko commission was "Special Commission for the Findings and Examination of the Circumstances Surrounding the Shooting by the German Fascist Invaders in the Katyn Forest of the *Prisoners of War*" [my emphasis].[3880]

In Furr's 2013 article, 'The "Official" Version of the Katyn Massacre Disproven? Discoveries at a German Mass Murder Site in Ukraine',[3881] much is made of the Burdenko commission supposedly refuting the official version of events in the Katyń forest. This it achieves, Furr asserts, because the Burdenko commission was a fair and impartial commission (despite its contrived nature implied in its official name),[3882] and he insists it was unlike the International Commission convened in April 1943 by the Fascist invaders.

To begin with, Furr mentions the so-called camps No. 1-ON, 2-ON, and 3-ON, where "ON" stood for "osobogo naznacheniia" (special purpose or assignment). Furr contends that these camps, located about 25 to 45 kilometres west of Smolensk, were special assignment camps for "road construction,"[3883] and that from the "testimony"[3884] of witnesses and "documentary"[3885] evidence, the Burdenko Commission established that after the outbreak of hostilities, and in view of the situation that arose, the camps could not be evacuated in time and all the Polish war prisoners, as well as some members of the guard and staffs of the camps, fell prisoner to the Germans. In Furr's mind, this version is given further "plausibility" by the fact that the Soviet government, in their very first response of April 16, 1943 to the discovery of the Katyń graves, claimed that Polish officers were involved in construction in the Smolensk area.

The Soviet government's response was made on April 16, 1943. However, this is where the Stalinist "truth" starts and ends. The Germans made the announcement of the discovery of the Katyń graves on April 13, 1943.[3886] Just three days later, the Soviets delivered their response, which Furr contends, implies the truth of their story,[3887] on the grounds that any contrived story would have taken much longer to fabricate. However, as documented earlier, these "ON" camps were a fiction of the NKVD-NKGB.[3888] They were never mentioned in the Polish-Soviet exchanges of 1941–1943, following the Barbarossa invasion, nor were they reported by any Pole in the USSR.[3889]

Moreover, on December 3, 1941, in Moscow, with the hypothermic German invaders at the city's gates,[3890] there was exchange between Stalin and Molotov on the Soviet side, and General Władysław Sikorski, veteran of the 1919-20 Polish Soviet War[3891] and head of the London Polish Government in exile,[3892] and General Władysław Anders, commanding officer of the Polish army in the Middle East and Italy during World War II. He became a leading figure among the anti-communist Poles, who wisely refused to return to their homeland after the war. Like Sikorski, a veteran of the 1919–20 Polish-Soviet War, Anders had been imprisoned by the Soviets in September 1939 before being released in August 1941, following Hitler's Barbarossa invasion in June 1941, and subsequent restoration of Polish-Soviet diplomatic ties.[3893] Also present was the Polish ambassador, Stanisław Kott.

Sikorski and Anders were pressing Stalin on the issue of 15,000 unaccounted Polish prisoners. In November, Kott had already confronted Stalin on this issue. In every instance, Stalin attempted to palm them off with feigned confusion, and never, at any stage, was mention made of the fictitious ON camps,[3894] as at that stage, Stalin would not yet have envisaged their necessity. On December 3, 1941, Stalin made the following statement: "I don't know where they are. Maybe they fled to Manchuria."[3895] Furr, in his 2013 article, makes no mention of these Polish-Soviet exchanges between the June 1941 Barbarossa invasion, and the German announcement of their discovery of the Katyń graves on April 13, 1943. Nor does he mention the dates of final entry in the victims' diaries,[3896] which clearly attest to NKVD guilt.

Furr does, however, make what appears at first to be a compelling argument, when he makes much of the discovery of badges of two Polish policemen, Józef Kuligowski and Ludwik Małowiejski, discovered in May 2011[3897] and September 2011[3898] respectively. They were unearthed during a joint 2011-12 Polish-Ukrainian archaeological dig of a mass execution site at the modern-day Ukrainian town of Volodymyr-Volyns'kiy (pre-war, the Polish town of Włodzimierz-Wołyński,[3899] and today, still only fifteen kilometres inside the Ukraine from the Polish border).[3900] This town is located in the modern-day Ukraine, which explains the reference to the Ukraine in the full title of Furr's 2013 article "The 'Official' Version of the Katyn Massacre Disproven? Discoveries at a German Mass Murder Site in Ukraine."[3901]

In 1997, a mass grave of NKVD victims from 1939–1941 was discovered. However, it was not until 2011, that Ukrainian archaeologists, examining the foundations of the castle of the Polish king, Casimir the Great, found traces of subsequent mass graves and numerous items suggesting that there may be Poles among the victims.[3902] Polish archaeologists were called in, and according to the Polish archaeologist, Adam Kaczyński, they were expecting to find victims of the NKVD, especially those murdered during the so-called liquidation of prisons during the first days of the German Barbarossa invasion. Then, the NKVD executed prisoners before evacuating eastwards from the relentless German advance.[3903] At the NKVD prison in Włodzimierz-Wołyński, for example, the NKVD executed 36 prisoners[3904] before they fled east. In the autumn of 2011, co-operation between Ukrainian and Polish archaeologists began, and continued into the summer and autumn of 2012. They managed to examine about twelve percent of the medieval stronghold's area.[3905]

However, to the amazement of the Poles, they discovered mass burials of the Jewish population murdered in 1941—1942, during the German occupation. Results of earlier excavations and available historical sources indicated that only the burials of NKVD victims should be located within the stronghold.[3906] The content of burial pits, the way the corpses were laid, and the huge number of women and children, clearly indicated that they were dealing with victims of the Nazi Holocaust. The first mass execution in the prison yard took place on July 5, 1941, when around 150 people were murdered.[3907] Further crimes in the prison took place from August to December 1941. However, the largest number of people were murdered during the liquidation of the Włodzimierz ghetto, which began on September 1, 1942. Within two weeks, 18,000 were killed, about four thousand in the ghetto, and the remainder from the outskirts of the city.[3908]

According to Adam Kaczyński, the Polish and Ukrainian reports do not differ in substantive content, but only in conclusions regarding the time and circumstances of the victims' murder.[3909] The report prepared by Polish archaeologists was, however, more complete because it contained anthropological analysis of the remains found and refers to the wider context of the entire find.[3910] This raises the question of why the Ukrainian conclusion diverges from the Polish one. Adam Kaczyński commented: "

> In Włodzimierz Wołyński lie the Poles and Ukrainians murdered by the NKVD in 1939—1941. [A fact omitted by Furr.] However, in addition to them, are also victims of the murders that were perpetrated during the German occupation. I see no reason why we should hide this fact and forcibly attribute Holocaust victims to executioners from the NKVD. In Włodzimi-

erz Wołyński, there was a situation where what archaeologists discovered does not meet the political expectations of their government, or the population in general, because it destroys the meticulously built myth about the heroism of the UPA (Ukrainian Nationalists). For many in the Ukraine, it is unacceptable that people who in 1943, deserted the Germans, and formed the UPA,[3911] had during the previous twelve or so months together with the Nazis, actively participated in the mass murder of the Jewish population. In this context, the efforts of Ukrainian journalists to cover up the whole matter and blame the executioners of the NKVD — even at the price of discrediting their own archaeologists — are fully understandable… Our main goal is to find victims of the NKVD, however, honesty and a universal approach requires that all victims of the war be dignified, regardless of their origin and nationality."[3912]

In his 2013 article, Furr makes no mention of the fact that some of the victims in the graves were ruled by both teams of archaeologists to be victims of the NKVD.[3913] On the other hand, he does mention the Ukrainians' motivation to attribute the crimes to the NKVD in order to sanitise the reputation of their UPA — Ukrainian Insurgent Army (Ukrainian: Українська повстанська армія, УПА, Ukrayins'ka Povstans'ka Armiya).[3914] This is favourable to Furr's case, since before the formation of the UPA in October 1942, many of its members collaborated with the Nazis.[3915] However, he fails to mention that the Polish archaeologists were at odds with their Ukrainian counterparts from the outset of Polish participation at the site.[3916] In other words, there never was any attempt by the Poles to fabricate any evidence to fit a predetermined story, which was indeed the case with the Burdenko commission[3917] — which Furr abundantly quotes to support his case.

Moreover, German and possible UPA guilt at Volodymyr-Volyns'kiy cannot, on its own, overturn Stalinist guilt at Katyń Wood. Nevertheless, when the badges of the Polish policemen were found in May and September of 2011 by the joint Polish-Ukrainian archaeological team, neo-Stalinists perceived an opportunity to revoke the official version of Katyń. In the process however, neo-Stalinists disregarded untainted exhumations in the 1990s and 2000s, especially the site at Mednoye, which the Germans never reached, and the fact that no neo-Stalinist denier could account for the fate of the missing 15,000 Polish POWs,[3918] which Sikorski and Anders spoke of to Stalin and Molotov in Moscow in early December 1941.[3919] All which point to NKVD guilt at Katyń in the spring of 1940. In other words, how can the two alleged anomalies disprove the mountainous remainder of evidence?[3920] Moreover, they disregard the fact that official police badges found during the exhumations in Volodymyr-Volyns'kiy were found not among human remains, but in the bulk layer above the graves.[3921]

This conundrum was solved in 2019 by Aleksandr Guryanov,[3922] mentioned earlier as one of the "Memorial" researchers of the mass grave site at Mednoye. Well before 2011, Mednoye was proven to be the place where the bodies of the two Polish police officers, Józef Kuligowski and Ludwik Małowiejski were buried — a site the Germans never reached. Furr, on other the hand, claimed the bodies of Kuligowski[3923] and Małowiejski[3924] were among those found at Volodymyr-Volyns'kiy in 2011. However, in 2019, revealing documentary data was unearthed by Aleksandr Guryanov. It was from The Main Administration for Affairs of Prisoners of War and Internees, the GUPVI, a department of the NKVD. In it was data stating that Ludwik Małowiejski was indeed in Volodymyr-Volyns'kyi, not in 1941, but in September 1939.[3925]

Ludwik Małowiejski was captured wounded in September 1939; after his arrival at the NKVD Shepetovka reception centre, he was placed in a hospital in Shepetovka, where he was kept until he was sent to the Ostashkov camp — the camp where all the Polish prisoners buried at Mednoye in May 1940 had been held in the months before.[3926] Documentary data on the date and place of the capture of Józef Kuligowski, as well as on where he was held as a prisoner of war until his arrival at the Ostashkov camp, are not available in the researched archive documents, but it can be assumed that he, like many other Polish soldiers and police, was captured in September 1939 in Volodymyr-Volyns'kyi; his police badge probably ended up in the bulk layer above the mass grave in Volodymyr-Volyns'kyi, in the same way as the badge of Ludwik Małowiejski[3927] As discussed earlier, since September 2019, the Memorial organisation, of which Aleksandr Guryanov is a member, has been barraged with fines associated with its status as a "foreign agent," a label applied by the Russian government to groups that receive foreign funding.[3928]

One more aspect of Furr's questionable 2013 narrative of neo-Stalinist propaganda, relating to the 1919-20 Polish Soviet War needs to addressed. It claims as follows: "

It is likely that a substantial number of the Polish POWs —
military officers, policemen, and guards of various kinds —
had been involved either in repression of or atrocities against
Soviet troops, communists, trade unionists, or workers, peasants, or Belorussian, Ukrainian, and Jewish schools or institutions. The Soviet Union would have prosecuted them. It is also
likely that some Polish POWs were sentenced to labor in areas
that were captured by the Germans when they invaded the
USSR in 1941, and subsequently executed, as Kuligowski and
Malowiejski were."[3929]

While Furr does not quite claim that every single Polish POW captured
by the Soviets in 1939 was involved in Polish-perpetrated war crimes in
the 1919-20 Polish-Soviet War, it seems to be implied by him that some
grossly exaggerated proportion was, in which he includes Józef Kuligowski and Ludwik Małowiejski.

It would be ludicrous to assert that Polish troops were entirely
guiltless during this brutal war, so typical of the power vacuum created
in the chaotic aftermath of the Great War. However, in order to sanitise
Soviet crimes against the Polish people during World War II, which
goes well beyond just Katyń, Furr makes no mention of Soviet atrocities during the 1919-20 Polish-Soviet war. In *White Eagle Red Star*,
Norman Davies mentions the instance of the Bolsheviks using Polish
prisoners for sabre practice.[3930] However, with an objective balance,
counter to the narrative of Furr, Davies comments as follows: "

> The end of the fighting brought a welcome term to the suffer-
> ing of the civilian population; it also brought a series of inves-
> tigations and attempts to apportion the blame. The Polish army
> was charged with repressive and brutal police measures, the
> Red Army with wanton anarchy and classicide; both armies
> were charged with anti-semitism, though in an area with a
> large Jewish population it is hard to say where common vio-
> lence ends and anti-semitism begins. The Warsaw and Moscow
> press competed with each other over their stories of the ene-
> my's frightfulness. Every pulpit in Poland reverberated weekly
> to tales of the 'Bolshevik horrors', of Soviet cannibalism, of
> the nationalization of women, and of the murder of priests.
> Pravda ran a daily column called Zhertva Panov ("Victims of
> the Polish Lords"). Despite the propaganda, there are well
> documented instances of atrocity... The agonies of innocent

civilians is an unsavoury subject which politicians and generals are not eager to air. It is not really surprising that [Soviet] Budyonny disowned Babel's Konarmiya [Soviet Cavalry] stories and denounced their author for "rooting around in the garbage of the army's backyard." Regrettably, most armies do have a "back-yard" where "garbage" invariably collects."[3931]

Hence, Furr's 2013 narrative cannot sanitise Soviet guilt for atrocities perpetrated on the Polish people in World War II and its aftermath. This includes the deportation of 1.7 million Borderland Poles to Siberian gulags, where half would perish in the frigid hell.[3932] Among them were infants, cripples, and the blind,[3933] all exiled into the vast abyss of the Siberian hell; the vast majority had nothing to do with any possible atrocities committed by Poles in the 1919-20 war. Moreover, Furr's assertion that: **"NOBODY CARES what happened to the Polish officers! Nobody, including the Poles."**[3934] (The uppercase letters and bold formatting are Professor Furr's.) does not hold true, as numerous documents and publications by Poles and non-Poles, and even Russian historians such as Natalia Lebedeva,[3935] and Aleksandr Guryanov, in his 2019 work documenting the victims executed in Kalinin, then buried in Mednoye,[3936] attest to.

Moreover, while I taught English in Poland for ten months from September 2004 to July 2005, evidence was all around me that Furr's assertion is anything but true. For one thing, Muzeum Powstania Warszawskiego (Warsaw Uprising Museum), which I visited in early October 2004, opened on July 31, 2004, marking the Rising's 60th anniversary. This implies that Poles will never forget Katyń.[lii] My boss told me of times during communist rule when people were forbidden to even mention Molotov-Ribbentrop, Katyń or the 1944 Rising, due to the inconvenient truth all embodied for their overlords in Moscow. A female director at another language school told me she was grateful that the collapse of Poland's communist regime in 1989 came just in time

---

[lii] The 1944 Warsaw General Uprising will be covered in the following appendix. Norman Davies in his book *Rising '44: The Battle for Warsaw*, published by Penguin Books; Reprint edition (October 4, 2005), ISBN-10: 0143035401, ISBN-13: 9780143035404, on page 48, states that Stalin personally signed the order for the Katyń executions, and gives an overview of Katyń to illustrate the acrimonious relationship between the Polish Government in Exile in London and the Soviet regime, due in no small part to Katyń. See for example, pages 44, 48 and 115 to 116.

for her to choose English as her second language, rather than the language of the Russian oppressor. She did not explicitly mention Katyń or the 1944 Rising, but they were implied between the lines.

On Saturday, April 10, 2010, a Tupolev Tu-154 aircraft of the Polish Air Force crashed near the Russian city of Smolensk, killing all 96 people on board. Among the victims were the President of Poland Lech Kaczyński and his wife Maria, the former President of Poland in exile (during the Cold War) Ryszard Kaczorowski, the chief of the Polish General Staff and other senior Polish military officers, the president of the National Bank of Poland, Polish Government officials, 18 members of the Polish Parliament, senior members of the Polish clergy and relatives of victims of the Katyń massacre. The group was arriving from Warsaw to attend an event commemorating the 70th anniversary of the Katyń massacre, which took place near Smolensk in western Russia.[3937]

Both the Russian and Polish official investigations found no technical faults with the aircraft, and concluded that the crew failed to conduct the approach in a safe manner in the given weather conditions. However, the British Air Crash Investigator, Frank Taylor, who was involved in the investigation into the losses of 1988 Lockerbie Pan Am Flight 103, and numerous other investigations,[3938] dismissed the official verdict of the Russian and Polish inquiries as a politically convenient fantasy, stating, "There is no doubt there were explosions on board before the aircraft hit the ground."[3939] In a subsequent interview, Taylor explained, "There is strong evidence that a few seconds later the door on the left side of the fuselage, just forward of the wing, was blown out and driven hard into the ground by another explosion in the fuselage." He added that the Kremlin investigation was a fraud: "Russian politicians took over the investigation, preventing the professional investigator from taking control of the accident site, from completing the full investigation, including a full reconstruction of the wreckage, and from writing the final accident report."[3940] All this seems reminiscent of the Burdenko Katyń commission.

Even if one were to dismiss the opinion of a highly credible investigator such as Frank Taylor, there are still disturbing incidents suggesting that the Kremlin was remarkably slipshod in its handling of the dead. Sent home in sealed coffins, many of the bodies had been swapped or misidentified. In 24 cases of re-examination in 2016, half of the coffins opened contained the wrong remains. Even the coffin of the Polish President Lech Kaczyński included the remains of two other victims.[3941] Such carelessness inevitably led to questions about what else the Russians had mishandled—or worse. One thing implied here is the deeply embedded Russian psyche of Stalinist Katyń denial.

According to a March 2013 poll, 11% of Poles were firmly convinced of Russian foul play, while another 22%, were open to such a possibility. In other words, one-third of Poles were, in March 2013, at least open to the theory of Russian foul play.[3942] Further fuelling the theories is the fact that Russia, in April 2013, had still not turned over the wreckage of the downed airliner to the Poles. Moscow stated it had not yet "completed its investigation," and would return the debris to Poland when it does.[3943] Moreover, even by April 2020, a decade following the accident,[3944], the Russian Federation was still maintaining possession of the plane wreckage, the black boxes with original flight data recordings and other materials of evidence. While copies, but not originals of flight data recordings and some material evidence have been transmitted to the Polish authorities, Poland has strongly insisted for years that the wreckage and all original materials be returned.[3945]

In all, from the mass graves at Katyń, Mednoye and near Kharkov, 21,892 Polish citizens were buried.[3946] The vast majority of them were Poles by nationality, but not all, as Poland was then a multinational state, which, in spite of its ethnic turmoil between the wars, in great part provoked by Moscow,[3947] possessed a multinational and multi-faith officer corps. As a result, many of the dead were Jews, ethnic Ukrainians, and Belarusians. About eight percent of the victims were Jews, corresponding to the proportion of Jews in Poland's Borderlands.[3948] Moreover, as mentioned earlier this chapter, there was the retired Professor of Neurology and Epileptology at the University of Berne, Kazimierz Karbowski, whose Jewish mother died in the Warsaw Ghetto, and father was executed at Katyń.[3949] As Timothy Snyder commented: "

> Fyodor Dostoevsky, the famous nineteenth century Russian novelist, had set a crucial scene of *The Brothers Karamazov* at the Optyn Hermitage in Kozelsk, which in 1939 and 1940 became the site of the Soviet administered prisoner-of-war camp. Here took place the most famous exchange in the book: a discussion between a young nobleman and a monastery elder about the possibility of morality without God. If God is dead, is everything permitted? In 1940, the real building where this fictional conversation took place, the former residence of some of the monks, housed the NKVD interrogators. They represented a Soviet answer to that question: only the death of God allowed for the liberation of humanity. Unconscious-ly, many

of the fervently religious Polish officers and reserves, possessing an intellect far surpassing that of the NKVD thugs, provided a different answer: that in a place where everything is permitted, God is a refuge. They saw their camps as churches, and prayed in them. Many of them attended Easter services[liii] before they were dispatched to their deaths."[3950]

As Stalin and Beria had come to realise, men of such integrity and intelligence, unlike their NKVD captors, would never become ideologically compliant Bolshevik puppets, and hence embodied a clear and present danger to the Stalinist subjugation of Poland.

Katyń, and the other sites of mass murder and burial such as Kalinin-Mednoye, that the term Katyń now embodies, were unequivocally acts of genocide. Admittedly, Katyń was not an extermination of an entire ethnic group on the scale of the Jewish Holocaust or Rwanda. However, it was the calculated and deliberate murder of a nation's elite,[3951] simultaneously embodying classicide,[3952] with the intention of obliterating its political and creative energy for the future.[3953] To these men such as Adam Solski,[3954] perceived as a clear and present danger to the Stalinist world view, this chapter is dedicated to ensure, that their memory, which embodies so much more than just Katyń itself, will not rot in the grave.[3955]

[liii] Easter Sunday in 1940 fell on March 24th. The early Easter implies that many of the victims would have attended Easter services just a fortnight or so before their deaths in early April. See the Calendar 12 website at https://www.calendar-12.com/holidays/easter/1940.

Polish WWII Supplement IV

AK and 1944 Warsaw General Uprising — Stalin's mass murder by German proxy

„Chcieliśmy być wolni i wolność sobie zawdzięczać"

"We wanted to be free and owe this freedom to nobody"[3956]

On the freezing cold, snow-swept evening of Tuesday December 26, 1939,[3957] in the south-eastern Warsaw district of Wawer, now three months into the German occupation of Warsaw, two common thugs refused to leave a snack bar at 85 Widoczna Street. They were Stanisław Dąbek and Marian Prasuła, who had, during the chaos and confusion of the German invasion, escaped the maximum security prison of Święty Krzyż (Holy Cross).[3958] Twelve hours earlier that day, the pair had shot and seriously wounded a Polish policeman in the nearby town of Otwock, just 15 kilometres south-east of Wawer.[3959]

In response to the refusal of the fugitives to leave his establishment, Antoni Bartoszek decided to summon the local Polish police. Upon his arrival at the scene, officer Rozwadowski recognised the pair and promptly requested support from the German Wehrmacht 538 Construction Battalion, which was stationed in Wawer. His request was fulfilled when two non-commissioned officers of the German reserve, described in the subsequent report as being "somewhat advanced in years" appeared,[3960] and engaged the fugitives in what turned out to be a fatal shoot-out for both the German NCOs, as they entered with guns slung over their shoulders.[3961] One was killed by the bandits on the spot, while the other died en route to hospital. The wife of the proprietor of the bar, Zofia Bartoszek, was also wounded[3962] before the fugitives escaped out the back door and through the yard, leaving footprints in the snow.[3963] From this point, whatever the fate was for these common thugs, remains unknown to this day.[liv] In any event, for the German oc-

---

[liv] I say this because, from all the sources I have read, there is nothing documented about what happened to these fugitives after the shoot-out at the snack bar in Wawer.

cupiers, the capture of the perpetrators seemed to be peripheral[3964] if not irrelevant in the National Socialist directive of terror enacted in disproportionate vengeance upon the Slavic *Untermensch*. In short, "The Poles perpetrated the killing, and the Poles must suffer the consequences."[3965]

Just before 11 p.m., "law enforcement" in the form of the Ordnungspolizei (Order Police) Regiment (also known as Polizei-Regiment Warschau — Warsaw Police Regiment) arrived in Wawer and the neighbouring district of Anin.[3966] The local community had given assurances to the German Police that they were willing to support them in apprehending the perpetrators, but instead, Lieutenant-Colonel Max Daume, fully aware of the circumstances surrounding the incident, issued orders for his subordinates to randomly arrest the men living in Wawer and Anin.[3967] In the majority of these arrests, the men were shaken from their sleep, so they had no way of knowing of the incident. A significant number were not from Wawer or Anin, as they were visiting for the Christmas holiday period. According to one of the few survivors of the subsequent massacre, the 120 detainees aged between 16 and 70 were gathered before the local police station; the Germans selected three men at a time for interrogation at the police headquarters.[3968] When they were exiting, the German police would hit them with their rifle butts.

The German mass murder began when the bar's proprietor, Antoni Bartoszek, was hanged near the bar's entrance.[3969] Just before 5.00 a.m., a "summary court" was convened at II Poprzeczna Street 3, where the surnames of the 114 arrestees were written down before they were sentenced to death. In justifying this verdict, the Germans incessantly bellowed; "The Poles perpetrated the killing, and the Poles must suffer the consequences."[3970] Stanisław Piegat, one who survived the massacre by "playing dead" amidst the pile of dead bodies,[3971] spoke later of the shock experienced by local residents. Yet the majority of the residents of Wawer and neighbouring townships were well aware of the atrocities committed by the German army during the September invasion.[3972] These atrocities took place in the course of military operations — which of course is no justification. However, in the case of Wawer in late December 1939, the deaths of the two German soldiers from the Construction Battalion were attributable directly to fugitive bandits, and hence the random repressions applied by the Germans were a manifestation of unprecedented barbarity.[3973] Stanisław Piegat observed: "At the time hardly anyone was aware that this was what the German occupation would look like."[3974]

The "trial" was presided over by Major Friedrich Wilhelm Wenzel, the commander of the two companies that took a direct part in the operation. The instigator of the whole undertaking, Lieutenant-Colonel Daume, was also present. However, neither would survive for long post-war. Daume would be identified by the Americans before being turned over to the Polish authorities and tried before the Supreme National Tribunal — a judicial body established in order to try, among others, German war criminals.[3975] On March 3, 1947, Daume was sentenced to death by hanging, and four days later, in the Warszawa-Mokotów Custody Suite at Rakowiecka Street, the execution order was duly performed. Four years later, Friedrich Wilhelm Wenzel was likewise sentenced to death.[3976]

Initially, the Germans had planned to execute 100 men for each German killed. However, during the operation, this figure was "reduced" to 60. The victims of the night time round-up were led through a tunnel running under the local narrow-gauge track to the square between Spiżowa and Błękitna streets, which was illuminated with headlights. In order to humiliate the arrestees, the Germans ordered them to take off their caps and kneel with their backs to the position of the machine-gun. However, according to witnesses, in a case of typical Polish defiance, the condemned refused to meekly comply; an atmosphere of patriotic elation could be sensed by those nearby.[3977] By around 6.00 a.m, the mass execution took place. According to Janina Przedlacka, one could hear patriotic shouts and the groans of the dying, as bullets were discharged from automatic weapons. The German bullets killed 106 of the 113 detained men; one managed to escape while being led to the execution site.[3978] Six, such as Stanisław Piegat,[3979] feigned death and survived, in spite of testimonies to the effect that the Germans subsequently finished off the wounded.[3980] Clearly, in their mop-up, the Germans were not entirely thorough.

In a curious ethnic twist, amongst those sentenced to death after spurning the German offer for clemency because of his German sounding name was Daniel Gering of Wawer. Three times, the Germans gave him 15 minutes to think things through and declare that he was a German, thereby avoiding death. Instead, on all three occasions, Gering defiantly declared: "I was born a Pole and I shall die a Pole, and I do not really care how my death will come about."[3981] As a result, he was executed along with the others. Later, it was determined that Daniel Gering was an employee of Bank Gospodarstwa Krajowego, and was indeed of German descent, and fluent in the invader's language. It has been conjectured that the perpetrators may have been concerned that they were dealing with a distant relative of Hermann Göring, the Chief of the Luftwaffe, and for this reason, as a witnesses later testified, they made an effort to "play it safe"— to spare a possible relative of one of the most powerful figures in Nazi Germany.[3982]

In the massacre's aftermath, the relatives and neighbours of the victims wished to take the bodies for a proper burial. However, the German police forbade this. Rather, in accordance with an administrative decision issued by the occupation authorities, they were buried in a temporary mass grave. Only towards the end of June 1940 was an exhumation ordered, accompanied by a full identification, which identified 106 of the victims, including Antoni Bartoszek, the bar's proprietor; he was hung just before the perpetration of the mass execution. One victim's identity could not be established.[3983] Support for the massacre among the various German authorities in occupied Poland was not unequivocal. General Johannes Blaskowitz, the Wehrmacht's Commander-in-Chief East, commented, in his report dated February 6, 1940: "This execution […] has deeply angered the Poles, for the murder had no connection at all to the civilian population; the motives for this crime were entirely criminal in nature."[3984]

On the first anniversary of the Wawer massacre, the Organizację Małego Sabotażu Wawer (Organisation of Minor Sabotage Wawer — OMS) was founded and codenamed to commemorate victims of the Wawer executions in late December 1939.[3985] It was subordinate to the Biuru Informacji i Propagandy okręgu warszawskiego (Information and Propaganda Bureau of the district of Warsaw) of the Związek Walki Zbrojnej (ZWZ — Union of Armed Struggle),[3986] itself the precursor to the Armia Krajowa (AK or Home Army) formed in early 1942.[3987] In the autumn of 1941, it was merged with the similar organisation, Palmiry. The Commandant and founder of the OMS was a well-known scout activist and editor of *Biuletynu Informacyjnego* (Information Bulletin) from November 1939 to October 1944, Alexander Kamiński (aka Kamyk Dąbrowski).[3988] Before 1942-1944, the OMS had several hundred members and it included four districts in Warsaw. Over half of its members were scouts from the Szare Szeregi (Gray Ranks),[3989] a codename for the underground paramilitary Polish Scouting Association.

The roles of the OMS were embodied in anti-Nazi propaganda, including the painting of pro-Polish slogans on walls, deforming German slogans, removing tablets with German inscriptions, anti-Nazi leaflets, hanging Polish flags on national anniversaries and the like.[3990] One of the slogans it adopted was *Pomścimy Wawer* ("We shall avenge Wawer"), soon to be abbreviated as "PW,"[3991] in reference to the Wawer massacre of late December 1939. Thanks to the actions of the OMS, the memory of the Wawer crime lasted throughout the German occupation and it was an unequivocal slogan for Polish resistance in the face of fascist oppression.[3992] The most visible of the activities of the OMS included drawings on walls of the letters P and W, or Wawer, Wawer, Wawer;[3993] drawings of Churchill's "V", symbolising victory; anti-German subtitles in public places; distribution of leaflets, and megaphone campaigns.[3994] In the process, these acts of minor sabotage, implemented by defiant Polish youth at risk of life and limb, gnawed on the psyche of the invader, while serving to sustain the morale of Poles and their faith in the final victory.[3995]

In February 1942, Europe's largest resistance movement, Związek Walki Zbrojnej (ZWZ — Union of Armed Struggle) became the Armia Krajowa (AK or Home Army, literally Nation's Army).[3996] The letters "PW" increasingly appeared in the city as a "signature" for acts of Polish resistance and sabotage; the AK, in early 1942, put out a call to design an emblem that could be easily printed. To this end, a design that superimposed the P and W into an anchor — the Kotwica (pronounced "kotveetsa") — was submitted by Anna Smoleńska (code name "Hania"),[3997] a member of OMS Wawer,[3998] and was chosen as the symbol of the underground.[3999] Smoleńska, an art history student at the underground University of Warsaw, was arrested in November 1942. She died of typhus in Auschwitz in March 1943 at the age of 23.[4000] Her brother was the only family member to survive post-war, before passing away in Warsaw in 1986.[4001] Though she and her brother did not live to see an independent Warsaw, the symbol she created has endured World War II,[4002] the Cold War and beyond, to symbolise a now free and independent Poland. In early 1942, in the wake of the founding of the Home Army, the letters PW had evolved from *Pomścimy Wawer* ("We shall avenge Wawer") to the more encompassing kotwica (anchor) of *Polska Walcząca* (Fighting Poland).[4003]

From its founding in February 1942, the Home Army was planning a national uprising against the German occupiers. In these initial plans made by the London based Polish government-in-exile in 1942, it was assumed that the western Allied invasion of Europe would compel the withdrawal of considerable German forces from the Eastern Front for the defence of the Reich. In turn, the Home Army would act to block the German troop transfer west, to allow British and American forces to seize Germany by breaking all communication links with the majority of German forces massed in the Soviet Union.[4004]

However, as 1943 wore on, it became apparent that the western Allied invasion of Europe would not come in time to liberate Poland before the arrival of the Soviet Red Army,[4005] with their own agenda virulently hostile to a free and independent post-war Poland.[4006] In February, 1943, General Stefan Rowecki ("Grot" — Spearhead) and commander-in-chief of the Home Army,[4007] amended the plan. The Uprising was to be started in three phases, the first being in the East, with main centres of resistance in Lwów and Wilno before the advancing Red Army. The second phase was to include armed struggle in the belt between the Vistula river and Curzon Line,[4008] while the third phase was to be a nationwide uprising in all of Poland.[4009]

In essence, this plan, codenamed "Tempest" (Polish: "*Burza*," sometimes translated as "Storm"), was a number of consecutive uprisings initiated in each area as the German retreat began, rather than a synchronised operation beginning in all areas simultaneously.[4010] The success of "Tempest" depended above all on timing, as premature engagement with the German forces could turn Polish attacks into a disaster.[4011] The Home Army had to wait for the last hours of the German retreat, and no operations were to be taken against the Soviet forces or the Polish army raised in the Soviet Union.[4012] The Home Army was to conduct its operations independently of the Red Army in view of the suspension of diplomatic relations between the London based Polish Government in exile, and the Soviet Union in April 1943.[4013] This was in the wake of the German discovery of the Katyń Wood massacre near Smolensk in western Russia, and contemptuous dismissal by the Stalinist regime of subsequent enquiries by the Polish Government in exile .[4014]

On June 30, 1943, Stefan Rowecki was arrested by the Gestapo, having been betrayed by three turncoat members of the Home Army.[4015] They were the lovers Ludwik Kalkstein and Blanka Kaczorowska, as well as Kalkstein's brother-in-law Eugeniusz Świerczewski, who had known Stefan Rowecki since 1920, during their days serving together in the 1919-20 Polish-Soviet war.[4016] On the last day in June 1943, Świerczewski had tailed Rowecki for some time before phoning the Gestapo. Minutes later Rowecki was arrested.[4017] Before plans for Rowecki's rescue could be attempted, he was removed to Berlin for interrogation, where he rejected outright any proposals that he should collaborate with the Third Reich against the Soviet Union, and was subsequently moved to Sachsenhausen concentration camp, where he was murdered on August 2, 1944.[4018] This was decided upon by the head of the SS, Heinrich Himmler, when he heard about the commencement of the Warsaw Uprising the evening before.[4019]

Blanka Kaczorowska, pseudonym "Sroka" was born on October 13, 1922 in Brest on the River Bug, now in modern-day Belarus. Initially, she was active in the intelligence service in Siedlce, about 90 kilometres east of Warsaw. In early November 1941, under the imminent threat of arrest, she fled to Warsaw, where, by an order of November 11, she was awarded the Polish Cross of Valour.[4020] As was Ludwik Kalkstein, born on March 13, 1920 in Warsaw, where in the spring of 1939, months before the invasion, he graduated from the gymnasium (senior high school). At the outbreak of war in September, he moved to Wilno (the modern-day Lithuanian capital of Vilnius), where, in all likelihood, he went underground before being posted back to Warsaw in January 1940, where he was engaged in the "Stragan" intelligence network.[4021]

In the spring of 1941, he began to organise an observation and intelligence group codenamed "Hanka." In this group, the deputy manager was his brother-in-law Eugeniusz Świerczewski, as well as his future wife Blanka Kaczorowska acting as secretary, typist and translator, and his cousin Jerzy Kopczewski "Krzysztof." This group, headed by Kalkstein, had 10 employees and about 150 informants, although according to Kalkstein's testimony post-war, the group had about seven people employed.[4022] Around the end of March to the beginning of April 1942, Kalkstein was arrested at Kopczewski's apartment. Six to seven weeks later, on May 15, Kalkstein's mother Ludwika née Kucińska was arrested, and then in June, so too was his sister Nina — Świerczewski's wife. On the night of April 27-28, 1942, Mieczysław Rutkowski "Goszczyński," the head of the Western section of the "Stall" group, was arrested.[4023]

According to Kalkstein's testimony post-war, it was only after four months of interrogation and torture that he broke down and handed over the names and addresses of twenty people of the "Stall" group.[4024] Moreover, when the Gestapo threatened his mother and sister with a similar fate, he told his interrogator in German: "

> Before you decide to bring my mother here, I wanted to say something without an interpreter. I grew up in Poland, went to a Polish school, I thought I had a duty to defend my new homeland. Now, after a deeper reflection, I think that I, as a German, can feel free of my oath. I feel German. I am a young man, please take into account the mistake and give me the op-

portunity to rehabilitate myself and my family in loyal service to the Third Reich."[4025]

His feeling of being German, being "nudged" by the showering of Nazi propaganda leaflets, highlighting his link to the Kalksteins of the East Prussian nobility.[4026]

Irena Chmielewicz, the translator and typist in the Warsaw Gestapo, claimed that, along with Kalkstein, about 52 people were arrested in the first wave. In November 1942, Kalkstein was released from the Gestapo's Szucha remand prison as agent "97," where he subsequently renewed contact with Świerczewski and Kaczorowska ; he married the latter in the village of Radość, north-east of Warsaw on November 14, 1942. Kaczorowska was codenamed "V-98" and used her former Home Army pseudonym "Sroka," while Świerczewski was assigned the codename "100" by the Gestapo. Both, on Kalkstein's persuasion, decided on this traitorous path.[4027]

Kalkstein worked in a Gestapo cell managed by SS-Untersturmführer Erich Merten, whose task was counter-intelligence to Home Army and British intelligence. With Kaczorowska's collaboration, at least fourteen people known to her from her work in Siedlce were arrested, five of whom were shot. Among those arrested were; Kazimierz Tomaszewski, Jerzy Brolski, Edward Kwaśniewski, Jadwiga Krasicka, Halina Skierska, Janusz Wituski, and Irena Wituska. On May 15, 1943, Captain Karol Trojanowski "Radwan," head of the Western offensive intelligence department "Stall" of the 2nd Division of the Home Army, was arrested on the corner of Rakowiecka Street and Niepodległości (Independence) Avenue. Thereafter, Kaczorowska introduced "Radwan" to Kalkstein, who persuaded "Radwan" to engage in betraying the intelligence and communications of the Home Army.[4028]

By war's end, this traitorous trio would be responsible for the betrayal of over 500 members of the Home Army.[4029] On March 25, 1944, the Special Military Court of the Home Army sentenced the trio of traitors to death. On June 20, 1944, Eugeniusz Świerczewski was hanged in a cellar of a house at Krochmalna Street, following interrogation by Stefan Ryś "Józef," deputy head of the Security and Counterintelligence Department of the Second Headquarters of the Home Army. Świerczewski admitted to betraying Rowecki; however, it's worth noting that the testimony of Stefan Ryś, given on March 24, 1954, makes no mention of the betrayal of Rowecki "Grot" by Świerczewski, but there was a long list of people betrayed who were employees of intelligence and communications of the Home Army.[4030]

With Kalkstein and Kaczorowska still to face justice, about a month later in mid-July, two weeks before the outbreak of the Warsaw Uprising and just days before the Valkyrie assassination attempt on Hitler at his Wolf's Lair in East Prussia,[4031] Ludwik Kalkstein got a new identity.[4032] He took the name Konrad Stark and was entitled to wear an SS uniform, and indeed, during the Warsaw Uprising, in the Waffen SS, he fought against his own family, mainly in the Mokotów district. However, by the end of August 1944 — about halfway through the uprising — he left Warsaw.[4033] Before war's end, the Home Army had the opportunity to liquidate Kaczorowska, but due to her pregnancy at the time, her death penalty was waived.[4034] Until war's end, the Gestapo kept her in hiding.[4035]

After the war, Kaczorowska remarried, and in the pragmatic collaborationist spirit, had become a member of the Polish Workers' Party — the party of the post-war communist regime. However, in December 1952, she was arrested, owing to her past collaboration with the Gestapo, and subsequently sentenced to life imprisonment.[4036] Nevertheless, her collaborationist mindset, embodied in her willingness to act as a stool pigeon — that is, to report on her fellow prisoners — again reaped fruit when her life sentence was commuted to time served on July 1, 1958.[4037] After her release, she continued working with the communist regime's counter-intelligence Department II, until the early 1970s.[4038] Some time later, she emigrated to France, where she died in 2002.[4039]

After the war, Kalkstein spent several months in Kraków. Later he lived in Koszalin, Przyborów and Szczecin under false names. He was detained twice, first in 1949 and then on August 20, 1953. In the sixties, he launched several appeals, and was released on July 12, 1965, which provoked protests by former Home Army soldiers, aired on Radio Free Europe.[4040] In the early 1980s, he moved to France,[4041] where his son to Blanka Kaczorowska was now living. In 1994, he died of cancer[4042] in Munich.[4043] Naturally, the names comprising this trio of traitors live on in Poland in disgrace and infamy.

The arrest of Stefan Rowecki, on the last day of June 1943, was a devastating blow to the Home Army. However, under very suspicious circumstances, a no lesser catastrophe for them took place at Gibraltar just four days later, in the late hours of the evening of July 4.[4044] Following an inspection tour of Polish forces in the Middle East, the head of the Polish government in exile, Władysław Sikorski and his only daughter Zofia Lesniowska,[4045] who served as his personal assistant, died when their American built B-24 Liberator aircraft crashed shortly after take-off from Gibraltar. Only the Czech pilot survived.[4046] The circumstances of the crash remain a mystery and the subject of much speculation as to possible Soviet involvement.[4047] While no assassination theory has ever been proven,[4048] the exact circumstances of his death have never been fully explained, especially when certain files have had their status extended as top secret for 100 years; the action of a third party has not been ruled out.[4049]

There are conspiracy theories that Churchill wanted Sikorski dead, owing to Sikorski's "inconvenient" request that the International Red Cross investigate the Katyń Forest massacre, in the process "angering"[4050] Stalin to the point of breaking off diplomatic relations with the London based Polish government in exile and annoying the western Allies, who wanted to bury the incident.[4051] There is even the notion that the most overtly anti-Soviet elements in the Polish exile government wanted Sikorski dead because of the agreement brokered in 1941 with the Soviets in the wake of the Barbarossa invasion. Yet Sikorski was one of the heroes during the August 1920 Battle of Warsaw, repelling Lenin's Bolsheviks at Warsaw's gates.[4052] Even the British discreetly blamed the Polish officers of the Intelligence department for what they perceived as Sikorski's pro-Soviet policy.[4053] Another notion was that Sikorski was willing to countenance concessions to Poland's eastern frontier post-war that would leave many soldiers, now under the command of Władysław Anders in the Middle East, and having experienced the hell of the Siberian gulags before Barbarossa,[4054] homeless post-war. Hence rumours even before he left for the Middle East, that an attempt would be made on his life by Poles.[4055] This friction between Sikorski and Anders prompted Sikorski to make this trip to raise this issue and other possible differences with Anders.[4056]

Naturally, there is a theory that the Soviets were responsible, involving the infamous British, pro-Soviet mole, Harold "Kim" Philby; he was in charge of security for the Gibraltar area and chief of British counter-intelligence for the Iberian Peninsula.[4057] As such, Philby could easily find out the date of Sikorski's visit to Gibraltar on his way back from the Middle East to London. In this version of events, the Soviets arranged for Maisky, their ambassador to London, who brokered the July 30 1941 agreement with Sikorski (The Sikorski-Maisky Agreement),[4058] to fly back to Moscow via Gibraltar,[4059] [lv] and to be in Gibraltar with the assigned Soviet saboteurs at the same time as General Sikorski. When the Liberator aircraft crashed, the occasion for ambassador Maisky's prophecy to be fulfilled had come; on March 31, 1941, in a conversation with the Czechoslovakian legate to the Soviet Union, Zdenek Fierlinger, Maisky stated that he "can guarantee that General Sikorski will never enter Warsaw again."[4060]

Unlike the incontrovertible evidence pointing to Stalinist guilt at Katyń in April 1940,[4061] Marek Kaminski does admit that direct evidence implying such guilt in the death of Sikorski is lacking.[4062] Nevertheless, among the members of the entire anti-Hitler alliance, Kaminski is of the opinion that the one who had the greatest motivation to assassinate Sikorski was Stalin, as his politics were always focused on the ultimate weakening of the legal London-based Polish government.[4063] According to Kaminski, in the first half of February 1943, following the capitulation of the German Field Marshal Friedrich Wilhelm von Paulus's Sixth Army in Stalingrad, Stalin decided to find the most convenient moment to break off diplomatic relations with the Polish government.[4064] With the German discovery of the mass graves at Katyń two months later in April 1943, he didn't have to wait long for that moment.[4065]

Be it conspiracy or pure accident, Sikorski's death was a devastating blow to the Polish cause[4066] and another coup for Stalin towards the weakening of the legal London-based Polish government.[4067] On July 14, a new government was formed under the civilian Stanisław Mikołajczyk, the leader of the Peasant Party.[4068] General Kazimierz Sosnkowski, like Sikorski, a veteran from the 1919-20 Polish Soviet War,[4069] was appointed as military Commander-in-Chief.[4070] In this way, the two functions performed by Sikorski were separated. Mikołajczyk continued to hold the policy of Sikorski in foreign affairs, hoping to reach an understanding with Stalin, which would allow his government to assume power in Poland with the help of the Polish resistance movement at the end of hostilities.[4071]

[lv] Maisky was recalled to Moscow by Stalin, where he was promoted to Deputy Commissar of Foreign Affairs. He would never return to Britain. See page 1476 to 1478 of *The Complete Maisky Diaries, Volume 3 Annals of Communism* by Ivan Mikhaĭlovich Maĭskiĭ, edited by Gabriel Gorodetsky, translated by Tatiana Sorokina and Oliver Ready, published by Yale University Press, 2017, ISBN 0300117825, 9780300117820.

Mikołajczyk believed in seeking to establish cordial relations with Moscow and abandon what he saw as the "demagogy of intransigence."[4072] In his mind, the calculations of the "hawks," such as Sosnkowski, were "illusory and dangerous," as they were based on a possible conflict between the Western Powers and Soviet Union following the crushing of Nazi Germany.[4073] He was aware that the Western Powers were not prepared to fight for the Polish eastern frontiers and that in the event of a crisis they would not support Poland. Rather, he envisaged that, in the event of a Russo-Polish understanding, Britain and the USA would be willing to guarantee Poland's independence. Certainly, Mikołajczyk's thinking embodied two naive hopes:[4074] firstly, conciliating Stalin to any notion of post-war Polish independence, and secondly, inducing the Western powers to support Polish independence[4075] in the face of Stalin's hostile agenda for Poland,[4076] and indeed, for the whole of eastern Europe. In regard to the former, the Katyń Wood massacre alone[4077] attested to how forlorn this hope was.

Sosnkowski on the other hand, was convinced that the government must defend the territorial and political integrity of Poland "in spite of all and against all."[4078] He was opposed to making concessions to Stalin, because, in his opinion, they would merely lead to the gradual "Sovietisation of Poland,"[4079] as they indeed did. He envisaged that the Western Powers sooner or later "might be compelled to face a showdown with Russian imperialism," for which reason there was no need to adopt a conciliatory attitude towards Moscow.[4080] He maintained that the London Poles could influence neither Soviet policy nor the outcome of military operations and were therefore left with no alternative except to defend their rights and "demand the same from the Western Powers."[4081] He wished to turn the Polish Question into a "problem for the conscience of the world,"[4082] a test case for the future of European nations. As Commander-in-Chief he believed that he was entitled to play an important role in politics.[4083]

Given the divergent views of the "dove" Mikołajczyk and the "hawk" Sosnkowski, the relations between the two were strained and unhappy,[4084] much, one would think, to the delight of Stalin.[4085] In Sosnkowski's mind, Mikołajczyk's hope of a conciliation with Stalin over post-war independence were naive to say the least, as events post-war indeed proved. However, Sosnkowski's notions were equally so, since, upon this card table, Stalin held all the trumps, if not indeed, all the cards. In short, for the west, if the obliteration of Hitler's National Socialist Germany compelled an understanding with Stalin that embodied Polish betrayal, and indeed the betrayal of all of eastern Europe to decades of oppressive Sovietisation, then so be it. Likewise, the hopes of the German conspirators for an understanding with the western Allies were, by this stage, equally forlorn.

On July 17, 1943,[4086] in the wake of Stefan Rowecki's betrayal and arrest on June 30 1943,[4087] Tadeusz Marian Komorowski ("Bór" — "Forest") assumed the role of Commander-in-Chief of the Home Army.[4088] He was born in Chorobrów (now Khorobriv or Хоробрів in the Lviv Oblast of the western Ukraine) on June 1, 1895. He began his military career in the cavalry of the Austro-Hungarian Army, subsequently fighting on the Eastern and Italian fronts during the Great War. In November 1918, immediately following the rebirth of Polish independence, he joined its emerging army[4089] at Dębica, in the country's south-east, where the Second Polish Regiment of Legionary Uhlans was being organised.[4090]

In 1919, he took part in the Polish-Ukrainian war, and then in the 1919-20 Polish-Soviet War, during which he commanded the 12th Uhlan Regiment. In particular, during the last great cavalry battle in Europe of Komarów, from late August to early September 1920,[4091] in spite of being wounded in action, he did not want to leave his soldiers on the battlefield, and fought on until the end of the fight.[4092] In the subsequent peace, ensuring the survival of the Second Polish Republic during the inter-war years, he served in cavalry garrisons and was a horse-riding instructor at cadets' schools. Such was his ability, that he took part in equestrian competitions, as well as representing Poland at the Paris 1924 and Hitler's Berlin 1936 Olympic Games.[4093]

At the latter Olympics, a photo was taken of Komorowski to the right, saluting Hitler, whilst awaiting to be acknowledged by him, following the Polish equestrian team's silver medal. Goebbels was shaking hands to the left of this photo, which was used by the Gestapo during the war in an unsuccessful attempt to track Komorowski down.[4094] For eleven years before the outbreak of WWII, Komorowski commanded the 9th Regiment of Lesser Poland Uhlans, and in 1939, with the rank of colonel, he commanded the Cavalry Training Centre in Grudziądz in the north of Poland; in light of the approaching war, the centre was moved south-east to Garwolin in August 1939.[4095]

Following the outbreak of war on September 1, 1939, he was ordered to assist in the creation of the Combined Cavalry Brigade under Colonel Adam Zakrzewski. In his ranks, he defended the Vistula River line near Góra Kalwaria, until the fighting in that region ceased on September 22 near Krasnobród.[4096] According to historian Andrzej Kunert on the Polish Radio broadcast "Characters of the 20th century," it was around this stage, until Poland's official surrender in early October 1939, that many future members of the Polish resistance, that avoided German capture, such as Komorowski, went underground.[4097] In his case, he managed to escape to Kraków, where, at the beginning of 1940, he joined the precursor of the Home Army — Union of Armed Struggle (*Związek Walki Zbrojnej* — ZWZ) and took command of the South-west or Kraków-Silesian region.[4098] In the same year he was promoted to the rank of Brigadier General.[4099] In July 1941,[4100] the commander of the ZWZ, general Stefan Rowecki-Grot ordered him to move to War-saw and take command of the Western District of the ZWZ.[4101] With Rowecki's betrayal in the middle of 1943, Komorowski assumed com-mand of the Home Army in mid-July.[4102]

Just two months later, in late September 1943, the Red Army, after more than two years, retook Smolensk and the nearby massacre site in the Katyń forest.[4103] By October, they were only 250 kilometres from the pre-war eastern Polish frontier[4104] when the Polish London-based government issued the Home Army with new directives to guide its activities during the envisaged approaching German retreat into pre-war Poland.[4105] The Polish exile government stated that it might at some future date order the resistance to stage "an insurrection" against the Germans, or alternatively to promote an "intensified sabotage diver-sion" operation according to the strategic and political situation.[4106] The aim of the rising was to free Poland from the Germans and assume po-litical power on behalf of the legitimate London-based government, of which an important condition would be Anglo-American help.

The Polish exile government, however, was in a quandary, be-cause it was unable to inform the resistance of what form, if any, such support would take.[4107] This especially so, given the obvious fact that western Allied forces were close to two thousand kilometres away over the sea, in Britain, or similarly distant on the Italian peninsula,[4108] as they progressed glacially in the mountainous terrain against stubborn and resolute German resistance.[4109] Moreover, on October 5, 1943 the British Foreign Secretary and pro-Stalinist appeaser, Anthony Eden, told the British War Cabinet that the question of supplying the Home Army with arms was difficult, and such an action, undertaken without consultations with the Russians, might "antagonise" them.[4110] In fact, from 1941 to 1945 the Home Army received just 600 tons of supplies from Anglo-American sources.[4111] Appeasement of Stalinist demands took precedence over support for the Polish Home Army; Stalin, in his objective to Sovietise Poland, did not wish to face a well-armed non-Communist Polish resistance. Less than a year later, this Stalinist objective would be brought to bear with catastrophic effect upon the people of Warsaw.[4112]

Hence, the conundrum: how should the Home Army act when the Soviet army crossed the pre-war eastern Polish frontier? The London government announced the directive that if Soviet-Polish diplomatic relations were still not restored by the time of the Soviet crossing of Poland's pre-war eastern frontier, (as if they ever would be following the German April 1943 revelation of the Katyń mass graves) the Home Army should only act behind the German lines and remain underground in the areas under Soviet control until further orders.[4113] In other words, Home Army units which had been involved in fighting the Germans were going underground again. This decision to conceal the Home Army was a dangerous proposition, because, in all probability, it would have led to an open clash with the Soviet security forces with tragic consequences.[4114]

For Komorowski, this course of going underground upon the arrival of Soviet troops was unacceptable, as he believed that the Home Army operations against the Germans would be credited by Soviet propaganda to the relatively tiny Polish communist Armia Ludowa ("People's" Army).[4115] In Warsaw in 1943, the Armia Ludowa numbered only 800 compared to the Home Army or Armia Krajowa (AK) of 40,330 men.[4116] Moreover, Norman Davies and Roger Moorhouse document the fact that the non-communist Polish Home Army was the largest underground movement in German-occupied Europe.[4117] Hence, Komorowski ordered his men of the Armia Krajowa, having engaged the Germans, to reveal themselves to the Soviet forces and "manifest the existence of Poland."[4118] This would embody Operation Tempest.

This would be akin to members of underground anti-Nazi resistance in western Europe appearing in the wake of liberation by American and British forces, manifesting their nation's reborn existence in liberation. However, the "elephant in the room" in this case, for Poland, was the hostile Stalinist position to any sort of meaningful Polish independence post-war.[4119] This in stark contrast to the American and British stance to respect the independence of nations of western Europe, as they assisted them in rebuilding from wartime devastation. Certainly, the brutal and oppressive Soviet occupation of Poland, embodying the Katyń Wood Massacre[4120] and the deportation of 1.7 million Poles to the gulags[4121] from September 1939, until the Barbarossa invasion of June 1941 show that the advancing Soviets in 1944 were anything but liberators in the cause of Polish independence.

Yet, even with the benefit of hindsight more than three-quarters of a century later, it is impossible to suggest any course of action that would have had any realistic chance of Polish post-war independence. With Stalin holding all the trumps, the only possibilities by this stage for Poland, and indeed the rest of eastern Europe, were: decades of existence under the direct rule of the Soviet jackboot, as was the case for the Baltic states; or being one of the compliant puppet states, as was the case for the "People's" Republic of Poland. However, now looking back in the light of the course chosen by Komorowski, one can at least say that the Home Army manifested the existence of a truly independent Poland during the months of their engagement of the Germans in Operation Tempest, culminating with their heroic 63 day Warsaw General Uprising from August 1 to October 2, 1944.[4122]

Operation Tempest began in February 1944 in the Wołyń region (Volhynia, today Ukrainian Волинь (Volyn)) on Poland's south-eastern pre-war frontier,[4123] and in the summer, during the Soviet Operation Bagration, the single greatest German defeat of World War II[4124] was extended to Wilno (now the modern-day Lithuanian capital of Vilnius), Lwów (now Ukrainian Lviv) and Lublin areas.[4125] During Tempest in Volhynia, a certain pattern of events emerged which was soon to reappear in other parts of Poland; it became apparent to all concerned, Russians, Germans and Poles alike, that immediately before the arrival of the Red Army into a particular area of the country, some of the local Home Army units would be mobilised, concentrated and thrown into battle against the Germans.[4126]

During the fighting, temporary contact and co-operation with the Soviets would be established, and initially relations between both sides would be cordial and friendly.[4127] However, when the battle concluded, those of the Home Army units that found themselves in Soviet-held territory would be disarmed, incorporated into the Polish Berling army subordinate to the Soviets, or deported to the gulags.[4128] As Tempest proceeded, it became clear that Stalin, in the malevolent spirit of the Katyń massacre and his deportation of Poles to the gulags from 1939 until June 1941[4129] just preceding Barbarossa, was not prepared to co-operate militarily and politically with the Home Army.[4130] Stalin knew that he held all the cards for post-war Soviet eastern European hegemony.[4131]

Initially, large towns and cities such as Warsaw, were excluded from Operation Tempest in order to spare mass populations suffering and loss of property. However, in July 1944, Komorowski reversed his decision, ordering his men to occupy large towns before the arrival of the Soviet troops, because he had finally realised that the capture of towns was essential to the policy of acting as hosts to the Soviet authorities.[4132] As Norman Davies commented: "

> He [Stalin] did not have to be swayed by the advice of his own marshals, let alone by the dispositions of an ally of allies [Poland and its Home Army] on just one sector of one front. The Polish Resistance leaders had seen how Stalin had shown no generosity during Operation Tempest when their colleagues had approached the Soviets in a spirit of partnership. So their chances of a better outcome could hardly be further reduced if they now aimed to deal from a position of local strength [in Warsaw]. If the whole democratic world were to learn that the Polish capital had been recaptured by Polish democrats, Stalin would really be straining the Grand Alliance if he subsequently tried to dislodge them by force."[4133]

In his memoirs post-war, Komorowski justified his decision to launch the Warsaw General Uprising, his only card available for possible post-war Polish independence, by explaining the expected consequences of inaction by the Home Army in the nation's capital: "

> That afternoon [Monday July 31, 1944], a communiqué of the Wehrmacht's High Command had announced [that] the Russians had launched "a general assault on Warsaw from the south-east." It also said that the commander of the [German] 73rd Infantry Division, stationed across the [Vistula] river from Warsaw, had been taken prisoner ... In my view, if we unleashed our struggle then, we would prevent the Germans from bringing up reserves and cut off their supply lines... If, on the other hand, the Germans were forced back across the river under Soviet pressure, as could be expected at any moment, their troops would crowd into the city in great numbers and would paralyse any chance of action by us. The city would become a battlefield between Germans and Russians, and would be reduced to ruins. [Hence], in my opinion, the right time for starting [the Uprising] had arrived . . ."[4134]

This decision was made by Komorowski at 6 p.m. on that sunny evening, in a safe apartment in the very heart of Warsaw. Present with Komorowski were his two deputies, General Leopold Okulicki (Niedźwiadek — Bear Cub)[4135] and General Tadeusz Pełczyński (Gregory — Grzegorz),[4136] and the Head of the AK's (Armia Krajowa or Home Army) Warsaw Region, General Antoni Chruściel (Monter).[4137] The Government Delegate was waiting in an adjacent room.[lvi] A notable absentee was the Head of AK Intelligence, Colonel Kazimierz Iranek-Osmecki (Heller), who had been delayed by a German roadblock. Nonetheless, since the Vistula bridges were heavily guarded but still open, Monter had been able to take a bicycle that afternoon and ride out for a few kilometres beyond the eastern suburbs [to the east of the Vistula]. He then reported that the Germans had withdrawn from several districts on the immediate outskirts of the city, and that Soviet tanks had been seen on the road to Praga. His report was duly noted, and Komorowski concluded that the time for the Warsaw Rising had come, advising that the state of "stand-by" should be instituted without delay.[4138]

General Monter was then asked to put the necessary order into writing for distribution to his subordinates. Teams of runners were at hand to carry the following order to every Underground unit in Warsaw:
"

> Alarm — by hand! 31 July, 1900hrs. I am fixing L-Hour [time for the Rising] for 5 p.m. on 1 August. My address, valid from L-Hour, is at 22 Ulica Jasna [Bright Street], apartment 20. Acknowledge receipt of this order."[4139]

As a last step, the civilian Chief Delegate Jan Stanisław Jankowski (Soból — Sable),[4140] was called in to give the order his blessing. After asking a few questions, he said: "Very well. Go ahead!"[4141]

---

lvi 4140 4297 4589 The Government Delegation for the Republic of Poland (Delegatura Rządu Rzeczypospolitej Polskiej na Kraj) was an agency of the London based Polish Government in Exile during World War II. It was the highest authority of the Polish Secret State in occupied Poland. It was headed by the Government Delegate for Poland, a de facto deputy Polish Prime Minister. The Government Delegation for Poland was intended as the first provisional government of war-torn Poland until the Exiled Polish Government in London could safely return from abroad to a liberated Poland. It was of course, not to be. See the online Polish *Encyklopedia WIEM* at https://zapytaj.onet.pl/encyklopedia/50872,,,,delegatura_rzadu_na_kraj,haslo.html and page 188 of *Rising '44: The Battle for Warsaw* Reprint Edition, by Professor Norman Davies, Penguin Books, Reprint edition (October 4, 2005). Also, page 653 which is appendix 11, describes the Polish Secret State in 1944 in a flow chart.

In a sense, the Rising commenced prematurely; at 1:50 p.m., in the suburb of Jolibord, a young Home Army captain, Zdzisław Sierpiński, known by the pseudonym Marek S[4142] (later to become a prominent music critic), while leading his company towards their rendezvous point, ran into a motorised German patrol. The Germans could not fail to notice them, and Marek S saw that they were calculating the pros and cons of engaging this group of youngsters, wearing half-concealed uniforms and carrying sub-machine guns under their coats. Ultimately, the Germans decided to engage them, but this turned into a fatal decision, as Marek S and his cohorts emerged unscathed, threw grenades into the German lorry, and ran across the street to take cover with the rest of their unit.[4143]

At five o'clock, as planned, the main German strong points were rushed, infiltrated, or bombarded by groups of daring young men wearing red-and-white armbands — the colours of the Polish flag. Civilians were still on the streets, and some were hit in the crossfire, or cut off from their homes for life. Soon the red-and-white banner was waving atop the Prudential Building, the city's tallest.[4144] A major German arsenal and storehouse were captured, along with the main post office, the power station, the railway office in Praga, among large swathes of the city. This, however, came at the cost of 2,500 lives, eighty percent of whom were from the Home Army — a similar total to Allied losses on the Normandy beaches on D-Day, just two months earlier.[4145] Moreover, the insurgents had met with little success in Castle Square (Rynek Zamkowy), in the Police district, and crucially, had failed to capture the airport, where they suffered heavy losses, and they failed to secure either ends of two bridges across the river.[4146]

However, on Thursday the 3rd, the insurgents of the Zośka (Sophie) Storm Battalion not only captured their first German tank, they repaired it and drove it into action against its former proprietors.[4147] The inmates of the SS "Farma Gęsiówka" — "Goose Farm" concentration camp were early beneficiaries. This camp, a satellite camp of the Majdanek concentration camp to the east near Lublin since April 1944,[4148] was located on the north-western fringe of the infamous former Ghetto, which spawned the heroic Jewish Ghetto Uprising in April 1943.[4149] It housed inmates who became responsible for the demolition and clearing of the old ghetto. Conditions were brutal, more so than in its parent camp in Majdanek. The area of the ghetto was to be levelled and made into a park after all sewer and cellar openings had been sealed.[4150] In the following month of May 1944, about 3,000 Hungarian Jews were brought in to work on the dismantling of the buildings and removal of ruins.[4151]

When the Zośka Storm Battalion liberated Goose Farm, its commander recalled hearing a voice cry out: "Attention. Eyes left," before one of the liberated prisoners proclaimed to the Zośka commander: "Sergeant Henryk Lederman, sir, and the Jewish Battalion ready for action."[4152] The Zośka commander's amazement and admiration for these people knew no bounds. Not only had they not been broken by Nazi barbarity, they had managed to organise themselves, despite the conditions of the camp, and to ready themselves as soon as an opportunity occurred.[4153] Before long, the Zośka commander was given permission to take these Jewish soldiers into his ranks. Many died in combat. During the liberation of Goose Farm, just two men from the Zośka Battalion were killed; they liberated 348 people, of whom 24 were women. Some survived the uprising, but the overall losses for the Zośka Battalion during the rest of the Rising were appalling. While it is true that KZ-Warschau (Concentration Camp Warsaw — Goose Farm) contained no gas chambers, conditions there were just as brutal as in other concentration camps, and the precise number of people who perished there remains unknown.[4154]

The capture of the German tank, and subsequent liberation of Goose Farm, was only the beginning of the resourceful actions of the heavily out-gunned and under-armed insurgents;[4155] only one in six were armed out of the 45,000 at the outbreak of the Rising.[4156] On the following night, the first RAF bombers appeared over Warsaw's skies,[4157] having flown from over 1300 kilometres away from Brindisi in southern Italy.[4158] They made successful drops over Krasiński Square and the western district of Wola, but the insurgents could not know how many other planes had taken off and had been lost.[4159] This indicated the critical failure in not taking the airport. Nevertheless, they took heart, as they had not been totally forgotten by the west.[4160] Over the entire sixty-three days of the Rising, with the Red Army on Warsaw's doorstep, no such Soviet support, at least of any meaningful value,[4161] would be forthcoming.[4162]

By Sunday the 6th, the sixth day of the Rising, the extreme limit of its envisaged duration by the Home Army had been reached. Ideally, it was supposed to have been just forty-eight hours. Certainly, they had taken much of the capital, but they had not driven the Germans out.[4163] At the time, German counter-attacks under the command of Walter Model, one of Hitler's ablest generals,[4164] were taking place east of the city against the Soviet army, but they had no idea how they were progressing.[4165] At the same time, they held what would turn out to be forlorn hopes for Premier Stanisław Mikołajczyk's "mission" to Moscow.[4166] Needless to say, the premier of the London-based Polish government, in "talks" with Stalin on his home turf, was always going to be like Neville Chamberlain with Hitler on his home turf in Munich in 1938.[4167] In short, hopelessly out his depth.

At the end of July, the decision by Komorowski to reverse the order excluding Warsaw from Operation Tempest embodied three critical elements.[4168] The first was the success of the Soviet summer offensive ,Operation Bagration. The second was the 20th July Valkyrie plot to assassinate Hitler, and the third was Walter Model's counter-offensive against the Red Army at the end of July 1944.[4169] Bagration was the single greatest Nazi defeat of World War II; the AK watched as the Red Army swept through Byelorussia towards Poland, seemingly indicating that the German Army was on the brink of collapse. This seemed to be confirmed in light of the failed Valkyrie attempt to assassinate Hitler. Thanks to the remarkable Soviet success of Bagration, Warsaw had been filled with bedraggled German soldiers trudging back to the west. As a result, the AK leadership believed that it would not be difficult to defeat this beaten army in Warsaw and welcome the Red Army as equals.[4170]

However, on the June 28, when even Hitler began to realise the sheer scale of Stalin's Bagration, he appointed the highly capable Walter Model as head of Army Group Centre. Model had amassed an impressive collection of troops and smashed into the unsuspecting Red Army at Razymin and Wolomin just to the east of Warsaw on July 31, 1944. The day Komorowski made his fateful decision he was not aware of this crucial fact.[4171] This was further exacerbated when the Home Army's Warsaw commander, General Monter, rushed into the final meeting before the Rising, with incorrect intelligence that Soviet tanks were in the eastern Praga district. Komorowski did not wait for verification and gave the order to begin the uprising at 5 p.m. on August 1, 1944.[4172]

As a result, there was no way that the Red Army could have reached Warsaw in the first week of August, and although this was only a temporary setback for the Red Army, Stalin used this setback to justify not going to the aid of the beleaguered Poles.[4173] Throughout the sixty-three days of the rising, the Germans were hardly challenged by the Soviets, allowing them to take murderous revenge on the Polish capital[4174] and eliminate Warsaw's Home Army, which would have been a thorn in Stalin's side in his agenda for Poland. On July 29 and 30, the

Moscow radio station "Kosciuszko" broadcast an appeal to Varsovians to "Fight against the Germans,"[4175] which suggests, that if Komorowski decided not to launch the Rising, Stalinist propaganda would have portrayed the Home Army as fascist collaborators and ineffective cowards.[4176] Either way, Stalin was on a winner. In the end, Komorowski's fateful decision would lead to the Stalinist mass murder of Warsaw by German proxy, aided and abetted by Red Army inaction on the Vistula's east bank, and coinciding with Premier Stanisław Mikołajczyk's forlorn and pointless "mission" to Moscow.

By the second week of August 1944, the first communications links through sewers were opened between the now isolated districts of Mokotów and the City Centre.[4177] Their isolation was due to a German thrust splitting the main Polish stronghold in half.[4178] Hence, the sewers serving as vital transportation and evacuation lines for the duration of the Uprising.[4179] Before long, "sewer paranoia" became prevalent among the Germans.[4180] SS General von dem Bach Zalewski reported that he never managed to convince his soldiers to descend into the sewers and engage the insurgents there.[4181] Rather, by late August, when the Germans realised the insurgents were using the sewers, the invaders resorted to throwing in hand grenades, pouring in acrid gas, laying mines, building obstacles, and dumping and igniting gasoline in order to disrupt the sewer traffic.[4182] At the end of September, 150 evacuating Mokotów defenders accidentally exited into a German-held area and were executed on the spot.[4183] Nevertheless, until the very end of the Warsaw Uprising, the Germans were not able to overcome this "underground" resistance in Warsaw. The sewer system remained solely the turf of the Polish underground fighters for the entire duration of the Warsaw Uprising.[4184]

The clearance of the passages varied. The smallest that could be negotiated were a metre or three feet high and sixty centimetres or two feet wide.[4185] In cases where the passages were high enough for adults to walk upright, the sludge level was significantly higher, exacerbated by a strong current. Moreover, the semicircular floor was very slippery and covered with debris and corpses. The insurgents controlled sewer traffic by issuing permits and guarding the manholes. Due to the limited width of the sewers that rendered passing impossible, all traffic was "one way," controlled by schedules to organise the flow.[4186] During the capitulation negotiations in early October, von dem Bach Zalewski admitted that the Germans did use the sewers, but to a very limited degree.[4187] This involved the transfer of Polish and Ukrainian collaborators, as well as ethnic Germans, back to the city through the smaller sewers under the Downtown district. Their planned destination was in German-held territory, to mix in with the exodus of the city's populace. However, many of them did not make it into German-held territory, but fell into the hands of the insurgents, as the major entrances to the sewers were guarded by the resistance gendarmerie, who questioned and carefully scrutinised the identity papers of every individual they met in the sewers or caught exiting them.[4188]

The bacteria-infested filth of the claustrophobic sewers was poison for even the most minor open wound.[4189] Komorowski reported:

"

> The level of the water was now lower, but the mud was thicker and progress no easier. I helped myself along by putting my hands on my knees. I had to find a new technique for advance in order not to cut my legs on the sharp scraps of rubbish lying at the bottom of the sewer. At one point the guide put his torch on for minute or two. In its light I could see the bodies of cats lying amongst the indescribable filth and excrement. The air was becoming steadily more fetid. Only below the open manholes could we fill our lungs with comparatively fresh air. At one point we had a longer rest. We could change our positions a bit, but it was, of course, impossible to stand upright. A few minutes of immobility made us chatter with cold. Soon we went slowly on again. Leg muscles and back ached intolerably."[4190]

While in the sewers, regardless of rank, the guide was in command.[4191] However, it was on Komorowski's initiative that staff were appointed to control traffic and plot passages in the sewers. Passage through the sewers was only allowed on written permission.[4192]

Meanwhile, AK partisans on the east bank of the Vistula, in Soviet-held territory, attempted to reinforce their compatriots on the other side. However, as had become standard Soviet practice during Tempest, these Home Army enlisted soldiers were arrested, and their officers usually executed.[4193][lvii] Indeed, if ever there was an instance of a three-sided conflict, the 1944 Warsaw General Uprising was it, with

---

[lvii] This Soviet policy during Operation Tempest is consistent with the April 1940 Katyń executions. While some officer orderlies (enlisted men) were among the victims, the vast majority were officers and civilian intelligentsia. See endnote [3643] of Polish WWII Supplement III "The Katyń Wood Massacre."

Stalin's Red Army in the primary role of spectator and occasional combatant, while becoming its sole and undisputed victor. In the mode as spectator, Stalin invoked propaganda that mouthpieces in the west were all too ready to assimilate. In the first week of the Rising, Komorowski commented how complete silence from Soviet radio stations prevailed on the subject of the Rising.[4194] This in contrast to the repeated appeals for an armed rising by the populace in broadcasts prior to August 1st.[4195] On August 7th, the London *Communist Daily Worker* repeated the view of the Soviet Press that the battle in Warsaw was a product of the imagination of Polish émigré circles in London.[4196]

Then suddenly, at 3:15 p.m. on the 8th, Moscow broadcast the assertion that, in spite of Soviet guns being silent, Soviet troops and the pro-Soviet Polish Berling Army were fighting at Warsaw's gates and the liberation of Warsaw was at hand.[4197] Moreover, they claimed that the Polish Armia Ludowa or communist "People's" Army, was playing a lone hand in the streets of the city, fighting the Germans while the Home Army lay idle, taking all the credit. To which Komorowski made the point that clearly, Moscow was trying to create the impression that the Warsaw rising was being fought solely by units of the Communist People's Army, in spite of the fact they could only deploy five platoons, as compared with over 600 platoons of the non-communist Home Army.[4198] In short, the presence of the communist "People's" Army or Armia Ludowa was as tenuous as the legitimacy of the post-war "People's" regime.[4199]

On August 11, SS units unleashed escalating terror tactics upon Warsaw's civilian population. Rather than simply continue the beatings and murders, the SS were rounding up Polish civilians and marching them in front of panzer and infantry attacks as human shields. Initially, AK soldiers watched with disbelief the sight of children, women and old men being marched at gunpoint at the head of German formations. The Polish human shields encouraged the insurgents to fire,[4200] preferring to die as participants in the liberation of Poland, rather than die an inevitable death later as helpless victims aiding and abetting the invaders. As the SS advanced behind the human shield, AK soldiers were faced with the terrible choice of being overrun and doomed to SS retribution, or to fire, with the horrible realisation that they would inevitably kill some of the people they were trying to liberate. On this occasion of August 11, the insurgents fired.[4201]

In these acts of unbridled SS brutality, it is plausible that the traitorous former Home Army officer Ludwik Kalkstein, now under the assumed identity of the Waffen SS officer Konrad Stark, was complicit, for he was in Warsaw for most of August 1944.[4202] In any event, these actions of wanton SS mass murder of civilians, in concert with their use as human shields continued. This prompted the Home Army in general to treat Wehrmacht and SS prisoners differently. Komorowski issued strict orders that the AK were not to retaliate against Wehrmacht prisoners,[4203] but in regard to SS prisoners, this rule was equivocal.

At the outbreak of the Rising, the AK were not recognised by the western Allies, Germans or Soviets as an official branch of the Polish Army. Indeed, in the minds of the latter two dictatorial regimes, the AK or Home Army were nothing more than bandits.[4204] Hence the imperative, that AK soldiers conducted themselves as professional soldiers to ensure those rights, in line with the Geneva convention, were accorded them.[4205] In short, not to be perceived as an unruly mob of retribution. However, in the case of the SS and Gestapo, who had brutalised the Polish populace throughout the war, no such rights were availed to them. In the eyes of the AK, they were war criminals, and so, upon the issuing of the requisite death sentences in the underground courts, were subsequently executed.[4206] One SS officer who had murdered Jews in the Ghetto offered a suitcase full of jewellery for his life. It was not accepted.[4207]

For Wehrmacht officers in general, they considered it beneath their dignity to suppress the Rising. Indeed, as General Walter Model commented: "This revolt is the result of the corruption and false treatment of the Polish population [by the SS and Gestapo]. My soldiers are too good for that!"[4208] General Model knew he could get away with this piece of effrontery, because Hitler was already praising him as the "Saviour of the Eastern Front," when Model pushed the Soviet Army back in the days just preceding the Rising.[4209] [lviii] As already discussed, this made direct Soviet Army assistance in the very early days of the Rising impossible. However, given the 63-day duration of the Rising, it's a major stretch to claim this as a valid excuse for nothing more than token Soviet assistance for the entirety of the Rising.[4210]

On Tuesday August 29, 1944, the governments of Britain and the United States took a major step in officially recognising the non-

---

[lviii] Model's relationship with Hitler would, however, break down after the German defeat at the Battle of the Bulge in Belgium in December 1944 to January 1945. In the aftermath of the encirclement and defeat of Army Group B at the Ruhr Pocket, Model committed suicide on April 21, 1945. See the online *Encyclopaedia Britannica* article at https://www.britannica.com/biography/Walther-Model.

communist Home Army as the official fighting force of occupied Poland. They issued separate but identically worded declarations granting combatant rights to the AK: "The Polish Home Army, which is now mobilised, constitutes a combatant force forming an integral part of the Polish Armed Forces."[4211] Moreover, on September 9, the British Government took this further in another declaration that effectively extended combatant rights to the civilians.[4212] These statements were extremely important to Bór-Komorowski and to "Monter,"[4213] because at the beginning of September, they had to decide whether or not to continue the uprising, which had already extended far beyond the week they had originally envisaged. Now they knew that, if the AK surrendered, the western allies would do their utmost to ensure that the AK soldiers would be treated as POWs under the accords of the Geneva convention, rather than be executed as common bandits.[4214] At least, that was the theory.

On September 10, the Red Army commenced its sporadic and token combatant role; Soviet artillery could be heard, and Soviet aircraft bombed German positions near Praga on the river's east bank.[4215] Due to Soviet inaction up to this point, the Home Army, with Komorowski's authorisation, had commenced surrender talks with the Germans. However, with the commencement of Soviet engagement of the Germans, which would never amount to more than token during the Rising, the Poles abandoned the surrender talks,[4216] and subsequently requested Soviet aid; the London-based Polish government lobbied the western Allies to pressure Stalin to aid the Warsaw defenders.[4217] At this point, the only means of radio communication the Home Army had with the Red Army on the opposite bank of the Vistula was via London.[4218]

Finally, on September 14, the Soviets did drop supplies into the city centre, but they were of questionable value.[4219] Jerzy Zagrodzki, then with the AK High Command, recalled this Soviet "help" was in the form of armaments simply dropped in potato sacks without parachutes from small aircraft coming in at low altitude. In the sacks, the components were packed out of order, making their reassembly almost impossible, and most of the ammunition were incompatible with the German and British manufactured weapons in use by the AK.[4220] The drops included some desperately needed canned food and bread, but in accordance with Stalin's agenda for Warsaw, it was in such small amounts that it hardly made a difference.[4221]

By this stage, even the turgid Plujka (spit) soup, made from wheat and barley, and so-named because you had to spit the husks out at every mouthful,[4222] ran out. The city's inhabitants and its defenders had resorted to eating horses and even rats. Mothers, unable to now produce milk, saw their babies die of starvation, as dysentery and all manner of disease ran rampant. Clean water was now all but non-existent.[4223] By September 15, the Red Army had taken control of the entire Praga district on the east bank, while Polish pleas for help to London, over a thousand kilometres away, and the Red Army at their doorstep, continued. That day two Soviet parachutists landed in the city centre, giving more false hope of meaningful Soviet assistance to the defenders. One would die in the bombing, but the other, for whatever it was worth, helped set-up radio cipher contact with the Red Army.[4224] More token Soviet airdrops continued, before two more Soviets parachuted in to act as artillery spotters. However, minimal Soviet barrages were fired, and of those fired, several landed on Polish positions, leading to speculation that the Red Army were deliberately targeting the Polish defenders.[4225]

In the Czerniaków district, the Home Army still held a bridgehead on the west bank of the river. Polish messengers crossed the river to establish direct contact with the Red Army; in response, the Soviets "promised" to bring reinforcements and supplies to the desperate Poles in the city centre.[4226] It took several days to materialise, but when it did, the hearts of the Polish insurgents sank even further. The reinforcements consisted of 500 men from the Soviet sponsored Polish army under the command of the opportunist,[4227] Zygmunt Berling. They were hardly fighting soldiers, but recently conscripted Polish peasant conscripts with little or no military training. For the AK, they were just 500 more mouths they felt obligated to protect and feed with what desperate little they had.[4228] The only consolation was that the peasant conscripts brought over some machine guns and antitank weapons. In spite of the Red Army being on the Polish defenders' doorstep, its "help" was never more than token in lip service to Anglo-American pressure.

On the night of Sunday September 17, 1944, following six weeks of pleas from Warsaw and its London-based exile government, a message was received by the beleaguered defenders that a large scale Allied airdrop would be flown over the city.[4229] The following day, 107 B-17 American flying fortresses appeared over Warsaw while German anti-aircraft artillery bellowed as parachutes fell from the sky.[4230] Initially, the defenders were elated, but the wind carried the vast majority of the supplies to the German side. Out of the 1,248 containers dropped, just 21 were recovered by the Home Army.[4231] Utterly dejected, Komorowski pondered what a difference such supplies would have made to the outcome of the battle had they arrived a month earlier when the AK held almost two-thirds of the city, when large parks and cemeteries were designated as drop zones.[4232] And what difference the capture of the airport would have made at the outbreak of Rising?[4233] As Komorowski commented: "

> Doubts as to whether the Russians had intended to cross the Vistula and take Warsaw in the near future were expressed more and more openly. Soviet policy might have been directed against the Polish Government [exile government in London], against me, or against a certain group of Polish people, but it was difficult to imagine that this policy would be opposed to their own interests. Such would be the case if they missed the opportunity offered by our hold on Warsaw to capture, without difficulty or losses, so powerful a bridgehead and at the same time increased the distrust of the population towards them in encouraging it to undertake a fight which,[4234] in view of their lack of support, they had condemned to hopelessness. For six weeks they had bridgeheads on the western bank of the Vistula, they now had Praga [on the river's east bank] in their hands, and our Rising provided them with diversionary activity right in the heart of the German lines; here then, was every condition favourable for the capture of Warsaw by an encircling movement from the south in conjunction with a frontal attack."[4235]

Airdrops were being attempted by the Western Allies from the air base at Brindisi in southern Italy, over one thousand kilometres distant, while the Soviets, on Warsaw's doorstep, only made the most token and virtually useless airdrops. Moreover, as recalled by Australian aircrew man Alan McIntosh[4236] of the RAF and South African Air Force squadrons of No. 205 Group, the Germans were not the only enemy they had to contend with while in transit to and from Warsaw. "

> On my crew's last sortie to Warsaw (night of 10/11 September 1944) we were engaged by Russian AA [Anti-aircraft] fire and Russian night fighters along much of the two-and-a-half hour route. Disenchanted by this, our South African pilots and Australian navigator, at about 12,000 feet [3,660 metres] and outside gun-range from Lublin, rapidly decided that if we survived the drop on Warsaw and were fated to be shot down on

the way home, it would be by the enemy and not by our Russian 'friends.' On climbing away from Warsaw, therefore we followed the direct route through enemy territory, rather than putting our Russian blood chits to the test. Some crews of our force were not so lucky. With the benefit of hindsight, one wonders what our masters knew (and how much they chose to tell) about our Russian 'Allies.'"[4237]

On August 25, Churchill sent Roosevelt the draft of a telegram which he proposed to send to Stalin on the subject of sending American planes from Britain to make an airdrop on Warsaw; it asked Stalin bluntly: "Why should they not land on the refuelling ground which has been assigned to us behind the Russian lines without enquiry as to what they have done on the way?"[4238] Roosevelt, always indifferent to the Polish cause and all too ready to appease Stalin, replied the following day that he was not willing to join Churchill in such a "bold" statement: "I do not consider it advantageous to the long-range general war prospect for me to join with you in the proposed message."[4239]

Without Roosevelt's support, Churchill did not send the telegram, but continued to apply pressure by other means. On September 4, 1944, the British Government sent a telegram to Molotov informing him that British public opinion was beginning to question why the Soviets were doing nothing to help the Poles in Warsaw.[4240] The Soviet embassy in London also noticed that the normally pro-Soviet British press was becoming embarrassed by Soviet inactivity.[4241] Churchill was so furious over Stalin's refusal to allow western Allied planes to land on Soviet airfields that he even suggested to Roosevelt that the western Allies should ignore the embargo and just go ahead and land on them anyway.[4242] Roosevelt, all too typically, was not prepared to risk Stalin's displeasure, especially since his chief of staff, Admiral William Leahy, had confused the fall of Warsaw's Old Town with the collapse of the entire Uprising.[4243]

John Ward, who was sending short news reports by radio to the British Press, had been captured by the Germans three years before, but had escaped and made it to Warsaw, where, together with a great many other British prisoners of war in hiding, he lived among the Polish people and took an active part in Underground work. Komorowski described Ward as a courageous young man; he was the only foreign correspondent in Warsaw and took an active part in the fighting. In recognition, Komorowski personally awarded him the Cross of Valour.[4244] On

September 10, John Ward described the appalling scenes in the beleaguered city as follows: "

> On every conceivable little piece of ground are graves of civilians and soldiers. Worst of all, however, is the smell of rotting bodies, which pervades over the whole centre of the city. Thousands of people are buried under the ruins … Soldiers defending their battered barricades are an awful sight. Mostly they are dirty, hungry and ragged. There are very few who have not received some sort of wound. And on and on, through a city of ruins, suffering and dead."[4245]

In the last week of August, news spread that the French Resistance had instigated an uprising in Paris, which in certain respects, closely paralleled the Home Army's rising in Warsaw.[4246] Not waiting for the arrival of the US Army, elements of the French Underground assaulted remnants of the German garrison on August 19th, which precipitated several days of chaotic and bitter street fighting. As in Warsaw, there had been no question of co-ordinated action with the advancing Allies, even when the Germans had begun to withdraw. In short, no pre-arranged plan. A general strike had broken out on the 18th and the French police rebelled against their German overlords. Before long, civilians joined in and barricades were thrown up. As the fighting spread, isolated German outposts were attacked. Later, it was revealed that the military Governor of Paris, German General von Choltitz, had ignored Hitler's orders to raze the city.[4247]

Even after their successful breakout from the Normandy beachhead in early August opened the road to Paris, Generals Dwight Eisenhower and Omar Bradley considered Paris an unnecessary detour that would slow the Allied advance towards Germany. They sought to avoid the type of house-to-house urban fighting that had ensnared the Germans at Stalingrad and did not want to have to feed the city's nearly two million residents.[4248]

However, for General Charles de Gaulle, the head of the London based Free French, and president of the Provisional Government of the French Republic, bypassing Paris was unthinkable. In a pure military sense, the city's objective value was limited, but de Gaulle, as a Frenchman, deeply understood its symbolic importance. Whoever liberated France's capital would gain a huge advantage in determining France's post-war political fate — and de Gaulle was determined that this advantage fall to the Free French Army, rather than to British or

American forces, or another French resistance group,[4249] such as the principal clandestine military organisation in Paris, the Forces Françaises de l'Intérieur (FFI), commanded by the Communist, Colonel 'Rol' Tanguy.[4250] For Charles de Gaulle, a military training instructor on the Polish side during the 1919-1920 Polish-Soviet War, and even attached briefly to a combat unit in July to August of 1920,[4251] such a notion would have been unthinkable.

As the Paris uprising progressed, Eisenhower, in spite of his reluctance to divert the Allied advance, was now unwilling to stand by and allow German forces to crush the Paris uprising,[4252] as they would, virtually unhampered, six weeks later in Warsaw. Hence, on August 22nd, he authorised the French 2nd Armoured Division[4253] under the command of General Leclerc to take the city.[4254] By the 25th, Paris was liberated amid an elated populace.[4255] Charles de Gaulle, delivered a resounding speech at the Hôtel de Ville: "

> Paris! Paris outraged! Paris broken! Paris martyred! But Paris liberated! Liberated by itself, liberated by its people with the help of the French armies, with the support and the help of all France, of the France that fights, of the only France, of the real France, of the eternal France!"[4256] [And with the help of American, British and Canadian troops, landing at Normandy in early June, and the Polish 1st Armoured Division in July.][4257]

The following day, a de Gaulle, standing at six feet, five inches (197 cm), led a procession of French troops down the Champs Elysées. Throughout he never ducked, making himself a ripe target for German snipers as they fired on the crowd![4258] Inevitably, close parallels with the Rising in Warsaw were noted with approval. As the *Biuletin Informacyjny* commented: "

> As in Warsaw, the French Underground did not wait for the moment when the capital would have been liberated by external forces. The people of Paris undertook the struggle on their own account, and brought it to a victorious conclusion after three days."[4259]

Moreover, Radio Lightning in Warsaw contrived to broadcast its congratulations in French: "

Comrades-in-arms! On this occasion, when Paris, the capital of Freedom and the heart of European civilisation, has cast off its shackles . . . We, the soldiers of Poland's Home Army, who have been fighting in Warsaw for three weeks, send you our most heartfelt felicitations."[4260]

For those who knew, the broadcast was all the more moving because it was read by the unlikeliest of broadcasters — a Belgian diamond smuggler, who had been accidentally trapped in Warsaw by the Rising, and who had now been pulled from his refuge in a cellar to give the message an authentic flavour. By all accounts, the smuggler adorned his performance with a fervour and passion worthy of a professional actor.[4261] Unfortunately for Varsovians and Polish hopes in general, the similarity between the respective uprisings from this point on ended. Warsaw's external and potential liberating army, unlike the case in Paris, was overtly hostile to the Polish cause. A free and independent Poland would not be reborn until decades later, in August 1989. [4262] On Wednesday September 27th, 1944, Komorowski and his closest subordinates, decided to cease fighting, in what was by now, a dire and hopeless situation.[4263] It had become obvious that the Soviets were not willing to cross the Vistula and "liberate" Warsaw,[4264] prompting Komorowski to place the remaining civilians and combatants, at the questionable mercy of the Germans.[4265] In the city centre alone, there were still over 300,000 people.[4266]

The following morning, Komorowski sent one more message to the Soviet commander, Marshal Konstanty Rokossovsky, who was of paternal Polish Borderland blood.[4267] In it, Komorowski briefly described the desperate situation of the civilians and the Home Army, declaring that hunger and German pressure could, even in these dire circumstances, still be endured for a further seventy-two hours. If, however, Soviet inaction continued, he informed Rokossovsky that he would be compelled to cease the fight.[4268] The Soviets did confirm receipt of the message, but apart from several more token airdrops of ammunition and *kasha* (eastern European porridge), Soviet forces persisted in not acting. As for the *kasha*, it burst on impact, scattering the contents, which were picked up to the last grain by the starved insurgents and inhabitants.[4269] By the 29th, Komorowski sent envoys to the German SS commander, Obergruppenführer Erich von dem Bach-Zelewski.[4270]

On the night of November 9-10th 1938, Bach-Zelewski was in command of the Reichskristallnacht (National Night of Broken Glass) in the Breslau region.[4271] In August 1941, in the aftermath of Barbarossa's launch, Einsatzgruppe members complained of the "psychological burden caused by shooting large numbers of women and children."[4272] With the invention of the gas vans, aside from their greater and more economical efficiency, the "battle fatigue and mental anguish" for the "heroic" Einsatzgruppe members diminished. The most vocal "complainants" on their behalf were Bach-Zelewski[4273] and Arthur Nebe,[4274] then commander of Einsatzgruppe B based in the Belarusian capital of Minsk,[4275] and perhaps the most questionable member in the entire German resistance. When the Nuremberg Trials began on November 20, 1945, von dem Bach made an appearance. In exchange for his testimony, the Americans, to whom he had given himself up in August 1945, did not hand him over to the Poles or the Soviet Union. He was never charged at Nuremberg, but his testimony heavily incriminated his comrades.[4276] Among them was Reichsmarschal Hermann Göring, one of the three most powerful men in Hitler's inner circle,[4277] who was later sentenced to death for crimes against humanity, among other charges, reacted indignantly, calling von dem Bach a "traitor," "bastard" and "the bloodiest murderer in this whole system."[4278]

While he was never charged at Nuremberg, von dem Bach was put under house arrest. Later, he worked as a night watchman. In 1961, he was sentenced to four and-a-half years in prison for ordering the murder of the SS officer Anton von Hohberg und Buchwald. A year later, he received a second sentence because of murders he committed in the 1930s.[4279] These included the murders he perpetrated in the 1934 Night of the Long Knives — the purge of Ernst Röhm's Sturmabteilung (SA or Brown Shirts),[4280] and the murder of six communists shortly after Hitler came to power in late January 1933.[4281] For this he was sentenced to life imprisonment. On March 8, 1972, he died in prison.[4282] In 1961, the German news magazine *Der Spiegel* reported that when von dem Bach was asked by the judges how he reconciled the ethos of a former Prussian lieutenant with helping Hitler's SS, he said: "I was Hitler's man to the end. I am still convinced of his innocence."[4283]

On August 5, just five days into the Rising, von dem Bach arrived in Warsaw to take charge of all anti-insurgent operations. His arrival coincided with the news of mass murders of civilians, the flight of refugees, and heavy bombardments.[4284] Most notorious of these was the Wola massacre, which began at 7 a.m. that day;[4285] it was perpetrated by the notorious Waffen SS Dirlewanger Convict Brigade in concert with the Kaminski renegade Soviet Brigade.[4286] In accordance with Himmler's orders, their skirmishes with Home Army defenders for two days became a sideline issue, as they concentrated on massacring every man, woman, and child in sight. No one was spared — not even nuns, nurses, hospital patients, doctors, invalids, or babies. Amidst this wanton orgy of genocide in the suburbs of Ohota and Wola, it has been estimated that the number of civilians executed, ranged from 20,000 to 50,000.[4287] The following day of the 6th, there were further mass executions, making it one of the worst massacres of World War II.[4288] According to Davies, however, von dem Bach-Zelewski instituted a new policy that day, whereby only men were to be shot, and captured civilians sent to a transit camp just created 16 kilometres (10 miles) outside the city in Pruszków.[4289] Given this history, one can understand the trepidation that Komorowski and his Home Army in general had in surrendering to the Germans.

Late on the night of September 30th, weary after protracted talks with his staff, Komorowski turned in to his quarters for a rest, and fell into a deep sleep almost immediately. In the next room, Agaton (Captain Stanisław Jankowski),[4290] commanding the security platoon, was on duty at the wireless. An hour later, an excited Agaton woke Komorowski up. The first thought that entered Komorow-ski's mind as he leapt off the bed was of news from the Soviets. Instead, Agaton, proclaimed the following news from London: "Sir, just a moment ago the BBC broadcast the news that you had been appointed Commander-in-Chief of the Polish armed forces."[4291] [Inside and outside of Poland. This for example, would include the Polish 2nd Corps fighting in Italy, and the Polish 1st Armoured Division engaged in France.] At first, Komorowski thought Agaton had gone mad. The news seem-ed preposterous. Nevertheless, hours later, in the early hours of October 1st, Komorowski received official confirmation in a message of appointment from the Polish President in London: "

> With effect from September 30th, 1944, according to Article 13 of the Constitution, I appoint you Commander-in-Chief, Polish Armed Forces. You will assume your rights and duties on arrival at the present seat of the highest Polish authorities."

(Signed) WŁADYSŁAW RACZKIEWICZ.[4292]

In his book, Komorowski commented as follows: "

> With the name of General Sosnkowski, the Commander-in-Chief now leaving office,[4293] was linked a fine tradition dating back to the early days of the present Polish Army [in the 1919-

20 Polish Soviet War].[4294] General Sosnkowski's dismissal, together with the fate of Warsaw, presented the morale of the Polish forces with a severe test. In those difficult days, President Raczkiewicz had doubtless tried to put forward a symbol which would unite all Poles. This symbol was Warsaw. I understood my appointment as a tribute to my soldiers in Warsaw."[4295]

With the realisation of now imminent surrender, Komorowski issued his final instructions. Outside Warsaw, the remainder of the Home Army was still operating on German-occupied territory, which could not be left without orders. In Komorowski's mind, the surrender of Warsaw was not to identified with the surrender of the entire Underground movement, which was compelled to carry on the resistance as long as there were Germans occupying Polish soil. As his replacement, he appointed General Okulicki as the new Commander of the Home Army. This was due to Okulicki having left Italy months before the Rising to be parachuted into Poland. This went unnoticed by the Gestapo, and even by this time, they were still ignorant of Okulicki's presence. He prepared his departure from the city and chose a small group of Staff officers, who had to leave Warsaw individually after agreeing on their later meeting point elsewhere in German occupied Poland.[4296]

At the same time, Komorowski appointed two couriers who were to reach Great Britain and report to the Polish Government on the events which had taken place in Warsaw. Two others were appointed by the Government delegate.[4297] From these four, it was expected that at least one would succeed in reaching London. That was indeed with the case; Captain Jan Nowak-Jeziorański was the only one to make it to London.[4298] He would survive post-war as a radio host for the Polish section of Radio Free Europe, and author of the book *Courier from Warsaw*. As this book's title implies, this was far from being his first run between Warsaw and London. He was honoured with his own photo and tablet in Warsaw's *Muzeum Powstania* (Uprising Museum), which I had the privilege to witness on my visit to the museum in October 2004.

At 8 p.m. on October 2nd, the surrender agreement was signed at von dem Bach's headquarters. Komorowski was not present, but was represented by the Home Army envoys Colonel Kazimierz Iranek-Osmecki (Heller) and Lieutenant Colonel Zygmunt Dobrowolski (Zyndram) whom he appointed on the 29th. For the second time in this war, Warsaw had to give way to the armed superiority of the enemy. However, the conditions in which fighting had transpired in September,

1939, were vastly different from those of 1944.[4299] Five years earlier, the Germans had been at the summit of their power, and the weakness of the Allies had made it impossible for them to help Warsaw. The fall of Warsaw in 1939 was the first in a long series of German victories; but in 1944 the situation was reversed. The German's star was setting, and Komorowski and his Home Army had a bitter feeling that the failure of the Rising would probably be the last significant German victory over the Allies. For Komorowski, history would perhaps show one day why Warsaw had been left this second time without relief.[4300]

At the time of writing more than three-quarters of a century later, this reason is self-evident for all those willing to study and acknowledge what was Stalin's mass murder of the Polish people by German Proxy. The most conservative figures put the civilian death toll for the Rising at 180,000.[4301] Out of the 40,000 Home Army combatants, 18,000 were seriously wounded, missing or killed in action, while the Germans suffered 20,000 dead and 9,000 wounded.[4302] This embarrassing truth was never acknowledged by the puppet regime of the so-called "People's" Republic of Poland. Any criticism of the Red Army and Stalinist inaction during the Rising was expressly forbidden.[4303] As was any mention of Stalinist guilt in the April 1940 Katyń Wood massacre.[4304] Neither fitted the narrative of a Soviet "liberator," to which Poland supposedly owed its eternal and sycophantic homage.

One aspect of the Rising that evokes heated debate, even among pro-post-war-independence Poles, the wisdom, or lack of it, of Komorowski's invocation of it. Among its strongest critics was Władysław Anders,[4305] who was imprisoned by the Soviets in September 1939.[4306] Following the Barbarossa invasion and subsequent Polish-Soviet Military Agreement in August 1941, he was released. In time, he would command the Polish 2nd Corps, made up of formerly Soviet incarcerated Borderland Poles. The Corps would distinguish itself, in particular, during the 1944 Battle of Monte Cassino in Italy.[4307] Naturally, Anders was a staunch anti-communist, and seeing the writing on the wall for Poland post-war, settled in Great Britain. Subsequently, he became a prominent leader of Polish exiles in the West.[4308]

On hearing of the outbreak of the Rising in early August 1944, Anders left his superiors in no doubt that he viewed the Rising as a catastrophe, even "a serious crime," and "madness." He maintained from the outset that the insurrection did not have "a remote chance of success" and that the capital would be "annihilated."[4309] Moreover, his views mirrored those of General Sosnkowski, the Commander-in-Chief of the London-based government, but not of the majority of Polish leaders there.[4310] Having suffered Soviet incarceration for almost two years,[4311] Anders perhaps foresaw the Stalinist abandonment of Poland. In London, Sosnkowski,[4312] like Anders[4313] and Komorowski,[4314] was a veteran of the 1919-20 Polish Soviet War, and with the German revelation of the Katyń Wood Massacre sixteen months earlier in April 1943,[4315] may well have had the same concern about Stalinist abandonment of the Rising. However, for the people in Warsaw at the time, including Komorowski,[4316] this seemed unthinkable — akin to the notion of General Eisenhower abandoning the Paris Uprising in late August 1944.[4317]

If Eisenhower had indeed done so, one can only imagine the eruption of French anger and rage at the US allowing the Germans a free hand in suppressing it, as Stalin did for the Germans in Warsaw. In a *Jerusalem Post* article in 2017, Soviet inaction at Warsaw was justified with the notion that the Soviets had more important objectives elsewhere[4318] — which Eisenhower to, in theory, could have used to justify the abandonment of Paris for the time being, in mid to late August 1944. Hence, the "nuance,"[4319] of Stalin having bigger fish to fry elsewhere, as Robert Cherry asserts in his Jerusalem Post article, can only hold true, if by logical extension, you assert that Eisenhower, in August 1944, should have abandoned Paris, for the same reason. For Eisenhower, a reasonable man of empathy, rigid adherence to original plans became unthinkable. On the other hand, catastrophically for Warsaw, to a rank sociopath, such a course of action was the only natural and logical choice.

In spite of Anders's feelings towards the Rising, he attended and escorted Komorowski's wife Irena at her husband's memorial service at London's Westminster Cathedral on October 20, 1966. This service was arranged and attended by Conservative politicians, such as former prime minister, Harold MacMillan, ex-foreign secretary Selwyn Lloyd, and the Leader of the House of Lords, Lord Longford.[4320] This service took place amidst outrage in the Polish émigré community when seven weeks earlier, on September 1st,[4321] in London,[4322] Harold Wilson's Labour government, unlike the French and Americans, refused to send a representative to Komorowski's funeral. Wilson's questionable justification in doing so, was not to antagonise the Soviet Union.[4323]

When Komorowski invoked the Uprising on Tuesday August 1, 1944, his reasoning was that if the Germans were forced back across the river under Soviet pressure, as could have been expected at any moment, their troops would crowd into the city in great numbers and would paralyse any chance of action by the Home Army. The city would then become a battlefield between Germans and Soviets, reducing the city to ruins. Hence the right time for invoking the Rising had arrived.[4324] A counter-argument to Komorowski's assessment is that Kraków, Poland's cultural capital, never invoked any uprising, and essentially remained undamaged. But this was not the case for Gdańsk, Poznań, and virtually every other city in Poland.

Kraków escaped damage partly because it was the capital of the German General Government for the occupied Polish Region, under the governorship of Hans Frank. In Poland's west, such as Poznań, the country had been absorbed into the German Reich proper. During the Cold War, the Soviet narrative was that the brilliance of the Soviet commander Ivan Konev, saved the city, and a statue was erected in Kraków in his honour.[4325] It seems that the legend of Marshal Konev heroically saving Kraków was needed for him personally as an asset in his rivalry with Marshal Georgy Zhukov, and aided Soviet plans of expansion.[4326] Moreover, with Poles accusing the Red Army of passivity and of letting the Warsaw Uprising bleed out in 1944, in January 1945, when they captured Kraków,[4327] they needed a narrative of taking proper care of Poland's cultural jewel, in order to mitigate unrest in Poland. Numerous Soviet-contrived historical dogmas made it all the way to 1989, and Konev's "rescue" of Kraków was one of them.[4328]

Post-Cold War research has proved that the Germans had little interest in defending Kraków, and that the threat of being encircled was more than likely. The Germans were well-prepared for the Soviets, and when they approached, the Germans blew up the bridges on the river Dunajec south of Kraków, securing a safe line of retreat for all their troops. They also closed the dam in Rożnów, so that the Dunajec rose by three metres, thus becoming almost impassable. The Germans had so much time for a full retreat that they not only managed to evacuate all their administration, but also transport away looted pieces of art[4329] — much, one would imagine, to the delight governor Hans Frank. For Ivan Konev, his monument was taken down and removed to Russia in 1991. The following year, his title of honorary citizen of Kraków, was duly revoked.[4330]

In Warsaw's case, if the Home Army remained passive, the populace would have been compelled to comply with the following order issued by the city's German governor, Ludwig Fischer, on July 27, 1944, just five days before the Rising, gratuitously appealing to Warsaw's spirit of August 1920: "

Poles! In 1920, outside this city, you repelled Bolshevism thereby demonstrating your anti-Bolshevik sentiments. Today Warsaw is again the breakwater for the Red flood and its contribution to the struggle shall be that 100,000 men and women should report for work to build defences. Gather on the main squares: Jolibord, Marszalstr., Lubliner Platz, etc. Those whose refuse will be punished."[4331]

This suggests that the Germans were not going to give Warsaw up without a fight, supporting Komorowski's fear of Home Army inaction with its consequences. In short, there was never going to be a bloodless solution for Warsaw. A cataclysm was coming for the city regardless. As mentioned earlier, on the June 28, when even Hitler began to realise the sheer scale of Stalin's Operation Bagration, he appointed the highly capable Walter Model as head of Army Group Centre. Model had amassed an impressive collection of troops and smashed into the unsuspecting Red Army at Razymin and Wolomin just to the east of Warsaw on July 31, 1944 — the day Komorowski made his fateful decision, unaware of this crucial fact.[4332] Moreover, accusations that Komorowski and the Home Army in general were incompetent[4333] because of their miscalculations at the outbreak of the Rising are not compatible with the fact that an underground Army, only envisaging a conflict lasting at the most six days[4334] against one of the most fearsome armies in the world, held out for more than ten times that period — 63 days.

Furthermore, the notion of Evan McGilvray that Komorowski, having endured and co-ordinated traffic in the sewers,[4335] was taken into "genteel" captivity as a privileged nobleman by the Germans, while his compatriots were subject to illegal captivity, slave labour, and death, is grossly unfair.[4336] Jan Nowak-Jeziorański, the legendary[4337] "Courier From Warsaw" and former head of the Polish section of Radio Free Europe in Munich, was one of several people to make a speech at the interment of Komorowski and his wife Irena in 1994 at Warsaw's Powązki Cemetery. He recalled how he met Komorowski after the war in London and asked him why, knowing she was expecting a baby, he had not warned his wife to leave Warsaw before the Uprising began. Komorowski replied:
"How many pregnant women do you think there were in Warsaw at the time? I couldn't warn them all. So I could not use my position to make an exception for my wife."[4338]

Komorowski's son, Adam, subsequently met President Lech Wałęsa at one of the receptions for the fiftieth anniversary of the Uprising. Wałęsa mused, "I wonder what the general would have to say if he could see us now?" Adam replied "that he would probably be as amazed as I am." To which Poland's first elected President post-war proclaimed: "Well let me tell you, without the Warsaw Uprising there would have been no Solidarity."[4339]

Solidarity, in Polish Solidarność, was a Polish trade union that in the early 1980s became the first independent labour union in a country belonging to the Soviet bloc. Solidarity was founded in September 1980, then forcibly suppressed by the Polish government in December 1981, when martial law was imposed. In 1989 however, it re-emerged to become the first opposition movement to participate in free elections in a Soviet-bloc nation. Lech Wałęsa, an electrician at Gdańsk's Lenin Shipyards, was the leader of this movement.[4340] His story suggests that the Rising became an icon of defiance, freedom and independence for Poles amidst the sterile desolation of what they perceived as the illegitimate "People's" Republic — in spite of 0.2 million Poles perishing in it. To which, one can argue, no Rising, still a similar death toll, but minus the iconic Cold War rallying point that was the Warsaw Uprising. Komorowski does not deserve to be labelled as culpable for these deaths. Culpability here is the domain of Stalin and his German (SS) proxy.

When Heller returned from negotiating the surrender agreement, he informed Komorowski of a curious aspect of his conversation with General von dem Bach-Zelewski. During the talks, the latter stated that the greatest interest of leading German circles had been evoked by the part played by Polish women in the Home Army, and indeed, in the fight in Warsaw. It had astonished the Germans; even the Führer had become so interested that von dem Bach had been summoned to Berlin, during the fighting, to inform Hitler personally of his experiences and opinion on the matter.[4341] In contrast, for the entire war, the Germans did not employ women in the factories.[4342] [lix] Only in the final months, when manpower became desperately short, they had women man the Flak — "Flug-Abwehr-Kanone" — or anti-aircraft batteries.[4343]

The key terms of the surrender agreement were as follows: "

[lix] ***It's true that female labour was exploited in the concentration camps, but German women would never work alongside civilian German males in the factories. Their place in National Socialist dogma was strictly in the home.***

Section I

5. ... Soldiers of the Home Army are entitled to the rights of the Geneva Convention dated August 27th, 1929, concerning the treatment of prisoners of war. Soldiers of the Home Army taken prisoner in the area of the city of Warsaw in the course of the struggle which began on August 1st, 1944, shall enjoy the same rights.

6. Those non-combatant persons accompanying the Home Army, within the meaning of Article 81 of the Geneva Convention on the treatment of prisoners of war without distinction of sex, are entitled to the rights of prisoners of war. This affects in particular women workers.

8. Persons being prisoners of war in the sense of the aforesaid articles shall not be persecuted for their military or political activities either during the period of struggle in Warsaw or in the preceding period. ...

9. In regard to the civilian population who were in the city of Warsaw during the period of struggle, collective responsibility shall not be applied. No person who was in Warsaw during the period of struggle shall be persecuted for functioning in time of war in the organisation of administrative or judiciary authorities. ...

10. The evacuation of the civilian population of the city of Warsaw requested by the German command will be executed at a time and in a manner which will cause minimal human suffering. They will facilitate the evacuation of items of artistic, cultural and religious value. The German authorities will do their utmost to protect remaining public and private property.[4344]

Section II

2. The Home Army Command will deliver to the German lines all German prisoners of war....

8. The evacuation of the wounded and sick soldiers of the Home Army, as also of medical material, will be determined by the Medical Head of the German forces in consultation with the Medical Head of the Home Army....

9. Soldiers of the Home Army shall be recognised by a white-and-red arm-band or pennons, or a Polish eagle....[4345]

Signatures:

Von dem Bach
Iranek, Casimir Colonel (Heller)
Dobrowolski Lieutenant Colonel (Zyndram)"[4346]

In the final order to his troops, Komorowski expressed his undying admiration for them. In spite of the seeming desolation of Polish hopes of post-war independence, Komorowski still asserted that the dream was alive, embodied in their heroism in the Rising, which would influence the destiny of their home land: "

Soldiers of Fighting Warsaw!

Our two months' struggle in Warsaw, which has been a chain of heroic actions on the part of the Polish soldiers, is fraught with dread, yet it is a solemn proof, above all, of our mighty striving for liberty. The valour of Warsaw is the admiration of the whole world. Our struggle in the capital under the blows of death and destruction, carried on with such tenacity by us, takes first place among the glorious deeds achieved by Polish soldiers during this war. By it, we have proved our spirit and our love of freedom... Our struggle will influence the destiny of our nation, because it is an unparalleled contribution of devoted valour in the defence of our independence...

... In agreeing that military operations shall terminate, I have endeavoured to ensure to the soldiers all rights due to them after the cessation of the struggle and to the civilian population such conditions of existence and protection as shall best save them from the cruelties of war...

You soldiers, my dearest comrades in these two months of fighting, one and all of whom have been to the very last moment constant in the will to fight on, I ask now to fulfil obediently such orders as arise from the decision to cease fighting. I call to the population to comply with the evacuation instructions issued by me, the city's Commander, and the civil authorities.

With faith in ultimate victory of our just cause, with faith in a beloved, great and happy country, we shall all remain soldiers and citizens of an independent Poland, faithful to the standard of the Polish Republic."[4347]

It would be easy to mock Komorowski's final address to his troops. Forty-five years later, in 1989, twenty-three years following his death, the fulfilment of Komorowski's bold but seemingly forlorn prophecy would be witnessed by his sons Adam and Jerzy. The latter was born on September 10, 1944, in the midst of the Rising.[4348] Adam was born two years earlier on December 12, 1942.[4349] Moreover, even during the decades of the Soviet puppet "People's" Republic, the Poles, unlike North Korea for example, with its God-like idolatrous worship of its supreme leaders, were never truly assimilated into the Stalinist-Soviet mindset in their minds and spirit.

Just before and after the formal German capitulation in early May 1945, there were instances of successful armed Polish resistance against the Soviet occupation of "liberation," such as The Battle of Miodusy Pokrzywne (in modern-day north-eastern Poland) on August 18, 1945. In this engagement, the battle culminated in the annihilation of a Soviet NKVD task force, which had been responsible for terrorising the population of the Bielsko Podlasie region.[4350] This battle, led by Zygmunt Błażejewicz, is considered one of the three greatest successes of the Polish armed anti-communist underground — next to the battle of Kuryłówka on May 7, 1945, fought by a branch of the National Military Organisation (NOW — Narodowej Organizacji Wojskowej). The third was the battle in Stockim Forest on May 24, 1945, where Major Marian Bernaciak "Orlik" led the partisans to victory.[4351] During the night of May 20-21, 1945, a unit led by Lieutenant Eugeniusz Wasilewski "Wichura" liberated an NKVD concentration camp in Rembertów, on Warsaw's eastern outskirts. During this operation, several hundred prisoners were able to escape. The NKVD organised a massive operation to recapture the escapees. From among those recaptured, the NKVD murdered around 100 individuals.[4352]

However, as the late 1940s wore on into the 1950s and beyond, with no outside help, unlike the case for the Afghan resistance during the Soviet occupation from 1979-89,[4353] Polish armed resistance gradually faded away. From this point, there were the workers' uprisings of Poznan and Radom in 1956 and 1976 respectively.[4354] More ubiquitous however, was the passive resistance embodied by the Catholic church, pivotal to the Polish consciousness since 966 AD,[4355] that kept the Polish dream of independence alive. In 1978, it was prodigiously enhanced by the Vatican's political master-stroke in electing Karol Wojtyła as pontiff to become the charismatic Pope John Paul II. Three million people greeted the Pontiff in Kraków on his unprecedented nine-day journey in June 1979. This triggered an anxious correspondence between Yuri Andropov, the Soviet Communist Party's General Secretary, and Edward Gierek, First Secretary of the Polish United Workers' Party.[4356] While John Paul II's words, "The tree was already rotten. I just gave it a good shake and the rotten apples fell" ring true, as Arragon Perrone comments: "Pope John Paul II's dynamic personality and anti-communist efforts impacted global events, revealing historical precedence for a religious leader who modifies international affairs."[4357] He presents a parallel to the decades of passive resistance invoked by Mahatma Gandhi, leading to Indian independence in 1947.[4358]

In a kind of irony, the last Communist prime minister of Poland, Mieczysław Rakowski, while pondering his country's history during an American PBS interview, felt he and the Pope shared a common view, which he described as follows: "

> You have to remember that Poland during the medieval years was a power to be reckoned with. The area of Poland was immense. It reached from the Baltic to the Black Sea. In the 18th century, Poland ceased to exist on the European map. The next five generations of Poles lived in slavery through partitioning. The nation developed this inferiority complex towards other nations. History became an obsession for the Poles, and whether you joined the Communist Party, as I did, or the Church like John Paul II, you were reacting to the national past."[4359]

This could well be true. However, in modern-day Poland, the population barely remembers, and then with derision, the names of old communists. In a stark contrast, the eulogising of Pope John Paul II is ubiquitous. In early April 2005, during my ten months of teaching English in Poland, Pope John Paul II passed away in the Vatican. The outpouring of grief, in the land of my paternal ancestors, was palpable.

Following the unrest of the 1956 Poznań uprising, Cardinal Stefan Wyszyński, the Roman Catholic Primate of Poland and second most revered Polish religious figure post-war,[4360] was a central figure in its resolution.[4361] Unlike the illegitimate puppet regime, he possessed the popular authority which they lacked;[4362] and by reaching a public understanding with Comrade Gomułka, he ensured that the People's Republic enjoyed a generation of relative stability. Essentially, the agreement between Church and state embodied a strategy of mutual restraint, whereby the Party would cease undermining the liberties of the Church, provided the Church refrained from questioning the "legitimacy" of the "People's" Regime.[4363] The Party Secretary agreed to the deal because, as a Marxist, he believed that the hold of the Church on an industrialising and modernising society was bound to wane.[4364]

On the other hand, the Primate's agreement was based on the equally confident belief that a Church free from political interference could actually strengthen its hold.[4365] In time, albeit eight years after his death in 1981,[4366] Stefan Wyszyński was vindicated. For a quarter-of-century, from 1956, he carefully nourished the religious and cultural life of the nation, teaching them that the battle of minds was more effective than battles on the streets.[4367] Certainly, with Poland in the midst of the Soviet bloc, isolated from any notion of western support, this was especially so, and in the process, he rapidly became the supreme moral authority in the country, attracting a degree of affection and admiration to which no party leader could ever aspire.[4368] So long as he lived, he wielded unparalleled influence. His was the archetypal positivist line — not to fight with sticks and stones, but to preserve and strengthen the essential spirit and sinews of the nation.[4369]

Cardinal Stefan Wyszyński died in 1981, but by this time, the younger Karol Wojtyła in Rome, with regular visits back to the homeland, was able to continue Stefan Wyszyński's legacy. In this way, Stefan Wyszyński and Karol Wojtyła, even in the sterile desolation of the "People's" regime, from a position of major weakness, remained as soldiers and citizens of an independent Poland, faithful to the standard of the Polish Republic.[4370] Seen in this context, Komorowski's words in his final address to his troops amidst the seemingly devastated hopes of the Rising's surrender, are anything but hollow.

Around the time of the signing of the surrender agreement, Komorowski received several suggestions that he should escape and try to get to London. His refusal of such notions was blunt to say the least. He felt obligated to share the fate of his men, and moreover, reasoned that his escape would have been looked upon by the Germans as a breach of the signed surrender agreement, with subsequent repercussions for his men and civilians.[4371] Only upon arrival at a POW camp, could he have contemplated escape, as then he would only have been responsible for himself. In any event, this proved impossible, as he was always too well guarded,[4372] probably due to his role as the Rising's commander.

On October 3rd, the day after the signing, in the early hours of the morning, dead silence reigned over the city after 63 days of fighting. Waves of people, pale and hungry, moved from their cellars and shelters towards the barricaded exits. In nearly every family there was someone who was unable to leave the city without help.[4373] All that Komorowski and his men knew, was that the evacuated people were being directed to a transit camp (Durchgangslager 121)[4374] at Pruszków,[4375] about 14 kilometres west of the city centre. Although the Germans had promised proper care, food, and no undue hurry in evacuation, no one had the slightest confidence in their promises. The insurgents, too, felt uneasy, since just days before, the Germans had been calling them "bandits" and shooting their comrades who had been taken prisoner.[4376]

The civilians passing through Durchgangslager 121 numbered 550,000 of the city's residents and approximately 100,000 from its outskirts. In all, 650,000.[4377] The security police and the SS segregated the deportees and decided their fate. Approximately 55,000 were sent to concentration camps, including 13,000 to Auschwitz.[4378] The remainder were consigned to slave labour in the Reich proper.[4379] Their fate would have been preferable to the KZ (Konzentrationslager), but nevertheless, their most likely fate, of being consigned to the ZAL or Zwangsarbeitslager (Forced Labour Camps)[4380] would still have been one of being housed in barracks and fed on the bare subsistence level,[4381] rather than the outright starvation levels for inmates of the KZ.[4382]

The one remaining possibility was for those consigned to the most "fortunate" classification of the Reicharbeitsdienst (German National Work Service). They were officially portrayed as volunteers, but in the vast majority of cases, they were the product of round-ups to meet quota-collections — which may have included some of the civilians in the round-up at Pruszków's Durchgangslager 121. At most, the element of choice was minimal, and of course, for the civilians passing through Pruszków, entirely non-existent. Initially, they were mainly young Polish men and women, but later, Balts, Ukrainians, Serbs and others were sent to Germany for designated jobs, where they were housed in private homes or hostels and paid the predictable pittance.[4383] The work was menial, such as that of domestic servants, unskilled factory workers, or farmhands, but clearly, they were the relatively lucky ones. For one thing, they were not on the starvation or subsistence rations characteristic of the KZ or ZAL.

Nevertheless, even for workers of the Reicharbeitsdienst, their existence was still a precarious and restrictive one, due to the fact that they were subjected to an endless list of prohibitions, which, if violated, would demand investigation by the Gestapo. One such Polish lady stated that she had to wear the armband with "P" and was not permitted to ride on trams, enter a church, restaurant, theatre, opera, circus, zoo, or botanical garden and more. Moreover, park benches would be marked "FÜR POLEN UND JUDEN SITZEN VERBOTEN" (For Poles and Jews sitting forbidden).[4384] Life was on a knife's edge, with the spectre of the ZAL or KZ forever in the forefront of their mind. For the deportees passing through Pruszków in early October 1944, and not sent to the KZ, it's more likely they were sent to the ZAL — Zwangsarbeitslager (Forced Labour Camps),[4385] on their designated subsistence rations, given the fate the Germans had in mind for Warsaw upon the forced evacuation of the city.[lx]

During the days around the time of the surrender, Komorowski lived in constant anxiety over the fate of his wife and son Adam. They had been in an area of the city now under German control, and Komorowski was grimly aware of the mass murders of civilians evacuated from captured areas of the city.[4386] Nevertheless, during the course of the Rising, he did not speak to anyone about this, as he knew such concerns were common to most his men, and feared that such disclosures on his part, as the commander-in-chief of the Home Army, may adversely affect their spirit and will to fight. Hence his relief and joy when, in the final days before surrender, he received a short radio message from one of his area commanders: "Bór's wife and both sons safe...."[4387] His relief and joy had been heightened by the birth of his second son Jerzy.[4388]

Following the signing of the surrender agreement, von dem Bach, through Zyndram, sent an invitation to Komorowski to meet him

---

[lx] This fate for Warsaw will be elaborated upon shortly.

at his H.Q. at Ozarów, about five kilometres north of Pruszków, around noon on Wednesday October 4th, to discuss "additional measures" to be taken in connection with the surrender and fate of the civilians. As well, Komorowski was invited to a lunch where all the heads of the German Army and civil administration would be present. He refused the lunch, but agreed to discuss the "fate of the population of Warsaw" with von dem Bach, and the problem of "improving the conditions of evacuation."[4389] Late that morning, Komorowski, accompanied by Heller and his interpreter, proceeded through a barricade, where two German cars awaited them the other side. The district through which they were driven had never been engulfed in the fight,[4390] but nevertheless, one side of the streets were blocked by the rubble of houses and ploughed up by shells, while the other, on which the cars were driven unhindered, was curiously untouched.[4391] Clearly, the German systematic destruction of what was left of Warsaw, in accordance with Hitler's directive, had already begun.[4392]

Thirty minutes later, the cars pulled up in front of a Polish country style house in Ozarów.[4393] In the hall, the German Chief of Staff drew Heller aside. Another German officer tried to do the same with Komorowski's interpreter Alfred Edward Korczyński (Sas),[4394] but the newly appointed commander of all Polish armed forces, ordered Sas to remain. Komorowski in fact, did speak German, but after years of little practice, he informed von dem Bach of his wish to have a reliable and trusted interpreter by his side.[4395] Komorowski described von dem Bach as "the living personification of the Prussian Junker type":[4396] tall, broad shoulders, aged about fifty, wearing gold-rimmed glasses, dressed in SS uniform, with the insignia of a Knight of the Iron Cross hung round his neck. His demeanour struck him as one of elaborately polite self-assurance, as he spoke in a very loud and distinct voice, which seemed characteristic of Nazi Party leaders.[4397] After shaking hands with a very disconsolate Komorowski,[4398] he opened the discourse with a series of compliments and tributes to the courage and fighting spirit of the defenders of Warsaw.[4399]

Promptly turning to political matters, he continued to flatter the bravery of the Poles, conveying his sympathy for their fate, realising the bitterness which the Home Army and civilians alike must feel for Russia and their western Allies. In his mind the Poles, could no longer harbour the slightest doubt of the hostile intentions of Soviet Russia, and the western Allies abandonment of them to their fate. As a consequence, Germany and Poland, in von dem Bach's mind, were now facing a common threat and foe. Hence, the Reich and Poland should cease their "squabbles" and go forward together, "shoulder to shoulder"[4400] as newly found "comrades in arms." The five previous years of mass murder, oppression, terror, concentration camps and apartheid could, as von dem Bach expressed it, be all forgiven by Poles, with a simple admission by Germans, of "past and serious mistakes."[4401]

This would not be the first of von dem Bach's fruitless overtures to Komorowski, who made it clear from the outset how he and the Home Army in general stood. In spite of the signed surrender agreement of Home Army units in Warsaw and his personal intention to honour it, he said, it had in no way effected a change in attitude of Poland towards Germany, with whom she had been at war since September 1, 1939.[4402] At this point, given Germany's desperate strategic plight, von dem Bach was eager to seek out what he perceived as potential new allies. To this end, with his very recent experience of the Warsaw Home Army's heroic resistance, he erroneously perceived an opportunity to secure a most worthy new ally. However, as was the case throughout the 1930s, when Hitler's Germany made repeated proposals to Poland for a Nazi-Polish alliance,[4403] von dem Bach's multiple overtures to Komorowski likewise came to nought.[4404]

Von dem Bach's reply readily conceded that Germans had committed a series of great "mistakes" towards the Poles. Moreover, von dem Bach further asserted that he had always been personally opposed to the policy of oppression and terror which had been adopted in Poland.[4405] Nevertheless, he proposed that there was still time to repair these "errors" and to undertake anti-Soviet activities together in a common interest.[4406] To which, the Polish commander-in-chief reiterated that Germany could expect nothing from him that would be in conflict with his conception of honour and his allegiance and fidelity to his authorities.[4407] For Komorowski, and his Home Army in general, a mere admission of past German "errors" in order to realise von dem Bach's notion of a post-Rising German-Polish alliance was not going to cut it.

Von dem Bach then made his second proposal. Komorwoski was asked to occupy a villa which had been prepared for him. Only a token sentry would be posted there, and von dem Bach suggested that Komorowski should relax there after the hardships of the fighting. He said that this would enable Komorowski to jointly supervise with him the evacuation of the population of the city.[4408] Komorowski thanked von dem Bach for the offer of rest, but refused this proposal as well. In essence, he was unable to accept different conditions from those of the other prisoners. Neither, in his mind, could he supervise the evacuation with the German if it was to be carried out by German military or police units. Komorowski expected that the German side would put into effect their commitments embodied in the agreement with regard to the civilian population, but he could not share with the German authorities the responsibility towards the Polish nation for the execution of that agreement.[4409] It is true that, under the terms of the surrender agreement, the Germans were solely responsible for the "orderly and humane" evacuation of the civilian population. However, in hindsight, perhaps Komorowski should have accepted von dem Bach's second proposal, at least in regard to joint supervision of the civilian evacuation.[lxi]

Von dem Bach then made one last proposal. He suggested that the armistice signed in Warsaw should be applied to all units of the Home Army operating in the part of Poland still under German occupation, in order to avoid further useless bloodshed. He considered this to be the only sensible solution, in view of the present political situation of Poland.[4410] Once more, Komorowski refused. After fulfilling their commitments as an Allied nation for five years, the Poles were certainly not going to default on the eve of victory. [At least in terms of unconditional surrender of the criminal state of the Third Reich to the Allied powers.] To which a still smiling von dem Bach cited his delusions, not only common to the likes of his ilk among the SS and elite of the Third Reich, but still in significant part, to great proportions of the civilian populace:[4411] "

> But, General, you and your compatriots are quite wrong. You are being unduly influenced by a temporary German setback. The future will bring surprises of which nobody has dreamed.[4412] German victory is absolutely certain. You will remember my words. Final victory in this war will be ours."[4413]

Komorowski, in turn, explained his disagreement,[4414] based on the self-evident reality of Germany's strategic plight. In May 1943,[4415] the famous German fighter ace, Adolf Galland, had flown the Messerschmitt 262 fighter jet — perhaps the most realistic and practical of all the conceived Wunderwaffe (Wonder Weapons). However, thanks to Hitler's obstinance when he insisted that time be spent transforming the practical jet fighter to a blitz-bomber, the jet fighter appeared too late to affect the course of the war. In mid-1943, it could have annihilated the Allied bombing raids that were devastating the cities and crippling the

---

[lxi] This point will be discussed in detail shortly.

industry of the Reich.[4416] Hitler, however, was myopic on paying back to Britain several times over by bombing raids which were always going to be beyond the industrial resources of the Reich. Galland, on the other hand, was full of admiration for Britain's heroic defence of its homeland by its fighter pilots in the 1940 Battle of Britain.[4417] This perception was beyond Hitler's rigid mindset.

As their parley was nearing its end, von dem Bach "promised" Komorowski that he would personally see to it that the civilians would not be expelled from Warsaw, "except for reason of military necessity," as per the surrender agreement.[4418] At this point, Komorowski had no idea that masses of civilians from the district conquered by the Germans during the fighting had been taken to concentration camps. He was only made aware of this following his liberation in 1945.[4419] His conversation with von dem Bach lasted nearly an hour; von dem Bach's disposition had transformed from elaborately polite self-assurance to cold disdain.[4420] This was reflected in the German treatment of civilians forcibly gathered at Pruszków's Durchgangslager 121. Leaving the house, Komorowski brushed aside the crowd of German cameramen and got into the car to take him back to the city centre. The march-out of the Home Army from Warsaw was scheduled for the following day, October 5, at 9.45 a.m. [4421]

During the Rising Komorowski appeared once or twice in a uniform which was a sort of home-made battle-dress made from a captured German material of light blue. However, in this meeting with von dem Bach, he was dressed in civilian clothes with a white-and-red armband, because a large proportion of the Home Army never had a uniform, and their only distinguishing mark was their red and white armband. He feared that the Germans would interpret the Hague Convention by according combatant rights only to those in uniform. Hence, his wish to demonstrate that an armband and an identity card of the Home Army was sufficient to prove military status.[4422]

The morning of the 5th, Komorowski's security platoon of 36, which had been 128 in the early days of the Rising,[4423] assembled for inspection. At once, Komorowski was struck by the scarcity of their arms. When he asked the officer for an explanation, he uneasily replied, that the men had buried most of their arms during the night to avoid handing them over to the Germans.[4424] As they marched to their rendezvous point, which was a barricade manned by SS troops, a woman in mourning emerged from the crowd, approached Komorowski, and handed him a medal. She said , "General, please accept this souvenir of the 1863 rising."[4425] Before he had time to thank her, she had disappeared back into the crowd. As the march progressed, he began singing the Polish national anthem, "*Jeszcze* Polska *nie Zginęta*" (Poland is not yet Lost),[4426] which the troops and civilian population at once took up. Upon arrival before the barricade, a chaplain, holding the Blessed Sacrament in his hands, made a cross in benediction over the departing troops and the gathered crowds.

As they passed through the barricade, they were surrounded by a cordon of German soldiers and the cars and motor-cycles of German police, whose automatic rifles were at the ready. Tanks and armoured cars were patrolling street crossings.[4427] As they entered the wide courtyard of the Military Technical Institute, the Home Army detachments gave up their arms, and a German colonel in command approached and asked Komorowski to enter one of the waiting police cars. The remaining cars were boarded by a designated group of several Polish officers and staff. As they were driven off, Komorowski bade his troops a final farewell as they stood at attention.[4428] An hour later, they arrived at Ozarów Station, where von dem Bach was waiting. Closely guarded by multiple SS guards, they boarded the middle car of the train, which promptly departed. At each compartment a guard was posted with an automatic rifle, and accompanied them to the toilet. At this stage, they had no idea where we were being taken, other than knowing they were heading in a westerly direction. En route, the Germans gave them breakfast, and for the first time in a month they tasted bread.[4429]

When the train pulled up at Sochaczew Station, the convoy's commander informed Komorowski that the commander of the 9th German Army, Wehrmacht General Nikolaus von Vormann,[4430] wished to speak to him. Together with Heller, Komorowski alighted, and after a few minutes' car ride they arrived at a nearby Polish country house. There, von Vormann awaited them in full regalia with his staff officers. Standing stiffly to attention, von Vormann, who had participated in the suppression of the Rising in its earliest days before the arrival of von dem Bach, declared: "

> From now on, General, you and all your soldiers who have been taken prisoner in Warsaw are under the protection of the Wehrmacht, which is responsible for ensuring that your treatment is in accordance with international conventions and those of the Ozarów surrender."[4431]

This declaration over, they exchanged stiff bows and returned to the train in Sochaczew.

The treatment of Home Army soldiers from the Rising as regular soldiers entitled to rights under the Geneva convention, and in accord with the surrender agreement, rather than common bandits, had been secured. As mentioned earlier, on Tuesday August 29, 1944, the governments of Britain and the United States took a major step in officially recognising the non-communist Home Army as the official fighting force of occupied Poland, in separate but identically worded declarations granting combatant rights to the Home Army.[4432] It is likely that this declaration played its part in ensuring that this point in the surrender agreement became more than just mere words.

At dusk, the train turned northwards. When night had fallen, a guard with an automatic rifle entered each compartment with orders to remain with the prisoners until dawn. At each stop the carriage was surrounded by guards, and at the large stations police in plain clothes could be seen. At daybreak they were in East Prussia and, finally, at the little station at Kruglanken, where the prisoners were ordered to alight. A cordon of fifty armed SS men then surrounded the party of twenty unarmed and weary prisoners, before cars took them to a Waffen SS camp, where they were housed in small huts. Exhausted, they went to bed almost immediately.[4433]

The following day of the 6th, General von dem Bach appeared in Komorowski's hut to inform him that afternoon he would take him to Hitler or Himmler, who were nearby at the German GHQ — Hitler's Eastern Front military headquarters,[4434] which was the site of the Valkyrie assassination attempt on July 20, 1944.[4435] In short, the Wolfsschanze (Wolf's Lair). Von dem Bach, however, never reappeared, and two days later, four SS men, armed with machine-guns, escorted Komorowski to a neighbouring barracks, where a Luftwaffe major and a Lieutenant-Colonel with the letters SD (Sicherheitsdienst — SS intelligence arm)[4436] on his sleeve were waiting. They explained that German GHQ wished to speak to him on the phone and that they were now trying to put the call through.

While putting the call through, they explained to Komorowski that Headquarters wished to confirm whether or not the signed capitulation of Warsaw applied only to the troops that took part in the battle for the capital, or to all detachments of the Home Army under Komorowski's command. Komorowski replied that the answer was contained in the text of the surrender agreement, which clearly stated that only the detachments which fought in Warsaw had surrendered.[4437] The officers then asked the same question that von dem Bach asked Komorowski two days earlier in Ozarów. That is, in view of this, would he now be willing to give orders for the cessation of hostilities and to negotiate a "discreet" laying-down of arms?

Komorowski replied: "

> I shall issue no such order. And even if I did, it would not be obeyed, because the whole of Poland knows that I am now in German hands, and my subordinates would understand that I had done so under pressure. Consequently, all such proposals are useless."[4438]

When the telephone call came through two hours later, the German major repeated Komorowski's answer to HQ, whereupon the "intransigent" prisoner was escorted back to the huts. Four days later on October 10th, he and his group were transferred to Berlin, where they spent twenty-four hours in the Reichssicherheitshauptamt (RSHA — Reich Main Security Office),[4439] supposedly waiting for Himmler.[4440]

The devastation of Berlin made the prisoners optimistic, that the end for the Reich at least, must be imminent. There was an air-raid alarm that night, followed by the arrival of British light Mosquito bombers, again postponing the talks with Hitler or Himmler. The next morning of the 11th, they were taken to a large prisoner-of-war camp, Oflag 73, in Langwasser, near Nuremberg, where they were isolated from other prisoners. Even members of the German camp personnel had to have a permit signed by the Camp Commander in order to enter the area of their huts.[4441] To confirm the German's hangover of sewer paranoia from the Rising,[4442] the manhole to the sewer nearest the camp was reinforced with iron bars and fitted with a large padlock, which was inspected with inordinate frequency.[4443]

At first, the excessive safety measures and restrictions amused the prisoners, but as time wore on, they become more irksome, even life threatening. When General Tadeusz (Grzegorz — Gregory) Pełczyński's wound was still festering, he was not permitted to go to the camp hospital, for fear he might make friendly contacts and succeed in escaping. Before long, the wound threatened to develop into blood-poisoning and his health deteriorated every day.[4444] It was not until Komorowski sent a sharp protest to German HQ that Grzegorz was finally transferred to the hospital, where he was placed in a room with barred windows and watched by two guards, one of whom stood at the window and the other at the door. Only once was Komorowski allowed to visit him, and even then he was accompanied by an escort consisting of one officer and two soldiers with guns, with an interpreter present throughout their conversation.[4445] For Komorowski, Pełczyński's plight was a personal one. Firstly, he was one of Komorowski's two deputies, and secondly, he was present at the meeting on the sunny summer evening of July 31, 1944, when the fateful decision was made for L-Hour — the invocation of the Rising at 5 p.m. the following day of August 1, 1944.[4446]

The Germans applied far more stringent rules to Komorowski than to the other prisoners. As a general, he was not permitted the privileges applicable to prisoners of that rank. He was not allowed to leave the barracks nor the little yard adjacent to it. At first, they did not allot any Red Cross parcels for himself and the others from his group, without which it was hard to make the starvation prison rations suffice. It was only after the personal intervention of a representative of the International Red Cross from Geneva that this was corrected. They were constantly searched, and their small pile of personal belongings ransacked. They were not allowed to contact anyone, nor to attend Sunday church service.[4447]

Their civilian clothes were taken away and replaced with old, worn-out Italian uniforms. The barracks in which they were confined was bitterly cold, as the wind blew through the cracks in the walls, and water in the buckets froze practically every day. As time dragged on, amidst the boredom of camp life, the two months of hunger in Warsaw and the effects of a camp diet began to make themselves felt — a glass of bitter soup extract and 250 grams of rye bread for lunch and supper, with the addition of a plate of turnips for lunch. Komorowski felt himself growing weaker and weaker.[4448] Such was the "genteel" captivity, for an "indulgently privileged" noble, asserted by Evan McGilvray,[4449] for Tadeusz Bór Komorowski.

At the beginning of November, the monotony of the camp was interrupted when, unexpectedly, the Camp Commander and two civilians turned up at Komorowski's hut. Immediately, it was obvious that the "civilians" were Gestapo agents. The camp commander introduced them as employees of the Reichssicherheitshauptampt (RSHA — Reich Main Security Office),[4450] who had arrived at Himmler's request to ask the same tired old questions and propositions. Co-operation against the Soviets, justified by the same worn-out clichés, was familiar to everyone who had read the Goebbels Press. Enormous forces in reserve, making them unconquerable, were coupled with new wonder weapons which would enable them to conquer, not only the Soviet Union, but also the western powers.[4451] This went on for two hours until they adjourned for lunch. After lunch, they proposed a secret armistice with the Home Army detachments in the provinces. For Komorowski, there was satisfaction in this proposal, since it was evident, from their propaganda show, that the Home Army was still active and making itself felt, as the Reich's strategic position worsened with every passing day.[4452]

During this discourse, one of Komorowski's Gestapo visitors, who Komorowski later learned was Harro Thomson, asked him if there was anything he wanted. To which, Komorowski inquired about the fate of his predecessor, General Grot Rowecki, who had been arrested in Warsaw on June 30, 1943,[4453] following his betrayal by the infamous traitors, Ludwik Kalkstein and Blanka Kaczorowska, as well as Kalkstein's brother-in-law Eugeniusz Świerczewski; he had known Stefan Rowecki since 1920 during their days serving together in the 1919-20 Polish-Soviet war.[4454] Harro Thomson admitted that he had been in charge of the case and interrogated Rowecki in the Gestapo headquarters in Berlin. He informed Komorowski that "General Rowecki showed the same senseless obstinacy which we are now encountering from you."[4455]

As mentioned earlier, however, Rowecki was executed on Himmler's order in the Sachsenhausen concentration camp on August 2, 1944 — the second day of the Rising.[4456] Komorowski did not learn of Rowecki's execution until the spring of 1948, when Harro Thomson revealed his end during interrogation in Britain.[4457] An August 1948 article by Tadeusz Pełczyński, one of Komorowski's deputies and fellow prisoners at Langwasser, asserts that, in contrast to Himmler's usual modus operandi of cold and calculated killing, he impulsively ordered Rowecki's execution. He had demanded that Rowecki be the first commander of the Home Army, a man of great authority in Poland, to sign an appeal for the uprising in Warsaw to cease. As Thomson told Komorowski, Rowecki was every bit as obstinate as his successor. Hence, Himmler's impulsive order to execute Rowecki in the very early days of the Rising, and subsequent desire to keep it secret.[4458]

From the camp, the prisoners had a grandstand view of two destructive night air raids on Nuremberg. Fragments were falling like hail and even hammering their roof. Some bombs fell close enough to shake the barracks to their foundation. The prisoners witnessed this scene in bitter cold from open windows, as flares lit up night like day, and anti-aircraft artillery bellowed with an incessant, deafening roar.[4459]

On February 5, 1945, after about four months in the Langwasser camp, they were suddenly ordered to pack their belongings, and were conveyed by rail, under heavy guard, to the POW camp of Colditz,[4460][lxii] near Leipzig in the former East Germany — located in an old castle of the Kings of Saxony. Since the castle is situated on a rocky outcrop above the River Mulde, the Germans believed it to be an ideal site for a high security prison.[4461] More than 300 prisoners were incarcerated there, mostly British, some free French from de Gaulle's army, a dozen exiled Czechs from the RAF, and a few Americans.[4462] For four British officers, their meeting with Komorowski and his fellow Poles was a reunion of sorts, as they had previously escaped from a camp in Poland before heading to Warsaw and living amidst Komorowski and co. for a significant time, until they were recaptured and sent to Colditz.[4463] The camp held many high profile figures, whom the Germans dubbed "prominent" prisoners. In every sense of the word, they were "Prominenten," as alluded to in earlier chapters.[lxiii] They included Captain John Alexander Elphinstone and Lieutenant Lord Lascelles, nephews of King George VI, Lieutenant John Winant, son of the United States Ambassador in London, and two relations of Winston Churchill.[4464]

With such illustrious figures in their midst, incarceration in Colditz, was a welcome relief for Komorowski and his fellow Poles from the deprivations of Langwasser.[4465] After Langwasser, Komorowski's incarceration possibly conformed with Evan MacGilvray's notion of "genteel" captivity; he shared a room with his former Chief of Staff and Deputy Commander, General Pełczyński, in a separate wing of the castle, reserved for the "prominent."[4466] Life in Colditz was well organised by the prisoners, and they had a wireless set in safe hiding, which all the efforts of the Abwehr never succeeded in disclosing, and it worked non-stop.[4467] Hence, for the first time since the Rising's surrender in early October, Komorowski was receiving news from the outside world. Moreover, their fellow prisoners, on their own initiative, replaced their tattered Italian uniforms and provided them with some shirts and underwear.[4468]

But during their benign existence there, they received news of what Komorowski dubbed their most painful blow, not from the hand of the enemy [Soviet Union], but from those whom they considered faithful friends. They learned the conditions of the infamous Yalta

---

[lxii] This was two days before Dietrich was transferred from Prinz-Albrecht-Strasse to Buchenwald. See endnotes [2053] and [2054] for Chapter 22 "Prinz-Albrecht-Strasse."

[lxiii] See for example endnotes [2708] to [2714] of Chapter 27 "The Prominenten and Miraculous Reprieves."

Agreement through their colleagues who listened to the BBC.[4469] It had been concluded six days after their departure from Langwasser. From February 4 to 11, 1945, in the Black Sea resort city of Yalta (modern-day Russia since 2014), on the Crimean Peninsula, the three chief Allied leaders, Roosevelt, Churchill and Stalin, met to discuss the final defeat of Nazi Germany and the post-war order for Europe.[4470] In terms of the future for Eastern Europe, Stalin could not have wished for more.

The Soviet Union was diametrically opposed to true post-war independence of Poland, as its meaningless token actions in the Rising had reaffirmed. At best, it would be a post-war puppet communist Poland, entirely subservient to the Kremlin's will, or even potentially, a Seventeenth Republic of the Soviet Union[4471] — as was the post-war fate of the Baltic states of Lithuania, Latvia and Estonia.[4472] Komorowski and his fellow Poles could not comprehend why the western Allies were giving up their most faithful and oldest ally of the war to slavery and major territorial annexation.[4473] Norman Davies in his book *Rising' 44*, repeatedly refers to Poland as the "First Ally."[4474] As Komorowski explained in his book: "

> Their decision erased and tore to bits all the principles of the Atlantic Charter and allowed brute force and violence to be inflicted on Poland — the "inspiration of nations" — and to prevail over right and justice. Poland was to give up 46 per cent of its pre-war territories, while a clique of usurpers and Kremlin agents, "supplemented" by "members of other parties" in a manner devoid of any practical effect or meaning were to be imposed on the nation as a government by the three signatories of the Yalta Pact. Moreover, these decisions were made with complete disregard for the existence of the body of legal Polish authorities, as well as of the wishes of the nation itself."[4475]

In the September 1938 Munich conference, Czechoslovakia, in its absence, was the sacrificial pyre for the expedient "peace" of appeasement.[4476] Munich 1938 was "about" them, but "without" them. Yalta signed a similar fate for Poland, and indeed, the rest of Eastern Europe in February 1945.

The Atlantic Charter mentioned by Komorowski refers to the meeting between Roosevelt and Churchill at sea in Placentia Bay off the coast of Newfoundland on Thursday August 14, 1941, just four months before the Japanese bombing of Pearl Harbour and the subsequent official US entry into the war. The President was aboard on the Augusta, the Prime Minister on the Prince of Wales, surrounded on deck by a numerous entourage of the highest-ranking military and naval dignitaries of both countries, and in the sea, by an imposing fleet and with a sky full of protecting war planes.[4477] When it ended, the President and the Prime Minister issued what they called a Joint Declaration. The most important parts of that document were the first three points and point six: "

> Point One: Their countries seek no aggrandisement, territorial or otherwise.

> Point Two: They desire to see no territorial changes that do not accord with the freely expressed wishes of the peoples concerned.

> Point Three: They respect the right of all peoples to choose the form of government under which they will live; and they wish to see self-government restored to those from whom it has forcibly been removed.

> Point Six: They hope to see established a peace, after the final destruction of the Nazi tyranny, which will afford to all nations the means of dwelling in security within their own boundaries, and which will afford assurance to all peoples that they may live out their lives in freedom from fear."[4478]

Initially, this agreement was only a statement of principles hastily drafted and agreed to by Churchill and Roosevelt. The term "Atlantic Charter" was later coined by a London newspaper (*The Daily Herald*) after the joint declaration had been published. The ideals expressed in the eight points of the agreement were so popular that the US Office of War Information in 1943 produced 240,000 posters of the full text.[4479] Three weeks after Pearl Harbor, in late December 1941, Roosevelt sent for all the representatives in America of Nazi occupied Europe and told them: "

> Be assured, gentlemen, that the restoration of the countries occupied by Germany and suffering under the Axis yoke is my greatest concern, which is shared in like degree by Mr.

Churchill. We promise that all will be done to insure the independence of these countries."[4480]

Churchill was present. He turned to the Polish Ambassador and said: "

We will never forget what glorious Poland has done and is doing nor what heroic Greece and Holland have done in this war. I hope I need not add that Great Britain has set herself the aim of restoring full independence and freedom to the nations that have been overrun by Hitler."[4481]

Before long, a handsome copy of it was made, bearing the names of Churchill and Roosevelt, and placed on exhibition in the National Museum in Washington, where crowds viewed it with reverence as one of the great documents of history.[4482] Before Pearl Harbor, and a month after the charter's proclamation on September 24, 1941, an inter-allied meeting was held in St. James Palace in London, where Ivan Maisky, the Soviet Ambassador to Great Britain, "professed": "

The Soviet was and is guided in its foreign policy by the principle of the self-determination of nations. Accordingly the Soviet defends the right of every nation to the independence and territorial integrity of its country and its right to establish such a social order as it deems opportune and necessary for the promotion of its economic and cultural prosperity."[4483]

With and without hindsight, as was the case for Poland, Lithuania, Latvia, Estonia and Finland,[4484] it is self-evident that Maisky's statement at the time was, for the Stalinist agenda, a politically expedient lie. As events in the Rising transpired, however, they proved no less hollow than the multiple assertions of Roosevelt.[lxiv]

Komorowski would have considered that points one, two, three, and most of all, point six of the charter were incinerated upon the pyre of political expedience. Never, in the history of the human race, has such a grandiose and idealistic document been so publicised, and yet become so hollow and meaningless. For Poland's commander-in-chief, Yalta blotted out their country's independence, and it shook him and his fellow Poles to the core. Their fellow Allied prisoners seemed perplexed and embarrassed by this unexpected turn of events. Most were

---

[lxiv] See for example endnotes [4238] and [4239] for this supplement.

openly ashamed when they met the Poles, and some even asked straight-out if they would still be inclined to shake hands with them.[4485]

During the first days at Colditz, Komorowski received his final overture from the Germans.[4486] By this stage, virtually all of pre-war Poland was under Soviet occupation.[4487] Komorowski was taken to a private room in the camp command offices, where an immaculately dressed civilian, introducing himself as Counsellor Benninghausen, was waiting for him. He opened the discourse by stating that he had arrived from Berlin on the authority of close friends, who were members of the pre-war German-Polish Association. Next, he claimed that himself and his boon fellows were united in their opposition to the years of "bad" treatment doled out to the Poles. In acknowledging this policy as "unfortunate," the Counsellor claimed that in a new dawn of Polish-German co-operation, these "errors" could be rectified.[4488] Especially now, in view of the Polish nation traditionally belonging to the West,[lxv] now confronted with a serious menace from the East.[4489] This notion, which flew in the face of years of National Socialist rhetoric vilifying the "*Untermensch* Slavs,"[4490] was motivated by the desperate strategic plight of the Third Reich.

Komorowski now correctly surmised that virtually all of pre-war Poland was under Soviet occupation. Given these circumstances, and the overwhelming evidence of Soviet hostility to Polish independence, in particular during the Rising, the Germans were hoping that Komorowski, with German help, would be willing to resume his underground fight, this time against the Soviets. The German offer involved Komorowski being released immediately with officers of his choosing, before transfer to Polish territory behind Soviet lines.[4491] To assist with their new underground resistance, the Germans would help with both money and arms, co-ordinating activities[4492] in a manner similar to the London-based Polish exile government's conduct since the 1939 invasion. The plan was far-reaching in its attempt to oppose the Soviets and their policy to Sovietise Europe.[4493] Of course, aside from the long-term moral and political implications for the Poles engaging in such an agreement, from a purely practical point of view, such support could hardly begin, let alone last, with a Reich now on life support.

[lxv] Poles are regarded as western Slavs, having, for the most part, embraced the western Catholicism of Rome. However, eastern Slavs, such as the Ukrainians and Russians, embraced eastern Orthodoxy. As such, Poland has traditionally regarded itself as more western in outlook.

Hence, Komorowski, had no desire to be beholden to Poland's first and now desperate invaders. Instead, he bluntly informed the Counsellor that he was merely wasting his time, pointing out to him the multiple German overtures he had already dismissed. Benninghausen, in a final act, informed Komorowski that he was prepared to stay for three or four days to give him time to consider the matter in depth. Komorowski, re-affirmed that his mind was already made-up, and that further consideration of such things was a waste of time. Benninghausen finally left.[4494]

By mid-April, the advancing American armies were approaching Saxony, and the heightened anxiety of the Germans clearly indicated to the prisoners that their time of liberation was near. During those days they lived from one wireless communiqué to another, hearing at the same time the sounds of approaching battle and expecting to see their liberators at the gates of the camp every day. Their situation, in many respects, mirrored that of Dietrich and his fellow prisoners earlier that month at Buchenwald, when the approaching artillery fire of the American Third Army of General George S. Patton was heard on Easter Sunday April 1 1945.[4495] However, to their disappointment, later that day, due to their status as "special prisoners,"[4496] they were ordered to move.[4497] Such was the case for Komorowski and his fellow "prominent prisoners." Just when liberation seemed so close, on April 13th, all the "prominent" group and Polish comrades were suddenly roused in the night and evacuated from the camp. Those who were to stay behind felt very anxious about them, because it looked as though they were to be treated as hostages and taken to "Hitler's fortress,"[4498] known also as the Southern or National Redoubt or Alpine Fortress (Alpenfestung).

This notion of a fortress had only ever existed on paper. However, Eisenhower's Supreme Headquarters, despite access to a considerable amount of intelligence to the contrary, including ULTRA (Allied code-breaking of German radio communications), nevertheless maintained its preconception that a stronghold in the mountains of Bavaria existed.[4499] The rumour was spread by Josef Goebbels and his propaganda ministry.[4500] The non-existence of the Alpenfestung would not be confirmed until the first week of May 1945, once soldiers from the Seventh US Army had captured the cities of Innsbruck, Berchtesgaden, and Salzburg with little organised resistance.[4501] Given this, it's not surprising that this notion was held by the prisoners of Colditz.

Instead of heading south, they were taken east-south-east to the medieval village fortress of Königstein,[4502] on the Elbe, where they were to have remained. However, after twenty-four hours they moved on again, this time southwards to a civilian internee camp at Laufen near the pre-war Austrian frontier.[4503] After vigorous protests against the internment of officers in a civilian camp, they were transferred twenty kilometres north to Tittmoning, a camp for Dutch prisoners.[4504] There, to the German's rage, one of the British prisoners succeeded in escaping, prompting the Germans to keep them in the courtyard the whole night. Meanwhile, the Gestapo pursued its search with the help of police dogs, turning everything upside down. The next day, with five times more guards than before, their submachine guns trained on them, the prisoners were taken back to Laufen.[4505]

In the distance, the prisoners could hear the first sound of American artillery and Allied planes appearring overhead.[4506] The civilian internees at Laufen, mostly British and American, with a few Poles, made contact with the new arrivals by bribing a German soldier.[4507] Using their own channels, they informed the Swiss Minister Feldscher, who was in the vicinity of Laufen; he wasted no time in travelling there to request the German guards to allow him to see them in accordance with his rights as a representative of the protecting power.[4508] After twenty-four hours of political wrangling, the Germans, in a much overdue acknowledgement that the Third Reich was in its death throes, allowed the prisoners to be transported 200 kilometres in several cars, flying large Red Cross and Swiss flags, to the Swiss frontier, via Innsbruck in Austria.[4509] During the night of May 5, 1945, they passed numerous routed German Army columns withdrawing in disarray to the east.[4510]

Komorowski had nothing but praise for their Swiss "guardian angel" Minister Feldscher.[4511] As it turned out, transport to the Swiss frontier became unnecessary, as Innsbruck had already been liberated by the 103rd American Infantry Division.[4512] In a charming hilltop tourist hotel, with an awe-inspiring view of the valley, the prisoners were able to enjoy a full rest. They were immensely grateful for the hospitality and goodwill of the command and troops of the 103rd Division, in stark contrast to what would have been the Soviet equivalent.[4513]

While there, Komorowski, by chance, met, for the first time, the French Generals Weygand (and his wife) and Gamelin, both released at the same time from German captivity. Weygand had been an observer during the August 1920 Battle of Warsaw during the Polish-Soviet war,[4514] when just weeks later,[4515] Komorowski fought in Europe's last great cavalry battle at Komarów.[4516] The French generals expressed their sincere admiration for Poland's effort in its battle against the Germans to Poland's commander-in-chief. They were particularly in awe, from the military point of view, of the Warsaw rising. Komorowski was deeply moved by their kind words and sympathy.[4517] Days later, Komorowski, via Paris, finally arrived in London. He would never see his beloved Poland again.

His safety was now assured, but his anxiety for his wife and family remained. In October 1945, he finally received news that his wife had arrived in the US occupied Zone in Germany, before flying with the children to Brussels.[4518] She, with the boys, escaped from Poland across the so-called "green frontier," organising the entire crossing to the western side of the Iron Curtain on her own initiative, with the Soviet NKVD on her tail. Her husband had been branded by the Stalinists as a war criminal.[4519] For Komorowski, her escape was awe inspiring, especially with two very young children. The youngest, Jerzy, after his birth on September 10, 1944[4520] outside of Warsaw,[4521] was close to death several times.[4522] While the parents would not live to see a truly liberated Poland, their sons Adam and Jerzy (George), much to their joy, would do so.

In the early days of the Rising, before Jerzy was born, Irena and Adam came close to being exploited by the SS as human shields at the head of tanks. The worst tribulation was the intolerable thirst; she described her capture by the Germans in the letter to her husband in October 1945: "

> The worst tribulation was the intolerable thirst. Our tongues were literally drying up. People were throwing themselves on buckets of filthy water from ponds. The baby [the elder son Adam, not yet two years old] had parched lips and I had nothing to give him. I saw a German [in all likelihood SS] standing by and asked him what was going to happen to us. He told me that two days before they drove the people out into the yard and shot them, but that probably we should merely be convoyed out and taken to Germany. I asked him whether they also shot the children? … He shrugged his shoulders. 'They did whatever was ordered.' … A young SS man came in and started with the announcement that everyone had to be punished because we were equally responsible for those 'bandits who are fighting us: it is all the dirty work of Jews.' He ended with the words: 'And the worst criminal of the lot is this one'— pointing to the figure of Christ on the ruined altar."[4523]

As he did so, he likely perceived Christ as being the "illegitimate son of a Jewish whore," a concept fundamental to the SS mindset.[4524] As the SS suppressed the Rising, especially in its earlier days, and continued their general programme of mass-genocide throughout Europe, they perceived that their mission of destiny was to save the world from the Jews and thereby redeem humanity. In their eyes, this is what "Christ failed to do."[lxvi]

As Irena and Adam were marched along the side streets, they could even see barricades manned by their Home Army insurgents, as the Germans took advantage of the cover which their march provided to bring up ammunition wagons. When they reached the station, they were crowded into cars bound for the wretched Pruszków Durchgangslager (Transit Camp), as they continued to suffer from searing thirst on this "beautiful" hot sunny day. Fortunately for them, their stay in Pruszków was brief, thanks in part to Irena being eight months pregnant.[4525]

Upon release from the camp, Irena was surprised by little Adam's reaction to their welcome release. As they left the dismal crowd and gates of the camp behind them, Adam joyfully rolled in the grass, in spite of fatigue, as if he were a little animal released from its cage. They stayed in the township of Pruszków for two days with some friends, and after that, stayed with some people they knew in the country. Not wishing to be an undue "burden" on their hosts, who were already hosting numerous refugees, they left two days before childbirth.[4526]

From there, they proceeded to what Irena dubbed one of those "pseudo-hospitals," where not even a a midwife was present, and a gynaecologist lived some three miles away. The one consolation was that there were some benches and clean sheets. Jerzy was born at midnight on September 9th to 10th,[4527] with no one to help except a nurse who knew next to nothing and did not even tie the umbilical cord. Thirty minutes later, the doctor arrived. In the first few days, Jerzy was terribly weak, and Irena had very little milk; she had infectious diarrhoea and there was a dire shortage of food. Yet somehow, they all pulled through. After six days, she was up and about. Two days before the capitulation in early October, Irena took her boys to her birthplace of Kraków,[4528] which, unlike Warsaw and the vast majority of Polish cities, had escaped major wartime damage.[lxvii]

---

lxvi See endnotes [312] to [313] for Chapter 2 "Ominous Clouds on the Horizon."
lxvii See endnotes [4325] to [4330] for this supplement.

In spite of the relative peace and safety in Kraków, for two months, little Jerzy was gravely ill and hardly gained any weight. By late January 1945, the Soviets subjected Kraków to a brief artillery and air bombardment[4529] before the entry of Marshal Ivan Konev's army.[4530] Around the same time, after almost six months occupation of its outskirts, the Soviet Army finally marched into a desolate and virtually deserted Warsaw.[4531] Kraków, on the other hand, following the requisite securing of plundered art works,[4532] was given up by the Germans with hardly a fight, owing to their fear of encirclement, rather than to any perceived strategic genius of Marshal Konev.[4533]

Irena had changed her address three times, and her name twice, following warnings that the NKVD were on her tail.[4534] In the last two months before escaping Poland, she spent time in a small village just outside the city, living in a tiny, picturesque, thatched cottage. But now the situation was deteriorating from day to day, as arrests of Home Army soldiers continued unabated and all administrative posts were gradually assimilated by local Communists,[4535] morally bankrupt opportunists,[4536] or Soviet agents.[4537] Irena felt the noose tightening around her neck, and realised escape from Poland was becoming imperative. Curiously, she found the escape from her motherland, less harrowing than she first envisaged: "

> By sheer luck, it was quite easy on the whole, and, apart from brief moments, I did not encounter any major difficulties. In spite of the security thus achieved, and joy at the prospect of seeing you again, the saddest moment came to me when I realised, on reaching this side, the extent of tragic abandonment in which Poland was left. Everyone there still strongly believed that it was merely temporary; they live only by that hope. The darkest and most terrible moments in the Underground now seem beautiful and happy compared with the present day, because we had faith in victory and a happy end, while today ..."[4538]

Tadeusz "Bór" Komarowski would be buried in London after passing away on August 24, 1966, aged 71.[4539] Irena Pelagia Maria Komorowska née Lamezan de Salins, died two years later on October 22, 1968,[4540] aged 64. At the time of writing this in April 2020, their sons Adam and Jerzy, both in their late seventies, are still living,[4541] having borne witness in 1989 to a truly independent Poland. From 1795[4542] until the Great War's end on November 11, 1918,[4543] Poland had ceased to "officially" exist, to be reborn in the subsequent post-Great War power vacuum as the Second Republic, lasting just twenty-one years until early October 1939. For the next fifty years, it had suffered under the Nazi and Soviet jackboots, meaning that for 194 years from 1795 until 1989, Poland, had only known 21 years of freedom. Now, in 2020, Poland's democratic Third Republic, has been in existence for more than three decades, and taken its rightful place in the NATO Alliance. During his English exile, Komorowski wrote: "

> The long years of strife and struggle and faith in the victory of a just cause, the loss of so many lives, the untold tragedies born with fortitude — all this seems to have been in vain. Germany fell defeated, but Poland did not gain the freedom for which she had paid such heavy toll. The Yalta Agreement shattered our justified expectations. In consequence of the decisions taken there, Europe has been divided into two spheres of influence, and Stalin—who in 1939 had helped Germany to launch the Second World War — could at last grasp the booty which, according to the secret clause of the Molotov-Ribbentrop Agreement,[4544] he was to have shared with Hitler. This time he received his prize from the hands of our own allies. …[4545]

> However, the people of Poland cannot forget that a thousand-year-old tradition links them to Western civilisation and the Western way of life. [Poland had for example embraced western Catholicism in 966 AD, rather than eastern Orthodoxy.][4546] Against all odds, they still believe that Poland's war effort and the sacrifices suffered for a common victory have not been wasted. Putting their trust in the future, they can only conceive it in a close union with the Western world, fully aware that the present artificial division of our continent will not stand the test of life and that in reality western and central-eastern Europe form one whole. …[4547]

> To construct world peace at the expense of injustice and wrong done to smaller nations is a dangerous experiment. It can only result in acute political tensions and a perpetual smouldering of grievances—a most precarious state of international affairs, so clearly demonstrated by our present times."[4548]

Hence, for many Poles, and peoples in general of eastern Europe, World War II did not end until 1989.[4549] On Wednesday August 23, 1989, the fiftieth anniversary of the signing of the Molotov-Ribbentrop pact, a human chain of 650 kilometres (400 miles), from Tallinn in Estonia, via Riga in Latvia, to the Lithuanian capital, Vilnius, held hands for fifteen minutes, galvanising the Baltic push for independence.[4550] This chain of two million citizens of the Baltic republics of the USSR[4551] was indicative of the changing mood throughout Eastern Europe, with the fall of the Berlin Wall in early November 1989,[4552] and a week later in Warsaw, when Poles tore down the statue of Felix Dzerzhinsky (Dzierżyński), the Polish founder of the first Soviet secret police (Cheka).[4553] In concluding the foreword to his father's book, Adam wrote the following: "

> My father wrote this book at the start of the 1950s. At the end of it he writes: "The darkest and most terrible moments in the Underground now seem beautiful and happy compared with the present day, because we had faith in victory and a happy end."[lxviii] He may not have lived to witness that end, but the sacrifices of his generation that experienced the Uprising, forged a determination that led the nation through Stalinism and decades of totalitarianism, to a free and democratic Poland, to membership of NATO and the European Union. Their sacrifice, though vast, was not in vain."[4554]

On the second Saturday in October 2004, among a party of fellow foreign English teachers and Polish friends, I made a day trip by train to Warsaw from Radom, about 90 kilometres south of the capital. This was four months before my weekend trip to Wrocław, when I photographed the bronze cross monument to Dietrich. The day was spent seeing many sites, memorials and monuments of this city, which was, in the aftermath of the Rising, almost obliterated in an act of systematic destruction by the Germans. Indeed post-war, such was the devastation, that Warsaw came close to never being rebuilt.[4555] One idea even countenanced the notion of Warsaw being left the way it was — a lunar landscape of ruins — as a war memorial for future generations. [4556]

The Royal Castle, near the city's Old Town, has been faithfully rebuilt, thanks in great part to donations by the Polish diaspora,[4557] but

---

lxviii This was first written by Adam's mother in her letter to her husband. Later, in the 1950s, Adam's father Tadeusz would quote this letter in his book. See endnotes [4523] to [4538] for this supplement.

its resurrection only commenced in 1971 and finally completed in 1988.[4558] Most significant in this restoration were the bloody events of December 1970 on the Baltic Coast in Gdańsk, which compelled the regime to meet certain social expectations in the sphere of traditional culture.[4559] The inordinate delay in the Royal Castle's rebuilding was due to ideological objections by the "People's" regime and their Soviet overlords, with undue priority given to Stalin's so called "gift to Poland" — the Palace of Science and Culture (Pałac Kultury i Nauki, also abbreviated PKiN), built from 1952 to 1955, which many Varsovians have dubbed Stalin's syringe,[4560] or more irreverently as *Chuj Stalina*" — Stalin's penis/dick (or in the literal word order "Dick Stalin").[4561] As this multi-purpose monolithic monstrosity towers above the city skyline from near the city's Centralna (Central) station, it does offer an impressive view of the city.

But the first of my indelible impressions of the people's spirit was the monument to the Rising in Krasiński Square (Plac Krasińskich), just half a kilometre west of the remarkably restored Old Town. Krasiński Square was itself a place of fierce fighting during the uprising. The monument there consists of two bronze sculptures, one called "insurgents," depicting soldiers ready to fight, and the other called "exodus," depicting soldiers and a priest overseeing one soldier disappearing into the entrance of a sewer.[4562] Behind and just rising above the insurgents are pillars depicting the icon that became synonymous with Polish Resistance — the kotwica (anchor) — created by the superimposing of the upper-case letters P and W, to resonate with *Pomścimy Wawer* ("We shall avenge Wawer"),[4563] in the aftermath of the late December 1939 Wawer Massacre. However, with the genesis of the Armia Krajowa (Home Army) in the first half of 1942, it came to epitomise the country as a whole — *Polska Walcząca* (Fighting Poland).[4564] This would not be my last sighting of the iconic anchor.

Half a kilometre north-west of Krasiński Square, at the entrance to the *kościół święty* Jana Bożego (Saint John of God church) are several plaques paying tribute, not only to the participants in the 1944 Rising, but also to two soldiers of the Home Army who fought in the heroic Jewish Ghetto Uprising about sixteen months earlier, which broke out on April 19, 1943 and lasted almost one month until May 16, 1943.[4565] These men were Eugeniusz Morawski and Józef Wilk, who perished on that very spot on the northern fringes of the ghetto. Some Jewish commentators have criticised the Home Army for not doing more to assist the Ghetto Uprising, and some have even suggested the Home Army, and indeed Warsaw's civilian population, got its just deserts, with 0.2 million perish-ing sixteen months later. However, the circumstances for the two insurgencies were radically different. To begin with, in 1944, there was a fully equipped Soviet Army for weeks on Warsaw's doorstep, with all resources imaginable at its disposal to assist the revolt, but it chose to remain idle and give the Germans a free hand in suppressing it. On the other hand, the Home Army in April 1943 was hardly capable of liberating the Ghetto in an all-out conflict with the Germans, given the vast separation of Warsaw from any of the Allied armies to the west or east.

Another plaque is in memory of 300 doctors and nurses at the nearby Bonifratrów convent-come hospital, who were executed by the Germans in late August 1944. Another three commemorate the fallen from three battalions of the Armia Krajowa (Home Army). They are the Miotła (Broom), Zośka (Sophie — which liberated the Goose Farm concentration camp in the early days of the Rising)[4566] and Pięść (Fist) from the Radosław group. Some of the fighters in these battalions were only kids from the Polish Boy Scouts (Szare Szeregi — Grey Ranks), who managed to exist clandestinely after the 1939 invasion.[4567] They acted as couriers for an underground postal service, risking their lives daily. Women, too, played their role, as memorialised in the plaque honouring the special women's detachment called DYSK (Dywersja i Sabotaż Kobiet — Women's Diversion and Sabotage) commanded by Major Wanda Gertz ("Kazik" or "Lena,") herself a veteran from the Polish Soviet War of 1919-20. Unlike many of her honoured subordinates, she survived the war; she was taken prisoner after the Uprising,[4568] but later liberated in Germany by the US 89th Division,[4569] whereupon she settled in London until her death in November 1958, aged 62.

Just a stone's throw to the west is the Monument for the Fallen and Murdered in the East, or Pomnik Poległym i Pomordowanym na Wschodzie. The motivation for this monument lies in the Soviet invasion of Eastern Poland on September 17, 1939, just sixteen days after the launch of Hitler's invasion. As mentioned earlier, this precipitated the deportation of 1.7 million eastern Borderland Poles to the Arctic Hell of the Siberian gulag, with half that number dying there.[4570] This memorial was only unveiled fifty-six years to the day after the Soviet invasion of Poland's Eastern Borderlands on September 17, 1995.[4571] It was created by sculptor Maksymilian Biskupski and was dedicated to all Polish citizens who had suffered during World War II as a result of Soviet aggression. Located on Muranowska Street, the bronze cast monument includes an authentic railway track and railway carriage such as those used by the Soviets for deportation. The carriage is filled with symbols that represent the diverse ethnic and religious mix of the Eastern Borderland peoples. Catholic and Orthodox crosses, Jewish Stars of David, and the Crescent of Islam: all stand side by side in the wagon. The tracks themselves are just as poignant as the transport, for each bronze sleeper carries the names of Siberian districts and cities to which Polish Citizens were deported and where many died — some executed.[4572]

The epitaph on the sculpture reads simply as:

Poległym i Pomordowanym na Wschodzie
Ofiarom Agresji Sowieckiej
17-09-1939
+
Naród
17-09-1995

Which translates to:

To the Fallen and the Murdered in the East
Victims of Soviet Aggression
17-09-1939
+
The Nation
17-09-1995[4573]

Less than a kilometre west of this monument is the Umschlagplatz (collection point or reloading point), a monument dedicated to the Jews who were deported from the Ghetto to the death camp of Treblinka II,[4574] on the River Bug on the eastern border of pre-war Poland. It lies on Stawki Street near the corner of Dzika Street, a location which was once the northern boundary of the Ghetto.[4575] From here, more than 300,000 Jews from the Ghetto were sent to their deaths on freight trains bound for Treblinka. The deportations started on July 23, 1942, the day after the round-up of residents in the Ghetto by SS and non-German auxiliaries.[4576] This action was in response to an order given by Heinrich Himmler at the Auschwitz concentration camp six days earlier: the Warsaw Ghetto must be depopulated in what he described as a "total cleansing," and the inhabitants deported to what was to become an extermination camp constructed at the railway village of Treblinka, 80 kilometres (50 miles) north-east of Warsaw.[4577]

The chairman of the Warsaw Jewish Council, Adam Czerniaków, was ordered by the Nazis to draw up lists for deportation on July 22. The following day, however, he committed suicide rather than become implicit in the deportations.[4578] The daily deportations continued until September 12, 1942,[4579] but less frequent deportations continued well into 1943, almost up to the time of the Ghetto Uprising in April 1943. In the 52-day period from July 23, 1942 until September 12, 1942, over 300,000 Jews were deported — equating to about 7,000 deportations daily. During this period as well, the Germans killed an estimated 925,000 Jews at the Treblinka II killing centre, as well as an unknown number of Poles, Roma, and Soviet POWs.[4580] While the killing centre was in operation, some of the arriving Jews were selected and transferred to Treblinka I, while Jews too weak to work at Treblinka I were periodically sent to Treblinka II to be killed.[4581]

In memory of the victims, tablets in Polish, Hebrew and English read as follows:

ALONG THIS PATH	TA DROGA
OF SUFFERING	CIERPIENIA I SMIERCI
AND DEATH	W LATACH 1942-1943
OVER 300,000 JEWS	Z UTWORZONEGO
WERE DRIVEN IN 1942-1943	W WARSZAWIE GETTA
FROM	PRZESZŁO
THE WARSAW GHETTO	DO HITLEROWSKICH
TO THE GAS CHAMBERS	OBOZÓW ZAGŁADY
OF THE NAZI	PONAD
EXTERMINATION CAMPS	300,000 ŻYDÓW

Next to the tablets on both walls are inscribed, with great symbolic significance, hundreds of Jewish first names, such as SAMUEL, SAUL, SZYFRA, MAJLECH, MAGARETA, PAWEŁ and PAULINA, to name a few.

Less than a hundred metres west across Dzika Street from the Umschlagplatz memorial is another memorial tablet to the 1944 Uprising, this time cast in a large rock. It commemorates the insurgents of Battalion Broom "Miotła," commanded by Major Francis Mazurkiewicz "Niebora", attempting to break through southwards between Wola and the Old Town towards the city centre on August 11 to 12 ; the heaviest fighting took place on that very spot on the corner of Stawki and Dzika streets, where 25 insurgents died, including Niebora.[4582] This was during the second week of the Rising, when the districts of Mokotów and the City Centre became isolated, due to a German thrust splitting the main Polish stronghold in half. The fire-fight that took the life of Niebora was in the midst of that German advance. As mentioned earlier, this prompted the insurgents to create the first communications links through the sewers, from Mokotów to the City Centre.[4583] Those who survived the engagement on Stawki and Dzika streets would continue the fight at further redoubts such as Muranow, the Old Town and Czerniaków.[4584]

The most indelible memorial for me that day was located two kilometres south of the Umschlag-platz memorial, near the city's trade centre: the Muzeum Powstania (Uprising Museum), dedicated of course to the Uprising of 1944. At the museum's south-eastern corner is its viewing tower, proudly displaying on its eastern face the symbol of Polish resistance — the iconic *kotwica* (anchor). All AK battalions had their own emblem, but the common thread in all is the presence in some form of the *kotwica*.[4585]

The idea of setting up the Museum was brought forward in 1981, when the Public Committee for Building the Warsaw Rising Museum was founded. For over twenty years, the idea never passed the project stage. In July 2003 the Mayor of Warsaw, Lech Kaczyński granted the land of the former tram power station for the location of the forthcoming museum. In November 2003, through a contest, an architectural concept of the museum was chosen, and in January 2004, the realisation of a permanent exhibition was decided upon. At the same time, insurgents' memorabilia were gathered, which enriched the museum's collection by a few thousand exhibits. On July 31 2004, one day before the 60th Anniversary of the invocation of the Uprising,[4586] only two months or so before my visit, the museum was opened. Tragically, in April 2010, as president of Poland, Lech Kaczyński and his wife, along with the entire cabinet of the Polish government, were among the 96 victims on the Tupolev Tu-154 aircraft of the Polish Air Force that crashed near the Russian city of Smolensk and the accursed Katyń forest. He was flying there to commemorate the 70th anniversary of the April 1940 Katyń Wood massacre.[4587] Indicative of the present-day mistrust between Poland and Russia, Lech's identical twin brother Jarosław, and much of the Polish populace, suspect foul play on Putin's part.[4588]

The Muzeum Powstania (Uprising Museum) gave me the impression of a combat headquarters from which the Home Army planned and coordinated the uprising. It had red brick walls that looked worn from the scars of battle and was not brightly lit, rather lit just well enough to view the exhibits and read documents. This gave me the atmosphere of being immersed in the Rising. As I approached the entrance, I photographed an austere iron plaque above it, which poignantly embodied in Polish and English the people's dream of reclaiming their freedom:

Chcieliśmy być wolni

i wolność sobie zawdzięczać

We wanted to be free
and owe this freedom to nobody

Jan Stanisław Jankowski | *Delegat Rządu na Kraj* (Government Delegate for Poland)[4589]
[This man, as the civilian Government Delegate for Poland, gave the final authorisation for the invoking of the Rising.][4590]

This brave and free state was to last only fleetingly for the sixty-three days of the Uprising, and would not reappear until forty-five years later in 1989. Many plaques in the museum are dedicated to the participants in the Uprising, all written in Polish and English. One titled FOR HIS COURAGE AND BRAVERY or ZA MĘSTWO I ODWAGĘ describes Corporal Witold Modelski (Warszawiak), who was honoured with the Cross of Valour for his courage and bravery. He was the youngest of the insurgents to be given this honour, aged only eleven! He died on September 20, 1944, defending one of the last insurgent redoubts in Czerniaków at 1 Wilanowska Street.[4591]

Melchior Czesław Szczubełek was captured by the Soviets during their invasion of Poland in 1939, but after being deported deep into the Soviet Union managed to escape from the transport and find his way back to Warsaw in October. He joined the Armia Krajowa in March 1942 and during the Uprising was the Commander of the Czerniakowski Fort, where he died during the bombardment on September 1.[4592]

Jan Nowak Jezierański was captured by the Germans during September 1939, but also managed to escape in 1941; he made his way to Warsaw, where he served as a courier between Warsaw and London. After the war, he emigrated to London, where he served as editor of the

Polish Section of the BBC from 1948-1952, and subsequently, until 1975, as the director of the Polish Section at Radio Free Europe.[4593] Just before the surrender, Nowak was one of the four couriers sent to London to inform the government in exile of the Rising's end. He was the only one to make it.[4594]

Nurses were, naturally, a key aspect of the Rising. They included Ewa Matuszewska, born in 1919; she began her medical studies in 1938, and in September 1939 worked in the dressing station of the Baby Jesus Hospital. During the occupation she continued her studies at the Clandestine Faculty of Medicine and participated in underground humanitarian actions, including the rescue of children from the Zamość Region. During the Uprising, she managed the health service in the 2nd Company of the "Baszta" Regiment in Mokotów. She set up a small field hospital in the rear, and on September 26, she died, shot by the Germans, holding a bandage in her hand. She is posthumously decorated with the Order of Virtuti Militari and the Cross of Valour.[4595]

Other displays try to illustrate life under the occupation, such as the multiple ghettos. The first ghetto was set up by the Germans as early as October 1939, soon followed by many more. The largest ghetto of all, the ghetto of the April-May 1943 Jewish Uprising, was not established until October 1940, incarcerating 450,000 Jews. From the outset, the Jews were forced to wear the Star of David Armbands.[4596] For the population in general, there is a photo of German troops shouldering arms with bayonets with the caption underneath in German: *"Nur für Deutsche"* — "Only for Germans."[4597] Another has notices — *obwieszczenie* (Polish) or *Bekanntmachung* (German) that the Germans posted on walls throughout the city to enforce laws designed to terrorise and intimidate the Polish population. Appropriately they were displayed under the heading of "TERROR."[4598]

More displays detail the lead-up to the Uprising. POLISH UNDERGROUND STATE or POLSKIE PAŃSTWO PODZIEMNE details its evolution from the aftermath of the invasion in 1939, from the birth of the Union for Armed Struggle (ZWZ Związek Walki Zbrojnej),[4599] to the genesis of the Home Army in February 1942. Politically, the Home Army leaned slightly to the left, but its agenda was one of liberty, equality and independence.[4600] OPERATION „BURZA" [TEMPEST] IN THE LUBLIN AREA or „BURZA" NA LUBELSZCZYŹNIE documents the state of affairs that became commonplace as the Soviet Army progressed through pre-war eastern Poland: in the Lublin region in July 1944, District Commander Colonel Kazimierz Tumidajski "Edward" mobilised the 3rd, 9th and a part of the 27th Infantry Divisions.

The Home Army troops inflicted considerable casualties on German forces as they liberated many villages without Soviet assistance. Afterwards, the Soviets demanded that Home Army troops be incorporated into the Berling (Pro-Soviet Polish) Army or be dissolved. On July 29, 1944, Colonel Tumidajski ordered the dissolution of his troops. Days later on August 4, three days following the invocation of the Rising, Colonel Tumidajski was arrested.[4601]

"BEFORE THE 'W-HOUR'" documents the messages on July 29 and 30, just two and one days before the Rising, broadcast by Moscow radio station "Kosciuszko", appealing to Varsovians to "Fight against the Germans."[4602] The implied promise in this message of Soviet assistance to the Poles was never, at any stage during the Rising, going to be honoured by Stalin. In COMPARISON OF FORCES or PORÓWNANIE SIŁ it states that, at the invocation of the Rising, Home Army soldiers numbered around 45,000. This was supplemented with soldiers from other resistance groups such as the National Armed Forces, Internal Security Corps, with the communist "People's" Army making up an additional 2,500. Their major shortcoming was lack of weapons, which meant that only one in six insurgents was armed.[4603] On the other hand, they had to face well-trained German formations of about 25,000, armed to the teeth and supported by artillery and tanks and air cover. Moreover, the Germans could call on extra troops as required.[4604]

Tablets titled RADOŚĆ PIERWSZYCH DNI or THE JOY OF THE VERY FIRST DAYS document the early days of the Rising, when, after nearly five years of brutal occupation, Warsaw was once again a free city. National flags were hung on buildings and patriotic songs were played boldly from loudspeakers. Armia Krajowa or Home Army Soldiers heard words of support at every turn. Varsovians provided them with food and cigarettes and handed out flowers as well as taking care of the wounded. They built barricades on the streets and pointed to enemy posts. "Warsaw began and led a deathly struggle in isolation, yet her soldiers were not left alone" wrote Adam Borkiewicz, the first historian of the Uprising.[4605]

The THEATRES or TEATRZYKI display documents how artists continued their mission during the battle. In the second half of August, a theatre was set up on Powiśle under the name of "Puppets under the Barricade." It was created by Krystyna Artyniewicz, Michał Dadletz and Zofia Rendzner. Actors prepared comedy shows picturing fighting with the Germans and making decorations themselves. Puppet shows, embellished with music, were presented in the courtyards and on the squares, and were watched by children and adults alike.[4606] Tragically, however, CIVILIAN'S FATE or LOS CYWILA documents the mass murder of civilians by the Germans in the early days of the Rising, including women and children, many of whom were burnt alive. Civilians were forced to march as human shields in front of tanks.[4607]

The display, SHRINES OF INSURGENT WARSAW or KAPLICZKI POWSTAŃCZEJ WARSZAWEJ, describes how religious life moved from the burned churches to the courtyards of tenements and into flats. Field masses were celebrated and worshippers gathered in services around yard shrines with statues of Christ, or more commonly, the Holy Virgin. Women had gathered around the shrines for rosary and novena, praying for relatives and friends fighting on the barricades.[4608]

The filming of the Rising is discussed in THE PALLADIUM CINEMA or KINO PALLADIUM, where extraordinary efforts of recording evidence were undertaken by the Field War Reporters of the Home Army High Command Bureau of Information and Propaganda. A group of cinematographers led by Antoni Bohdziewicz shot over 30,000 metres of film. These were reports from insurgents' fighting put together in the form of an Insurgents' Film Chronicle. Three insurgents' chronicles were produced under the title "Warsaw is Fighting." They were shown in the Palladium Cinema on Złota Street. The first showing of the Insurgents' Film Chronicle took place on Sunday August 13, 1944.[4609]

Six days later, as documented in CONQUEST OF THE PAST or ZDOBYCIE PAST-y, it was on the night of August 19 to 20 that insurgent troops, under the command of Cavalry Captain Henryk Roycewicz "Leliwa," attacked the building of the Polish Telephone Company Limited — PAST — on 37/39 Zielna Street. After a dozen or so hours of bitter engagement, the insurgents annihilated the enemy's strong point, inflicting upon them 38 casualties, many wounded and burned, and taking 121 prisoners. Among the insurgents, at least 17 were killed. In the process of fighting, they captured a large cache of weapons. Almost every day, a cameraman or photographer was on duty near the building to ensure the assault on the PAST was well documented.[4610]

But by the end of September, as documented on CAPITULATION or KAPITULACJA, there was no hope for the insurgents. As given on the copies of the agreement in English and Polish, the suspension of warfare operations in Warsaw was signed in Ożarów, about thirteen kilometres west of the Warsaw Centrum on October 2. Home Army soldiers were deported to POW camps and the civilian population passed through a temporary camp in Pruszków, about five kilometres south of Ożarów. More than 18,000 insurgents and 180,000 civilians died in the Uprising. The Germans broke several resolutions of the capitulation treaty and carried out the long-planned action of destroying Warsaw. They systematically destroyed most of the Warsaw monuments, schools, churches and libraries, including the Royal Castle. Archives and works of art were turned into ashes.[4611] In the DECISION OF GENERAL „BÓR" or DECYZJA GEN. „BÓRA," his decision to be taken captive rather than escape and risk further punishments of his men and civilians is documented.[4612]

In EXODUS, it is documented that, early in the Rising, on August 5, 1944, the Germans created in Pruszków a transit camp for civilians — Dulag 121. The first transport arrived on August 6. As mentioned earlier, the living conditions in the Dulag were appalling; approximately 650,000 people, including 550,000 Varsovians passed through it, including Komorowski's wife Irena and their two-year-old son Adam. While there, the people were compelled to go through a selection process. About 150,000 people were sent to compulsory work in the Reich proper or concentration camps. About 100,000, including Irena and her son Adam were released, while others were smuggled out.[4613]

The display, THE DEATH OF THE CITY or ŚMIERĆ MIASTA, chronicles how, following the mass exodus of civilians and insurgents from the city, the Germans implemented its systematic destruction. The Germans started by dividing the city into regions and numbering the corner buildings. On the walls they put instructions concerning the method of destruction. They blew up the walls of the Royal Castle and a section of the Palace in Łazienki Park. They destroyed monuments, burnt to ashes the largest libraries. They converted into ruins and ashes the archives and museums and their collections. The Old Town became a sea of ruins.[4614]

Finally, in spite of the mass exodus of the population out of the city, there were, as stated in THOSE WHO STAYED or CI, KTÓRZY POZOSTALI the "Robinsonowie warszawscy" — "Warsaw Robinsons" who stayed and went into hiding amongst the rubble. The Germans called them "rats"; the majority were Jews, but there were also Christian Poles and Russians among them. The dangers that presented themselves included the possible discovery by Germans and the gruesome prospect of being trapped in rubble as the systematic destruction of the city was being implemented. Not to mention the chronic shortage of food and water. All this is what faced the famous Polish pianist

Władysław Szpilman, the central character of the major award-winning 2002 movie "The Pianist."[4615] For the expelled general population of Warsaw, the Soviet "liberation" of their city in January 1945 was virtually meaningless. However, for the Robinsonowie, liberation from the dangers and tribulations they faced in the freezing cold of winter had some tangible sense or feel.[4616]

The final tragedy of the Uprising was the defeat of Polish aspirations for independence, which were decisively crossed out by resolutions of the Yalta Conference,[4617] months later in early February 1945.[4618] The virtual inaction of the Soviets during the weeks of the Rising, allowing the Germans a free hand in destroying Warsaw, which was potentially the biggest centre of resistance against the new occupation by the Soviets, made it easier to impose the communist system of power and to Sovietise Polish society, as stated at the end of the display, CAPITULATION. At the time, and right up to this day, for me, the tablets of "BEFORE THE 'W-HOUR'"[4619] and "CAPITULATION" synthesise a damning indictment of Soviet inaction during the 63 days of the Rising.

Before my October 2004 visit to Warsaw's Uprising Museum, I was well aware of the April 1940 Katyń Wood massacre,[4620] but I was barely aware that the Rising ever took place. Hence, this visit was most enlightening in regard to this most pivotal and cataclysmic event in Polish history. In particular, the betrayal is embodied in the radio messages from Moscow in late July, ordering the populace of Warsaw to rise up,[4621] and then, by the time of the capitulation, the overwhelming evidence that Stalin never had any intention of delivering upon the implied promise of meaningful assistance for the Rising in those broadcasts.[4622] Hence, I was given more a sense of the rank illegitimacy of the post-war "People's" regime, which in no way represented the people's hopes and aspirations of the "freedom owing to nobody."[4623] [lxix] The tyranny of the Third Reich was gone, only to be replaced by another. Officially, Poland was one of the victors of World War II, but never was a "victory" so hollow and meaningless.

[lxix] The Poles especially did not want their liberation to be owing to Stalin. Komorowski's hope, in invoking the Rising, was for the Home Army to liberate Warsaw before the arrival of the Red Army. With the world watching, the political fallout for Stalin from the Red Army arresting or liquidating the city's Home Army would have been significant. Komorowski's invocation of the Rising was the Home Army's final card, played in their hope to achieve a free and independent Poland post-war. See endnotes [4132] to [4134] for this supplement.

Before, during and after the Rising, Stalin was on a winner, regardless of whether Komorowski took the active or passive option. Unlike Kraków,[4624] the Germans were never going to give up Warsaw easily. The city's German governor, Ludwig Fischer, on July 27, 1944, just five days before the Rising, gratuitously appealed to Warsaw's spirit of August 1920, calling its populace to report for duty in defence of the city from the "Bolshevik horde."[4625] Had they complied with Fischer's order, the Home Army and the city's populace in general would have been portrayed in Stalinist propaganda as fascist collaborators and ineffective cowards,[4626] and still be confronted with a devastated city. On the other hand, as Komorowski chose the proactive option, he unwittingly invoked Stalin's choice of abandoning the Rising, giving the Germans a free hand to suppress it, and in the process, greatly simplified Stalin's agenda of Sovietising Poland post-war.[4627]

More than three-quarters of a century later, however, with Stalin long dead and the re-birth of a truly independent Poland post-Cold War, the Stalinist cause is off the table. Unlike Yalta in early February 1945, appeasement of this agenda is no longer required. Hence, Stalin's true agenda of rendering 0.2 million Varsovians to be expendable canon fodder to a German proxy, all in the name of expanding global communism, can be made bare for all the world to see. As the memory of the 20,000 plus victims of Katyń will not rot in the grave,[4628] neither will the sacrifice of Varsovians for 63 days be in vain. At the harbour fortress of Tobruk on the Libyan coast in 1941, Polish exiles fought alongside the legendary Aussie Rats of Tobruk.[4629] Hence, by an Aussie of proud Polish descent, it is to them, on this ANZAC day of 2020, Lest We Forget, and beyond, this chapter is dedicated.[4630]

SOURCES AND END-NOTES

Preface - Birth and Memory upon the Lesser Known Fault Line of History

2 3482 4542 Concerning the three stages of Poland's partitioning in 1772, 1793 and 1795, see the book, *God's Playground A History of Poland: Volume 1: The Origins to 1795*, by Norman Davies, published by Oxford University Press Oxford, 2005, ISBN 0199253390, 9780199253395, in particular, page 386. As well, page 245 onwards of the book *The Polish Way* by Adam Zamoyski (a friend of Norman Davies), published by John Murray Publishers Limited, 1989, ISBN 10: 0719546745 ISBN 13: 9780719546747.

3 Page 324 of *The Polish Way* by Adam Zamoyski.

4 Concerning Hitler's invasion of Poland on September 1 1939, followed by Stalin's invasion sixteen days later on the 17th, see Polish WWII Supplement I "The Molotov-Ribbentrop Pact"3268 and pages 361 and 385 of the book *Lenin, Stalin and Hitler* by Robert Gellately, published by Vintage 2008, ISBN 9780712603577. See also, the Washington Post online article by Eugene Volokh, dated September 2, 2016 at https://www.washingtonpost.com/news/volokh-conspiracy/wp/2016/09/02/saying-that-the-ussr-and-nazi-germany-jointly-invaded-poland-is-a-crime-in- russia/?noredirect=on&utm_term=.2a88ae8b2663. See also the English language online article at http://khpg.org/en/index.php?id=1472775460 on the website of *Human Rights in Ukraine — Website of the Kharkiv Human Rights Protection Group* also dated September 2, 2016, which documents the danger of stating the fact of the Soviet September 1939 invasion of Poland in Putin's Russia. Both links accessed on Saturday July 25, 2020.

5 For information on the 1920 "Miracle on the Vistula" — "*Cud na Wisła*" see page 225 of *White Eagle Red Star*, by Professor Norman Davies, published in 2003 by Pimlico, Random House UK Limited, ISBN 9780712606943 and the book *Warsaw 1920, Lenin's Failed Conquest of Europe*, by Adam Zamoyski, paperback published by William Collins 2014, ISBN 9780007225538.

6 658 2356 3362 Page 8 of the book *Recovered Territory: A German-Polish Conflict over Land and Culture, 1919-1989* by Peter Polak-Springer, published by Berghahn Books, 2015, ISBN 1782388885, 9781782388883. See also the map on page xix.

7 Position 636.2 of the ebook *Bonhoeffer: Pastor, Martyr, Prophet, Spy A righteous Gentile vs, the Third Reich*, by Eric Metaxas, published by Thomas Nel-

son Nashville Tennessee, 2010, ISBN 9781595551382, 9781595553188(IE), 9781595552464(TP).

[8] Pages 14 to 15 of the book *Matriarch of Conspiracy : Ruth von Kleist 1867-1945* by Jane Pejsa, originally published by Kenwood Publishing, Minneapolis, Minnesota 1991 and in 1992 by The Pilgrim Press, Cleveland Ohio 44115, ISBN 0829809317 document Ruth's ancestral home in Silesia, while page 213 writes of Ruth sharing the same birthday as Dietrich. Moreover, page 213 also states that this date of February 4 was the date of her wedding anniversary in 1886.

[9] Position 46.5 of the ebook *Dietrich Bonhoeffer 1906-1945: Martyr, Thinker, Man of Resistance* by Ferdinand Schlingensiepen, translated by Isabel Best, first published in 2010 by Continuum, but since 2011, Bloomsbury T&T Clark, ePub-ISBN 9780567217554, ePDF-ISBN 9780567357755.

[10] The numerous variants of the name for Wrocław over the ages is given on page 2 of the paper *Wrocław — Cultural Semantics of the Contemporary Urban Embedding* by Marcin R. Odelski, MA High School NR 2, Wrocław, Poland. It can be downloaded from http://journals.univ-danubius.ro/index.php/communication/article/view/144/137/144-555-1-PB.pdf from the journals repository of the Danubius University of Galati in Romania. Accessed on Saturday July 25, 2020. Moreover, the cover of the ebook *Microcosm: A Portrait of a Central European City*, by Norman Davies and Roger Moorhouse, published by Jonathan Cape 2002, Epub ISBN 9781448114085, gives nine variants of the city's name over the ages.

[11] The fall of Festung Breslau (Fortress Breslau) on the May 6 1945, is documented on page 265 of the book *Red Storm on the Reich: The Soviet March on Germany, 1945* by Christopher Duffy, published by Atheneum, 1991, ISBN 0689120923, 9780689120923. As does position 1112.0 of Microcosm. Position 1118.0 states that peace was declared in Europe on May 8 1945. In regards to the fall of Berlin, see page 13 of the book *Berlin 1945: End of the Thousand Year Reich*, by Peter Antill, published by Osprey Publishing, 2005, ISBN 1841769150, 9781841769158 which gives a timeline stating the surrender of Berlin taking place on May 2 1945. That being, four days before the surrender of Breslau.

[12] Pages 13 to 14 of the book *Cuius regio? Ideological and Territorial Cohesion of the Historical Region of Silesia (c. 1000-2000) Volume 1* edited by Lucyna Harc, Przemysław Wiszewski, Rościsław Żerelik. This **Volume 1** is entitled *The Long Formation of the Region Silesia (c. 1000—1526)* edited by Przemysław Wiszewski, translated by Katarzyna Hussar. published by eBooki.com.pl, ISBN 9788392713210 (print) ISBN 9788392713227 (online). It can be viewed online at http://www.bibliotekacyfrowa.pl/Content/49790/Cuius_regio_vol_1.pdf or downloaded from the University of Wrocław at http://www.slasknasz.uni.wroc.pl/Cuius-Regio-Ideological-and-Territorial-

Cohesion-Historical-Region-Silesia-c-1000-2000-vol-1-Long. Both links accessed on Saturday July 25, 2020.

[13] Ibid. The Odra (German Oder) River, is the dominant river of this region.

[14] The online *Encyclopaedia Britannica* article on Mieszko I at https://www.britannica.com/biography/Mieszko-I states that Mieszko I was born in 930, and died on May 25, 992. Accessed on Saturday July 25, 2020.

[15] "*Ostrów Tumski*" from Old Polish translating to "Cathedral Island" in modern English, literally translates to modern English as "Island Cathedral." The modern Polish translation is "*Wyspa Katedralna*," with a clear similarity to modern English. See http://www.britannica.com/place/Wroclaw and http://library.eb.com.au/levels/adults/article/77571. They also mention the founding of the city in the 10th century, along with the fortifications on Ostrów Tumski ("Cathedral Island") built by Bolesław I (the Brave) when he founded the Bishopric in 1000. Both links accessed on Saturday July 25, 2020.

[16] Page 14 of the book *Cuius regio? Ideological and Territorial Cohesion of the Historical Region of Silesia (c. 1000-2000) Volume 1* edited by Lucyna Harc, Przemysław Wiszewski, Rościsław Żerelik. This **Volume 1** is entitled *The Long Formation of the Region Silesia (c. 1000—1526)* edited by Przemysław Wiszewski, translated by Katarzyna Hussar. published by eBooki.com.pl, ISBN 9788392713210 (print) ISBN 9788392713227 (online).

[17] Position 82.6 of the ebook *Genghis Khan & the Mongol Conquests 1190-1400* by Stephen Turnbull, published by Osprey Publishing Limited 2003. ISBN 9781472810212.

[18] I visited these fascinating 90 metre subterranean mines in June 2008, which since their cessation of mining operations in 1996, now attract over one million tourists annually. Dating back over 7 centuries, the present day tourist section only covers 1% of the original mining operations and its magnificent underground salt (literally) cathedral, ninety (90) metres below the surface, is a sight to behold. A timeline of the Wieliczka Salt Mine can be found its official website at http://www.wieliczka-saltmine.com/about-the-mine/the-mine-of-the-past-and-of-today. Accessed on Saturday July 25, 2020.

[19] Pages 173-174 of the book *Historia małych krajów Europy (The history of the small countries of Europe)*, by Józef Łaptos, published by Zakład Narodowy im. Ossolińskich, 2007, ISBN-10: 8304049376, ISBN-13: 9788304049376.

[20] Position 307.2 of the ebook *Microcosm: A Portrait of a Central European City*, by Norman Davies and Roger Moorhouse, published by Jonathan Cape 2002, Epub ISBN 9781448114085.

[21] Position 307.9 of *Microcosm*.

[22] Position 309.0 of *Microcosm*.

[23] Position 399.3 of *Microcosm*.

[24] Positions 400.3 and 400.8 respectively of *Microcosm*.

[25] [1001] See position 369.3 to 369.9 of Microcosm for details of these unspeakable atrocities in Breslau in May and July 1453. See also position 513.7 in regard to their restricted access and existence in the city.

[26] Position 368.5 of *Microcosm.*

[27] Page 410 onwards of Chapter 24 "The Fall" in *BYZANTIUM THE DECLINE AND FALL* by John Julius Norwich, published by Penguin Books London 1996, ISBN 0140114491, 9780140114492.

[28] See article on the Hussites at https://www.britannica.com/topic/Hussite.

[29] Position 369.4 of *Microcosm.*

[30] Position 369.5 of *Microcosm.*

[31] [1001] Position 369.6 to 369.9 of *Microcosm.*

[32] Position 513.7 of *Microcosm.*

[33] Position 513.8 of *Microcosm.*

[34] Position 514.2 of *Microcosm.*

[35] Position 515.0 of *Microcosm.*

[36] Position 514.8 of *Microcosm.*

[37] Position 714.1 of the ebook *Dietrich Bonhoeffer 1906-1945: Martyr, Thinker, Man of Resistance* by Ferdinand Schlingensiepen, translated by Isabel Best, first published in 2010 by Continuum, but since 2011, Bloomsbury T&T Clark, ePub-ISBN 9780567217554, ePDF-ISBN 9780567357755 documents the decree of German Jews being compelled to wear the Star of David from September 1941, followed by deportations east the following month. See https://www.britannica.com/topic/Star-of-David for more information on the "Star of David." Accessed on Saturday July 25, 2020.

[38] See also pages 11 to 12 of *Lenin, Stalin and Hitler The Age of Social Catastrophe* by Robert Gellately, published by Vintage 2008, ISBN 9780712603577.

[39] Ibid page 12.

[40] https://www.britannica.com/event/Holocaust#ref716460 by Michael Berenbaum. Accessed on Saturday July 25, 2020.

[41] Ibid. See also pages 164 to 169 of Jane Pejsa and endnote [718] in Chapter 9 "The von Kleists and the Prophecy."

[42] [3580] Pages 33 to 34 of the book *Symphonia Catholica: The Merger of Patristic and Contemporary Sources in the Theological Method of Amandus Polanus (1561-1610), Volume 30 of Reformed Historical Theology* by Byung Soo Han, published by Vandenhoeck & Ruprecht, 2015, ISBN 3525550855, 9783525550854.

[43] https://visitwroclaw.eu/historia-wroclawia (in Polish) from the official municipal website of the city of Wrocław in an article by Krzysztof Popiński, Ph.D, accessed on Saturday July 25, 2020, dealing with the history of Wrocław, states the rule over the city by the Austrian Catholic House of Habsburg commencing in 1526. However, the article also mentions the continuation of Protestant dominance of the city for centuries to come even in the face of

Catholic Habsburg rule. See also position 431.0 onwards of Chapter Four of *Microcosm* "Presslaw under the Habsburg Monarchy."

[44] [3580] Position 480.8 of Microcosm.

[45] Positions 580.5, 581.9 and 582.5 of Microcosm. This will not be the last time the Miracle of Brandenburg will be mentioned in this Preface.

[46] Messalina Valeria, third wife of the Roman emperor Claudius, notorious for licentious behaviour and instigating murderous court intrigues. See https://www.britannica.com/biography/Messalina-Valeria. Accessed on Saturday July 25, 2020.

[47] [141] [719] [2837] Page 457 of *Frederick the Great: King of Prussia* by David Fraser, published by Fromm International, 2001, ISBN 0880642610, 9780880642613.

[48] Position 580.6 of Microcosm.

[49] Position 474.6 onwards of Microcosm implies the Swedish and Saxon occupation of Breslau during the Thirty Year's War (1618-1648).

[50] Position 462.1 of Microcosm.

[51] Position 448.1 of Microcosm. Note as well the authors' use of "Presslaw" for the spelling of the city's name during this period of history.

[52] See the family tree given on page xxiv of the book *Young Wilhelm: The Kaiser's Early Life, 1859-1888* by John C. G. Röhl, translated by Jeremy Gaines, Rebecca Wallach, published by Cambridge University Press, 1998, ISBN 0521497523, 9780521497527. The son of Wilhelm I and the father of Wilhelm II, namely Frederick III and referred to here as Crown Prince Frederick William, only reigned for ninety-nine days in the Year of Three Emperors — 1888. As well, Kaiser Wilhelm II was the grandson of Britain's Queen Victoria, having been the son of her eldest child Victoria.

[53] Position 601.6 of *Microcosm*.

[54] Position 601.9 of *Microcosm*.

[55] Position 602.1 of *Microcosm*.

[56] Position 602.3 of *Microcosm*.

[57] Position 602.7 of *Microcosm*.

[58] Position 587.5 to 596.5 of *Microcosm* describes Breslau's Napoleonic episode from November 1806 to around June 1813.

[59] Position 603.8 of *Microcosm*.

[60] [506] Pages 148 to 149 of Jane Pejsa.

[61] Page 133 of the book *Bismarck* by A.J.P. Taylor, published by Knopf Doubleday Publishing Group, 2011, ISBN 0307787427, 9780307787422.

[62] The prosperity of Germany in the years just preceding the Great War, is documented on page 325, of the book *Health and Welfare during Industrialization* by Richard H. Steckel and Roderick Floud, editors, published in January 1997 by University of Chicago Press, © 1997 by the National Bureau of Economic Research, ISBN 0226771563. This being Chapter 8, "Heights and Living Standards in Germany, 1850-1939: The Case of Wurttemberg" by Sophia Twarog. This book can be downloaded from the website of National Bureau of

Economic Research at http://papers.nber.org/books/stec97-1, while its Chapter 8 can be downloaded from http://www.nber.org/chapters/c7434.pdf. Both links accessed on Saturday July 25, 2020. Position 770.7 of Microcosm states how the economy of Silesia, with Breslau at its hub, grew exponentially in the decades following the founding of the German Empire (Second Reich) in 1871.

[63] 537 542 606 Pages 24 and 29 of the book *Yugoslavism: Histories of a Failed Idea, 1918-1992* by Dejan Djokić, published by C. Hurst & Co. Publishers, 2003, ISBN 1850656630, 9781850656630.

[64] 538 540 541 543 The online article entitled the *July Crisis 1914* on the website of the International Encyclopedia of the First World War at https://encyclopedia.1914-1918-online.net/article/july_crisis_1914, by Annika Mombauer, documents and describes the events that led to the outbreak of war in 1914. The credentials of this website can be viewed at https://encyclopedia.1914-1918-online.net/project/overview/. Both links accessed on Saturday July 25, 2020.

[65] 677 721 1337 1351 2293 2909 Position 886.0 of *Microcosm* in the last paragraph of Chapter 6 "Breslau in the German Empire, 1871—1918."

[66] Position 760.2 of *Microcosm*

[67] Position 886.0 of *Microcosm*.

[68] 556 The *Encyclopaedia Britannica* article on the Treaties of Brest-Litovsk at https://library.eb.com.au/levels/adults/article/treaties-of-Brest-Litovsk/16373 describes the position of major weakness for Bolshevik Russia and its eventual compelled acceptance of the treaty's humiliating terms. The text of the peace treaty can be read online on the website of Avalon Project of the Yale Law School at http://avalon.law.yale.edu/20th_century/brest.asp, while a brief summary of its dire implications for Bolshevik Russia is given at http://avalon.law.yale.edu/20th_century/bl36.asp. All links accessed on Saturday February 27, 2021.

[69] Position 887.7 of Microcosm.

[70] 677 721 1337 1351 2293 2909 See pages 83, 414, 427 and 568 of *Lenin, Stalin and Hitler The Age of Social Catastrophe* by Robert Gellately, published by Vintage 2008, ISBN 9780712603577, in regard to Hitler's perception of the synonymous Jews and left-wing of politics.

[71] Pages 118-120 of the book *The Second Reich: Kaiser Wilhelm II and his Germany Macdonald library of the 20th century*, by Harold Kurtz, published by Macdonald in the British Commonwealth, and by American Heritage Press in the USA, both in 1970, ASIN: B008T15I7M, ISBN-10: 007035653X ISBN-13: 9780070356535, detail the Kaiser eventually abdicating at the German Army Headquarters in the Belgium town of Spa, in early November 1918, followed by his flight to neutral Holland by train. See also the beginning of Chapter 7 "Breslau before and during the Second World War, 1918—45" in Microcosm from position 887.0.

[72] Page 144 of Jane Pejsa.

[73] Position 887.5 of Microcosm.

[74] Position 888.1 of Microcosm.

[75] Position 888.2 of *Microcosm*.

[76] Page 30 of *Dietrich Bonhoeffer: A Biography* by Eberhard Bethge, edited by Victoria J. Barnett, published by Fortress Press, 2000, ISBN 0800628446, 9780800628444.

[77] 254 3208 Oma is the German diminutive of grandmother and it will not be the last time it is used in this book.

[78] 254 3208 Page 30 of *Dietrich Bonhoeffer: A Biography* by Eberhard Bethge, edited by Victoria J. Barnett, published by Fortress Press, 2000, ISBN 0800628446, 9780800628444.

[79] 254 3697 Pages 85 to 86 of *Lenin, Stalin and Hitler The Age of Social Catastrophe* by Robert Gellately, published by Vintage 2008, ISBN 9780712603577.

[80] 635 The "Golden Age of Weimar" being from 1924 to 1929 is documented at J. Llewellyn et al, at http://alphahistory.com/weimarrepublic/golden-age-of-weimar/. The academics that contribute to the website are listed here: http://alphahistory.com/alpha-history-authors/. Both links accessed on Saturday July 25, 2020.

[81] 3583 Positions 901.2, 901.3 and 901.9 of *Microcosm*.

[82] Position 901.3 of *Microcosm*.

[83] Documented at http://acienciala.faculty.ku.edu/hist557/lect11.htm from the Lecture Notes 11 from the History 557 Lecture Notes website of Anna Maria Cienciala at the University of Kansas. Accessed on Saturday July 25, 2020. As well, page 141 of *White Eagle Red Star*, by Professor Norman Davies, published in 2003 by Pimlico, Random House UK Limited, ISBN 9780712606943, documents the Bolshevik attack on Poland ready by July 1920, after four months of preparation (beginning in March 1920) and the recapture of Kiev and the rest of the western Ukraine by the Bolsheviks in June.

[84] Position 900.5 of *Microcosm*.

[85] Page 116 of John Brown Mason's book *The Danzig Dilemma; a Study in Peacemaking by Compromise* published by Stanford University Press, 1946, ISBN 080472444X, 9780804724449. At the top of page 118, it is stated that this led to Poland's determination to build the port at nearby Gdynia.

[86] Position 900.9 of *Microcosm*.

[87] The Times (London), August 28 1920, page 9 and position 901.7 of *Microcosm*.

[88] Position 902.0 of *Microcosm*.

[89] Position 902.6 of *Microcosm*.

[90] 3583 Position 904.1 of *Microcosm*.

[91] Online *Encyclopaedia Britannica* article at https://www.britannica.com/biography/Adolf-Hitler. Accessed on Saturday July 25, 2020.

92 132 461 784 901 1407 1613 1748 1919 2182 3565 4280 3143 3067 3130 3242 Position 924.3 of *Microcosm*.

93 Position 923.9 of *Microcosm*.

94 Position 924.3 of *Microcosm*.

95 Page 320 of *Nemesis of Power: The German Army in Politics 1918-1945* by Sir John Wheeler-Bennett and Richard Overy, published by Springer, 1964, ISBN 1349002216, 9781349002214. This also appears on page 320 of the much later published Palgrave Macmillan UK, 2005 edition, ISBN 1403918120, 9781403918123. The exact dates of the beginning and end of the purge are given at https://encyclopedia.ushmm.org/content/en/article/roehm-purge on the website United States Holocaust Museum Memorial Encyclopaedia. Accessed on Saturday February 20, 2021.

96 Position 924.3 onwards of Microcosm gives an account of the purge in Silesia.

97 Position 924.6 of Microcosm.

98 Position 924.6 of Microcosm.

99 Position 920.6 of Microcosm.

100 Position 925.0 of Microcosm.

101 The United States Holocaust Memorial Museum's online article about the Röhm Purge at https://www.ushmm.org/wlc/en/article.php?ModuleId=10007885.

102 The United States Holocaust Memorial Museum's online article on the *German Churches and the Nazi State* at https://www.ushmm.org/wlc/en/article.php?ModuleId=10005206. Accessed on Saturday July 25, 2020.

103 Pages 200 to 202 of Jane Pejsa. See also endnote 784 in Chapter 9 "The von Kleists and the Prophecy" in regard to Ewald von Kleist's narrow escape during the 1934 Röhm purge.

104 Online *Encyclopaedia Britannica* article on von Papen at https://www.britannica.com/biography/Franz-von-Papen. Accessed on Saturday July 25, 2020.

105 3132 3133 Page 470 of the book *Hitler* by Joachim C. Fest, published by Harcourt Incorporated, 2002, ISBN 0156027542, 9780156027540.

106 Online *Encyclopaedia Britannica* article at http://www.britannica.com/biography/Paul-von-Hindenburg. Accessed on Saturday July 25, 2020.

107 132 461 784 901 1407 1613 1748 1919 2182 3565 4280 3143 3067 3130 3242 Article about the Röhm Purge at https://www.ushmm.org/wlc/en/article.php?ModuleId=10007885. Accessed on Saturday July 25, 2020.

108 This nationwide pogrom will be covered in detail in Chapter 14 "Reichskristallnacht."

109 Position 925.9 of *Microcosm*. This will be described in greater detail in Chapter 14 "Reichskristallnacht."

[110] Position 927.3 of *Microcosm*.

[111] Position 928.3 of *Microcosm*.

[112] Page 30 of *The Third Reich in Power* by Richard J. Evans, published by Penguin Books, 2006, ISBN 0143037900, 9780143037903.

[113] Position 730.3 of Metaxas and position 926.3 to 927.4 of Microcosm.

[114] The Giant Mountains, the natural barrier between Silesia and the ethnic German Sudetenland of then Czechoslovakia, with their names in several languages are given on the Czech Tourist Portal web site at http://www.czecot.com/?id_region=20 (English), http://www.czecot.cz/?id_region=20 (Czech), http://www.czecot.pl/?id_region=20 (Polish) and http://www.czecot.de/?id_region=20 (German). In Czech they are they are the "Krkonoše," in Polish "Karkonosze" and in German "Riesengebirge." All links accessed on Saturday July 25, 2020.

[115] Pages 421-422 *Rise And Fall Of The Third Reich: A History of Nazi Germany* by William L. Shirer, published by Simon and Schuster, 1990, ISBN 0671728687, 9780671728687. See also endnote [950] of Chapter 13 "Flight and the Tumultuous Appeasement of Evil" in regard to the crippling of Czech industry brought on by the Munich 1938 appeasement. That chapter will deal with this episode of appeasement in detail.

[116] [124] The United Press International Archives website at http://www.upi.com/Archives/1939/03/15/Crowds-defiant-in-Prague-as-Hitler-crosses-Czech-frontier/8148408176316/, accessed on Saturday July 25, 2020, gives the date of Wednesday March 15 1939 when Hitler's troops marched into the Czech capital of Prague. As does position 742.0 near the beginning of Chapter 21 "The Great Decision" of the ebook *Bonhoeffer: Pastor, Martyr, Prophet, Spy A righteous Gentile vs, the Third Reich*, by Eric Metaxas, published by Thomas Nelson Nashville Tennessee, 2010, ISBN 9781595551382, 9781595553188(IE), 9781595552464(TP) and page 640 of *Dietrich Bonhoeffer: A Biography* by Eberhard Bethge, edited by Victoria J. Barnett, published by Fortress Press, 2000, ISBN 0800628446, 9780800628444.

[117] Position 935.3 of *Microcosm*.

[118] Position 934.6 of *Microcosm*.

[119] Article with map at https://www.britannica.com/place/Austria-Hungary. Accessed on Saturday July 25, 2020.

[120] Position 934.8 of *Microcosm*.

[121] The *Encyclopaedia Britannica* article on the Sudetenland at https://library.eb.com.au/levels/adults/article/Sudetenland/70151. Accessed on Saturday February 27, 2021.

[122] Page 1843 of *The Czechs and the Lands of the Bohemian Crown* by Hugh LeCaine Agnew, published by Hoover Press, 2004, ISBN 0817944923, 9780817944926. Charles IV is one of the greatest Czech kings — indicative of which, is the fact that Prague's most iconic bridge over its Vltava river, is

named after him. My wife and I visited it in September 2014. See the online *Encyclopaedia Britannica* article on him at https://www.britannica.com/biography/Charles-IV-Holy-Roman-emperor. Accessed on Saturday July 25, 2020.

[123] Ibid page 1828.

[124] See endnote [116] for this preface in regard to Hitler's March 1939 annexation of the remainder of what was left of Czechoslovakia.

[125] [3330] Position 1103.3 of *Microcosm* states that the non-communist Polish Home Army (AK — Armia Krajowa) was the largest underground movement in Nazi occupied Europe. See also page 183 of *Rising '44: The Battle for Warsaw* Reprint Edition, (October 4, 2005), ISBN-10: 0143035401, ISBN-13: 9780143035404, where it documents the underwhelming figure for the communist Armia Ludowa (AL) of 800 in Warsaw in 1943, as compared to the Home Army (AK — Armia Krajowa) with 40,330 men!

[126] Positions 1040.2 and 1043.7 of *Microcosm*.

[127] [2312] [2438] *SS*, abbreviation of Schutzstaffel (German: "Protective Echelon" or "Protective Squadron"), were the black-uniformed elite corps and self-described "political soldiers" of the Nazi Party. Founded by Adolf Hitler in April 1925 as a small personal bodyguard, the SS grew with the success of the Nazi movement and, gathering immense police and military powers, became virtually a state within a state. Several child entities would spawn from it such as the SD — Sicherheitsdienst — its intelligence arm and the Waffen SS, its military wing. See https://library.eb.com.au/levels/adults/article/SS/69325. https://encyclopedia.ushmm.org/content/en/article/waffen-ss states that the number of Waffen SS troops numbered half-a-million at its peak. It could well have been more. All links accessed on Saturday July 25, 2020.

[128] [1104] [3561] [3564] [3711] [4436] [4439] [4450] *Einsatzgruppen*, (German: "deployment groups") were units of the Nazi security forces composed of members of the SS, the Sicherheitspolizei (Sipo; "Security Police"), and the Ordnungspolizei (Orpo; "Order Police") that acted as mobile killing units during the German invasions of Poland (1939) and the Soviet Union (1941). From https://www.britannica.com/topic/Einsatzgruppen. Accessed on Saturday July 25, 2020.

[129] Position 1048 of Microcosm and page 42 of *Hitlers Einsatzgruppen* by Helmut Krausnick, Frankfurt-am-Main, 1985.

[130] [3711] Concerning the *Einsatzgruppen* being resurrected following the Barbarossa invasion of June 1941, see position 812.0 of the ebook *Bonhoeffer: Pastor, Martyr, Prophet, Spy A righteous Gentile vs, the Third Reich*, by Eric Metaxas, published by Thomas Nelson Nashville Tennessee, 2010, ISBN 9781595551382, 9781595553188(IE), 9781595552464(TP), page 660 of *The Rise and Fall of the Third Reich* by William L. Shirer, Edition reprint, reissue, annotated, published by Simon and Schuster, 2011, ISBN 1451651686, 9781451651683 and page 30 of *The Waffen SS: Hitler's Elite Guard at War,*

1939-1945 by George H. Stein, published by Cornell University Press, 1984, ISBN 0801492750, 9780801492754.

[131] [1119] In regard to the acts of mass murder perpetrated by Breslau's Udo von Woyrsch, see position 1048.7 onwards of *Microcosm*. His date of birth of the June 24 1895 is given on the online database of the Reichstag at http://www.reichstag-abgeordnetendatenbank.de/selectmaske.html?pnd=121027562&recherche=ja, while his dates of birth and death can be seen on a photo at https://ww2gravestone.com/people/woyrsch-udo-gustav-wilhelm-egon-von/ on the website of the World War II Gravestones. All links accessed on Saturday July 25, 2020. Footnote #39 on page 11 of the book *War, Pacification, and Mass Murder, 1939: The Einsatzgruppen in Poland* by Jürgen Matthäus, Jochen Böhler, Klaus-Michael Mallmann, published by Rowman & Littlefield, 2014, ISBN 1442231424, 9781442231429, documents how this mass murderer lived on decades following World War II!

[132] Position 924.3 of *Microcosm*. See also endnotes [92] to [107] of this Preface in regard to the 1934 Röhm Purge.

[133] [1104] Position 1049.0 of *Microcosm*.

[134] [2725] [2728] Position 741.0 of the ebook *Bonhoeffer: Pastor, Martyr, Prophet, Spy A righteous Gentile vs, the Third Reich* by Eric Metaxas, published by Thomas Nelson Nashville Tennessee, 2010, ISBN 9781595551382, 9781595553188(IE), 9781595552464(TP). See also endnote [1992] of Chapter 21 "Valkyrie's Wake" in regard to the "Chronicle of Shame" files.

[135] This is essentially true but not in the strictest sense. Breslau was bombed on November 13 1941 by the British with ten people killed. However, this seems to be the only instance, and in comparison to the devastation of German cities west of it, it was certainly regarded as a safe haven for the vast majority of the war until the Soviet siege of March 1945. Certainly it seems to have been outside of effective Western Allied bombing range. See page 23 of the book *Lower Silesia From Nazi Germany To Communist Poland 1942-49*, by Sebastian Siebel-Achenbach, published by Springer, 1994, ISBN 1349232165, 9781349232161.

[136] Position 86.6 of *Microcosm*.

[137] Position 71.6 of *Microcosm*.

[138] In regard to German-Polish names for these fortress towns/cities, go to the website of the *Verein für Computergenealogie e.V. (Association for Computer Genealogy e.V.)* starting at say http://wiki-de.genealogy.net/Ratibor. Accessed on Saturday July 25, 2020. A search on *Encyclopaedia Britannica* will give the German names for some of these now modern-day Polish towns/cities. NOTE however, that Kaliningrad/Königsberg is now in the Russian enclave located in north-eastern Poland.

[139] Position 73.2 of *Microcosm*.

[140] [719] [2420] [2837] Evidence of Hitler holding out for a re-visitation of Frederick the Great's "Miracle of Brandenburg" can be found in the book *The Last Days of Hitler* by Hugh Redwald Trevor-Roper, published by Pan 1999, ISBN 1743298889, 9781743298886. Look for reference #141 or see Google Books online at https://books.google.com.au/books?id=OyjvAgAAQBAJ&printsec=frontcover &dq=The+Last+Days+of+Hitler,+Hugh+Trevor-Roper,&hl=en&sa=X&redir_esc=y#v=onepage&q=frederick&f=false. Accessed on Saturday July 25, 2020.

[141] [719] [2421] [2837] In regard to the 1762 "Miracle of Brandenburg" itself, see endnote [47] for this preface, and position 580.2 to 582.5 of *Microcosm* and page 457 of *Frederick the Great: King of Prussia* by David Fraser, published by Fromm International, 2001, ISBN 0880642610, 9780880642613.

[142] Position 115.3 of Microcosm.

[143] [2438] Position 95.7 of Microcosm states that the rape carried out by Soviet soldiers was indiscriminate of ethnicity.

[144] [2438] The fate of Soviet POWs in German captivity and post war, with Stalin's perception of them being traitors is documented from pages 242-249 in the book *The Gulag Archipelago, Parts I and II* by Alexander Solzhenitsyn, translated from Russian by Thomas P. Whitney, first published in Australia 1974 simultaneously by Collins/Harvill Press and Fontana, ISBN 0006336426.

[145] Position 71.6 of *Microcosm*.

[146] Page 1131 of the book *Rise And Fall Of The Third Reich: A History of Nazi Germany* by William L. Shirer, published by Simon and Schuster, 1990, ISBN 0671728687, 9780671728687.

[147] Position 1108.5 of Microcosm documents the suicide of Hitler on the 30th April 1945, and the surrender of Festung Breslau at 6pm on May 6 1945, with the very soon to follow signing of the Nazi unconditional surrender by General Jodl in Rheims.

[148] Page 13 of the book *Berlin 1945: End of the Thousand Year Reich*, by Peter Antill, published by Osprey Publishing, 2005, ISBN 1841769150, 9781841769158 gives a timeline stating the surrender of Berlin taking place on the May 2 1945. This being four days before the surrender of Breslau.

[149] Position 1108.5 of *Microcosm*.

[150] Position 1118.8 of *Microcosm*.

[151] Position 1119.1 of *Microcosm*.

[152] [2617] Position 1119.4 of *Microcosm*.

[153] Position 1119.5 of *Microcosm*.

[154] [2359] [2617] [3360] [4008] Position 1119.8 of *Microcosm*.

[155] Position 1124.1 of *Microcosm*.

[156] [3360] [4008] In regard to the Spa-London-Moscow telegram, including its dormancy in between the wars and the inordinate importance given to it by the Soviets during World War II, with subsequent western Allied appeasement, see

pages 168 to 172 of *White Eagle Red Star*, by Professor Norman Davies, published in 2003 by Pimlico, Random House UK Limited, ISBN 9780712606943. Also position 353.6 to 364.7 of the ebook edition — Epub ISBN 9781446466865, also published in 2003 by Pimlico Random House UK. This telegram also became known as the Curzon Line telegram, named after the then British Foreign Secretary Lord Curzon, who had in fact, nothing to do with its creation. See pages 169 to 170 of *White Eagle Red Star* and position 358.1 of the ebook.

[157] Page 168 of *White Eagle Red Star*. Also, positions 354.2 and 355.4 of the ebook edition.

[158] Page 168 of *White Eagle Red Star*. Also, positions 354.2 and 355.4 of the ebook edition.

[159] Page 170 of *White Eagle Red Star* and position 358.7 of the ebook edition. See also the second map and legend given before the foreword in the book and at position 7.0 in the ebook. The map is titled "The Riga Settlement."

[160] End of page 169 of *White Eagle Red Star* and position 357.9 in the ebook.

[161] Page 169 to 170 of *White Eagle Red Star* and position 358.0 in the ebook.

[162] Page 170 of *White Eagle Red Star* and positions 358.4 and 358.9 in the ebook.

[163] Pages 171 to 172 of *White Eagle Red Star* and positions 360.4 and 362.3 of the ebook.

[164] See page 7 of the book *Warsaw 1920, Lenin's Failed Conquest of Europe* by Adam Zamoyski, paperback published by William Collins 2014, ISBN 9780007225538. See also http://acienciala.faculty.ku.edu/hist557/lect11.htm from the Lecture Notes 11 from the History 557 Lecture Notes website of Anna Maria Cienciala at the University of Kansas. Accessed on Saturday July 25, 2020.

[165] See pages 265 to 266 of *White Eagle Red Star* and position 568.3 to 571.9 in the ebook, when Lenin states his regrets over the 1919-20 Polish Soviet War to German communist Clara Zetkin soon after the Riga Armistice of March 18, 1921. (See page 261 of the book and position 561.7 of the ebook).

[166] Bottom of page 170 of *White Eagle Red Star* and position 360.0 of the ebook.

[167] [2359 2617 3360 4008] The last paragraph at https://www.britannica.com/event/Curzon-Line, accessed on Saturday July 25, 2020, explicitly states that Curzon Line was never proposed as a permanent boundary. The Curzon Line, the spawn of the Spa-London-Moscow telegram, was named after the then British Foreign Secretary Lord Curzon, who had in fact, nothing to do with its creation. See pages 169 to 170 of *White Eagle Red Star* or position 358.1 of the ebook.

[168] [4470 4618] *Encyclopaedia Britannica* at https://www.britannica.com/event/Yalta-Conference. For the location of Yalta, see Google Maps at

https://www.google.com/maps/place/Yalta/@44.5017106,34.1251114,13z/data=!3m1!4b1!4m13!1m7!3m6!1s0x4094cfaddbf966fb:0x3349b71a0a56e918!2s Yal-ta+City+Council!3b1!8m2!3d44.495205!4d34.166301!3m4!1s0x4094c9077c8 d204b:0x7c5f808a64d487ae!8m2!3d44.4911175!4d34.1530609. All links accessed on Saturday July 25, 2020.

[169] 2356 3362 4470 4618 The last paragraph at https://www.britannica.com/event/Curzon-Line. Accessed on Saturday July 25, 2020.

[170] Position 1125.6 of *Microcosm*.

[171] 658 963 2356 3023 1 3362 3364 Refer to the publication *The Oder-Neisse line as Poland's western border: As postulated and made a reality*, appearing in the periodical *Geographia Polonica Vol. 88 No. 1 (2015)*, pages 77-105, author Piotr Eberhardt (1935-), published by IGiPZ PAN Warsaw 2015, downloaded from the Digital Repository of Scientific Institutes at http://rcin.org.pl/Content/53298/WA51_72321_r2015-t88-no1_G-Polonica-Eberhardt.pdf. Accessed on Saturday July 25, 2020. On page 20 it documents that the proposed border changes for Poland in 1945, which became a reality in 1946, meaning a territorial loss in Poland's east to the Soviet Union of 180,000 square kilometres. While this was offset somewhat with gained German territories of about 100,000 square kilometres, Poland still lost 80,000 square kilometres of territory overall, and 7 million of its population. On page 26, there is a map illustrating Polish frontiers in 1939 just before the outbreak of war, overlaid with the modified frontiers by 1946. However, it must be said, that the opinion of the author is that Poland still benefited overall due to fact that it inherited areas with much more advanced German infrastructure (Albeit, most of it devastated as the Red Army advanced). The question though, was this worth the resulting mass human suffering, both German and Polish? (See endnotes [188] to [197] in this Preface in regard to the German suffering and endnotes [197] to [220] in regard to the Polish suffering caused by this upheaval of forced mass migration.) On the map on page 26, note the changing sovereignties of Lwów and Breslau/Wrocław. The opening page of this document, in the introduction, states how the post-war Polish frontiers roughly coincided with those at the end of the 10th century. See also the comparative map on page 372 of the book *The Polish Way* by Adam Zamoyski (a friend of Norman Davies), published by John Murray Publishers Limited, 1989, ISBN 10: 0719546745 ISBN 13: 9780719546747. Read also Adam Zamoyski's comments from pages 371 to 372.

[172] Position 1124.1 to 1125.3 of *Microcosm*.

[173] 658 2356 3362 Position 1121.7 of *Microcosm*.

[174] Position 1122.1 of *Microcosm*.

[175] Position 1122.6 of *Microcosm*.

[176] Position 1123.2 of *Microcosm*.

[177] Position 1123.2 of *Microcosm*.

[178] See the article *The Riel Value of Money: How the World's Only Attempt to Abolish Money Has Hindered Cambodia's Economic Development* by Sheridan T. Prasso on the East-West Center website at https://www.eastwestcenter.org/system/tdf/private/api049.pdf?file=1&type=node&id=31779, issue #49, dated January 2001. Accessed on Saturday July 25, 2020.

[179] Position 1123.4 of *Microcosm*. See also page 183 of the book *Rising '44: The Battle for Warsaw*, by Professor Norman Davies, published by Penguin Books; Reprint edition (October 4, 2005), ISBN-10: 0143035401, ISBN-13: 9780143035404. Note the underwhelming figure for the communist *Armia Ludowa* (AL) of 800 in Warsaw in 1943, as compared to the Home Army (AK — *Armia Krajowa*) with 40,330 men!

[180] See for example, pages 105 to 106 of *Warsaw 1920, Lenin's Failed Conquest of Europe* by Adam Zamoyski, paperback published by William Collins 2014, ISBN 9780007225538, documenting the massacre perpetrated by the *konkorpus* (cavalry) of Ghaia Dmitriyevich (born as Gaik Bzhishkian, at Tabriz in Persia in 1887, the eldest son of an exiled Armenian socialist — see page 51) in the picturesque Polish Renaissance town of Płock on August 18 1920.

[181] [3930] See the description for photo #60 after page 220 in *White Eagle Red Star* and position 635.8 in the ebook.

[182] In regard to Katyń, see Polish WWII Supplement III "The Katyń Wood Massacre"[3618] and pages 44, 48, 115 to 116 of Norman Davies' book *Rising '44: The Battle for Warsaw*, published by Penguin Books; Reprint edition (October 4, 2005), ISBN-10: 0143035401, ISBN-13: 9780143035404. On page 48, Davies states that Stalin personally signed the order for their execution. The article at https://library.eb.com.au/levels/adults/article/Katyn-Massacre/44867, states that in all likelihood, over 20,000 were executed. See also the Central Intelligence Agency report online by Benjamin B. Fischer at https://www.cia.gov/library/center-for-the-study-of-intelligence/csi-publications/csi-studies/studies/winter99-00/art6.html. All links accessed on Saturday July 25, 2020.

[183] Position 1123.6 of *Microcosm*.

[184] Position 1123.7 of *Microcosm*.

[185] Page 100 of the publication The Oder-Neisse line as Poland's western border: As postulated and made a reality, appearing in the periodical Geographia Polonica Vol. 88 No. 1 (2015), author Piotr Eberhardt (1935-), published by IGiPZ PAN Warsaw 2015, downloaded from the Digital Repository of Scientific Institutes at http://rcin.org.pl/Content/53298/WA51_72321_r2015-t88-no1_G-Polonica-Eberhardt.pdf. Accessed on Saturday July 25, 2020.

[186] See the comparative map on page 372 of the book *The Polish Way* by Adam Zamoyski, published by John Murray Publishers Limited, 1989, ISBN 10:

0719546745 ISBN 13: 9780719546747. Read also the author's comments from pages 371 to 372.

[187] [215] Page 217 of *Minority Rights and Humanitarianism: The International Campaign for the Ukrainians in Poland, 1930—1931* by Stefan Dyroff in the Journal of Modern European History / Zeitschrift Für Moderne Europäische Geschichte / Revue D'histoire Européenne Contemporaine 12, no. 2 (2014): pages 216-30. It can be viewed online at JSTOR at https://www.jstor.org/stable/26266131. Accessed on Saturday July 25, 2020. During the early 1930s, their were acts of terrorism perpetrated by the Organisation of Ukrainian Nationalists (OUN), with the subsequent retribution of Polish authorities.

[188] See the opening page and page 81 of the publication *The Oder-Neisse line as Poland's western border: As postulated and made a reality*, appearing in the periodical *Geographia Polonica Vol. 88 No. 1 (2015)*, author Piotr Eberhardt (1935-), published by IGiPZ PAN Warsaw 2015, downloaded from the Digital Repository of Scientific Institutes at http://rcin.org.pl/Content/53298/WA51_72321_r2015-t88-no1_G-Polonica-Eberhardt.pdf. Accessed on Saturday July 25, 2020.

[189] Position 1140.7 of *Microcosm*.

[190] [963] [3023] See for example endnotes [1115] to [1120] of Chapter 16 "Homecoming to Outbreak of War."

[191] See for example endnotes [3950] to [3955] of Polish WWII Supplement III "The Katyń Wood Massacre" and endnote [3443] of Polish WWII Supplement I "The Molotov-Ribbentrop Pact."

[192] Position 1150.4 of *Microcosm*.

[193] Position 1151.7 of *Microcosm*.

[194] Position 1152.1 of *Microcosm*.

[195] Page 383 in the Epilogue of Jane Pejsa. This will be covered in detail in Chapter 25 "Old Prussia Gone With The Wind."

[196] Position 1152.5 of *Microcosm*.

[197] [658] [2356] [3362] Position 1161.2 of *Microcosm*.

[198] Position 1164.1 of *Microcosm*.

[199] Page 35 of *White Eagle Red Star* and position 58.0 of the ebook.

[200] Page 35 of *White Eagle Red Star* and position 58.2 of the ebook.

[201] Page 35 of *White Eagle Red Star* and position 58.7 of the ebook.

[202] [3024] Page 35 of *White Eagle Red Star* and position 57.8 of the ebook.

[203] Pages 345-346 from the book *God's Playground A History of Poland: Volume 1: The Origins to 1795* by Norman Davies, published by Oxford University Press, ISBN 0199253390, 9780199253395, documents the 1610 to 1612 Polish occupation of Moscow. It states the Polish garrison surrendered on the October 22 1612, but this was according to the Old Julian Calendar used in Russia. This was on November 4 1612 according to the modern Gregorian calendar.

²⁰⁴ ^{206 958 980 1377 2528 3367 3932 4054 4121 4129 4570} Page 22 of the book *The Polish Underground 1939-1947 Campaign chronicle*, by David G Williamson, Published by Pen and Sword, 2012, ISBN 1848842813, 9781848842816, states that 1.7 million Poles were deported to Siberia by the Soviets. As does page 348 of K.O.R. (Oakland Project Series Issue 1 of Studies in society and culture in East-Central Europe), by Jan Józef Lipski, published by University of California Press, 1985, ISBN 0520052439, 9780520052437 and page 123 of *The Secret Army: The Memoirs of General Bor-Komorowski* by Tadeusz Bor-komorowski, published by Frontline Books, 2011, ISBN 1848325959, 9781848325951. See also the film *A forgotten Odyssey* written and directed by Jagna Wright née Rafp; produced by Jagna Wright née Rafp, Aneta Naszyńska, narrated by Stephen Wright, released 1990. The VHS can be purchased from TROVE National Library of Australia at https://trove.nla.gov.au/work/28569419?q&versionId=34730839. See also the Kresy Memorial website at http://kresy-siberia.org/hom/files/9/Jagna_Memorial.pdf honouring Jagna Wright née Rafp the producer, writer and director of this film. The funding partners for Kresy include the Polish Ministry of Foreign Affairs can be viewed at http://kresy-siberia.org/museum/en/support/funding-partners/. All links accessed on Saturday July 25, 2020. See also page 107 of the book *No Greater Ally, The Untold Story of Poland's Forces in World War II* by Kenneth K. Koskodan, published by Osprey Publishing 2011, ISBN-13: 9781849084796. It states that 0.25 million military personnel were imprisoned by Poland's future "Liberators" but that up to as many as 1.5 million more civilians were imprisoned. Read on until page 120 for further information on the way Poles were treated by their future "Liberators." See also pages 26 to 28 and page 372 of *The Murderers of Katyń* by Vladimir Abarinov published by Hippocrene Books, 1993 ISBN 0781800323, 9780781800327 while page 387 of the book *Lenin, Stalin and Hitler* by Robert Gellately, published by Vintage 2008, ISBN 9780712603577, gives figures ranging from 760,000 to 1.25 million and higher. On page 644, Robert Gellately in note #10 for Chapter 25 "The Soviet Response" states that the lower number is given for three deportations by Józef Garliński in his book *Poland in the Second World War (London, 1985)* on pages 36 to 37, while the higher number is given by Gross in his book *Revolution from Abroad* on page 194. This is because Gross adds the deportation that took place in June 1941 — the month when Hitler launched Operation Barbarossa — his invasion of the Soviet Union. See page 429 of Gellately's book.

²⁰⁵ Position 1161.6 of *Microcosm*.

²⁰⁶ ³⁹³³ See the film *A forgotten Odyssey* written and directed by Jagna Wright née Rafp; produced by Jagna Wright née Rafp, Aneta Naszyńska, narrated by Stephen Wright, released 1990, as stated in the recent endnote.²⁰⁴

²⁰⁷ In regard to Katyń, see Polish WWII Supplement III "The Katyń Wood Massacre."³⁶¹⁸

[208] Position 1162.4 of *Microcosm*.

[209] Position 1162.5 of *Microcosm*.

[210] See Polish WWII Supplement I "The Molotov-Ribbentrop Pact."[3268]

[211] Position 1046.8 of *Microcosm*.

[212] Position 1162.8 of *Microcosm*.

[213] Position 1163.5 of *Microcosm*.

[214] [3024] Position 1163.2 of *Microcosm*.

[215] In regard to the ethnic violence in the inter-war Second Polish Republic, see endnote [187] for this Preface.

[216] Position 1163.5 of *Microcosm*.

[217] Position 1163.7 of *Microcosm*.

[218] Position 1164.4 of *Microcosm*.

[219] Position 1164.8 of *Microcosm*.

[220] [658 2356 2357 2358 1 2616 2617 3362] Position 1198.9 of *Microcosm*.

[221] Position 1270.4 of *Microcosm*.

[222] [3375] The *Encyclopaedia Britannica* article on Bolesław Bierut at https://www.britannica.com/biography/Boleslaw-Bierut, the "Stalin" of Poland, accessed on Saturday July 25, 2020, gives the date of his death being March 12 1956 in Moscow.

[223] Position 1244.4 of *Microcosm*. Position 1243.5 onwards describes Poland's infamous Stalinist period from 1949-1956.

[224] Position 1249.8 of *Microcosm*.

[225] Position 1249.9 of *Microcosm*.

[226] Position 1198.7 of *Microcosm*.

[227] See page 387 in the Epilogue of Jane Pejsa and the end of Chapter 26 "Oma Ruth's Progeny After Death" in regard to the cemetery post-war at Kieckow (now Polish Kikowo).

[228] Position 1172.4 of *Microcosm*.

[229] Position 1245.6 and 1220.6 of *Microcosm*. The latter describes conditions in 1946.

[230] Position 1243.5 onwards describes the Stalinist period from 1949-1956.

[231] See the online *Encyclopaedia Britannica* article on Bolesław Bierut at https://www.britannica.com/biography/Boleslaw-Bierut, accessed on Saturday July 25, 2020. It states that Bierut was "Always a loyal follower of party directives from Moscow."

[232] Position 1276.3 to 1277.1 of *Microcosm*.

[233] See endnote [4262] for Polish WWII Supplement IV "AK and 1944 Warsaw General Uprising — Stalin's mass murder by German proxy."

[234] See the photos and description on page 403 of the book *Uprooted: How Breslau Became Wroclaw during the Century of Expulsions* by Gregor Thum, published by Princeton University Press, 2011, ISBN 1400839963, 9781400839964.

[235] See the last page before the contents in Jane Pejsa. It reads; *"This book is dedicated to men and women in every age and place who have acted to uphold decency and honor amid indecency and dishonor, and especially to those who, in so doing, have perished."*

Chapter 1 - Roots, Genesis and Moulding of the Pastor

[236] Position 35.5 in the ebook *Bonhoeffer: Pastor, Martyr, Prophet, Spy A righteous Gentile vs, the Third Reich,* by Eric Metaxas, published by Thomas Nelson Nashville Tennessee, 2010, ISBN 9781595551382, 9781595553188(IE), 9781595552464(TP).

[237] Position 52.9 of the ebook *Dietrich Bonhoeffer 1906-1945: Martyr, Thinker, Man of Resistance* by Ferdinand Schlingensiepen, translated by Isabel Best, first published in 2010 by Continuum, but since 2011, Bloomsbury T&T Clark, ePub-ISBN 9780567217554, ePDF-ISBN 9780567357755.

[238] Position 1100.0 in "Appendix 6: Bonhoeffer Family Tree" of Schlingensiepen.

[239] Position 45.3 of Schlingensiepen.

[240] Position 45.4 of Schlingensiepen.

[241] Position 45.6 of Schlingensiepen

[242] Position 77.4 of Schlingensiepen.

[243] Position 65.2 of Schlingensiepen.

[244] Position 71.8 of Schlingensiepen.

[245] Google Book review at https://books.google.com.au/books?id=fjBtDwAAQBAJ&dq, of the book *The Scientific World of Karl-Friedrich Bonhoeffer* — Palgrave studies in the history of science and technology, by Kathleen L. Housley, published by Springer, 2018, ISBN 3319958011, 9783319958019 accessed on Saturday July 25, 2020.

[246] Page 36 of *Dietrich Bonhoeffer: A Biography* by Eberhard Bethge, edited by Victoria J. Barnett, published by Fortress Press, 2000, ISBN 0800628446, 9780800628444.

[247] Page 28 of Bethge.

[248] Position 79.0 of Schlingensiepen.

[249] Position 905.3 of the ebook *Microcosm: A Portrait of a Central European City,* by Norman Davies and Roger Moorhouse, published by Jonathan Cape 2002, Epub ISBN 9781448114085.

[250] Pages 33 and 34 of Bethge's biography of Dietrich.

[251] Page 34 of Bethge's biography of Dietrich.

[252] Page 33 of Bethge's biography of Dietrich.

[253] 3207 Oma is the German diminutive of grandmother and it will not be the last time it is used in this book.

254 3208 Page 30 of Bethge's biography of Dietrich. See also endnotes 77, 78 and 79 for the Preface "Birth and Memory upon the Lesser Known Fault Line of History."

255 Position 85.2 of Schlingensiepen.

256 The *About Catholics* and *Merriam-Webster dictionary* web sites at http://www.aboutcatholics.com/beliefs/meaning-of-the-term-catholic/ and http://www.merriam-webster.com/dictionary/catholic, concerning the meaning of "Catholic." Both links accessed on Saturday July 25, 2020.

257 Position 95.9 of Schlingensiepen.

258 *Encyclopaedia Britannica* at https://library.eb.com.au/levels/adults/article/Martin-Luther/108504 and the Martin Luther portal on the Christ and the Church websites at http://martinluther.ccws.org/journey/index.html. Both links accessed on Saturday July 25, 2020.

259 *Encyclopaedia Britannica* on indulgences at https://www.britannica.com/topic/indulgence#ref176957. Accessed on Saturday July 25, 2020.

260 Position 93.0 of Schlingensiepen.

261 Position 107.1 of Schlingensiepen.

262 2939 Position 178.0 of Metaxas and page 3 of the book *Authentic Faith: Bonhoeffer's Theological Ethics in Context* by Heinz Eduard Todt, published by Wm. B. Eerdmans Publishing, 2007, ISBN 0802803822, 9780802803825.

263 2962 Position 154.0 of Metaxas.

264 2962 The *Internationale Bonhoeffer-Gesellschaft (IBG), Deutschsprachige Sektion* (*International Bonhoeffer Society IBG*), at https://www.dietrich-bonhoeffer.net/bonhoeffer-umfeld/gerhard-leibholz/ details the life of Gerhard Leibholz in German. Documented, is their permanent return to Germany in 1947. Link accessed on Saturday July 25, 2020.

265 Position 131.0-172.9 in Schlingensiepen describes how Bonhoeffer arrived at the decision to become a pastor's assistant in Barcelona, and his time there.

266 Position 140.0 of Schlingensiepen and position 199.3 of Metaxas. Also pages 77 and 123 of the book *Barcelona, Berlin, New York, 1928-1931, Volume 10 of Dietrich Bonhoeffer Works*, by Dietrich Bonhoeffer, editor Clifford J. Green, translated by Douglas W. Stott, published by Fortress Press, 2008, ISBN 0800683307, 9780800683306.

267 Position 197.3 of Metaxas.

268 Position 187.3 of Metaxas.

269 Position 191.7 of Metaxas and page 100 of Bethge.

270 Position 150.1 of Schlingensiepen. Position 1087.0 documents his time in Barcelona as a pastoral assistant from February 1928 to February 1929. Position 907.7 of *Microcosm* gives the approximate time of the Wall Street crash in October 1929.

271 Position 151.5 of Schlingensiepen.

272 Page 26 of Bethge.

273 Position 154.9 of Schlingensiepen.

274 The timeline from position 1087.0 of Schlingensiepen.

275 2938 Page 138 of Bethge and position 226.0 of Metaxas.

276 Page 138 of Bethge.

277 1279 See page 150 of Bethge, position 1380.3 of Metaxas in the Reading Group Guide for Chapters 7 to 9 and the timeline for Dietrich Bonhoeffer on the *US Public Broadcasting* web site at http://www.pbs.org/bonhoeffer/timeline.html. Accessed on Saturday July 25, 2020.

278 Timeline for Dietrich Bonhoeffer on the *US Public Broadcasting* web site at http://www.pbs.org/bonhoeffer/timeline.html, positions 265.8 and position 1380.1 of Metaxas, and page 150 of Bethge. Accessed on Saturday July 25, 2020.

279 Official *American Civil War Trust* website at http://www.civilwar.org/battlefields/appomattox-courthouse.html. Accessed on Saturday July 25, 2020.

280 Position 263.4 of Metaxas.

281 Position 264.0 of Metaxas.

282 Position 264.0 of Metaxas and page 150 of Bethge.

283 A perfect case in point being Poland's deep and resilient Catholic faith, withstanding centuries of oppression in both its distant and not so distant history. In Radom for example, where I taught English for 10 months from early September 2004 to late June 2005, churches in this city of 300,000, about 90Km south of Warsaw, would hold about seven services a day, with nearly all, filled at least to near capacity.

284 The online article at https://ous.wisc.edu/2016/02/04/the-search-for-truth/, dated the 4th of February 2016 entitled *The Search for Truth* on the University of Wisconsin website. Accessed on Saturday July 25, 2020. Also positions 259.5 and 265.2 of Metaxas.

285 Pages 202 to 203 of Bethge.

286 Position 246.8 of Metaxas. See also page 157 of Bethge which states how Dietrich was forever irritated by the American lack of concern for the genuine problems of theology.

287 Page 94 of *The Scientific World of Karl-Friedrich Bonhoeffer — Palgrave studies in the history of science and technology*, by Kathleen L. Housley, published by Springer, 2018, ISBN 3319958011, 9783319958019. See also position 267.5 of Metaxas.

288 Page 96 of Kathleen L. Housley, page 151 of Bethge, and a condensed text at position 268.9 of Metaxas.

289 Page 96 of Kathleen L. Housley, page 151 of Bethge, and a condensed text at position 268.9 of Metaxas.

290 Position 269.2 of Metaxas.

[291] The website of the *Journal of the Abraham Lincoln Association* at https://quod.lib.umich.edu/j/jala/2629860.0013.104?view=text;rgn=main. Accessed on Saturday July 25, 2020.

[292] Article entitled *Slavery and Emancipation in the Nation's Capital* by Damani Davis in the Spring 2010, Volume 42, No 1 issue of Prologue Magazine. It can be viewed online on the website of the *US National Archives* at https://www.archives.gov/publications/prologue/2010/spring/dcslavery.html. Accessed on Saturday July 25, 2020.

[293] *Encyclopaedia Britannica* at https://www.britannica.com/science/physical-chemistry. Accessed on Saturday July 25, 2020.

[294] Review of Kathleen L. Housley's book on *Google Books* at https://books.google.com.au/books?id=fjBtDwAAQBAJ&dq. Accessed on Saturday July 25, 2020.

[295] Position 278.1 of Metaxas and pages 190 to 191 of *Understanding Bonhoeffer* by Peter Frick, published by Mohr Siebeck, 2017, ISBN 3161547233, 9783161547232.

[296] Position 284.9 of Metaxas.

[297] Page 152 of Bethge.

[298] See position 279.5 of Metaxas.

Chapter 2 - Ominous Clouds on the Horizon

[299] [2927] Postion 287.0 of Metaxas. The dates of the birth and death of Karl Barth in Basel Switzerland are given at https://www.britannica.com/biography/Karl-Barth.

[300] [724] [3424] Positions 906.9 and 911.1 of *Microcosm*.

[301] [724] Position 290.3 onwards of Metaxas and page 404 of *A testament to freedom: the essential writings of Dietrich Bonhoeffer* by Dietrich Bonhoeffer, edited by Geffrey B. Kelly and F. Burton, published by HarperSanFrancisco, 1990, ISBN 0060608137, 9780060608132.

[302] [2927] [3424] Position 290.8 of Metaxas.

[303] Pages 221-222 of Bethge and page 209 of *What Will A Man Give In Exchange For His Soul?* by George D. Johnson, published by Xlibris Corporation, 2011, ISBN 1465380981, 9781465380982.

[304] Page 214 of *The Cross of Reality: Luther's Theologia Crucis and Bonhoeffer's Christology* by H. Gaylon Barker, published by Fortress Press, 2015, ISBN 1506400493, 9781506400495.

[305] Position 292.0 of Metaxas.

[306] Position 291.7 of Metaxas.

[307] Position 292.4 of Metaxas.

[308] Position 914.3 of *Microcosm* documents Breslau's spiralling violence in the summer of 1932. This was documented in *The Times* (London), of June 24, June 27, August 4 and August 8 1932.

309 Position 293.7 of Metaxas.

310 Position 141.3 of Metaxas.

311 Position 1088.1 of Schlingensiepen.

312 2771 2806 xxxiii 4524 lxvi For information on this famous battle from antiquity, see the article on the Smithsonian Institute website at http://www.smithsonianmag.com/history/the-ambush-that-changed-history-72636736/. This article also mentions Peter S. Wells book *The Battle that Stopped Rome: Emperor Augustus, Arminius, and the Slaughter of the Legions in the Teutoburg Forest* published by W.W. Norton 2004, ISBN 0393326438, 9780393326437.

313 2771 2809 xxxiii 4524 lxvi Page 21 of *Preaching in Hitler's Shadow: Sermons of Resistance in the Third Reich* by Dean G. Stroud, published by Wm. B. Eerdmans Publishing, 2013, ISBN 0802869025, 9780802869029.

314 2770 2804 Page 22 of Dean G. Stroud.

315 327 2770 2804 Page 22 of Dean G. Stroud.

316 Page 23 of Dean G. Stroud.

317 Pages 177 to 178 of Bethge.

Chapter 3 - Evil's Storm Descends

318 The make-up of Hitler's first cabinet in late January 1933, is given on page 3 of the New York newspaper *The Jewish Daily Bulletin* dated Tuesday the 31st of January 1933. It can be downloaded from the website of the Jewish Telegraphic Agency at http://pdfs.jta.org/1933/1933-01-31_2464.pdf?_ga=2.168216929.1504613013.1533967459-202169450.1533967459. Only four out of eleven were Nazis, namely Hitler himself, Hermann Göring, Franz Seldte and Wilhelm Frick. See also http://www.iiipublishing.com/blog/2018/04/hitler_cabinet.html, the blog of American writer and activist, William P. Meyers. Both links accessed on Saturday July 25, 2020.

319 Position 330.0 of Metaxas. See also position 331.5 of Schlingensiepen and source note #32 on page 280 of *Berlin: 1932-1933: Dietrich Bonhoeffer Works, Volume 12* of Dietrich Bonhoeffer Works Series, by Dietrich Bonhoeffer, edited by Larry L. Rasmussen, translated by Isabel Best, David Warren Simons Higgins, published by Fortress Press, 2009, ISBN 1451406657, 9781451406658. The most latter source states exactly when the speech was cut-off. See also position 331.7 of Schlingensiepen.

320 Position 332.3 of Metaxas.

321 Position 334.3 of Metaxas.

322 Position 334.5 of Metaxas.

323 Position 336.2 of Metaxas.

324 Position 336.4 of Metaxas.

325 Position 332.8 of Metaxas.

[326] Position 340.0 of Metaxas.

[327] See endnote [315] for Chapter 2 "Ominous Clouds on the Horizon."

[328] The three quotes from Hitler's speech made after barely 48 hours in power, can be found from position 340.9 of Metaxas and pages 115 to 116 of *The Holy Reich: Nazi Conceptions of Christianity, 1919—1945* by Richard Steigmann-Gall, published by Cambridge University Press, 2003, ISBN 1107393922, 9781107393929. While the latter source does not make any contention against Hitler making this speech, it contends that Hitler was making this speech as an impassioned and devout Catholic, rather than as a pragmatic and cynical politician. However, in an online review of Steigmann-Gall's book by John S. Conway from the Department of History, University of British Columbia on the website of the *Humanities and Social Sciences* at https://www.h-net.org/reviews/showrev.php?id=7658, dated June 2003, the late Conway logically de-constructs this notion. Accessed on Saturday July 25, 2020. See also position 332.7 onwards of Schlingensiepen, where the author alludes to the fact that too many people were seduced by such language, and as such, failed to hear or discern the speech's false undertones.

[329] Position 341.5 of Metaxas.

[330] [3072] [3098] Page 85 of *Burning the Reichstag: An Investigation Into the Third Reich's Enduring Mystery* by Benjamin Carter Hett, published by OUP USA, 2014, ISBN 0199322325, 9780199322329.

[331] [1608] [2059] Page 193 of *Rise And Fall Of The Third Reich: A History of Nazi Germany* by William L. Shirer, published by Simon and Schuster, 1990, ISBN 0671728687, 9780671728687. Hitler was born on April 20, 1889 in Braunau am Inn, Austria, near the border with the German state of Bavaria. See the article on Hitler at https://www.britannica.com/biography/Adolf-Hitler. Accessed on Saturday August 8, 2020.

[332] [3073] Position 349.8 of Metaxas and pages 191 to 192 William L. Shirer.

[333] Position 350.8 to 353.4 of Metaxas and pages 264-265 of Bethge.

[334] Hans von Dohnányi was born in Vienna on the January 1 1902 as the son of the Hungarian pianist and conductor Ernö von Dohnányi and the pianist Elisabeth von Dohnányi (née Kunwald). Upon the separation of his parents in 1913, he grew up in Berlin, where he attended the liberal Grunewald Gymnasium, from which blossomed, his friendship with Dietrich and Klaus Bonhoeffer. See the timeline in German on the website of the *German Historical Museum (Deutsches Historisches Museum)* at https://www.dhm.de/lemo/biografie/hans-dohnanyi. Accessed on Saturday July 25, 2020.

[335] Page 142 of Benjamin Carter Hett and the online article from the *Monthly Review* website, an independent American socialist magazine, by Michael E. Tigar and John Mage at http://monthlyreview.org/2009/03/01/the-reichstag-fire-trial-1933-2008-the-production-of-law-and-history/. Accessed on Saturday July 25, 2020.

336 3342 Page 22 of *The Forming of the Communist International* by James W. Hulse, published by Stanford University Press, 1964, ISBN 0804701768, 9780804701761, quotes the manifesto of the Comintern from its First Congress in March 1919.

337 Page 193 of William L. Shirer, states that Ernst Torgler, the parliamentary leader of the communists, gave himself up the day after the fire, due to the fact that he heard that Göring had implicated him.

338 3342 Pages 91-93 of the book *Biographical Dictionary of the Comintern, Volume 340 of Hoover Institution publication*, published by Hoover Press, 1986, ISBN 0817984038, 9780817984038, gives a brief biography of Georgi Dimitrov. Pages 92-93 include his appointment as the director of the West European Bureau of the Comintern in 1929, and his subsequent settlement in Berlin under the assumed identity of Doctor Hediger. Page 93 gives the date of his arrest as the March 9 1933, while page 459 states likewise for Vasil Tanev, and page 371 for Simon Popov.

339 Position 351.4 of Metaxas and page 265 of Bethge.

340 Position 351.9 of Metaxas.

341 Pages 108-109 of *The Reichstag Fire* by Fritz Tobias, with an Introduction by A. J. P. Taylor, first American edition 1964, English translation 1963 by Martin Secker & Warburg Limited, first published in Germany under the title Der Reichstagsbrand, by G. Grotesche Verlagsbuchhandlung.

342 Page 169 of William L. Shirer.

343 Position 355.8 of Metaxas.

344 Page 45 of *In the Name of the Volk: Political Justice in Hitler's Germany* by H. W. Koch, published by I.B.Tauris, 1997, ISBN 1860641741, 9781860641749, documents the Nazi cabinet meeting of the March 23 1934 and the subsequent official founding of the *Volksgerichtshof* (People's" Court) one month later.

345 Ibid.

346 Pages 45 to 46 of *In the Name of the Volk: Political Justice in Hitler's Germany*.

347 4340 3264 3202 Position 356.8 of Metaxas. See also pages 265 to 266 of Bethge.

348 Position 921.1 of *Microcosm*.

349 Page 266 of Bethge. In the line after, Bethge states that the National Socialists only secured 44% of the national vote. This agrees closely with the figure of 43.2% given at position 921.1 in *Microcosm*.

350 3033 3076 3099 Page 11 of the book *Berlin: 1932-1933: Dietrich Bonhoeffer Works, Volume 12* by Dietrich Bonhoeffer, edited by Larry L. Rasmussen, translated by Isabel Best, David Warren Simons Higgins, published by Fortress Press, 2009, ISBN 1451406657, 9781451406658.

351 4340 3034 3099 Position 357.0 of Metaxas.

352 3264 3202 Pages 266 to 267 of Bethge.

[353] Position 358.0 of Metaxas. Postition 341.0 of Schlingensiepen states that it was passed in the Reichstag on April 1933, but Metaxas states that it came into effect days later on April 7.

[354] [2941] Page 273 of Bethge and position 359.1 of Metaxas.

[355] Position 361.5 of Metaxas.

[356] Position 360.5 of Metaxas.

[357] Position 369.0 of Metaxas. See also the Bible Gateway website at https://www.biblegateway.com/passage/?search=Galatians+3%3A28&version =NLT.Accessed on Saturday July 25, 2020.

[358] Position 366.8 of Metaxas and page 275 of Bethge.

[359] Position 373.6 of Metaxas, position 61.9 of Schlingensiepen and page 11 of Bethge.

[360] Position 372.8 Metaxas and page 80 of *The Other Victims: First-Person Stories of Non-Jews Persecuted by the Nazis* by Ina R. Friedman, published by Houghton Mifflin Harcourt, 1990, ISBN 0395745152, 9780395745151.

[361] Position 372.9 Metaxas and see the photo on page 534 of *History of World War II* by the Marshall Cavendish Corporation, published by Marshall Cavendish, 2004, ISBN 076147482X, 9780761474821.

[362] Position 374.0 Metaxas.

[363] Position 374.7 onwards of Metaxas documents the German Christian's conference and the visit by Paul and Marion Lehmann at the same time. Page 268 of Bethge also mentions the visit by the Lehmanns, but makes no mention of George Bell's presence in Berlin at the same time, which was erroneously attested to at position 376.8 of Metaxas.

[364] Position 376.6 of Metaxas.

[365] Position 378.1 of Metaxas and page 367 of Bethge.

[366] Position 379.8 to 385.2 of Metaxas and pages 275 to 276 of Bethge.

[367] [3100] Position 381.4 of Metaxas.

[368] [3101] Position 381.4 of Metaxas. See also position 350.5 of Schlingensiepen.

[369] Positions 375.5 and 385.9 of Metaxas.

[370] [3113] Position 389.5 of Metaxas. See also the article on the United States Holocaust Memorial Museum website at https://www.ushmm.org/exhibition/book-burning/burning.php in regard to the book burning in general. Accessed on Saturday July 25, 2020.

[371] Page 21 of *Preaching in Hitler's Shadow: Sermons of Resistance in the Third Reich* by Dean G. Stroud

[372] Position 424.6 of Metaxas.

[373] Position 426.7 to 428.0 of Metxas. Also, position 372.1 of Schlingensiepen and page 295 of Bethge document the name of Rudolf Diels for the Gestapo Chief.

[374] See *The Third Reich in Power, 1933 - 1939: How the Nazis Won Over the Hearts and Minds of a Nation by Richard J. Evans*, published by Penguin UK, 2012, ISBN 0718196813, 9780718196813. Accessed on Saturday February 27, 2021.

[375] Page 258 of *Leaders and Personalities of the Third Reich: Their Biographies, Portraits, and Autographs* by Charles Hamilton, published by R. James Bender Publishing, 1984, ISBN 0912138270, 9780912138275.

[376] Position 427.4 of Metaxas.

[377] Position 428.4 of Metaxas, page 291 of Bethge and position 370.6 of Schlingensiepen.

[378] Position 430.3 of Metaxas, position 372.9 of Schlingensiepen and page 297 of Bethge.

[379] [3060] [3064] [3068] [3225] [3244] Article in the UK Guardian by Harriet Sherwood, dated Saturday September 22, 2018 at https://www.theguardian.com/world/2018/sep/22/vatican-pope-francis-agreement-with-china-nominating-bishops. Accessed Monday August 3, 2020.

[380] Article by Michael Sainsbury, dated September 24, 2018, on the website of the *National Catholic Reporter* at https://www.ncronline.org/news/opinion/vaticans-deal-china and article in the UK Guardian by Harriet Sherwood, dated Saturday September 22, 2018 at https://www.theguardian.com/world/2018/sep/22/vatican-pope-francis-agreement-with-china-nominating-bishops. Both accessed Monday August 3, 2020.

[381] https://www.theguardian.com/world/2018/sep/22/vatican-pope-francis-agreement-with-china-nominating-bishops and https://www.ncronline.org/news/opinion/vaticans-deal-china. Both accessed Monday August 3, 2020.

[382] https://www.ncronline.org/news/opinion/vaticans-deal-china. Accessed Monday August 3, 2020.

[383] https://www.theguardian.com/world/2018/sep/22/vatican-pope-francis-agreement-with-china-nominating-bishops. Accessed Monday August 3, 2020.

[384] https://www.theguardian.com/world/2018/sep/22/vatican-pope-francis-agreement-with-china-nominating-bishops. Accessed Monday August 3, 2020.

[385] https://www.theguardian.com/world/2018/sep/22/vatican-pope-francis-agreement-with-china-nominating-bishops and the article in the Chinese Communist Party's English language mouthpiece the *Global Times*, dated November 28, 2017, by Liu Caiyu at http://www.globaltimes.cn/content/1077696.shtml. Both links accessed Tuesday August 4, 2020.

[386] [694] https://www.ncronline.org/news/opinion/vaticans-deal-china.

[387] Interview of Drew Pavlou conducted by the YouTube channel *China Unscripted* at https://www.youtube.com/watch?v=_o1sZefER0E, from 27 minutes in. It was uploaded on May 18, 2020.

388 The Sixty Minutes story aired on Channel 9 in Brisbane Queensland Australia on Sunday night July 19, 2020 from 18 minutes in. It can be viewed on YouTube at https://www.youtube.com/watch?v=OyLO9-riykU.

389 Ibid.

390 694 3200 Page 150 of *The China Tribunal Judgment* released on March 1, 2020, chaired by Sir Geoffrey Nice QC. It can downloaded from *The China Tribunal* website at https://chinatribunal.com/wp-content/uploads/2020/03/ChinaTribunal_JUDGMENT_1stMarch_2020.pdf. Accessed Monday August 3, 2020.

391 Ibid. This is discussed repeatedly in this document.

392 3201 Article on the *Australian Broadcasting Commission* website titled *China imposes forced abortion, sterilisation on Uyghurs, investigation shows*, posted Tuesday June 30, 2020 at 1:42p.m at https://www.abc.net.au/news/2020-06-30/china-forces-birth-control-on-uyghurs-to-suppress-population/12404912. Accessed Monday August 3, 2020.

393 https://www.theguardian.com/world/2018/sep/22/vatican-pope-francis-agreement-with-china-nominating-bishops. Accessed Monday August 3, 2020.

394 Article by Elise Ann Allen on the *Crux Now* Catholic website at https://cruxnow.com/vatican/2020/06/vatican-agreement-with-china-likely-to-be-renewed-archbishop-says/ dated June 8, 2020. Accessed Monday August 3, 2020.

395 3060 3064 3068 3225 3244 The Reuter's News Agency article dated July 29, 2020 at https://www.reuters.com/article/us-china-vatican-cyber/u-s-cybersecurity-firm-says-beijing-linked-hackers-target-vatican-ahead-of-talks-idUSKCN24U0PC and the article on the British Columbia Catholic website, dated July 30, 2020 at https://bccatholic.ca/news/world/the-holy-see-and-beijing-vatican-s-computers-reportedly-hacked. Both links accessed on Wednesday August 5, 2020.

396 2941 Position 432.0 of Metaxas and pages 298 to 299 of Bethge.

397 Implied on page 299 of Bethge.

398 Position 432.0 of Metaxas

399 2941 Position 418.9 of Metaxas documents the ordination of Franz Hildebrandt on the June 18 1933. Position 422.5 states the resignation of Bishop Friedrich von Bodelschwingh later that same month, while from position 432.0, his Bethel community in Biesenthal is given a brief history starting with its founding by his father in the 1860s.

400 Position 433.8 of Metaxas.

401 Position 930.8 onwards of *Microcosm* documents the heinous "T-4 Aktion."

402 Schlingensiepen states that the vast majority of church social service institutions did by then, cave in to Nazi pressure to surrender those deemed by the regime to be "unfit for life." In regard to patients at other institutions in 1940 being "saved" from death by gassing, only to still die from lethal injection or being left to die by starvation, see note #20 of Chapter 10 "In the Resistance

(1939—1943)" of Schlingensiepen at position 1039.1 — which is linked to note #20 at position 687.7. This is a testament to Bethel being an oasis of peace and the very best of German Christian culture. Schlingensiepen, in an online article writes on the official Bonhoeffer Center website at http://thebonhoeffercenter.org/index.php?option=com_content&view=article&id=37:schlingensiepen-on-metaxas-and-marsh: "Bethel was the only institution of its kind that did not become part of this programme. Not one of its patients was murdered." In this article, Schlingensiepen, while critical on some grounds of Metaxas, including Metaxas erroneously asserting that Bethel ultimatley caved into Nazi pressure, he is absolutely scathing in regard to the book by Charles Marsh on Dietrich Bonhoeffer. Given his friendship with Eberhard Bethge for over fifty years, this article carries a great deal of weight. Accessed on Saturday July 25, 2020.

[403] Page 298 of Bethge and position 377.2 of Schlingensiepen.

[404] Position 437.2 of Metaxas, position 382.0 of Schlingensiepen and pages 302 and 325 of Bethge.

[405] [2941] Position 370.3 of Schlingensiepen

[406] The timeline given on the website of the Saint Stephen Presbyterian Church in Fort Worth Texas at https://ststephenpresbyterian.com/timeline-bonhoeffer-and-church-based-attempts-to-resist-hitler-1933-39/, accessed on Saturday August 15, 2020 and page 256 of the book *Approaches to Auschwitz: The Holocaust and Its Legacy* by Richard L. Rubenstein and John K. Roth, published by Westminster John Knox Press, 2003, ISBN 0664223532, 9780664223533.

[407] [2941] Position 441.0 of Metaxas and page 256 of the book *Approaches to Auschwitz: The Holocaust and Its Legacy* by Richard L. Rubenstein and John K. Roth, published by Westminster John Knox Press, 2003, ISBN 0664223532, 9780664223533. See also https://ststephenpresbyterian.com/timeline-bonhoeffer-and-church-based-attempts-to-resist-hitler-1933-39/, accessed on Saturday August 15, 2020.

[408] Position 441.6 of Metaxas.

[409] [2746] [2941] Position 443.1 of Metaxas and page 309 of Bethge.

[410] [2941] Position 416.0 of Metaxas.

[411] Position 416.0 of Metaxas and page 78 of *I was in Hell with Niemoeller* by Leo Stein, published by Fleming H. Revell Company, 1942, (no ISBN given). It can be viewed on Google Books at https://books.google.com.au/books?redir_esc=y&id=y34cAAAAMAAJ&focus=searchwithinvolume&q=1932. Accessed on Saturday July 25, 2020.

[412] Position 443.0 of Metaxas and pages 304 and 311 of Bethge.

[413] [2951] Section II "The Story" of Chapter 2 "A Story of Friendship: Bell and Bonhoeffer" in the book *Politics in Friendship: A Theological Account, T & T Clark theology* by Guido de Graaff, published by Bloomsbury Publishing, 2014, ISBN 0567655628, 9780567655622 and on Goolge Books at https://books.google.com.au/books?id=D0uCBAAAQBAJ&pg=PT236&dq=IS

BN+0567655628,+9780567655622&hl=en&sa=X&ved=0ahUKEwi7xf3flKX
bAhXFEbwKHfKEDsAQ6AEIKTAA#v=onepage&q=Novi%20Sad&f=false.
Accessed on Saturday July 25, 2020.

[414] [2951] Position 445.9 of Metaxas.

[415] See the timeline given on page 41 of the book *Brethren in Adversity: Bishop George Bell, the Church of England and the Crisis of German Protestantism, 1933-1939* by George Kennedy Allen Bell, edited by Andrew Chandler, published by Boydell Press, 1997, ISBN 0851156924, 9780851156927

[416] Page 47 of the book *George Bell, Bishop of Chichester: Church, State, and Resistance in the Age of Dictatorship* by Andrew Chandler, published by Wm. B. Eerdmans Publishing, 2016, ISBN 0802872271, 9780802872272.

[417] Page 47 of Andrew Chandler.

[418] Page 51 of Andrew Chandler.

[419] The Martin Luther portal on the Christ and the Church websites at http://martinluther.ccws.org/theses/index.html and https://www.britannica.com/event/Ninety-five-Theses. Accessed on Saturday July 25, 2020.

[420] [2941] Page 68 of *Dietrich Bonhoeffer: A Life in Pictures*, editors Renate Bethge (wife of Eberhard) and Christian Gremmels, translated by Brian McNeil, published by Fortress Press, ISBN 1451416563, 9781451416565. This also gives an account of the conferences at Novi Sad and Sofia in September 1933.

[421] [2941] Page 355 of Bethge which contradicts Metaxas at position 449.5, which claims it was in Magdeburg Cathedral.

[422] [2948] Position 382.0 of Schlingensiepen, pages 302 and 325 of Bethge and position 437.9 of Metaxas.

[423] Position 450.9 of Metaxas. See also position 399.0 of Schlingensiepen.

[424] Position 452.2 of Metaxas and page 323 of Bethge.

[425] [2941] Position 453.3 of Metaxas and page 323 of Bethge.

[426] [3211] Pages 305-306 of the book *Piłsudski: A Life For Poland* by Wacław Jędrzejewicz, published by Hippocrene Books, New York, 1982, ISBN 9780870527470.

[427] [2941] Position 454.4 of Metaxas. See also the article on Martin Niemöller on the website of the United States Holocaust Memorial Museum https://www.ushmm.org/wlc/en/article.php?ModuleId=10007392. Accessed on Saturday July 25, 2020.

[428] [2746] [2874] [2891] Positions 626.7 onwards and position 746.8 of the ebook *The Venlo Incident* by Sigismund Payne Best, published by Frontline Books, an imprint of Pen & Sword Books Limited, 47 Church Street, Barnsley, S. Yorkshire, S70 2AS, ISBN 9781848325586. See also a comprehensive list of the prisoners by nationality, and an account of their odyssey, albeit in German, online at http://www.mythoselser.de/niederdorf.htm#liste, the website of the *Georg-Elser-Arbeitskreis*, edited by Peter Koblank since 2005 with the largest

online archive worldwide for a resistance fighter against the Third Reich. Accessed on Saturday July 25, 2020.

[429] [3211] See the official website of War Resisters' International at https://www.wri-irg.org/en/story/2007/wri-and-nonviolent-intervention. Accessed on Saturday July 25, 2020.

[430] Position 455.9 of Metaxas.

[431] Position 457.2 to 458.0 of Metaxas, position 408.7 of Schlingensiepen and page 335 of Bethge. These sources also document the negative consequences of this rally for the German Christians.

[432] Position 458.0 of Metaxas and pages 249 to 250 of *A Church Undone: Documents from the German Christian Faith Movement, 1932-1940*, translated by Mary M. Solberg. These pages contain the author's commentary on the speech of Reinhold Krause.

[433] Page 335 of Bethge and position 408.8 of Schlingensiepen.

[434] Page 256 of *A Church Undone: Documents from the German Christian Faith Movement, 1932-1940*, translated by Mary M. Solberg, published by Fortress Press, 2015, ISBN 1451496664, 9781451496666. This is from the full text of Reinhold Krause's speech given in this book from page 251.

[435] Position 458.0 of Metaxas and *Twisted Cross: The German Christian Movement in the Third Reich* by Doris L. Bergen, published by University of North Carolina Press, 2000, ISBN 0807860344, 9780807860342 on Google Books at https://books.google.com.au/books?id=5f31b4fe46EC&pg=PT30&dq=debilita ting+remnant+of+Judaism,+unacceptable+to+National+Socialists!&hl=en&sa =X&ved=0ahUKEwjtwsmklP7pAhXm6nMBHQ-hCOAQ6AEIQjAD#v=onepage&q=debilitating%20remnant%20of%20Judais m%2C%20unacceptable%20to%20National%20Socialists!&f=false. Accessed on Saturday July 25, 2020. See also page 260 of Mary M. Solberg.

[436] Page 256 of Mary M. Solberg.

[437] Position 458.0 of Metaxas and page 256 of Mary M. Solberg, published by Fortress Press, 2015, ISBN 1451496664, 9781451496666. This is from the full text of Reinhold Krause's speech given in this book from page 251.

[438] Position 458.0 of Metaxas and the full text of the speech given from page 251 of Mary M. Solberg.

[439] Position 458.0 of Metaxas and pages 249 to 250 of *A Church Undone: Documents from the German Christian Faith Movement, 1932-1940*, translated by Mary M. Solberg. These pages document the author's impression of the speech made by Reinhold Krause, and the fallout of the speech for the German Christians in the wake of the speech.

[440] Position 458.0 of Metaxas. This is also implied on page 23 of *Preaching in Hitler's Shadow: Sermons of Resistance in the Third Reich* by Dean G. Stroud, published by Wm. B. Eerdmans Publishing, 2013, ISBN 0802869025, 9780802869029.

441 Page 22 of Dean G. Stroud.

442 Position 519.9 of Metaxas, position 444.2 of Schlingensiepen and page 367 of Bethge.

443 Position 529.9 of Metaxas and the online article on the 1517 website at https://1517.org/1517blog/grant-confessingchurch.

444 https://www.britannica.com/event/Synod-of-Barmen#ref41332. Accessed on Saturday July 25, 2020.

445 German History in Documents and Images (GHDI) website at http://germanhistorydocs.ghi-dc.org/sub_image.cfm?image_id=2060. Accessed on Saturday July 25, 2020. Although, in Chapter 7 "Women in the Manly Movement" of the book *Twisted Cross: The German Christian Movement in the Third Reich* by Doris L. Bergen, published by University of North Carolina Press, 2000, ISBN 0807860344, 9780807860342, its states the contention of Müller's wife Paula that he died of heart attack. Source note #17 for that chapter also states the same contention by Müller's sister.

446 2948 Position 382.0 of Schlingensiepen, pages 302 and 325 of Bethge and position 437.9 of Metaxas.

Chapter 5 - London Pastorate and the Fanø Conference

447 Position 400.0 to 403.0 of Schlingensiepen.

448 Position 402.8 of Schlingensiepen.

449 Position 465.0 of Metaxas and page 135 *London: 1933-1935, vol. 13, Dietrich Bonhoeffer Works*, edited by Keith Clements, translated by Isabel Best, published by New York: Fortress Press, 2007, ISBN 0800683137, 9780800683139. See also page 326 of Bethge.

450 Position 407.3 of Schlingensiepen.

451 2949 Position 478.0 of Metaxas.

452 Position 478.5 of Metaxas and is implied at position 470.1 of Schlingensiepen.

453 Position 507.2 of Metaxas and page 365 of Bethge.

454 2746 Page 327 of Bethge, position 407.7 of Schlingensiepen and position 473.7 of Metaxas.

455 Concerning the inappropriate friendship and sympathies Edward VIII and his wife Wallis Simpson had for the Third Reich, they are widely documented, but examples can be found on page 49 of the book *The House of Windsor, Volume 6 of A royal history of England* by Andrew Roberts, edited by Antonia Fraser, published by University of California Press, 2000, ISBN 0520228030, 9780520228030 when he and Wallis Simpson were welcomed at Berchtesgaden and page 72 of *Inside the Third Reich* by Albert Speer, Edition illustrated, reprint, reissue, published by Simon and Schuster, 1997, ISBN 0684829495, 9780684829494.

456 Position 468.5 of Metaxas and page 40 of Andrew Chandler.

457 Page 414 of Bethge.

458 Position 471.6 of Metaxas.

459 Position 600.5 of Metaxas and pages 414 to 415 of Bethge.

460 Position 479.2 of Metaxas and page 414 of Bethge.

461 In regard to the 1934 Röhm purge, see endnotes [92] to [107] of the Preface "Birth and Memory upon the Lesser Known Fault Line of History."

462 Position 456.7 of Schlingensiepen states Hindenburg's death being at Neudeck, and his dates of birth and death are given at https://www.britannica.com/biography/Paul-von-Hindenburg. The exact date of the assassination of Engelbert Dollfuß by Austrian Nazis is given at https://www.britannica.com/biography/Engelbert-Dollfuss. Both accessed on Saturday July 25, 2020.

463 In regard to Neudeck now being modern-day Polish Ogrodzieniec, see the online article dated December 3, 2003 on the website of *Castles of Poland* at https://www.castlesofpoland.com/prusy/ilawa_stories01.htm. Also, from the web page of the archaeologist Bogumił Wiśniewski at http://www.bogumil.wisniewski.ckj.edu.pl/15.html, hosted on the website of the Kwidzyn Cultural Centre at https://kck.ckj.edu.pl/. All links accessed on Saturday August 8, 2020.

464 Position 206.2 of the ebook *The Dictators* by Richard Overy, published by Penguin Books Ltd 2005, 80 Strand, London WC2R 0RL England, ISBN 9780141912240.

465 [621] Position 456.9 of Schlingensiepen. This Tannenberg Mausoleum and memorial will be covered in more detail in Chapter 6 "Old Prussia — Birth of Ruth to Precarious Survival."

466 [621] Position 457.3 of Schlingensiepen.

467 See "Appendix 5: Chronology" in Schlingensiepen at position 1092.0.

468 Ascension Day is the 40th day of Easter or 40th day after Easter Sunday, which means it always falls on a Thursday. It is a religious holiday that commemorates the ascension of Jesus Christ into heaven. See the article on the website of the United Methodist Church at http://www.umc.org/what-we-believe/why-ascension-day-matters-to-united-methodists.

469 Position 462.6 of Schlingensiepen. Accessed on Saturday July 25, 2020.

470 [1046] Position 558.4 of Metaxas and page 92 of *I Knew Dietrich Bonhoeffer*, editors Wolf-Dieter Zimmermann and Ronald Gregor Smith, published by Harper & Row, 1967, no ISBN given. Information on Dietrich's student Wolf-Dieter Zimmermann can be found at https://www.dietrich-bonhoeffer.net/bonhoeffer-umfeld/wolf-dieter-zimmermann/ on the website of International Bonhoeffer Society. Accessed on Saturday 23rd January, 2021.

471 [2811] Position 568.7 of Metaxas.

472 Position 464.6 of Schlingensiepen.

473 [2811] Position 569.1 of Metaxas and page 385 of Bethge.

474 Position 553.6 of Metaxas.

[475] Position 465.8 of Schlingensiepen. Also page 307 of *Volume 13 of Dietrich Bonhoeffer Works in English (London 1933-1935).*

[476] Position 554.1 of Metaxas and page 390 of Bethge.

[477] Position 553.8 of Metaxas.

[478] Position 118.4 of Metaxas and page 48 of Bethge.

[479] Position 555.5 of Metaxas.

[480] The fate of conscientious objectors in the Third Reich is given in *The German War: A Nation Under Arms, 1939—45* by Nicholas Stargardt, published by Random House, 2015, ISBN 1473523737, 9781473523739. See passages of selected text on Google Books at https://books.google.com.au/books?id=7drvCAAAQBAJ&printsec=frontcover &dq=History+books+The+German+War+by+Nicholas+Stargardt&hl=en&sa= X&ved=0ahUKEwit5LzogPvcAhULzbwKHQIcCwUQ6AEIKTAA#v=onepag e&q=112&f=false and https://books.google.com.au/books?id=5fe6gbDyDhEC&pg=PA425&lpg=PA4 25&dq=fate+of+conscientious+objectors+in+Nazi+Germany&source=bl&ots =RvAz_2Tdlx&sig=Djw27Jv40botNT6gDGx251isRMA&hl=en&sa=X&ved= 2ahUKEwi1kfDt7_rcAhWMAIgKHQU0BZoQ6AEwB3oECAMQAQ#v=one page&q=fate%20of%20conscientious%20objectors%20in%20Nazi%20Germa ny&f=false. Both links accessed on Saturday July 25, 2020.

[481] Position 753.8 of Metaxas. Moreover, at position 975.4, Metaxas states that in November 1942, Walter Haeften (see endnote [1765] of Chapter 20 "Valkyrie II") had broached this same question to Dietrich. See also the sermon by Michael Banner at Trinity College Cambridge on Remembrance Sunday on November 10 2013 on page 3 which can be downloaded on the Trinity College website at http://trinitycollegechapel.com/media/filestore/sermons/BannerBonhoeffer101 113.pdf and the online review by Cliff Vaughn, dated October 9 2003, of the 2003 Documentary *Bonhoeffer*, directed and produced by Martin Doblmeier on the website of the Nashville based Baptist Center for Ethics at https://www.ethicsdaily.com/bonhoeffer-cms-3209/. Both links accessed on Saturday July 25, 2020.

[482] Position 631.4 of Schlingensiepen.

[483] The term "cheap grace" can be traced back to a book written by Dietrich, entitled *The Cost of Discipleship*, (In German *Nachfolge* which literally translates to simply "Discipleship") published in 1937. In it, Dietrich defined "cheap grace" as *"the preaching of forgiveness without requiring repentance, baptism without church discipline. Communion without confession. Cheap grace is grace without discipleship, grace without the cross, grace without Jesus Christ."* Fundamental to Dietrich's definition of cheap grace is what is de-emphasised, with the benefits of Christianity being reaped without the costs involved; hence, the adjective cheap to describe it. See the *Got Questions Ministries website* at https://www.gotquestions.org/cheap-grace.html. Accessed on

Saturday July 25, 2020. In the case of pointless peace agreements with Hitler in the 1930s, such as the Czech-Sudeten crisis in 1938 (see Chapter 13 "Flight and the Tumultuous Appeasement of Evil), the "benefit" of what would in time, prove to be a fleeting peace, always came with the indulgence of the easy way out embodied by abject appeasement.

[484] Pages 361 and 385 of the book *Lenin, Stalin and Hitler* by Robert Gellately, published by Vintage 2008, ISBN 9780712603577.

[485] Position 570.1 to 571.0 of Metaxas documents the visits Dietrich made after Fanø before returning to London.

[486] Position 570.8 of Metaxas and page 88 of *The Bonhoeffers; portrait of a family* by Sabine Leibholz-Bonhoeffer, published by Sidgwick and Jackson, 1971, no ISBN given.

[487] Position 571.0 of Metaxas and page 89 of Sabine Leibholz-Bonhoeffer.

[488] Position 279.9 of Metaxas.

[489] Position 468.0 of Schlingensiepen and volume 13, section 152 of Dietrich Bonhoeffer Works in English, by Dietrich Bonhoeffer, edited by Keith W. Clements, published by Augsburg Fortress Publishing, 2007, ISBN 0800683137, 9780800683139.

[490] Position 601.0 of Metaxas and position 468.7 of Schlingensiepen.

[491] Position 469.1 of Schlingensiepen and page 74 of *I Knew Dietrich Bonhoeffer*, editors Wolf-Dieter Zimmermann and Ronald Gregor Smith, published by Harper & Row, 1967, no ISBN given.

[492] See footnote #30 at position 468.9 of Schlingensiepen.

[493] [613] The terms of the Versailles Treaty for the Saar Region are stipulated in Part III articles 45 to 50 of Section IV. See http://avalon.law.yale.edu/imt/partiii.asp.Accessed on Saturday July 25, 2020.

[494] http://markcallagher.com/history/ww2readings/8_Germany%20reoccupies%20Rhineland_%20Japan%20invades%20China/page_03.htm on the website of Mark Callagher. Accessed on Saturday July 25, 2020.

[495] Article on *20th-century international relations* at https://library.eb.com.au/levels/adults/article/20th-century-international-relations/105970. Accessed on Saturday July 25, 2020.

[496] Position 482.0 of Schlingensiepen.

[497] Article on *20th-century international relations* at https://library.eb.com.au/levels/adults/article/20th-century-international-relations/105970. Accessed on Saturday July 25, 2020.

[498] Position 454.3 of Schlingensiepen.

[499] Position 454.5 of Schlingensiepen.

[500] The article on the outcome of the January 1935 Saar plebiscite, dated Tuesday January 29, 1935 in Kalgoorlie's *Western Argus* can be viewed on the Trove National Library of Australia website at

https://trove.nla.gov.au/newspaper/article/34731990. Accessed on Saturday July 25, 2020.

[501] The website of the Australian War Memorial at https://www.awm.gov.au/articles/atwar/first-world-war.

Chapter 6 - Old Prussia — Birth of Ruth to Precarious Survival

[502] Pages 7 to 10 of Jane Pejsa.

[503] [608] In regard to the notion of the "Second Reich," see the book *The Second Reich: Kaiser Wilhelm II and his Germany* Macdonald library of the 20th century, by Harold Kurtz, published by Macdonald in the British Commonwealth, and by American Heritage Press in the USA, both in 1970, ASIN: B008T15I7M, ISBN-10: 007035653X ISBN-13: 9780070356535.

[504] Position 732.1 onwards of Microcosm at the start of Chapter 6 "Breslau in the German Empire,1871—1918" describes when and how the unified Germany was formed in the wake of the Franco-Prussian War in the palace of Versailles in January 1871.

[505] The online article on Otto von Bismarck on the BBC History website at http://www.bbc.co.uk/history/historic_figures/bismarck_otto_von.shtml. Accessed on Saturday July 25, 2020.

[506] Pages 148 to 149 of Jane Pejsa. See also endnote [60] of the Preface "Birth and Memory upon the Lesser Known Fault Line of History" in regard to Oma Ruth's father and future father-in-law witnessing this ceremony. NOTE however, that the notion of the succession of Reichs was only born about a decade or so before Hitler's rise to power in 1933. As such, Oma Ruth's father and then future father-in-law, would not have recognised such a term. See article at https://www.britannica.com/story/why-was-nazi-germany-called-the-third-reich. Accessed on Saturday July 25, 2020.

[507] Pages 118-120 of the book *The Second Reich: Kaiser Wilhelm II and his Germany*, Macdonald library of the 20th century, by Harold Kurtz, published by Macdonald in the British Commonwealth, and by American Heritage Press in the USA, both in 1970, ASIN: B008T15I7M, ISBN-10: 007035653X ISBN-13: 9780070356535.

[508] [608] On page 262 of Jane Pejsa, the author makes a brief note of the Kaiser's death in June 1941, with the news hardly registering a beat among the Junkers, in spite of the military funeral that took place in Berlin. See also endnote [709] for Chapter 9 "The von Kleists and the Prophecy."

[509] Page 30 of Jane Pejsa.

[510] See article on Prussia at https://library.eb.com.au/levels/adults/article/Prussia/61665. Accessed on Saturday July 25, 2020. The circumstances leading to the official end of Prussia's existence, in particular, the only way of life Oma Ruth knew, will be discussed in Chapter 25 "Old Prussia Gone With The Wind."

511 [1397] Pages 16 to 17 of Jane Pejsa.

512 Page 22 of Jane Pejsa.

513 Page 23 of Jane Pejsa.

514 [1397] See the family tree on page 394 of Jane Pejsa.

515 [2512] Page 40 of Jane Pejsa.

516 Page 40 of Jane Pejsa.

517 Page 65 of Jane Pejsa. See also the family tree on page 394.

518 Page 69 of Jane Pejsa.

519 Page 69 of Jane Pejsa.

520 Page 69 of Jane Pejsa.

521 Article on Szczecin/Stettin at https://www.britannica.com/place/Szczecin. Accessed on Saturday July 25, 2020.

522 [2512] Pages 80 to 81, pages 84 to 85 and pages 124 to 126 of Jane Pejsa.

523 [637] See the Family Search web page on Prince Joachim of Prussia at https://ancestors.familysearch.org/en/KFBM-3S8/joachim-franz-humbert-hohenzollern-prince-of-prussia-1890-1920. Accessed on Saturday July 25, 2020. Prince Joachim was the seventh child, but two years later in 1892, Viktoria, the second daughter and youngest was born.

524 Page 21 of *Zwölf Jahre am deutschen Kaiserhof (Twelve years at the German imperial court)* by Robert Graf Zedlitz-Trützschler (Ruth's brother), published by BoD — Books on Demand, 2012 and Salzwasser Verlag, Paderborn Germany, ISBN 3846008788, 9783846008782. The original was published in April 1924. See page 156 and note #14 on page 397 of Jane Pejsa.

525 Pages 72 to 73 of Jane Pejsa.

526 Page 80 of *Daisy, Princess of Pless, 1873-1943: A Discovery* by W. John Koch, published by BOOKS by W. JOHN KOCH PUBLISHING, 2003, ISBN 0973157909, 9780973157901 and page 93 of Jane Pejsa.

527 Pages 93 to 94 of Jane Pejsa.

528 Page 107 of Jane Pejsa.

529 Page 107 of Jane Pejsa.

530 See page 156 and note #14 on page 397 of Jane Pejsa.

531 Page 115 of Jane Pejsa.

532 The online article on Otto von Bismarck on the BBC History website at http://www.bbc.co.uk/history/historic_figures/bismarck_otto_von.shtml. Accessed on Saturday July 25, 2020.

533 Ibid.

534 Page 117 of Jane Pejsa.

535 Pages 117 to 118 of Jane Pejsa.

536 Page 118 of Jane Pejsa. Ruthchen is the German diminutive of Ruth that Jane Pejsa uses to address Ruth's youngest child.

537 See endnote [63] for the Preface "Birth and Memory upon the Lesser Known Fault Line of History."

[538] See endnote [64] for the Preface "Birth and Memory upon the Lesser Known Fault Line of History."

[539] [xix] [4490] Admittedly, Lithuanians are not Slavs. However, Slavs do include Russians, Ukrainians, Belorussians, Czechs, Slovakians, Serbs, Croats and Poles. See https://www.britannica.com/topic/Slav. Accessed on Saturday July 25, 2020. Remember, that in Hitler's mind, Slavs were barely one rung above the Jews in his racial hierarchy. Hence the use of the Einsatzgruppen in Poland and later in the Soviet Union. See also, endnotes [1231] to [1233] of Chapter 17 "Pastor and Spy" and pages 426 to 428 of *Lenin, Stalin and Hitler* by Robert Gellately, published by Vintage 2008, ISBN 9780712603577 in regard to Hitler's infamous and racially charged Commissar Order just preceding Barbarossa. (The invasion of the Soviet Union in June 1941).

[540] [637] See endnote [64] for the Preface "Birth and Memory upon the Lesser Known Fault Line of History."

[541] See endnote [64] for the Preface "Birth and Memory upon the Lesser Known Fault Line of History."

[542] See endnote [63] for the Preface "Birth and Memory upon the Lesser Known Fault Line of History."

[543] See endnote [64] for the Preface "Birth and Memory upon the Lesser Known Fault Line of History."

[544] Pages 126 to 127 of Jane Pejsa.

[545] Pages 124 to 125 of Jane Pejsa.

[546] Page 124 of Jane Pejsa.

[547] Page 125 of Jane Pejsa.

[548] Page 129 of Jane Pejsa.

[549] Page 130 of Jane Pejsa.

[550] See pages 135 to 136 of Jane Pejsa.

[551] Page 130 of Jane Pejsa.

[552] Article on the 1916 Battle of Verdun at https://www.britannica.com/event/Battle-of-Verdun. Accessed on Saturday July 25, 2020.

[553] Pages 118 to 119 of Jane Pejsa.

[554] [616] Article *WHAT WAS THE FEBRUARY REVOLUTION?* on the website of the Imperial War Museum at https://www.iwm.org.uk/history/what-was-the-february-revolution. Accessed on Saturday July 25, 2020.

[555] [559] The article on the website of the *Atlantic* Magazine archive at https://www.theatlantic.com/magazine/archive/1928/03/the-last-days-of-the-romanovs/303877/. This article was written in March 1928. The *Atlantic* Magazine was founded in 1857. See https://www.theatlantic.com/history/. See also the article on Tsar Nicholas II at https://www.britannica.com/biography/Nicholas-II-tsar-of-Russia. All links accessed on Saturday July 25, 2020.

556 See endnote 68 for the Preface "Birth and Memory upon the Lesser Known Fault Line of History."

557 The website of the International Encyclopedia of the First World War at https://encyclopedia.1914-1918-online.net/article/brest-litovsk_treaty_of by Susanne Schattenberg, documents and describes the Treaty of Brest-Litovsk. A map of the vast territory ceded by Bolshevik Russia is also given. Links accessed on Saturday July 25, 2020.

558 Ibid.

559 See endnote 555 for this chapter.

560 Page 135 of Jane Pejsa.

561 For all intents and purposes, the USA by 1917, was a super-power. Economically, it surpassed Britain, and while its armed forces were numerically inferior to Britain in April 1917, that would rapidly change upon the official entry of the US into WWI. See for example, https://www.vox.com/2015/5/20/8615345/america-global-power-maps on the website of Vox media, https://www.theatlantic.com/international/archive/2014/12/the-real-story-of-how-america-became-an-economic-superpower/384034/ on the website of the Atlantic. Even by 1890, the United States had by far the world's most productive economy. American industry produced twice as much as its closest competitor Britain. See http://www.digitalhistory.uh.edu/disp_textbook.cfm?smtid=2&psid=3159 on the Digital History website. All web sites accessed on Saturday July 25, 2020. All links accessed on Saturday July 25, 2020.

562 616 See the online article *VOICES OF THE FIRST WORLD WAR: ARRIVAL OF THE AMERICAN TROOPS* on the Imperial War Museum at https://www.iwm.org.uk/history/voices-of-the-first-world-war-arrival-of-the-american-troops. Accessed on Saturday July 25, 2020.

563 See pages 135 to 136 of Jane Pejsa.

564 Page 132 to 133 of Jane Pejsa.

565 Page 133 of Jane Pejsa.

566 Page 135 of Jane Pejsa.

567 The mobile nature of the Great War in its very early stages and final eight months is documented on the first two pages of "Chapter 8 World War I" by Michael S. Neiburg in the book *The Cambridge History of War: Volume 4, War and the Modern World*, edited by Roger Chickering, Dennis Showalter and Hans van de Ven, published by Cambridge University Press, 2012, ISBN 1316175928, 9781316175927.

568 Ibid. See also the map on Google Books at https://books.google.com.au/books?id=nXphBAAAQBAJ&printsec=frontcover&dq=ISBN+1316175928,+9781316175927&hl=en&sa=X&ved=0ahUKEwivq-

zI9bnpAhVDWysKHb80DScQ6AEIKDAA#v=onepage&q=The%20tactics%20that%20were&f=false. All links accessed on Saturday July 25, 2020.

[569] The online articles on the website of the Australian War Memorial titled *Hamel: the textbook Victory - 4 July 1918* at https://www.awm.gov.au/visit/exhibitions/1918/battles/hamel and *General John Monash* at https://www.awm.gov.au/collection/P11013307, accessed on Saturday July 25, 2020.

[570] Page 139 of Jane Pejsa.

[571] Pages 139 to 141 of Jane Pejsa.

[572] Page 141 of Jane Pejsa.

[573] Page 139 of Jane Pejsa.

[574] See endnotes [774] onwards of Chapter 9 "The von Kleists and the Prophecy" in regard to Franz von Papen.

[575] See the online article *WHAT YOU NEED TO KNOW ABOUT THE BRITISH NAVAL BLOCKADE OF THE FIRST WORLD WAR* dated Monday 8 January 2018, by Paul Cornish on the website of the Imperial War Museum at https://www.iwm.org.uk/history/what-you-need-to-know-about-the-british-naval-blockade-of-the-first-world-war. To the Germans' great resentment, it continued until June 1919 — following the signing of the humiliating Versailles Treaty. Accessed on Saturday July 25, 2020.

[576] Pages 141 to 142 of Jane Pejsa.

[577] Page 142 of Jane Pejsa.

[578] Page 139 of Jane Pejsa.

[579] Page 142 of Jane Pejsa.

[580] Page 142 of Jane Pejsa.

[581] Page 142 of Jane Pejsa.

[582] Page 143 of Jane Pejsa.

[583] Page 143 of Jane Pejsa.

[584] Page 144 of Jane Pejsa.

[585] Position 887.0 of Jane Pejsa.

[586] Pages 118 to 120 of the book *The Second Reich: Kaiser Wilhelm II and his Germany, Macdonald library of the 20th century*, by Harold Kurtz, published by Macdonald in the British Commonwealth, and by American Heritage Press in the USA, both in 1970, ASIN: B008T15I7M, ISBN-10: 007035653X ISBN-13: 9780070356535, detail the Kaiser eventually abdicating at the German Army Headquarters in the Belgium town of Spa.

[587] Page 144 of Jane Pejsa.

[588] Page 144 of Jane Pejsa.

[589] Page 262 of Jane Pejsa.

[590] Page 144 of Jane Pejsa.

[591] Page 144 of Jane Pejsa.

[592] Page 144 of Jane Pejsa.

[593] Pages 144 to 145 of Jane Pejsa.

594 Page 145 of Jane Pejsa.

595 The website of the Armistice Museum at https://armistice-museum.com/understanding-the-history/the-armistice-of-1918/, accessed on Saturday July 25, 2020.

596 Ibid.

597 See the final minutes of the BBC documentary *The Last Day of World War 1 - Michael Palin* - As Seen on BBC1 [DVD], released on October 27 2014, ASIN: B00MXXJ0PI.

598 Ibid.

599 Ibid.

600 Page 145 of Jane Pejsa.

601 Page 146 of Jane Pejsa.

602 Pages 146 to 147 of Jane Pejsa.

603 Pages 153 to 154 of Jane Pejsa.

604 Page 148 of Jane Pejsa.

605 Page 148 of Jane Pejsa.

606 See endnote 63 for the Preface "Birth and Memory upon the Lesser Known Fault Line of History."

607 See the online *Encyclopaedia Britannica* article on the Versailles Treaty at https://www.britannica.com/event/Treaty-of-Versailles-1919. Accessed on Saturday July 25, 2020.

608 See endnotes 503 to 508 for this chapter.

609 Pages 148 to 149 of Jane Pejsa.

610 See position 899.0 of Microcosm.

611 See the online *Encyclopaedia Britannica* article on the Rhineland at https://www.britannica.com/place/Rhineland. Accessed on Saturday July 25, 2020.

612 The online article *The Ruhr Occupation* by Jennifer Llewellyn and Steve Thompson, published by Alpha History at https://alphahistory.com/weimarrepublic/ruhr-occupation/ on September 25, 2019, accessed on Saturday July 25, 2020.

613 See endnotes 493 onwards for Chapter 5 "London Pastorate and the Fanø Conference" in regard to the 1935 Saar Plebiscite.

614 Page 149 of Jane Pejsa. In regard to Germany being forbidden military aircraft, see page 1 of *The First and the Last* by the highly decorated German WWII fighter ace, Adolf Galland, English edition published by Metheun and Company Limited London 1955, translated by Mervyn Savill from the German *DIE ERSTEN UND DIE LETZEN*, published by Franz Schneekluth in 1953.

615 See pages 148 to 151 of Jane Pejsa. In regards to the agricultural strike, see page 149.

616 Article on the Treaties of Brest-Litovsk at http://library.eb.com.au/levels/adults/article/16373 describes the position of major weakness for Bolshevik Russia and its eventual compelled acceptance of

the treaty's humiliating terms. The text of the peace treaty can be read at http://avalon.law.yale.edu/20th_century/brest.asp, while a brief summary of its dire implications for Bolshevik Russia is given at http://avalon.law.yale.edu/20th_century/bl36.asp. All links accessed on Saturday July 25, 2020. See also endnotes [554] to [562] for this chapter.

[617] The modern-day Polish name for Tannenberg is given at http://gov.genealogy.net/item/show/TANERGKO03BM on the website of the *Verein für Computergenealogie e.V. (Association for Computer Genealogy e.V.)*. Its credentials can be viewed online at http://compgen.de/?Ueber_uns. It's modern-day Polish name Stębark is pronounced "Stenbark." All links accessed on Saturday July 25, 2020.

[618] Page 162 of The First World War by John Keegan, published by Random House, 2011, ISBN 1407064126, 9781407064123.

[619] Article *The Tannenberg myth in history and literature, 1914—1945* by Jan Vermeiren (2018) in the European Review of History: Revue européenne d'histoire Volume 25, NO. 5, 778—802. View online at https://www.tandfonline.com/doi/full/10.1080/13507486.2018.1497010. Accessed on Saturday July 25, 2020.

[620] Page 230 of *Studies: An Irish Quarterly Review*, volume 26, no. 102, June 1937, pages 223—242 in the article *Paul Von Hindenburg 1847-1934* by Professor Daniel A. Binchy M.A., PH.D., Irish Minister to Germany 1929-1932. It can be viewed online at https://www.jstor.org/stable/30097404?seq=8#metadata_info_tab_contents. Accessed on Saturday July 25, 2020.

[621] Position 456.9 of Schlingensiepen describes the funeral ceremony. See also endnotes [465] and [466] for Chapter 5 London Pastorate and the Fanø Conference.

[622] The Tannenberg Denkmal (Monument) website at http://www.tannenberg-denkmal.com/en/20_pomnik_rozproszony_1.php. Accessed on Saturday July 25, 2020.

[623] Page 107 of *From Monuments to Traces: Artifacts of German Memory, 1870-1990* by Rudy Koshar, published by University of California Press, 2000, ISBN 0520922522, 9780520922525.

[624] http://www.tannenberg-denkmal.com/en/20_pomnik_rozproszony_2.php. Accessed on Saturday July 25, 2020.

[625] Page 130 of *White Eagle Red Star* by Norman Davies.

[626] Ibid page 275.

[627] [3428] Page 433 of the *World War I Almanac*, by David R. Woodward, Infobase Publishing, 2009, ISBN 1438118961, 9781438118963, as well as position 617.2 of the ebook *Paris 1919: Six Months That Changed the World*, by Margaret MacMillan, published by John Murray Publishing London UK, 2001, ISBN 9781848546684. She in turn states her source as page 396 of Norman Davies' book *God's Playground A History of Poland: Volume II: 1795 to the*

Present, published by Oxford University Press Oxford, 2005, ISBN 0199253404, 9780199253401.

[628] See pages 265 to 267 of White Eagle Red Star, by Professor Norman Davies, published in 2003 by Pimlico, Random House UK Limited, ISBN 9780712606943 and page 73 of Lenin, Stalin and Hitler The Age of Social Catastrophe by Robert Gellately, published by Vintage 2008, ISBN 9780712603577.

[629] See http://acienciala.faculty.ku.edu/hist557/lect11.htm accessed on Saturday July 25, 2020.

[630] [4490] Admittedly, Lithuanians are not Slavs. However, Slavs do include Russians, Ukrainians, Belorussians, Czechs, Slovakians, Serbs, Croats and Poles. See https://www.britannica.com/topic/Slav. Accessed on Saturday July 25, 2020. Remember, that in Hitler's mind, Slavs were barely one rung above the Jews in his racial hierarchy. Hence the use of the Einsatzgruppen in Poland and later in the Soviet Union. See also, endnotes [1231] to [1233] of Chapter 17 "Pastor and Spy" and pages 426 to 428 of *Lenin, Stalin and Hitler* by Robert Gellately, published by Vintage 2008, ISBN 9780712603577 in regard to Hitler's infamous and racially charged Commissar Order just preceding Barbarossa. (The invasion of the Soviet Union in June 1941).

[631] See the BBC documentary *Armistice* narrated by Professor David Reynolds, from 7 minutes and 35 seconds. The DVD was released on July 14 2014, ASIN: B00JDATTPK. See the description on Amazon at https://www.amazon.co.uk/WW1-Armistice-World-presented-Reynolds/dp/B00JDATTPK. Accessed on Saturday July 25, 2020.

[632] For the Poles, this medieval battle, is known as the Battle of Grunwald. See https://www.britannica.com/event/Battle-of-Grunwald-1410. Accessed on Saturday July 25, 2020.

[633] Article *The Tannenberg myth in history and literature, 1914—1945* by Jan Vermeiren (2018) in the European Review of History: Revue européenne d'histoire Volume 25, NO. 5, 778—802. View online at https://www.tandfonline.com/doi/full/10.1080/13507486.2018.1497010. Accessed on Saturday July 25, 2020.

[634] Pages 18 to 19 of *Hindenburg: Power, Myth, and the Rise of the Nazis* by Anna von der Goltz, published by OUP Oxford, 2009, ISBN 0199570329, 9780199570324. See also https://www.britannica.com/event/Battle-of-Grunwald-1410. All links accessed on Saturday July 25, 2020.

[635] In regard to Weimar Germany's "Golden Years," see endnote [80] for the Preface "Birth and Memory upon the Lesser Known Fault Line of History."

[636] Page 156 of Jane Pejsa. Note #14 on page 397 states that this book was entitled *Zwölf Jahre am Deutschen Kaiserhof* (Twelve Years at the Imperial German Court).

[637] See endnotes [523] to [540] for this chapter in regard to Robert Junior's years in the Kaiser's Imperial Court.

[638] [2821] Pages 169 to 170 of Jane Pejsa. See also the family trees on pages 391 and 395.

[639] Page 170 of Jane Pejsa.

[640] See the family tree on page 391 of Jane Pejsa.

Chapter 7 - Zingst and Finkenwalde

[641] Position 604.0 to 604.3 of Metaxas.

[642] See https://www.britannica.com/place/Szczecin. Accessed on Saturday July 25, 2020.

[643] Position 620.4 of Metaxas.

[644] [3580] Albrecht Schönherr was born in 1911 in Katscher in Silesia and died in Potsdam in 2009. In 1969, he was elected Bishop of Berlin-Brandenburg which was in East Germany, but had included West Berlin, which was cut off by the wall after 1961. During that time he was instrumental in forming the Federation of Protestant Churches in the German Democratic Republic, which would, during the next 20 years, right up until the collapse of the Berlin wall, grow in self-confidence to make a significant contribution to the world church. This, after all, was the heartland of the Lutheran reformation. See the online obituary on the website of *The Guardian* at https://www.theguardian.com/world/2009/apr/03/obituary-bishop-albrecht-schonherr and *Independent* at https://www.independent.co.uk/news/obituaries/albrecht-schonherr-evangelical-bishop-in-communist-east-germany-1648289.html, which states his birthplace. Both links accessed on Saturday July 25, 2020.

[645] Position 624.5 of Metaxas.

[646] Position 624.9 of Metaxas and page 429 of Bethge.

[647] Position 625.2 of Metaxas.

[648] Position 625.8 of Metaxas.

[649] Position 619.1 of Metaxas.

[650] Page 705 of Bethge.

[651] Page 429 of Bethge.

[652] Position 619.3 of Metaxas.

[653] Position 612.5 of Metaxas and page 431 of Bethge.

[654] Position 394.8 of Metaxas. See also the documentary on Himmler; *True Evil: The Making Of A Nazi Season 1 Episode 3 — Himmler* aired on SBS Australia in Brisbane at 5:30pm on Sunday the October 14 2018, which repeatedly makes reference to Himmler's overtly anti-Christian and pagan ancient Germanic mindset.

[655] Position 615.4 of Metaxas.

[656] Position 617.8 of Metaxas and the bottom of page 427 of Bethge.

[657] The article on Pomerania in The Columbia Encyclopedia, Sixth Edition, 2001-07. It can be viewed online at

https://web.archive.org/web/20080829002114/http://www.bartleby.com/65/po/Pomerani.html and mentions the numerous changes in sovereignty down through the centuries including the immediate aftermath of World War II. Accessed on Saturday July 25, 2020.

[658] Position 1123.9 of *Microcosm*. For a map of the entire "Recovered Territories" with pre-war German-Polish borders, see the map on page xix of the book *Recovered Territory: A German-Polish Conflict over Land and Culture, 1919-1989* by Peter Polak-Springer, published by Berghahn Books, 2015, ISBN 1782388885, 9781782388883. Note the presence of Stettin-Szczecin and Breslau-Wrocław in the north and south of the Recovered territories respectively. See also endnote [6] and endnotes [171] to [173] and [197] to [220] of the Preface "Birth and Memory upon the Lesser Known Fault Line of History" in regard to the so-called "Recovered Territories" and post WWII twin displacement west of eastern Germans and eastern Poles.

[659] [750] https://www.britannica.com/topic/Junker. Accessed on Saturday July 25, 2020.

[660] Position 911.1 of Microcosm documents the results of the 1930 Reichstag election including the election of the Nazi Party candidate for Breslau, Helmuth Brückner. As is the staggering increase for support of the Nazi Party since the 1928 election, especially in the Silesian capital of Breslau. In Bavaria, Hitler's failed 1923 Beer Hall Putsch took place in the state capital of Munich, while in another Bavarian city, namely Nuremberg, was where the so-named rallies took place in the 1930s. See https://www.britannica.com/event/Beer-Hall-Putsch, accessed on Saturday July 25, 2020, in regard to the former, and for the latter, see Chapter 8 "Institutionalised Hatred — The Nuremberg Laws."

[661] Pages 439 to 440 of Bethge.

[662] Position 636.7 of Metaxas.

[663] [750] Position 639.4 of Metaxas.

[664] These circumstances will be covered early on in Chapter 9 "The von Kleists and the Prophecy."

[665] Pages 207 to 210 of Jane Pejsa. On page 208, note the photo taken in the Stettin flat of six of Oma Ruth's grandchildren.

[666] Position 638.3 of Metaxas.

[667] Pages 465 to 466 of Bethge and position 633.7 of Metaxas.

[668] Position 4.5 in the credits for Metaxas states that Eberhard Bethge was the author of the Bonhoeffer biography *Dietrich Bonhoeffer: Man of Vision, Man of Courage (1970)*.

[669] Position 490.6 of Schlingensiepen.

[670] Position 490.0 of Schlingensiepen.

[671] Position 490.2 of Schlingensiepen.

[672] Page 290 of Jane Pejsa. This letter will be covered in more detail in Chapter 18 "Romance, Plots and Arrest."

[673] Position 637.8 to 642.0

[674] Position 640.0 of Metaxas and page 438 of Bethge.

[675] Position 642.0 of Metaxas.

Chapter 8 - **Institutionalised Hatred — The Nuremberg Laws**

[676] The website *Traces of Evil* http://www.tracesofevil.com/ by David Heath, history teacher at the Bavarian International School, accessed on Saturday July 25, 2020. In a touch of irony post-war, Nuremberg would be the venue for the anti-Nazi trials. Position 522.2 of Schlingensiepen also states that Hitler announced the laws on in the September 15 1935 at the national party rally.

[677] Position 887.7 of Microcosm. See also endnotes [65] to [70] of the Preface "Birth and Memory upon the Lesser Known Fault Line of History."

[678] Alpha History website article accessed on Saturday July 25, 2020 at https://alphahistory.com/nazigermany/law-for-the-protection-of-german-blood-1935/, with the text of "The Law for the Protection of German Blood and German Honour" which was one of the two Nuremberg Laws, unveiled by Adolf Hitler at the 1935 Nuremberg rally and implemented in September that year. The other Nuremberg Law passed was the "The Reich Citizenship Law." See also pages 463-467 of the book *Documents on Nazism 1919-1945* by Jeremy Noakes and Geoffrey Pridham. NY: Viking Press, 1975, ISBN 0670275840, 9780670275847.

[679] http://www.tracesofevil.com/. Accessed on Saturday July 25, 2020. This was also stated by my tour guide in September 2014 when I visited the Nuremberg Rally grounds.

[680] https://www.britannica.com/story/why-was-nazi-germany-called-the-third-reich, clarifies the notion of the three Reiches, as well as fact that it was only born around 1923 — about a decade or so before Hitler's rise to power. Accessed on Saturday July 25, 2020.

[681] http://www.tracesofevil.com/ by David Heath. Accessed on Saturday July 25, 2020.

[682] My father told me of this fact as he was showing me family birth certificates going back well into the 19th century.

[683] Position 993.9 of Microcosm documents the role of the American firm IBM in supplying the punch card machines for cross-referencing genealogical data and their search for the requisite skilled demographers. This is written about in detail in the books *IBM and the Holocaust: The Strategic Alliance Between Nazi Germany and America's Most Powerful Corporation-Expanded Edition*, published by Dialog Press; Expanded edition (February 16, 2012), ISBN-10: 0914153277, ISBN-13: 9780914153276 and in German *Die restlose Erfassung. Volkszählen, Identifizieren, Aussondern im Nationalsozialismus (The residue-free detection. People counting, identifying, segregating in National Socialism)*,

by Götz Aly and Karl Heinz Roth, published by Fischer Paperback; Edition: 2 (June 1, 2000), ISBN-10: 3596147670, ISBN-13: 9783596147670.

[684] Position 925.9 of Microcosm.

[685] The United States Holocaust Memorial Museum's online article at https://www.ushmm.org/outreach/en/article.php?ModuleId=10007695. It also gives a detailed account of the Nuremberg Laws and key dates. Accessed on Saturday July 25, 2020.

[686] Position 649.8 of Metaxas and for the text of Paul's letter to the Romans 13:1—5, see the Bible Gateway with text of the New International Version at https://www.biblegateway.com/passage/?search=Romans+13%3A1-5&version=NIV. Accessed on Saturday July 25, 2020.

[687] Position 649.9 of Metaxas.

[688] Position 366.8 of Metaxas and page 275 of Bethge.

[689] Position 649.4 of Metaxas. See also page 607 of Bethge, which states that it is more likely Dietrich made this statement in 1935 rather than in November 1938 in the wake of *Reichskristallnacht* (Night of Broken Glass).

[690] Position 650.3 of Metaxas and page 488 of Bethge.

[691] Position 651.1 of Metaxas and pages 489 to 490 of Bethge.

[692] Postition 499.9 of Schlingensiepen.

[693] Position 499.7 to 500.6 of Schlingensiepen.

[694] For a disturbing modern-day parallel, see endnotes [386] to [390] of Chapter 4 "The Aryan Paragraph."

[695] Position 651.9 to 652.6 of Metaxas.

[696] Position 652.9 of Metaxas and page 490 of Bethge. In regards to Julie Bonhoeffer's defiance of SA thugs in April 1933, see position 373.6 of Metaxas, position 61.9 of Schlingensiepen and page 11 of Bethge.

[697] Position 654.0 of Metaxas, and page 83 of the book *The Bonhoeffers; portrait of a family* by Sabine Leibholz-Bonhoeffer.

Chapter 9 - The von Kleists and the Prophecy

[698] Page 212 of Jane Pejsa.

[699] Pages 212 to 213 of Jane Pejsa.

[700] Page 199 of Jane Pejsa.

[701] Pages 65 to 66 of Jane Pejsa.

[702] Page 26 of Jane Pejsa.

[703] Page 213 of Jane Pejsa.

[704] Page 214 of Jane Pejsa, position 530.0 of Schlingensiepen, position 654.9 of Metaxas and page 506 of Bethge.

[705] Page 214 of Jane Pejsa.

[706] Page 214 of Jane Pejsa, although Bethge on page 507 states that German nationals were allowed to take the equivalent of one pound sterling in foreign

exchange out of the country. In any event, the amount allowed was for all intensive purposes, nil.

[707] Page 215 of Jane Pejsa.

[708] Pages 7 to 10 of Jane Pejsa.

[709] [508] Pages 118-120 of the book *The Second Reich: Kaiser Wilhelm II and his Germany*, Macdonald library of the 20th century, by Harold Kurtz, published by Macdonald in the British Commonwealth, and by American Heritage Press in the USA, both in 1970, ASIN: B008T15I7M, ISBN-10: 007035653X ISBN-13: 9780070356535, detail the Kaiser eventually abdicating at the German Army Headquarters in the Belgium town of Spa, in early November 1918, followed by his flight to neutral Holland by train. See also the beginning of Chapter 7 "Breslau before and during the Second World War, 1918—45" in *Microcosm* from position 887.0. Page 144 of Jane Pejsa, documents the abject sense of betrayal felt by Ruth von Kleist-Retzow and her fellow Junkers, while on page 262, the author makes a brief note of the Kaiser's death in June 1941, with the news hardly registering a beat among the Junkers, in spite of the military funeral that took place in Berlin.

[710] Pages 215 to 216 of Jane Pejsa.

[711] Page 59 of Jane Pejsa.

[712] Page 216 of Jane Pejsa.

[713] Pages 232 to 233 and page 237 of Jane Pejsa.

[714] Pages 155 to 156 of Jane Pejsa.

[715] The book was entitled *Die Soziale Krisis und die Verantwortung des Gutsbesitzes* (*The social crisis and the responsibility of landowning*) by Carl Schweitzer and Ruth von Kleist-Retzow. In truth, Ruth was the true author, as Carl merely wrote a brief foreword. Ruth most charitably stated that the name of Pastor Carl helped in getting the book, published, but Ruth's admirers did not share her charitable perspective. See pages 161 to 163 of Jane Pejsa.

[716] Page 162 of Jane Pejsa.

[717] In invoking this comparison, I must make it clear that the Prussian feudal system of which Ruth von Kleist-Retzow née von Zedlitz-Trützschler was born into, in no shape or form, practised slavery like the American Confederacy. However, in both cases, after major cataclysms, both ways of life were indeed "Gone with the Wind."

[718] [41 1117 1689 2384 2580 2825 3435 3201] See pages 164 to 169 of Jane Pejsa for a record of the discourse taking place at this prophetic meeting.

[719] [2837] Hitler was obsessively enamoured with Friedrich (Frederick) the Great. He would often look up to his picture of Friedrich during his final days in the Berlin bunker in April 1945, hoping desperately for a reincarnation of Friedrich's "Miracle of Brandenburg" 183 years earlier. See endnotes [47], [140], and [141] for the Preface "Birth and Memory upon the Lesser Known Fault Line of History."

[720] The Reich's greatest battleship, was named after the great 19th century statesman Otto von Bismarck. It would be sunk by the British in the Atlantic as early as July 1940. See pages 258-260 of *A Man Called Intrepid The Secret War 1939-1945* by William Stevenson, first published by Macmillan London Ltd 1976, published by Sphere Books Ltd 1977, reprinted twice in 1977, ISBN 0722181574, 9780722181577, reprinted twice in 1978, and again in 1979, which covers the covert American assistance in the sinking of the Bismarck. See also the account of Leonard B. Smith, Ensign, U.S. Navy online at the archive of the Library of Congress (loc) at http://webarchive.loc.gov/all/20101205192505/http%3A//www.history.navy.mil/faqs/faq118-3.htm dated June 9 1941 — six months before America's official entry into WWII. Accessed on Saturday July 25, 2020.

[721] See endnotes [65] to [70] of the Preface "Birth and Memory upon the Lesser Known Fault Line of History."

[722] Page 168 of Jane Pejsa.

[723] [2825] Ibid.

[724] See endnotes [300] and [301] for Chapter 2 "Ominous Clouds on the Horizon."

[725] [3435] [3201] Page 216 of Jane Pejsa.

[726] Position 911.3 of Microcosm.

[727] The online article on Weimar political parties on the Facing History website at https://www.facinghistory.org/weimar-republic-fragility-democracy/readings/weimar-political-parties, by by Professor Paul Bookbinder, University of Massachusetts Boston, documents the political parties of Weimar, stating that as many as thirty parties at times existed within it. See also https://www.britannica.com/topic/Weimar-Republic. All links accessed on Saturday July 25, 2020.

[728] Page 188 of Jane Pejsa.

[729] [2459] Page 177 of Jane Pejsa. A portrait of Raba is shown on page 179.

[730] Page 98 of Jane Pejsa.

[731] Page 177 of Jane Pejsa.

[732] Page 177 of Jane Pejsa.

[733] Pages 177 to 178 of Jane Pejsa.

[734] Page 180 of Jane Pejsa.

[735] Page 180 of Jane Pejsa.

[736] Pages 83 to 84 of Jane Pejsa. See also page 180 which in a paragraph there highlights the fond memories Ruth had of the Wödtke Estate.

[737] Page 181 of Jane Pejsa.

[738] Page 181 of Jane Pejsa.

[739] Page 181 of Jane Pejsa.

[740] Page 181 of Jane Pejsa.

[741] Page 181 of Jane Pejsa.

[742] Page 181 of Jane Pejsa.

[743] Pages 181 to 182 of Jane Pejsa.

744 Page 182 of Jane Pejsa.

745 Page 182 of Jane Pejsa.

746 Page 182 of Jane Pejsa and note #27 on page 397 for the original German text.

747 Page 182 of Jane Pejsa.

748 Pages 182 to 183 of Jane Pejsa.

749 Pages 182 to 183 of Jane Pejsa.

750 See position 269.0 onwards of Metaxas, which states the Bonhoeffers were raised in the affluent Berlin neighbourhood of Grunewald, dominated with its academics and cultural elites, of which a third were Jewish. See also position 653.4 of Metaxas which states they *moved from their vast home on 14 Wangenheimstrasse in Grunewald (the house number of "14" is given at position 497.3) to a new house that they had built in Charlottenburg."* Both districts were adjoining, hence their new home in Charlottenburg at 43 Marienburgeralle was just two or so kilometres north-west of their former home. See also page 28 and page 491 of Bethge. Note that at the time of February 1931, Dietrich had not yet met the Pomeranian Junkers. That would not take place until four years later in 1935. See endnotes [659] to [663] of Chapter 7 "Zingst and Finkenwalde."

751 Page 182 of Jane Pejsa.

752 Page 183 of Jane Pejsa.

753 Page 183 of Jane Pejsa.

754 Page 183 of Jane Pejsa.

755 Page 183 of Jane Pejsa.

756 Page 183 of Jane Pejsa.

757 Page 183 of Jane Pejsa.

758 Page 183 of Jane Pejsa.

759 See pages 161 to 163 of Jane Pejsa. It was entitled *Die Soziale Krisis und die Verantwortung des Gutsbesitzes* (The social crisis and the responsibility of landowning) by Carl Schweitzer and Ruth von Kleist-Retzow.

760 Pages 183 to 184 of Jane Pejsa.

761 Page 184 of Jane Pejsa.

762 Page 184 of Jane Pejsa.

763 Page 184 of Jane Pejsa.

764 Page 184 of Jane Pejsa.

765 Page 184 of Jane Pejsa.

766 Page 184 of Jane Pejsa.

767 Page 184 of Jane Pejsa.

768 Pages 184 to 185 of Jane Pejsa.

769 In regard to Raba's Jewish ancestry, see the footnote on page 185 of Jane Pejsa and as stated in note #28 on page 397, the interview of Raba in the Jerusalem Post dated June 8, 1989. See also *Indexes and Supplementary Materials: Dietrich Bonhoeffer Works, Volume 17* by Dietrich Bonhoeffer, editors Victoria

J. Barnett and Barbara Wojhoski, published by Fortress Press, 2014, ISBN 1451489544, 9781451489545 on Google Books at https://books.google.com.au/books?id=ZR7qAwAAQBAJ&pg=PR56&lpg=PR56&dq=ruth+roberta+stahlberg+heckscher&source=bl&ots=7G6x08Tupf&sig=hS9vGflvfjhAz4_A9K6DhXgQMYM&hl=en&sa=X&ved=2ahUKEwiFjbyd85HfAhVYdCsKHciYBxEQ6AEwCXoECAgQAQ#v=onepage&q=Heckscher%2C%20Ruth%20Roberta%20(Raba)&f=false. Accessed on Saturday July 25, 2020.

[770] [2459] Page 385 of Jane Pejsa in the Epilogue, documents Raba's emigration to Israel in 1986, and her conversion to Judaism in 1989, and that every Friday, she worked as a volunteer at Jerusalem's Yad Vashem Holocaust Museum. See also, albeit in German, pages 141 to 142 of the book *Die Studentinnen an der Universität München 1926 bis 1945: Auslese, Beschränkung, Indienstnahme, Reaktionen* (The Students at the University of Munich 1926 to 1945: Selection, Restriction, Intervention, Reactions) by Petra Umlauf, published by Walter de Gruyter GmbH & Co KG, 2016, ISBN 3110446626, 9783110446623.

[771] Page 186 of Jane Pejsa. Pages 186 to 194 of Jane Pejsa documents events in the ten or so months from March 1932 until Hitler's rise to power at the end of January 1933.

[772] Pages 186 to 188 of Jane Pejsa.

[773] Page 188 of Jane Pejsa.

[774] [574] https://www.britannica.com/biography/Franz-von-Papen. Accessed on Saturday July 25, 2020.

[775] Page 190 of Jane Pejsa.

[776] Pages 190 to 191 of Jane Pejsa.

[777] Pages 189 to 190 of Jane Pejsa.

[778] Page 191 of Jane Pejsa. Also documented is Gert and Henning von Tresckow's support of Hitler at the time — albeit it not lasting that far into Hitler's reign.

[779] Page 17 of *The Second World War: Ambitions to Nemesis* by Bradley Lightbody, published by Psychology Press, 2004, ISBN 0415224047, 9780415224048.

[780] Page 192 of Jane Pejsa.

[781] Page 192 of Jane Pejsa.

[782] Page 193 of Jane Pejsa.

[783] Page 193 of Jane Pejsa.

[784] [103] Pages 200 to 202 of Jane Pejsa. See also endnotes [92] to [107] in the Preface "Birth and Memory upon the Lesser Known Fault Line of History" in regard to the 1934 Röhm purge.

[785] Page 193 of Jane Pejsa and the book *Selbsterlebte wichtige Begebenheiten aus den Jahren 1933 und 1934* (Self-important events from the years 1933 and 1934) which Ewald von Kleist-Schmenzin wrote in 1934. See Jane Pejsa's note #29 on page 397.

[786] Pages 193 to 194 of Jane Pejsa.

[787] [3071 3092] Page 17 of the book *The Second World War: Ambitions to Nemesis* by Bradley Lightbody, published by Psychology Press, 2004, ISBN 0415224047, 9780415224048 and J. Llewellyn et al, *Hitler becomes chancellor* Alpha History, at http://alphahistory.com/nazigermany/hitler-becomes-chancellor/, accessed on Saturday July 25, 2020.

[788] https://www.britannica.com/biography/Kurt-von-Schleicher, accessed on Saturday July 25, 2020. Schleicher would be the last chancellor of Weimar.

[789] https://www.britannica.com/biography/Franz-von-Papen. Accessed on Saturday July 25, 2020.

[790] This article can be read on Trove on the website of the National Library of Australia at https://trove.nla.gov.au/newspaper/article/48419481. Accessed on Saturday July 25, 2020.

[791] Page 194 of Jane Pejsa.

Chapter 10 - Swedish trip and the Brethren Houses

[792] Page 216 of Jane Pejsa.

[793] Pages 289 to 290 of William L. Shirer.

[794] Page 295 of William L. Shirer.

[795] Page 295 of William L. Shirer.

[796] Online *Encyclopaedia Britannica* articles at https://www.britannica.com/biography/Engelbert-Dollfuss and https://library.eb.com.au/levels/adults/article/20th-century-international-relations/105970. Accessed on Saturday July 25, 2020.

[797] Pages 295 to 296 of William L. Shirer.

[798] Pages 63, 74 and 82 of the book *Fortress Europe: European Fortifications of World War II* by Robert M. Jurga, translated by J. E. Kaufmann, Edition illustrated, published by Greenhill, 1999, ISBN 1853673412, 9781853673412 and the online *Encyclopaedia Britannica* article at https://www.britannica.com/topic/Siegfried-Line. Accessed on Saturday July 25, 2020. I visited a remnant of this defensive wall near the Belgium/Dutch/German border in late August 2004, before I started my ten month stint of teaching English in Poland.

[799] Page 295 of William L. Shirer.

[800] The online *Encyclopaedia Britannica* article on the Rhineland at https://www.britannica.com/place/Rhineland. Accessed on Saturday July 25, 2020.

[801] Page 226 of Jane Pejsa.

[802] Page 237 of Jane Pejsa.

[803] The United Press International Archives website at http://www.upi.com/Archives/1939/03/15/Crowds-defiant-in-Prague-as-Hitler-crosses-Czech-frontier/8148408176316/, accessed on Saturday July 25, 2020,

gives the date of Wednesday March 15 1939 when Hitler's troops marched into the Czech capital of Prague.

[804] Pages 226 to 227 of Jane Pejsa.

[805] Page 237 of Jane Pejsa.

[806] Pages 232 to 233 of Jane Pejsa.

[807] Position 532.1 to 532.7 of Schlingensiepen documents the positive outcomes of the Swedish visit.

[808] Position 532.8 to 535.1 of Schlingensiepen reveals the consequences of the trip once Theodor Heckel became aware of it.

[809] Position 533.7 of Schlingensiepen.

[810] Position 532.8 to 535.1 of Schlingensiepen.

[811] Pages 216 to 217 of Jane Pejsa.

[812] Page 218 of Jane Pejsa.

[813] Page 217 of Jane Pejsa.

[814] Pages 216 to 219 of Jane Pejsa document the establishment of the Brethren Houses.

[815] Page 217 of Jane Pejsa.

[816] Page 218 of Jane Pejsa.

[817] Page 218 of Jane Pejsa.

[818] Pages 200 to 202 of Jane Pejsa.

[819] Page 218 of Jane Pejsa.

[820] Page 219 of Jane Pejsa.

Chapter 11 - Memo to Hitler and his Olympics

[821] Position 536.8 of Schlingensiepen.

[822] Position 536.1 of Schlingensiepen.

[823] Position 538.6 to 540.0 of Schlingensiepen, documents the memo's seven main sections, which the author sourced from pages 132 to 137 of *Kirchliches Jahrbuch für den Evangelische Kirche in Deutschland (Church Yearbook for the Protestant Church in Germany) 1933—1944, 2nd edition* edited by Joachim Beckmann, published in 1976 by Gütersloh Bertelsmann.

[824] Position 539.1 of Schlingensiepen.

[825] Position 539.9 of Schlingensiepen.

[826] [2521] Position 541.3 of Schlingensiepen.

[827] Position 541.3 of Schlingensiepen documents Dietrich being the one to uncover the individuals responsible for leaking the memo to the foreign press. The article on Werner Koch at https://www.evangelischer-widerstand.de/html/view.php?type=kurzbiografie&id=56&l=de, documents the life of Werner Koch, including his first meeting with Dietrich in 1931, where he shared the same view as Dietrich in regards to the ominous political developments in Germany. Accessed on Saturday July 25, 2020.

[828] [2521] Position 542.0 of Schlingensiepen.

829 The dates for the beginning and end of the 1936 Berlin Olympics are given on the official website of the International Olympic Committee at https://www.olympic.org/berlin-1936. Accessed on Saturday July 25, 2020.

830 https://www.olympic.org/berlin-1936, documents the medal count for individual athletes, in which Jesse Ownes topped with four gold medals. For the medal count for individual nations, which Germany topped, see the Australian Olympic Committee site at http://olympics.com.au/games/berlin-1936. Note the not so auspicious count for Australia. All links accessed on Saturday July 25, 2020.

831 The TIME magazine article by Emma Ockerman at http://time.com/4432857/hitler-hosted-olympics-1936/, updated on Monday August 1 2016. Accessed on Saturday July 25, 2020.

832 The TIME magazine article by Emma Ockerman.

833 The TIME magazine article by Emma Ockerman.

834 The official Olympic Games website at https://www.olympic.org/news/alfred-nakache-swimming accessed on Saturday July 25, 2020.

835 Page 83 of the paper *Avery Brundage and American Participation in the 1936 Olympic Games* by Carolyn Marvin University of Pennsylvania, cmarvin@asc.upenn.edu, dated 1st of April 1982, documents how Avery Brundage felt that America should applaud the New Germany for halting Communist gains in Western Europe. More than likely, Brundage was referring to Hitler's support for Franco in the Spanish Civil War that broke out the previous month.

836 https://alphahistory.com/nazigermany/spanish-civil-war/, accessed on Saturday July 25, 2020.

837 Page 103 of *The Franco Regime, 1936—1975* by Stanley G. Payne, published by University of Wisconsin Press, 2011, ISBN 0299110737, 9780299110734.

838 Page 47 of the book *De Gaulle: Lessons in Leadership from the Defiant General* by Michael E. Haskew, published by St. Martin's Press, 2011, ISBN 0230340563, 9780230340565.

839 Page 95 of *White Eagle Red Star* by Professor Norman Davies, published in 2003 by Pimlico, Random House UK Limited, ISBN 9780712606943.

840 Pages 128 to 129 of *White Eagle Red Star*.

841 Pages 101 to 104 of *White Eagle Red Star*.

842 4514 Page 221 of *White Eagle Red Star*.

843 The TIME magazine article by Emma Ockerman.

844 The United States Holocaust Memorial Museum at https://www.ushmm.org/exhibition/olympics/?content=continuing_persecution&lang=en, accessed on Saturday July 25, 2020 and the Time magazine article by Emma Ockerman.

[845] Page 216 of the book *Hitler's Olympics: The Story of the 1936 Nazi Games* by Anton Rippon, published by Pen and Sword, 2006, ISBN 1781597375, 9781781597378.

[846] Page 12 of the Sydney Morning Herald, Friday August 21 1936 or see the online record at Trove on the website of the National Library of Australia at https://trove.nla.gov.au/newspaper/article/17262966. Accessed on Saturday July 25, 2020.

[847] [864] Position 542.4 of Schlingensiepen.

[848] Position 542.6 of Schlingensiepen.

[849] Page 219 of Jane Pejsa.

[850] Page 238 of Jane Pejsa.

[851] Page 219 of Jane Pejsa,

[852] Pages 219 to 220 of Jane Pejsa.

[853] Position 544.0 of Schlingensiepen and page 536 of Bethge.

[854] General Francisco Franco's recognition as the Generalissimo and Chief of State of the Nationalist zone just two-and-a-half months into the Spanish Civil War on the 1st of October 1936 is documented in the chronology on page xv of the book *The Franco Regime, 1936—1975* by Stanley G. Payne, published by University of Wisconsin Press, 2011, ISBN 0299110737, 9780299110734. For Hitler's military, albeit somewhat clandestine support of Franco during the Spanish Civil War, see pages 23 to 36 of the book *The First and the Last* by the highly decorated German WWII fighter ace, Adolf Galland, English edition published by Metheun and Company Limited London 1955, translated by Mervyn Savill.

[855] Page 537 of Bethge.

[856] For background information on superintendent Otto Dibelius see page 304 of *Dietrich Bonhoeffer Works, Volume 17* by Dietrich Bonhoeffer, edited by Gerhard Ludwig Müller, Albrecht Schönherr, Clifford J. Green, Hans-Richard Reuter, Geoffrey B. Kelly, Victoria J. Barnett, published by Augsburg Fortress Publishers, 1996, ISBN 1451469330, 9781451469332.

[857] Position 1093.8 of Schlingensiepen in the chronology in Appendix 5.

[858] Pages 212 to 213 of Jane Pejsa. See also the beginning of Chapter 9 "The von Kleists and the Prophecy."

[859] Page 537 of Bethge.

[860] Position 545.0 of Schlingensiepen.

[861] Page 203 of the book *Hitler's Olympics: The Story of the 1936 Nazi Games* by Anton Rippon, published by Pen and Sword, 2006, ISBN 1781597375, 9781781597378, gives the date of August 16 1936 for the closing ceremony.

[862] Page 537 of Bethge.

[863] Position 545.6 of Schlingensiepen.

[864] See endnote [847] for this chapter.

Chapter 12 - The Sammelvikariats

[865] Position 688.5 to the end of Chapter 19 "Scylla and Charybdis" in Metaxas describe the end of Finkenwalde and the establishment of the Sammelvikariat or collective pastorates in its place, in the far north-eastern corner of then German Pomerania. As well, the end of Chapter 7 "Finkenwalde (1935—1937)" in Schlingensipen at position 565.0 states the closure of Finkenwalde in September 1937 while Dietrich and Bethge were on leave.

[866] The arrest of Martin Niemöller is covered from position 683.5 of Metaxas and position 554.3 of Schlingensiepen. See also endnote [2746] of Chapter 28 "Memory Transcending Executioners' Legal but Criminal Flights from Justice."

[867] In regard to Martin Niemöller's ultimate liberation in the German speaking Italian village of Niederdorf in the Tyrol region on April 30, 1945, see positions 626.7 onwards and position 746.8 of the ebook *The Venlo Incident* by Sigismund Payne Best, published by Frontline Books, an imprint of Pen & Sword Books Limited, 47 Church Street, Barnsley, S. Yorkshire, S70 2AS, ISBN 9781848325586. See also a comprehensive list of the prisoners by nationality, and an account of their odyssey, albeit in German, online at http://www.mythoselser.de/niederdorf.htm#liste, edited by Peter Koblank since 2005. Accessed on Saturday July 25, 2020. See also endnotes [2708] onwards of Chapter 27 "The Prominenten and Miraculous Reprieves" which focuses on two other prisoners liberated at Niederdorf.

[868] [2940] [2942] See position 687.5 to 688.2 of Metaxas and position 555.0 of Schlingensiepen, with both making mention of Dietrich's family being instrumental in Hildebrandt's successful flight from Germany.

[869] Position 691.6 of Metaxas at the end of Chapter 19 "Scylla and Charybdis" describes the founding of the first two Sammelvikariats at Köslin and Schlawe, as well as the rambling, wind-battered parsonage in Gross-Schlönwitz, on the boundary of the church district of Schlawe, where the ordinands of Schlawe lived.

[870] Page 594 of Bethge.

[871] Page 594 of Bethge. Chapter 15 "New York — Troubled Revisiting," will cover Dietrich's second but troubled sojourn to New York.

[872] The modern-day Polish names for Köslin and Schlawe being Koszalin and Sławno respectively, can be found at http://gov.genealogy.net/item/show/object_162914 and http://gov.genealogy.net/item/show/object_884851 respectively on the website of the *Verein für Computergenealogie e.V. (Association for Computer Genealogy e.V.)*. Both links accessed on Saturday July 25, 2020.

[873] NOTE: Today, Gross-Schlönwitz is Słonowice, just inside the Pomeranian Voivodeship to the east of the boundary with the West Pomeranian Voivodeship, which is not to be confused with the Słonowice in the centre of the West Pomeranian Voivodeship which is located 106 kilometres south-west of the

former. See http://gov.genealogy.net/item/show/SCHITZJO84KJ. Accessed on Saturday July 25, 2020.

[874] Position 692.8 of Metaxas.

[875] Position 570.5 of Schlingensiepen and page 591 of Bethge. Both also document the even more primitive conditions at the Sigurdshof house at Tychow, in comparison to their former accommodation at Gross-Schlönwitz.

[876] Page 591 of Bethge.

[877] NOTE: The then German village of Tychow is now Tychowo in Sławno County. See http://gov.genealogy.net/item/show/TYCHOWJO84JI. Note however in modern-day Poland, there are two other villages within 160 kilometres of the same name.

[878] Page 591 of Bethge.

[879] In regard to the modern-day Polish name for the Wipper River, download the document *WYKAZ NAZW WÓD PŁYNĄCYCH" — "LIST OF NAMES OF FLOWING WATERS* from http://ksng.gugik.gov.pl/pliki/hydronimy1.pdf, then do a word search for "Wieprza," and with the latitude and longitude given along the way of this river, and the latitude and longitude for Tychowo given at http://gov.genealogy.net/item/show/TYCHOWJO84JI, it can be inferred that Bethge in his description of the Sigurdshof house backing onto the then German Wipper River on page 591 of his book, was referring to what is today the Polish *"Rzeka Wieprza."* Both links accessed on Saturday July 25, 2020.

[880] Position 570.5 of Schlingensiepen and page 591 of Bethge.

[881] Position 696.0 of Metaxas and pages 591 to 592 of Bethge.

[882] Position 624.3 of Schlingensiepen.

[883] Position 651.6 of Schlingensiepen and page 592 of Bethge.

[884] Position 651.9 of Schlingensiepen.

Chapter 13 - Flight and the Tumultuous Appeasement of Evil

[885] Position 706.6 of Metaxas.

[886] Pages 597 to 598 of Bethge and position 697.0 of Metaxas.

[887] Page 598 of Bethge and position 698.5 of Metaxas.

[888] [2058] https://library.eb.com.au/levels/adults/article/Hjalmar-Schacht/66070 documents the life of Hjalmar Schacht, including his role in halting the rampant inflation of the early 1920s, and the friction he had with Göring. It also states how Göring became a virtual economic dictator of the German economy from 1936. Accessed on Saturday February 27, 2021.

[889] See the document from the American Library of Congress at https://www.loc.gov/rr/frd/Military_Law/pdf/NT_Vol-XIII.pdf. Accessed on Saturday July 25, 2020.

[890] See pages 9-10 of Ibid.

891 See http://www.cvce.eu/content/publication/1997/10/13/3e38f437-48ba-4a5d-8846-68fc8550f442/publishable_en.pdf on page 2. Accessed on Saturday July 25, 2020.

892 2058 *The Anatomy of the Nuremberg Trials* by Telford Taylor, Edition una-bridged, published by Knopf Doubleday Publishing Group, 2012, ISBN 0307819817, 9780307819819. See Google Books online at https://books.google.com.au/books?id=hEH7KcpN-OcC&printsec=frontcover&dq=ISBN+0307819817,+9780307819819&hl=en&sa=X&ved=0ahUKEwj6gp7D7-XgAhXPbCsKHey-VCAgQ6AEIKjAA#v=onepage&q=until%20the%20end%20of%201950&f=false. Accessed on Saturday July 25, 2020.

893 Position 587.4 of Schlingensiepen and position 699.3 of Metaxas.

894 See http://library.eb.com.au/levels/adults/article/Anschluss/7719 and http://www.upi.com/Archives/1939/03/15/Crowds-defiant-in-Prague-as-Hitler-crosses-Czech-frontier/8148408176316/ accessed on Saturday July 25, 2020 and position 742.0 near the beginning of Chapter 21 "The Great Decision" of Metaxas.

895 See https://www.britannica.com/biography/Engelbert-Dollfuss and https://library.eb.com.au/levels/adults/article/Anschluss/7719. All links accessed on Saturday July 25, 2020.

896 2388 The second and final footnote at the end of Chapter 18 "Zingst and Finkenwalde" at position 642.0 in Metaxas, and pages 235 to 239 of Jane Pejsa.

897 Position 707.2 of Metaxas.

898 Position 701.4 of Metaxas.

899 1189 Position 703.0 to 709.2 of Metaxas describes the Fritsch affair. As does pages 314 to 321 of The Rise and Fall of the Third Reich by William L. Shirer. See also the German History in documents website at http://ghdi.ghi-dc.org/sub_document.cfm?document_id=1541. All links accessed on Saturday July 25, 2020.

900 1327 2121 Position 703.7 of Metaxas.

901 See also endnotes 92 to 107 of the Preface "Birth and Memory upon the Lesser Known Fault Line of History" in regard to the 1934 Röhm Purge.

902 Position 588.6 of Schlingensiepen, position 705.4 of Metaxas and page 317 of William L. Shirer.

903 Position 589.1 of Schlingensiepen.

904 Position 707.1 of Metaxas. See also pages 627 to 628 of Bethge, which document Fritsch's hesitation.

905 1327 2121 3553 Position 708.2 of Metaxas.

906 1189 Position 708.7 of Metaxas.

907 Position 708.9 of Metaxas.

908 1189 https://library.eb.com.au/levels/adults/article/Anschluss/7719, accessed on Saturday July 25, 2020.and pages 325 to 330 of William L. Shirer.

[909] [1189] Page 350 of William L. Shirer.

[910] Page 599 of Bethge and position 710.7 of Metaxas.

[911] Page 599 of Bethge and position 711.1 of Metaxas.

[912] Position 712.6 of Metaxas and pages 298 to 299 of *Encyclopedia of Martin Luther and the Reformation, Volume 2*, edited by Mark A. Lamport, contributors Bruce Gordon and Martin E. Marty, published by Rowman & Littlefield, 2017, ISBN 1442271590, 9781442271593.

[913] Page 599 of Bethge and position 712.8 of Metaxas.

[914] In 1935, Barth lost his position as professor in Bonn when was forced to leave Germany because he refused to swear a pledge to Adolf Hitler without adding the qualification *"to the extent that I responsibly am able as a Protestant Christian."* See http://barth.ptsem.edu/karl-barth/biography accessed on Saturday July 25, 2020.

[915] Page 602 of Bethge and position 713.6 of Metaxas.

[916] Position 714.1 onwards of Metaxas and page 227 to 228 of Jane Pejsa.

[917] Position 715.0 of Metaxas. Position 1240.0 of Metaxas documents Maria's death from cancer in 1977 and the death of Maria in 1977 is also documented in the New York Times online article at https://www.nytimes.com/1977/11/17/archives/maria-von-wedemeyerweller-at-53.html?_r=0, dated November 17 1977. Accessed on Saturday July 25, 2020.

[918] Position 715.1 of Metaxas. See also the description of the photo on page 228 of Jane Pejsa.

[919] [4167] Page 365 of William L. Shirer and position 716.0 of Metaxas.

[920] [1935] While this was during the period of Churchill's "Wilderness years" from 1929-39 where he was excluded from political office, in 1935, the then PM, Stanley Baldwin granted him the exceptional privilege of membership in the secret committee on air-defence research, thus enabling him to work on some vital national problems. See https://www.britannica.com/biography/Winston-Churchill under the heading *Exclusion from office, 1929—39*. See also the website of the Churchill society at https://winstonchurchill.org/the-life-of-churchill/wilderness-years/ and in particular, https://winstonchurchill.org/the-life-of-churchill/wilderness-years/1935-1939/, focussing more on the 1938 Munich crisis. Accessed on Saturday July 25, 2020. Note there, the inverted commas for Chamberlain's *"mission of peace"* in September 1938.

[921] See page 380 of *Rise And Fall Of The Third Reich: A History of Nazi Germany* by William L. Shirer, published by Simon and Schuster, 1990, ISBN 0671728687, 9780671728687 and pages 235 to 237 of Jane Pejsa.

[922] Page 235 of Jane Pejsa.

[923] [1935] Position 725.6 of Metaxas and page 367 of William L. Shirer.

[924] Position 717.1 of Metaxas.

[925] Position 716.7 of Metaxas. See also page 631 of Bethge.

[926] The details of Gerhard and Sabine Leibholzes flight from Germany in 1938 is documented from position 716.6 to 721.5 of Metaxas. Also, albeit in lesser detail, from position 592.5 to 593.5 of Schlingensiepen. See also pages 631 to 632 of Bethge. On page 587, Bethge states that he and Dietrich spent the final days of September 1938 staying at the Leibholzes house in Göttingen where Dietrich spent time in the study writing his book *Life Together.* As does position 721.6 of Metaxas.

[927] Position 717.6 of Metaxas.

[928] Position 717.8 of Metaxas.

[929] Position 718.4 of Metaxas and pages 97 to 98 of *The Bonhoeffers; portrait of a family* by Sabine Leibholz-Bonhoeffer, published by Sidgwick and Jackson, 1971 (No ISBN given).

[930] Position 718.9 of Metaxas and page 98 of *The Bonhoeffers; portrait of a family*.

[931] Position 720.7 of Metaxas and pages 97 to 98 of *The Bonhoeffers; portrait of a family*.

[932] Page 587 of Bethge.

[933] Position 722.0 of Metaxas and page 587 of Bethge. See also the description of this book on Amazon at https://www.amazon.com.au/Life-Together-Dietrich-Bonhoeffer/dp/0060608528. Accessed on Saturday July 25, 2020.

[934] Page 587 of Bethge.

[935] Position 722.3 of Metaxas.

[936] Pages 421-422 of William L. Shirer state the catastrophic consequences of the Sudeten annexation for the Czech industrial economy.

[937] Page 359 of William L. Shirer.

[938] Page 359 of William L. Shirer.

[939] Page 359 to 360 of William L. Shirer.

[940] Position 722.8 of Metaxas and position 579.2 of Schlingensiepen.

[941] [3468] This is implied on page 382 of William L. Shirer.

[942] Page 380 of William L. Shirer. Strangely however, page 237 of Jane Pejsa states that it was not until days later, following Ewald's return to Berlin, that Ewald received this letter via diplomatic channels. Moreover, in his footnote, Shirer states that he found evidence that the German Foreign Office knew about this letter as early as the 6th of September 1938! It was marked: "*Extract from a letter of Winston Churchill to a German confidante.*" This perhaps implies that Pejsa's version is true.

[943] Position 724.4 of Metaxas and page 631 of Bethge.

[944] [2802] Concerning Chamberlain's declaration of "Peace for/in our time," see page 420 William L. Shirer. Albeit, Chamberlain, as in numerous other sources, is misquoted by Shirer as saying "Peace in our time" when he is supposed to have said "Peace for our time." See also the official UK government website at https://www.gov.uk/government/history/past-prime-ministers/neville-

chamberlain. In any event, the gist of either quote is undoubtedly identical. All links accessed on Saturday July 25, 2020.

[945] Position 726.8 of Metaxas. This is confirmed on the International Churchill Society website at https://winstonchurchill.org/the-life-of-churchill/wilderness-years/1935-1939/the-munich-crisis/. All links accessed on Saturday July 25, 2020.

[946] In regard to the reuniting of the Germanic peoples of Silesia and the Sudetenland after 198 years, see position 937.3 of Microcosm which states the unopposed occupation of the Sudetenland by the Wehrmacht as well as the likewise unopposed occupation five months later of the Czech capital of Prague.

[947][3468] For the names of the Giant Mountains in various languages, see their official website at http://www.giant-mountains.info/ and click on the box at top right with various language versions. Accessed on Saturday July 25, 2020.

[948] Pages 421-422 of William L. Shirer.

[949] *Untermensch* literally underman, sub-man, subhuman; plural: *Untermenschen* is a term that became infamous when the Nazis used it to describe non-Aryan "inferior people" often referred to as "the masses from the East," that is Jews, Roma, and Slavs — mainly Poles, Serbs, and later also Russians. See page 219 of *Poland Under Nazi Occupation* (First edition) by Janusz Gumkowski and Kazimierz Leszczynski, translated by Edward Rothert 1961, published by Polonia Publishing House, ASIN B0006BXJZ6.

[950][115][4476] Pages 421-422 of William L. Shirer.

[951][4167] Position 727.3 of Metaxas.

[952][3397] Page 388 of William L. Shirer.

[953] Page 421 of William L. Shirer.

[954] BUTTIN, FÉLIX. *The Polish-Czechoslovak Conflict over Teschen Silesia (1918—1920): a Case Study.* Perspectives, no. 25, 2005, pp. 63—78. JSTOR, https://www.jstor.org/stable/23616032. Page 65 gives the date of January 23 1919 when Czechoslovakia invaded Poland. Accessed on Saturday July 25, 2020.

[955] Page 75 of *Germany and European Order: Enlarging NATO and the EU* by Adrian Hyde-Price, published by Manchester University Press, 2000, ISBN 0719054281, 9780719054280, quotes Churchill's written statement post Great War; *"The war of giants has ended, the wars of the pygmies begin."* As does page 21 of *White Eagle Red Star* and position 27.6 of the ebook.

[956] Page 421 of William L. Shirer.

[957] See the transcript of the English language interview on Spiegel Online at http://www.spiegel.de/international/germany/post-war-myths-the-logic-behind-the-destruction-of-dresden-a-607524.html, dated February 13 2009. Accessed on Saturday July 25, 2020.

[958] See endnote [204] in the Preface "Birth and Memory upon the Lesser Known Fault Line of History" in regard to the deportation of Borderland Poles to the Gulag.

[959] [1258] In regard to the Katyń Wood Massacre, see Polish WWII Supplement III "The Katyń Wood Massacre"[3618] and pages 44, 48, 115 to 116 of Norman Davies' book *Rising '44: The Battle for Warsaw*, published by Penguin Books; Reprint edition (October 4, 2005), ISBN-10: 0143035401, ISBN-13: 9780143035404. On page 48, Davies states that Stalin personally signed the order for their execution. See also the online *Encyclopaedia Britannica* article at https://library.eb.com.au/levels/adults/article/Katyn-Massacre/44867, which states that in all likelihood, over 20,000 Polish officers were executed, and the Central Intelligence Agency report online by Benjamin B. Fischer at https://www.cia.gov/library/center-for-the-study-of-intelligence/csi-publications/csi-studies/studies/winter99-00/art6.html. All links accessed on Saturday July 25, 2020.

[960] See Polish WWII Supplement I "The Molotov-Ribbentrop Pact."[3268]

[961] See Polish WWII Supplement I "The Molotov-Ribbentrop Pact"[3268] and pages 356 to 359 of the book *Lenin, Stalin and Hitler* by Robert Gellately, published by Vintage 2008, ISBN 9780712603577.

[962] See page 316 of *Rising '44*. In regard to the Polish death toll of 200,000, see page 622 of *Rising '44* and pages 220 to 221 of *No Greater Ally, The Untold Story of Poland's Forces in World War II* by Kenneth K. Koskodan, published by Osprey Publishing 2011, ISBN-13: 9781849084796. See also endnotes [4301] to [4302] of Polish WWII Supplement IV "AK and 1944 Warsaw General Uprising — Stalin's mass murder by German proxy."

[963] See endnote [190] in the Preface "Birth and Memory upon the Lesser Known Fault Line of History" in regard to the Stalinist perpetrated post-war displacement of eastern Germans and Borderland Poles.

[964] See position 1237.3 of Microcosm.

[965] See page 221 of *No Greater Ally, The Untold Story of Poland's Forces in World War II* by Kenneth K. Koskodan.

[966] [3397] Position 1103.3 of Microcosm states that the non-communist Polish Home Army (AK — Armia Krajowa) was the largest underground movement in Nazi occupied Europe. See also page 183 of *Rising '44: The Battle for Warsaw* Reprint Edition (October 4, 2005), ISBN-10: 0143035401, ISBN-13: 9780143035404 where it documents the underwhelming figure for the communist Armia Ludowa (AL) of 800 in Warsaw in 1943, as compared to the Home Army (AK — Armia Krajowa) with 40,330 men!

[967] Page 423 of William L. Shirer. The reassessment of Hitler to Dr. Burckhardt post-Munich is given in the footnote on page 424.

[968] Page 424 of William L. Shirer.

[969] Page 424 of William L. Shirer.

[970] The footnote on page 424 of William L. Shirer. Shirer quotes page 5 of *The Gravediggers of France: Gamelin, Daladier, Reynaud, Pétain, and Laval: Military Defeat, Armistice, Counter-revolution* by André Géraud and Pertinax,

Edition revised, published by Doubleday, Doran, Incorporated, 1944 (no ISBN given).

[971] Pages 426 to 427 of William L. Shirer.

[972] Page 426 of William L. Shirer.

[973] Page 423 of William L. Shirer.

[974] Page 50 of *The Gathering Storm, 1948 Volume 1 of Winston S. Churchill The Second World War*, by Winston S. Churchill, published by Rosetta Books, 2010, ISBN 0795308329, 9780795308321.

[975] Page 423 of William L. Shirer.

[976] See Quora at https://www.quora.com/Did-Churchill-ever-read-Mein-Kampf. Accessed on Saturday July 25, 2020.

[977] https://www.britannica.com/event/Beer-Hall-Putsch/The-Munich-Putsch. Accessed on Saturday July 25, 2020.

[978] Page 50 of *The Gathering Storm, 1948 Volume 1 of Winston S. Churchill The Second World War*, by Winston S. Churchill, published by Rosetta Books, 2010, ISBN 0795308329, 9780795308321.

[979] See Polish WWII Supplement I "The Molotov-Ribbentrop Pact."[3268]

[980] See endnote [204] in the Preface "Birth and Memory upon the Lesser Known Fault Line of History" in regard to the deportation of Borderland Poles to the Gulags.

[981] [2117] The period of the Nanking Massacre is documented at http://news.bbc.co.uk/2/hi/asia-pacific/7126455.stm, http://www.independent.co.uk/news/world/asia/the-scars-of-nanking-memories-of-a-japanese-outrage-764827.html, and http://www.pacificwar.org.au/JapWarCrimes/TenWarCrimes/Rape_Nanking.html. All links accessed on Saturday July 25, 2020.

[982] Position 727.7 of Metaxas and page 632 of Bethge.

[983] Position 728.0 of Metaxas and page 633 of Bethge.

[984] Clive Staples Lewis (1898—1963) born in Belfast, was a former atheist, who converted to Christianity in September 1931. From the official website of C.S. Lewis at http://www.cslewis.com/us/about-cs-lewis/, accessed on Saturday July 25, 2020.

Chapter 14 - Reichskristallnacht

[985] http://www.yadvashem.org/odot_pdf/Microsoft%20Word%20-%206321.pdf and http://www.holocaustresearchproject.org/holoprelude/grynszpan.html Both links accessed on Saturday July 25, 2020.

[986] Ibid.

[987] Metaxas does not name the young assassin, and Metaxas' contention that the young assassin instead intended to murder the German Ambassador Count Johannes von Welczeck, is stated at position 729.7. However, most sources

now state this was a Nazi fabrication of evidence, as is stated on page 358 of the book *1938: Hitler's Gamble* by Giles MacDonogh, Edition large print, published by ReadHowYouWant.com, 2011, ISBN 1459620399, 9781459620391. Page 167 of the book *The Day the Holocaust Began* by Gerald Schwab, published by Praeger, 1990, ISBN 0275935760, 9780275935764 also contradicts Metaxas' contention.

[988] Position 268.9 of Metaxas.

[989] For the distinction between German Jews and *Ostjuden* (Eastern Jews), see the article on the University of Chicago website at https://www.lib.uchicago.edu/collex/exhibits/exeej/. See also the online Oxford dictionaries at https://en.oxforddictionaries.com/definition/ostjuden which defines the term Ostjuden. Both links accessed on Saturday July 25, 2020.

[990] For Heydrich's role in the 1934 Night of the Long Knives (Nacht der langen Messer) see page 30 of *The Third Reich in Power* by Richard J. Evans, published by Penguin Books, 2006, ISBN 0143037900, 9780143037903.

[991] For Heydrich's role in the Final Solution, see page 166 of *The Destruction of the European Jews, Volume 2* by Raul Hilberg, Edition abridged, illustrated, revised, published by Lynne Rienner, 1985, ISBN 0841909105, 9780841909106.

[992] [3565] For Heydrich's role in Reichskristallnacht see position 730.3 of Metaxas and position 926.3 to 927.4 of *Microcosm*.

[993] Position 730.5 of Metaxas.

[994] The document about Herschel Grynszpan on the Yad Vashem website at http://www.yadvashem.org/odot_pdf/Microsoft%20Word%20-%206321.pdf. Accessed on Saturday July 25, 2020.

[995] Position 730.6 of Metaxas gives 1:20am as the time that Heydrich sent urgent teletype messages to every Gestapo station across the country to implement *Kristallnacht* (Night of Broken Glass). Position 926.6 of Microcosm gives the time of 1:09am on the morning of November 10 1938 as the date and time that the SS commanding officer in Breslau, Erich von dem Bach-Zelewski, was given the order to place an urgent call to a hotel in Munich, where Reinhard Heydrich was staying. By 2am in Breslau, the destruction was well under way.

[996] Position 926.1 of *Microcosm*.

[997] Position 926.5 of *Microcosm*. Erich von dem Bach-Zelewski would, almost six years later, be in command of the brutal suppression of the 1944 Warsaw General Uprising. See endnote [4271] of Polish WWII Supplement IV "AK and 1944 Warsaw General Uprising — Stalin's mass murder by German proxy."

[998] Position 926.7 of *Microcosm*.

[999] Position 926.8 of *Microcosm*.

[1000] Position 927.1 of *Microcosm*.

[1001] See endnotes [25] to [31] of the Preface "Birth and Memory upon the Lesser Known Fault Line of History" in regard to the May to July 1453 inquisition lead by Brother John Capistrano in Breslau's market square.

[1002] Position 927.4 of *Microcosm*.

[1003] Position 927.7 of *Microcosm*.

[1004] Position 927.8 of *Microcosm*.

[1005] Position 928.4 of *Microcosm*.

[1006] Page 607 of Bethge and position 731.3 of Metaxas.

[1007] Page 607 of Bethge.

[1008] Position 731.4 of Metaxas.

[1009] Position 732.1 of Metaxas and page 607 of Bethge.

[1010] The commentary of Matthew Henry from the Bible Hub at http://biblehub.com/commentaries/psalms/74-8.htm. Accessed on Saturday July 25, 2020.

[1011] Position 733.2 of Metaxas and page 607 of Bethge.

[1012] Position 733.9 of Metaxas and page 607 of Bethge.

[1013] Page 607 of Bethge.

[1014] Page 607 of Bethge.

[1015] Position 649.4 of Metaxas.

[1016] Position 580.6 to 583.5 of Schlingensiepen.

[1017] Position 581.2 of Schlingensiepen.

[1018] Position 711.1 of Metaxas and page 599 of Bethge.

[1019] Position 581.5 of Schlingensiepen and page 462 of *Kampf und Zeugnis der Bekennenden Kirche* (Struggle and Witness of the Confessing Church), by Wilhelm Niemöller (older brother of Martin), published by L. Bechauf, 1948.

[1020] Position 582.4 of Schlingensiepen.

[1021] Page 193 of the book *Was hätten Sie getan?: die Flucht der Familie Kahle aus Nazi-Deutschland **UND** Die Universität Bonn vor und während der Nazi-Zeit (1923-1939)* (What would you have done ?: The escape of the Kahle family from Nazi Germany **AND** The University of Bonn before and during the Nazi period (1923-1939)), Volume 7 of Edition Rheinische Bibliothek, Authors Marie Kahle AND Paul Kahle, Editors John H. Kahle, Wilhelm Bleek, Edition 2, published by Bouvier, 1998, ISBN 3416028066, 9783416028066, is actually two books in one by Marie Kahle and her husband Paul Kahle. Marie covers the family's escape to England in 1939, while her husband Paul covers the time at the University in Bonn from 1923 until 1939.

[1022] Position 583.2 of Schlingensiepen and page 193 of *Was hätten Sie getan?: die Flucht der Familie Kahle aus Nazi-Deutschland **UND** Die Universität Bonn vor und während der Nazi-Zeit (1923-1939)*.

[1023] Position 735.9 of Metaxas and page 91 of *Selected Writings* by Dietrich Bonhoeffer, edited by Edwin Hanton Robertson, published by Fount, 1995, ISBN 0006279309, 9780006279303 quotes Dietrich's Advent letter of 1938

and how disheartened he was with the Confessing Church being unable to mount any effective resistance to Hitler. See also pages 610 to 611 of Bethge.
[1024] The incredible courage of Alexander Krzyżanowski is documented in the article on the Polish History Portal website at http://dzieje.pl/postacie/aleksander-krzyzanowski-wilk-1895-1951 which states his treacherous arrest on July 17 1944 by the NKVD and the fact that he never gave into torture by the infamous UB post-war. Concerning the Polish Communist Secret Police, namely the Urząd Bezpieczeństwa (UB), see the English language version of the Doomed Soldiers website at http://www.doomedsoldiers.com/polish-secret-police.html. Both links accessed on Saturday July 25, 2020.
[1025] Page 89 of the book *Between Hitler and Stalin* by Archibald L. Patterson, published by Dog Ear Publishing, 2010, ISBN 1608445631, 9781608445639, quotes Józef Piłsudski, as does the back cover of the book *Piłsudski: A Life For Poland*, by Wacław Jędrzejewicz, published by Hippocrene Books, New York, 1982, ISBN 9780870527470.

Chapter 15 - New York — Troubled Revisiting

[1026] Position 742.0 of Metaxas and page 634 of Bethge.
[1027] The fate of conscientious objectors in the Third Reich is given in *The German War: A Nation Under Arms, 1939—45* by Nicholas Stargardt, published by Random House, 2015, ISBN 1473523737, 9781473523739. See passages of selected text on Google Books at https://books.google.com.au/books?id=7drvCAAAQBAJ&printsec=frontcover&dq=History+books+The+German+War+by+Nicholas+Stargardt&hl=en&sa=X&ved=0ahUKEwit5LzogPvcAhULzbwKHQIcCwUQ6AEIKTAA#v=onepage&q=112&f=false and https://books.google.com.au/books?id=5fe6gbDyDhEC&pg=PA425&lpg=PA425&dq=fate+of+conscientious+objectors+in+Nazi+Germany&source=bl&ots=RvAz_2Tdlx&sig=Djw27Jv40botNT6gDGx251isRMA&hl=en&sa=X&ved=2ahUKEwi1kfDt7_rcAhWMAIgKHQU0BZoQ6AEwB3oECAMQAQ#v=onepage&q=fate%20of%20conscientious%20objectors%20in%20Nazi%20Germany&f=false. Both links accessed on Saturday July 25, 2020.
[1028] Position 600.2 of Schlingensiepen and position 742.6 of Metaxas.
[1029] Position 599.4 of Schlingensiepen, position 743.2 of Metaxas and page 638 of Bethge.
[1030] The United Press International Archives website at http://www.upi.com/Archives/1939/03/15/Crowds-defiant-in-Prague-as-Hitler-crosses-Czech-frontier/8148408176316/ gives the date of Wednesday March 15 1939 when Hitler's troops marched into the Czech capital of Prague. As does position 742.0 near the beginning of Chapter 21 "The Great Decision" of Metaxas and page 640 of Bethge. Accessed on Saturday July 25, 2020.

[1031] Position 743.6 of Metaxas and position 607.0 of Schlingensiepen.

[1032] See pages 22-23 of *No Greater Ally, The Untold Story of Poland's Forces in World War II*, by Kenneth K. Koskodan, published by Osprey Publishing 2011, ISBN-13: 9781849084796. Page 41 describes how the Poles, had never expected to fight a protracted campaign on their own against Germany, and as it turned out, against the Soviets on their eastern frontier.

[1033] Page 219 of *Hitler's Pre-emptive War: The Battle for Norway, 1940* by Henrik O. Lunde, published by Casemate Publishers, 2009, ISBN 1932033920, 9781932033922.

[1034] Ibid page 3.

[1035] See Chapter 2 "French Misfortunes: The Phony War and the Defense of France" from pages 42-58 of Koskodan.

[1036] Page 55 of Koskodan.

[1037] [2943] Position 746.2 to 749.1 of Metaxas describes Dietrich's stay in England from March 11 and his return to Berlin on April 18. See also position 599.8 of Schlingensiepen in regard to Dietrich's March 1939 meeting with Franz Hildebrandt.

[1038] [1150] Position 600.7 of Schlingensiepen.

[1039] Position 746.8 of Metaxas, position 600.4 of Schlingensiepen and page 639 of Bethge.

[1040] Position 747.0 of Metaxas and a more detailed quote at pages 644 to 645 of Bethge.

[1041] Page 645 of Bethge. On this page, a most relevant and critical excerpt from the manifesto is quoted.

[1042] Position 748.2 of Metaxas and position 601.9 of Schlingensiepen and pages 646 to 647 of Bethge.

[1043] Page 648 of Bethge, position 749.0 of Metaxas and page 114 of *Dietrich Bonhoeffer: A Life in Pictures* edited by Renate Bethge and Christian Gremmels, translated by Brian McNeil, published by Fortress Press Minneapolis 2006, ISBN 1451416563, 9781451416565.

[1044] Position 750.5 of Metaxas. See also position 608.0 of Schlingensiepen and page 648 of Bethge.

[1045] Page 211 of *The Way to Freedom: Letters, Lectures and Notes, 1935-1939, from the Collected Works of Dietrich Bonhoeffer Volume 2*, by Dietrich Bonhoeffer, edited by Edwin Hanton Robertson, published by Collins, 1966, no ISBN given.

[1046] See endnote [470] of Chapter 5 "London Pastorate and the Fanø Conference."

[1047] Page 212 of *The Way to Freedom: Letters, Lectures and Notes, 1935-1939, from the Collected Works of Dietrich Bonhoeffer Volume 2*, by Dietrich Bonhoeffer, edited by Edwin Hanton Robertson, published by Collins, 1966, no ISBN given and position 751.2 of Metaxas.

[1048] Position 751.4 of Metaxas and page 211 of *The Way to Freedom: Letters, Lectures and Notes, 1935-1939, from the Collected Works of Dietrich Bonhoef-*

fer Volume 2, by Dietrich Bonhoeffer, edited by Edwin Hanton Robertson, published by Collins, 1966, no ISBN given.

[1049] Position 751.7 of Metaxas.

[1050] Position 722.8 of Metaxas, position 579.2 of Schlingensiepen and pages 605 to 606 of Bethge. In September 1938, Barth wrote this letter from Basel to his colleague in Prague, Professor Josef Hromádka. Eventually, it became public.

[1051] [1764] [3006] Position 753.7 of Metaxas quoting the interview of Otto Dudzus, by Martin Doblmeier, the creator of the 2003 documentary film *Bonhoeffer: Pastor, Pacifist, Nazi Resister* (See position 1260.0 in the notes of Metaxas). See this documentary's online review by Cliff Vaughn, dated October 9 2003, on the website of the Nashville based Baptist Center for Ethics at https://www.ethicsdaily.com/bonhoeffer-cms-3209/. Also see the documentary review on the Internet Movie Database at https://www.imdb.com/title/tt0371583/. As well, the sermon by Michael Banner at Trinity College Cambridge on Remembrance Sunday on November 10 2013 on page 3 which can be downloaded on the Trinity College website at http://trinitycollegechapel.com/media/filestore/sermons/BannerBonhoeffer101 113.pdf. All links accessed on Saturday July 25, 2020.

[1052] Position 753.8 of Metaxas. The fact that Bethge accompanied Dietrich in escorting the Leibholzes part of the way to the Swiss border around the time of the 1938 Czech-Sudeten crisis, also implies this. See Chapter 13 "Flight and the Tumultuous Appeasement of Evil."

[1053] Position 754.0 of Metaxas.

[1054] The BBC online article *Attack on Nice: Who was Mohamed Lahouaiej-Bouhlel?* dated August 19 2016 at https://www.bbc.com/news/world-europe-36801763. Accessed on Saturday July 25, 2020.

[1055] Position 754.3 of Metaxas.

[1056] Position 609.7 of Schlingensiepen.

[1057] Page 649 of Bethge.

[1058] Page 649 of Bethge. See also pages 115 to 116 of *Dietrich Bonhoeffer: A Life in Pictures* edited by Renate Bethge and Christian Gremmels, translated by Brian McNeil, published by Fortress Press Minneapolis 2006, ISBN 1451416563, 9781451416565.

[1059] This is implied on page 650 of Bethge.

[1060] Position 608.0 of Schlingensiepen.

[1061] Position 609.7 of Schlingensiepen.

[1062] Page 68 of *The Oxford Handbook of Dietrich Bonhoeffer*, editors Michael Mawson, Philip G. Ziegler, published by Oxford University Press, 2019, ISBN 0191067423, 9780191067426 and position 759.5 of Metaxas.

[1063] Position 610.1 of Schlingensiepen, position 760.2 of Metaxas and pages 649 to 651 of Bethge.

[1064] Position 795.0 of Metaxas.

[1065] Position 760.7 of Metaxas and page 650 of Bethge.

[1066] Position 761.1 of Metaxas.

[1067] Position 760.8 of Metaxas.

[1068] Position 763.6 of Metaxas and and page 493 of *A testament to freedom: the essential writings of Dietrich Bonhoeffer* by Dietrich Bonhoeffer, edited by Geoffrey B. Kelly, F. Burton Nelson, published by Harper San Francisco, 1990, ISBN 0060608137, 9780060608132.

[1069] Position 93.1 of Schlingensiepen mentions Dietrich's meetings with the royal family, Mussolini and even Pope Pius XI. However, it also states that he did not regard these meetings as the highlight of his visit to the Eternal city. Rather, it would be Saint Peter's that would unequivocally hold that distinction.

[1070] Position 774.7 of Metaxas and position 613.5 of Schlingensiepen.

[1071] Position 776.0 of Metaxas. See also pages 653 to 654 of Bethge and position 614.0 to 614.8 of Schlingensiepen.

[1072] See position 768.7 of Metaxas. The footnote states that he was a main proponent in appeasing Hitler. This is implied in the article *Harry Emerson Fosdick's role in the war and pacifist movements* by David P. King, dated June 22 2006, published by Baptist History and Heritage, ISSN: 0005-5719. It can be read online at https://www.thefreelibrary.com/_/print/PrintArticle.aspx?id=155475841. Accessed on Saturday July 25, 2020.

[1073] Position 771.2 of Metaxas and page 495 of *A testament to freedom: the essential writings of Dietrich Bonhoeffer* by Dietrich Bonhoeffer, edited by Geoffrey B. Kelly, F. Burton Nelson, published by Harper San Francisco, 1990, ISBN 0060608137, 9780060608132. See also page 658 of Bethge.

[1074] Positions 776.5 of Metaxas. See also page 653 of Bethge and position 614.3 of Schlingensiepen.

[1075] Position 776.7 of Metaxas and page 93 of *I Knew Dietrich Bonhoeffer*, editors Wolf-Dieter Zimmermann and Ronald Gregor Smith, published by Harper & Row, 1967 (No ISBN given).

[1076] Position 776.9 of Metaxas.

[1077] Positions 778.0 of Metaxas. One of the works of Julius August Bewer was *The Literature of the Old Testament in its Historical Development* published in New York by Columbia University Press 1924. It can be downloaded at the US Archive at https://ia802504.us.archive.org/22/items/literatureofoldt00bewe/literatureofold t00bewe.pdf. Accessed on Saturday July 25, 2020. Near the beginning of this book, it is stated that he graduated with a Ph.D., Columbia and D.Theol., Göttingen — where the Leibholzes lived and father/husband Gerhard lectured before their flight to Switzerland in September 1938.

[1078] A photo of Julius August Bewer and Dietrich among other students and professors at Union in 1930 can be found at position 196.6 of Schlingensiepen.

[1079] Position 782.7 of Metaxas and page 655 of Bethge.

[1080] Position 788.6 of Metaxas.

[1081] Position 795.0 of Metaxas and position 615.5 of Schlingensiepen.

[1082] Position 790.9 of Metaxas and page 656 of Bethge.

[1083] Position 791.5 of Metaxas.

[1084] While I could not find any sources to confirm this, one can likely infer that Paul Lehmann would have given his farewell to Karl-Friedrich as well. However, most of Paul Lehmann's time at the pier would have been spent talking to Dietrich.

[1085] See letter #129 in *Theological Education Underground, 1937-1940, Volume 15 of Dietrich Bonhoeffer Works Series* by Dietrich Bonhoeffer, editors Victoria Barnett and Dirk Schulz, published by Fortress Press, 2011, ISBN 1451406835, 9781451406832. Also, see position 742.0 at the beginning of Chapter 21 "The Great Decision" in Metaxas.

[1086] This can be implied from position 790.9 of Metaxas and page 656 of Bethge, where Karl-Friedrich declined the lucrative safety of an offer of a professorship in Chicago.

[1087] Position 620.8 of Schlingensiepen.

[1088] 2944 Position 796.5 of Metaxas and page 661 of Bethge.

[1089] Pages 661 to 662 of Bethge, position 796.9 of Metaxas and position 621.0 of Schlingensiepen. Page 50 of the book *Confront!: Resistance in Nazi Germany* by editor John J. Michałczyk, published by Peter Lang, 2004, ISBN 0820463175, 9780820463179 gives the exact date of execution as the July 18 1939.

[1090] Page 662 of Bethge and position 621.0 of Schlingensiepen at the end of "Chapter 9 New York (1939)."

Chapter 16 - Homecoming to Outbreak of War

[1091] Position 620.8 of Schlingensiepen at the end of "Chapter 9 New York (1939)" mentions Dietrich's visits to Dortmund and Elberfeld on his way back to Berlin. Included, is the tragic story of Hermann and his son Helmuth Hesse of Elberfeld.

[1092] Position 797.4 of Metaxas.

[1093] Position 797.4 of Metaxas at the end of Chapter 21 the "Great Decision." See also pages 118 to 119 of *Behind Valkyrie: German Resistance to Hitler, Documents*, contributor Peter Hoffmann, published by McGill-Queen's Press - MQUP, 2011, ISBN 0773587152, 9780773587151 concerning Hellmut Traub's account of Dietrich's return from New York.

[1094] Ibid.

[1095] Position 798.0 of Metaxas at the end of Chapter 21 the "Great Decision" and page 662 of Bethge.

[1096] See Polish WWII Supplement II "The Gleiwitz (Gliwice) Incident"3537.

[1097] Position 803.5 of Metaxas, position 624.1 of Schlingensiepen and pages 665 to 666 of Bethge.

[1098] Pages 591 to 592 of Bethge and position 651.6 of Schlingensiepen.

[1099] Position 623.0 of Schlingensiepen

[1100] Position 622.6 of Schlingensiepen, position 804.1 of Metaxas and page 663 of Bethge.

[1101] Position 803.7 of Metaxas.

[1102] Position 632.2 of Schlingensiepen.

[1103] Position 632.4 of Schlingensiepen.

[1104] See endnotes [128] to [133] in the Preface "Birth and Memory upon the Lesser Known Fault Line of History" in regard to the Einsatzgruppen deployed during the invasion of Poland.

[1105] Position 812.0 of Metaxas, page 660 of William L. Shirer and page 30 of *The Waffen SS: Hitler's Elite Guard at War, 1939-1945* by George H. Stein, published by Cornell University Press, 1984, ISBN 0801492750, 9780801492754.

[1106] Page 30 of *The Waffen SS: Hitler's Elite Guard at War, 1939-1945* by George H. Stein, published by Cornell University Press, 1984, ISBN 0801492750, 9780801492754. See also position 808.4 of Metaxas, although, Metaxas makes no mention of Wehrmacht officers attempting to prosecute the perpetrators.

[1107] Position 636.7 of Schlingensiepen and page 671 of Bethge.

[1108] *Oskar Schindler: The Untold Account of His Life, Wartime Activites, and the True Story Behind the List* by David Crowe, published by Hachette UK, 2007, ISBN 0465008496, 9780465008490 on Google Books at https://books.google.com.au/books?id=aMQ_DgAAQBAJ&dq=ISBN+046500 8496%2C+9780465008490&q=Blaskowitz#v=snippet&q=Blaskowitz&f=fals e. Accessed on Saturday July 25, 2020.

[1109] The indifference of Keitel during his meeting with Canaris in Hitler's armoured train in Upper Silesia on September 12 1939 is documented in *Oskar Schindler: The Untold Account of His Life, Wartime Activites, and the True Story Behind the List*, by David Crowe, published by Hachette UK, 2007, ISBN 0465008496, 9780465008490 under the section "Krakow and the Early Months of the German Occupation," or see Google Books at https://books.google.com.au/books?id=aMQ_DgAAQBAJ&printsec=frontcov er&dq=ISBN+0465008496,+9780465008490&hl=en&sa=X&ved=0ahUKEwi 7jr73pvHdAhXZZt4KHUmADAoQ6AEIKTAA#v=snippet&q=Keitel&f=fals e. This section contains both of Keitels statements, while Metaxas at position 812.8 contains just the former statement; "The Führer has already decided on this matter." Accessed on Saturday July 25, 2020.

[1110] [2059] Ibid.

[1111] Page 31 of The Waffen SS: Hitler's Elite Guard at War, 1939-1945 by George H. Stein, published by Cornell University Press, 1984, ISBN 0801492750, 9780801492754.

[1112] Ibid.

[1113] Position 814.6 of Metaxas

[1114] Position 807.6 of Metaxas and position 631.3 of Schlingensiepen.

[1115] [190] Position 810.6 of Metaxas.

[1116] Position 811.7 of Metaxas.

[1117] See pages 80-81 of Chapter 4 "The Mind of Hitler and the Roots of the Third Reich" in the book *The Rise and Fall of the Third Reich: A History of Nazi Germany* by William L. Shirer. See also pages 164 to 169 of Jane Pejsa and endnote [718] in Chapter 9 "The von Kleists and the Prophecy."

[1118] Position 809.4 of Metaxas.

[1119] An example of an Einsatzgruppe mass murderer is given from position 1048.7 of Microcosm. He being, Breslau's Udo von Woyrsch. See also endnote [131] from the Preface "Birth and Memory upon the Lesser Known Fault Line of History" in regard to this individual.

[1120] [190] [2803] Position 807.4 of Metaxas.

[1121] [3610] Position 631.2 of Schlingensiepen and pages 668 to 669 of Bethge.

[1122] [2803] Position 636.2 of Schlingensiepen and page 671 of Bethge in regard to Hitler's violation in 1940 of his pledge to respect Dutch and Belgian neutrality — thus rendering pointless, all convoluted and indulgent overtures for peace while Hitler remained in power.

[1123] [1214] Position 930.8 onwards of Microcosm documents the heinous "T-4 Aktion."

[1124] Position 819.2 of Metaxas.

[1125] Position 818.6 of Metaxas.

[1126] Position 932.8 of Microcosm and position 818.8 of Metaxas.

[1127] [1214] See note #20 of Chapter 10 "In the Resistance (1939—1943)" of Schlingensiepen at position 1039.1 — which is linked to note #20 at position 687.7.

[1128] Page 672 of Bethge and position 821.5 of Metaxas.

[1129] Page 671 of Bethge and position 821.8 of Metaxas .

[1130] Position 822.0 of Metaxas and page 641 of William L. Shirer.

[1131] Ibid.

[1132] Position 823.0 of Metaxas.

[1133] Position 641.3 of Schlingensiepen.

[1134] Article on the website of the Holocaust Education & Archive Research Team at http://www.holocaustresearchproject.org/holoprelude/RSHA/rsha.html. See also the quick facts page on the various SS and other Nazi leaders at http://www.holocaustresearchproject.org/holoprelude/ssleaders.html. Both links accessed on Saturday July 25, 2020.

[1135] Position 641.8 of Schlingensiepen.

[1136] [2059] Position 642.9 of Schlingensiepen.

[1137] A map of the frontlines in Europe at the time of the assassination plot on Hitler on July 20 1944 can be found on page vi of the book *Countdown to Valkyrie: The July Plot to Assassinate Hitler* by Nigel Jones, published by Casemate Publishers, 2008, ISBN 1848325088, 9781848325081. Also at position 13.8 of the ebook of the same title and author, published in 2008 by Frontline Books, Digital Edition ISBN 9781783407811. The name Adolf is a contraction of the Old German "Adelwolf," meaning "Noble Wolf," hence the naming of Hitler's East Prussian headquarters as Wolfsschanze (Wolf's Lair). (See position 1094.9 of Metaxas and position 25.9 of Nigel Jones). Likewise the naming of his headquarters during the Battle of France as Wolfsschlucht (Wolf's Gorge), and the forward eastern headquarters at Vinnitsa in the Ukraine as Werwolf (Werewolf), which by July 1944, was well and truly under the Red Army's control. No doubt, as Metaxas put it; "the wild carnivorous and Darwinian ruthlessness of the beast appealed to him." (See position 1094.9 of Metaxas). However, the most famous or infamous of Hitler's lupine retreats was the East Prussian Lair.

[1138] Position 643.5 of Schlingensiepen.

[1139] See page iv of the book *Dietrich Bonhoeffer: Man of Vision, Man of Courage* by Eberhard Bethge, published by Harper & Row Publishers Inc. New York and William Collins Sons and Co Ltd London, 1970. It can be viewed on Google Books at https://books.google.com.au/books?id=0BNDAAAAIAAJ&q=Dietrich+Bonhoeffer:+Man+of+Vision,+Man+of+Courage%E2%80%9D+by+Eberhard+Bethge,+published+by+Harper+%26+Row+Publishers+Inc.+New+York+and+William+Collins+Sons+and+Co+Ltd+London,+1970&dq=Dietrich+Bonhoeffer:+Man+of+Vision,+Man+of+Courage%E2%80%9D+by+Eberhard+Bethge,+published+by+Harper+%26+Row+Publishers+Inc.+New+York+and+William+Collins+Sons+and+Co+Ltd+London,+1970&hl=en&sa=X&ved=0ahUKEwjJ7Ia404HjAhXCeisKHUvdD5AQ6AEIMDAB. Accessed on Saturday July 25, 2020.

[1140] Position 645.0 of Schlingensiepen.

[1141] Position 644.0 of Schlingensiepen.

[1142] Concerning Dutch neutrality during the Great War, see the online article at http://www.waroverholland.nl/index.php?page=holland-wwi-and-the-international-relations, by the Dutch historian Allert M.A. Goossens. Accessed on Saturday July 25, 2020.

[1143] Position 632.4 of Schlingensiepen.

[1144] Position 644.6 of Schlingensiepen and page 675 of Bethge.

[1145] Position 647.9 of Schlingensiepen.

[1146] Position 647.5 of Schlingensiepen.

[1147] https://www.britannica.com/event/Vichy-France. Accessed on Saturday July 25, 2020.

[1148] https://www.britannica.com/biography/Philippe-Petain. Accessed on Saturday July 25, 2020.

[1149] Position 649.0 of Schlingensiepen.

[1150] Position 600.7 of Schlingensiepen. See also endnote [1038] from Chapter 15 "New York — Troubled Revisiting" in regard to Dietrich's fruitless meetings with ecumenical contacts in England during his March-April 1939 visit to England.

[1151] Position 649.1 of Schlingensiepen.

[1152] Position 648.8 of Schlingensiepen.

[1153] Position 651.6 of Schlingensiepen and page 592 of Bethge.

[1154] Position 651.7 of Schlingensiepen.

[1155] Between the world wars, East Prussia had been isolated from Germany proper by the Polish or Danzig/Gdańsk corridor as a consequence of Versailles, in order to give Poland access to the sea. See https://www.britannica.com/place/Polish-Corridor and https://www.britannica.com/place/East-Prussia. While a source of bitterness for Germans in the wake of Versailles, it must be mentioned, as stated in the former article, that the territory was historically Polish (that is, before the partitions of Poland in the late 18th century) and was inhabited by a Polish majority, not to mention the 13th provision of U.S. President Woodrow Wilson's Fourteen Points, for giving Poland "a free and secure access to the sea" and indeed its only access. The full text of Woodrow Wilson's Fourteen Points can be accessed on the Yale Law School Avalon Project website at http://avalon.law.yale.edu/20th_century/wilson14.asp. All links accessed on Saturday July 25, 2020.

[1156] Position 651.9 of Schlingensiepen.

[1157] Concerning the Dunkirk evacuation, see https://www.britannica.com/event/Dunkirk-evacuation and the supplement to the London Gazette dated Tuesday July 15 1947, downloaded from http://www.ibiblio.org/hyperwar/UN/UK/LondonGazette/38017.pdf. Both links Accessed on Saturday July 25, 2020.

[1158] Position 652.0 of Schlingensiepen.

[1159] Position 652.1 of Schlingensiepen.

[1160] Position 653.5 of Schlingensiepen, page 681 of Bethge and page 255 of Jane Pejsa.

[1161] Position 832.5 of Metaxas.

[1162] Page 681 of Bethge.

[1163] Page 255 of Jane Pejsa.

Chapter 17 — Pastor and Spy

[1164] See the online *Encyclopaedia Britannica* article on Kaliningrad at https://www.britannica.com/place/Kaliningrad, accessed on Saturday August 8, 2020.

[1165] Position 653.7 of Schlingensiepen and page 697 of Bethge.

[1166] Position 654.4 of Schlingensiepen.

[1167] Position 655.6 of Schlingensiepen.

[1168] Position 655.9 of Schlingensiepen.

[1169] Position 656.9 of Schlingensiepen.

[1170] Position 670.8 of Schlingensiepen.

[1171] Position 655.2 of Schlingensiepen.

[1172] Position 655.6 of Schlingensiepen and page 700 of Bethge.

[1173] Position 658.3 of Schlingensiepen.

[1174] Page 700 of Bethge.

[1175] New York times online article on Paul Ernst Fackenheim at https://www.nytimes.com/1985/12/29/books/the-jew-who-spied-for-th-nazis.html dated December 29 1985. Accessed on Saturday July 25, 2020.

[1176] See the article on the website of Elly Kleinman at http://ellykleinman.com/nazis-jewish-spy/. Accessed on Saturday July 25, 2020.

[1177] Ibid.

[1178] Ibid.

[1179] [1251] Ibid and https://www.nytimes.com/1985/12/29/books/the-jew-who-spied-for-th-nazis.html dated December 29 1985. Accessed on Saturday July 25, 2020. While this case is an instance of a Jew working for the Abwehr, I have not been able to find a similar instance of a communist working for the Abwehr. However, considering the fact that National Socialist dogma perceived Jews and Communism as synonymous, perhaps in one sense, this fully explains the notion of Jews and Communists being employed by the Abwehr. See pages 83, 414, 427 and 568 of *Lenin, Stalin and Hitler The Age of Social Catastrophe* by Robert Gellately, published by Vintage 2008, ISBN 9780712603577, in regard to the National Socialist perception of the "synonymous" Jews.

[1180] [1251] Position 298.8 of Nigel Jones.

[1181] [3290] [3561] [3564] [3717] [4436] [4439] [4450] Article on the website of the Holocaust Education & Archive Research Team at http://www.holocaustresearchproject.org/holoprelude/aboutthess.html. Accessed on Saturday July 25, 2020.

[1182] Article on the website of the Holocaust Education & Archive Research Team at http://www.holocaustresearchproject.org/holoprelude/RSHA/rsha.html. See also the quick facts page on the various SS and other Nazi leaders at http://www.holocaustresearchproject.org/holoprelude/ssleaders.html. Both accessed on Saturday July 25, 2020.

[1183] [2889 3290 3561 3564 3551 3717 4436 4439 4450] A diagram of the competing intelligence agencies in Hitler's Reich is given at position 209.0 of the ebook *Hitler's Spy Chief The Wilhelm Canaris Mystery* by Richard Bassett, published by The Orion Publishing Group Limited, a Hachette UK company, ISBN 9780297865711. Note the Abwehr being separate to the RSHA under Himmler.

[1184] This most questionable individual will be mentioned in Chapter 20 "Valkyrie II."

[1185] Position 177.8 of the ebook *Hitler's Spy Chief The Wilhelm Canaris Mystery* by Richard Bassett.

[1186] The Global Security website at https://www.globalsecurity.org/military/world/europe/de-reichsmarine.htm and the German Armed Forces Research 1918-1945 website at https://www.feldgrau.com/WW1-German-Reichsmarine. Both links accessed on Saturday July 25, 2020. Both accessed on Saturday July 25, 2020.

[1187] Position 191.4 of the ebook *Hitler's Spy Chief The Wilhelm Canaris Mystery* by Richard Bassett.

[1188] Position 179.1 of the ebook *Hitler's Spy Chief The Wilhelm Canaris Mystery* by Richard Bassett. See also position 229.2 onwards where Canaris' Abwehr closely co-operated with the SD in 1935 as an instrument of "internal" repression — position 229.7. During the March 1936 Rhineland crisis, Canaris assured Hitler that the French and British would not take military action if German troops occupied the demilitarised Rhineland in violation of the Versailles Treaty. Hitler not surprisingly, regarded this as a major intelligence coup for Canaris and his Abwehr. See also the beginning of Chapter 10 "Swedish trip and the Brethren Houses" for this book.

[1189] Position 277.7 of the ebook *Hitler's Spy Chief The Wilhelm Canaris Mystery* by Richard Bassett. In regard to the Austrian Anschluss, see endnotes [908] and [909], and for the Fritsch Affair, see endnotes [899] to [906], all from Chapter 13 "Flight and the Tumultuous Appeasement of Evil."

[1190] Position 659.9 of Schlingensiepen.

[1191] Position 661.5 of Schlingensiepen.

[1192] Position 661.5 of Schlingensiepen which states 30,000 miles which is around 50,000 kilometres.

[1193] Page 682 of Bethge.

[1194] Bottom of page 683 of Bethge.

[1195] Pages 682 to 683 of Bethge.

[1196] Page 684 of Bethge.

[1197] Page 684 of Bethge.

[1198] Position 664.2 of Schlingensiepen.

[1199] Position 664.7 of Schlingensiepen.

[1200] Position 648.8 of Schlingensiepen.

[1201] Position 653.3 onwards in Schlingensiepen and page 681 of Bethge.

[1202] Position 671.5 of Schlingensiepen.

[1203] Position 672.8 of Schlingensiepen.

[1204] Page 686 of Bethge.

[1205] Position 858.3 of Schlingensiepen.

[1206] Detrich's foreign contacts are listed in part at position 823.0 of Metaxas at the end of Chapter 22, "The End of Germany." In regard to Willem A. Visser 't Hooft, see Schlingensiepen at position 748.2 and at position 510.0 where it states Visser 't Hooft's position as the Ecumenical General Secretary, appointed in 1939. This being just before Dietrich's meeting with Visser 't Hooft at Paddington Station, while just after that same meeting, at position 604.9, Schlingensiepen states; *When Bonhoeffer later made contact with the ecumenical offices in Geneva on behalf of the Resistance movement, he had in Visser 't Hooft, from the first moment, a dependable colleague and friend.*

[1207] Page 686 of Bethge.

[1208] Page 264 at the start of Chapter 5 "Ecumenical Dialogue or 'The War Behind the War'" and pages 273 to 274 of *German Resistance Against Hitler: The Search for Allies Abroad, 1938-1945* by Klemens Von Klemperer, published by Ebsco Publishing, 1994, ISBN 0191513342, 9780191513343.

[1209] Page 267 of *German Resistance Against Hitler: The Search for Allies Abroad, 1938-1945*.

[1210] Position 694.7 of Schlingensiepen.

[1211] Position 695.5 of Schlingensiepen.

[1212] Position 868.4 of Metaxas and page 727 of Bethge.

[1213] Position 693.0 of Schlingensiepen.

[1214] Position 871.6 of Metaxas talks of Dietrich revealing the euthanasia (T-4 Aktion) measures and persecution of Confessing Church ministers. In regard to the heinous T-4 Aktion see endnotes [1123] to [1127] of Chapter 16 "Homecoming to Outbreak of War."

[1215] Position 693.8 of Schlingensiepen.

[1216] Position 695.8 of Schlingensiepen.

[1217] Position 694.6 of Schlingensiepen and page 728 of Bethge.

[1218] Position 871.6 of Metaxas.

[1219] Position 698.3 of Schlingensiepen.

[1220] Position 698.7 of Schlingensiepen. The story of this brave French village is documented in the book *Lest Innocent Blood be Shed: The Story of the Village of Le Chambon, and how Goodness Happened There* by Philip Paul Hallie, published by Harper & Row, 1985, ISBN 006132051X, 9780061320514.

[1221] Position 697.8 to 700.9 of Schlingensiepen.

[1222] Position 699.3 of Schlingensiepen.

[1223] Position 699.4 of Schlingensiepen.

[1224] Position 699.6 of Schlingensiepen.

[1225] Position 700.5 of Schlingensiepen.

[1226] Position 695.1 of Schlingensiepen.

[1227] Position 696.6 of Schlingensiepen.

[1228] Position 696.9 of Schlingensiepen.

[1229] Position 697.2 of Schlingensiepen.

[1230] Pages 717 to 718 of Bethge.

[1231] [539 630 2364 3711] The date of March 30 1941 for Hitler's notorious "Commissar Order," is given at position 701.4 of Schlingensiepen, page 732 of Bethge and page 33 of the book *War of Annihilation: Combat and Genocide on the Eastern Front, 1941* by Geoffrey P. Megargee, published by Rowman & Littlefield, 2007, ISBN 0742544826, 9780742544826. While some sources give June 4 1941, just preceding the invasion as the date for the issuing of the Commissar Order, this was the official issuing of it by the German High Command (OKW). The date of March 30 1941 was when Hitler addressed the most important commanders and staff officers that would lead the invasion into the Soviet Union. Hence the conjecture over when it was issued — either Hitler's rant in late March, or in June by OKW just preceding the invasion, as stated at position 877.7 of Metaxas and pages 426 to 428 of *Lenin, Stalin and Hitler* by Robert Gellately, published by Vintage 2008, ISBN 9780712603577. In any event, no one denies the existence of the order and what it embodied, nor its ultimate progenitor. See also page 38 of Geoffrey P. Megargee.

[1232] [3366] https://www.britannica.com/event/Operation-Barbarossa. Accessed on Saturday July 25, 2020.

[1233] [539 630 3435 3711] Position 701.7 of Schlingensiepen.

[1234] Position 701.8 of Schlingensiepen.

[1235] Position 702.2 of Schlingensiepen.

[1236] Position 702.5 of Schlingensiepen.

[1237] Position 703.7 of Schlingensiepen.

[1238] Position 703.6 of Schlingensiepen.

[1239] Position 703.3 of Schlingensiepen.

[1240] Page 736 of Bethge. See also position 704.6 of Schlingensiepen. Bell's book was published by Penguin in 1940 during the war, as stated on page 736 of Bethge.

[1241] Position 705.7 of Schlingensiepen.

[1242] Position 705.6 of Schlingensiepen.

[1243] Dietrich's meeting with a group of people, including Visser 't Hooft at Zürich's famous Pestalozzi Bibliotek is documented from position 712.2 of Schlingensiepen and page 744 of Bethge. The official website of the Pestalozzi-Bibliothek Zürich, is at http://www.pbz.ch/. Their is also the website for the Pestalozzi Children's Foundation at https://www.pestalozzi.ch/en/our-mission. Both links accessed on Saturday July 25, 2020.

[1244] [3205 3206 3414] Position 712.8 of Schlingensiepen and page 744 of Bethge.

[1245] [1577 3205 3206 3414] In regard to the original German publishing of Bethge's biography of Bonhoeffer in 1967 in Munich by the München Christian Kaiser Verlag, see page iv of *Dietrich Bonhoeffer: Man of Vision, Man of Courage* by Eberhard Bethge, published by Harper & Row Publishers Inc. New York and

William Collins Sons and Co Ltd London, 1970 and page iv of *Dietrich Bonhoeffer: A Biography* by Eberhard Bethge, edited by Victoria J. Barnett, published by Fortress Press, 2000, ISBN 0800628446, 9780800628444. For the original German title *Dietrich Bonhoeffer - Eine Biographie* see the German website https://www.booklooker.de/B%C3%BCcher/Eberhard-Bethge+Dietrich-Bonhoeffer-Eine-Biographie/id/A01xAkhK01ZZe. Accessed on Saturday July 25, 2020.

[1246] Position 714.1 of Schlingensiepen and position 893.6 of Metaxas. See also https://www.britannica.com/topic/Star-of-David for more details on the "Star of David." Accessed on Saturday July 25, 2020.

[1247] Position 714.4 of Schlingensiepen.

[1248] Position 546.4 of Schlingensiepen.

[1249] Position 714.6 of Schlingensiepen.

[1250] Position 714.9 of Schlingensiepen.

[1251] Page 747 of Bethge. This was not the only operation where the Abwehr used this pretext. See endnotes [1179] and [1180] for this chapter.

[1252] Page 747 of Bethge.

[1253] Position 719.9 of Schlingensiepen.

[1254] Position 1100.7 of Microcosm documents the best known German resistance organisation in Silesia, namely the *Kreisauer Kreis*, or "Kreisau circle," including their gruesome fate following the July 1944 assassination attempt on Hitler. The relationship of the estate's owner, Count Helmuth James von Moltke to the famous Moltke military dynasty is stated at position 276.3 of the ebook *Traitors or Patriots?: A Story of the German Anti-Nazi Resistance*, by Louis R. Eltscher, published by McNidder & Grace Carmarthen UK 2020, Ebook ISBN 9780857162045. Position 276.4 to 279.9 document his repugnance to the Nazi regime and his reluctant approval for Hitler's July 1944 attempted assassination. See also pages 117-118 and page 121 of the paper book of the same title, by Louis R. Eltscher, published by iUniverse, 2013, ISBN 1475981422, 9781475981421.

[1255] Position 720.6 of Schlingensiepen.

[1256] Pages 127-128 of the book *Dietrich Bonhoeffer: Called by God* by Elizabeth Raum, published by Bloomsbury Publishing USA, 2003, ISBN 1441167838, 9781441167835.

[1257] Positions 721.6 and 723.4 of Schlingensiepen.

[1258] Smolensk is near Katyń Wood, where the Stalinist perpetrated massacre of 4,000 plus Polish officers, took place from April to May 1940. The order for this action was signed and ordered by Stalin on March 5 1940. The Germans however would not discover the mass grave until April 1943, which will be covered in the next chapter. For a more detailed account of Katyń, see Polish WWII Supplement III "The Katyń Wood Massacre"[3618] and endnote [959] for Chapter 13 "Flight and the Tumultuous Appeasement of Evil."

[1259] [2820] Position 728.2 of Schlingensiepen.

[1260] Pages 84-86 of the book *Operation Barbarossa 1941 (1): Army Group South* by Robert Kirchubel, published by Bloomsbury Publishing, 2012, ISBN 1846036518, 9781846036514.

[1261] Ibid.

[1262] Page 173 of the book *The War Aims and Strategies of Adolf Hitler* by Oscar Pinkus, published by McFarland, 2005, ISBN 0786420545, 9780786420544 states that von Bock was the commander of Army Group Centre.

[1263] The advance of the German Army stalling at Moscow is documented at position 728.7 of Schlingensiepen, while position 899.7 of Metaxas documents it in greater detail, stating that advanced German units came to within fourteen miles (22.5 kilometres) of the Kremlin to glimpse its golden spires, as well as documenting the extreme cold and its consequences for German troops.

[1264] Page ccxiii (207) in Chapter 5 "Kicking in the Door: June-December 1941" of the book *The Storm of War: A New History of the Second World War* by Andrew Roberts, published by Penguin UK, 2009, ISBN 0141938862, 9780141938868.

[1265] Ibid.

[1266] Position 728.5 of Schlingensiepen.

[1267] Position 729.3 of Schlingensiepen.

[1268] Online article accessed on Saturday July 25, 2020 on the History Reader website at http://www.thehistoryreader.com/modern-history/december-111941-hitler-arguably-insane-pivotal-decision-history/ by Stephen Frater. It gives a detailed account of Hitler's declaration of war on the US in the Reichstag on December 11 1941 in the wake of Pearl Harbour. It also states that Hitler was in his Wolf's Lair in East Prussia when he gleefully received the news of the Japanese bombing of Pearl Harbour on the 7th. It also states that three-quarters of a million German soldiers died in the Russian winter of 1941-42.

[1269] The text of the Tripartite Pact at http://avalon.law.yale.edu/wwii/triparti.asp. Accessed on Saturday July 25, 2020.

[1270] Page 662 of *Hitler: A Study in Tyranny* by Alan Bullock, published in London by Penguin in 1962, ISBN 0140135642.

[1271] Online article on the History Reader website at http://www.thehistoryreader.com/modern-history/december-111941-hitler-arguably-insane-pivotal-decision-history/ by Stephen Frater. Accessed on Saturday July 25, 2020.

[1272] See the book *The war with Japan: A Concise History edition 2* by Charles Bateson, published by Michigan State University Press, 1968, no ISBN given. In particular see pages 58-59 in Chapter three "THE FALL OF THE PHILIPPINES" where General MacArthur along with almost every other Allied leader, military and civilian was guilty, and pages 88-89 in Chapter four "THE CONQUEST OF MALAYA," where the prevalence of complacency and wishful thinking in Singapore of the British, both military and civilian, is stated.

[1273] Page 248 of *A War To Be Won: fighting the Second World War* edition revised, by Williamson Murray and Allan Reed Millett, published by Harvard University Press, 2009, ISBN 0674041305, 9780674041301. Dönitz would briefly succeed Hitler when he committed suicide in his bunker on the 30th April 1945. See https://www.britannica.com/biography/Karl-Donitz. Accessed on Saturday July 25, 2020.

[1274] The BBC online article *The Battle of the Atlantic: The U-boat peril* at http://www.bbc.co.uk/history/worldwars/wwtwo/battle_atlantic_01.shtml. Accessed on Saturday July 25, 2020.

[1275] Page 32 of *Operation Drumbeat: the dramatic true story of Germany's first U-boat attacks along the American coast in World War II* by Michael Gannon, published by Harper & Row, 1990, ISBN 0060161558, 9780060161552.

[1276] In regard to the sinking of U-158, look for the date "June 30 Tuesday 1942" in *The Official Chronology of the U.S. Navy in World War II* by Robert Cressman, published by Naval Institute Press, 2016, ISBN 1682471543, 9781682471548. The Google Book link for its sinking is https://books.google.com.au/books?id=K6D1DAAAQBAJ&printsec=frontcover&dq=ISBN+1682471543,+9781682471548&hl=en&sa=X&ved=0ahUKEwjg1oH6797lAhXA4HMBHdnpC-wQ6AEIKTAA#v=onepage&q=west-southwest%20of%20Bermuda&f=false, while for the havoc it wrought before its sinking on June 30 1942, see the Google Book link at https://books.google.com.au/books?id=K6D1DAAAQBAJ&printsec=frontcover&dq=ISBN+1682471543,+9781682471548&hl=en&sa=X&ved=0ahUKEwjg1oH6797lAhXA4HMBHdnpC-wQ6AEIKTAA#v=snippet&q=U-158&f=false. Both accessed on Saturday July 25, 2020.

[1277] The online article by Stephen Frater on the History Reader website at http://www.thehistoryreader.com/modern-history/december-111941-hitler-arguably-insane-pivotal-decision-history/ quotes excerpts of Hitler's rant in the Reichstag on December 11 1941, where he formalised Germany's declaration of War on the US. Accessed on Saturday July 25, 2020.

[1278] Ibid.

[1279] Pages 661-664 of *Hitler: A Study in Tyranny* by Alan Bullock, published in London by Penguin in 1962, ISBN 0140135642. Note that Dietrich purchased a prodigious collection of Negro music, which he brought back to Germany in 1931. See endnote [277] for Chapter 1 "Roots, Genesis and Moulding of the Pastor."

[1280] [3344] The online article by Stephen Frater on the History Reader website at http://www.thehistoryreader.com/modern-history/december-111941-hitler-arguably-insane-pivotal-decision-history/. Accessed on Saturday July 25, 2020.

[1281] Ibid.

[1282] [3344] Ibid.

[1283] Position 731.4 of Schlingensiepen and pages 135-136 of *Ethics Volume 6 of Dietrich Bonhoeffer Works* by Dietrich Bonhoeffer, edited by Clifford J.

Green, edition annotated, published by Fortress Press, 2008, ISBN 1451406754, 9781451406757.

[1284] Position 731.9 of Schlingensiepen and page 139 of *Ethics Volume 6 of Dietrich Bonhoeffer Works*.

[1285] Position 736.9 of Schlingensiepen and page 704 of Bethge.

[1286] Position 741.5 of Schlingensiepen and page 251 of the book *Conspiracy and Imprisonment, 1940-1945 (Dietrich Bonhoeffer Works, Vol. 16)* by Dietrich Bonhoeffer, edited by Mark S Brocker, translated by Lisa E Dahill, published by Fortress Press; 1st English-language edition (June 27, 2006), ISBN-10: 0800683161 ISBN-13: 9780800683160.

[1287] Position 736.3 of Schlingensiepen.

[1288] Position 744.5 of Schlingensiepen.

[1289] Page 44 of *Quisling: A Study in Treachery* by Hans Fredrik Dahl, edition abridged, illustrated, reprint, published by Cambridge University Press, 1999, ISBN 0521496977, 9780521496971, documents Vidkun Quisling's humanitarian work in Russia and the Ukraine in the early 1920s.

[1290] Ibid.

[1291] Ibid page 69.

[1292] Ibid.

[1293] Ibid page 76.

[1294] Ibid page 84 gives the date of death for Peter Kolstad.

[1295] Ibid page 84 states that Quisling was retained as Minister of Defence upon Kolstad's death.

[1296] Ibid page 69.

[1297] Ibid pages 94 to 95.

[1298] Page 529 of the book *Hitler's Pre-emptive War: The Battle for Norway, 1940* by Henrik O. Lunde, published by Casemate Publishers, 2009, ISBN 1932033920, 9781932033922 gives the date of June 10 1940 for the Norwegian capitulation.

[1299] Time Magazine at http://content.time.com/time/magazine/article/0,9171,764097,00.html.

[1300] Page 219 of the book *Hitler's Pre-emptive War: The Battle for Norway, 1940* by Henrik O. Lunde, gives 2315 hours on April 8 1940, as the date and time for the launch of the German invasion of Norway. Accessed on Saturday July 25, 2020.

[1301] The Collins English Dictionary website at http://www.dictionary.com/browse/quisling states that the term "quisling" was first used in the London Times of April 15, 1940. Accessed on Saturday July 25, 2020.

[1302] Position 744.7 of Schlingensiepen.

[1303] Ibid.

[1304] [1394] Position 748.5 of Schlingensiepen.

[1305] Position 630.7 of Schlingensiepen.

[1306] Position 748.7 of Schlingensiepen.

[1307] Position 748.8 of Schlingensiepen.

[1308] [1394] Position 749.5 of Schlingensiepen.

[1309] Ibid.

[1310] Position 749.9 of Schlingensiepen. See also page 38 of *Memories of Kreisau and the German Resistance* by Freya von Moltke, translated by Julie M. Winter, edition illustrated, reprint, published by Univeristy of Nebraska Press, 2005, ISBN 0803296258, 9780803296251.

[1311] Position 750.1 of Schlingensiepen.

[1312] Position 750.0 of Schlingensiepen and page 755 of Bethge.

[1313] Position 751.3 of Schlingensiepen.

[1314] Position 750.2 of Schlingensiepen.

[1315] Position 750.4 of Schlingensiepen.

[1316] Position 750.7 of Schlingensiepen.

[1317] Position 752.0 of Schlingensiepen.

[1318] Position 753.3 of Schlingensiepen and page 755 of Bethge.

[1319] Position 753.6 of Schlingensiepen.

[1320] Position 761.2 of Schlingensiepen and page 754 of Bethge.

[1321] Position 753.9 of Schlingensiepen.

[1322] Page 38 of Memories of Kreisau and the German Resistance by Freya von Moltke and page 755 of Bethge.

[1323] Position 754.3 of Schlingensiepen.

[1324] Position 755.6 of Schlingensiepen and page 259 of *Ethics Volume 6 of Dietrich Bonhoeffer Works* by Dietrich Bonhoeffer, edited by Clifford J. Green, edition annotated, published by Fortress Press, 2008, ISBN 1451406754, 9781451406757.

[1325] Author of the ebook *Dietrich Bonhoeffer 1906-1945: Martyr, Thinker, Man of Resistance* by Ferdinand Schlingensiepen, translated by Isabel Best, first published in 2010 by Continuum, but since 2011, Bloomsbury T&T Clark, ePub-ISBN 9780567217554, ePDF-ISBN 9780567357755.

[1326] Position 755.7 of Schlingensiepen.

[1327] See endnotes [900] to [905] of Chapter 13 "Flight and the Tumultuous Appeasement of Evil" in regard to the Fritsch Affair.

[1328] Position 755.4 of Schlingensiepen and page 494 of *Letters and Papers from Prison*, Volume 8 of Dietrich Bonhoeffer Works by Dietrich Bonhoeffer, editors Christian Gremmels and John W. De Gruchy, published by Fortress Press, 2010, ISBN 1451406789, 9781451406788.

[1329] Position 755.2 of Schlingensiepen.

[1330] Position 756.0 of Schlingensiepen.

[1331] Position 756.3 of Schlingensiepen.

[1332] Position 761.3 of Schlingensiepen and page 754 of Bethge.

[1333] The Norwegian Biographical Archives online article on Eivind Josef Berggrav at https://nbl.snl.no/Eivind_Berggrav. Accessed on Saturday July 25, 2020.

[1334] Page 3 of *Quisling: A Study in Treachery* by Hans Fredrik Dahl, edition abridged, illustrated, reprint, published by Cambridge University Press, 1999, ISBN 0521496977, 9780521496971.

[1335] Time magazine article on Bishop Berggrav dated Christmas Day 1944, entitled *Religion: The Bishop and the Quisling* can be found online at http://content.time.com/time/magazine/article/0,9171,791745-1,00.html. Accessed on Saturday July 25, 2020.

[1336] Page 38 of *Memories of Kreisau and the German Resistance* by Freya von Moltke, translated by Julie M. Winter, edition illustrated, reprint, published by Univeristy of Nebraska Press, 2005, ISBN 0803296258, 9780803296251.

[1337] See endnotes [65] to [70] of the Preface "Birth and Memory upon the Lesser Known Fault Line of History."

[1338] Position 759.5 of Schlingensiepen.

[1339] Page 38 of *Memories of Kreisau and the German Resistance* by Freya von Moltke.

[1340] Ibid.

[1341] Ibid page 39.

[1342] Position 907.0 of Metaxas and the online article *Moral legacy of Nazi resister takes root in Germany — and abroad* at https://www.csmonitor.com/2007/0312/p01s04-woeu.html in The Christian Science Monitor, by Robert Marquand dated March 12 2007. Accessed on Saturday July 25, 2020. See also page 6 of *Helmuth James Graf von Moltke: Völkerrecht im Dienste der Menschen : Dokumente (Deutscher Widerstand 1933-1945)* (International Law in the Service of Humans: Documents (German Resistance 1933-1945)) by Helmuth-James-Moltke, published by Siedler Verlag 1986, edited by G van Roon, Letter to sons (in German), ISBN-10: 3886801543 ISBN-13: 9783886801541.

[1343] Ibid.

[1344] Page 308 of *Europe at War: 1939-1945 : No Simple Victory* by Norman Davies, published by Macmillan, 2006, ISBN 0333692853, 9780333692851. This will not be the last mention of this air raid in this book.

[1345] The official website of the Freya von Moltke Foundation for the New Kreisau is at http://www.fvms.de/willkommen.html in German and at http://www.fvms.de/en/welcome.html in English. Its current flyer in German can be downloaded at http://www.fvms.de/fileadmin/freya/content/PDF/fvms_flyer_2012.pdf. Excerpts of letters written by her husband from Tegel Prison before his trial can be downloaded in English from http://www.fvms.de/fileadmin/freya/content/PDF/Die_Stiftung/freya-von-moltke-helmuth-james-von-moltke-selection-of-farewell-letters-with-introduction-english-version.pdf. The page on Freya's life story is at http://www.fvms.de/en/foundation/freya-von-moltke.html in English. All links accessed on Saturday July 25, 2020.

[1346] On page 38, Freya states: *"By the end of the year [1944] he had been in Brussels, Paris, The Hague, Oslo, Stockholm, Copenhagen, and twice in Istanbul. As always on these trips, he connected his two professions--that of the office with the High Command of the Armed Forces and that of the conspiracy."* While Oslo is mentioned, nothing specific in the book is mentioned, including no references to Dietrich or their April 1942 mission.

[1347] Pages 117-118 and page 121 of *Traitors or Patriots?: A Story of the German Anti-Nazi Resistance*, by Louis R. Eltscher, published by iUniverse, 2013, ISBN 1475981422, 9781475981421. Also, position 276.4 to 279.9 of the ebook of the same title published by McNidder & Grace Carmarthen UK 2020, Ebook ISBN 9780857162045.

[1348] Position 726.9 of Schlingensiepen.

[1349] Page 122 of *Traitors or Patriots?: A Story of the German Anti-Nazi Resistance* by Louis R. Eltscher, published by iUniverse, 2013, ISBN 1475981422, 9781475981421. Also position 287.9 of the ebook of the same title published by McNidder & Grace Carmarthen UK 2020, Ebook ISBN 9780857162045.

[1350] Page 188 of Jane Pejsa.

[1351] In regard to the Dolchstosslegende, see endnotes [65] to [70] of the Preface "Birth and Memory upon the Lesser Known Fault Line of History."

[1352] J. Llewellyn et al, *Weimar Republic timeline 1921-23*, Alpha History, accessed Sunday March 13 2016 at http://alphahistory.com/weimarrepublic/weimar-republic-timeline-1921-23/ documents the 1923 right-wing putsches of Küstrin and Munich as well as the communist takeover of Hamburg on the 23rd October 1923, but also the eventual stabilisation of the Germany currency via the introduction of the Rentenmark in mid-November 1923. Accessed on Saturday July 25, 2020. See also position 262.0 of the ebook *Lenin, Stalin and Hitler*, by Robert Gellately, published by Vintage 2008, Epub ISBN 9781448138784.

[1353] Position 763.4 of Schlingensiepen.

[1354] Position 765.1 of Schlingensiepen.

[1355] Position 765.7 of Schlingensiepen. The text of the Anglo-Soviet Treaty at http://avalon.law.yale.edu/wwii/brsov42.asp. Accessed on Saturday July 25, 2020.

[1356] Page 152 of the book *Heydrich: The Face of Evil* by Mario R. Dederichs, published by Casemate Publishers, 2009, ISBN 1935149121, 9781935149125.

[1357] [2714] Position 765.6 of Schlingensiepen.

[1358] Schlingensiepen discusses Dietrich's visit to Stockholm from position 766.6 to 772.0. See also pages 757 to 761 of Bethge.

[1359] [1475] Page 220 of the book *History of the German Resistance, 1933-1945* by Peter Hoffmann, published by McGill-Queen's Press - MQUP, 1996, ISBN 0773566406, 9780773566408. See also page 760 of Bethge.

[1360] The chronic wavering of Kluge in the aftermath of the July 1944 Valkyrie plot will be covered in Chapter 20 "Valkyrie II." See page 25 *Operation Valkyrie: The German Generals' Plot Against Hitler* by Pierre Galante, Eugene Silianoff, translated by Mark Howson, published by Rowman & Littlefield, 2002, ISBN 0815411790, 9780815411796. Also, from position 67.8 of the ebook edition, ISBN-13: 9780815411796. Also from position 494.4 of the ebook *Countdown to Valkyrie: The July Plot to Assassinate Hitler* by Nigel Jones, published in 2008 by Frontline Books, Digital Edition ISBN 9781783407811 and pages 220 to 221 of the paper book published by Casemate Publishers, 2008, ISBN 1848325088, 9781848325081.

[1361] Position 766.7 of Schlingensiepen.

[1362] See the timeline at position 1097.3 of Schlingensiepen.

[1363] Position 662.2 of Schlingensiepen.

[1364] Position 768.7 of Schlingensiepen.

[1365] Position 768.8 of Schlingensiepen.

[1366] Position 768.6 of Schlingensiepen and pages 97 to 98 of *George Bell, Bishop of Chichester: Church, State, and Resistance in the Age of Dictatorship* by Andrew Chandler, published by Wm. B. Eerdmans Publishing, 2016, ISBN 0802872271, 9780802872272. See also page 761 of Bethge.

[1367] Position 771.2 of Schlingensiepen and page 761 of Bethge.

[1368] Position 771.4 of Schlingensiepen.

[1369] Pages 508 to 509 of Bethge and position 921.5 of Metaxas.

[1370] Position 918.1 of Metaxas.

[1371] Page 97 of *George Bell, Bishop of Chichester: Church, State, and Resistance in the Age of Dictatorship* by Andrew Chandler, published by Wm. B. Eerdmans Publishing, 2016, ISBN 0802872271, 9780802872272.

[1372] Ibid page 98 and position 920.9 of Metaxas.

[1373] Page 19 of the book *German Resistance Against Hitler: The Search for Allies Abroad, 1938-1945* by Klemens Von Klemperer, published by Ebsco Publishing, 1994, ISBN 0191513342, 9780191513343.

[1374] While this is true, it's not the full story. For one thing, Stalin's agenda was hardly one of liberty and freedom, and he could hardly have expected to defeat Hitler on his own. The incessant American and British aerial bombardment of Germany, chronically disrupting German industry, being a case in point.

[1375] In regard to Katyń, see Polish WWII Supplement III "The Katyń Wood Massacre"[3618] and pages 44, 48, 115 to 116 of *Rising '44: The Battle for Warsaw*, published by Penguin Books; Reprint edition (October 4, 2005), ISBN-10: 0143035401, ISBN-13: 9780143035404. On page 48, Davies states that Stalin personally signed the order for their execution. See also the Central Intelligence Agency report online by Benjamin B. Fischer at https://www.cia.gov/library/center-for-the-study-of-intelligence/csi-publications/csi-studies/studies/winter99-00/art6.html.

[1376] Pages 246 to 247 *No Greater Ally, The Untold Story of Poland's Forces in World War II,* by Kenneth K. Koskodan, published by Osprey Publishing 2011, ISBN-13: 9781849084796. Admittedly, the British insisted on Polish Airmen — heroes from the 1940 Battle of Britain, be allowed to march, but no ground forces were allowed to do so. As Ed Bucko put it: *At that parade all those God-damned shit countries [eg Mexico and Argentina] who didn't even barely participate, didn't even shoot at the Germans, they were a big deal...big heroes. [We] were nobody.* As such, the Polish Air Force in protest over the exclusion of the ground forces, refused their invitation to march.

[1377] See endnote [204] in the Preface "Birth and Memory upon the Lesser Known Fault Line of History" in regard to the deportation of Borderland Poles to the Gulag.

[1378] Page 115 of *No Greater Ally, The Untold Story of Poland's Forces in World War II*, by Kenneth K. Koskodan, published by Osprey Publishing 2011, ISBN-13: 9781849084796.

[1379] Professor Norman Davies in his book, *Rising '44: The Battle for Warsaw Reprint Edition*, published by Penguin Books; Reprint edition (October 4, 2005), ISBN-10: 0143035401, ISBN-13: 9780143035404, repeatedly refers to the Poles as the "First Ally." However, pages 54-57 are a perfect examples.

[1380] Page 276 of *The Other Europe: Eastern Europe to 1945* by E. Garrison Walters, published by Syracuse University Press, 1988, ISBN 0815624409, 9780815624400. The Polish Government in Exile in London alone commanded more than 0.5 million men.

[1381] Position 929.8 of Metaxas, page 174 of *The sword and the umbrella* by James Graham-Murray, published by Times Press, 1964, (no ISBN given), and page 183 of *True patriotism; 1939-45: from the collected works of Dietrich Bonhoeffer*, by Dietrich Bonhoeffer, Edwin Hanton Robertson, edited by Edwin Hanton Robertson, published by Collins, 1973, (no ISBN given) all document Anthony Eden's letter to George Bell dated August 4, 1942.

[1382] Pages 298-300 of *Rising '44: The Battle for Warsaw Reprint Edition* by Professor Norman Davies. See also Polish WWII Supplement IV "AK and 1944 Warsaw General Uprising — Stalin's mass murder by German proxy," In particular, endnotes [4131] to [4630].

[1383] Position 16.6 of the ebook *The Secret War Against Hitler* by Fabian von Schlabrendorff, published by Routledge, 2018, ISBN 0813321905, ISBN 13: 9780813321905 (paperback), states that this meeting took place in 1949, with Schlabrendorff recalling his then conversation with Churchill; *"Reviewing the years that lay between our two meetings, he [Churchill] told me that he realised afterwards that during the war he had been misled by his assistants about the considerable strength and size of the German anti-Hitler resistance."*

[1384] Page 286 of Jane Pejsa.

[1385] Pages 619-620 of *Rising '44: The Battle for Warsaw Reprint Edition* by Professor Norman Davies. In regard to the 1944 Warsaw General Uprising (not the 1943 Jewish Ghetto Uprising), see Polish WWII Supplement IV "AK and 1944 Warsaw General Uprising — Stalin's mass murder by German proxy." In particular, endnotes [4131] to [4630].

Chapter 18 — Romance, Plots and Arrest

[1386] Page 287 of Jane Pejsa.

[1387] Page 278 of Jane Pejsa.

[1388] Position 932.0 of Metaxas and position 772.9 of Schlingensiepen. See also pages 787 to 790 of Bethge under the section "The Engagement."

[1389] Position 774.2 of Schlingensiepen.

[1390] Position 773.6 of Schlingensiepen and page 224 of Jane Pejsa. The latter makes it abundantly clear as to why Dietrich regarded Maria as then being too young or perhaps immature to take on the serious responsibility of confirmation.

[1391] Dietrich's joyful letter to Maria dated Sunday January 17 1943, can be read from page 383 of *Conspiracy and Imprisonment, 1940-1945 (Dietrich Bonhoeffer Works, Vol. 16)* Hardcover — June 12, 2006 by Dietrich Bonhoeffer (Author), Lisa E Dahill (Editor), Mark Brocker (Editor), published by Fortress Press; 1st English-language edition (June 12, 2006), ISBN-10: 9780800683160 ISBN-13: 9780800683160, ASIN: 0800683161 and from position 966.3 of Metaxas.

[1392] Position 177.4 of Metaxas.

[1393] Page 290 of Jane Pejsa.

[1394] Page 279 to 280 of Jane Pejsa. See also endnotes [1304] to [1308] for Chapter 17 "Pastor and Spy."

[1395] Page 278 of Jane Pejsa.

[1396] Page 290 of Jane Pejsa.

[1397] Page 46 of Jane Pejsa. See also endnotes [511] to [514] for Chapter 6 "Old Prussia — Birth of Ruth to Precarious Survival."

[1398] Position 175.9 of Metaxas and page 208 of *Love letters from cell 92: Dietrich Bonhoeffer, Maria von Wedemeyer, 1943-1945*.

[1399] Page 208 of *Love letters from cell 92: Dietrich Bonhoeffer, Maria von Wedemeyer, 1943-1945*.

[1400] Position 176.8 of Metaxas.

[1401] Position 178.0 of Metaxas. Dietrich's relationship with Elisabeth is hardly covered in his biographies, with Eric Metaxas being one of the very few that gives her more than the barest mention. A more detailed account of this relationship is given in Diane Reynolds' book *The Doubled Life of Dietrich Bonhoeffer: Women, Sexuality, and Nazi Germany*, published by James Clarke, 2017, ISBN 022790608X, 9780227906088. On page 56, the author states: "*With his twin [Sabine] married, Dietrich now turned to Elisabeth Zinn, a third cousin who had grown up in Grunewald in a house opposite the Bonhoeffers', and bore 'a shadowy and indefinable resemblance to Sabine. '"* In Schlingen-siepen, the author only mentions Elisabeth twice, albeit with some significance, in that the author from position 275.1, quotes a letter written by Dietrich to Elisabeth, where Dietrich states most forthrightly, how he became a Christian. In Eberhard Bethge, Elisabeth is barely mentioned — namely in one sentence on pages 137 to 138.

[1402] Position 791.1 of Schlingensiepen, position 935.5 of Metaxas and page 288 of Jane Pejsa.

[1403] Page 288 of Jane Pejsa.

[1404] Page 189 of Jane Pejsa.

[1405] See page 17 of the book *The Second World War: Ambitions to Nemesis* by Bradley Lightbody, published by Psychology Press, 2004, ISBN 0415224047, 9780415224048.

[1406] Position 934.3 of Metaxas and page 248 of *Love letters from cell 92: Dietrich Bonhoeffer, Maria von Wedemeyer, 1943-1945*, authors Dietrich Bonhoeffer, Ruth-Alice von Bismarck, Maria von Wedemeyer, Ulrich Kabitz, Edition illustrated, published by HarperCollins, 1994, ISBN 0006278035, 9780006278030. See also position 791.3 of Schlingensiepen.

[1407] Position 934.5 of Metaxas and page 248 of *Love letters from cell 92: Dietrich Bonhoeffer, Maria von Wedemeyer, 1943-1945*. Von Papen however narrowly escaped. See https://www.britannica.com/biography/Franz-von-Papen. Accessed on Saturday July 25, 2020. In regard to the Night of the Long Knives, see endnotes [92] to [107] of the Preface "Birth and Memory upon the Lesser Known Fault Line of History."

[1408] Page 249 of *Love letters from cell 92: Dietrich Bonhoeffer, Maria von Wedemeyer, 1943-1945* and position 128.5 to 130.4 of the ebook *The Secret War Against Hitler* by Fabian von Schlabrendorff, published by Routledge, 2018, e-ISBN 0813321905, ISBN 13: 9780813321905 (paperback). See also position 791.5 of Schlingensiepen.

[1409] Position 791.8 of Schlingensiepen.

[1410] Position 792.1 of Schlingensiepen and page 224 of Jane Pejsa.

[1411] Position 792.1 of Schlingensiepen. Ruth von Wedemeyer née von Kleist was the youngest child of Ruth von Kleist.

[1412] Position 800.0 of Schlingensiepen.

[1413] Position 793.1 of Schlingensiepen.

[1414] Position 953.4 of Metaxas quotes Dietrich's letter to Maria on November 13 1942. This letter can also be read from pages 369 to 371 of the book *Conspiracy and Imprisonment, 1940-1945 (Dietrich Bonhoeffer Works, Vol. 16)* Hardcover — June 12, 2006, by Dietrich Bonhoeffer (Author), Lisa E Dahill (Editor), Mark Brocker (Editor), published by Fortress Press; 1st English-language Edition (June 12, 2006), ISBN-10: 9780800683160 ISBN-13: 9780800683160, ASIN: 0800683161.

[1415][1518] Pages 374 to 375 of *Conspiracy and Imprisonment, 1940-1945 (Dietrich Bonhoeffer Works, Vol. 16)* from source note #1, page 294 of Jane Pejsa, position 801.8 of Schlingensiepen and page 790 of Bethge.

[1416] Page 374 of *Conspiracy and Imprisonment, 1940-1945 (Dietrich Bonhoeffer Works, Vol. 16)*.

[1417] Position 813.6 of Schlingensiepen.

[1418] Positions 950.4 and 965.7 of Metaxas and page 383 of *Conspiracy and Imprisonment, 1940-1945 (Dietrich Bonhoeffer Works, Vol. 16)*.

[1419][2720][2721][3620] Position 978.1 of Metaxas and page 176 of *Operation Valkyrie: The German Generals' Plot Against Hitler* by Pierre Galante, Eugene Silianoff, translated by Mark Howson, published by Rowman & Littlefield, 2002, ISBN 0815411790, 9780815411796 and position 418.8 of the ebook, ISBN-13: 9780815411796.

[1420] See the family trees given on pages 394 to 395 and 391 of Jane Pejsa.

[1421] Position 979.3 of Metaxas and pages 690 to 691 of Bethge. Position 819.2 onwards of Schlingensiepen also describes the assassination plots of March 1943.

[1422] Position 978.5 to 992.0 of Metaxas describes the two failed March 1943 assassination plots, as does position 819.2 onwards of Schlingensiepen and pages 778 to 780 of Bethge. As well, Chapter 16 "The First Assassination Attempt" from position, 380.0 onwards of *The Secret War Against Hitler* by Fabian von Schlabrendorff, published by Routledge, 2018, ISBN 0813321905, ISBN 13: 9780813321905 (paperback).

[1423] Position 561.3 of the ebook *Killing Hitler The Third Reich and the Plots against the Führer* by Roger Moorhouse, published by Vintage 2007 (The Random House Group Limited), ISBN 9781446485842 documents how the Abwehr seized plastic explosives and associated mechanisms from failed British SOE operations. Albeit, the author does so in describing the July 1944 Valkyrie assassination plot. As does position 298.8 of Nigel Jones.

[1424] Position 981.3 of Metaxas and page 779 of Bethge.

[1425] Position 388.1 of *The Secret War Against Hitler* by Fabian von Schlabrendorff and position 981.7 of Metaxas.

[1426] Position 389.0 of *The Secret War Against Hitler* by Fabian von Schlabrendorff and position 982.0 of Metaxas.

[1427][1783] Position 391.1 of *The Secret War Against Hitler* by Fabian von Schlabrendorff and position 983.5 of Metaxas.

[1428] Page 57 of *They almost killed Hitler: based on the personal account of Fabian von Schlabrendorff*, edited by Gero von Gaevernitz, published by Macmillan Co., 1947, no ISBN given and position 984.4 of Metaxas.

[1429] Position 392.0 of *The Secret War Against Hitler* by Fabian von Schlabrendorff and position 984.7 of Metaxas. A more recent edition of *They almost killed Hitler* is published by Arcole Publishing, 2017, ISBN 1787207188, 9781787207189.

[1430] Position 393.4 of *The Secret War Against Hitler* by Fabian von Schlabrendorff and position 985.4 of Metaxas.

[1431] Page 122 of the *Słownik etymologiczny nazw geograficznych Polski* (*Etymological dictionary of geographical names of Poland*) by Maria Malec, published by Naukowe PWN, 2002. (No ISBN given)

[1432] Position 394.7 of *The Secret War Against Hitler* by Fabian von Schlabrendorff and position 821.1 of Schlingensiepen.

[1433] [1783] Position 395.4 of *The Secret War Against Hitler* by Fabian von Schlabrendorff and position 986.6 of Metaxas.

[1434] [2105] [3620] Position 396.9 of *The Secret War Against Hitler* by Fabian von Schlabrendorff, position 987.5 of Metaxas and page 779 of Bethge.

[1435] Position 539.2 of the ebook *Killing Hitler The Third Reich and the Plots against the Führer* by Roger Moorhouse, published by Vintage 2007 (The Random House Group Limited), ISBN 9781446485842 and position 989.1 of Metaxas.

[1436] Position 822.7 of Schlingensiepen, position 989.7 of Metaxas and pages 779 to 780 of Bethge.

[1437] Position 538.5 of *Killing Hitler The Third Reich and the Plots against the Führer* by Roger Moorhouse and position 991.1 of Metaxas.

[1438] https://www.britannica.com/biography/Karl-Donitz documents Dönitz briefly succeeding Hitler when the latter committed suicide in his bunker on April 30, 1945. Accessed on Saturday July 25, 2020.

[1439] Position 539.5 of *Killing Hitler The Third Reich and the Plots against the Führer* by Roger Moorhouse and position 991.6 of Metaxas.

[1440] Position 540.2 of *Killing Hitler The Third Reich and the Plots against the Führer* by Roger Moorhouse and position 999.2 of Metaxas.

[1441] Position 44.9 of the autobiographical ebook *Soldier in the Downfall: A Wehrmacht Cavalryman in Russia, Normandy, and the Plot to Kill Hitler*, by Rudolf-Christoph von Gersdorff (Author), Anthony Pearsall (Translator), published by The Aberjona Press (25 March 2013), ASIN: B00C6FYGP2, ISBN 13: 9780977756377.

[1442] [3620] Ibid position 342.1. In regard to Katyń, see Polish WWII Supplement III "The Katyń Wood Massacre."[3618]

[1443] Position 992.0 of Metaxas.

[1444] Page 785 of Bethge.

[1445] Ibid and position 824.0 of Schlingensiepen and position 993.4 of Metaxas.

[1446] [2105] [2720] [2721] Position 992.0 of Metaxas and position 824.0 of Schlingensiepen .

[1447] Page 785 of Bethge and position 992.0 of Metaxas.

[1448] Position 992.0 of Metaxas, page 134 of *Dietrich Bonhoeffer: A Life in Pictures*, editors Renate Bethge, Christian Gremmels, translated by Brian McNeil, published by Fortress Press, ISBN 1451416563, 9781451416565 and page 785 of Bethge.

[1449] [2722] [xxxii] *Reichskriegsgericht* (RKG — War Court) was in Nazi Germany, the highest German military court. While it was separate to the dreaded *Volksgerichtshof* (People's Court), Manfred Roeder one must think, would have been perfectly at home in either. A document in German describing the RKG from the *Österreichische Nationalbibliothek* (Austrian National Library) can be viewed online at http://alex.onb.ac.at/cgi-content/alex?aid=dra&datum=1939&page=1691&size=45. Accessed on Saturday July 25, 2020.

[1450] [2722] Position 825.0 to 830.5 of Schlingensiepen. See also pages 785 to 786 of Bethge.

[1451] Page 786 of Bethge and position 829.5 of Schlingensiepen. See also page 784 of Bethge.

[1452] Page 786 of Bethge and position 830.2 of Schlingensiepen.

[1453] Page 784 of Bethge.

[1454] Position 670.8 of Schlingensiepen.

[1455] Page 784 of Bethge.

[1456] Position 821.9 of Schlingensiepen.

[1457] [3622] Page 784 of Bethge.

[1458] Position 835.5 of Schlingensiepen.

[1459] Position 830.5 of Schlingensiepen.

[1460] Position 830.4 of Schlingensiepen.

[1461] Position 833.8 of Schlingensiepen. Most confusingly, this prison is also referred to as Moabit Prison, having been located in the Berlin locality of Moabit. Then and today, there is also in Moabit, a remand prison. See endnote [2026] from Chapter 22 "Prinz-Albrecht-Strasse" for clarification of this confusion.

[1462] Position 833.9 of Schlingensiepen.

[1463] [3017] Position 834.4 of Schlingensiepen and position 993.6 of Metaxas.

[1464] Position 993.9 of Metaxas.

[1465] Position 834.4 of Schlingensiepen.

[1466] Position 834.6 of Schlingensiepen.

[1467] Position 994.3 of Metaxas.

[1468] Position 834.7 of Schlingensiepen.

[1469] [3622] Position 1003.7 of Metaxas documents the various prisons in Berlin the arrested people were sent to.

[1470] Position 834.8 of Schlingensiepen and position 1001.2 of Metaxas.

[1471] Position 835.3 of Schlingensiepen and position 1001.8 of Metaxas.

[1472] Position 835.2 of Schlingensiepen and position 1002.0 of Metaxas.

[1473] Position 1002.4 of Metaxas and see also position 803.9 of Schlingensiepen.

[1474] Position 836.1 of Schlingensiepen.

[1475] [xxxii] Page 220 of the book *History of the German Resistance, 1933-1945* by Peter Hoffmann, published by McGill-Queen's Press - MQUP, 1996, ISBN 0773566406, 9780773566408. See also page 760 of Bethge and endnote [1359] for Chapter 17 "Pastor and Spy."

Chapter 19 — The Tormentor Tormented

[1476] [2723 xxxii] Position 807.2 of Schlingensiepen.

[1477] See the start of Chapter III "THE SCHMIDHUBER AFFAIR" of "PART TWO" of *The Canaris Conspiracy: The Secret Resistance to Hitler in the German Army* by Roger Manvell and Heinrich Fraenkel, published by Simon and Schuster, 2019, ISBN 1510739793, 9781510739796.

[1478] Position 971.5 of Metaxas.

[1479] Position 807.2 of Schlingensiepen.

[1480] [2723 xxxii] Position 972.0 of Metaxas.

[1481] Position 836.8 of Schlingensiepen.

[1482] Sonderegger worked for the plain clothes Kriminalpolizei (Kripo; "Criminal Police"), which with the likewise civilian attired Geheime Staatspolizei (Gestapo; "Secret State Police"), formed two sub-departments of Sicherheitspolizei (SiPo; "Security Police"). The structure of the police departments in Nazi Germany was extremely complex and convoluted, but in the context of describing the arrests in April 1943, the Kriminalpolizei, like the closely related Gestapo, ultimately came under Himmler's control. An online description can be found at http://www.holocaustresearchproject.org/holoprelude/RSHA/rsha.html on the website of the Holocaust Research Project, by Dr Matthew Feldman, Senior Lecturer in History School of Social Sciences, University of Northampton. A photo of Sonderegger can be found at position 828.9 of Schlingensiepen, while for Roeder, one is given at position 833.6, along with a brief description of their respective roles.

[1483] Position 837.8 of Schlingensiepen.

[1484] See the preface of the ebook at position 10.0 of *Resisting Hitler: Mildred Harnack and the Red Orchestra* by Shareen Blair Brysac, published by Oxford University Press, 2000, ISBN-13: 9780195152401 which describes how the Harnacks and the Red Orchestra in general remained practically non-existent in Western sources during the Cold War. Moreover, the author describes how she was able to, post Cold War, to obtain documents shedding much overdue light on the Harnacks and the Red Orchestra in general.

[1485] See the article on Eva-Maria Buch on the official website of the *Gedenkstätte Deutscher Widerstand* (Memorial of the German Resistance) at http://www.gdw-berlin.de/en/recess/topics/biographies-topics/view-bio/eva-maria-buch/?no_cache=1. In this brief article, it states that throughout her short life, she remained deeply rooted in the Catholic faith.

[1486] Position 9.0 of *Resisting Hitler: Mildred Harnack and the Red Orchestra* by Shareen Blair Brysac, published by Oxford University Press, 2000, ISBN-13: 9780195152401.

[1487] Emmi Delbrück was married to Dietrich's elder brother Klaus. See the Bonhoeffer Family Tree at position 1100 of Schlingensiepen. In her book, Shareen Blair Brysac mentions the Bonhoeffers on numerous occasions.

[1488] Position 154.5 of Shareen Blair Brysac.

[1489] Ibid position 154.0.

[1490] Position 620.7 of Shareen Blair Brysac.

[1491] Page 25 of *Der Judenmord in Polen und die deutsche Ordnungspolizei 1939-1945* (The murder of Jews in Poland and the German *Ordnungspolizei* 1939-1945) by Wolfgang Curilla, published by Ferdinand Schöningh Paderborn, 2011, ISBN 3506770438, 9783506770431 in footnote #32 states that the *Ordnungspolizei* existed from 1936 to 1945. See also the bottom of the first page of Chapter 2 "The Order Police" in the book *Ordinary Men: Reserve Police Battalion 101 and the Final Solution in Poland* by Christopher R. Browning, published by HarperCollins, 2017, ISBN 0062303031, 9780062303035.

[1492] Position 16.3 in the preface of the ebook *The Red Orchestra: The Soviet Spy Network Inside Nazi Europe* by V. E. Tarrant, published by John Wiley & Sons Inc, 1996, ISBN-10: 0471134392, ISBN-13: 9780471134398.

[1493] Ibid position 71.6.

[1494] Ibid position 134.1.

[1495] Ibid position 135.0.

[1496] Position 838.2 of Schlingensiepen.

[1497] Ibid.

[1498] Ibid.

[1499] The surrender of the German Sixth Army in Stalingrad is documented at https://www.britannica.com/event/Battle-of-Stalingrad. Accessed on Saturday July 25, 2020.

[1500] Position 795.5 of Shareen Blair Brysac.

[1501] Position 688.9 of Schlingensiepen.

[1502] Position 721.0 of Schlingensiepen — although the author does not state whether or not these Nazi party zealots within the Abwehr, were successful in leaking documents pertaining to Operation 7 to SS headquarters. However, given the arrests of Dietrich and Dohnányi in relation to Operation 7, it seems probable that at least some documents were successfully leaked to SS headquarters.

[1503] Position 16.8 of Tarrant. Tarrant's assertion is rather contentious to say the least.

[1504] https://www.britannica.com/place/Volgograd-Russia. Accessed on Saturday July 25, 2020.

[1505] https://library.eb.com.au/levels/adults/article/Volga-River/106071. Accessed on Saturday July 25, 2020.

[1506] Position 104.3 of Tarrant.

[1507] Ibid position 104.5.

[1508] Ibid position 134.1.

[1509] Ibid position 135.0.

[1510] Page 227 of the book *Germany at War: 400 Years of Military History [4 volumes]: 400 Years of Military History* edited by David T. Zabecki Ph.D, published by ABC-CLIO, 2014, ISBN 1598849816, 9781598849813, documents the commencement on June 28 of Case Blue (*Fall Blau*), the second German campaign against the Soviet Union in the summer of 1942.

[1511] Position 661.6 of Brysac.

[1512] Position 16.8 of Tarrant.

[1513] Ibid position 106.0.

[1514] Footnote #69 at position 948.2 of Brysac.

[1515] Position 859.0 of Schlingensiepen.

[1516] Page 813 of Bethge.

[1517] Page 813 of Bethge.

[1518] Pages 374 to 375 of *Conspiracy and Imprisonment, 1940-1945 (Dietrich Bonhoeffer Works, Vol. 16)* from source note #1, documents Dietrich's letter to Eberhard Bethge on November 27 1942, where Dietrich states his somewhat reluctant intention to comply with Ruth von Wedemeyer's terms. This letter was written just three days following Dietrich's meeting with Ruth von Wedemeyer. See also page 294 of Jane Pejsa, position 801.8 of Schlingensiepen, page 790 of Bethge and endnote [1415] for Chapter 18 "Romance, Plots and Arrest."

[1519] Position 839.3 of Schlingensiepen and position 1014.5 of Metaxas.

[1520] Position 841.5 of Schlingensiepen.

[1521] Position 841.6 of Schlingensiepen.

[1522] Position 841.8 of Schlingensiepen.

[1523] Position 842.1 of Schlingensiepen.

[1524] Position 862.7 of Schlingensiepen.

[1525] Position 863.2 of Schlingensiepen.

[1526] Page 340 of Schlingensiepen's book in the original German text *Dietrich Bonhoeffer, 1906-1945: eine Biographie* by Ferdinand Schlingensiepen, published by C.H. Beck, 2005, ISBN 3406534252, 9783406534256. This can be viewed on Google Books at https://books.google.com.au/books?id=GlNxZsZLuwAC&printsec=frontcover&dq=ISBN+3406534252,+9783406534256&hl=en&sa=X&ved=0ahUKEwjqwZGQ6ozgAhUFK48KHdM6A0YQ6AEIKjAA#v=onepage&q=erkennt&f=false in the second window of text. Accessed on Saturday July 25, 2020.

[1527] Position 852.1 of Schlingensiepen and page 343 of *Letters and Papers from Prison, Volume 8 of Dietrich Bonhoeffer Works* by Dietrich Bonhoeffer, editors Christian Gremmels and John W. De Gruchy, published by Fortress Press, 2010, ISBN 1451406789, 9781451406788.

[1528] Position 855.4 of Schlingensiepen.

[1529] Position 855.6 of Schlingensiepen.

1530 Page 567 of *Letters and Papers from Prison, Volume 8 of Dietrich Bon-hoeffer Works* and position 857.4 of Schlingensiepen. See also pages 810 to 812 of Bethge.

1531 See page 342 of Jane Pejsa in regards to a similar situation and remarkable outcome for Oma Ruth's eldest son Hans Jürgen, while he was incarcerated, along with Dietrich, in Berlin's infamous Prinz-Albrecht-Strasse Gestapo prison in December 1944. This episode will be covered in Chapter 25 "Old Prussia Gone With The Wind."

1532 Position 858.2 of Schlingensiepen.

1533 Position 858.6 of Schlingensiepen.

1534 Position 858.8 of Schlingensiepen and page 811 of Bethge.

1535 2952 Position 862.5 of Schlingensiepen.

1536 Position 837.5 and 837.6 of Schlingensiepen.

1537 Position 864.6 of Schlingensiepen.

1538 Position 864.9 of Schlingensiepen.

1539 2954 Position 863.6 of Schlingensiepen. See also page 811 of Bethge.

1540 Position 863.8 of Schlingensiepen.

1541 Page 347 of Bethge. The report itself, dated November 28, 1943, can be found on page 205 of *Letters and Papers from Prison Volume 8 of Dietrich Bonhoeffer Works*.

1542 Page 347 of Bethge.

1543 Page 13 of *Letters and Papers from Prison Volume 8 of Dietrich Bonhoeffer Works* documents that it was in November 1943 that this "illegal correspondence" commenced. This page also documents that Corporal Knobloch was the conduit for the "illegal correspondence." See also page xv in the preface of Bethge.

1544 Position 1007.9 of Metaxas and position 867.8 of Schlingensiepen.

1545 Position 1027.4 of Metaxas.

1546 Position 1028.6 of Metaxas.

1547 Position 1028.8 of Metaxas.

1548 Position 1127.6 to 1131.6 of Metaxas and page 827 of Bethge.

1549 Pages 827 to 828 of Bethge and position 1127.6 to 1131.6 of Metaxas.

1550 2954 Ibid.

1551 1637 Position 848.8 to 850.2 of Schlingensiepen.

1552 This air raid of November 26 1943, was the one that Dietrich wrote his report for on November 28 1943. That it caused the brain embolism for Hans von Dohnányi, see APPENDIX 1 CHRONOLOGY 1942—1945 of *Letters and Papers from Prison Volume 8 of Dietrich Bonhoeffer Works* from page 597.

1553 Position 849.1 of Schlingensiepen.

1554 1637 Position 849.3 of Schlingensiepen.

1555 Position 849.9 of Schlingensiepen and page 808 of Bethge.

1556 Position 850.0 of Schlingensiepen.

1557 2952 Position 879.7 of Schlingensiepen.

[1558] In regard to the German, Polish and Ukrainian names for Lwów, see the book *Lemberg, Lwów, and L'viv 1914-1947: Violence and Ethnicity in a Contested City* by Christopher Mick, published by Purdue University Press, 2016, ISBN 1557536716, 9781557536716.

[1559] Position 879.9 of Schlingensiepen.

[1560] Position 879.5 to 880.6 of Schlingensiepen.

[1561] Position 880.9 of Schlingensiepen and page 809 of Bethge.

[1562] Position 881.3 of Schlingensiepen. See also page 809 of Bethge.

[1563] Position 881.5 of Schlingensiepen, although this account is not entirely accurate, as the two young men were involved in separate attempts. See position 377.5 of Nigel Jones *Countdown to Valkyrie* for von dem Bussche's attempt, and position 380.0 for Ewald Heinrich Kleist-Schmenzin's (son of Ewald) attempt. Both of which being aborted suicide assassination attempts. Both of these young men would ironically, like Gersdorff, survive the war.

[1564] Position 1039.4 of Metaxas and page 111 of *Letters and Papers from Prison Volume 8 of Dietrich Bonhoeffer Works*. The latter quotes the letter Dietrich had been in the process of writing to his parents both before and after Maria's visit on June 24 1943. Schlingensiepen, incorrectly it seems, at position 885.3, gives the date of June 26 1943 for this meeting, but given page 111 of *Letters and Papers from Prison Volume 8 of Dietrich Bonhoeffer Works*, I have used the timeline of Metaxas, which gives instead the date of June 24 1943 in agreement with *Letters and Papers from Prison Volume 8 of Dietrich Bonhoeffer Works*.

[1565] Position 1040.0 of Metaxas and footnote #16 on page 111 of *Letters and Papers from Prison Volume 8 of Dietrich Bonhoeffer Works*.

[1566] The footnote at position 1039.5 of Metaxas (click on the asterix "*"), gives the dates of the visits in 1943 as 24th June, 30th July, 26th August, 7th October, 10th and 26th November, December 10th and 22nd, while in 1944, they were on 1st and 24th of January, 4th of February (his 38th birthday), 30th March, 18th and 25th April, 22nd of May, 27th June, and finally 23rd August. The visit on the November 26 1943 was made with the accompaniment of Dietrich's parents and Eberhard Bethge, as stated at position 1084.0 and in APPENDIX 1 CHRONOLOGY 1942—1945 from page 597 of *Letters and Papers from Prison Volume 8 of Dietrich Bonhoeffer Works*. This also being the date of the air raid where Hans von Dohnányi suffered a brain embolism and Dietrich submitted his report on two days later, as stated in the chronology from page 597 of *Letters and Papers from Prison Volume 8 of Dietrich Bonhoeffer Works*. In all, there were 17 visits, with all, except for the first one in the War Court, made at Tegel Prison. Schlingensiepen in "Appendix 5: Chronology," at position 1097.9 states that there were 18 visits by Maria to Tegel, with some dates that conflict with Metaxas. However, Metaxas' timeline is the one consistent with *Letters and Papers from Prison Volume 8 of Dietrich Bonhoeffer Works* on page 111 and in APPENDIX 1 CHRONOLOGY 1942—1945 from page 597.

1567 Position 1040.7 of Metaxas.

1568 Position 881.8 of Schlingensiepen.

1569 Position 77.4 of Schlingensiepen, page 36 of *I Knew Dietrich Bonhoeffer* as told by Fabian von Schlabrendorff, edited by Wolf-Dieter Zimmermann, Ronald Gregor Smith published by Harper & Row, 1967, page 36 of Bethge and position 105.6 of Metaxas.

1570 Position 882.7 of Schlingensiepen and page 77 of *Letters and Papers from Prison Volume 8 of Dietrich Bonhoeffer Works*.

1571 Position 884.0 of Schlingensiepen.

1572 Position 915.9 of Schlingensiepen.

1573 Position 917.0 of Schlingensiepen.

1574 Position 919.8 of Schlingensiepen.

1575 Position 917.2 of Schlingensiepen.

1576 Position 917.4 of Schlingensiepen and page 283 of *Letters and Papers from Prison Volume 8 of Dietrich Bonhoeffer Works*.

1577 See endnote 1245 from Chapter 17 "Pastor and Spy" in regard to the publishing of the original German and later English editions of Bethge's biography of Dietrich.

1578 Page iv of *Letters and Papers from Prison Volume 8 of Dietrich Bonhoeffer Works*.

1579 See footnote #23 at position 918.3 of Schlingensiepen.

1580 Position 919.2 of Schlingensiepen.

1581 Page 199 of *Letters and Papers from Prison Volume 8 of Dietrich Bonhoeffer Works* which documents Dietrich's letter written to Eberhard that day of November 26 1943, following the visit by Maria, Dietrich's parents and Eberhard.

1582 The visit on the November 26 1943 was made with the accompaniment of Dietrich's parents and Eberhard Bethge, as stated at position 1084.0 of Metaxas and in APPENDIX 1 CHRONOLOGY 1942—1945 from page 597 of *Letters and Papers from Prison Volume 8 of Dietrich Bonhoeffer Works*.

1583 Pages 13 to 14 of *Letters and Papers from Prison Volume 8 of Dietrich Bonhoeffer Works*.

1584 Ibid.

1585 Position 946.2 of Schlingensiepen.

1586 Position 946.4 of Schlingensiepen.

1587 Position 1085.8 of Metaxas.

1588 Position 558.0 onwards of the ebook *Hitler's Spy Chief The Wilhelm Canaris Mystery* by Richard Bassett, published by The Orion Publishing Group Limited, 2011, a Hachette UK company, ISBN 9780297865711.

1589 3565 On May 29 1942, Radio Prague announced that Reinhard Heydrich, Reichsprotektor of Bohemia and Moravia, was dying; assassins had wounded him fatally. On the 6th of June he died. See the online Central Intelligence Agency Report on the Assassination of Reinhard Heydrich at https://www.cia.gov/library/center-for-the-study-of-intelligence/kent-csi/vol4no1/html/v04i1a01p_0001.htm, approved for release by the CIA Historical Review Program September 22 1993. Heydrich was also the mastermind behind the November 1938 Reichskristallnacht (see position 730.3 of *Metaxas* and position 926.3 to 927.4 of *Microcosm*) and the 1934 Röhm purge (page 30 of *The Third Reich in Power* by Richard J. Evans, published by Penguin Books, 2006, ISBN 0143037900, 9780143037903) among others, which included his role as chairman at the January 1942 Wannsee Conference in implementing the Final Solution. See https://www.yadvashem.org/holocaust/about/final-solution-beginning/wannsee-confer-ence.html?gclid=Cj0KCQjwvdXpBRCoARIsAMJSKqI4PKe2JydoRekuBww0sjAipR0oya4UuzheRLvJHDMS_RuZ6yhPcg8aAj0kEALw_wcB on the website of Yad Vashem — The World Holocaust Memorial Center. All links accessed on Saturday July 25, 2020.

[1590] Ibid position 558.9.

[1591] https://www.britannica.com/topic/SS. Accessed on Saturday July 25, 2020.

[1592] Position 1101.8 of Microcosm documents the hanging of conspirators on meat-hooks in a Gestapo execution chamber being filmed for the Führer's pleasure.

Chapter 20 — Valkyrie II

[1593] Page 168 of *German Resistance to Hitler* by Peter Hoffmann, published by Harvard University Press, 1988, ISBN 0674350863, 9780674350861.

[1594] [xxiv] Page 11 of *Countdown to Valkyrie: The July Plot to Assassinate Hitler* by Nigel Jones, published by Casemate Publishers, 2008, ISBN 1848325088, 9781848325081. Also at position 42.2 of the ebook published in 2008 by Frontline Books, Digital Edition ISBN 9781783407811.

[1595] Page 22 and position 69.4 of Nigel Jones.

[1596] Page 12 and position 45.1 of Nigel Jones.

[1597] Page 13 and position 16.0 of Nigel Jones.

[1598] See https://www.cia.gov/library/center-for-the-study-of-intelligence/kent-csi/vol4no1/html/v04i1a01p_0001.htm, approved for release by the CIA Historical Review Program September 22 1993. Accessed on Saturday July 25, 2020.

[1599] This was discussed in Chapter 17 "Pastor and Spy." See also position 766.6 to 772.0 of Schlingensiepen and pages 757 to 761 of Bethge.

[1600] The article by Peter Hoffmann, *Colonel Claus Von Stauffenberg in the German Resistance to Hitler: Between East and West* on page 631 of The Historical Journal, vol. 31, no. 3, 1988, pp. 629—650. JSTOR, www.jstor.org/stable/2639760, states that during the 1940 French campaign,

Captain Count von Stauffenberg had been transferred to army high command. Accessed on Saturday July 25, 2020.

[1601] [1955] Page 133 and position 302.8 of Nigel Jones.

[1602] [3565] In regard to Heydrich's role at the Wannsee Conference, and the conference in general, see https://www.ushmm.org/wlc/en/article.php?ModuleId=10005477 and the book *The Wannsee Conference and the Final Solution: A Reconsideration* by Mark Roseman, published by St Martins Press, 2003, ISBN 0312422342, 9780312422349. See also http://www.holocaustresearchproject.org/holoprelude/Wannsee/wannseeconference.html. All links accessed on Saturday July 25, 2020.

[1603] Page 133 and position 302.8 of Nigel Jones.

[1604] Page 133 of and position 305.2 of Nigel Jones.

[1605] Position 306.0 of Nigel Jones.

[1606] [3434] Pages 34 to 35 of Russel H. S. Stolfi, *Barbarossa Revisited: A Critical Reappraisal of the Opening Stages of the Russo-German Campaign (June-December 1941), The Journal of Modern History 54, no. 1 (Mar., 1982): 27-46.* It can be downloaded at https://core.ac.uk/download/pdf/36736381.pdf. Accessed on Sunday May 16, 2021.

[1607] [3433] Position 306.5 of Nigel Jones.

[1608] [2059] Position 306.8 of Nigel Jones. It was Halder who, four or so years later at the Nuremberg trials, stated Göring's admission of responsibility for the February 1933 Reichstag Fire. See page 193 of *Rise And Fall Of The Third Reich: A History of Nazi Germany* by William L. Shirer, published by Simon and Schuster, 1990, ISBN 0671728687, 9780671728687 and endnote [331] for Chapter 3 "Evil's Storm Descends."

[1609] Position 307.0 of Nigel Jones.

[1610] Position 327.9 of Nigel Jones.

[1611] Position 305.6 of Nigel Jones.

[1612] Pages 158-159 of *VOICES FROM STALINGRAD: UNIQUE FIRST-HAND ACCOUNTS FROM WORLD WAR II'S CRUELLEST BATTLE* paperback, by Jonathan Bastable, published by DAVID & CHARLES; 2nd Revised edition edition (September 28, 2007), ISBN-10: 0715327259 ISBN-13: 9780715327258.

[1613] See endnotes [92] to [107] in the Preface "Birth and Memory upon the Lesser Known Fault Line of History" in regard to the 1934 Röhm Purge.

[1614] Position 333.3 of Nigel Jones.

[1615] Position 333.9 of Nigel Jones.

[1616] Position 334.1 of Nigel Jones. NOTE however that the article by historian Joel S. A. Hayward states that the die had already been cast in regards to the Stalingrad Airlift, regardless of Göring's vainglorious entry. An entry which had more to do with Göring's forlorn hope of ingratiating himself with Hitler, as German cities were being devastated by the relentless Allied bombing. Nevertheless, Hayward makes numerous references to the ribald strategic reckless-ness of Hitler's assertion that the Sixth Army could be supplied from the air. This article can be downloaded at http://www.joelhayward.org/An-Examination-of-.pdf. Accessed on Saturday July 25, 2020. In particular, see pages 32, 35 and the conclusion on page 36. That said, in terms of the narrative for Valkyrie, with Stauffenberg as its central and leading character, his fervent belief that Göring's assurance to Hitler was pivotal in the Stalingrad airlift go-ing ahead, is what matters.

[1617] Position 334.5 of Nigel Jones.

[1618] Position 632.1 of Nigel Jones in the Dramatis Personae.

[1619] Position 307.5 of Nigel Jones.

[1620] Position 979.3 of Metaxas.

[1621] Position 339.3 of Nigel Jones.

[1622] Position 335.8 of Nigel Jones.

[1623] Frau Burker was the daughter of Field Marshal Blomberg, the war minister disgraced and dismissed in the Fritsch scandal of 1938 (See Chapter 12). Her two brothers, Henning and Axel, had both been killed in Northern Africa and the Middle East. See position 335.6 of Nigel Jones.

[1624] Position 336.2 of Nigel Jones.

[1625] Position 339.4 of Nigel Jones.

[1626] Position 339.5 of Nigel Jones.

[1627] Position 340.0 of Nigel Jones.

[1628] Position 340.2 of Nigel Jones.

[1629] Position 339.7 of Nigel Jones.

[1630] Position 344.1 of Nigel Jones.

[1631] Position 343.5 of Nigel Jones.

[1632] Position 344.2 of Nigel Jones.

[1633] Position 344.3 of Nigel Jones.

[1634] Position 344.5 of Nigel Jones.

[1635] Position 344.6 of Nigel Jones.

[1636] Position 346.4 of Nigel Jones.

[1637] Seven to eight months later, following the air raid on Berlin on November 26 1943, Hans von Dohnányi, until January 1944, would be under the care of Ferdinand Sauerbruch in Berlin's Charité Hospital, where Dietrich's father Karl had worked. See endnotes [1551] to [1554] for Chapter 19 "The Tormentor Tor-mented."

[1638] Position 346.7 of Nigel Jones.

[1639] Position 346.8 of Nigel Jones.

[1640] Position 346.9 of Nigel Jones.

[1641] Position 347.1 of Nigel Jones.

[1642] Position 360.8 of Nigel Jones.

[1643] Position 347.3 of Nigel Jones.

[1644] Position 347.5 of Nigel Jones.

[1645] Position 347.6 of Nigel Jones.

[1646] Position 354.8 of Nigel Jones.

[1647] [2822] Position 361.9 of Nigel Jones.

[1648] See the family trees given an pages 394 to 395 and 391 of Jane Pejsa.

[1649] Position 978.0 of Metaxas.

[1650] Position 362.4 of Nigel Jones.

[1651] Position 362.3 of Nigel Jones.

[1652] Position 365.0 of Nigel Jones.

[1653] Position 365.3 of Nigel Jones.

[1654] Position 1062.8 onwards of Microcosm describes the tiered system for foreign workers in Breslau, which applied throughout the Reich.

[1655] Position 1063.4 of Microcosm and page 4 of *Niewolnicy w Breslau, wolni we Wrocławiu* (Slaves in Breslau, free in Wrocław) by Anna Kosmulska, published by Wratislavia, 1995 (No ISBN given). See Google Books at https://books.google.com.au/books?id=4-mAAAAAI-AAJ&dq=Niewolnicy+w+Breslau%2C+wolni+w+Wroc%C5%82awiu&focus=searchwithinvolume&q=sitzen. Accessed on Saturday July 25, 2020.

[1656] Position 1064.4 of Microcosm.

[1657] Position 365.8 of Nigel Jones.

[1658] [4342] Position 365.7 of Nigel Jones.

[1659] Position 366.1 of Nigel Jones.

[1660] Page 61 of *Comparative Studies in History of Religions: Their Aim, Scope, and Validity*, Editors Erik Reenberg Sand, Jørgen Podemann Sørensen, Edition illustrated, published by Museum Tusculanum Press, 1999, ISBN 8772895330, 9788772895338. The goddess Freyja mentioned on this page is a good example of the role of the Valkyrie.

[1661] Position 365.9 of Nigel Jones.

[1662] Position 366.1 of Nigel Jones.

[1663] Position 366.5 of Nigel Jones.

[1664] Position 367.7 of Nigel Jones.

[1665] [2919] Position 368.0 of Nigel Jones.

[1666] Position 367.8 of Nigel Jones.

[1667] [2919] Position 368.3 of Nigel Jones. Indeed, dare one dub Friedrich Fromm a "Fromm Flip Flopp"?

[1668] Position 370.4 of Nigel Jones.

[1669] Position 370.5 of Nigel Jones.

[1670] Position 370.6 of Nigel Jones.

[1671] Position 371.0 of Nigel Jones.

[1672] Position 371.1 of Nigel Jones. This sounded so preposterous that I had to get this confirmed by another source. That being page 27 of *Luck of the Devil: The Story of Operation Valkyrie*, by Ian Kershaw, published by Penguin, 2009, ISBN 0141040068, 9780141040066. Carl Goerdeler was the former mayor of

Leipzig and friend of Dietrich Bonhoeffer. Position 753.8 of Schlingensiepen states the opposing views that Dietrich and Helmuth von Moltke had of Carl Goerdeler.

[1673] Position 371.2 of Nigel Jones.

[1674] Position 371.3 of Nigel Jones.

[1675] Position 371.5 of Nigel Jones.

[1676] Position 371.9 of Nigel Jones. See also position 339.2.

[1677] Position 375.0 of Nigel Jones.

[1678] Position 378.0 of Nigel Jones.

[1679] Position 378.3 of Nigel Jones.

[1680] Page 51 of the book Axel von dem Bussche by Gevinon von Medem in German, published by Hase und Koehler, 1994, ISBN 377581311X, 9783775813112.

[1681] [1728] Position 378.8 of Nigel Jones.

[1682] Position 307.6 of the ebook *Killing Hitler The Third Reich and the Plots against the Führer* by Roger Moorhouse, published by Vintage 2007 (The Random House Group Limited), ISBN 9781446485842.

[1683] Position 420.9 of Nigel Jones.

[1684] Page 350 of *The Trial of the Germans: An Account of the Twenty-two Defendants Before the International Military Tribunal at Nuremberg* by Eugene Davidson, published by University of Missouri Press, 1997, ISBN 0826211399, 9780826211392.

[1685] [1728] Position 379.0 of Nigel Jones.

[1686] Position 379.2 of Nigel Jones.

[1687] Position 379.6 of Nigel Jones.

[1688] Position 379.8 of Nigel Jones. See also page 380 of *Rise And Fall Of The Third Reich: A History of Nazi Germany* by William L. Shirer, published by Simon and Schuster, 1990, ISBN 0671728687, 9780671728687, position 716.4 of Metaxas, page 631 of Bethge and page 236 of Jane Pejsa. The most latter, states that Ewald initially intended to meet Chamberlain. However, as Chamberlain was "unavailable," Ewald instead met with Churchill.

[1689] Pages 164 to 169 of Jane Pejsa. See also endnote [718] in Chapter 9 "The von Kleists and the Prophecy."

[1690] Position 379.9 of Nigel Jones.

[1691] Position 380.1 of Nigel Jones and page 315 of Jane Pejsa.

[1692] Hans-Bernd Haeften was in Dietrich's 1922 confirmation class in Grunewald. See position 975.3 of Metaxas, and the end of pages 36 and 193 of Bethge.

[1693] Position 380.9 of Nigel Jones.

[1694] Position 380.9 of Nigel Jones.

[1695] Position 381.3 of Nigel Jones.

[1696] Position 381.4 of Nigel Jones.

[1697] Position 381.6 of Nigel Jones.

[1698] Position 381.9 of Nigel Jones.

[1699] Position 382.1 of Nigel Jones.

[1700] Position 382.5 of Nigel Jones.

[1701] Position 382.6 of Nigel Jones.

[1702] Position 382.7 of Nigel Jones.

[1703] See the online genealogy site at https://www.geni.com/people/Eberhard-von-Breitenbuch/6000000027022469353. Accessed on Saturday July 25, 2020.

[1704] Position 388.5 of Nigel Jones.

[1705] Position 388.6 of Nigel Jones. See also the end of Chapter 19 "The Tormentor Tormented."

[1706] [1881] [1912] Position 389.7 of Nigel Jones.

[1707] [2822] Position 390.6 of Nigel Jones.

[1708] Position 396.1 of Nigel Jones.

[1709] Position 396.3 of Nigel Jones.

[1710] Position 396.8 of Nigel Jones.

[1711] Position 397.2 of Nigel Jones.

[1712] During my "rookies" training in 1984 at RAAF Base Edinburgh near Adelaide in South Australia, the Flight Lieutenant (female) base intelligence officer drummed into us the cardinal intelligence axiom of "need to know."

[1713] For the invocation of the ancient "Sippenhaft" law on the Stauffenberg family in the aftermath of the failed Valkyrie plot, see pages 140-142 of the book *Family Punishment in Nazi Germany: Sippenhaft, Terror and Myth* by R. Loeffel, Edition illustrated, published by Springer, 2012, ISBN 1137021837, 9781137021830. In this law, the family of a party deemed guilty automatically assumed that guilt as well. A perfect modern-day example being the militant North Korean communist regime. In regards to the life of Countess Nina von Stauffenberg see the online newspaper articles of the Scotsman and UK Telegraph respectively at https://www.scotsman.com/news/obituaries/countess-nina-von-stauffenberg-1-489609 and http://www.telegraph.co.uk/news/obituaries/1514824/Countess-von-Stauffenberg.html. Accessed on Saturday July 25, 2020.

[1714] Position 397.5 of Nigel Jones.

[1715] Position 397.5 of Nigel Jones.

[1716] Position 397.8 of Nigel Jones.

[1717] Position 395.5 of Nigel Jones.

[1718] Position 399.2 of Nigel Jones.

[1719] See positions 393.8 to 394.6 of Nigel Jones.

[1720] Position 399.3 of Nigel Jones.

[1721] Position 398.1 of Nigel Jones.

[1722] Position 398.2 of Nigel Jones.

[1723] Position 398.3 of Nigel Jones.

[1724] Position 398.6 of Nigel Jones.

[1725] Position 398.8 of Nigel Jones.

[1726] Position 399.0 of Nigel Jones.

[1727] Position 399.6 of Nigel Jones.

[1728] Position 400.4 of Nigel Jones. Note; this was not to be a suicide attempt. Like the attempt on the 20th, they were to contrive an excuse to leave the meeting, as they left the briefcase with the time bomb in it in the conference room. See also endnotes [1681] to [1685] for this chapter, where in late December 1943, following his first visit to Hitler's Wolfsschanze, Stauffenberg suggested to Beck and Olbricht upon his return to Berlin, that he could carry out a suicide bomb plot in Hitler's bunker. However, Beck and Olbricht objected on the grounds that the sacrifice of such a brilliant mind and charismatic personality would be too great a waste for Germany, as it needed Stauffenberg alive. See Position 379.0 of Nigel Jones.

[1729] Position 404.9 of Nigel Jones.

[1730] Position 405.3 of Nigel Jones.

[1731] Position 405.7 of Nigel Jones.

[1732] Position 406.4 of Nigel Jones.

[1733] Position 406.4 of Nigel Jones.

[1734] Position 404.4 of Nigel Jones.

[1735] Position 409.7 of Nigel Jones.

[1736] See the description of the photo at position 409.4 of Nigel Jones.

[1737] Position 410.0 of Nigel Jones.

[1738] Position 410.4 of Nigel Jones.

[1739] Position 411.0 of Nigel Jones.

[1740] Position 411.4 of Nigel Jones.

[1741] Position 411.7 of Nigel Jones.

[1742] Position 412.1 of Nigel Jones.

[1743] Position 412.7 of Nigel Jones.

[1744] Page 131 of *Rising '44: The Battle for Warsaw Reprint Edition*, by Norman Davies, published by Penguin Books; Reprint edition (October 4, 2005), ISBN-10: 0143035401, ISBN-13: 9780143035404.

[1745] Position 412.8 of Nigel Jones.

[1746] [1818] Position 578.9 of Nigel Jones. This led to Rommel's secretive cyanide capsule suicide on October 14 1944, three months after the Valkyrie attempt. He was given a state funeral with full military honours and full widow's pension for his wife, to avoid the public disgrace and slow painful death of a show trial and imprisonment. Hitler himself would "solemnly" lay the largest wreath, with Goebbels' propaganda explaining away Rommel's death as due to multiple war wounds.

[1747] Position 413.1 of Nigel Jones.

[1748] See endnotes [92] to [107] in the Preface "Birth and Memory upon the Lesser Known Fault Line of History" in regard to the 1934 Röhm Purge.

[1749] Position 413.3 of Nigel Jones.

[1750] Position 413.7 of Nigel Jones.

[1751] Position 415.2 of Nigel Jones.

[1752] Position 415.3 of Nigel Jones.

[1753] Position 415.7 of Nigel Jones.

[1754] Position 415.9 of Nigel Jones.

[1755] [1758] Position 1089.2 of Metaxas documents Major-General Paul von Hase visiting Dietrich in Tegel Prison for five hours on June 30 1944. Included is Dietrich's writing in a letter to Bethge of how guards at Tegel treated his famous uncle with sycophantic deference. See also page 449 of *Letters and Papers from Prison Volume 8 of Dietrich Bonhoeffer Works* by Dietrich Bonhoeffer, editors Christian Gremmels, John W. De Gruchy, published by Fortress Press, 2010, ISBN 1451406789, 9781451406788 which documents Dietrich's letter to Eberhard Bethge on June 30 1944 and page 604 in the APPENDIX 1 CHRONOLOGY 1942—1945.

[1756] Ibid.

[1757] Positions 400.0 and 409.4 respectively of Nigel Jones.

[1758] Page 826 of Bethge. That the date this was written by Dietrich was July 7, 1944, is implied by Bethge stating that Dietrich wrote this a week following the five hour visit by his Uncle Paul. This visit took place on June 30, 1944 — see endnote [1755] for this chapter.

[1759] Page 826 of Bethge.

[1760] Page 826 of Bethge and page 474 of *Letters and Papers from Prison Volume 8 of Dietrich Bonhoeffer Works*.

[1761] Page 223 of *Operation Valkyrie: The German Generals' Plot Against Hitler* by Pierre Galante, Eugene Silianoff, translated by Mark Howson, published by Rowman & Littlefield, 2002, ISBN 0815411790, 9780815411796 and position 531.0 of the ebook ISBN-13: 9780815411796. Also, position 1095.6 of Metaxas.

[1762] The location of the now abandoned Rangsdorf Airport just south of Berlin is given on Google Maps at https://www.google.de/maps/place/52%C2%B016'59.8%22N+13%C2%B025'45.6%22E/@52.1910855,12.818939,98537m/data=!3m1!1e3!4m5!3m4!1s0x0:0x0!8m2!3d52.2832778!4d13.4293333?hl=en = and more information on it can be found online at the Abandoned Berlin website at http://www.abandonedberlin.com/2015/10/flugplatz-rangsdorf-stauffenberg-hitler-july-20-plot-soviet-airfield.html written by Ciarán Fahey and author of the bilingual book *Verlassene Orte / Abandoned Berlin* published by be.bra Publishing House (http://www.bebraverlag.de/), ISBN-10: 381480208X, ISBN-13: 9783814802084. Ciarán Fahey states that this was airport where Stauffenberg boarded the flight for Rastenburg in East Prussia, near the Wolfsschanze. All links accessed on Saturday July 25, 2020.

[1763] [2908] Position 1096.1 of Metaxas and pages 5 to 6 of Pierre Galante and Eugene Silianoff and position 24.1 of the ebook, ISBN-13: 9780815411796.

1764 Position 753.8 of Metaxas. See endnote 1051 from Chapter 15 "New York — Troubled Revisiting."

1765 481 2004 3009 3011 Position 975.4 of Metaxas states that twenty months before Valkyrie (in November 1942), Haeften had broached the same question as Stauffenberg to Bonhoeffer. See also pages 140 to 141 of *Dietrich Bonhoeffer: Reality and Resistance* by Larry L. Rasmussen, published by Westminster John Knox Press, 1970, ISBN 066422704X, 9780664227043. See also pages 190 to 192 of *I Knew Dietrich Bonhoeffer* by Wolf-Dieter Zimmermann and Ronald Gregor Smith, published by Harper & Row, 1967 (No ISBN given) on Google Books at https://books.google.com.au/books?id=Xn2ZvgEACAAJ&dq=I+Knew+Dietrich+Bonhoeffer&focus=searchwithinvolume&q=thereafter. Accessed on Saturday July 25, 2020.

1766 See footnote #2 at the bottom of page 6 of the book *Operation Valkyrie: The German Generals' Plot Against Hitler* by Pierre Galante, Eugene Silianoff and at position 24.0 of the ebook ISBN-13: 9780815411796.

1767 This cavalry regiment was Stauffenberg's first military unit, which he joined way back in 1926, aged just eighteen. See page 22 and position 69.4 of Nigel Jones.

1768 This implied at position 671.3 of the ebook *Church of Spies: The Pope's Secret War Against Hitler* by Mark Riebling, published by Scribe Publications 2015, ISBN 9781925307139, where Mark Riebling talks of "Galante and Silianoff in *Operation Valkyrie: The German Generals' Plot Against Hitler*, asserting (without source) that Stauffenberg met with Chaplain Hermann Wehrle, but likely conflating an episode in December 1943, when Wehrle learned of Stauffenberg's plots through an intermediary." This intermediary referred to by Mark Riebling, can be inferred as being Major Ludwig Freiherr (Baron) von Leonrod.

1769 The Roman Christendom blogspot, dated Tuesday January 19 2010 at http://romanchristendom.blogspot.com/2010/01/father-hermann-wehrle-sj-martyr-priest.html. Accessed on Saturday July 25, 2020.

1770 The official website of the *Gedenkstätte Deutscher Widerstand* (Memorial of the German Resistance) at https://www.gdw-berlin.de/en/recess/biographies/index_of_persons/biographie/view-bio/ludwig-freiherr-von-leonrod/?no_cache=1. Accessed on Saturday July 25, 2020.

1771 2908 Page 111 of *After Valkyrie: Military and Civilian Consequences of the Attempt to Assassinate Hitler* by Don Allen Gregory, published by McFarland, 2018, ISBN 1476634475, 9781476634470.

1772 Page 6 of Pierre Galante and Eugene Silianoff (position 25.5 of the ebook) and position 1096.5 of Metaxas.

1773 2908 4031 4435 Pages 7 to 17 of Pierre Galante and Eugene Silianoff (position 26.4 to 51.0 of the ebook) and position 1096.8 to 1106.3 of Metaxas, which uses the former as its source, describe the events of July 20 1944 from Stauffenberg's arrival at Rastenburg airport until the immediate aftermath of the bomb blast. Again, their accounts differ in some respects to Nigel Jones, such as Jones claiming that Haeften, Stieff and Roll parted ways with Stauffenberg at Rastenburg airport, with Stauffenberg meeting back up with Haeften at 11:30 a.m. at positions 420.8. I have used the accounts of the former two sources, which are in essential agreement. Although, Pierre Galante and Eugene Silianoff on page 7 give the arrival time for the plane at Rastenburg airport being at 10:15 a.m. rather than 10 a.m. in Metaxas.

[1774] Position 1097.7 of Metaxas and position 422.9 of Nigel Jones. See also positions 312.6 and 510.0 of Pierre Galante and Eugene Silianoff.

[1775] [2908] Nigel Jones at position 421.9 claims that Keitel stated that the conference *originally scheduled for 12 noon, was "put off" half-an-hour later, and rescheduled for 12:30 p.m.*, due to preparations for the Duce's arrival around mid-afternoon. However, Page 8 (position 29.5 of the ebook) of Pierre Galante, Eugene Silianoff, states that the conference was *moved forward* — due also to the Duce's arrival around mid-afternoon! Again, I have used the account of Pierre Galante and Eugene Silianoff. Ultimately, both do agree with the time the conference was held, and hence, the time when the bomb exploded. Page 8 of Pierre Galante & Eugene Silianoff and position 424.9 of Nigel Jones, document the walk from the meeting with Keitel to the conference.

[1776] Page 8 (position 29.9 of the ebook) of Pierre Galante and Eugene Silianoff.

[1777] Page 16 (position 49.4 of the ebook) of Pierre Galante & Eugene Silianoff gives the account of Traudl Junge, the secretary to write Hitler's final will and testament (see https://www.britannica.com/biography/Traudl-Junge accessed on Saturday July 25, 2020.) in his final days, which confirms that the conference was initially meant to take place in the bunker, but on the advice of Hitler's valet Heinz Linge, it was moved to the Lagebaracke due to the arrival of the Duce at 3pm. She states, that as such, Stauffenberg had no way of being aware of this change before his arrival at the Wolfsschanze. This contradicts assertions that the conference was always meant to take place in the Lagebaracke. Also, when Mussolini arrived, Hitler showed him the devastation caused by the bomb blast.

[1778] Pages 7 to 8 (position 28.5 of the ebook) of Pierre Galante and Eugene Silianoff.

[1779] Pages 7 to 8 (position 28.4 of the ebook) of Pierre Galante and Eugene Silianoff.

[1780] Page 8 (position 28.4 of the ebook) of Pierre Galante and Eugene Silianoff.

[1781] Page 8 (position 30.8 of the ebook) of Pierre Galante & Eugene Silianoff and position 424.9 of Nigel Jones.

[1782] Page 10 (position 34.2 of the ebook) of Pierre Galante & Eugene Silianoff and position 427.3 of Nigel Jones.

[1783] See endnotes [1427] to [1433] of Chapter 18 "Romance, Plots and Arrest" and position 982.8 of Metaxas, position 425.4 of Nigel Jones and position 389.6 of

The Secret War Against Hitler by Fabian von Schlabrendorff, published by Routledge, 2018, ISBN 0813321905, ISBN 13: 9780813321905 (paperback).

[1784] Position 34.8 of Pierre Galante & Eugene Silianoff and position 427.7 of Nigel Jones.

[1785] Position 1099.9 of Metaxas gives the dimensions of the heavy oaken table as 18 feet by 5 feet with its pillars being almost as wide as the table. Five feet is equal to 5 x 30 cm = 150 cm = 1.5 metres. A schematic diagram of the table with dimensions in metres is given at position 429.5 of Nigel Jones.

[1786] Position 435.8 of Nigel Jones.

[1787] See position 445.4 of Nigel Jones and page 13 (position 42.3 of the ebook) of Pierre Galante & Eugene Silianoff.

[1788] Position 442.3 of Nigel Jones shows a photo of the unused explosive thrown from their car by Stauffenberg and Haeften as they fled. The author then asks the question: "would it have made the difference?"

[1789] Position 433.6 of Nigel Jones.

[1790] Position 1101.1 of Metaxas and page 15 (position 47.7 of the ebook) of Pierre Galante & Eugene Silianoff. Gertraud Junge would type Hitler's dictation of his final will and testament in his Berlin bunker, just before his suicide in late April 1945, and yet claimed ignorance of the Holocaust. See https://www.theguardian.com/news/2002/feb/14/guardianobituaries.humanities. She passed away on February 10 2002. Accessed on Saturday July 25, 2020.

[1791] Position 434.0 of Nigel Jones.

[1792] Position 1102.0 of Metaxas. See also position 438.8 of Nigel Jones and the photo above and position 941.7 of Schlingensiepen.

[1793] [2908] Position 442.0 of Nigel Jones.

[1794] Position 445.0 of Nigel Jones.

[1795] Page 12 (position 40.0 of the ebook) of Pierre Galante & Eugene Silianoff.

[1796] [2908] Page 12 (position 41.1 of the ebook) of Pierre Galante & Eugene Silianoff.

[1797] Page 11 and position 37.5 of Pierre Galante & Eugene Silianoff and position 436.0 of Nigel Jones.

[1798] Page 13 and position 43.3 of Pierre Galante & Eugene Silianoff.

[1799] Position 501.7 of Nigel Jones and page 32 and position 85.9 of Pierre Galante & Eugene Silianoff.

[1800] Position 502.0 of Nigel Jones.

[1801] Position 505.5 of Nigel Jones.

[1802] As stated on page 14 and position 44.0 of Pierre Galante & Eugene Silianoff.

[1803] Position 413.3 of Nigel Jones.

[1804] Pages 225 to 226 and position 536.3 of Pierre Galante & Eugene Silianoff.

[1805] Page 225 and position 534.1 of Pierre Galante & Eugene Silianoff.

[1806] Position 415.8 of Nigel Jones.

[1807] Page 225 and position 535.8 of Pierre Galante & Eugene Silianoff.

[1808] Page 226 and position 536.7 of Pierre Galante & Eugene Silianoff.

[1809] Page 226 and position 537.5 of Pierre Galante & Eugene Silianoff.

[1810] [2919] Page 228 and position 542.1 of Pierre Galante & Eugene Silianoff.

[1811] Page 228 and position 542.6 of Pierre Galante & Eugene Silianoff.

[1812] Page 252 and position 598.2 of Pierre Galante & Eugene Silianoff.

[1813] The date of Dietrich's execution being April 9 1945 is stated in the chronology on page 1027 of Bethge. This being three weeks following Fromm's execution on March 19 1945.

[1814] The biography of Werner von Haeften on the official website of the *Gedenkstätte Deutscher Widerstand* (Memorial of the German Resistance) at https://www.gdw-berlin.de/en/recess/biographies/index_of_persons/biographie/view-bio/werner-von-haeften/. A complete index of the anti-Hitler conspiracy is given at https://www.gdw-berlin.de/en/recess/biographies/complete_index/. Both links accessed on Saturday July 25, 2020.

[1815] [2919] The official website of the *Gedenkstätte Deutscher Widerstand* (Memorial of the German Resistance) at https://www.gdw-berlin.de/en/memorial_center/history/. Accessed on Saturday July 25, 2020.

[1816] [2919] Position 501.7 of Nigel Jones and page 32 and position 85.9 of Pierre Galante & Eugene Silianoff states the arrests and imprisonment of SS officers on the evening of July 20 1944 in Paris. This being unmatched elsewhere in the Reich proper and Nazi occupied Europe.

[1817] Pages 22 to 23 and position 62.6 of Pierre Galante & Eugene Silianoff.

[1818] Positions 38.3 and 412.8 of Nigel Jones and page 23 and position 63.5 of Pierre Galante & Eugene Silianoff. The former states the Rommel's staff car was strafed by American fighters, while the latter said it was strafed by British planes. Hence, I use the more general term "Allied." In regard to the dispute as to the name and nationality of the pilot responsible for strafing Rommel's staff car in Normandy on July 17 1944, see the online UK Telegraph obituary article for the Canadian fighter pilot Flight Lieutenant Charley Fox at https://www.telegraph.co.uk/news/obituaries/3381986/Flight-Lieutenant-Charley-Fox.html dated 11:11PM GMT 04 Nov 2008. Accessed on Saturday July 25, 2020. In regard to Rommel's forced suicide post-Valkyrie, see endnote [1746] for this chapter.

[1819] Page 30 and position 81.2 of Pierre Galante & Eugene Silianoff, where the vacillating Kluge is quoted venting his rage over Karl Heinrich von Stülpnagel ordering the arrests of SS personnel in Paris without his authority.

[1820] Page 23 and position 64.0 of Pierre Galante & Eugene Silianoff.

[1821] Page 24 and position 65.9 of Pierre Galante & Eugene Silianoff.

[1822] Page 29 and position 78.4 of Pierre Galante & Eugene Silianoff.

[1823] Page 25 and position 67.9 of Pierre Galante & Eugene Silianoff and position 494.4 of Nigel Jones.

[1824] Page 25 and position 67.9 of Pierre Galante & Eugene Silianoff and position 494.5 of Nigel Jones.

[1825] Page 25 and position 68.8 of Pierre Galante & Eugene Silianoff and position 494.9 of Nigel Jones.

[1826] Page 25 and position 69.5 of Pierre Galante & Eugene Silianoff and position 495.2 of Nigel Jones.

[1827] Page 26 and position 71.6 of Pierre Galante & Eugene Silianoff.

[1828] Page 29 and position 78.6 of Pierre Galante & Eugene Silianoff and position 497.1 of Nigel Jones.

[1829] Page 30 and position 80.8 of Pierre Galante & Eugene Silianoff.

[1830] Page 31 and position 82.9 of Pierre Galante & Eugene Silianoff and position 498.9 of Nigel Jones.

[1831] Page 31 and position 83.1 of Pierre Galante & Eugene Silianoff and position 499.1 of Nigel Jones.

[1832] Page 31 and position 83.1 of Pierre Galante & Eugene Silianoff and position 499.2 of Nigel Jones.

[1833] [2919] Page 31 and position 83.9 of Pierre Galante & Eugene Silianoff and position 499.5 of Nigel Jones.

[1834] Pages 237 to 238 and position 562.3 of Pierre Galante & Eugene Silianoff and position 532.6 of Nigel Jones.

[1835] Position 500.9 of Nigel Jones.

[1836] In regard to the "Sippenhaft" law, see pages 140-142 of the book *Family Punishment in Nazi Germany: Sippenhaft, Terror and Myth* by R. Loeffel, Edition illustrated, published by Springer, 2012, ISBN 1137021837, 9781137021830. In this law, the family of a party deemed guilty automatically assume that guilt as well. A perfect modern-day example being the militant North Korean communist regime. See the Liberty in North Korea website at https://www.libertyinnorthkorea.org/learn-nk-challenges/ under the title "Collective Punishment." See also page VIII of the publication *The Hidden Gulag Second Edition The Lives and Voices of "Those Who are Sent to the Mountains" Exposing North Korea's Vast System of Lawless Imprisonment* by David Hawk, A Report by the Committee for Human Rights in North Korea, published by Committee for Human Rights in North Korea 1001 Connecticut Avenue, NW Suite 435 Washington, DC 20036, ISBN 0615623670, Library of Congress Control Number: 2012939299. It can be downloaded at https://www.hrnk.org/uploads/pdfs/HRNK_HiddenGulag2_Web_5-18.pdf on the website of the Committee for Human Rights in North Korea. Both links accessed on Saturday July 25, 2020.

[1837] Position 565.3 of Pierre Galante & Eugene Silianoff.

[1838] Page 239 and position 566.1 of Pierre Galante & Eugene Silianoff.

[1839] Position 577.0 of Nigel Jones.

[1840] [2504] Position 576.9 to 577.2 of Nigel Jones.

[1841] Page 308 of *Europe at War: 1939-1945 : No Simple Victory* by Norman Davies, published by Macmillan, 2006, ISBN 0333692853, 9780333692851.

[1842] Position 577.1 of Nigel Jones.

[1843] [4411] Page 243 and position 574.0 of Pierre Galante & Eugene Silianoff and position 656.7 of Nigel Jones.

[1844] Page 255 and position 603.0 of Pierre Galante & Eugene Silianoff.

[1845] [4411] Position 577.3 of Nigel Jones and the CIA declassified file online at https://www.cia.gov/library/readingroom/docs/HEUSINGER,%20ADOLF_00 06.pdf which states his surrender to American forces in May 1945.

[1846] https://www.britannica.com/place/Kaliningrad-city-Kaliningrad-oblast-Russia. Both links accessed on Saturday July 25, 2020.

[1847] Page 238 and position 563.9 of Pierre Galante & Eugene Silianoff.

[1848] Page 238 and position 564.4 of Pierre Galante & Eugene Silianoff.

[1849] Page 233 and position 555.0 of Pierre Galante & Eugene Silianoff.

[1850] Page 242 and position 568.8 of Pierre Galante & Eugene Silianoff.

[1851] Pages 225 and 186 of the book *The liberation of Paris* by Willis Thornton, published by Harcourt, Brace & World, 1962 (No ISBN given), give the date of August 25 1944 for the liberation of Paris. As does page 163 of *The Liberation of Paris: How Eisenhower, de Gaulle, and von Choltitz Saved the City of Light* by Jean Edward Smith, published by Simon and Schuster, 2019, ISBN 1501164929, 9781501164927.

[1852] Page 242 and position 570.9 of Pierre Galante & Eugene Silianoff and position 575.1 of Nigel Jones.

[1853] Page 231 and position 550.8 of Pierre Galante & Eugene Silianoff.

[1854] Position 525.5 of Nigel Jones.

[1855] Page 1069 of *The Rise and Fall of the Third Reich* by William L. Shirer, Edition reprint, reissue, annotated, published by Simon and Schuster, 2011, ISBN 1451651686, 9781451651683.

[1856] Position 468.7 of Nigel Jones quotes Mussolini's declaration of Providence to Hitler while being shown the bomb damage to the conference room, just three hours after the explosion. Note the photo immediately below.

[1857] Dönitz would briefly succeed Hitler when he committed suicide in his bunker on April 30 1945. See https://www.britannica.com/biography/Karl-Donitz. Accessed on Saturday July 25, 2020.

[1858] Position 528.7 of Nigel Jones. Note the photo just above with Hitler and others watching Dönitz broadcast the navy's loyalty on the night of 20/21 July 1944.

[1859] Pages 242-243 and position 571.6 of Pierre Galante & Eugene Silianoff.

[1860] See the book *Rising '44: The Battle for Warsaw Reprint Edition*, by Professor Norman Davies,published by Penguin Books; Reprint edition (October 4, 2005), ISBN-10: 0143035401, ISBN-13: 9780143035404. Page 427 gives the officially declared duration of the Warsaw Rising being from August 1 1944 to October 2 1944. Page 13 also gives the date of August 1 1944 as the date of the message officially informing the British of the commencement of the Warsaw General Uprising. See also Polish WWII Supplement IV "AK and 1944 Warsaw General Uprising — Stalin's mass murder by German proxy," in particular, endnote [4344] and endnotes [4373] to [4376].

[1861] In regard to Jacques de Lesdain himself, see page 104 of *Les intellectuels et l'occupation, 1940-1944: collaborer, partir, résister* (Intellectuals and occupation, 1940-1944: collaborators, sufferers and resisters), Issue 106 of Collection Mémoires by Albrecht Betz, Stefan Martens, Hans Manfred Bock, published by Autrement, 2004, ISBN 2746705400, 9782746705401. See also the Bibliothèque nationale de France (National Library of France) online at http://data.bnf.fr/11649900/jacques_de_lesdain/ which details a book written by him about his adventures in Tibet, as well as his role in exile in Sigmaringen. See also page 212 of the book *National Regeneration in Vichy France: Ideas and Policies, 1930—1944* by Debbie Lackerstein, published by Routledge, 2016, ISBN 1317089987, 9781317089988 for the author's insight into the mindset of this collaborator.

[1862] Position 608.2 of Nigel Jones.

[1863] Position 613.9 of Nigel Jones.

[1864] Position 614.5 of Nigel Jones.

[1865] Position 609.8 of Nigel Jones.

[1866] Position 610.0 of Nigel Jones.

[1867] Position 611.1 to 611.6 of Nigel Jones.

[1868] Position 612.1 of Nigel Jones.

[1869] Position 613.4 of Nigel Jones. Position 612.6 of Nigel Jones documents the arrival of Great Aunt Alexandrine in Bad Sachsa to arrange a bus to take the children back to the Stauffenberg country home in Lautlingen. NOTE: While the date given is July 11 1945 for the arrival of Great Aunt Alexandrine in Bad Sachsa, by inference, it must really be the June 11 1945, because it is stated that Great Aunt Alexandrine and the children arrived afterwards in Lautlingen on June 13 1945. Moreover, at position 613.4, it is stated that in early July 1945, they became aware of the whereabouts of Nina in a village near Hof.

[1870] The online UK Telegraph article at http://www.telegraph.co.uk/news/obituaries/1514824/Countess-von-Stauffenberg.html, dated 12:01AM BST 05 Apr 2006, states in its penultimate paragraph, the view of Nina that the heroic failure of the plan resonated more down the years than a successful coup might have done. In the online article of the Scotsman at https://www.scotsman.com/news/obituaries/countess-nina-von-stauffenberg-1-489609, dated Monday 10 April 2006, in its penultimate paragraph, Nina is quoted as saying that she always supported her husband's actions. In the same paragraph, it is stated that Nina raised her children in the Catholic faith. Both links accessed on Saturday July 25, 2020.

[1871] Position 80.5 of Nigel Jones.

[1872] Position 615.0 of Nigel Jones.

[1873] Implied at position 615.2 of Nigel Jones.

[1874] Position 615.4 of Nigel Jones.

[1875] Position 617.1 of Nigel Jones.

[1876] Position 617.3 of Nigel Jones. Berthold's famous aviator Aunt will be covered later on in this chapter.

[1877] See the family trees given on pages 394 to 395 and 391 of Jane Pejsa.

[1878] Page 26 and position 71.6 of Pierre Galante & Eugene Silianoff.

[1879] The gruesome fate of General Stieff, and his resilience in the face of it, is stated at position 637.0 of Nigel Jones in the Dramatis Personae. Also, given the fact that Kluge phoned Stieff on the evening of July 20 1944, it can easily be inferred that Stieff must have been arrested within just a few hours of this phone conversation.

[1880] [2006] [2007] Position 562.7 of Nigel Jones and position 734.7 of the ebook *Traitors or Patriots?: A Story of the German Anti-Nazi Resistance* by Louis R. Eltscher, published by McNidder & Grace Carmarthen UK 2020, Ebook ISBN 9780857162045.

[1881] See endnote [1706] for this chapter.

[1882] Position 638.1 of Nigel Jones in the Dramatis Personae.

[1883] Position 582.0 of the ebook *Killing Hitler The Third Reich and the Plots against the Führer* by Roger Moorhouse, published by Vintage 2007 (The Random House Group Limited), ISBN 9781446485842.

[1884] Page 336 of Jane Pejsa.

[1885] See the Genealogy website at https://www.geni.com/people/Erika-von-Falkenhayn/6000000021470617332. Accessed on Saturday July 25, 2020.

[1886] Position 371.7 of Nigel Jones.

[1887] Position 1145.9 to 1148.3 of Metaxas and page 914 of Bethge document the demise of Roland Freisler and the circumstances in which it took place — including the scale of the bombing by the American Eighth Air Force on Saturday February 3 1945.

[1888] Position 635.0 of Nigel Jones in the Dramatis Personae. This remarkable episode of survival will be elaborated upon further in Chapter 25 "Old Prussia Gone With The Wind."

[1889] Position 572.5 of Nigel Jones.

[1890] See endnotes [2713] onwards from the start of Chapter 27 "The Prominenten and Miraculous Reprieves" for a detailed explanation of the "Prominenten."

[1891] [2034] Page xi of *Hostage of the Third Reich: the story of my imprisonment and rescue from the SS*, by Fey Von Hassell, edited by David Forbes-Watt, published by Scribner, 1989, ISBN 068419080X, 9780684190808, lists Fabian von Schlabrendorff as one of the hostages. Also see the online resource http://www.mythoselser.de/niederdorf.htm, edited by Peter Koblank, which gives a list of the hostages liberated by nationality. Accessed on Saturday July 25, 2020. As does position 725.6 onwards of the ebook *The Venlo Incident* by Sigismund Payne Best, published by Frontline Books, an imprint of Pen &

Sword Books Limited, 47 Church Street, Barnsley, S. Yorkshire, S70 2AS, ISBN 9781848325586.

[1892] Position 635.3 of Nigel Jones in the Dramatis Personae. A more detailed account of Fabian von Schlabrendorff's miraculous survival post-war, is given in Chapter 27 "The Prominenten and Miraculous Reprieves." The meaning of the term "Prominenten" is given at the beginning of that chapter. See endnotes [2708] onwards for that chapter.

[1893] http://www.mythoselser.de/niederdorf.htm. Accessed on Saturday July 25, 2020. As does position 725.6 onwards of the ebook *The Venlo Incident* by Sigismund Payne Best, published by Frontline Books, an imprint of Pen & Sword Books Limited, 47 Church Street, Barnsley, S. Yorkshire, S70 2AS, ISBN 9781848325586.

[1894] See endnotes [2708] onwards from the start of Chapter 27 "The Prominenten and Miraculous Reprieves" for a detailed explanation of the "Prominenten."

[1895] As stated by historians in the dramatised documentary *Hostages of the SS*.

[1896] [2034] See the end of Episode 2 of the dramatised documentary *Hostages of the SS*.

[1897] See the online article on the Wannsee Conference at https://www.ushmm.org/wlc/en/article.php?ModuleId=10005477. Accessed on Saturday July 25, 2020. See also endnote [3565] of Polish WWII Supplement II "The Gleiwitz (Gliwice) Incident."

[1898] Position 546.5 of Nigel Jones.

[1899] Page 1070 of *Rise And Fall Of The Third Reich: A History of Nazi Germany* by William L. Shirer, published by Simon and Schuster, 1990, ISBN 0671728687, 9780671728687 and page 223 of *The Holocaust: An Encyclopedia and Document Collection [Volume 1 (A - K) of 4]*, editors Paul R. Bartrop, Michael Dickerman, published by ABC-CLIO, 2017, ISBN 1440840849, 9781440840845, in an article by Eve E. Grimm. See also position 519.8 of the ebook *The Secret War Against Hitler* by Fabian von Schlabrendorff, published by Routledge, 2018, e-ISBN 0813321905, ISBN 13: 9780813321905 (paperback).

[1900] Pages 223 to 224 of *The Holocaust: An Encyclopedia and Document Collection [Volume 1 (A - K) of 4]*, editors Paul R. Bartrop, Michael Dickerman, published by ABC-CLIO, 2017, ISBN 1440840849, 9781440840845, in an article by Eve E. Grimm.

[1901] Pages xvi and 220 of *Hitler's Hitmen* by Guido Knopp, published by Sutton, 2002, ISBN 0750926023, 9780750926027.

[1902] Position 546.9 of Nigel Jones.

[1903] Positions 544.8 and 547.4 of Nigel Jones and position 25.3 of the ebook *The Secret War Against Hitler* by Fabian von Schlabrendorff, published by Routledge, 2018, e-ISBN 0813321905, ISBN 13: 9780813321905 (paperback).

[1904] Page 223 of *The Holocaust: An Encyclopedia and Document Collection [Volume 1 (A - K) of 4]*.

[1905] Position 547.0 of Nigel Jones.

[1906] See position 519.8 of the ebook *The Secret War Against Hitler* by Fabian von Schlabrendorff, published by Routledge, 2018, e-ISBN 0813321905, ISBN 13: 9780813321905 (paperback).

[1907] Position 594.5 of *Killing Hitler The Third Reich and the Plots against the Führer* by Roger Moorhouse, published by Vintage 2007 (The Random House Group Limited), ISBN 9781446485842.

[1908] Position 595.1 of *Killing Hitler The Third Reich and the Plots against the Führer*.

[1909] Positions 415.9 and 416.8 of Nigel Jones.

[1910] Position 595.5 of *Killing Hitler The Third Reich and the Plots against the Führer*.

[1911] Position 594.2 of *Killing Hitler The Third Reich and the Plots against the Führer*. Cited from page 134 of *Until the Final Hour* (London, 2003) by Gertraud (Traudl) Junge and Melissa Müller.

[1912] Position 389.7 of Nigel Jones and endnote [1706] for this chapter.

[1913] The online UK Telegraph article at http://www.telegraph.co.uk/news/obituaries/1514824/Countess-von-Stauffenberg.html, dated 12:01AM BST 05 Apr 2006. Accessed on Saturday July 25, 2020.

[1914] Position 334.6 of Nigel Jones.

[1915] Position 307.0 of Nigel Jones.

[1916] Position 335.5 of Nigel Jones.

[1917] Position 308.7 of Nigel Jones.

[1918] Position 272.6 of Nigel Jones.

[1919] Position 274.1 of Nigel Jones and page 191 of Jane Pejsa. In regard to the Röhm purge in 1934, see endnotes [92] to [107] in the Preface "Birth and Memory upon the Lesser Known Fault Line of History."

[1920] Position 274.9 of Nigel Jones.

[1921] Not to mention Dietrich as a young high school student in 1922, during the era of hyper-inflation, engaging in a protracted argument with a Nazi sitting next to him on a train during his school holidays. See page 33 of Bethge.

[1922] Page 17 of *The Second World War: Ambitions to Nemesis* by Bradley Lightbody, published by Psychology Press, 2004, ISBN 0415224047, 9780415224048. Also, the online source J. Llewellyn et al, *Hitler becomes chancellor*, Alpha History, accessed on Saturday July 25, 2020 at http://alphahistory.com/nazigermany/hitler-becomes-chancellor/.

[1923] Position 906.7 to 911.1 of Microcosm.

[1924] See position 929.8 of Metaxas, page 174 of *The sword and the umbrella* by James Graham-Murray, published by Times Press, 1964, (no ISBN given), and page 183 of *True patriotism; 1939-45: from the collected works of Dietrich Bonhoeffer*, by Dietrich Bonhoeffer, Edwin Hanton Robertson, edited by Edwin Hanton Robertson, published by Collins, 1973, (no ISBN given) all documenting Anthony Eden's letter to George Bell dated August 4 1942.

[1925] In regard to Katyń, see Polish WWII Supplement III "The Katyń Wood Massacre"[3618] and pages 48 to 49 of *Rising '44: The Battle for Warsaw Reprint Edition* (October 4, 2005), ISBN-10: 0143035401, ISBN-13: 9780143035404 by Professor Norman Davies, which documents the Western denial of the Stalinist perpetrated Katyń massacre. As well the Central Intelligence Agency report online by Benjamin B. Fischer at https://www.cia.gov/library/center-for-the-study-of-intelligence/csi-publications/csi-studies/studies/winter99-00/art6.html. Accessed on Saturday July 25, 2020.

[1926] Pages 298 to 300 of *Rising '44: The Battle for Warsaw Reprint Edition* (October 4, 2005), ISBN-10: 0143035401, ISBN-13: 9780143035404 by Professor Norman Davies, describes Eden's similar attitude to the Polish Government in exile just before and during the Warsaw General Uprising of 1944. See also endnote [4110] of Polish WWII Supplement IV "AK and 1944 Warsaw General Uprising — Stalin's mass murder by German proxy."

[1927] Page 826 of Bethge and position 1105.5 of Metaxas.

[1928] Page 192 of *Disobedience and Conspiracy in the German Army, 1918-1945* by Robert B. Kane, published by McFarland, 2008, ISBN 0786437448, 9780786437443 on Google Books at https://books.google.com.au/books?id=PP7uMQdgv5AC&pg=PA192&dq=to+kid-nap+or+kill+the+head+of+the+German+state+and+commander+in+chief+of+the+Army&hl=en&sa=X&ved=0ahUKEwjrrKLehvfjAhVJLY8KHT0fAboQ6AEIKjAA#v=onepage&q=to%20kidnap%20or%20kill%20the%20head%20of%20the%20German%20state%20and%20commander%20in%20chief%20of%20the%20Army&f=false. Accessed on Saturday July 25, 2020.

[1929] https://www.ushmm.org/information/exhibitions/online-exhibitions/special-focus/liberation-of-auschwitz, gives the date of January 27 1945 for the liberation of the Auschwitz concentration camp. Accessed on Saturday July 25, 2020.

[1930] Page 2 of *On the Road to the Wolf's Lair: German Resistance to Hitler* by Theodore S. Hamerow and G P Gooch, published by Harvard University Press, 1997, ISBN 0674636805, 9780674636804. Also page 108 of *Resistance and Conformity in the Third Reich* (Routledge Sources in History) by Martyn Housden, published by Routledge, 2013, ISBN 1134808461, 9781134808465 and position 1106.3 of Metaxas.

[1931] New South Books website at http://www.newsouthbooks.com/bkpgs/detailauthor.php?author_id=73840. Accessed on Saturday July 25, 2020.

[1932] Page 192 of *Disobedience and Conspiracy in the German Army, 1918-1945* by Robert B. Kane, published by McFarland, 2008, ISBN 0786437448, 9780786437443.

[1933] Page 180 of *The Bonhoeffers; Portrait of a Family* by Sabine Leibholz-Bonhoeffer, published by Sidgwick and Jackson, 1971, no ISBN given. Sabine had fled Germany with her husband Gerhard for Switzerland, and ultimately England, in September 1938. See Chapter 13 "Flight and the Tumultuous Appeasement of Evil."

[1934] Page 423 of *Rise And Fall Of The Third Reich: A History of Nazi Germany* by William L. Shirer, published by Simon and Schuster, 1990, ISBN 0671728687, 9780671728687. See also the documented assessment by General Beck on page 367.

[1935] Page 380 of *Rise And Fall Of The Third Reich: A History of Nazi Germany* by William L. Shirer. In regard to Ewald's meeting with Churchill in August 1938, see endnotes [920] to [923] of Chapter 13 "Flight and the Tumultuous Appeasement of Evil."

[1936] Footnote on page 380 of *Rise And Fall Of The Third Reich: A History of Nazi Germany* by William L. Shirer, published by Simon and Schuster, 1990, ISBN 0671728687, 9780671728687.

[1937] https://www.britannica.com/biography/Nevile-Meyrick-Henderson. Accessed on Saturday July 25, 2020.

[1938] Page 380 of *Rise And Fall Of The Third Reich: A History of Nazi Germany* by William L. Shirer.

[1939] Page 380 of *Rise And Fall Of The Third Reich: A History of Nazi Germany* by William L. Shirer.

[1940] Most curiously, page 237 of Jane Pejsa states that it was not until days later, following Ewald's return to Berlin, that Ewald received this letter via diplomatic channels. Moreover, in a footnote on page 380, Shirer states that he himself, discovered that the German Foreign Office knew about this letter as early as September 6 1938! This being from a German Foreign Office memorandum that Shirer found marked as: "Extract from a letter of Winston Churchill to a German confidante." This perhaps implies that Jane Pejsa's version is true — namely that Ewald received this letter upon his return Berlin. However, the question still remains: How did the Nazis become aware of this letter as early as September 6 1938?

[1941] Pages 329 to 330 of Jane Pejsa and pages 185 to 186 of *Bodyguard of Lies Volume II* by Anthony Brown, published by Harper and Row, Publishers, Incorporated, 10 East 53rd Street New York, NY, 10022 and simultaneously in Canada by Fitzhenry and Whiteside Limited, Toronto (No ISBN given). This letter is also quoted in part on page 380 of *Rise And Fall Of The Third Reich: A History of Nazi Germany* by William L. Shirer.

[1942] See endnote [3384] of Polish WWII Supplement I "The Molotov-Ribbentrop Pact" in regard to when the last Polish forces surrendered following the joint German-Soviet September-October 1939 invasion of Poland.

[1943] Page 3 of *Hitler's Pre-emptive War: The Battle for Norway, 1940* by Henrik O. Lunde, published by Casemate Publishers, 2009, ISBN 1932033920,

9781932033922 documents the desperate hope Neville Chamberlain held for the German people overthrowing Hitler during the appropriately dubbed "Phoney War."

[1944] In the book *War of Extermination: The German Military in World War II, 1941-1944*, edited by Hannes Heer, Klaus Naumann, Volume 3 of Berghahn Series, Volume 3 of Studies on war and genocide, published by Berghahn Books, 2000, ISBN 1571812326, 9781571812322. Christian Gerlach contributes Chapter 6, "MEN OF 20 JULY AND THE WAR IN THE SOVIET UNION" starting on page 127. His credentials can be viewed at http://www.suche.unibe.ch/index_en.php?eingabe=Christian+Gerlach on the University of Bern website. Accessed on Saturday July 25, 2020.

[1945] Klaus Jochen Arnold wrote the essay *Verbrecher aus eigener Initiative? Der 20. Juli 1944 und die Thesen Christian Gerlachs* (Criminals on their own initiative? The 20th of July 1944 and the theses of Christian Gerlach) while Peter Hoffman in his article entitled *Tresckow und Stauffenberg: Ein Zeugnis aus dem Archiv des russischen Geheimdienstes* (Tresckow and Stauffenberg: A testimony from the archive of the Russian secret service) published in the *Frankfurter Allgemeine Zeitung*, on July 20 1998, accuses Gerlach and other such investigators of intentional distortion of evidence. Arnold's essay can be downloaded at http://www.zeitgeschichte-online.de/sites/default/files/media/20juli_arnold.pdf on the Zeitgeschichte-online (History online) website. The profile of which can be viewed at http://www.zeitgeschichte-online.de/profil. Klaus Jochen Arnold's credentials can be viewed online at http://www.kas.de/wf/de/37.4228/ on the Konrad Adenauer Stiftung (Foundation) website, while for Peter Hoffman, they can be viewed online at http://www.mcgill.ca/history/peter-hoffmann on the McGill University website. See also the essay of Danny Orbach which can be downloaded online at https://www.academia.edu/4312992/Criticism_Reconsidered_The_German_Resistance_to_Hitler_in_Critical_German_Scholarship. In particular, note page 10 of Danny Orbach's essay which quotes Hoffman's criticism of Christian Gerlach, and in footnote 17 at the bottom of this page, gives the source as an article Hoffman had written in the *Frankfurter Allgemeine Zeitung*, on July 20 1998. It also documents the criticism of other German historians of Gerlach, such as Joachim Fest, the author of numerous works on the Nazi era, and indeed, Klaus Jochen Arnold. All links accessed on Saturday July 25, 2020.

[1946] Position 333.9 of Nigel Jones.

[1947] See the Deutsche Welle online article in English, about halfway down at http://www.dw.com/en/germany-remembers-operation-valkyrie-the-plot-to-kill-hitler/a-1271174 dated July 20 2011, which states that some view Stauffenberg acting more out of self-interest and less out of benevolent concern for the plight of the Jews and other victims of Nazi war crimes. Accessed on Saturday July 25, 2020.

[1948] Page 127 of *War of Extermination: The German Military in World War II, 1941-1944*.

[1949] Position 394.2 of Nigel Jones states that the ultra-conservative Goerdeler was the conspirators' official choice for the post of post-putsch Chancellor. See also position 624.1 which gives a profile of Carl Goerdeler in the Dramatis Personae. It seems that Goerdeler's greatest flaws were his bad judgement of character, and poor grasp on reality, exemplified with his naive hopes of Germany retaining its territorial gains seized by the Nazis.

[1950] Page 103 of *Der lange Weg nach Westen: Deutsche Geschichte vom 'Dritten Reich' bis zur Wiedervereinigung* (The long way to the west: German history from the "Third Reich" to reunification), Volume 2, by Heinrich August Winkler, published by C.H.Beck, 2000, ISBN 340646002X, 9783406460029.

[1951] Page 13 of *Rising '44: The Battle for Warsaw Reprint Edition*, by Norman Davies, published by Penguin Books; Reprint edition (October 4, 2005), ISBN-10: 0143035401, ISBN-13: 9780143035404 gives August 1 1944 at 1700 hours as the date of the commencement of the Warsaw Uprising. Page 678 gives the translated English text of the Capitulation Agreement between the German Army and the Home Army, giving the date of capitulation as the "2 X 1944" (October 2 1944). This being a duration of 63 days for the Uprising. See also Polish WWII Supplement IV "AK and 1944 Warsaw General Uprising — Stalin's mass murder by German proxy," in particular endnote [4344] and endnotes [4373] to [4376].

[1952] Page xxii of *Inside a Gestapo Prison: The Letters of Krystyna Wituska, 1942-1944* by Krystyna Wituska, Irene Tomaszewski Wayne State University Press, 2006 - Biography & Autobiography, ISBN 0814332943, 9780814332948.

[1953] In regard to the three stages of Poland's partitioning in 1772, 1793 and 1795, see page 386 of *God's Playground A History of Poland: Volume 1: The Origins to 1795*, by Norman Davies, published by Oxford University Press Oxford, 2005, ISBN 0199253390, 9780199253395. As well, page 245 onwards of the book *The Polish Way: A Thousand Year History of the Poles and Their Culture* by Adam Zamoyski (a friend of Norman Davies), published by John Murray Publishers Limited, 1989, ISBN 10: 0719546745 ISBN 13: 9780719546747.

[1954] [3565] See the online Central Intelligence Agency Report on the Assassination of Reinhard Heydrich at https://www.cia.gov/library/center-for-the-study-of-intelligence/kent-csi/vol4no1/html/v04i1a01p_0001.htm, approved for release by the CIA Historical Review Program September 22 1993. Accessed on Saturday July 25, 2020.

[1955] Page 133 and position 302.8 of Nigel Jones. See also endnote [1601] for this chapter.

[1956] [3565] See https://www.cia.gov/library/center-for-the-study-of-intelligence/kent-csi/vol4no1/html/v04i1a01p_0001.htm. Accessed on Saturday July 25, 2020.

[1957] [3565] In regards to the Wannsee Conference, see https://www.ushmm.org/wlc/en/article.php?ModuleId=10005477 and the book *The Wannsee Conference and the Final Solution: A Reconsideration* by Mark Roseman, published by St Martins Press, 2003, ISBN 0312422342, 9780312422349. See also http://www.holocaustresearchproject.org/holoprelude/Wannsee/wannseeconference.html. All links accessed on Saturday July 25, 2020.

[1958] Page 134 and position 305.8 of Nigel Jones.

[1959] Position 303.3 of Nigel Jones.

[1960] Position 303.7 of Nigel Jones.

[1961] In regard to Japan holding the clear ascendency at this time in the war in the Pacific and South-East Asian theatre, see the early chapters of the book *The war with Japan: A Concise History edition 2* by Charles Bateson, published by Michigan State University Press, 1968. In particular see pages 58-59 in Chapter three "THE FALL OF THE PHILIPPINES" where General MacArthur along with almost every other Allied leader, military and civilian was guilty of dangerous complacency, and pages 88-89 in Chapter four "THE CONQUEST OF MALAYA," where the prevalence of complacency and wishful thinking in Singapore of the British, both military and civilian, is stated.

[1962] See the later chapters of *The war with Japan: A Concise History edition 2* by Charles Bateson.

[1963] [2204] [2925] [4274] Page 164 of *Withstanding Hitler* by Michael Balfour, published by Routledge, 2013, ISBN 1136088601, 9781136088605 and http://www.holocaustresearchproject.org/othercamps/nebe.html. Accessed on Saturday July 25, 2020.

[1964] Page 205 of *The Nazi Persecution of the Gypsies* by Guenter Lewy, published by Oxford University Press, USA, 2000, ISBN 0195125568, 9780195125566 and http://www.holocaustresearchproject.org/othercamps/nebe.html. Accessed on Saturday July 25, 2020.

[1965] Pages 164-165 of *Withstanding Hitler* by Michael Balfour, published by Routledge, 2013, ISBN 1136088601, 9781136088605.

[1966] Page 165 of *Withstanding Hitler* by Michael Balfour, published by Routledge, 2013, ISBN 1136088601, 9781136088605.

[1967] Footnote (1) in the online article at http://aircrewremembered.com/williams-john-edwin-ashley.html on the Aircrew Remembered website. Accessed on Saturday July 25, 2020. In March 1944, Nebe drew up the list of fifty escapees to be shot in the wake of the famous "Great Escape," immortalised in Hollywood folklore with the requisite embellishments. This list included John Williams from the Sydney northern beach side suburb of Manly. In April 2017, I listened to the story of John Williams, recounted by his niece Louise on the ABC Radio show "Conversations" hosted by Richard Vidler on ABC-612 in Brisbane.

[1968] Page 165 of *Withstanding Hitler* by Michael Balfour, published by Routledge, 2013, ISBN 1136088601, 9781136088605.

[1969] Footnote (1) in the online article at http://aircrewremembered.com/williams-john-edwin-ashley.html on the Aircrew Remembered website and http://www.holocaustresearchproject.org/othercamps/nebe.html on the website of the Holocaust Education & Archive Research Team. Both links accessed on Saturday July 25, 2020.

[1970] [2204] [2925] [4274] Footnote (1) in the online article at http://aircrewremembered.com/williams-john-edwin-ashley.html on the Aircrew Remembered website and http://www.holocaustresearchproject.org/othercamps/nebe.html. Both links accessed on Saturday July 25, 2020.

[1971] Page 208 of *The Nazi Persecution of the Gypsies* by Guenter Lewy, published by Oxford University Press, USA, 2000, ISBN 0195125568, 9780195125566.

[1972] Ibid.

[1973] Ibid.

[1974] Ibid.

[1975] Page 250 of *Burning the Reichstag: An Investigation Into the Third Reich's Enduring Mystery* by Benjamin Carter Hett, published by OUP USA, 2014, ISBN 0199322325, 9780199322329.

[1976] Ibid.

[1977] This likely figure of 5,000 being executed due to the Valkyrie plot, is given on page 258 of *Withstanding Hitler* by Michael Balfour, published by Routledge, 2013, ISBN 1136088601, 9781136088605. Although Balfour qualifies this figure of 5,000 by stating that probably no more than 200 were closely associated with the plot or in sheltering those who had been. In August 1944, 5,000 people had been rounded up, but the majority of these were later released, with Konrad Adenauer, the first West German Chancellor post-war, being released in November 1944.

[1978] Position 598.0 of the ebook *Killing Hitler The Third Reich and the Plots against the Führer* by Roger Moorhouse, published by Vintage 2007 (The Random House Group Limited), ISBN 9781446485842.

[1979] Ibid page 76.

[1980] Ibid page 77. Cited from page 68 of *The Last Days of Hitler*, Edition 3 revised. by Hugh Redwald Trevor-Roper, published by Macmillan, 1962.

[1981] Ibid page 77.

[1982] Page 105 of *Inside the Third Reich* by Albert Speer, published by Simon and Schuster, 1970, ISBN 0684829495, 9780684829494.

[1983] See position 648.8 of Schlingensiepen which states that Compiègne was a classical example of evil thriving on pseudo-justice. It also quotes Paul in his second letter to the Corinthians, chapter 11, verse 14; "Satan appearing in the form of an angel of light."

Chapter 21 — Valkyrie's Wake

[1984] Page 485 of *Letters and Papers from Prison Volume 8 of Dietrich Bonhoeffer Works* by Dietrich Bonhoeffer, editors Christian Gremmels, John W. De Gruchy, published by Fortress Press, 2010, ISBN 1451406789, 9781451406788. Footnote #3 on this page states that the Daily Text for Thursday, July 20, was Psalm 20:8 in Luther's Bible, which is verse 7 in the NRSV: "Some take pride in chariots, and some in horses, but our pride is in the name of the LORD our God"; and Romans 8:31: "If God is for us, who is against us?" For Friday, July 21, 1944, footnote #4 states they were Psalm 23:1: "The LORD is my shepherd, I shall not want"; and John 10:14: "I am the good shepherd. I know my own and my own know me." See also position 1107.3 of Metaxas.

[1985] Pages 512-513 of *Letters and Papers from Prison Volume 8 of Dietrich Bonhoeffer Works*.

[1986] Eucharistic Celebration Homily of his Holiness John Paul II at Oriole Park at Camden Yards, Baltimore, Sunday October 8 1995. This can be viewed online at https://w2.vatican.va/content/john-paul-ii/en/homilies/1995/documents/hf_jp-ii_hom_19951008_baltimore.html on the official Vatican website. Accessed on Saturday July 25, 2020.

[1987] Position 1114.9 of Metaxas. This can also be implied from positions 563.0 and 564.2 of the ebook *Hitler's Spy Chief The Wilhelm Canaris Mystery* by Richard Bassett, published by The Orion Publishing Group Limited, 2011, a Hachette UK company, ISBN 9780297865711.

[1988] Position 1115.0 of Metaxas and position 523.7 of Nigel Jones.

[1989] Position 1116.8 of Metaxas and position 625.7 of Nigel Jones in the Dramatis Personae. See also the online article on the official website of the *Gedenkstätte Deutscher Widerstand* (Memorial of the German Resistance) at https://www.gdw-berlin.de/en/recess/biographies/index_of_persons/biographie/view-bio/paul-von-hase/. Accessed on Saturday July 25, 2020.

[1990] In early 1944, Hans von Dohnányi begged Christine to poison the food she brought to him in order to infect him with diphtheria, and supposedly avoid further Gestapo interrogations. Christine finally agreed to do it, and it succeeded in that he was transferred to the epidemic hospital in Potsdam. However, when his son Christoph visited him secretly and for the last time, he noticed that his father's fingers were taped — a sure sign of torture. See the online Boston Globe article at https://www.bostonglobe.com/arts/music/2013/10/12/legacy-resisitance-recalling-life-and-struggle-hans-von-dohnanyi/s30Pu3ftHhz7AWYOMl4yNN/story.html by Jeremy Eichler dated October 12, 2013, 6:00 p.m. The online article on Hans von Dohnányi on the official website of the Yad Vashem World Holocaust Remembrance Center at http://db.yadvashem.org/righteous/family.html?language=en&itemId=4018107 also mentions his diphtheria being self inflicted, albeit without the help of his wife Chritine. Both links accessed on Saturday July 25, 2020.

[1991] Page 810 of Bethge and position 1116.9 of Metaxas.

[1992] [134] [2726] [2728] [2729] Position 1117.0 of Metaxas states that the *Chronicle of Shame files* were discovered in Zossen on September 20 1944. However, position 942.1 of Schlingensiepen gives September 22 1944, as does note #32 on page 583 of the book *History of the German Resistance, 1933-1945*, Canadian electronic library: Books collection EBSCO ebook academic collection, by Peter Hoffmann, published by McGill-Queen's Press - MQUP, 1996, ISBN 0773515313, 9780773515314. Page 810 of Bethge, gives both these dates as possible dates for the discovery of the Zossen files by Criminal Commissioner Franz-Xaver Sonderegger. Metaxas at position 741.0, first mentions the *Chronicle of Shame files*, later to be known as the Zossen Files upon their discovery in September 1944, which Dohnányi started writing in the wake of the invasion of Poland in September 1939.

[1993] [2729] Position 942.9 onwards of Schlingensiepen.

[1994] Position 942.1 of Schlingensiepen.

[1995] Google Maps at https://www.google.com.au/maps/place/Zossen,+Germany/@52.1378776,13.3279621,9z/data=!4m5!3m4!1s0x47a86b0cf890eedf:0xa4b91c817603e69c!8m2!3d52.2169747!4d13.453792. Accessed on Saturday July 25, 2020.

[1996] Position 942.0 of Schlingensiepen.

[1997] Central Intelligence Agency declassified document *The Last Days of Ernst Kaltenbrunner*, dated September 22 1993, which can be viewed online at https://www.cia.gov/library/center-for-the-study-of-intelligence/kent-csi/vol4no2/html/v04i2a07p_0001.htm. Accessed on Saturday July 25, 2020.

[1998] Position 942.0 of Schlingensiepen.

[1999] The online article on Hans von Dohnányi on the official website of the Yad Vashem World Holocaust Remembrance Center at http://db.yadvashem.org/righteous/family.html?language=en&itemId=4018107. Accessed on Saturday July 25, 2020. Note however, this article refers to Prinz-Albrecht-Strasse as simply Berlin's Gestapo prison, which it indeed was. See the next chapter, Chapter 22 "Prinz-Albrecht-Strasse."

[2000] Position 942.8 of Schlingensiepen.

[2001] Position 943.1 of Schlingensiepen.

[2002] Page 239 of Pierre Galante & Eugene Silianoff also describes Hofacker's arrest on July 25 1944, and the extraordinary courage and resilience of Cäsar von Hofacker, with his execution being on December 20 1944, once the Gestapo had realised he was not going to talk under any circumstances. It's also stated that Hofacker was the final victim of the July 20 plot in Paris. Position 576.9 to 577.2 of Nigel Jones documents Hofacker's brave belligerence in Freisler's court, with his dauntless refusal to be cowed by Freisler's rants.

[2003] Page 192 of *Ewald von Kleist-Schmenzin: ein Konservativer gegen Hitler : Biographie* (Ewald von Kleist-Schmenzin: a Conservative against Hitler : Biography) by Bodo Scheurig, published by Propyläen, 1994, ISBN 354905324X, 9783549053249.

[2004] See position 975.4 of Metaxas. Note to, that in November 1942, Werner had met Dietrich, posing the question of tyrannicide — see again position 975.4 of Metaxas which states that twenty months before Valkyrie (in November 1942), Haeften had broached the same question as Stauffenberg to Bonhoeffer. See also endnote [1765] of Chapter 20 "Valkyrie II."

[2005] Position 1117.6 of Metaxas and position 736.1 of the ebook *Traitors or Patriots?: A Story of the German Anti-Nazi Resistance* by Louis R. Eltscher, published by McNidder & Grace Carmarthen UK 2020, Ebook ISBN 9780857162045.

[2006] Position 562.6 of Nigel Jones. See also endnote [1880] for Chapter 20 "Valkyrie II."

[2007] Position 562.8 of Nigel Jones and position 734.6 of the ebook *Traitors or Patriots?: A Story of the German Anti-Nazi Resistance* by Louis R. Eltscher, published by McNidder & Grace Carmarthen UK 2020, Ebook ISBN 9780857162045.. See also endnote [1880] for Chapter 20 "Valkyrie II."

[2008] [2223] Position 947.6 to 948.6 of Schlingensiepen.

[2009] Position 915.9 of Schlingensiepen and position 1118.3 of Metaxas.

[2010] Position 1119.3 of Metaxas and page 214 of the book *Love letters from cell 92: Dietrich Bonhoeffer, Maria von Wedemeyer, 1943-1945* by Dietrich Bonhoeffer, Ruth-Alice von Bismarck, Maria von Wedemeyer, Ulrich Kabitz, published by Harper Collins, 1994, ISBN 0006278035, 9780006278030.

[2011] Page 149 of *Letters and Papers from Prison: New edition, with a new introduction by Samuel Wells Position*, by Dietrich Bonhoeffer, contributor Samuel Wells, edition abridged, published by SCM Press, 2018, ISBN 0334055083, 9780334055082 and position 1126.9 of Metaxas.

[2012] Position 943.5 onwards of Schlingensiepen and position 1127.3 onwards of Metaxas document Dietrich's ultimately aborted escape attempt from Tegel. As does pages 827 to 828 of Bethge.

[2013] Position 1130.5 of Metaxas. See also top of page 828 of Bethge.

[2014] Position 1129.6 of Metaxas, position 944.6 of Schlingensiepen and page 828 of Bethge.

[2015] Pages 827 to 828 of Bethge and position 1130.3 of Metaxas.

[2016] Top and one-third down of page 828 of Bethge.

[2017] [3018] Page 828 of Bethge, position 944.7 of Schlingensiepen and position 1129.8 of Metaxas.

[2018] Page 828 of Bethge.

[2019] Page 828 of Bethge.

[2020] [2892] Page 204 of *Bonhoeffer, Christ and Culture*, Wheaton Theology Conference Series, edited by Keith L. Johnson, Timothy Larsen, published by InterVarsity Press, 2013, ISBN 0830827161, 9780830827169 and page 106 of *The Collected Sermons of Dietrich Bonhoeffer* by Dietrich Bonhoeffer, edited by Isabel Best, published by Fortress Press (July 1, 2012), ISBN-10: 0800699041 ISBN-13: 9780800699048. See also position 1217.0 of Metaxas.

[2021] Position 945.6 of Schlingensiepen, page 828 of Bethge and position 1131.5 of Metaxas.

Chapter 22 — Prinz-Albrecht-Strasse

[2022] [2818] Page 228 of *I Knew Dietrich Bonhoeffer* as told by Fabian von Schlabrendorff, edited by Wolf-Dieter Zimmermann, Ronald Gregor Smith published by Harper & Row, 1967 and position 1142.7 of Metaxas. See also position 524.1 of the ebook The Secret War Against Hitler by Fabian von Schlabrendorff, published by Routledge, 2018, e-ISBN 0813321905, ISBN 13: 9780813321905 (paperback).

[2023] The English language online article on Spiegel online at http://www.spiegel.de/international/zeitgeist/new-third-reich-monument-in-berlin-revealing-the-young-bureaucrats-behind-the-nazi-terror-a-693373.html, dated the May 6 2010, documents how the Prinz Albrecht precinct of Berlin was transformed into the very nerve centre for the administration and co-ordination of terror throughout the Third Reich and its occupied territories. Link accessed on Saturday July 25, 2020.

[2024] Page 907 of Bethge and position 1132.2 of Metaxas.

[2025] Position 1132.3 of Metaxas.

[2026] [1461] [2101] [2389] [2395] [2565] *Lehrter Strasse* is in the Berlin locality of Moabit. Hence Moabit Prison referred to in literature about the German Resistance is the same as *Lehrter Strasse* Prison. Schlingensiepen, Metaxas and Bethge refer to this prison as *Lehrter Strasse*, while Jane Pejsa and other sources refer to it as Moabit. Although, on page 932 in Bethge, Karl-Friedrich Bonhoeffer in a letter to his children, mistakenly refers to Moabit and Lehrte Strasse prisons as different prisons, when they were in fact, in the context of the story of the German Underground, the same prison — near the then Lehrte Strasse Bahnhof (Railway Station) which today, is Berlin's Hauptbahnhof (Main or Central Railway Station). See the online article by Roderick Miller at https://www.frankfallaarchive.org/prisons/moabit-prison/ on the website of the Frank Falla Archive. Click on the map image thumbnail to the right hand side of the article, with an explanation clarifying the confusion. This confusion, is due to the existence during and before the Third Reich of the *Unter-suchungsgefängnis Moabit* — Moabit Detention or Remand Centre about 800 metres to the west-south-west as stated in the article on the website of the Frank Falla Archive — still in existence and use today. See the online Berlin Stadt Portal in German at https://www.berlin.de/justizvollzug/anstalten/jva-moabit/die-anstalt/. Today, on the location of what was during the Third Reich and before, the *Zellengefängnis* (Solitary Confinement) *Lehrter Strasse*; today better known as *Zellengefängnis Moabit* on Lehrter Strasse, is now Moabit Memorial Park (*Geschichtspark Ehemaliges Zellengefängnis*) and dedicated in 2007 with an award-winning design by the Berlin architecture firm Glasser und Dagenbach. Zellengefängnis translates literally into English as "Cell prison" which implies "solitary confinement." The co-ordinates for the present day remand prison are 52°31'29.69'N 13°21'18.76"E, while the location of the present day memorial park, where the *Lehrter Strasse Wehrmacht* Prison, relevant to this story, was located, are 52°31'38.00"N 13°21'58.25"E. See Google Maps. Both links accessed on Saturday July 25, 2020.

[2027] [2184] The New York Times online article at http://www.nybooks.com/articles/2012/10/25/tragedy-dietrich-bonhoeffer-and-hans-von-dohnanyi/, dated October 25 2012, documents that Eberhard Bethge was imprisoned at the Lehrterstrasse prison at the time, along with Rüdiger Schleicher and Klaus Bonhoeffer. See also positions 946.0 and 978.6 of Schlingensiepen and footnote #4 on page 563 and footnote #5 on page 552 of *Letters and Papers from Prison Volume 8 of Dietrich Bonhoeffer Works* by Dietrich Bonhoeffer, editors Christian Gremmels, John W. De Gruchy, published by Fortress Press, 2010, ISBN 1451406789, 9781451406788. Accessed on Saturday July 25, 2020.

[2028] Position 568.5 of the ebook *Hitler's Spy Chief The Wilhelm Canaris Mystery* by Richard Bassett, published by The Orion Publishing Group Limited, 2011, a Hachette UK company, ISBN 9780297865711.

[2029] [2962] Ibid position 568.7.

[2030] The English language article on Spiegel online at http://www.spiegel.de/international/zeitgeist/new-third-reich-monument-in-berlin-revealing-the-young-bureaucrats-behind-the-nazi-terror-a-693373.html, dated May 6 2010.

[2031] The Stern Magazine (German general interest weekly magazine — similar to Der Spiegel) online article at https://www.stern.de/politik/deutschland/topographie-des-terrors-horst-koehler-eroeffnet-dokumentationszentrum-in-berlin-3098054.html, dated May 6 2010, documents the opening of the *Topographie des Terrors* (Topography of Terror) in Berlin. Both links accessed on Saturday July 25, 2020.

[2032] The website of Topographie des Terrors at https://www.topographie.de/en/the-historic-site/the-terrain-of-the-topography-of-terror/. Accessed on Saturday July 25, 2020.

[2033] Position 1133.0 of Metaxas and pages 338 to 339 of Jane Pejsa.

[2034] See endnotes [1891] to [1896] of Chapter 20 "Valkyrie II." These "Hostages of the SS" will be discussed again in Chapters 23 and 26.

[2035] Position 1134.4 of Metaxas writes of the sole letter Dietrich was able to write to Maria from *Prinz-Albrecht-Strasse* just before Christmas 1944. Position 1137.4 onwards quotes the poem *Powers of Good* that Dietrich enclosed with this letter, including the fame that this poem attained post-war. See also pages 246 to 247 of *The Cost of Moral Leadership: The Spirituality of Dietrich Bonhoeffer* by Geoffrey B. Kelly, F. Burton Nelson, published by Wm. B. Eerdmans Publishing, 2003, ISBN 0802805116, 9780802805119 and page 343 of Jane Pejsa.

[2036] Position 848.8 to 850.2 of Schlingensiepen documents how Hans von Dohnányi's imprisonment was a time of abject suffering in contrast to most of the 18 months Dietrich spent at Tegel prison. Position 849.1 tells of the Allied air raid on November 26 1943 that fire-bombed Dohnányi's cell which caused his embolism. The typical antics of Roeder are also covered, as are the "*impeccable*" National Socialist credentials of Professor Max de Crinis.

[2037] Boston Globe article at https://www.bostonglobe.com/arts/music/2013/10/12/legacy-resisitance-recalling-life-and-struggle-hans-von-dohnanyi/s30Pu3ftHhz7AWYOMl4yNN/story.html, dated October 12 2013, which states that Dohnányi begged his wife Christine to contaminate the food she brought him with diphtheria, in order for him to avoid further interrogation at the hands of the Gestapo. See also position 1133.6 of Metaxas and position 957.5 of Schlingensiepen. Accessed on Saturday July 25, 2020.

[2038] https://www.bostonglobe.com/arts/music/2013/10/12/legacy-resisitance-recalling-life-and-struggle-hans-von-dohnanyi/s30Pu3ftHhz7AWYOMl4yNN/story.html. Accessed on Saturday July 25, 2020.

[2039] Position 962.2 of Schlingensiepen.

[2040] [2818] [2956] Position 1143.8 of Metaxas and page 228 of *I Knew Dietrich Bonhoeffer* as told by Fabian von Schlabrendorff, edited by Wolf-Dieter Zimmermann, Ronald Gregor Smith published by Harper & Row, 1967.

[2041] [2184] [2427] [2501] [2503] [2817] [2826] [2955] Page 914 of Bethge and position 1146.1 of Metaxas. Page 259 of *Mission to Berlin: The American Airmen Who Struck the Heart of Hitler's Reich* by Robert F. Dorr, published by Voyageur Press, 2011, ISBN 0760338981, 9780760338988 documents the approximate weight of bombs dropped that day on Berlin — 6.9 million pounds which is well over 3,000 metric tons. Pages 304 to 305 give a brief biography of Lewis E. Lyle (1916 — 2008), the commander of the February 3 1945 mission to Berlin. He completed sixty-nine combat missions and became deeply involved in the establishment and expansion of the Eighth Air Force Museum in Savannah Georgia.

[2042] [2503] [2504] [2826] [2955] Position 622.4 of Nigel Jones in the Dramatis Personae and page 18 of *Mission to Berlin: The American Airmen Who Struck the Heart of Hitler's Reich* by Robert F. Dorr. The latter gives the more precise date and details of the American bombing raid that day, while the former states that Freisler's demise occurred while he was "conducting" Fabian von Schlabrendorff's case. Jane Pejsa on page 355 gives a more detailed account of events in the court room that morning around 10 a.m. Curiously, just moments before calling Fabian to the stand, Freisler had angrily dismissed a belligerent Ewald von Kleist.

[2043] https://www.ushmm.org/wlc/en/article.php?ModuleId=10005477. Accessed on Saturday July 25, 2020.

[2044] [2104] Page 914 of Bethge and position 962.9 of Schlingensiepen.

[2045] Position 576.9 to 577.2 of Nigel Jones.

[2046] Page 914 of Bethge.

[2047] Page 914 of Bethge.

[2048] Top of page 915 of Bethge and position 1148.3 of Metaxas.

[2049] Pages 914 to 915 of Bethge and position 1148.1 of Metaxas.

[2050] Footnote #4 on page 563 of *Letters and Papers from Prison Volume 8 of Dietrich Bonhoeffer Works* by Dietrich Bonhoeffer, editors Christian Gremmels, John W. De Gruchy, published by Fortress Press, 2010, ISBN 1451406789, 9781451406788. In regard to Klaus and Rüdiger being surreptitiously shot, see the online English language article on on Klaus Bonhoeffer on the official website of the *German Resistance Memorial Centre* at https://www.gdw-berlin.de/en/recess/biographies/index_of_persons/biographie/view-bio/klaus-bonhoeffer/. Accessed on Saturday July 25, 2020.

[2051] Position 963.0 of Schlingensiepen and page 915 of Bethge.

[2052] Page 555 of *Letters and Papers from Prison Volume 8 of Dietrich Bonhoeffer Works* by Dietrich Bonhoeffer, editors Christian Gremmels, John W. De Gruchy, published by Fortress Press, 2010, ISBN 1451406789, 9781451406788.

[2053] [2708] [2815] [2829] [lxii] This is implied at position 977.9 of Schlingensiepen, where in early April 1945, Schlingensiepen documents Hans von Dohnányi transfer from Berlin's state hospital to the Sachsenhausen concentration camp for his execution.

[2054] [2708] [2815] [2816] [2823] [2829] [lxii] This is implied at position 963.0 of Schlingensiepen at the end of Chapter 11 "In Prison (1943—1945)." Note that Fabian had the hearing of his case interrupted by the air raid on February 3. See also page 917 of Bethge.

[2055] The date of the March 12 1938 for the Austrian Anschluss is given at https://www.britannica.com/event/Anschluss. Accessed on Saturday July 25, 2020.

[2056] [2713] These prisoners were also known as "Special Prisoners" or "Prominenten — Prominent Prisoners." For a more detailed explanation of these terms, see endnotes [2708] onwards of Chapter 27 "The Prominenten and Miraculous Reprieves."

[2057] For more information on the von Schuschnigg family, see the book *When Hitler Took Austria: A Memoir of Heroic Faith by the Chancellor's Son* by Kurt von Schuschnigg Junior and Janet Von Schuschnigg, published by Ignatius Press, 2012, ISBN 1586177095, 9781586177096. See also http://www.mythoselser.de/niederdorf.htm#liste which gives the list of prisoners in German by nationality liberated in Niederdorf on April 30 1945. Accessed on Saturday July 25, 2020. As does position 740.6 of the ebook *The Venlo Incident* by Sigismund Payne Best, published by Frontline Books, 2009, an imprint of Pen & Sword Books Limited, 47 Church Street, Barnsley, S. Yorkshire, S70 2AS, ISBN 9781848325586, albeit, this one in English, but again by nationality.

[2058] See endnotes [888] to [892] of Chapter 13 "Flight and the Tumultuous Appeasement of Evil" in regard to Doctor Hjalmar Schacht.

[2059] In regard to Franz Halder, see endnote [331] for Chapter 3 "Evil's Storm Descends," endnotes [1110] and [1136] for Chapter 16 "Homecoming to Outbreak of War" and endnote [1608] for Chapter 20 "Valkyrie II."

[2060] [2709] [2710] Page 917 of Bethge and position 1149.9 of Metaxas give the full list of prisoners that were leaving Prinz-Albrecht-Strasse on February 7, 1945.

[2061] Page 917 of Bethge.

[2062] Position 421.1 of the ebook *The Venlo Incident* by Sigismund Payne Best, published by Frontline Books, 2009, an imprint of Pen & Sword Books Limited, 47 Church Street, Barnsley, S. Yorkshire, S70 2AS, ISBN 9781848325586. Page 917 of Bethge documents that General von Falkenhausen's governorship also encompassed northern France.

[2063] Position 508.7 of the ebook *The Venlo Incident* by Sigismund Payne Best.

[2064] [2709] Page 917 of Bethge and position 1149.9 of Metaxas give the full list of prisoners that were leaving Prinz-Albrecht-Strasse on February 7, 1945.

[2065] [3613] Ibid position 512.0.

[2066] Position 80.1 of the ebook *Church of Spies: The Pope's Secret War Against Hitler* by Mark Riebling, published by Scribe Publications 2015, ISBN 9781925307139. Mark Riebling is one of the historians making several appearances in the National Geographic documentary *Pope Vs Hitler*. As is Eric Metaxas. This dramatised documentary will be discussed in the final Chapter 28 "Memory Transcending Executioners' Legal but Criminal Flights from Justice." It was released on September 4 2016, written and directed by Christopher Cassel. See also the Internet Movie Database at https://www.imdb.com/title/tt6142740/. Accessed on Saturday July 25, 2020.

[2067] [2819] Position 1150.8 of Metaxas.

[2068] Page 918 of Bethge.

[2069] Page 918 of Bethge and position 1151.0 of Metaxas.

[2070] [2819] Page 918 of Bethge.

[2071] Position 964.0 of Schlingensiepen.

[2072] Position 956.7 of Schlingensiepen.

[2073] *Einsatzgruppen*, (German: "deployment groups") were units of the Nazi security forces composed of members of the SS, the Sicherheitspolizei (Sipo; "Security Police"), and the Ordnungspolizei (Orpo; "Order Police") that acted as mobile killing units during the German invasions of Poland (1939) and the Soviet Union (1941). From https://www.britannica.com/topic/Einsatzgruppen. Accessed on Saturday July 25, 2020.

[2074] Pages 202-203 of the book *Historical Dictionary of German Intelligence* by Jefferson Adams, published by Scarecrow Press, 2009, ISBN 0810863200, 9780810863200.

[2075] Ibid. See also the online description of the documentary *Trial of Nazi SS prosecutor in 1950s* Film | Accession Number: 2014.526 | RG Number: RG-60.1547 | Film ID: 4113, on the website of the United States Holocaust Memorial Museum at https://collections.ushmm.org/search/catalog/irn1004825. As well, the book *Walter Huppenkothen* by Jesse Russell, Ronald Cohn, published by Book on Demand, 2012, ISBN 5511656321, 9785511656328; the online Munzinger archive in German at https://www.munzinger.de/search/go/document.jsp?id=00000005131; and page 188 onwards of the book *Das juristische Erbe des 'Dritten Reiches'* (The legal Legacy of the Third Reich) by Joachim Perels, published by Campus Verlag, 1999, ISBN 3593363186, 9783593363189. Both links accessed on Saturday July 25, 2020.

Chapter 23 — Buchenwald

[2076] Position 1152.0 of Metaxas.

[2077] Position 1152.0 of Metaxas gives a general description of the barbarity that was Buchenwald. Metaxas' claim however that the fatty tissue of humans was used to make soap, has been refuted in online articles such as http://hlrecord.org/books-bound-in-human-skin-lampshade-myth/ on the Harvard Law Record website and at http://holocaustcontroversies.blogspot.com.au/2017/11/nazi-shrunken-heads-human-skin.html on the Holocaust Controversies blogspot. Nevertheless, what is shown on the one minute silent video at https://www.ushmm.org/wlc/en/media_fi.php?ModuleId=10005198&MediaId=159 on the United States Holocaust Memorial Museum website is gruesome enough. Moreover, the Holocaust Controversies website does state unequivocally, the production of various articles from human skin, and states the plethora of documentation available in regards to the exploitation of human hair of concentration camp victims. This article also documents the order from Buchenwald of human hair on the 31st January 1945. All links accessed on Saturday July 25, 2020.

[2078] National Geographic documentary *Hitler's G.I. Death Camp* aired on SBS Australia in Brisbane at 5:30 p.m. on Sunday December 3 2017. It was first released in the US on December 18 2011. See the Internet Movie Database at http://www.imdb.com/title/tt2179849/?ref_=ttrel_rel_tt, accessed on Saturday July 25, 2020.

[2079] Position 611.1 to 611.6 of Nigel Jones.

[2080] Position 1152.3 of Metaxas, position 964.0 of Schlingensiepen and page 918 of Bethge.

[2081] Position 964.0 of Schlingensiepen and page 918 of Bethge.

[2082] Position 964.8 of Schlingensiepen.

[2083] Position 964.7 of Schlingensiepen.

[2084] Position 965.0 of Schlingensiepen. See also page 919 of Bethge.

[2085] Position 1153.5 of Metaxas.

[2086] The list of *Hostages of the SS* liberated in Niederdorf on April 30 1945 can be viewed online at http://www.mythoselser.de/niederdorf.htm#liste and position 725.6 at the end of Payne Best. See also endnotes [2708] onwards of Chapter 27 "The Prominenten and Miraculous Reprieves." This explains the notion of the "Hostages of the SS," also known as "Special Prisoners" or "Prominenten — Prominent Prisoners." Accessed on Saturday July 25, 2020.

[2087] [3613] Position 1153.4 of Metaxas and position 965.5 of Schlingensiepen.

[2088] Position 510.2 of the *Venlo Incident* by Sigismund Payne Best. Note, in his book, Payne Best spells Dietrich's surname with the umlaut "ö" and other variations as "Bonnhöfer" rather than the generally accepted Bonhoeffer.

[2089] The online English article on the official website of the German Resistance Memorial Centre at https://www.gdw-berlin.de/en/recess/biographies/index_of_persons/biographie/view-bio/friedrich-von-rabenau/. Accessed on Saturday July 25, 2020. See also page 919 of Bethge.

[2090] Ibid and pages 919 to 920 of Bethge.

[2091] Position 510.3 of Payne Best.

[2092] Page 920 of Bethge and position 966.3 of Schlingensiepen.

[2093] Position 510.7 of Payne Best.

[2094] Page 920 of Bethge and position 966.4 of Schlingensiepen.

[2095] Page 920 of Bethge and position 966.7 of Schlingensiepen.

[2096] Rabenau biography on the official website of the Buchenwald Memorial at https://www.buchenwald.de/en/1245/.

[2097] Page 919 of Bethge. Accessed on Saturday July 25, 2020.

[2098] Rabenau biography on the official website of the Buchenwald Memorial at https://www.buchenwald.de/en/1245/.

[2099] Page 920 of Bethge. Accessed on Saturday July 25, 2020.

[2100] Page 920 of Bethge.

2101 See endnote 2026 for an explanation of Moabit and Lehrterstrasse prisons being the same prison — at least in regard to this narrative.

2102 Rabenau biography on the official website of the Buchenwald Memorial at https://www.buchenwald.de/en/1245/. Accessed on Saturday July 25, 2020.

2103 Ibid.

2104 Position 510.7 of Payne Best. A more condensed version at position 967.3 of Schlingensiepen.

2105 Position 822.7 of Schlingensiepen, position 989.7 of Metaxas and pages 779 to 780 of Bethge. See endnotes 1434 to 1446 for Chapter 18 "Romance, Plots and Arrest" in regard to the second of two failed plots of March 1943, just preceding Dietrich and Hans von Dohnányi's arrests in early April.

2106 Position 1081.7 of Schlingensiepen in Appendix 4.

2107 Position 507.5 of Payne Best.

2108 Page 919 of Bethge and position 1177.2 of Metaxas.

2109 Page 919 of Bethge.

2110 Position 532.5 of Payne Best and position 1178.7 of Metaxas.

2111 Pages 128, 153, 185, 186, 448, 574 and 618 of *The Gulag Archipelago, Parts I and II* by Alexander Solzhenitsyn, translated from Russian by Thomas P. Whitney, first published in Australia 1974 simultaneously by Collins/Harvill Press and Fontana, ISBN 0006336426.

2112 Position 519.2 of Payne-Best.

2113 Page 57 of *Who's Who in Nazi Germany* by Robert S. Wistrich, published by Routledge, 2013, ISBN 1136413812, 9781136413810.

2114 Ibid and position 519.3 of Payne Best.

2115 Ibid.

2116 Position 520.0 of Payne Best.

2117 See endnote 981 of Chapter 13 "Flight and the Tumultuous Appeasement of Evil" in regard to the Nanking Massacre.

2118 Page 57 of *Who's Who in Nazi Germany* by Robert S. Wistrich.

2119 Position 520.8 of Payne Best.

2120 Position 521.1 of Payne Best.

2121 Position 521.9 of Payne Best. In regard to the Fritsch Affair, see endnotes 900 to 905 of Chapter 13 "Flight and the Tumultuous Appeasement of Evil."

2122 Position 523.0 of Payne Best.

2123 In regard to Qian Xiuling (錢秀玲), and her relationship to General Freiherr von Falkenhausen, see the online articles at http://www.china.org.cn/english/2002/Apr/30512.htm on the China Internet Information Center, and http://www.womenofchina.cn/womenofchina/html1/people/history/1409/552-1.htm on the Women of China website. Accessed on Saturday July 25, 2020.

2124 Women of China website at http://www.womenofchina.cn/womenofchina/html1/people/history/1409/552-1.htm. Accessed on Saturday July 25, 2020.

[2125] [2896] [2897] Position 504.6 Payne Best.

[2126] Portrait of Waldemar Hoven as a defendant in the Medical Case Trial at Nuremberg at https://collections.ushmm.org/search/catalog/pa1036615. Click on "Expand All" to read the details, including the date of his death on June 2 1948. Accessed on Saturday July 25, 2020.

[2127] Portrait of Waldemar Hoven as a defendant in the Medical Case Trial at Nuremberg online at https://collections.ushmm.org/search/catalog/pa1036615. Click on "Expand All" to read the details of the verdict. Accessed on Saturday July 25, 2020.

[2128] Details of the Dutch Communist politician Leendert (Leen) Seegers can be viewed online at https://www.parlement.com/id/vg09ll8aejvg/l_leen_seegers on the Dutch Parliament and Politics website (Parlement & Politiek). Accessed on Saturday July 25, 2020.

[2129] Pages 125-126 of *HLSL Nuremberg Document #613*. This is the "Closing brief for Waldemar Hoven" and can be downloaded online at http://nuremberg.law.harvard.edu/documents/613-brief-closing-brief-for-waldemar?q=defendant:%22Waldemar+Hoven%22#p.1 on the Harvard University Law website for the Nuremberg Trials. Accessed on Saturday July 25, 2020.

[2130] http://nuremberg.law.harvard.edu/transcripts/1-transcript-for-nmt-1-medical-case?seq=4795&q=I+am+very+glad+to+be+in+a+position+to+answer+this+question+with+yes. This is page 4731 of the transcript for the Nuremberg Military Tribunal (NMT) — NMT 1: Medical Case. Accessed on Saturday July 25, 2020.

[2131] These 24 drawings are catalogued on the website of the Los Angeles Museum of the Holocaust at http://lamoth.info/?p=collections/findingaid&id=15&q=&rootcontentid=2478. Accessed on Saturday July 25, 2020.

[2132] Page 4729 at http://nuremberg.law.harvard.edu/transcripts/1-transcript-for-nmt-1-medical-case?seq=4793&q=It+is+remarkable+how+Dr.+Hoven+on+many+occasions+faked%2C. Accessed on Saturday July 25, 2020. Also *HLSL Nuremberg Document #613* page 140.

[2133] *HLSL Nuremberg Document #613* bottom of page 140.

[2134] [2144] Page 4728 of Transcript for *NMT 1: Medical Case*. This can also be viewed online at http://nuremberg.law.harvard.edu/transcripts/1-transcript-for-nmt-1-medical-case?seq=4792&q=%2AHoven+saw+to+it+that+an+exception+was+made+and+saw+to+it+that+these+people+were+cared+for+properly+in+the+hospital%2A. Accessed on Saturday July 25, 2020.

[2135] Page 8604-8605 of Transcript for NMT 1: Medical Case. Online at http://nuremberg.law.harvard.edu/transcripts/1-transcript-for-nmt-1-medical-

case?seq=8751&q=%2Awho+had+no+right++to+live+in+the+National%2A.
Accessed on Saturday July 25, 2020.

[2136] Page 127 of *HLSL Nuremberg Document #613* and
http://nuremberg.law.harvard.edu/transcripts/1-transcript-for-nmt-1-medical-
case?seq=10032&q=If+you+had+ever+been+in+a+concentration+camp+and+
knew+the+actual+conditions+there%2C+you+wouldn%27t+ask+that+questio
n on page 9883. Accessed on Saturday July 25, 2020.

[2137] Details of Dutch nobleman Philip Dirk, Baron van Pallandt can be found
on page 125 of *HLSL Nuremberg Document #613*, where the Baron states that
he was arrested on October 7 1940 as a hostage for the Germans being held by
the Dutch in the then Dutch East Indies, now Indonesia. For further details on
the Baron, see the online article at
https://www.canonvannederland.nl/nl/overijssel/salland/ommen/van-pallandt
on the website of the Nederlands Openluchtmuseum (Netherlands Open Air
Museum.) Accessed on Saturday July 25, 2020. In this article, it states that the
Baron was an inmate of Buchenwald for nine months. Thus, one can infer his
release from Buchenwald in July 1941.

[2138] Page 126-127 of *HLSL Nuremberg Document #613* and online at
http://nuremberg.law.harvard.edu/transcripts/1-transcript-for-nmt-1-medical-
case?seq=10033&q=render+harmless on pages 9884-9885. Accessed on Saturday July 25, 2020.

[2139] Page 125 of *HLSL Nuremberg Document #613* and online at
http://nuremberg.law.harvard.edu/transcripts/1-transcript-for-nmt-1-medical-
case?seq=10034&q=Quakers+in+my+manor. Accessed on Saturday July 25,
2020.

[2140] See pages 4744-4745 online at
http://nuremberg.law.harvard.edu/transcripts/1-transcript-for-nmt-1-medical-
case?seq=4808&q=phenol+Hoven. Accessed on Saturday July 25, 2020.

[2141] Bottom of the online article on Oscar Schindler on the Yad Vashem website
at http://www.yadvashem.org/righteous/stories/schindler.html. Accessed on
Saturday July 25, 2020.

[2142] http://nuremberg.law.harvard.edu/transcripts/1-transcript-for-nmt-1-
medical-case?seq=1486&q=Roemhild on page 1470 states that Ferdinand
Roemhild was a witness for the prosecution. Accessed on Saturday July 25,
2020.

[2143] Bottom of page 127 of *HLSL Nuremberg Document #613* and online at
http://nuremberg.law.harvard.edu/transcripts/1-transcript-for-nmt-1-medical-
case?seq=11433&q=it+would+have+been+impossible+to+save. Accessed on
Saturday July 25, 2020.

[2144] See endnote [2134] for this chapter.

[2145] Portrait of Waldemar Hoven as a defendant in the Medical Case Trial at
Nuremberg online at https://collections.ushmm.org/search/catalog/pa1036615

on the website of the United States Holocaust Memorial Museum. Click on "Expand All" to read the details. Accessed on Saturday July 25, 2020.

[2146] Position 1162.2 of Metaxas and http://nuremberg.law.harvard.edu/transcripts/1-transcript-for-nmt-1-medical-case?seq=10105&q=The+skull+was+prepared+as+ordered+and+delivered+to on page 9956. Accessed on Saturday July 25, 2020.

[2147] Position 1307.3 of Metaxas.

[2148] http://nuremberg.law.harvard.edu/transcripts/1-transcript-for-nmt-1-medical-case?seq=10105&q=The+skull+was+prepared+as+ordered+and+delivered+to on page 9956. Accessed on Saturday July 25, 2020.

[2149] See pages 10654-10655 online at http://nuremberg.law.harvard.edu/transcripts/1-transcript-for-nmt-1-medical-case?seq=10803&q=Josef+Ackermann. Accessed on Saturday July 25, 2020.

[2150] Page 337 of the book *Bericht über das Konzentrationslager Buchenwald bei Weimar* (The Buchenwald Report) edited and translated by David A. Hackett, Allied Forces. Supreme Headquarters. Psychological Warfare Division. Intelligence Team, published by Westview Press, 1995, ISBN 0813317770, 9780813317779.

[2151] [2896] [2897] http://nuremberg.law.harvard.edu/transcripts/1-transcript-for-nmt-1-medical-case?seq=54&q=professional+diary on page 39 and http://nuremberg.law.harvard.edu/transcripts/1-transcript-for-nmt-1-medical-case?seq=1099&q=Ding+Schuler on page 1081. Accessed on Saturday July 25, 2020.

[2152] [2897] Position 526.3 of Payne Best which states: "I should say here that Rascher gave at least half a dozen different reasons for his imprisonment, and no one ever discovered what he really had done."

[2153] Position 526.0 of Payne Best.

[2154] Position 525.8 of Payne Best.

[2155] Position 523.4 of Payne Best.

[2156] Position 524.3 of Payne Best.

[2157] Position 524.5 of Payne Best.

[2158] Position 524.7 of Payne Best.

[2159] Position 525.5 of Payne Best.

[2160] Position 525.6 of Payne Best.

[2161] Position 525.7 of Payne Best.

[2162] Position 526.0 of Payne Best.

[2163] Position 525.9 of Payne Best.

[2164] Position 526.1 of Payne Best.

[2165] Position 525.6 of Payne Best.

[2166] [2897] See the article by Peter Tyson on the website of the US Public Broadcasting Service (PBS) at http://www.pbs.org/wgbh/nova/holocaust/experiside.html, which documents the various types of medical experiments carried out by the Third Reich. Rascher's name is mentioned in the freezing and high altitude experiments. Photos of Rascher's high altitude experiments on humans can be viewed online at http://nuremberg.law.harvard.edu/documents/27-photographs-of-sigmund-raschers?q=author:%22Sigmund+Rascher%22#p.1. This being document *HLSL Nuremberg Document #27 pages 1-41.pdf*. BEWARE, THESE PHOTOS ARE TERRIBLY DISTURBING. All accessed on Saturday July 25, 2020.

[2167] [2897] http://nuremberg.law.harvard.edu/transcripts/1-transcript-for-nmt-1-medical-case/search?q=I+particularly+recommended+to+you+for+your+consideration+the+work+of+a+certain+SS on page 225. Accessed on Saturday July 25, 2020.

[2168] Page 178 of the book *Lives of Hitler's Jewish Soldiers: Untold Tales of Men of Jewish Descent who Fought for the Third Reich* by Bryan Mark Rigg, published by University Press of Kansas, 2009, ISBN 0700616381, 9780700616381, documents Milch's Jewish heritage and Göring's intervention to compel the Gestapo to drop the case.

[2169] Ibid page 183.

[2170] Position 1176.3 of Metaxas.

[2171] Position 526.5 to 527.1 of Payne Best.

[2172] Position 527.1 of Payne Best.

[2173] The book *The Master Plan: Himmler's Scholars and the Holocaust* by Heather Pringle, published by Hachette UK, 2006, ISBN 1401383866, 9781401383862, viewed on Google Books at https://books.google.com.au/books?id=-GlrAwAAQBAJ&printsec=frontcover&dq=SS+Geiseln+in+Der+Alpenfestung,+Hans-Guenter+Ricardi,+Bolzano:+Raetia,+2015,+Loc+4644&hl=en&sa=X&ved=0ahUKEwjV1fD8v5baAhXFWbwKHdyGDpoQ6AEISDAF#v=snippet&q=Ravensbr%C3%Bcck&f=false. Accessed on Saturday July 25, 2020.

[2174] Ibid.

[2175] Position 516.4 to 518.2 of Payne Best.

[2176] Position 517.2 of Payne Best.

[2177] Position 517.3 of Payne Best.

[2178] Position 517.3 of Payne Best.

[2179] Position 517.4 of Payne Best.

[2180] Position 924.3 of Microcosm.

[2181] Page 320 of the book *Nemesis of Power: The German Army in Politics 1918-1945*, by Sir John Wheeler-Bennett and Richard Overy, published by Springer, 1964, ISBN 1349002216, 9781349002214. Also on page 320 of the much later published Palgrave Macmillan UK, 2005 edition, ISBN 1403918120, 9781403918123.

[2182] See endnotes [92] to [107] in the Preface "Birth and Memory upon the Lesser Known Fault Line of History" in regard to the 1934 Röhm Purge.

[2183] Position 518.1 of Payne Best.

[2184] Position 518.0 of Payne Best. NOTE: Payne Best incorrectly states that von Petersdorff was incarcerated in the Lehrterstrasse prison before it was destroyed by bombing on February 3 1945. However, the prison destroyed on that day, as already discussed was the Prinz-Albrecht-Strasse prison which was actually, the Gestapo prison. See endnote [2041] of Chapter 22 "Prinz-Albrecht-Strasse" and page 917 of Bethge. Furthermore, the Lehrterstrasse prison had still incarcerated Rudiger Schleicher and Klaus Bonhoeffer until the middle of April 1945. See pages 929 to 930 of Bethge.

[2185] Position 532.6 of Payne Best. Nigel Jones in the Dramatis Personae of *Countdown to Valkyrie: The July Plot to Assassinate Hitler* at position 626.9 gives additional details of Erich Hoepner.

[2186] Position 533.3 of Payne Best.

Chapter 24 — Dietrich's Final Days

[2187] [2715] [2829] [4495] Position 534.5 of Payne Best mentions the thunder of American artillery. Details of the US "Sixth Armored Division," which was part of General George S. Patton's Third Army, are given on the website of the United States Holocaust Memorial Museum at https://encyclopedia.ushmm.org/content/en/article/the-6th-armored-division. Accessed on Saturday July 25, 2020.

[2188] [4497] Position 534.8 of Payne Best

[2189] Position 534.8 of Payne Best and position 1180.3 of Metaxas.

[2190] The story of the American GIs of Berga and their liberation can be found at https://collections.ushmm.org/search/catalog/irn42602 which states the liberation of one group of prisoners by the American 11th Armored Division on April 23 1945, while the Geni genealogy website at https://www.geni.com/projects/Berga-an-der-Elster/24471 describes the liberation of both groups of prisoners by the American 90th Infantry Division on April 20 1945, and the second by the American 11th Armored Division on April 23 1945. Both links accessed on Saturday July 25, 2020. The respective liberations are also given at position 319.1 and 344.9 of the ebook *Given Up For Dead, American GIs in the Nazi Concentration Camp at Berga* by Flint Whitlock, published by Basic Books — a member of the Perseus Books Group New York, 2006, eBook ISBN 9780786736645.

[2191] The Geni genealogy website at https://www.geni.com/projects/Berga-an-der-Elster/24471, accessed on Saturday July 25, 2020, and position 358.1 of Flint Whitlock.

[2192] The Geni genealogy website at https://www.geni.com/projects/Berga-an-der-Elster/24471. In regard to Tony Acevedo, see the National Geographic documentary *Hitler's G.I. Death Camp* aired on SBS Australia in Brisbane at 5:30 p.m. on Sunday December 3 2017. It was first released in the US on December 18 2011. See the Internet Movie Database at http://www.imdb.com/title/tt2179849/?ref_=ttrel_rel_tt. Both links accessed on Saturday July 25, 2020.

[2193] The United States Holocaust Memorial Museum website at https://collections.ushmm.org/search/catalog/irn42602. Accessed on Saturday July 25, 2020. A possible explanation for this enforced silence, mentioned by Flint Whitlock in his book, is that: *"Dr. Patricia Wadley, national historian for the American Ex-Prisoners of War organization, who has studied POWs for years, believes that a secret agreement made at Yalta in February 1945 between the United States, Britain, and the Soviet Union regarding repatriation of POWs holds the key, but as of 2004 the text of such an agreement has not become available."* Click on the asterisk footnote at position 359.4 to view.

[2194] [2829] Position 536.1 of Payne Best, pages 921 to 922 of Bethge and position 1181.0 of Metaxas.

[2195] The online article on the Buchenwald concentration camp at https://www.ushmm.org/wlc/en/article.php?ModuleId=10005198, documents its liberation, including the fact that the prisoners did so before the entry of American 6th Armored Division. Accessed on Saturday July 25, 2020.

[2196] Position 1182.3 onwards of Metaxas describes the motley assortment of the seventeen special prisoners crammed into the *Grüne Minna* (Green Minnie), dubbed as such at position 1190.9. As well, their abandonment in the van while the air raid siren sounded.

[2197] Payne Best from position 561.2 gives his account, as well as the account of Isa Vermehren, of the mysterious woman Payne Best knew as Miss Heidi. Included is the infatuation Wassilli Kokorin developed for her, and his depression when separated from her. On the website of von Peter Koblank at http://www.mythoselser.de/niederdorf.htm#liste, accessed on Saturday July 25, 2020, her name is given as Heidel Nowakowski. Footnote #12 has an account of her in German, which does include the accounts given by Payne Best and Isa Vermehren. The latter being not among the special prisoners at Buchenwald, but among those liberated at Niederdorf on the 30th April 1945, of which Miss Heidi, Isa Vermehren and Payne Best were among. These special prisoners were also known as "Prominenten — Prominent Prisoners" or "Hostages of the SS." See endnotes [2708] onwards from the start of Chapter 27 "The Prominenten and Miraculous Reprieves."

[2198] Position 1182.3 onwards of Metaxas and position 535.3 of Payne Best.

[2199] Position 1183.2 of Metaxas and position 535.1 of Payne Best.

[2200] Position 524.7 of Payne Best.

[2201] Page 286 of *Moscow: Governing the Socialist Metropolis*, Volume 88 of Russian Research Center Cambridge, Massachusetts: Russian Research Center studies, by Timothy J. Colton, published by Harvard University Press, 1998,

ISBN 0674587499, 9780674587496 and page 200 of *Night of Stone: Death and Memory in Twentieth-Century Russia* by Catherine Merridale, published by Penguin, 2002, ISBN 0142000639, 9780142000632.

[2202] [4272] Page 142 of *The Final Solution: Origins and Implementation* edited by David Cesarani, published by Routledge, 2002, ISBN 1134744218, 9781134744213. Also, page 110 of the book *The Path to Genocide: Essays on Launching the Final Solution Canto original series*, by Christopher R. Browning, published by Cambridge University Press, 1995, ISBN 0521558786, 9780521558785, and the article at https://www.ushmm.org/wlc/en/article.php?ModuleId=10005220. Accessed on Saturday July 25, 2020.

[2203] [4273] Position 926.6 of Microcosm documents the role of Erich von dem Bach-Zelewski in co-ordinating *Reichkristallnacht* in Breslau. For his involvement in the ruthless suppression of the 1944 Warsaw General Uprising, see the Yad Vashem online article at https://www.yadvashem.org/odot_pdf/Microsoft%20Word%20-%205937.pdf. Davies also mentions him in his book Rising '44, however, just as Erich von dem Bach. See also http://www.holocaustresearchproject.org/einsatz/bach-zelweski.html and endnotes [4270] to [4289] and [4390] to [4421] of Polish WWII Supplement IV "AK and 1944 Warsaw General Uprising — Stalin's mass murder by German proxy." Both links accessed on Saturday July 25, 2020.

[2204] See endnotes [1963] to [1970] of Chapter 20 "Valkyrie II" in regard to Arthur Nebe.

[2205] [4275] Page 205 of The Nazi Persecution of the Gypsies by Guenter Lewy, published by Oxford University Press, USA, 2000, ISBN 0195125568, 9780195125566 and http://www.holocaustresearchproject.org/othercamps/nebe.html. Accessed on Saturday July 25, 2020.

[2206] Position 1183.9 of Metaxas and position 535.6 of Payne Best.

[2207] Position 1184.1 of Metaxas and position 535.8 of Payne Best.

[2208] Position 973.1 of Schlingensiepen.

[2209] Position 973.4 of Schlingensiepen.

[2210] Position 536.5 of Payne Best and position 973.5 of Schlingensiepen.

[2211] Position 1186.0 of Metaxas and position 537.1 of Payne Best.

[2212] Position 538.4 of Payne Best.

[2213] Position 1186.6 of Metaxas.

[2214] Position 1187.9 of Metaxas.

[2215] Position 1187.9 of Metaxas and position 538.6 of Payne Best.

[2216] Position 973.7 of Schlingensiepen.

[2217] Position 540.2 of Payne Best.

[2218] [2750] Position 539.5 of Payne Best.

[2219] Page 922 of Bethge.

[2220] Ibid.

[2221] https://www.gdw-berlin.de/en/recess/biographies/index_of_persons/biographie/view-bio/ludwig-gehre/?no_cache=1 on the website of the German Resistance Memorial Centre. Accessed on Saturday July 25, 2020.

[2222] Ibid and position 511.3 of Payne Best.

[2223] Position 511.5 of Payne Best. At this position however, Payne Best erroneously states that Gehre was condemned to death by a People's Court. The reason this assertion is wrong, is given from position 947.6 to 948.6 of Schlingensiepen. In short, members of the Abwehr, Dietrich included, were never hauled before Freisler's most public People's Court. See also endnote [2008] for Chapter 21 "Valkyrie's Wake."

[2224] [2752] Position 516.3 of Payne Best.

[2225] [4499] Position 515.9 of Payne Best.

[2226] [2713] [4499] Position 516.8 of Payne Best.

[2227] Page 922 of Bethge and position 1189.3 of Metaxas.

[2228] Position 510.8 to 511.3 of Payne Best.

[2229] [2750] Position 539.6 of Payne Best.

[2230] Position 540.0 of Payne Best, position 1191.1 of Metaxas and position 974.7 of Schlingensiepen.

[2231] The book *The Master Plan: Himmler's Scholars and the Holocaust* by Heather Pringle, published by Hachette UK, 2006, ISBN 1401383866, 9781401383862, viewed on Google Books at https://books.google.com.au/books?id=-GlrAwAAQBAJ&printsec=frontcover&dq=SS+Geiseln+in+Der+Alpenfestung,+Hans-Guenter+Ricardi,+Bolzano:+Raetia,+2015,+Loc+4644&hl=en&sa=X&ved=0ahUKEwjV1fD8v5baAhXFWbwKHdyGDpoQ6AEISDAF#v=snippet&q=Ravensbr%C3%Bcck&f=false, states that Sigmund Rascher was executed at Dachau just days before its liberation. The date of April 29 1945 is given as the date of the liberation for the Dachau concentration camp at https://www.ushmm.org/learn/timeline-of-events/1942-1945/liberation-of-dachau, and states that American forces were approaching on the 26th, which more than likely, is the date that Sigmund Rascher was executed. Both links accessed on Saturday July 25, 2020.

[2232] See Google Maps at https://www.google.com.au/maps/place/Regensburg,+Germany/@49.043913,12.0058665,12.22z/data=!4m5!3m4!1s0x479fc19872222ef7:0x41d25a40937cb10!8m2!3d49.0134297!4d12.1016236. Accessed on Saturday July 25, 2020. The Regen flows into the Danube to the north of the town, while the Naab flows into the Danube just six or so kilometres to the west of this junction.

[2233] The article on the official Regensburg website at https://www.regensburg.de/welterbe/en/world-heritage-site. Accessed on Saturday July 25, 2020.

[2234] https://www.regensburg.de/welterbe/en/world-heritage-site/restoration-and-development. Accessed on Saturday July 25, 2020.

[2235] https://www.regensburg.de/welterbe/en/world-heritage-site/about-regensburg/history. Accessed on Saturday July 25, 2020.

[2236] Online article on the website of the Ukrainian Weekly at http://www.ukrweekly.com/old/archive/2001/050120.shtml. Accessed on Saturday July 25, 2020.

[2237] [2864] Position 541.5 of Payne Best and position 1193.2 of Metaxas.

[2238] Position 554.1 of Payne Best.

[2239] Position 554.4 of Payne Best.

[2240] Position 554.6 to 554.7 of Payne Best. What Payne Best called the "Free German Movement" was more precisely known as the Soviet sponsored "Nationalkomitee Freies Deutschland" — NKFD (National Free German Committee). After the catastrophic German defeat in Stalingrad in early February 1943, the numbers joining the Soviet sponsored NKFD swelled, with its most notable recruit being Field Marshal Friedrich Paulus. He being none other than the commander of the German Sixth Army surrendering to the Soviets in Stalingrad. See pages 91-92 of the book *Family Punishment in Nazi Germany: Sippenhaft, Terror and Myth* by R. Loeffel, Edition illustrated, published by Springer, 2012, ISBN 1137021837, 9781137021830. In spite of his collaboration with the Soviets, Paulus would not be repatriated until 1953, retiring to Dresden in communist East Germany, where he passed away just four years later in 1957. See the translator's note at the beginning of the book *With Paulus at Stalingrad* by Wilhelm Adam, translated by Tony Le Tissier, published by Pen and Sword, 2017, ISBN 1526723506, 9781526723505. The author was Paulus' adjutant in Stalingrad, and like his superior, joined the NKFD and settled in East Germany post-war. As such, the translator's note needs to be read, which states that the book is devoid of any criticism of the Soviet Union. Furthermore, while Adam does mention his wife and daughter pre-Stalingrad, he never mentions them after his repatriation, which as Tony Le Tissier alludes to, prompts one to think that his wife and daughter, most wisely, decided not to join him in the newly founded Germanic worker's "utopia." Nevertheless, it looks like an intriguing account of how a decorated Wehrmacht soldier became a devoted disciple of the Soviet coerced communist "utopia" post-war.

[2241] In regard to the year of death for Alexander Stauffenberg, see the bottom of page 17 of the PDF document at http://www.schwaben-kultur.de/pdfs/2003-3.pdf on the *Schwaben-kultur* website, which also gives the date of execution for Berthold. Accessed on Saturday July 25, 2020. Also page 9 and pages 62 to 84 of the book *Der andere Stauffenberg: der Historiker und Dichter Alexander von Stauffenberg* (The other Stauffenberg: the historian and poet Alexander von Stauffenberg) by Karl Christ, published by C.H. Beck, 2008, ISBN 3406569609, 9783406569609.

[2242] For a list of special prisoners liberated in Niederdorf see position 752.0 of Payne Best and http://www.mythoselser.de/niederdorf.htm#liste. Accessed on Saturday July 25, 2020. These special prisoners were also known as "Prominenten — Prominent Prisoners" or "Hostages of the SS." See endnotes [2708] onwards from the beginning of Chapter 27 "The Prominenten and Miraculous Reprieves."

[2243] See the online biography of Isa Vermehren on the Rate Your Music website at https://rateyourmusic.com/artist/isa_vermehren. This gives the dates and places of birth and death for Isa Vermehren. See also the biographical index of the book *Swansong 1945: A Collective Diary from Hitler's Last Birthday to VE Day* by Walter Kempowski, published by Granta Books, 2014, ISBN 184708642X, 9781847086426 on Google Books in the at https://books.google.com.au/books?id=jlW5BAAAQBAJ&pg=PT353&lpg=PT353&dq=Society+of+Sisters+of+the+Sacred+Heart+of+Jesus+Isa+VERMEHREN&source=bl&ots=2q-mGoL-shf&sig=ACfU3U2byaxd2zlNACYXsRFX34ez8Iqfyg&hl=en&sa=X&ved=2ahUKEwiAtaG5nc_kAhUHeysKHaT3D2EQ6AEwDnoECAkQAQ#v=onepage&q=VERMEHREN&f=false. Because the original German version of this book was published in 2005, before her death in 2009, it does not document her date and place of death. See also the online article at http://holocaustmusic.ort.org/places/camps/central-europe/ravensbruck/vermehrenisa/ on the *Music and Holocaust* website, which includes an account of her 1944 arrest. It however, does not list the date and place of her death, suggesting it was published before 2009. All links accessed on Saturday July 25, 2020.

[2244] Position 1195.8 of Metaxas.

[2245] Position 460.1 of Payne Best and the online article on the website of the UK Independent dated Monday May 2 2005 at https://www.independent.co.uk/news/obituaries/erich-vermehren-491468.html and the online archived story in the New York Times at https://www.nytimes.com/1944/02/10/archives/nazi-deserter-identified-erich-vermehren-was-clerk-in-reich-embassy.html. Both links accessed on Saturday July 25, 2020. See also position 556.5 to 558.2 of the ebook *Hitler's Spy Chief The Wilhelm Canaris Mystery* by Richard Bassett, published by The Orion Publishing Group Limited, 2011, a Hachette UK company, ISBN 9780297865711.

[2246] The online article at http://holocaustmusic.ort.org/places/camps/central-europe/ravensbruck/vermehrenisa/ on the *Music and Holocaust* website. Accessed on Saturday July 25, 2020.

[2247] The online article at http://holocaustmusic.ort.org/places/camps/central-europe/ravensbruck/vermehrenisa/ on the *Music and Holocaust* website. Accessed on Saturday July 25, 2020.

[2248] The online article *My mother Fey von Hassell (1919-2010)* at https://www.castellodibrazza.com/fey-von-hassell?lang=en on the website of the Castello di Brazzà (Castle of Brazà located in the north-east of Italy near the modern-day Slovenian border) located near Venice Italy. Accessed on Saturday July 25, 2020.

[2249] The book *Hostage of the Third Reich: the story of my imprisonment and rescue from the SS*, by Fey von Hassell, edited by David Forbes-Watt, published by Scribner, 1989, ISBN 068419080X, 9780684190808.

[2250] This can be inferred on pages ix and xv of ibid.

[2251] Details of the German Bismarck class Battleship "Tirpitz" can be found on page 247 of the book *Battleships: Axis and Neutral Battleships in World War II* by William H. Garzke, Robert O. Dulin, edition illustrated, reprint, revised, published by Naval Institute Press, 1985, ISBN 0870211013, 9780870211010.

[2252] The online article *My mother Fey von Hassell (1919-2010)* at https://www.castellodibrazza.com/fey-von-hassell?lang=en on the website of the Castello di Brazzà, accessed on Saturday July 25, 2020.

[2253] Ibid.

[2254] http://avalon.law.yale.edu/wwii/italy01.asp gives the text of the Armistice agreement, signed at Fairfield Camp in Sicily. http://www.navy.mil/submit/display.asp?story_id=9445 on the US Navy website gives the village of Cassible in Sicily where the Armistice was signed. Taken together, these sources imply that Fairfield Camp was near the village of Cassible in Sicily. Both links accessed on Saturday July 25, 2020.

[2255] http://news.bbc.co.uk/onthisday/hi/dates/stories/september/8/newsid_3612000/3612037.stm from the BBC News website and http://www.navy.mil/submit/display.asp?story_id=9445 on the US Navy website. Both links accessed on Saturday July 25, 2020.

[2256] http://www.navy.mil/submit/display.asp?story_id=9445. Accessed on Saturday July 25, 2020.

[2257] *The Day Of Battle: The War in Sicily and Italy 1943-44 Liberation Trilogy* by Rick Atkinson, published by Hachette UK, 2013, ISBN 1405527250, 9781405527255 on Google Books at https://books.google.com.au/books?id=KqCi3wuskFkC&printsec=frontcover&dq=Howard+McGaw+Smyth,+%22The+Armistice+of+Cassibile%22,+Military+Affairs+12:1+(1948),+12%E2%80%9335.&hl=en&sa=X&ved=0ahUKEwjv7tvV4c_aAhUH5bwKHRjIBywQ6AEIQzAE#v=onepage&q=twenty%20rounds%20per%20gun&f=false. Accessed on Saturday July 25, 2020.

[2258] Ibid on Google Books at https://books.google.com.au/books?id=KqCi3wuskFkC&printsec=frontcover&dq=Howard+McGaw+Smyth,+%22The+Armistice+of+Cassibile%22,+Militar

y+Affairs+12:1+(1948),+12%E2%80%9335.&hl=en&sa=X&ved=0ahUKEwj
v7tvV4c_aAhUH5bwKHRjIBywQ6AEIQzAE#v=onepage&q=Italian%20garr
isons&f=false. Accessed on Saturday July 25, 2020.

[2259] Page 1351 of *World War II in Europe: An Encyclopedia Military History of the United States* by David T. Zabecki, published by Routledge, 2015, ISBN 1135812497, 9781135812492.

[2260] Ibid.

[2261] The New Zealand government history website at https://nzhistory.govt.nz/war/the-italian-campaign/timeline. Accessed on Saturday July 25, 2020.

[2262] Page 1351 of *World War II in Europe: An Encyclopedia Military History of the United States*.

[2263] [4109] See https://www.cia.gov/library/readingroom/docs/CIA-RDP70-00058R000300010031-3.pdf from the Central Intelligence Agency (CIA) online library. Accessed on Saturday July 25, 2020.

[2264] [3743] Page 1351 of *World War II in Europe: An Encyclopedia Military History of the United States* and the BBC News website at http://news.bbc.co.uk/2/hi/world/monitoring/media_reports/1243615.stm, dated Monday March 26 2001. Accessed on Saturday July 25, 2020.

[2265] [3743] George Duncan's *Massacres and Atrocities of World War II* web page at http://members.iinet.net.au/~gduncan/massacres.html on his website *Historical Facts of World War II* at http://members.iinet.net.au/~gduncan/ accessed on Sunday September 15 2019. Page 106 of the book *Forgotten Battles: Italy's War of Liberation, 1943-1945* by Charles T. O'Reilly, published by Lexington Books, 2001 gives the figure in a table of 6,504 Italian deaths on the Greek Island of Cephalonia in September 1943. Compare this with the figure of over 20,000 for the Soviet perpetrated March 1940 Katyń Wood massacre — see Polish WWII Supplement III "The Katyń Wood Massacre"[3618] and https://www.britannica.com/event/Katyn-Massacre and the Central Intelligence Agency report online by Benjamin B. Fischer at https://www.cia.gov/library/center-for-the-study-of-intelligence/csi-publications/csi-studies/studies/winter99-00/art6.html. All links accessed on Saturday July 25, 2020.

[2266] The online article *My mother Fey von Hassell (1919-2010)* at https://www.castellodibrazza.com/fey-von-hassell?lang=en on the website of the Castello di Brazzà, accessed on Saturday September 14 2019.

[2267] Page 206 of *Hostage of the Third Reich: the story of my imprisonment and rescue from the SS*, by Fey von Hassell, edited by David Forbes-Watt, published by Scribner, 1989, ISBN 068419080X, 9780684190808. Also, the article on Ulrich von Hassell at https://www.gdw-berlin.de/en/recess/biographies/index_of_persons/biographie/view-bio/ulrich-von-hassell/?no_cache=1. Both links accessed on Saturday July 25, 2020.

[2268] Page 110 of *Hostage of the Third Reich: the story of my imprisonment and rescue from the SS*, by Fey von Hassell, edited by David Forbes-Watt, published by Scribner, 1989, ISBN 068419080X, 9780684190808.

[2269] Page 331 of *The von Hassell diaries, 1938-1944: the story of the forces against Hitler inside Germany* by Ulrich von Hassell, published by H. Hamilton, 1948, no ISBN given. Note, at position 555.2 of Payne Best, the author incorrectly states that Fey was arrested while visiting her mother in Germany. However, Payne Best's statement that her two small boys were taken from her, is true. The taking of Fey's boys in Innsbruck is dramatised at the beginning of the documentary *Hostages Of The SS Season 1 Episode 1 Journey Into The Unknown*, screened on SBS in Brisbane at 5:30 p.m. on Sunday December 10 2017.

[2270] The romance that Fey had with Alexander von Stauffenberg is documented in the online UK Daily Mail article at http://www.dailymail.co.uk/femail/article-1114668/The-Valkyrie-lovers-How-passionate-bond-relatives-plotters-defied-Fuhrers-vengeance.html, dated the 14th of January 2009 and accessed on Sunday April 23 2018. It is written by David Stafford, author of the book *Endgame 1945: Victory, Retribution, Liberation*, which can viewed in part on Google Books at https://books.google.com.au/books/about/Endgame_1945.html?id=xeWd-Vc8tRQC&redir_esc=y. Both links accessed on Saturday July 25, 2020.

[2271] Ibid.

[2272] Page 184 of *Hostage of the Third Reich: the story of my imprisonment and rescue from the SS*, by Fey von Hassell, edited by David Forbes-Watt, published by Scribner, 1989, ISBN 068419080X, 9780684190808.

[2273] Melitta's date of birth being January 9 1903, is given at position 33.0 of Clare Mulley. Her date of death being April 8 1945, can be inferred from position 679.8 to 688.0 of Clare Mulley.

[2274] The ebook *The Women Who Flew for Hitler, The True Story of Hitler's Valkyries* by Clare Mulley, published by Pan Macmillan London, 2018, ISBN 9781447274247.

[2275] The birth date of March 29 1912 for Hanna Reitsch is given at position 80.2 of Clare Mulley. Her date of death of August 24 1979 is given at position 801.4.

[2276] Position 714.8 of Clare Mulley.

[2277] Position 131.2 of Clare Mulley. In regard to Moses Schiller being Melitta's paternal grandfather, see https://www.geni.com/people/Michael-Schiller/6000000034489001832 on the Geni genealogy website. Accessed on Saturday July 25, 2020.

[2278] Position 131.3 of Clare Mulley.

[2279] Position 132.3 of Clare Mulley. In this book, see also Chapter 8 "Institutionalised Hatred — The Nuremberg Laws."

[2280] Position 134.8 of Clare Mulley.

2281 Position 561.9 of Clare Mulley.

2282 Position 645.5 of Clare Mulley onwards documents Melitta's flight to Buchenwald in mid-March 1945 to see Alexander for what would be the last time.

2283 Position 686.1 of Clare Mulley.

2284 Position 688.0 of Clare Mulley.

2285 Position 556.8 of Payne Best and position 1195.7 of Metaxas.

2286 Position 975.6 of Schlingensiepen and position 1196.0 of Metaxas.

2287 Ibid.

2288 Position 557.2 of Payne Best, position 1196.2 of Metaxas and position 975.9 of Schlingensiepen.

2289 Position 557.4 of Payne Best.

2290 Position 557.8 of Payne Best.

2291 2719 Position 976.7 of Schlingensiepen.

2292 2724 Position 942.0 of Schlingensiepen.

2293 In regard to the Dolchstosslegende (Stab in the back myth), see endnotes [65] to [70] of the Preface "Birth and Memory upon the Lesser Known Fault Line of History."

2294 2719 2724 Position 976.6 of Schlingensiepen.

2295 Position 977.3 of Schlingensiepen.

2296 Position 977.4 of Schlingensiepen.

2297 Listen to the comments of Clare Mulley, the author of *The Women Who Flew for Hitler, The True Story of Hitler's Valkyries* in the dramatised documentary *Adolf & Eva: Love & War (2016)* produced by UK Channel 5, released on the September 3 2016. In particular, Mulley's comments at 1 minute 37 seconds, 12 minutes 19 seconds, 1 hour 29 minutes 4 seconds and 1 hour 32 minutes and 59 seconds. This documentary was aired on SBS Australia in Brisbane on Sunday April 8 2018 at 8:30 p.m.

2298 Position 977.9 of Schlingensiepen.

2299 Position 1212.8 of Metaxas.

2300 2730 2731 3816 Position 977.9 of Schlingensiepen and page 925 of Bethge.

2301 Page 930 of Bethge.

2302 Position 979.0 of Schlingensiepen.

2303 Page 930 of Bethge.

2304 Position 558.0 of Payne Best, position 1197.3 of Metaxas, position 979.3 of Schlingensiepen and page 923 of Bethge.

2305 Position 558.1 of Payne Best, position 1197.3 of Metaxas and page 923 of Bethge.

2306 Position 558.4 of Payne Best.

2307 Position 558.5 of Payne Best, position 1197.6 of Metaxas and page 923 of Bethge.

2308 Position 558.8 of Payne Best.

2309 Position 559.0 of Payne Best.

[2310] Position 559.1 of Payne Best.

[2311] Position 559.3 of Payne Best and position 1199.1 of Metaxas and page 923 of Bethge.

[2312] Position 559.4 of Payne Best and position 1199.3 of Metaxas and page 923 of Bethge. The SD were the intelligence arm of the SS. See endnote [127] for the Preface "Birth and Memory upon the Lesser Known Fault Line of History" for an explanation of the various child entities of the SS.

[2313] Position 559.6 of Payne Best and position 1199.6 of Metaxas.

[2314] Position 559.8 of Payne Best and position 1199.8 of Metaxas.

[2315] Position 979.9 of Schlingensiepen and page 923 of Bethge.

[2316] Position 560.1 of Payne Best and position 1200.7 of Metaxas.

[2317] Position 560.4 of Payne Best and position 1201.6 of Metaxas.

[2318] [2716] Note that Payne Best uses the incorrect spelling of "Schöneberg" as opposed to the correct spelling of "Schönberg" in Schlingensiepen, Metaxas and Bethge's biography of Dietrich. This is confirmed in Google Maps when you type in "Schönberg, Bavaria, Germany." Schöneberg is a suburb in Berlin.

[2319] [2716] Page 924 of Bethge.

[2320] Position 564.1 of Payne Best.

[2321] Position 564.4 of Payne Best position 1202.3 of Metaxas.

[2322] Position 980.3 of Schlingensiepen.

[2323] Position 564.0 of Payne Best and position 1203.9 of Metaxas.

[2324] [2872] See the dramatised documentary *Hostages Of The SS Season 1 Episode 2 - On a razor's edge* televised on SBS Australia in Brisbane at 5:30 p.m. on Sunday December 17 2017 at 34 minutes and 36 seconds in. Episode 1 *Journey Into The Unknown* was televised exactly one week earlier. See also the Internet Movie Database at https://www.imdb.com/title/tt4554406/. Accessed on Saturday July 25, 2020.

[2325] Position 564.8 of Payne Best and position 1204.5 of Metaxas.

[2326] Position 564.3 of Payne Best.

[2327] Position 565.3 of Payne Best.

[2328] Position 567.0 of Payne Best and position 1207.5 of Metaxas.

[2329] Position 570.6 of Payne Best.

[2330] Position 570.7 of Payne Best.

[2331] Position 980.7 of Schlingensiepen, position 1206.2 of Metaxas and page 924 of Bethge.

[2332] Position 981.7 of Schlingensiepen.

[2333] [2733] See the article on the Flossenbürg concentration camp at https://www.ushmm.org/wlc/en/article.php?ModuleId=10005537 in regard to SS Drumhead Court Martials. Accessed on Saturday July 25, 2020. It also documents the specific case of Dietrich and his fellow Abwehr conspirators on Monday April 9 1945.

[2334] Position 982.6 of Schlingensiepen. See also pages 925 to 926 of Bethge and position 586.4 of Payne Best.

[2335] Position 982.9 of Schlingensiepen.

[2336] Position 586.5 of Payne Best and position 983.2 of Schlingensiepen.

[2337] Position 983.1 of Schlingensiepen.

[2338] [2735] This date of April 9 1945, can be inferred from position 572.5 of Payne Best — when Bader informs Best, von Falkenhausen and Kokorin to get ready to leave, and position 571.9, which describes Dietrich's arrest late the previous morning of Sunday April 8, 1945 in Schönberg.

[2339] [2733] Position 591.4 of Payne Best and page 926 of Bethge.

[2340] Position 983.8 of Schlingensiepen and page 926 of Bethge.

[2341] [2849] Position 984.1 of Schlingensiepen and page 926 of Bethge.

[2342] Position 984.6 of Schlingensiepen and page 926 of Bethge.

[2343] On the website of New York Times best selling author Martha Hall Kelly at http://www.marthahallkelly.com/which-ravensbruck-commandant-was-more-despicable-koegel-or-suhren/. Accessed on Saturday July 25, 2020.

[2344] Page 926 of Bethge and position 984.6 of Schlingensiepen.

[2345] Position 984.8 of Schlingensiepen, position 1207.6 of Metaxas and pages 926 to 927 of Bethge.

[2346] Position 984.9 of Schlingensiepen and pages 926 to 927 of Bethge.

[2347] [2717] Position 571.5 of Payne Best.

[2348] [2957] Position 571.6 of Payne Best and position 1209.2 of Metaxas.

[2349] Position 1209.7 of Metaxas and position 1076.2 of Schlingensiepen. This letter was written by Payne Best to reply to a letter he had already received from the Leibholz's in regards to their most favourable account of his book.

[2350] Position 1210.0 of Metaxas and page 927 of Bethge.

[2351] Position 1210.0 of Metaxas and position 988.0 of Schlingensiepen. However, Metaxas describes it in greater detail.

[2352] Position 572.4 of Payne Best.

[2353] [2717] Position 526.5 of Payne Best.

Chapter 25 — Old Prussia Gone with the Wind

[2354] https://library.eb.com.au/levels/adults/article/Prussia/61665. Accessed on Saturday July 25, 2020.

[2355] [2617] Pages 7 to 10 of Jane Pejsa document the christening of Ruth in her Lower Silesian ancestral home of Grossenborau in 1867.

[2356] See endnote [6] and endnotes [171] to [173] and [197] to [220] of the Preface "Birth and Memory upon the Lesser Known Fault Line of History" in regard to the so-called "Recovered Territories" and post WWII twin displacement west of eastern Germans and eastern Poles.

[2357] Position 1198.9 of *Microcosm*. See also endnote [220] of the Preface "Birth and Memory upon the Lesser Known Fault Line of History" in regard to the so-called "Recovered Territories" and post WWII twin displacement west of eastern Germans and the eastern Poles.

²³⁵⁸ ²²⁰ Ibid.

²³⁵⁹ ²⁶¹⁷ See endnotes ¹⁵⁴ to ¹⁶⁷ of the Preface "Birth and Memory upon the Lesser Known Fault Line of History" in regard to the Spa-London-Moscow telegram in July 1920 during the 1919-20 Polish-Soviet War. Stalin and Molotov used this obscure, dormant and tampered telegram (while in transit in London) to justify the Soviet invasion of eastern Poland in September 1939, and then post-war, the displacement of the eastern Borderland Poles westwards into the former eastern lands of the pre-war Reich.

²³⁶⁰ Article on the American Civil War at https://www.britannica.com/event/American-Civil-War/ states the duration of the American Civil War from April 12 1861 to April 26 1865. Accessed on Saturday July 25, 2020.

²³⁶¹ Ibid.

²³⁶² See the online Washington Post article by Alyssa Rosenberg, dated July 1 2015 at https://www.washingtonpost.com/news/act-four/wp/2015/07/01/why-we-should-keep-reading-gone-with-the-wind/. Accessed on Saturday July 25, 2020. The book's author Margaret Mitchell, was a native Georgian writing the fictional story from a Confederate standpoint. Moreover, at the beginning of the 1939 movie, there is a romanticising epitaph to the way of life "Gone With the Wind." Alyssa Rosenberg in her article, puts it this way: *These sentiments don't have direct racist sting of Confederate general and early Ku Klux Klan member Nathan Bedford Forrest's declaration that "I am not an enemy of the negro. We want him here among us; he is the only laboring class we have."* But the implication is clear. Furthermore: *I'm sure by this point in this piece, you'll notice that I haven't discussed how the characters in "Gone With The Wind" think about race. The answer is that neither Scarlett nor her antagonists pay much attention to the subject, even as their comfort depends on a race-based system of slavery, and the cataclysm of their lives centers on the destruction of that system.* Nevertheless, one must take notice of the title of Alyssa Rosenberg's article — "Why we should keep reading 'Gone With The Wind'." For myself, in spite of my reservation in regard to the movie's introductory epitaph romanticising the Old Southern way of life, I found the movie to be a great work of cinema.

²³⁶³ See page 344 onwards of Jane Pejsa. In particular, the last letter received by anybody from Oma Ruth as quoted on pages 372 to 373.

²³⁶⁴ Page 410 of *Lenin, Stalin and Hitler The Age of Social Catastrophe* by Robert Gellately, published by Vintage 2008, ISBN 9780712603577. See also endnote ¹²³¹ for Chapter 17 "Pastor and Spy" in regard to Hitler's notorious "Commissar Order."

²³⁶⁵ Page 132 of *Lenin, Stalin and Hitler The Age of Social Catastrophe* by Robert Gellately, published by Vintage 2008, ISBN 9780712603577. See https://www.britannica.com/event/Emancipation-Manifesto, which while stat-

ing in theory, the serfs were emancipated in 1861, they were still very much beholden to their landlords. Accessed on Saturday July 25, 2020.

[2366] This is abundantly clear from reading Jane Pejsa. For example, page 89 talks of Ruth making her monthly visit to the village in June 1899, where she visits and takes time to chat and present flowers to a mother who recently gave birth. This is followed by her visiting another household where the man is facing death, with her words of great solace to he and his family. This being two years following the death of her dearly beloved husband Jürgen.

[2367] See the later chapters of *The war with Japan: A Concise History edition 2* by Charles Bateson, published by Michigan State University Press, 1968, in regard to the tide of the war turning against Japan by 1943.

[2368] Pages 312 to 314 of Jane Pejsa.

[2369] Page 312 of Jane Pejsa.

[2370] Ibid.

[2371] Ibid.

[2372] See Chapter 27 "WAR OF EXTERMINATION AS NAZI CRUSADE" of *Lenin, Stalin and Hitler The Age of Social Catastrophe* from page 413 by Robert Gellately, published by Vintage 2008, ISBN 9780712603577.

[2373] Page 313 of Jane Pejsa.

[2374] The fate of Soviet POWs in German captivity and post war, with Stalin's perception of them as traitors is documented from pages 242-249 in *The Gulag Archipelago, Parts I and II 1918 - 1956* by Alexander Solzhenitsyn, translated from Russian by Thomas P. Whitney, first published in Australia 1974 simultaneously by Collins/Harvill Press and Fontana, ISBN 0006336426.

[2375] For an article on William Joyce, byname Lord Haw-haw, see https://www.britannica.com/biography/William-Joyce. Accessed on Saturday July 25, 2020.

[2376] Page 242 of Solzhenitsyn.

[2377] Around 2007, Sonia and I visited the Lutheran church in Rochedale in the south of suburban Brisbane. The thing that struck us was the absence of icons, with only a large cross visible behind the altar. That said, some Lutheran churches do contain icons and there is a debate over whether or not Lutherans in general are iconoclasts. Ultimately however, the veneration of icons in the Catholic Church is far more predominant in general. See Google Images at https://www.google.com.au/search?q=Lutheran+Churches+with+icons&tbm=isch&tbo=u&source=univ&sa=X&ved=2ahUKEwjLyKmIkLfeAhXF6Y8KHUgNCqMQsAR6BAgDEAE. In particular, the website of the Trinity Evangelical Lutheran Church, a congregation of the Southern Ohio Synod of the Evangelical Lutheran Church in America at http://www.oldtrinity.com/. See also the article on the website of the Web Gallery of Art at https://www.wga.hu/tours/german/iconocla.html. Its credentials can be viewed on it homepage at https://www.wga.hu/. All links accessed on Saturday July 25, 2020.

2378 Page 313 of Jane Pejsa.

2379 Throughout her book, Jane Pejsa addresses Oma Ruth's youngest child Ruth (Maria's mother), as the diminutive "Ruthchen." See the family tree on page 394. Pages 313 to 314 document the intense dislike Ruthchen developed towards the German soldiers guarding the Soviet prisoners on her land.

2380 Pages 313 to 314 of Jane Pejsa.

2381 Position 881.3 of Schlingensiepen documents the then latest assassination plot — that being another suicide attack, with the protagonists supposedly both being Axel von dem Bussche and Ewald Heinrich von Kleist, the eldest son of Ewald von Kleist-Schmenzin. However, Schlingensiepen's account is not entirely accurate. See position 377.5 of Nigel Jones *Countdown to Valkyrie* for von dem Bussche's attempt, and position 380.0 for Ewald Heinrich Kleist-Schmenzin's attempt. Both of which being aborted suicide assassination attempts. Both would ironically, like Gersdorff, survive the war. These attempts were covered in detail in Chapter 20 "Valkyrie II." Moreover, Jane Pejsa's account from page 320 of Ewald Heinrich Kleist-Schmenzin's attempt in February 1944 being in concert with Axel von dem Bussche, is wrong, as Axel von dem Bussche was badly wounded in December 1943, upon which, he had to have a leg amputated and thus, never took any further part in the conspiracy — as stated in Nigel Jones. It is true however, as Jane Pejsa stated on page 315, that Ewald Heinrich did seek counsel with his father on the Schmenzin estate on New Year's Eve, 1943. See position 380.3 and 629.0 of Nigel Jones.

2382 While at position 629.0, Nigel Jones writes that Ewald Heinrich was the very last of the surviving plotters at the time of writing (2008), he has since passed away at age ninety in 2013. See the official website of the *Gedenkstätte Deutscher Widerstand* (Memorial of the German Resistance) at https://www.gdw-berlin.de/en/recess/biographies/index_of_persons/biographie/view-bio/ewald-heinrich-von-kleist/?no_cache=1 and the Yahoo article at https://www.yahoo.com/news/last-survivor-plot-kill-hitler-dies-90-180118395.html, dated March 13 2013, by David Rising of Associated Press. Accessed on Saturday July 25, 2020.

2383 Pages 328 to 329 of Jane Pejsa.

2384 See endnote [718] in Chapter 9 "The von Kleists and the Prophecy." This describes the meeting in September 1925, where Ewald summoned Oma Ruth and Hans Jurgen to a meeting in Oma Ruth's cottage to discuss the recently published work of Adolf Hitler; *Mein Kampf* (My Struggle).

2385 Page 329 of Jane Pejsa.

2386 Page 261 of Jane Pejsa in Chapter VI "The Pastor's Friend 1939-1943" already talks of the "prostrate" Confessing Church.

2387 Page 329 of Jane Pejsa.

2388 Pages 329 to 330 of Jane Pejsa. This was during the time of Churchill's "Wilderness Years," where in the 1930s, it appeared Churchill's political career had ended, never to be resurrected. See the online article *The Churchill Wilderness Years* History on the Net © 2000-2019, Salem Media. Accessed on September 28, 2019 at https://www.historyonthenet.com/churchill-wilderness-years. This website's credentials can be viewed at https://www.historyonthenet.com/about-historyonthenet. Both links accessed on Saturday July 25, 2020. See also endnote [896] for Chapter 13 "Flight and the Tumultuous Appeasement of Evil" in regard to Ewald's meeting with Churchill in August 1938.

[2389] See endnote [2026] in regard to Moabit Prison being the same as Lehrter Strasse Prison — at least in the context of the narrative of the anti-Hitler German Resistance.

[2390] Page 337 of Jane Pejsa.

[2391] Page 339 of Jane Pejsa.

[2392] Position 945.6 of Schlingensiepen, page 828 of Bethge and position 1131.5 of Metaxas.

[2393] See the family tree on page 394 of Jane Pejsa.

[2394] Page 339 of Jane Pejsa.

[2395] Page 339 of Jane Pejsa gives the list of prisoners incarcerated at the time at Prinz-Albrecht-Strasse. However, Jane Pejsa includes Rüdiger Schleicher, Klaus Bonhoeffer and Eberhard Bethge among the incarcerated at Prinz-Albrecht-Strasse, but this contradicts other sources such as Schlingensiepen at position 978.7, Bethge on page 932 and the New York Times online article at http://www.nybooks.com/articles/2012/10/25/tragedy-dietrich-bonhoeffer-and-hans-von-dohnanyi/ which documents their imprisonment at the *Lehrterstrasse* (Moabit) prison at the time. Accessed on Saturday July 25, 2020. See endnote [2026] for Chapter 22 "Prinz-Albrecht-Strasse," in regard to the two different names of Moabit and Lehrterstrasse for what was then the same prison in Berlin.

[2396] Page 339 of Jane Pejsa.

[2397] Advent is the preparation for the celebration of the birth of Jesus Christ at Christmas and also of preparation for the Second Coming of Christ. In Western churches, Advent begins on the Sunday nearest to the 30th of November (St. Andrew's Day) and is the beginning of the liturgical year. See https://www.britannica.com/topic/Advent. All links accessed on Saturday July 25, 2020.

[2398] The article on Ewald Heinrich's father Ewald at https://www.gdw-berlin.de/en/recess/biographies/index_of_persons/biographie/view-bio/ewald-von-kleist-schmenzin/?no_cache=1, on the on the website of the German Resistance Memorial Centre. All links accessed on Saturday July 25, 2020. That said, it does contradict Jane Pejsa, in that it contends that Ewald Heinrich, upon his release, returned to his unit at the front, rather than go underground.

[2399] The remote relative of the Kleist clan of Oma Ruth, that was Field Marshal Paul Ludwig Ewald von Kleist, would die on October 10 1954 in the Soviet

Vladimir prison. See pages 127 to 128 of *The Lesser Terror: Soviet State Security, 1939-1953* by Michael Parrish, published by Greenwood Publishing Group, 1996, ISBN 0275951138, 9780275951139. He had actually been promoted to Field Marshal in 1943. See https://www.britannica.com/biography/Paul-Ludwig-Ewald-von-Kleist. All links accessed on Saturday July 25, 2020. Page 341 of Jane Pejsa states how Hitler authorised the release of Ewald's son Ewald Heinrich, under the misconception that Ewald Heinrich was a son of the said field marshal.

[2400] The official website of the *Gedenkstätte Deutscher Widerstand*" (Memorial of the German Resistance) at https://www.gdw-berlin.de/en/recess/biographies/index_of_persons/biographie/view-bio/ewald-heinrich-von-kleist/?no_cache=1 and the Yahoo article at https://www.yahoo.com/news/last-survivor-plot-kill-hitler-dies-90-180118395.html, dated March 13 2013, by David Rising of Associated Press. Both links accessed on Saturday July 25, 2020. These sources contradict Jane Pejsa's claim on page 341 that Ewald Heinrich went underground upon his release.

[2401] Ewald's first wife Anning died of scarlet fever back in May 1937. See the family tree on page 395 and page 221 of Jane Pejsa.

[2402] Page 342 of Jane Pejsa. For the original German text, see page 275 of *Ewald von Kleist-Schmenzin: ein Konservativer gegen Hitler : Biographie* (Ewald von Kleist-Schmenzin: a Conservative against Hitler : Biography) by Bodo Scheurig, published by Propyläen, 1994, ISBN 354905324X, 9783549053249.

[2403] Page 342 of Jane Pejsa.

[2404] Page 342 of Jane Pejsa.

[2405] [2952] Page 343 of Jane Pejsa.

[2406] [2952] Position 765.4 of Schlingensiepen and page 220 of *History of the German Resistance, 1933-1945* by Peter Hoffmann, published by McGill-Queen's Press - MQUP, 1996, ISBN 0773566406, 9780773566408.

[2407] Position 1134.4 of Metaxas writes of the sole letter Dietrich was able to write to Maria from Prinz-Albrecht-Strasse just before Christmas 1944. Position 1137.4 onwards quotes the poem *Powers of Good* that Dietrich enclosed with this letter, including the fame that this poem attained post-war. See also pages 246 to 247 of *The Cost of Moral Leadership: The Spirituality of Dietrich Bonhoeffer* by Geoffrey B. Kelly, F. Burton Nelson, published by Wm. B. Eerdmans Publishing, 2003, ISBN 0802805116, 9780802805119 and page 343 of Jane Pejsa.

[2408] Pages 343 to 344 of Jane Pejsa.

[2409] Page 344 of Jane Pejsa.

[2410] See page 316 of *Rising '44: The Battle for Warsaw Reprint Edition*, by Professor Norman Davies, published by Penguin Books; Reprint edition (October 4, 2005), ISBN-10: 0143035401, ISBN-13: 9780143035404 which states, that already by early August 1944, there was no serious military obstacle to crossing the Vistula River and rescuing the Rising. For a map of the Soviet "advance" into Warsaw's Praga district, see the map in Appendix 27 on page 676. See also endnote [4235] of Polish WWII Supplement IV "AK and 1944 Warsaw General Uprising — Stalin's mass murder by German proxy."

[2411] The site at http://www.warsawuprising.com/timeline.htm with a timeline of the 1944 Warsaw General Uprising, documents Stalin's refusal to let Allied aircraft use Soviet controlled airfields east of Warsaw for supply air drops to the Rising, coupled with his blatant refusal for Soviet pilots to do likewise. In it are numerous references of orchestrated Soviet inaction with only the odd crumb of token assistance. On their "frequently asked questions page" at http://www.warsawuprising.com/faq.htm under the title: "The main reasons for the Uprising's failure:" it gives the three main reasons for the Uprising's failure. They centre on the deliberate and calculated Soviet inaction, motivated in part by the lawful Polish Government in exile in London having demanded in 1943 a Red Cross investigation into the Soviet perpetrated Katyń Wood Massacre sanctioned by Stalin in March 1940, while Stalin was aligned with Hitler. Both links accessed on Saturday July 25, 2020. In regard to Katyń, see Polish WWII Supplement III "The Katyń Wood Massacre."[3618] See also Polish WWII Supplement IV "AK and 1944 Warsaw General Uprising — Stalin's mass murder by German proxy."[3956] The site "warsawuprising.com" is maintained by Project InPosterum [Latin — for the future], a non-profit, public benefit corporation established in 2004 in California with the purpose to organise for the specific purpose of preserving and popularising selected subjects of World War II history and its aftermath with a focus on Central and Eastern Europe. It's not the official website of the Rising, however, it uses reliable sources which include by permission, Norman Davies *Rising '44: The Battle for Warsaw Reprint Edition*, published by Penguin Books; Reprint edition (October 4, 2005), ISBN-10: 0143035401, ISBN-13: 9780143035404.

[2412] See note #12 on page 730 of *Rising '44: The Battle for Warsaw Reprint Edition*, by Professor Norman Davies, published by Penguin Books; Reprint edition (October 4, 2005), ISBN-10: 0143035401, ISBN-13: 9780143035404.

[2413] [4162] Pages 308-309 of *Rising '44: The Battle for Warsaw Reprint Edition*, by Professor Norman Davies, published by Penguin Books; Reprint edition (October 4, 2005), ISBN-10: 0143035401, ISBN-13: 9780143035404. See also endnote [4237] of Polish WWII Supplement IV "AK and 1944 Warsaw General Uprising — Stalin's mass murder by German proxy." Davies states that this was from a personal recollection written in 2002 by Mr Alan McIntosh, Australia: to the author on 23 June 2003.

[2414] See the battle front maps from August 1, 1944 to February 1, 1945 from pages 57 to 81 of the *Atlas of the World Battle Fronts in Semimonthly Phases, to August. 15, 1945*, produced for the Chief of Staff of the United States Army in 1945 by the United States War Department General Staff, published by the

Army Map Service, 1945. This digitised document can be downloaded from the Wikimedia website at https://upload.wikimedia.org/wikipedia/commons/4/42/Atlas_of_the_World_Battle_Fronts_in_Semimonthly_Phases_to_August_15%2C_1945.pdf. Accessed on Saturday July 25, 2020.

[2415][4162][4555] The article on the Polish culture website (the flagship brand of the Adam Mickiewicz Institute https://iam.pl/en, https://culture.pl/en) at http://culture.pl/en/article/how-warsaw-came-close-to-never-being-rebuilt by Mikołaj Gliński, a graduate of cultural studies at Warsaw University, dated February 4, 2015. Both links accessed on Saturday July 25, 2020.

[2416] Page 344 of Jane Pejsa.

[2417] https://www.britannica.com/event/Battle-of-the-Bulge. Accessed on Saturday July 25, 2020.

[2418] Page 344 of Jane Pejsa.

[2419] Article on the Battle of the Bulge at https://www.britannica.com/event/Battle-of-the-Bulge. Accessed on Saturday July 25, 2020.

[2420] See endnote [140] of the Preface "Birth and Memory upon the Lesser Known Fault Line of History" for evidence of Hitler holding out for a re-visitation of Frederick the Great's "Miracle of Brandenburg."

[2421] In regard to the 1762 "Miracle of Brandenburg" itself, see endnote [141] of the Preface "Birth and Memory upon the Lesser Known Fault Line of History."

[2422] Position 87.1 of Microcosm.

[2423] See the map for February 15 1945 on page 83 of the *Atlas of the World Battle Fronts in Semimonthly Phases, to August. 15, 1945*, produced for the Chief of Staff of the United States Army in 1945 by the United States War Department General Staff, published by the Army Map Service, 1945. This digitised document can be downloaded from the Wikimedia website at https://upload.wikimedia.org/wikipedia/commons/4/42/Atlas_of_the_World_Battle_Fronts_in_Semimonthly_Phases_to_August_15%2C_1945.pdf. Accessed on Saturday July 25, 2020. See also the map for Germany from 1920 to 1933 showing the location of all the Kleist estates and estates of related families on page 145 of Jane Pejsa. Note however, that the region around the Kleist estates to the north, but still east of the Oder River, was still holding out against the Soviet advance.

[2424] Pages 350 to 351 of Jane Pejsa. By the end of January 1945, the Red Army was on the threshold of the von Wedemeyer's Pätzig estate. See the map for February 1 1945 on page 81 of the *Atlas of the World Battle Fronts in Semimonthly Phases, to August 15, 1945*, produced for the Chief of Staff of the United States Army in 1945 by the United States War Department General Staff, published by the Army Map Service, 1945, and the map for Germany from 1920 to 1933 showing the location of all the Kleist estates and estates of related families on page 145 of Jane Pejsa.

[2425] Pages 7 to 10 of Jane Pejsa document the christening of Ruth in her Lower Silesian ancestral home of Grossenborau in 1867.

[2426] [2489] https://www.ushmm.org/information/exhibitions/online-exhibitions/special-focus/liberation-of-auschwitz gives the date of January 27 1945 for the liberation of the Auschwitz concentration camp. Accessed on Saturday July 25, 2020.

[2427] See endnote [2041] for Chapter 22 "Prinz-Albrecht-Strasse" in regard to the bombing raid that day on Berlin by the American Eighth Air Force.

[2428] Page 347 of Jane Pejsa.

[2429] This can be inferred from positions 1122.8 and 1125.1 of Metaxas. See also page 221 of *Love letters from cell 92: Dietrich Bonhoeffer, Maria von Wedemeyer, 1943-1945* by Dietrich Bonhoeffer, Ruth-Alice von Bismarck, Maria von Wedemeyer, Ulrich Kabitz, published by Harper Collins, 1994, ISBN 0006278035, 9780006278030.

[2430] Bottom of page 346 of Jane Pejsa.

[2431] The details of Maria and the party she led over the Oder River in late January to early February 1945 are given on pages 403-404 of *The Doubled Life of Dietrich Bonhoeffer: Women, Sexuality, and Nazi Germany* by Diane Reynolds, published by James Clarke, 2017, ISBN 022790608X, 9780227906088. See also page 347 of Jane Pejsa.

[2432] Page 349 of Jane Pejsa.

[2433] Page 427 in Appendix 1 of the book *The Doubled Life of Dietrich Bonhoeffer: Women, Sexuality, and Nazi Germany*, by Diane Reynolds, published by James Clarke, 2017, ISBN 022790608X, 9780227906088.

[2434] [2489] Article on the Bergen-Belsen concentration camp at https://www.ushmm.org/wlc/en/article.php?ModuleId=10005224, states that this camp was located just 11 miles (18km) north of Celle, and liberated by the British on April 15 1945. It can thus be inferred that Celle ended up in the British occupied zone of post-war Germany. This liberation by the British 11th Armoured Division is described in greater detail in the article at https://www.ushmm.org/wlc/en/article.php?ModuleId=10006188 which states the peaceful surrender of the camp, which we can infer to have been the case for the nearby town of Celle. Both links accessed on Saturday July 25, 2020.

[2435] Pages 403-404 of Diane Reynolds.

[2436] Page 351 of Jane Pejsa.

[2437] Page 351 of Jane Pejsa.

[2438] Numerous such instances will be covered later in this chapter. However, see also endnotes [143] and [144] of the Preface "Birth and Memory upon the Lesser Known Fault Line of History" describing the aftermath of the siege of Festung (Fortress) Breslau. In regard to arbitrary SS terror on its own people during this siege, see position 115.3 of Microcosm and the story of Cilli Steindörfer from position 117.4 of Microcosm. Note that the Sicherheitspolizei or Sicherheitsdienst referred to here, were arms of the SS. See endnote [127] for the Preface "Birth and Memory upon the Lesser Known Fault Line of History."

[2439] Page 361 of Jane Pejsa. See also position 117.4 of Microcosm from the previous note.

[2440] Page 404 of Diane Reynolds.

[2441] Page 352 of Jane Pejsa.

[2442] Page 352 of Jane Pejsa.

[2443] Page 352 of Jane Pejsa.

[2444] Page 352 of Jane Pejsa.

[2445] This is what happens about two months later in Kieckow — see page 369 of Jane Pejsa.

[2446] Pages 352 to 353 of Jane Pejsa.

[2447] Page 353 of Jane Pejsa.

[2448] Page 353 of Jane Pejsa.

[2449] Page 361 of Jane Pejsa. See also position 117.4 of Microcosm for the story of sixteen year-old Cilli Steindörfer.

[2450] [2487] Page 353 of Jane Pejsa.

[2451] [2487] Page 353 of Jane Pejsa.

[2452] See the text of Maria's letter to her mother following her fruitless search for Dietrich in mid-February 1945 on page 556 of the book *Letters and Papers from Prison Volume 8 of Dietrich Bonhoeffer Works* by Dietrich Bonhoeffer, editors Christian Gremmels, John W. De Gruchy, published by Fortress Press, 2010, ISBN 1451406789, 9781451406788. The alternative source which is consistent with this letter is page 427 in Appendix 1 of *The Doubled Life of Dietrich Bonhoeffer: Women, Sexuality, and Nazi Germany*, by Diane Reynolds, published by James Clarke, 2017, ISBN 022790608X, 9780227906088. Schlingensiepen and Jane Pejsa contradict these sources, but it is difficult to go past *Letters and Papers from Prison Volume 8 of Dietrich Bonhoeffer Works*.

[2453] [4343] See the text of Maria's letter to her mother on page 556 of the book *Letters and Papers from Prison Volume 8 of Dietrich Bonhoeffer Works* by Dietrich Bonhoeffer, editors Christian Gremmels, John W. De Gruchy, published by Fortress Press, 2010, ISBN 1451406789, 9781451406788. Footnote #2 at the bottom of this page states what Maria meant by our "Pätzig friends" and footnote #3 describes what the acronym "Flak" stood for.

[2454] [4343] Position 366.0 of Nigel Jones.

[2455] [xxviii] See http://wiki-de.genealogy.net/GOV:Object_1136073 in regard to German Oppeln now being Polish Opole. Accessed on Saturday July 25, 2020.

[2456] Page 14 of Jane Pejsa.

[2457] [2679] Page 344 of Jane Pejsa.

[2458] [xxviii] Page 345 of Jane Pejsa and the family tree on page 394.

[2459] The story of the young university student Raba, discovering her Jewish ancestry in 1931, and its subsequent fallout, is discussed from endnotes [729] to [770] of Chapter 9 "The von Kleists and the Prophecy."

[2460] Page 291 of Jane Pejsa.

[2461] Family tree on page 394 of Jane Pejsa.

[2462] Pages 344 to 345 of Jane Pejsa.

[2463] Position 339.1 of Nigel Jones.

[2464] Pages 344 to 345 of Jane Pejsa.

[2465] Page 345 of Jane Pejsa.

[2466] Family tree on page 394 of Jane Pejsa.

[2467] Page 345 of Jane Pejsa.

[2468] Page 345 of Jane Pejsa.

[2469] Page 345 of Jane Pejsa.

[2470] Page 345 of Jane Pejsa.

[2471] Page 345 of Jane Pejsa.

[2472] Page 345 of Jane Pejsa.

[2473] Page 345 of Jane Pejsa.

[2474] The family tree on page 391 of Jane Pejsa.

[2475] Page 346 of Jane Pejsa.

[2476] Page 346 of Jane Pejsa.

[2477] Page 346 of Jane Pejsa.

[2478] Page 346 of Jane Pejsa.

[2479] The family tree on page 394 of Jane Pejsa. Note, Jane Pejsa's book was published in 1992, and gives no year of death for Ruthi born in 1926. If still alive at the time of this writing in October 2019, she would be aged ninety-two or ninety-three.

[2480] Page 385 of Jane Pejsa in the epilogue.

[2481] See the map of Germany for 1920-1933 on page 145 of Jane Pejsa.

[2482] Page 331 of Jane Pejsa.

[2483] Page 336 of Jane Pejsa.

[2484] See the Genealogy website at https://www.geni.com/people/Erika-von-Falkenhayn/6000000021470617332. Accessed on Saturday July 25, 2020.

[2485] Page 334 of Jane Pejsa.

[2486] Page 334 of Jane Pejsa.

[2487] Page 353 of Jane Pejsa. See also endnotes [2450] and [2451] for this chapter in regard to Ruthchen's eventual flight west.

[2488] Pages 350 to 351 of Jane Pejsa.

[2489] Page 349 of Jane Pejsa. See also endnotes [2426] to [2434] for this chapter in regard to Maria leading a wagon party over the frozen Oder River in late January 1945.

[2490] Page 352 of Jane Pejsa.

[2491] See the family tree on page 395 of Jane Pejsa.

[2492] Page 350 of Jane Pejsa.

[2493] Pages 350 to 351 of Jane Pejsa.

[2494] [2526] The online digitised New York Times article, dated April 21 1995 by Serge Schmemann at https://www.nytimes.com/1995/04/21/obituaries/milovan-djilas-yugoslav-critic-of-communism-dies-at-83.html. Accessed on Saturday July 25, 2020. [2495] In regard to Stalin blithely viewing women in effect as "the spoils of war," see page 49 of the book *War Crimes Against Women: Prosecution in International War Crimes Tribunals* by Kelly Dawn Askin, Edition illustrated, published by Martinus Nijhoff Publishers, 1997, ISBN 9041104860, 9789041104861. See also footnote #172 on the same page. This complaint was made by the former Yugoslav/Serbian communist Milovan Djilas, and one time Stalin supporter, who would later proclaim Stalin to be the *"the greatest criminal in history."* It seems he was instrumental in getting Tito to pursue a communism independent of Stalin and the Soviet Bloc. See the online digitised New York Times article, dated April 21 1995 by Serge Schmemann at https://www.nytimes.com/1995/04/21/obituaries/milovan-djilas-yugoslav-critic-of-communism-dies-at-83.html. See also page 19 of the document *Secret Intelligence Service (C-I) On the Treatment and Maltreatment of Women Room 15. Discussion Notes On the MASS RAPE of GERMAN WOMEN During and following WW2* downloaded from the Secret Intelligence Service (C-I) website at https://www.secretintelligenceservice.org/wp-content/uploads/2016/04/BRUTAL-MASS-RAPE-OF-GERMAN-WOMEN-During.pdf. See also the poem by Alexander Solzhenitsyn on page 7. It must be mentioned however, that Western Allied troops were far from entirely innocent in this regard, which this document does cover. That said, it was not of the magnitude perpetrated by Soviet troops in Germany, but nevertheless, still very disturbing. See also the book *Why Did I Have To Be A Girl?* by Gabriele Koepp, with an article on it and the author in the Sydney Morning Herald dated March 2 2010 which can be viewed online at https://www.smh.com.au/world/german-woman-breaks-taboo-on-soviet-rapes-20100301-pdic.html. While the number of rapes perpetrated by the Red Army in Yugoslavia were not of the magnitude of what was seen in Germany, due in great part to the Yugoslavs being seen as fellow communists for the most part, they still occurred. See the document which can be downloaded from the Cambridge University website at https://www.cambridge.org/core/services/aop-cambridge-core/content/view/8D212624135E340F6DAF0E8298776464/S003767790015 5287a.pdf/red_army_in_yugoslavia_19441945.pdf. This article dated January 20 2017, appeared in the Slavic Review and was entitled *The Red Army in Yugoslavia, 1944—1945* and written by Vojin Majstorović. Its description can be viewed at https://www.cambridge.org/core/journals/slavic-review/article/red-army-in-yugoslavia-19441945/8D212624135E340F6DAF0E8298776464. All links accessed on Saturday July 25, 2020. The first page of this article makes the point that the rapes in Yugoslavia perpetrated by the Red Army seemed to have been more of the magnitude committed by Western Allied troops, rather than of those perpetrated by Soviets in Germany, which had been seen as the shrine of Fascism and perpetrator of four years of horrific crimes in the Soviet Union. As such, the just aforementioned Sydney Morning Herald article and *Secret Intelligence Service (C-I) On the Treatment and Maltreatment of Women Room 15 — Discussion Notes On the MASS RAPE of GERMAN WOMEN During and following WW2* estimates that around two million German women were raped by Soviet troops. The latter however estimates that around ten million rapes were perpetrated by German soldiers on Soviet soil.

[2496] The online digitised New York Times article, dated April 21 1995 by Serge Schmemann at https://www.nytimes.com/1995/04/21/obituaries/milovan-djilas-yugoslav-critic-of-communism-dies-at-83.html. Accessed on Saturday July 25, 2020.

[2497] Ibid.

[2498] Ibid.

[2499] Ibid.

[2500] [2526] Ibid.

[2501] [2824] In regard to the scale of this bombing and it leading to Freisler meeting his maker, see position 1145.9 to 1148.3 of Metaxas and page 914 of Bethge. See also endnote [2041] for Chapter 22 "Prinz-Albrecht-Strasse."

[2502] [2824] Page 355 of Jane Pejsa and page 192 of *Ewald von Kleist-Schmenzin: ein Konservativer gegen Hitler : Biographie* (Ewald von Kleist-Schmenzin: a Conservative against Hitler : Biography) by Bodo Scheurig, published by Propyläen, 1994, ISBN 354905324X, 9783549053249, quote Ewald's brave and belligerent impudence in the face of Freisler and his court, just minutes before Freisler's death from the imminent bombing of Berlin by the American Eight Air Force.

[2503] See position 1145.9 to 1148.3 of Metaxas, page 914 of Bethge and page 355 of Jane Pejsa. See also endnotes [2041] and [2042] for Chapter 22 "Prinz-Albrecht-Strasse" in regard to this bombing raid on Berlin in early February 1945.

[2504] [2827] Position 593.3 of Nigel Jones. See also the ironic quote from endnote [1840] for Chapter 20 "Valkyrie II."

[2505] Bottom of page 355 of Jane Pejsa.

[2506] Page 356 of Jane Pejsa.

[2507] See the map for February 15 1945 on page 83 of the *Atlas of the World Battle Fronts in Semimonthly Phases, to August 15, 1945*, produced for the Chief of Staff of the United States Army in 1945 by the United States War Department General Staff, published by the Army Map Service, 1945, and the map for Germany from 1920 to 1933 showing the location of all the Kleist estates and estates of related families on page 145 of Jane Pejsa. The digitised US Army Atlas can be downloaded from the Wikimedia website at https://upload.wikimedia.org/wikipedia/commons/4/42/Atlas_of_the_World_Battle_Fronts_in_Semimonthly_Phases_to_August_15%2C_1945.pdf. Accessed on Saturday July 25, 2020.

[2508] Page 356 of Jane Pejsa. Spes was Oma Ruth's first daughter but second eldest child. Hans Jürgen was Oma Ruth's eldest. See the family tree on page 394 of Jane Pejsa.

[2509] Page 357 of Jane Pejsa.

[2510] Page 360 of Jane Pejsa.

[2511] Pages 360 to 361 of Jane Pejsa.

[2512] Pages 360 to 361 of Jane Pejsa. See also endnotes [515] to [522] for Chapter 6 "Old Prussia — Birth of Ruth to Precarious Survival."

[2513] Page 361 of Jane Pejsa.

[2514] Page 387 of Jane Pejsa. This will be elaborated upon in the next chapter.

[2515] Page 361 of Jane Pejsa.

[2516] Page 374 of Jane Pejsa states that Konstantin was captivity at the time, while pages 320 to 321 document Konstantin being shipped across the Atlantic to American captivity in March 1944. Post war, Konstantin would serve fourteen years as a Lutheran missionary and pastor in the black townships of South Africa. See page 385 in the epilogue and the photo on page 215 of himself seated alongside Dietrich and Oma Ruth to his right on the Kieckow lawn in March 1936.

[2517] Page 361 and the family tree on page 394 of Jane Pejsa. Hans Jürgen's eldest child and daughter Ferdinande had died in July 1924 aged just ten in a wagon accident, in which her brother Konstantin survived physically unscathed. See pages 157 to 158.

[2518] Page 361 of Jane Pejsa.

[2519] See *Gauleiter: Herbert Albrecht-H. Wilhelm Huttmann* Volume 1 of *Gauleiter: The Regional Leaders of the Nazi Party and Their Deputies, 1925-1945* by Michael D. Miller and Andreas Schulz, published by R. James Bender Publishing, 2012, ISBN 1932970215, 9781932970210.

[2520] Page 361 of Jane Pejsa.

[2521] In regard to Werner Koch, see positions 542.4 and 543.6 of Schlingensiepen and pages 219 and 238 of Jane Pejsa. See also endnotes [826] to [828] for Chapter 11 "Memo to Hitler and his Olympics."

[2522] Pages 361 to 362 of Jane Pejsa.

[2523] See page 13 in the introduction to *Lenin, Stalin and Hitler The Age of Social Catastrophe* from page 413 by Robert Gellately, published by Vintage 2008, ISBN 9780712603577.

[2524] See Chapter 27 "WAR OF EXTERMINATION AS NAZI CRUSADE" of *Lenin, Stalin and Hitler The Age of Social Catastrophe* from page 413 by Robert Gellately, published by Vintage 2008, ISBN 9780712603577. This chapter sums up how Hitler explained to his generals how Operation Barbarossa — the invasion of the Soviet Union launched on June 22 1941, would be a campaign vastly different to the one in Western Europe, where commanders would be compelled to sacrifice their personal scruples, owing to Hitler's assertion that international law and military traditions should not be applied to the war against "Jewish Bolshevism."

[2525] See the maps for February 1 and February 15 1945 on pages 81 and 83 respectively of the *Atlas of the World Battle Fronts in Semimonthly Phases, to August 15, 1945*, produced for the Chief of Staff of the United States Army in 1945 by the United States War Department General Staff, published by the Army Map Service, 1945, and the map for Germany from 1920 to 1933 showing the location of all the Kleist estates and estates of related families on page 145 of Jane Pejsa. The digitised US Army Atlas can be downloaded from the Wikimedia website at https://upload.wikimedia.org/wikipedia/commons/4/42/Atlas_of_the_World_Battle_Fronts_in_Semimonthly_Phases_to_August_15%2C_1945.pdf. Accessed on Saturday July 25, 2020.

[2526] This is clearly implied from endnotes [2494] to [2500] for this chapter.

[2527] See Polish WWII Supplement I "The Molotov-Ribbentrop Pact"[3268] in regard to how Hitler and Stalin had agreed in late August 1939, to divide the spoils of Eastern Europe between themselves, in their pacts "Secret Protocol."

[2528] See endnote [204] in the Preface "Birth and Memory upon the Lesser Known Fault Line of History" in regard to the deportation of Borderland Poles to the Gulag. See also endnotes [3367] to [3373] of Polish WWII Supplement I "The Molotov-Ribbentrop Pact."

[2529] In regard to Katyń, see Polish WWII Supplement III "The Katyń Wood Massacre."[3618]

[2530] Article on Joseph Stalin at https://www.britannica.com/biography/Joseph-Stalin by Ronald Francis Hingley, former lecturer in Russian, University of Oxford and author of Chekhov: A Biographical and Critical Study. In particular, see the section titled "The Young Revolutionary." Accessed on Saturday July 25, 2020.

[2531] See endnote [3618] of Polish WWII Supplement III "The Katyń Wood Massacre."

[2532] https://www.britannica.com/biography/Joseph-Stalin which explicitly mentions "Caucasian blood-feud tradition." Accessed on Saturday July 25, 2020. See also the introduction to the critically acclaimed book and ebook *Young Stalin* by Simon Sebag Montefiore, published by The Orion Publishing Group Ltd Orion House 5 Upper Saint Martin's Lane London WC2H 9EA, a Hachette UK Company, eISBN : 9780297863847, from position 31.

[2533] Position 108.0 of *Young Stalin*. This being near the beginning of Chapter 2 "CRAZY BESO" — Stalin's abusive father. See also page 131 of *Lenin, Stalin and Hitler The Age of Social Catastrophe* by Robert Gellately.

[2534] https://www.britannica.com/biography/Joseph-Stalin. Accessed on Saturday July 25, 2020.

[2535] Ibid and positions 598.5 and 599.6 of *Young Stalin* by Simon Sebag Montefiore.

[2536] Position 89.2 of Microcosm. My father's benevolent treatment by the British in a POW camp in Egypt, from 1943 until 1948, is testament to this fact. It was during this time, that he took advantage of English lessons given by German officers. By 1945, he could easily converse with the British guards, albeit, with the typical mistakes of native German speakers speaking English. No doubt, a hangover from lessons given by German officers.

[2537] Page 362 of Jane Pejsa. This would have been identical to the prohibition imposed on travel for Hans Jürgen and his party in late February 1945 by their Gauleiter (local or regional Nazi leader).

[2538] Page 363 of Jane Pejsa.

[2539] Page 363 of Jane Pejsa. Considering the fact that Mecklenburg would ultimately come under the Soviet zone of occupation, it would have been most wise to continue their journey further west to Celle. See https://www.britannica.com/place/Mecklenburg-historical-region-Germany. Accessed on Saturday July 25, 2020.

[2540] Page 363 of Jane Pejsa.

[2541] Page 363 of Jane Pejsa.

[2542] Pages 363 to 364 of Jane Pejsa.

[2543] Pages 360 to 361 of Jane Pejsa.

[2544] Bottom of page 363 of Jane Pejsa.

[2545] Chapter 12 verse 1 of Genesis in the New International Version (NIV) from the Bible Gateway website at https://www.biblegateway.com/passage/?search=Genesis+12%3A1-3&version=NIV. Accessed on Saturday July 25, 2020. Jane Pejsa's quote of it on page 364 has somewhat different wording, but the essential meaning is still the same.

[2546] See the context summary on the Bible Reference website at https://www.bibleref.com/Genesis/12/Genesis-12-1.html. Accessed on Saturday July 25, 2020.

[2547] Page 364 of Jane Pejsa.

[2548] Pages 364 to 365 of Jane Pejsa.

[2549] Pages 365 to 366 of Jane Pejsa.

[2550] See the family tree on page 394 of Jane Pejsa. As such, Maria Bismarck née von Kleist Retzow was Maria von Wedemeyer's aunt. The latter being of course, Dietrich's fiancée.

[2551] Pages 71 to 80 of Jane Pejsa.

[2552] Page 365 of Jane Pejsa.

[2553] Page 365 of Jane Pejsa.

[2554] Page 365 and note #7 on page 397 of Jane Pejsa.

[2555] Page 365 of Jane Pejsa.

[2556] Page 366 of Jane Pejsa.

[2557] The remote relative of Hans Jürgen that was Field Marshal Paul Ludwig Ewald von Kleist, would die on October 10 1954 in the Soviet Vladimir prison.

See pages 127 to 128 of the book *The Lesser Terror: Soviet State Security, 1939-1953* by Michael Parrish, published by Greenwood Publishing Group, 1996, ISBN 0275951138, 9780275951139. He had actually been promoted to Field Marshal in 1943. See https://www.britannica.com/biography/Paul-Ludwig-Ewald-von-Kleist. Accessed on Saturday July 25, 2020.

[2558] Page 341 of Jane Pejsa. See also position 629.0 of Nigel Jones and the official website of the German Resistance at https://www.gdw-berlin.de/en/recess/biographies/index_of_persons/biographie/view-bio/ewald-heinrich-von-kleist/?no_cache=1 and the Yahoo article at https://www.yahoo.com/news/last-survivor-plot-kill-hitler-dies-90-180118395.html, dated March 13 2013, by David Rising of Associated Press. Both links accessed on Saturday July 25, 2020.

[2559] Page 366 of Jane Pejsa.

[2560] Page 366 of Jane Pejsa.

[2561] Page 366 of Jane Pejsa.

[2562] Pages 366 to 367 of Jane Pejsa.

[2563] Page 367 of Jane Pejsa.

[2564] Page 367 of Jane Pejsa.

[2565] The bottom of page 367 of Jane Pejsa documents Ewald's final words to Eberhard Bethge, just prior to his execution on the 9th of April 1945 — the very date of Dietrich's execution at Flossenbürg. The online article on Ewald von Kleist-Schmenzin on the website of the German Resistance Memorial Centre at https://www.gdw-berlin.de/en/recess/biographies/index_of_persons/biographie/view-bio/ewald-von-kleist-schmenzin/?no_cache=1, states that Ewald was executed at Plötzensee prison, which was near the Moabit prison. Accessed on Saturday July 25, 2020. That Eberhard Bethge was incarcerated at the Moabit (*Lehrterstrasse*) Prison, see position 978.5 of Schlingensiepen. See endnote [2026] for Chapter 22 "Prinz-Albrecht-Strasse," in regard to the two different names of Moabit and Lehrterstrasse for what was then the same prison in Berlin.

[2566] See the Timeline early on in the book *After Hitler: The Last Days of the Second World War in Europe* by Michael Jones, published by Hachette UK, 2015, ISBN 1848544979, 9781848544970. This can be viewed on Google Books at https://books.google.com.au/books?id=fzyqjnmpD_4C&printsec=frontcover&dq=ISBN+1848544979,+9781848544970&hl=en&sa=X&ved=0ahUKEwiPrbue5IPhAhWbV30KHaWlBZcQ6AEIKjAA#v=onepage&q=Timeline&f=false. Accessed on Saturday July 25, 2020.

[2567] [2872] Page 369 of Jane Pejsa.

[2568] Page 369 of Jane Pejsa.

[2569] [2736] In regard to Georg Thomas' role in the infamous "Hunger Plan," see pages 477 to 478 of the book *The wages of destruction: the making and breaking of the Nazi economy* by Adam Tooze, published by Allen Lane, 2006. See also the ebook published by Penguin in 2007, ISBN 9780141040929, from position 1166.4 to 1170.3 and https://books.google.com.au/books?id=ECkVAQAAMAAJ&dq=The+wages+ of+destruction%3A+the+making+and+breaking+of+the+Nazi+economy%E2 %80%9D+by+Adam+Tooze%2C+published+by+Allen+Lane%2C+2006&foc us=searchwithinvolume&q=be+described+as+secret and https://books.google.com.au/books?id=ECkVAQAAMAAJ&dq=The+wages+ of+destruction%3A+the+making+and+breaking+of+the+Nazi+economy%E2 %80%9D+by+Adam+Tooze%2C+published+by+Allen+Lane%2C+2006&foc us=searchwithinvolume&q=quibble on Google Books. See also the list of special prisoners on Peter Koblank's website at http://www.mythoselser.de/niederdorf.htm#liste and position 725.2 of Payne Best in the Appendix of that book. The name of Georg Thomas does indeed appear on both of these lists. Given his instrumental role in the infamous "*Hunger Plan*," the presence of this cynical opportunist on the on the website of *Die Gedenkstätte Deutscher Widerstand* (German Resistance Memorial Centre) at https://www.gdw-berlin.de/en/recess/biographies/index_of_persons/biographie/view-bio/georg-thomas/?no_cache=1, seems rather inappropriate. These special prisoners were also known as "Prominenten — Prominent Prisoners" or "Hostages of the SS." See endnotes [2708] onwards from the start of Chapter 27 "The Prominenten and Miraculous Reprieves." All links accessed on Saturday July 25, 2020.

[2570] See page 20 of *Hitler's Commanders: Officers of the Wehrmacht, the Luftwaffe, the Kriegsmarine, and the Waffen-SS, Edition 2, illustrated* by Samuel W. Mitcham Junior and Gene Mueller, published by Rowman & Littlefield Publishers, 2012, ISBN 1442211547, 9781442211544.

[2571] [2872] [2876] [2877] Page 369 of Jane Pejsa.

[2572] Page 369 of Jane Pejsa.

[2573] Page 370 of Jane Pejsa. See there the map of post-war Germany and Poland, where Old Prussian Belgard is now Polish Białogard, and in Silesia, German Breslau is now Wrocław, and German Oppeln is now Polish Opole. Compare this with the map on page 145 of Germany from 1920 to 1933.

[2574] Page 370 of Jane Pejsa.

[2575] Page 371 of Jane Pejsa.

[2576] Page 371 of Jane Pejsa.

[2577] Page 371 of Jane Pejsa.

[2578] Bottom of page 371 of Jane Pejsa.

[2579] Page 372 of Jane Pejsa.

[2580] As Ewald von Kleist of Schmenzin prophesied during his meeting with Ruth and Hans Jürgen in Ruth's Klein Krössin cottage in September 1925. See pages 164 to 169 of Jane Pejsa and endnote [718] in Chapter 9 "The von Kleists and the Prophecy."

[2581] Page 373 of Jane Pejsa.

[2582] Page 373 of Jane Pejsa.

[2583] In September 1945, Ruthchen was living near the Thuringian mountains, as stated at the bottom of page 373 of Jane Pejsa. This mountain range was in the Soviet occupied zone — however, Ruthchen in the then American occupied zone, as stated on page 375, must have been just to their southern foot in northern Bavaria. A map of the Allied occupied zones of Germany post World War II can be found near the back of the Webster's Dictionary unabridged, published by the World Publishing Company Cleveland and New York 1959 and at https://www.themaparchive.com/allied-occupation-zones-of-germany-may-1945.html on the Map Archive. The co-ordinates for the Thuringian Forest are 50°35'39.11"N 10°46'30.68"E as seen on Google Earth. Note the boundary between the modern-day states of Thuringia and Bavaria. See also the article on Thuringia at https://www.britannica.com/place/Thuringia. Both links accessed on Saturday July 25, 2020.

[2584] Pages 373 to 374 of Jane Pejsa.

[2585] Page 375 of Jane Pejsa.

[2586] Page 375 of Jane Pejsa.

[2587] Position 1132.9 of Microcosm.

[2588] See the comparative map on page 372 of the book *The Polish Way* by Adam Zamoyski, published by John Murray Publishers Limited, 1989, ISBN 10: 0719546745 ISBN 13: 9780719546747. Read also the author's comments from pages 371 to 372.

[2589] Page 376 of Jane Pejsa.

[2590] Page 376 of Jane Pejsa.

[2591] Page 376 of Jane Pejsa.

[2592] Page 376 of Jane Pejsa.

[2593] Page 377 of Jane Pejsa.

[2594] Page 377 of Jane Pejsa.

[2595] Page 377 of Jane Pejsa.

[2596] Page 377 of Jane Pejsa.

[2597] The remarkable 1948-49 Berlin airlift is described at https://www.britannica.com/event/Berlin-blockade-and-airlift. Accessed on Saturday July 25, 2020.

[2598] Page 378 of Jane Pejsa.

[2599] Page 378 of Jane Pejsa also describes Ruthchen's visit to the *Marienburgerallee* to see Dietrich's parents. By this time, the Bonhoeffer home would have been in the British occupied zone of Berlin. This can be inferred by typing in "43 Marienburgeralle (Berlin), Berlin, Germany" into Google Earth, then by viewing a Berlin Wall map at http://maps-berlin.com/berlin-wall-map#&gid=1&pid=1 on the website of Maps-Berlin and a map of the occupied zones of Berlin at https://i0.wp.com/www.insidersberlin.com/wp-content/uploads/2016/12/30249103203_b0502a62cb_o.jpg, on the website of the "Insiders Berlin," which contains declassified CIA maps of the German capital. Both links accessed on Saturday July 25, 2020.

[2600] Page 335 of Jane Pejsa.

[2601] Page 379 of Jane Pejsa.

[2602] Pages 379 to 380 of Jane Pejsa.

[2603] Page 379 of Jane Pejsa.

[2604] https://www.britannica.com/place/Szczecin. Accessed on Saturday July 25, 2020.

[2605] Page 379 of Jane Pejsa.

[2606] Page 379 of Jane Pejsa.

[2607] Page 380 of Jane Pejsa.

[2608] Page 380 of Jane Pejsa.

[2609] Such signs I saw while visiting the Warsaw Uprising Museum in October 2004, just months after its opening.

[2610] Page 380 of Jane Pejsa.

[2611] Page 380 of Jane Pejsa.

[2612] See http://gov.genealogy.net/item/show/BELARDJO74XA. Accessed on Saturday July 25, 2020.

[2613] Page 380 of Jane Pejsa.

[2614] Page 380 of Jane Pejsa.

[2615] Page 380 of Jane Pejsa.

[2616] See endnote [220] of the Preface "Birth and Memory upon the Lesser Known Fault Line of History."

[2617] [2359] See endnotes [152] to [220] of the Preface "Birth and Memory upon the Lesser Known Fault Line of History" in regard to the two or so decades dormant July 1920 Spa-London-Moscow Telegram and the subsequent Stalinist engineered displacement of eastern Poles and eastern Germans post-war. For a condensed version, see endnotes [2355] to [2359] at the beginning of this chapter.

[2618] Page 380 of Jane Pejsa.

[2619] The latitude and longitude for Belgard (Białogard) and Bublitz (Bobolice) are given at http://gov.genealogy.net/item/show/BELARDJO74XA and http://gov.genealogy.net/item/show/BUBITZJO83GW respectively. Plugged into Google Earth or Google Maps, this shows that Bublitz (Bobolice) is just under forty kilometres east-south-east from Belgard (Białogard). Both links accessed on Saturday July 25, 2020.

[2620] Now Polish Tychowo. See http://gov.genealogy.net/item/show/TYCHOWJO83DW. Accessed on Saturday July 25, 2020.

[2621] Page 381 of Jane Pejsa.

[2622] Pages 350 to 351 of Jane Pejsa.

[2623] Page 381 of Jane Pejsa.

[2624] Page 381 of Jane Pejsa.

[2625] Page 381 of Jane Pejsa.

[2626] Pages 381 to 382 of Jane Pejsa.

[2627] Page 382 of Jane Pejsa.

[2628] Page 382 of Jane Pejsa. Klaus von Bismarck was the husband of Rutchen's daughter Ruth-Alice. See the family tree on page 394.

[2629] Page 382 of Jane Pejsa.

[2630] Page 382 of Jane Pejsa.

[2631] Page 382 of Jane Pejsa.

[2632] Page 382 of Jane Pejsa.

Chapter 26 — Oma Ruth's Progeny After Death

[2633] The exact date of death for Oma Ruth is given at https://www.geni.com/people/gr%C3%A4fin-Ruth-von-Zedlitz-Tr%C3%Bctzschler/6000000010383910393. From this, and pages 381 to 382 of Jane Pejsa, we can infer that Oma Ruth died the day following her youngest child's revelation to her of Dietrich's execution just shy of six months earlier.

[2634] Pages 135 to 136 of Jane Pejsa document the family's impression that Ruth's second son Konstantin was the most gifted of all her children and the Matriarch's favourite. Page 383 at the start of the epilogue, states that Oma Ruth was buried between her husband Jürgen and son Konstantin.

[2635] Konstantin would survive the 1916 Battle of Verdun, but would die in October 1917 after just three months training as a replacement aviator. See pages 130 to 134 of Jane Pejsa and the family tree on page 394. Oma Ruth's son Konstantin is not to be confused with her grandson of the same name. He was born in 1919 as the second child and first son of Hans Jürgen. The younger Konstantin saw out World War II in American captivity, and would post-war, serve as a pastor in the black townships of South Africa. See page 385 in the epilogue and the photo on page 215 in Jane Pejsa of himself seated alongside Dietrich and Oma Ruth to his right on the Kieckow lawn in March 1936. In regard to his American captivity, see page 374.

[2636] Page 383 of Jane Pejsa and the online article dated June 20 2003 on the Three Towns (Gdańsk, Gdynia, Sopot) Polish Gazetta Wyborcza website at http://trojmiasto.wyborcza.pl/trojmiasto/1,35612,1538963.html?disableRedirects=true.

[2637] Page 383 of Jane Pejsa.

[2638] Page 383 of Jane Pejsa.

[2639] Pages 313 to 314 of Jane Pejsa.

[2640] See the family tree on page 394 of Jane Pejsa.

[2641] [3363] Page 383 of Jane Pejsa.

[2642] See the post-war map on page 387 of Jane Pejsa.

[2643] See the links at http://wiki-de.genealogy.net/GOV:KIEKOWJO83DV and http://wiki-de.genealogy.net/GOV:KROSINJO83DW.

[2644] [3363] Page 383 of Jane Pejsa. Again, not to be confused with Oma Ruth's second son.

[2645] This eastern German city on the river Oder is not to be confused with the much larger western German city of Franfurt am Main. During the Cold War, they were respectively in East and West Germany. See articles at https://www.britannica.com/place/Frankfurt-an-der-Oder and https://www.britannica.com/place/Frankfurt-am-Main.

[2646] Page 383 of Jane Pejsa. Verse 6 of the Psalm in the New International Version reads as: "Those who go out weeping, carrying seed to sow, will return with songs of joy, carrying sheaves with them."

[2647] [3209] Bottom of page 383 of Jane Pejsa.

[2648] [3210] Page 342 of Jane Pejsa describes how Hans Jürgen prepared himself for but then remarkably escaped torture while being incarcerated at Prinz-Albrecht-Strasse.

[2649] See the translator's note at the beginning of the book *With Paulus at Stalingrad* by Wilhelm Adam, translated by Tony Le Tissier, published by Pen and Sword, 2017, ISBN 1526723506, 9781526723505. The author was Paulus' adjutant in Stalingrad, and like his superior, joined the NKFD and settled in East Germany post-war. As such, the translator's note needs to be read, which states that the book is devoid of any criticism of the Soviet Union. Furthermore, while Adam does mention his wife and daughter pre-Stalingrad, he never mentions them after his repatriation, which as Tony Le Tissier alludes to, prompts one to think that his wife and daughter, most wisely, decided not to join him in the newly founded Germanic worker's "*utopia.*"

[2650] Page 247 of Rüdiger Overmans.

[2651] [2784] The online articles on the websites of *Die Deutsche Geschichte in Dokumenten und Bildern (DGDB)* — (German History in Documents and Images (GHDI)) at http://ghdi.ghi-dc.org/sub_image.cfm?image_id=2562 and the Rare Historical Photos webiste at https://rarehistoricalphotos.com/adenauer-returns-cologne-prisoners-1955/. Also, page 258 of *Soldaten hinter Stacheldraht: Deutsche Kriegsgefangene des Zweiten Weltkriegs* (Soldiers behind barbed wire: German prisoners of war of the Second World War) Edition 2 by Rüdiger Overmans and Ulrike Goeken-Haidl, published by Propyläen Verlag, 2000, ISBN 3549071213, 9783549071212. Although in this source, the authors talk of the agreement to release the remaining 10,000 *Kriegsverurteilten* (condemned prisoners of war) in the Soviet Union. The figure of 15,000 from the Rare Historical Photos website includes civilians and prisoners of war.

[2652] Page 277 of Rüdiger Overmans.

[2653] Table 198 in *Россия и СССР в войнах XX века: потери вооруженных сил : статистическое исследование* (Russia and the USSR in the wars of the 20th century: loss of armed forces: a statistical study) by Г. Ф Кривошеев (G. F Krivosheev), published by ОЛМА-Пресс, 2001 (OLMA-Press, 2001), ISBN 5224015154, 9785224015153.

2654 Page 246 of Rüdiger Overmans.

2655 2784 Page 246 of Rüdiger Overmans.

2656 Page 188 of Jane Pejsa.

2657 Page 260 of Jane Pejsa.

2658 Page 252 of Jane Pejsa.

2659 Pages 259 to 260 of Jane Pejsa.

2660 Page 384 of Jane Pejsa.

2661 Page 384 of Jane Pejsa.

2662 Page 384 of Jane Pejsa. The book on Ewald von Kleist is *Ewald von Kleist-Schmenzin: ein Konservativer gegen Hitler : Biographie* (Ewald von Kleist-Schmenzin: a Conservative against Hitler : Biography) by Bodo Scheurig, published by Propyläen, 1994, ISBN 354905324X, 9783549053249.

2663 See family tree on page 394 of Jane Pejsa.

2664 Page 384 of Jane Pejsa.

2665 Page 384 of Jane Pejsa and the closing "AFTERWORD" section of Metaxas from position 1240.0 onwards summarise Maria's life post-war in the US.

2666 Ibid.

2667 Position 1244.0 of Metaxas.

2668 The book *Love letters from cell 92: Dietrich Bonhoeffer, Maria von Wedemeyer, 1943-1945* by Dietrich Bonhoeffer, Ruth-Alice von Bismarck, Maria von Wedemeyer, Ulrich Kabitz, published by Harper Collins, 1994, ISBN 0006278035, 9780006278030.

2669 That this visit was made in 2008, can be inferred from the year of publication for his book, which was 2010, as given at position 16.0, and that Metaxas states that he made this visit two years earlier at the time of writing.

2670 Position 642.0 of Metaxas.

2671 The dates of birth and death for Ruth-Alice can be found at https://www.geni.com/people/Ruth-Alice-von-Bismarck/6000000010384100251 on Geni: A Genealogy Website.

2672 Page 384 of Jane Pejsa.

2673 In regard to Maria's younger sister Christine, see the New York Times online article at https://www.nytimes.com/2018/01/19/obituaries/christine-beshar-trailblazing-lawyer-dies-at-88.html and the bottom of page 384 of Jane Pejsa.

2674 Page 385 of Jane Pejsa.

2675 Page 385 of Jane Pejsa and in *Indexes and Supplementary Materials: Dietrich Bonhoeffer Works, Volume 17* by Dietrich Bonhoeffer, editors Victoria J. Barnett and Barbara Wojhoski, published by Fortress Press, 2014, ISBN 1451489544, 9781451489545 on Google Books at https://books.google.com.au/books?id=ZR7qAwAAQBAJ&pg=PR56&lpg=PR56&dq=ruth+roberta+stahlberg+heckscher&source=bl&ots=7G6x08Tupf&sig=hS9vGflvfjhAz4_A9K6DhXgQMYM&hl=en&sa=X&ved=2ahUKEwiFjbyd

85HfAhVYdCsKHciYBxEQ6AEwCXoECAgQAQ#v=onepage&q=Heckscher
%2C%20Ruth%20Roberta%20(Raba)&f=false.

[2676] In *Indexes and Supplementary Materials: Dietrich Bonhoeffer Works, Volume 17* by Dietrich Bonhoeffer, editors Victoria J. Barnett and Barbara Wojhoski, published by Fortress Press, 2014, ISBN 1451489544, 9781451489545.

[2677] See the footnote on page 185 of Jane Pejsa.

[2678] Page 385 of Jane Pejsa.

[2679] Hans Conrad Stahlberg, son of Oma Ruth's headstrong first daughter Spes, (see page 98 of Jane Pejsa) was marrying Maria von Loesch, a descendant from a branch of the Zedlitz family. (Oma Ruth's maiden name was Gräfin von Zedlitz-Trützschler). The wedding was a Zedlitz family reunion, oblivious, at least for the time being, to the implacable advance of the Red Army. See endnote [2457] of Chapter 25 "Old Prussia Gone With The Wind."

[2680] Page 385 of Jane Pejsa.

[2681] Alla's memoir is *Die verdammte Pficht, Erinnerungen 1932 bis 1945* published in 1987 by Ullstein, Berlin, and in English as *Bounden Duty, The Memoirs of German Officer, 1932-45*, published in 1990 by Maxwell London. Also published by Brassey's, 1990 ISBN 0080367143, 9780080367149. See also note #48 on page 398 of Jane Pejsa.

[2682] Page 385 of Jane Pejsa.

[2683] See pages 31 and 157 to 158 of Jane Pejsa.

[2684] Page 385 of Jane Pejsa documents Konstantin's life post-war. He being the second child of Hans Jürgen and Mieze. See also page 130 of the book *Dietrich Bonhoeffer: A Life in Pictures*, editors Renate Bethge and Christian Gremmels, translated by Brian McNeil, published by Fortress Press, ISBN 1451416563, 9781451416565, which contains a photo of Konstantin with Oma Ruth in discussion with Dietrich at Kieckow in 1942. As does page 215 of Jane Pejsa.

[2685] Pages 118 to 119 of Jane Pejsa describe how Oma Ruth's second son Konstantin met Wilhelm Merton in 1912. Wilhelm's son Richard took over the firm upon his father's death in 1916. See pages 130 to 131 and pages 222 to 223.

[2686] Page 385 of Jane Pejsa. In regard to the death of Konstantin — Oma Ruth's second son during the Great War, see pages 132 to 133.

[2687] See the family tree on page 395 and page 221 of Jane Pejsa.

[2688] Page 386 of Jane Pejsa.

[2689] Page 386 of Jane Pejsa.

[2690] Page 386 of Jane Pejsa documents the author's impression of Oma Ruth's ancestral home of Grossenborau — now in the Polish village of Borów Wielki (pronounced "Boroov Vielkee").

[2691] Page 386 of Jane Pejsa.

[2692] See articles at https://www.britannica.com/place/Lubuskie on the Lubusz voivodeship and https://www.britannica.com/place/Dolnoslaskie on the Dolny

Śląsk (Lower Silesia, or in German, Niederschlesien) voivodeship — both established in 1999.

[2693] Look up these these co-ordinates of "51°40'44.71"N, 15°38'3.06"E" on Google Earth or Google Maps.

[2694] See the link at http://wiki-de.genealogy.net/GOV:KIEKOWJO83DV for Kieckow becoming Kikowo.

[2695] See the link at http://gov.genealogy.net/item/show/BELARDJO74XA for Belgard becoming Białogard.

[2696] The Kikowo old stone roads lined with linden, chestnut, oak and maple trees can be viewed in Google Street View on Google Earth or Google Maps, at co-ordinates 53°53'2.00"N 16°16'37.00"E.

[2697] Page 386 of Jane Pejsa.

[2698] Page 387 of Jane Pejsa.

[2699] See pages 360 to 361, page 40 and pages 68 to 69 of Jane Pejsa.

[2700] See for example pages 133 to 134 of *Warsaw 1920, Lenin's Failed Conquest of Europe* by Adam Zamoyski.

[2701] That every displaced Borderland Pole from the east, with their still fresh and terrible memories of the war and the even more recent ordeal of their Stalinist perpetrated displacement, being bereft of any will to acknowledge for example, the history of German Breslau, but rather to declare that every brick in their newly Polish Wrocław *"only lived and spoke Polish,"* see position 1198.7 of Microcosm.

[2702] The Geni genealogy website at http://gov.genealogy.net/item/show/TYCHOWJO83DW.

[2703] Pages 387 to 388 of Jane Pejsa.

[2704] The date of Heinrich's death was published in the Frankfurter Allgemeine Zeitung on August 29, 2014. This was accessed on the newspaper's website at https://lebenswege.faz.net/unternehmensnachrufe/heinrich-von-kleist-retzow/39495738 on Sunday February 17, 2019. However, this link is now broken.

[2705] See the family tree on page 394 of Jane Pejsa.

[2706] The Geni genealogy website at https://www.geni.com/people/Ruth-von-Wedemeyer/6000000010383922436.

[2707] See the last page before the contents in Jane Pejsa. It reads; *"This book is dedicated to men and women in every age and place who have acted to uphold decency and honor amid indecency and dishonor, and especially to those who, in so doing, have perished."*

Chapter 27 — The Prominenten and Miraculous Reprieves

[2708] 867 1892 1894 2056 2086 xxvii 2197 2242 2569 2756 lxiii 4496 See endnotes [2053] to [2054] for Chapter 22 "Prinz-Albrecht-Strasse."

[2709] See endnote [2064] for Chapter 22 "Prinz-Albrecht-Strasse."

[2710] See endnote [2060] for Chapter 22 "Prinz-Albrecht-Strasse."

[2711] Position 18.8 of *Hitler's last plot: the 139 VIP hostages selected for death in the final days of World War II* by Ian Sayer and Jeremy Dronfield, published by Da Capo Press, an imprint of Perseus Books, LLC, a subsidiary of Hachette Book Group, New York April 2019, ebook ISBN 9780306921575.

[2712] Ibid.

[2713] [2056] See endnote [2226] for Chapter 24 "Dietrich's Final Days."

[2714] xxvii lxiii See endnote [1357] for Chapter 17 "Pastor and Spy."

[2715] See endnote [2187] for Chapter 24 "Dietrich's Final Days."

[2716] See endnotes [2318] and [2319] for Chapter 24 "Dietrich's Final Days."

[2717] See endnotes [2347] to [2353] for Chapter 24 "Dietrich's Final Days."

[2718] See the chronology at position 1099.0 of Schlingensiepen. Their deaths and the aftermath will be discussed in the next chapter.

[2719] See endnotes [2291] to [2294] for Chapter 24 "Dietrich's Final Days."

[2720] See endnotes [1419] to [1446] for Chapter 18 "Romance, Plots and Arrest" in regard to the two March 1943 assassination plots.

[2721] See endnotes [1419] to [1446] for Chapter 18 "Romance, Plots and Arrest" in regard to the two March 1943 assassination plots.

[2722] See endnotes [1449] and [1450] for Chapter 18 "Romance, Plots and Arrest."

[2723] See endnotes [1476] to [1480] for Chapter 19 "The Tormentor Tormented" in regard to the Schmidhuber affair that led to the arrests on April 5, 1943.

[2724] See endnotes [2292] and [2294] for Chapter 24 "Dietrich's Final Days."

[2725] See endnote [134] for the Preface "Birth and Memory upon the Lesser Known Fault Line of History."

[2726] See endnote [1992] for Chapter 21 "Valkyrie's Wake."

[2727] See endnote [134] for the Preface "Birth and Memory upon the Lesser Known Fault Line of History."

[2728] See endnote [1992] for Chapter 21 "Valkyrie's Wake."

[2729] See endnote [1993] for Chapter 21 "Valkyrie's Wake."

[2730] See endnote [2300] for Chapter 24 "Dietrich's Final Days."

[2731] See endnote [2300] for Chapter 24 "Dietrich's Final Days."

[2732] Flossenbürg would be liberated a fortnight later by the 90th US Infantry Division on April 23, 1945. See endnote [2914] for Chapter 24 "Dietrich's Final Days."

[2733] SS Obersturmführer (Second Lieutenant) Gogalla was in charge of one the convoys transporting special prisoners south. As well, he was responsible for conveying "Reich Secret Business" files to Flossenbürg, Schönberg and Dachau that contained instructions about who was to be killed and moved further south. See pages 925 to 926 of Bethge and endnotes [2333] to [2339] for Chapter 24 "Dietrich's Final Days."

[2734] [2894] Page 927 of Bethge.

[2735] See endnote [2338] for Chapter 24 "Dietrich's Final Days," as well as position 572.9 and 591.4 of Payne Best and page 926 of Bethge. SS Obersturmführer

(Second Lieutenant) Gogalla, was known to Payne Best since the earliest days of his incarceration in 1939 (position 479.2).

[2736] In regard to General Georg Thomas, see endnote [2569] for Chapter 25 "Old Prussia Gone With The Wind."

[2737] At https://www.gdw-berlin.de/en/recess/biographies/index_of_persons/biographie/view-bio/georg-thomas/. Accessed on Saturday July 25, 2020.

[2738] Page 20 of *Hitler's Commanders: Officers of the Wehrmacht, the Luftwaffe, the Kriegsmarine, and the Waffen-SS, Edition 2, illustrated* by Samuel W. Mitcham Junior and Gene Mueller, published by Rowman & Littlefield Publishers, 2012, ISBN 1442211547, 9781442211544.

[2739] Position 607.0 of Payne Best. However, Payne Best misspells Halder's name as "Haider."

[2740] Ibid.

[2741] Ibid.

[2742] Position 583.1 of Payne Best.

[2743] [2865] This date can be inferred by reading the text from position 631.2 to 632.7 of Payne Best.

[2744] Position 647.3 of Payne Best.

[2745] Position 617.2 of Payne Best.

[2746] [3212] In regard to Martin Niemöller's connection to Dietrich, see endnotes [409] to [428] of Chapter 4 "The Aryan Paragraph" and [454] of Chapter 5 "London Pastorate and the Fanø Conference." The arrest of Martin Niemöller in 1937 is discussed from position 683.5 of Metaxas, position 554.3 of Schlingensiepen and in endnote [866] of Chapter 12 "The Sammelvikariats."

[2747] Position 618.7 of Payne Best.

[2748] [2856] Position 618.2 of Payne Best.

[2749] [2856] This can be inferred from page 930 of Bethge.

[2750] See endnotes [2218] to [2229] for Chapter 24 "Dietrich's Final Days" in regard to the remaining prisoners in the Grüne Minna believing that Müller, Gehre and Liedig were being taken to their certain deaths.

[2751] Position 618.7 of Payne Best.

[2752] See endnote [2224] for Chapter 24 "Dietrich's Final Days."

[2753] Accessed on the Deutscher Marinen (German Naval) website at http://www.marine.de/portal/poc/marine?uri=ci%3Abw.mar.ueberuns.geschichte.reichsundkriegsmarine.widerstand&de.conet.contentintegrator.portlet.current.id=01DB070000000001%7C6FHKR3496INFO on Sunday March 17, 2019. However, this link is now broken.

[2754] The Memorial of the German Resistance at https://www.gdw-berlin.de/en/recess/biographies/index_of_persons/biographie/view-bio/josef-mueller/. Accessed on Saturday July 25, 2020.

[2755] Ibid and https://www.britannica.com/topic/Christian-Social-Union.

[2756] The list at position 732.4 of Payne Best. See also the list of special prisoners on Peter Koblank's website at http://www.mythoselser.de/niederdorf.htm#liste. Accessed on Saturday July 25, 2020. These special prisoners were also known as "Prominenten — Prominent Prisoners" or "Hostages of the SS." See endnotes [2708] onwards from the start of Chapter 27 "The Prominenten and Miraculous Reprieves."

[2757] In regard to how Josef Müller was spared at the last moment, see the National Geographic documentary *Pope Vs Hitler*, released on September 4 2016, written and directed by Christopher Cassel, from 1 hour and 18 minutes to 1 hour and 24 minutes. See also the Internet Movie Database at https://www.imdb.com/title/tt6142740/, accessed on Saturday July 25, 2020 and positions 482.2 and 482.9 of *Church of Spies: The Pope's Secret War Against Hitler* by Mark Riebling, published by Scribe Publications 2015, ISBN 9781925307139. Mark Riebling is one of the historians making several appearances in the documentary *Pope Vs Hitler*.

[2758] Position 942.0 of Schlingensiepen.

[2759] Ibid.

[2760] Ibid.

[2761] Position 442.6 of Mark Riebling.

[2762] Central Intelligence Agency declassified document *The Last Days of Ernst Kaltenbrunner*, dated September 22 1993, which can be viewed online at https://www.cia.gov/library/center-for-the-study-of-intelligence/kent-csi/vol4no2/html/v04i2a07p_0001.htm. Accessed on Saturday July 25, 2020.

[2763] Ibid.

[2764] Position 942.0 of Schlingensiepen.

[2765] Position 442.8 of *Church of Spies: The Pope's Secret War Against Hitler* by Mark Riebling, published by Scribe Publications 2015, ISBN 9781925307139.

[2766] Position 443.0 of Mark Riebling.

[2767] Article on Heinrich Himmler at https://www.britannica.com/biography/Heinrich-Himmler. Accessed on Saturday July 25, 2020.

[2768] Position 85.7 of Mark Riebling.

[2769] Position 87.1 of Mark Riebling.

[2770] See endnotes [314] and [315] of Chapter 2 "Ominous Clouds on the Horizon" in regard to Dietrich agreeing with the overt anti-Christians, such as Himmler, in the National Socialist movement, that Christianity and National Socialism were inherently incompatible.

[2771] See endnotes [312] and [313] of Chapter 2 "Ominous Clouds on the Horizon" in regard to Heinrich Himmler being overtly anti-Christian and desiring of Germany embracing its ancient pagan past. Unlike the German Christians, Himmler had no interest in even the most bastardised form of Christianity, made palatable to National Socialist dogma.

[2772] Position 87.3 of Mark Riebling.

[2773] Position 87.4 of Mark Riebling. Joey the Ox being Josef Müller — in reference to his resilience and tough stocky physical stature.

[2774] Position 87.5 of Mark Riebling.

[2775] Position 85.7 to 87.7 of Mark Riebling.

[2776] Position 402.2 of *Guarding Hitler: THE SECRET WORLD OF THE FÜHRER* by Mark Felton, published by PEN & SWORD MILITARY an imprint of Pen & Sword Books Ltd 2014, Barnsley South Yorkshire S70 2AS, ISBN 9781781593059 eISBN 9781473838383.

[2777] Position 404.5 of *Guarding Hitler: THE SECRET WORLD OF THE FÜHRER* by Mark Felton. Position 402.5 states that only three of the originally intended ten groups ultimately left the bunker.

[2778] Position 402.6 of *Guarding Hitler: THE SECRET WORLD OF THE FÜHRER* by Mark Felton.

[2779] Position 404.8 of *Guarding Hitler: THE SECRET WORLD OF THE FÜHRER* by Mark Felton.

[2780] Page 183 of *Hitler's Death: Russia's Last Great Secret from the Files of the KGB* by V. K. Vinogradov, contributors J. F. Pogonyi, Andrew Roberts, N V Teptzov, published by Chaucer, 2005, ISBN 1904449131, 9781904449133.

[2781] Ibid.

[2782] Page 184 of *Hitler's Death: Russia's Last Great Secret from the Files of the KGB* by V. K. Vinogradov. See this on Google Books at https://books.google.com.au/books?id=bOygAAAAMAAJ&dq=ISBN+19044 49131%2C+9781904449133&focus=searchwithinvolume&q=other+Reich+lea ders. Accessed on Saturday July 25, 2020.

[2783] Ibid on Google Books at https://books.google.com.au/books?id=bOygAAAAMAAJ&dq=ISBN+19044 49131%2C+9781904449133&focus=searchwithinvolume&q=1955. Accessed on Saturday July 25, 2020.

[2784] See endnotes [2651] to [2655] of Chapter 26 "Oma Ruth's Progeny After Death" in regard to Konrad Adenauer's initiative in 1955, to get the Soviet Union to release Germans still interred there.

[2785] *Hitler's Death: Russia's Last Great Secret from the Files of the KGB* on Google Books at https://books.google.com.au/books?id=bOygAAAAMAAJ&dq=ISBN+19044 49131%2C+9781904449133&focus=searchwithinvolume&q=1957. Accessed on Saturday July 25, 2020.

[2786] *Hitler and Hitler Youth in last newsreel* viewed on the website of the United States Holocaust Memorial Museum at https://collections.ushmm.org/search/catalog/irn1004475 on Saturday July 25, 2020.

[2787] Pages 891 to 892 of *The Devil's Disciples: Hitler's Inner Circle* by Anthony Read, published by W.W. Norton, 2005, ISBN 0393326977, 9780393326970.

[2788] Central Intelligence Agency declassified document *The Last Days of Ernst Kaltenbrunner*, dated September 22 1993, which can be viewed online at https://www.cia.gov/library/center-for-the-study-of-intelligence/kent-csi/vol4no2/html/v04i2a07p_0001.htm. Accessed on Saturday July 25, 2020.

[2789] Ibid.

[2790] Ibid. See also the Avalon Project Yale Law School website page on the Nuremberg Trial Proceedings Volume 12 ONE HUNDRED AND FOURTEENTH DAY, Thursday April 25 1946, at http://avalon.law.yale.edu/imt/04-25-46.asp, where Abwehr conspirator Dr. Hans Bernd Gisevius gives his disturbing impressions of Ernst Kaltenbrunner. Accessed on Saturday July 25, 2020.

[2791] Central Intelligence Agency declassified document *The Last Days of Ernst Kaltenbrunner*, dated September 22 1993, which can be viewed online at https://www.cia.gov/library/center-for-the-study-of-intelligence/kent-csi/vol4no2/html/v04i2a07p_0001.htm. Accessed on Saturday July 25, 2020.

[2792] For Pope Pius XII's joyful meeting with Josef Müller on June 1 1945, see the National Geographic documentary *Pope Vs Hitler*, released on September 4, 2016, written and directed by Christopher Cassel, from 1 hour and 22 minutes, while at 1 hour and 23 minutes and 18 seconds, listen to Müller's response to the pontiff's question; "What have you learned?." See also the Internet Movie Database at https://www.imdb.com/title/tt6142740/ for a description of this documentary. Accessed on Saturday July 25, 2020.

[2793] Position 618.2 of Payne Best.

[2794] Position 619.5 of Payne Best.

[2795] National Geographic documentary *Pope Vs Hitler* from 48 minutes and 39 seconds and from 1 hour and 24 minutes.

[2796] The New Zealand government history website at https://nzhistory.govt.nz/war/the-italian-campaign/timeline. Accessed on Saturday July 25, 2020.

[2797] https://www.irishcentral.com/roots/history/vatican-honor-world-war-ii-irish-priest-who-saved-thousands-video, dated May 13 2016 at 02:05 a.m. IrishCentral is the leading Irish digital media company in North America, providing political, current affairs, entertainment, and historical commentary to the worldwide Irish diaspora. See also the Internet Movie Database at https://www.imdb.com/title/tt0086251/?ref_=fn_al_tt_1, in regard to the 1983 movie, *The Scarlet and the Black*, starring Gregory Peck as Monsignor Hugh O'Flaherty. All links accessed on Saturday July 25, 2020.

[2798] National Geographic documentary *Pope Vs Hitler* from 48 minutes and 39 seconds and 1 hour and 24 minutes for Geoffrey Robertson QC and from 1 hour and 24 minutes and 42 seconds for Rabbi Shmuley Boteach.

[2799] [2814] National Geographic documentary *Pope Vs Hitler* from 1 hour and 24 minutes and 42 seconds to 1 hour and 25 minutes.

[2800] Ibid from 48 minutes and 38 seconds to 49 minutes.

[2801] The United Press International Archives website at http://www.upi.com/Archives/1939/03/15/Crowds-defiant-in-Prague-as-Hitler-crosses-Czech-frontier/8148408176316/ gives the date of Wednesday March 15 1939 when Hitler's troops marched into the Czech capital of Prague. As does position 742.0 near the beginning of Chapter 21 "The Great Decision" of Metaxas and page 640 of Bethge. Link accessed on Saturday July 25, 2020.

[2802] In regard to Chamberlain's declaration of "Peace for/in our time," see page 420 of the book *Rise And Fall Of The Third Reich: A History of Nazi Germany* by William L. Shirer, published by Simon and Schuster, 1990, ISBN 0671728687, 9780671728687. Albeit, Chamberlain, as in numerous sources is misquoted as saying "Peace in our time" when he is supposed to have said "Peace **for** our time." See also the official UK government website at https://www.gov.uk/government/history/past-prime-ministers/neville-chamberlain. In any event, the gist of either quote is undoubtedly identical. Link accessed on Saturday July 25, 2020. See also endnote [944] for Chapter 13 "Flight and the Tumultuous Appeasement of Evil."

[2803] As stated from position 636.1 of Schlingensiepen, already by September 27 1939, the day of Poland's surrender, Hitler ordered his general staff to plan invasions of the Netherlands and Belgium in preparation for attacking France. See also pages 2 to 3 of the book *Hitler's Pre-emptive War: The Battle for Norway, 1940* by Henrik O. Lunde, published by Casemate Publishers, 2009, ISBN 1932033920, 9781932033922 and endnotes [1120] to [1122] of Chapter 16 "Homecoming to Outbreak of War."

[2804] Page 22 of *Preaching in Hitler's Shadow: Sermons of Resistance in the Third Reich* by Dean G. Stroud, published by Wm. B. Eerdmans Publishing, 2013, ISBN 0802869025, 9780802869029 documents how Hitler and his closest cohorts did not care much for Christianity, even in the bastardised version created by the pro-Hitler and so-called "German Christian" movement, in attempting to make Christ, compatible with National Socialist dogma. See also endnotes [314] to [315] for Chapter 2 "Ominous Clouds on the Horizon."

[2805] That Heinrich Himmler, the head of the SS was in nostalgic awe of the Germanic victory over the Roman legions in the Teutoburg Forest in 9AD, thus longing for a reversion to the old pagan traditions, is mentioned in the documentary *Nazi Megastructures, Season 2, Episode 4, Himmler's SS*, aired on SBS Australia in Brisbane at 5:30 p.m. on Sunday November 13 2016. Another documentary, specifically on Himmler; *True Evil: The Making Of A Nazi Season 1 Episode 3 — Himmler* aired on SBS Australia in Brisbane at 5:30 p.m. on Sunday October 14 2018, repeatedly makes reference to Himmler's overtly anti-Christian and pagan ancient Germanic mindset.

2806 See endnote 312 for Chapter 2 "Ominous Clouds on the Horizon" for more information on this famous battle from antiquity.

2807 390 In regard to the mindset of the SS, see the 2002 documentary *Die Waffen SS* directed by Christian Fey, English version narrated by Stephen Rashbrook, production company Story House Productions for ZDF - Zweites Deutsches Fernsehen in co-operation with Channel Four, The History Channel and ZDF Enterprises, from 5 minutes and 11 seconds. Thirty-three seconds later, at 5 minutes and 44 seconds is the SS claim; "Christ was the illegitimate son of a Jewish whore."

2808 390 From 5 minutes and 32 seconds in the 2002 documentary *Die Waffen SS* directed by Christian Fey, English version narrated by Stephen Rashbrook.

2809 390 See the bottom of page 21 of *Preaching in Hitler's Shadow: Sermons of Resistance in the Third Reich* by Dean G. Stroud, published by Wm. B. Eerdmans Publishing, 2013, ISBN 0802869025, 9780802869029 and endnote 313 for Chapter 2 "Ominous Clouds on the Horizon" in regard to the Nazis perceiving the cross as a symbol of shame, weakness and synonymous humility, and as such, their new Germany being the one to achieve what Christ failed to do.

2810 National Geographic documentary *Pope Vs Hitler* from 1 hour and 25 minutes and 14 seconds. See also, immediately following, the assessment of the pontiff by Robert M. Edsel, the author of *Saving Italy* and Chairman of the Board for The Monuments Men Foundation For the Preservation of Art. Their website is at https://www.monumentsmenfoundation.org/about-the-foundation/directors-page. Accessed on Saturday July 25, 2020.

2811 The fact that the passing of the resolution in favour of Bell's "Ascension Day Message" was a hollow one in the long term is documented at positions 568.7 and 569.1 of Metaxas and position 464.6 of Schlingensiepen. See also page 385 of Bethge, which states that later, Dietrich had to admit that Fanø was nothing more than a short-lived climax. See also endnotes 471 to 473 for Chapter 5 "London Pastorate and the Fanø Conference."

2812 National Geographic documentary *Pope Vs Hitler* from 9 minutes and 31 seconds to 10 minutes and 9 seconds.

2813 National Geographic documentary *Pope Vs Hitler* from 51 minutes and 53 seconds to 52 minutes and 36 seconds.

2814 See endnote 2799 for this chapter.

2815 See endnotes 2053 and 2054 for Chapter 22 "Prinz-Albrecht-Strasse."

2816 See endnote 2054 for Chapter 22 "Prinz-Albrecht-Strasse."

2817 See endnote 2041 for Chapter 22 "Prinz-Albrecht-Strasse."

2818 See endnotes 2022 and 2040 for Chapter 22 "Prinz-Albrecht-Strasse."

2819 See endnotes 2067 and 2070 for Chapter 22 "Prinz-Albrecht-Strasse."

2820 See endnote 1259 for Chapter 17 "Pastor and Spy."

2821 See endnote 638 for Chapter 6 "Old Prussia — Birth of Ruth to Precarious Survival."

2822 See endnotes [1647] and [1707] of Chapter 20 "Valkyrie II."

2823 See endnote [2054] for Chapter 22 "Prinz-Albrecht-Strasse."

2824 See endnotes [2501] and [2502] of Chapter 25 "Old Prussia Gone With The Wind."

2825 To see how close Ruth and her eldest son Hans Jürgen were to Ewald von Kleist of Schmenzin, see endnotes [718] to [723] of Chapter 9 "The von Kleists and the Prophecy."

2826 See endnotes [2041] and [2042] for Chapter 22 "Prinz-Albrecht-Strasse" in regard to this bombing raid on Berlin in early February 1945.

2827 See endnote [2504] of Chapter 25 "Old Prussia Gone With The Wind."

2828 Position 533.8 of the ebook *The Secret War Against Hitler* by Fabian von Schlabrendorff, published by Routledge, 2018, ISBN 0813321905, ISBN 13: 9780813321905 (paperback).

2829 See endnotes [2053] and [2054] for Chapter 22 "Prinz-Albrecht-Strasse," which gives the date of February 7, 1945 when Dietrich's party left Prinz-Albrecht-Strasse for Buchenwald, and then endnotes [2187] to [2194] of Chapter 24 "Dietrich's Final Days," which give the first days of April 1945, when Dietrich's party left Buchenwald.

2830 Position 533.9 of the ebook *The Secret War Against Hitler* by Fabian von Schlabrendorff, published by Routledge, 2018, ISBN 0813321905, ISBN 13: 9780813321905 (paperback).

2831 Ibid position 533.9.

2832 Ibid position 534.0.

2833 Ibid.

2834 Ibid.

2835 Ibid.

2836 Ibid.

2837 [719] Hitler was obsessively enamoured with Frederick the Great. See for example endnotes [47], [140] and [141] for the Preface "Birth and Memory upon the Lesser Known Fault Line of History."

2838 Position 534.0 of *The Secret War Against Hitler* by Fabian von Schlabrendorff,

2839 Ibid.

2840 Ibid.

2841 Ibid position 535.0.

2842 Ibid.

2843 Ibid.

2844 Ibid position 535.8.

2845 Ibid position 536.0.

2846 Ibid position 535.8.

2847 Ibid position 535.2.

2848 Ibid position 536.1.

2849 Ibid position 536.5. See also endnote 2341 for Chapter 24 "Dietrich's Final Days."

2850 Ibid position 536.8.

2851 Ibid position 536.9.

2852 Ibid position 537.1.

2853 Ibid position 537.2.

2854 Ibid position 537.7.

2855 Ibid position 538.0.

2856 See endnotes 2748 to 2749 for this chapter.

2857 2875 2900 Jørgen Lønborg Friis Mogensen, had a brief but most interesting account of his life given on the website of the Embassy of the Republic of Poland in Copenhagen at http://www.kopenhaga.msz.gov.pl/en/bilateral_cooperation/historical_relations/famous_people/j_rgen_l_nborg_friis_mogensen;jsessionid=B2C54E453A9F0090DC10FFC1C131E8D5.cmsap2p, accessed on March 16, 2019. This link however, is now broken.

2858 2900 Ibid. However, this link however, is now broken.

2859 Position 538.2 of the ebook *The Secret War Against Hitler* by Fabian von Schlabrendorff, published by Routledge, 2018, ISBN 0813321905, ISBN 13: 9780813321905 (paperback).

2860 Ibid position 538.5.

2861 Ibid position 538.8.

2862 Ibid position 538.9.

2863 Position 539.3 of the ebook *The Secret War Against Hitler* by Fabian von Schlabrendorff, published by Routledge, 2018, ISBN 0813321905, ISBN 13: 9780813321905 (paperback).

2864 See endnote 2237 of Chapter 24 "Dietrich's Final Days."

2865 See endnote 2743 for this chapter.

2866 Position 540.8 of the ebook *The Secret War Against Hitler* by Fabian von Schlabrendorff, published by Routledge, 2018, ISBN 0813321905, ISBN 13: 9780813321905 (paperback).

2867 Ibid position 541.0.

2868 Position 649.3 of Payne Best.

2869 See positions 540.8 to 543.0 of the ebook *The Secret War Against Hitler* by Fabian von Schlabrendorff, published by Routledge, 2018, ISBN 0813321905, ISBN 13: 9780813321905 (paperback).

2870 Positions 402.2 and 423.5, as well as the description of the photo at position 239.0 of *Guarding Hitler: THE SECRET WORLD OF THE FÜHRER* by Mark Felton, published by PEN & SWORD MILITARY an imprint of Pen & Sword Books Ltd 2014, Barnsley South Yorkshire S70 2AS, ISBN 9781781593059 eISBN 9781473838383.

[2871] Position 537.4 of the ebook *The Secret War Against Hitler* by Fabian von Schlabrendorff, published by Routledge, 2018, ISBN 0813321905, ISBN 13: 9780813321905 (paperback).

[2872] Fabian's liberation in Niederdorf is covered in more detail in endnotes [2567] to [2571] for Chapter 25 "Old Prussia Gone With The Wind." See also endnote [2324] of Chapter 24 "Dietrich's Final Days," in regard to their liberation by Wehrmacht forces, involving a confrontation with SS commander Untersturmführer (Second Leiutenant) Ernst Bader at gunpoint. Bear in mind, that Fabian in his book, at position 543.0, incorrectly gives the name of this German speaking village in the Italian Tyrol, as Niedernhausen — which is a German village just west of Frankfurt am Main. He is correct however, in saying at position 543.0, that it is in the Puster valley south of the Brenner Pass.

[2873] For the languages spoken in the South Tyrol region see the South Tyrol information web page at https://www.suedtirol.info/en/this-is-south-tyrol/people/languages. Accessed on Saturday July 25, 2020.

[2874] [2900] [3212] See endnote [428] for Chapter 4 "The Aryan Paragraph" for lists of the Prominenten liberated in Niederdorf on April 30, 1945.

[2875] See endnote [2857] for this chapter.

[2876] Position 548.0 of *The Secret War Against Hitler* by Fabian von Schlabrendorff, published by Routledge, 2018, ISBN 0813321905, ISBN 13: 9780813321905 (paperback). See also endnote [2571] of Chapter 25 "Old Prussia Gone With The Wind."

[2877] Position 548.0 of *The Secret War Against Hitler*. See also endnote [2571] of Chapter 25 "Old Prussia Gone With The Wind."

[2878] Ibid.

[2879] Position 635.3 of Nigel Jones in the Dramatis Personae.

[2880] Pages 385 to 386 of Jane Pejsa.

[2881] The dates of birth and death for Luitgarde, the wife of Fabian von Schlabrendorff, are documented at https://www.geni.com/people/Luitgarde-von-Schlabrendorff/6000000015672813962 on Geni: A Genealogy Website. Likewise for her husband at https://www.geni.com/people/Fabian-Ludwig-v-Schlabrendorff/6000000015672978316. Both links accessed on Saturday July 25, 2020.

[2882] Ibid.

Chapter 28 — Memory Transcending Executioners ' Legal but Criminal Flights from Justice

[2883] Position 1215.9 of Metaxas. While Schlingensiepen at position 988.0 states that Dietrich was accompanied by Friedrich von Rabenau to Flossenbürg, it now seems likely that Rabenau was taken from Schönberg three days later on April 11, and executed in Flossenbürg on April 15. See the online article *The Murder of General Friedrich von Rabenau When, Where and How Did It Hap-*

pen? by Frode Weierud, dated April 2005, on his Crypto Cellar website at https://cryptocellar.org/Rabenau/index.html. The German language presentation by Professor Dr. Eberhard Dünninger, mentioned by Frode Weierud, and confirming the latter's conclusions, can be accessed online on the Wayback Machine at https://web.archive.org/web/20070924232823/http://www.bayerischer-wald-verein.de/archiv/archivbaywald/2001/01/bonhoeffer.htm. All links accessed Saturday July 25, 2020. Frode Weierud is a retired Norwegian electronics engineer formerly employed by the European Organisation for Particle Physics (CERN) in Geneva, with cryptography being his main interest for close to 50 years.

[2884] Page 927 of Bethge.

[2885] Position 988.0 of Schlingensiepen.

[2886] See Polish WWII Supplement II "The Gleiwitz (Gliwice) Incident."[3537]

[2887] In regard to the Gleiwitz incident on August 31 1939, see Polish WWII Supplement II "The Gleiwitz (Gliwice) Incident"[3537] and position 938.1 of Microcosm and *Nuremberg Trial Proceedings Volume 4 TWENTY-FOURTH DAY Thursday December 20 1945 Morning Session*, which can be viewed at http://avalon.law.yale.edu/imt/12-20-45.asp. Accessed on Saturday July 25, 2020. The latter source makes mention of the major involvement of Reinhard Heydrich, head of the SD and Chief of the Security Police, in the operation.

[2888] See Chapter 17 "'Cleansing' the Soviet Elite" of Part 5 "Stalin's Reign of Terror" from page 267 onwards of *Lenin, Stalin and Hitler The Age of Social Catastrophe* by Robert Gellately, published by Vintage 2008, ISBN 9780712603577.

[2889] A diagram of the competing intelligence agencies in Hitler's Reich is given at position 209.0 of the ebook *Hitler's Spy Chief The Wilhelm Canaris Mystery* by Richard Bassett, published by The Orion Publishing Group Limited, 2011, a Hachette UK company, ISBN 9780297865711. Note the Abwehr being separate to RSHA under Himmler. See also endnote [1183] for Chapter 17 "Pastor and Spy."

[2890] Page 927 of Bethge and position 1215.2 of Metaxas. From this point on, these sources make no mention of Friedrich von Rabenau. Also, the Danish prisoner and former intelligence officer Colonel Lunding, would be among the liberated in Niederdorf in late April.

[2891] [3212] See endnote [428] for Chapter 4 "The Aryan Paragraph" for lists of the Prominenten liberated in Niederdorf on April 30, 1945.

[2892] See endnote [2020] for Chapter 21 "Valkyrie's Wake." This gives the unabridged quote.

[2893] Pages 512-513 of the book *Letters and Papers from Prison Volume 8 of Dietrich Bonhoeffer Works* by Dietrich Bonhoeffer, editors Christian Gremmels, John W. De Gruchy, published by Fortress Press, 2010, ISBN 1451406789, 9781451406788, quotes Dietrich's poem *"Stations on the Way to*

Freedom." Footnote #2 on page 512 states that this poem was probably written to Bethge on August 14 1944.

[2894] Pages 927-928 of Bethge and position 1218.3 of Metaxas. The latter however, mentions General Thomas in this list, which is not possible, as he survived the war. See endnote [2734] for Chapter 27 "The Prominenten and Miraculous Reprieves."

[2895] Page 228 of *I Knew Dietrich Bonhoeffer* as told by Fabian von Schlabrendorff, edited by Wolf-Dieter Zimmermann, Ronald Gregor Smith published by Harper & Row, 1967 (No ISBN given). This can also be accessed online at Google Books at https://books.google.com.au/books?redir_esc=y&id=TaSPAAAAMAAJ&focus=searchwithinvolume&q=Dohnányi. Accessed on Saturday July 25, 2020. See also position 1141.8 of Metaxas.

[2896] For the curious case of SS Totenkopf (Death's Head) doctor Waldemar Hoven, see endnotes [2125] to [2151] of Chapter 23, "Buchenwald."

[2897] Waldemar Hoven was, until 1943, the SS camp doctor at Buchenwald and originally, one of Dietrich's fellow inmates at Buchenwald. At the Nuremberg trails, many former inmates would testify they owed their survival to him. When Sigmund Rascher appeared at Buchenwald among Dietrich's fellow special prisoners, he gave Payne Best an account of the numerous medical experiments he unashamedly carried out on human subjects. See endnotes [2125] to [2151] for Chapter 23 "Buchenwald" in regard to Waldemar Hoven and endnotes [2152] to [2167] in regard to Sigmund Rascher. In particular, endnote [2166], contains a link to Nuremberg trial documents which contain photos of the experiments carried out by Sigmund Rasher. BEWARE, THESE PHOTOS ARE TERRIBLY DISTURBING.

[2898] Page 311 of the book *Von guten Mächten wunderbar geborgen... "Dietrich Bonhoeffer.: Theologe, Pastor und Dichter im Widerstand gegen Hitler. Mit einem `Who is Who` zu Dietrich Bonhoeffer und seiner Zeit* (By loving forces wonderfully sheltered... Dietrich Bonhoeffer: theologian, pastor and poet in the resistance against Hitler. With a Who's Who to Dietrich Bonhoeffer and his time) by Thomas O. H. Kaiser, Edition 3, published by BoD — Books on Demand, 2014, ISBN-10 3735762255, ISBN-13 9783735762252.

[2899] Sammlung Rüter, Volume XIII, no. 436 — *Sammlung Rüter, Bd. XIII, Lfd. Nr. 436* https://www.expostfacto.nl/junsv/ncot/brdeng/vols01.html **(Note: Click on number 436 in the left panel)** on the website for the historical legal project *Foundation for Research on National-Socialist Crimes, Amsterdam — (Justiz und NS-Verbrechen).* Its credentials can be viewed at https://www.expostfacto.nl/about.html. Both links accessed on Saturday July 25, 2020. See also page 29 of the book *Der "Prozess" gegen Dietrich Bonhoeffer und die Freilassung seiner Mörder* (The "trial" against Dietrich Bonhoeffer and the release of his murderers) by Christoph Ulrich Schminck-Gustavus, published by J.H.W. Dietz Nachfolger, 1995, (no ISBN given).

[2900] In regard to Jørgen Lønborg Friis Mogensen, see endnotes [2857], [2858] and [2874] and footnote [xxxiv] for Chapter 27 "The Prominenten and Miraculous Reprieves."

[2901] Position 988.0 of Schlingensiepen. Then click on the link at footnote #9.

[2902] The *Foundation for Research on National-Socialist Crimes, Amsterdam* website at https://www.junsv.nl/cgi/t/text/text-idx?c=justizw&cc=justizw&idno=w13&type=boolean&lang=en&rgn=div3&q1=unmittelbar&op2=and&q2=Canaris&op3=and&q3=, about two-thirds of the way down. As does https://www.expostfacto.nl/junsv/ncot/brdeng/vols01.html. See also http://www.tenhumbergreinhard.de/taeter-und-mitlaeufer/dokumente/das-standgericht-in-flossenbuerg.html on the website of the *Familie Tenhumberg*. All links accessed on Saturday July 25, 2020.

[2903] The National Geographic documentary *Pope Vs Hitler*, released on September 4 2016, written and directed by Christopher Cassel, from 1 hour and 16 minutes and 38 seconds to 1 hour and 16 minutes and 51 seconds. See also the Internet Movie Database at https://www.imdb.com/title/tt6142740/. Accessed on Saturday July 25, 2020.

[2904] Ibid from 1 hour and 17 minutes and 27 seconds to 1 hour and 17 minutes and 37 seconds.

[2905] Ibid from 1 hour and 17 minutes and 45 seconds to 1 hour and 18 minutes and 35 seconds.

[2906] Position 1217.8 of Metaxas and pages 927 to 928 of Bethge.

[2907] Fischer's year of birth is given as 1883 at https://www.junsv.nl/cgi/t/text/text-idx?type=simple;rgn=full%20text;lang=en;c=justizw;cc=justizw;idno=w13;q1=Fischer;submit=Go;view=reslist;subview=detail;didno=w13;start=31;size=10 on the website for Foundation for Research on National-Socialist Crimes, Amsterdam. Accessed on Saturday July 25, 2020.

[2908] See for example endnotes [1763] to [1771], [1773] to [1775] and [1793] to [1796] of Chapter 20 "Valkyrie II" in regard to various sources giving conflicting versions of events.

[2909] See endnotes [65] to [70] of the Preface "Birth and Memory upon the Lesser Known Fault Line of History."

[2910] Page 928 of Bethge and position 1219.1 of Metaxas.

[2911] Position 447.0 of Mark Riebling.

[2912] Ibid.

[2913] Position 988.0 of Schlingensiepen.

[2914] [2732] The article on the Flossenbürg concentration camp at https://www.ushmm.org/wlc/en/article.php?ModuleId=10005537. Accessed on Saturday July 25, 2020.

[2915] Page 930 of Bethge. Three inaccuracies in the telegram; Klaus being supposedly murdered in Clossburg, Dietrich supposedly being executed on April 15 1945, rather than the 9th, and the incorrect spelling of "Clossburg" in the telegram must be referring to Flossenbürg. However, the gist is true — both Bonhoeffer brothers by that time were dead. See also page 126 of *George Bell, Bishop of Chichester: Church, State, and Resistance in the Age of Dictatorship*" by Andrew Chandler, published by Wm. B. Eerdmans Publishing, 2016, ISBN 0802872271, 9780802872272.

[2916] Page 184 of *The Bonhoeffers; Portrait of a Family* by Sabine Leibholz-Bonhoeffer, published by Sidgwick and Jackson, 1971, no ISBN given, and position 1220.3 of Metaxas.

[2917] Page 184 of *The Bonhoeffers; Portrait of a Family* by Sabine Leibholz-Bonhoeffer and position 1220.6 of Metaxas.

[2918] Page 185 of *The Bonhoeffers; Portrait of a Family* by Sabine Leibholz-Bonhoeffer and position 1221.5 of Metaxas.

[2919] See endnotes [1665] to [1667] and [1810] to [1815] in regard to Fromm and endnotes [1816] to [1833] for Kluge from Chapter 20 "Valkyrie II."

[2920] Page 185 of *The Bonhoeffers; Portrait of a Family* by Sabine Leibholz-Bonhoeffer and position 1221.9 of Metaxas.

[2921] Page 186 of *The Bonhoeffers; Portrait of a Family* by Sabine Leibholz-Bonhoeffer and position 1222.2 of Metaxas.

[2922] Page 186 of *The Bonhoeffers; Portrait of a Family* by Sabine Leibholz-Bonhoeffer and position 1222.6 of Metaxas.

[2923] In regard to Katyń, see Polish WWII Supplement III "The Katyń Wood Massacre"[3618] and pages 44, 48, 115 to 116 of Norman Davies' book *Rising '44: The Battle for Warsaw*, by Professor Norman Davies, published by Penguin Books; Reprint edition (October 4, 2005), ISBN-10: 0143035401, ISBN-13: 9780143035404. On page 48, Davies states that Stalin personally signed the order for their execution. See also https://library.eb.com.au/levels/adults/article/Katyn-Massacre/44867 which states that in all likelihood, over 20,000 Poles were executed. Accessed on Saturday July 25, 2020.

[2924] See endnote [4110] of Polish WWII Supplement IV "AK and 1944 Warsaw General Uprising — Stalin's mass murder by German proxy" in regard to Eden's attitude of appeasement towards the Soviets.

[2925] In regard to perhaps the most cynical German conspirator of all, Arthur Nebe, see endnotes [1963] to [1970] of Chapter 20 "Valkyrie II."

[2926] See position 333.0 onwards of Nigel Jones.

[2927] Position 290.3 onwards of Metaxas and page 404 of *A testament to freedom: the essential writings of Dietrich Bonhoeffer* by Dietrich Bonhoeffer, edited by Geffrey B. Kelly and F. Burton, published by HarperSanFrancisco, 1990, ISBN 0060608137, 9780060608132. See also endnotes [299] and [302] for Chapter 2 "Ominous Clouds on the Horizon."

[2928] Page 930 of Bethge.

[2929] Position 623.3 in the Dramatis Personae of Nigel Jones. See also position 404.9.

[2930] Position 1223.5 of Metaxas.

[2931] Page 930 of Bethge, position 1226.7 of Metaxas and page 188 of *The Bonhoeffers; Portrait of a Family* by Sabine Leibholz-Bonhoeffer.

[2932] Page 930 of Bethge.

[2933] Position 1226.7 of Metaxas and page 930 of Bethge.

[2934] Page 115 of *Doctor Franz Hildebrandt Mr-Valiant-for-Truth* by Amos S. Cresswell, Maxwell G. Tow, published by Gracewing Publishing, 2000, ISBN 0852443226, 9780852443224.

[2935] Page 188 of *The Bonhoeffers; Portrait of a Family* by Sabine Leibholz-Bonhoeffer and position 1225.9 of Metaxas.

[2936] Page 189 of *The Bonhoeffers; Portrait of a Family* by Sabine Leibholz-Bonhoeffer and position 1231.7 of Metaxas.

[2937] Page 189 of *The Bonhoeffers; Portrait of a Family* by Sabine Leibholz-Bonhoeffer and position 1231.9 of Metaxas.

[2938] See endnote [275] of Chapter 1 "Roots, Genesis and Moulding of the Pastor" in regard to Dietrich's first meeting with Franz Hildebrandt.

[2939] Position 178.0 of Metaxas and page 3 of *Authentic Faith: Bonhoeffer's Theological Ethics in Context* by Heinz Eduard Todt, published by Wm. B. Eerdmans Publishing, 2007, ISBN 0802803822, 9780802803825. See also endnote [262] of Chapter 1 "Roots, Genesis and Moulding of the Pastor" in regard to Dietrich's graduation with "summa cum laude" — highest honours.

[2940] The successful flight of Franz Hildebrandt to Switzerland and ultimately to London is covered from position 687.5 to 688.2 of Metaxas and position 555.0 of Schlingensiepen, with both making mention of Dietrich's family being instrumental in his successful flight from Germany. See also endnote [868] of Chapter 12 "The Sammelvikariats."

[2941] See endnotes [354], [396], [399], [405], [407], [409], [410], [420], [421], [425] and [427] of Chapter 4 "The Aryan Paragraph" in regard to Dietrich and Franz Hildebrandt being it seems, the only voices in 1933 speaking out against the Aryan Paragraph.

[2942] See endnote [868] of Chapter 12 "The Sammelvikariats."

[2943] Position 599.8 of Schlingensiepen and position 746.2 of Metaxas. See also endnote [1037] for Chapter 15 "New York — Troubled Revisiting."

[2944] Position 796.5 of Metaxas, page 661 of Bethge and endnote [1088] for Chapter 15 "New York — Troubled Revisiting" for Dietrich's final ever meeting with Franz Hildebrandt.

[2945] Position 1232.3 of Metaxas. That this was the reading chosen by Franz Hildebrandt, for his eulogy in honour of Dietrich, is also documented on page 114 of *Doctor Franz Hildebrandt Mr-Valiant-for-Truth* by Amos S. Cresswell, Maxwell G. Tow, published by Gracewing Publishing, 2000, ISBN 0852443226, 9780852443224.

[2946] For the various English translations of the theme for Franz Hildebrandt's sermon from the Old Testament Second Book of Chronicles, chapter 20, verse 12, see the Bible Study Tools website at https://www.biblestudytools.com/2-

chronicles/20-12.html which has the translation according to the New Living Translation (NLV), while https://www.biblestudytools.com/bible-versions/ gives a description of the various Bible versions and translations. Also, the Bible Gateway at https://www.biblegateway.com/versions/New-Living-Translation-NLT-Bible/ gives a similar description of the NLV. All links accessed on Saturday July 25, 2020.

[2947] Page 114 of *Doctor Franz Hildebrandt Mr-Valiant-for-Truth* by Amos S. Cresswell, Maxwell G. Tow, published by Gracewing Publishing, 2000, ISBN 0852443226, 9780852443224.

[2948] The drafting of the "Bethel Confession" by Dietrich and Hermann Sasse for three weeks in August 1933, followed by its watering down by theologians nationwide to a document supine to the National Socialist regime, is stated from position 437.2 of Metaxas onwards, position 382.0 of Schlingensiepen and pages 302 and 325 of Bethge. Schlingensiepen states that this was a major factor in Dietrich ultimately taking up his eighteen month London pastorate. This is also strongly implied in Bethge. See also endnotes [422] and [446] for Chapter 4 "The Aryan Paragraph."

[2949] Position 465.0 of Metaxas and page 135 London: 1933-1935, vol. 13, Dietrich Bonhoeffer Works, edited by Keith Clements, translated by Isabel Best, published by New York: Fortress Press, 2007, ISBN 0800683137, 9780800683139. See also page 326 of Bethge and endnote [451] of Chapter 5 "London Pastorate and the Fanø Conference."

[2950] See positions 437.9, 450.9, 465.0 and 478.0 of Metaxas and positions 382.0 and 399.0 of Schlingensiepen.

[2951] See endnotes [413] and [414] for Chapter 4 "The Aryan Paragraph" in regard to Dietrich's first meeting with George Bell.

[2952] Position 862.5 of Schlingensiepen and page 813 of Bethge. See also endnotes [1535] and in particular, [1557] of Chapter 19 "The Tormentor Tormented" in regard to how Dietrich and Hans von Dohnányi never implicated anybody in the Resistance. As well, endnotes [2405] and [2406] of Chapter 25 "Old Prussia Gone with the Wind."

[2953] See endnote [2029] of Chapter 22 "Prinz-Albrecht-Strasse" for a similar instance where Admiral Canaris, the head of the Abwehr, likewise confounded his tormentors.

[2954] See endnotes [1539] to [1550] of Chapter 19 "The Tormentor Tormented" in regard to how Dietrich's time at Tegel prison became relatively routine.

[2955] See endnotes [2041] and [2042] for Chapter 22 "Prinz-Albrecht-Strasse" in regard to this bombing raid on Berlin in early February 1945.

[2956] In regard to Dietrich's conversation with Hans von Dohnányi while returning from the air raid shelter at Prinz-Albrecht-Strasse on Fenruary 3 1945, see position 1143.8 of Metaxas. See also page 228 of the book *I Knew Dietrich Bonhoeffer* as told by Fabian von Schlabrendorff, edited by Wolf-Dieter Zimmermann, Ronald Gregor Smith published by Harper & Row, 1967, no ISBN given. That this took place on February 3 1945 while the air raid siren was blaring, see position 957.4 of Schlingensiepen. See also endnote [2040] of Chapter 22 "Prinz-Albrecht-Strasse."

[2957] In regard to how Dietrich calmly faced his arrest at Schönberg on Sunday April 8 1945, see position 571.6 of Payne Best, position 1209.2 of Metaxas and endnote [2348] of Chapter 24 "Dietrich's Final Days."

[2958] In regard to Holocaust denial, see the online article *HOLOCAUST DENIAL TIMELINE* at https://www.ushmm.org/wlc/en/article.php?ModuleId=10008003. Accessed on Saturday July 25, 2020.

[2959] Position 1239.0 of Metaxas. This quote can also be found on page xv of *On Faith: Lessons from an American Believer* by Antonin Scalia, edited by Christopher J. Scalia and Edward Whelan, contributor Justice Clarence Thomas, published by Crown Publishing Group, 2019, ISBN 1984823329, 9781984823328.

[2960] Position 1239.0 of Metaxas.

[2961] Pages 114 to 115 of *Doctor Franz Hildebrandt Mr-Valiant-for-Truth* by Amos S. Cresswell, Maxwell G. Tow, published by Gracewing Publishing, 2000, ISBN 0852443226, 9780852443224.

[2962] The Internationale Bonhoeffer-Gesellschaft (IBG), Deutschsprachige Sektion (International Bonhoeffer Society IBG), at https://www.dietrich-bonhoeffer.net/bonhoeffer-umfeld/gerhard-leibholz/ details the life of Gerhard Leibholz in German. Accessed on Saturday July 25, 2020. See also endnotes [263] and [264] of Chapter 1 "Roots, Genesis and Moulding of the Pastor."

[2963] Page 115 of *Doctor Franz Hildebrandt Mr-Valiant-for-Truth* by Amos S. Cresswell, Maxwell G. Tow, published by Gracewing Publishing, 2000, ISBN 0852443226, 9780852443224.

[2964] Ibid page 206. See also The Internationale Bonhoeffer-Gesellschaft (IBG), Deutschsprachige Sektion (International Bonhoeffer Society IBG), at https://www.dietrich-bonhoeffer.net/bonhoeffer-umfeld/franz-hildebrandt/. Accessed on Saturday July 25, 2020.

[2965] The date for the unveiling of the statues being Thursday July 9 1998 is given at the very top of the BBC online article at http://news.bbc.co.uk/2/hi/uk_news/129587.stm. See also the year of 1998 given on the Westminster homepage for the Modern Martyrs at https://www.westminster-abbey.org/about-the-abbey/history/modern-martyrs/. On this web page, a link to the BBC article is given. Both links accessed on Saturday July 25, 2020.

[2966 2992] Position 989.0 of Schlingensiepen, at the start of the epilogue, documents that Dietrich's statue is among the statues of the "Ten Martyrs of the 20th Century" above the west portal of London's Westminster Cathedral. His statue being the seventh from the left holding the open bible. See the photo just below. A view of all ten martyrs can be seen on Google Maps Street View at https://www.google.com.au/maps/@51.4994904,-0.128975,3a,15y,93.91h,100.6t/data=!3m6!1e1!3m4!1sFdTN4l2OZm20HxLEnfY0Vw!2e0!7i13312!8i6656, where Dietrich, with bible in his right hand, as seen in Schlingensiepen's photo, is the seventh from the left. Photos of all ten martyrs above the western portal can also be found on the official Westminster Abbey website at https://www.westminster-abbey.org/about-the-abbey/history/modern-martyrs/. On this page, links are given for more information on the individual lives of the ten martyrs. All links accessed on Saturday July 25, 2020. However, the order of these links given does not match the actual order of the statues from left to right, which is as follows:

i) Saint Maximilian Kolbe of Poland
ii) Manche Masemola of South Africa
iii) Janani Luwum of Uganda
iv) Grand Duchess Elizabeth of Russia
v) Martin Luther King Junior of the USA
vi) Blessed Oscar Romero of El Salvador
vii) Dietrich Bonhoeffer of Germany
viii) Esther John, born in British India in 1929, murdered in Pakistan in 1960.
ix) Lucian Tapiedi of Papua New Guinea
x) Wang Zhiming of China

This order can be inferred from photos of all ten statues above Westminster Abbey's west portal, as well as photos of individual statues on the official website of Westminster Abbey at https://www.westminster-abbey.org/about-the-abbey/history/modern-martyrs/. This link accessed on Saturday July 25, 2020.

[2967] Page 346 of *Westminster Abbey: The Lady Chapel of Henry VII* edited by T. W. T. Tatton-Brown and Richard Mortimer, published by Boydell & Brewer, 2003, ISBN 184383037X, 9781843830375 and *Westminster Abbey: Official Guide*, contributors E. D. Nixon, Westminster Abbey, published by Dean and Chapter of Westminster, documents the cathedral's restorative work from 1973 to 1995. See also https://www.westminster-abbey.org/abbey-commemorations/commemorations/st-maximilian-kolbe under the section at the beginning entitled "Introduction to the ten modern martyr statues." Accessed on Saturday July 25, 2020.

[2968] Photos of all ten martyrs above the western portal can also be found on the official Westminster Abbey website at https://www.westminster-abbey.org/about-the-abbey/history/modern-martyrs/. On this page, links are given for more information on the individual lives of the ten martyrs. Accessed on Saturday July 25, 2020.

[2969] Ibid.

[2970] Starting from the Westminster Abbey homepage for the Ten Modern Martyrs at https://www.westminster-abbey.org/about-the-abbey/history/modern-martyrs/, brief articles on all ten martyrs can be found. However, in the case of the Polish martyr Saint Maximilian Kolbe at https://www.westminster-abbey.org/abbey-commemorations/commemorations/st-maximilian-kolbe/, the Auschwitz prison number given for him, namely "16770," is incorrect. The correct number being "16670." Put another way, the correct number is the number containing double six "66," not double seven "77." The correct Auschwitz prison numbers can be searched on the official Auschwitz Museum website at http://auschwitz.org/en/museum/auschwitz-prisoners/. Try Googling "Prisoner 16670" then "Prisoner 16770" and find the numerous articles which erroneously assign this latter prison number to Maximilian Kolbe, including the aforementioned Westminster Abbey article. Moreover, two photos I took in 2005 and 2008 of the painting of Maximilian Kolbe in his chapel in Poland's holiest shrine of Jasna Góra in Częstchowa — dating back to 1382, clearly show the correct prisoner number of "16670." All links accessed on Saturday July 25, 2020.

[2971] The article on Maximilian Kolbe on the Westminster Abbey website at https://www.westminster-abbey.org/abbey-commemorations/commemorations/st-maximilian-kolbe after the section at the beginning entitled "Introduction to the ten modern martyr statues." Accessed on Saturday July 25, 2020.

[2972] Position 103.6 of the ebook *Maximilian Kolbe* by Elaine Murray Stone, illustrated by Patrick Kelley, published by Paulist Press, 1997, ISBN 0809166372, 9780809166374, documents his first arrest by the Nazis on September 19 1939.

[2973] Position 95.0 of the ebook *Maximilian Kolbe* by Elaine Murray Stone, illustrated by Patrick Kelley, published by Paulist Press, 1997, ISBN 0809166372, 9780809166374, states the name of the Friary being Niepokalanów. Note: The correct Polish spelling is Niepokalanów — not the Anglicised Niepokalanow. See the friary official website at https://niepokalanow.pl/sanktuarium/kaplica-sw-maksymiliana/. Accessed on Saturday July 25, 2020.

[2974] Ibid position 109.3. Note: The Feast of the Immaculate Conception is held in early December. Position 103.6 documents his first arrest by the Nazis on September 19 1939, while at https://www.britannica.com/topic/Immaculate-Conception-Roman-Catholicism, states the date of this feast being the 8th of December. Accessed on Saturday July 25, 2020.

[2975] Position 113.2 of the ebook *Maximilian Kolbe* by Elaine Murray Stone, illustrated by Patrick Kelley, published by Paulist Press, 1997, ISBN 0809166372, 9780809166374.

[2976] Ibid position 114.7.

[2977] Ibid position 125.0.

[2978] Ibid.

[2979] Ibid.

[2980] Ibid.

[2981] Type in prisoner number 5659 at http://auschwitz.org/en/museum/auschwitz-prisoners/ on the official website of the Auschwitz Museum. Franciszek Gajowniczek was born on November 15 1901, while Father Kolbe was born on January 8 1894. For Kolbe, type in Prisoner number 16670. Accessed on Saturday July 25, 2020.

[2982] Position 138.5 of the ebook *Maximilian Kolbe* by Elaine Murray Stone, illustrated by Patrick Kelley, published by Paulist Press, 1997, ISBN 0809166372, 9780809166374.

[2983] The DK Holocaust website article on Father Maximilian Kolbe article states that Kolbe was thrown down the stairs of Building 13 to starve to death, when the article on the official Auschwitz website at http://auschwitz.org/en/history/punishments-and-executions/starvation-to-death states that it was Block 11. See also on the official Auschwitz website for the article about the 75th anniversary of the Kolbe's death at http://auschwitz.org/en/museum/news/75th-anniversary-of-the-martyrdom-of-st-maximilian-kolbe,1218.html which was in August 2016. Elaine Murray Stone, the author of *Maximilian Kolbe* and Mary Craig, author of the article *St. Maximilian Kolbe, Priest Hero of a Death Camp* on the Eternal Word Television Network, Inc. (EWTN) website at https://www.ewtn.com/catholicism/library/st-maximilian-kolbe-priest-hero-of-a-death-camp-5602 state that the starvation block was block 13. I have decided to go with the Auschwitz Museum version, which states the starvation block was block 11. Links accessed on Saturday July 25, 2020.

[2984] Position 141.0 of Elaine Murray Stone.

[2985] Position 141.7 of Elaine Murray Stone.

[2986] Position 142.5 of Elaine Murray Stone.

[2987] The DK Holocaust website article on Father Maximilian Kolbe at http://www.auschwitz.dk/Kolbe.htm and the Polish genealogical website (MORE MAIORUM Miesięcznik Genealogiczny — Genealogical Monthly) at http://www.moremaiorum.pl/114-lat-temu-urodzil-sie-franciszek-gajowniczek/. Both links accessed on Saturday July 25, 2020.

[2988] The Polish genealogical website (MORE MAIORUM Miesięcznik Genealogiczny — Genealogical Monthly) at http://www.moremaiorum.pl/114-lat-temu-urodzil-sie-franciszek-gajowniczek/ and the wikidot article at http://maksymilian.wikidot.com/swiadek — a testimony of Franciszek Gajowniczek. Both links accessed on Saturday July 25, 2020.

[2989] Position 14.0 of Elaine Murray Stone and the Westminster Abbey website article on Father Kolbe at https://www.westminster-abbey.org/abbey-commemorations/commemorations/st-maximilian-kolbe/. Accessed on Saturday July 25, 2020.

[2990] The UK Independent online obituary article on Franciszek Gajowniczek dated Thursday March 23, 1995 at https://www.independent.co.uk/news/people/obituary-francziszek-gajowniczek-1612377.html, which states his service to his country during the 1920 Battle of the Vistula against the Bolsheviks. It also correctly states his Auschwitz prison number of "5659." Accessed on Saturday July 25, 2020.

[2991] The wikidot article at http://maksymilian.wikidot.com/swiadek — a testimony of Franciszek Gajowniczek. Accessed on Saturday July 25, 2020.

[2992] See endnote [2966] for this chapter for a list of the martyrs from left to right.

[2993] See pages 199, 200, 247 and 248 of *Eyewitness to Genocide: The Operation Reinhard Death Camp Trials, 1955-1966* by Michael Bryant, published by University of Tennessee Press, 2014, ISBN 1621900495, 9781621900498. Pages 247 and 248 are a chronology of events.

[2994] Otto Thorbeck's date of death, being October 10 1976, is given on page 105 of *Bonhoeffer und seine Richter: ein Prozess und sein Nachspiel* (Bonhoeffer and his judges: a trial and its aftermath) by Elke Endrass, published by Kreuz, 2006, ISBN 3783127459.

[2995] The online review of the film *Der Prozess Huppenkothen — Trial of Nazi SS prosecutor in 1950s*, Film | Accession Number: 2014.526 | RG Number: RG-60.1547 | Film ID: 4113 at https://collections.ushmm.org/search/catalog/irn1004825, gives the year of death for Walter Huppenkothen being 1978. Accessed on Saturday July 25, 2020.

[2996] See position 1145.9 to 1148.3 of Metaxas and page 914 of Bethge.

[2997] Bottom of page 199 of *Eyewitness to Genocide: The Operation Reinhard Death Camp Trials, 1955-1966* by Michael Bryant, published by University of Tennessee Press, 2014, ISBN 1621900495, 9781621900498.

[2998] The Iliad is a famous Ancient Greek text written around 800 BC by Homer, relating to the Siege of Troy. A text only version can be downloaded from the website of the Massachusetts Institute of Technology at http://classics.mit.edu/Homer/iliad.mb.txt while the approximate time of its writing can be viewed at http://classics.mit.edu/Homer/iliad.html. Both links accessed on Saturday July 25, 2020.

[2999] The article on the Humanities Texas website at https://www.humanitiestexas.org/news/articles/new-home-humanities, dated October 29 2010, states how closely associated Dietrich and Otto Thorbeck were at university. Accessed on Saturday July 25, 2020.

[3000] Ibid.

[3001] In regard to Dietrich's poem the *Death of Moses*, written while incarcerated at Tegel prison, see the online article by Paul Axton on the Forging Ploughshares website, affiliated with Outreach International, at https://forgingploughshares.org/2018/01/25/hope-for-getting-through-the-dark-night-of-the-soul/#more-943. A review of Paul Axton's book *The Psychotheol-*

ogy of Sin and Salvation: An Analysis of the Meaning of the Death of Christ in Light of the Psychoanalytical Reading of Paul on Amazon at https://www.amazon.com/Psychotheology-Sin-Salvation-Analysis-Psychoanalyti-cal/dp/0567659402/ref=sr_1_7?ie=UTF8&qid=1473478822&sr=8-7&keywords=psychoanalytical+theology states: "Paul Axton spent 20 years in Japan as an educator and missionary. He presently directs Ploughshares Bible Institute and the work of Forging Ploughshares, a ministry aimed at cultivating peace. He blogs at forgingploughshares.org under 'Walking Truth' at http://forgingploughshares.org/category/walking-truth/." All links accessed on Saturday July 25, 2020.

[3002] Position 993.9 of Schlingensiepen and page 540 of *Letters and Papers from Prison Volume 8 of Dietrich Bonhoeffer Works* by Dietrich Bonhoeffer, edited by Christian Gremmels, John W. De Gruchy, published by Fortress Press, 2010, ISBN 1451406789, 9781451406788. The entire poem is given from page 531 onwards.

[3003] See position 993.9 of Schlingensiepen and page 531 of the book *Letters and Papers from Prison Volume 8 of Dietrich Bonhoeffer Works* by Dietrich Bonhoeffer, edited by Christian Gremmels, John W. De Gruchy, published by Fortress Press, 2010, ISBN 1451406789, 9781451406788.

[3004] Position 572.0 of Payne Best, position 988.0 of Schlingensiepen and position 1207.4 of Metaxas.

[3005] See page 186 of *The Power to Comprehend with All the Saints: The Formation and Practice of a Pastor-Theologian* edited by Wallace M. Alston Junior and Cynthia A. Jarvis, published by Wm. B. Eerdmans Publishing, 2009, ISBN 0802864724, 9780802864727 and page 87 of *Bonhoeffer in a World Come of Age* by Paul Matthews Van Buren, edited and compiled by Peter Vorkink, published by Fortress Press, 1967 (No ISBN given). See Google Books at https://books.google.com.au/books?id=YE9DAAAAIAAJ&dq=Bonhoeffer+in+a+world+come+of+age&focus=searchwithinvolume&q=unprofitable. Accessed on Saturday July 25, 2020.

[3006] See endnote [1051] of Chapter 15 "New York — Troubled Revisiting."

[3007] Position 1096.1 of Metaxas and pages 5 to 6 of Pierre Galante and Eugene Silianoff and position 24.1 of the ebook, ISBN-13: 9780815411796.

[3008] Position 975.3 of Metaxas. See also page 140 of *Dietrich Bonhoeffer: Reality and Resistance* by Larry L. Rasmussen, published by Westminster John Knox Press, 1970, ISBN 066422704X, 9780664227043.

[3009] Position 975.4 of Metaxas state that twenty months before Valkyrie (in November 1942), Haeften had broached the same question as Stauffenberg to Bonhoeffer. See also endnote [1765] of Chapter 20 "Valkyrie II."

[3010] Position 825.0 to 830.5 of Schlingensiepen. See also pages 785 to 786 of Bethge.

3011 Page 140 of *Dietrich Bonhoeffer: Reality and Resistance* by Larry L. Rasmussen, published by Westminster John Knox Press, 1970, ISBN 066422704X, 9780664227043. See also endnote [1765] of Chapter 20 "Valkyrie II."

3012 Ibid.

3013 Online article of Father James Wallace entitled *A Bold Venture of Faith* on the website of Chicago's Saint Juliana's Parish at https://stjuliana.org/faith-life/item/157-tassel16oct16. Accessed on Saturday July 25, 2020.

3014 The *Internationale Bonhoeffer-Gesellschaft (IBG), Deutschsprachige Sektion* (International Bonhoeffer Society (IBG), at https://www.dietrich-bonhoeffer.net/bonhoeffer-umfeld/gerhard-leibholz/ details the life of Gerhard Leibholz in German stating his return to Germany in 1947. See also the article on his wife and Dietrich's twin sister Sabine at https://www.dietrich-bonhoeffer.net/bonhoeffer-umfeld/sabine-leibholz-bonhoeffer/. This website's credentials can be viewed at https://www.dietrich-bonhoeffer.net/ibg/ueber-uns/. All links accessed on Saturday July 25, 2020.

3015 See Appendix 6: Bonhoeffer Family Tree at position 1100.0 of Schlingensiepen.

3016 See Appendix 6: Bonhoeffer Family Tree at position 1100.0 of Schlingensiepen.

3017 Position 834.4 of Schlingensiepen and position 993.6 of Metaxas. See also endnote [1463] of Chapter 18 "Romance, Plots and Arrest" in regard to Dietrich's *letzten herzhaftes Mittagessen* (final hearty lunch).

3018 Page 828 of Bethge, position 944.7 of Schlingensiepen and position 1129.8 of Metaxas. See also endnote [2017] of Chapter 21 "Valkyrie's Wake" in regard to Ursula's regret over talking Klaus out of committing suicide before his arrest during Valkyrie's aftermath.

3019 See Appendix 6: Bonhoeffer Family Tree at position 1100.0 of Schlingensiepen.

3020 See Appendix 6: Bonhoeffer Family Tree at position 1100.0 of Schlingensiepen.

3021 See footnote #4 on page 563 of *Letters and Papers from Prison Volume 8 of Dietrich Bonhoeffer Works* by Dietrich Bonhoeffer, editors Christian Gremmels, John W. De Gruchy, published by Fortress Press, 2010, ISBN 1451406789, 9781451406788. In regard to Klaus and Rüdiger being surreptitiously shot, see the online English language article on Klaus Bonhoeffer on the official website of the German Resistance Memorial Centre at https://www.gdw-berlin.de/en/recess/biographies/index_of_persons/biographie/view-bio/klaus-bonhoeffer/. Accessed on Saturday July 25, 2020.

3022 New York Times online obituary article dated April 18 2000 at https://www.nytimes.com/2000/04/18/world/eberhard-bethge-90-writer-theologian-and-biographer.html. Accessed on Saturday July 25, 2020.

[3023] See endnote [190] in the Preface "Birth and Memory upon the Lesser Known Fault Line of History" in regard to the Stalinist perpetrated post-war displacement of eastern Germans and Borderland Poles.
[3024] See endnotes [202] to [214] in the Preface "Birth and Memory upon the Lesser Known Fault Line of History" in regard to horrific wartime experiences of the Borderland Poles under both Stalinist and Nazi overlords.
[3025] Position 1198.7 of Microcosm.
[3026] At position 46.4 of Schlingensiepen, the author's exact wording of his quip is: " *'True Berliners come from Silesia' — people used to say, and this applies to Dietrich Bonhoeffer.*" In spite of the fact that Dietrich was only six when the family left Breslau in 1912 for Berlin, he still remembered Breslau as *"a paradise for children."*

Chapter 29 — Dietrich and Ruth and their Times Relevance for America in 2020-21 — Lessons of History

Note that in this time of growing mass censorship in America and indeed elsewhere, it's possible that some source endnote links, since the time of writing in late February 2021, have been removed. For articles, it may be possible to still retrieve them on the WayBack Machine or Web Archive at https://archive.org/web/. Just type or paste the link into the dialogue box. In the case of videos, especially YouTube videos, given YouTube's mass censorship, I have as much as possible, given links to these videos on alternative platforms such as *The Epoch Times* Youmaker platform at https://www.youmaker.com/. Indeed, some links already given by me, are via the Web Archive. See for example, the final footnote (not endnote) for this chapter. YouTube videos can also be retrieved on the Internet Archive with the Youtube code for the video. For example; Joshua Philipp's Question and Answer on December 19, 2020 still on YouTube at https://youtu.be/El4zqaRG-sk, can also be accessed on the Internet Archive at https://archive.org/details/youtube-El4zqaRG-sk. At 45 minutes and 30 seconds, Joshua answers a question of mine where I use the pseudonym "kulturedyobbo."

[3027] "Slogans in 1984: Meaning & Analysis." *Study.com*, 28 January 2021, http://study.com/academy/lesson/slogans-in-1984-meaning-analysis.html. Accessed Saturday March 6, 2021. Also, page 33 of the book *1984*, by George Orwell, published by Houghton Mifflin Harcourt, 1983, ISBN 0547249640, 9780547249643.
[3028] https://www.thebonhoeffercenter.org/index.php?option=com_content&view=article&id=37:schlingensiepen-on-metaxas-and-marsh titled *Making Assumptions About Dietrich: How Bonhoeffer was Made Fit for America.* Accessed on Sunday February 14, 2021.

3029 https://www.dtv.de/autor/ferdinand-schlingensiepen-4773/ albeit in German. Accessed on Sunday February 14, 2021.

3030 Ibid.

3031 See for example https://www.youtube.com/watch?v=WGRnhBmHYN0 or on the Internet archive at https://archive.org/details/youtube-WGRnhBmHYN0. See also Joshua Philipp's documentary *2020 Election Investigative Documentary: Who's Stealing America?* from 1 hour 22 minutes and 40 seconds in at https://www.youmaker.com/video/73bbe59a-0850-4b10-a132-ffdaa5beb240. All accessed on Sunday March 14, 2021.

3032 https://www.abc.net.au/news/2020-12-27/covid-dominated-2020-democracy-at-a-crossroads/13010694. Accessed on Sunday February 14, 2021.

3033 Page 11 of the book *Berlin: 1932-1933: Dietrich Bonhoeffer Works, Volume 12* by Dietrich Bonhoeffer, edited by Larry L. Rasmussen, translated by Isabel Best, David Warren Simons Higgins, published by Fortress Press, 2009, ISBN 1451406657, 9781451406658. See also endnote [350] of Chapter 3 "Evil's Storm Descends."

3034 Position 357.0 of Metaxas. See also endnote [351] of Chapter 3 "Evil's Storm Descends."

3035 https://www.newsweek.com/bernie-sanders-rigged-hillary-clinton-dnc-lawsuit-donald-trump-president-609582. See also https://www.politico.com/story/2016/04/arizona-primary-voter-problems-dnc-lawsuit-221957 and https://www.rasmussenreports.com/public_content/political_commentary/commentary_by_ted_rall/hillary_cheated. All accessed on Sunday February 14, 2021.

3036 [3159] https://fresnoalliance.com/opinion-our-elections-are-a-mess-and-only-leftists-care-enough-to-fix-them/ accessed on Saturday March 13, 2021.

3037 [3159] Ibid accessed on Saturday March 13, 2021.

3038 https://www.bbc.com/news/world-us-canada-41850798 accessed on Saturday March 13, 2021.

3039 https://time.com/5936036/secret-2020-election-campaign/ or on the Internet Archive at https://web.archive.org/web/20210312150232/https://time.com/5936036/secret-2020-election-campaign/. Accessed on Sunday March 14, 2021.

3040 https://www.theepochtimes.com/time-magazine-article-points-to-a-controlled-election_3688393.html. Accessed on Sunday February 14, 2021.

3041 Ibid.

3042 https://time.com/5936036/secret-2020-election-campaign/. Accessed on Sunday February 14, 2021.

3043 [3151] https://gellerreport.com/2020/11/why-did-six-battleground-states-with-democrat-governors-all-pause-counting-on-election-night-and-how-was-this-coordinated.html/, https://www.thegatewaypundit.com/2020/11/six-battleground-states-democrat-governors-pause-counting-election-night-coordinated/, https://www.wnd.com/2020/11/great-election-night-pause-vote-counting/. It is poignant to note, that I obtained these sources from the first search results for the term "counting stopped in Michigan and Wisconsin election night" on the French search engine Qwant. On the other hand, Google gave search results almost exclusively from pro-leftist mainstream sources, not inclined in any way to seriously explain obvious voting irregularities. All accessed on Sunday February 14, 2021. As well, Joshua Philipp's excellent documentary *2020 Election Investigative Documentary: Who's Stealing America?* at https://www.youmaker.com/video/73bbe59a-0850-4b10-a132-ffdaa5beb240 from four minutes in. All accessed on Sunday March 7, 2021.

[3044] https://www.youtube.com/watch?v=keANzinHWUA. See also Joshua Philipp's documentary *2020 Election Investigative Documentary: Who's Stealing America?* at https://www.youmaker.com/video/73bbe59a-0850-4b10-a132-ffdaa5beb240 from 25 minutes and 50 seconds in and the *American Thinker* article at https://www.americanthinker.com/blog/2020/12/does_a_surveillance_video_prove_georgia_election_fraud.html. Also the *Zooming In* video at https://zoomingin.tv/en/investigative-reports/will-georgias-suitcase-ballots-incident-change-the-prospect-of-trumps-lawsuits/. All accessed on Sunday March 7, 2021.

[3045] Joshua Philipp's Q & A video December 5, 2020 at https://www.youmaker.com/video/ddd708b6-25cb-4e8c-bbe4-27a715368ce5 from 2 minutes and 30 seconds in. See also the American Thinker article at https://www.americanthinker.com/blog/2020/12/does_a_surveillance_video_prove_georgia_election_fraud.html. Also as viewed by myself on the NTD (sister media of The Epoch Times) YouTube channel at https://www.youtube.com/watch?v=Ak1p_yv5JhQ&t=26645s at around 3:15 p.m. in Brisbane Australia on Wednesday November 4, 2020, which was just after midnight on the US east coast.

[3046] Near the end of https://www.youtube.com/watch?v=keANzinHWUA. See also Joshua Philipp's documentary *2020 Election Investigative Documentary: Who's Stealing America?* at https://www.youmaker.com/video/73bbe59a-0850-4b10-a132-ffdaa5beb240 from 26 minutes and 30 seconds in. Both accessed on Sunday March 7, 2021.

[3047] Joshua Philipp's documentary *2020 Election Investigative Documentary: Who's Stealing America?* at https://www.youmaker.com/video/73bbe59a-0850-4b10-a132-ffdaa5beb240 from 26 minutes and 45 seconds in.

[3048] https://uselectionatlas.org/RESULTS/national.php. Accessed on Sunday March 7, 2021.

[3049] xxxvii See https://www.theepochtimes.com/facebook-fact-checker-funded-by-chinese-money-through-tiktok_3610009.html and https://web.archive.org/web/20201230120813if_/https://www.tiktok.com/safety/resources/covid-19?lang=en (Why did Tik Tok remove the latter from their

website around New Year's? Thank goodness for the WayBack Machine!)
NOTE: Contrary to what mainland Chinese companies like Huawei assert, if the Chinese Communist Party (CCP) demanded they hand over network data, they would be compelled to do so because of espionage and national security laws in the "People's" Republic of China. See https://www.cnbc.com/2019/03/05/huawei-would-have-to-give-data-to-china-government-if-asked-experts.html. This of course, is not the case in western democracies, although, given the path already taken by the Biden-Harris regime, how much longer will this be the case in the US? All links accessed on Sunday March 14, 2021.

[3050] https://leadstories.com/hoax-alert/2020/12/fact-check-video-from-ga-does-not-show-suitcases-filled-with-ballots-pulled-from-under-a-table-after-poll-workers-dismissed.html. Accessed on Sunday February 14, 2021.

[3051] As heard by myself on Joshua's Q and A video on his YouTube *Crossroads* channel on December 5, 2020. YouTube have since removed it, but it can still be viewed on the *The Epoch Times* Youmaker platform at https://www.youmaker.com/video/ddd708b6-25cb-4e8c-bbe4-27a715368ce5 from 2 minutes and 30 seconds in.

[3052] https://leadstories.com/hoax-alert/2020/12/fact-check-video-from-ga-does-not-show-suitcases-filled-with-ballots-pulled-from-under-a-table-after-poll-workers-dismissed.html.

[3053] https://www.theepochtimes.com/fulton-county-board-votes-to-fire-elections-director-richard-barron_3698907.html accessed on Saturday March 6, 2021.

[3054] Documentary *ABSOLUTE PROOF Exposing Election Fraud and the Theft of America by Enemies Foreign and Domestic* hosted at https://michaeljlindell.com/ from 1 hour and 37 minutes. Accessed on Sunday February 14, 2021.

[3055] Ibid from 1 hour and 39 minutes.

[3056] See the beginning of https://www.youtube.com/watch?v=FqsC5vIeoGw&feature=youtu.be. However, if YouTube take it down, see it on bitchute at https://www.bitchute.com/video/6KIrGRQQhBcr/.

[3057] Ibid.

[3058] [3067] https://www.theepochtimes.com/mkt_breakingnews/xi-jinpings-adviser-outlines-plan-for-ccp-to-defeat-us-including-manipulating-elections_3748196.html and the Chinese text of the speech can be viewed on the Archive Today website at https://archive.is/z5RMg. Both accessed on Saturday March 27, 2021.

[3059] [3067] Ibid.

[3060] See endnotes [379] to [395] of Chapter 4 "The Aryan Paragraph."

[3061] See for example https://www.japantimes.co.jp/opinion/2020/12/10/commentary/world-

commentary/joe-biden-foreign-policy-china/ and
https://www.foxnews.com/politics/biden-joe-hunter-china-tony-bobulinski-
dan-crenshaw. Accessed on Friday February 26, 2021.

[3062] Page 1 of Document *491038048 Ratcliffe Views on Intelligence Community Election SecurityAnalysis* downloaded from
https://www.scribd.com/document/491038048/Ratcliffe-Views-on-
Intelligence-Community-Election-Security-Analysis#from_embed and
https://www.2020votingresults.com/china/national-intelligence-director-china-
sought-interfere-2020-election-cia-management-pressured-analysts-downplay-
46246264. All accessed on Sunday February 14, 2021.

[3063] Ibid page 3.

[3064] See endnotes [379] to [395] of Chapter 4 "The Aryan Paragraph."

[3065] And see for example
https://www.japantimes.co.jp/opinion/2020/12/10/commentary/world-
commentary/joe-biden-foreign-policy-china/ and
https://www.foxnews.com/politics/biden-joe-hunter-china-tony-bobulinski-
dan-crenshaw. Accessed on Friday February 26, 2021.

[3066] https://www.nationalreview.com/2020/11/why-beijing-hopes-for-a-biden-
win/. Accessed on Friday February 26, 2021.

[3067] The translated speech can be seen on Joshua Philipp's documentary *2020
Election Investigative Documentary: Who's Stealing America?* at
https://www.youmaker.com/video/73bbe59a-0850-4b10-a132-ffdaa5beb240
from 55 minutes and 30 seconds to 63 minutes in. Accessed on Friday February 26, 2021. See also endnotes [3058] and [3059] for this chapter for a speech by
another CCP advisor/professor from Beijing's Renmin university given in July
2016.

[3068] See endnotes [379] to [395] of Chapter 4 "The Aryan Paragraph."

[3069] And see for example
https://www.japantimes.co.jp/opinion/2020/12/10/commentary/world-
commentary/joe-biden-foreign-policy-china/ and
https://www.foxnews.com/politics/biden-joe-hunter-china-tony-bobulinski-
dan-crenshaw. Accessed on Friday February 26, 2021.

[3070] Article on von Papen at https://www.britannica.com/biography/Franz-von-
Papen. Accessed on Wednesday February 17, 2021.

[3071] Page 17 of the book *The Second World War: Ambitions to Nemesis* by
Bradley Lightbody, published by Psychology Press, 2004, ISBN 0415224047,
9780415224048 and J. Llewellyn et al, *Hitler becomes chancellor* Alpha History, at http://alphahistory.com/nazigermany/hitler-becomes-chancellor/, accessed on Friday February 26, 2021. See also endnote [787] of Chapter 9 "The
von Kleists and the Prophecy."

[3072] See endnote [330] of Chapter 3 "Evil's Storm Descends."

[3073] Position 349.8 of Metaxas and pages 191 to 192 William L. Shirer. See
also endnote [332] of Chapter 3 "Evil's Storm Descends."

[3074] Page 49 of *Midnight in Sicily* by the Australian author Peter Robb, published by Random House, 2015, ISBN 009959580X, 9780099595809. I read this book in 2020 and remember the author discussing this point.

[3075] [3083] American conservative Jewish academic Dennis Prager interviewed on January 14, 2021 in New York by Jan Jekielek, senior editor of *The Epoch Times* from 1 minute in. See the video at https://www.theepochtimes.com/video-dennis-prager-this-is-the-reichstag-fire-relived_3657503.html. Also on the Epoch Times sister channel NTD at https://www.ntd.com/dennis-prager-this-is-the-reichstag-fire-relived_553875.html and https://www.youmaker.com/video/6c5a5e96-d512-4693-7319-d49502edd8a3. All accessed on Sunday March 14, 2021.

[3076] Page 11 of the book *Berlin: 1932-1933: Dietrich Bonhoeffer Works, Volume 12* by Dietrich Bonhoeffer, edited by Larry L. Rasmussen, translated by Isabel Best, David Warren Simons Higgins, published by Fortress Press, 2009, ISBN 1451406657, 9781451406658. See also endnote [350] of Chapter 3 "Evil's Storm Descends."

[3077] https://www.theepochtimes.com/trump-offered-to-deploy-10000-national-guard-troops-in-dc-ahead-of-jan-6-mark-meadows_3690294.html. Accessed on Sunday February 21, 2021.

[3078] The beginning of Fox News Tucker Carlson at https://www.youtube.com/watch?v=M0l7xH5zbIg just before January 20, 2021 and *The Epoch Times* articles at https://www.theepochtimes.com/biden-sworn-in-as-46th-president-of-the-united-states_3664308.html, https://www.theepochtimes.com/no-security-incidents-involving-national-guard-on-inauguration-day-spokesperson_3666110.html and https://www.theepochtimes.com/rep-jeff-van-drew-mass-national-guard-deployment-during-inauguration-was-overkill_3667066.html. All accessed on Sunday 21, February 2021.

[3079] Fox News Tucker Carlson at https://www.youtube.com/watch?v=M0l7xH5zbIg just before January 20, 2021 from 3 minutes and 50 seconds in. Note it takes footage of the CNN interview of Stephen Cohen. See also https://www.theepochtimes.com/texas-governor-decries-vetting-of-national-guard_3662510.html. All accessed on Sunday February 21, 2021.

[3080] [3214] https://www.thedailybeast.com/after-the-capitol-riots-can-us-spy-agencies-stop-white-terror accessed on Sunday February 21, 2021.

[3081] https://www.britannica.com/topic/Stasi accessed on Sunday February 21, 2021.

[3082] https://www.military.com/join-armed-forces/swearing-in-for-military-service.html. Accessed on Friday February 26, 2021.

[3083] See video referred to in endnote [3075] for this chapter from within the first five minutes. Accessed on Sunday March 14, 2021.

3084 https://www.theepochtimes.com/poll-challenger-dominion-contractor-say-voting-machines-in-detroit-were-connected-to-internet_3597825.html. Accessed on Thursday February 25, 2021.

3085 https://www.bbc.com/news/world-latin-america-40804812 which discusses the Venezuelan election of August 2017. Accessed on Sunday February 14, 2021.

3086 https://gellerreport.com/2020/11/why-did-six-battleground-states-with-democrat-governors-all-pause-counting-on-election-night-and-how-was-this-coordinated.html/, https://www.thegatewaypundit.com/2020/11/six-battleground-states-democrat-governors-pause-counting-election-night-coordinated/, https://www.wnd.com/2020/11/great-election-night-pause-vote-counting/. It is poignant to note, that I obtained these sources from the first search results for the term "counting stopped in Michigan and Wisconsin election night" on the French search engine Qwant. On the other hand, Google gave search results almost exclusively from pro-leftist mainstream sources. All accessed on Sunday February 14, 2021.

3087 https://www.theepochtimes.com/dr-paul-kengor-the-pennsylvania-voting-curve-doesnt-line-up_3569060.html. Accessed on Sunday February 14, 2021.

3088 https://www.theepochtimes.com/biden-asked-national-intelligence-director-to-assess-domestic-extremism_3667645.html. Accessed on Sunday February 14, 2021.

3089 https://www.britannica.com/topic/Red-Guards accessed on Wednesday February 17, 2021.

3090 *Monthly Harvard-Harris Poll: February 2021* as viewed at https://harvardharrispoll.com/wp-content/uploads/2021/03/February2021_HHP_Topline_RV.pdf. Accessed on Thursday March 4, 2021.

3091 Ibid.

3092 https://www.theepochtimes.com/congress-put-itself-above-the-law-in-trump-impeachment-dershowitz_3687699.html. Accessed on Thursday February 18, 2021.

3093 https://www.theepochtimes.com/trump-impeachment-attorney-canceled-by-law-school-civil-rights-law-group_3700521.html. Accessed on Friday February 26, 2021.

3094 https://www.theepochtimes.com/home-of-trump-attorney-van-der-veen-vandalized-with-graffiti_3695878.html. Accessed on Friday February 26, 2021.

3095 https://www.theepochtimes.com/home-of-trump-attorney-van-der-veen-vandalized-with-graffiti_3695878.html. Accessed on Friday February 26, 2021.

3096 https://www.youmaker.com/video/d6bf3e18-4315-4ee7-8a16-5d3f59038bd5 from 15 minutes and 30 seconds in and NTD news at https://www.youmaker.com/video/0f5db8d8-9021-4a93-91b4-c56de4ae7c87 from 7 minutes in and https://www.youmaker.com/video/ac90a779-3fb5-4829-

997e-4d9f7571c271 from 1 minute and 10 seconds. Accessed on Friday February 26, 2021.

[3097] https://www.theepochtimes.com/congress-put-itself-above-the-law-in-trump-impeachment-dershowitz_3687699.html. Accessed on Thursday February 18, 2021.

[3098] See endnote [330] of Chapter 3 "Evil's Storm Descends."

[3099] See also endnotes [350] and [351] of Chapter 3 "Evil's Storm Descends."

[3100] Position 381.4 of Metaxas. See also endnote [367] of Chapter 4 "The Aryan Paragraph."

[3101] Position 381.4 of Metaxas. See also position 350.5 of Schlingensiepen and endnote [368] of Chapter 4 "The Aryan Paragraph."

[3102] https://www.dailymail.co.uk/news/article-9170237/Protesters-gather-damage-Democratic-headquarters-Oregon.html. Accessed on Sunday February 14, 2021.

[3103] https://www.theepochtimes.com/black-lives-matter-antifa-march-through-dc-chant-burn-it-down_3688149.html and https://twitter.com/MrAndyNgo/status/1358213357271195649 and https://www.washingtonexaminer.com/news/blm-antifa-washington-dc-burn-it-down. All accessed on Sunday February 14, 2021.

[3104] https://www.theepochtimes.com/self-proclaimed-revolutionary-eggs-on-capitol-intruders-as-he-records-them-publishes-video_3649617.html with the story of the BLM activist John Sullivan well and truly involved in the Capitol Hill breach. The video he shot under the moniker "Jayden X" is at https://www.youtube.com/watch?v=PfiS8MsfSF4&bpctr=1612010912. Accessed on Friday February 26, 2021.

[3105] https://www.theepochtimes.com/cnn-nbc-paid-antifa-activist-for-footage-from-capitol-breach_3700090.html. The invoices can be downloaded from https://assets.documentcloud.org/documents/20485309/invoices-for-john-earle-sullivan.pdf. Accessed on Friday February 26, 2021.

[3106] https://www.youmaker.com/video/73a30d31-b9ce-4982-5dcc-d3c40a4341ca from to 10 to 11 minutes. Interview by *The Epoch Times* senior editor Jan Jekielek of Andy Ngo. Accessed on Sunday February 14, 2021.

[3107] https://youtu.be/yJjwKGSppYM or https://www.youmaker.com/video/ebfd74f2-8ef4-4cba-5032-51d830ff9d68 within the first five minutes. Interview by *The Epoch Times* journalist Joshua Philipp on January 26, 2021. All accessed on Sunday February 14, 2021.

[3108] https://www.youmaker.com/video/73a30d31-b9ce-4982-5dcc-d3c40a4341ca from 33 to 35 minutes. Accessed on Sunday February 14, 2021.

[3109] [3171] See footnote #15 on page 5 of the article *E.P. Thompson and the rule of law: Qualifying the unqualified good* by Douglas Hay, Osgoode Hall Law School of York University, 2020 from https://digitalcommons.osgoode.yorku.ca/cgi/viewcontent.cgi?article=3798&context=scholarly_works. Accessed on Sunday February 14, 2021.

[3110] https://ocasio-cortez.house.gov/. Accessed on Sunday February 14, 2021.

[3111] https://www.vox.com/policy-and-politics/2018/6/27/17509604/alexandria-ocasio-cortez-democratic-socialist-of-america. Accessed on Friday February 26, 2021.

[3112] https://www.youtube.com/watch?v=g0BKdRywTcg at one minute and also 23 minutes in. Accessed on Sunday February 14, 2021.

[3113] See endnote [370] of Chapter 3 "Evil's Storm Descends."

[3114] https://www.theepochtimes.com/chinese-regime-burns-religious-books-jails-believers-in-war-against-faith_3709244.html.

[3115] https://www.youtube.com/watch?v=SLsaZwC3P-k. However, see how the independent journalist Andy Ngo describes it from 29 minutes in at https://www.youmaker.com/video/73a30d31-b9ce-4982-5dcc-d3c40a4341ca. All accessed on Sunday February 14, 2021.

[3116] https://www.q13fox.com/news/chop-seattle-mayor-walks-back-summer-of-love-comment. Accessed on Sunday February 14, 2021.

[3117] Ibid. See also https://www.nytimes.com/2020/06/29/us/seattle-protests-CHOP-CHAZ-autonomous-zone.html, https://www.wsj.com/articles/goodbye-summer-of-love-11607898398 and https://www.youmaker.com/video/73a30d31-b9ce-4982-5dcc-d3c40a4341ca from 27 minutes. All accessed on Sunday February 14, 2021.

[3118] https://www.youmaker.com/video/73a30d31-b9ce-4982-5dcc-d3c40a4341ca from around 5 minutes. In regard to Wheeler being a Democrat, see https://www.bizjournals.com/portland/stories/2010/05/17/daily23.html. All accessed on Sunday February 14, 2021.

[3119] https://www.youtube.com/watch?v=6PnWpOOoHNo or on Rumble at https://rumble.com/vempl3-freedom-road-socialist-organization-exposed.html. See also https://frso.org/?s=Yorek and https://frso.org/statements/minnesota-frso-may-day-celebration-we-are-up-against-a-real-monster-a-system-called-capitalism/. All accessed on Sunday March 14, 2021.

[3120] https://frso.org/main-documents/looking-back-at-tiananmen-square-the-defeat-of-counter-revolution-in-china/. Accessed on Sunday March 14, 2021.

[3121] See for example https://www.reuters.com/article/us-minneapolis-police-biden-bail-idUSKBN2360SZ. Accessed on Sunday February 14, 2021.

[3122] https://frso.org/statements/frso-spring-fundraising-drive-100000-plus-needed-for-great-leap-forward/ accessed on Saturday May 15, 2021.

[3123] *The Devil and Karl Marx: Communism's Long March of Death, Deception, and Infiltration* by Paul Kengor, published by Tan Books, 2020, ISBN 1505120055, 9781505120059. See also the YouTube interview of Paul Kengor by Joshua Philipp at https://www.youtube.com/watch?v=_8T11VSHg1U or *The Epoch Times* Youmaker platform at https://www.youmaker.com/video/90620a5c-ee6f-4e2a-bbb3-9de912ebb7b7 from 1 minute and 37 seconds. As well, from the Marxist mouthpiece itself at https://www.marxists.org/archive/marx/works/1848/communist-manifesto/ch04.htm. All accessed on Sunday February 14, 2021.

[3124] See https://www.wnd.com/2020/02/1619-vs-1776-battle-truth/. In this article, it is stated; "Many historians have spoken out against the 1619 Project. And now several of the nation's pre-eminent black scholars, pastors and activists are pushing back too, and speaking up for America through what they are calling '1776.'" See also the book *Debunking Howard Zinn Exposing the Fake History That Turned a Generation Against America* by Mary Grabar on Google Books at https://www.google.com/books/edition/Debunking_Howard_Zinn/VniHDwA AQBAJ?hl=en&gbpv=0.

[3125] https://www.theepochtimes.com/medias-obsession-with-jan-6-extremely-frustrating-to-law-enforcement-retired-sergeant_3688471.html Accessed on Sunday February 14, 2021.

[3126] Ibid.

[3127] https://www.youmaker.com/video/73a30d31-b9ce-4982-5dcc-d3c40a4341ca from around 20 minutes. Interview by *The Epoch Times* senior editor Jan Jekielek of Andy Ngo: Infiltrating CHAZ; Antifa's Plot to Destroy America; New Book "Unmasked" | American Thought Leaders. Accessed on Sunday February 14, 2021.

[3128] See https://www.youtube.com/watch?v=UaWsYjBOXdg.

[3129] See for example https://www.reuters.com/article/us-minneapolis-police-biden-bail-idUSKBN2360SZ. Accessed on Sunday February 14, 2021.

[3130] See endnotes [92] to [107] of the Preface "Birth and Memory upon the Lesser Known Fault Line of History".

[3131] The exact dates of the beginning and end of the purge are given at https://encyclopedia.ushmm.org/content/en/article/roehm-purge on the website United States Holocaust Museum Memorial Encyclopaedia. Accessed on Saturday February 20, 2021.

[3132] Page 470 of the book *Hitler* by Joachim C. Fest, published by Harcourt Incorporated, 2002, ISBN 0156027542, 9780156027540. See also endnote [105] of the Preface "Birth and Memory upon the Lesser Known Fault Line of History."

[3133] See endnote [105] of the Preface "Birth and Memory upon the Lesser Known Fault Line of History."

[3134] https://www.theepochtimes.com/attempts-to-impeach-trump-would-be-dangerous-unsuccessful-lindsey-graham_3649037.html. Note that before the Capitol breach and protests, Trump called on supporters at the rally to remain peaceful and not attack the U.S. Capitol Police. After that, the president released a video message calling on the demonstrators to "go home in peace" before it was deleted by Facebook and Twitter. Accessed on Sunday February 14, 2021.

3135 3231 See https://www.france24.com/en/live-news/20210310-russia-disrupting-twitter-over-illegal-content, https://www.msn.com/en-us/news/world/russia-attacks-twitter-for-donald-trump-ban-after-platform-raises-censorship-concerns/ar-BB1eu4FY and https://www.rt.com/russia/517688-twitter-slowed-down-block/.

3136 See for example https://www.youtube.com/watch?v=WGRnhBmHYN0 or on the Internet archive at https://archive.org/details/youtube-WGRnhBmHYN0. See also Joshua Philipp's documentary *2020 Election Investigative Documentary: Who's Stealing America?* from 1 hour 22 minutes and 40 seconds in at https://www.youmaker.com/video/73bbe59a-0850-4b10-a132-ffdaa5beb240. All accessed on Sunday March 14, 2021.

3137 xxxvii https://web.archive.org/web/20201230120813if_/https://www.tiktok.com/safety/resources/covid-19?lang=en. This article was removed from Tik Tok's website between Christmas and New Year, but can still be accessed on the Web Archive. **NOTE:** Contrary to what mainland Chinese companies like Huawei assert, if the Chinese Communist Party (CCP) demanded they hand over network data, they would be compelled to do so because of espionage and national security laws in the "People's" Republic of China. See https://www.cnbc.com/2019/03/05/huawei-would-have-to-give-data-to-china-government-if-asked-experts.html. This of course, is not the case in western democracies, although, given the path already taken by the Biden-Harris regime, how much longer will this be the case in the US? All links accessed on Sunday March 14, 2021.

3138 https://leadstories.com/hoax-alert/2020/11/fact-check-joe-biden-did-not-admit-he-put-togethe-voter-fraud-organization-he-was-talking-about-preventing-voter-fraud.html. Accessed on Sunday February 14, 2021.

3139 https://www.digitalhistory.uh.edu/disp_textbook.cfm?smtID=3&psid=1123. Accessed on Sunday February 14, 2021.

3140 See for example https://www.reuters.com/article/us-minneapolis-police-biden-bail-idUSKBN2360SZ. Accessed on Sunday February 14, 2021.

3141 https://www.youtube.com/watch?v=NTg1ynIPGls from 5 minutes and 20 seconds in. Accessed on Sunday March14, 2021.

3142 https://www.theepochtimes.com/trump-offered-to-deploy-10000-national-guard-troops-in-dc-ahead-of-jan-6-mark-meadows_3690294.html. Accessed on Sunday February 14, 2021.

3143 https://www.theepochtimes.com/congress-put-itself-above-the-law-in-trump-impeachment-dershowitz_3687699.html. Accessed on Sunday February 14, 2021.

3144 3226 https://www.vanityfair.com/news/2019/06/alan-dershowitz-donald-trump-joe-biden. Accessed on Sunday February 14, 2021.

3145 https://www.speaker.gov/newsroom/11221-0. Accessed on Sunday February 14, 2021.

[3146] https://libertyangle.com/2020/12/25/breaking-swalwells-chinese-honeypot-was-a-paid-democrat-employee/. Accessed on Sunday February 14, 2021.

[3147] See for example the first five minutes of Joshua Philipp's Q & A on February 12, 2021 at https://www.youtube.com/watch?v=85wl8HEoJL8 or https://www.youmaker.com/video/d6a222ed-5141-47d8-b3e1-4a5ded9935f0 titled *Live Q&A: Trump Team Exposes Impeachment Hypocrisy | Crossroads*. He also elaborates on Trump's "separation" of children of illegal immigrants from their "parents." Often these "parents" are not the parents, but rather human traffikers. All accessed on Sunday February 14, 2021.

[3148] https://www.theepochtimes.com/trump-acquitted-in-second-impeachment-trial_3695836.html. Accessed on Friday February 26, 2021.

[3149] https://www.theepochtimes.com/house-democrats-try-pressuring-tv-carriers-to-stop-hosting-fox-oan-and-newsmax_3706639.html. Accessed on Friday February 26, 2021.

[3150] The beginning of the Documentary *ABSOLUTE PROOF Exposing Election Fraud and the Theft of America by Enemies Foreign and Domestic* hosted at https://michaeljlindell.com/. Accessed on Friday February 26, 2021.

[3151] See endnote [3043] for this chapter.

[3152] https://news.northeastern.edu/2020/11/04/the-polls-were-still-way-off-in-the-2020-election-even-after-accounting-for-2016s-errors/. As well, the now embarrassing article by *The Atlantic* just days before the election on October 29, 2020 at https://www.theatlantic.com/ideas/archive/2020/10/five-reasons-to-believe-2020-wont-be-a-2016-sequel/616896/ claiming that the 2020 election, unlike 2016, would vindicate the pollsters. Accessed on Friday February 26, 2021.

[3153] As viewed by myself on the NTD (sister media of The Epoch Times) YouTube channel at https://www.youtube.com/watch?v=Ak1p_yv5JhQ&t=28060s at around 3:15 p.m. in Brisbane Australia on Wednesday November 4, 2020, which was just after midnight on the US east coast.

[3154] https://www.theepochtimes.com/these-models-predicted-trumps-victory-in-2016-heres-what-they-say-for-2020_3533139.html.

[3155] Joshua Philipp's documentary *2020 Election Investigative Documentary: Who's Stealing America?* From 42 minutes and 55 seconds to 45 minutes in at https://www.youmaker.com/video/73bbe59a-0850-4b10-a132-ffdaa5beb240. Accessed on Sunday March 7, 2021.

[3156] https://www.npr.org/2020/12/22/949294173/dominion-voting-systems-employee-sues-trump-campaign-and-allies-for-defamation. Accessed on Sunday February 14, 2021.

[3157] In the first presidential debate, Biden made the ridiculous assertion that Antifa is just an idea. See https://www.youtube.com/watch?v=UaWsYjBOXdg. However, the article by Roger L. Simon at https://www.theepochtimes.com/encountering-antifa-in-front-of-the-marriott_3579646.html is a must read for that incognisant and vapid fool of a leftist mouthpiece. Accessed on Sunday February 14, 2021.

[3158] https://opslens.com/eric-coomer-dominion-voting-ties-to-german-antifa-is-foreign-interference/ and https://www.thegatewaypundit.com/2020/11/dominion-voting-systems-officer-strategy-security-eric-coomer-admitted-2016-vendors-election-officials-access-manipulate-vote/. Both contain archived copies of Coomer's pro-Antifa-anti-Trump Facebook rant on June 2, 2020. This post has now been deleted from Facebook. All accessed on Sunday February 14, 2021.

[3159] https://www.clintonfoundation.org/clinton-global-initiative/commitments/delian-project-democracy-through-technology accessed Friday March 12, 2021. See also endnotes [3036] and [3037] for this chapter.

[3160] https://www.theamericanconservative.com/articles/the-extremist-at-dominion-voting-systems/ accessed Saturday March 13, 2021.

[3161] https://alumnius.net/university_of_califo-7940-1020#id23242501 accessed Saturday March 13, 2021.

[3162] https://www.washingtonexaminer.com/red-alert-politics/even-liberals-dont-want-to-speak-at-uc-berkeley, https://www.nytimes.com/2017/08/04/education/edlife/antifa-collective-university-california-berkeley.html, https://www.berkeleyside.com/2019/05/10/11-years-of-radical-thought-and-action-in-berkeley-led-to-creation-of-peoples-park and https://searcharchives.library.gwu.edu/agents/corporate_entities/977. All accessed Saturday March 13, 2021.

[3163] https://www.ajc.com/politics/fix-upcoming-to-georgia-touchscreens-to-restore-missing-senate-candidates/ASEWAGDAR5DFPGW2OPULV4N3JY/ accessed Friday March 12, 2021.

[3164] Joshua Philipp's documentary *2020 Election Investigative Documentary: Who's Stealing America?* from 45 minutes and 25 seconds in at https://www.youmaker.com/video/73bbe59a-0850-4b10-a132-ffdaa5beb240. Accessed on Saturday March 13, 2021.

[3165] Joshua Philipp's documentary *2020 Election Investigative Documentary: Who's Stealing America?* from 46 minutes in at https://www.youmaker.com/video/73bbe59a-0850-4b10-a132-ffdaa5beb240. Accessed on Sunday March 7, 2021.

[3166] https://money.yahoo.com/fact-check-no-joe-bidens-180145435.html. Note; the fact-check article by the global MSM mouthpiece Yahoo, emphasises in the headline that Biden's brother-in-law Stephen Owens does not own Dominion. However, it later admits the following: "Dominion Voting Systems is part-owned by Stephen Owens, who co-runs the private equity firm Staple Street Capital. Staple Street Capital and Dominion's management team acquired Dominion in 2018, according to a news release." Curiously, the beginning of this sentence contradicts the headline. Accessed Tuesday 2nd March 2021.

[3167] The company involved in the transaction was New York based UBS Securities LLC. Initially my listed source was https://www.bloomberg.com/profile/company/5766Z:US. At the time of transaction, three of the four board members of UBS Securities LLC were originally from China, with one still residing in Hong Kong. However, since that time, there has been a major shake up of the board. See the archive of the Bloomberg web page at https://archive.is/https://www.bloomberg.com/profile/company/5766Z:US. All accessed on Sunday February 14, 2021.

[3168] https://www.theepochtimes.com/dominions-parent-company-arranges-400-million-placement-1-month-before-election-sec-filing_3604287.html and https://thejewishvoice.com/2020/12/is-dominion-voting-systems-connected-to-ccp-money/. See also https://www.theepochtimes.com/400-million-sec-filing-links-dominion-ubs-and-china_3605748.html. All accessed on Sunday February 14, 2021.

[3169] This first question is raised by Joshua Philipp in his documentary *2020 Election Investigative Documentary: Who's Stealing America?* from 54 to 56 minutes in at https://www.youmaker.com/video/73bbe59a-0850-4b10-a132-ffdaa5beb240. The latter question is raised at https://thejewishvoice.com/2020/12/is-dominion-voting-systems-connected-to-ccp-money/. Both accessed on Sunday March 7, 2021.

[3170] Joshua Philipp's *2020 Election Investigative Documentary: Who's Stealing America?* from 44 to 46 minutes in at https://www.youmaker.com/video/73bbe59a-0850-4b10-a132-ffdaa5beb240. Accessed on Sunday March 7, 2021.

[3171] See endnote [3109] for this chapter.

[3172] See https://legalinsurrection.com/2021/01/capitol-hill-riot-doj-arrest-reports-focus-on-facebook-youtube-twitter-barely-mention-parler/ and https://www.justice.gov/usao-dc/press-release/file/1351946/download both accessed on Friday March 12, 2021.

[3173] https://ocasio-cortez.house.gov/. All accessed on Sunday February 14, 2021.

[3174] https://www.youtube.com/watch?v=q2fDsam9-Pw from within the first two minutes. Accessed on Sunday February 14, 2021.

[3175] https://www.vox.com/policy-and-politics/2018/6/27/17509604/alexandria-ocasio-cortez-democratic-socialist-of-america. Accessed on Wednesday February 17, 2021.

[3176] https://checkyourfact.com/2019/05/29/fact-check-democracy-jefferson-adams-franklin-hamilton/. Accessed on Sunday February 14, 2021.

[3177] https://www.whitehouse.gov/about-the-white-house/presidents/john-adams. Adams was also the first vice-president under George Washington. Accessed on Sunday February 14, 2021.

[3178] https://founders.archives.gov/documents/Adams/99-02-02-6371. Accessed on Sunday February 14, 2021.

[3179] https://books.google.com.au/books?id=z_oVEAAAQBAJ&dq=Tyranny+of+Big+Tech and see the interview of Josh Hawley at https://www.youtube.com/watch?v=ugwezczQM-8 from 14 minutes in. All accessed on Sunday February 14, 2021.

[3180] https://www.theepochtimes.com/hawley-plans-lawsuit-after-simon-schuster-cancels-publication-of-his-book_3648793.html. Accessed on Sunday February 14, 2021.

[3181] Ibid.

[3182] https://www.theepochtimes.com/sen-josh-hawley-says-antifa-threatened-wife-newborn-daughter_3643789.html and https://twitter.com/HawleyMO/status/1346308783325253633. See also the interview of Josh Hawley at https://www.youtube.com/watch?v=ugwezczQM-8 from 12 minutes in. All accessed on Sunday February 14, 2021.

[3183] [3218] The movie *The Plot Against The President* https://patpmovie.com/. See also Joshua Philipp's documentary *2020 Election Investigative Documentary: Who's Stealing America?* at https://www.youmaker.com/video/73bbe59a-0850-4b10-a132-ffdaa5beb240 from 1 hour and 22 minutes in. Both accessed on Sunday March 7, 2021.

[3184] Joshua Philipp's documentary *2020 Election Investigative Documentary: Who's Stealing America?* at https://www.youmaker.com/video/73bbe59a-0850-4b10-a132-ffdaa5beb240 from 1 hour 27 minutes and 30 seconds in. Accessed on Sunday March 14, 2021.

[3185] https://www.theepochtimes.com/supreme-court-refuses-to-hear-trumps-last-remaining-election-challenge_3724913.html. As to the motives of the US Supreme Court, see the transcript of an interview conducted by Attorney Lin Wood of Ryan D. White on Saturday January 9, 2021 at https://www.scribd.com/embeds/497646937/content. Search for key terms such as "Supreme," "Roberts" and "Pence" to name a few. Both accessed on Sunday March 14, 2021.

[3186] See again the second source of ibid.

[3187] Joshua Philipp's documentary *2020 Election Investigative Documentary: Who's Stealing America?* at https://www.youmaker.com/video/73bbe59a-0850-4b10-a132-ffdaa5beb240 from 1 hour and 22 minutes in. Accessed on Sunday March 7, 2021.

[3188] https://www.nbcnews.com/politics/2020-election/hillary-clinton-says-biden-should-not-concede-2020-election-under-n1238156. Accessed on Friday February 26, 2021.

[3189] https://www1.cbn.com/cbnnews/entertainment/2021/january/katie-couric-says-trump-supporters-need-to-be-deprogrammed. See also https://www.dailywire.com/news/dnc-member-rants-deprogram-75-million-trump-supporters. All accessed on Sunday February 14, 2021.

[3190] https://www.theepochtimes.com/rejoining-paris-climate-deal-will-have-devastating-economic-consequences-experts-say_3665887.html. Accessed on Sunday February 14, 2021.

[3191] https://ourworldindata.org/grapher/annual-co2-emissions-per-country?tab=chart&time=1800..latest&country=AUS~CHN~FRA~POL~RUS~GBR~USA&region=World. Accessed on Sunday February 14, 2021.

[3192] https://www.theguardian.com/world/2010/apr/17/smolensk-crash-katyn-accident-of-history. Accessed on Sunday February 14, 2021. See also endnotes [3951] to [3953] of Polish WWII Supplement III "The Katyń Wood Massacre."

[3193] https://www.history.com/topics/china/cultural-revolution. Accessed on Sunday February 14, 2021.

[3194] See endnotes [3957] to [3983] of Polish WWII Supplement IV "AK and 1944 Warsaw General Uprising — Stalin's mass murder by German proxy."

[3195] See endnotes [4214] to [4319] of Polish WWII Supplement IV "AK and 1944 Warsaw General Uprising — Stalin's mass murder by German proxy."

[3196] https://ocasio-cortez.house.gov/. Accessed on Sunday February 14, 2021.

[3197] https://www.youtube.com/watch?v=q2fDsam9-Pw. Accessed on Sunday February 14, 2021.

[3198] See for example https://www.dsausa.org/democratic-left/red-scare-rising-a-new-cold-war-with-china/. Accessed on Sunday February 14, 2021.

[3199] https://www.vox.com/policy-and-politics/2018/6/27/17509604/alexandria-ocasio-cortez-democratic-socialist-of-america. Accessed on Wednesday February 17, 2021.

[3200] Position 930.8 onwards of the e-book *Microcosm: A Portrait of a Central European City*, by Norman Davies and Roger Moorhouse, published by Jonathan Cape 2002, Epub ISBN 9781448114085.

[3201] See for example endnotes [718] to [725] of Chapter 9 "The von Kleists and the Prophecy."

[3202] See endnotes [347] to [352] of Chapter 3 "Evil's Storm Descends."

[3203] https://www.theepochtimes.com/poll-challenger-dominion-contractor-say-voting-machines-in-detroit-were-connected-to-internet_3597825.html. Accessed on Sunday February 14, 2021.

[3204] Ibid.

[3205] I am recalling the story I discussed back in Chapter 17 "Pastor and Spy." See endnotes [1244] and [1245] for this chapter.

[3206] See endnotes [1244] and [1245] of Chapter 17 "Pastor and Spy."

[3207] Oma is the German diminutive of grandmother. See also endnote [253] of Chapter 1 "Roots, Genesis and Moulding of the Pastor."

[3208] Page 30 of *Dietrich Bonhoeffer: A Biography* by Eberhard Bethge, edited by Victoria J. Barnett, published by Fortress Press, 2000, ISBN 0800628446, 9780800628444. See also endnotes [77] and [78] of the Preface "Birth and Memory upon the Lesser Known Fault Line of History" and endnote [254] of Chapter 1 "Roots, Genesis and Moulding of the Pastor."

[3209] See endnote [2647] of Chapter 26 "Oma Ruth's Progeny After Death."

[3210] See endnote [2648] of Chapter 26 "Oma Ruth's Progeny After Death."

[3211] Position 454.4 of Metaxas. See also the article on Martin Niemöller at https://www.ushmm.org/wlc/en/article.php?ModuleId=10007392. Accessed on Saturday July 25, 2020. See also endnotes [426] to [429] of Chapter 4 "The Aryan Paragraph."

[3212] [2746] [2874] [2891] Positions 626.7 onwards and position 746.8 of the ebook *The Venlo Incident* by Sigismund Payne Best, published by Frontline Books, an imprint of Pen & Sword Books Limited, 47 Church Street, Barnsley, S. Yorkshire, S70 2AS, ISBN 9781848325586. See also a comprehensive list of the prisoners by nationality, and an account of their odyssey, albeit in German, online at http://www.mythoselser.de/niederdorf.htm#liste, the website of the *Georg-Elser-Arbeitskreis*, edited by Peter Koblank since 2005 with the largest online archive worldwide for a resistance fighter against the Third Reich. Accessed on Friday February 26, 2021.

[3213] See the official website of War Resisters' International at https://www.wri-irg.org/en/story/2007/wri-and-nonviolent-intervention. Accessed on Saturday July 25, 2020.

[3214] See endnote [3080] for this chapter.

[3215] https://www.britannica.com/biography/George-Santayana and https://plato.stanford.edu/entries/santayana/.

[3216] As photographed by the author during a visit to Poland's Auschwitz Concentration Camp Museum on Tuesday June 28, 2005.

[3217] See the chat window from 1 hour and 3 minutes into the video at https://www.youtube.com/watch?v=aIfF8QG7w0w. Accessed at around 1:30 p.m. Brisbane Queensland Australia time on Monday May 3, 2021. This was 11:30 p.m. on Sunday May 2, 2021 on the US East Coast. Joshua Philipp is *The Epoch Times* senior investigative reporter in New York and owner of the YouTube Crossroads Channel, which is one of dozens under the umbrella of *The Epoch Times*. Zygmunt (Ziggy) Staszewski is a Polish Diaspora activist and member of Stowarzyszenie Wolnego Słowa (Free Words Association.) See https://www.youtube.com/watch?v=slLC-LHk6Kc&list=PLElKrBDtiaEmf77MggQ5xnqODcxnPCbHa and https://www.youtube.com/watch?v=hLdm1RjdAUw&list=PLElKrBDtiaEmf77MggQ5xnqODcxnPCbHa. In the latter, published on November 10, 2020, Staszewski in an interview in Polish, discusses the electoral irregularities in the November 3, 2020 US federal election.

[3218] See endnote [3183] for this chapter.

[3219] https://www.theepochtimes.com/house-democrats-try-pressuring-tv-carriers-to-stop-hosting-fox-oan-and-newsmax_3706639.html. Accessed on Friday February 26, 2021.

3220 https://www.theepochtimes.com/house-democrats-try-pressuring-tv-carriers-to-stop-hosting-fox-oan-and-newsmax_3706639.html. Accessed on Friday February 26, 2021.

3221 Ibid.

3222 Ibid.

3223 See also endnotes [350] and [351] of Chapter 3 "Evil's Storm Descends."

3224 https://freedomhouse.org/report/special-report/2020/beijings-global-megaphone for information on Chinese media spreading CCP censored news globally. Accessed on Friday February 26, 2021.

3225 See endnotes [379] to [395] of Chapter 4 "The Aryan Paragraph."

3226 See endnote [3144] for this chapter.

3227 https://www.theepochtimes.com/alan-dershowitz-all-americans-need-to-fight-cancel-culture_3722191.html accessed on Saturday March 6, 2021.

3228 http://www.clearharmony.net/articles/a45540-Looking-Back-on-July-20-1999.html and https://thediplomat.com/2019/07/in-july-1999-the-ccp-created-exactly-what-it-had-feared/ accessed on Sunday February 14, 2021.

3229 https://www.theepochtimes.com/about-us. Accessed on Sunday February 14, 2021.

3230 For example, https://twitter.com/i/status/1298833929160593409 and from 1 minute and 50 seconds in at https://www.youmaker.com/video/1a0eb407-8a4b-44d6-bdeb-3998e83c72dd. See also the article at https://unherd.com/2020/07/the-ugly-truth-about-the-blm-protests/. All accessed on Thursday February 25, 2021.

3231 For another poignant example, see endnote [3135] for this chapter.

3232 https://www.latimes.com/politics/story/2020-07-16/kamala-harris-joe-biden-vice-president-debate-clash second paragraph. Accessed on Sunday February 14, 2021.

3233 Video from 7 minutes in on *The Epoch Times* Youmaker platform at https://www.youmaker.com/video/2b9b0685-b4ea-4969-b586-97aedd276f50. Accessed on Sunday February 14, 2021. The YouTube video at https://www.youtube.com/watch?v=TQ0imduTI1Y had been taken down by Sunday February 14, 2021.

3234 https://web.archive.org/web/20200917194804/https://blacklivesmatter.com/what-we-believe/. This is from September 17, 2020. The following day of the 18th, this page was removed. See https://web.archive.org/web/20200918033916/https://blacklivesmatter.com/what-we-believe/. Why is this so? Both accessed on Friday February 26, 2021.

3235 https://www.youtube.com/watch?v=p7C6tNjiRKY from 35 seconds in. Also on the Internet Archive at https://archive.org/details/youtube-p7C6tNjiRKY. Accessed on Sunday March 14, 2021.

3236 https://www.abc.net.au/news/2020-11-03/former-democrat-insider-backs-donald-trump/12844328 states her civil rights activism during the 1960s. Accessed on Sunday February 14, 2021.

[3237] https://www.heraldsun.com.au/blogs/andrew-bolt/heineback-from-democrat-to-trump-defender/news-story/f10c631175b7890335b7e8f57907fc0b. Accessed on Sunday February 14, 2021.

[3238] The Sky News video aptly titled *Democrats have been pushing Joe Biden and his 'cognitive issues' across the line* at https://www.youtube.com/watch?v=PJnw-ztF6kU from 5 minutes and 19 seconds. Accessed on Sunday February 14, 2021.

[3239] https://www.theepochtimes.com/lara-logan-propagandists-political-assassins-have-infected-the-media_3816309.html. See the video from 17 minutes in. This interview by Jan Jakielek, the Senior Reporter of the Epoch Times, is a fascinating interview of a brave journalist summoning the will to break free from the insidious global MSM programming. Myself, after decades of feeling beholden to the MSM agenda, and now finally recognising them for what they truly are, is as Lara alludes to; liberating!

[3240] https://www.youtube.com/watch?v=vzDDIvoOV20 or on *The Epoch Times* sister media NTD at https://www.ntd.com/the-nation-speaks-jan-2-rep-vernon-jones-on-whats-at-stake-in-georgia-what-polling-can-tell-us-about-ga-runoff-elections-2020-year-in-review_548054.html from 12 minutes and 30 seconds in. All accessed on Sunday February 14, 2021.

[3241] See for example Jan Jakielek's interview of Vernon Jones at the Conservative Political Action Conference (CPAC) in Orlando Florida in early March 2021 at https://www.youmaker.com/video/67cf2baf-5fad-4eec-be7e-3bc1419c2973.

[3242] See endnotes [92] to [107] of the Preface "Birth and Memory upon the Lesser Known Fault Line of History."

[3243] The Chinese Doctor Li Wenliang passed away on February 7, 2020 after he warned his colleagues on social media in late December 2019 about a mysterious virus that would become known as the coronavirus/COVID 19 epidemic. Rather than take the appropriate counter-measures, Dr Li was detained by police in Wuhan on January 3rd for "spreading false rumours", before he was forced to sign a police document to admit he had breached the law and had "seriously disrupted social order." See https://www.theguardian.com/global-development/2020/feb/07/coronavirus-chinese-rage-death-whistleblower-doctor-li-wenliang. This of course, is just the tip of the iceberg in regard to the CCP cover-up, whether it be by incompetence or malevolent intent. See also Joshua Philipp's video at https://www.youtube.com/watch?v=Gdd7dtDaYmM or https://rumble.com/v93vzx-1st-documentary-movie-on-the-origin-of-ccp-virus.html titled *1st documentary movie on the origin of CCP virus, Tracking Down the Origin of the Wuhan Coronavirus*. As well, Simone Gao's *The Coverup of the Century | Zooming In's one-hour documentary movie* at https://zoomingin.tv/en/investigative-reports/the-coverup-of-the-century-zooming-ins-one-hour-documentary-movie/ or https://www.epochbase.com/video/9052d8c4-d3de-4f7b-7f26-81c3620fb3c9.

On the other hand, note the remarkable containment of the virus, without lock-down, by the democratic ethnic Chinese island nation of Taiwan. On island half the size of Tasmania, or one-quarter the size of Florida, with a population of 24 million, Taiwan has had only ten deaths, thanks to them not trusting the CCP and its mouthpiece the WHO. See https://www.worldometers.info/coronavirus/country/taiwan/ and https://www.abc.net.au/news/2020-05-30/taiwans-coronavirus-strategy-healthcare-and-location-data/12296948. All accessed on Sunday March 7, 2021.

[3244] See endnotes [379] to [395] of Chapter 4 "The Aryan Paragraph."

[3245] https://radiopatriot.net/2021/02/12/lin-wood-to-lead-defense-in-sidney-powell-suit-against-dominion/.

[3246] https://www.huffpost.com/entry/exclusive-on-heels-of-die_b_620084 titled *EXCLUSIVE: On Heels of Diebold/Premier Purchase, Canadian eVoting Firm Dominion Also Acquires Sequoia, Lies About Chavez Ties in Announcement.* Hugo Chavez was the president of Venezuela from 1999 until his death in 2013. He was succeeded by Nicolás Maduro. Under these two socialist presidents, Venezuela has been mired in electoral fraud. See for example https://www.bbc.com/news/world-latin-america-44187838 and https://www.thedialogue.org/analysis/venezuelas-questionable-election-observers/ during Maduro's presidency and https://journals.plos.org/plosone/article?id=10.1371/journal.pone.0100884 in regard to fraud during Chavez's presidency. All accessed on Sunday March 7, 2021.

[3247] https://www.msn.com/en-us/news/politics/democratic-senators-warned-of-potential-vote-switching-by-dominion-voting-machines-prior-to-2020-election/ar-BB1aZAYf in an article dated after the election on November 13, 2020 and https://wbsm.com/warren-deserves-credit-for-work-on-voting-opinion/. Both accessed on Sunday March 7, 2021.

[3248] https://www.theepochtimes.com/pre-election-concerns-over-dominion-voting-systems-highlighted-in-georgia-lawsuit_3576863.html.

[3249] See Joshua Philipp's documentary *2020 Election Investigative Documentary: Who's Stealing America?* from 33 to 39 minutes in at https://www.youmaker.com/video/73bbe59a-0850-4b10-a132-ffdaa5beb240.

[3250] https://www.theepochtimes.com/dominion-part-of-council-that-disputed-election-integrity-concerns-in-dhs-statement_3581659.html. Accessed on Sunday March 7, 2021.

[3251] https://www.theepochtimes.com/trump-says-voting-machines-may-have-been-breached-by-solarwinds-hack-during-election_3625553.html. Accessed on Sunday March 7, 2021.

[3252] https://www.theepochtimes.com/trump-says-voting-machines-may-have-been-breached-by-solarwinds-hack-during-election_3625553.html. Accessed on Sunday March 7, 2021.

3253 https://dvsfileshare.dominionvoting.com/Web%20Client/Mobile/Mlogin.htm. Accessed on Sunday March 7, 2021.

3254 http://web.archive.org/web/20201214235952/http://dvsfileshare.dominionvoting.com/Web%20Client/Mobile/Mlogin.htm. Accessed on Sunday March 7, 2021.

3255 https://dvsfileshare.dominionvoting.com/Common/Images/Mclient_RS_Logo.png. Accessed on Saturday May 15, 2021.

3256 https://www.theepochtimes.com/dominion-part-of-council-that-disputed-election-integrity-concerns-in-dhs-statement_3581659.html. Accessed on Sunday March 7, 2021.

3257 Ibid and https://www.cisa.gov/government-facilities-election-infrastructure-charters-and-membership then **click on "Membership."** Accessed on Sunday March 7, 2021.

3258 https://www.sos.texas.gov/elections/forms/sysexam/oct2019-sneeringer.pdf.

3259 https://www.theepochtimes.com/dominion-voting-systems-sues-mypillow-ceo-mike-lindell_3706214.html.

3260 The sworn affidavit of Melissa Carone at https://beta.documentcloud.org/documents/20404633-dominion-contractor-affidavit. Accessed on Sunday February 14, 2021.

3261 https://onenewsnow.com/legal-courts/2020/11/11/dems-dismiss-them-but-affidavits-mean-something-to-courts. See also *Here is the Evidence* at https://hereistheevidence.com/. Both accessed on Sunday March 14, 2021.

3262 https://www.theepochtimes.com/poll-challenger-dominion-contractor-say-voting-machines-in-detroit-were-connected-to-internet_3597825.html. Accessed on Sunday February 14, 2021.

3263 https://www.mypillow.com/mikes-story. Accessed on Sunday February 14, 2021.

3264 See the Google search at https://www.google.com/search?q=ceo+mike+lindell&oq=CEO+Mike+Lindell. Accessed on Sunday February 14, 2021.

3265 https://www.newsweek.com/donald-trumps-736-million-popular-votes-over-7-million-more-any-sitting-president-history-1548742. Accessed on Friday February 26, 2021.

3266 See the first five minutes of https://www.youtube.com/watch?v=F6sWD45TQFE where Trump rightly asserts that nations have the right to chart their own futures — not globalists, in his speech to the UN in late September 2019. Accessed on Sunday February 14, 2021.

3267 https://web.archive.org/web/20210120151726/https://www.whitehouse.gov/trump-administration-accomplishments/. Note; the Biden administration removed this article from the White House website by January 23, 2021, just three days following Biden's "inauguration." See https://web.archive.org/web/20210123094108/https://www.whitehouse.gov/trump-administration-accomplishments/ and https://web.archive.org/web/*/https://www.whitehouse.gov/trump-administration-accomplishments/. All accessed on Friday February 26, 2021.

Polish WWII Supplement I — The Molotov-Ribbentrop Pact

[3268] [4] [210] [960] [961] [979] [2527] [3555] [3719] [3744] [3750] [4544] Positions 9.6 and 340.5 of *Case White The Invasion of Poland, 1939* by Robert Forczyk, published by Osprey Publishing 2019, eISBN 9781472834942.

[3269] Page 154 of *Molotov: A Biography* by Derek Watson, published by Springer, 2005, ISBN 0230514529, 9780230514522.

[3270] The online article on Lavrentiy P. Beria on the website of the Atomic Heritage Foundation at https://www.atomicheritage.org/profile/lavrentiy-p-beria. Accessed on Saturday July 25, 2020. By early 1940, Beria orchestrated the execution of NKVD chief Nikolai Yezhov and then assumed his predecessor's position.

[3271] Articles on Lavrentiy P. Beria at https://www.britannica.com/biography/Lavrenty-Beria and on the website of the Atomic Heritage Foundation at https://www.atomicheritage.org/profile/lavrentiy-p-beria. Both links accessed on Saturday July 25, 2020.

[3272] Page 356 of *Lenin, Stalin and Hitler* by Robert Gellately, published by Vintage 2008, ISBN 9780712603577.

[3273] Page 155 of *Molotov: A Biography* by Derek Watson, published by Springer, 2005, ISBN 0230514529, 9780230514522.

[3274] Ibid. See also page 356 of *Lenin, Stalin and Hitler* by by Robert Gellately, published by Vintage 2008, ISBN 9780712603577.

[3275] [3405] Page 153 of *Molotov: A Biography* by Derek Watson, published by Springer, 2005, ISBN 0230514529, 9780230514522.

[3276] [3404] Page 356 of *Lenin, Stalin and Hitler* by by Robert Gellately, published by Vintage 2008, ISBN 9780712603577.

[3277] [3404] Page 356 of *Lenin, Stalin and Hitler* by by Robert Gellately, published by Vintage 2008, ISBN 9780712603577.

[3278] Page 524 of *Rise And Fall Of The Third Reich: A History of Nazi Germany* by William L. Shirer, published by Simon and Schuster, 1990, ISBN 0671728687, 9780671728687.

[3279] Page 525 of William L. Shirer.

[3280] The Deutsche Biographie (German Biographical) website at https://www.deutsche-biographie.de/sfz117245.html. Accessed on Saturday July 25, 2020.

[3281] Page 524 of William L. Shirer.

[3282] [3323] [3535] Page 524 of William L. Shirer.

[3283] https://www.britannica.com/event/German-Soviet-Nonaggression-Pact. See also the German text of the pact/treaty on the 1000 Documents for German

History website at https://www.1000dokumente.de/index.html?c=dokument_de&dokument=0025_pak&object=translation&st=&l=de. This also contains the controversial Secret Additional Protocol. Both links accessed on Saturday July 25, 2020.

[3284] Page 525 of William L. Shirer.

[3285] Ibid.

[3286] Ibid.

[3287] Position 361.2 of *Case White The Invasion of Poland, 1939* by Robert Forczyk, published by Osprey Publishing 2019, eISBN 9781472834942.

[3288] Position 9.0 of the ebook *The Second World War: Ambitions to Nemesis* by Bradley Lightbody, published by the Taylor & Francis e-Library, 2004, eISBN 9781134592722.

[3289] Position 362.7 of Robert Forczyk.

[3290] See endnotes [1181] to [1183] of Chapter 17 "Pastor and Spy" for clarification on the various intelligence agencies within the Third Reich.

[3291] Position 362.7 of Robert Forczyk.

[3292] Ibid position 361.4.

[3293] Ibid.

[3294] Ibid position 363.0

[3295] Page 527 of William L. Shirer.

[3296] Page 12 of *World War II - Behind Closed Doors: Stalin, the Nazis and the West* by Laurence Rees, published by Random House, 2009, ISBN 184607794X, 9781846077944.

[3297] [3404] Page 533 of William L. Shirer.

[3298] https://www.theguardian.com/world/from-the-archive-blog/2019/jul/24/molotov-ribbentrop-pact-germany-russia-1939. Accessed on Saturday July 25, 2020.

[3299] Ibid.

[3300] Page 43 of *The Lure of Neptune: German-Soviet Naval Collaboration and Ambitions, 1919-1941* by Tobias R. Philbin, published by University of South Carolina Press, 1994, ISBN 0872499928, 9780872499928.

[3301] http://wiki-de.genealogy.net/Kaliningrad. Accessed on Saturday July 25, 2020.

[3302] Page 49 of William L. Shirer.

[3303] Position 50.2 of *The Devils' Alliance: Hitler's Pact with Stalin, 1939—41* by Roger Moorhouse, published by The Bodley Head 2014 (of the Random House Group), Epub ISBN 9781448104710.

[3304] https://www.britannica.com/biography/Eva-Braun. Accessed on Saturday July 25, 2020.

[3305] Position 50.2 of *The Devils' Alliance: Hitler's Pact with Stalin, 1939—41.*

[3306] Position 51.6 of *The Devils' Alliance: Hitler's Pact with Stalin, 1939—41.*

[3307] Position 51.8 of *The Devils' Alliance: Hitler's Pact with Stalin, 1939—41* and page 55 of *Zwischen Hitler und Stalin, 1939-1945: Aufzeichnungen (Be-*

tween Hitler and Stalin, 1939-1945: Records) by Peter Kleist, published by Athenäum-Verlag, Bonn 1950, no ISBN given. See also Google Books at https://books.google.com.au/books?id=V54fAAAAMAAJ&dq=Peter+Kleist%2C+Zwischen+Hitler+und+Stalin%2C+1939%E2%80%931945&focus=search withinvolume&q=kultur. Accessed on Saturday July 25, 2020.

[3308][3778][3781] Positions 49.0 and 690.9 of *The Devils' Alliance: Hitler's Pact with Stalin, 1939—41*. Albeit, Roger Moorhouse uses the political metaphor "ideological gymnastics." See also pages 10 to 12 of *World War II - Behind Closed Doors: Stalin, the Nazis and the West* by Laurence Rees, published by Random House, 2009, ISBN 184607794X, 9781846077944.

[3309] Position 52.4 of *The Devils' Alliance: Hitler's Pact with Stalin, 1939—41*.

[3310] L'Internationale, (French), English The International, Russian Internatsional (Интернационал), former official socialist and communist song. It was the anthem of the First, Second, and Third (Communist) Internationals and, from 1918 to 1944, the national anthem of the Soviet Union. See https://www.britannica.com/topic/LInternationale. Accessed on Saturday July 25, 2020.

[3311] Position 53.0 of *The Devils' Alliance: Hitler's Pact with Stalin, 1939—41*.

[3312] Position 105.8 of *The Devils' Alliance: Hitler's Pact with Stalin, 1939—41*.

[3313] Position 105.9 of *The Devils' Alliance: Hitler's Pact with Stalin, 1939—41*.

[3314] Position 106.4 of *The Devils' Alliance: Hitler's Pact with Stalin, 1939—41* and page 161 of *Inside the Third Reich* by Albert Speer, published by Simon and Schuster, 1970, ISBN 0684829495, 9780684829494.

[3315][3693] Position 106.8 of *The Devils' Alliance: Hitler's Pact with Stalin, 1939—41*.

[3316] Position 107.1 of *The Devils' Alliance: Hitler's Pact with Stalin, 1939—41*.

[3317] Position 107.5 of *The Devils' Alliance: Hitler's Pact with Stalin, 1939—41* and page 10 of *World War II - Behind Closed Doors: Stalin, the Nazis and the West* by Laurence Rees, published by Random House, 2009, ISBN 184607794X, 9781846077944.

[3318] This refers to the April 24 1926 Treaty of Berlin (Neutrality Contract) between Weimar Germany and the Soviet Union. See the website *100(0) Schlüsseldokumente zur deutschen Geschichte im 20. Jahrhundert* (100 (0) Key Documents on German History in the 20th Century) at https://www.1000dokumente.de/index.html?c=dokument_de&dokument=0020_ber&st=VERTRAG%20BERLIN%201926&l=de. Accessed on Saturday July 25, 2020.

[3319] From the website *100(0) Schlüsseldokumente zur deutschen Geschichte im 20. Jahrhundert* (100 (0) Key Documents on German History in the 20th Century) at https://www.1000dokumente.de/index.html?c=dokument_de&dokument=0025_pak&object=translation&st=&l=de. Accessed on Saturday July 25, 2020.

3320 3688 Position 107.8 of *The Devils' Alliance: Hitler's Pact with Stalin, 1939—41*.

3321 Position 108.0 of *The Devils' Alliance: Hitler's Pact with Stalin, 1939—41*.

3322 Position 108.1 of *The Devils' Alliance: Hitler's Pact with Stalin, 1939—41*.

3323 See endnote 3282 for this supplement.

3324 Position 108.4 of *The Devils' Alliance: Hitler's Pact with Stalin, 1939—41*.

3325 Position 108.5 of *The Devils' Alliance: Hitler's Pact with Stalin, 1939—41*.

3326 Page 28 of *At Hitler's Side: The Memoirs of Hitler's Luftwaffe Adjutant* by Nicolaus von Below, published by Frontline Books, 2010, ISBN 1848325851, 9781848325852 and position 109.6 of *The Devils' Alliance: Hitler's Pact with Stalin, 1939—41*.

3327 3356 Position 110.4 of *The Devils' Alliance: Hitler's Pact with Stalin, 1939—41* and page 28 of *At Hitler's Side: The Memoirs of Hitler's Luftwaffe Adjutant* by Nicolaus von Below.

3328 Page 28 of *At Hitler's Side: The Memoirs of Hitler's Luftwaffe Adjutant* by Nicolaus von Below.

3329 3492 From 1921-39, Vilnius was Polish Wilno. See the map on page 338 of *The Polish Way* by Adam Zamoyski, published by John Murray Publishers Limited, 1989, ISBN 10: 0719546745 ISBN 13: 9780719546747. This city was hotly disputed by both Poland and Lithuania, and immediately following Poland's carve-up in October 1939, it was granted to Lithuania (see the map at position 11 of *The Devils' Alliance: Hitler's Pact with Stalin, 1939—41*), and post-war, it was the capital of the Soviet Republic of Lithuania. Note, it was not until June 1940, that the Soviet Union annexed all three Baltic states of Lithuania, Latvia and Estonia. This will be discussed later in this supplement.

3330 From Poland's surrender in September-October 1939 to the end of the war and just beyond, no formally independent Polish state existed. Hence this point of the Secret Protocol is mute. However, a Polish Underground state, the largest in Nazi occupied Europe, certainly did exist. See endnote 125 of the Preface "Birth and Memory upon the Lesser Known Fault Line of History" and *The Polish Underground 1939-1947 Campaign chronicle*, by David G Williamson, Published by Pen and Sword, 2012, ISBN 1848842813, 9781848842816.

3331 Bessarabia was then part of Romania. Ten months later on June 26 1940, the Soviet Union demanded that Romania cede Bessarabia and the northern portion of Bukovina. The Romanian government complied, after which, Soviet troops entered the region on June 28. See the online *Encyclopaedia Britannica* article at https://www.britannica.com/place/Bessarabia. Accessed on Saturday July 25, 2020.

3332 https://www.1000dokumente.de/index.html?c=dokument_de&dokument=0025_pak&object=translation&st=&l=de. Accessed on Saturday July 25, 2020.

3333 Ibid.

[3334] Pages 482 to 485 of Chapter 32 "Between Surrender and Defiance" of *Lenin, Stalin and Hitler* by by Robert Gellately, published by Vintage 2008, ISBN 9780712603577. See also page 509 of the same book, which states how one year later, in late 1942, the situation had made a 180 degree turn, with Ribbentrop, proposing that Hitler now make peace with Stalin.

[3335] Ibid page 509.

[3336] Position 117.1 of *The Devils' Alliance: Hitler's Pact with Stalin, 1939—41*.

[3337] Page 18 of *World War II - Behind Closed Doors: Stalin, the Nazis and the West* by Laurence Rees, published by Random House, 2009, ISBN 184607794X, 9781846077944.

[3338] Ibid and position 117.5 of *The Devils' Alliance: Hitler's Pact with Stalin, 1939—41*.

[3339] Page 19 of *World War II - Behind Closed Doors: Stalin, the Nazis and the West* and position 118.0 of *The Devils' Alliance: Hitler's Pact with Stalin, 1939—41*.

[3340] [3778] [3781] Page 18 of *World War II - Behind Closed Doors: Stalin, the Nazis and the West* and position 118.0 of *The Devils' Alliance: Hitler's Pact with Stalin, 1939—41*.

[3341] Positions 9.6 and 340.5 of *Case White The Invasion of Poland, 1939* by Robert Forczyk, published by Osprey Publishing 2019, eISBN 9781472834942.

[3342] In regard to the Comintern (Communist International), see endnotes [336] to [338] of Chapter 3 "Evil's Storm Descends."

[3343] Page 358 of *Lenin, Stalin and Hitler* by by Robert Gellately, published by Vintage 2008, ISBN 9780712603577.

[3344] In regard to the prevailing public opinion and policy of US isolationism at the time, see endnotes [1280] to [1282] of Chapter 17 "Pastor and Spy."

[3345] Page 358 of *Lenin, Stalin and Hitler* by by Robert Gellately, published by Vintage 2008, ISBN 9780712603577.

[3346] Page 358 to 359 of *Lenin, Stalin and Hitler* by by Robert Gellately, published by Vintage 2008, ISBN 9780712603577.

[3347] Position 582.1 of *Mao: The Unknown Story* by Jung Chang and Jon Halliday, published by Vintage of the Random House Group, 2007, Epub ISBN 9781448156863.

[3348] Page 359 of *Lenin, Stalin and Hitler* by by Robert Gellately, published by Vintage 2008, ISBN 9780712603577.

[3349] Position 581.1 of *Mao: The Unknown Story* by Jung Chang and Jon Halliday, published by Vintage of the Random House Group, Epub ISBN 9781448156863.

[3350] Position 583.1 of *Mao: The Unknown Story* by Jung Chang and Jon Halliday, published by Vintage of the Random House Group, Epub ISBN 9781448156863.

[3351] Page 359 of *Lenin, Stalin and Hitler* by by Robert Gellately, published by Vintage 2008, ISBN 9780712603577.

[3352] Position 580.1 of *Mao: The Unknown Story* by Jung Chang and Jon Halliday, published by Vintage of the Random House Group, Epub ISBN 9781448156863.

[3353] [3778] [3781] Ibid position 580.5.

[3354] These dates can be found in "APPENDIX C: CHRONOLOGY" of *Case White The Invasion of Poland, 1939* by Robert Forczyk, published by Osprey Publishing 2019, eISBN 9781472834942 from position 904.0.

[3355] https://avalon.law.yale.edu/20th_century/sesupp.asp and *Secret Supplementary Protocols of the Molotov-Ribbentrop Non-Aggression Pact, 1939*, September, 1939, History and Public Policy Program Digital Archive, Published in Nazi-Soviet Relations, 1939-1941: Documents from the Archives of the German Foreign Office at the Wilson Center Digital Archive at https://digitalarchive.wilsoncenter.org/document/110994. All links accessed on Saturday July 25, 2020.

[3356] See endnote [3327] for this supplement.

[3357] The timetable for Ribbentrop's second visit to Moscow from https://avalon.law.yale.edu/20th_century/ns086.asp. Accessed on Saturday July 25, 2020.

[3358] Online article *Nazis and communists divvy up Poland at* https://www.history.com/this-day-in-history/nazis-and-communists-divvy-up-poland, by History.com Editors, published by A&E Television Networks, last updated September 25, 2019, original publication date November 16, 2009. See also the Wilson Center Digital Archive at https://digitalarchive.wilsoncenter.org/document/110994 and https://avalon.law.yale.edu/20th_century/sesupp.asp. All links accessed on Saturday July 25, 2020.

[3359] The Wilson Center Digital Archive at https://digitalarchive.wilsoncenter.org/document/110994 and https://avalon.law.yale.edu/20th_century/sesupp.asp. Both links accessed on Saturday July 25, 2020.

[3360] See endnotes [154] to [167] of the Preface "Birth and Memory upon the Lesser Known Fault Line of History" in regard to the two or so decades dormant July 1920 Spa-London-Moscow Telegram, also known as the Curzon Line telegram — see endnote [156].

[3361] Bottom of page 170 of *White Eagle Red Star* and position 360.0 of the ebook.

[3362] See endnote [6] and endnotes [171] to [173] and [197] to [220] of the Preface "Birth and Memory upon the Lesser Known Fault Line of History" in regard to the so-called "Recovered Territories" and post WWII twin displacement west of eastern Germans and eastern Poles.

[3363] See endnotes [2641] to [2644] of Chapter 26 "Oma Ruth's Progeny After Death" in regard to the deportation of eastern Germans post-war.

[3364] See endnote [171] in the Preface "Birth and Memory upon the Lesser Known Fault Line of History."

[3365] [3688] See the comparative map on page 372 of *The Polish Way* by Adam Zamoyski (a friend of Norman Davies), published by John Murray Publishers Limited, 1989, ISBN 10: 0719546745 ISBN 13: 9780719546747, then read Adam Zamoyski's comments from pages 371 to 372.

[3366] See endnote [1232] of Chapter 17 "Pastor and Spy."

[3367] [2528] [3372] [3388] [3536] [3932] [4054] [4121] [4129] [4570] See endnote [204] in the Preface "Birth and Memory upon the Lesser Known Fault Line of History" in regard to the deportation of Borderland Poles to the Gulag.

[3368] [3933] See the film *A forgotten Odyssey* written and directed by Jagna Wright née Rafp; produced by Jagna Wright née Rafp, Aneta Naszyńska, narrated by Stephen Wright, released 1990. The VHS can be purchased from TROVE National Library of Australia at https://trove.nla.gov.au/work/28569419?q&versionId=34730839. Accessed on Saturday July 25, 2020.

[3369] Pages 511 to 522 in Chapter 34 "ETHNIC CLEANSING IN WARTIME SOVIET UNION" of *Lenin, Stalin and Hitler* by by Robert Gellately, published by Vintage 2008, ISBN 9780712603577. Bear in mind, that even after the launch of Barbarossa, many of the deported Borderland Poles, were still not released — as stated in the film *A forgotten Odyssey*.

[3370] Pages 62 to 63 and pages 167 to 174 of *Lenin, Stalin and Hitler* by by Robert Gellately, published by Vintage 2008, ISBN 9780712603577.

[3371] [3933] The film *A forgotten Odyssey* written and directed by Jagna Wright née Rafp; produced by Jagna Wright née Rafp, Aneta Naszyńska, narrated by Stephen Wright, released 1990.

[3372] [3933] From endnote [3367] to here, see the film *A forgotten Odyssey* written and directed by Jagna Wright née Rafp; produced by Jagna Wright née Rafp, Aneta Naszyńska, narrated by Stephen Wright, released 1990. The VHS can be purchased from TROVE National Library of Australia at https://trove.nla.gov.au/work/28569419?q&versionId=34730839. Accessed on Saturday July 25, 2020.

[3373] [2528] [3388] [3536] [3932] [4054] [4121] [4129] [4570] Ibid.

[3374] Position 1244.4 of *Microcosm*.

[3375] See endnote [222] of the Preface "Birth and Memory upon the Lesser Known Fault Line of History" in regard to this speech and the mysterious death of the Polish "Stalin" Bolesław Bierut that time in Moscow during the 20th Congress. See also position 1244.5 of *Microcosm*.

[3376] [3389] Page 388 of *Lenin, Stalin and Hitler* by by Robert Gellately, published by Vintage 2008, ISBN 9780712603577.

[3377] [3389] Ibid.

[3378] Ibid.

[3379] Page 387 of Ibid.

[3380] [3878] Article by Grover Furr at https://msuweb.montclair.edu/~furrg/research/furr_katyn_2013.pdf on the website of Montclair State University. See his profile at https://www.montclair.edu/profilepages/view_profile.php?username=furrg. In regard to the Stalinist perpetrated Katyń Wood Massacre, see Polish WWII Supplement III "The Katyń Wood Massacre."[3618] Both links accessed on Saturday July 25, 2020.

[3381] Article by Grover Furr at https://msuweb.montclair.edu/~furrg/research/mlg09/did_ussr_invade_poland.html. Accessed on Saturday July 25, 2020.

[3382] The timeline at position 738.8 of *Case White The Invasion of Poland, 1939* by Robert Forczyk, published by Osprey Publishing 2019, eISBN 9781472834942.

[3383] [3395] Page 115 of the article *THE FOREIGN POLICY OF JÓZEF PIŁSUDSKI AND JÓZEF BECK, 1926-1939: MISCONCEPTIONS AND INTERPRETATIONS* by Anna M. Cienciala, published in The Polish Review, Vol. LVI, Nos. 1-2, 2011:111-152. Here, two crucial facts must be mentioned. Firstly, as also stated on page 115, this pact was balanced by The Polish-German Declaration of Non-Aggression of January 26, 1934, valid for ten years. Secondly, unlike the Molotov-Ribbentrop pact, these pacts contained no secret protocols, as stated on pages 117 to 118. For more information on these pacts, see endnotes [3471] to [3479] for this supplement.

[3384] [1942] These dates can be found in "APPENDIX C: CHRONOLOGY" of *Case White The Invasion of Poland, 1939* by Robert Forczyk, published by Osprey Publishing 2019, eISBN 9781472834942 from position 904.0.

[3385] Article on the website of *Human Rights in Ukraine — Website of the Kharkiv Human Rights Protection Group* at http://khpg.org/en/index.php?id=1472775460. Accessed on Saturday July 25, 2020.

[3386] [3879] Article *Decision to commence investigation into Katyn Massacre*, dated November 30 2004 at https://ipn.gov.pl/en/news/77,dok.html on the website of the Polish INSTITUTE OF NATIONAL REMEMBRANCE. Accessed on Saturday July 25, 2020.

[3387] [3878] Position 746.1 of *Case White The Invasion of Poland, 1939* by Robert Forczyk.

[3388] See endnotes [3367] to [3373] for this supplement.

[3389] See endnotes [3376] and [3377] for this supplement.

[3390] Position 746.4 of *Case White The Invasion of Poland, 1939* by Robert Forczyk.

[3391] Position 130.5 of *The Devils' Alliance: Hitler's Pact with Stalin, 1939—41*.

[3392] Ibid.

³³⁹³ Position 342.0 of the autobiographical ebook *Soldier in the Downfall: A Wehrmacht Cavalryman in Russia, Normandy, and the Plot to Kill Hitler*, by Rudolf-Christoph von Gersdorff (Author), Anthony Pearsall (Translator), published by The Aberjona Press (25 March 2013), ASIN: B00C6FYGP2, ISBN 13: 9780977756377.

³³⁹⁴ Position 746.5 of *Case White The Invasion of Poland, 1939* by Robert Forczyk.

³³⁹⁵ See endnote ³³⁸³ for this supplement.

³³⁹⁶ Position 747.0 of *Case White The Invasion of Poland, 1939* by Robert Forczyk.

³³⁹⁷ ˣˡⁱⁱⁱ ³⁵²⁷ For more information on this episode of the Teschen district, see endnotes ⁹⁵² to ⁹⁶⁶ of Chapter 13 "Flight and the Tumultuous Appeasement of Evil."

³³⁹⁸ The article *Turning Back Time: Putting Putin's Molotov-Ribbentrop Defense Into Context* by By Robert Coalson, dated May 15, 2015 06:49 GMT on the website of Radio Free Europe at https://www.rferl.org/a/putin-russia-molotov-ribbentrop-pact/27017723.html. Accessed on Saturday July 25, 2020.

³³⁹⁹ Page 421 of William L. Shirer.

³⁴⁰⁰ BUTTIN, FÉLIX. *The Polish-Czechoslovak Conflict over Teschen Silesia (1918—1920): a Case Study.* Perspectives, no. 25, 2005, pp. 63—78. JSTOR, https:www.jstor.org/stable/23616032. Page 65 gives the date of January 23 1919 when Czechoslovakia invaded Poland. Accessed on Saturday July 25, 2020.

³⁴⁰¹ Page 75 of *Germany and European Order: Enlarging NATO and the EU* by Adrian Hyde-Price, published by Manchester University Press, 2000, ISBN 0719054281, 9780719054280, quotes Churchill's written statement post Great War; *"The war of giants has ended, the wars of the pygmies begin."* As does page 21 of *White Eagle Red Star* and position 27.6 of the ebook.

³⁴⁰² Page 421 of William L. Shirer.

³⁴⁰³ ˣˡⁱⁱⁱ ³⁵²⁷ Position 1103.3 of Microcosm states that the non-communist Polish Home Army (AK — Armia Krajowa) was the largest underground movement in Nazi occupied Europe. See also page 183 of *Rising '44: The Battle for Warsaw* Reprint Edition (October 4, 2005), ISBN-10: 0143035401, ISBN-13: 9780143035404 where it documents the underwhelming figure for the communist Armia Ludowa (AL) of 800 in Warsaw in 1943, as compared to the Home Army (AK — Armia Krajowa) with 40,330 men!

³⁴⁰⁴ See endnotes ³²⁷⁶ and ³²⁷⁷ near the beginning for this supplement, as well as endnote ³²⁹⁷ in regard to Stalin's months of negotiations with Anglo-French missions from March to August 1939.

³⁴⁰⁵ See endnote ³²⁷⁵ near the beginning for this supplement in regard to the sacking of Maxim Litvinov.

³⁴⁰⁶ See Shirer's quote of Stalin to Churchill, during the latter's visit to Moscow in August 1942 on page 526.

3407 Position 112.0 to 112.2 of *The Devils' Alliance: Hitler's Pact with Stalin, 1939—41*, quoting the conversation between Ribbentrop and Stalin, following the conclusion of talks on August 23 1939 in regard to the Secret Protocol.

3408 Position 276.2 of *The Devils' Alliance: Hitler's Pact with Stalin, 1939—41*.

3409 Ibid position 600.6.

3410 Ibid positions 379.5 and 311.2 and position 417.1 of *Bloodlands* by Timothy Snyder, published by The Bodley Head of the Random House Group 2010, ISBN 9781407075501.

3411 Pages 95 to 96 of the essay *The Reception of William L. Shirer's the Rise and Fall of the Third Reich in the United States and West Germany, 1960—62* by Gavriel D. Rosenfeld, a doctoral candidate of the University of California. It can be viewed on the website of the University of California Santa Barbara at http://marcuse.faculty.history.ucsb.edu/classes/201/articles/94RosenfeldShirerJCH.pdf. Accessed on Saturday July 25, 2020.

3412 3528 Book review by Bryan Hiatt on the World War II Database at https://ww2db.com/read.php?read_id=75. Accessed on Saturday July 25, 2020. See also page 595 of *Berlin Diary: The JOURNAL of a Foreign Correspondent 1934-1941* by William L. Shirer, published by ALFRED A. KNOPF New York 1942, where Shirer describes his final and nervous broadcast from Berlin on the evening of December 3, 1940.

3413 *Berlin Diary: The JOURNAL of a Foreign Correspondent 1934-1941* by William L. Shirer, published by ALFRED A. KNOPF New York 1942. The book's title has "JOURNAL" in upper-case.

3414 See also endnotes [1244] and [1245] of Chapter 17 "Pastor and Spy" in reference to my September 2014 visit to the old Nazi Rally grounds in Nuremburg, where I record the impressions of our German guide, and how his father and granfather had difficulty coming to terms with Germany's Nazi past.

3415 Pages 117 to 118 of the essay *The Reception of William L. Shirer's the Rise and Fall of the Third Reich in the United States and West Germany, 1960—62* by Gavriel D. Rosenfeld.

3416 Ibid pages 115 to 116.

3417 Ibid.

3418 Article on Oswald Mosley at https://www.britannica.com/biography/Oswald-Mosley. Accessed on Saturday July 25, 2020.

3419 In regard to Dietrich's 1930-31 trip to America, see endnotes [277] to [298] of Chapter 1 "Roots, Genesis and Moulding of the Pastor."

3420 Pages 116 to 117 of the essay *The Reception of William L. Shirer's the Rise and Fall of the Third Reich in the United States and West Germany, 1960—62* by Gavriel D. Rosenfeld.

[3421] See the photo on page 86 of *White Robes and Burning Crosses: A History of the Ku Klux Klan from 1866* by Michael Newton, published by McFarland, 2016, ISBN 1476617198, 9781476617190.

[3422] Page 85 of *White Robes and Burning Crosses: A History of the Ku Klux Klan from 1866* by Michael Newton, published by McFarland, 2016, ISBN 1476617198, 9781476617190.

[3423] See endnotes [287] to [290] of Chapter 1 "Roots, Genesis and Moulding of the Pastor."

[3424] See endnotes [300] to [302] of Chapter 2 "Ominous Clouds on the Horizon."

[3425] Page 533 of *Rise And Fall Of The Third Reich: A History of Nazi Germany* by William L. Shirer.

[3426] Ibid page 536.

[3427] Ibid pages 533 to 538.

[3428] See endnote [627] of Chapter 6 "Old Prussia — Birth of Ruth to Precarious Survival."

[3429] Ibid.

[3430] The online article *80th Anniversary of a Poisonous Partnership: Hitler and Stalin* by Peter Kenez, emeritus professor of history at the University of California at Santa Cruz, dated August 5, 2019 on the website of Law and Liberty at https://www.lawliberty.org/liberty-forum/80th-anniversary-of-a-poisonous-partnership-hitler-and-stalin/. Accessed on Saturday July 25, 2020.

[3431] See the online *Encyclopaedia Britannica* article on the Holodomor at https://www.britannica.com/event/Holodomor by the 2004 Pulitzer Prize winning author Anne Applebaum. Accessed on Saturday July 25, 2020.

[3432] The online article *80th Anniversary of a Poisonous Partnership: Hitler and Stalin* by Peter Kenez, emeritus professor of history at the University of California at Santa Cruz, dated August 5, 2019 on the website of Law and Liberty at https://www.lawliberty.org/liberty-forum/80th-anniversary-of-a-poisonous-partnership-hitler-and-stalin/. Accessed on Saturday July 25, 2020.

[3433] See endnote [1607] of Chapter 20 "Valkyrie II."

[3434] See endnote [1606] of Chapter 20 "Valkyrie II."

[3435] See also endnote [1233] of Chapter 17 "Pastor and Spy" and endnotes [718] to [725] of Chapter 9 "The von Kleists and the Prophecy."

[3436] Page 481 of *Lenin, Stalin and Hitler The Age of Social Catastrophe* by Robert Gellately.

[3437] Page 42 of *Warsaw 1920, Lenin's Failed Conquest of Europe* by Adam Zamoyski, paperback published by William Collins 2014, ISBN 9780007225538.

[3438] [4091] [4516] Ibid pages 117 to 119 and page 226 of *White Eagle Red Star*, by Professor Norman Davies, published in 2003 by Pimlico, Random House UK Limited, ISBN 9780712606943.

[3439] Page 226 of *White Eagle Red Star*, by Professor Norman Davies, published in 2003 by Pimlico, Random House UK Limited, ISBN 9780712606943.

[3440] [3846] Article of Joseph Stalin at https://www.britannica.com/biography/Joseph-Stalin by Ronald Francis Hingley, former lecturer in Russian, University of Oxford and author of *Chekhov: A Biographical and Critical Study*. Accessed on Saturday July 25, 2020.

[3441] Pages 265 to 267 of *White Eagle Red Star*, by Professor Norman Davies, published in 2003 by Pimlico, Random House UK Limited, ISBN 9780712606943 and page 73 of *Lenin, Stalin and Hitler The Age of Social Catastrophe* by Robert Gellately. The latter states the scale of Lenin's illusions was monumental.

[3442] The article on the Poland Today website at https://poland-today.pl/echoes-of-the-past/. Accessed on Saturday July 25, 2020.

[3443] [191] [3367] [3846] Pages 133 to 134 of *Warsaw 1920, Lenin's Failed Conquest of Europe* by Adam Zamoyski.

[3444] Position 729.8 of *Case White The Invasion of Poland, 1939* by Robert Forczyk.

[3445] Page 583 of *Lenin, Stalin and Hitler The Age of Social Catastrophe* by Robert Gellately.

[3446] Ibid pages 169 to 172.

[3447] Ibid pages 227 to 239 in Chapter 14 "FIGHT AGAINST THE COUNTRYSIDE."

[3448] Ibid page 275.

[3449] Ibid pages 267 to 281 of Chapter 17 "'CLEANSING' THE SOVIET ELITE."

[3450] Ibid page 250.

[3451] Ibid.

[3452] Ibid page 583 in the EPILOGUE.

[3453] Ibid page 583 in the EPILOGUE.

[3454] Ibid pages 583 to 584 in the EPILOGUE and position 471.5 of The Gulag Archipelago 1918—56: An Experiment in Literary Investigation, by Aleksandr Solzhenitsyn, published by Vintage Publishing London 2018, Epub ISBN 9781448128624.

[3455] Page 584 of *Lenin, Stalin and Hitler The Age of Social Catastrophe* in the EPILOGUE.

[3456] Ibid page 584 in the EPILOGUE.

[3457] Website of Anne Applebaum at https://www.anneapplebaum.com/anne-applebaum/ and the Pulitzer website at https://www.pulitzer.org/prize-winners-by-year/2004 and bookspot at http://www.bookspot.com/lists/pulitzer04.htm. All links accessed on Saturday July 25, 2020.

[3458] Ibid page 584 in the EPILOGUE and position 1449.8 of *Gulag: A History of the Soviet Camps* by Anne Applebaum, published by Penguin Books Limited, ISBN 9780141975269.

[3459] Page 584 of *Lenin, Stalin and Hitler The Age of Social Catastrophe* in the EPILOGUE.

[3460] Ibid page 252. See also page 278 of *Molotov Remembers: Inside Kremlin Politics* by V. M. Molotov, Feliz Chuev, edited by Albert Rees, published by Ivan R. Dee, 2007, ISBN 1461694914, 9781461694915. This book is the edited English translation of *Sto sorok besed s Molotovym: Iz dnevnika F. Chueva (Сто сорок бесед с Молотовым: Из дневника Ф. Чуева) — One Hundred and Forty Conversations with Molotov: From the Diary of F. Chuev*, paperback published by Terra Publishing Centre in Moscow 1991. This was the source used by Robert Gellately.

[3461] Page 353 of *The Polish Way* by Adam Zamoyski, published by John Murray Publishers Limited, 1989, ISBN 10: 0719546745 ISBN 13: 9780719546747.

[3462] Page 354 of *The Polish Way* by Adam Zamoyski.

[3463] See pages 22 to 23 of *No Greater Ally, The Untold Story of Poland's Forces in World War II*, by Kenneth K. Koskodan, published by Osprey Publishing 2011, ISBN-13: 9781849084796. Page 41 describes how the Poles, had never expected to fight a protracted campaign on their own against Germany, and as it turned out, against the Soviets on their eastern frontier.

[3464] Page 353 of *The Polish Way* by Adam Zamoyski, published by John Murray Publishers Limited, 1989, ISBN 10: 0719546745 ISBN 13: 9780719546747.

[3465] Position 365.1 of *Bloodlands* by Timothy Snyder, published by The Bodley Head of the Random House Group 2010, ISBN 9781407075501.

[3466] Page 219 of *Hitler's Pre-emptive War: The Battle for Norway, 1940* by Henrik O. Lunde, published by Casemate Publishers, 2009, ISBN 1932033920, 9781932033922.

[3467] Ibid page 3.

[3468] See endnotes [941] to [947] of Chapter 13 "Flight and the Tumultuous Appeasement of Evil" in regard to Chamberlain's appeasement of Hitler at Munich in late September 1938.

[3469] See Chapter 2 "French Misfortunes: The Phony War and the Defense of France" from pages 42-58 of Koskodan.

[3470] [3528] Page 55 of Koskodan.

[3471] [3383] [4403] Page 115 of the article *THE FOREIGN POLICY OF JÓZEF PIŁSUDSKI AND JÓZEF BECK, 1926-1939: MISCONCEPTIONS AND INTERPRETATIONS* by Anna M. Cienciala, published in The Polish Review, Vol. LVI, Nos. 1-2, 2011:111-152.

[3472] Ibid pages 117 to 118.

[3473] [3692] Position 70.6 of *The Devils' Alliance: Hitler's Pact with Stalin, 1939—41* and position 298.0 of *Bloodlands* by Timothy Snyder, published by The Bodley Head of the Random House Group 2010, ISBN 9781407075501.

[3474] Page 336 of *Piłsudski: A Life For Poland*, by Wacław Jędrzejewicz, published by Hippocrene Books, New York, 1982, ISBN 9780870527470.

[3475] Ibid page 347.

[3476] Ibid. The port of Gdańsk (Danzig) was where a German Battleship fired the first shots of WWII. See endnote [3539] of Polish WWII Supplement II "The Gleiwitz (Gliwice) Incident." In regard to the legal status of the then Free City of Danzig/Gdańsk, see endnotes [3543] to [3067], also in Polish WWII Supplement II "The Gleiwitz (Gliwice) Incident."

[3477] Page 118 of the article *THE FOREIGN POLICY OF JÓZEF PIŁSUDSKI AND JÓZEF BECK, 1926-1939: MISCONCEPTIONS AND INTERPRETATIONS* by Anna M. Cienciala, published in The Polish Review, Vol. LVI, Nos. 1-2, 2011:111-152.

[3478] [3383] Ibid page 118.

[3479] [3383] Page 354 of *The Polish Way* by Adam Zamoyski, published by John Murray Publishers Limited, 1989, ISBN 10: 0719546745 ISBN 13: 9780719546747.

[3480] Position 69.3 of *The Devils' Alliance: Hitler's Pact with Stalin, 1939—41*.

[3481] Ibid position 70.1.

[3482] See endnote [2] from the Preface "Birth and Memory upon the Lesser Known Fault Line of History" in regard to the partitioning of Poland in 1795 between the empires of Tsarist Russia, Prussia and Austria.

[3483] [3692] [4403] Position 70.5 of *The Devils' Alliance: Hitler's Pact with Stalin, 1939—41*.

[3484] On the website of America's library at http://www.americaslibrary.gov/jb/jazz/jb_jazz_wwi_1.html. Accessed on Saturday July 25, 2020.

[3485] Pages 58 to 59 of *Piłsudski: A Life For Poland*, by Wacław Jędrzejewicz, published by Hippocrene Books, New York, 1982, ISBN 9780870527470.

[3486] See Chapter 4 "NAZISM AND THE THREAT OF BOLSHEVISM" from page 81 of *Lenin, Stalin and Hitler* by by Robert Gellately, published by Vintage 2008, ISBN 9780712603577.

[3487] Ibid page 318.

[3488] Ibid.

[3489] Ibid pages 359 to 369.

[3490] [3682] [4484] Position 205.5 of *The Devils' Alliance: Hitler's Pact with Stalin, 1939—41*.

[3491] Ibid position 248.5.

[3492] Ibid position 247.6. See endnote [3329] for this supplement for clarification on the changing sovereignty of Wilno/Vilnius.

[3493] [3682] Ibid position 204.7.

[3494] Ibid position 247.9.

[3495] Ibid position 251.0.

[3496] Ibid position 251.4.

[3497] Ibid position 253.4.

[3498] Ibid position 209.0.

[3499] Ibid position 208.6.

[3500] Ibid position 253.4.

[3501] See https://www.jstor.org/stable/43211534. JSTOR provides access to more than 12 million academic journal articles, books, and primary sources in 75 disciplines. See https://about.jstor.org/. Both links accessed on Saturday July 25, 2020. Both links accessed on Saturday July 25, 2020.

[3502] Position 206.2 of *The Devils' Alliance: Hitler's Pact with Stalin, 1939—41.*

[3503] [4484] Ibid position 206.7

[3504] Article *REFLECTIONS ON THE HOLOCAUST IN LITHUANIA: A NEW BOOK BY ALFONSAS EIDINTAS* by Alfred E. Senn of the University of Wisconsin in the LITHUANIAN QUARTERLY JOURNAL OF ARTS AND SCIENCES, Volume 47, No. 4 - Winter 2001, Editor of this issue: M. Gražina Slavėnas, ISSN 0024-5089, LITUANUS Foundation, Inc.

[3505] Ibid.

[3506] Ibid.

[3507] Ibid. See also page 170 of Menachim Begin's book *White Nights: The Story of a Prisoner in Russia*, published by Macdonald, 1957, no ISBN given.

[3508] Article on Menachem Begin at https://www.britannica.com/biography/Menachem-Begin. Accessed on Saturday July 25, 2020.

[3509] Position 684.4 of *The Devils' Alliance: Hitler's Pact with Stalin, 1939—41.*

[3510] Page 161 of *Estonia and the Estonians: Second Edition* by Toivo U. Raun, published by Hoover Press, 2002, ISBN 0817928537, 9780817928537.

[3511] Ibid.

[3512] Ibid page 167.

[3513] [3664] [3673] See the online *Encyclopaedia Britannica* article on Finland at https://www.britannica.com/place/Finland. Accessed on Saturday July 25, 2020.

[3514] Position 231.3 of *The Devils' Alliance: Hitler's Pact with Stalin, 1939—41.*

[3515] The Central Intelligence Agency report online titled *The Katyń Controversy: Stalin's Killing Field* by Benjamin B. Fischer at https://www.cia.gov/library/center-for-the-study-of-intelligence/csi-publications/csi-studies/studies/winter99-00/art6.html. Accessed on Saturday July 25, 2020.

[3516] Position 217.3 of *The Devils' Alliance: Hitler's Pact with Stalin, 1939—41.*

[3517] [3674] Online *Encyclopaedia Britannica* article on the Russo-Finnish War at https://www.britannica.com/event/Russo-Finnish-War. Accessed on Saturday July 25, 2020.

[3518] [3674] Ibid.

[3519] [3664] [3673] Ibid.

[3520] [4472] [4484] [4549] [4550] The online articles on the BBC website at https://www.bbc.com/news/world-europe-49446735 titled *Molotov-Ribbentrop: Five states remember 'misery' pact victims* and the website of *The Atlantic* at https://www.theatlantic.com/ideas/archive/2019/08/molotov-ribbentrop-pact/596596/ titled *The Lasting Lesson of the Molotov-Ribbentrop Pact* by Nicholas Burns Former U.S. ambassador to NATO, dated August 23 2019. Both links accessed on Saturday July 25, 2020. See also the description of the photo of part of the human chain from position 746.0 of *The Devils' Alliance: Hitler's Pact with Stalin, 1939—41*.

3521 4472 4484 4551 Ibid.

3522 4552 Article on the Berlin Wall at https://www.britannica.com/topic/Berlin-Wall.

3523 4553 Online article and photo in the Wall Street Journal at https://www.wsj.com/articles/SB124051894535749519, updated April 24, 2009 and the online poll on the Polish History Museum website at http://muzhp.pl/en/polls/206. See also the online *Encyclopaedia Britannica* article on Feliks Edmundovich Dzerzhinsky, (Polish Feliks Dzierżyński) at https://www.britannica.com/biography/Feliks-Edmundovich-Dzerzhinsky. All links accessed on Saturday July 25, 2020.

3524 The online article on the website of *The Atlantic* at https://www.theatlantic.com/ideas/archive/2019/08/molotov-ribbentrop-pact/596596/ titled *The Lasting Lesson of the Molotov-Ribbentrop Pact* by Nicholas Burns Former U.S. ambassador to NATO, dated August 23 2019. Accessed on Saturday July 25, 2020.

3525 Ibid.

3526 Position 340.9 of *Case White The Invasion of Poland, 1939* by Robert Forczyk.

3527 See endnotes 3397 to 3403 for this supplement for Vladimir Putin's view of the 1938 Polish annexation of the Teschen region justifying the Soviet annexation of eastern Poland in September to October 1939.

3528 See endnotes 3412 to 3470 for this supplement in regard to the reasons why Poland did not voluntarily allow Soviet troops on its soil in 1939.

3529 Position 340.2 of *Case White The Invasion of Poland, 1939* by Robert Forczyk.

3530 Ibid position 340.5.

3531 Ibid position 9.6.

3532 Ibid position 340.6.

3533 Ibid position 340.8.

3534 On the Harvard University Law website for the Nuremberg Trials at http://nuremberg.law.harvard.edu/documents/4926-secret-protocol-supplementing-the-german-soviet?q=Molotov-Ribbentrop#p.1. Accessed on Saturday July 25, 2020.

3535 4549 See endnote 3282 for this supplement in regard to Ribbentrop's telegram from the Berghof to the German ambassador in Moscow on Friday August 18 1939, where Ribbentrop mentions the discussion of "sphere's of interest."

3536 See endnotes 3367 to 3373 for this supplement.

Polish WWII Supplement II — The Gleiwitz (Gliwice) Incident

[3537] [1096] [2886] [2886] [2887] See the link at http://gov.genealogy.net/item/show/GLIICEJO90IH for German Gleiwitz becoming Polish Gliwice post WWII. Accessed on Saturday July 25, 2020.

[3538] See endnote [3556] for this supplement.

[3539] [3476] [3608] Position 9.0 of the ebook *The Second World War: Ambitions to Nemesis* by Bradley Lightbody, published by the Taylor & Francis e-Library, 2004, eISBN 9781134592722. In April 2005, I visited the ruins of the Westerplatte Fort.

[3540] The extract "Free city of Danzig" from pages 382 to 387 of *Ten Years of World Cooperation* (League of Nations, 1930), Document symbol: A/AC.25/Com.Jer/W.6. It can viewed on the United Nations website at https://www.un.org/unispal/document/auto-insert-210766/. Accessed on Saturday July 25, 2020.

[3541] *THE FREE CITY OF DANZIG: BORDERLAND, HANSESTADT OR SOCIAL DEMOCRACY?* by Elizabeth Morrow Clark in *The Polish Review*, volume 42, no. 3, 1997, page 262. This article can be viewed online at JSTOR, https://www.jstor.org/stable/25779004. Accessed on Saturday July 25, 2020.

[3542] Position 154.4 of the ebook *The Second World War: Ambitions to Nemesis* by Bradley Lightbody.

[3543] [3476] Positions 11.5 and 997.6 of the ebook *Case White The Invasion of Poland, 1939* by Robert Forczyk, published by Osprey Publishing 2019, eISBN 9781472834942.

[3544] Position 13.6 of the ebook *Case White The Invasion of Poland, 1939* by Robert Forczyk.

[3545] Page 85 of *No Greater Ally, The Untold Story of Poland's Forces in World War II*, by Kenneth K. Koskodan, published by Osprey Publishing 2011, ISBN-13: 9781849084796. This for example, correctly contradicts the assertion of Bradley Lightbody in *The Second World War: Ambitions to Nemesis* from positions 155.6 to 155.9.

[3546] Positions 835.5 and 857.0 of the ebook *Case White The Invasion of Poland, 1939* by Robert Forczyk. The former refers to the first Allied Air Ace of WWII, Stanisław Skalski. See the ebook *Skalski Against All Odds: The First Allied Ace of the Second World War* by Franciszek Grabowski, published by Fonthill Media Limited, 2017, eISBN 9781781555491.

[3547] Position 15.2 of the ebook *Case White The Invasion of Poland, 1939* by Robert Forczyk. Again, this correctly contradicts the assertion of Bradley Lightbody in *The Second World War: Ambitions to Nemesis* from positions 155.6 to 155.9.

[3548] Position 156.0 to 156.4 of the ebook *The Second World War: Ambitions to Nemesis* by Bradley Lightbody and position 573.8 to 576.8 of *Case White The Invasion of Poland, 1939* by Robert Forczyk.

[3549] Position 153.0 of the ebook *The Second World War: Ambitions to Nemesis* by Bradley Lightbody.

[3550] Ibid position 155.4.

[3551] Position 371.0 of Robert Forczyk. In regard to the various Intelligence agencies within the Third Reich, see endnote [1183] of Chapter 17 "Pastor and Spy."

[3552] Position 154.9 of Bradley Lightbody.

[3553] In regard to the obsequious character of Wilhelm Keitel, see endnote [905] from Chapter 13 "Flight and the Tumultuous Appeasement of Evil."

[3554] Page 518 of *Rise And Fall Of The Third Reich: A History of Nazi Germany* by William L. Shirer, published by Simon and Schuster, 1990, ISBN 0671728687, 9780671728687.

[3555] See Polish WWII Supplement I "The Molotov-Ribbentrop Pact."[3268]

[3556] [3538] [3617] Position 34.9 of the ebook *First to Fight: The Polish War 1939* by Roger Moorhouse, published by Penguin Books Limited, ISBN 9781473548220.

[3557] Ibid position 39.8.

[3558] Ibid position 40.2.

[3559] Ibid position 40.5.

[3560] Ibid position 41.0.

[3561] In regard to the various departments of the Reich Security Main Office (*Reichssicherheitshauptamt* — RSHA), see endnotes [1181] to [1183] of Chapter 17 "Pastor and Spy" and endnote [128] of the Preface "Birth and Memory upon the Lesser Known Fault Line of History."

[3562] [3576] Page 519 of *Rise And Fall Of The Third Reich: A History of Nazi Germany* by William L. Shirer, published by Simon and Schuster, 1990, ISBN 0671728687, 9780671728687.

[3563] [3576] [3612] Nuremberg Trial Proceedings Volume 4 TWENTY-FOURTH DAY Thursday, 20 December 1945 which can be viewed online on the website of the Avalon Project of the Yale Law School at https://avalon.law.yale.edu/imt/12-20-45.asp. Accessed on Saturday July 25, 2020.

[3564] In regard to the various departments of the Reich Security Main Office (*Reichssicherheitshauptamt* — RSHA), see endnotes [1181] to [1183] of Chapter 17 "Pastor and Spy" and endnote [128] of the Preface "Birth and Memory upon the Lesser Known Fault Line of History."

[3565] [1897] See endnotes [1589] from Chapter 19 "The Tormentor Tormented," and [1602], [1897] and [1957] from Chapter 20 "Valkyrie II" in regard to Reinhard Heydrich chairing the 1942 Wannsee Conference. As stated in endnote [1589], Heydrich was also the chief co-ordinator of the nationwide Röhm Purge in June/July 1934 (see endnotes [92] to [107] of the Preface "Birth and Memory upon the Lesser Known Fault Line of History") and the nationwide Reichskristallnacht pogrom in November 1938 (see endnote [992] of Chapter 14 "Reichskristallnacht"). Heydrich would die in Prague in early June 1942, following and assassination attempt by the Czech underground in late May. The German recriminations unleashed upon the Czechs, were monstrously disproportionate to say the least. See endnotes [1954] and [1956] of Chapter 20 "Valkyrie II."

[3566] Document 2751-PS — Exhibit USA-482 — the affidavit of Alfred Helmut Naujocks, dated November 20, 1945, from Nuremberg Trial Proceedings Volume 4, TWENTY-FOURTH DAY Thursday, 20 December 1945 Morning Session, which can be viewed at https://avalon.law.yale.edu/imt/12-20-45.asp. Accessed on Saturday July 25, 2020.

[3567] Ibid.

[3568] Position 364.1 of *Case White The Invasion of Poland, 1939* by Robert Forczyk gives the disposition of Polish and German forces on Friday September 1 1945. See also pages 361 and 385 of the book *Lenin, Stalin and Hitler* by Robert Gellately, published by Vintage 2008, ISBN 9780712603577.

[3569] Document 2751-PS — Exhibit USA-482 — the affidavit of Alfred Helmut Naujocks, dated November 20, 1945, from Nuremberg Trial Proceedings Volume 4, TWENTY-FOURTH DAY Thursday, 20 December 1945 Morning Session, which can be viewed online on the website of the Avalon Project of the Yale Law School at https://avalon.law.yale.edu/imt/12-20-45.asp. Accessed on Saturday July 25, 2020.

[3570] Ibid.

[3571] Ibid. At Gleiwitz, as will be discussed later, there was only one victim, and unlike the victims elsewhere, he was not dressed in a Polish military uniform, but in civilian clothes. The was because he was already widely known in the district as a pro-Polish agitator. He had been arrested for this purpose on August 30, and since Naujocks meeting with Heinrich Müller, according to Naujocks's affidavit, took place between the 25th and the 31st, it is not certain if the Gleiwitz victim, Franciszek Honiok, was already among these 12 to 13 condemned mentioned by Heinrich Müller. In any event, by the 30th, with his arrest, Franciszek Honiok's fate was sealed.

[3572] Ibid.

[3573] Document 2751-PS — Exhibit USA-482 — the affidavit of Alfred Helmut Naujocks, dated November 20, 1945, from Nuremberg Trial Proceedings Volume 4, TWENTY-FOURTH DAY Thursday, 20 December 1945 Morning Session.

[3574] [3604] Ibid.

[3575] Position 40.9 of the ebook *First to Fight: The Polish War 1939* by Roger Moorhouse, published by Penguin Books Limited, ISBN 9781473548220.

[3576] See endnotes [3562] and [3563] for this supplement in regard to the affidavit of Alfred Helmut Naujocks.

[3577] [3612] Ibid.

[3578] [3591] The article by Bob Graham in the UK Telegraph *World War II's first victim*, dated 7:00AM BST 29 Aug 2009. It can be viewed online at https://www.telegraph.co.uk/history/world-war-two/6106566/World-War-Iis-first-victim.html. Accessed on Saturday July 25, 2020. See also position 30.9 of the ebook *First to Fight: The Polish War 1939* by Roger Moorhouse, published by Penguin Books Limited, ISBN 9781473548220. Although, this states that Honiok at the time was 41 years-old rather than 43.

[3579] Page 140 of *Between Hitler and Stalin: The Quick Life and Secret Death of Edward Smigly Rydz, Marshal of Poland* by Archibald L. Patterson, published by Dog Ear Publishing, 2010, ISBN 1608445631, 9781608445639.

[3580] The eastern region of Germany was the heartland of the Reformation. See the UK Guardian article mentioned in endnote [644] from Chapter 7 "Zingst and Finkenwalde." See also endnote [42] from the Preface "Birth and Memory upon the Lesser Known Fault Line of History" in which Johann Heß, a fervent follower of Martin Luther, publicly professed the Lutheran faith for Silesian Breslau in 1524, in the midst of the Reformation, as well as endnote [44] from the Preface. Not to mention the fact that Oma Ruth was a native of Silesia and of course, a fervent Lutheran.

[3581] Page 140 of *Between Hitler and Stalin: The Quick Life and Secret Death of Edward Smigly Rydz, Marshal of Poland* by Archibald L. Patterson and the article by Bob Graham in the UK Telegraph *World War II's first victim.*

[3582] The article by Bob Graham in the UK Telegraph *World War II's first victim.*

[3583] The article by Bob Graham in the UK Telegraph *World War II's first victim.* See also endnotes [81] to [90] from the Preface "Birth and Memory upon the Lesser Known Fault Line of History" in regard to the three Silesian Uprisings in the years just following the Great War. Honiok may well have been involved in at least one of them.

[3584] The article by Bob Graham in the UK Telegraph *World War II's first victim.*

[3585] [3591] See the link at http://gov.genealogy.net/item/show/object_189954 for German Pohlam becoming Polish Połomia post WWII. Accessed on Saturday July 25, 2020.

[3586] Position 41.9 of the ebook *First to Fight: The Polish War 1939* by Roger Moorhouse, published by Penguin Books Limited, ISBN 9781473548220.

[3587] The article by Bob Graham in the UK Telegraph *World War II's first victim*, dated 7:00AM BST 29 Aug 2009. It can be viewed online at https://www.telegraph.co.uk/history/world-war-two/6106566/World-War-Iis-first-victim.html. Accessed on Saturday July 25, 2020.

[3588] Position 46.0 of the ebook *First to Fight: The Polish War 1939* by Roger Moorhouse, published by Penguin Books Limited, ISBN 9781473548220.

[3589] Ibid position 42.0.

[3590] Ibid position 42.5.

[3591] See endnotes [3578] to [3585] for this supplement.

[3592] Position 42.6 of the ebook *First to Fight: The Polish War 1939* by Roger Moorhouse, published by Penguin Books Limited, ISBN 9781473548220.

[3593] Ibid position 43.0.

3594 Ibid position 41.9.

3595 Ibid position 43.5.

3596 Ibid position 43.8.

3597 Ibid position 44.3.

3598 Ibid position 44.6.

3599 Ibid position 45.2.

3600 Ibid position 46.0.

3601 The article by Bob Graham in the UK Telegraph *World War II's first victim*.

3602 Position 46.0 of the ebook *First to Fight: The Polish War 1939* by Roger Moorhouse, published by Penguin Books Limited, ISBN 9781473548220.

3603 Ibid.

3604 See endnote 3574 for this supplement in regard to the affidavit of Naujocks.

3605 Position 46.0 of the ebook *First to Fight: The Polish War 1939* by Roger Moorhouse, published by Penguin Books Limited, ISBN 9781473548220.

3606 The article by Bob Graham in the UK Telegraph *World War II's first victim*.

3607 The article by Bob Graham in the UK Telegraph *World War II's first victim*. See also position 573.0 onwards of Chapter 6 "Total War" in the ebook *Case White The Invasion of Poland, 1939* by Robert Forczyk, published by Osprey Publishing 2019, eISBN 9781472834942.

3608 See endnote 3539 for this supplement.

3609 Position 574.7 of *Case White The Invasion of Poland, 1939* by Robert Forczyk.

3610 Ibid position 575.5. For another example of the appeasing nature of Lord Halifax, see endnote 1121 of Chapter 16 "Homecoming to Outbreak of War."

3611 The article by Bob Graham in the UK Telegraph *World War II's first victim*.

3612 See endnotes 3563 to 3577 for this supplement.

3613 Page 519 of *Rise And Fall Of The Third Reich: A History of Nazi Germany* by William L. Shirer, published by Simon and Schuster, 1990, ISBN 0671728687, 9780671728687. In regard to the Venlo Incident, see endnote 2065 of Chapter 22 "Prinz-Albrecht-Strasse" and endnote 2087 of Chapter 23 "Buchenwald."

3614 Ibid.

3615 The article by Bob Graham in the UK Telegraph *World War II's first victim*.

3616 Position 288.6 of *The SS: A New History* by Adrian Weale, published by Hachette UK, 2010, ISBN 9780748125517.

3617 See endnote 3556 for this supplement.

Polish WWII Supplement III — The Katyń Wood Massacre

3618 182 207 959 1258 1375 1442 1925 2265 2411 2529 2531 2923 3380 3696 3764 3807 3935 4014 4061 4077 4120 4304 4620 See pages 132 to 133 of *Warsaw 1920, Lenin's Failed Conquest of Europe* by Adam Zamoyski, paperback published by William Collins 2014, ISBN 9780007225538. See also the final paragraph of the online New York Times article titled *Russian Files Show Stalin Ordered Massacre of 20,000 Poles in 1940* by Celestine Bohlen, dated October 15, 1992 at https://www.nytimes.com/1992/10/15/world/russian-files-show-stalin-ordered-massacre-of-20000-poles-in-1940.html. This states the agreement of the Soviet historian Natalya Lebedeva, with Adam Zamoyski. Accessed on Saturday July 25, 2020.

[3619] [3955] [4628] Adapted from the online article *Totuus ei mätäne haudassa (The truth will not rot in the grave)* at https://www.savonsanomat.fi/paakirjoitukset/Totuus-ei-mätäne-haudassa/632263 dated April 20, 2010 in the Finnish daily newspaper *Savon Sanomat* by Seppo Kononen. Accessed on Saturday July 25, 2020.

[3620] In regard to these plots, see endnotes [1419] to [1434] for the plot on March 13th, and [1434] to [1442] for the plot on March 21st of Chapter 18 "Romance, Plots and Arrest."

[3621] See positions 194.6 to 198.8 and 213.7 of the autobiographical ebook *Soldier in the Downfall: A Wehrmacht Cavalryman in Russia, Normandy, and the Plot to Kill Hitler*, by Rudolf-Christoph von Gersdorff (Author), Anthony Pearsall (Translator), published by The Aberjona Press (25 March 2013), ASIN: B00C6FYGP2, ISBN 13: 9780977756377.

[3622] See endnotes [1457] to [1469] of Chapter 18 "Romance, Plots and Arrest."

[3623] Position 635.0 of the ebook *Countdown to Valkyrie: The July Plot to Assassinate Hitler* by Nigel Jones, published in 2008 by Frontline Books, Digital Edition ISBN 9781783407811, in the Dramatis Personae gives the years of birth and death for Fabian von Schlabrendorff as 1907 and 1980 respectively.

[3624] Ibid position 623.0 in the Dramatis Personae gives the years of birth and death for Rudolf-Christoph von Gersdorff as 1905 and 1980 respectively.

[3625] See pages 24 to 25 of *Military Intelligence, Volume 15, Issue 1*, contributors United States Army Intelligence Center & School, U.S. Army Intelligence Center, Fort Huachuca (Arizona), published by U.S. Army Intelligence Center & School, 1989 which briefly describes the role of the German G-2 intelligence service.

[3626] Position 508.1 of the autobiographical ebook *Soldier in the Downfall: A Wehrmacht Cavalryman in Russia, Normandy, and the Plot to Kill Hitler*, by Rudolf-Christoph von Gersdorff (Author), Anthony Pearsall (Translator), published by The Aberjona Press (25 March 2013), ASIN: B00C6FYGP2, ISBN 13: 9780977756377. See also Gersdorff's affidavit in English, *The Truth About "Katyn,"* Document #6032179 at https://www.ifz-muenchen.de/archiv/zs/zs-0047_3.pdf on the website of the Munich Leibnitz Institute for German Contemporary History (*Institut für Zeitgeschichte*). Accessed on Saturday July 25, 2020. This written statement appears in the appendix of Gersdorff's autobiography.

[3627] Ibid Position 340.6. The text of endnote #29 for the chapter "Soldier and Traitor," states that this discovery was made in early April 1943.

[3628] Position 341.0 of *Soldier in the Downfall*.

[3629] [3809] Position 341.2 of *Soldier in the Downfall*.

[3630] [3639] [3651] li This railway station is approximately 12 to 13 kilometres east of the Smolensk Central station. In Russian Cyrillic text it is Гнёздово, which in Polish is Gniezdowo — pronounced "G-niez-dovo." In English spelling, as is often the case when Romanisation of Cyrillic text is applied, confusing variants are the result. In the body of his autobiography, in the English translation at least, the spelling "Nyezdova" is used, while in his written 1946 statement to the Nuremberg Tribunal, in the English translated document at least, "Gniezdovo," which closely resembles the Polish spelling, was used. (In Polish, the "w" is pronounced like the English "v." In Polish, there are no letters "q," "v" or "x.") The most common English spelling seems to be "Gnezdovo." In my book, in the interests of clarity and consistency, I have decided to use the Polish spelling.

[3631] Position 341.8 of *Soldier in the Downfall*. See also Gersdorff's 1946 affidavit in English, *The Truth About "Katyn,"* Document #6032179 at https://www.ifz-muenchen.de/archiv/zs/zs-0047_3.pdf on the website of the Munich Leibnitz Institute for German Contemporary History (*Institut für Zeitgeschichte*). This written statement appears in the appendix of his autobiography. Both links accessed on Saturday July 25, 2020.

[3632] Position 342.0 of *Soldier in the Downfall*. See also pages 1 to 2 of Gersdorff's 1946 affidavit in English, *The Truth About "Katyn,"* Document #6032179 at https://www.ifz-muenchen.de/archiv/zs/zs-0047_3.pdf. Accessed on Saturday July 25, 2020.

[3633] [3809] [4315] Page 2 of Gersdorff's 1946 affidavit.

[3634] [3652] [3751] [3765] Position 342.2 of *Soldier in the Downfall*. Note that in the body of the book, Gersdorff refers to the perpetrators as the NKVD — who were indeed Stalin's Secret Police at the time. However, in his 1946 written statement to the Nuremberg Tribunal, as stated in an endnote at position 597.3 of his autobiography, he called them the GPU — who were the predecessor to the NKVD. See the US Library of Congress (LOC) webpage titled *Revelations from the Russian Archives Internal Workings of the Soviet Union* at https://www.loc.gov/exhibits/archives/intn.html and https://www.loc.gov/exhibits/archives/secr.html and the "Abbreviations and Glossary" on pages xi to xii of *Lenin, Stalin and Hitler* by by Robert Gellately, published by Vintage 2008, ISBN 9780712603577. In 1934, the NKVD superseded the GPU, which in turn, in 1954, following Stalin's death in March 1953, was superseded by the KGB. See the online *Encyclopaedia Britannica* article on the KGB at https://www.britannica.com/topic/KGB. All links accessed on Saturday July 25, 2020.

[3635] Position 342.3 of *Soldier in the Downfall* and page 2 of Gersdorff's 1946 affidavit.

[3636] Page xiii of *Operation Barbarossa and Germany's Defeat in the East* by David Stahel, published by Cambridge University Press, 2009, ISBN 0521768470, 9780521768474.

[3637] Position 342.7 of *Soldier in the Downfall*, page 2 of Gersdorff's 1946 affidavit and the photo and description on the web page of the Imperial War Museum at https://www.iwm.org.uk/collections/item/object/205075618. Accessed on Saturday July 25, 2020.

[3638] Page 578 of the 2012 publication *Mass Murderers Discover Mass Murder: the Germans and Katyn, 1943* by Kenneth F. Ledford, Professor of Law, School of Law, Associate Professor and Chair, Department of History, College of Arts and Sciences at Case Western Reserve University Cleveland Ohio. It can be viewed online at https://scholarlycommons.law.case.edu/cgi/viewcontent.cgi?article=1089&context=faculty_publications. Accessed on Saturday July 25, 2020.

[3639] To clarify the confusing Romanised spelling of this village, see endnote [3630] for this supplement.

[3640] Position 345.0 of *Soldier in the Downfall*.

[3641] [4315] Position 345.1 of *Soldier in the Downfall*.

[3642] Page 2 of Gersdorff's 1946 affidavit.

[3643] [lvii] Ibid.

[3644] Ibid.

[3645] [3836] [3837] Ibid.

[3646] Ibid.

[3647] Ibid.

[3648] See endnotes [3650] to [3654] for this supplement.

[3649] [3849] The document signed by Stalin and others in the Politburo, authorising the execution, can be viewed on the World War II Today web site at http://ww2today.com/stalin-orders-the-katyn-forest-murders. Accessed on Saturday July 25, 2020. See also position 348.7 of *Bloodlands* by Timothy Snyder, published by The Bodley Head of the Random House Group 2010, ISBN 9781407075501.

[3650] [3648] [3896] Pages 2 to 3 of Gersdorff's 1946 affidavit. See also the map and narrative at position 354.2 of *Bloodlands*.

[3651] [3805] [3834] To clarify the confusing Romanised spelling of this village, see endnote [3630] for this supplement.

[3652] See endnote [3634] for this supplement in regard to the name of this NKVD holiday resort.

[3653] Gersdorff assumed the Polish officers were murdered in the wood. (See pages 2 to 3 of his 1946 statement to the Nuremberg Tribunal.) However, according to Timothy Snyder, author of *Bloodlands*, it appears that the executions took place on the nearby grounds of the NKVD holiday resort, before the bodies of the victims were taken to the wood for burial in a mass grave. See endnote [3655] for this supplement. Gersdorff in his 1946 statement to the Nuremberg tribunal, naturally assumed the executions took place in the wood itself, as was the case with Einsatzgruppen massacre near Kiev in late September 1941, which became known as the infamous Babi Yar massacre — one of the largest single massacres of the Holocaust. (See https://www.britannica.com/place/Babi-Yar-massacre-site-Ukraine). Accessed on Saturday July 25, 2020. However, this does not change the essence of Gersdorff's written statement. Namely, that the Katyń murders were perpetrated by the NKVD, more than a year before Hitler's Barbarossa invasion. Gersdorff did in fact mention the then former NKVD holiday resort, which since September 1941, had been the HQ for the German Army Group Signals regiment. (See page 1 of Gersdorff's 1946 statenment to the Nuremberg tribunal and position 342.2 of his autobiography.)

[3654 3954 3648 3896] Top of page 3 of Gersdorff's 1946 affidavit.

[3655 3653 3805 3954 3834] Position 354.6 of *Bloodlands* by Timothy Snyder, published by The Bodley Head of the Random House Group 2010, ISBN 9781407075501.

[3656] Page 3 of Gersdorff's 1946 affidavit.

[3657] Page 578 of the 2012 publication *Mass Murderers Discover Mass Murder: the Germans and Katyn, 1943* by Kenneth F. Ledford, Professor of Law, School of Law, Associate Professor and Chair, Department of History, College of Arts and Sciences at Case Western Reserve University Cleveland Ohio. It can be viewed online at https://scholarlycommons.law.case.edu/cgi/viewcontent.cgi?article=1089&context=faculty_publications. Accessed on Saturday July 25, 2020.

[3658] Page 3 of Gersdorff's 1946 affidavit.

[3659] Page 3 of Gersdorff's 1946 affidavit.

[3660] Page 3 of Gersdorff's 1946 affidavit.

[3661] Page 3 of Gersdorff's 1946 affidavit.

[3662 3741 4184 4187 4374 4585] As stated in the document: *International Katyn Commission Findings. Der Massenmord in Walde von Katyn Ein Tatsachenbericht (the Mass-Murder in the Katyn Forest, a Documentary Account of Evidence). Germany, 1943.* This English Language translated document can be viewed online at http://www.warsawuprising.com/doc/katyn_documents1.htm. Accessed on Saturday July 25, 2020. This site is maintained by Project InPosterum [Latin — for the future], a non-profit, public benefit corporation established in 2004 in California with the purpose to organise for the specific purpose of preserving and popularising selected subjects of World War II history and its aftermath with a focus on Central and Eastern Europe. It's not the official website of the Rising, however, it uses reliable sources which include by permission, Norman Davies *Rising '44: The Battle for Warsaw Reprint Edition*, published by Penguin Books; Reprint edition (October 4, 2005), ISBN-10: 0143035401, ISBN-13: 9780143035404. At the bottom of this document, signed in Smolensk on April 30, 1943, is a jpeg image of signatures of all twelve medical university professors, attesting to the fact, that the massacre took place in the months of March and April 1940. The bottom of the original German language document, with signatures is given on page 47 of the 2004 paper *Professeur François Naville (1883 - 1968) Son rôle dans l'enquête sur le massacre de Katyn (His role in the investigation into the Katyn massacre)* by Kazimierz Karbowski, Professor of Neurology and Epileptology, University of Berne on pages 41 to 61 of Issue #1 of the 2004 *Bulletin de la Société des sciences médicales du Grand-Duché de Luxembourg* (Bulletin of the Society of Medical Sciences of the Grand Duchy of Luxembourg). The paper is in French, however, the abstract on page 41 is in English. It can be downloaded on the Wayback machine at https://web.archive.org/web/20091128020305/http://www.ssm.lu/pdfs/bssm_0 4_1_8.pdf. Accessed on Saturday July 25, 2020.

[3663] Ibid.

[3664] See endnotes [3513] to [3519] of Polish WWII Supplement I "The Molotov-Ribbentrop Pact."

[3665] Article on the Ustaša regime at https://www.britannica.com/topic/Ustasa. Accessed on Saturday July 25, 2020.

[3666] Article on the Axis powers at https://www.britannica.com/topic/Axis-Powers. Accessed on Saturday July 25, 2020.

[3667] [3748] The 2004 paper *Professeur François Naville (1883 - 1968) Son rôle dans l'enquête sur le massacre de Katyn (His role in the investigation into the Katyn massacre)* by Kazimierz Karbowski, Professor of Neurology and Epileptology, University of Berne on pages 41 to 61 of Issue #1 of the 2004 *Bulletin de la Société des sciences médicales du Grand-Duché de Luxembourg* (Bulletin of the Society of Medical Sciences of the Grand Duchy of Luxembourg). The paper is in French, however, the abstract on page 41 is in English, which is what is quoted here. It can be downloaded on the Wayback machine at https://web.archive.org/web/20091128020305/http://www.ssm.lu/pdfs/bssm_0 4_1_8.pdf. For the credentials of Kazimierz Karbowski, see the memorial article in German titled *In memoriam Prof. Kazimierz Karbowski* which can be downloaded at https://sanp.ch/article/doi/sanp.2012.02368 on the website of the Swiss Archives of Neurology, Psychiatry and Psychotherapy. Both links accessed on Saturday July 25, 2020.

[3668] Ibid.

[3669] That Mikhail Gorbachev was in power in 1989 in the Soviet Union, see https://www.britannica.com/biography/Mikhail-Gorbachev. Accessed on Saturday July 25, 2020.

[3670] [3949] The memorial article in German titled *In memoriam Prof. Kazimierz Karbowski* which can be downloaded at https://sanp.ch/article/doi/sanp.2012.02368 on the website of the Swiss Archives of Neurology, Psychiatry and Psychotherapy. Accessed on Saturday July 25, 2020.

[3671] Page 53 of the 2004 paper *Professeur François Naville (1883 - 1968) Son rôle dans l'enquête sur le massacre de Katyn (His role in the investigation into the Katyn massacre)* by Kazimierz Karbowski, Professor of Neurology and Epileptology, University of Berne on pages 41 to 61 of Issue #1 of the 2004 *Bulletin de la Société des sciences médicales du Grand-Duché de Luxembourg* (Bulletin of the Society of Medical Sciences of the Grand Duchy of Luxembourg). This paper can be downloaded on the Wayback Machine at https://web.archive.org/web/20091128020305/http://www.ssm.lu/pdfs/bssm_0 4_1_8.pdf. For the credentials of Kazimierz Karbowski, see the memorial article in German titled *In memoriam Prof. Kazimierz Karbowski* which can be downloaded at https://sanp.ch/article/doi/sanp.2012.02368 on the website of the Swiss Archives of Neurology, Psychiatry and Psychotherapy. All links accessed on Saturday July 25, 2020.

[3672] See for example the so-called Swedish language *mythcracker* website at http://www.mythcracker.com/katyn/. Accessed on Saturday July 25, 2020.

[3673] See endnotes [3513] to [3519] of Polish WWII Supplement I "The Molotov-Ribbentrop Pact."

[3674] See endnotes [3517] and [3518] of Polish WWII Supplement I "The Molotov-Ribbentrop Pact."

[3675] The Central Intelligence Agency report online titled *The Katyń Controversy: Stalin's Killing Field* by Benjamin B. Fischer at https://www.cia.gov/library/center-for-the-study-of-intelligence/csi-publications/csi-studies/studies/winter99-00/art6.html. Accessed on Saturday July 25, 2020.

[3676] Page 7 of the US Congress, House of Representatives, Select Committee on the Katyn Forest Massacre. The Katyn Forest Massacre: Hearings before the Select Committee on Conduct an Investigation of the Facts, Evidence and Circumstances of the Katyn Forest Massacre, 82d Congress, 1951-52, Document 100-183. It can be downloaded on the Kresy-Siberia website, dedicated to the Borderland Polish family and victims of Stalinist oppression at http://kresy-siberia.com/1952_Katyn_report_to_Congress.pdf. Accessed on Saturday July 25, 2020.

[3677] Position 1118.0 of Microcosm.

[3678] [3698] The Central Intelligence Agency report online titled *The Katyń Controversy: Stalin's Killing Field* by Benjamin B. Fischer and page 7 of the US Congress, House of Representatives, Select Committee on the Katyn Forest Massacre. The Katyn Forest Massacre: Hearings before the Select Committee on Conduct an Investigation of the Facts, Evidence and Circumstances of the Katyn Forest Massacre, 82d Congress, 1951-52, Document 100-183. It can be downloaded on the Kresy-Siberia website, dedicated to the Borderland Polish family and victims of Stalinist oppression at http://kresy-siberia.com/1952_Katyn_report_to_Congress.pdf. Accessed on Saturday July 25, 2020.

[3679] Page 387 of the book *The war with Japan: A Concise History edition 2* by Charles Bateson, published by Michigan State University Press, 1968.

[3680] Position 1118.0 of Microcosm.

[3681] Page 276 of *The Other Europe: Eastern Europe to 1945* by E. Garrison Walters, published by Syracuse University Press, 1988, ISBN 0815624409, 9780815624400. The Polish Government in Exile in London alone commanded more than 0.5 million men.

[3682] [4014] See endnotes [3490] to [3493] of Polish WWII Supplement I "The Molotov-Ribbentrop Pact" .

[3683] In regard to aerial Battle of Britain, following the fall of France, see https://www.britannica.com/event/Battle-of-Britain-European-history-1940. Accessed on Saturday July 25, 2020.

[3684] The online article *THE POLISH PILOTS WHO FLEW IN THE BATTLE OF BRITAIN* by Mariusz Gasior dated Tuesday 9 January 2018 on the website of the Imperial War Museum at https://www.iwm.org.uk/history/the-polish-pilots-who-flew-in-the-battle-of-britain. Accessed on Saturday July 25, 2020.

[3685] [4065] [4630] Page 276 of *The Other Europe: Eastern Europe to 1945* by E. Garrison Walters, published by Syracuse University Press, 1988, ISBN 0815624409, 9780815624400. The Polish Government in Exile in London alone commanded more than 0.5 million men.

[3686] [4630] Professor Norman Davies in his book, *Rising '44: The Battle for Warsaw Reprint Edition*, published by Penguin Books; Reprint edition (October 4, 2005), ISBN-10: 0143035401, ISBN-13: 9780143035404, repeatedly refers to the Poles as the "First Ally." However, pages 54-57 are perfect examples.

[3687] See the online article *Katyn: the long cover-up* by Dariusz Tolczyk, Associate Professor of Slavic Languages and Literatures at The University of Virginia, dated May 2010, at https://newcriterion.com/issues/2010/5/katyn-the-long-cover-up, accessed on Saturday July 25, 2020, on the website of *The New Criterion*. This article appeared in *The New Criterion, Volume 28 Number 9*, on page 4.

[3688] See endnotes [3320] to [3365] of Polish WWII Supplement I "The Molotov-Ribbentrop Pact."

[3689] Page 115 of *Rising '44: The Battle for Warsaw Reprint Edition* (October 4, 2005), ISBN-10: 0143035401, ISBN-13: 9780143035404 by Professor Norman Davies.

[3690] [4474] Professor Norman Davies in his book, *Rising '44: The Battle for Warsaw Reprint Edition*, published by Penguin Books; Reprint edition (October 4, 2005), ISBN-10: 0143035401, ISBN-13: 9780143035404, repeatedly refers to the Poles as the "First Ally." However, pages 54-57 are a perfect examples.

[3691] Not to be confused with the August to October 1944 Warsaw General Uprising. See Polish WWII Supplement IV "AK and 1944 Warsaw General Uprising — Stalin's mass murder by German proxy."[3956] Both nevertheless, were heroic acts of defiance against an inexorably more powerful and ruthless enemy. Both were about sixteen months apart. In regard to the April-May 1943 Warsaw Jewish Ghetto Uprising, see endnote [4565] of Polish WWII Supplement IV "AK and 1944 Warsaw General Uprising — Stalin's mass murder by German proxy."

[3692] [4014] [4065] Pages 115 to 116 of *Rising '44: The Battle for Warsaw Reprint Edition*, published by Penguin Books; Reprint edition (October 4, 2005), ISBN-10: 0143035401, ISBN-13: 9780143035404. In regard to the Polish inter-war "doctrine of two enemies," see endnotes [3473] and [3483] of Polish WWII Supplement I "The Molotov-Ribbentrop Pact."

[3693] See endnote [3315] of Polish WWII Supplement I "The Molotov-Ribbentrop Pact."

[3694] Pages 482 to 484 of *Lenin, Stalin and Hitler*.

[3695] Pages 484 to 485 of *Lenin, Stalin and Hitler*.

[3696] See endnote [3618] for this supplement.

[3697] See endnote [79] for the Preface "Birth and Memory upon the Lesser Known Fault Line of History" in regard to Lenin's dream of spreading the Soviet revolution to the rest of the world.

[3698] See endnote [3678] for this supplement.

[3699] [3788] Pages 36 to 37 of the US Congress, House of Representatives, Select Committee on the Katyn Forest Massacre. The Katyn Forest Massacre: Hearings before the Select Committee on Conduct an Investigation of the Facts, Evidence and Circumstances of the Katyn Forest Massacre, 82d Congress, 1951-52, Document 100-183. It can be downloaded on the Kresy-Siberia website, dedicated to the Borderland Polish family and victims of Stalinist oppression at http://kresy-siberia.com/1952_Katyn_report_to_Congress.pdf. Accessed on Saturday July 25, 2020.

[3700] Ibid. Also JSTOR at https://www.jstor.org/stable/25779772?readnow=1&refreqid=excelsior%3Ae376df3d2c9677c5caf708d3adb41a0a&seq=23#page_scan_tab_contents. Accessed on Saturday July 25, 2020.

[3701] Page 37 of the US Congress, House of Representatives, Select Committee on the Katyn Forest Massacre.

[3702] Page 37 of the US Congress, House of Representatives, Select Committee on the Katyn Forest Massacre.

[3703] Page 36 of the US Congress, House of Representatives, Select Committee on the Katyn Forest Massacre.

[3704] Page 37 of the US Congress, House of Representatives, Select Committee on the Katyn Forest Massacre.

[3705] [3832] Page 36 of the US Congress, House of Representatives, Select Committee on the Katyn Forest Massacre.

[3706] [3832] Page 3 of Gersdorff's 1946 affidavit.

[3707] Page 37 of the US Congress, House of Representatives, Select Committee on the Katyn Forest Massacre.

[3708] Page 2 of Gersdorff's 1946 affidavit.

[3709] The climatic graph for Smolesnk at https://en.climate-data.org/asia/russian-federation/smolensk-oblast/smolensk-413/#climate-graph on the Climate-Data website. See also the table at https://www.eldoradoweather.com/climate/europe/russia/Smolensk.html on the website of El Dorado Weather. Both accessed on Saturday July 25, 2020.

[3710] [3788] The Warfare History Network website article by Victor Kamenir at https://warfarehistorynetwork.com/2016/07/29/operation-barbarossa-holding-the-line-at-smolensk/. Accessed on Saturday July 25, 2020.

[3711] In regard to the Einsatzgruppen/Einstazkommandos, see endnotes [128] to [130] of The Preface "Birth and Memory upon the Lesser Known Fault Line of History" and endnotes [1231] to [1233] of Chapter 17 "Pastor and Spy."

[3712] Page 1 of Gersdorff's 1946 affidavit.

[3713] [3789] Page 3 of Gersdorff's 1946 affidavit.

[3714] [3789] Page 3 of Gersdorff's 1946 affidavit.

[3715] Bottom of page 3 of Gersdorff's 1946 affidavit. Gersdorff stated that with this discovery, an estimate of 10,000 to 12,000 executed at Katyń was certainly not too high. However, this was an overestimate, and was in fact used in the Soviet Burdenko Commission in January 1944. See position 433.9 of the ebook *Katyn and the Soviet Massacre of 1940: Truth, justice and memory* by George Sanford, published by Routledge 2005, ISBN13: 978113430299-4 (ePub ISBN). The Burdenko Commission will be covered in detail later on in this supplement.

[3716] Bottom of page 3 of Gersdorff's 1946 affidavit.

[3717] Page 4 of Gersdorff's 1946 affidavit. In regard to the differentiation between the Wehrmacht and SS, see endnotes [1181] to [1183] of Chapter 17 "Pastor and Spy."

[3718] [3855] See for example the so-called Swedish language *mythcracker* website at http://www.mythcracker.com/katyn/. Accessed on Saturday July 25, 2020.

[3719] [3857] See Polish WWII Supplement I "The Molotov-Ribbentrop Pact."[3268]

[3720] [3744] [3857] Position 348.4 Gersdorff's autobiography, *Soldier in the Downfall*

[3721] [3858] Position 308.1 of *Katyn and the Soviet Massacre of 1940: Truth, justice and memory* by George Sanford, published by Routledge 2005, ISBN13: 978113430299-4.

[3722] The so-called Swedish language *mythcracker* website at http://www.mythcracker.com/katyn/. Accessed on Saturday July 25, 2020.

[3723] Position 434.3 of *Katyn and the Soviet Massacre of 1940: Truth, justice and memory* by George Sanford.

[3724] Page 1 of Gersdorff's 1946 affidavit.

[3725] Position 348.9 of *Soldier in the Downfall*.

[3726] Position 348.9 of *Soldier in the Downfall*.

[3727] [3810] Position 593.0 of *Soldier in the Downfall*.

[3728] Position 348.6 of *Soldier in the Downfall*.

[3729] Position 348.7 of *Soldier in the Downfall*.

[3730] Position 439.3 of *Katyn and the Soviet Massacre of 1940: Truth, justice and memory* by George Sanford, published by Routledge 2005, ISBN13: 978113430299-4.

[3731] Position 439.3 of *Katyn and the Soviet Massacre of 1940: Truth, justice and memory* by George Sanford.

[3732] Position 348.8 of *Soldier in the Downfall*.

[3733] Position 409.6 of *Katyn and the Soviet Massacre of 1940: Truth, justice and memory* by George Sanford.

[3734] The first name of this Katyń investigator is given on page 79 of the publication *ENCOUNTER WITH KATYN The wartime and postwar story of Poles who saw the Katyn site in 1943* by Tadeusz Wolsza, originally published as *Dotyk Katynia. Wojenne i powojenne losy Polaków wizytujących Katyń w 1943 roku*, Poznań: Zysk i S-ka Wydawnictwo, 2018, Translated from the Polish by Teresa Bałuk-Ulewiczowa, Marta Kapera, Piotr Pieńkowski, The Janusz Kurtyka Foundation al. Waszyngtona 39/25 04-015 Warszawa, Poland. It can be downloaded at http://fundacjakurtyki.pl/images/Encounter-with-Katyn_print2.pdf. Accessed on Saturday July 25, 2020.

[3735] Page 9 of the statement of František Šubík in the Central Intelligence Agency document CIA-RDP80-00810A001000670008-9 dated May 12, 1953. It can be downloaded on the CIA website at https://www.cia.gov/library/readingroom/docs/CIA-RDP80-00810A001000670008-9.pdf. Accessed on Saturday July 25, 2020. See also the 2014 Polish Documentary *Poświęcając życie prawdzie (Dedicating Life to the Truth)* aired on Telewizja Polska S.A. (TVP S.A., or Polish Television), which is the Polish public service broadcaster and the largest Polish television network. This documentary is dedicated to the story of the twelve doctors, specialists and experts in forensic medicine who made up the International Medical Commission appointed by the Germans to investigate the murder in Katyń. More information on this documentary can be found on the Polish Film website at http://filmpolski.pl/fp/index.php?film=1236402. Accessed on Saturday July 25, 2020.

[3736] See for example the so-called Swedish language *mythcracker* website at http://www.mythcracker.com/katyn/. Accessed on Saturday July 25, 2020.

[3737] [3810] See the description of the 2014 Polish Documentary *Poświęcając życie prawdzie (Dedicating Life to the Truth)* aired on Telewizja Polska S.A. (TVP S.A., or Polish Television) on the Polish Film website at http://filmpolski.pl/fp/index.php?film=1236402. Accessed on Saturday July 25, 2020.

[3738] See for example the so-called Swedish language *mythcracker* website at http://www.mythcracker.com/katyn/. Accessed on Saturday July 25, 2020.

[3739] Bottom of page 1601 of *The Katyn Forest Massacre: Hearings Before the Select Committee to Conduct an Investigation of the Facts, Evidence and Circumstances of the Katyn Forest Massacre, Eighty-second Congress, First-*

[second] Session, on Investigation of the Murder of Thousands of Polish Offic-ers in the Katyn Forest Near Smolensk, Russia, by the United States Congress House Select Committee to Conduct an Investigation and Study of the Facts, Evidence, and Circumstances on the Katyn Forest Massacre, published by the U.S. Government Printing Office, 1952, original from the University of Minnesota, digitised December 1, 2014. See also Google Books at https://books.google.com.tw/books?id=PWJFAQAAMAAJ&printsec=frontcover&source=gbs_ge_summary_r&cad=0#v=onepage&q=1601&f=false. Accessed on Saturday July 25, 2020.

[3740] Hitler proclaimed this "protectorate" on March 16, 1939 following German troops marching into Prague without a shot being fired. See the JOURNAL ARTICLE *Three Years of the Protectorate of Bohemia and Moravia* by Moses Moskowitz in the Political Science Quarterly Vol. 57, No. 3 (Sep., 1942), pp. 353-375 Published by: The Academy of Political Science DOI: 10.2307/2144345, It can be downloaded at https://www.jstor.org/stable/2144345. Accessed on Saturday July 25, 2020.

[3741] [3742] František Šubík was Professor of Pathological Anatomy at the University of Bratislava and Slovakian Chief of State Public Health Works. See the document: *International Katyn Commission Findings. Der Massenmord in Walde von Katyn Ein Tatsachenbericht (the Mass-Murder in the Katyn Forest, a Documentary Account of Evidence). Germany, 1943* at http://www.warsawuprising.com/doc/katyn_documents1.htm on the website of the Warsaw 1944 Uprising. See this website's credentials at endnote [3662] for this supplement.

[3742] See endnote [3741] for this supplement.

[3743] See for example, endnotes [2264] and [2265] of Chapter 20 "Valkyrie II," in regard to the Cephalonia massacre.

[3744] See endnote [3720] for this supplement, where Gersdorff explains how the NKVD came into possession of German manufactured ammunition used for the Katyń massacre. In regard to the Molotov-Ribbentrop pact, see endnote [3268] of Polish WWII Supplement I "The Molotov-Ribbentrop Pact."

[3745] [3769] This is a distortion of the truth, used by František Šubík to placate and/or stall his communist overlords. Dr. André Costedoat was merely sent by the head of the Vichy French government to observe the work of the Commission. See pages 1402 and 1423 of *The Katyn Forest Massacre: Hearings Before the Select Committee to Conduct an Investigation of the Facts, Evidence and Circumstances of the Katyn Forest Massacre, Eighty-second Congress, First-[second] Session, on Investigation of the Murder of Thousands of Polish Officers in the Katyn Forest Near Smolensk, Russia*, by the United States Congress House Select Committee to Conduct an Investigation and Study of the Facts, Evidence, and Circumstances on the Katyn Forest Massacre, published by the U.S. Government Printing Office, 1952, original from the University of Minnesota, digitised December 1, 2014. See also Google Books at

https://books.google.com.tw/books?id=PWJFAQAAMAAJ&pg=PA1402&lpg
=PA1402&dq=Dr.+Costedoat,+Medical+Inspector,&source=bl&ots=5sWJHz
A_VZ&sig=ACfU3U2rythpcsdgp9CGoQo1c4Br6kzUYw&hl=en&sa=X&ved
=2ahUKEwjQp5KHsZfnAhVFL6YKHWYiDJQQ6AEwAHoECAgQAQ#v=o
nepage&q=Costedoat&f=false. Accessed on Saturday July 25, 2020.

[3746] Again, another fabrication for the benefit of Vincent NECAS. See for example the testimony of Dr. Orsos on pages 1600 to 1601 of ibid.

[3747] Pages 8 to 9 of the statement of František Šubík in the Central Intelligence Agency document CIA-RDP80-00810A001000670008-9 dated May 12, 1953. It can be downloaded on the CIA website at https://www.cia.gov/library/readingroom/docs/CIA-RDP80-00810A001000670008-9.pdf. Accessed on Saturday July 25, 2020.

[3748] See endnote [3667] for this supplement.

[3749] Page 25 of the 2009 Italian paper *KATYŃ una verità storica negata: La Perizia di V.M. Palmieri (Katyń a historical truth denied: The Expertise of V.M. Palmieri)* by Luigia Melillo, University of Naples 2009. It can downloaded at https://www.scribd.com/document/150269981/Katyn-una-verita-storica-negata-La-perizia-di-Vincenzo-Maria-Palmieri. Accessed on Saturday July 25, 2020.

[3750] In regard to the Molotov-Ribbentrop pact, see endnote [3268] of Polish WWII Supplement I "The Molotov-Ribbentrop Pact."

[3751] Note that at the time, the KGB, with Stalin still alive, did not yet exist. It was not until 1954, in the year following Stalin's death, with Nikita Khrushchev in power, that the NKVD was superseded by the KGB. See endnote [3634] for this supplement in regard to the succession of Soviet secret police agencies. In the context of this story, whether the perpetrators were the NKVD or the KGB, is only of peripheral importance at most.

[3752] Pages 24 to 25 of the 2009 Italian paper *KATYŃ una verità storica negata: La Perizia di V.M. Palmieri (Katyń a historical truth denied: The Expertise of V.M. Palmieri)* by Luigia Melillo, University of Naples 2009. It can downloaded at https://www.scribd.com/document/150269981/Katyn-una-verita-storica-negata-La-perizia-di-Vincenzo-Maria-Palmieri. Accessed on Saturday July 25, 2020.

[3753] The article by Lauri Saxén: *Saxén, Arno (1895—1952) Suomen kansallisbiografia (Finnish National Biography)*, Volume 8, pages 720—721. Helsinki: Suomalaisen Kirjallisuuden Seura (Finnish Literature Society), 2006. ISBN 9517464495. Online version of the book on the Finnish National Biography website at https://kansallisbiografia.fi/kansallisbiografia/henkilo/6900/. Lauri Saxén was a son of Arno. See the Geni genealogical website at https://www.geni.com/people/Arno-Saxén/6000000000001127960. All links accessed on Saturday July 25, 2020.

[3754] The online article *Totuus ei mätäne haudassa (The truth will not rot in the grave)* at https://www.savonsanomat.fi/paakirjoitukset/Totuus-ei-mätäne-haudassa/632263 dated April 20, 2010 in the Finnish daily newspaper *Savon Sanomat* by Seppo Kononen, accessed on Saturday July 25, 2020 and page 7 of *Finland's Search for Security through Defence, 1944—89* by Penttilä R.E.J. (1991) in Chapter 1 "'The Years of Danger', 1944—47," published by Palgrave Macmillan, London 1991, ebook ISBN 9781349116362.

[3755] Page 6 of *Finland's Search for Security through Defence, 1944—89* by Penttilä R.E.J. (1991) in Chapter 1 "'The Years of Danger', 1944—47," published by Palgrave Macmillan, London 1991, ebook ISBN 9781349116362.

[3756] The article by Lauri Saxén: *Saxén, Arno (1895—1952) Suomen kansallisbiografia (Finnish National Biography)*, Volume 8, pages 720—721. Helsinki: Suomalaisen Kirjallisuuden Seura (Finnish Literature Society), 2006. ISBN 9517464495. Online version of the book on the Finnish National Biography website at https://kansallisbiografia.fi/kansallisbiografia/henkilo/6900/. See also the online article *Totuus ei mätäne haudassa (The truth will not rot in the grave)* at https://www.savonsanomat.fi/paakirjoitukset/Totuus-ei-mätäne-haudassa/632263 dated April 20, 2010 in the Finnish daily newspaper *Savon Sanomat* by Seppo Kononen. Both links accessed on Saturday July 25, 2020.

[3757] The article by Lauri Saxén: *Saxén, Arno (1895—1952), Suomen kansallisbiografia (Finnish National Biography)*, Volume 8, pages 720—721. Helsinki: Suomalaisen Kirjallisuuden Seura (Finnish Literature Society), 2006. ISBN 9517464495. Online version of the book on the Finnish National Biography website at https://kansallisbiografia.fi/kansallisbiografia/henkilo/6900/. Accessed on Saturday July 25, 2020.

[3758] Page 6 to 7 of *Finland's Search for Security through Defence, 1944—89* by Penttilä R.E.J. (1991) in Chapter 1 "'The Years of Danger', 1944—47," published by Palgrave Macmillan, London 1991, ebook ISBN 9781349116362.

[3759 3855] The online article *Totuus ei mätäne haudassa (The truth will not rot in the grave)* at https://www.savonsanomat.fi/paakirjoitukset/Totuus-ei-mätäne-haudassa/632263 dated April 20, 2010 in the Finnish daily newspaper *Savon Sanomat* by Seppo Kononen. Accessed on Saturday July 25, 2020.

[3760] The article by Lauri Saxén: *Saxén, Arno (1895—1952), Suomen kansallisbiografia (Finnish National Biography)*, Volume 8, pages 720—721. Helsinki: Suomalaisen Kirjallisuuden Seura (Finnish Literature Society), 2006. ISBN 9517464495. Online version of the book on the Finnish National Biography website at https://kansallisbiografia.fi/kansallisbiografia/henkilo/6900/. Accessed on Saturday July 25, 2020.

[3761] Page 7 of the article *Professor Arno Saxén w sprawie polskiej / część trzecia (ostatnia)* (Professor Arno Saxén on the Polish Matter / Part 3 (last)), in: Polonia-Finlandia, number 4, 2008, by Zdzisław Mackiewicz. It can be downloaded on the Polonia-Finlandia website at http://www.polonia-finlandia.fi/biuletyny/2008-4.pdf. Accessed on Saturday July 25, 2020.

[3762] Page 83 of the publication *ENCOUNTER WITH KATYN The wartime and postwar story of Poles who saw the Katyn site in 1943* by Tadeusz Wolsza, originally published as *Dotyk Katynia. Wojenne i powojenne losy Polaków wizytujących Katyń w 1943 roku*, Poznań: Zysk i S-ka Wydawnictwo, 2018, Translated from the Polish by Teresa Bałuk-Ulewiczowa, Marta Kapera, Piotr Pieńkowski, The Janusz Kurtyka Foundation al. Waszyngtona 39/25 04-015 Warszawa, Poland. It can be downloaded at http://fundacjakurtyki.pl/images/Encounter-with-Katyn_print2.pdf. See also Yrjö Meurman (1954) Arno Saxén: In Memoriam, Acta Oto-Laryngologica, 44:2, 189-190, DOI: 10.3109/00016485409139627 or view at Taylor and Francis Online at https://www.tandfonline.com/doi/abs/10.3109/00016485409139627. The latter also makes reference to his sudden death. Both links accessed on Saturday July 25, 2020.

[3763] https://www.britannica.com/biography/Joseph-Stalin. Accessed on Saturday July 25, 2020.

[3764] [3935] See endnote [3618] for this supplement.

[3765] [3859] Page 7 of the article *Professor Arno Saxén w sprawie polskiej / część trzecia (ostatnia)* (Professor Arno Saxén on the Polish Matter / Part 3 (last)), in: Polonia-Finlandia, number 4, 2008, by Zdzisław Mackiewicz. It can be downloaded on the Polonia-Finlandia website at http://www.polonia-finlandia.fi/biuletyny/2008-4.pdf. Accessed on Saturday July 25, 2020. Note that at the time, the KGB, with Stalin still alive, did not yet exist. It was not until 1954, in the year following Stalin's death, with Nikita Khrushchev in power, that the NKVD was superseded by the KGB. See endnote [3634] for this supplement in regard to the succession of Soviet secret police agencies. In the context of this story, whether the perpetrators were the NKVD or the KGB, is only of peripheral importance at most.

[3766] Ibid page 8.

[3767] Ibid page 8.

[3768] The article dated April 12, 2019 by Feliks Koperski titled *Lektura na weekend: Naoczni świadkowie Katynia — Reading for the weekend: Eyewitnesses of Katyn* on the website of *Kresy24* at https://kresy24.pl/lektura-na-weekend-naoczni-swiadkowie-katynia/. Accessed on Saturday July 25, 2020. Kresy24 is an information portal run by the "Fundacja Wolność i Demokracja" — "Freedom and Democracy Foundation." Full name of the website: *Kresy24.pl - Wschodnia Gazeta Dnia — Kresy24.pl Eastern Newspaper of the Day*. It publishes news from Belarus, Lithuania, Ukraine, Russia, Asia and the Caucasus. The Freedom and Democracy Foundation is an independent, non-party non-governmental organisation. Since its foundation in 2005, the Foundation has been operating in two main areas: helping Poles in the East and supporting democratic changes in the former Soviet Union. The impetus for the foundation of the Foundation was the closing of two independent Polish magazines related to the Union of (ethnic) Poles in Belarus in summer 2005 by the Belarusian authorities. The need to publish magazines in exile and to raise funds for this purpose led to the creation of the Foundation. See their statement online at http://wid.org.pl/kim-jestesmy/. Accessed on Saturday July 25, 2020.

[3769] See endnote [3745] for this supplement in regard to Dr. André Costedoat's role at Katyń.

[3770] Page 79 of the publication *ENCOUNTER WITH KATYN The wartime and postwar story of Poles who saw the Katyn site in 1943* by Tadeusz Wolsza, originally published as *Dotyk Katynia. Wojenne i powojenne losy Polaków wizytujących Katyń w 1943 roku*, Poznań: Zysk i S-ka Wydawnictwo, 2018, Translated from the Polish by Teresa Bałuk-Ulewiczowa, Marta Kapera, Piotr Pieńkowski, The Janusz Kurtyka Foundation al. Waszyngtona 39/25 04-015 Warszawa, Poland. It can be downloaded at http://fundacjakurtyki.pl/images/Encounter-with-Katyn_print2.pdf. Accessed on Saturday July 25, 2020.

[3771] The article dated April 12, 2019 by Feliks Koperski titled *Lektura na weekend: Naoczni świadkowie Katynia"* — *"Reading for the weekend: Eyewitnesses of Katyn* on the website of Kresy24 at https://kresy24.pl/lektura-na-weekend-naoczni-swiadkowie-katynia/. Kresy24 is an information portal run by the "Fundacja Wolność i Demokracja" — "Freedom and Democracy Foundation." Accessed on Saturday July 25, 2020.

[3772] The article dated April 12, 2019 by Feliks Koperski titled *Lektura na weekend: Naoczni świadkowie Katynia"* — *"Reading for the weekend: Eyewitnesses of Katyn* on the website of Kresy24 at https://kresy24.pl/lektura-na-weekend-naoczni-swiadkowie-katynia/. Kresy24 is an information portal run by the "Fundacja Wolność i Demokracja" — "Freedom and Democracy Foundation." See also, page 83 of the publication *ENCOUNTER WITH KATYN The wartime and postwar story of Poles who saw the Katyn site in 1943* by Tadeusz Wolsza, originally published as *Dotyk Katynia. Wojenne i powojenne losy Polaków wizytujących Katyń w 1943 roku*, Poznań: Zysk i S-ka Wydawnictwo, 2018, Translated from the Polish by Teresa Bałuk-Ulewiczowa, Marta Kapera, Piotr Pieńkowski, The Janusz Kurtyka Foundation al. Waszyngtona 39/25 04-015 Warszawa, Poland. It can be downloaded at http://fundacjakurtyki.pl/images/Encounter-with-Katyn_print2.pdf. Both links accessed on Saturday July 25, 2020.

[3773] Page 83 of Tadeusz Wolsza.

[3774] The online article dated April 12, 2019 by Feliks Koperski.

[3775] The online article dated April 12, 2019 by Feliks Koperski.

[3776] The online article dated April 12, 2019 by Feliks Koperski. See also page 83 of Tadeusz Wolsza. This latter source does not give the name of the victim, but it still states that the victim was from Kraków.

[3777] The online article dated April 12, 2019 by Feliks Koperski.

[3778] In regard to international communist ideological acrobatics in the wake of the signing of the Molotov-Ribbentrop pact, see endnotes [3308] and [3340] to [3353] of Polish WWII Supplement I "The Molotov-Ribbentrop Pact."

[3779] The online article dated April 12, 2019 by Feliks Koperski.

[3780] The online article dated April 12, 2019 by Feliks Koperski.

[3781] In regard to international communist ideological acrobatics in the wake of the signing of the Molotov-Ribbentrop pact, see endnotes [3308] and [3340] to [3353] of Polish WWII Supplement I "The Molotov-Ribbentrop Pact."

[3782] See the online *Encyclopaedia Britannica* article on the Korean War at https://www.britannica.com/event/Korean-War. Accessed on Saturday July 25, 2020.

[3783] The online article dated April 12, 2019 by Feliks Koperski.

[3784] The online article dated April 12, 2019 by Feliks Koperski.

[3785] Page 83 of Tadeusz Wolsza and the online article dated April 12, 2019 by Feliks Koperski.

[3786] The online article dated April 12, 2019 by Feliks Koperski. See also pages 83 to 84 of Tadeusz Wolsza.

[3787] [3832] Page 36 of the US Congress, House of Representatives, Select Committee on the Katyn Forest Massacre.

[3788] [3832] See endnotes [3699] to [3710] for this supplement.

[3789] See the maps for September 15, 1943 and October 1, 1943 on pages 15 and 17 respectively of the Atlas of the World Battle Fronts in Semimonthly Phases, to August 15, 1945, produced for the Chief of Staff of the United States Army in 1945 by the United States War Department General Staff, published by the Army Map Service. Analysis of these maps, infer the Soviet capture of Smolensk by the Soviet Army sometime in September 1943. The digitised US Army Atlas can be downloaded from the Wikimedia website at https://upload.wikimedia.org/wikipedia/commons/4/42/Atlas_of_the_World_B attle_Fronts_in_Semimonthly_Phases_to_August_15%2C_1945.pdf. Accessed on Saturday July 25, 2020. See also endnotes [3713] and [3714] for this supplement concerning the approximate time of withdrawal of the Germans from Smolensk.

[3790] Position 428.8 of *Katyn and the Soviet Massacre of 1940: Truth, justice and memory* by George Sanford.

[3791] [4051] This date was actually January 22, 1944 as stated on page 687 of the article *The Birth and Persistence of the Katyn Lie* by Witold Wasilewski, written in 2012 and published in 2013 in Volume 45, issue 3 of *Case Western Reserve Journal of International Law*. This article can be downloaded on the website of the *Case Western Reserve Journal of International Law* at https://scholarlycommons.law.case.edu/jil/vol45/iss3/3/. Accessed on Saturday July 25, 2020.

[3792] [3825] [4051] Pages 109 to 110 of Tadeusz Wolsza. He in turn cites J. Tebinka, 'Dyplomacja brytyjska wobec sprawy katyńskiej w latach 1943—1945, ('British diplomacy in the Katyn case in 1943—1945')' in *Z dziejów Polski i emigracji (1939—1989) (From the history of Poland and emigration (1939—1989))*. Book dedicated to the former President of the Republic of Poland

Ryszard Kaczorowski, by M. Szczerbiński and T. Wolsza, editors. See also J. Tebinka, *Wielka Brytania dotrzyma lojalnie swojego słowa. Winston Churchill a Polska* (*Great Britain will keep its word. Winston Churchill and Poland*), published by Warszawa: Wydawnictwo Neriton, 2013. (Warsaw: Neriton Publishing House, 2013), in the chapter entitled 'Katyń,' 134—148.

[3793] Position 434.1 of *Katyn and the Soviet Massacre of 1940: Truth, justice and memory* by George Sanford.

[3794] Ibid.

[3795] Ibid.

[3796] Position 427.6 of *Katyn and the Soviet Massacre of 1940: Truth, justice and memory* by George Sanford.

[3797] https://www.britannica.com/biography/Aleksey-Nikolayevich-Graf-Tolstoy. Accessed on Saturday July 25, 2020.

[3798] Position 428.6 of *Katyn and the Soviet Massacre of 1940: Truth, justice and memory* by George Sanford.

[3799] [4103] Page 677 of the article *The Birth and Persistence of the Katyn Lie* by Witold Wasilewski, written in 2012 and published in 2013 in Volume 45, issue 3 of *Case Western Reserve Journal of International Law*. This article can be downloaded on the website of the *Case Western Reserve Journal of International Law* at https://scholarlycommons.law.case.edu/jil/vol45/iss3/3/. Accessed on Saturday July 25, 2020.

[3800] Ibid. That NKVD meant "People's Commissariat for Internal Affairs" see page 672.

[3801] Ibid.

[3802] Ibid.

[3803] [3885] Ibid page 678.

[3804] Ibid page 678.

[3805] See endnotes [3651] to [3655] for this supplement.

[3806] Page 678 of the article *The Birth and Persistence of the Katyn Lie* by Witold Wasilewski.

[3807] [3885] [3935] Ibid page 678. See also the third page of the undated document *Katyn Massacre* by the Russian historian Natalia S. Lebedeva, explaining the establishment of the Burdenko Commission. It is available on the website of Princeton University at http://press.princeton.edu/chapters/pons/s5_9143.pdf. Accessed on Saturday July 25, 2020. See also endnote [3618] for this supplement.

[3808] [3884] Ibid pages 678 to 679.

[3809] See endnotes [3629] to [3633] for this supplement.

[3810] See endnotes [3727] to [3737] for this supplement.

[3811] Page 680 of *The Birth and Persistence of the Katyn Lie* by Witold Wasilewski.

[3812] [3888] [3894] Position 430.5 of *Katyn and the Soviet Massacre of 1940: Truth, justice and memory* by George Sanford.

[3813] Page 681 of *The Birth and Persistence of the Katyn Lie* by Witold Wasilewski.

[3814] Ibid.

[3815] [3880] [3882] [3917] Ibid page 682.

[3816] Position 977.9 of Schlingensiepen and page 925 of Bethge. See also endnote [2300] for Chapter 24 "Dietrich's Final Days" in regard to the sentencing and execution of Hans von Dohnányi on Monday April 9 1945 — the same date as Dietrich's execution.

[3817] Page 684 of *The Birth and Persistence of the Katyn Lie* by Witold Wasilewski.

[3818] Page 690 to 691 of *The Birth and Persistence of the Katyn Lie* by Witold Wasilewski.

[3819] Ibid pages 684 to 685.

[3820] Ibid.

[3821] Ibid page 691.

[3822] Ibid page 687.

[3823] Position 433.9 of *Katyn and the Soviet Massacre of 1940: Truth, justice and memory* by George Sanford.

[3824] Position 434.2 of *Katyn and the Soviet Massacre of 1940: Truth, justice and memory* by George Sanford.

[3825] Pages 109 to 110 of Tadeusz Wolsza. See also endnote [3792] for this supplement.

[3826] As discussed in Witold Wasilewski's article *The Birth and Persistence of the Katyn Lie*.

[3827] Position 434.8 of *Katyn and the Soviet Massacre of 1940: Truth, justice and memory* by George Sanford.

[3828] As discussed in Witold Wasilewski's article *The Birth and Persistence of the Katyn Lie*.

[3829] Position 435.0 of *Katyn and the Soviet Massacre of 1940: Truth, justice and memory* by George Sanford.

[3830] Page 683 of *The Birth and Persistence of the Katyn Lie* by Witold Wasilewski gives the full name and title of Vladimir Potemkin, who was one of the eight members of the Burdenko commission.

[3831] Pages 688 to 689 of *The Birth and Persistence of the Katyn Lie* by Witold Wasilewski.

[3832] See endnotes [3705], [3706], [3787] and [3788] for this supplement.

[3833] Pages 688 to 689 of *The Birth and Persistence of the Katyn Lie* by Witold Wasilewski.

[3834] See endnotes [3651] to [3655] for this supplement.

[3835] See footnote #97 on page 690 of *The Birth and Persistence of the Katyn Lie* by Witold Wasilewski.

[3836] See endnote [3645] for this supplement.

[3837] See endnote [3645] for this supplement.

[3838] Position 435.5 of *Katyn and the Soviet Massacre of 1940: Truth, justice and memory* by George Sanford.

[3839] Ibid position 435.9.

[3840] Ibid position 436.2.

[3841] Pages 132 to 134 of *Katyń: the Untold Story of Stalin's Polish Massacre* by Allen Paul, published by Macmillan Publishing Company New York, First Edition, First Printing edition (August 1, 1991), ISBN-10: 0684192152, ISBN-13: 9780684192154.

[3842] Position 436.4 of *Katyn and the Soviet Massacre of 1940: Truth, justice and memory* by George Sanford.

[3843] Position 353.8 to 357.4 of *Bloodlands* by Timothy Snyder, published by The Bodley Head of the Random House Group 2010, ISBN 9781407075501. Note the map given for the location of the three massacres of Polish officers committed by the NKVD.

[3844] [3847] [3947] Pages 76 to 77 of the English language article (translated from Polish by Iwona Ewa Waldzińska (State School of Higher Education in Oświęcim (Auschwitz))) *Katyn Massacre — Basic Facts* published in the periodical of *Uniwersytetu Papieskiego Jana Pawła II* (Pontifical University of John Paul II in Kraków, Faculty of Theology, Section in Tarnów — http://www.wt.diecezja.tarnow.pl/dzia%C5%82alno%C5%9B%C4%87-naukowa/czasopisma-naukowe/the-person-and-the-challenges) *The Person and the Challenges,* Volume 3 (2013) Number 2. It can be downloaded at the Instytut Pamięci Narodowej (the Polish Institute of National Remembrance) at https://ipn.gov.pl/en/news/1105,Katyn-Massacre-Basic-Facts.html. Its authors are Monika Komaniecka, Institute of National Remembrance, Kraków, Poland; Krystyna Samsonowska, Jagiellonian University, Kraków, Poland; Mateusz Szpytma, Institute of National Remembrance, Kraków, Poland; and Anna Zechenter Institute of National Remembrance, Kraków, Poland. Both links accessed on Saturday July 25, 2020.

[3845] Ibid.

[3846] See endnotes [3440] to [3443] of Polish WWII Supplement I "The Molotov-Ribbentrop Pact" in regard to the Stalinist objective in 1939-41 of wiping Poland from existence on the map of Europe.

[3847] Page 72 of *Katyn Massacre — Basic Facts* published in the periodical *The Person and the Challenges,* Volume 3 (2013) Number 2. It can be downloaded at the Instytut Pamięci Narodowej (the Polish Institute of National Remembrance) at https://ipn.gov.pl/en/news/1105,Katyn-Massacre-Basic-Facts.html. Accessed on Saturday July 25, 2020. For full information on this source, see endnote [3844] for this supplement.

[3848] Ibid.

[3849] See endnote [3649] for this supplement.

[3850] Pages 65 to 66 of *Katyn Massacre — Basic Facts* published in the periodical *The Person and the Challenges,* Volume 3 (2013) Number 2.

[3851] Ibid.

[3852] Page 48 of the publication *The WAR & MYTH UNKNOWN WWII 1939 1945,* by Igor Bigun, Sergii Butko, Volodymyr Viatrovych, Kyrylo Halushko, Serhii Horobets, Sergii Gromenko, Oleksandr Zinchenko, Olesia Isaiuk, Bogdan Korolenko, Maksym Maiorov, Vasyl Pavlov, Rostyslav Pyliavets, Yana Prymachenko, Sergii Riabenko, Viktoria Iaremenko, under the editorship of: Oleksandr Zinchenko, Volodymyr Viatrovych, Maksym Maiorov, published by the Ukrainian Institute of National Remembrance, 2018, ISBN 966136558X, 978966136558.

[3853] Page ccvii (207) in Chapter 5 "Kicking in the Door: June-December 1941" of the book *The Storm of War: A New History of the Second World War* by Andrew Roberts, published by Penguin UK, 2009, ISBN 0141938862, 9780141938868.

[3854] Page 48 of the publication *The WAR & MYTH UNKNOWN WWII 1939 1945.*

[3855] See endnote [3718] for this supplement.

[3856] Page 48 of the publication *The WAR & MYTH UNKNOWN WWII 1939 1945.*

[3857] See endnotes [3719] and [3720] for this supplement.

[3858] See endnote [3721] for this supplement.

[3859] See endnote [3765] for this supplement. It was in 1954, in the year following Stalin's death, with Nikita Khrushchev in power, that the NKVD was superseded by the KGB.

[3860] The article by Matthew Luxmoore, dated December 22, 2019 on the website of Radio Free Europe at https://www.rferl.org/a/russia-katyn-massacre-rewriting-history-removal-plaques/30338487.html. "Memorial" is is an international historical and civil rights society that operates in a number of post-Soviet states. It focuses on recording and publicising the Soviet Union's totalitarian past, but also monitors human rights in Russia and other post-Soviet states. Its website is at https://www.memo.ru/en-us/. Both links accessed accessed on Saturday July 25, 2020.

[3861] Ibid.

[3862] Ibid.

[3863] Ibid.

[3864] Ibid.

[3865] Ibid.

[3866] Ibid.

[3867] The questionable research of this neo-Stalinist historian will be dealt with in the coming pages.

[3868] The article by Matthew Luxmoore, dated December 22, 2019 on the website of Radio Free Europe at https://www.rferl.org/a/russia-katyn-massacre-rewriting-history-removal-plaques/30338487.html. Accessed on Saturday July

25, 2020. The article provides a youtube link to a clip one of these neo-Stalinist propaganda movies.

3869 Ibid.

3870 Ibid.

3871 Ibid.

3872 See the English language online article by Halya Coynash at http://khpg.org/en/index.php?id=1588896084 on the website of *Human Rights in Ukraine — Website of the Kharkiv Human Rights Protection Group* dated May 8, 2020. Accessed on Saturday July 25, 2020.

3873 The article by Matthew Luxmoore, dated December 22, 2019 on the website of Radio Free Europe at https://www.rferl.org/a/russia-katyn-massacre-rewriting-history-removal-plaques/30338487.html. Accessed on Saturday July 25, 2020.

3874 Ibid.

3875 Ibid.

3876 3928 Ibid.

3877 From Grover Furr's university profile page at https://www.montclair.edu/profilepages/view_profile.php?username=furrg. Accessed on Saturday July 25, 2020.

3878 See endnotes 3380 to 3387 of Polish WWII Supplement I "The Molotov-Ribbentrop Pact" in regard to this spurious claim.

3879 See endnote 3386 of Polish WWII Supplement I "The Molotov-Ribbentrop Pact."

3880 See endnote 3815 for this supplement.

3881 3901 The 2013 article by Grover Furr *The "Official" Version of the Katyn Massacre Disproven? Discoveries at a German Mass Murder Site in Ukraine*, published in the periodical *Socialism and Democracy*, 2013 Vol. 27, No. 2, 96—129. It can be downloaded at http://dx.doi.org/10.1080/08854300.2013.795268. Accessed on Saturday July 25, 2020.

3882 See endnote 3815 for this supplement which documents the sycophantic and official title for the Burdenko commission.

3883 3894 Page 115 of the 2013 article by Grover Furr *The "Official" Version of the Katyn Massacre Disproven? Discoveries at a German Mass Murder Site in Ukraine*.

3884 In regard to the questionable testimony gathered by the Burdenko commission, see endnote 3808 for this supplement.

3885 In regard to the questionable documentary evidence gathered by the Burdenko commission, see endnotes 3803 to 3807 for this supplement.

3886 https://www.britannica.com/event/Katyn-Massacre. Accessed on Saturday July 25, 2020.

[3887] Page 115 of The 2013 article by Grover Furr *The "Official" Version of the Katyn Massacre Disproven? Discoveries at a German Mass Murder Site in Ukraine.*

[3888] See endnote [3812] for this supplement and position 430.5 of *Katyn and the Soviet Massacre of 1940: Truth, justice and memory* by George Sanford.

[3889] Ibid.

[3890] Pages ccx to ccxi (210 to 211) in Chapter 5 "Kicking in the Door: June-December 1941" of the book The Storm of War: A New History of the Second World War by Andrew Roberts, published by Penguin UK, 2009, ISBN 0141938862, 9780141938868.

[3891] That Sikorski was a major figure in the 1920 Battle of Warsaw, see page 84 and the map on page 85 of *Warsaw 1920, Lenin's Failed Conquest of Europe* by Adam Zamoyski.

[3892] That General Władysław Sikorski headed the Polish Government in Exile in London after the Nazi invasion of Poland in September 1939, see page 34 of *Rising '44: The Battle for Warsaw Reprint Edition,* by Professor Norman Davies, published by Penguin Books; Reprint edition (October 4, 2005), ISBN-10: 0143035401, ISBN-13: 9780143035404.

[3893] [4306] [4308] [4311] [4313] In regard to Władysław Anders, see the online *Encyclopaedia Britannica* article at https://www.britannica.com/biography/Wladyslaw-Anders. Accessed on Saturday July 25, 2020.

[3894] See endnote [3812] for this supplement and position 430.5 of *Katyn and the Soviet Massacre of 1940: Truth, justice and memory* by George Sanford in regard to the fictitious "ON" camps. See also, the implausible claim by Grover Furr at endnote [3883] for this supplement, who maintains that they did exist, in spite of the fact that they were never found and never mentioned in Polish-Soviet exchanges from 1941 to 1943, preceding the discovery of the Katyń mass graves.

[3895] [3919] Page 73 of the publication *KATYŃ - ZBRODNIA BEZ SĄDU I KARY (KATYŃ - A CRIME WITHOUT JUDGMENT AND PENALTIES)* by Jacek Trznadel, published by Antyk Marcin Dybowski Warszawa (Warsaw) 1997, ISBN 8390587718, ISSN: 14264064. See also page 180 of *The Eagle Unbowed: Poland and the Poles in the Second World War* by Halik Kochanski, published by Harvard University Press, 2012, ISBN 0674068165, 9780674068162 and page 363 of *God's Playground A History of Poland: Volume II: 1795 to the Present*, by Norman Davies, published by Oxford University Press, 2005, ISBN 0199253404, 9780199253401.

[3896] See endnotes [3650] to [3654] for this supplement in regard to the significance of the diaries of the Katyń victims.

[3897] Page 103 of the 2013 article by Grover Furr *The "Official" Version of the Katyn Massacre Disproven? Discoveries at a German Mass Murder Site in Ukraine.*

[3898] Ibid page 110.

[3899] See the official website of the modern-day eastern Polish town of Hrubieszów at https://www.miasto.hrubieszow.pl/page/w%C5%82odzimierz-wo%C5%82y%C5%84ski-ukraina for the article regarding the cooperation agreement between the cities of Włodzimierz Wołyński and Hrubieszów, which was signed on May 19, 1995. The agreement extending cooperation for an indefinite period was signed on February 24, 2011 in Włodzimierz Wołyński (Ukrainian: Володимир-Волинський which Romanised is Volodymyr-Volyns'kiy). The website for for modern-day Volodymyr-Volyns'kiy is at http://volodymyrrada.gov.ua/. Both accessed on Saturday July 25, 2020.

[3900] Ibid.

[3901] See endnote [3881] for this supplement.

[3902] The online article *Kontrowersje wokół ekshumacji we Włodzimierzu Wołyńskim* (Controversy around exhumation in Włodzimierz Wołyński), dated April 18, 2013 on the website the bi-weekly magazine Kurier Galicyjski (Galician Courier) at https://kuriergalicyjski.com/rozmaitosci/2033-kontrowersje-wok-ekshumacji-we-wodzimierzu-woyskim. The magazine was first published on August 15, 2007, with its purpose to inform Poles living in Ukraine about the cultural and political life of the Polish community, as well as Polish-Ukrainian relations. The editors devote a lot of attention to historical, social and regional issues. In February 2018, the magazine received a special award of the Polish Minister of Culture and National Heritage. See the article at https://www.kuriergalicyjski.com/actualnosci/report/6631-nagroda-specjalna-ministra-kultury-i-dziedzictwa-narodowego-rp-dla-kuriera-galicyjskiego. Both links accessed on Saturday July 25, 2020.

[3903] See for example the online article on the website of Ukrainian Euro Maidan Press at http://euromaidanpress.com/2016/07/01/lists-of-nkvd-victims-killed-in-mass-executions-in-1941-published-online/. In this article, the original NKVD document list of prisoners for Lviv (Polish Lwów) prison #4 which carries the resolution of the local NKVD chief: "I authorize the execution of the enemies of the nation." Euromaidan Press (EP) is an online English-language independent newspaper launched in 2014 by Ukrainian volunteers. EP focuses on events covering Ukraine and provides translations of Ukrainian news and expert analysis as well as independent research. Through its work, EP strives to bridge Ukraine with the English-speaking world. See their "About page" at http://euromaidanpress.com/about/. Both links accessed on Saturday July 25, 2020.

[3904] See the Figure 1 map on page 24 of the publication, *The Great West Ukrainian Prison Massacre of 1941* edited by Ksenya Kiebuzinski and Alexander Motyl, published by Amsterdam University Press 2017, ISBN 9789089648341 e-ISBN 9789048526826 (pdf) doi: 10.5117/9789089648341 nur: 689. It gives the number of 36 for Volodymyr-Volyns'kiy (Polish: Włodzimierz- Wołyński).

[3905] April 18, 2013 article on the website the bi-weekly magazine Kurier Galicyjski (Galician Courier) at https://kuriergalicyjski.com/rozmaitosci/2033-kontrowersje-wok-ekshumacji-we-wodzimierzu-woyskim. Accessed on Saturday July 25, 2020.

[3906] Ibid.

[3907] Ibid.

[3908] Ibid.

[3909] Ibid.

[3910] Ibid.

[3911] For more information on the UPA see the article *Interventions: Challenging the Myths of Twentieth-Century Ukrainian History* by John-Paul Himka from the Department of History and Classics, Winner of the J. Gordin Kaplan Award for Research Excellence University of Alberta. Text based on an address delivered at the 2nd annual Celebration of Research and Creative Work Faculty of Arts, March 28, 2011. It can be viewed and downloaded at http://www.viaevrasia.com/documents/celebration_jph_march28.pdf. Accessed on Saturday July 25, 2020.

[3912] April 18, 2013 article on the website the bi-weekly magazine Kurier Galicyjski (Galician Courier) at https://kuriergalicyjski.com/rozmaitosci/2033-kontrowersje-wok-ekshumacji-we-wodzimierzu-woyskim. Accessed on Saturday July 25, 2020.

[3913] Ibid. In particular, see the earlier quoted statement of the Polish Archaeologist Adam Kaczyński.

[3914] Page 109 of Grover Furr's 2013 article. He refers to them as the "Ukrainian Nationalist" forces.

[3915] April 18, 2013 article on the website the bi-weekly magazine Kurier Galicyjski (Galician Courier) at https://kuriergalicyjski.com/rozmaitosci/2033-kontrowersje-wok-ekshumacji-we-wodzimierzu-woyskim. Accessed on Saturday July 25, 2020. In particular, see the earlier quoted statement of the Polish Archaeologist Adam Kaczyński.

[3916] Ibid. In particular, see the earlier quoted statement of the Polish Archaeologist Adam Kaczyński.

[3917] See endnote [3815] for this supplement which documents the sycophantic and official title for the Burdenko commission.

[3918] The Holocaust Controversies Blogspot at https://holocaustcontroversies.blogspot.com/2020/01/looking-for-katyn-lighthouses.html. Accessed on Saturday July 25, 2020. This source later makes reference to, and gives a link to Alexandr Gurynov's work documenting the names of Polish victims buried at Mednoye in May 1940, and explaining the reason for the badges of two Poles buried at Mednoye, being found at Volodymyr-Volyns'kiy.

[3919] See endnote [3895] for this supplement.

[3920] The Holocaust Controversies Blogspot at https://holocaustcontroversies.blogspot.com/2020/01/looking-for-katyn-lighthouses.html. Accessed on Saturday July 25, 2020.

[3921] [3936] Ibid and pages 79 to 81 and 620 of *УБИТЫ В КАЛИНИНЕ, ЗАХОРОНЕНЫ В МЕДНОМ* (*Ubity v Kalinine, zakhoroneny v Mednom — Killed in Kalinin, buried in Mednoye) 2019, volume 1* by Alexandr Guryanov, published by Издательство «Бослен» Москва (Boslen Publishing House Moscow), ISBN 9785604192146 (т.1), for Международный Мемориал 127051 Москва, Малый Каретный пер, (International Memorial 127051 Moscow, Maly Karetny https://www.memo.ru). Accessed on Saturday July 25, 2020. This work has been compiled with the help of numerous assistants, among which Polish historians figure prominently.

[3922] The Holocaust Controversies Blogspot at https://holocaustcontroversies.blogspot.com/2020/01/looking-for-katyn-lighthouses.html. Accessed on Saturday July 25, 2020.

[3923] Pages 103 to 104 of Furr's 2013 article.

[3924] Ibid pages 110 to 111.

[3925] Pages 79 to 81 of *УБИТЫ В КАЛИНИНЕ, ЗАХОРОНЕНЫ В МЕДНОМ* (*Ubity v Kalinine, zakhoroneny v Mednom — Killed in Kalinin, buried in Mednoye) 2019, volume 1* by Alexandr Guryanov.

[3926] Ibid and The Holocaust Controversies Blogspot at https://holocaustcontroversies.blogspot.com/2020/01/looking-for-katyn-lighthouses.html. Accessed on Saturday July 25, 2020.

[3927] Page 620 of *УБИТЫ В КАЛИНИНЕ, ЗАХОРОНЕНЫ В МЕДНОМ* (*Ubity v Kalinine, zakhoroneny v Mednom — Killed in Kalinin, buried in Mednoye) 2019, volume 1* by Alexandr Guryanov and The Holocaust Controversies Blogspot at https://holocaustcontroversies.blogspot.com/2020/01/looking-for-katyn-lighthouses.html. Accessed on Saturday July 25, 2020.

[3928] See endnote [3876] for this supplement.

[3929] Pages 122 to 123 of the 2013 article by Grover Furr *The "Official" Version of the Katyn Massacre Disproven? Discoveries at a German Mass Murder Site in Ukraine.*

[3930] See the description for photo #60 after page 220 in White Eagle Red Star and position 635.8 in the ebook. See also endnote [181] of The Preface "Birth and Memory upon the Lesser Known Fault Line of History."

[3931] Position 510.5 of White Eagle Red Star in the ebook and pages 238 to 239 of the paperback published in 2003 by Pimlico, Random House UK Limited, ISBN 9780712606943.

[3932] See endnotes [3367] to [3373] of Polish WWII Supplement I "The Molotov-Ribbentrop Pact" in regard to the deportation of Borderland Poles to the Gulag. See also endnote [204] in the Preface "Birth and Memory upon the Lesser Known Fault Line of History."

[3933] See endnote [206] of The Preface "Birth and Memory upon the Lesser Known Fault Line of History" and endnotes [3368], [3371] and [3372] for Polish WWII Supplement I "The Molotov-Ribbentrop Pact."

[3934] Cited on Grover Furr's Katyn discussion page *The Katyn Forest Whodunnit* at https://msuweb.montclair.edu/~furrg/pol/discuss_katyn041806r.html. Accessed on Saturday July 25, 2020.

[3935] See endnotes [3618], [3764] and [3807] for this supplement.

[3936] See endnote [3921] for this supplement.

[3937] [4587] Final Report from the examination of the aviation accident no 192/2010/11 involving the Tu-154M airplane, tail number 101, which occurred on April 10th, 2010 in the area of the SMOLENSK NORTH airfield (https://wayback.archive-it.org/all/20120906032711/http://mswia.datacenter-poland.pl/FinalReportTu-154M.pdf) (PDF). Committee for Investigation of National Aviation Accidents. 29 July 2011. Archived from the original (http://mswia.datacenter-poland.pl/FinalReportTu-154M.pdf). Both links accessed on Saturday July 25, 2020.

[3938] Online article in the New York Observer at https://observer.com/2018/05/evidence-shows-russia-had-role-in-smolensk-crash-killed-kaczynski/, dated May 15, 2018 by John Schindler, security expert and former National Security Agency analyst. Accessed on Saturday July 25, 2020.

[3939] Online article in the New York Observer at https://observer.com/2018/05/evidence-shows-russia-had-role-in-smolensk-crash-killed-kaczynski/, dated May 15, 2018 by John Schindler, security expert and former National Security Agency analyst. Accessed on Saturday July 25, 2020.

[3940] Online article in the New York Observer at https://observer.com/2018/05/evidence-shows-russia-had-role-in-smolensk-crash-killed-kaczynski/, dated May 15, 2018 by John Schindler, security expert and former National Security Agency analyst. Accessed on Saturday July 25, 2020.

[3941] The online article on the website of Reuters at https://www.reuters.com/article/us-poland-smolensk-kaczynski/poland-finds-other-body-parts-in-coffin-of-president-killed-in-2010-crash-prosecutors-idUSKBN18S620, dated June 2, 2017 and the article in the New York Observer at https://observer.com/2018/05/evidence-shows-russia-had-role-in-smolensk-crash-killed-kaczynski/, dated May 15, 2018 by John Schindler, security expert and former National Security Agency analyst. Both links accessed on Saturday July 25, 2020.

[3942] Online article on the website of Aljazeera by Natalia Ojewska, dated April 11, 2013, https://www.aljazeera.com/indepth/features/2013/04/2013410113411207111.html. The results of the Polish poll can be downloaded given at https://www.cbos.pl/SPISKOM.POL/2013/K_025_13.PDF. The homepage of CBOS, the Polish survey firm, is at https://www.cbos.pl/PL/home/home.php. All links accessed on Saturday July 25, 2020.

[3943] Online article on the website of Aljazeera by Natalia Ojewska, dated April 11, 2013.

[3944] See the online article *Poland Marks 10 Years Since Smolensk Plane Crash Killed Top Officials in Russia* on the website of Radio Free Europe, dated April 10, 2020 at https://www.rferl.org/a/poland-smolensk-kaczynski-10-yearsplane-crash-russia/30546535.html. Accessed on Saturday July 25, 2020.

[3945] The June 2018 report of the Council of Europe on the April 2010 Smolensk air disaster on its website at http://www.assembly.coe.int/LifeRay/JUR/Pdf/TextesProvisoires/2018/201806 25-PolishCrash-EN.pdf. Its "about us" page is at https://www.coe.int/en/web/about-us/who-we-are. Accessed on Saturday July 25, 2020.

[3946] Position 360.9 of *Bloodlands* by Timothy Snyder, published by The Bodley Head of the Random House Group 2010, ISBN 9781407075501. Note the map given for the location of the three massacres of Polish officers committed by the NKVD at position 350.7.

[3947] After 1921, following the conclusion of the 1919-20 Polish Soviet War, small, specially trained groups of Ukrainian and Belarusian Bolsheviks and Red Army soldiers slipped across the border from the Soviet Union. They attacked police stations, civilians, clerks and set fire to forests. The Creation of the Border Protection Corps in 1924 gradually restricted the penetration of these agents and terrorists. See Pages 66 to 67 of the English language article (translated from Polish by Iwona Ewa Waldzińska (State School of Higher Education in Oświęcim (Auschwitz)) *Katyn Massacre — Basic Facts* published in the periodical *The Person and the Challenges,* Volume 3 (2013) Number 2. It can be downloaded at the Instytut Pamięci Narodowej (the Polish Institute of National Remembrance) at https://ipn.gov.pl/en/news/1105,Katyn-Massacre-Basic-Facts.html. Accessed on Saturday July 25, 2020. For full information on this source, see endnote [3844] for this supplement.

[3948] Position 361.1 of *Bloodlands* by Timothy Snyder.

[3949] The memorial article in German titled *In memoriam Prof. Kazimierz Karbowski* which can be downloaded at https://sanp.ch/article/doi/sanp.2012.02368 on the website of the Swiss Archives of Neurology, Psychiatry and Psychotherapy. Accessed on Saturday July 25, 2020. See also endnote [3670] for this supplement.

[3950] [191] Position 358.2 of *Bloodlands* by Timothy Snyder.

[3951] [3192] Online article by Neal Ascherson on the website of the UK Guardian at https://www.theguardian.com/world/2010/apr/17/smolensk-crash-katyn-accident-of-history, dated Saturday 17 April, 2010, which was just one week after the Smolensk air disaster. Accessed on Saturday July 25, 2020.

[3952] Norman Davies uses this term at position 509.5 of *White Eagle Red Star* in the ebook, and page 238 in the paperback published in 2003 by Pimlico, Random House UK Limited, ISBN 9780712606943.

[3953] [3192] Online article by Neal Ascherson on the website of the UK Guardian.

[3954] See position 358.2 of *Bloodlands* by Timothy Snyder for the account of Adam Solski. Or see endnotes [3654] and [3655] for this supplement.

[3955] [191] See endnote [3619] for this supplement.

Polish WWII Supplement IV — AK and 1944 Warsaw General Uprising — Stalin's mass murder by German proxy

[3956] [2411] [3691] Austere iron plaque in Polish and English, placed above the entrance to Warsaw's *Muzeum Powstania* (Uprising Museum), embodying the people of Warsaw's dream in August 1944, in reclaiming their freedom, as seen and photographed by me on Saturday October 9, 2004.

[3957] [3194] [4563] See page 14 of the publication *EGZEKUCJA LUDNOŚCI CYWIL-NEJ W WAWRZE 27 GRUDNIA 1939 (EXECUTION OF THE CIVIL POPU-LATION IN WAWER DECEMBER 27, 1939)* by Jan Tyszkiewicz, published by Urząd m.st. Warszawy Wydział Kultury dla Dzielnicy Wawer (City Hall Warsaw Department of Culture for the Wawer District), ISBN 9788392169062. It can be downloaded at http://mbc.cyfrowemazowsze.pl/Content/57749/00061734%20-%20Tyszkiewicz%20J%20-%20Egzekucja%20ludn%20cyw%20w%20Wwrze%2027%2012%2039%20-%20V-2-2.pdf on the website of the *Mazowiecka Biblioteka Cyfrowa* (Mazovian Digital Library) at http://mbc.cyfrowemazowsze.pl/dlibra. Both links accessed on Sunday July 26, 2020.

[3958] The online English language article titled *A Bloody Night in Wawer* by Przemysław Mazur at https://www.zapisyterroru.pl/dlibra/context?id=context2 on the website of the *39-45 Chronicles of Terror*. Chronicles of Terror is one of the largest collections of civilian testimonies from occupied Europe and features hundreds of accounts submitted by Polish citizens, who suffered immense hardship at the hands of the German and Soviet totalitarian regimes during the Second World War. See https://www.zapisyterroru.pl/dlibra. One of its several partners is the *Instytut Pamięci Narodowej* (Polish Institute of National Remembrance) at https://ipn.gov.pl/en/. See also, the Polish language online article at http://polska-zbrojna.pl/home/articleshow/29927 on the website of *Polska Zbrojna* (Armed Poland — the website of the Polish Armed Forces). Its partners include the *Ministerstwo Obrony Narodowej* (Ministry of National Defence). All links accessed on Sunday July 26, 2020.

[3959] Ibid.

[3960] The online English language article titled *A Bloody Night in Wawer* by Przemysław Mazur at https://www.zapisyterroru.pl/dlibra/context?id=context2

on the website of the *39-45 Chronicles of Terror*. Accessed on Sunday July 26, 2020. See also pages 15 to 16 of *EGZEKUCJA LUDNOŚCI CYWILNEJ W WAWRZE 27 GRUDNIA 1939 (EXECUTION OF THE CIVIL POPULATION IN WAWER DECEMBER 27, 1939)* by Jan Tyszkiewicz..

[3961] Page 15 of *EGZEKUCJA LUDNOŚCI CYWILNEJ W WAWRZE 27 GRUDNIA 1939 (EXECUTION OF THE CIVIL POPULATION IN WAWER DECEMBER 27, 1939)* by Jan Tyszkiewicz.

[3962] Ibid.

[3963] Ibid.

[3964] Page 16 of *EGZEKUCJA LUDNOŚCI CYWILNEJ W WAWRZE 27 GRUDNIA 1939 (EXECUTION OF THE CIVIL POPULATION IN WAWER DECEMBER 27, 1939)* by Jan Tyszkiewicz. This page implies that the collection of "hostages" by the Germans took precedence over apprehending the perpetrators.

[3965] [3970] Ibid page 19 and the online English language article titled *A Bloody Night in Wawer* by Przemysław Mazur at https://www.zapisyterroru.pl/dlibra/context?id=context2 on the website of the *39-45 Chronicles of Terror*. Accessed on Sunday July 26, 2020.

[3966] The online English language article titled *A Bloody Night in Wawer* by Przemysław Mazur at https://www.zapisyterroru.pl/dlibra/context?id=context2 on the website of the *39-45 Chronicles of Terror*. Accessed on Sunday July 26, 2020.

[3967] Ibid.

[3968] Ibid.

[3969] Ibid and the description of the photo on page 41 *EGZEKUCJA LUDNOŚCI CYWILNEJ W WAWRZE 27 GRUDNIA 1939 (EXECUTION OF THE CIVIL POPULATION IN WAWER DECEMBER 27, 1939)* by Jan Tyszkiewicz.

[3970] See endnote [3965] for this supplement.

[3971] [3979] The account of Stanisław Piegat at https://zapisyterroru.pl/dlibra/show-content?id=172& on the website of the *39-45 Chronicles of Terror*. All links accessed on Sunday July 26, 2020.

[3972] The online English language article titled *A Bloody Night in Wawer* by Przemysław Mazur at https://www.zapisyterroru.pl/dlibra/context?id=context2 on the website of the *39-45 Chronicles of Terror*. All links accessed on Sunday July 26, 2020.

[3973] Ibid.

[3974] Ibid.

[3975] Ibid.

[3976] Ibid.

[3977] Ibid.

[3978] Ibid.

[3979] See endnote [3971] for this supplement.

[3980] The online English language article titled *A Bloody Night in Wawer* by Przemysław Mazur at https://www.zapisyterroru.pl/dlibra/context?id=context2 on the website of the *Chronicles of Terror*. All links accessed on Sunday July 26, 2020.

[3981] Ibid.

[3982] Ibid.

[3983] [3194] Ibid.

[3984] Ibid and page 32 of *EGZEKUCJA LUDNOŚCI CYWILNEJ W WAWRZE 27 GRUDNIA 1939 (EXECUTION OF THE CIVIL POPULATION IN WAWER DECEMBER 27, 1939)* by Jan Tyszkiewicz. Note in the latter source, the date given as "6.II.1940" means 6th of February 1940, as "II" is the Roman numeral for the second month of February. In many Polish texts, the month in a date, is given in Roman numerals.

[3985] Page 81 of the paper *ORGANIZACJA MAŁEGO SABOTAŻU WAWER W WARSZAZWIE (1940—1944)* (Organisation of Minor Sabotage Wawer in Warsaw (1940—1944)), by Władysław Bartoszewski, published in the 1966 edition of the yearbook *NAJNOWSZE DZIEJE POLSKI, 1939—1945* (Recent Polish History, 1939—1945). It can be downloaded from https://rcin.org.pl/dlibra/show-content/publication/edition/44795?id=44795 on the website of Repozytorium Cyfrowe Instytutów Naukowych (Digital Repository of Scientific Institutes). Accessed on Sunday July 26, 2020.

[3986] Page 35 of *EGZEKUCJA LUDNOŚCI CYWILNEJ W WAWRZE 27 GRUDNIA 1939 (EXECUTION OF THE CIVIL POPULATION IN WAWER DECEMBER 27, 1939)* by Jan Tyszkiewicz.

[3987] See page 171 of *Rising '44: The Battle for Warsaw*, published by Penguin Books; Reprint edition (October 4, 2005), ISBN-10: 0143035401, ISBN-13: 9780143035404.

[3988] Page 35 of *EGZEKUCJA LUDNOŚCI CYWILNEJ W WAWRZE 27 GRUDNIA 1939 (EXECUTION OF THE CIVIL POPULATION IN WAWER DECEMBER 27, 1939)* by Jan Tyszkiewicz. See also pages 52 and 54 of the book *Wojna warszawsko-niemiecka (The Warsaw-German War)* by Czesław Michalski, published by Czytelnik (Reader), 1974. It documents the Wawer massacre of late December 1939 and the aftermath one year later with underground boy scout groups creating it as "*Pomścimy Wawer*" — "We'll avenge Wawer."

[3989] Page 35 of *EGZEKUCJA LUDNOŚCI CYWILNEJ W WAWRZE 27 GRUDNIA 1939 (EXECUTION OF THE CIVIL POPULATION IN WAWER DECEMBER 27, 1939)* by Jan Tyszkiewicz.

[3990] Ibid.

[3991] [4563] The online article dated March 20, 2019 on the website of "Poland in," the English language portal of *Telewizja Polska* (Poland's national television network) at https://polandin.com/41828137/77-years-of-fighting-poland-emblem. All links accessed on Sunday July 26, 2020. See also pages 54 and 67 of the book *Wojna warszawsko-niemiecka (The Warsaw-German War)* by Czesław Michalski, published by Czytelnik (Reader), 1974. It documents the Wawer massacre of late December 1939 and the aftermath one year later with underground boy scout groups creating it as "*Pomścimy Wawer*" — "We'll avenge Wawer."

[3992] Page 35 of *EGZEKUCJA LUDNOŚCI CYWILNEJ W WAWRZE 27 GRUDNIA 1939 (EXECUTION OF THE CIVIL POPULATION IN WAWER DECEMBER 27, 1939)* by Jan Tyszkiewicz. All links accessed on Sunday July 26, 2020.

[3993] Page 81 of the paper *ORGANIZACJA MAŁEGO SABOTAŻU WAWER W WARSZAZWIE (1940—1944)* (Organisation of Minor Sabotage Wawer in Warsaw (1940—1944)), by Władysław Bartoszewski, published in the 1966 edition of the yearbook *NAJNOWSZE DZIEJE POLSKI, 1939—1945* (Recent Polish History, 1939—1945). It can be downloaded from https://rcin.org.pl/dlibra/show-content/publication/edition/44795?id=44795 on the website of Repozytorium Cyfrowe Instytutów Naukowych (Digital Repository of Scientific Institutes). Accessed on Sunday July 26, 2020.

[3994] Ibid page 104.

[3995] Ibid page 104.

[3996] [4564] Page 171 of *Rising '44: The Battle for Warsaw*, by Norman Davies, published by Penguin Books; Reprint edition (October 4, 2005), ISBN-10: 0143035401, ISBN-13: 9780143035404.

[3997] The online article *Decoding Warsaw: A Guide to the City's Sights and Symbols* by by Alena Aniskiewicz, dated August 5, 2015, on the Polish Culture website at https://culture.pl/en/article/decoding-warsaw-a-guide-to-the-citys-sights-and-symbols. This article summarises the various icons of Warsaw. Pages 93 to 94 of the paper *ORGANIZACJA MAŁEGO SABOTAŻU WAWER W WARSZAZWIE (1940—1944)* (Organisation of Minor Sabotage Wawer in Warsaw (1940—1944)), by Władysław Bartoszewski, also documents Anna Smoleńska being the author of the Kotwica. Link accessed on Sunday July 26, 2020.

[3998] See the online article dated March 20, 2019 on the website of "Poland in," the English language portal of *Telewizja Polska* (Poland's national television network) at https://polandin.com/41828137/77-years-of-fighting-poland-emblem. Accessed on Sunday July 26, 2020.

[3999] The online article *Decoding Warsaw: A Guide to the City's Sights and Symbols* by by Alena Aniskiewicz, dated August 5, 2015, on the Polish Culture website at https://culture.pl/en/article/decoding-warsaw-a-guide-to-the-citys-sights-and-symbols. This article summarises the various icons of Warsaw. All links accessed on Sunday July 26, 2020.

[4000] See the online article commemorating Anna's birth a century on, dated February 27, 2020, by Stuart Dowell at https://www.thefirstnews.com/article/the-woman-who-created-iconic-wwii-fighting-poland-symbol-was-born-100-years-ago-today-10748 on the website of *The First News*, a Polish English language news service owned by the PAP, the Polish Press Agency. See its "about page" at https://www.thefirstnews.com/page/about-us. All links accessed on Sunday July 26, 2020.

[4001] See the online article commemorating Anna's birth a century on, dated February 27, 2020, by Stuart Dowell at https://www.thefirstnews.com/article/the-woman-who-created-iconic-wwii-fighting-poland-symbol-was-born-100-years-ago-today-10748 on the website of *The First News*, a Polish English language news service owned by the PAP, the Polish Press Agency. See its "about page" at https://www.thefirstnews.com/page/about-us. All links accessed on Sunday July 26, 2020.

[4002] Ibid.

[4003] [4564] The online article dated March 20, 2019 on the website of "Poland in," the English language portal of *Telewizja Polska* (Poland's national television network) at https://polandin.com/41828137/77-years-of-fighting-poland-emblem. Accessed on Sunday July 26, 2020.

[4004] Chapter 24 "The struggle for freedom; lost hopes and further betrayal" of the online book *The second Polish Republic, 1918 - 1939 - 1945 - and after* by Henryk Hil. This chapter can be viewed online at https://sites.google.com/site/secondpolishrepublik/trabajos-de-la-fii/chapter-01. A full content list of the book can be found at https://secondpolishrepublic.wixsite.com/19181939-and-after/dedicated-to-cznf. See also the online transcript of the Interview conducted by the National WWII Museum in New Orleans of Dr. Alexandra Richie, Author of *Warsaw 1944* on Wednesday January 22, 2020 at https://www.nationalww2museum.org/war/articles/interview-dr-alexandra-richie-author-warsaw-1944. All links accessed on Sunday July 26, 2020. In this interview, Richie states that "The Poles had always planned to rise up against the Germans ... ."

[4005] Chapter 24 "The struggle for freedom; lost hopes and further betrayal" of the online book *The second Polish Republic, 1918 - 1939 - 1945 - and after* by Henryk Hil. This chapter can be viewed online at https://sites.google.com/site/secondpolishrepublik/trabajos-de-la-fii/chapter-01. Accessed on Sunday July 26, 2020.

[4006] See the article *Another 'warning from history'? Stalin's Plan for The Destruction of Pro-Western Democratic Forces in Poland* by Dr Andrzej Slawinski, published: 15 February 2002 on the website of the Polish Resistance at http://www.polishresistance-ak.org/7%20Article.htm. For the credentials of this website, see its Author's and Sponsors page at http://www.polishresistance-ak.org/Authors.htm. See also the page listing of articles on this site at http://www.polishresistance-ak.org/Essays.htm. Accessed on Sunday July 26, 2020. Two of the authors of these articles include Norman Davies and Roger Moorhouse, mentioned a number of times in the sources for this book.

[4007] See the online article *"KALKSTEIN I KACZOROWSKA W ŚWIETLE AKT UB"* (KALKSTEIN AND KACZOROWSKA IN LIGHT OF COLLABORATION WITH THE UB — Urząd Bezpieczeństwa — post-war Polish Communist Secret Police), from number 8-9/2004 Biuletynu IPN (Instytut Pamięci Narodowej — Institute of National Remembrance) at https://pamiec.pl/pa/teksty/artykuly/13916,KALKSTEIN-I-KACZOROWSKA-W-SWIETLE-AKT-UB.html. Accessed on Sunday July 26, 2020.

[4008] See endnotes [154] to [167] of the Preface "Birth and Memory upon the Lesser Known Fault Line of History" in regard to the two or so decades dormant July 1920 Spa-London-Moscow Telegram, also known as the Curzon Line telegram — see endnote [156]. The Vistula River is Poland's mightiest river, running from the mountains on its southern frontier, to the Vistula Lagoon just off the Baltic Sea in the north.

[4009] The envisaged three stages of the national uprising, as conceived by Stefan Rowecki, are documented in Chapter 24 The chapter "The struggle for freedom; lost hopes and further betrayal" of the online book *The second Polish Republic, 1918 - 1939 - 1945 - and after* by Henryk Hil. This chapter can be viewed online at https://sites.google.com/site/secondpolishrepublik/trabajos-de-la-fii/chapter-01. Accessed on Sunday July 26, 2020.

[4010] See the article *Operation 'Tempest' - a general outline* by Professor Jan Ciechanowski, published: 15 February 2002 on the website of the Polish Resistance at http://www.polishresistance-ak.org/9%20Article.htm. Accessed on Sunday July 26, 2020.

[4011] Ibid.

[4012] Ibid.

[4013] Ibid.

[4014] In regard to the Stalinist perpetrated massacre of Polish officers in Katyń Wood, see Polish WWII Supplement III "The Katyń Wood Massacre."[3618] In particular, see endnotes [3682] to [3692] of that appendix.

[4015][4087][4453] The *Polska Times* online article *Blanka Kaczorowska i Ludwik Kalkstein. Kochankowie, którzy wydali Grota-Roweckiego* dated June 30, 2017 by Jakub Szczepański https://polskatimes.pl/blanka-kaczorowska-i-ludwik-kalkstein-kochankowie-ktorzy-wydali-grotaroweckiego/ar/12184897 and the online article *"KALKSTEIN I KACZOROWSKA W ŚWIETLE AKT UB"* (KALKSTEIN AND KACZOROWSKA IN LIGHT OF COLLABORATION WITH THE UB — Urząd Bezpieczeństwa — post-war Polish Communist Secret Police), from number 8-9/2004 Biuletynu IPN (Instytut Pamięci Narodowej — Institute of National Remembrance) at https://pamiec.pl/pa/teksty/artykuly/13916,KALKSTEIN-I-

KACZOROWSKA-W-SWIETLE-AKT-UB.html. Both links accessed on Sunday July 26, 2020.

[4016] [4454] Ibid.

[4017] [4454] Ibid.

[4018] [4456] Position 227.1 of *The Polish Underground 1939-1947 Campaign chronicle*, by David G Williamson, published by Pen and Sword, 2012, ISBN 1848842813, 9781848842816.

[4019] [4456] The online article dated June 24, 2017, by Jakub Szczepański at https://plus.gazetalubuska.pl/kochankowie-agenci-gestapo-ktorzy-wydali-az-500-osob-z-ak/ar/12207875 on the website of Gazeta Lubuska. Accessed on Sunday July 26, 2020.

[4020] The online article *"KALKSTEIN I KACZOROWSKA W ŚWIETLE AKT UB"* (KALKSTEIN AND KACZOROWSKA IN LIGHT OF COLLABORATION WITH THE UB — Urząd Bezpieczeństwa — post-war Polish Communist Secret Police), from number 8-9/2004 Biuletynu IPN (Instytut Pamięci Narodowej — Institute of National Remembrance) at https://pamiec.pl/pa/teksty/artykuly/13916,KALKSTEIN-I-KACZOROWSKA-W-SWIETLE-AKT-UB.html. Accessed on Sunday July 26, 2020.

[4021] Ibid.

[4022] Ibid.

[4023] Ibid.

[4024] Ibid.

[4025] The *Polska Times* online article *Blanka Kaczorowska i Ludwik Kalkstein. Kochankowie, którzy wydali Grota-Roweckiego* dated June 30, 2017 by Jakub Szczepański https://polskatimes.pl/blanka-kaczorowska-i-ludwik-kalkstein-kochankowie-ktorzy-wydali-grotaroweckiego/ar/12184897. Accessed on Sunday July 26, 2020.

[4026] Ibid.

[4027] The online article *"KALKSTEIN I KACZOROWSKA W ŚWIETLE AKT UB"* (KALKSTEIN AND KACZOROWSKA IN LIGHT OF COLLABORATION WITH THE UB — Urząd Bezpieczeństwa — post-war Polish Communist Secret Police), from number 8-9/2004 Biuletynu IPN (Instytut Pamięci Narodowej — Institute of National Remembrance) at https://pamiec.pl/pa/teksty/artykuly/13916,KALKSTEIN-I-KACZOROWSKA-W-SWIETLE-AKT-UB.html. Accessed on Sunday July 26, 2020.

[4028] Ibid.

[4029] The *Polska Times* online article *Blanka Kaczorowska i Ludwik Kalkstein. Kochankowie, którzy wydali Grota-Roweckiego* dated June 30, 2017 by Jakub Szczepański https://polskatimes.pl/blanka-kaczorowska-i-ludwik-kalkstein-kochankowie-ktorzy-wydali-grotaroweckiego/ar/12184897. Also, by the same author, dated June 24, 2017 at https://plus.gazetalubuska.pl/kochankowie-agenci-gestapo-ktorzy-wydali-az-500-osob-z-ak/ar/12207875 on the website of Gazeta Lubuska. Accessed on Sunday July 26, 2020.

[4030] [4032] [4033] [4036] [4037] [4038] Ibid and the online article *"KALKSTEIN I KACZOR-OWSKA W ŚWIETLE AKT UB"* (KALKSTEIN AND KACZOROWSKA IN LIGHT OF COLLABORATION WITH THE UB from number 8-9/2004 Biuletynu IPN (Instytut Pamięci Narodowej — Institute of National Remembrance) at https://pamiec.pl/pa/teksty/artykuly/13916,KALKSTEIN-I-KACZOROWSKA-W-SWIETLE-AKT-UB.html. Accessed on Sunday July 26, 2020.

[4031] See endnote [1773] of Chapter 20 "Valkyrie II," which gives the date of July 20, 1944 for the Valkyrie assassination attempt.

[4032] [4202] See endnote [4030] for this supplement.

[4033] [4202] See endnote [4030] for this supplement.

[4034] The *Polska Times* online article *Blanka Kaczorowska i Ludwik Kalkstein. Kochankowie, którzy wydali Grota-Roweckiego* dated June 30, 2017 by Jakub Szczepański https://polskatimes.pl/blanka-kaczorowska-i-ludwik-kalkstein-kochankowie-ktorzy-wydali-grotaroweckiego/ar/12184897. Also, by the same author, dated June 24, 2017 at https://plus.gazetalubuska.pl/kochankowie-agenci-gestapo-ktorzy-wydali-az-500-osob-z-ak/ar/12207875 on the website of Gazeta Lubuska. Both links accessed on Sunday July 26, 2020.

[4035] Blogspot of *Zbrodniarze i oprawcy Polaków 1939-45 // War Criminals in occupied Poland 1939-45* at http://morro-zbrodniarze.blogspot.com/2011/12/blanka-kaczorowska.html. Accessed on Sunday July 26, 2020.

[4036] See endnote [4030] for this supplement.

[4037] See endnote [4030] for this supplement.

[4038] See endnote [4030] for this supplement.

[4039] Blogspot of *Zbrodniarze i oprawcy Polaków 1939-45 // War Criminals in occupied Poland 1939-45* at http://morro-zbrodniarze.blogspot.com/2011/12/blanka-kaczorowska.html. Accessed on Sunday July 26, 2020.

[4040] https://plus.gazetalubuska.pl/kochankowie-agenci-gestapo-ktorzy-wydali-az-500-osob-z-ak/ar/12207875. Accessed on Sunday July 26, 2020.

[4041] The online article *"KALKSTEIN I KACZOROWSKA W ŚWIETLE AKT UB"* (KALKSTEIN AND KACZOROWSKA IN LIGHT OF COLLABORATION WITH THE UB from number 8-9/2004 Biuletynu IPN (Instytut Pamięci Narodowej — Institute of National Remembrance) at https://pamiec.pl/pa/teksty/artykuly/13916,KALKSTEIN-I-KACZOROWSKA-W-SWIETLE-AKT-UB.html. Accessed on Sunday,July 26, 2020.

[4042] Online article on the website of *Tygodnik Siedlecki* at https://tygodniksiedlecki.com/t7819-

nowe.informacje.na.temat.blanki.kaczorowskiej.htm. Accessed on Sunday July 26, 2020.

[4043] Online article on the website of *Gazeta Lubuska* at https://plus.gazetalubuska.pl/kochankowie-agenci-gestapo-ktorzy-wydali-az-500-osob-z-ak/ar/12207875. Accessed on Sunday July 26, 2020.

[4044] Page 101 of *The Polish Underground Army, the Western Allies, and the Failure of Strategic Unity in World War II* by Michael Alfred Peszke, published by McFarland, 2005, ISBN 078642009X, 9780786420094.

[4045] Ibid.

[4046] Ibid.

[4047] Article on the website of the World War II Database, dated December 2005, by John Radzilowski, Professor of History Arts and Sciences - Social Sciences University of Alaska Southeast at https://ww2db.com/person_bio.php?person_id=151. The credentials of the author are displayed on the website of the University of Alaska Southeast at http://www.uas.alaska.edu/dir/jtradzilowski.html. See also the online article on Sikorski on the Ognisko Polskie — The Polish Hearth Club website at http://www.ogniskopolskie.org.uk/about/the-four-generals/general-w%C5%82adys%C5%82aw-sikorski.aspx. Its "about" page can be viewed at http://www.ogniskopolskie.org.uk/about.aspx. All accessed on Sunday July 26, 2020.

[4048] Accessed on Sunday July 26, 2020.

[4049] The online article on Sikorski on the Ognisko Polskie — The Polish Hearth Club website at http://www.ogniskopolskie.org.uk/about/the-four-generals/general-w%C5%82adys%C5%82aw-sikorski.aspx. Accessed on Sunday July 26, 2020.

[4050] See endnote [4065] for this supplement, which explains how Stalin's "anger" in this instance, was in all likelihood, part of an act to seize the opportunity to politically isolate the Poles.

[4051] See endnotes [3791] and [3792] of Polish WWII Supplement III "The Katyń Wood Massacre."

[4052] That Sikorski was a major figure in the 1920 Battle of Warsaw, see page 84 and the map on page 85 of *Warsaw 1920, Lenin's Failed Conquest of Europe* by Adam Zamoyski.

[4053] Page 103 of *The Polish Underground Army, the Western Allies, and the Failure of Strategic Unity in World War II* by Michael Alfred Peszke, published by McFarland, 2005, ISBN 078642009X, 9780786420094.

[4054] See endnotes [3367] to [3373] of Polish WWII Supplement I "The Molotov-Ribbentrop Pact" in regard to the deportation of Borderland Poles to the Gulag. See also endnote [204] in the Preface "Birth and Memory upon the Lesser Known Fault Line of History." In regard to Władysław Anders, and his imprisonment by the Soviet NKVD, see https://www.britannica.com/biography/Wladyslaw-Anders. Accessed on Sunday July 26, 2020.

[4055] Page 346 of *The Eagle Unbowed: Poland and the Poles in the Second World War* by Halik Kochanski, published by Harvard University Press, 2012, ISBN 0674068165, 9780674068162.

[4056] Page 101 of *The Polish Underground Army, the Western Allies, and the Failure of Strategic Unity in World War II* by Michael Alfred Peszke, published by McFarland, 2005, ISBN 078642009X, 9780786420094.

[4057] Page 297 of *Edvard Beneš kontra gen. Władysław Sikorski: polityka władz czechosłowackich na emigracji wobec rządu polskiego na uchodźstwie 1939-1943* (*Edvard Beneš versus General Władysław Sikorski: policy of the Czechoslovak authorities in exile towards the Polish government in exile 1939-1943*) by Marek K. Kamiński, published by Neriton, Inst. Historii PAN, 2005, ISBN 8389729113, 9788389729118. Also, page 103 of Michael Alfred Peszke.

[4058] In regard to this agreement, see the timeline for 1941-42 on the Polish History of New Zealand website at https://polishhistorynewzealand.org/1941-2/. Accessed on Sunday July 26, 2020. This also contains the text of the agreement, which concludes with the following paragraph: "The Soviet Government grants 'amnesty' to all Polish citizens now detained on Soviet territory either as prisoners of war or on other sufficient grounds, as from the resumption of diplomatic relations." Aside from the obvious question of "amnesty from what?," according to Komorowski, out of the 1.5 million deported Borderland eastern Poles, whom the Soviets had committed themselves to free, only 115,000 Polish citizens had regained their liberty. All extraordinary efforts of the Polish authorities to discover the whereabouts of the remainder had failed. See page 123 of *The Secret Army: The Memoirs of General Bor-Komorowski* by Tadeusz Bor-komorowski, published by Frontline Books, 2011, ISBN 1848325959, 9781848325951.

[4059] Page 1476 of *The Complete Maisky Diaries, Volume 3 Annals of Communism* by Ivan Mikhaĭlovich Maĭskiĭ, edited by Gabriel Gorodetsky, translated by Tatiana Sorokina and Oliver Ready, published by Yale University Press, 2017, ISBN 0300117825, 9780300117820. Maisky was recalled to Moscow by Stalin, where he was promoted to Deputy Commissar of Foreign Affairs.

[4060] Page 297 of *Edvard Beneš kontra gen. Władysław Sikorski: polityka władz czechosłowackich na emigracji wobec rządu polskiego na uchodźstwie 1939-1943* (*Edvard Beneš versus General Władysław Sikorski: policy of the Czechoslovak authorities in exile towards the Polish government in exile 1939-1943*) by Marek K. Kamiński, published by Neriton, Inst. Historii PAN, 2005, ISBN 8389729113, 9788389729118.

[4061] See Polish WWII Supplement III "The Katyń Wood Massacre."[3618]

[4062] Page 297 of *Edvard Beneš kontra gen. Władysław Sikorski: polityka władz czechosłowackich na emigracji wobec rządu polskiego na uchodźstwie 1939-1943* (*Edvard Beneš versus General Władysław Sikorski: policy of the Czechoslovak authorities in exile towards the Polish government in exile 1939-1943*) by Marek K. Kamiński, published by Neriton, Inst. Historii PAN, 2005, ISBN 8389729113, 9788389729118.

[4063] [4067] [4085] Ibid page 295.

[4064] Ibid page 274.

[4065] [4050] [4085] See endnotes [3685] to [3692] of Polish WWII Supplement III "The Katyń Wood Massacre." This explains how Goebbels envisaged propaganda gold mine of the Katyń Wood Massacre turned into an anti-climax, and was politically and strategically a disaster for the Poles. On the other hand, for Stalin, it was the propitious moment he was waiting for to politically isolate the Poles.

[4066] The conclusion of the online article on Sikorski on the Ognisko Polskie — The Polish Hearth Club website at http://www.ogniskopolskie.org.uk/about/the-four-generals/general-w%C5%82adys%C5%82aw-sikorski.aspx. Accessed on Sunday July 26, 2020.

[4067] See endnote [4063] for this supplement.

[4068] See the article *Operation 'Tempest' - a general outline* by Professor Jan Ciechanowski, published: 15 February 2002 on the website of the Polish Resistance at http://www.polishresistance-ak.org/9%20Article.htm. Accessed on Sunday July 26, 2020.

[4069] [4294] [4312] See for example, page 194 of *White Eagle Red Star*, by Professor Norman Davies, published in 2003 by Pimlico, Random House UK Limited, ISBN 9780712606943. See also position 414.0 of the ebook, Epub ISBN 9781446466865, also published in 2003 by Pimlico Random House UK.

[4070] [4293] See the article *Operation 'Tempest' - a general outline* by Professor Jan Ciechanowski, published: 15 February 2002 on the website of the Polish Resistance at http://www.polishresistance-ak.org/9%20Article.htm. Accessed on Sunday July 26, 2020.

[4071] Ibid.

[4072] See the article *Operation 'Tempest' - a general outline* by Professor Jan Ciechanowski, published: 15 February 2002 on the website of the Polish Resistance at http://www.polishresistance-ak.org/9%20Article.htm. Accessed on Sunday July 26, 2020.

[4073] Ibid.

[4074] Ibid.

[4075] Ibid.

[4076] See the article *Another 'warning from history'? Stalin's Plan for The Destruction of Pro-Western Democratic Forces in Poland* by Dr Andrzej Slawinski, published: 15 February 2002 on the website of the Polish Resistance at http://www.polishresistance-ak.org/7%20Article.htm. Accessed on Sunday July 26, 2020.

[4077] See Polish WWII Supplement III "The Katyń Wood Massacre."[3618]

[4078] See the article *Operation 'Tempest' - a general outline* by Professor Jan Ciechanowski, published: 15 February 2002 on the website of the Polish Resistance at http://www.polishresistance-ak.org/9%20Article.htm and accessed on Sunday July 26, 2020.

[4079] Ibid.

[4080] Ibid.

[4081] Ibid.

[4082] Ibid.

[4083] Ibid.

[4084] Ibid.

[4085] See endnotes [4063] to [4065] for this supplement.

[4086] [4102] Page 483 of *Biographical Dictionary of Central and Eastern Europe in the Twentieth Century* by Wojciech Roszkowski and Jan Kofman, published by Routledge, 2016, ISBN 1317475941, 9781317475941.

[4087] See endnote [4015] for this supplement in regard to the date of arrest for Stefan Rowecki.

[4088] The online article on Tadeusz Marian Bór-Komorowski on the Polish Radio website at https://www.polskieradio.pl/39/156/Artykul/855583,Gen-Tadeusz-BorKomorowski-To-on-wydal-rozkaz-o-rozpoczeciu-Powstania-Warszawskiego. It was last updated on August 24, 2019 and accessed on Sunday July 26, 2020.

[4089] Ibid.

[4090] Page 483 of *Biographical Dictionary of Central and Eastern Europe in the Twentieth Century* by Wojciech Roszkowski and Jan Kofman, published by Routledge, 2016, ISBN 1317475941, 9781317475941.

[4091] [4515] In regard to the Battle of Komarów, which had also been the first cavalry battle since 1813 during the Napoleonic era, see endnote [3438] of Polish WWII Supplement I "The Molotov-Ribbentrop Pact."

[4092] [4314] [4515] The online article on Tadeusz Marian Bór-Komorowski on the Polish Radio website at https://www.polskieradio.pl/39/156/Artykul/855583,Gen-Tadeusz-BorKomorowski-To-on-wydal-rozkaz-o-rozpoczeciu-Powstania-Warszawskiego. It was last updated on August 24, 2019 and accessed on Sunday July 26, 2020.

[4093] Ibid.

[4094] Page 112 of *The Secret Army: The Memoirs of General Bor-Komorowski* by Tadeusz Bor-komorowski, published by Frontline Books, 2011, ISBN 1848325959, 9781848325951.

[4095] The online article on Tadeusz Marian Bór-Komorowski on the Polish Radio website at https://www.polskieradio.pl/39/156/Artykul/855583,Gen-Tadeusz-BorKomorowski-To-on-wydal-rozkaz-o-rozpoczeciu-Powstania-Warszawskiego. It was last updated on August 24, 2019 and accessed on Sunday July 26, 2020.

[4096] Ibid.

[4097] Ibid.

[4098] Ibid and page 483 of *Biographical Dictionary of Central and Eastern Europe in the Twentieth Century* by Wojciech Roszkowski and Jan Kofman, published by Routledge, 2016, ISBN 1317475941, 9781317475941.

[4099] https://www.polskieradio.pl/39/156/Artykul/855583,Gen-Tadeusz-BorKomorowski-To-on-wydal-rozkaz-o-rozpoczeciu-Powstania-Warszawskiego. It was last updated on August 24, 2019 and accessed on Sunday July 26, 2020.

[4100] Page 483 of *Biographical Dictionary of Central and Eastern Europe in the Twentieth Century* by Wojciech Roszkowski and Jan Kofman, published by Routledge, 2016, ISBN 1317475941, 9781317475941.

[4101] https://www.polskieradio.pl/39/156/Artykul/855583,Gen-Tadeusz-BorKomorowski-To-on-wydal-rozkaz-o-rozpoczeciu-Powstania-Warszawskiego. Accessed on Sunday July 26, 2020. It was last updated on August 24, 2019.

[4102] See endnote [4086] for this supplement.

[4103] In regard to the Soviets retaking Smolensk and the Katyń forest in late September 1943, see endnote [3799] of Polish WWII Supplement III "The Katyń Wood Massacre."

[4104] [4108] See the maps for October 15, 1943 and November 1, 1943 on pages 19 and 21 of the *Atlas of the World Battle Fronts in Semimonthly Phases, to August. 15, 1945*, produced for the Chief of Staff of the United States Army in 1945 by the United States War Department General Staff, published by the Army Map Service, 1945. This digitised document can be downloaded from the Wikimedia website at https://upload.wikimedia.org/wikipedia/commons/4/42/Atlas_of_the_World_B attle_Fronts_in_Semimonthly_Phases_to_August_15%2C_1945.pdf. Accessed on Sunday July 26, 2020.

[4105] See the article *Operation 'Tempest' - a general outline* by Professor Jan Ciechanowski, published: 15 February 2002 on the website of the Polish Resistance at http://www.polishresistance-ak.org/9%20Article.htm. Accessed on Sunday July 26, 2020.

[4106] Ibid.

[4107] Ibid.

[4108] See endnote [4104] for this supplement.

[4109] See endnote [2263] of Chapter 24 "Dietrich's Final Days" in regard to the mountainous Italian peninsula lending itself to stubborn or almost impregnable defence. See also the maps from July 1, 1943 to May 15, 1943 from pages 5 to 95 of the *Atlas of the World Battle Fronts in Semimonthly Phases, to August. 15, 1945*, produced for the Chief of Staff of the United States Army in 1945 by the United States War Department General Staff, published by the Army Map Service, 1945. This digitised document can be downloaded from the Wikimedia website at https://upload.wikimedia.org/wikipedia/commons/4/42/Atlas_of_the_World_B

attle_Fronts_in_Semimonthly_Phases_to_August_15%2C_1945.pdf. Accessed on Sunday July 26, 2020. Even in early May 1945, the Germans were still in control of a significant amount of northern Italy.

[4110] [1926] [2924] See the article *Operation 'Tempest' - a general outline* by Professor Jan Ciechanowski, published: 15 February 2002 on the website of the Polish Resistance at http://www.polishresistance-ak.org/9%20Article.htm. Accessed on Sunday July 26, 2020.

[4111] Ibid.

[4112] This will become clear when the Warsaw Uprising itself is described later on in this supplement.

[4113] See the article *Operation 'Tempest' - a general outline* by Professor Jan Ciechanowski, published: 15 February 2002 on the website of the Polish Resistance at http://www.polishresistance-ak.org/9%20Article.htm. Accessed on Sunday July 26, 2020.

[4114] Ibid.

[4115] Ibid.

[4116] [4199] See page 183 of Rising '44: The Battle for Warsaw Reprint Edition (October 4, 2005), ISBN-10: 0143035401, ISBN-13: 9780143035404.

[4117] [4199] Position 1103.3 of Microcosm.

[4118] See the article *Operation 'Tempest' - a general outline* by Professor Jan Ciechanowski, published: 15 February 2002 on the website of the Polish Resistance at http://www.polishresistance-ak.org/9%20Article.htm. Accessed on Sunday July 26, 2020. See also pages 206 to 208 of Rising '44: The Battle for Warsaw Reprint Edition (October 4, 2005), ISBN-10: 0143035401, ISBN-13: 9780143035404 in regard to the divergent views of action of Komorowski and the London based government. Note that Davies, in the interest of ease of reading and pronunciation for native English speaking readers, uses English translated pseudonyms for members of the Home Army. In Komorowski's case, it is inaccurate, as he designates him with "Boor," which is pronounced similarly to the true Polish spelling "Bór" meaning in English "Forest." Komorowski, of noble Polish stock, it must be said, was anything but a "boor" or uncouth individual. Nor by any stretch of the imagination, the opposite extreme of a snob.

[4119] See the article *Another 'warning from history'? Stalin's Plan for The Destruction of Pro-Western Democratic Forces in Poland* by Dr Andrzej Slawinski, published: 15 February 2002 on the website of the Polish Resistance at http://www.polishresistance-ak.org/7%20Article.htm. Accessed on Sunday July 26, 2020.

[4120] See Polish WWII Supplement III "The Katyń Wood Massacre."[3618]

[4121] See endnotes [3367] to [3373] of Polish WWII Supplement I "The Molotov-Ribbentrop Pact" in regard to the deportation of Borderland Poles to the Gulag. See also endnote [204] in the Preface "Birth and Memory upon the Lesser Known Fault Line of History."

⁴¹²² See the book *Rising '44: The Battle for Warsaw Reprint Edition*, by Professor Norman Davies, published by Penguin Books; Reprint edition (October 4, 2005), ISBN-10: 0143035401, ISBN-13: 9780143035404. Page 427 gives the officially declared duration of the Warsaw Rising being from August 1 1944 to October 2 1944. Page 13 also gives the date of August 1 1944 as the date of the message officially informing the British of the commencement of the Warsaw General Uprising.

⁴¹²³ See the maps for February 1 and 15, 1944 on pages 33 and 35 of the *Atlas of the World Battle Fronts in Semimonthly Phases, to August. 15, 1945*, produced for the Chief of Staff of the United States Army in 1945 by the United States War Department General Staff, published by the Army Map Service, 1945. This digitised document can be downloaded from the Wikimedia website at https://upload.wikimedia.org/wikipedia/commons/4/42/Atlas_of_the_World_B attle_Fronts_in_Semimonthly_Phases_to_August_15%2C_1945.pdf. Accessed on Sunday July 26, 2020.

⁴¹²⁴ In regard to Operation Bagration, see the online transcript of the interview *Interview with Dr. Alexandra Richie, Author of 'Warsaw 1944'* dated January 22, 2020, on the website of the World War II Museum in New Orleans at https://www.nationalww2museum.org/war/articles/interview-dr-alexandra-richie-author-warsaw-1944. Accessed on Sunday July 26, 2020.

⁴¹²⁵ See the article *Operation 'Tempest' - a general outline* by Professor Jan Ciechanowski, published: 15 February 2002 on the website of the Polish Resistance at http://www.polishresistance-ak.org/9%20Article.htm. Accessed on Sunday July 26, 2020. See also the maps for July 1 and 15, 1944 on pages 53 and 55, and maps for August 1 and 15, 1944 on pages 57 and 59 of the *Atlas of the World Battle Fronts in Semimonthly Phases, to August. 15, 1945*.

⁴¹²⁶ See the article *Operation 'Tempest' - a general outline* by Professor Jan Ciechanowski, published: 15 February 2002 on the website of the Polish Resistance at http://www.polishresistance-ak.org/9%20Article.htm. Accessed on Sunday July 26, 2020.

⁴¹²⁷ Ibid. See also pages 219 to 221 of *Rising '44: The Battle for Warsaw Reprint Edition*, by Professor Norman Davies, published by Penguin Books; Reprint edition (October 4, 2005), ISBN-10: 0143035401, ISBN-13: 9780143035404.

⁴¹²⁸ Ibid.

⁴¹²⁹ See endnotes ³³⁶⁷ to ³³⁷³ of Polish WWII Supplement I "The Molotov-Ribbentrop Pact" in regard to the deportation of Borderland Poles to the Gulag. See also endnote ²⁰⁴ in the Preface "Birth and Memory upon the Lesser Known Fault Line of History."

⁴¹³⁰ See the article *Operation 'Tempest' - a general outline* by Professor Jan Ciechanowski, published: 15 February 2002 on the website of the Polish Re-

sistance at http://www.polishresistance-ak.org/9%20Article.htm. Accessed on Sunday July 26, 2020.

4131 1382 1385 This is implied on page 221 of *Rising '44: The Battle for Warsaw Reprint Edition*, by Professor Norman Davies, published by Penguin Books; Reprint edition (October 4, 2005), ISBN-10: 0143035401, ISBN-13: 9780143035404, where Davies states that "Operation Tempest was doomed before it began."

4132 lxix See the article *Operation 'Tempest' - a general outline* by Professor Jan Ciechanowski, published: 15 February 2002 on the website of the Polish Resistance at http://www.polishresistance-ak.org/9%20Article.htm. Accessed on Sunday July 26, 2020.

4133 Page 230 of *Rising '44: The Battle for Warsaw Reprint Edition*, by Professor Norman Davies, published by Penguin Books; Reprint edition (October 4, 2005), ISBN-10: 0143035401, ISBN-13: 9780143035404.

4134 4324 lxix Ibid page 232. Davies had cited this from page 215 of *Armia podziemna* (*Underground Army*), published by Veritas London, 1967, by T. Bór-Komorowski himself.

4135 4446 See page 691 of Appendix 35 "Guide to Modified Names Used in the Text" in *Rising '44: The Battle for Warsaw Reprint Edition*, by Professor Norman Davies. This appendix runs from pages 691 to 705.

4136 Ibid page 692.

4137 4213 Ibid page 693.

4138 4446 Ibid page 232.

4139 Ibid.

4140 Ibid page 693. For a description of "The Government Delegation for the Republic of Poland," see footnote lvi for this supplement.

4141 4590 Ibid page 233 and page 271 of *Armia podziemna* (*Underground Army*), published by Bellona 1983, by T. Bór-Komorowski himself. Also, page 216 of the London 1967 edition.

4142 Ibid page 693.

4143 Ibid page 245.

4144 Ibid.

4145 Ibid.

4146 4233 Ibid page 247.

4147 4566 Ibid.

4148 The Holocaust Research Project online article on the Farma Gęsiówka (Goose Farm) at http://www.holocaustresearchproject.org/othercamps/gesiowka.html. Accessed on Sunday July 26, 2020.

4149 Ibid.

4150 Ibid.

4151 Ibid.

4152 Ibid.

[4153] Ibid.

[4154] [4566] Ibid.

[4155] Page 248 of *Rising '44: The Battle for Warsaw Reprint Edition*, by Professor Norman Davies, published by Penguin Books; Reprint edition (October 4, 2005), ISBN-10: 0143035401, ISBN-13: 9780143035404.

[4156] [4603] Ibid page 419 under the side story "LOGISTICS." This attempts to answer how the insurgents were able to make the Rising last for sixty-three days.

[4157] Ibid page 248.

[4158] Ibid page 307 states that Warsaw was 1,311 kilometres or 815 miles from the RAF base in Brindisi in Apulia, which is in southern Italy.

[4159] Ibid page 248.

[4160] Ibid page 248.

[4161] See pages 216 to 217 of *No Greater Ally, The Untold Story of Poland's Forces in World War II*, by Kenneth K. Koskodan, published by Osprey Publishing 2011, ISBN-13: 9781849084796. On these pages, the author describes the virtually worthless air drops, in small aircraft, made by the Soviets in mid-September 1944.

[4162] [2413] [2415] This will become clear as this supplement progresses. For now, see endnote [4173] for this supplement, which implies the Soviets never had any intentions to make any air drops over Warsaw during the Rising. This unlike the western Allies over a thousand kilometres away from Warsaw. See also endnote [4237] for this supplement for the account of Australian flight navigator Alan McIntosh. This appears on pages 308 to 309 of Norman Davies' book *Rising '44: The Battle for Warsaw Reprint Edition*.

[4163] [4334] Ibid page 248.

[4164] The online transcript of the interview *Interview with Dr. Alexandra Richie, Author of 'Warsaw 1944'* dated January 22, 2020, on the website of the World War II Museum in New Orleans at https://www.nationalww2museum.org/war/articles/interview-dr-alexandra-richie-author-warsaw-1944. Accessed on Sunday July 26, 2020.

[4165] Page 248 of *Rising '44: The Battle for Warsaw Reprint Edition*, by Professor Norman Davies.

[4166] Ibid.

[4167] See endnotes [919] to [951] of Chapter 13 "Flight and the Tumultuous Appeasement of Evil."

[4168] The online transcript of the interview *Interview with Dr. Alexandra Richie, Author of 'Warsaw 1944'* dated January 22, 2020, on the website of the World War II Museum in New Orleans at https://www.nationalww2museum.org/war/articles/interview-dr-alexandra-richie-author-warsaw-1944. Accessed on Sunday July 26, 2020.

[4169] Ibid.

[4170] Ibid.

[4171] [4209] [4332] Ibid.

[4172] Ibid.

[4173] [4162] [4210] Ibid.

[4174] [4210] Ibid.

[4175] [4195] [4234] [4602] This statement was cited by the author on a plaque in Warsaw's *Muzeum Powstania* or Uprising Museum on Saturday October 9, 2004.

[4176] [4626] See Chapter 24 "The struggle for freedom; lost hopes and further betrayal" of the online book *The second Polish Republic, 1918 - 1939 - 1945 - and after* by Henryk Hil. This chapter can be viewed online at https://sites.google.com/site/secondpolishrepublik/trabajos-de-la-fii/chapter-01. Accessed on Sunday July 26, 2020.

[4177] [4562] [4583] The timeline from http://www.warsawuprising.com/timeline.htm. Accessed on Sunday July 26, 2020. This site is maintained by Project InPosterum [Latin — for the future], a non-profit, public benefit corporation established in 2004 in California with the purpose to organise for the specific purpose of preserving and popularising selected subjects of World War II history and its aftermath with a focus on Central and Eastern Europe. It's not the official website of the Rising, however, it uses reliable sources which include by permission, Norman Davies *Rising '44: The Battle for Warsaw Reprint Edition*, published by Penguin Books; Reprint edition (October 4, 2005), ISBN-10: 0143035401, ISBN-13: 9780143035404.

[4178] Page 204 of *No Greater Ally, The Untold Story of Poland's Forces in World War II*, by Kenneth K. Koskodan, published by Osprey Publishing 2011, ISBN-13: 9781849084796.

[4179] The timeline from http://www.warsawuprising.com/timeline.htm. Accessed on Sunday July 26, 2020.

[4180] [4442] The account by Jan Rossman "Wacek," a member of the top leadership of the Szare Szeregi [Gray Ranks, Polish Scouting] during the war, and an officer in the command of the Polish Home Army "Zośka" (Sophie) battalion at http://www.warsawuprising.com/paper/warsaw_sewers.htm. Translated by Łukasz Nogalski and accessed on Sunday July 26, 2020.

[4181] Ibid.

[4182] The article on sewer use by the insurgents from http://www.warsawuprising.com/paper/sewers.htm. Accessed on Sunday July 26, 2020.

[4183] [4583] The article on sewer use by the insurgents from http://www.warsawuprising.com/paper/sewers.htm. Accessed on Sunday July 26, 2020.

[4184] The account by Jan Rossman "Wacek," a member of the top leadership of the Szare Szeregi [Gray Ranks, Polish Scouting] during the war, and an officer in the command of the Polish Home Army "Zośka" (Sophie) battalion, documented at http://www.warsawuprising.com/paper/warsaw_sewers.htm. Accessed on Sunday July 26, 2020. Translated by Łukasz Nogalski. For this website's credentials, see endnote [3662] for Polish WWII Supplement III "The Katyń Wood Massacre."

[4185] The article on sewer use by the insurgents from http://www.warsawuprising.com/paper/sewers.htm. Accessed on Sunday July 26, 2020.

[4186] Ibid.

[4187] The account by Jan Rossman "Wacek," a member of the top leadership of the Szare Szeregi [Gray Ranks, Polish Scouting] during the war, and an officer in the command of the Polish Home Army "Zośka" (Sophie) battalion, documented at http://www.warsawuprising.com/paper/warsaw_sewers.htm. Translated by Łukasz Nogalski and accessed on Sunday July 26, 2020. For this website's credentials, see endnote [3662] for Polish WWII Supplement III "The Katyń Wood Massacre."

[4188] Ibid.

[4189] [4335] Page 204 of *No Greater Ally, The Untold Story of Poland's Forces in World War II*, by Kenneth K. Koskodan, published by Osprey Publishing 2011, ISBN-13: 9781849084796.

[4190] Ibid pages 204 to 205 which Koskodan cited on pages 307 to 308 of *The secret army* by Tadeusz Komorowski, published by Battery Press, 1984, ISBN 0898390826, 9780898390827. Also on the same pages of *The Secret Army: The Memoirs of General Bor-Komorowski* by Tadeusz Bor-komorowski, published by Frontline Books, 2011, ISBN 1848325959, 9781848325951.

[4191] Ibid page 205 of Koskodan.

[4192] [4335] [4562] Ibid.

[4193] Pages 205 to 206 of *No Greater Ally, The Untold Story of Poland's Forces in World War II*, by Kenneth K. Koskodan, published by Osprey Publishing 2011, ISBN-13: 9781849084796.

[4194] Page 258 of *The Secret Army: The Memoirs of General Bor-Komorowski* by Tadeusz Bor-komorowski, published by Frontline Books, 2011, ISBN 1848325959, 9781848325951.

[4195] See endnote [4175] for this supplement in regard to the broadcasts of July 29 and 30, from the Moscow radio station "Kosciuszko," appealing to Varsovians to rise up against the Germans.

[4196] Page 258 of *The Secret Army: The Memoirs of General Bor-Komorowski* by Tadeusz Bor-komorowski, published by Frontline Books, 2011, ISBN 1848325959, 9781848325951.

[4197] Ibid.

[4198] Ibid.

[4199] In further regard to the underwhelming numbers of the communist Armia Ludowa in comparison to the non-communist Home Army, see endnotes [4116] and [4117] for this supplement.

[4200] Page 208 of Koskodan which he cited on pages 232 to 233 of *The secret army* by Tadeusz Komorowski, published by Battery Press, 1984, ISBN

0898390826, 9780898390827. Also on the same pages of *The Secret Army: The Memoirs of General Bor-Komorowski* by Tadeusz Bor-komorowski, published by Frontline Books, 2011, ISBN 1848325959, 9781848325951.

[4201] Ibid.

[4202] See endnotes [4032] to [4033] for this supplement.

[4203] Page 201 of Koskodan.

[4204] Ibid.

[4205] Ibid.

[4206] Ibid.

[4207] Page 407 of *The Eagle Unbowed: Poland and the Poles in the Second World War* by Halik Kochanski, published by Harvard University Press, 2012, ISBN 0674068165, 9780674068162.

[4208] [4430] Page 99 of *The German Defeat in the East: 1944-45* by Samuel W. Mitcham Junior, published by Stackpole Books, 2007, ISBN 146175187X, 9781461751878.

[4209] See endnote [4171] for this supplement.

[4210] [4430] See endnotes [4173] and [4174] for this supplement.

[4211] [4432] Page 413 of *The Eagle Unbowed: Poland and the Poles in the Second World War* by Halik Kochanski.

[4212] Ibid.

[4213] General Antoni Chruściel (pseudonym Monter), was the Head of the AK's (Armia Krajowa or Home Army) Warsaw Region. See endnote [4137] for this supplement.

[4214] [3195] [4432] Page 413 of *The Eagle Unbowed: Poland and the Poles in the Second World War* by Halik Kochanski, published by Harvard University Press, 2012, ISBN 0674068165, 9780674068162.

[4215] Page 216 of *No Greater Ally, The Untold Story of Poland's Forces in World War II*, by Kenneth K. Koskodan, published by Osprey Publishing 2011, ISBN-13: 9781849084796.

[4216] Page 340 of *The Secret Army: The Memoirs of General Bor-Komorowski* by Tadeusz Bor-komorowski, published by Frontline Books, 2011, ISBN 1848325959, 9781848325951.

[4217] Page 216 of *No Greater Ally, The Untold Story of Poland's Forces in World War II*, by Kenneth K. Koskodan, published by Osprey Publishing 2011, ISBN-13: 9781849084796.

[4218] Pages 339 and 344 of *The Secret Army: The Memoirs of General Bor-Komorowski* by Tadeusz Bor-komorowski, published by Frontline Books, 2011, ISBN 1848325959, 9781848325951.

[4219] Page 216 of *No Greater Ally, The Untold Story of Poland's Forces in World War II*, by Kenneth K. Koskodan, published by Osprey Publishing 2011, ISBN-13: 9781849084796.

[4220] Ibid.

[4221] Ibid pages 216 to 217.

[4222] Pages 357 to 358 of *The Secret Army: The Memoirs of General Bor-Komorowski* by Tadeusz Bor-komorowski, published by Frontline Books, 2011, ISBN 1848325959, 9781848325951.

[4223] Page 217 of *No Greater Ally, The Untold Story of Poland's Forces in World War II*, by Kenneth K. Koskodan, published by Osprey Publishing 2011, ISBN-13: 9781849084796.

[4224] Ibid.

[4225] Ibid.

[4226] Ibid.

[4227] Ibid page 120.

[4228] Ibid page 217.

[4229] Ibid.

[4230] Ibid pages 217 to 218.

[4231] Ibid page 218.

[4232] Ibid. Koskodan cited this on page 350 of *The secret army* by Tadeusz Komorowski, published by Battery Press, 1984, ISBN 0898390826, 9780898390827. Also on the same pages of *The Secret Army: The Memoirs of General Bor-Komorowski* by Tadeusz Bor-komorowski, published by Frontline Books, 2011, ISBN 1848325959, 9781848325951.

[4233] See endnote [4146] for this supplement.

[4234] [4602] See endnote [4175] for this supplement.

[4235] [2410] [4316] Pages 350 to 351 of *The Secret Army: The Memoirs of General Bor-Komorowski* by Tadeusz Bor-komorowski, published by Frontline Books, 2011, ISBN 1848325959, 9781848325951.

[4236] See note #12 on page 730 of *Rising '44: The Battle for Warsaw Reprint Edition*, by Professor Norman Davies, published by Penguin Books; Reprint edition (October 4, 2005), ISBN-10: 0143035401, ISBN-13: 9780143035404.

[4237] [2413] [4162] Pages 308-309 of *Rising '44: The Battle for Warsaw Reprint Edition*, by Professor Norman Davies, published by Penguin Books; Reprint edition (October 4, 2005), ISBN-10: 0143035401, ISBN-13: 9780143035404. Davies states that this was from a personal recollection written in 2002 by Mr Alan McIntosh, Australia: to the author on 23 June 2003. See also endnote [2413] for Chapter 25 "Old Prussia Gone With The Wind."

[4238] [lxiv] Page 413 of *The Eagle Unbowed: Poland and the Poles in the Second World War* by Halik Kochanski, published by Harvard University Press, 2012, ISBN 0674068165, 9780674068162.

[4239] [lxiv] Ibid.

[4240] Ibid.

[4241] Ibid.

[4242] Ibid.

[4243] Ibid.

[4244] Page 351 of *The Secret Army: The Memoirs of General Bor-Komorowski* by Tadeusz Bor-komorowski, published by Frontline Books, 2011, ISBN 1848325959, 9781848325951.

[4245] Page 414 of *The Eagle Unbowed: Poland and the Poles in the Second World War* by Halik Kochanski, published by Harvard University Press, 2012, ISBN 0674068165, 9780674068162. This report was cited in the London Times on September 10, 1944.

[4246] Page 305 of *Rising '44: The Battle for Warsaw Reprint Edition*, by Professor Norman Davies, published by Penguin Books; Reprint edition (October 4, 2005), ISBN-10: 0143035401, ISBN-13: 9780143035404.

[4247] Ibid and online article dated August 2019 on the Liberation of Paris at https://origins.osu.edu/milestones/the-liberation-of-paris-wwii on the website of *ORIGINS Current Events in Historical Perspective* by Lauren A. Henry, published by the History Departments at The Ohio State University and Miami University. Accessed on Sunday July 26, 2020.

[4248] Online article dated August 2019 on the Liberation of Paris at https://origins.osu.edu/milestones/the-liberation-of-paris-wwii on the website of *ORIGINS Current Events in Historical Perspective* by Lauren A. Henry, published by the History Departments at The Ohio State University and Miami University. Accessed on Sunday July 26, 2020.

[4249] Ibid.

[4250] Page 305 of *Rising '44: The Battle for Warsaw Reprint Edition*, by Professor Norman Davies.

[4251] Page 95 of *White Eagle Red Star* by Norman Davies, published in 2003 by Pimlico, Random House UK Limited, ISBN 9780712606943. See also positions 193.1 to 193.6 of the ebook, Epub ISBN 9781446466865, also published in 2003 by Pimlico Random House UK.

[4252] [4317] Online article dated August 2019 on the Liberation of Paris at https://origins.osu.edu/milestones/the-liberation-of-paris-wwii on the website of *ORIGINS Current Events in Historical Perspective* by Lauren A. Henry, published by the History Departments at The Ohio State University and Miami University. Accessed on Sunday July 26, 2020.

[4253] Ibid.

[4254] Page 305 of *Rising '44: The Battle for Warsaw Reprint Edition*, by Professor Norman Davies.

[4255] Online article dated August 2019 on the Liberation of Paris at https://origins.osu.edu/milestones/the-liberation-of-paris-wwii. Accessed on Sunday July 26, 2020.

[4256] Ibid.

[4257] See pages 136 to 147 of Chapter 6 "A Bloody Job Well Done: 1st Amored Division" of *No Greater Ally, The Untold Story of Poland's Forces in World War II*, by Kenneth K. Koskodan, published by Osprey Publishing 2011, ISBN-13: 9781849084796.

[4258] Online article dated August 2019 on the Liberation of Paris at https://origins.osu.edu/milestones/the-liberation-of-paris-wwii. Accessed on Sunday July 26, 2020.

[4259] Page 306 of *Rising '44: The Battle for Warsaw Reprint Edition*, by Professor Norman Davies.

[4260] Ibid.

[4261] Ibid pages 306 to 307.

[4262] 233 New York Times online article dated August 15, 1989 by John Tagliabue at https://www.nytimes.com/1989/08/15/world/poland-s-premier-offering-to-yield-to-non-communist.html. Accessed on Sunday July 26, 2020.

[4263] Page 361 of *The Secret Army: The Memoirs of General Bor-Komorowski* by Tadeusz Bor-komorowski, published by Frontline Books, 2011, ISBN 1848325959, 9781848325951.

[4264] Ibid.

[4265] Ibid page 362

[4266] Ibid.

[4267] Page 125 of *Rising '44: The Battle for Warsaw Reprint Edition*, by Professor Norman Davies, published by Penguin Books; Reprint edition (October 4, 2005), ISBN-10: 0143035401, ISBN-13: 9780143035404.

[4268] Page 362 of *The Secret Army: The Memoirs of General Bor-Komorowski* by Tadeusz Bor-komorowski, published by Frontline Books, 2011, ISBN 1848325959, 9781848325951.

[4269] Ibid.

[4270] 2203 Ibid pages 362 to 363.

[4271] See endnote 997 of Chapter 14 "Reichskristallnacht" and position 926.5 of Microcosm.

[4272] See endnote 2202 of Chapter 24 "Dietrich's Final Days."

[4273] See endnote 2203 of Chapter 24 "Dietrich's Final Days."

[4274] See endnotes 1963 to 1970 of Chapter 20 "Valkyrie II" in regard to Arthur Nebe.

[4275] See endnote 2205 of Chapter 24 "Dietrich's Final Days."

[4276] Deutsche Welle online English language article titled *'Daddy was a man of honor,' daughter of Nazi SS officer insists* dated January 2, 2020 at https://www.dw.com/en/daddy-was-a-man-of-honor-daughter-of-nazi-ss-officer-insists/a-51853837. Accessed on Sunday July 26, 2020.

[4277] The article *Hitler's Inner Circle: The 10 Most Powerful Men in Nazi Germany* on the online history channel History Hit at https://www.historyhit.com/hitlers-inner-circle/ by Tina Gale, dated August 8, 2018. Accessed on Sunday July 26, 2020.

[4278] Deutsche Welle online English language article titled *'Daddy was a man of honor,' daughter of Nazi SS officer insists* dated January 2, 2020 at https://www.dw.com/en/daddy-was-a-man-of-honor-daughter-of-nazi-ss-officer-insists/a-51853837. Accessed on Sunday July 26, 2020.

[4279] Deutsche Welle online English language article titled *'Daddy was a man of honor,' daughter of Nazi SS officer insists* dated January 2, 2020 at https://www.dw.com/en/daddy-was-a-man-of-honor-daughter-of-nazi-ss-officer-insists/a-51853837. Accessed on Sunday July 26, 2020.

[4280] In regard to the 1934 Night of the Long Knives (Nacht der Langen Messer of Röhm Purge), see endnotes [92] to [107] of the Preface "Birth and Memory upon the Lesser Known Fault Line of History."

[4281] Page 182 of *The Routledge Companion to Nazi Germany* by Roderick Stackelberg, published by Routledge, 2007, ISBN 1134393865, 9781134393862. This documents his role in the 1934 Night of the Long Knives and in the murder of six communists just following Hitler's rise to power. In regard to the exact date of Hitler's rise to power, see the online *Encyclopaedia Britannica* article on Hitler at https://www.britannica.com/biography/Adolf-Hitler. Accessed on Sunday July 26, 2020.

[4282] Deutsche Welle online English language article titled '*Daddy was a man of honor,' daughter of Nazi SS officer insists* dated January 2, 2020 at https://www.dw.com/en/daddy-was-a-man-of-honor-daughter-of-nazi-ss-officer-insists/a-51853837. Accessed on Sunday July 26, 2020.

[4283] Deutsche Welle online English language article titled '*Daddy was a man of honor,' daughter of Nazi SS officer insists* dated January 2, 2020 at https://www.dw.com/en/daddy-was-a-man-of-honor-daughter-of-nazi-ss-officer-insists/a-51853837. Accessed on Sunday July 26, 2020.

[4284] Page 248 of *Rising '44: The Battle for Warsaw Reprint Edition*, by Professor Norman Davies, published by Penguin Books; Reprint edition (October 4, 2005), ISBN-10: 0143035401, ISBN-13: 9780143035404. Note that, in this book, Davies just refers to von dem Bach Zelewski as von dem Bach. However, at positions 926.5 and 1017.0 of *Microcosm*, he and Roger Moorhouse, refer to him as von dem Bach-Zelewski.

[4285] Deutsche Welle online English language article titled *'Daddy was a man of honor,' daughter of Nazi SS officer insists* dated January 2, 2020 at https://www.dw.com/en/daddy-was-a-man-of-honor-daughter-of-nazi-ss-officer-insists/a-51853837. Accessed on Sunday July 26, 2020.

[4286] *The Waffen-SS (4): 24. to 38. Divisions, & Volunteer Legions* by Gordon Williamson, published by Bloomsbury Publishing, 2012, ISBN 178096577X, 9781780965772. See Google Books at https://books.google.com.au/books?id=ZoWICwAAQBAJ&dq=isbn%3A178096577X&q=Dirlewanger#v=snippet&q=Dirlewanger&f=false. Accessed on Sunday July 26, 2020.

[4287] Page 252 of *Rising '44: The Battle for Warsaw Reprint Edition*, by Professor Norman Davies, published by Penguin Books; Reprint edition (October 4, 2005), ISBN-10: 0143035401, ISBN-13: 9780143035404. The Deutsche Welle online English language article gives the figure of 20,000 to 45,000.

[4288] Deutsche Welle online English language article titled *'Daddy was a man of honor,' daughter of Nazi SS officer insists* dated January 2, 2020 at https://www.dw.com/en/daddy-was-a-man-of-honor-daughter-of-nazi-ss-officer-insists/a-51853837. Accessed on Sunday July 26, 2020.

[4289] [2203] Pages 252 to 253 of *Rising '44: The Battle for Warsaw Reprint Edition*, by Professor Norman Davies, published by Penguin Books; Reprint edition (October 4, 2005), ISBN-10: 0143035401, ISBN-13: 9780143035404.

[4290] Ibid page 691.

[4291] Page 364 of *The Secret Army: The Memoirs of General Bor-Komorowski* by Tadeusz Bor-komorowski, published by Frontline Books, 2011, ISBN 1848325959, 9781848325951.

[4292] Ibid. The office of President of the London Exile Government was separate to the office of Premier, which was held by Stanisław Mikołajczyk. See the index entries on page 746 for Raczkiewicz and page 743 for Mikołajczyk in *Rising '44: The Battle for Warsaw Reprint Edition*, by Professor Norman Davies, published by Penguin Books; Reprint edition (October 4, 2005), ISBN-10: 0143035401, ISBN-13: 9780143035404.

[4293] See endnote [4070] for this supplement.

[4294] See endnote [4069] for this supplement.

[4295] Page 365 of *The Secret Army: The Memoirs of General Bor-Komorowski* by Tadeusz Bor-komorowski, published by Frontline Books, 2011, ISBN 1848325959, 9781848325951.

[4296] Page 365 of *The Secret Army: The Memoirs of General Bor-Komorowski* by Tadeusz Bor-komorowski, published by Frontline Books, 2011, ISBN 1848325959, 9781848325951.

[4297] For a description of "The Government Delegation for the Republic of Poland," see footnote [lvi] for this supplement.

[4298] [4594] Page 365 of *The Secret Army: The Memoirs of General Bor-Komorowski* by Tadeusz Bor-komorowski.

[4299] Ibid page 369.

[4300] Ibid.

[4301] [962] Pages 220 to 221 of *No Greater Ally, The Untold Story of Poland's Forces in World War II*, by Kenneth K. Koskodan, published by Osprey Publishing 2011, ISBN-13: 9781849084796.

[4302] [962] Page 220 of *No Greater Ally, The Untold Story of Poland's Forces in World War II*, by Kenneth K. Koskodan, published by Osprey Publishing 2011, ISBN-13: 9781849084796.

[4303] Page 230 of *Bitwa o prawdę: historia zmagań o pamięć Powstania Warszawskiego 1944-1989* (Battle for the truth: a history of struggles for the memory of the Warsaw Uprising 1944-1989) by Jacek Zygmunt Sawicki, published by "DiG," 2005, ISBN 837181366X, 9788371813665.

[4304] See the online article titled *The Black Book of Polish Censorship* published in Volume 83, Issue 4 of the Michigan Law Review. It can be downloaded at https://repository.law.umich.edu/cgi/viewcontent.cgi?article=2577&context=mlr. See also the online Shwarz Report June 2012 at http://www.schwarzreport.org/uploads/schwarz-report-pdf/schwarz-report-2012-06.pdf and Polish WWII Supplement III "The Katyń Wood Massacre."[3618] All links accessed on Sunday July 26, 2020.

[4305] Position 731.4 of *Trail of Hope, The Anders Army, An Odyssey Across Three Continents* by Norman Davies, published by Osprey Publishing, part of Bloomsbury Publishing 2015, ePub ISBN 9781472816054.

[4306] See endnote [3893] of Polish WWII Supplement III "The Katyń Wood Massacre."

[4307] Position 333.8 of *Trail of Hope, The Anders Army, An Odyssey Across Three Continents* by Norman Davies, published by Osprey Publishing, part of Bloomsbury Publishing 2015, ePub ISBN 9781472816054.

[4308] See endnote [3893] of Polish WWII Supplement III "The Katyń Wood Massacre."

[4309] Position 731.4 of *Trail of Hope, The Anders Army, An Odyssey Across Three Continents* by Norman Davies, published by Osprey Publishing, part of Bloomsbury Publishing 2015, ePub ISBN 9781472816054.

[4310] Ibid position 731.5.

[4311] See endnote [3893] of Polish WWII Supplement III "The Katyń Wood Massacre."

[4312] See endnote [4069] for this supplement.

[4313] See endnote [3893] of Polish WWII Supplement III "The Katyń Wood Massacre."

[4314] See endnote [4092] for this supplement.

[4315] See endnotes [3633] to [3641] of Polish WWII Supplement III "The Katyń Wood Massacre."

[4316] See Komorowski's shock, and indeed that of the Warsaw populace in general, at Soviet inaction documented in endnote [4235] for this supplement.

[4317] See endnote [4252] for this supplement.

[4318] Online article in the Jerusalem Post by Robert Cherry, dated July 12, 2017 at https://www.jpost.com/opinion/1944-warsaw-uprising-why-a-nuanced-history-is-rejected-499533. Accessed on Sunday July 26, 2020.

[4319] [3195] Ibid.

[4320] Page xxiii and photos between pages 240 to 241 of *The Secret Army: The Memoirs of General Bor-Komorowski* by Tadeusz Bor-komorowski, published by Frontline Books, 2011, ISBN 1848325959, 9781848325951.

[4321] Ibid.

[4322] *Find a Grave* website at https://www.findagrave.com/cemetery/859637/gunnersbury-cemetery, accessed on Saturday July 11, 2020. Since 2013, it has been a wholly owned subsidiary of *Ancestry*. See their "about" web page at https://www.findagrave.com/about. Both links accessed on Sunday July 26, 2020.

[4323] *Berlin Games: How Hitler Stole the Olympic Dream* by Guy Walters, published by Hachette UK, 2012, ISBN 1848547498, 9781848547490. See Google Books at
https://books.google.com.au/books?id=vFYti_djZYEC&printsec=frontcover&dq=Berlin+Games+-+How+Hitler+stole+the+Olympic+Dream&hl=en&sa=X&ved=2ahUKEwia0OCG58PqAhUhyjgGHXGzAaYQ6AEwAHoECAYQAg#v=onepage&q=lead%20the%20Polish%20Home%20Army&f=false. Accessed on Sunday July 26, 2020.

[4324] [4530] See endnote [4134] for this supplement.

[4325] [4624] [lxvii] The online article by Wojciech Oleksiak, published on May 23, 2015 on the Polish Culture website at https://culture.pl/en/article/how-krakow-made-it-unscathed-through-wwii. Accessed on Sunday July 26, 2020.

[4326] Ibid.

[4327] [4531] See the maps for January 15 and February 1, 1945 on pages 79 and 81 of the *Atlas of the World Battle Fronts in Semimonthly Phases, to August. 15, 1945*. This document was produced for the Chief of Staff of the United States Army in 1945 by the United States War Department General Staff, published by the Army Map Service, 1945. This digitised document can be downloaded from the Wikimedia website at
https://upload.wikimedia.org/wikipedia/commons/4/42/Atlas_of_the_World_Battle_Fronts_in_Semimonthly_Phases_to_August_15%2C_1945.pdf. Accessed on Sunday July 26, 2020.

[4328] The online article by Wojciech Oleksiak, published on May 23, 2015 on the Polish Culture website at https://culture.pl/en/article/how-krakow-made-it-unscathed-through-wwii. Accessed on Sunday July 26, 2020.

[4329] [4532] Ibid.

[4330] [4624] [lxvii] Ibid.

[4331] [4625] Page 117 of *Rising '44: The Battle for Warsaw Reprint Edition*, by Professor Norman Davies, published by Penguin Books; Reprint edition (October 4, 2005), ISBN-10: 0143035401, ISBN-13: 9780143035404.

[4332] See endnote [4171] for this supplement.

[4333] Position 533.1 of *Anders' Army General Władysław Anders and the Polish Second Corps 1941-46* by Evan McGilvray, published by Pen & Sword Military an imprint of Pen & Sword Books Ltd Barnsley South Yorkshire, 2018, eISBN 9781473889750.

[4334] [4530] See endnote [4163] for this supplement.

[4335] See endnotes [4189] to [4192] for this supplement. These indicate anything but an incompetent and overtly privileged noblman.

[4336] [4449] [4466] Position 533.4 of *Anders' Army General Władysław Anders and the Polish Second Corps 1941-46* by Evan McGilvray, published by Pen & Sword

Military an imprint of Pen & Sword Books Ltd Barnsley South Yorkshire, 2018, eISBN 9781473889750.

[4337] Page xxiv of *The Secret Army: The Memoirs of General Bor-Komorowski* by Tadeusz Bor-komorowski, published by Frontline Books, 2011, ISBN 1848325959, 9781848325951. This is from the Foreword by Adam Komorowski — the son of Tadeusz Bor-Komorowski.

[4338] Page xxiv of *The Secret Army: The Memoirs of General Bor-Komorowski* by Tadeusz Bor-komorowski, published by Frontline Books, 2011, ISBN 1848325959, 9781848325951. This is from the Foreword by Adam Komorowski — the son of Tadeusz Bor-Komorowski.

[4339] Ibid.

[4340] See https://www.britannica.com/topic/Solidarity. Accessed on Sunday July 26, 2020. The article states that in 1989, Solidarity re-emerged to become the first opposition movement to participate in free elections in a Soviet-bloc nation since the 1940s. However, I omitted the reference to "the 1940s," as this was in Poland's immediate post-war aftermath. In the 1946 referendum, the unfavourable results for the communists, were given a statistical "massage" by the "Department of Electoral Mathematics." In the full elections seven months later in January 1947, the communists revealed how much they had "learned" from the June 1946 referendum. In wishing to drastically reduce the role played by the "Department of Electoral Mathematics," the communists took no chances, with measures including open examination of people's ballot papers being rampant, while the names of people attempting to place their vote in envelopes were written down by voting officials. Two million voters had been struck from the voting register by government controlled committees while factory workers were marched to the polls by their foremen and instructed to vote for the communist government under the threat of losing their jobs. See page 426 of *God's Playground A History of Poland: Volume II: 1795 to the Present*, by Norman Davies, published by Oxford University Press, 2005, ISBN 0199253404, 9780199253401, position 1222.5 of Microcosm and pages 242-243 *No Greater Ally, The Untold Story of Poland's Forces in World War II*, by Kenneth K. Koskodan, published by Osprey Publishing 2011, ISBN-13: 9781 849084796. The 1947 election, was in essence, identical to the German election in early March 1933, just weeks after Hitler taking power. See endnotes [347] to [351] of Chapter 3 "Evil's Storm Descends."

[4341] Page 368 of *The Secret Army: The Memoirs of General Bor-Komorowski* by Tadeusz Bor-komorowski, published by Frontline Books, 2011, ISBN 1848325959, 9781848325951.

[4342] See endnote [1658] of Chapter 20 "Valkyrie II."

[4343] See endnotes [2453] to [2454] for Chapter 25 "Old Prussia Gone with the Wind."

[4344] [1860] [1951] [4409] On this point, I have used the full text given in Davies *Rising '44: The Battle for Warsaw Reprint Edition* on page 679.

[4345] Page 370 of *The Secret Army: The Memoirs of General Bor-Komorowski* by Tadeusz Bor-komorowski, published by Frontline Books, 2011, ISBN 1848325959, 9781848325951. The full translated text of the surrender agreement, by Wanda Wyporska, is given in Appendix 29 on pages 678 to 680 of *Rising '44: The Battle for Warsaw Reprint Edition*, by Professor Norman Davies, published by Penguin Books; Reprint edition (October 4, 2005), ISBN-10: 0143035401, ISBN-13: 9780143035404.

[4346] Page 680 of *Rising '44: The Battle for Warsaw Reprint Edition*, by Professor Norman Davies.

[4347][4370] Page 371 of *The Secret Army: The Memoirs of General Bor-Komorowski* by Tadeusz Bor-komorowski, published by Frontline Books, 2011, ISBN 1848325959, 9781848325951.

[4348][4388][4520][4541] See the information page for Jerzy Komorowski at http://www.sejm-wielki.pl/b/psb.12319.6 on the website of *Genealogy of the descendants of the Great Sejm* (Polish Parliament). Accessed on Sunday July 26, 2020.

[4349][4541] For information on the elder brother Adam, see the same website at http://www.sejm-wielki.pl/b/psb.12319.5. Accessed on Sunday July 26, 2020.

[4350] The online article on *The Doomed Soldiers* website at http://www.doomedsoldiers.com/battle-of-Miodusy-Pokrzywne.html. This English language article, translated by Magdalena Nogal, with additional Editing by Jan Czarniecki, is based on the Polish language book *"Łupaszka," "Młot," "Huzar": działalność 5 i 6 Brygady Wileńskiej AK : (1944-1952)* *("Łupaszka," "Hammer," "Huzar": activities of the 5th and 6th Vilnius Brigade AK (1944-1952))* by Kazimierz Krajewski, published by Oficyna Wydawnicza Volumen, 2002 (Volumen Publishing House, 2002), ISBN 8372330190, 9788372330192. As well, the Polish history portal at https://dzieje.pl/artykuly-historyczne/nkwd-kompletnie-rozbite-zwycieska-bitwa-5-brygady-wilenskiej-w-miodusach-pokrzywnych. Both links accessed on Sunday July 26, 2020.

[4351] The Polish history portal at https://dzieje.pl/artykuly-historyczne/nkwd-kompletnie-rozbite-zwycieska-bitwa-5-brygady-wilenskiej-w-miodusach-pokrzywnych. All links accessed on Sunday July 26, 2020.

[4352] The online introductory article on *The Doomed Soldiers* website at http://www.doomedsoldiers.com/introduction.html. Accessed on Sunday July 26, 2020.

[4353] John Prados. *Notes on the CIA's Secret War in Afghanistan The Journal of American History*, vol. 89, no. 2, 2002, pp. 466—471. JSTOR, http://www.jstor.org/stable/3092167. Accessed April 10, 2020. See also the University of Western Canada's timeline on the conflict at http://publish.uwo.ca/~acopp2/historyofwar/coldwar/militaryconflicts/sovietafghanwar/timeline.html. Both links accessed on Sunday July 26, 2020.

[4354] A Radio Free Europe Report titled *Polish Workers Commemorate their Past Struggles* RAD Background Report/192 (Poland), by J. B. de Weydenthal, published on July 7, 1981. It can be viewed online at https://libcom.org/library/poznan-1956-radom-1976 on the *Libertarian Communist* website. The Radom uprising is also documented on the Polish Government history website at http://www.poland.gov.pl/history/history-poland/june-1976-and-workers-defence-committee/ and the Poznań uprising in the online *Encyclopaedia Britannica* article at https://www.britannica.com/event/Poznan-Riots. All links accessed on Sunday July 26, 2020.

[4355] [4546] See the online article by Mikołaj Gliński, published on March 16, 2016 on the Polish Culture website at https://culture.pl/en/article/historical-facts-about-the-baptism-of-poland in regard to Poland becoming embracing western Catholicism in 966 AD. Accessed on Sunday July 26, 2020.

[4356] The Honors Scholars thesis, by Arragon Perrone, University of Connecticut OpenCommons@UConn Honors Scholar Theses Honors Scholar Program, titled *Pope John Paul II's Role in the Collapse of Poland's Communist Regime: Examining a Religious Leader's Impact on International Relations* dated May 6, 2012. It can viewed online at https://opencommons.uconn.edu/cgi/viewcontent.cgi?article=1244&context=srhonors_theses. Accessed on Sunday July 26, 2020.

[4357] Ibid at the end of the introduction.

[4358] The online *Encyclopaedia Britannica* article at https://www.britannica.com/biography/Mahatma-Gandhi. Accessed on Sunday July 26, 2020.

[4359] American Public Broadcasting Service (PBS) online biographical article of John Paul II, by Jane Barnes and Helen Whitney at https://www.pbs.org/wgbh/pages/frontline/shows/pope/etc/bio.html. Accessed on Sunday July 26, 2020.

[4360] At Poland's six century old holiest shrine of Jasna Góra in Częstohowa, there a statue of John Paul II. However, on the grounds just outside the main entrance, is an imposing statue of Stefan Wyszyński.

[4361] Page 582 of *Rising '44: The Battle for Warsaw Reprint Edition*, by Professor Norman Davies, published by Penguin Books; Reprint edition (October 4, 2005), ISBN-10: 0143035401, ISBN-13: 9780143035404. Most poignantly, this is in Chapter VIII "ECHOES OF THE RISING 1956-2000."

[4362] Ibid.

[4363] Ibid.

[4364] Ibid pages 582 to 583.

[4365] Ibid page 583.

[4366] See the online *Encyclopaedia Britannica* article on Stefan Wyszyński at https://www.britannica.com/biography/Stefan-Wyszynski. Accessed on Sunday July 26, 2020.

[4367] Page 583 of *Rising '44: The Battle for Warsaw Reprint Edition*, by Professor Norman Davies

[4368] Ibid.

[4369] Ibid.

[4370] See endnote [4347] for this supplement.

[4371] Page 371 of *The Secret Army: The Memoirs of General Bor-Komorowski* by Tadeusz Bor-komorowski, published by Frontline Books, 2011, ISBN 1848325959, 9781848325951. Also, the tablet titled 'DECISION OF GENERAL „BÓR"' cited inside the Warsaw Uprising Museum (Muzeum Powstania) by the author on Saturday October 9th 2004.

[4372] Page 371 of *The Secret Army: The Memoirs of General Bor-Komorowski* by Tadeusz Bor-komorowski, published by Frontline Books, 2011, ISBN 1848325959, 9781848325951.

[4373] [1860] [1951] Page 372 of *The Secret Army: The Memoirs of General Bor-Komorowski* by Tadeusz Bor-komorowski, published by Frontline Books, 2011, ISBN 1848325959, 9781848325951.

[4374] [4377] [4378] http://www.warsawuprising.com/paper/auschwitz_museum.htm. This was reprinted from Auschwitz-Birkenau Memorial and Museum website: http://www.auschwitz.org.pl on the sixtieth anniversary of the Warsaw Uprising and from the book *Księga Pamięci. Transporty Polaków z Warszawy do KL Auschwitz 1940-1945 (Book of Remembrance. Transports of Poles from Warsaw to KL Auschwitz 1940-1945)*. Both links accessed on Sunday July 26, 2020. For the former website's credentials, see endnote [3662] for Polish WWII Supplement III "The Katyń Wood Massacre."

[4375] Page 372 of *The Secret Army: The Memoirs of General Bor-Komorowski* by Tadeusz Bor-komorowski, published by Frontline Books, 2011, ISBN 1848325959, 9781848325951.

[4376] [1860] [1951] Page 372 of *The Secret Army: The Memoirs of General Bor-Komorowski* by Tadeusz Bor-komorowski, published by Frontline Books, 2011, ISBN 1848325959, 9781848325951.

[4377] See endnote [4374] for this supplement.

[4378] [4374] Page 372 of *The Secret Army: The Memoirs of General Bor-Komorowski* by Tadeusz Bor-komorowski.

[4379] The online transcript of the interview *Interview with Dr. Alexandra Richie, Author of 'Warsaw 1944'* dated January 22, 2020, on the website of the World War II Museum in New Orleans at https://www.nationalww2museum.org/war/articles/interview-dr-alexandra-richie-author-warsaw-1944. Accessed on Sunday July 26, 2020.

[4380] Position 1060.1 of *Microcosm*. This passage gives a detailed description of the various categories of forced labour within the Reich and its occupied territories. That ZAL stands for Zwangsarbeitslager and KZ for Konzentrationslager are documented respectively at http://www.deathcamps.org/occupation/plaszow.html which is the official web site for Aktion Reinhard Camps, and at https://www.dhm.de/lemo/kapitel/ns-regime/ausgrenzung/kz/ on the German Historical Museum web site in German. Both links accessed on Sunday July 26, 2020.

[4381] Position 1062.3 of *Microcosm*.

[4382] Position 1062.4 of *Microcosm*.

[4383] Position 1063.2 of *Microcosm*.

[4384] Position 1063.8 of *Microcosm*.

[4385] Position 1060.1 of *Microcosm*.

[4386] Page 373 of *The Secret Army: The Memoirs of General Bor-Komorowski* by Tadeusz Bor-komorowski, published by Frontline Books, 2011, ISBN 1848325959, 9781848325951.

[4387] [4521] Ibid.

[4388] [4521] For the name and date of birth of Komorowski's second son, see endnote [4348] for this supplement.

[4389] Page 373 of *The Secret Army: The Memoirs of General Bor-Komorowski* by Tadeusz Bor-komorowski, published by Frontline Books, 2011, ISBN 1848325959, 9781848325951.

[4390] [2203] Ibid.

[4391] Ibid pages 373 to 374.

[4392] The tablet titled "CAPITULATION" cited inside the Warsaw Uprising Museum (Muzeum Powstania) by the author on Saturday October 9th 2004.

[4393] Page 374 of *The Secret Army: The Memoirs of General Bor-Komorowski* by Tadeusz Bor-komorowski, published by Frontline Books, 2011, ISBN 1848325959, 9781848325951.

[4394] In Komorowski's book on page 374, he just referred to his interpreter by his pseudonym "Sas." His real name of Alfred Edward Korczyński, is given on the website of the Muzeum Powstania (Uprising Museum) at https://www.1944.pl/powstancze-biogramy/alfred-korczynski,22487.html. Accessed on Sunday July 26, 2020.

[4395] Page 374 of *The Secret Army: The Memoirs of General Bor-Komorowski* by Tadeusz Bor-komorowski, published by Frontline Books, 2011, ISBN 1848325959, 9781848325951.

[4396] Ibid.

[4397] Ibid.

[4398] See the photos between pages 374 and 375 of *Rising '44: The Battle for Warsaw Reprint Edition*, by Professor Norman Davies, published by Penguin Books; Reprint edition (October 4, 2005), ISBN-10: 0143035401, ISBN-13: 9780143035404.

[4399] Page 374 of *The Secret Army: The Memoirs of General Bor-Komorowski* by Tadeusz Bor-komorowski, published by Frontline Books, 2011, ISBN 1848325959, 9781848325951.

[4400] Pages 374 to 375 of *The Secret Army: The Memoirs of General Bor-Komorowski* by Tadeusz Bor-komorowski, published by Frontline Books, 2011, ISBN 1848325959, 9781848325951.

[4401] Ibid page 375.

[4402] Ibid.

[4403] See endnotes [3471] to [3483] for Polish WWII Supplement I "The Molotov-Ribbentrop Pact." It is important to note here, the difference between a non-aggression pact and outright collaboration — which the secret protocols of the Molotov-Ribbentrop Pact certainly embodied.

[4404] See pages 374 to 376 of *The Secret Army: The Memoirs of General Bor-Komorowski* by Tadeusz Bor-komorowski, published by Frontline Books, 2011, ISBN 1848325959, 9781848325951.

[4405] Page 375 of *The Secret Army: The Memoirs of General Bor-Komorowski* by Tadeusz Bor-komorowski, published by Frontline Books, 2011, ISBN 1848325959, 9781848325951.

[4406] Ibid.

[4407] Ibid.

[4408] Ibid.

[4409] Ibid. See also Section I, paragraph 10 of the surrender agreement in Appendix 29 "Capitulation Agreement between the German Army and the Home Army" on page 679 of *Rising '44: The Battle for Warsaw Reprint Edition*, by Professor Norman Davies, published by Penguin Books; Reprint edition (October 4, 2005), ISBN-10: 0143035401, ISBN-13: 9780143035404 See also endnote [4344] for this supplement.

[4410] Page 375 of *The Secret Army: The Memoirs of General Bor-Komorowski* by Tadeusz Bor-komorowski, published by Frontline Books, 2011, ISBN 1848325959, 9781848325951.

[4411] In regard to the delusions of even common Germans in regard to the course of the war towards its end, see for example endnotes [1843] to [1845] for Chapter 20 "Valkyrie II."

[4412] See page 368 of *The Secret Army: The Memoirs of General Bor-Komorowski* by Tadeusz Bor-komorowski, published by Frontline Books, 2011, ISBN 1848325959, 9781848325951 in regard to the German V1 and V2 weapons. In regard to the "Wunderwaffe" or wonder weapons in general, see the Quora discussion at https://www.quora.com/What-were-the-most-and-least-practical-of-the-Wunderwaffe-of-Nazi-Germany, accessed on Sunday July 26, 2020 and the paperback *The Truth About The Wunderwaffe* by Igor Witkowski, published by RVP Press (January 15, 2013), ISBN-10: 1618613383 ISBN-13: 9781618613387.

[4413] Page 375 of *The Secret Army: The Memoirs of General Bor-Komorowski* by Tadeusz Bor-komorowski.

[4414] Ibid.

[4415] See page 330 and Chapter 35 "THE JET FIGHTER TRAGEDY" from pages 334 to 346 of *The First and the Last* by the highly decorated German WWII fighter ace, Adolf Galland, English edition published by Metheun and Company Limited London 1955, translated by Mervyn Savill from the German *DIE ERSTEN UND DIE LETZEN*, published by Franz Schneekluth in 1953.

[4416] Ibid.

[4417] Ibid page 189.

[4418] Page 376 of *The Secret Army: The Memoirs of General Bor-Komorowski* by Tadeusz Bor-komorowski, published by Frontline Books, 2011, ISBN 1848325959, 9781848325951.

[4419] Ibid.

[4420] Ibid.

[4421] [2203] Ibid.

[4422] Ibid.

[4423] Ibid page 378.

[4424] Ibid.

[4425] Ibid.

[4426] Ibid page 379 .

[4427] Ibid.

[4428] Ibid.

[4429] Ibid page 380.

[4430] Komarowski stated that the name of the Wehrmacht general was "General von Lützow, Commander of the 2nd German Army." However, that cannot be right, as he had already been captured by the Soviets during Operation Bagration, which concluded in the middle of August during the first-half of the Rising. See page 274 of *A Writer at War: Vasily Grossman with the Red Army, 1941-1945* by Vasiliĭ Semenovich Grossman, edited and translated by Antony Beevor, Luba Vinogradova, published by Pantheon Books, 2005, ISBN 0375424075, 9780375424076. Moreover, the Wehrmacht General that Komorowski met would have been the commander of the German 9th Army, in charge of the Warsaw sector, his name being Nikolaus von Vormann. See page 100 of *The German Defeat in the East: 1944-45* by Samuel W. Mitcham Junior, published by Stackpole Books, 2007, ISBN 146175187X, 9781461751878. Moreover, on page 99, Mitcham states that at the commencement of the Rising, von Vormann was briefly involved in its suppression before the arrival of von dem Bach-Zelewski. Curiously, as stated on pages 99 to 100, Wehrmacht generals considered it beneath their dignity to suppress the Rising. See endnotes [4208] to [4210] for this supplement.

[4431] Page 380 of *The Secret Army: The Memoirs of General Bor-Komorowski* by Tadeusz Bor-komorowski, published by Frontline Books, 2011, ISBN 1848325959, 9781848325951.

[4432] See endnotes [4211] to [4214] for this supplement.

[4433] Page 380 of *The Secret Army: The Memoirs of General Bor-Komorowski* by Tadeusz Bor-komorowski.

[4434] Ibid.

[4435] See endnote [1773] of Chapter 20 "Valkyrie II," which gives the date of July 20, 1944 for the Valkyrie assassination attempt.

[4436] In regard to the various departments of the Reich Security Main Office (*Reichssicherheitshauptamt* — RSHA), see endnotes [1181] to [1183] of Chapter 17 "Pastor and Spy" and endnote [128] of the Preface "Birth and Memory upon the Lesser Known Fault Line of History."

[4437] Pages 380 to 381 of *The Secret Army: The Memoirs of General Bor-Komorowski* by Tadeusz Bor-komorowski, published by Frontline Books, 2011, ISBN 1848325959, 9781848325951.

[4438] Ibid page 381.

[4439] In regard to the various departments of the Reich Security Main Office (*Reichssicherheitshauptamt* — RSHA), see endnotes [1181] to [1183] of Chapter 17 "Pastor and Spy" and endnote [128] of the Preface "Birth and Memory upon the Lesser Known Fault Line of History."

[4440] Page 381 of *The Secret Army: The Memoirs of General Bor-Komorowski* by Tadeusz Bor-komorowski, published by Frontline Books, 2011, ISBN 1848325959, 9781848325951.

[4441] Ibid.

[4442] See endnote [4180] for this supplement.

[4443] Pages 381 to 382 of *The Secret Army: The Memoirs of General Bor-Komorowski* by Tadeusz Bor-komorowski.

[4444] Ibid page 382.

[4445] Ibid.

[4446] See endnotes [4135] to [4138] for this supplement.

[4447] Page 382 of *The Secret Army: The Memoirs of General Bor-Komorowski* by Tadeusz Bor-komorowski, published by Frontline Books, 2011, ISBN 1848325959, 9781848325951.

[4448] Ibid page 382.

[4449] See endnote [4336] for this supplement.

[4450] In regard to the various departments of the Reich Security Main Office (*Reichssicherheitshauptamt* — RSHA), see endnotes [1181] to [1183] of Chapter 17 "Pastor and Spy" and endnote [128] of the Preface "Birth and Memory upon the Lesser Known Fault Line of History."

[4451] Page 383 of *The Secret Army: The Memoirs of General Bor-Komorowski* by Tadeusz Bor-komorowski, published by Frontline Books, 2011, ISBN 1848325959, 9781848325951.

[4452] Ibid.

[4453] Ibid. See also endnote [4015] for this supplement.

[4454] See endnotes [4016] to [4017] for this supplement.

[4455] Page 383 of *The Secret Army: The Memoirs of General Bor-Komorowski* by Tadeusz Bor-komorowski, published by Frontline Books, 2011, ISBN 1848325959, 9781848325951.

[4456] Ibid page 384 and endnotes [4018] and [4019].

[4457] Page 384 of *The Secret Army: The Memoirs of General Bor-Komorowski* by Tadeusz Bor-komorowski, published by Frontline Books, 2011, ISBN 1848325959, 9781848325951.

[4458] This Polish language article by Tadeusz Pełczyński, can be viewed online at http://retropress.pl/wiadomosci/jak-zginal-stefan-rowecki/, accessed on Sunday July 26, 2020, on the Polish RetroPress website, dedicated to selected press articles published in the former Polish-language press - from the partitions, through the Second Polish Republic, the emigration press to the years of early "People's" Republic. Columns, reports, interviews, trivia, memories; from ambitious and opinion-forming press to tabloids. From the extreme left to the extreme right; also national minority press published in Polish. Accessed on Sunday July 26, 2020.

[4459] Page 384 of *The Secret Army: The Memoirs of General Bor-Komorowski* by Tadeusz Bor-komorowski, published by Frontline Books, 2011, ISBN 1848325959, 9781848325951.

[4460] Ibid.

[4461] See the UK Department of Engineering article at http://www.eng.cam.ac.uk/news/escape-colditz. Accessed on Sunday July 26, 2020. The conceived escape of prisoners by glider never took place as the castle was liberated just before the planned implementation of the escape. Nevertheless, the glider had been completed.

[4462] Page 384 of *The Secret Army: The Memoirs of General Bor-Komorowski* by Tadeusz Bor-komorowski, published by Frontline Books, 2011, ISBN 1848325959, 9781848325951.

[4463] Ibid pages 384 to 385.

[4464] Ibid page 385.

[4465] Ibid.

[4466] See endnote [4336] for this supplement.

[4467] Page 385 of *The Secret Army: The Memoirs of General Bor-Komorowski* by Tadeusz Bor-komorowski, published by Frontline Books, 2011, ISBN 1848325959, 9781848325951.

[4468] Ibid.

[4469] Ibid.

[4470] See endnotes [168] and [169] for the Preface "Birth and Memory upon the Lesser Known Fault Line of History."

[4471] Page 385 of *The Secret Army: The Memoirs of General Bor-Komorowski* by Tadeusz Bor-komorowski, published by Frontline Books, 2011, ISBN 1848325959, 9781848325951.

[4472] See endnotes [3520] and [3521] of Polish WWII Supplement I "The Molotov-Ribbentrop Pact."

[4473] Page 385 of *The Secret Army: The Memoirs of General Bor-Komorowski* by Tadeusz Bor-komorowski, published by Frontline Books, 2011, ISBN 1848325959, 9781848325951.

[4474] See endnote [3690] for Polish WWII Supplement III "The Katyń Wood Massacre."

[4475] Page 386 of *The Secret Army: The Memoirs of General Bor-Komorowski* by Tadeusz Bor-komorowski, published by Frontline Books, 2011, ISBN 1848325959, 9781848325951.

[4476] See endnote [950] for Chapter 13 "Flight and the Tumultuous Appeasement of Evil."

[4477] Position 705.0 onwards at the beginning of Chapter 5 "THE ATLANTIC CHARTER" in the ebook *The Roosevelt Myth* by John Thomas Flynn, published by Ludwig von Mises Institute, 1956, ISBN 9781610161497. See also the UN website at https://www.un.org/en/sections/history-united-nations-charter/1941-atlantic-charter/index.html and https://cdn.un.org/unyearbook/yun/pdf/1946-47/1946-47_37.pdf. As well, "THE ATLANTIC CHARTER," a framed original U.S. Office of War Information Poster can be viewed online at Chartwell Booksellers at https://www.chartwellbooksellers.com/product/the-atlantic-charter/. All links accessed on Sunday July 26, 2020.

[4478] Page 2 of the document from the UN website at https://cdn.un.org/unyearbook/yun/chapter_pdf/1946-47YUN/1946-47_P1_SEC1.pdf. Accessed on Sunday July 26, 2020.

[4479] Chartwell Booksellers at https://www.chartwellbooksellers.com/product/the-atlantic-charter/ documents the printing by the U.S. Office of War Information in 1943 of 240,000 posters of the full text. Accessed on Sunday July 26, 2020.

[4480] Position 714.0 of *The Roosevelt Myth* by John Thomas Flynn, published by Ludwig von Mises Institute, 1956, ISBN 9781610161497.

[4481] Ibid.

[4482] Ibid position 714.0

[4483] Ibid position 796.3.

[4484] See endnotes [3490] to [3503] and [3520] to [3521] of Polish WWII Supplement I "The Molotov-Ribbentrop Pact."

[4485] Page 386 of *The Secret Army: The Memoirs of General Bor-Komorowski* by Tadeusz Bor-komorowski, published by Frontline Books, 2011, ISBN 1848325959, 9781848325951.

[4486] Ibid.

[4487] Pages 81 and 83 of the maps for February 1 and February 15, 1945 on pages 81 and 83 of the *Atlas of the World Battle Fronts in Semimonthly Phases, to August. 15, 1945*. This document was produced for the Chief of Staff of the

United States Army in 1945 by the United States War Department General Staff, published by the Army Map Service, 1945. This digitised document can be downloaded from the Wikimedia website at https://upload.wikimedia.org/wikipedia/commons/4/42/Atlas_of_the_World_B attle_Fronts_in_Semimonthly_Phases_to_August_15%2C_1945.pdf. Accessed on Sunday July 26, 2020.

[4488] Page 386 of *The Secret Army: The Memoirs of General Bor-Komorowski* by Tadeusz Bor-komorowski, published by Frontline Books, 2011, ISBN 1848325959, 9781848325951.

[4489] Ibid.

[4490] [539] See endnote [630] of Chapter 6 "Old Prussia — Birth of Ruth to Precarious Survival" for an explanation on what nationalities are considered Slavs.

[4491] Page 386 of *The Secret Army: The Memoirs of General Bor-Komorowski* by Tadeusz Bor-komorowski, published by Frontline Books, 2011, ISBN 1848325959, 9781848325951.

[4492] Ibid pages 386 to 387.

[4493] Ibid page 387.

[4494] Ibid.

[4495] See endnote [2187] for Chapter 24 "Dietrich's Final Days."

[4496] For a more detailed explanation of the concept of special prisoners, also known as "Prominenten — Prominent Prisoners" or "Hostages of the SS," see endnotes [2708] onwards from the start of Chapter 27 "The Prominenten and Miraculous Reprieves."

[4497] See endnote [2188] for Chapter 24 "Dietrich's Final Days."

[4498] Page 387 of *The Secret Army: The Memoirs of General Bor-Komorowski* by Tadeusz Bor-komorowski, published by Frontline Books, 2011, ISBN 1848325959, 9781848325951.

[4499] See the thesis by Marvin L. Meek on *ULTRA AND THE MYTH OF THE GERMAN "NATIONAL REDOUBT"* on the website *All World Wars* at https://www.allworldwars.com/Ultra-and-The-Myth-of-the-National-Redoubt-by-Marvin-Meek.html. Accessed on Sunday July 26, 2020. Payne Best in his book, also refers to this mythical fortress in his book. See endnotes [2225] and [2226] of Chapter 24 "Dietrich's Final Days."

[4500] The thesis by Marvin L. Meek on *ULTRA AND THE MYTH OF THE GERMAN "NATIONAL REDOUBT"*.

[4501] Ibid.

[4502] Page 387 of *The Secret Army: The Memoirs of General Bor-Komorowski* by Tadeusz Bor-komorowski, published by Frontline Books, 2011, ISBN 1848325959, 9781848325951.

[4503] Ibid page 387.

[4504] Ibid page 387.

[4505] Ibid page 387.

[4506] Ibid page 387.

[4507] Ibid pages 387 to 388.

[4508] Ibid page 388.

[4509] Ibid page 388.

[4510] Ibid pages 388 to 389.

[4511] Ibid page 388.

[4512] Ibid page 389.

[4513] Ibid page 292. On this page, Komorowski refers to how the Stalinist regime had, during the Rising, branded him a war criminal. Hence, the self-evident difference of American and Soviet reception.

[4514] See endnote [842] of Chapter 11 "Memo to Hitler and his Olympics."

[4515] In regard to Komorowski's gallantry in the 1920 Battle of Komarów, see endnotes [4091] to [4092] for this supplement.

[4516] In regard to the Battle of Komarów, see endnote [3438] of Polish WWII Supplement I "The Molotov-Ribbentrop Pact."

[4517] Page 389 of *The Secret Army: The Memoirs of General Bor-Komorowski* by Tadeusz Bor-komorowski, published by Frontline Books, 2011, ISBN 1848325959, 9781848325951.

[4518] Ibid page 390.

[4519] Ibid page 292.

[4520] In regard to the name and date of birth for the Komorowskis' second son, see endnote [4348] for this supplement.

[4521] See endnotes [4387] and [4388] for this supplement.

[4522] Pages 394 to 396 of *The Secret Army: The Memoirs of General Bor-Komorowski* by Tadeusz Bor-komorowski, published by Frontline Books, 2011, ISBN 1848325959, 9781848325951.

[4523] [lxviii] Page 393 of *The Secret Army: The Memoirs of General Bor-Komorowski* by Tadeusz Bor-komorowski, published by Frontline Books, 2011, ISBN 1848325959, 9781848325951.

[4524] See the bottom of page 21 of *Preaching in Hitler's Shadow: Sermons of Resistance in the Third Reich* by Dean G. Stroud, published by Wm. B. Eerdmans Publishing, 2013, ISBN 0802869025, 9780802869029 and endnotes [312] to [313] for Chapter 2 "Ominous Clouds on the Horizon" in regard to the Nazis perceiving the cross as a symbol of shame, weakness and synonymous humility, and as such, their new Germany being the one to achieve what Christ failed to do.

[4525] Page 394 of *The Secret Army: The Memoirs of General Bor-Komorowski* by Tadeusz Bor-komorowski, published by Frontline Books, 2011, ISBN 1848325959, 9781848325951.

[4526] Ibid.

[4527] Ibid page xvii and page 394. See also the information page for Jerzy Komorowski at http://www.sejm-wielki.pl/b/psb.12319.6 on the website of *Genealogy of the descendants of the Great Sejm* (Polish Parliament). Accessed on

Sunday July 26, 2020. From these three pieces of information, it can be inferred that Jerzy was born at midnight on the 9th to 10th of September 1944.

[4528] Pages 394 to 395 of *The Secret Army: The Memoirs of General Bor-Komorowski* by Tadeusz Bor-komorowski. That Kraków was her birthplace, see the Geni genealogical website at https://www.geni.com/people/Irena-Komorowska/6000000012481095700. Accessed on Sunday July 26, 2020.

[4529] Page 395 of *The Secret Army: The Memoirs of General Bor-Komorowski* by Tadeusz Bor-komorowski.

[4530] See endnotes [4324] to [4334] for this supplement in regard to the easy Soviet capture of Kraków in January 1945.

[4531] See endnote [4327] for this supplement. The fact that Warsaw was virtually deserted in January 1945, when the Soviet Army entered Warsaw, will soon be covered in greater detail. The battle front maps from July 1944 until February 1945, illustrate the virtual Soviet inaction on Warsaw's outskirts from late July 1944 until late January 1945.

[4532] See endnote [4329] for this chapter.

[4533] Ibid.

[4534] Page 395 of *The Secret Army: The Memoirs of General Bor-Komorowski* by Tadeusz Bor-komorowski, published by Frontline Books, 2011, ISBN 1848325959, 9781848325951.

[4535] Ibid.

[4536] See position 1123.0 of Microcosm, describing the need and indeed lack qualms for the post-war Stalinist regime in Poland, to recruit the dregs of Polish Society.

[4537] Page 395 of *The Secret Army: The Memoirs of General Bor-Komorowski* by Tadeusz Bor-komorowski, published by Frontline Books, 2011, ISBN 1848325959, 9781848325951.

[4538] [lxviii] Ibid.

[4539] See the Geni genealogical website at https://www.geni.com/people/Tadeusz-B%C3%B3r-Komorowski/6000000012481066824. Accessed on Sunday July 26, 2020. All links accessed on Sunday July 26, 2020.

[4540] See the Geni genealogical website at https://www.geni.com/people/Irena-Komorowska/6000000012481095700.

[4541] For Adam, see endnote [4349], and for Jerzy, see endnote [4348] from this supplement. Accessed on Sunday July 26, 2020.

[4542] In regard to the three stages of the partitioning of Poland in 1772, 1793 and 1795, see endnote [2] of the Preface "Birth and Memory upon the Lesser Known Fault Line of History."

[4543] The article by Marek Kępa, published on November 5. 2018 on the Polish culture website (the flagship brand of the Adam Mickiewicz Institute https://iam.pl/en, https://culture.pl/en) at https://culture.pl/en/article/why-does-poland-celebrate-independence-day-on-11th-november describes the significance of Polish Independence day celebrated on November 11. All links accessed on Sunday July 26, 2020.

[4544] See Polish WWII Supplement I "The Molotov-Ribbentrop Pact."[3268]

[4545] Page 395 of *The Secret Army: The Memoirs of General Bor-Komorowski* by Tadeusz Bor-komorowski, published by Frontline Books, 2011, ISBN 1848325959, 9781848325951.

[4546] See endnote [4355] for this supplement.

[4547] Page 396 of *The Secret Army: The Memoirs of General Bor-Komorowski* by Tadeusz Bor-komorowski, published by Frontline Books, 2011, ISBN 1848325959, 9781848325951.

[4548] Ibid.

[4549] See for example endnotes [3520] to [3535] for Polish WWII Supplement I "The Molotov-Ribbentrop Pact."

[4550] See endnote [3520] for Polish WWII Supplement I "The Molotov-Ribbentrop Pact."

[4551] See endnote [3521] for Polish WWII Supplement I "The Molotov-Ribbentrop Pact."

[4552] See endnote [3522] for Polish WWII Supplement I "The Molotov-Ribbentrop Pact."

[4553] See endnote [3523] for Polish WWII Supplement I "The Molotov-Ribbentrop Pact."

[4554] Page xxiv of *The Secret Army: The Memoirs of General Bor-Komorowski* by Tadeusz Bor-komorowski, published by Frontline Books, 2011, ISBN 1848325959, 9781848325951.

[4555] See endnote [2415] for Chapter 25 "Old Prussia Gone with the Wind."

[4556] Ibid.

[4557] The online English language article on the official website of the Royal Castle in Warsaw at https://www.zamek-krolewski.pl/en/your-visit/permanent-exhibitions/the-royal-castle-from-destruction-to-reconstruction. Accessed on Sunday July 26, 2020.

[4558] Ibid.

[4559] The online Polish language article on the official website of the Royal Castle in Warsaw, edited by Piotr Majewski at https://www.zamek-krolewski.pl/historia/historia/zamek-krolewski-po-1939-roku-zniszczenie-i-odbudowa. Accessed on Sunday July 26, 2020.

[4560] See the online article on the UK Construction News website, dated December 5, 2017, by Tom Fitzpatrick at https://www.constructionnews.co.uk/buildings/project-reports/communist-relics-erased-in-europes-regen-hotspots-05-12-2017/. Accessed on Sunday July 26, 2020.

[4561] See for example the article *Today's Warsaw* dated September 7, 2014 on Rick Steve's travel blog at https://blog.ricksteves.com/blog/todays-warsaw/. Also, about halfway through Rick Steve's book, *Rick Steves Eastern Europe* by Rick Steves and Cameron Hewitt, Edition 9, published by Hachette UK, 2017, ISBN 1631216147, 9781631216145. See Google Books at https://books.google.com.au/books?id=Q3NuDgAAQBAJ&pg=PT595&lpg=PT595&dq=Stalin%27s+penis&source=bl&ots=Zhn5bV099T&sig=ACfU3U1bAiZ-txXAw_8yN92y4zPieXuDfgA&hl=en&sa=X&ved=2ahUKEwiR9a6frvPoAhVdyDgGHc4EB0Q4FBDoATADegQICxAu#v=onepage&q=Stalin's%20penis&f=false. Both links accessed on Sunday July 26, 2020.

[4562] In regard to the use of the sewers by the insurgents during the Rising, see endnotes [4177] to [4192] for this supplement.

[4563] See endnote [3991] for this supplement. In regard to the Wawer Massacre itself, see the beginning for this supplement.[3957]

[4564] See endnotes [3996] to [4003] for this supplement.

[4565] [3691] The online article on the website of the United States Holocaust Memorial Museum at https://encyclopedia.ushmm.org/content/en/article/the-warsaw-ghetto-uprising, which gives the dates for the outbreak and brutal suppression of the Ghetto Rising, as opposed to the 1944 General Uprising. Accessed on Sunday July 26, 2020.

[4566] See endnotes [4147] to [4154] for this supplement.

[4567] Pages 176 to 177 of *Rising '44: The Battle for Warsaw Reprint Edition*, by Professor Norman Davies, published by Penguin Books; Reprint edition (October 4, 2005), ISBN-10: 0143035401, ISBN-13: 9780143035404.

[4568] In regard to Wanda Gertz, see the following:

(a) http://www.1944.pl/historia/powstancze-biogramy/Wanda_Gertz from the official website of the 1944 Warsaw Uprising in Polish. Accessed on Sunday July 26, 2020.

(b) http://www.polacyzwyboru.pl/bohaterowie/biogramy/wanda-gertz from the website: *Polacy z wyboru Rodziny pochodzenia niemieckiego w Warszawie w XIX i XX wieku* — Poles of choice for families of German origin in Warsaw in the nineteenth and twentieth centuries. Accessed on Sunday July 26, 2020.

[4569] In regard to the liberation of Wanda Gertz in April 1945, specifically by the US 89th Infantry Division, see the World War II Database at https://ww2db.com/person_bio.php?person_id=893 and the online booklet *Rolling Ahead!: The Story of the 89th Infantry Division* by the United States Army — Forces in the European Theater, published by P. Dupont, 1945. The text can be viewed at http://www.lonesentry.com/gi_stories_booklets/89thinfantry/index.html on the website of *Lone Sentry — Photos, Articles, & Research on the European Theater in World War II*. Both links accessed on Sunday July 26, 2020.

[4570] See endnotes [3367] to [3373] of Polish WWII Supplement I "The Molotov-Ribbentrop Pact" in regard to the deportation of Borderland Poles to the Gulag.

See also endnote [204] in the Preface "Birth and Memory upon the Lesser Known Fault Line of History."

[4571] http://www.kresy-siberia.com/memorial/warszawa_memorial.html from the Kresy-Siberia Virtual Museum documents the history behind the Monument for the Fallen and Murdered in the East, or *Pomnik Poległym i Pomordowanym na Wschodzie.* http://kresy-siberia.org/galleries/soviet-tyranny/katyn/ documents the Katyń Wood Massacre. The reference sources for this website can be viewed at http://www.kresy-siberia.com/reference.html and its funding partners, which include the Polish Ministry of Foreign Affairs can be viewed at http://kresy-siberia.org/museum/en/support/funding-partners/. All links accessed on Sunday July 26, 2020.

[4572] Ibid.

[4573] Ibid.

[4574] The online article *Treblinka* on the website of the United States Holocaust Memorial Museum at https://encyclopedia.ushmm.org/content/en/article/treblinka. Treblinka I was the forced labour camp that was already functioning at the time. Accessed on Sunday July 26, 2020.

[4575] See the Warsaw Ghetto map at http://www.deathcamps.org/occupation/pic/bigwarsawmap.jpg of the Aktion Reinhard Camps (ARC) group. Accessed on Sunday July 26, 2020.

[4576] The online article *DEPORTATIONS TO AND FROM THE WARSAW GHETTO* on the website of the United States Holocaust Memorial Museum at https://encyclopedia.ushmm.org/content/en/article/deportations-to-and-from-the-warsaw-ghetto. Accessed on Sunday July 26, 2020.

[4577] The online article *Deportations from Warsaw ghetto to Treblinka begin* by History.com Editors on the HISTORY website at https://www.history.com/this-day-in-history/deportations-from-warsaw-ghetto-to-treblinka-begin, published by A&E Television Networks on November 5, 2009, last updated July 28, 2019, accessed on Sunday July 26, 2020.

[4578] The online article *DEPORTATIONS TO AND FROM THE WARSAW GHETTO* on the website of the United States Holocaust Memorial Museum at https://encyclopedia.ushmm.org/content/en/article/deportations-to-and-from-the-warsaw-ghetto. Accessed on Sunday July 26, 2020.

[4579] The Holocaust Explained website, affiliated with the London Wiener Holocaust Library, in the article titled *Warsaw Ghetto* at https://www.theholocaustexplained.org/the-camps/the-warsaw-ghetto-a-case-study/conditions-inside-the-warsaw-ghetto/. Accessed on Sunday July 26, 2020.

[4580] The online article *Treblinka* on the website of the United States Holocaust Memorial Museum at https://encyclopedia.ushmm.org/content/en/article/treblinka. Accessed on Sunday July 26, 2020.

[4581] Ibid.

[4582] As stated on the plaque.

[4583] See endnotes [4177] to [4183] for this supplement.

[4584] As stated on the plaque.

[4585] The Home Army battalion emblems are displayed at http://www.warsawuprising.com/doc/emblem.htm. For this website's credentials, see endnote [3662] for Polish WWII Supplement III "The Katyń Wood Massacre."

[4586] Museum tablet photographed by the author on Saturday October 9, 2004.

[4587] See endnote [3937] for Polish WWII Supplement III "The Katyń Wood Massacre."

[4588] Online article in the New York Observer at https://observer.com/2018/05/evidence-shows-russia-had-role-in-smolensk-crash-killed-kaczynski/, dated May 15, 2018 by John Schindler, security expert and former National Security Agency analyst. Accessed on Sunday July 26, 2020.

[4589] [4623] Plaque above the entrance to Warsaw's Muzeum Powstania (Uprising Museum) as photographed by the author on Saturday October 9, 2004. For a description of "The Government Delegation for the Republic of Poland," see footnote [lvi] for this supplement.

[4590] See endnote [4141] for this supplement.

[4591] Museum tablet titled FOR HIS COURAGE AND BRAVERY and ZA MĘNSTWO I ODWAGĘ as photographed by the author Saturday October 9, 2004.

[4592] Museum tablet with photograph of Melchior Czesław Szczubełek "Jaszczur" — "Saurian" (large reptile) as photographed by the author Saturday October 9, 2004.

[4593] Museum tablet with photograph of Jan Nowak Jezoriański as photographed by the author Saturday October 9, 2004.

[4594] See endnote [4298] for this supplement.

[4595] Museum tablet with photograph of Ewa Mataszewska "Mewa" — "Seagull" as photographed by the author on Saturday October 9, 2004.

[4596] Museum tablet titled GHETTO OR GETTO as photographed by the author on Saturday October 9, 2004.

[4597] As photographed by the author on Saturday October 9, 2004.

[4598] As photographed by the author on Saturday October 9, 2004.

[4599] Page xx of *God's Playground A History of Poland: Volume II: 1795 to the Present*, by Norman Davies, published by Oxford University Press, 2005, ISBN 0199253404, 9780199253401. This is in the abbreviations section, documenting the existence of the ZWZ from 1939 to 1942.

[4600] Museum tablet titled POLISH UNDERGROUND STATE or POLSKIE PAŃSTWO PODZIEMNE as photographed by the author on Saturday October 9, 2004.

[4601] Museum tablet titled OPERATION „BURZA" [TEMPEST] IN THE LUBLIN AREA or „BURZA" NA lUBELSZCZYŹNIE and photo of Colonel Kazimierz Tumidajski "Edward" as photographed by the author on Saturday October 9, 2004.

[4602] [4619] [4621] Museum tablet titled BEFORE THE 'W-HOUR as photographed by the author on Saturday October 9, 2004. See also endnotes [4175] and [4234] for this supplement.

[4603] See endnote [4156] for this supplement.

[4604] Museum tablet titled COMPARISON OF FORCES or PORÓWNANIE SIŁ as photographed by the author on Saturday October 9, 2004.

[4605] Museum tablet titled RADOŚĆ PIERWSZYCH DNI or THE JOY OF THE VERY FIRST DAYS as photographed by the author on Saturday October 9, 2004.

[4606] Museum tablet titled THEATRES or TEATRZYKI as photographed by the author on Saturday October 9, 2004.

[4607] Museum tablet titled CIVILIAN'S FATE or LOS CYWILA as photographed by the author on Saturday October 9, 2004.

[4608] Museum tablet titled SHRINES OF INSURGENT WARSAW or KAPLICZKI POWSTAŃCZEJ WARSZAWEJ as photographed by the author on Saturday October 9, 2004.

[4609] Museum tablet titled THE PALLADIUM CINEMA or KINO PALLADIUM as photographed by the author on Saturday October 9, 2004.

[4610] Museum tablet titled CONQUEST OF THE PAST or ZDOBYCIE PAST-y as photographed by the author on Saturday October 9, 2004.

[4611] Museum tablet titled CAPITULATION or KAPITULACJA as photographed by the author on Saturday October 9, 2004.

[4612] Museum tablet titled DECISION OF GENERAL „BÓR" or DECYZJA GEN. „BÓRA" as photographed by the author on Saturday October 9, 2004.

[4613] Museum tablet titled EXODUS as photographed by the author on Saturday October 9, 2004.

[4614] Museum tablet titled THE DEATH OF THE CITY or ŚMIERĆ MIASTA as photographed by the author on Saturday October 9, 2004.

[4615] Museum tablet titled THOSE WHO STAYED or CI, KTÓRZY POZOSTALI as photographed by the author on Saturday October 9, 2004.

[4616] See the online transcript of the interview conducted by the National WWII Museum in New Orleans of Dr. Alexandra Richie, Author of *Warsaw 1944* on Wednesday January 22, 2020 at https://www.nationalww2museum.org/war/articles/interview-dr-alexandra-richie-author-warsaw-1944. Accessed on Sunday July 26, 2020.

[4617] Museum tablet titled CAPITULATION or KAPITULACJA as photographed by the author on Saturday October 9, 2004.

[4618] In regard to the dates of the period in which the Yalta Conference was held, and where Yalta is located, see endnotes [168] and [169] for the Preface "Birth and Memory upon the Lesser Known Fault Line of History."

[4619] See endnotes [4602] and [4621] for this supplement.

[4620] See endnote [3618] for Polish WWII Supplement III "The Katyń Wood Massacre."

[4621] [4619] [4602] Museum tablet titled BEFORE THE 'W-HOUR as photographed by the author on Saturday October 9, 2004.

[4622] Museum tablet titled CAPITULATION or KAPITULACJA as photographed by the author on Saturday October 9, 2004.

[4623] See endnote [4589] for this supplement.

[4624] In regard to the easy Soviet capture of Kraków in January 1945, see endnotes [4325] to [4330] for this supplement.

[4625] See endnote [4331] for this supplement.

[4626] See endnote [4176] for this supplement.

[4627] Museum tablet titled CAPITULATION or KAPITULACJA as photographed by the author on Saturday October 9, 2004.

[4628] See endnote [3619] for Polish WWII Supplement III "The Katyń Wood Massacre."

[4629] The online Australian War Memorial article, by Peter Burness, Senior Historian in the Military History Section of the Australian War Memorial at https://www.awm.gov.au/wartime/49/burness_tobruk. Accessed on Sunday July 26, 2020.

[4630] [1382] [1385] In numerous Anzac day marches I have witnessed in Brisbane's city centre, albeit, not of course in 2020, members of the Polish diaspora always marching near the end of the procession. As do the diasporas of other nations such as Serbia, Greece and Vietnam. Moreover, it's again worth mentioning, that the Polish exile Army, was the fourth largest of the Allied coalition after Britain, USA and the Soviet Union. See endnotes [3685] and [3686] for Polish WWII Supplement III "The Katyń Wood Massacre."